The River
Road

Other Books by

FRANCES PARKINSON KEYES

FICTION

ALSO THE HILLS

CRESCENT CARNIVAL

ALL THAT GLITTERS

FIELDING'S FOLLY

THE GREAT TRADITION

PARTS UNKNOWN

HONOR BRIGHT

THE SAFE BRIDGE

SENATOR MARLOWE'S DAUGHTER

LADY BLANCHE FARM

QUEEN ANNE'S LACE

THE CAREER OF DAVID NOBLE

THE OLD GRAY HOMESTEAD

NON-FICTION

THE GRACE OF GUADALUPE

THE SUBLIME SHEPHERDESS:
The Life of St. Bernadette of Lourdes

ALONG A LITTLE WAY

WRITTEN IN HEAVEN:
The Life of the Little Flower of Lisieux

CAPITAL KALEIDOSCOPE

SILVER SEAS AND GOLDEN CITIES

LETTERS FROM A SENATOR'S WIFE

POETRY

THE HAPPY WANDERER

FRANCES PARKINSON KEYES

The River Road

GROSSET & DUNLAP
Publishers
NEW YORK, N. Y.

PUBLISHED BY JULIAN MESSNER, INC.
8 WEST 40TH STREET, NEW YORK 18, N. Y.

PRINTED IN THE UNITED STATES OF AMERICA

Contents

Author's Note

SOMETIMES TITLES are written to books and sometimes books are written to titles. I have done the latter twice now. In both instances I found my title, as a little girl, on the New England countryside. But I waited many years for the discovery of the right story to go with it, and finally found it "a far piece"—as they say in Louisiana—from the place where I originally sought it.

While I was writing *Crescent Carnival,* my lifelong friend, Jean Darling, who spent that winter with me in New Orleans, reminded me of a childhood episode I had entirely forgotten. "One day when you and I were walking down the lane at the Oxbow," she said, referring to the road which runs between the meadows back of my mother's house near Newbury, Vermont, "you called my attention to the fields of flowering Queen Anne's lace. And then you remarked thoughtfully, 'Queen Anne's lace—that would be a good title for a book. When I grow up, I'll write one and name it that.'"

As Jean recalled this incident, I remembered it perfectly, though I could not have told, before then, when and where I first conceived the title of *Queen Anne's Lace* for my first political novel. And the reminder served to shift the memory of a similar episode from the recesses of my mind to its forefront: once while jogging along the dusty highway between Haverhill and Orford, New Hampshire, in the horse and buggy days, I noticed a tottering wooden sign, half-hidden by overhanging brambles, and inscribed in fading letters with the words "The River Road." I turned off the highway and followed the winding course of the Connecticut River for several miles. It was a drowsy sort of day, phenomenally warm for New England even in midsummer, and though the sign had diverted me, I was not seeking adventure or even attune to it. So I was not disappointed because I met no one along the way, and saw nothing beyond neat hay fields, patches of stony pasture, a red schoolhouse, a white church, and a few farmhouses attached to their barns. No seasoned New Englander, accustomed to the rural scene, would have expected to find anything more arresting on such a secluded byway. But somehow I felt that the sign had been significant, that because of it I would watch for other river roads, and that some day I would find one that belonged to a story.

Shortly after Jean's reminder, I found it in Louisiana.

At first I hardly dared believe that the search of years had been so richly rewarded. I turned the idea over and over in my mind, until it reached the point where it could not be suppressed any longer. This happened to occur on a terrifically hot June night, when I had already been working for some fifteen hours on end, but when the latter part of my labors had been somewhat lightened by the presence and assistance of Hermann Deutsch, Associate Editor of the *New Orleans Item*. I wiped the perspiration from my streaming face, detached my fingers from the smudgy sheets beneath them, and spoke with more firmness than I felt.

"Hermann, I've got an idea for another Louisiana novel. I think I have to come here again and write it."

"Good grief! Suppose you finish this one first!"

There was certainly something in what he said. The manuscript of *Crescent Carnival* was overdue and grim reminders to that effect had been coming in by air mail and telegraph from my publishers.

"No, but listen," I persisted. "I want to write a story about the River Road—the one that used to be the main thoroughfare between Baton Rouge and New Orleans, with all those big sugar plantations on it. Then the air line was cut through, and traffic and trade were diverted. Most of the old families felt they couldn't hang on any longer, in their huge houses, under changed labor and living conditions."

"Well?"

He had picked up a cigarette and had begun to smoke quietly. He did not interrupt and he did not try to hurry me. Those were both such unusually good signs that I was encouraged.

"Well, but some of them did hang on. I'd like to tell the story of a family that managed to."

I went on talking and Hermann went on smoking. At last I stopped and he laid down his cigarette.

"I think maybe you've got something there," he said briefly.

"I think so too. But it would be a hard story to write, Hermann, harder even than *Crescent Carnival* has been. I'd have to put endless work into it, I'd have to do an enormous amount of research, I'd have to go and live on the River Road myself or I couldn't get the feel of it. Even so, I couldn't write a novel like that without help. Would you help again, if I came back to Louisiana to write?"

"Yes. I'd be willing to help, in parts where I can, because you do work hard. All right, you're coming back to Louisiana to write *The River Road*. Now that's settled, we might get on where we left off before you started this subject. My alarm goes off at five."

So after a year in Washington I did come back and he has helped—he and so many others that I cannot shake off the fear of failing to include all the names which should be on my long list of those who have given me invaluable assistance and information. But first of all, unquestionably, I should record my gratitude and indebtedness to the

viii

men who have been good enough to share with me as much of their own great knowledge of sugar and its production as my limited powers would absorb. Among these are the Honorable Edward J. Gay, manager and president of the St. Louis plantation, a valued friend of many years' standing; all the Supples of Catherine Plantation, newer friends, but equally kind and helpful; the William B. Burkenroads, Senior and Junior, and the Edward Lafayes, Senior and Junior, partners in the great coffee importing firm of J. Aron and Son and owners of the Supreme Sugar Factory and Refinery, where the pleasant guest house affords an ideal center for conference and research, and where the genial manager, Mr. J. T. Landry, is always ready for both; Mr. Richard C. Plater, Jr., of Acadia, another plantation where I am always sure of a welcome; Mr. Clifford G. LeBlanc, Chief Chemist of Cora Texas, under whose guidance I first experienced the pleasures of a sugar-house party; Mrs. Florence B. McGowen, who recalled many other festive observances connected with sugar making, and whose recollections served to send me in search of them; Mr. George M. Murrell, Manager of Tally-Ho, the factory with the mellow brick façade and graceful fanlight which inspired the description of my fictional sugar house; Mr. George C. Pitcher, President and Manager of Alma Plantation; Mr. Feltus B. Leake, Factory Superintendent of Poplar Grove, and Mr. S. J. Gianelloni, Jr., owner of Longwood. Thanks to the never-failing hospitality of these persons and their families I have been able to visit Louisiana's sugar factories, both in and out of season, and to observe many angles of the activities which take place there. And it has also been my privilege to listen, not only to historical facts, statistics and definitions connected with the sugar business, but to the legends which have grown up around it and around the men whose characters and careers, to such an astonishing degree, are interwoven with it.

No one possessing the most superficial acquaintance with the history of Louisiana sugar could fail to recognize, in my fictional account of the experiments with Java cane at Belle Heloise, the great factual contribution made to the industry at Southdown Plantation by such measures. But for the benefit of those who lack any such acquaintance, I am happy to quote from *One Hundred Great Years,* by Thomas Ewing Dabney, one of the most enlightening as well as one of the most enjoyable books on Louisiana which I have consulted:

"In this century, Louisiana's sugar swung still closer to extinction [than in the last] and this time there seemed to be no hope, for the land apparently had lost the ability to produce. . . . In 1926 it had sunk to 42,000 long tons. That year the yield of the entire sugar belt was worth only $5,000,000, the value of the strawberry crop in one or two Parishes. The cane harvested just about equaled the seed planted.
"The falling sickness Dr. E. W. Brandes of the United States De-

partment of Agriculture in 1919 diagnosed as mosaic disease, which had already swept through the cane fields of Puerto Rico and Argentina. The only cure, he said, was to plant new varieties, disease-resistant, as those countries had done. But the Louisiana planters paid no heed—they were no longer the careful farmers they had been when their principal concentration was upon the growing of cane, and sugar-making was a routine chore with equipment which cost a few thousand dollars; now the involved and costly manufacturing process consumed most of their attention. They did not have time to read farm bulletins. Too cold, too hot, too wet, too dry, land worked out, they said, and there was nothing they could do about it. Anyway, there was no new cane they could get, for the United States prohibited the importation of seed for general planting purposes.

"On Southdown Plantation near Houma, however, there were three men who read what Dr. Brandes had written, and pondered. They were David Pipes, Charles Krumbhaar, and Elliot Jones, who divided the financial, manufacturing, and production management of the plantation. From Dr. Brandes, they secured, in 1922, twenty-one eyes (seed) of a cane new to this country but proved mosaic-proof in Argentina.

"This was P.O.J. 234—the 234th seedling evolved in the cross-pollenization experiments in Proefstation Oest Java; but scoffing planters in Louisiana said the letters meant Poor Old Jones.

"The Southdowners planted that tiny row of P.O.J. Strong and green grew the stalks—no sign of mosaic, though they were surrounded by fields pale and droopy with the disease. They planted the entire yield. Next year, they did the same, and the next, and they kept this up until by 1927 they had enough new cane for their seven thousand acres, and to give the rest of the cane belt a start."

In trying to interpret various phases of life along the River Road I needed guidance and enlightenment on many subjects besides the production of sugar, and sport, as locally pursued, was foremost among these, for this is a great hunting country. After receiving my first helpful hint from Hermann Deutsch about the prevalence of cat hunting, I conferred with my neighbor, Mr. S. J. Gianelloni, Jr. of Longwood Plantation, to whom I have already referred, and who has shown a co-operative spirit every time I have consulted him, no matter what the subject. I guessed that he might be a devotee of cat hunting and I was right; I had hardly put my question to him before he and his wife, his son and his daughter, had all embarked on enthusiastic accounts of the cat hunts they had enjoyed, and from there they went on to tell tall tales of squirrel hunting and 'possum hunting, too. But they knew a much greater authority, they assured me: their friend Elemore Morgan, who, by a happy chance, was coming to Longwood that evening with some photographs he had just taken of the place—he was one of the finest photographers anywhere around, didn't I know? Look, we would just have another drink and a few more sandwiches, and by that time Elemore and Dorothy would be there. . . .

The meeting was a happy one for me in every respect. For Elemore Morgan proved to be not only a fine photographer—as anyone who reads this book will be able to see for himself!—and an authority on cat hunting, but a person of such varied knowledge and wide acquaintance that he was able to supplement his own store of information by help from several other authentic quarters; and the hunters with whom I came in touch through him, like the planters I had previously met, not only taught me facts but told me stories, which in turn I have tried to retell.

As a matter of fact, while all the characters with whom I have peopled *The River Road* are wholly imaginary—except in the case of well-known political and historical figures, whose real names have been used throughout with no attempt to disguise them, and Angus Holt, who actually lived and labored at "The Cottage" for many years—many of the stories which I have woven around them or caused them to relate are wholly or largely true. These stories have come to me from many different sources, on many different occasions. It was Mrs. C. A. Dupuy, the mother of my friend Wilma Supple, who told me the story of the reluctant bride, when we were relaxing after a duck dinner at Catherine Plantation. It was Hewitt Bouanchaud who told me the story of the wolf who fell in love with a dog, at one of those expansive buffet suppers which abound in New Roads. It was Mrs. Corinne Favrot Hart of New Orleans who told me about the dance at Doiron's, and made me see the girls' gay cretonne dresses and their escorts' matching blouses as clearly as if I had seen them myself. It was Lewis Gottlieb of Baton Rouge who told me about the speech to the deaf-mutes, at his camp on the Amite River, between the snatches of songs which Meadows, his own dusky "Admirable Crichton," was playing to the accompaniment of a banjo. He also acted as the intermediary through whom I met Major Felix Spiller and Captain J. C. Floyd, whose reminiscences supplied me with valuable material. Other incidents were suggested by the notable overseas exploits of Lt. Col. Eberhard P. Deutsch and Paul Kalman. If these stories, and others too numerous to specify, do not carry conviction with them, it is less because they are not as real as the River Road itself than because of my own lack of skill as a raconteuse.

Besides the persons who have told me specific stories, there are many who, because of their peculiar fitness to do so, have helped me to understand—and I hope interpret—atmosphere and develop character. Among these are Mrs. Lucille Bourgeois Dutton, now Chief of Central Files at Standard Oil, who was born and reared at "Stonewall" near New Roads, and Miss Marie Conrad, a niece of the owner of "The Cottage," whose stories of their childhood have made me more conscious than ever of the happy lot of boys and girls who grew up on plantations in the Deep South. Miss Marie's father, Mr. Frederick D. Conrad, has helped me, too, tramping over every inch of the property on Conrad Point with me, so that I could mentally recreate all the buildings which once stood here. Her cousin, Mr. Joseph A. Loret—formerly Assistant Attorney General of Puerto Rico and now Special Assistant Attorney for the Louisiana Highway Department—has furnished invaluable local color, too; he remembered all about the shrimp and beer parties they used to have on the batture, and all about the men who used to come to them. Through the good offices of Monsignor H. Joseph Jacobi I have met his friends the Cangemis of Baton Rouge and Father Gardino, Chaplain of the St. John Berchman's Home in New Orleans, and we have all taken counsel together as to how best to develop the characters of my Italian peddler and his family and to reproduce their dialect. Through the good offices of Mr. E. P. Simmons, President of Sangers in Dallas, I familiarized myself with many department store details, hitherto unknown to me. Through the good offices of Mr. W. B. Cotton, Jr., Director of Public Relations, and Mr. Claude F. Reynaud, Assistant Manager and General Superintendent Inland Waterways, Louisiana Division of the Standard Oil, I have met Sherman Banta and Leland Le Normand, two of the real captains on the "McDougall," and groped my way towards the creation of another imaginary character, incidentally using another true incident in doing so. Through the good offices of Lucille Bourgeois Dutton I met her visiting sister, Corinne Bourgeois Bienvenu, whose husband, Graham Bienvenu, is the manager of a large sugar central in Cuba, and revived my own pleasant memories of that delightful island! And acting on my own initiative, I have met Captain William B. Smith, Assistant Director, Division of Student Life, at Louisiana State University, who has put me in touch with Mrs. Thomas W. Fort, whose husband's heroic career, typical of the finest product of L.S.U., furnished me with the details I needed to describe Riccardo's. (The real winner of the Kemper Williams Saber in 1937 was Cadet Colonel Henry Holt Frisbee of Springfield, Massachusetts, now stationed at the Port of Embarkation in Boston with the rank of Major; but the action in the Pacific, which I have attributed to Riccardo, was all Major Fort's.) A mutual friend brought Colonel W. G. Schauffler, Jr., then Commandant of Harding Field, to a party I was giving to celebrate the publication of Harnett Kane's *Deep Delta Country,* and Vail's war record was gradually established from this meeting, with the added help of Colonel Paul E. Todd, Captain Robert C. Camaish, Lieutenant John E. O'Loughlin, and Captain Frank P. Agnost, Headquarters E.A.T.C., Maxwell Field, Alabama. (And speaking of Harnett Kane, if I could do for Louisiana—or for any other state—in fiction what he has done for it in *The Bayous of Louisiana* and *Deep Delta Country* I should feel I had achieved the ultimate for which any novelist could hope!)

Miss Thekla Hollingsworth, now a staff writer on the *New York Times,* who has long been recognized as a leading interpreter and adapter of Southern spirituals, wrote two of the lyrics which appear in this book, and helped me to arrange various versions of another which has long been locally sung at the end of the grinding season. The rest of the Negro songs which I have quoted have been taught me by my own colored staff at "The Cottage," and are part of their own tradition. And let me gratefully say in passing that they have contributed in many other ways besides in teaching me their songs!

My friend, Frances Meredith Richard, librarian of Iberville Parish Library Association and a staff writer on the *Iberville South,* did much of the research and furnished many of the reminiscences which enabled me to describe the Plaquemine Sugar Festival of 1936; she was ably assisted by her brother, Dr. John Alvery Richard, Jr., and her friend, Mrs. Samuel Daigre. Incidentally, the high-school essay contest described in Part IX really did take place, and the actual winner of the prize awarded in New Roads was Anne Louise Hewes of the Poydras High School. To New Roads also goes the honor of claiming as a citizen Allan Ramsey Wurtele, whose mechanical inventions—attributed in this novel to Mortimer Prescott—have revolutionized the harvesting of sugar cane. The home of Mr. and Mrs. Chester D. Folkes in Baton Rouge furnished me with the prototype of the one I "gave" to Fabian d'Alvery; and though Folkeses have a pleasant garden of their own, I transplanted the one which actually belongs to Mr. and Mrs. Thomas Moody, also of Baton Rouge, from St. Charles Street to Somerulos Street and attached it to the d'Alvery house!

Besides isolated articles, editorials and pamphlets too numerous for mention, I have read with care and attention *The Year Book of the Louisiana Sugar Planters Association* for 1917 and for 1921–1924, inclusive; the 1939 *Year Book of the Louisiana Sugar Industry; the Story of Louisiana Sugar Cane* issued in 1939 by the Educational Committee of the American Sugar Cane League; *The Cane Sugar Handbook* by Guilford L. Spencer and George P. Meade; the spring issue of *The Louisiana Tourist* for 1939; and the series of ten articles, variously titled but all dealing with the problems precipitated by mosaic disease, written by Thomas Ewing Dabney and published in the *New Orleans Item* during the spring of 1927. With the same care and attention which I have given the official records of the sugar industry, I have read the official journal of the proceedings of the Louisiana Senate and House of Representatives of 1930, and numerous diaries kept by planters, both past and present, in this region. Most of these diaries are privately owned. Two, however—*The Scrapbook and Diary of E. J. Capell* and *The Diary of Mrs. Isaac J. Hilliard*—both in manuscript form, are in the archives of the Louisiana State University; and one, *Plantation Life in the Florida Parishes of Louisiana,* as reflected in the diary of Bennett H. Barrow, has been edited by Edwin Adams Davis and is published by the Columbia University Press.

G. G. Gerbing's *Camellias;* Harnett Kane's *Louisiana Hayride!* Elma Godchaux' *Stubborn Roots;* Frazier Smith's *White Pillars;* Hermann de Bachelle Seebold's *Old Louisiana Plantation Homes and Family Trees;* William A. Read's *Louisiana French;* Lizzie Carters McVoy's *Louisiana in the Short Story;* and the *Louisiana State Guide* of the State Guide series published by Hastings House are among the many books, besides those already mentioned, which I have found especially illuminating. The article *Old Man River is Rolling on to War,* published in the February 21, 1943 issue of *Parade,* first stimulated the interest in river traffic which the location of The Cottage has further awakened, and part of Frances Belle's reflections in Chapter XLVII are based on certain paragraphs of this article. I am greatly indebted to *Parade* for permission to use them in this way. I have also consulted the files of the *New Orleans Item,* the *Baton Rouge Advocate* and *State Times,* and the *Lake Charles American Press* with good results.

Louisiana is a law unto herself literally as well as figuratively; she is the only State in the Union governed by the Napoleonic Code instead of the English Common Law, just as she is the only State which is divided into Parishes instead of Counties; and lest through my own lack of legal knowledge I should err in my references to the inheritance of property and other important questions I have consulted Charles Cecil Bird, Esq., of Baton Rouge and obtained his valuable legal advice. Mr. Lewis Gottlieb, Vice-President of the City National Bank of Baton Rouge, has been equally patient in explaining some of the complex relations between bankers and planters, whose "yearly meetings were generally dreaded to an equal degree by both" during the depression period, though current conditions are happily very different. Steele Burden, Landscape Architect of Louisiana State University, has revealed to me the mysteries of many an old garden, enabling me, in the end, to recreate a real one as well as several imaginary ones.

Though Jean Darling, the lifelong friend I mentioned near the beginning of this note, came with me on my first Louisiana venture, Clara Wilson, the faithful housekeeper who had ministered to my wants and needs for so many years, simultaneously decided she could not face the alien atmosphere of the Deep South. I missed her very much during my own absence from more accustomed ground and I am happy to feel she missed me a little, too. At all events, she was waiting to welcome me home, and when I told her that the Washington scene was to be only an interlude then between sojourns in Louisiana, she said that the next time she would come, too. She was as good as her word, and I think she has had her reward. She freely states that "The Cottage" is the most beautiful place she has ever seen, and her kindly ways and culinary skill have won new friends for her as well as for me. These friends, to whom she is "Miss Clara," are scattered up and down the River Road, throughout the Teche country, and all over the city of New Orleans. Indeed, who knows if without the refreshment and sustenance of her incomparable mint juleps, her onion soups, corn chowders and dewberry pies, my various assistants would have the endurance to persevere in helping me throughout our long hard task?

Among these assistants, I must not fail to mention my secretary, Marion Ridinger Hunter, who certainly needed perseverance and endurance in order to keep abreast of her share of my work, but who somehow managed to do it, often against heavy odds. She is by all means the best woman driver I have ever seen, and as she represented my only means of transportation most of the time, was an important consideration. Being decorative, as well as efficient, not the least of her contributions to *The River Road* was in posing with Mr. James J. Bailey, one of the heirs to "The Cottage," and my dog Lucky, as the photograph which Elemore Morgan took on this occasion furnished the basis for Mr. Norman Reeves' jacket drawing. From these examples, it will be readily understood that "Little Hunter's" activities in behalf of the book have extended in many directions. Katharine McKiever, of the N.C.W.C. News Service, whose dependability in the matter of research is as great as ever; Mary Lester of the *New Orleans Item;* and Lucille Dutton, mentioned before, have all supplemented Marion's efforts in various ways and also deserve a hand.

Every word in this author's note will serve to reveal the fact that "I have received advice and help from many quarters." But then, as Thomas Ewing Dabney adds after making the same admission in *One Hundred Great Years* . . . "What careful reporter does not?" And anyway "This was in clarifying obscure developments," not in creative work. Many developments in Louisiana, among them political developments, require clarification, if the product of an outsider's imagination is to have an indispensable seal of authenticity in the end, and this is one of the many ways in which Hermann's help has meant so much. Moreover, the mere mechanics of living have been difficult, and on that account also I have needed all the encouragement and succor I could secure from every source. While plying a profession peculiarly dependent upon communication, I have had to get along without a telephone, without mail service, without delivery of any commodity, even a newspaper. All this has taken some adjustment to meet, especially as the intermittent absence of water, roads which at times have been almost impassable, the ruin of two victory gardens —one through drought and one through seepage—and several long hard illnesses have further complicated the picture. I have found everything from snakes to skunks on my doorstep, and I have been obliged to combat mosquitoes and other insects which found no difficulty in boring their way through two sets of screens and a mosquito bar. After Mrs. Hunter's departure at six in the evening I have been absolutely cut off from the outside world. There has been no way of summoning help in an emergency, and no way of getting out for change and diversion since a spinal difficulty prevents me from driving a car myself and there was no one else on the place who could do so. I have been separated from all my family and most of my friends—never has my isolation been so complete in any place where I have visited. At one time I was seriously tempted to give up trying to cope with all these handicaps and resume my role of foreign correspondent, which I came to believe would entail fewer difficulties! But I resisted the temptation because, even in my moments of greatest depression, I knew down deep in my heart that the beauty of my surroundings, the wealth of available material, the boon of my opportunity, and the faith of those friends who believed that I could "crown my gifts with grace to persevere" were far more significant than any obstacle in my path. Holding fast to this knowledge, I eventually found I could go on with an ever-deepening sense of purpose, of fulfillment, and of joy. In discovering the River Road which belonged to my story, I have proven again to myself that in life there is no such thing as a blind alley. Every impasse which looks like one leads, after all, to another magic highway.   F. P. K.

"The Cottage," River Road,
Baton Rouge, Louisiana.
December 1943–September 1945.

PART I

"Hail the Conquering Hero Comes"

April 1919

"The description which I have given of a sugar estate, with its vast level fields, like emerald plains, its stately *sucrerie,* its snow-white Negro village, its elegant chateau buried in trees, will answer for that of the hundreds which continuously line the two shores of the Mississippi, between Baton Rouge and New Orleans. . . . A few yards from the water *runs a beautiful road,* bordered on one side by gardens and houses, and on the other by the River. . . . The whole line of shore, for the one hundred and fifty miles, is a continued unbroken street. . . . This . . . is *the river road,* following in and out every curve of the embanked shore, and level as a race horse track. Thus, one riding along this road has constantly the green bank, or Levee, on one side, with the mile-wide River flowing majestically by, bearing huge steamers past on its tawny bosom. On the other hand are hedges separating gardens, lawns, cottages, villas, and emerald cane fields, with groups of live oaks, magnolias, lemon, and banana trees interspersed. For miles, all the day long, the traveler can ride through a scene of beauty and ever lively interest."

—Taken from "The Sunny South, or The Southerner at Home: Letters embracing five years experience of a northern governess in the land of sugar and cotton" . . . Edited by Professor G. H. Ingraham of Mississippi. Published by G. G. Evans, Philadelphia—1860.

"Hail the Conquering Hero Comes"

April 1919

CHAPTER I

I

"THERE'S NO USE going to the window yet, Merry. It's barely five, and you know these things never start on time. I don't believe the parade's left the campus yet."

"I don't suppose it has. But I like standing here where I can see the flags and festoons. Come here and look at them, too."

"I've looked at 'em already. Anyway, our own show windows have got all the other decorations licked to a standstill and we can't see those from here. That backdrop of the battleship with the eagle hovering over her is a knockout."

"Yes, it is. And I like the way the war relics are arranged in front of it between the Victory Loan posters. But the other stores have good displays, too, Hazel, and all this bunting floating in the air gives me a big thrill. So do the crowds. I never saw so many people on Third Street. The parade'll be along presently. I don't mind waiting."

"I know you don't. But at that, it doesn't usually get a girl anywhere."

Hazel Wallace spoke in a tone slightly tinged with sarcasm. Everyone in Goldenberg's store knew that Meredith Randall, Mr. Goldenberg's private secretary, had waited and waited for Gervais d'Alvery to come back from France and marry her. As far as that went, everyone in Baton Rouge knew it, and almost everyone had thought that her waiting would be in vain. But Merry, as they all called her, did not seem to mind. She did not mind having people know that she was waiting, she did not mind having people speak of it, she did not even mind having them feel that her confidence was misplaced. To be sure, she did not air her patience and her trust, she did not bring up Gervais d'Alvery's name of her own accord. But her faith in him was so supreme that her very bearing bespoke it; her love for him had such a shining quality that its glow pervaded her being. Lately, since the grudging but general admission that her confidence had not been misplaced after all, and the further unmistakable evidence that she had reason not only to trust his integrity but to glory in his prowess, this glow had expanded to include everyone around her and actually to transform the drab surroundings of herself and her fellow workers. Gervais d'Alvery had won promotion for gallant conduct in the face of the enemy; in spite of serious wounds, he had successfully led his men against Hun machine-gun emplacements; after his recovery, the United States Government had conferred the Distinguished Service Cross upon him, and the French Government the Croix de Guerre. His home coming, late the previous week, had been the occasion of the greatest demonstration that had ever taken place at the Baton Rouge station. Now in the Victory Loan Parade which was about to begin he was the object of excited and concentrated attention. Nearly one hundred officers and men, recently returned from overseas, were to march in the parade. But none of them had made such a record as Gervais d'Alvery; none so dashingly embodied the popular conception of a "hero"; and none, by birth and background, was so logically predestined to become the local idol.

No wonder that Hazel, sauntering over to the dingy window of the crowded cubbyhole where she and Merry did their typing at adjacent clattering machines, said to herself, rather resentfully, that her sarcasm seemed to fall flat. Merry could certainly afford to ignore it. Because everyone had now seen the meeting of her and Gervais at the station. Everyone had known from the avidity with which he seized her in his arms and pressed his face down against hers, and from the lingering reluctance with which he finally released her, with what fervor and intensity he returned her love. Everyone knew that he would rather have gone straight home with her to the jerrybuilt little bungalow on St. Napoleon Street, where she lived with her shrewish mother, and their eccentric lodger, Miss Mittie Alden, than to have been borne away on the shoulders of cheering men to the music of a big brass band. In fact, a good many people said afterwards that it was a shame the official banquet to which Gervais had so triumphantly been taken had lasted so long, that the Governor and the Mayor and the Secretary of State had all made such long speeches. Because, when these were finally over, it had been too late for Gervais to see Merry again that night. He had been obliged to go straight on to his plantation, Belle Heloise, and the cheering men and the brass band had accompanied him all the way down the River Road. Not that anyone doubted he had managed to get back to see Merry since then. . . .

The door leading from Mr. Goldenberg's private office into the cubbyhole opened quietly, and Mr. Goldenberg came out—a thickset, gray-haired man, immaculate of appearance and formal of manner. He spoke to the girls civilly but conventionally.

"I see you've finished your letters, Miss Meredith. Mrs. Goldenberg and my mother, with two or three of their friends, have come down to my office to watch the parade, and Mrs. Goldenberg has suggested that perhaps you would like to join us. She'd be very glad to have you, if you would. Miss Hazel may come, too, if Mr. Sears can spare her."

Mr. Sears, the merchandise manager, whose office was on the other side of the cubbyhole, was a notorious martinet, and Mr. Goldenberg never interfered with his subordinates' discipline. Hazel had been pouting all the afternoon over the amount of work which he had left her to plow through when he went out. But after all, he had gone. He was going to march in the parade himself, with other members of the Victory Loan Committee. If he did not find all his letters written when he came back the next morning he could stew and stew, but there would be nothing he could do about it then. Hazel accepted Mr. Goldenberg's invitation with gushing alacrity.

"Oh, Mr. Goldenberg, that's simply sweet of you! I mean it's simply sweet of Mrs. Goldenberg. I'd adore to watch the parade from your office windows. Wouldn't you, Merry?"

"It is very kind of Mrs. Goldenberg to ask us. But I think perhaps I ought to wait here for Miss Mittie. I told her this was where she'd find me. She wouldn't know where to look for me, if I left."

"I will keep someone else here, in your place, Miss Meredith, to tell your friend that you're in my office. Of course, Mrs. Goldenberg and I will be very pleased to have her join us there, too, when she arrives."

As if the matter were settled, Mr. Goldenberg opened the door of his office again, and the two girls walked in. The cubicles occupied by the minor officials of the store were drab and cluttered, and great naked-looking white water coolers stood in their corners, between the olive-green files. The floors in most of these cubicles were bare, though Mr. Sears had somehow contrived to achieve a shabby, mousecolored carpet. The desks were badly battered and perpetually heaped with untidy piles of papers, escaping from beneath glass paperweights, and other miscellaneous packages littered the straightbacked chairs. The walls were undecorated except for dog-eared sales charts, felt bulletin boards defaced by pricking, and mammoth calendars issued by insurance companies. But Mr. Goldenberg's office was entirely different, and Hazel, who seldom had occasion to enter it, was much impressed. A brightly colored rug covered the floor, and reproductions of Mr. Maxfield Parrish's exotic paintings adorned the walls. There were no files, and instead of the objectionable water cooler, a shining thermos jar, precisely placed with two neat glasses on a matching tray, invited refreshment. The glassed-over desk was orderly and sparsely covered, and the only calendar in the room was a small one, neatly encased in a frame of tooled leather, which matched the frame containing the photograph of Mrs. Goldenberg in full but restrained evening dress which stood on the opposite side of the unblemished blotter, near a silver bud vase containing a lonely crimson rose. Merry was a pretty lucky girl, Hazel thought, to spend so much of her time in an office like this, working for a perfect gentleman like Mr. Goldenberg, instead of being cooped up in a horrid little pen with a sourpuss like Mr. Sears. Just the same, she did not think Merry had been invited to come to this office, socially, before. She knew, for a fact, that nothing of the sort had happened on Armistice Day, because she and Merry had watched the parade together then. It was that million-volt kiss at the depot which had got Merry this invitation. Mrs. Goldenberg knew perfectly well that Captain Gervais d'Alvery of Belle Heloise would not have kissed Meredith Randall of St. Napoleon Street like that, for all the world to see, if he had not meant to marry her; and now that Merry's days as Mr. Goldenberg's secretary were numbered, and her position as the chatelaine of Belle Heloise assured, Mrs. Goldenberg felt very differently towards her.

Mrs. Goldenberg came forward to meet the girls and to introduce them to her mother-in-law and her friends. She was a dark handsome woman dressed in dark handsome clothes, which were a little heavy-looking for late spring, but nevertheless as elegant as they were costly. Before the World War, Mrs. Goldenberg had gone to Paris every year to buy her clothes, and she was already planning to resume these pleasant pilgrimages; meanwhile she had done very well in New York. A sable stole was draped over her satin-sheathed shoulders, and a diamond bar pin sparkled in the smooth folds of the shining material drawn down over her ample breast. There were diamonds on her fingers, too, not many of them, but enormous, Hazel noticed, and beyond a doubt the large pearls around her neck were real. There were advantages in marrying a rich storekeeper after all, whatever stuck-up girls who would have nothing to do with anyone "in trade" might say about it. Hazel was sure Merry would never have diamonds to compare with Mrs. Goldenberg's, just heirloom jewelry in heavy settings, cameos and garnets probably, and maybe some seed pearls. Hazel had noticed the insignificant little ring which Merry had been wearing the last few days, and though she had it on her right hand instead of her left, Hazel had no doubt that Gervais had given it to her. It was just the sort of ring Hazel would have expected of him, made of twisted gold and studded with turquoises, some of them slightly discolored. The d'Alverys were not poverty-stricken, like so many of the old River families who looked down on the townsfolk and spoke of them sneeringly as "catfish aristocracy," because when the Mississippi receded after it had risen, quantities of catfish were left on the banks beside Baton Rouge. But they were not wealthy either.

As far as Hazel knew, Fabian d'Alvery was the only one of Gervais' kin who was really prosperous, and he had not lived on a plantation in a long time, but in a cute house on Somerulos Street. This was right on the edge of "Catfish Town," but no one made disparaging remarks about Fabian for living there, because he was a d'Alvery. He was also a lawyer, and furthermore he was making money fast. Of course he had something queer the matter with his spine, which had prevented him from going to war, and he had been very bitter about that; but he had kept on getting richer and richer just the same. And he was one of the best speakers in the Parish; he had been in constant demand as a "Four-Minute Man" in every one of the Liberty Loan Drives. He was going to speak that very afternoon, on the corner of Convention and Third Street, when the parade halted on purpose to admit such addresses. Probably he had done just as much good, raising money by making speeches and giving away a lot himself besides to the Red Cross and other good causes, as Gervais had done getting wounded and killing Huns. Only he did not think so, and Merry did not seem to think so either. That was another reason why Fabian was embittered. Merry respected Fabian and pitied him, but she adored Gervais. And if Merry had only felt just a little differently, or would have pretended that she did, she could have been married at the beginning of the war, when nearly all the other girls were doing it, and given wonderful parties on Somerulos Street for visiting celebrities, and worn diamonds as big as Mrs. Goldenberg's. . . .

"This is my husband's mother, Miss Randall," Mrs. Goldenberg was saying smoothly, breaking in on Hazel's reverie. "She enjoys a parade beyond anything, so I hope you'll stand right here beside her, and explain everything to her. I'm afraid I don't understand the program very well. But it begins at the University, doesn't it?"

"Yes, on the campus. The parade must have started already. I think it's headed by the mounted police. If we listen we'll hear the horses coming presently. And the music. There are going to be three bands."

Without self-consciousness or awkwardness, Merry had taken the indicated place beside the elder Mrs. Goldenberg. The old lady looked at her shrewdly, and, at first, rather sharply; but apparently she was pleased with what she saw. Merry's big brown eyes met hers candidly, and there was something so trustful in their gaze that her own glance softened as she continued her scrutiny. She had heard that this girl was a beauty, and she had suffered occasional pangs of maternal uneasiness in thinking of her son's secretary. But now she knew the pangs were needless. There was an almost childlike quality, not only in Merry's guileless gaze, but in the fresh bloom of her skin, and in the dimples which deepened in her cheeks when she smiled. Her hair, which she wore bound with a ribbon and falling in loose waves over her shoulders, enhanced the illusion of extreme youth; it must have been honey-colored when she was a little girl, for though it was brown now, it was still full of golden glints. But the old lady who was so carefully appraising all this likewise saw that beneath its masses of shining hair the girl's head was shapely and erect, and she sensed that beneath the fair flesh the bodily structure was very strong. Here before her was something more than beauty and better than beauty. She could feel Merry's generous vitality flowing out towards her, warming her aged limbs and reanimating her wary spirit, and in like measure she was aware of the girl's integrity and intelligence and steadfastness. She smothered a little sigh, knowing that her son would lose a great deal when he lost the cheer and challenge of such a presence. Then she smiled and gave Merry's hand a little pat, as her daughter-in-law went on with the introductions, belatedly including Hazel in them.

"Mrs. Silver, you've met my husband's invaluable little secretary before, haven't you? Really? Why I thought— And this is her friend Miss—oh, yes—of course, Miss Wallace! Mrs. Wayland, Miss Randall and Miss Wallace. Mrs. Bourdonnay, Miss Randall and Miss Wallace. It's delightful, isn't it, that we could have some charming young girls added to our little group? I asked Miss d'Alvery and her friend Miss Hathaway to join us, because I really think you can get a better view of a parade from this office than from any other point. But it seems they'd already been invited to the Mansion. Governor and Mrs. Pleasant are having a small coffee party. You know Miss Cresside d'Alvery, of course, Miss Randall?"

"No, I haven't met her yet. But I'm hoping to."

Funny that she can talk like that about Gervais' sister, Hazel thought, as if it did not matter at all that Cresside d'Alvery, who was as snooty as she was fast, had gone out of her way to avoid meeting Merry. And as for Cresside's bosom friend, Regine Hathaway, she had told all over town that there was nothing in the rumored engagement, that Gervais had never intended to marry a nobody like Meredith Randall. The scene at the station had put an abrupt stop to her spiteful talk, and Hazel, for one, was glad of it. But still she wasn't easy in her mind about Regine Hathaway; she thought Regine would try to get even with Merry yet. Because, of course, Regine had wanted Gervais herself—almost as much as Cresside wanted Regine's friend, Sylvestre Tremaine, who was up from New Orleans visiting at Hathaway Hall now, and who must have gone with them to the Mansion. Sylvestre Tremaine hadn't been in the war either, though the reason wasn't as obvious as it was in Fabian d'Alvery's case. As far as anyone knew, there wasn't anything the matter with Sylvestre's spine. That is, not really. Though Hazel seemed to remember she had heard someone refer to him as "that spineless slacker."

Hazel's contemptuous reflections were interrupted at this point by the properly heralded arrival of Miss Mittie Alden. No one in Baton Rouge knew much about the Randalls' lodger, beyond the fact that she was an excellent teacher and a strict disciplinarian, and she was generally considered to be as mysterious as she was peculiar. She was a wiry little woman, with unkempt hair and hands, whose clothes were an eyesore, and whose nose always looked as if it were very cold, even in the warmest weather. Among her few friends, she had a way of expressing herself that was both quaint and effective, but when she went out among strangers, she was silent and constrained, and her cold nose quivered all the time, like a rabbit's. It quivered now, as she made her miserable rounds of the Goldenbergs and their friends, meanwhile casting an accusing eye at Merry, and muttering angrily under her breath, as if to blame the girl for the agonizing experience to which she was being subjected. But Merry, seemingly more and more at ease, blithely ignored this. She made sure that Miss Mittie was placed where there would be the best possible view of the parade, and then herself went on talking to old Mrs. Goldenberg.

"I can hear the music now, can't you? Listen!"

Old Mrs. Goldenberg leaned forward. She was growing a little deaf, but the strains which had so quickly reached Merry's alert ears sounded thrillingly, if dimly, in her own.

> "Buy a bond, buy a bond, buy a bond,
> Help the boys across the pond.
> They are fighting there for you,
> Yes, they're dying for you too,
> Buy a bond, buy a bond, buy a bond!"

"Well they're not dying now," Merry said thankfully, pressing old Mrs. Goldenberg's hand. "The song doesn't fit that way any more. But, of course, we still ought to buy bonds—that's the whole point of this parade. So in that way the song does fit, doesn't it? And it's a grand tune!" She began to hum the song herself, under her breath.

> "'Help the boys across the sea,
> Far away in sunny France,
> Where they take a hero's chance,
> Buy a bond, buy a bond for liberty!'"

The music was coming nearer and nearer. Merry interrupted herself to tell Mrs. Goldenberg about something else, now that the stimulus of the song was no longer a surprise. "We'll be seeing the mounted police any moment. And then the Red Cross nurses, and the canteen workers, and the Boy Scouts——"

"And the Victory Loan Committee," interposed Hazel, speaking up, in spite of herself, for the absent Mr. Sears.

"Yes, the Victory Loan Committee, and hundreds of Standard Oil employees. The Standard Oil has a wonderful band of its own, Mrs. Goldenberg. A man named Sylvester Smith leads it. And there's the fife and drum corps, too. Price Mitchell leads that. And the University Band——"

"You're not going to forget to mention the Overseas Contingent, are you, Miss Meredith, while you're talking to my mother?"

Mr. Goldenberg still spoke civilly and conventionally in addressing Merry but somehow it was evident that she had contrived to please him very much. Hazel did not know whether this was because Merry was being so nice to his mother, to whom he was devoted; or whether it was because she was so natural and simple in the presence of his wife and the other important ladies, though a little graver than usual; or whether it was because he too had realized the import as well as the impact of that million-volt kiss at the station. If it were the kiss that had changed his estimate of Merry, however, Hazel felt that the underlying reasons for this were not the same as the underlying reasons for his wife's cordiality. He would not be moved by Merry as the prospective mistress of Belle Heloise; in fact, he would probably go out of his way to indicate that this would make no difference to him, for Mr. Goldenberg was a very proud person in his own right, much prouder than Mrs. Goldenberg, and toadied to no one. But he might well be moved by Merry as a human being devotedly loving and passionately beloved. . . .

When the Overseas Contingent swung into sight, led by Gervais d'Alvery, lean, bronzed, handsome, wearing his captain's uniform and all his medals, Hazel, watching the expression of Mr. Goldenberg's face, knew that in her last surmise she had not guessed wrong.

II

"If you fellows really want to see anything of this parade, you better stop talking politics for a few minutes and come on out. There's the Red Cross unit starting up the street right now and the Overseas Division's right behind it."

"I don't give a damn about the Overseas Division. I can't go anywhere these days that I don't find the streets blocked by a parade. What I came down here from Caddo to find out, and what I haven't found out yet——"

"I know, Tack, I know. In fact, Jim and I both know why you came down here from Caddo. So does Carruth, for that matter. Just the same, this is only April, and the election doesn't come off till next January. So there's still a little time to spare. We've been talking politics quite a while now to please you. Maybe you'd be willing to humor the rest of us by taking a half-hour off to see the parade. It couldn't do any harm."

Three of the four men who had paused in front of the cash register at "Izzy's" moved unhurriedly towards the sidewalk, and after an instant's hesitation the fourth one, Tack Evans, reluctantly decided to join them. At his invitation the others had been drinking small blacks and eating L.S.U. cream cheese at the counter which ran the length of the tunnel-like room, constituting the politicians' favorite meeting place: "Jim" Bailey, the Secretary of State who had spoken first; George Favrot, the Congressman from the sixth district, who had retorted to Tack so drily, and Carruth Jones, an attorney and legislator of East Baton Rouge Parish, whose high-pitched voice seemed to be momentarily silenced. On their way out they had stopped to speak to the beaming, baldheaded proprietor of the little café. Izzy always presided personally at the cash register, in front of a large photograph of himself which was fastened up against a shelf and inscribed across the forehead with the words FAMOUS FOR HIS BRAINS. He was a very short man, so that physically the cash register almost concealed him; the tufts of gray hair encircling his shiny dome and the cleanshaven contour of his rubicund countenance were barely visible above it. But nothing could obscure Izzy's radiant personality or dim the luster of his fame. Orleanians often said, rather sneeringly, that Izzy's was the only place in Baton Rouge where civilized food could be had. But not one of them denied that you could get it there.

"The Congressman's right, Mr. Evans," he now said encouragingly, noticing that the outsider still hesitated. "You don't want to miss seeing this Overseas Division. It's going to be a great sight. More'n a hundred men in it, all from Baton Rouge. And this young fellow who's leading it, Gervais d'Alvery, he's made a fine record. We're all mighty proud of him in this section. He was in here Saturday, eating some of my specialties, relishing 'em, too. Mary's Lamb and Izzy's Yam, that's what I served him. Well, I'm going to have another look at that boy myself. I believe he's going far." While Izzy was still speaking, three or four white-jacketed, white-aproned Negro waiters shot past towards the door with unaccustomed alacrity, and Izzy beamed more broadly than ever. "I might just as well," he said. "There won't be any cash coming in to ring up until those boys of mine get back. My customers are out on the sidewalk already. Everybody wants to see Captain d'Alvery at the head of that Division."

He might as well give up the struggle, Tack Evans said to himself, though he stood still for a moment longer, impatiently jiggling the large monogram hanging from his watch chain, and listening unmoved to strains of "Over There." As he had previously remarked, he had not come down from Caddo to see a parade; he had come down because he wanted to know what was brewing in the political pot, who was going to support whom, what the score was on the governorship. He assumed that the man backed by Behrman, the mayor of New Orleans, would get in; Behrman had backed Pleasant, and Pleasant had got in, so very likely it would be the same next time. But he wanted to be sure. At the same time, he wanted to be on good terms with the three men who had just been his guests, because as far as Baton Rouge was concerned, the right side was whatever side they were on. In other words, the gubernatorial candidate they didn't support might be elected, but never the local representatives; and Tack had to stand in with the local representatives, too, if he intended to make a mark for himself. That was just what he did intend, now that his field had proved up, after he had got that grand drilling contract. And he couldn't make his mark if he made mistakes. He had to try to run with the hare and hunt with the hounds. It was all very complicated.

Moving slowly forward, Tack abandoned the monogrammed watch chain, and lighted a cigarette. Jim Bailey was smoking a cigar now, he noticed, Carruth Jones a pipe, and George Favrot was unobtrusively chewing tobacco. Tack pushed his way through the crowd and joined them at the edge of the sidewalk, towering above them all. Bailey

11

was a tall man, too, but Evans was long and rangy, built more like the traditional Texan than the typical Louisianian. He was proud of his size, as he was of his record, but he knew that neither impressed this triumvirate whose good will it was so essential he secure. He was only a hillbilly to them; the others all "belonged."

The Red Cross unit was directly in front of Izzy's now, the first section of it being in the form of a living "Old Glory," woven by nurses. Some were dressed entirely in white, others entirely in red; these two divisions made up the stripes of the flag. The field effect was given by stars in the caps of another division of marchers. The nurses swung rapidly along, their pretty faces alight, their trim persons swaying to the strains of "Keep the Home Fires Burning":

> "Keep the Home Fires Burning,
> While your hearts are yearning,
> Though the lads are far away
> They dream of home.
> There's a silver lining, through the dark clouds shining,
> Turn the dark clouds inside out
> Till the boys come home."

Behind the section forming "Old Glory" was another forming the Red Cross, and this was followed by still another forming a big blue V to typify the Fifth Loan. These animate flags were all greeted with tremendous applause, in which Bailey, Favrot and Jones all joined heartily, while Evans continued to stare moodily out towards the street. The Red Cross unit was followed by a huge white float, with a beautiful girl enthroned at one end. She was dressed in a flowing Grecian robe, and carried an enormous American flag; at her feet, in attitudes of appropriate admiration, were grouped several sailors, soldiers and marines. Jim Bailey looked the girl over appraisingly, and nodded his approval.

"Corinne Bourgeois does right well as Miss America," he said to Favrot. Then he gave a soft chuckle. "Just the same, the general effect would be a whole lot better if that brass eagle on the top of her flag didn't keep getting caught in the electric wires. Someone ought to have measured it beforehand."

"You're a great one, Jim, always telling what someone else ought to do. Why didn't you ever think of that yourself, until just now?"

"I can't think of everything, can I? I've got enough to do running an office, running for re-election to that office, and not minding other people's business. Well, here's what we've been waiting for. Suppose we stop arguing and take it all in."

The "Miss America" float had been the direct precursor of the Overseas Division. Preceded by a band playing "Over There," more than a hundred recently discharged soldiers and sailors were now coming up Third Street. Most of them marched jauntily, responding gaily to the prolonged cheers with which they were greeted; but a few looked straight ahead of them as they marched, their white faces set in grim lines. Several were minus an arm, and several others walked with a limp, struggling and skipping to keep up with the smart pace of their comrades. Here and there three gold stripes, representing a year and a half of service overseas, glittered in the sunshine; here and there a medal gleamed, proclaiming its wearer a hero of the Argonne or St. Mihiel; and taken by and large, the men's uniforms were fresh and neat. Some, however, were stained and shabby, some were incomplete, and in still other instances, the men were even wearing civilian dress, placarded with circular cards bearing the legend "Veteran, World War." Many wore a white rose, previously pinned upon their persons by the pretty girls who made up the animate flags in the Red Cross Division. But it was obvious that no special effort had been made to achieve conformity in appearance among the ranks; the men had only recently returned from overseas, singly and in small groups and they represented many different types of service; it was something of a triumph to have got so many together on such short notice, in a small city, without trying to do more.

What the division as a whole lacked in dash, however, its leaders supplied in abundant measure: Gervais d'Alvery, clad in the field uniform of a Captain of Artillery was an arresting figure. He was only a little above medium height, and slenderly built; but he carried himself so proudly and erectly that he gave the effect of being a tall and powerful man. He had the high cheek bones, fine features and clear olive complexion characteristic of a Creole aristocrat, and his tan accentuated the fine quality of his skin instead of detracting from it. A small black mustache, closely clipped, shadowed his upper lip, and his rather heavy brows were black, too; both added to the striking quality of his handsome face. His magnetism, like his vitality, was inescapable.

"If I only had that young fellow up in Shreveport, I'd know what to do. I wouldn't have to be studying who to send down here," Evans remarked at last, his eyes following the trim figure of Captain d'Alvery with reluctant admiration.

"Aren't you getting pretty biggity, talking about 'sending down'? If you've elected anyone yet, I haven't happened to hear of it. Not outgrowing your breeches, are you, Evans?"

Bailey was invariably soft-spoken, but his pleasant voice could be oddly at variance with his pointed words. Evans flushed angrily at the sound of it now. Before he could frame an effective retort, however, George Favrot broke in.

"It's not impossible, you know, that the Parish of East Baton Rouge may know what to do with Gervais d'Alvery. Caddo isn't the only place where his qualities could be appreciated."

"That's so. Besides, it might be a good thing if the other representative from this Parish were a planter."

Carruth Jones was joining in the discussion at last, somewhat self-consciously. His high-pitched voice broke in a slight squeak, and he took his pipe from between his teeth and turned to look covertly at each of his companions in turn. Jim Bailey laughed, easily.

"I suppose you think you're elected already, Carruth."

"Well, same to you, Jim. You think you've got a mortgage on your job. Some time Louisiana might decide it actually wanted another Secretary of State."

"Yes, it might. But I'll begin to worry about that when it happens. Meanwhile, I'm not so sure about running soldiers as candidates, especially officers," Jim Bailey replied. He still spoke with easy good nature, but a more thoughtful note had crept into his voice. "Right now, everyone's shouting 'Hooray' just like we are. But every buck private who's had to salute and say, 'Yes sir'!—'No sir'!—'Oh sir'! for two years will be laying in the gap to catch even."

"I can't agree with you there, Jim." Tack Evans was jiggling his monogrammed watch chain again, while he rather dourly regarded a large truck that was lumbering by, placarded with the inscription WE HELPED TAKE THE GERM OUT OF GERMANY AND THE HELL OUT OF WILHELM. The truck, along with others bearing similar captions, was a feature of the division sponsored by the Standard Oil, and it seemed to rouse a special feeling of animosity in him. Under his breath Evans was damning the Standard Oil as an organization, and even its products listed on the side of another truck as war-winning commodities. But the watch chain had always given him a feeling of importance; now it seemed partly to restore the right to authoritative speech of which the genial Secretary of State kept robbing him. "A hero is a hero," Evans ended stentoriously.

"I think you've got something there, Tack. Besides, if one of our representatives is going to have a name like Jones—" George Favrot paused, chuckling and glancing slyly in the direction of the attorney—"it wouldn't do any harm if we picked somebody with a name like d'Alvery for the other. I don't need to tell you we have to think of things like that in South Louisiana."

"I suppose you do." Though the remark had not been addressed to Tack Evans, he picked it up as if it had. "But can you always get men like this captain of yours to run for office, even if you do think of it? The d'Alverys are a pretty proud bunch, aren't they? Inclined to believe politics too damned dirty for them?"

"You may think you know the d'Alvery breed, Tack, but you don't. Not as well as I do, anyway. You've never been thrown with the River families any to speak of, so far, have you?" Again the soft-spoken Secretary of State was putting the hillbilly in his place; again Tack Evans felt the angry flush rising from his ruddy forehead to the roots of his sandy hair. "I'll admit you couldn't get him to run for a job like sheriff or assessor," Bailey went on pleasantly. "He wouldn't be interested in the patronage side of politics. But he'd be glad to do anything he thought would help his friends and neighbors, especially his fellow planters." Jim Bailey looked thoughtfully down Third Street,

14

as if he could still see Gervais d'Alvery marching at the head of the Overseas Division. "In fact, I'd be glad to bet on it, if anyone would care to take me up." Again his face brightened with his winning smile, and he nodded across the clearing sidewalk in the direction of Izzy's. The beaming proprietor had resumed his place behind the cash register, and the white-jacketed, white-aproned Negro waiters were unhurriedly beginning to serve the customers who were drifting back towards the stools lining the long counter. "The parade seems to be about over, the part we're interested in, anyway," he said. "Why don't we have another round of small blacks, on me this time? We can go to work now on whatever Tack came all the way down from Caddo to get off his chest."

III

"'Oh, it isn't cheerful to see a man, the marvelous work of God,
   Crushed in the mutilation mill, crushed to a smeary clod;
Oh, it isn't cheerful to hear him moan; but it isn't that I mind,
   It isn't the anguish that goes with him, it's the anguish he leaves
      behind.
For his going opens a tragic door that gives on a world of pain,
   And the death he dies, those who live and love, will die again and
      again.'"

Fabian d'Alvery raised one arm slowly and shook his hand from left to right as he quoted this verse from a poem by Robert Service. The gesture had seemed both appropriate and effective when he practiced it before his bedroom mirror; but somehow, here in the street, it did not go over so well. Besides, he could feel the little wooden stand underneath him teetering as he gesticulated. The stand had been provided to assure him extra height and consequence, raising him above the crowd and setting him apart from it; he needed it, for unlike his kinsman, Gervais d'Alvery, he was unable to cut a fine figure. He had been born with a spinal deformity which not only prevented him from walking in a normal way, but also gave him a hunched appearance when he was standing or sitting. However, at this moment he would willingly have sacrificed the height of the stool if he could have felt the solidity of the sidewalk under his feet. He persevered, fully aware that his position was precarious.

"Today's parade is an appeal to help provide for those who are left behind," he said, trying to speak impressively. His voice was earnest and so was his face. But he did not speak loudly enough, and his gray eyes, which were his finest feature, were wise and honest rather than impelling; aside from them, his thin, refined face was at first glance unremarkable. "Thank God, men are no longer being crushed to smearing clods in mutilation mills," he went on laboriously. "But it is all too true that when they died they opened tragic doors on a world of pain, and that thousands of others, who still survive, are facing destruction and devastation which is a living death."

15

Beyond the mob jostling around him and making his position more precarious every minute, Fabian was conscious of the derisive countenance of "College," the Italian who kept the fruit stand on the opposite side of Convention Street. College, whose real name was Tony Cangelosi, had acquired his nickname while he was selling peanuts, chewing gum, soft drinks and cheap candy from a much less pretentious stand out at the University, which was then still run on a military basis, so that the students were subject to strict discipline. Fabian, who had spent a year at L.S.U. before going to Princeton, himself had become a patron of College at that period, sometimes more or less surreptitiously. Now, in the wide grin which enlivened the huge Italian's jolly face and in the shrug which shook his broad shoulders, Fabian seemed to discern the humiliating mockery of an older man who has known a younger one since his salad days and has consequently never grown accustomed to regarding an erstwhile prankish student as either authoritative or mature. As usual, College was wearing no necktie and his collar was unbuttoned at his throat, which was thrown back a little, adding to the effect of merriment which he gave; his hands were thrust impudently under his exposed suspenders. Everything about his enormous figure, framed with the bunches of bananas hanging in succulent abundance on either side of his wooden shack, bespoke ease, content and amusement. As Fabian unwillingly met his twinkling eye, his own discomfiture increased apace. But he went doggedly on with what he had to say.

"If we do not rescue these sad survivors from their living death, the heroes who have fallen will have died in vain," he declared. " 'They will not sleep though poppies grow in Flanders Field.' This is a war which has been fought to make the world safe—safe for democracy, as our great President has so often reminded us, and safe in all other ways as well. The dead have done their part. Now we must do ours, in this tumultuous postwar period upon which we are just entering. We must do it in both tangible and intangible ways. We must be as ready to prove our patriotism now as we were in the darkest days of the war."

This time he felt he had really put his idea over and that his words had been respectfully received. He did not glance in the direction of College again, but kept his eyes fixed on the division of the parade which had halted, according to schedule, at Convention and Third. It was a large division, extending far down the street, and consisting of a group of boys and girls in their teens. The group was not in uniform, yet strangely enough there was a certain uniformity in the bearing and expression of these boys and girls, and they gave a greater effect of accustomed unity than many which had passed by. They were not rollicking and roisterous either, like many of the others, but grave and attentive, as if they understood the basic solemnity and importance of the occasion. A great wave of gratitude and recompense welled up in Fabian's heart as he looked at them, and he leaned forward to see the

16

inscription on the banner which their sober young leaders were carrying with so much circumspection. The banner was fluttering in the crisp breeze, and he could not instantly make out the lettering, because it was partially concealed by the shifting folds. Then, with horrible suddenness, it leaped out at him:

STATE SCHOOL FOR THE DEAF AND DUMB

The deaf mutes! The unfortunate boys and girls, educated at public expense, who could not hear a word that he or anyone else said to them and could not have responded even if they did! Their apparent attention had been a mockery, just as the Italian's grin and shrug had been; their steadfast gaze had been inspired by no efforts of his, but by their anxious watchfulness for the signal to proceed. Unless their alertness was unremitting, they might miss this, for no sharp command, no blaring bugle, could penetrate the tragic and perpetual silence to which they were doomed. Fabian was still staring at them, with a gaze almost as fixed as theirs, when they caught sight of the awaited signal and began to move, not freely and joyously, but in that monotonous unison which no longer puzzled him. He did not wait to see who would follow after them. He stepped down from his wooden stand, giving it a vicious kick as he escaped from it, and plunged into the crowd. The corroding knowledge that his disappointment was puerile in no way assuaged his overpowering sense of chagrin.

He was still plowing ahead without any reason or objective, other than avoiding the direction of the fruit stand, when he caught sight of Meredith Randall and Miss Mittie Alden, less than half a block away from him. The girl's arm was linked in that of her queer companion, and she was chattering gaily. Miss Mittie's own expression was glum, but she was obviously exercising considerable will power to keep it so; every now and then it relaxed into a reluctant smile. Finally Fabian heard her laugh and give utterance to one of her favorite sayings, in a voice which for some inexplicable reason was audible above the surrounding hubbub.

"Well, I haven't seen anything to equal it since Hector was a pup, and now he's a full-grown dog," she admitted. "I'm telling you, Merry, when I saw that American flag spread out flat and held up by those four pretty girls, it did something to me. I'd have thrown the last cent I had to my name into it, if I'd have had the cash with me. I guess maybe it's just as well I didn't have but two-seventy-eight in my purse. Not but what I'm planning to go down to the bank tomorrow."

"Oh, Miss Mittie, I felt just the same way! When I thought of all that Gervais had suffered and of the others who had died, and realized that we were only being asked for *money!* . . . Besides, I wanted to give a thank offering because he'd come home safe and well to me after all."

Fabian worked his way sidewise through the crowd towards the curbstone. If he could reach it, he could forge forward fast enough to catch up with Merry; and if he could do that, then the day would not be a failure after all. No day could be a failure that was crowned with her presence, no matter what had happened through the burden and heat of it. He called out to her; if he could hear her and Miss Mittie above the noise, surely they ought to be able to hear him.

"Hi, there, Merry! What's your hurry? Wait a sec, can't you?"

He saw her pause and turn her head, trying to locate the source of his call, but unsuccessfully. He had not been able to reach the curbstone yet; he was still swallowed up by his turbulent surroundings. But a substantial matron who was in front of him had heard him, too. She elbowed out a small circle and turned herself around in it.

"*Why, Fabian!*" she exclaimed delightedly. "I *thought* I recognized your voice! Of course, you have such a *wonderful* voice that I couldn't very well help it! I'm *so* glad to have a chance to speak to you! I want to tell you that your talk was simply *marvelous!*"

"It's terribly kind of you to say so, Mrs. Ingledew. But I know it wasn't really. I know it was an awful flop. I'd rather not talk about it if you don't mind, especially just now——"

"Why, Fabian, how can you *say* such a thing! It was the most marvelous speech I ever heard in my *life!* Everyone said, when you were in high school, that by and by you would be L.S.U.'s most outstanding orator. When I think of all those debates you were in, about sugar and tariffs and serious subjects like that, and then of your *beautiful* valedictory——"

With desperate determination, Fabian had reached the curb, in spite of Mrs. Ingledew. Once there, as he had foreseen, he had no trouble in plunging forward. But meanwhile Merry and Miss Mittie must have turned a corner, for they were nowhere to be seen. Fabian sang out again, but the only response to his words came from astonished strangers. Suddenly he felt very tired, and his back hurt him almost unbearably. He could not understand how he had dared to hope, even for a moment, that the day might not be a failure after all. This was not his day. It belonged to his cousin, who could go to war because he did not have a bad spine. Who had been wounded, to be sure, but afterwards decorated for conspicuous gallantry. Who had now come home to be acclaimed as the hero of Louisiana and was the accepted suitor of Meredith Randall. His cousin, Gervais d'Alvery.

IV

"It's good to feel the sun so warm, isn't it, Pascal?"

"Why not? It belongs to be warm in April, don't it, Max? And somehow another it still puts me in mind of Appomattox, even after all this long a time."

"Reckon I might feel the same as you, if I'd been there. But I never did get back into the fight, after I was wounded at Donaldsonville. I

18

never even heard what went on at Appomattox till a week after it was all over. Did you, Pres?"

"Yes, I heard. But that's not like I'd been there."

The parade was still coming down Third Street. It would turn presently beside the stereotyped Confederate Monument where these aged veterans were waiting to see it come, and swing up North Boulevard, where it would disband a few blocks beyond the Executive Mansion. But the music from Sylvester Smith's Band and Price Mitchell's Fife and Drum Corps was still distant; the strains of BUY A BOND, BUY A BOND, BUY A BOND! were not so loud that the three old friends could not hear each other as they rambled on, talking about old days and comparing these to new ones.

It was the principal pleasure they had left in life. Two of them—Pascal Tremblet and Preston Vicknair—lived in Baton Rouge, Pascal with his married granddaughter, Preston with his bachelor grandson. They were equally in the way and equally aware of it; the wooden bench beside the shell-strewn walk which encircled the monument represented almost their only haven of escape. They came to it every pleasant morning and sat there indefinitely, engaged in endless bickering, contented as long as they could keep it up, saddened when they parted to return to the meals for which they knew they must not be late. Max Stoetzner was more fortunately placed; he had saved a little money when he was younger and more vigorous, and this, with his pension of fifteen dollars a month, enabled him to live peacefully alone, in a small shack ornamented with wooden scrollwork, on the outskirts of Port Allen. When he crossed the River to Baton Rouge, he made a great occasion of it, arraying himself in his faded gray uniform which had been made for him at the time the United Confederate Veterans attended the dedication of the Albert Sidney Johnson Memorial in New Orleans. He took immense pride in the fact that it still fitted him, though this was largely because he could afford no bounty at his bare and lonely table. The uniform set him slightly apart from the others, who always wore the same dingy black suits.

"You know this fellow everyone's making such a fuss about, don't you, Pascal?" Max asked, stroking his goatee softly as he spoke. Since he had the advantage of his uniform, he felt he should accord his friends some advantage also, and he did this by tacitly acknowledging that their acquaintance with local figures and local conditions must necessarily be more thorough than that of a man who lived on the west side of the River, even if this habitation were only four miles away.

"Positively, yes. I know all the d'Alverys, me. They're kin to us in a way. Philogene d'Alvery's sister, Sybelle, married the second cousin of my mother. Philogene was Gervais' father—well, you know about that, at least. But I tell you frankly I don't know Gervais like I know Fabian, or like I knew their grandfather, Lucien Estrade. You take when I was a young boy, nobody called Belle Heloise the d'Alvery

Place. It was the Estrade Plantation, then. The Estrades been living there, them, ever since 1824."

"They was there a long time, I grant you that," interrupted Pres belligerently, stabbing at the dusty white shells before their bench with his gnarled cane. "But that house wasn't built in no 1824. Nearer 1830, if you ask me, when old man François Estrade, that always lived in New Orleans himself, gave it to his son for a wedding present."

"He gave it to his son for a wedding present, yes, but that was in 1824," Pascal retorted, glowering. "I ain't forgot, even if you have, Pres, how Lafayette got off the boat, him, and visited my kin at Belle Heloise. And that was in January 1825 when he made his voyage from New Orleans to Baton Rouge. I tell you frankly, I don't like the way you ignore history, my friend."

Preston Vicknair muttered something unintelligible, his head bowed over the clasped hands fondling the gnarled cane. Resentfully, he felt himself unequal to the task of challenging history.

"I haven't got used till yet hearing people talk about the d'Alvery Plantation," Pascal continued in triumph; it was not often Pres would admit an error, even tacitly. "Philogene d'Alvery never was more'n a poor relation, taken in out of charity, if he did marry Isabelle Estrade. Sybelle, his sister that I'm kin to, never had so much as a dowry. But I got to admit, me, those d'Alverys always had a way with them, paupers or not paupers. This boy's just running true to form. That's the onliest reason he's gone so far, him."

"He's a mighty handsome young buck. He hasn't just got a way with him. He's got looks, too," volunteered Max.

"He must 'a had something else, too, if he killed all them Huns. I reckon Pascal won't go so far 's to deny he did kill 'em. Medals like he's got ain't handed out for nothin'," Pres added, recovering his spirits.

"Oh, I grant you, me, he's got medals and all the other trimmin's," Pascal Tremblet retorted, with some bitterness. "People fall mighty hard for heroes nowadays, from the President down. But I can remember when things was different, yes. They never had no parade when Lucien Estrade come home after the War." He did not identify the war. In his mind, and those of his hearers, there was still only one war that really counted, changing the destinies of men and the aspects of civilization. "He was on Beauregard's staff, too," Pascal went on, flattered by his friends' attention. "So, like you see, he way outranked that grandson of his. But no bands, my friends, not so much as one trumpet. Lucien Estrade never even came into the depot, no. He just picked up a little old brown mule that the damn Yankees must of overlooked, God knows how, and he rode into Baton Rouge like that. Minnie, the mule's name was, and I inform you, there has always been one mule named Minnie at Belle Heloise ever since, out of respect to General Estrade."

"A hell of a mark of respect, should you ask me," jeered Pres, tapping with his cane. Pascal ignored the interruption.

"Minnie carried the General all the way from Natchez down to Woodville and through Bayou Sarah to hit the River Road at Baton Rouge," he continued loftily. "She deserves respect. But they wasn't nobody to meet Lucien Estrade nowhere, and he never expected it, no. Besides, nobody could tell when a man in that War would get home, or how. But the General wasn't studying on parades anyway. All he had on his mind was finding his wife and children and putting Minnie to plow. The poor, poor fellow hadn't got the news till yet how both the little boys were already dead and buried, them. Malarial fever, the summer before. Isabelle was born after he got back."

"Seem like a sickly lot, the d'Alverys or the Estrades, whichever way you want to call their name. Isabelle, she lost a couple of children, too, before Gervais, and another before Cresside came along."

"Well, not to say sickly, no. Overbred, maybe. They've all been marrying their cousins, as far back as I can remember. I tell you frankly, it would do no harm to get some fresh blood into that strain."

"I hear Gervais's got a sweetheart right here in Baton Rouge, and I don't call to mind she's any cousin."

"Nothing of the sort, Pres. You've got everything turned around, same as usual. He is to marry one of the Hathaways, him. Regine, the girl's name is, and handsome? I assure you, my friends—a picture! But I never thought so much of Hathaway Hall, me. Built by Carolinians, if I am not mistaken, or maybe it was just Virginians. I rather see Gervais marry a Louisiana girl. Not so much on account of the d'Alverys. But on account of the plantation. I tell you something, Belle Heloise was a fine place once, and lots of fine people stayed there in the old days, yes. Not just Lafayette either. Henry Clay—Zachary Taylor— Judah P. Benjamin—Jefferson Davis——"

The old voice faltered and trailed wistfully to a pause. The approaching band music swelled and stopped.

"So little was left of the place when Lucien Estrade came home," Pascal continued sadly. "I give you my word of honor, not even gear for Minnie. And I don't know as I would say it ever came back to what it was before the War." Again he did not identify the war. "But it could. The land's rich and there's lots of it." He paused with a chuckle which ended in a sad sigh. "Three thousand arpents altogether and twenty-five just in the 'Small Yard.' That was where they took the passengers from the *Princess* when she busted a boiler in midstream."

"It wasn't the *Princess* busted her boiler in midstream, Pascal. It was the *Mattie Belle.*"

"The *Mattie Belle!*" Pascal exclaimed scornfully. "The *Mattie Belle* never had no explosion, her. It was the *Princess,* I assure you, loaded with sightseers watching the famous race between the *Nachez* and the *Robert E. Lee.* Poor, poor people! There was a tragic end to their merry-making. But the passengers fished out of the water were each and every-one laid down on sheets spread in the Small Yard. I do not recollect, me, how many barrels they broke open to roll those poor scalded people in flour on the sheets. One did not buy a little poke of flour in those days, no. One kept it by the barrel."

"Much good it did to bust up all those flour barrels," Pres said in feeble mockery. "The most of those people died anyway."

"And was that the fault of the Estrades, then?" bristled Pascal. "No, never. In fact, the Estrades gave those that died decent burial right there at Belle Heloise, yes, in the cedar grove alongside the Yankees that died of smallpox, when the Federals used the house as a hospital. They tried to drive the family away but they didn't succeed— Madame Estrade stood her ground and dared them to put her and her children out. They didn't succeed in shelling the house from the river either— the damned Yankee Commodore who tried to do that was some kind of kin to Lucien, but kinship didn't stop him, darn his rotten hide. Lots of Yankees died on the place though, and their consciences must have hurt them, robbers and usurpers that they were, them. They can't rest too easy in their grave. If I believed in ghosts, me, I could say frankly that many would haunt that place."

"I do not believe in such things either," said Max, looking up at the square crenelated towers of the capitol the Yankees had burned in '62. "But I have many times heard Belle Heloise was haunted."

"Oh, that!" replied Pascal. "That's Angus Holt."

"Never knew of no family by the name of Holt on the River Road," Pres challenged at once. "And I'd have heard of them if they'd amounted to shucks."

"Angus Holt was no family, him," Pascal explained loftily. "He was just a Scotch tramp came up the levee at sunset one night, and asked at Belle Heloise for a drink of water. After he got the water, he asked could he have a hot dinner, and after he got the dinner, he asked for a night's lodging. Imagine it, he never left the place again, no, not until he died. Not even then, at least, for he is buried right there in the garden he tended. What a gardener, my friends! No other could touch him. But he was a man of learning, too. He could make anything grow that had a root, him, and he knew the roots of all the languages, too. He taught them to Lucien Estrade and Lucien Estrade's children— why he even taught Lucien how to speak *English!*"

Pascal was warming to his subject. Here was a story that was actually all new to his hearers, which Max could not supplement and which Pres could not dispute.

"Philogene d'Alvery—a wild young buck, that rascal!—used to dress in a sheet, and go prowling around to frighten everybody, pretending he was a ghost of Angus Holt. He was no more than pestering his rich wife's family, I assure you, but his pranks started old women to telling it about that Belle Heloise was haunted. Maybe Angus does really haunt the downstairs room he slept in. The Garden Room it has been called ever since, because it leads right into the garden he laid out."

"Then he would haunt that, too, for certain."

"Maybe." Pascal no longer cared to dispute with Pres. His eyes were fixed on the approaching troops, his foot tapping time to the band music. "I'm not denying, me, Angus Holt might have some kind of a part in the past which goes with an old River house like Belle Heloise," he admitted. "But if he does, he's got a part in the future, too—a future that's coming towards us this very minute along with that brass band that's playing 'Over There.'" Softly, in his quavering voice, he began to hum.

> " 'So prepare, say a prayer,
> Send the word, send the word
> To beware . . .
> We'll be over, we're coming over,
> And we won't come back 'til it's
> Over, over there.' "

He could not go on. His voice cracked and broke. He coughed regretfully and rose. "I could have managed all right if it had only been 'Dixie,'" he said in an apologetic way. "I've been waiting for that, but it looks as if I'd have to wait a while longer. And I can still salute. Shall we, my friends? I'm not saying Gervais d'Alvery is any such soldier as Lucien Estrade. But I figure we could owe him that much anyway, for his grandfather's sake."

v

"Well, it certainly was a fine parade. But that seems to be the last of it. Suppose we come into the dining room and have a little coffee!"

The governor's wife rose, looking at her guests with a comprehensive smile and addressing them as a group. They had been sitting on the lower gallery of the Executive Mansion, a large, rather boxlike white house situated on a street corner at one end of a long lawn. A few japonica bushes bordered the walk between the house and the street, but the bushes were small and the walk was short; the visitors had enjoyed an unobstructed view of the parade as it swung up North Boulevard; they had also enjoyed discussing its principal features with each other.

"Weren't those Negro pipestill cleaners from the Standard Oil a scream? I mean the ones that made up the last unit, dressed in their regular cleaning togs, wooden shoes with canvas uppers and all the rest of the paraphernalia."

"Yes, I know the ones you mean—the men carrying umbrellas and wearing blankets over their heads. Ridiculous, I thought—calling out all the time that they couldn't stand the heat of the sun, when their regular work is in the blazing hot stills of the plant! I don't wonder the bystanders were all laughing at them."

"Well, I got a great kick out of seeing them, and I think Mr.

23

McClelland was a mighty good sport to lead them. Though when it comes to wearing wooden shoes himself, I think perhaps that was going a bit too far. . . . Listen, did you notice that Britisher marching with the Overseas Contingent? He stood out among the others because he had on an English uniform, and I believe he got more applause than anyone except Gervais d'Alvery, of course. I don't know who he is though."

"He isn't a Britisher, he's an American. I heard someone say his name was Spyker and that he'd been in the Army four years, joining the Canadian Forces first. That's a good deal longer than any of the other men served. I think he deserved all the attention he got."

"Well, I'm not in favor of having American boys fight the Britishers' battles for them. You mark my words, there's been too much of that sort of thing already, and there's bound to be more in the future."

Some of the guests were so intensively engaged in conversation of this type that they were only vaguely aware of their hostess's suggestion; though they rose, politely, when she did, they made no immediate move to follow her and some of them went on talking among themselves.

"I'm afraid we ought not to linger too long. I'm sure some of you will want to hear Colonel Prescott's stirring address at the conclusion of the parade and it's going to disband just a few blocks from here."

The governor's wife still spoke smilingly, but there was a little more insistence in her voice this time; she plainly wished to shepherd her guests into the dining room without further delay. A slim dark girl, exceptionally chic, but piquant rather than pretty, who was perched on a railing at the further end of the gallery, somewhat apart from most of the other visitors, made a slight grimace as she slid from her seat, and linked her arm in that of another young girl who was standing near her.

"Listen to the old battleaxe, will you, Regine?" she murmured. "Much she cares whether we hear Colonel Prescott's stirring address or not. All she wants is to get us out of the house. Well, I don't think we'll be delayed long in the dining room—we'll get one small black and one small cookie apiece, if the impending feast is anything like the others I've been to here. I don't think this outfit ever heard of gin, much less champagne. But come on, let's get the orgy over with. I want to go down to the river to see those four submarine destroyers that have just come in from the New Orleans Navy Yard."

"But what have they come for?"

"To advertise this Loan we're all getting so hot and bothered about. Gervais says they're on the first leg of the run up to Memphis. . . . After I've given them the once over, I'd like to go down to the block dance in front of the Istrouma. Wouldn't you? There may be a little life to that!"

"Hush, Cresside! I do wish you wouldn't talk like that! Someone might overhear and tell. Then you'd never be invited to the Mansion again."

The second girl spoke in a fluttering way which was oddly at variance with her statuesque appearance. Someone had told Regine Hathaway, in her very early youth, that she bore a marked resemblance to the Empress Eugénie; ever since then she had cultivated this resemblance with phenomenal success, considering the handicaps imposed on her by modern fashion. Her hair was always arranged in ringlets, and her carefully planned costumes were always characterized by some touch of elegance suggesting the Third Empire. But evidently it had not occurred to her that her appearance made her manner of speaking seem doubly silly. This had, however, often occurred to Cresside d'Alvery, and though Regine was her best friend, it annoyed her excessively. She made no effort to conceal this annoyance as she answered.

"Now wouldn't I break right down and cry if that happened! You talk as if a coffee party at the Mansion were in the same class as a Carnival ball! Doesn't she, Sylvestre?"

Cresside turned from Regine to a young man, immaculately dressed in the height of fashion, who was standing near them. He had handsome features, a fine figure and a beguiling manner. But it was his coloring which made his appearance especially striking; he had very red cheeks, very blue eyes and very black hair. He smiled engagingly at Cresside, and a look of intimate and ardent understanding flashed swiftly between them. But though he answered lightly and pleasantly, there was a guarded undertone to his voice.

"Oh, I wouldn't go so far as to say that! Besides, there have been some mighty fine parties here in the past, Cresside, and there'll probably be a lot more in the future. It's just as well to keep in with the crowd that's automatically invited to the Mansion in every administration, whether you care for the present one or not. And at the moment we're the guests of the governor's wife. I think we'd be very wise to go on into the dining room!"

They swung into the end of the line which was now advancing through the wide hallway dividing the double drawing rooms on one side of it from the governor's study and the dining room on the other. Their temporary absence had passed unobserved in the midst of the animated chatter which still preoccupied their fellow guests. But now a few of these detached themselves from their special affinities long enough to speak to Cresside about her brother.

"Honey, I should think you'd be so proud you'd be about to burst! I declare, I get teary myself when I think that one of our own hometown boys got two promotions for gallant conduct in the face of the enemy and medals from two different Governments!"

"Well, I haven't shed any tears over it yet. I still think Gervais 's a stuffed shirt, just like I always did. I haven't got used to all this hero business yet!"

"You're not looking for Captain d'Alvery to leave here any time soon, are you, Miss Cresside? It would be a great loss to the community if he did. He's got so much to contribute! This state needs men like him. It hasn't got too many."

"I don't know how much he'll contribute, but I reckon he's here to stay. Anyway, I'm afraid so. He's going around Belle Heloise giving Army orders right and left."

Determined to put an end to this sort of thing, Cresside slipped adroitly through the crowd, abandoning Sylvestre and Regine to the gushing enthusiasts who were uncertain just what to say or do next. They had shared the general impression that there was an "understanding" between Regine Hathaway and Gervais d'Alvery. But now the whole town was buzzing with talk about the way he had greeted another girl at the depot, and here was Regine herself, escorted by that handsome young Tremaine from New Orleans. That is, at one moment he appeared to be her escort; but the next he appeared to be Cresside's. It was all very confusing. Perhaps it would be better to say nothing more, after all. Murmuring something incoherent, the puzzled ladies hurried on to the dining room, leaving Regine and Sylvestre behind them.

"Let's go into the parlor for a minute," Regine whispered. "No one noticed when Cresside delayed us, so I don't believe anyone would notice if we slipped off now. We haven't had a minute to ourselves all day, Sylvestre."

"Are you telling me? I don't know that we can prove much though, just going into those great open spaces."

It was true that the double drawing rooms at the Executive Mansion did not provide a very cosy or secluded spot for an interval of surreptitious love making. The "front parlor" and the "back parlor," furnished identically in tapestried Victorian furniture, led into each other through wide folding doors. The large gilt-framed mirrors which hung over the twin fireplaces, not only reflected a formidable expanse of room, but everything which took place there. Regine and Sylvestre sat down on one of the stiff sofas ranged between rows of still stiffer chairs, and after glancing carefully about, achieved an uneasy embrace. Then, as no disturbing element appeared to interrupt them, they permitted themselves to unbend a little more. But their period of relaxation was brief. Unanticipated sounds at the front door proclaimed the arrival of a tardy visitor and they had hardly time to get to their feet when Fabian d'Alvery walked unconcernedly into the drawing room.

"Why, hello there!" he said. "Is the party over, except for you two? I know it's late. To tell the truth, I forgot until just a few minutes ago that I was supposed to come here after I finished my speech. I was almost home, but I turned around and came back. Evidently it wasn't worth the trouble after all."

"I don't know whether you'll think it worth the trouble or not,"

26

Regine said with a giggle. "It hasn't been much of a party. You should have heard Cresside raging on about it. But it isn't over. Everyone else is in the dining room. We came back here a moment ago to—to look for my handkerchief." Regine giggled again. "It was one of my very best embroidered ones, and I couldn't bear to lose it."

"I see," Fabian remarked rather drily. "Well, now that you've found it, suppose we join the others in the dining room. You *have* found it, haven't you?"

"Oh, yes! Look!"

Regine produced a wisp of muslin and lace from her petit-point hand-bag and held it up for Fabian's inspection. He took it from her and regarded it solicitously.

"Yes, that would have been quite a loss," he agreed gravely, handing it back to her. Then, at the sound of light footsteps, he glanced to the rear of the room and saw that Cresside was coming towards them. "Did you lose your handkerchief, too?" he inquired.

"I lose on an average of three a day," she said. "I can't find any place to put them in the clothes we wear now. But I don't know what that's got to do with this lousy party—no, don't bother to tell me. How did your speech go off, Fabian?"

"It was a lousy speech—thanks for supplying me with just the right adjective. It sounded all right when I got it off in the privacy of my own apartment, but, of course, no one heard it there." He stopped, grinning again. "No one heard it on Third Street either," he said. "I thought at first I had a very attentive audience. Then I found out that the division I was so eloquently addressing was a group from the State School for the Deaf."

"Oh, Fabian, you didn't!"

For the first time, there was no flippancy in Cresside's voice when she spoke, and none in her pert, provocative little face either. This had softened suddenly, and the expression with which she looked at Fabian was full of sympathy and affection. He regarded her gratefully but whimsically.

" 'Pride cometh before a fall and a haughty spirit before destruction,' " he said. "I thought I was quite an orator once, but I know better now. The speech really was lousy, Cresside. I tried talking down to my listeners and that's an insult to any crowd. It's a good thing nobody heard me. It took me a few minutes to realize that, too, but eventually came the dawn. I think the whole thing's darn funny, when you get right down to it. And I had another funny experience afterwards."

"I want to hear."

"Well, I saw Merry Randall in the crowd and tried to catch up with her. But who do you think got me into her clutches? That outstanding clubwoman and public-spirited citizen, Mrs. Ivy Mae Ingledew. She stopped me and——"

They strolled back to the dining room, while Fabian told them about

27

his encounter with Mrs. Ingledew, making a good story out of it. Cresside was laughing unrestrainedly before he finished and presently he laughed, too.

"You see it just wasn't my day," he said. "Not that there's any reason why I should ever have thought it was. Where is the hero of the family, Cresside? I was sure I'd find him here. Hasn't he done his duty to the Great Cause by this time?"

"I reckon so. But he was going straight home to mother after the parade. With a grim purpose, unless I miss my guess. We tried to get him to stay in town for the block dance, but he wouldn't. All the gang is going, and later on we'll probably go somewhere else. You wouldn't come with us, would you, Fabian?"

"Thanks a lot. But you know I'm not much of an addition, when it comes to dancing."

The merriment had suddenly gone from his manner. He turned away to speak to his hostess, and presently he was swallowed up in a group of other acquaintances. When he looked for Cresside again, she had disappeared; so had Regine and Sylvestre. As he walked downtown, half an hour later, he heard the band playing for the block dance, and for a moment he thought of going over to the Istrouma after all, to see who else was in his cousin's party. Then he decided against it. There was a fellow named Erlo Vicknair that Cresside trained with a lot, who was not a bad sort; probably he was looking after her—though Fabian could not help feeling, despite the scene in the drawing room of the Executive Mansion, that Cresside had expected Sylvestre to do this, and that Regine still believed Gervais would show up sooner or later. He went home alone, telling himself that of course everything would be all right and wondering why he did not believe it.

CHAPTER II

GERVAIS D'ALVERY WAS devoutly thankful that no banquet had been planned after the parade, and that he was free to start for home as soon as it was over. Swinging into the River Road, he was acutely conscious, as he always had been when he made the turn, of the immediacy with which the capital merged into the country. The black fields pierced by the tender green of young cane; the flat muddy stretches which later would be rich with rice; the sturdy cattle ranging over the banks of the clover-covered levee; the Negro horsemen riding along its ridge; the turbaned women sauntering through the twilight with fagots on their heads; the rickety cabins surrounded by thrifty garden patches; the fluttering fowl and rooting hogs and plodding mules—all these, no

28

less than the sudden coming of quietude, were the unmistakable symbols of the region's abrupt and complete detachment from the city scene. The sky, lightly veiled with small clouds, had the soft color of pale amethysts. A fluttering breeze scattered the fragrance of the clover. The great River flowed imperturbably on, concealed by the levee, yet omnipresent as any other invisible deity. Gervais could feel its force, its immensity, its continuance. Here, at last, by its shores, was beauty after ugliness, harmony after discord, tranquility after turmoil, peace after war. . . .

Peace in as far as the countryside could give it, and that was abundantly; still it would not suffice unless the hearthstone which was the core of the countryside was beatified by it, too. Instinctively, Gervais glanced away from the levee and saw the immense façade of Hathaway Hall, glistening among the greens and grays of the grove which encircled it. The house was one of the handsomest on either side of the River, both inside and out: the stateliness of its situation, the majesty of its proportions, the delicacy of its carved ornamentation—all this gave it a grandeur which made the simpler attributes of Belle Heloise seem almost humble in comparison. Yet Hathaway Hall, for him, lacked the final quality of charm which would have made it irresistible, either in itself or as a setting for his love. He tried to tell himself that this was because it was not essentially Louisianian in feeling and expression; its builder had been a Carolinian who had not constructed it on the scale and in the style of either his native or his adopted state, but in a manner which he conceived to be a glorification of both. The result was impressive but it was not enchanting, at least to Gervais, though it was suited to Regine and she to it. This was the sort of house to which she inevitably belonged, quite as much as it was the sort of house which inevitably belonged to her. Even as a child, she had preferred playing alone in its great galleries to paddling with the others on the sandy shores of the old barrow pit at the bend of the River near Belle Heloise. Declining the honors of a Carnival queen, she had made her debut in the White Ball Room; she would be married in it, too, disdaining the solemnity of the Church; and after her marriage she would abide at Hathaway Hall and reign there. She would never follow her husband spontaneously to his home, or merge her life instinctively with his.

Gervais smiled a little wryly and shook his head, thinking of all this. The role of Prince Consort at Hathaway Hall had never appealed to him; there was not money enough in the world, let alone on one plantation, to tempt him to repeat his father's mistake. He knew that Philogene d'Alvery had come to Belle Heloise as the poor relation, the charming wastrel who had not the stamina or the purpose to strike out for himself; and the kinsfolk who hastened to give him shelter, also hastened to give him their daughter, conniving to keep her with them. Gervais knew that this case was different; but still it was comparable. Strange that his mother, who must know that he was more her son

29

than Philogene's, had never admitted it, that she had always assumed—or at all events pretended to assume—that eventually he and Regine would be married. Very possibly it had been part of her plan that he *would* leave Belle Heloise, and that it would be Cresside, and Cresside's future husband, who would stay with her. The wry smile hardened into a straight line, and he shook his head again, thinking of this. . . .

A small cemetery, dominated by a latticed tower built to house a tolling bell, lay at the outskirts of Hathaway Hall. Philogene d'Alvery was buried there, in the same lot with the kinsfolk who had found him so convenient to kidnap. Even in death he had not escaped any of the respectable responsible relatives who had remained at Belle Heloise from one generation to another, while his branch of the family went wandering; and the family tombs of the Tremaines and Hathaways were divided from those of the Estrades and the d'Alverys by only the width of a lot, suggesting another unchangeable and unbreakable tie. Gervais slowed down his car as he approached the cemetery, and the general appearance of weediness and neglect which it presented from the road moved him to get out and walk down the unkempt *allée* towards his father's grave, to inspect the condition of this. Formerly his mother had been prone to make a cult of the dead, but evidently this mourning phase was past. Everywhere the grass was rank and long, making it impossible to tell where the lots ended and the pathway began, except in the cases where the former were surrounded by rusty iron railings, most of them in a state of extreme decrepitude; Gervais walked warily and watchfully, keeping a sharp lookout for snakes as he went forward. He had an antipathy for these so great that it amounted almost to a phobia, and Cresside, who did not share it, had always delighted in playing on his fear. He was thankful that she was not with him, for the prevailing eeriness of the place had served to rouse it.

The newer tombs were nearest the road, and starkly uniform in appearance; they rose in great rectangular blocks, white as chalk above the green grass and against the green trees. Further back were several which rose in uneven tiers of crumbling red brick, their haphazard construction suggesting casual additions to an original block whenever another member of a disappearing family died. Still more to the rear was a heterogeneous collection of mossy monuments more pretentious in character: there was a square stone slab sheltered by a square stone canopy which had once been supported at the four corners by columns; now two of the columns were tottering, and in consequence the canopy was grotesquely tilted. Near this pitiful wreck of stability was a draped urn surmounting a fluted pillar, both so badly chipped that it looked as if one side had been actually hacked off. The Estrades' lot was dominated by a small Gothic chapel, the Hathaways' by a female figure whose hands were devoutly clasped, but who had managed to bend only one knee, while the simpering expression on her upturned face indicated complacency rather than resignation or grief.

30

The slabs which surrounded her were for the most part severely plain, as if to further accentuate her importance; but the head of one was decorated with a small recumbent lamb, so sharply chiseled as to make it appear that its sculptor had been thinking of quills instead of fleece when he carved it. Gervais had always hated this lamb, which marked the grave of the great-aunt for whom Regine had been named, and whom she was said to resemble. But he could not avoid passing the Hathaway tombs if he were to reach his father's, and involuntarily he glanced at the repulsive little stone creature as he went by it. To his surprise, he saw that it was not alone on the slab; something circular, which looked like a coiled rope, lay beside it; and a flat, evil-looking head reared up in the midst of the spiral, which quivered and commenced to unwind. Horror stricken, Gervais recoiled as a snake slithered off the stone and vanished in the tall grass which he had almost forgotten to regard with suspicion.

Gervais forced himself to go on towards his father's tomb. All this treacherous grass should be cut early the next morning, he vowed; and hereafter there should be fresh flowers for the little Gothic chapel or none at all; savagely he flung out the dark brown blossoms drooping in front of him and emptied the slimy water in the vase that had held them. The cornice should be repaired, too, the inscriptions cleaned and clarified, the iron railing mended and painted. Most of the tombs he had passed had once belonged to families who long ago had left the River Road—the Comerfords, the Simoneaux, the Bovards, the Surcliffes. Some of them had lost their homes through fire or flood, others through mere neglect, others through poverty or indifference. The Faith Estate, Chelmsford, Cedar Grove—all these places which had once been such proud plantations were only names now; there was no one left on them to care for either the living or the dead. Only Hackberry Lodge, recently bought by a Bostonian named Charles Boylston, had been redeemed; the general neglect of the cemetery was all too easy to explain. But he would not permit it to continue; henceforth it must take its tone from the families who had possessed the stamina to survive disaster and decay, and stubbornly he excluded the Hathaways and their kin from this category. It was nothing to him what happened to their simpering statues and their prickly lambs; but there should be no more snakes slithering through the grass near the place where the Estrades and the d'Alverys were buried.

Still raging with resentment, he walked slowly back towards the road. The light was changing fast; the tottering tiers of brick were already engulfed by the shadows of the cedars which surrounded them, and even the chalk-white tombs looked gray against the grass. But there were still patches of sunshine on his path, and looking down, as inadvertently as he had glanced at the lamb half an hour earlier, he saw a four-leaf clover in the midst of a common cluster. Like most Creoles, he was extremely superstitious, though he himself would have vehemently denied this; and here, at last, was a good omen, after the evil one which had so badly shaken him. He picked the four-leaf clover and folded it carefully away in his wallet; he would have it enclosed in a little gold-rimmed glass locket and give it to Merry. The best luck he had ever had lay in his meeting with her. Now he wanted to share this token of it.

Thanks to his cheering discovery, he left the cemetery happier than he had entered it, after all. And he brightened still further when he heard a joyous shout and saw an old favorite of his, Luigi Tramonte, hastening forward to meet him. Luigi was an Italian peddler, who carried his picayune wares in a deep coarse-woven basket strapped to his shoulders. He had been a familiar figure along the River Road ever since Gervais could remember; his arrival was always hailed with delight in the quarters of all the plantations and he was not infrequently summoned courteously, if condescendingly, into the mansions also. His principal stock in trade was a sort of syrup candy, called Johnny Crooks, into which fresh shredded cocoanut had been stirred before it was shaped into balls; but he also dealt in two other specialties of the region: stage planks—four by eight slabs of hard gingerbread with thin white icing on one side; and sauerkraut candy—a brown sugar sweetmeat flavored with vinegar and vanilla; also in taffy, licorice, peanuts, bananas, peppermint sticks and other delicacies of like nature. All in all, his sweetmeats made so substantial a burden that his basket was very heavy, and he wore large tufted pads on his shoulders to prevent the wide leather straps which held it in place from cutting into his flesh. He was also adept in shifting the weight of his load, so that it should never rest too long in one place, and his manner of doing it had developed into a motion resembling a violent and habitual shrug. He shrugged now, in a series of powerful contortions, before waving his broad-brimmed hat several times around his dark head and lumbering forward to meet Gervais.

"'Allo, 'allo, *Capitano*," he shouted delightedly. "Watta good luck I have to meeta you this day! I wanta shaka your hand!"

Suiting his actions to his words he hitched over to the car, which Gervais had brought to a standstill, and pumped the young officer's arm up and down with unabating vehemence. "We go to the depot to see you come in," he continued. "Me and my wife, Netta, and my bambino, too. I gotta me a beautiful bambino, *Capitano,* while you were at the war. Fifteen years we been married, me and Netta, never I getta me a bambino before. But Netta, she pray plenty to Santo Amico, and now I gotta him. We tooka him to the depot, so he coulda say, bimeby, when he's bigga man, in war himself maybe, he see *Capitano* d'Alvery coma back from France. You stay in France alla time, eh, *Capitano?* You no go to Italy?"

"No, I didn't go to Italy, I'm sorry to say. But I hope I'll get there some day yet. All the men who did go there were crazy about it. . . . So you got you a fine bambino while I was away, did you, Luigi? What's his name?"

"His name Riccardo. *Si, si,* one very fine bambino. I holda him up high at the depot, but you no see him because you're looking alla time at one very pretty young lady, eh, *Capitano?*"

Luigi, who was as habitually jolly as he was habitually heavy-laden, laughed heartily, throwing back his head and showing his gleaming white teeth. Encumbered though he was with his big basket, he managed, amidst his merriment, to poke Gervais jestingly in the ribs. But this familiarity, coming from Luigi, somehow lacked the quality which would have made Gervais regard it as presumptuous, coming from almost anyone else. Gervais laughed, too.

"I'm afraid you're right, Luigi," he said. "I didn't see the fine bambino this time. I *was* pretty preoccupied. But I hope to see him some other time, very soon."

"I bringa him to Belle Heloise myself, one day," Luigi said proudly. "I gonna teach him my trade. Soon like he can walk, he gonna go 'long with me on the River Road. Then maybe, bimeby, we make so much money, Riccardo he don' have just a basket with candy in—see?— toting it alla day long like his papa. He have nice littla store, sell fancy groceries, all sorts fancy groceries. Well, I gotta go 'long, *Capitano.* I know you wanna get home, and I gotta get to the quarters by Hathaway before sundown. But you leta me give you a package of Johnny Crooks for gooda luck. Next time, when I come to Belle Heloise you buy two stage planks to make up, eh, *Capitano?*"

Gervais laughed again, telling Luigi he had just found a four-leaf clover and that he would be glad to add the Johnny Crooks to it; then with a more serious show of gratitude, he accepted the squashy package which the Italian offered him. Having hitched his heavy basket into position, Luigi stood in the middle of the road waving his hat and cheering as the Captain drove off. Gervais did not have much further to go now. A stranger, approaching Belle Heloise for the first time, might easily have missed the myrtle-bordered driveway into which Gervais turned. This driveway, leading off the River Road at a sharp angle, was narrow as well as short; and the entrance to it was nearly hidden by clusters of wild palmetto, which likewise almost concealed the squat wooden posts on either side of it; it was as inconspicuous as it was unpretentious, and with the labor shortage which had come during the war, it was also unkempt. The cattle-gap between the posts rattled as Gervais went over it, and he smiled contentedly—the same old rattle, always the first of the familiar home sounds! The next was the cooing of the doves in the twin *pigeonniers;* these quaint, conical structures, surrounded by overgrown shrubbery, were the singing towers of Belle Heloise. Sometimes, when Gervais was coming in, doves flew across his face in whirring pursuit of each other, or lighted, with a gentle flutter of wings, upon his shoulders. Not when it was as late as this, however; they were now settled in their cotes for the night; only the mild music which they made, drifting drowsily towards him, revealed their continual presence.

The straightaway of the drive ended as abruptly as it had begun; it swerved to the right in order to skirt a tall tangle of overgrown privet now in the fullness of its feathery white bloom, which marked the beginning of the flagstone walk to the front door, and which looked as forbidding and impenetrable as the thorny thickets which allegedly guarded the Sleeping Beauty. As a matter of fact, a hole was periodically hacked in the midst of the privet growth to form a crude and narrow archway. But this was so seldom used that prickly boughs quickly enclosed it again; by force of habit almost everyone took the turn that Gervais was taking now, skirting the privet trees and winding into the small grove of oaks at the side of the house. Some of the moss-draped branches made a frame for the cream-colored colonnade; but there was no imposing *allée,* no studied and formal plan of planting. At Belle Heloise it was the ancient house itself, not its approach or its surroundings, which really counted.

A Negro boy who had been drowsing by the pump came forward to take the car and put it in the dilapidated shed which served as a garage. This was Amen, the youngest son of Selah the butler, who had always taken the reins from his master when Gervais came back from riding the crops, pridefully leading the palomino back to the stables for special grooming. Now he took charge of the battered automobile with much the same air. Gervais was fond of Amen, and ordinarily he would have stopped to chat with the boy: but for the moment he was bent on seeing his mother with the least possible delay; there had been no chance for a serious talk with her amidst the first hurly-burly of his homecoming, but he was determined that there should be no procrastination in clarifying his position with Merry. So he responded abstractedly to Amen's cheerful greeting, and freed himself impatiently from the two dogs who leaped about him, barking with excitement and delight. This was another of the old familiar sounds, but it failed to evolve such fond memories as the rattle of the cattle-gap and the cooing of the doves. He did not see why they had ever had dogs like these at Belle Heloise in the first place, he told himself irritably, momentarily forgetting his own youthful attachment to Snow, the aging white collie, and Cornet, the crippled fox terrier; they should have had a *real* dog like Fabian's spaniel Belizaire. He called out after the disappearing Negro boy, voicing his irritation after failing to voice any kindliness.

"How many times have I told you to keep the cockleburrs out of Snow's hair? He looks as if he had been rolling in them. Have him combed out by morning or tell me the reason why. And Cornet's as badly maimed as if he'd been fighting a tiger. You'd better get him to the veterinary before he loses a leg."

Amen stopped the car noisily and stuck his wooly head out of the side. "Yessuh, Mr. Gervais. Ah didn't disremember what you told me, but Ah'se done had a fever in mah back." The look of beaming expectancy with which he had come forward to meet Gervais had gone, and a hangdog expression of dejection had taken its place. Ordinarily

Gervais would have felt compunction for such a change, knowing himself responsible for it. But now he spoke even more sharply the second time.

"Well, then, you'd better go to the doctor yourself when you take Cornet to the veterinary. But get him there. I'm working up a fever, too, and it isn't just in one place, either——"

The family cat, a tortoiseshell named Miss Larcella, whose bulging form belied her right to a maidenly title, came padding towards him, purring sonorously and rubbing her sleek sides against his ankles. Again he freed himself, even more irritably than from the dogs, but less easily, for Miss Larcella instantly dug her claws into his skin, clinging to his leg and mewing piteously. Another silly, superfluous animal, Gervais thought savagely, restraining with difficulty the impulse to toss the persistent pet out into the shrubbery, as he strode off towards the colonnade forming the gallery that surrounded three sides of the house. It was paved with the same type of mellow brick which made the walls, and his footsteps tapped out a signal of approach on this pavement as he crossed it. But even without the signal Gervais knew that Selah would be watching for him from the doorway. The sight of the old butler's bent figure, standing between the fluted pillars, was another integral part of home coming. Selah was not the formal butler of tradition, given to platitudes and pomposity; he stumbled a little as he walked, and his clothes were always slightly askew; he gave a general effect of apology and shabbiness. But he belonged. He was as much a part of Belle Heloise as the colonnade, and it never occurred to Gervais that he might not be as permanent.

"Good evening, Selah. Has Lucie told you how Madame's feeling tonight?"

Contrary to local custom, none of the servants had continued to call his mother Miss Isabelle after her marriage. She had been Madame to them from the time she became Philogene's wife. Gervais had never heard them address her otherwise, and never referred to her himself in any other way.

"Yessuh, Mr. Gervais. She's po'ly, jes lak she alluz is. There ain't no difference. . . . The parade was mighty grand, wasn't it, Mr. Gervais? Ah reckon there ain't never been anything in Baton Rouge to equal it."

"Well, it seemed to go off all right. . . . Madame is awake, isn't she?"

"Yessuh, she's awake. Lucie don' tole me she waked up extra early this ebenin'. Seems lak she's restless, waitin' for you and Miss Cresside to git home and tell her all about the parade."

"I don't think Miss Cresside will be home until pretty late, Selah. She went to a party at the Mansion this afternoon, with Miss Regine and Mr. Sylvestre, and I have an impression they're going on to another somewhere else after that. Tell Lou Ida not to hold up dinner for her. I'm hungry myself. But I'm going up to see Madame before I eat."

He handed his cap to the old butler, nodded, a trifle less abstractedly

35

than when he had left Amen, and started across the immense hall. It ran the entire length of the house, dividing the library, music room and garden room on one side from the parlor, dining room and service quarters on the other. Though the door at either end of it habitually stood open, the colonnade so shaded it that it was really radiant only during the brief period of sunset; now it was already engulfed in evening shadows. Gervais was used to its dimness, but suddenly this irked him; never had he felt so strongly that the house lacked light and warmth and the simple kindly humanity that was as alien to his sister's flippant coquetry as it was to his mother's arrogant reserve. Light and warmth were what Merry would bring to the house, if he could only get her there without such a struggle that it spoiled the spontaneity of her single-hearted love for him. Those were the qualities that would stamp her as its chatelaine, if he could persuade his mother to step aside for his wife. He had no delusions about the difficulties and delays which confronted him; but because it seemed as if he could not stand the dimness and the cold another moment, he turned sharply, and gave an abrupt order to Selah from the stairway, aware, as he did so, that the fulfillment of his command would alter only the face of the established order, and not its spirit.

"Do turn on the gas, Selah. Tonight and every night. I hate to come home to a dark house. And light some fires. I don't like to freeze to death either, and it's still mighty chilly in the evenings."

"Yessuh, Mr. Gervais. Madame, she's in her room all de time, and Miss Cresside, she's out all de time. It ain't hardly seemed worthwhile——"

"Well, I'm home again now, and I like a bright house and a warm one. I've had enough gloom and cold in France to last me all the rest of my life. Don't forget. I like a clean one, too. And there are cobwebs and dirt-daubers' nests in practically every corner of this place."

"They comes right overnight, Mr. Gervais. Ah cleans 'em out in de ebenin', and there they is again, first thing de nex' mornin'."

"Well, clean them out again the next morning, too, then."

He went on up the stairs, slightly ashamed of himself for having spoken so sharply to the old servant who was conscientiously trying to save gas and fuel, and who had long lacked anyone to set household standards for him. On the landing he paused briefly, and from force of reviving habit, rather than from any devout impulse, muttered the first few words of an old Latin prayer. There was a niche beside the landing, where an ancient Spanish statue of the Virgin and Child was enshrined. It was a beautiful wooden image, exquisitely carved and lavishly gilded, which had originally been brought to Louisiana from Seville, among the belongings of a royal governor. The first mistress of Belle Heloise, who was a descendant of this functionary, had brought it with her when she came to the plantation as a bride, and ever since it had stood in this niche, which had been built on purpose to receive it. Vigil lights were always kept burning in front of it, and on special feast days taller candles were lighted there, too, while jeweled crowns and rich robes were placed upon the figures, and flowers on either side of them. The statue was the family's most prized possession, and every succeeding generation was taught to pray before it. Gervais and Cresside had knelt there together countless times, while their mother stood behind them, a detaining hand on the shoulder of each, a meticulous voice prompting their impatient patter. Gervais could not remember that his father had ever stood there, too. Philogene d'Alvery had usually been out hunting in the fields or sipping brandy in the gallery while his wife guided the children through their reluctant prayers. But Gervais could feel his mother's hand on his shoulder still. He tried to shake it off as he went on up the stairs and knocked at her door. Speaking in French, she told him to come in, and he entered her room.

Like all other rooms at Belle Heloise, this one had high blank walls of white plaster and dark massive furniture. Downstairs, the brocade draperies and Aubusson rugs, the portraits and porcelains, did much to relieve the severity of the walls and the somber quality of the furniture; but in Madame d'Alvery's room there was no such relief. The curtains at the wide windows and on the mammoth four-poster were made of plain white muslin, and except for a dark braided rug beside the bed, the floor was bare. The mantel shelf was unadorned by vases, and a realistic crucifix, instead of a pleasing portrait, hung over it. Madame d'Alvery herself sat propped up among huge square pillows, the fine linen of her nightgown closing tightly in around her neck and wrists, her hair covered with a fine linen cap. Her long, veined hands lay folded over the smooth sheet in deadly impassivity; they would be folded like that when she lay in her coffin. But her black eyes, which had been the greatest of her many beauties in her youth, glowed from her pale face like dark fire. She waited, silent and motionless, for her son to approach her and address her.

"Hello, *maman*," he said with forced cheerfulness. "How are you this fine evening? Feeling better?"

"There is no change in my condition, Gervais. I have no hope that there will be. I shall never recover from my crushing loss. But I do not complain. I await in long-suffering a Heavenly reunion with your dear father."

She sighed, patiently, and Gervais smothered an ejaculation which was considerably less resigned. He had been puzzled, at the time of his father's death, by his mother's complete prostration; she had never impressed him as a woman whose being was so interlocked with her husband's that the two could not be wrenched apart without disaster to the survivor. In fact he had always felt that Philogene d'Alvery— improvident, charming, inconsequential—was completely under the dominion of his handsome and imperious wife, and that the only real difference caused by Philogene's elimination from Belle Heloise lay in Isabelle's grievance over having one vassal the less. His bewilderment at his mother's collapse deepened into distrust when the family physician, Dr. Champagne, after a succession of more tactful utterances, abruptly announced one day that he could not deprive those who were really suffering of his services or consume valuable time traveling back and forth over the River Road, merely because it was Madame d'Alvery's whim to lie abed, visited by no one except her doctor and her confessor. If her heart really had been broken—the physician's tone betrayed his skepticism on this point—it would mend again in time, like any other woman's under similar circumstances. As for her body, that was as strong as steel.

At the time this unfeeling pronouncement had been made, Gervais was still willing to give his mother the benefit of the doubt; he at first suggested a consultation of physicians, and upon her indignant refusal to sanction this, asked her to let him seek out someone else who would be willing to take over her case; he was sure that a younger man, less preoccupied and harassed than Dr. Champagne, would be glad to give her all the attention she needed. Madame d'Alvery had proudly replied that she did not propose to have an unskilled youth experiment upon her, furthering his career at her expense; and, in any case, the heartlessness and carelessness of Dr. Champagne had so disillusioned her that she had lost faith in all physicians. From then on, she would bear her afflictions without any attempt to alleviate them. The gravity of these afflictions had long since become a matter of mistrust to her son and of indifference to her daughter; but she herself fostered it with the same relentlessness which marked her every other purpose.

"Your sister did not return with you?" she inquired now, having allowed an effective interval to elapse after the sigh.

"No, I believe she and Regine were going on to some party or other after the parade."

He had been impatient when Selah pleaded with him for an account of the parade, because he was in a hurry to get to his mother and talk to her about Merry. Now, illogically, he wished his mother would ask him some questions. And yet, it was not so illogical, after all, for a man to desire his mother to share his hour of triumph, to reveal pride and pleasure in his achievement. Madame d'Alvery dismissed the parade by asking an irrelevant question.

"Unescorted?"

"Not by a long shot. When you see either of those girls unescorted, you'll see a white blackbird. They had about a dozen boys buzzing around. Besides, of course Sylvestre, in attendance with his usual gallantry."

"I should have said, unescorted by you. I should have thought, Gervais, that you would have wished to remain with your sister—and her friend."

Madame d'Alvery stressed the last three words. The emphasis was unnecessary. Without it, Gervais knew that it was not because Regine was Cresside's friend that his mother wanted him to act as the girl's escort, but because she was predestined as his wife. He decided to plunge into his subject without more delay.

"No, I didn't, especially. As I said, Sylvestre was along. It seems he's visiting at Hathaway Hall again. And if there's one man I can't stomach, it's he. But at least he provides the figure of the protective male that you think is so important. And I was in a hurry to get home. I wanted to talk to you."

"I am very much gratified by your filial devotion. At the same time——"

"I've got something a lot more important on my mind than taking Cresside and Regine to some tame tea. I'm going to get married."

For the first time, the long slim hands which were folded over the white sheet fluttered slightly. Then almost immediately they were still again. But the great eyes burned with increasing intensity in the white face.

"Get married? This is very sudden, my son."

"It isn't at all sudden. It's been going on for years. If I'd had any sense at all, I'd have got married before I went to France. Then I'd have had a wife and child to come home to, like the other men I know. I wouldn't have come back to a great shadowy empty house that my sister won't stay in and my mother withdraws from. I'd have had someone besides the butler waiting to welcome me. Well, I'm going to have someone, from now on!"

Again Madame d'Alvery's hands fluttered momentarily. But she spoke with complete control.

"You are very vehement, Gervais, and very critical. I see no good reason for you to be either. Surely you know that I shall put no impediment in the way of your marriage—if you have made a proper choice. I never would have done so. You could have married two years ago as easily as now. As for the emptiness of the house, I cannot help my infirmities, and it is natural, at Cresside's age, that she should be pleasure-loving."

"Well, suppose we pass over the condition of the house for a moment—especially as I propose to change that. But I don't know whether you will think I have made a proper choice. Not that there's any sound reason why you shouldn't—in fact you ought to be thankful that a girl of any real caliber will have me. I haven't so much to offer her. . . . I don't need to have you tell me, though, what your idea of a proper choice is. And it isn't the same as mine."

"Then I am very sorry, Gervais. I had hoped you would be guided by my wishes."

"Usually I have been, haven't I?"

"Yes. That is why I am the more amazed—and the more distressed—that you should not be, in this all-important instance."

"You chose all my friends while I was growing up. You chose my college and my career. At least you might let me choose my own wife. I *have* chosen her."

"Who is this wife you have chosen, Gervais?"

"Her name's Meredith Randall."

"I do not recall any Randalls among our acquaintances. Has her family ever visited with ours?"

"Not that I know of."

"Then where did you meet her?"

"On the *River Queen.*"

"The *River Queen?*"

"Yes. The dance boat that comes down from St. Louis every winter. You must have heard about it dozens of times."

"If I have, I have forgotten. You met this girl you want to make your wife at a public dance?"

"Good God, don't talk about it in that tone of voice! Everyone in Baton Rouge—at least everyone young—dances aboard the *River Queen* when it's anchored there. There's nothing disgraceful or furtive about it. You make up your own crowd, and it's a good crowd. The same goes for Plaquemine and Donaldsonville that goes for Baton Rouge. Someone in my crowd asked Meredith Randall—I forget now who. As a matter of fact, I think it was Fabian. It's of no consequence anyway. It was the first time she'd ever been aboard the *River Queen,* or to a big dance anywhere—she was just a kid, a sophomore at the Baton Rouge High School. And, gosh, did she eat it all up! Everyone wanted to dance with her, because she was having such a swell time herself that it did something contagious to her dancing. I never saw a girl who had so much vitality!"

He paused, his resentment against his mother momentarily swallowed up in vivid reminiscence. He was remembering the two searchlights stabbing upward through the river mists, visible for miles away and none the less effective because their manipulation was a clever advertising trick. He was remembering the screaming calliope, drowning out the crackling calls of the tree frogs and the shrill notes of the crickets chirping along the river bank. He was remembering the old-fashioned landing stage leading from the foot of the levee to the boiler deck, and the ornamental white fretwork banister of the stairway that led to the upper deck where the dance floor was, and where the orchestra began to tune up as soon as the calliope stopped playing. He was remembering the gleaming dance floor itself, not flat, but concave, sloping markedly upward at the bow end. He was remembering the first time he had served notice on the rest of the "bunch" that there wasn't to be any more cutting in when he was dancing with Merry, and the special tune that he and Merry had begun to look upon as their own soon after this—"We'll Go On a Chinese Honeymoon," the name of it was. He was remembering the couples who parked in adjoining chairs on the dark deck outside which was supposedly brightly illumined, but where someone always thoughtfully extinguished most of the overhead incandescents, which were pretty dim at best, by unscrewing them part way in their sockets. He was remembering some of these couples were frequently fused in the single silhouette of a long kiss; and he was remembering, with chagrin mingled with admiration, that when he had tried to draw Merry into such an embrace, she had eluded him, not coyly but almost gravely, and that afterwards she had told him very earnestly how she would have to feel about a man before she would let him kiss her or want to kiss him in return. It was that kiss he had not succeeded in getting which had made him want desperately to hold her in his arms, not as an interlude in an evening's outing, but as a fulfillment and a reward. . . . His mother's measured voice cut coolly across his warm reverie.

"This girl received her education at the Baton Rouge High School?"

"Now that you know what her name is, suppose you refer to her as Meredith. Or Merry—that's what I call her. Yes . . . is there anything wrong with the Baton Rouge High School?"

"I believe not. I believe it does a very worthy work in supplying instruction to a great many young middle-class persons who would otherwise have none."

"I suppose you'd have felt better if I'd have told you Merry went to Convent or Grand Coteau?"

"Much better. It would have assured me that even if she were not a Catholic herself, she had been surrounded by excellent influences. Incidentally, is she a Catholic?"

"No. She isn't."

"There has never been a Protestant at Belle Heloise, Gervais."

"There is going to be one now."

Defiantly, the two pairs of dark eyes met. To his mother's surprise and chagrin, Gervais was able to outstare her. His gaze was as stubborn as it was piercing. Reluctantly, Madame d'Alvery lowered her white lids, unable to endure the challenge any longer. Aware that he had won the first round, Gervais relaxed.

"I think I'll light the fire. There's no use sitting and shivering, if we're in for a long discussion. What else would you like to have me tell you about Merry?"

Without waiting for an answer, he rose and walked over to the fireplace. The grate was already neatly laid with coal and small kindling, and when he set a match to these, the flame leapt up instantly, alternately illuminating the blank white walls with its radiance and darkening them with its shadow. The eerie quality of the grim crucifix over the marble mantel, and of the still figure on the mahogany bed was intensified in the weird light.

"And the candles, too, while I'm about it," Gervais went on. "There's no use talking in the dark either. I told Selah when I came in that I hated a gloomy house. Of course, you'll do as you please about your own room. But I'd appreciate your letting me brighten it up a little when I am in it. Do you mind very much if I smoke?"

Madame d'Alvery made a deprecatory gesture, designed to indicate that in her opinion the suggestion was unworthy of a true Creole gentleman, but that, of course, he would do as he pleased. She contrived to make this gesture so eloquent that Gervais could almost hear her saying that never, in all the years of their marriage, had her husband smoked in her bedchamber. Gervais reseated himself, crossed his knees, and repeated his question, lighted cigarette in hand.

"What else would you like me to tell you about Merry?"

"I should like to know something about her family and her background, if that is not asking too much."

"Of course it isn't asking too much. She's an only child. At least she is now. She had two brothers, Malcolm and Vail, but they were both killed in the war—one at St. Mihiel and the other at Montfaucon. I reckon they were good fellows, though I don't believe they were quite in Merry's class. They both married girls from out of town. I don't know anything about their wives. Merry's mother's a widow. She and Merry live in a little house on St. Napoleon Street—you know, the kind that has two front doors, though the façade's so narrow it's taken some planning to get them side by side. The extra door is for the convenience of the lodger."

"The lodger?"

"Yes. Nearly everyone around there has a lodger who occupies the front room. The extra door leads directly into this room, and the lodger goes in and out through it, without disturbing the family. It is a very sensible arrangement."

"And the Randall family takes in lodgers?"

"Not lodgers, just one of them. And you wouldn't call it taking in, exactly. There's no coming and going. Miss Mittie's lived with the Randalls for years—ever since I've known them, and long before that, too, I reckon. She's quite a character. Came from New England originally. Teaches Latin at the High School. Has an inexhaustible fund of wise sayings and a droll way of getting them off. Dotes on Merry."

Madame d'Alvery actually raised one hand, as a signal to her son that she did not desire to hear anything more about the peculiar Miss Mittie. But she asked another question about the Randalls themselves.

"Since they're obliged to share their home with a lodger, I gather that this family with whom you have become—" She hesitated, quailed for the second time before her son's accusing gaze, and substituted "acquainted" for "entangled," at least aloud. "I gather that this family with whom you have become acquainted is in straitened circumstances."

"I'm afraid they are. I don't know much about the late Mr. Randall. I believe he was some kind of a minor railroad official. Anyway, it's obvious he didn't leave his widow very well provided for. She and

Merry live very simply. And Merry's worked ever since she got through High School."

"She *works!*"

"Yes. She's a stenographer at Goldenberg's store. Or, rather, she's risen now to be Mr. Goldenberg's private secretary. I reckon she's made herself pretty nearly invaluable to him. It's going to be an awful shock for the old codger to lose her. I'm sure he figured that if he didn't, at the beginning of the war hysteria, when practically every girl in town was getting married over night, he never would. Well, of course, he should have lost her then. That's when I ought to have married her, as I said before. I don't deserve the luck I've got in having her wait for me."

"And what withheld you then, since you are not withheld now?"

"I'm ashamed to say so, but I suppose it was the same sort of silly inhibition that's cluttering up your mind—the deep-rooted conviction that great River families and mere catfish town nobility shouldn't mix their blood. That I was the last of my line, and that when it came to marriage, it behooved me to make a suitable alliance—with Regine Hathaway, or at least some girl like her, exactly as you'd planned. That, of course, I was entitled to a few light love affairs before I settled down, but that when I did——"

"And that was what this was before you went to war? A light love affair with a stenographer?"

"No. This was never a light love affair, *ma mère*. I must ask you to be very sure that you do not make any mistake about that."

Suddenly his voice was steely, as his eyes had been already, and for the first time in his life he was calling her *"ma mère"* instead of *maman*. Madame d'Alvery was horribly aware that this change in address was not accidental, and that its meaning was grave. He went on, inexorably.

"There were a few light love affairs in France," he said. "And a few others before I ever knew Merry at all. I'm not at all proud of the fact. It isn't worthy of me or of her. I only mention it in passing to try to show you the difference. . . . I was attracted to Merry the first time I met her, that night on the *River Queen*. I told you, it was her vitality I noticed first. There was something about her enjoyment—the spontaneity and freshness of it—that affected her dancing and made it different from any other girl's. It was so natural and un-affected. Her laugh was that way, too, and she laughed a lot. I got so I listened for it, and waited for it. Of course I liked her looks, too. She's very lovely to look at. She has rosy cheeks, with deep dimples in them, and beautiful white teeth and big brown eyes. Her hair's brown, too, but there are golden lights in it. She's more than lovely looking. She looks warm-hearted and tender and true, and she is. She's the soul of honor and steadfastness."

Gervais paused, but his mother made no comment. He walked over to the fire and laid more coals on it, and again the flames leapt up, transfiguring the cold walls and the suffering Christ and the bed-bound woman. When he came back, he did not reseat himself. He stood over his mother and looked down at her.

"I knew all that before I went to France," he said. "The first dance on the *River Queen* was only one incident in our—association. I saw a lot of her after that at dances and elsewhere. And every time I saw her, I liked her better than I had the time before. But, of course, she was just a kid. And she went to the Baton Rouge High School and lived on St. Napoleon Street and there was a lodger in the house. And by and by she graduated at the head of her class and went to work in Goldenberg's store as a stenographer. By that time I wasn't merely attracted to her, I was in love with her. But still I didn't have the guts to ask her to marry me. I was a hidebound fool. But at least I wasn't enough of a fool to suggest an affair. And at least I had enough sense, before I went away, to ask her if she'd wait for me.

"She said she would, and she kissed me good-by—it was the first time she ever had kissed me. I realized then how much I meant to her, because—well, because I'd tried to get her to do it before, and she wouldn't. She wrote to me, but we didn't get our mail very regularly, and the letters were sort of shy, especially at first. But from the ones I did get, I knew there must have been others, and gradually they grew less and less reserved. She wasn't afraid, after a while, to tell me just how she felt, and I could see that she felt plenty. But what touched me most of all was her loyalty and her trust. It never occurred to her to look at another man, from the time I asked her to wait for me and she said she would, and it never occurred to her that I wouldn't marry her as soon as I got back. That I wouldn't want to. I do want to. I want to more than I want anything else in the world. If I haven't learned another damn thing in France, I've learned something about values. I'm going to marry her right away, without wasting any more precious time."

Suddenly he smiled, as if the very thought of marrying Meredith Randall made him so happy that he forgot he had set out to be stubborn and stern or that there was any reason why he should be. Then he leaned over and kissed his mother on the forehead.

"You'll enjoy having her in the house," he said. "She'll be pleasant company for you. She'll take the responsibility of the housekeeping off your shoulders. It must have worried you to feel things were being neglected, when you couldn't look after them yourself. She might even help you get well. I thought we'd keep my old room for ours—then you and Cresside could both stay where you are, on this side of the hall, and if Merry and I need to expand later on, we'll have all the space on the other side to do it in. We ought to be able to tuck away any number of grandchildren for you! Is there anything more I can do for you, *maman,* before I go down to dinner?"

CHAPTER III

THE BELATED DINNER which Gervais ate alone in the big square dining room was very good, and he did full justice to it. A week or so earlier Amen had caught a huge turtle which had been lumbering unconcernedly along the River Road where it skirted the Small Yard, and Selah had snatched it away from him and saved it for Gervais, whose arrival they knew was impending. Gervais had always been inordinately fond of turtle soup, and Lou Ida had put forth her best efforts in making the one into which the unwary traveler had been transformed. Selah set down the tureen with solemnity, and then removed the cover with a flourish. Gervais sniffed in the steaming fragrance from the succulent dish as he ladled it out into the heated soup plate of gold-banded china which Selah had previously placed on the spotless damask cloth between the neatly laid silverware.

"There's not a soup in France that can touch this, Selah, and they have mighty fine soups there, too," Gervais said enthusiastically. Now that he had spoken his mind and indicated his will to his mother, he was much less tense. Moreover, he was sincerely sorry for his earlier abruptness, and eager to make amends for it by a special show of geniality. He had always talked, incidentally, to Selah when he was eating alone, though he never did so if there were guests, or if Cresside were with him; but this time he talked by deliberate intent. "I stayed in one place where we had a different kind twenty-seven nights in succession; but at that, turtle soup wasn't one of the varieties. And there isn't any turtle soup like *this* anywhere in the world except at Belle Heloise. You may tell Lou Ida I said so."

"Yessuh, Mr. Gervais, Ah sholy shall. Ah wish you coulda seen ole Mr. Turtle befo' he went into dat soup, though, Mr. Gervais—crawlin' along down de road lak he never had a care in de world, when Amen cotched him. Ah disremember Ah ever seen a turtle big lak he was. He was marked handsome, too."

"I'll see plenty of turtles along the River Road from now on. I'm home to stay this time . . ."

"Ah'm proud to hear dat, Mr. Gervais."

Selah removed the tureen ceremoniously, in the same manner that he had brought it in, and substituted a hot dinner plate for the soup plate which Gervais had now emptied twice. Then he reappeared, bearing an immense ham, its sugar coating spiked with cloves, its pink substance pushed through with herb pockets.

"Lou Ida felt real bad she didn't get to cook your dinner the night you come home, 'cause you wuz to dat banquet. She broilin' a steak for yo', too, Mr. Gervais, but it ain't quite ready. She didn't want it to get to lookin' lak a piece of shoe leather while you wuz enjoyin' your soup, and she thut you mought lak to try dis ham while you wuz waitin'. Our hogs, they'se cured moughty good this year."

"I'm pleased to hear it, but I'm still more interested in our birds. What about those? Any left for next fall's shooting?"

"Yessuh, Mr. Gervais, you gwine to have plenty birds, mebbe more 'an you know what to do with. Ain't hardly nobody bothered them all de time you'se been gone. Mr. Fabian, he done come out dove-huntin' once or twice, but not bird-huntin'. An' he's a sure enough sorry shot, even on doves."

Having made his disparaging remark, he disappeared quickly in the direction of the kitchen, as if aware that Gervais might resent his reflection on the prowess of any member of his family, and that it might be wisest to retreat. When he returned, he brought with him the steak, now broiled to a turn and imbedded in enormous mushrooms.

"Good Lord, Selah, how do you think I'm ever going to eat that steak when you've filled me full of ham, and on top of that turtle soup, too?"

"Go 'long, Mr. Gervais, you never see de time you couldn't eat steak, 'specially right after Lent, when you done been filled up wid fish for five weeks. This here a mighty fine steak, too. Our beef cattle, they done just as good as our hogs. De grazin's never been better on de levee than this year past. Grass stayed green most all winter, and de clover, it started comin' out in February."

Stifling a mock groan, Gervais helped himself liberally to the steak. Besides the mushrooms, and the mound of flaky rice which automatically accompanied all gravied dishes, there were crimson beets cooked with their own greens, and asparagus heaped on toast in a jade-colored pile; also a bottle of St. Emilion. As he sipped his sound red wine, Gervais lighted a cigarette and asked Selah for an ash tray. Though the old butler gave it to him without demur, his expression changed, reverting to almost the same look of scorn as when he had spoken of Fabian's marksmanship. He knew that nicotine, like hard liquor, dulled the sense of taste, and he privately considered it an insult to Lou Ida's dinner to do this. But again he changed the plates, this time bringing in an unheated one of fragile porcelain, painted with fruit and flowers; and when Gervais had set aside his finger bowl, Selah offered him mammoth strawberries from a silver basket ornamented around the side with a berry design, and a large silver spoon embellished with a similar design at the end of the handle, with which to scoop them up.

"Good Lord, Selah!" Gervais said again. "The berry-patch must be doing as well as the hogs and the beef cattle. Those strawberries are as big as crabapples."

"Yessuh, Ah specks so. Ain't never seen no crabapples. The milch cows is doin' well, too. Ah done had to bring 'nother of Madame's strawberry spoons to git the cream outin de pitchur with."

46

Selah spoke gloatingly and truthfully. The cream in the little pitcher of garnet-colored Bohemian glass, ornamented with clear spots surrounded by blue stippling, was so thick that it could not possibly be poured. Gervais took the second precious old strawberry spoon and ladled it out, not avidly, as he had ladled out the turtle soup, but with leisurely appreciation and admiration. When the strawberries were almost covered with it, and with the snowy sugar which he sifted slowly over the cream from an antique muffineer, he looked up at Selah with his charming smile.

"This has been a wonderful dinner, Selah. There's only one trouble with it, and that isn't your fault, or Lou Ida's. I've had to eat it alone."

"Yessuh, Mr. Gervais, Ah knows. Mebbe Ah's got a misconviction, and mebbe Ah ought not to say it no ways. But Ah believes Madame might pearten up a mite, if she'd jes let herself. And Ah believes Miss Cresside mought have her a nice time right here at Belle Heloise, effen she'd ask nice lady people and nice gentlemen people all to come here, 'stead of goin' out other places wid dem all de time."

"I believe you're right. I've often thought the same thing myself, Selah. But unfortunately neither Madame nor Miss Cresside agrees with us. However——"

The charming smile did not wholly fade from Gervais' face. But as he went on, he spoke with increasing gravity, befitting a serious and highly important subject.

"However, I don't believe I shall have to eat many more meals alone. I'm expecting to be married very soon, Selah. So of course my wife will be at this table with me, hereafter. I'm sure you'll take pride in serving her as well as you always have me, and in making the silver shine as it never did before by the time she gets here. I'm sure you'll understand now why I want the house to be clean and bright and warm, always. I'm sure you'll be glad to know Belle Heloise is going to have a beautiful young mistress to grace it again."

"Ah is, Mr. Gervais, Ah sholy is. Lordy, if dat ain't de bes' news Ah's heard since Ah done foun' out de war ober dere in France done got ended, and you wuz comin' home. Is it Miss Regine gwine be de beautiful bride, Mr. Gervais?"

"No, Selah, it isn't Miss Regine. It's a Miss Merry—a Miss Merry Randall."

"Den she libes ober on de west side of de River, don't she, Mr. Gervais? Ah ain't neber heard of any Randall place on our side."

"She doesn't live on a plantation at all, Selah. She lives in Baton Rouge—like Mr. Fabian, you know."

"Yessuh, yessuh. Right in de town? Well, Ah sholy wishes yo' all de happiness in de world, Mr. Gervais, both you and de young lady dat's gwine be our new mistress. You don't mind effen Ah tells Lou Ida de good news right away, does you, Mr. Gervais?"

Gervais gave his consent gladly, and Selah, having served the coffee, returned to the kitchen to spread the glad tidings. The tall clock in the hall struck nine sonorously while Gervais was still eating strawberries, and immediately afterwards the ornate gilt timepiece which stood under a *silene* of oval glass on the drawing-room mantel tinkled out a silly tune. When Gervais and Cresside were little, Philogene had told them that whenever this happened, the heartless girl who leaned provocatively over the dial on the mantelpiece was mocking the poor old grandfather encased in the hall, and the children had believed him. Gervais had disliked that gilded girl from childhood, and he detested her doubly now that she reminded him it was too late for him to go back to town and see Merry again that night. Both Mrs. Randall and Miss Mittie had conservative ideas about male callers, even callers whose intentions were honorable, definite and urgent, and Merry respected these. She had told Gervais that if he could not get back to town before nine, she would not expect him. She had not said this resentfully or hintingly; that was not Merry's way. She had not asked him to supper either, after the parade. She knew that he must have time to talk to his mother, without any sense of pressure, and her own mother liked to have supper promptly at six o'clock. She had suggested that perhaps he would telephone if he were not coming, but then she had remembered, before he reminded her, that there was no telephone at Belle Heloise. She had said something soothing when he remarked, explosively, that it was ridiculous he should not be able to get a telephone installed within a few miles of the state capital, when he had used field telephones from one end of France to the other; it was just another example of the way the politicians ran things in Louisiana; after he got into the legislature, he was going to get all that changed, or know the reason why.

In spite of his disappointment, however, his deep irritation did not return. As he went from the dining room through the parlor and across the hall on his way to the library, he stopped at the open door of the house and looked out, drawing in the scented air with deep breaths. The Satsumas were in full bloom just then, and though they were located beyond the kitchen wing, at the side of the house, their fragrance was so strong that it came to him in great waves. But it was not only the smell of the orange blossoms which was so delicious. The sweet olive and night jasmine were blooming, too, and the privet and magnolia fuscata and honeysuckle; and besides all these, there was the indistinguishable scent which betokens the presence of no special flower, but which is the very essence of spring itself, pervading the grass and the shrubs and the trees and floating up to the very heavens. The Easter moon, at the height of its glory, added the element of radiance to this element of reviving freshness. Across the pavement of the gallery, the reflection of the columns slanted as white as snow between shafts of blackness, and the raftered ceiling above them was black, too, with a strange impenetrable darkness; but beyond the colonnade, the walk which led to the further end of the driveway at its final curve, was strangely luminous. The amaryllis, which had succeeded the azaleas blooming along this path earlier in the season, was at the fullness of its splendor now. So was the yucca which Amen, steeped in the lore which Angus Holt had handed down, trained to curve, when it reached its full height, to form a graceful archway. The crimson majesty of the amaryllis, the snowy bells of the yucca, formed a contrast so striking that it was almost breath-taking.

Gervais left the shelter of the gallery and walked slowly down the gorgeous illuminated pathway. This should have been his wedding night, he thought, and Merry should have been walking with him through this magic, scented arch, which might well have served as the aisle leading to an altar. His resolution that his marriage must take place immediately crystallized as he paced slowly back and forth, picturing Merry as his bride. Involuntarily, he thought of a story about Isabelle Estrade and Philogene d'Alvery which he had inevitably heard over and over again, since it was the sort of story which no man would choose to hear about his own father and mother: after their marriage had been arranged by Isabelle's parents, it was also arranged that they should not take a wedding trip, but spend their honeymoon in the *garçonnière* at the rear of the garden where Philogene had made his quarters during his prolonged visit to his rich relatives. In the dead of night, however, long after the departure of the last wedding guest who had made the event so convivial an occasion, Lucien and Evaline Estrade had been startled by having their daughter burst into their own stately conjugal chamber, clad only in her long-sleeved, high-necked nightgown, and crying out to them in hysterical resentment and rage:

"Je ne peux pas me coucher avec ce cochon là! Il veut m'enlever la chemise!"

Somehow they had quieted her, somehow, at that untimely hour, they had belatedly explained to her the rights and privileges of a husband; and before Philogene could start in pursuit of her, Lucien Estrade had himself led her back to the *garçonnière,* after Evaline had wrapped a cashmere dressing gown around her as she murmured a few last words of counsel and consolation in her daughter's ear. As a matter of fact, Philogene had not had the slightest idea of pursuing her. He awaited her return, the circumstances of which he had no difficulty in divining, without undue impatience and with considerable amusement; and, to do him justice, he took no advantage of the shamed and rebellious mood in which his bride was returned to him, either then or later. Philogene, who loved to make a jest of everything, even his own destitution, never derided his wife for the sorry role she had played at the moment which should have represented supreme fulfillment to her. Gervais realized this, for he understood his father better than most persons, and loved him better than anyone. But he had always been ashamed of the episode himself. Now he reveled in the realization that his fate would be so different from his father's, that his bride would not only accept his right of dominance and her destiny of surrender without question, but that she would receive him radiantly as well as trustfully, glorifying their union through her ardor even as she quickened it through her acquiescence.

For a long time, as he paced back and forth, in the strange luminescence of the colonnade, he could think only of Merry, and of this rapturous consummation of his marriage to her. The very conviction that this was at last so close at hand, however, that his long pent-up passion for her would so soon be assuaged, steadied him instead of increasing his restlessness and impatience; he began to think more quietly about other aspects of their life together. He took immense satisfaction in the knowledge that he would be able to give Merry a home and a tradition so superior to those she had hitherto possessed; he looked forward to seeing her live at leisure amidst surroundings distinguished by taste and tradition, in settings of great natural beauty. He visualized her presiding at the head of his table, pouring coffee in his parlor, sauntering through his garden, and—instinctively reverting to his earlier visions—enthroned on his bed. Mentally, he saw her exquisitely arrayed as well as adorably disrobed, adorned with the jewels and laces that had been his grandmother's and his great-grandmother's, tucking camellias and jasmine in the ribbon which bound the shining masses of her hair and the tulle that veiled the whiteness of her bosom. He saw her, too, as she would look when she was great with child, bearing herself with such dignity and composure that her condition enhanced her queenliness; and he saw her with the newborn child at her breast, not daunted or prostrated by her travail, but triumphantly nourishing the new life from her own abundant supply of vitality. . . .

Though these visions exhilarated him, they did not blind him, however. He knew that Belle Heloise, beautiful as it was, had escaped only by a hair's breadth the insidious decadence which in the end had destroyed not only countless houses which had been the glory of the River Road, but also hundreds of the men and women who had peopled them. Merry would help him, of course, to avert such a catastrophe here; but if she were to do justice to the part which he yearned to see her play, she must not be handicapped from the start by problems and burdens which lay essentially in a man's province and not his wife's. He must safeguard both the position she would adorn and the home which she would glorify. Still pacing back and forth in the slanting black and white shadows, he seriously considered first the state in which he had found the plantation, and then his general standing in the community. At last, finding that his thoughts were beginning to take him around and around in circles, he went into the library, and, at random, selected one volume after another from the row of old diaries on the top shelf of the breakfront bookcase. These were uniform in style, size and shape, and were all inscribed in block letters on the black cloth bindings with the words

50

Inside there was the same identity of format. Each page provided for a week's chronicle, being evenly divided into seven small rectangles under the general caption RECORD OF PASSING EVENTS ON THE ——— PLANTATION FOR THE WEEK BEGINNING—. The name of the plantation and the date were written in the blank spaces left for this purpose, and nearly every day's record began with a comment on the weather: "A cloudy foggy morning and fine day"—"A fine cold day with considerable frost this morning"—"A very warm day with thunder and rain after noon." Only births, deaths and important visits were recorded above such statements, and these were generally written in red ink, to set them apart from the rest. The next entry was generally on the subject of health or illness: "All well except Philogene who has a sore throat"—"I hear of no sickness in the Parish"—"I have several Negroes sick with several kinds of diseases the Dr. attending them" —"One boy lying up with sore eyes and one woman with her breast" —"Two women in childbed"—"More Negroes sick than ever before, Measles, Fever and everything else they can have." Next came comments of general character, mostly about working and crop conditions. Gervais had not previously realized, or if he did he had forgotten, that female slaves did such heavy work on the plantation, or that so many different kinds of activity had been the rule rather than the exception. He read, with astonishment, that "the women" were clearing ground, making fences, rolling logs, raking up manure; with equal amazement that "the boys" were making baskets, shoes and fences, cutting up new-ground logs, getting in tanbark, setting out peach trees and Irish potatoes, and building corn houses.

At first he found little to differentiate the books kept by his grandfather and his great-grandfather. They both attended the races in St. Francisville, they were both sworn in as Police Jurors in Baton Rouge. They both went fishing in the streams and hunting in the swamps and forests, taking bass, deer, ducks and in fact game of every sort. They both kept dogs, which they rubbed with linseed oil, turpentine and sulphur. They both entertained their friends, offering them such modest meals as those comprising "gumbo, boned turkey, young rooster, beef tongue, guava jelly, vegetables, plumb(sic) pudding and syllabub." But gradually Gervais came upon observations in Lucien's diary which had never appeared in François': "War is all the talk" —"Everything at exorbitant prices"—"The most dreadful time known to man." Even the vital statistics changed in character: "Many deaths in the Parish. Typhoid fever and pneumonia seem to be the prevalent diseases brought in by the Army."

Gervais shut the volume bearing the telltale date of 1862, put it back in the bookcase, and flung himself into a barrelback chair. The old entries no longer intrigued him; they revolted him. He did not want to read or hear or think about a war, even a war which was now only a part of history. He felt irritable and restless again, as he had earlier in the evening. But he was tired, too, and presently he realized that without knowing it, he must have dozed in front of the fire, for he had not heard a car coming in, or a horse's hoofs in the driveway, and the servants had long since gone to bed; yet there were footsteps in the gallery now, and the murmur of voices. The footsteps were dilatory, indicating a reluctance to go forward, and the murmur was so low that it suggested secrecy. Every now and then both ceased entirely, and somehow the silences suggested embraces, which seemed to become more and more lingering as they took place closer and closer to the front door. He would have risen and gone to the door himself, if he had not felt that any gesture of welcoming a guest might savor of spying on his sister; so he sat still, involuntarily listening, and increasingly uncomfortable as the silences became more and more intensified. He had almost decided that he could not stand them any longer, no matter how maladroit his manner of terminating them might seem, when there was a long-drawn-out good night, punctuated by unmistakable kisses. A moment later Cresside tiptoed into the hall alone.

"Don't trip, trying to keep quiet," Gervais called to her. "I can hear you, all right. I can also hear your cavalier cautiously retreating Why didn't he come in with you? Was he afraid I'd shoot him?"

"You sound mighty silly, Gervais, when you get smart-alecky. It's a little late, isn't it, to go visiting? And how were we to know you were here, anyway?"

"Thanks for the delicate compliment. I reckon that no matter how I get, I don't sound any sillier than you do, when you go creeping along like a cat, or when you stand out on the gallery smacking somebody else's lips along with your own. If you're going to quibble, I'd say it was a little late to be coming in, and I shouldn't think it would take a Sherlock Holmes to guess that if there were a light in the library at this hour, I might be the person who was using it. I don't suppose the servants have taken to literature, while I was in France. And as far as I know *maman* hasn't been down the stairs in over two years."

"Oh, for Pete's sake! Haven't you had enough fighting without trying to pick a quarrel with me all the time? You haven't done anything else but, so far."

Cresside swung herself into a chair sideways and lighted a cigarette, nonchalantly tossing the match, when she had done so, down on the Aubusson carpet. Gervais rose, rather pointedly, and, walking over to the place where the match lay, picked it up, and carried it to the fireplace.

"You've got to be terribly prissy since you went into the Army, do you know it?" Cresside said scornfully.

"No, I don't know that. But I do know that this carpet cost two thousand dollars, and that we couldn't find another like it anywhere, even if we could afford to buy another—which we can't."

"Well, I can remember when you used to throw matches around yourself, like nobody's business, and flick ashes on the carpet, too."

Cresside flicked ashes on the carpet now as she spoke, and began to swing her beautiful legs, delicately encased in silk stockings, back and forth over the arm of the chair. Her feet, unserviceably but attractively shod in gay high-heeled slippers, were also exquisitely noticeable. Apparently she had gone somewhere and changed her clothes after leaving the Executive Mansion, for she was now wearing a sleeveless beaded evening dress, which came barely to her knees and clung closely to her flat little figure. Gervais was conscious of a fleeting feeling of amazement that a girl, otherwise provocatively feminine, should have fallen so completely under the influence of the current craze for a "boyish form." But this seemed to him a cause for mild amusement rather than genuine concern; it was her face rather than her figure which really disquieted him. She used more makeup than Regine or any other girl he had seen in Baton Rouge who came into the comfortable category of ladies; but usually she applied it skillfully, if dashingly. Now it gave her a blurred look; the pearly glow of her skin seemed muddied under the rouge, the curving line of her mouth hardened by her lipstick. Her hair, usually so shiny and sleek, was also disordered. She saw him looking at it and tossed back the loose locks.

"All set to play the heavy elder brother, Gervais?"

"No. Just the same I'd be interested in knowing who brought you home."

"Well, just to show you what a sweet little sister I really am I'll tell you. It was Sylvestre."

"Good God, you don't mean to tell me you've really fallen for that muffin hound?"

"I'm sorry you don't appreciate him. In fact, it makes me damn mad. Just as mad as it makes you to have *maman* raise hell about Merry. So you ought to know how I feel."

"I wouldn't compare Merry with Sylvestre, if I were you. And I wouldn't swear quite so much either, if I were a presumably nice girl."

"Well, you're not a presumably nice girl. You're a conquering hero with all the privileges that go with it. Just the same, you might cut out the 'presumably' when you're talking about me. I don't care much for your dirty digs."

"And I don't care much about having you going in for heavy necking with a specimen like Sylvestre. If you think the nature of the tender passages out on the gallery escaped me, you're damn-well mistaken."

"No, I don't think so. I think you'd be bound to recognize them. After all, you're in pretty good practice yourself."

53

Cresside's last remark ended jerkily, not because of any voluntary change in the venomed honey of her tones, but because her brother was shaking her. The impudent swinging of her legs had ceased because he had pulled her abruptly to her feet; neither could she continue her spoken insults with any degree of effectiveness, because she could not get her breath, which she had lost from amazement as well as fury. Gervais had always been a kind and complaisant brother; even when they were children, he had very seldom teased her, and never before in his life had he touched her roughly. Now, when he stopped shaking her, he continued to grip her shoulders and to force her to look at him.

"See here," he said sternly. "All this nonsense is going to stop. From now on you're going to behave yourself. Who's supposed to be looking out for you, anyhow?"

"Lucie looks after me. She's my maid as much as she is *maman's*. She's a good one, too."

"I'm not talking about a maid, and you know it. Who looks after you in *maman's* place?"

"Mrs. Hathaway. She says it's just as easy for her to look after two girls as one. She's been mighty kind about it. *Maman's* very grateful to her."

"She may have been kind, but I'd say she's been damn careless, if tonight's a sample of the way she looks after you. I think I'd better have a little talk with her. I'll tell her that when you go out with her daughter, I'd like to have you *stay* with her daughter, and not come streaking in with her house guest at two in the morning. If I weren't going to get married right away, I'd see if one of our own kinswomen who's got a sharp eye and a strong constitution wouldn't come and make us a prolonged visit. As it is, I don't believe that's necessary. I'll look after you myself until Merry gets here to help me do it. And I'll begin my guardianship with the statement that you can stop this pretty little flirtation of yours before it goes any further."

"It's no more of a flirtation than yours is."

"I'm engaged to Meredith. Are you engaged to Sylvestre?"

"More or less."

"That's not quite definite enough to suit me. Has Sylvestre asked you to marry him?"

"Practically."

"That's not definite enough to suit me either. Unless he's said, in so many words, that he wants you to be his wife, I think it will be very healthy for both of you to stop seeing each other alone."

"Well, he has—in so many words."

"Do you mean what I mean by that, or do you mean rather vague words which you've slanted to suit yourself?"

"I don't see why I should tell you exactly what Sylvestre said to me when he proposed. I bet Merry doesn't go around telling everyone what you said to her when you proposed."

54

"This isn't a case of telling everyone. It's a case of telling me. You don't have to tell me exactly what he said either. All I want is your word of honor that he has proposed."

"All right. He has proposed."

Cresside's defiant eyes did not drop before her brother's accusing ones, as his mother's had dropped earlier in the evening. She continued to stare at him, boldly, as long as he confronted her. When at last he loosened his hold on her shoulders, she gave a little mocking laugh.

"Now that you've found that out, Paul Pry, suppose you let me go to bed. I could do with a little sleep."

"Yes, you look as if you could. These tense episodes quite often have exhausting after-effects. Well, I won't keep you. But I'll run over to Hathaway Hall tomorrow morning and have a little chat with Sylvestre. As long as he's going to be my brother-in-law, worse luck, we might just as well understand each other at the outset. And one of the things I don't want any *mis*understanding about is a fiancé's prerogatives, as the d'Alverys interpret them."

"Well, of course you're the soul of tact, but I shouldn't think, myself, that a conversation of the sort you have in mind would exactly pave the way for brotherly love. And I don't know just how pleased Mrs. Hathaway would be to have you make a scene in her house. She goes in for dignity with a capital D, and she seems to be feeling a little cool towards you right now. In fact, I shouldn't wonder if she said something to *you* about a proposal, if you gave her the right kind of an opening. I think she rather expected it. Oh, not for herself, of course, but for her dear daughter. You didn't by any chance ever take Regine home on a moonlight night, did you, and loiter for a little while on the way?"

"I've hardly seen Regine since I got home. You know that."

"Yes, but didn't you see her sometimes before you went away? Without the whole family sitting around? Now, now! Don't talk to me about men who raise false hopes in the fluttering breasts of innocent maidens!"

"Don't talk to me like a fool!" Gervais said sharply.

There was no sound reason why Gervais should have been so disquieted. He had never said anything to Regine, in that prewar period when after all they were both just kids, which she could truthfully have told her mother was "fresh"—that was the way it would have been expressed then. He did not know how the incoming crop of youngsters would define this particular type of conduct, if indeed there was any term of opprobrium connected with it; as far as he could see, almost anything went now. If he had ever tried to kiss Regine, either against her will or because she seemed to expect it, the caress had been so casual that he had completely forgotten it. The match-making schemes had been hatched between her mother

55

and his; if Regine had accepted them complacently—and he had an uneasy feeling that she might have—he had never furthered them, at least not consciously. Naturally, he had taken her home from a few parties, since they ran with the same crowd. Probably he had paid her some silly compliments and sent her insignificant little presents from time to time. But none of that amounted to a last year's bird's nest. It had nothing to do with his triumphant love for Merry, or with the unfortunate infatuation of Cresside for Sylvestre. There was no reason why he should not go to Hathaway Hall the first thing in the morning and have a plain talk with that skunk. He had half a notion that Cresside had lied to him about the proposal, in spite of the fact that she had given her word of honor, that she was telling the truth. Well, he would soon find out. . . .

He was unaccountably restless all night, disquieted not only by his own tumultuous thoughts, but by a variety of nocturnal sounds: the cricketlike chirp of toad-frogs, engaged on their amorous occasions in the disused sugar kettle beneath his window; the liquid trill of the mockingbird which had found daylight all too short for its throat-bursting jubilance; the lonesome wail of a freight engine hauling its mixed string of box and tank cars northward towards Vicksburg; the asthmatic chuff of the *John D. Grace* churning downstream from Baton Rouge to Plaquemine; and sharpening all these, the vicious whine of mosquitoes beyond the bars. Such sounds had once helped lull him to sleep; but for a long time the sounds he had listened to at night had been different; the chatter of machine guns at St. Mihiel; the roistering at Dufour's *estaminet* in Lille; the rhythmic crash of waters riven by the stem of a transport. The mockingbird's joyousness seemed ill-timed now, the toad-frog's lovenote offensive; they irritated and disturbed him. At last, tired of tossing from one side of the bed to the other, he rose and going to the plantation desk in the corner of the room, unlocked the dropleaf front which slanted across the pigeonholes and took out his own diary, which he had left there when he went to France. It fell open at the last entry:

"April 6, 1917. Heavy rainfall. Much needed after long spell dry weather but still too cool for young cane. *Maman* worse, sent for Dr. Champagne. Cresside came home from Convent for Easter holidays. War declared against Germany. Shall be off tomorrow to enlist."

"There certainly is a deadly monotony about the records the men in this family have kept," he said half aloud. "Maybe I'd better start in again along different lines." He hesitated, almost tempted to begin the new record then and there. It seemed an absurd thing to do, however, in the middle of the night, and presently he shoved the old diary back into its pigeonhole, relocked the desk, and got into bed again. But still he could not sleep, and eventually, abandoning the effort, he got up and dressed, long before his usual hour. As he stepped from his room into the upper hallway, Lucie opened the shutter door opposite his, leading into his mother's bedchamber. The mulatto maid was wearing her inevitable *tignon;* she was carrying the customary coffee tray; but there was an unwonted expression of bewilderment on her usually placid face. Gervais noticed it with concern. When Lucie looked like that, it was portentous.

"Good morning, Lucie," he said pleasantly. "How's Madame, this morning? I hope I didn't tire her, talking to her so long last evening."

Lucie curtsied. She was very fond of Gervais, and she had enormous respect for him. She had long regarded him as the head of the house, and now that he had come home from the war in heroic guise, his importance in her estimation was still further enhanced.

"No, sah, Mr. Gervais," she said respectfully. "You didn't tire her out none. I don't know when I seen her so pert like she is this morning. She done tole me she thought she mought try to get out of de bed, after while, and lay herself down on de couch in de boudoir instead. She must be feelin' pert if she's aimin' to do that. You knows yourself, Mr. Gervais, that Madame ain't been out of de bed before, not once, since poor Mr. Philogene done died."

CHAPTER IV

THE PLANTATION BELL calling the field hands to work was still ringing when Gervais went down the stairs and into the rear of the lower gallery. It was a great bronze bell, suspended from a wooden standard near the corn crib, and its tone, at once impelling and melodious, had increased in richness with age; it could be heard at least five miles away. Like the statue on the stairs, this bell was ancient and honorable and closely associated with the annals of the family. It not only gave the summons to daily toil; it warned of flood and fire, heralded births, pealed for weddings, tolled for the dead. All these functions were habitual on every great sugar estate; the bell was literally the voice of the plantation. But the one at Belle Heloise had served in even more homely and intimate ways; as a child, Lucien Estrade had learned most of his letters from its inscriptions, identifying them, one by one, under the painstaking direction of Angus Holt.

"J stands for justice, Laddie. And A for authority, P for patience, another P for peace, another A for amenity, R for rule, T for toil, I for ingenuity, E for energy, N for nobility. Repeat that after me now, and mind you don't forget what I've told you either, you scatterbrain you!"

When he had learned his lesson properly, Lucien was permitted to ring the bell for "quitting time," and to this reward he looked forward with eagerness. Then, strangely enough, Philogene d'Alvery had been the one to continue the custom the Scotchman had started; he taught Gervais the alphabet by the bell, too, less patiently but more gaily than Angus had taught his pupil, permitting him to peal it often without rhyme or reason, a practice which threw everyone into confusion. To Gervais, the sound of his father's drollery was forever intermingled with the peal of the bell.

"*J pour joie, A pour amour, P pour passion, encore de la passion quand nous trouvons P la deuxième fois, encore de l'amour avec le second A, R pour ravir, T pour tempter, I pour ivresse, E pour extase —dis donc, Gervais, a tu compris?*"

In those days Gervais had always shaken his head, smiling, and Philogene, shaking his head and smiling too, had continued the lesson in a slightly more serious vein. Now, stopping before the bell which still swayed though it had ceased to sound, Gervais smiled again at the remembrance of those strange lessons, tracing the inscription with his forefinger while he studied it afresh. The bell was ornamented at top and bottom with elaborate scrollwork, and beneath the upper scroll was a plaque, inscribed among further ornamentation with the words:

J'APPARTIEN

A MONSIEUR

FRANÇOIS ESTRADE

It was while pointing to that first word, *J'appartien*—I belong—that Philogene had told his son J stood for joy and E for ecstasy; but Gervais had known for a long time that there had been little joy and less ecstasy in his father's life, and the mockery in Philogene's voice, which still rang through the peal of the bell, always had a note of bitterness in it. But the bitterness had never silenced his wry jesting for long; after a temporary lapse into gravity, he usually continued his lesson in the same vein that he had begun it, as he went on to the second inscription on the bell, the one which encircled it below the plaque and above the lower scroll:

FONDUE A L'ATELIER DE THIAC-MAIGNAN DURAND NOUVELLE ORLEANS

LE 21 JUIN 1824

Gervais had often wondered about Thiac-Maignan Durand, the man who had cast this bell in his workshop nearly a hundred years before. He had asked Philogene what sort of an artisan Thiac probably was; and Philogene, in his droll way, had said Thiac must have been the sort who put everything hind side foremost, because all the Ns on the inscription were cast backwards, and were weirdly presented as Иs. Ns presented that way, Philogene told Gervais, did not stand for anything, which was the reason he had to skip the last letter in *J'appartien,* the incomplete word making it all too pointed that he, at any rate, did *not* belong; whereas, if the Ns had been properly presented, they might have stood for *normalcie*. It was too bad they didn't, because a little *normalcie* would not have been amiss at Belle Heloise and would have helped Philogene to belong. . . .

Gervais was still staring at the bell and thinking about his father when Lezine Sance, his overseer, came up to speak to him. Sance was a short wiry man, sallow faced in spite of his outdoor life, with an inverted crescent of a mustache, and thin straggling brown hair. As usual, he was wearing a khaki-colored shirt, open at the throat, a heavy leather belt, cloth riding breeches, and well-cut though rugged brown boots. The back of his neck was ravined from the sun and his sleeves were rolled up above the elbow. One shirt pocket was bulging with cigars, while from the other protruded an enormous silver watch with a minuscule trace chain attached to it at one end and looped through a buttonhole at the other. His hat, worn at a jaunty angle, was a coarsely plaited affair of palmetto straw, shaped into a somewhat dandified fedora model. He was leading his horse, a small cobby plantation pony, which would never have taken any ribbons on the tanbark, but which carried him interminably along ditch-banks and over headlands under the broiling Louisiana sun without showing any hint of fatigue, moving in a comfortable little rack equally easy on mount and rider.

"Good morning, Captain d'Alvery," he said agreeably. The air was crisp, but from force of habit he removed the pseudo-fedora and vigorously wiped first its sweatband and then his own unbeaded brow with his big bandana. "Regular Easter weather, isn't it? I don't recollect a year when the mornings haven't been chilly at Easter, whatever time of year that came. But it'll be plenty warm later in the day. . . . Anything you'd like to tell me before I go out into the fields?"

"Yes. I'd like to tell you that the fence to the mule yard looks in mighty bad condition to me. I'd be willing to bet that the mules and pigs have been breaking out and eating the corn sprouts."

"Well, Captain, you get me the bob-wire and posts and staples I need, and I'll see that the mules and pigs don't get out."

"Very well. I'll take care of that in Baton Rouge today. But your mule shed is in bad shape, too. A good many shingles are missing and half the doors from the catchpen are sagging on their hinges."

"Captain, I just haven't been able to get the materials, with the war going on. There are lots of things I'd like to see different myself. For instance, the rats are running wild in the corn cribs, and I need money for traps, and authority to offer bounty to Lou Ida's little boys for every dead one they bring me. Madame wouldn't give me the money or the authority either."

"Well, I'll do it. You can depend on having everything you need from now on. But get that leaking molasses trough fixed right away. All you need for that is a new plug."

While they were talking they had covered the ground between the

59

corn crib close to the bell and the harness-house where the field hands were whistling while preparing the mules to go into the fields. Thirty or more teams were already harnessed for the day's work and the trace chains were jingling with the singing sound peculiarly their own. By and large the teams presented a fine sight. But Gervais was ready to pick flaws in their appearance also.

"I wouldn't say those mules had been curried any too regularly, and if their manes and tails have been trimmed, I wouldn't know when."

"This time I have to admit I've got no alibi. But it's been too long since there's been anyone around that's shown interest. It'll be different from now on, I promise you, Captain."

"That's the stuff. And maybe in the fall I can take a run up to Missouri and get us some better mules. A lot of these don't even look like cane mules. They're not much bigger than cotton mules."

"The stock has run down some, for a fact, and I don't mind saying it's good hearing to know there'll be a change now that the bossman's come back."

While Gervais and the overseer were talking, the Negroes had begun to move out along the headland with their teams, some of them chanting as they went. One of them, a lanky loose-jointed teen-ager, paused to call out to the near mule of his team in the midst of his carol.

"Get along there, you old Susan you! You'se pure slow this mornin'."

"Susan!" echoed Gervais, turning to Lezine. "Isn't that our head Minnie?"

Lezine chuckled. "Why, Captain, you haven't forgot, have you, that the boys have two names for all these mules? Minnie's that one's stable name, all right; but out in the field she goes by Susan. You take that scrubby one she's teamed up with, too; her name's Mattie in the mule lot, but as soon as she gets outside the door, she's Kate."

"I do remember now," Gervais said laughing. "But I had forgotten for the moment." Then he added, as an afterthought, "And it wouldn't do not to have a mule named Minnie at Belle Heloise, you know."

The subject of the mules being logically terminated at this point, for the time being at least, Lezine, nodding a friendly farewell, swung one leg over the side of his cobby little pony, preparatory to trotting off in the wake of the field hands. Gervais made a detaining gesture.

"Just a minute more, Lezine. I hate to start off by so much variegated fault finding, but I was a good deal shocked at the state I found the cemetery in yesterday. If you can spare a couple of men, I wish you'd send them down there this morning to cut the grass, and hereafter I'd like it to be kept cut, regularly. A big snake was coiled up on one of the tombs in the Hathaway lot. I shouldn't be surprised if there was a regular nest of them there. Anyway, that long grass is a pretty good place for one. I want it cleaned up."

"Yes, Captain, I see how you feel." For the first time the overseer spoke hesitantly. "I'll get two or three of the boys down there just as soon as I can. But I may as well tell you that I'll have to offer them some kind of inducement or reward. The niggers are scared of that cemetery. It's not just graveyard fright either, like they generally have. There *are* a lot of those snakes, and the niggers are superstitious about them. They say old Miss Regine, that your young lady's named for, used to keep one in her room. The servants kept hearing a queer rustling sound there and it seems that after she died, when they started opening her dresser drawers, there was a snake skin in the place where she kept her paper patterns. The niggers believe that the snake followed her to her grave. . . . Well, you could see how it would all work out. Plumb foolishness, of course. But that kind of foolishness is hard to get around."

"I do see that it might present difficulties. But I believe you can get around it. I believe you're good at that sort of thing. And incidentally, the present Miss Regine isn't my young lady. I've just told my mother, and I'd like to tell you, that I'm engaged to Miss Meredith Randall in town."

"Well, that's fine. The best of luck to you, Captain. And now I'd really better get after those field hands if there's to be any work done today. But you can count on me. I'll see to everything we've talked about."

They had gone forward, spasmodically, as they talked, and now Gervais was almost opposite the sugar house, where he knew his engineer, Étienne Plauché, would be expecting him, for this was the beginning of the repair season and he had not yet been out to inspect the machinery. The sugar house had been built at the same time as the mansion, and though its equipment had been gradually modernized, its appearance, unlike that of any other mill in the vicinity, was essentially unaltered. Its low façade was made of mellow brick, and its simple doorway, flanked on either side by small rectangular windows, was handsomely paneled and surmounted by an ornamental fanlight. At both ends, wide wings of well-weathered wood stretched out beyond the brick, and above it a gabled roof closed down over a spreading triangle of clapboards. The whole effect was quaint, spacious and dignified to a degree more typical of a mansion than of a mill. Even the two square elevations, added to accommodate gigantic new machinery, and rising ungracefully, one over the other, above the gable, did not seriously impair this effect. A line drawing of the sugar mill was stamped on every bag of sugar that went out from Belle Heloise, for its owners had always been nearly as proud of the mill itself as they were of its product.

When Gervais opened the door to the mill room, he saw Plauché standing beside the big engine which drove all six rollers, and as he expected, the engineer, a swarthy, thickset man, whose blue denim

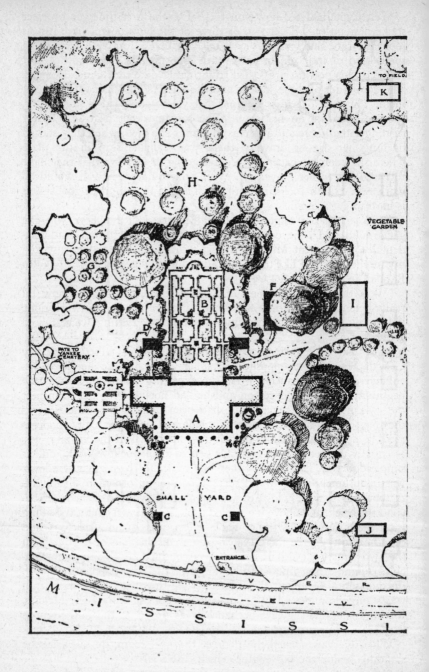

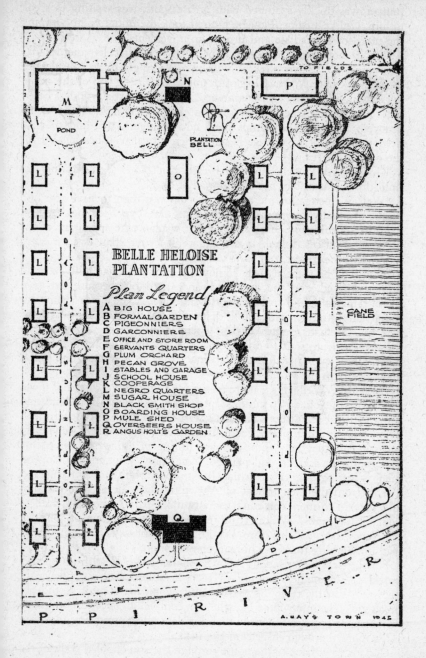

BELLE HELOISE PLANTATION

Plan Legend

A BIG HOUSE
B FORMAL GARDEN
C PIGEONNIERS
D GARCONNIERE
E OFFICE AND STORE ROOM
F SERVANTS QUARTERS
G PLUM ORCHARD
H PECAN GROVE
I STABLES AND GARAGE
J SCHOOL HOUSE
K COOPERAGE
L NEGRO QUARTERS
M SUGAR HOUSE
N BLACK SMITH SHOP
O BOARDING HOUSE
P MULE SHED
Q OVERSEERS HOUSE
R ANGUS HOLT'S GARDEN

TO FIELDS

POND

PLANTATION BELL

CANE FIELD

MISSISSIPPI RIVER

A. HAYS TOWN 1945

jumper was thickly spattered with grease spots, was waiting to speak to him. Unlike Lezine, Plauché himself took the initiative in outlining the need for immediate and urgent improvements.

"Good morning, Captain. I hoped you wouldn't let another day pass before going over the mill with me. We've got to do considerable repair work here. We had lots of trouble towards the end of the grinding season. Why, this very engine here should have the cylinders bored out! The last mill needs new shells and the front mill should be regrooved. Some of the pumps need new plungers, too, and they all need new Garlock packing. Besides, there are new tubes needed for the double effect and—"

"Good Lord, Plauché, stop for breath, can't you? You certainly are unloading a lot of bad news on me all at once!"

"Well, it's better for me to unload it on you than to have you find it out gradually for yourself and think that I've been negligent. I want to get things in shape here so that we can take advantage of the high sugar prices. I look to see sugar hit better than twenty cents, within the next year."

"You may be right at that. I know the Belgian sugar mills have all been destroyed, and the ones in France hard hit, because I've seen them. There's bound to be a world shortage. It's a damn shame we didn't go into Germany, and destroy the best factories there the way the Germans destroyed their enemies'. We've been too easy on those Huns from start to finish and some day we're going to be sorry. They've got every particle of machinery they've ever had, and it's as good as any in the world."

"Is that so? Well, all the more reason for trying to get ahead of them. . . . Now, if you don't mind, Captain, I'd like to walk around and show you just how things are. Let's start in the clarifying department. These heaters are in pretty good shape, but we should have some extra tubes in case they have to be changed during grinding. All the settlin' tanks must be scraped and painted. You know, Captain, the Government is getting mighty particular. Just to show you the way things are, a man from the Department of Agriculture was here the other day, and he said to me, 'You can't use any more paint containing lead in your settlin' tanks.' We can't use red lead, even in making a joint for our pipes, because the Pure Food Department says you can't have lead in anything that's for human consumption."

For the next hour Gervais followed the engineer's lead from one department to another, finding in each its own peculiar evidence of necessity. Finally, realizing the morning would be gone if he did not break away, he interrupted Plauché in a complaint concerning the state of the sugar room, and hastily took his departure, promising to return for a more thorough inspection the next day.

Gervais went back to the house through the sun-dappled walk of the pergola which bounded Angus Holt's garden on the south side. Besides providing an ideal retreat for lovers, this pergola, richly garlanded with foliage at every season of the year except midwinter, had long served as a promenade where the feminine contingent of the family took its genteel and unfatiguing exercise—indeed, Gervais believed that Cresside was the first to rebel against the tameness of the traditional "constitutional." Certainly his mother, up to the time of her widowhood, had regularly paced up and down there every pleasant morning, for a period carefully marked by an hourglass, except during those intervals vaguely described to him when he was a child as "certain days when ladies kept quiet." He could still see her, with her rosary between her white fingers, and her stiff skirt brushing the pebbles on the walk, as clearly as he could see Philogene bending laughingly over the letters on the bell. If what Lucie had told him about his mother were true, he might really see her walking like that again, with precision and restraint and elegance. But there could be no re-creation of Philogene in his far more appealing guise. That is, unless—Gervais' heart leapt suddenly at the thought—he himself some time had a son who was like his lost father, a second Philogene, happier than the first, in whose lightheartedness there would be no mockery and in whose charm there would be no bitterness. It would not be strange, after all, if such a boy should be born at Belle Heloise, for Merry would be his mother, and Merry's own charm and lightheartedness were like that. . . .

It would do no harm, he thought, to speak to his mother again about Merry before he started for Hathaway Hall. It was still early, by Sylvestre's standards, and Gervais had sense enough to realize that nothing would be gained by bursting in on his future brother-in-law with criticisms of his conduct and imperative demands that this should be rectified, before this wastrel was half awake. Gervais' deep-rooted aversion to Sylvestre and all his ways mounted as he pictured this sluggard lolling among his pillows at a time when any healthy man with an atom of initiative would have been up and doing for hours. Why, in heaven's name, should Cresside, who could have had her pick of the countryside, have made such a sorry selection? And how, again in heaven's name, could she have bestowed her favors so recklessly on the last man who was worthy of either her admiration or her trust?

There was no answer, of course, to either question, and as far as that went, Gervais was guided by instinct rather than knowledge in gaging the degree of his sister's indiscretion. But he was increasingly convinced that his instincts were not playing him false, and increasingly disturbed by his convictions. He strode through the hall almost unseeingly, and failed to salute the statue as he went up the stairs. The shutter doors of his mother's room stood open, and when he entered it, he saw, as he expected, that the great bed was empty: the white covers were drawn tight across its immense width and its square pillows were smooth. The wide shutters, flanked on either side by gigantic armoires, and dividing Madame d'Alvery's chamber from Cresside's, were tightly closed, and he gathered that his sister was still asleep, or pretending to be. But the smaller door beyond the fireplace, leading into Madame d'Alvery's boudoir, was ajar, and before he could reach it and knock, his mother's voice came to him from beyond it.

"You may enter, Gervais. I was expecting you to come and find out for yourself whether Lucie had told you the truth. Well, you will see that she has."

Madame d'Alvery spoke from a couch covered with dark brocade, on which she lay propped up by brocaded cushions. A purple comfort covered her, and a black satin *peignoir* concealed her linen nightgown. From the black lace cap that covered her hair depended long satin streamers, crossed and fastened under her chin with a diamond and onyx brooch. Her appearance, though still somber, was infinitely more regal than when she had been engulfed by the whiteness of her big bed, and it was also infinitely more suggestive of action. Her son was quick to feel the pulse of reviving power.

"Yes, I see that she has. Not that I doubted her word. But naturally I was anxious to witness this miracle for myself. You have made a most remarkable recovery, *ma mère.*"

"I have made a superhuman effort, because circumstances seemed to necessitate it."

"I'm not sure that I understand you."

"On the contrary, I am certain that you do."

Again, as on the previous evening, the two pairs of dark eyes challenged each other. This time it was Madame d'Alvery who triumphed in her gaze.

"I regret that you have obliged me to remind you this is my house. I cannot prevent you from bringing a bride to it. But I can, I hope, preclude its mismanagement by an inexperienced outsider."

"You can prevent me from bringing a bride to this house by ordering me out of it, if you care to do so."

"I resent that retort, my son. It is unbecoming of you to suggest that I would stoop to such a course, merely because the law would permit it."

"It was you who brought up the question of my legal status in this house to begin with. But apparently I care more for the place than you do—it has certainly suffered from lack of supervision during my absence. Moreover, I can assure you Belle Heloise would never be mismanaged by my wife, and I must remind you, in my turn, that whatever your other rights may be, you are not justified in referring to my fiancée as an outsider."

"I do not feel equal, at this point, to another prolonged argument with you, Gervais."

"I didn't intend to begin one. Just the same, I don't intend to let you speak about Merry like that, either."

"Shall we talk about someone else, perhaps?"

"No. You had better not overtax your strength. I'm just leaving for

Hathaway Hall anyhow. Is there anything I can do for you before I go?"

"Nothing. I hope you will enjoy your visit with the Hathaways. Please give them affectionate greetings from me."

"I'm not going to Hathaway Hall to visit the Hathaways. I'm going there to tell that skunk, Sylvestre Tremaine, exactly what I think of him."

"Isn't that somewhat superfluous as well as distinctly uncivil? You never concealed your dislike for our neighbors' friend, even when you were a child."

"It may be uncivil but I don't think it's superfluous. I think it's important Sylvestre should know what I think of him right now and why. It has nothing to do with the way I felt about him when he and I were both children. But we won't argue about that, either."

He left her abruptly, and stopping at Cresside's shutter door, knocked and called to her. But there was no answer, and after twice repeating his summons, he went on downstairs and out of the house. Amen had taken his car from the garage and was waiting patiently beside it, just as he had been accustomed to waiting beside the palomino. He gazed towards Gervais with a grin that was hesitant rather than wholehearted, but Gervais chose to disregard its shrinking quality.

"What are you so cheerful about this morning, Amen?"

"Ah's happy about de good news, Mr. Gervais."

"What news?"

"Selah done tole us you's fixin' to get married, Mr. Gervais."

"Does that make you happy, too?"

"Sure it do, Mr. Gervais. We's all happy when you's happy, and we grieves when you does."

Amen was telling the truth and Gervais knew it. It was his own brusqueness that had given the boy that hangdog look the night before and the memory of it that kept his smile so faltering now. Genuinely contrite, Gervais strove to make amends by a special show of geniality.

"You better hurry on and get married yourself. I want to dance at your wedding. Which means you've got to get married out of the book, you rascal, and not just take up."

"Yessuh, Mr. Gervais. That's what Ah's fixin' to do, sho' nuff. Ah don' hold with no takin' up myself."

The boy's grin was no longer hesitant; it reached almost from ear to ear. Gervais climbed into his car, smiling too, and started down the driveway, while Amen stood watching him out of sight. It was a glorious morning, bright with sparkling sunshine now, but still crisp enough to be tonic. As Gervais approached the overgrown privet hedge, a whirr of wings sounded above him, and two cock blue jays shot zigzagging through the air, one in desperate flight from the other. He looked up to follow the duel with his eyes, fully aware that from the concealing foliage near by a motionless little blue jay hen was watching it, too. Eventually one of the brawlers drove off his adversary, and with a perceptible swagger flew back to the nest which he had just successfully defended or invaded. The brawling was over, and tranquility reigned again in the hedge.

The animals on the levee, however, were no longer quiescent, as they had been the evening before. Along its crest, a colt was tearing forward at breakneck though aimless speed, and a flock of geese, with goslings trailing and cheeping behind them, quacked and waddled and clapped their wings. On its slope several calves cavorted with such absurd friskiness that Gervais laughed as he looked at them. Countless other calves were suckling their mothers, and little black-faced lambs, which looked as if they were grinning, were capering around the rotund ewes. As he passed a rickety cabin with butter-colored roses in its dusty yard and chinaberry trees bursting into bloom above its sagging roof, a young Negress lifted the length of cotton hanging at the doorless entrance and came out on the teetering porch. A small pickaninny crept after her, crowing, and as she stooped to pick him up, Gervais saw that she must be very near her time. Holding her child in her arms, she called out in surprise and delight, as she recognized the returning hero; her white teeth made a dazzling bar in her dark face, and she lifted the baby's hand, moving it back and forth until he began to wave it uncertainly of his own accord. Gervais waved back gaily, forgetful of snakes and tombs, and reached the driveway of Hathaway Hall almost before he knew it, a sense of joyous productiveness strong within him. And not the productiveness of spring alone. There was an old saying among the Louisiana French that the Mississippi itself had a special property which induced fecundity in every creature and every spot which it reached. It was the great river and the road that bounded it, even more than the season, which was responsible for the surge within him.

As Gervais walked up the great curving staircase which led, in two graceful branches railed with exquisite ironwork, to the vast galleries of Hathaway Hall, he was struck, as he had been so many times before, by the difference between the atmosphere in this house and his own. Hathaway Hall dominated its surroundings as an entity in itself; Belle Heloise was a part of them—an integral part, without which they could not have survived, any more than the human body could survive unless the heart sent its life blood coursing through all the members; but still only the heart and not the whole. Gervais felt that if the magnificence of Hathaway Hall were diminished or its luster dimmed, the entire plantation would lose its power and its prestige. But Belle Heloise would somehow triumph over shabbiness and neglect, even over decay. After all, the heart was essentially sound; it would keep on beating till the bitter end. . . .

The gallery which he entered now was empty, but the door leading into the house stood wide open, and Gervais whistled and went in, as he had hundreds of times before. He received a more immediate response than he had anticipated, for, unexpectedly, he found Mrs. Hathaway standing just inside the Ball Room at the right of the front door, and she instantly came forward to greet him. It was hard for him to realize that she was only a few years younger than his mother, whom he had long since regarded as an elderly woman. Not a single white hair was visible in Mrs. Hathaway's modish coiffure, nor a line in her handsome, expressionless face. Her figure was firm and faultless, and she carried herself erectly and moved briskly; she gave an effect of energy which was somewhat surprising, considering her background and tradition, and this effect detracted from the air of ease and elegance which would have seemed more natural under all the circumstances. She not only looked like a woman with a purpose, but like a woman whose pursuit of her purpose might be relentless. She regarded Gervais politely, but without warmth.

"Why, good morning, Gervais!" she said in a civil tone. "I didn't hear you coming up the steps. I must have been completely wrapped in thought. Come in here and give me your advice. You know that when Regine made her debut, she and I stood here, just inside this first door. But I have been thinking that if I were planning another important function, I should do it differently. I believe I should emphasize the space beyond the archway and the columns. What do you think?"

Gervais regarded the vast vacant space before him unenthusiastically. The White Ball Room was appropriately named. The twin mantels, the carved cornice, the high ceiling and the wide walls were all white; so was the graceful arch framed with fluted pillars, to which Mrs. Hathaway had just referred, and which divided the room in two well-proportioned parts. Even the floor had been treated to resemble white tiles, though this effect had actually been achieved by putting paint and lacquer over cypress. The room had never been furnished, and its emptiness added to its immensity. When it was decorated for a function and filled with people it lost this air of emptiness, and in the evening, when the great crystal chandeliers glittered and shone, it acquired a resplendent quality. But in the unrelieved light of morning it looked cold and meaningless. Sumptuously furnished as a drawing room and constantly chosen as the center for lavish hospitality, it would have been permeated with genuine splendor; as it was, Gervais felt that its beauty was engulfed in barrenness.

"Perhaps you're right," he said noncommittally. "Of course it would depend on what kind of function you had in mind."

"Well—a ceremony. And afterwards a reception. I think the participants in the—ceremony should enter through this door, and file down between the guests into the further end of the room where the ceremony would take place. Then after this was over, they would receive there, and the guests would file down in their turn. I think it would be very effective. Don't you agree with me?"

"Are you by any chance talking about a wedding ceremony, Mrs. Hathaway?"

"You've become very direct since you've been in the Army, haven't you, Gervais? It's a quality I've always greatly admired, and if you'll forgive me for saying so, it wasn't among your outstanding characteristics when you were younger. Well, since you've put the question to me so bluntly, I'll answer it bluntly, too. Yes, I was talking about a wedding ceremony."

"I always had a feeling Regine would want to be married in the White Ball Room, but I didn't know she's begun to make definite plans for it already. Would it be impertinent for me to ask the name of the lucky man?"

"Surely you must have guessed, Gervais!"

"I'm afraid I haven't. You know I've been gone for a long time, and I've been rather preoccupied. I haven't kept abreast of local love affairs as well as I should have. I'd begun to realize that already. I'll have to ask you to enlighten me."

"No one has given you a hint?"

"No, not a hint."

"Why, it's Sylvestre, Gervais!"

Mrs. Hathaway's handsome, unwrinkled face was still expressionless as she turned from her surveyal of the White Ball Room to look more closely at her caller, and her tone of voice was still even and polite. But there was now an unaccustomed glitter in her hard eyes.

"They've always been greatly attached to each other, you know that, from the time they were children. But I never gave the matter a second thought, as probably you didn't either. My own suspicions weren't aroused until it dawned on me that they were depending almost wholly on each other for companionship. These last two years they've been almost inseparable."

"I see. When all the other men Regine knew had gone to war, it was natural for her to turn to the one who remained at home."

"Why, Gervais! I hope you're not intimating that Sylvestre wouldn't have been glad to go to war, if he hadn't been prevented by grave physical handicaps, not to mention great financial responsibility! You almost sound as if you were jealous of him."

"No, I'm not jealous of him, and I didn't mean to intimate anything I wouldn't say straight out. Just the same, I did have an idea that he and Regine both had other interests."

"Why, Gervais!" Mrs. Hathaway said again. The exclamation had no vehemence, but by this time her hard eyes were gleaming like agates. "You told me, just a minute ago, that you'd been so preoccupied, during your long absence, that you hadn't had any chance to keep abreast of local love affairs."

"That's perfectly true. But I'll have to admit, after all, that since my return——"

"You've been somewhat preoccupied since your return, too, haven't you, Gervais?"

"Yes, somewhat. But that hasn't prevented me from——"

"I'm afraid it has prevented you from being as observant as usual, Gervais," remarked Mrs. Hathaway, who seemed bent on interrupting him. "Otherwise you certainly would have noticed the exceptional degree of congeniality between Regine and Sylvestre. Of course they're both too well-bred to be publicly demonstrative—in fact, I'm sure Sylvestre behaves with complete circumspection towards Regine at all times. He couldn't do otherwise, considering how greatly he respects her. Possibly you've been misled because they didn't seem more romantically inclined. But they are genuinely attached to each other, and very sensibly they have decided——"

"Yes, it does sound sensible, all around, as you outline it," Gervais said, interrupting in his turn. "The Hathaways seem to have lots of sense—I only wish I could say as much for the d'Alverys. Well, congratulations! I must have been blind, as you say, not to notice the drift of things. But I mustn't keep you standing here like this. You'll be all tired out. As a matter of fact, I really came over to see Sylvestre this morning, though of course, I hoped I'd have a glimpse of you and Regine, too. Could you tell me where I could find him? Then I won't detain you any longer."

"I'm not in the least tired," Mrs. Hathaway assured him. "It never tires me to stand. I stand a great deal. And I never lie down. In the daytime, I mean, of course. By the way, how is your dear mother? It's distressing to think of her languishing month after month, with no prospect of improvement."

"Thank you, she's better. She actually got up on her couch this morning for the first time in two years."

"Not really. And Cresside? I hope dear little Cresside didn't get overtired last night. She is so intense about everything she does," Mrs. Hathaway observed, lightly dismissing the subject of Cresside's mother without any apparent surprise at the bed-ridden woman's apparent improvement.

"She was going strong when I last saw her, which was around three this morning. But I do think that's a trifle late for her to be getting in. I waited up for her and suggested as much to her. I hope you won't mind if I suggest the same thing to you. I understand that you've been chaperoning her along with Regine, and it's very kind of you. But I think we'd better have some sort of understanding about the hours she keeps from now on, and also about the matter of escorts. Doubtless you know that Sylvestre brought Cresside home. A very suitable courtesy on the part of her friend's fiancé. But it seems to me it would have been just a shade more suitable if Regine had come along too, and if the whole expedition had taken place a few hours earlier. Of

71

course, Cresside must understand exactly how congenial Regine and Sylvestre are at this point——"

"Of course she must," Mrs. Hathaway said, speaking sharply for the first time.

"Yes, there can't be any difference of opinion about that. But she's rather intense, as you said yourself, and the d'Alverys aren't as sensible as the Hathaways, as *I* said *myself*. Suppose we let it go at that. . . . Where did you say you thought I'd find Sylvestre?"

"Why, Gervais, you've been talking so fast about all sorts of irrelevant things that you haven't given me a chance to tell you! Sylvestre left early this morning."

"He *left!* Where did he go?"

"Why, he went back to New Orleans, of course! He was very sorry not to remain for the banquet in honor of the officers on the submarine chasers. He and Regine had planned to go to the canteen ball afterwards, too. But they knew they could count on you and Cresside to take Regine with you, just as Cresside went to the Mansion with Sylvestre and Regine yesterday."

"I'm sorry, but I'm afraid they can't. I've asked Miss Meredith Randall to go to the canteen dance with me. I haven't any idea what arrangements Cresside's made. . . . When is Sylvestre coming back?"

"Really, Gervais, I don't know. After all, he has very extensive business interests. I assume he'll have to give up a good deal of time to them the next few weeks. He's been Mr. Pereira's right-hand man in that huge coffee importing house. And you know when a man's planning to be married——"

Mrs. Hathaway turned her bright gaze from her guest's face and again looked towards the graceful arch and the white pillars at the further end of the White Ball Room. Obviously, she already visualized the brilliant ceremony of which it was soon to be the scene. Gervais himself could see Regine, caparisoned in point lace and diamonds, as the central figure in this scene, with Sylvestre, sleek and safe, on one side of her, and Mrs. Hathaway, satisfied and smug, on the other. He could hear a priest declaring marriage to be a sacrament, and guests murmuring about the wonders of a true-love match. He could even smell the surfeit sweetness of gardenias and tuberoses, garlanding the room. Momentarily, his bafflement and rage were so submerged in nausea that his head swam. As it cleared, he could hear Mrs. Hathaway still talking brightly.

"Especially when he's planning to wind up all his affairs. He and Regine are going to live at Hathaway Hall. We talked it over, and he agreed with Regine and me that this would be suitable, too. So, you see, we'll have a real neighborhood here presently. Your dear mother, and little Cresside, and that nice girl who lives on St. Napoleon Street —Meredith Randall did you say her name was?—and my daughter and her husband, and you and I. It's nice to think it won't be as lonely on the River Road in the future as it's been in the past, isn't it?"

CHAPTER V

BEFORE DOGGEDLY ENTERING Goldenberg's, Gervais had never been in an emporium catering predominantly to feminine cut-price trade. As he walked down the center aisle towards the elevators, he registered a savage vow that he would never do so again. On one side, the counters were littered with mussy piles of pink silk underwear, placarded at intervals with such alluring signs as "Flat Fits reduced from $2.25 to $1.98"—"Our Step-ins Are a Step in the Right Direction"—"Girdles for Girlies"—"Our Up-to-Date Garments for Up-to-Date Occasions." Hordes of women were hovering over these, jostling each other belligerently, snatching at the soiled frippery and screaming at the salesgirls, who, in their turn, were either answering with impudence or turning a deaf ear to the shrill importunities, as they examined their fingernails, renewed their make-up and patted their new permanents more securely into place. The undiscussed lingerie of a lady, according to Gervais' standards, was made of fine white linen by nuns, whose seclusion was scarcely more complete than the privacy in which their delicate handiwork was selected and worn. He had never seen his own sister in her chemise since she was a small child, and now that the unwelcome idea was forced upon him, he thought that Cresside had probably discarded chemises for just such garments as these that littered the counters.

Turning away from the repugnant sight, he was confronted, on the other side of the aisle, by a special display of cosmetics, in charge of a henna-haired demonstrator who was almost mobbed by the drab customers ready to accept as Gospel truth her statement that the face creams, tissue builders, chin supports, scalp tonics, and reducing salts which she was extolling would transform them overnight into irresistible charmers.

His storming of the store was, at best, a last and desperate venture. From Hathaway Hall, he had driven straight to St. Napoleon Street, where he found Mrs. Randall calmly sweeping her small front porch. All the women on that block of St. Napoleon Street were sweeping their small front porches at this hour, unless they had paused from their labors long enough to cross the street or the yard and chat with their neighbors who were similarly engaged; the one exception was an eccentric who year in and year out sat rocking and crocheting, while her porch went unswept. Fortunately for Gervais, Mrs. Randall was, at the moment, undiverted from her sweeping by neighborhood gossip and Gervais plunged at once into his subject.

"Good morning, Mrs. Randall. Is Merry home? Could I talk to her for a moment?"

"Good mornin', Captain d'Alvery. I didn't expect to see you this early. I sure enough didn't. No, Merry isn't home. You know she's at the store daytimes, all but Sunday. She seldom ever gets home until six o'clock."

In his perturbation, Gervais had completely forgotten about the store and its demands upon Merry. For a moment he was nonplussed.

"It was mighty stupid of me to forget about the store, but I did. Well, I wonder if I could talk to you for a few minutes?"

Mrs. Randall looked rather longingly across the street. She had been expecting her friend, Mrs. Resendez, whose husband was part owner of the Fiesole Restaurant, to come over at almost any moment and tell her about a recipe for ravioli which a cousin who had just come home from Italy had brought to her, and which was said to excel anything of the sort which had ever been eaten in Baton Rouge. She had set her heart on trying out this recipe herself, that very night for supper, and surprising Miss Mittie and Merry with it. However, she knew her duty under the circumstances. If Captain d'Alvery had something serious to say to her, she must listen, for her daughter's sake.

"Why, of co'se, Captain d'Alvery, come on into the livin' room. I'm ashamed to have you see it, the way it looks, but I can't get around to do everything myself, and Miss Mittie and Merry, they both have to start out so early, they can't be any help to me. An' I can't get me any other help, not to save my life. Naturally, I always kept a servant, until the war, but you can't get one now for love nor money. I don't know what we're comin' to, or where all the niggers have gone to. There isn't a woman on this block who's had one workin' for her, as a regular thing, since I can remember. And the wages they ask, at that! Right up to four dollars a week."

Mrs. Randall could not refrain from sighing as she looked across the street, and saw Mrs. Resendez leaning expectantly on her broom. Besides discussing the ravioli recipe, they were to have discussed the servant shortage, which like female weaknesses, both physical and moral, and the ruinous cost of living, was a topic of never-flagging mutual interest. She thought that perhaps if Captain d'Alvery noticed her glance, it would suggest the advisability of brevity. But he did not even see it. He followed Mrs. Randall into the disordered living room, which lay directly beyond the front door, and plunged at once into his subject.

"Mrs. Randall, you know that Merry and I are very fond of each other. In fact, we're engaged. But so far, we hadn't discussed a definite time for the wedding. I want to discuss it with her and with you both. I'd like to get married at once. Well, at least as soon as it could conveniently be arranged."

The final sentence was a concession to the look of dismay, amounting almost to fright, which Gervais had seen on Mrs. Randall's face. As she stared at him dumbly, obviously unable to frame an adequate answer, he went on, trying to speak with less urgency.

"I know a girl needs a little time to get ready. But Merry's so sensible, she won't attach all that much importance to a trousseau, or a big wedding, or anything of the sort. And there's no reason why we should wait. I don't need to tell you I have a beautiful home I can take her to, or that I can support her properly. I hope I don't need to tell you I'll do my level best to make her happy, that I'll try hard to be a good husband. I don't know why I shouldn't succeed. I love her with all my heart and soul. I've loved her for years already. There's nothing on earth I want so much as to have her for my wife."

As he went on, his voice had grown more and more urgent after all, and Mrs. Randall stared at him in greater and greater alarm. But since he could think of nothing more that needed saying, he stopped as abruptly as he had begun, and waited for her to answer him. She opened her mouth, but no sound came out of it. She appeared too paralyzed for speech, until the approaching clang of a bell, ringing agreeably but insistently, roused her to relieved utterance.

"That's my vegetable man a-comin'," she said. "And less I rush out the minute he gets opposite this house, he goes right on and he won't turn back. He's peculiar that way. If you'll excuse me, Captain d'Alvery, I'll see what he has this mornin'. It'll save me walkin' all the way to market and back to do my grocery shoppin'."

Mrs. Randall hurried from the living room, leaving the front door open behind her. Gervais was certain she had welcomed the diversion, though he was beginning to feel slightly aggrieved and greatly amazed. It had not occurred to him that Merry's mother, as well as his own, might be averse to the marriage, and there was certainly nothing in Mrs. Randall's manner to suggest that she was eager to receive him as a son-in-law. He watched her while she crossed the small porch, flew down the steps and across the sidewalk, and began to bargain with the shabby Negro whose unpainted pushcart was piled with wilted vegetables. Life had dealt harshly with Mrs. Randall, and everything about her appearance betrayed this. It was obvious, not only that she did not have much money to spend on her personal appearance but that she had long since ceased to feel this mattered. Her iron-gray hair was gathered up into an untidy knot surrounded by sidecombs, placed more or less at random. Her morning dress, which was hardly more than a wrapper, was also iron-gray and hung unevenly over the dingy petticoat which protruded beneath it. Her shapeless shoes were down at the heel. As she argued with the vegetable man, she raised one hand in expostulation, and even at a distance, Gervais could see how worn and misshapen it was from neglect and toil; her wide, flat wedding ring, gleaming in the morning sunshine, accentuated its roughness and redness. Gervais thought of his mother's long slim fingers, folded marble-like over her white sheet, and suddenly the contrast between her hands and Mrs. Randall's seemed to symbolize all the difference between Merry's traditions and his own. Never before had he thought of them in that light; never before had they seemed so irreconcilable.

Eventually, Mrs. Randall stopped browbeating the vegetable man, and extracting a small shabby purse from the folds of her gray ging-ham dress, counted out a few coins, and grudgingly handed them to him one by one. Then she took a bunch of the wilted vegetables from him, and went over to speak to Mrs. Resendez, who was not buying vegetables that morning, and who was still leaning expectantly on her broom. The conversation between the two women went on and on. Gervais began to think that his future mother-in-law had resorted to this expedient in order to terminate the one with him. But at last she turned, with a slowness which contrasted oddly with the speed that had marked her departure, and came back to the living room and sat down again, placing the wilted vegetables on the table beside her.

"He didn't have anything but carrots and cabbages," she said, referring contemptuously to the disappearing man, whose bell had now become a mere tinkle in the distance. "He seldom ever does. There's another one comes along a little later though, with a horse and wagon. He generally has more of a variety." She gazed longingly out of the door, as if hoping that the second vegetable man might come into view and thus furnish another diversion. Then she sighed again, and forced herself to look at Gervais.

"You've sorta taken me by surprise, Captain d'Alvery, and that's a fact," she said. "Of course I knew you and Merry were keeping com-pany, but I didn't feel so sure it would ever come to anything. I thought if you were really set on marrying her, you'd have done it before you went to France. Merry's never said anything. That isn't her way. But I reckon she was disappointed not to be a war bride, like some of the girls she went with. It's natural for a girl to want to do the same thing other girls are doing." Fleetingly Gervais thought of Cresside, remem-bering that he tried to excuse her conduct on a similar theory, and the comparison grated. "Why, one girl Merry knew got to go to England, to marry her beau," Mrs. Randall went on. "He was a nice fellow, too. I think Merry was his first choice. But she did have a crush on you, Captain d'Alvery, from the first time she ever saw you."

"Yes. And I had one on her, too. But I had an idea it wasn't fair to marry her before I went away."

"Maybe you're right and I wouldn't say you're not sincere. Most generally though, I have noticed that when men talk about it not being fair to marry girls, they're figurin' that's the best kind of excuse they can think up. If they really want to get married, they're not so self-sacrificin' but what they'll do it. They don't stop to think whether it's fair to the girl or not. They're too busy thinkin' of what they'll get out of it themselves, that they can't get any ways else."

Mrs. Randall no longer spoke with shyness and hesitation, but with the increasing confidence inspired by the courage of her convictions. Gervais was annoyed to feel himself flushing.

"I'm sorry I made such a mistake. I realize now that it was a mistake. But I didn't make it because I didn't love her, or because I hadn't always wanted to marry her. And I'm not going to make a mistake like

76

that a second time. I've told you already that I'd like to be married right away. . . . Do you think you could manage a wedding here at the end of this week? Not a large wedding, of course, just the two families and a few intimate friends."

He spoke in the casual way natural to a man whose household has always adapted itself almost automatically to entertaining. It did not occur to him that for women in Mrs. Randall's category, any kind of a party, but most of all a wedding, represented a complete upheaval in their normal manner of living, even if their hearts were in the project, which obviously hers was not in this case. She had not told him that except for Merry's disappointment, she would have been glad of his procrastination and that she would have been still more pleased if his intentions had continued to be indefinite. But the growing certainty of this increased his discomfiture.

"I don't see how I could," Mrs. Randall was saying firmly. "I never was one to entertain much, even when I had help. And now without any, I wouldn't know how to swing it. Miss Mittie and Merry are both gone all day, like I told you, and they're mighty tired when they get in at night. Besides, maybe you forget we're in mournin'. I'm not lucky, like your mother, gettin' her son back covered with medals. I lost both of mine."

"I know you did, Mrs. Randall, and of course it's men like your sons who are the real heroes of this war. Malcolm and Vail both were mighty fine fellows, and you've a right to feel proud of them. No one knows that any better than I do or realizes more keenly what a great loss you've had. Of course, I wouldn't expect you to feel like having a large wedding for Merry, so soon after her brothers' death. I'm sure she wouldn't want it herself and I tried to explain before that I didn't have an elaborate function in mind. But——"

"There isn't space in this house even for a small company," Mrs. Randall said firmly. "It's as much as we can do to find chairs for half a dozen people, when they drop in for Sunday night supper. I don't encourage 'em to do it, but once in a while Merry puts something over on me. We've got quite a lot of kin, and I presume you have, too. I don't know how we'd accommodate 'em. . . . Would your mother be able to come? Seems to me I've heard she was puny."

"She's been a bedridden invalid for some years," Gervais said rather coldly. "I'm afraid she couldn't possibly. Aside from her, my sister Cresside's my only close kin. I'd rather like to ask Fabian d'Alvery, but it really isn't necessary—he's only a second cousin. So you see, the family wouldn't take up much room."

"But you'd want to ask your friends, people like the Hathaways, wouldn't you?" persisted Mrs. Randall. "Most everyone in Baton Rouge thought it was that Hathaway girl you meant to marry. I've heard it said dozens of times. Why, Mrs. Resendez was telling me just now——"

"Like lots of other rumors, that one didn't have a grain of truth in it. As a matter of fact, Regine Hathaway's engaged to someone else."

"I reckon she got engaged to someone else after she found out there wasn't any doubt but what you were engaged to Merry," Mrs. Randall said, again with her deadly air of conviction. "If we were to have a wedding party, I'd ask the Hathaways if I didn't ask another living soul. Well, we could make room for your sister all right, of course. But then she'd naturally want to ask her intended. His name's Sylvestre Tremaine, isn't it?"

The last person whom Gervais wished to discuss with Mrs. Randall was Sylvestre. But he could see all too well that Sylvestre must be invited to the wedding, not on account of Cresside, but on account of Regine. While he was trying to frame an appropriately evasive answer, Mrs. Randall went relentlessly on.

"Maybe you could have the marriage ceremony performed at the parsonage," she said, "and then have a wedding breakfast at Fiesole's Restaurant afterwards. Of course, we'd have to make it small, to keep down the cost; but Fiesole's in the habit of catering to wedding parties. There's a private dining room there, and everything. They even arrange for the decorations, big tissue-paper bells and place cards with cupids on them—I'm sure they'd take a special interest in this case, because you see my friend Mrs. Resendez——"

"I hope very much you'll give up the idea of having a wedding breakfast at Fiesole's," Gervais said almost curtly. "It doesn't appeal to me at all. In fact, it ties in with a mental picture of wedding guests tearing through the town in open automobiles, headed by the bride and groom all tooting their horns and singing at the top of their lungs. It may be a good old Italian custom, but it isn't the way the d'Alverys do things. And Merry's going to be a d'Alvery, from now on."

"Merry's a Randall through and through," her mother retorted fiercely. "She'll never be anything different. *She's* got backbone." Mrs. Randall had begun to rock, and the sound of the rockers formed a squeaky accompaniment to her strident voice. "I didn't mean to mention it, but since you're so bound and determined that I should go to all the trouble of having a wedding in this house, I may as well tell you that I haven't had a drop of running water since last Saturday. There's something the matter with the pipe between this house and the Serensky's, next door. I reckon it's rotted out. Anyway, I can't get it fixed. It isn't as if we had a public water supply in Baton Rouge, like I hear they do in most places up North, even small places. I can't get the water company to fix it. They claim they're not responsible for the leak, because the pipe's in the driveway and not in the street. I can't get a private plumber either. You ought to know how it is these days— as much as your life is worth to find a mechanic. They're even scarcer than servants. And if you ask me, I think it would be mighty embarrassing, if some of the guests should want to use the bathroom and we had to tell 'em to go next door to the Serenskys. I wouldn't think of asking the Serenskys to the wedding ordinarily, but of course I'd have to if my guests used their bathroom, and that's what Miss Mittie and

78

Merry and I been doin' ever since last Saturday. Except that of course at night, we've——"

"I'll speak to the President of the Water Company. I know him quite well," Gervais announced, cutting in again before Mrs. Randall could go into further details concerning makeshift sanitary arrangements. "And I'll find a 'private plumber,' too. I guarantee you'll have your pipe fixed before night, by someone. I don't know who, but someone. So let's consider that point settled. However, there's another I think we'll have to take up. You spoke, a few moments ago, of having the marriage ceremony performed at the 'parsonage.' I don't know quite what you meant by that, but perhaps I ought to remind you that Merry and I will have to be married by a priest."

"I'd never consent to that, never in this world," Mrs. Randall declared. "You'll be married by our minister, Mr. Hawkins, or you won't be married at all."

"We wouldn't be married at all, according to my faith, if Mr. Hawkins, whoever he is, performed a dozen ceremonies."

"Mr. Hawkins is the pastor of the First Baptist Church. Merry and I have been regular attendants there for years and years. I reckon a girl's got a right to be married by the minister of the church she's always attended if she wants to. What do you mean, you wouldn't be married at all? Of course you'd be married. I'd see to it that you were, all right."

"I'm going to see to it that we are, all right. If you don't think I'm telling you the truth, you might ask your friends, Mrs. Resendez and Mrs. Serensky, what happens sometimes under the sort of arrangement you're suggesting. It's perfectly regular, of course, if the bride and groom are both Protestants. But if the groom's a Catholic, and the bride isn't, he often finds a Protestant ceremony a mighty convenient excuse later on."

"Well, if you're beginning to think up convenient excuses again, Captain d'Alvery—of course, you thought of a considerable number before you went to France, and if you've started all over——"

She rose, bristling with rage. Gervais, no less enraged, also jumped up. But his furious retort was drowned by the clanging of a bell. The second vegetable man, the one who was the proud possessor of a horse and wagon instead of a hand cart, was now coming down the street. Mrs. Randall rushed out to meet him, in her haste knocking the wilted vegetables she had already purchased from the little table where she had placed them. Gervais stepped on them as he strode after her. If she saw him, as he followed her down the steps, and turned in the direction of North Boulevard, she gave no sign of it. She was already deep in vituperative argument with the second vegetable man.

It was this appalling encounter with his future mother-in-law that had driven Gervais to the doors of Goldenberg's. He was determined to see Merry and to see her at once. He did not care where she was working or for whom; he meant to get her away and take her to some place where he could talk to her, privately, urgently and immediately. As he charged past the "Flat-Fits Reduced" and the henna-haired demonstrator, he belatedly realized that he could not go rushing through the store at random, expecting that sooner or later he would fortuitously come face to face with her. He did not see a floorwalker anywhere, and the complete absence of such functionaries served to remind him that floorwalkers were now as scarce as plumbers, and that he had not yet done anything about the Randalls' rusty pipes. Finally he asked the slatternly elevator girl, who sat straddling a stool, staring into space and chewing gum, if she could tell him how he could find Miss Meredith Randall.

"Ah only come yestiddy. Ah dunno where anything is yet."

"She's Mr. Goldenberg's private secretary. Don't you know where Mr. Goldenberg's office is?"

"No, suh. Ah jus' don' tol' you, Ah only come yestiddy. Ah dunno where anything is."

Her lack of information seemed to be a thing of complete unconcern to her. Her gaze became more and more blank as she continued to chew gum and stare into space, though eventually she condescended to set the elevator in motion. Gervais decided that his only possible course would be to get out on every floor and keep on inquiring, with the hope that he might eventually encounter someone who had been in the store longer than a day.

He had reached the sixth floor, and a stage of infuriated desperation, when the unbelievable happened; he saw Merry herself going down the aisle ahead of him. Her back was towards him and she was yards away; but the sheen of her hair, the set of her head, and the grace of her carriage were all unmistakable. He did not know another girl who held herself like that or who walked like that, so uprightly yet so harmoniously; no other girl in all the world had so Biblical a "crown of glory." He hurried after her and caught up with her, putting a detaining hand on her shoulder.

"Merry!" he said breathlessly. "Merry, I thought I'd never find you!"

"Why, hello, Gervais! What's the matter? Why did you specially want to find me, in the middle of the morning?"

She looked at him delightedly, without any effort to conceal her joy in seeing him; but there was gaiety as well as gladness in her brown eyes. Her blithe disregard of the possibility that any serious trouble could have instigated his search was soothing in itself. Nevertheless, he continued to speak excitedly.

"All kinds of things are the trouble. I've got to talk to you about them right away."

"But you can't. I'm in the middle of dictation, I just went out to get the proofs of tomorrow's ads for the *State-Times*. Mr. Goldenberg always o.k.'s them himself, the last thing." She glanced down at the sheaf of papers she was carrying, directing Gervais' glance towards them, too. "But when I've taken them back to the Advertising Manager, we've got to go on with the letters."

"You've got to get time off to talk to me."

"I'll talk to you this evening. I thought you were coming to see me this evening anyway."

"Well, I was. But I decided, last night, that I'd better come to see you before that. And this morning I decided that the earlier I saw you the better."

He spoke not only with increasing urgency, but with increasing harshness. Merry had often heard him speak urgently, but she had never before heard him speak harshly. She continued to look at him lovingly, but a little of the gaiety went out of her look and she regarded him more thoughtfully.

"I'm fairly serious about this, Merry. In fact, I'm in deadly earnest. I want to talk to you right away."

"All right. Let's go to Mr. Goldenberg's office together, and tell him so. Perhaps he'll let someone else take the letters. Anyway, we can ask him."

She started down the aisle again, straightening the papers she was carrying as she went. The Department of Draperies and Floor Coverings was in front of the Executive Offices, and several scatter rugs were cluttering up the aisle. Gervais could hardy resist kicking them out of his way, and he was doubly ashamed of this impulse when Merry, who had apparently guessed it, stooped down and put them back in their proper place, folding them neatly. Since there was not a clerk in sight, no one except Gervais appreciated this service.

"We're terribly short-handed," she said, repeating the popular theme song so pleasantly that it sounded inoffensive for once. "But I reckon we won't be, much longer. I hear a boy applied for a job, this very morning." She smiled, and stretching out her hand, caught his in a sudden squeeze. "Don't worry, Gervais," she said softly. "Of course, I don't know what the matter seems to be, but I am sure we can straighten it out, between us. . . . This is where we turn," she said, nodding towards a huge pulsating red arrow suspended overhead, which pointed towards a corridor running at a right angle from the Department of Draperies and Floor Coverings. "We have to go through the dingiest part of the store to get to Mr. Goldenberg's office. But I'm used to it so I don't mind it. I hope you won't mind it too much either."

It certainly was dingy, Gervais agreed, and though he did not say so, he found it as depressing as he had found the first floor distasteful. One side of the unpainted wall was lined with a long row of steel lockers; on the other side was a large gaping hole, evidently the opening of the freight elevator, since harsh and creaking sounds seemed to herald its approach; beyond was an adjustment bureau, where several portly, vituperative women were arguing with harassed clerks about merchandise they wished to take back. Turning again, Merry led Gervais past the fire escape, and several small glassed-in cubicles labeled in black letters with the names and titles of the functionaries to whom they were allotted. Then, pausing before a sign which read NO VISITORS ALLOWED, she pressed his hand hard, before releasing hers from his grip with gentleness but determination.

"This is my little cubbyhole, and that's Mr. Goldenberg's office just beyond," she said. "We mustn't go in there holding hands. It wouldn't be the best approach. . . . We'll do it again afterwards, though," she added with a momentary return of gaiety. Then she opened the door. "Mr. Goldenberg," she said, without any preamble whatever, "this is my fiancé, Captain d'Alvery. I don't think you've met him before. He's sorry to burst in on you like this and I'm sorry to have him. But it's very important for him to have a chance to talk to me for a few minutes. I'd be grateful if he could have it. Perhaps you'd let Hazel take your letters. I don't think she's gone out to lunch yet. I just saw her, when I went down for the ads. And Mr. Sears *has* gone out. Captain d'Alvery and I could step into his office if you don't think he'd mind, and if you wouldn't yourself."

The thickset gray-haired man, who had the look of being shaved by an expert barber and manicured by a meticulous operator, turned in his swivel chair and looked appraisingly at his visitor. Gervais noticed that he was dressed with the precision so frequently affected by those who have not had the opportunity of wearing good clothes casually, early in life. His high stiff collar had a glazed look. His dark suit was so expertly tailored and so carefully pressed that it gave the effect of being cautiously worn and for the first time. Gervais had the impression that Mr. Goldenberg would much rather have worn loud sporting checks and a pink silk shirt, not to mention a diamond stickpin and a carbuncle ring, and that his conservative costume represented considerable will power and a high regard for the conventional and the correct. At the same time he was astute enough to guess and just enough to admit that Mr. Goldenberg's natural tastes were essentially alien rather than essentially vulgar. They were the logical ones of his race and background, and displayed in their indigenous setting they would have been fitting and harmonious. Suddenly Gervais seemed to see the executive as he might have appeared wearing the rich robes of a Levantine merchant, presiding with dignity and distinction over an establishment where gold-threaded brocades and jewel-colored rugs were sold, as they had been in the same place and under similar auspices for centuries. It was a pleasing and impressive picture. Gervais also noticed that his host's eyes had mercifully escaped this thorough process of control and transformation. They were very dark, slightly bloodshot, roving and expressive. They missed nothing within the range of their vision, and there were those who were convinced that somehow they saw far beyond it. Gervais himself immediately had this feeling, and it was not an entirely comfortable one.

"I am very glad to have an opportunity of meeting Captain d'Alvery,"

82

Mr. Goldenberg said agreeably. "Naturally I went to the station to see his triumphant return. And, as you know, I also watched the parade. But that is not like a personal meeting." His manner was courteous, but somehow he contrived to convey the impression that while he recognized the returning hero in Gervais, he remembered that the d'Alverys and the Goldenbergs had never mingled socially, and that since this was the case, he would not be the first to indicate any desire for a change. He did not rise, himself, and he did not ask his visitor to sit down; his black bloodshot eyes traveled slowly from Gervais to Merry and back again. "Please accept my congratulations, Captain d'Alvery," he went on at last. "I'd heard rumors, but I confess I hadn't listened to them—perhaps because I didn't want to. Miss Meredith's been with me a long time. I don't need to tell you that I consider her services invaluable. Under the circumstances, I suppose I ought to be thankful that you are asking to interrupt them only temporarily. . . . By all means, send Miss Hazel in to me, Miss Meredith."

CHAPTER VI

In determining to see Merry at once, and to take her some place where he could talk to her urgently, Gervais had formed no clear mental picture of what this place should be or could be. But certainly he had not visualized a glass-enclosed cubicle beside a public corridor in a department store. There was neither comfort nor privacy in the disorderly little office to which Merry led the way, sitting down in the straight-backed chair which was evidently provided for Mr. Sears' stenographer, and indicating the one by the little old desk for Gervais, after removing a pile of papers from it. Having done this much, she took no further initiative, but sat smiling at him expectantly, waiting for him to speak. His own rebellious impulse to protest against the inadequacy and unsuitability of the setting was curbed only by the certainty that there was no alternative to it, and that he must accept it and make the best of it.

"Merry," he said, and stopped. If they only had been safe from intrusion, if he only could have put his arm around her or even taken her hand, it would not have been so hard, it would not all have seemed so ugly and crude, in spite of the water cooler and the insurance calendars and the misshapen racks standing beside the steel files and hung with limp sample dresses. But he could see two giggling girls pausing to peer into the cubicle as they passed by it, and after they went on, their giggles grew louder and were interspersed with whispers. Merry must have heard them, too, but they did not seem to upset her as much as they did Gervais.

"Yes, honey?" she said. "What is it, Gervais? How can I help you if you don't tell me what the matter is?"

"I'm trying to tell you. But it's damn hard to do it in a place like this. I get all balled up. I know I'm going to say the wrong thing, because everything else is all wrong."

"I know. You'd like to say it under the colonnade at Belle Heloise in the moonlight. But don't you think we care enough for each other, Gervais, to forget the kind of place we're in, so long as we can be in it together?"

"You make me feel like a fool when you put it like that. Hell, the reason I hate all this so is because of you, and the way I feel about you. If you can't see my point, perhaps I'd better not go on."

"I do see your point. But I can't believe it's the most important one, just now. The most important point was that you wanted to have a chance to talk to me immediately. Well, you've got it. So I think you'd better go on."

"All right. I want you to marry me."

"But I *am* going to marry you. *I* want to marry *you.*"

"Enough to marry me right away?"

"Why, I reckon so. What do you mean by 'right away,' honey?"

"I want you to marry me today."

"Why, Gervais?"

She did not shrink away from the bald statement, but her steady eyes grew more searching as she looked at him. He answered with increasing vehemence.

"Because I'm afraid if you don't you won't marry me at all."

"Yes, I will. I promise I will. But I won't marry you today either. If you hadn't completely lost your head you'd know I couldn't do that."

"I haven't lost my head yet. But so many other people seem to be losing theirs that I'm likely to, any minute."

"Is that why you want me to marry you today, Gervais? Because so many people are losing their heads?"

"Yes, partly. Yours is always so clear. You'd help to clarify the others."

"Then what you really mean is that you need me, or think you do? Not that you want me?"

"Good God, Merry, don't talk like that! As if I'd wounded your vanity! I told you I knew I'd do this all wrong. But hell——"

"You haven't wounded my vanity. You don't really think I'm vain, do you, Gervais? Of course you don't. You know I'm not. But I do want to get this straight. I can't help you if I don't understand. If you want me more today than yesterday, I'd like to know why. And if you don't, if you only need me more than you did yesterday, I'd like to know that, too. I'd marry you just as quickly if I thought you needed

84

me more as I would if I thought you wanted me more. But you'd have to tell me the truth about it first."

"All right. The truth is I'm facing a very ugly, complicated situation. If you were my wife, you could help me straighten it out. You'd be in a position to, you'd have a right to. You're not and you haven't as long as you're only engaged to me."

"Can you tell me what this situation is, Gervais?"

"I can outline it for you. I can't go into details."

"Very well. Outline it for me."

"Primarily it concerns my sister. I'm very much disturbed about her."

For the first time Merry glanced away from Gervais, resting her face on her hand and looking thoughtfully towards the door of the cubicle. The two girls who had passed down the corridor a few minutes earlier were clattering back again now, giggling harder and whispering more brazenly than before. Merry nodded to them, and then spoke to them, briefly but pleasantly. Their bold silly conduct obviously did not upset her, and their untimely appearance did not seem to interrupt her train of thought. When they had gone, their babble dying away in the distance, Merry turned back to Gervais with her steady smile.

"I'm sorry," she said simply. Her tone carried conviction, but no curiosity. Gervais had an idea that this was not only because Merry was incurious by disposition, but also because she was not especially surprised. She probably knew a good deal about Cresside already, and as far as that went, about Regine too, and he experienced a momentary relief at the thought that he would not have to dwell on Regine's part in the picture, at least not immediately. "I'm very sorry, Gervais," Merry said again. "But I don't know that I could be helpful, just because I'm sorry. I don't think Cresside wants anyone to interfere with her, do you? I don't think she'd let anyone do it."

"No, I don't think she wants anyone to interfere with her. But I do think she may want someone to stand by her. Another woman."

"She has your mother, Gervais."

"My mother's been a recluse ever since my father died. I thought I'd told you that. Anyway, she's been so preoccupied with herself that she's overlooked Cresside's problems. They can't be overlooked much longer. Someone has got to help her solve them."

Again Merry glanced away. This time Gervais went on without waiting for her to make any comments.

"I told my mother, when I went home yesterday, that I was going to marry you. This morning I saw her maid, Lucie, for a moment, and she said *maman* was getting up—for the first time in two years. That means she intends to resume control of Belle Heloise. Before you can supplant her as its chatelaine."

"She doesn't want me there, Gervais?"

"You've asked for the truth, so I'm going to give it to you. No, she doesn't. She'll make trouble for you, Merry, she'll make trouble for both of us. We can't prevent her making some. But if we get married right away, if you simply step in before she can stop you and begin to take charge before she can get her strength back, we'll avert a good deal. I'll make it as easy for you as I can, and I can make it a good deal easier if we start the struggle right away. That's the second reason why I'm urging you to marry me at once."

"I see. That is, I think I do."

"Do you really? Gosh, I can't tell you how thankful I am. Merry, you may think I don't realize my own luck, but I do. You're wonderful to take it like this. There isn't a girl in a thousand who could."

"Of course there is. Any girl would, who loved the man she was going to marry as much as I love you. . . . Is there anything else, Gervais?"

"Yes. Yes." His words were coming in a rush now, his need of her piling higher and higher upon his yearning. "A third reason is that your mother's dead set against our marriage, too. I can't understand why she should be, but she is. And I don't know how much opposition you can buck without breaking under it, but I should think there might be a limit, if it went on and on. We'd have to put an end to it some time anyhow. It better be right away. It's got to be."

"I beg pardon. Is Mr. Sears out? He told me to let him see this as soon as I could get it ready. He wants to be sure the goods go out this afternoon."

A weedy-looking shipping clerk was standing in the doorway, holding a bill of lading in his hands. Gervais sprang up, swearing under his breath. Merry rose, too, and walked over to the door.

"I'm sorry, Tim," she said quietly. "Mr. Sears hasn't come back from lunch yet. But if you'll leave that with me, I'll see that he gets it, as soon as he does come in." She reached out her hand for the bill of lading, and after a moment's hesitation, the weedy-looking boy gave it to her, muttering something under his breath as he turned away. Merry laid the bill of lading carefully on the table under a glass paperweight; then she went to the door of the cubicle, closed it, locked it, and came back to Gervais. She did not take his hand again, but she stood so close to him that her nearness was like an embrace.

"I think you're right. I think it has got to be," she said gently. "That is, it's got to be as soon as it can without hurting anyone else more than we have to. I'm afraid it's going to hurt your mother so much anyway that it won't matter when we do it. So, as you say, it better be right off, as far as she's concerned. But I've got to think about my own mother. Not about her opposition. I can buck that, whatever you believe, and I will. But about her needs. You see, I support her. I've got obligations and problems, too. If I stop earning money, she won't have enough to live on. She hasn't a clear title to our house—it's mortgaged, and Miss Mittie only pays sixteen dollars a month for her room. If there wasn't any other way to manage, would you let me ask my mother to live with us? Of course, I wouldn't do it except as a last resort, because I don't think it would be a good plan. But would you, if I thought I had to?"

"I don't think it would be a good plan either. Not that I'd begrudge her a home, you know that. And there's plenty of room at Belle Heloise. I know it wouldn't work out well though." With merciless clarity he foresaw the clash of temperaments between Merry's mother and his own. But he gritted his teeth. "I'll let you do anything you want—I mean anything you think best, if you'll only marry me today," he said desperately.

"Please don't talk as if you were bribing me to marry you, honey," she said. She still spoke gently, but there was a hint of quiet reproof in her tone. "You know I'm not trying to bargain with you. I'm only trying to be fair with everybody. I've got to think of Mr. Goldenberg, too. He's always been very kind to me, and very generous. I can't suddenly leave him in the lurch, without anyone to do his work. I'll have to tell him, straight from the shoulder, what you want me to do, and make him understand, without going into detail, that it's important I should. If he says he can spare me, I'll go right to my desk and pick up my things. If he says he can't, I'll have to give him a few days' notice."

"You mean that if Mr. Goldenberg comes across you *will* marry me today?"

"Why, that's what you asked me to do, isn't it? That's what you want, isn't it? We *could* get married today, couldn't we? That is, there isn't any law about waiting after you get a license, or red tape of any other sort that would prevent it?"

"No," he said hoarsely. "No—that is, I don't think so. Or if there is, there's probably some way of getting around it, when there's a good reason why anyone should. There's a priest here in town I know very well. Father Navarre, his name is. He's a darn good scout. Comes from the swamp country, but he's been a chaplain in the war, and just now he's in Baton Rouge. I believe he'd understand, if I explained to him. Yes, I'm almost sure he would. Most priests are very understanding, Merry. You'll find that out."

"I'm sure I shall. And you mustn't mind, Gervais, if mother is bitter about your religion. She can't help being. It's just the way she's made. Of course, I'm going to ask her if she won't come with us, to see us married. I think I ought to do that. But if she says no, I'll go with you to see Father Navarre, just the same. We'll do what he tells us to."

Merry glanced towards the closed door and listened intently. There was no one in sight, and there was no sound of footsteps in the corridor either. She came still closer to him.

"I think it would be all right for us to kiss each other now," she said. "And I think it would be nice if we did, too, don't you?"

It was not until hours later, when they were on their way to Belle

Heloise, that Gervais was able to put into words his feeling for what she had done. Merry listened lovingly to what he said as they drove along the River Road in the twilight, with his arm tight around her waist and her head resting quietly on his shoulder. The words sounded very sweet to her, and she was happy to have him speak them; like every other woman, she wanted to hear the man she loved keep on telling her he was certain that no man had ever loved his wife so much before or with so much reason. But she did not require the assurance. No eloquent declaration of passion spoken in the scented moonlight, under the mystic colonnade, could have carried with it the force of the desperate plea which Gervais had made to her in the dingy little cubicle of the merchandising manager. If he had so besought her holding her closely embraced in some bower of beauty, she might have hesitated, fearing that her own stirred senses had confused her to such a degree that she could not see an involved issue clearly, or act on it wisely. But there had been no withstanding a supplication so starkly set apart from romantic appeal. She knew his need of her for what it was, and she could measure it, not by faltering or failure on his part, but by her own need of him.

She moved a little, lifting her head. It had been downcast because at first she had been so overcome by the prodigality of his praise that she could not bring herself to face him. Now she was calmer, and joyously accepting his tribute, she raised adoring eyes to his. Momentarily she had forgotten there was anyone else in the world except her husband and herself. But as she looked up, she became aware of the place they were passing, where a vast house rose like a white palace beyond the green grace of its encircling grove, and of a beautiful girl, who looked like a white-robed queen, standing in the gallery and watching them. Gervais did not see the motionless and mocking figure of Regine. He had bent over to kiss Merry again, and he was still forgetful that there was anyone else in the world. But Merry had already emerged from her fairyland of dreams to confront the menace of reality.

PART II

"Come, Haste to the Wedding"

June 30, 1919

"Come, haste to the wedding, ye friends and ye neighbors!
　The lovers their bliss shall no longer delay;
Forget all your sorrow, your care, and your labours,
　And let ev'ry heart beat with rapture today.
　　　　Ye votaries all
　　　　Attend to my call. . . .
　　　　And come at our bidding
　　　　To this happy wedding!"

—This was a favorite selection for festivals along the River Road. Eliza MacHatton-Ripley, who lived at "Arlington," wrote in her book of memoirs: ". . . The 'plantation band' with the inspiring airs of 'Monie Musk' and 'Come, Haste to the Wedding,' put wings to the giddy feet— how the happy moments fled!" It is found in Songs of England, *edited by J. L. Hatton and Eaton Faning.*

PART II

"Come, Haste to the Wedding"

June 30, 1919

CHAPTER VII

MEREDITH D'ALVERY STIRRED sleepily in her big bed and, almost subconsciously, stretched out her arms. It was their emptiness that awakened her. But she was beginning to remember now. . . . Gervais had risen, as usual, when the plantation bell rang. He had done it quietly, trying not to disturb her, and as she half opened her eyes and he had seen her looking at him drowsily but adoringly, he had come to the bedside, telling her to lie down again, like a good girl, and go back to sleep. She had lain down again because he had asked her to; she did everything he requested, not tamely, but exultantly, for nothing made her so happy as to feel she was contributing in any way to his contentment; and she had gone back to sleep again immediately, because nowadays she was unable to set any limits on her hours of slumber. It no longer seemed strange to her to lie in bed, late in the morning, after Gervais was up, as it had in the beginning. If it had not been for that joyous tractability of hers, she would have rebelled when he first told her this was what she was expected to do. But lately it not only seemed natural for her to luxuriate in early morning idleness; it seemed inevitable. She could not rouse herself if she tried. Over and over again she was engulfed by the prolonged, profound slumber of early pregnancy.

She was temporarily emerging from the depths of this gulf now, and in a few minutes she would ring for Creassy, who was Lou Ida's daughter and her own maid, assigned to her on the very evening of her arrival at Belle Heloise. The house servants all had their own bells, which hung in a row on the wall of the back gallery, near the kitchen. Each of these bells had a different sound, and the servants could tell by the tone, when they heard one ringing, whether it was for them or not.

These little tinkling house bells had not the great importance of the huge bronze bell by the mule shed, which had been cast by Thiac-Maignon Durand in 1824 and was duly inscribed to that effect. But they had their own small and significant place in plantation life just the same.

After Merry rang for her maid, Creassy would bring her coffee and draw her bath and lay out her clothes, and after she had drunk the coffee she would rise and dress in a leisurely way; then she would do a variety of inconsequential, unexacting things until dinner time. But after dinner she would go to sleep again. She would come back to this beautiful bed, which Creassy would have made up freshly and turned down invitingly; she would stretch out between the linen sheets which were so cool against her skin and drift quietly away into unconsciousness. The room was very restful in the afternoon. There was something about the artificial dimness which Creassy created by excluding the sunlight with shutters which made it seem even more tranquil than it was at night. Its darkness then was different, less uniform, less sheltering and enclosed, more thrilling and provocative. The shutters were swung wide at the open windows then, the moonlight streamed in, the fireflies flitted through the live oaks and camphor trees in the Small Yard, the lights on the riverboats flashed above the levee. Merry could see the fireflies and the boat lights without raising herself from her pillows, and often the moonlight seemed to saturate the very sheets.

These luminous aspects of the night were inescapable. But the afternoon sunshine could not prevail against Creassy's ingenuity. For long hours Merry was oblivious of its quivering intensity. She woke refreshed to face an evening enlivened by the presence of Gervais and an occasional visitor, but otherwise as uneventful as the morning. And then Gervais, who, unlike Merry, had been up early, was ready for bed early, too. She was back in the big square shuttered chamber and this time Gervais was with her.

This was one of the reasons, of course, why the darkness of the night was so different from the dusk of afternoon. She was not alone in the darkness, she was not watching the fireflies and the riverboats by herself, the moonlight did not bathe her in solitary state. And though Gervais' early rising was a convenient parlor pretext for an early bedtime, his pretense of weariness scarcely saw him up the stairs. He was an eager and demanding lover, assured and triumphant from the very first. The unprotesting acceptance of his dominance, which he himself had foreseen, had freed him from all those compunctions which a bride less rapt but more reluctant might have roused, and Merry was unresentfully aware of this. She could have exacted more restraint and gentleness, but in so doing she would have forfeited some of the glory she had gained. Untutored as she was in the ways of love, she knew that this was so; increasingly she rejoiced in the unquenched passion which she now could so ardently return. The darkness of her room at night was the majestic cloak enfolding her with her beloved.

92

No thought of a child had crossed her mind during the first blissful weeks of her marriage; it had been overflowing with thoughts of Gervais, with love for him, with thanksgiving for the fulfillment he had brought her. But now that she knew she was pregnant, she was doubly happy at the realization that she could take her place with all the other proud women whose passion had been productive and whose children were the visible symbol and proof of shared rapture and secret communion. More than this: having been brought, as an outsider, into surroundings where productiveness was the universal rule, she knew she would have remained indefinitely an alien unless she could have met existing standards and set new ones. Now she was not only the expectant mother of an heir to a great heritage, and as such entitled to the homage which no barren wife could have commanded; she was conscious of a mystic bond with the joyous fecundity which she saw on every side.

Even the drowsiness against which she no longer struggled had been a safeguard and support. Prostrated as she was by it, she could not supplant her mother-in-law aggressively or offensively. The course of action on which Gervais, in his anger, had been determined, was perforce delayed, and meanwhile the gradual readjustment of the household was taking place with far less friction than if he had been able to carry out his original wilful purpose. Defiantly, he had placed Merry at the head of the table when he brought her home after their precipitate marriage, and she had sat there, frightened but firm, watching with anxious eyes a ceremonial which was wholly unfamiliar to her. She knew she must not shame him before his sister and his servants; and how was he to guess that never before in her life had she seen a table set with shaded candles and silver ornaments, that she had never given a signal for changing plates or displaced a finger bowl? He had not given a thought to such matters, because they seemed so natural and trivial to him, and he would have been astonished and amused to learn that they could puzzle or agitate his bride. He would have been equally astonished and amused if he had realized that even her joy in him had not saved her from chagrin because she had gone straight to his house wearing the cheap little dress into which she had hastily changed after leaving the store, a dress in no way better than the one in which she had worked all day, except that it was fresh. She had flung two or three similar dresses and some clean, flimsy underwear into a suitcase that had belonged to her brother Vail, who had been killed at St. Mihiel, and these had constituted her trousseau. She could not have had much of an outfit in any case. But with a little time—enough to draw her small savings from the bank, enough to look around for bargains at Goldenberg's, enough to do some sewing herself—she could at least have had something that would have passed for one.

To her surprise, it was Cresside who came to her rescue. Gervais had not been able to reach his sister before the stark little ceremony which Father Navarre had been prevailed upon to perform; it had been witnessed only by Mrs. Randall, grim and rebellious, by Mr. and Mrs. Goldenberg, who vainly strove to create a less rigid atmosphere, and by Fabian, who aided and abetted their attempts with more success than they achieved themselves. But Cresside happened to be at home when Gervais and Merry arrived at Belle Heloise, and she shared that first dreadful dinner with them. After it was over, Gervais went up to his mother's room to tell her that he was married, and that he would bring his bride to see her, either that evening or the following morning, whichever she preferred; and then Cresside put her arms impulsively around Merry and kissed hei.

"Look here," she said. "I like you. I didn't think I was going to, but I do. I think you've got lots of spunk coming here like this. Not crust—that's what Gervais has bringing you this way. I'd have told him to go straight to hell, if I'd been you. But I still think you're swell because you didn't. At that, I know you haven't had time to take a long breath, much less get clothes together or anything. Would you think I was too darn fresh for words if I offered to step into the breach?"

"I'd think you were very kind. It has all been—well, pretty sudden. I don't suppose a man realizes. . . . But I'm afraid I don't understand just what you mean."

"I've got oodles of new clothes," Cresside explained. "A big boxful came in from New Orleans just yesterday. I don't see why I ever bought so many, but I go haywire like that about once in so often. Wouldn't you let me give you some of them for a wedding present? Of course, I want to give you something, and there's no use buying you silver, or furniture, or anything like that, with all the junk there is in the house already. Come along into the Garden Room. I've got my stuff stacked up in there. And no one will ever know—*maman* or the servants or that boob Gervais—that the things didn't belong to you in the first place. We're about the same size, though I'm a little more on the skinny side. Just the same, I think you can get into everything I have, the way clothes are cut nowadays. You've heard that silly riddle, haven't you, about waistlines? What two French cities they make you think of? No? Toulouse and Toulon! It isn't much of a joke, but it fits. . . . Hell, I didn't mean to make a bad pun on top of telling a bad joke. Come on in and change before that dumb brother of mine gets back. He probably won't even see that you've got a different dress on, but *maman*'ll notice you look exactly right, and she'll be impressed. Of course, she won't show that she is or even admit it to herself. But, believe me, Xantippe, it'll have its effect just the same."

So, thanks to Cresside, Merry had gone into her mother-in-law's room dressed in a soft and simple white chiffon which had been fashioned by a master hand; and even Madame d'Alvery's hard eyes, scanning her appraisingly from head to foot, had found nothing to evoke the cold criticism with which she desired to crush the girl. Her son's bride looked like a lady, and what was even more astonishing and disappointing, she acted like one. Her manner was not bold, as Madame d'Alvery uncharitably hoped it would be; but while it was deferential, it was not servile either; this strange little shop girl was respectful to her husband's mother, but not to the degree that would detract from her own self-respect. The first visit was characterized by cool courtesy on both sides, concealing rage on the one and trepidation on the other; and during each succeeding visit which Merry made to her mother-in-law's room, Madame d'Alvery continued to wait watchfully for the errors in conversation or conduct which did not occur. The girl carried herself with dignity, and though to be sure she did not talk much, on the other hand she did not say the wrong thing, and she was the first to lose her sense of constraint. The day came when she took her sewing into Madame d'Alvery's boudoir, and sitting down beside the regal couch, stitched away quietly for an hour or so before gathering up the fine linen on which she had been working and taking her leave with the same apparent ease with which she had come. Gervais was out on the plantation most of the time, Cresside dashing from one festivity to another in town; but Merry, intent on learning the ways of the house, stayed for the most part within its walls. When her drowsiness first came upon her, so that she could no longer spend so much time with her mother-in-law, Madame d'Alvery caught herself, more than once, glancing involuntarily towards the door for the pleasing young figure that failed to appear.

Meanwhile Madame d'Alvery was rapidly regaining her own strength. Vitiated as this was by the years during which she had so stubbornly lain in bed, it was basically indestructible. She began to walk to her couch unsupported, and, before long, to circulate through the second-story rooms, making caustic suggestions as to their rearrangement, and to pace slowly back and forth on the upper gallery, issuing an occasional peremptory order to the laborers in the Small Yard. When Gervais was available, she imperiously demanded his support; but after all, Gervais, like Cresside, was seldom in evidence at such times. And Lucie was growing old; her feeble footsteps were oftentimes even more faltering than those of her strong-willed mistress. When Merry offered for the first time to walk with her, Madame d'Alvery did not make her refusal quite as haughty and definite as she intended; and when Merry offered the second time, Madame d'Alvery accepted. So it happened that it was Merry who supported her when at last she went over the stairs, and who urged her to stay down for dinner. Gervais, coming in a little late, found his mother already ensconced at the head of the table again. But his protest was stilled because Merry reached quickly for his hand and caught it under the long white cloth, pressing it hard.

"You don't know how much I like sitting by you," she said. She did not whisper; she spoke so that not only Gervais, but Madame d'Alvery and Cresside and Selah could all hear her, too. "It's what I've wanted

95

to do, all the time. Only you never asked me! And I suppose that somebody did have to sit at the other end of this huge table until Madame Mère was well enough to come down again. But I've felt ever so far away from you, all this time."

It had been her own idea to call her mother-in-law Madame Mère, and the chance choice had been a happy one. She knew only a little schoolgirl French, which she had never put to spoken use; but having hit upon the regal title, she began to try out brief phrases, and to ask her mother-in-law for help in making them more fluent and idiomatic. She was honestly eager to learn, and though now it required real effort to try, she kept on doing so, not as intensively as she had at first, but at least intermittently, during those late morning hours that were filled with such a variety of inconsequential unexacting things. . . .

Her mother-in-law would be waiting for her now, she supposed. It was high time that she had her coffee and rose and dressed. But she put off ringing for Creassy, partly because she was still so sleepy, and partly because there was a good chance that Gervais might come back to their room, and she did not want to risk any distraction from the intimacy they might enjoy. He very often did come back about that time, for he had generally finished riding the crops by then and liked to have his second cup of coffee with her, the first one having been taken alone. It was superb coffee, a blend specially selected and roasted for him by one of his close friends, Billy Pereira, whose father headed the famous coffee-importing firm of Pereira Ltd., in New Orleans. Merry thought nothing else had ever tasted so good to her. She sat up in bed, beguilingly arrayed in one of the exquisite nightgowns that Cresside had given her, and drank her coffee from a daintily spread tray, while Gervais, still in riding togs, drank his from a small tilt-top table, easily drawn up by the bedside. This was his chosen period for telling her how things were going on the plantation, and for discussing his plans and projects with her. His mother was always with them at dinner and supper now, and, more frequently than in the beginning, Cresside as well; there was no chance for private conversation then, or in the evenings when they all sat in the parlor; and at bedtime Gervais was never in a mood for practical or serious discussion. It was this morning period, which constituted the breathing space between his manifold activities, that seemed ideally suited for such discussions, and that had caused them to become more or less habitual.

It was while they were chatting in this way, a month or so earlier, that he had first spoken to her about wanting to entertain at Belle Heloise. Until then, he had been not only satisfied, but eager, to spend every possible moment alone with her. She tried to tell herself she did not mind that this was no longer the case, to make him feel that if the time had come when he craved more conviviality in his home, she would be the first to encourage it. To a greater degree than most brides, under similar circumstances, she had succeeded.

"I've been thinking, Merry, that I'd like to have a few people in for dinner. Not many. Six or so. You won't need to bother about it at all. Lou Ida and Selah will look after everything."

"It wouldn't be a bother. I'd enjoy it." She could say this more sincerely now that candlelight and finger bowls had ceased to appall her; but still, she had so loved having him to herself! "Do you want to have a party for Regine and Sylvestre? I thought from something your mother said that perhaps you might."

"Hell, no! Why should I want to have a party for them?"

"Well, they're both old friends, aren't they? And Regine's always been a near neighbor besides. And they've both been very nice to us since we were married. It's customary for the friends of engaged couples to give parties for them, isn't it? I mean, when they *stay* engaged long enough to make that possible. Not when they rush off headlong to a priest the way we did!"

She spoke with appealing archness, and usually Gervais would have responded enthusiastically to such an approach. To her surprise, he answered almost abruptly.

"There wasn't anything the matter with the way we got married. Come right down to it, I'm glad we escaped all that special brand of foolishness. And I certainly don't intend to go in for it now, as far as Regine and Sylvestre are concerned. What do you mean, both old friends? I never could endure the sight of that bastard."

"Why do you always call Sylvestre a bastard, Gervais? I thought the Tremaines were very nice people."

"Good Lord, don't take me so literally! I wasn't trying to cast any aspersions on his family. I can call him a skunk, if you like that any better."

"But that isn't complimentary to his family either, is it?"

"I said, don't take me so literally. . . . Incidentally, I'm pretty sure that Sylvestre's sudden decision to become a planter isn't based on a yearning for life on the River Road, or even an abject desire to satisfy Regine's ambition to keep her husband tied to her apron strings. I think he's been fired from Pereira's, the coffee-importing house where he's been since he faded away from Tulane about halfway through his course. It's a fine old firm, with pretty high standards, and he never did measure up to them. He wouldn't have got into it in the first place, if the Tremaines hadn't been very nice people, as you put it. Now all that family influence hasn't been powerful enough to keep him there. He'd have had to leave there with his tail between his legs if the magnificence of Hathaway Hall hadn't saved his face. Well, I seem to be getting a little mixed in my metaphors, but at least they boil down to the plain statement that he's no friend of mine, and that I don't want him at my table, now or ever."

"Do you know I actually guessed that about five minutes ago? You haven't told me yet who it is you do want though."

"I thought I'd like to have a stag dinner with poker afterwards. You know I've been in town two or three times to play—not as often as if there hadn't been a powerful counterattraction right here." He set down his coffee cup and leaned over, pulling her clustering curls and kissing her upturned face. "But still I've gone. Now I think it's coming my turn. Besides, I couldn't have a better chance to put over the idea that I'd like to run for the legislature than after a good dinner at my own house. And believe me, we'd have a good dinner. I'd send some of the hands up to the barrow pit for bass, and the river shrimp ought to be at their best pretty soon. Then we'd have one of the gobblers from the yard and watermelon with champagne poured into it before it's chilled. Some of the 1901 Montrachet with the fish and—well, I'll go the whole hog!—1892 Ponte Canet with the turkey."

"I never heard of those wines before, but just the same it makes me hungry and thirsty to listen to you. However, I'd still like to know who's going to eat and drink all this."

"Well, Jim Bailey, if I can get him, and George Favrot. I'll find out what night they're free first. Then I thought I'd ask the president of the Cotton Factors National Bank, Melvin Bisbee, and that Yankee planter, Charles Boylston, who bought the old Surcliffe place, Hackberry Lodge, a piece down the road, while I was over in France. He's a member of the Police Jury now, and I've liked what I've seen of him. And I suppose I ought to ask Fabian. Anyhow, he's better company than you'd guess, when he gets with a group like that."

"I think Fabian's always good company. I like him."

"Well, he liked you plenty, too, if half I've heard happens to be true. I reckon it would be just as well if I didn't encourage him to come here too often." Again he paused to pull her curls and to kiss her. "But this time you won't be much in evidence, you know. Just long enough to say hello to all these hairy males before you fade gracefully away into the background."

"Won't Cresside say hello to them, too? And Madame Mère?"

"Oh, Cresside without a doubt! Cresside wouldn't miss a chance to say something, no matter what, to half a dozen men, no matter who. I couldn't keep her in her room unless I locked her up there, and I don't believe I'll bother to do that. I should think *maman* might just as well skip it. No one expects a social resurrection from a woman who's been several years on her deathbed."

"She'll enjoy it, honey, just as much as Cresside will. Not the same way, but just as much."

"Well, I shouldn't have thought so, but I'll take your word for it. You seem to have sized her up better than I ever could and to get along with her better, too. And naturally I shan't try to lock her in her room either. But, personally, I'd be just as glad if there was no one besides you with me in the parlor when the guests arrive."

Merry was pleased and proud because he said this and because she knew he meant it. But, personally, she was glad to have Madame d'Alvery on one side of her and Cresside on the other, when the

Secretary of State and the Congressman came in together, both easy-mannered and pleasant-spoken, but somehow a little awe-inspiring just the same. She was grateful to Cresside for giving her another of the pretty dresses from that seemingly inexhaustible supply, a rose-colored one this time, which Cresside said exactly matched her cheeks. She went into Cresside's room, with Creassy in attendance, to get ready for the party, because Cresside always had some bright ideas about adjusting bows or shifting flowers; and as she looked at her sister-in-law, she thought that Cresside had really been wise not to choose this particular dress for herself, because it certainly would not have matched *her* cheeks. Cresside was very pale, and though she sat longer than usual in front of her vanity, putting on variegated make-up, none of the cosmetics she so skillfully applied wholly concealed her pallor.

"Don't you feel well, Cresside?" Merry finally asked, unable to suppress her concern any longer.

"Of course. What makes you think I don't?"

"You don't look well."

"I haven't got the skin you love to touch, like you have, if that's what you mean. Don't rub it in."

"You know I didn't mean that. You've got lovely skin. I think it's even lovelier when you let it alone. But it's lovely anyway. And that's a mighty pretty spangled dress you're putting on. It's another new one, isn't it?"

"Yep. It's another new one."

"Whatever did you think you could do with so many new dresses, Cresside?"

"Oh, I don't know. I told you I went haywire about clothes every once in so often. When I do, I get dresses by the dozen, just the way some people get eggs. Come on, it's time to go downstairs. All the state officials will be foregathered before we get there, if we don't. I think Jim Bailey must have been mighty cute when he was young, don't you?"

Well, cute was not the right word for the Secretary of State, of course, but Merry herself thought that he was still very attractive, and she was sorry she could not have laughed and joked with him and with Gervais' other guests as easily and wittily as Cresside did, or addressed them with her mother-in-law's dignity and composure. She was a little afraid that Gervais would change his mind about wishing she could have received this group alone, because she felt that she made such an inadequate showing, and she thought a good deal about Cresside's sprightliness and about Madame d'Alvery's poise after she had gone upstairs to bed. Madame d'Alvery had gone to bed, too, more exhausted by the effort she had made than she would admit, and Cresside had started off "on a hunt of her own," as she had said jokingly when she bade Merry good night: Gervais might think he had corralled every man that was really worth having, but she knew better; there were still plenty at large if you knew where to look for them. She did know, and she had a swell date on at The Willows. She would tell Merry all about it in the morning.

Merry knew that Cresside would not tell her all about it in the morning, that she probably would not mention it again of her own accord, and that she would laugh off any specific questions about it. Merry had never been to The Willows herself, but the little she knew about the place did not help to make her happy in realizing that Cresside went there fairly frequently. It was a small café on the short stretch of batture near town, where the willows beyond the levee grew in great luxuriance. A number of small square openings had been cut in these, around one larger clearing where the bar was located. Each of the small clearings was barely large enough to accommodate a little table and some tin chairs, and each was thickly enclosed with abundant growth. Drinks and sandwiches were served in these caches upon request, but when no demand for these was made, the occupants of the little openings were not disturbed. Rightly or wrongly the café had acquired a bad name. It made Merry miserable to think that Cresside, who was so kind to her, and so gallant and gay, should frequent The Willows. . . .

But she could not go on thinking about Cresside indefinitely. Most of her thoughts centered on Gervais, as they always did, and the sound of his laughter kept drifting up to her now, together with the aroma of fine cigars and fragments of the talk around the poker table. The early June night was warm, and the shutter doors leading from her chamber into the guest room behind it and into the upper hall were all open; as to the doors downstairs, those were never closed.

It was Fabian's whimsical voice which she recognized first, as he jested with George Favrot, who had evidently taken in a fat pot. "Have you forgotten that we're all constituents of yours, George?" Fabian was saying. "Just for the look of things, you ought to let one of us win a pot now and then, or we'll organize the district against you."

The broad A's of the Bostonian were easily recognizable also: "Somebody better tip off a bank examiner to go over to the Cotton Factors National if Bisbee keeps on losing. It isn't in the realm of reason that any banker could keep on getting rid of his own money without putting up more of a squawk than he's doing. As for myself, I'd like to know if it isn't tough enough on a Yankee to be running for an office that the infidels around here call a police juryship. In all Christian parts of the world it's called a county commissioner's."

There was a pleasant pause, broken first by the tinkle of ice and the hiss of charged water and then by an inquiry, interested rather than anxious, from Boylston: "How are you fixed with prohibition coming along in a few weeks, d'Alvery? Ought we to go easy on this?" Gervais' answer was reassuring: "I haven't even bothered to make a complete check of what I have on hand since I came home. But I don't think we'll ever have to resort to Opelousas corn in this house. My father

100

always kept a fine cellar whatever else he went without. So I know there's enough to last me and my friends until that crazy law's been repealed. It stands to reason it can't last forever. . . . Here, let me fill that up!"

"Thanks. And let's talk about something besides politics for a change. The campaign won't start for months."

"Is that so?" inquired Bailey, rumbling in on Bisbee's pinched squeak. "Why, in just a few weeks now all six candidates for governor are going to talk at a Fourth of July rally at Hot Well."

"And where the hell is Hot Well, may I ask?"

The significant silence which followed this question indicated that Bisbee was apparently not the only member of the group who did not know, and Bailey continued chaffingly: "I'm surprised to see all you good Democrats look as blank as that. Not long ago some druggist decided that a hot water spring near Boyce would cure everything from the pip to a broken leg, and built him a little haywire and string health resort. That's Hot Well. This Fourth of July rally is his way of publicizing the place."

"Did you say six candidates were going to speak there?" Gervais inquired, and George Favrot interrupted sarcastically: "Yes, but candidates in name only. They'll never be anybody's political bedfellows."

"What about Phanor Breazeale?" asked Bisbee. "He's got the whole Liberty League behind him."

"Yes, both the members," Bailey retorted scornfully. "What's more I'll bet anybody that not one of the names of those six speakers will be on the tickets my office prints for the election."

A murmur of mild surprise greeted this announcement, but it was soon swallowed up by a further suggestion for fresh drinks. As he dispensed them, apparently with great liberality, Gervais seized the occasion to make the remark for which Merry had been listening.

"As a matter of fact I'm not so much interested in the gubernatorial race at the moment as I am in my own chances."

Boylston laughed. His laugh, like his voice, was pleasant, but usually it was not characterized by much heartiness; now it had a real ring to it and his amusement sounded through his mock oratory.

"Little as I know about politics in Louisiana, and grateful as I am that your conservation laws include Republicans, and unable as I may be to comprehend how any sugar planter can ever vote anything but a Republican ticket, I can still give you the answer to that one, neighbor. With your war record, all of these little local cliques will be honeying up to you instead of the other way around."

"Hey there, Boylston, stop poaching on our preserves!"

"Nonsense, Congressman, it's true, isn't it?"

"Of course it's true, but that's no reason for spoiling our little game, which was to keep Gervais on the anxious seat a while and get a handsome campaign contribution out of him in return for doing something we'd all made up our minds to do long ago. You damn

Yankees haven't changed a particle since you stabled your horses in the University buildings."

In the midst of the laughter and badinage which followed this accusation, Merry drifted off to sleep again; after all she had heard that Gervais' election was practically assured, and this was what most mattered to her. There was no reason why she should stay awake any longer. But the next morning Gervais brought up the subject again himself when he came to have coffee with her, greatly pleased with the results of his stag party.

"I was mighty proud of you, honey," he told her. "You looked just the way I hoped you would, and acted just the way I hoped you would, too. I can tell you it made a real impression on all the folks, from Jim Bailey right down the line. And it set me to thinking what an impression you'd make when I took you to the Mansion for parties, and had you beside me on the floor of the House."

"Oh, Gervais, you're not going to do that, are you?"

"You're darn right I am! Why, you must have known we'd be invited to the Mansion! And haven't you heard that every member of the legislature is allowed to have an extra chair set up right beside his?"

"Yes, I reckon I must have. But I never thought I'd be sitting in one of them."

"Well, then, you'd better begin to think of it, because you will be. And you won't be watching parades from the window of a department store, either. You'll be on the Governor's reviewing stand. You're not going to spend the rest of your life snoozing, you know."

"No. Though I suppose——"

"You suppose this isn't the only time you'll ever be in a delicate condition? Well, I hope you're right about that. I hope we'll have a lot of children, Merry, if you're strong enough to stand it, and it looks as if you would be. But far enough apart so that you and I can do things together, too. Do you realize the only party you've been to with me this spring was that one given for the officers of the sub-chaser that came up the River? Next year I want to take you to a lot of them, and have a lot of them here, too. And I want you to ride around over the plantation with me. My, but we've got a good stand of plant cane this year! I wish you could see it."

"I'll see next year's stand and I'll love doing that. I'd rather learn about our crops than go to the parties, Gervais."

"Well, I want you to care about both. I suppose it's too much to hope that you'll be interested in machinery, but I can tell you, I'm tickled to death with the new tractor we're trying out, and I think the cultivator we're using now is going to be fine. You know I tried to explain about that before. You see, darling, we can't put too much dirt into the cane now, because by and by each stalk will raise its own little family of stalks. 'Suckers' we call them. Cane's a sociable plant. It likes lots of company. Perhaps that's why sugar planters are a sociable lot, too. Living close to the land the way they do, they get habits just like their own suckers."

"I don't think I like to hear you compare yourself to any kind of a sucker, honey, even those that are just little stalks of cane."

"Shucks, I told you before not to be so literal! What I was trying to explain to you is that one stalk comes up first and that presently there are a dozen small shoots around it, making a stool that has to be nourished and fed. That's why we must do so much fertilizing at this time of year. Of course, we've got the richest soil in Louisiana right here, because the cream of all that comes from the states draining into the Mississippi Valley has been deposited on the banks of the River. But still we have to use a good deal of nitrogen to hasten growth and phosphate to give early maturity. You know how Lou Ida and Creassy are trying to 'tempt' you right now, because you've got to 'eat for two'? Well, it's just the same with plant life as it is with human beings. Sugar has to be nourished to support its own family. When it is, you wouldn't believe what quick results you get. You can almost see its color changing from pale jade to emerald green."

"I'd love to see it. It sounds beautiful, the way you talk about it. I never thought of cane starting a family, just the way we are, Gervais."

"Well, I want you to, honey. Because that's what it does. And next to our own family, I care more about that cane family than anything else in the world."

She went back to sleep, thinking about the dozen small shoots that came up around the one big stalk and needing to be nourished; and after that she never said no when Lou Ida and Creassy tried to "tempt" her. She remembered, too, that cane was a sociable plant, and she encouraged Gervais to have more company and made the required effort to go out with him the next time he asked her to. But she herself was secretly most content when they were by themselves, and when there were no extraneous diversions to enliven the monotony of the slumberous prescient days. She still preferred to let time drift past her while she remained sheltered and enclosed by the great shuttered room.

"Well, sleepy-head! If you keep on the way you're doing, presently you won't wake up at all. When I kiss you three times before it takes effect, one of us is certainly slowing up."

So she had not rung for Creassy at all that morning, she had not drunk her coffee, she had gone back to sleep a second time. And here was Gervais bending over her and pretending to shake her, while he looked at her teasingly. She sat up suddenly, rubbing her heavy eyes and shaking her tumbled curls away from her forehead. Then she blinked at him, catching her breath a little, and buried her rosy face against his shoulder.

"You better hide your head in shame!" he said, still teasingly. He had his arm around her now and his fond voice was in itself a caress. "Here it is only a little over two months since I practically had to hold you down, to keep you in bed mornings, and now I have to handle you roughly in order to rouse you at ten o'clock. I told Creassy to bring your coffee up with mine. Maybe I ought to tell Billy Pereira to add a little strychnine to the blend for a while in order to stimulate you. . . . Seriously, honey, I didn't mean to startle you so. I didn't suppose you really were all that sound asleep. I'm sorry I made you spring up like that. I don't believe you ought to move around so suddenly now. Hasn't Dr. Champagne told you not to?"

"No. He said I couldn't be getting along better. There's nothing he's forbidden me to do." She raised her face, and shifting her position so that her head was no longer hidden but rested easily on his shoulder, she looked up at him, her loving expression tinged with anxiety. "Do you know, Gervais, I think Cresside really needs a doctor a lot more than I do?" she said. "She doesn't look a bit well to me."

"She might look better if she'd stop running around nights," Gervais said shortly. "She could use a little extra sleep herself. But there's nothing the matter with her, any more than there was ever anything the matter with *maman*. You've got to take care of yourself, though. Because that means taking care of Philogene, too."

He had confidently assumed, from the beginning, that the expected child would be a boy, and he had already announced his intention of naming it after his father. He almost never spoke of "the baby," but nearly always of Philogene. It amused and delighted Merry to hear him.

"I'm interested in taking care of Philogene, too, Gervais."

"Then don't jump around in bed and don't waste worry on Cresside."

"I hate for you to talk about Cresside the way you do, Gervais. I'm mighty fond of her. She couldn't have been any kinder to me if she'd been my own sister."

"She better be kind to you. But that doesn't alter the fact that she lied to me. I don't see how anyone who's the soul of truthfulness, like you are, can stand up for a liar."

"Is it all right for me to ask you what she lied to you about, Gervais?"

"Yes. She lied to me about Sylvestre Tremaine. She told me that he'd asked her to marry him, and all the time he was actually engaged to Regine Hathaway."

"Had you said something critical to Cresside about Sylvestre, Gervais?"

"You're damn right I had. And I'd told her to stop staying out half the night with him."

"Well, but Cresside may have loved Sylvestre very much, Gervais. And if she did, naturally she'd defend him. If she really had been engaged to him, that would have made it all right for her to stay out late with him. Wouldn't it? She must have told you she was engaged so that you wouldn't think so ill of him."

"Merry, you're crazy, arguing it out that way."

"No, I'm not. I'd have done exactly the same thing myself if anyone had spoken critically to me about you."

104

"But, good God, I *wasn't* engaged to someone else!"

"Cresside couldn't have known that Sylvestre was either. It must have been a terrible shock to her when she found it out. I think she's being very brave about not showing how badly she feels. Of course, I'm sorry she chooses the way she does to cover it up. But I think it's just a phase. I'm sure she won't go on for long running around like she does now, with a fast crowd. She really doesn't care about that fast crowd, honey. She *couldn't*. She's not that kind. But she's out to show the world, just now, that it doesn't mean a thing to her that she misunderstood Sylvestre."

"*Misunderstood!*"

"Why, yes! She must have thought he was in love with her, honey. She must have thought he meant to propose, pretty soon. She was hoping so hard that he would, she misunderstood, that's all. Plenty of girls make mistakes like that. Because some men say such a lot when they don't mean a thing. Just like some of them mean such a lot, and never seem to be able to open their mouths."

"And you were thinking of just whom, when you said that?"

"Well, I was thinking of Sylvestre, for the first kind, naturally. And of Fabian for the other. I sure enough wasn't thinking of you, honey. You say plenty, but you mean plenty, too."

Gervais muttered something unintelligible. This was the first time he and Merry had talked so seriously or at any length about Cresside. A dozen times before, when he had been on the point of saying something, an innate aversion to discussing his sister, even with his wife, had withheld him. Now that the secret had been brought into the open, he felt immeasurably relieved. Merry had presented a point of view that was entirely novel to him, and at the same time, infinitely reassuring; in explaining Cresside's conduct to him, she had, in a measure, succeeded in excusing it. The day before, he had heard Merry patiently practicing her halting French under his mother's direction, and one of the trite proverbs she had been repeating was "*Tout comprendre c'est tout pardonner.*" At the time he had wondered, elatedly, if his mother had perception enough to realize how applicable the old saw was in her own case. Now that she was beginning to understand how wise his choice of a wife had been, she was also beginning to forgive him for having made it, though there were still no prospects that she would admit this. Belatedly he saw that the proverb was applicable in his case and in his sister's also. . . .

"I'm mighty lucky, you know, Gervais, not even to be having morning sickness," he heard Merry saying. Apparently she had decided, on her own initiative, that for the moment they had discussed Cresside enough, that there was no sense in running the subject into the ground. He followed her lead with the good cheer which sprang from relief.

"I reckon you are at that. And I'm lucky, too. I shouldn't think it would add to the general aura of romance surrounding a young couple for the bride to begin the day by up-chucking all over the place."

"Gervais, sometimes I think Cresside's right when she says that Army life didn't improve you. You shouldn't say things like that when you're talking about romance."

"I suppose I shouldn't. But you don't really mind, do you? You ought not to, as a matter of fact. If you don't ever hear me say anything worse than that, you'll be even luckier than you've been in escaping morning sickness."

There was a gentle knock at the shutter door and Creassy entered, watchfully carrying a porcelain coffee service on a silver tray. Without self-consciousness, Gervais released Merry from his embrace, and sat down at the small bedside table, while Creassy arranged Merry's pillows and straightened her coverings. Merry looked up at her smilingly.

"Thanks, Creassy. It's a lovely day for Miss Regine's wedding, isn't it?"

"Yes, Miss Merry, it sure is. Such days is well accepted."

"I love to hear you say that, Creassy, the first thing in the morning. It always makes a day begin better for me."

"Ah's proud to hear it, Miss Merry. Could Ah get you somethin' else before Ah goes downstairs?"

"I think we've got everything, but I'll let you know if we haven't." Then, as the maid left the room, beaming, Merry added, handing Gervais his cup, "I hope you're not going to say, like Miss Mittie does, that you wouldn't have minded if it had rained 'cats, dogs and billy goats' on Regine's wedding day, honey. Regine isn't to blame for what happened. We oughtn't to forget that, no matter how sorry we feel for Cresside."

"I'm not so sure. I think Regine *is* partly to blame. I think Sylvestre might have come across, if Regine hadn't snatched at him. Not that I wouldn't have hated like hell to have him for a brother-in-law. But just the same——"

Involuntarily, he was reverting to the subject of Cresside after all. This time Merry followed his lead.

"Just the same, you think he ought to have proposed to her. I know. But Cresside wouldn't have been happy, not in the long run, with Sylvestre, honey. She wouldn't be happy with any man who didn't love her as much as she loved him. No girl is. And Sylvestre isn't good enough for Cresside. He isn't much better than the men in this crowd she's running with now. Of course, I wouldn't go so far as you do and call him a—a——"

"A bastard? Or just a skunk?"

"I wouldn't call him any bad names. But I'm glad I don't have to call him kin, either. I'm glad it's Regine he's marrying and not Cresside."

"May I come in? Is this billing and cooing I hear mostly verbal? Or is Gervais back in bed, the middle of the morning? I don't want to burst in on anything a nice young girl ought to learn only from the birds and bees, God forbid!"

The shutter door leading into the hall opened slowly again, and this time Cresside came into the room. Gervais, glancing at her covertly to see if there could possibly be any basis for Merry's anxiety, was startled to notice, for the first time, that Cresside's face was not only pale, but haggard, under her make-up, and that there were violet circles around her eyes. As usual, however, she was as smart as paint. Her short linen dress was crisp and spotless and her scarlet belt and shoes matched her lipstick. She greeted her brother with a nonchalant nod; but she bent over to hug Merry with undisguised affection.

"How are you this morning, precious? Well, I don't need to ask. Dewy with sleep and rosy with kisses! I'd say that marriage and maternity were equally becoming to you. I just dropped in to tell you I'm going over to Hathaway Hall to help with the flowers, and I didn't want you to start dragging the River for me if you found I was missing from the old homestead. Besides, I thought maybe you'd come with me. But I promised I'd be there by ten-thirty, and you won't be as far as the tub by then, from the present look of things."

"Yes, I will. I'd like to come with you, Cresside. I'll hurry. Gervais was just going out again, anyway. Weren't you, honey?"

"Well, I wasn't in any particular hurry to get away from you. But now that I see you're eager to get rid of me, so that you can go and gloat over the near-by nuptial garlands, I can take a hint and clear out."

He grinned, kissed her once more and went off, nodding to Cresside with the same nonchalance that had marked her own greeting. But as the morning wore on, he found he could not get her out of his mind. For once the enchanting vision of Merry which was so constantly before him was obscured by the image of his sister's white face, with its scornful scarlet lips and its great violet-ringed eyes. Certainly a healthy young girl should not look as haggard as that, no matter how much running around she was doing. Merry was probably right, as usual. Cresside must be ill, and he would drive into town that afternoon, and ask Dr. Champagne to come out and have a look at her. No, curse it, he could not go that afternoon, because he would have to arrive early and stay late at Hathaway Hall. Sylvestre had asked him to be one of the ushers at the wedding, and he had not been able to think up any plausible pretext for declining. Well, anyway, all the Champagnes would be at the wedding and he would manage to draw the doctor aside and get in a word with him edgewise. Then the doctor would come out to Belle Heloise the first thing the next morning and find out what in hell was the matter with Cresside, and give her something that would pep her up. He still could not believe it was anything serious. It was just that she was taking the double-dealing of that bastard too hard. Much too hard. Too damn hard. . . .

He was roused from his reverie by the sound of the plantation bell. There was no logical reason why it should ring at this hour. It was not time for the field hands' dinner. Listening intently, he recognized the special signal which had occasionally been used, before he went to

France, to summon him from the fields: three long loud peals, then a pause and two short softer ones. This signal had very seldom been given and he had almost forgotten it. But as he hurried towards the house, he remembered that the last time he had heard it had been the morning when his father was suddenly and mortally stricken. And as he came quickly into the Small Yard, Amen ran excitedly out to meet him, with Snow and Cornet barking at his heels.

"Miss Cresside's been bad hurt, Mr. Gervais."

"What do you mean, bad hurt?"

"She was up on a ladder, fixin' flowers in de White Ball Room, and she must of had a swimmin' in de head from bein' up so high, caise she fainted. She done fell down and hurt herself bad."

"Stop saying she's hurt herself bad. Perhaps she's only stunned by the fall," Gervais said sharply. But he quickened his pace, covering the great expanse of the Small Yard in swift strides. Amen, still jabbering excitedly, trotted after him, followed by the dogs.

"No, suh, she ain't stunned no mo'. She done come out of her faint. She don' cry out, but you can tell she's bad hurt."

"Who got her home?"

"Mr. Sylvestre, he brung her home. Looks like he done forgot he was goin' to marry Miss Regine dis very evenin'. He carried Miss Cresside upstairs hisself, and put her on de bed, and stood there lookin' at her for de longes'."

"Is he still there?"

"No, suh, he done gone caise Miss Cresside, she make him. De doctor's dere now. Mr. Fabian come out to see what all he could do to help befo' de wedding, happenin' in jes' when Miss Cresside fell offen de ladder. So he done go for de doctor and brung him back here befo' noon."

The front door opened quietly, and Fabian shuffled down the circular brick stairs and limped towards them. His gait, as usual, was slow and awkward because of his deformity, and he made no evident effort to hurry. He was smiling in his customary wry way.

"Why don't you take those dogs out to the shed, Amen?" he asked pleasantly. "Their barking might disturb Miss Cresside. I'm afraid she's in for a good deal of pain and we've each got to do our part to see that she isn't disturbed." Then as the Negro hastened to follow his suggestion, with the joyous feeling of helpfulness rather than the one of shame which would have been caused by a harsh rebuke, Fabian turned to Gervais. "I'm afraid you've had a nasty jolt, perhaps unnecessarily," he said quietly. "Tante Isabelle insisted on having the bell rung. But I was against it myself. There's nothing you can do for Cresside at the moment. Dr. Champagne isn't even through examining her—she seems to have hurt her back, falling, but he doesn't know yet just how badly. And Merry's with her. Merry was the only person she asked for."

"I don't want Merry upset, just now. You ought to know that."

"I do know that. But Merry isn't upset. She's perfectly calm and collected. And Dr. Champagne himself said he'd like to have her stick around. He wouldn't have done that if he'd thought it would hurt her. Come on into the library, Gervais, and have a drink. I've got one ready for you."

"Damn white of you. But I'd rather get along to my sister."

"Well, of course, if you insist. But she'd rather you didn't. I heard her myself, saying, 'You keep Gervais out of here.' It was almost as final as what I heard her saying to Sylvestre."

"And what was that, damn his rotten hide?"

"She said, 'This is your wedding day, Sylvestre. Regine will be waiting for you.' He would've stayed if she'd let him. In fact, he'd have given anything on earth for a chance to stay. You should have seen his face—and hers. He knows at last what a damn fool he's been, just as well as you and I do. Because Cresside's a great girl, and he might have married her, instead of that alabaster image hung with diamonds that he's chained to instead. But Cresside's through with Sylvestre, Gervais. She found him out, too. She wouldn't marry him if he were the last man on earth. Don't you worry about her, though. She's got the guts to come out all right, by herself."

PART III

High, Wide and Handsome

May 8, 1920 to June 20, 1920

"Every great war has left in its wake a period of suffering and misery for the vanquished; of extravagance and waste on the part of the victors. The problems to be solved by the world today are complex, and cover nearly every phase of human endeavor. . . .

"As your incoming governor, my earnest appeal to every man and woman in Louisiana is to take a deep interest in public affairs. Remember, it is not only your welfare and happiness, but the future of your children and your children's children which is dependent upon efficient government."

—*From Inaugural address of John M. Parker, Governor of Louisiana, delivered May 17, 1920.*

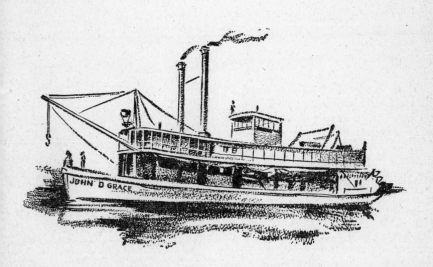

High, Wide and Handsome

May 8, 1920–June 20, 1920

CHAPTER VIII

"I HOPE WE won't have to wait much longer for d'Alvery. I'd like to get this thing clinched before that New Orleans crowd gets in on the ten forty-five."

"They ought to be here any minute now, Governor. It was about eight when I got hold of Fabian. He was just finishing his breakfast and he said he'd strike right out for Belle Heloise."

This pronouncement was made, with some pomposity, by Melvin Bisbee, who was extremely flattered at having been asked to help with the conference that was now taking place. He was answered by Hewitt Bouanchaud, the Lieutenant Governor Elect, a small dark man with jet black hair and a rubicund countenance, so markedly Gallic in appearance that the absence of any accent or colloquialism in his speech came as a surprise.

"Maybe he wasn't as nearly through as he said. If he wasn't, I wouldn't blame him if he took time out to eat before he started. Fabian d'Alvery keeps a good cook. Besides, it may take him longer than we figure to get down to his cousin's. I don't know what shape the River Road's in just now, but it's been pretty near impassable with mud most of the winter, and now it's just the season for seepage. Fabian may have got stuck and had to find a pair of horses to pull him out. What's more, we lost a lot of time because we couldn't get hold of Gervais direct. It's a damn nuisance there's no telephone at Belle Heloise. The place is almost as isolated as if it were in the middle of the Atchafalaya Swamp."

"It's isolated all right but that's the way for a farmer to live. I won't let them put a telephone on my place at Bayou Sara. I stayed at Belle Heloise several times during the campaign, and I like it there. I like this young fellow who owns it, too, and I as good as know he's with us. But I want to be sure how that new representative from somewhere in the seventh district, Gaston Daigle, is going to stand on the speakership vote, and d'Alvery can take care of that better than any man I know."

Having emphasized this point, John Parker, Governor Elect of Louisiana, resumed his study of the legislative list, which he had previously been engaged in checking. He was a well-built man, inordinately proud of the flat stomach which he had succeeded in retaining despite advancing years, partly, doubtless, because he was so disdainful of Creole cookery, his favorite fare being mustard greens and buttermilk. He had a ruddy face, iron-gray hair and an iron-gray mustache, and in manner and general appearance was curiously like a country merchant wearing "store-bought clothes" with apparent self-consciousness, though he was an outstanding member of the Boston Club in New Orleans, and belonged by both background and breeding in the top social bracket. At the moment he was in his shirt sleeves, seated on the side of the garish squeaky brass bed which dominated a musty little room in the Hotel Istrouma at Baton Rouge. The principal conferees were Hewitt Bouanchaud of New Roads, and the boss of the third ward in New Orleans, John P. Sullivan, both of whom had settled themselves more or less stably; various others came and went, among them Bisbee and Harry Gamble, who had been Parker's campaign manager.

In spite of the open window, the air was heavy and the room was full of smoke; Sullivan's cigar, one of the sleek Havanas manufactured especially for him, would alone have made this condition almost inevitable. Seated in a mission-style rocker of fumed oak, Sullivan puffed away contentedly while Parker studied his check list. The others were all clad in seersucker or white linen, in varying degrees of dishevelment, but Sullivan was magnificently arrayed in superbly tailored Shantung, and wore a Sulka cravat embellished with a diamond and emerald stickpin which the Elks had given him when he was their Grand Exalted Ruler. He was an enormous man, whose great height was overpowering even when he was seated, and whose vast shoulders seemed to fill the inadequate little room. In his youth he had been known as the only plebe at West Point who was never hazed, because he chose the alternative of fighting any upperclassman who was sent against him, and had fought and beaten twenty-seven of them on as many consecutive nights, "the Sabbath and Lord's Day only excepted!" This exploit had been followed by many others, both physical and political, which were scarcely less prodigious; some five years earlier he had broken with Behrman, the mayor of New Orleans, and organized his own city crowd, which had supported Parker for Governor during the recent campaign. Now he was riding the jubilant crest of victory and adroitly preparing to supplant Behrman with a man of his own. But for the moment his interest was centered on a matter of more immediate importance.

114

"I'm inclined to agree with the Governor on one point. I don't doubt that d'Alvery will vote for our program straight down the line," he said. If the other conferees had been strangers to him instead of boon companions, they would inevitably have been startled by the rolling basso with which he made his simple announcement, for he had a voice compared to which the percussion of a bass drum sounded like a shrill treble. "I only hope he has as much influence with Daigle as the Governor seems to think. But Daigle was elected on the Stubbs ticket, and while we've got a majority for our man Walker, what we're after is a unanimous vote. And if our side looks strong enough, Hamley won't even go to the post."

"Hold up a second, will you, John? I think someone's at the door now. But I can't half hear when you bear down on that fog horn."

Harry Gamble walked over to the door and flung it open, to disclose Fabian and Gervais standing on the threshold. As always, when the cousins appeared together, Fabian's deformity seemed the more marked. Nevertheless, it was he who entered first, his crooked smile enlivening the somberness of his expression.

"Sorry we took so long to get here," he said pleasantly. "I've never seen the seepage as bad as it's been this spring. Two or three cars were stuck in that soft spot just below McGregor's store. We had to turn back and go all round Robin Hood's barn to reach town."

"I told the crowd you were probably bogged down," Bisbee responded. "Sorry you were put to so much trouble, but after all, you River Roaders ought to gang up on the police jury and make them do something about it. . . . Good morning, Captain. Glad to see you. I don't need to introduce you to the Governor, of course. He's just been telling us how much he's enjoyed being your guest. You know Lieutenant Governor Bouanchaud, too, don't you?"

"Sure. I've known the Captain ever since he was knee-high to a *poule d'eau*," Bauanchaud broke in. "As a matter of fact, his father and I were friends before he was born. How are you these days, Gervais? Still up to mischief? Or had I better ask Fabian to testify on that point? Though you've probably sobered down now, with all your new responsibilities." He turned to the others in the room. "Possibly the rest of you don't know that Captain d'Alvery's the father of twins."

"Why, you don't say!" The Governor laid down his check list, and rising from the squeaky bed, went over to Gervais and heartily shook his hand. "That's bully. Gives me quite a fellow feeling. My son John has twins, too, and incidentally, I'm a twin myself. Let the grandfather of twins congratulate the father of twins! Both boys, are they?"

"No, a boy and a girl."

"I suppose the boy's a junior? Or did you name him after your father?" Bouanchaud inquired with genuine interest.

"We didn't do either. Both of my wife's brothers were killed in the war, and she wanted to name the boy for them—Malcolm Vail. We call him Vail. The girl's named for my father's sister, Sybelle, and it seemed fair that each side of the family should be represented, when it came to a christening."

"I agree with you. Plenty of time for the second Philogene yet, if you ask me." And as Gervais met his eye, laughing, Bouanchaud also laughed loudly and slapped him on the shoulder. "So it's that way already, is it? How old are the twins?"

"They were born in January."

"And this is only May! Well, you're certainly not losing any time! And how's that pretty sister of yours? I was sorry to hear she'd an accident of some kind."

"Yes, a bad fall. She injured her back pretty seriously. But I'm glad to say she's better now."

"Young fathers are proverbially garrulous, I know," Fabian remarked, sardonically. "In fact, they're usually even more tiresome than young mothers. But this is a political meeting, Gervais, it isn't a baby party. I can't believe the Governor interrupted my breakfast and sent me down the River Road to get you, in spite of its horrible condition, merely because you're the father of twins. I think he'd probably like to get along with whatever's on his mind, if you'd give him a chance."

Sullivan, still puffing away placidly at his cigar, shot a surreptitious glance at the speaker. The wry smile, which had made Fabian's face so vivid and winning at first, had completely faded; without this, it was not only somber but bitter. *A queer bird,* Sullivan said to himself; *something's eating him, not just his deformity at that. But he's nobody's fool; he's a smart man, a damn sight smarter than this showy cousin of his that everyone's making such a fuss about. Finer fibered, too. Not just because of the d'Alvery heritage or the Princeton polish either; because of something inside of him that no other man in the room has got. Not even John Parker. . . . certainly not John Sullivan.* Parker, more bent on action than analysis, broke in on his colleague's contemplation.

"You're right, Fabian. I asked you to bring your cousin here for a very special purpose. Won't you both sit down?"

The one vacant chair in the room had a straight back and a stamped leather seat, and stood near the washstand of poisonous pink marble. Gervais promptly seated himself in it. Involuntarily, Fabian met Sullivan's alert eye and a look of swift understanding and instantaneous liking passed between the two men who were so dissimilar. Then the former limped over to a small bent-legged table, and leaned against it. Parker also walked over to it and poured himself a drink of ice water from a sweating pitcher standing on a japanned tray.

"I thought perhaps you'd talk to Gaston Daigle," he said, emptying his glass. "We'd like to clinch his vote on the speakership."

"I don't know Daigle too well. And anyway, I'm not so sure I'd have all that influence with him."

"We thought you might have, both of you being planters and both of you being from sugar parishes," suggested Sullivan pleasantly.

116

"Well, supposing I had. How do you know I'd influence him the way you want? Seems to me you've taken my vote pretty much for granted."

Gervais' voice had the edginess which characterized it when he felt or fancied anyone had presumed upon his independence. Sullivan, with an amused glint in his eye, glanced first at Bouanchaud and then at Fabian over his cigar. Parker, rising from the squeaky bed, on which he had seated himself a second time, hooked his thumbs in his belt and drew in the flat stomach of which he was so proud.

"Yes, Captain, I think I may tell you I did take it for granted. But not for political reasons," he said, somewhat rhetorically. "Listen, son: you're an L.S.U. man. You know one of the things I've promised to do is build a real university, and by that I mean one that would include a first-class scientific agricultural school. That ought to appeal to you both as a planter and as an L.S.U. alumnus. I'm a practical farmer myself, and you know I want to write a new constitution for this state so that we won't have to use the patchwork of two constitutions we're trying to operate under now."

Still holding his audience with his beady eyes, he bit off a corner from the plug of tobacco which he took from his pocket, and rolled it deliberately around in his mouth before proceeding; he rather liked to parade this habit. "I want to institute a real system of highways for this state, too," he continued. "I want to take this state out of the mud. I can't do it unless those legislators who feel the same way I do about it uphold my hands. Unless you give me a Speaker who is my friend and who will appoint my friends to the important committee posts. That's why I venture to take your vote for granted, Captain d'Alvery."

"Well, of course, if you put it that way—" Gervais' voice was no longer arrogant; it was not even reluctant. Without any of the traditional artifices of a spellbinder, without even a struggle, Parker had succeeded in winning his point. "Naturally, I don't want to be an administration rubber stamp," Gervais added. "But I see what you mean. You may count on me to help in any way I can."

"Fine! I tell you, us ancestors of twins has got to stick together. There aren't but a few of us."

"No, you're right. There aren't."

Parker rose again and again shook Gervais' hand with great heartiness. "Another thing, we're riding high, wide and handsome right now, with sugar at twenty-six cents. But I don't need to tell you, for all that, that this new mosaic disease which is just beginning to creep in may constitute a terrible problem. We've got to get away from all one-crop systems."

Sullivan's deep laugh suddenly boomed through the room. "That's a great John Parker, isn't he?" the big man chuckled. "He'll be talking about his silos, next. But what the hell's mosaic disease, will somebody tell me?"

"It's a disease of the leaf, which is the lung of a plant. When cane's

117

afflicted with it, there's the same terrible results as when a human being is afflicted with tuberculosis, and it leaves other deadly afflictions, just as tuberculosis does—root rot, or red rot, as some call it, for instance. The two almost always go together and root rot is just as disastrous as mosaic disease. I've heard there were some evidences that it was beginning to creep in along your part of the River Road already."

"There are some signs of it at Hathaway Hall right near us, though I'm glad to say we haven't had any of it ourselves."

"Well, you can't put a coffee importer in charge of a sugar plantation and expect too much, especially if he didn't make a go of it in the coffee business. Thanks again for coming, Captain."

The leave-taking was genial, but as Gervais and his cousin went down the dingy hall to the antiquated elevator, Fabian murmured: "The oration of John Parker to the d'Alvery Philistines. That man couldn't talk about the weather without getting a stump to do it."

"I'm no Philistine, whatever you are, and he wasn't up on a stump. This isn't the first time he's talked to me about the future of L.S.U. He told me about his plans for it when he spent the night at Belle Heloise during the campaign. It's about time someone showed a little interest in it, too, though I wouldn't expect a Princetonian like you to realize it, or care. The Law School's the only department now that has any standing, and the Pentagon Buildings still look more like the cavalry post the Yankees used to stable their horses in than a place for students to live and learn."

"My God, are you going to start making speeches, too? You'll be kissing babies next, and I don't mean Sybelle and Vail either."

"Oh, shut up! It doesn't matter to a lawyer, I suppose, whether we get an experimental station here or not, but I can tell you it matters a lot to a planter. I'll admit I'm sitting pretty right now, as Parker said, with sugar at twenty-six. But if this darn disease does get in generally, I'm going to be up against it."

"And you really think there are signs of it at Hathaway Hall?"

"There isn't a doubt of it. But again, it's like Parker said: why in hell should anyone expect a moron who's made a failure in coffee to be a success in sugar? Especially when he spends the entire winter basking on the Riviera instead of looking after his crops? . . . Well, what do you say we go over to Izzy's and snatch a small black?"

"Very good idea."

They crossed Third Street to Izzy's, where they found the jovial proprietor ensconced, as usual, behind his cash register. He hurried forward to meet them, wreathed in smiles.

"Why, good morning, Captain! Good morning, Mr. d'Alvery," he said with great heartiness. "It's a pleasant surprise, seeing you gentlemen so early in the day. I'd like to take this occasion to tell you I voted for you, Captain, and I think I may say I was responsible for several other votes that were cast for you, too."

"That's fine, Izzy. I'm very much obliged to you and I'll try to

118

see that you'll never regret it. . . . How's about a couple of small blacks?"

"Right away, Captain, right away." Izzy turned to signal one of the white-coated waiters, but that functionary was already drawing coffee from a highly nickeled urn into two tiny white cups. "Sure there isn't anything else you'd like?" Izzy inquired, as the two cousins seated themselves at one of the alabastine-topped tables opposite the counter.

"No, thanks. It isn't long enough since breakfast. . . . All set for the big crowd that'll be battering down your doors when the legislature opens Monday, Izzy?"

"Oh, that!" Izzy made a deprecatory gesture, as if the opening of the legislature were almost too trivial an incident to merit his attention. "Why that won't be anything—mostly people from right here in town. The real headache'll begin when folks start coming in from Shreveport, Lake Charles and New Orleans, for the inauguration. But am I fixed for them? . . . Bring me a couple of those new bill-of-fares, the ones that have just been run off on the ditto machine," he called to another waiter. Then he handed one menu to Gervais and the other to Fabian, pointing with bursting pride to a small ornamentally boxed announcement at the top of each:

INAUGURATION SPECIAL

LOIN AND LAMB GET TOGETHER

35¢

"Oh, Izzy! Tampering with Holy Writ!" chuckled Fabian. "And you the son or grandson of a pious rabbi, no doubt!"

"Well, sir," replied the little restaurateur defensively, "Parker has brought all sides together, hasn't he? But you couldn't expect me to serve real lion, so I got the next best thing by just changing two letters. . . . And I expect the Lord'll forgive me, seeing as how it's a good cause."

"Don't let him get your goat, Izzy." Gervais' voice did not indicate the same relish in the situation as his cousin's and he changed the subject, without actual abruptness, but with understandable finality. "By the way, you haven't happened to see anything of Mr. Gaston Daigle around here, have you?"

"No, Captain. I wouldn't, not this early in the morning. But he seldom ever misses an evening, when he's in town. Drop in here again about six o'clock and you'll pretty near be sure to find him."

"I'll do that. And if he gets here before I do, please tell him I'd be much obliged if he'd wait for me, unless he's in a special hurry."

"Certainly, Captain. Another small black? No? Well, don't forget about that new specialty of mine. I want to get your opinion on it." Izzy nodded and meandered back towards his cash register, stopping to speak to patrons at several other tables as he did so. Fabian looked after him with friendly amusement.

"Quite a character."

"Yes—and if there's better coffee than this, I don't know where, except of course, at Belle Heloise." Gervais put down his drained cup slowly, still savoring its contents. "I'm glad Parker sent you out for me," he said. "Otherwise, Lord knows when I'd have seen you. You're quite a stranger these days."

"Didn't you ever hear the old saying that the law's a jealous mistress?"

"Yes. Personally, I never put too much stock in it. But then I'm not an authority on mistresses," Gervais answered, grinning. "If you're all that busy, I suppose it wouldn't do any good to suggest that you might spend the day at Belle Heloise when you take me back," he added as they rose. "I think the road will be patched up well enough to last the day out, and I'd like to have you, if you could. It's a long time since you've been to see us."

"Dying to show off your twins, I suppose?" Fabian inquired, suddenly speaking in the same sardonic tone with which he had broken in at the conference. Then, as if instantly sorry for his satire, he added quickly, "As a matter of fact, I'd like very much to come, and Saturday is always a slack day at the office. The only hitch is I've got guests coming to midday dinner myself."

"Who are they? Couldn't you bring them along, too?"

"They'd be tickled to death to be asked, but I don't know how Tante Isabelle would take it. I'm afraid she'd consider them the sort who ought to eat, with gratitude, at the second table."

"Why should she, for God's sake? You're asking them to yours, aren't you?"

"Yes, but I have all sorts at mine. It's one of the many advantages of being an orphan and a bachelor and an eccentric—you can have anyone you like, any time. As a matter of fact, one of these men is a distant kinsman of ours—his second cousin, Cenas Tremblet, married your father's sister, Sybelle. He'd be tickled to death to see the baby that's named after her."

"Funny I never ran across him. But of course *maman's* parents never had much to do with any of us d'Alvery's, except the one they captured for their daughter. God, but my father led a miserable life! . . . How did you happen to find Aunt Sybelle's second cousin by marriage?"

"I don't suppose you've ever noticed two old men who spend most of their time sitting on a bench by the Veterans' Monument, quarreling with each other, have you? This Pascal Tremblet's one of them; the other one's name is Preston Vicknair. . . . They've got a third crony, Max Stoetzner, but he lives over in Port Allen, and only crosses the River on great occasions. Tremblet and Vicknair both live with reluctant relatives, so I've got into the habit of having them to my place once in a while, on Saturdays. They know they're really welcome there. We play fantan, and they enjoy putting Belizaire through his tricks. Well, it just seems a generally satisfactory arrangement."

"I'd be glad to have them at Belle Heloise and so would Merry. Cresside won't care one way or the other, but she'll be civil. If *maman* doesn't want to meet them, she can always have dinner in her boudoir. That's what she does when Merry's mother or Miss Mittie comes out —imaginary ill health certainly furnishes a hell of a lot of excuses for anything a woman doesn't want to do! But, as a matter of fact, I shouldn't be surprised if *maman* did come down today. Miss Mittie's all tied up with this suffrage racket she and so many other women have gone crazy over, or you might find her there—Saturday and Sunday are her only free days, of course, on account of her school teaching, and Merry rather makes a point of getting her to Belle Heloise at least twice a month. On the other hand, Charles Boylston is dining with us today, and he's probably *maman's* greatest favorite among my friends, even if he is a Yankee."

"He's a nice fellow. I gathered he was at Belle Heloise a good deal. Is he making any headway?"

"With Cresside? Not a bit. She likes him, too, but it doesn't seem to get him anywhere. . . . What do we do, pick up the two old birds at the Monument?"

"Yes, we'll go there first and see how they react to our plan of taking them down to the Plantation. Of course, secretly they'll be delighted, but they may want to put on a show of reluctance for effect. We can't just kidnap them offhand. That wouldn't set just right, even though it's true, as I said, that old Pascal would give his eyeteeth to see little Sybelle! Then, if they agree, I think we'd better stop by at Somerulos Street for a minute, too. It's only fair to tell Carmelite I won't be home for dinner with two guests, and incidentally, I'd like to get Belizaire. It wouldn't seem just right to deprive Tremblet and Vicknair of the fun they're looking forward to having with him."

"To say nothing of depriving his master of the fun *he's* looking forward to having! You're a fool about that dog, Fabian."

"Well, after all, I haven't got twins, you know."

"If you don't mind, I wish you'd quit talking about the twins in that tone of voice. What's the matter with twins?"

"Nothing, I suppose, when they're yours. But let's drop the subject, as you suggest."

They rose, simultaneously, and drifted towards the door, their progress halted by the exchange of several hearty greetings and by their stop at the cash register. As they reached the threshold, Fabian hailed another friend, a young man who walked with even more difficulty than he did himself, but was proceeding with apparent buoyancy down Third Street, accompanied by a pretty girl carrying a market basket.

"Hello, Happy!" he called out. "What's your hurry? Can't you stop long enough to say hello to a fellow cripple? Hello, Rett!"

The young couple stopped and laughingly shook hands. Happy's compensation had been late, they said, and they had been living on bread and cheese and kisses for several days; but now the Government check had come in, and they were off to buy out Third Street. Their blithe and carefree attitude was infectious; almost everyone who passed by smiled back at them.

"Well, the next time that check's late, if you don't come over to Somerulos Street and let Carmelite and me feed you, we'll both consider it a personal insult," Fabian warned them. "So long, and good hunting!" Then, as his friends took their merry departure, he said to Gervais, "Do you mean to say you hadn't met the Seviers before?"

"No, I don't think so. But they're all right. Tell me about them."

"There isn't so much to tell. Happy was in the war, wounded three times. That's why he walks crooked—not because he was born crippled." Fabian paused for a moment, looking after Happy, whose arm was now linked in his young wife's, and whose very hobble was jaunty. "You can see he's still pretty badly bunged up," Fabian went on. "But I think he's coming out of it all right. He and Rett were sweethearts from the time they were kids. They were married before he went to France, and she stayed with her folks while he was gone; now they're living in a pocket-size apartment around the corner from me, while he finishes his interrupted law course. They haven't a blessed thing to come and go on, but they're having the time of their lives." Again he paused, trying to follow the Seviers with his eyes. But they had apparently turned in at some shop, for they were no longer to be seen. "Well, shall we go on and pick up our old men?" he asked, changing the subject abruptly.

"Yes, let's do."

The cousins found the two old veterans eagerly watching for Fabian's approach, and as he had predicted, there was a slight demur from them on the subject of going to Belle Heloise. But their objections, though garrulous, were feeble and easily overruled, and Carmelite made none at all. She was a handsome mulattress, possessed of private plans, to which the dinner at any case had been a distinct encumbrance; she was delighted to see it abandoned. The prospect of an outing was also delightful to Belizaire. Having first been informed by Fabian that he could not go with his master, he drooped pathetically. Then, at the reassuring words, "All right, if you really want to, you may come along!" he barked and bounded about with joy, shooting through the front door and catapulting himself into the car. Fabian watched him with an affectionate amusement which he made no effort to conceal, as he hoisted himself awkwardly into the front seat and drew the excited animal down between himself and Gervais, who took the wheel for his cousin, as Fabian always found it difficult to drive. Pascal and Preston, to whom a ride in an automobile was in itself a great event, sat very erect on the back seat, endeavoring to mask, with assumed nonchalance, their pleasure in the expedition, which was actually quite as great as Belizaire's. Until they approached Hathaway Hall, they were fairly successful. But at the sight of the vast façade, rising so majestically before them, Preston's enthusiasm got the better of his assumed indifference.

"Say what you will, that's the handsomest place on the River Road," he remarked in an awed voice, gazing at it intently. Pascal dug him indignantly in the ribs.

"You'd better mind your manners, my friend," he muttered in a stage whisper. "Seemingly, you do not recollect, no, that we are on our way to a finer one this minute, one we're invited to, us, which is more than we ever was to that one. I never saw anything so handsome about it anyway, me. Looks more like a picture in a magazine than a real home. The folks that own it don't live in it enough, and that, my friend, is bound to show up, in any house. I hear they were in France most of the winter."

"Are they back now?" inquired Preston, feeling properly rebuked, but still unable to suppress his excited interest in Hathaway Hall.

"Yes, they're back now, but only just, and the rumor is they're going to Hot Springs for most of the summer."

"Miss Regine's been married almost a year, hasn't she? Any prospects in that family?"

"Absolutely not that I have heard of, me. I tell you very frankly, all I did hear was, the crops are not doing so good, no. Mosaic disease."

"Mosaic disease?"

"Yes. You assuredly do not mean to tell me, Pres Vicknair, you have never heard of that?"

Less lyrically but quite as accurately as John Parker had described it to his hearers earlier that morning, Pascal Tremblet embarked upon an exposition for the benefit of his old crony. He was still deep in his subject when he realized that Captain d'Alvery was stopping the car in order to speak to someone on the road. Peering out, Pascal saw that they had overtaken a somewhat grotesque but immensely jolly man, obviously a peddler, who was pushing a cart hung with all sorts of small gaudy wares, in the midst of which was sitting a rather dirty but very beautiful little boy, who had enormous eyes and clustering black curls and who was sucking a long stick of peppermint candy.

"Hello, Luigi," Captain d'Alvery was saying genially. "So you've graduated from a basket to a cart, have you? I suppose that fancy grocery store must be almost around the corner. Just the same, I hope you haven't given up the Johnny Crooks! And no doubt this is the famous bambino I've heard so much about. I'm glad to see him at last."

"Howdado, *Capitano!* Howdado, Mr. d'Alvery! Howdado, gentlemen!" Luigi responded, saluting the entire group with great heartiness. "Yes, sir, I gotta me a cart now. I have the Johnny Crooks same as always, taffy and sauerkraut candy and stage planks, too. But I no carry justa candy no more. I gotta kitchenware—fancy dress goods —julery!" In rapid succession he seized various samples of his wares, finally dangling a string of red glass beads before Gervais' eyes. "You taka those for a present to the Missus, please, *Capitano*," he said. "You buya some beads for your sister, too, next time I come to the mansion to make up. I gonna go to the quarters today at Belle Heloise but maybe I don'ta come to the Big House, you get so much company already. . . . *Si, si,* this is my Riccardo. Only he's no bambino no more. He's a bigga boy. Ain't you, Riccardo?"

The beautiful child removed the stick of candy from his grimy little mouth, smiled beatifically, and answered his father with the respect that bespoke excellent home discipline.

"Yes, Papa," he said. "I'm bigga boy now. I'm three and a half."

"That'sa right," Luigi said encouragingly. "And when you maka four years, what you gonna do then, Riccardo?"

"I'm not gonna ride in the cart. I'm gonna help push it."

"Good for you, Riccardo. In the meantime, I'm sorry I can't give you and your papa both a lift, especially as the mud's so bad. But my car seems to be pretty full already."

"It is, it is, *Capitano*," agreed Luigi. "And we don't wanna any lift, Riccardo and me. I always walk and pretty soon he's gonna walk, too, with me. We donna mind the mud. But sure we sava money for the fancy grocery store all the time, *Capitano*."

"I'm glad to hear it. Mind you don't ever let it run low on sugar. Well, so long, Luigi. So long, Riccardo. Come to the Big House soon, even if you don't get there today, won't you?"

An exchange of farewells was characterized by much good will on all sides, and then the motor car started again, leaving the peddler and his child and his cart behind. The "singing towers" of Belle Heloise were already in sight, and the automobile had turned into the blind driveway before either of the old men was aware of it. Even the rattle of the cattle-gap might have passed unnoticed, if Gervais had not turned and spoken to them as the motor clattered over it.

"That rattle gives the signal of my approach, gentlemen. In a second you'll hear our two old dogs, Snow and Cornet, and they'll be jumping all over the car, too. But don't let that bother you—they're both perfectly harmless, and after a minute they'll be trying to pick a fight with Belizaire anyway, and forget all about you. My wife generally comes out to meet me, too, so in just about a minute you'll be in the bosom of the family."

The predicted barking began before he had finished speaking and the next instant the screen of the front door swung open, and a young and very lovely woman appeared between the fluted columns that flanked it, hastened down the brick demilune and across the gallery. In the comparatively brief period since she had come, so precipitately,

124

to Belle Heloise, Merry had changed, in some respects, very markedly. She now wore beautiful and becoming clothes as a matter of course, and her manner, always warm and friendly, had gained immeasurably in poise and graciousness. Her greeting to her husband was unself-conscious, but it was a salutation of welcome rather than an invitation to a prolonged embrace. She freed herself almost immediately to receive her guests with unaffected cordiality.

"Why, Fabian, I can't tell you how glad I am to see you! It seems like months since you've been here. . . . So this is another kinsman, is it? I'm glad to meet you, Cousin Pascal. Fabian's often spoken to me about you. And this is your friend, Mr. Vicknair? No, Belizaire, I didn't forget you. I was only speaking to your betters first. Won't you all come out on the rear gallery? That's where we seem to be assembled."

Still chatting pleasantly, she led the way to the front door and through the big hall that bisected the house, with great square rooms opening from it on either side. Essentially, the place was unchanged: the same draperies and furniture, the same portraits and ornaments, which had been there for so many years were still disposed as Madame d'Alvery and, before her, a long succession of Estrade ladies had always kept them. But there were more flower-filled vases scattered about, more doors and windows opened to admit air and sunshine. The slight mustiness that had formerly pervaded it was gone and freshness flowed through it; and while it still retained its air of elegance, its formality seemed inexplicably tempered. Pascal and Preston, treading cautiously over the soft carpet, cast awed and surreptitious glances into the parlor, the library, the dining room and the music room as they passed, hoping against hope that they would have a better look at these glories. Merry, as if reading their thoughts, paused reassuringly.

"We'll come back into the house by and by," she said. "But, of course, I can't wait to show off my family first. You don't mind, do you?"

Somewhat mendaciously, they assured her they did not, and she went on, next swinging open the door to the rear gallery. The old veterans, admitted to Belle Heloise for the first time, had no standards of comparison; but Fabian was quick to notice that here, at least, a tremendous change had taken place. Philogene d'Alvery, to be sure, had spent a good deal of time in the rear gallery, lounging about and sipping brandy; but nothing had ever been done to make the place attractive or appealing to him. At one end, it had served as a repository for brooms, mops and brushes, thrust out from the kitchen door; at the other, for hoes, rakes, and similar implements, which the uninspired successors of Angus Holt still seemed to feel should be near the Garden Room; in between, there had been a haphazard and heterogeneous collection of wicker chairs and tables and of broken iron flower stands, relegated to oblivion from more conspicuous places. The spacious width, paved with mellow brick, flanked on one side by the house itself and framed, on the other, by the noble columns supporting the upper gallery, had never before been utilized for living quarters. Yet it was ideally suited for this purpose, shielded as it was from the intensity of the sun, but full of the essence of sunlight, and facing the sweep of lawn which merged gradually into the blossoming woods beyond. Now, at last, the delightful possibilities of this gallery, which actually seemed more like a patio, had been recognized and turned to account. Ferns and other plants were scattered about, some hanging, some rising from long boxes, and still others clustering in graceful jars. At one end a refectory table with benches on either side, painted green to match the shutters which enlivened the white walls, suggested that it was frequently used as an alfresco dining room; while at the other end, some spruce rattan furniture, cushioned in bright chintz, indicated its unmistakable habitability as a living room. Dominating the rest of its equipment was an enormous double cradle in which two bouncing babies were sitting, propped up with pillows, and delightedly, if aimlessly, waving pink and blue rattles. A buxom colored woman, picturesquely dressed, who rose respectfully at the approach of the visitors, had been sitting watchfully beside this cradle; while bending over it, less quick to look up, was a dark graceful girl, whose face, even though half hidden, revealed a piquant, almost elfin quality of charm, while her extreme slenderness gave an obtrusive effect of fragility. Fabian went over and put his arm around her shoulder, Belizaire following closely behind him.

"Hello, Cresside!" he said. His flexible voice, which so quickly betrayed the varying moods his somber face might have masked, took on a new tone when he spoke. It was genial, and at the same time it was curiously gentle. "I brought another worshiper to the shrine. A cousin of Mr. Tremblet's here married our Aunt Sybelle. He wants to see the young lady that's named for her."

"He'll see a mighty fine baby then. . . . But where have you been all this time, you old wretch?" The latter remark, obviously addressed to Fabian, was made as Cresside straightened up, and when she had done so, the excessive thinness of her pretty, pointed little face became more noticeable. Her heavily fringed eyes, large out of all proportion to the rest of her features, still further accentuated this emaciation. But her elfin smile was extremely attractive, and she held out her hand with great cordiality.

"How are you, Mr. Tremblet?" she said. "Take a good look at a Carnival Queen of 1938. . . . And incidentally at her brother. He's nice, too," she added, stooping again to divert a rattle which seemed headed straight for the girl twin's eye. "Oh, I'm sorry! I didn't see you had a friend with you. Mr. Vicknair? I used to run around a lot with a boy named Erlo Vicknair. Could it possibly have been a relative of yours? Your *grandson*? *You live with him?* Well, that is a coincidence, isn't it. Give him my best, won't you? Here, let me get out of the way, so that you can see the twins, too."

The two old men bent delightedly over the double cradle. The twins, after staring for a moment doubtfully at the strangers, smiled beguilingly and resumed their gurgling and kicking. Merry had turned back to speak to Gervais, but Cresside and Fabian stood behind the veterans, looking down at the cradle, too. The Negro nurse, her capable, kindly hands folded quietly over her white apron, continued to watch from a respectful distance.

"I tell you frankly, I never saw a prettier pair of babies, me," Pascal announced at length. "I think you must be a true prophet, Miss Cresside. Most assuredly little Sybelle will be a Carnival Queen when she grows up. And you may say, my friends, it is all imagination, but I think, me, she favors her great aunt, the young lady that married my cousin. But she does not resemble her brother, no. I thought twins always looked alike, but she is fair, yes, and he is dark."

"You don't mean to tell me, Pascal, you ain't never heard that there's identical twins and non-identical twins?" Preston demanded, bridling indignantly. "These here are non-identical twins. That is always the case when one twin is a boy and the other a girl."

"How clever of you, Mr. Vicknair, to know all about that and to notice it right away!" Merry had come up now, her arm linked in Gervais', who was holding her hand. But again she freed herself easily, and picking up little Sybelle, tossed her high in the air, while the baby crowed with glee. "They're identical when it comes to being hungry, though," Merry added. "And it's almost their dinner time now. I think I'd better take them away before they start howling and spoil the good impression they've made. They can begin to scream right in the middle of a gurgle, if they think they're not getting their rights. Especially Vail. Sybelle is quite ladylike even when she cries—if she can keep on that way, it'll be a great asset to her later! But Vail bellows. . . . Take him please, Dinah," she added, turning to the nurse, who immediately gathered the little boy into her comfortable arms. "And excuse us, the rest of you, will you, please, for a little while? We won't be gone long. You'll find out what our guests would like to drink, won't you, Gervais? And I think we'll have dinner out here, unless anyone would rather go into the dining room!"

"I'd much rather have it here," Fabian said heartily. "This patio is swell, Merry. I hadn't seen it since you'd fixed it up."

"That's your own fault, isn't it? I've been puttering in it all the spring. I do that instead of sleeping, this time!"

She laughed, and Fabian joined in Gervais' laughing response as Merry left them, quiet, assured, radiant, her baby girl in her arms. The veterans, puzzled but polite, endeavored to laugh too. Cresside went over to Dinah, and taking the responsive Vail from her, smoothed down his little dress, which had been hunched up around him when he was lifted from the cradle. Then she handed him back again, and the Negro nurse, with a dignity comparable to that of her mistress, followed after Merry, carrying the little boy. Cresside sat down in one of the bright wicker chairs, and, lighting a cigarette, looked fixedly out towards the garden, her black eyes bigger than ever in her white face.

"I suppose it is my fault. I'll try not to let it happen again. 'Time is too slow for those who wait,' you know," Fabian said, answering Merry by speaking to Cresside. "By the way, where's Tante Isabelle?"

"I believe she's having dinner in her boudoir today. The heat, you know."

There was nothing prostrating about the pleasant warmth of May, and again the veterans found it hard to conceal their polite puzzlement. Fabian, however, nodded understandingly.

"And what about Boylston? I thought Gervais said he was coming today, too."

"Oh, he's here all right. He arrived before we were through breakfast."

"Cresside, he didn't do anything of the sort. He wasn't here when I went to town with Fabian."

"Well, it seems to me as if he'd been here forever. I can stand that Boston accent just so long and then it gets me down. Anyway, after listening to an exhilarating conversation for at least two hours, I suggested that he should go and see *maman*. That's where he is now. For all I know he may be reading St. Augustine's Sermons aloud."

"A good Unitarian from Boston? Now, now Cresside!" rallied Fabian.

"Being an invalid for such a long time didn't cure Cresside of a habit of mockery, Fabian," Gervais said, rather shortly. "I'll let Boylston know we're here, and I'm sure he'll be right down. If this is one of *maman's* bad days, she ought not to tire herself by talking too long anyway. What will you gentlemen have, a julep or a highball?"

Pascal and Preston eyed each other doubtfully. Cresside answered for them.

"I'm going to make you each one of my special juleps," she said. "You tell me truly afterwards if you don't think it's the best you ever tasted. Then while you're sipping it, why don't we play a game or something? There are five of us—six if the honorable Charles can tear himself away from *maman*. We can play poker. That is, unless there's something you'd rather do."

Again the two old men exchanged glances. Both were still somewhat bound by timidity, but Cresside's breezy friendliness was beginning to take effect, especially on Preston. He was the first to summon courage to speak, unexpectedly finding, once he had begun, that it was easy to go on.

"We wouldn't like to make all that work for you, Miss Cresside, when you've been sick so long," he said apologetically. "Anyone can see you're still puny. We'd enjoy the juleps, of course, but a highball would do just as well, and it wouldn't be half as much trouble. We'd enjoy a game of poker, too. We play fantan at Fabian's house; it's been some time though since we've been out in company where there was enough for poker. But maybe you'd like to rest in the bed a while before dinner, and maybe there's something your brother and Mr. Boylston would rather do, too. Me and Pascal, we could walk out and see where those Yanks are buried, them that died of smallpox during the War Between the States. I've always had a hankering to see that graveyard——"

"Then you'd better let Miss Cresside show it to you, and I want to come along and see it, too," Fabian broke in. "But not until later in the day, when it gets cooler. Let's have that game of poker now, with the juleps, as she suggests. . . . Didn't I hear something about your fixing up that little old cemetery, Cresside?" he asked, turning to her. "Getting a rustic bridge built over the gully that used to be impassable in wet weather? And then having the stones, that were all broken and battered, straightened and mended? And so on?"

"I don't know what you've heard. I haven't any special affinity for graveyards," Cresside said diffidently. "I only started to do something on the one between here and Hathaway Hall because Gervais wanted it cleaned up and none of the Negroes would go near it. As far as that is concerned, Gervais wouldn't either. He's afraid of snakes. I'm not. Then after I cleaned out the nest in the Hathaway's lot, so that ours would be free of them, I started in to see what I could do for the Yanks. I've always felt sort of sorry for them—outliers like that. No relatives ever coming with flowers, or fellow veterans with bands, or ladies' patriotic societies putting up markers. So I worked down there while Merry was fixing up the patio, and by and by we met in Angus Holt's garden. Maybe that was symbolic or something. I don't know. But I'd be very glad to take Mr. Tremblet and Mr. Vicknair down there later on if they'd really like to go."

"And can't I come?"

Cresside rose again from her wicker chair, pulling down her belt with the same show of gaiety with which she had adjusted the baby's dress, and once more Fabian was shocked by the revelation of abnormal slenderness. "Oh, you can tag along," she said carelessly. "That is, if you're really intrigued about my handiwork, and not just putting on an act, the way that damn Bostonian is most of the time. Set up a table and get out the cards and chips while I make the juleps, will you, Fabian? Gervais'll have to go upstairs and take another look at the young mother and her offspring before he'll be good for anything else."

CHAPTER IX

THE PATIO WAS so peaceful and pleasant that the afternoon was over before anyone could believe that its mellow hours had slipped away. The superlative juleps, presented in great silver goblets and encrusted with frost, had taken a long time to consume; then dinner, served informally but lavishly at the refectory table, had been a leisurely meal, beginning with fish aspic followed by fried chicken and "fixin's," and ending with peach ice cream and angel-food cake. There was coffee afterwards, and brandy with the coffee, the coffeepot and brandy bottle remaining within convenient reach of everyone. Preston and Pascal were both intermittently nodding a little and then rousing themselves in a startled way, when Gervais remarked casually that he always took a snooze after dinner and that perhaps they would like to do the same; if they would, the Garden Room, where a day bed supplemented the four-poster, was entirely at their disposal. They gratefully accepted his suggestion, and after he had shown them their quarters, by the simple process of opening the door which led directly into these from the patio, he took his leave of the other guests with equal informality, while mounting the adjacent outdoor stairway. Without either apology or explanation, Merry accompanied him; she obviously took it for granted that everyone would expect her to share her husband's siesta. Cresside, left behind with Fabian and Charles Boylston, looked from one to the other with her elfin smile.

"There are three or four more vacant beds in the house," she remarked. "Not to mention any number of stiff sofas. If either or both of you would like to lie down, too, it can very easily be managed."

Both men laughingly declined the invitation. Boylston had never succeeded in forming the siesta habit, he said; he did not get up as early as most of his neighbors, but once he *was* up, it was for the day. Fabian had been born with the habit, he drawled; but the war, which had evidently not been carried on with a view of making things easy for civilians, had interfered with it; since he never could brook interference, he had decided to give up the habit. But what about Cresside herself? She looked to him as if she could do with a little sleep.

"I can—very little," she retorted. "Don't make such unflattering remarks, Fabian—no girl likes to hear them, even from a mere cousin. . . . It's too bad there wasn't one more person in this gathering, besides us, who could keep awake. If there only had been, we might have a nice game of bridge."

"What about the Tremaines? Wouldn't they join us? I could run over and find out, if you like. It wouldn't take me ten minutes."

"Thanks, Charles. But you may be sure they're both asleep now, too.
130

And anyway, if they came, we'd have one too many, which is just as bad as having one too few. Why don't you two go ahead and play chess while I do some baby sewing? We're never caught up with that nowadays."

They settled down companionably with ash trays on either side of Cresside's work basket and a tall pitcher of iced tea within easy reach. Cresside sewed with surprising deftness and daintiness; but the chess game suffered somewhat, because, as they played, Boylston watched Cresside and Fabian watched Boylston. He had liked the little he had seen of the Bostonian, but he had never before had the occasion or taken the trouble to observe him closely. Now he found it interesting to scrutinize the outsider's appearance and to speculate on his character. Boylston's eyes were gray, very clear and cool, his thin straight hair the somewhat lifeless shade of brown into which a child's pretty flaxen locks so often darken with maturity. He was lean rather than slender, and he carried himself with poise rather than grace. His color was healthy, though it lacked ruddiness, and his skin indicated almost fastidious cleanliness; his hands were shapely and dexterous. He wore tweeds better than any other planter along the River Road; but he was less distinguished looking in linens; apparently he had never become wholly reconciled to the Louisiana custom of wearing these from May to October. In conversation he was agreeable, intelligent and cultured; he could hold his own in any group, even if he could not dominate it. He was never profane himself, but profanity did not seem to offend him; he had picked up no colloquialisms during his southern sojourn, and his Boston accent was still wholly unsoftened. Visitors to his house were greatly impressed by the number and quality of his framed diplomas, and his study also contained some very fine family portraits, and a large collection of valuable books; but he himself seldom referred to his education or his background, and then only in the most casual way. No one knew why he had come to Louisiana in the first place, or what had caused him to stay. But he fitted surprisingly well into the local picture; furthermore, he was a man of wealth, an accomplished host and a delightful guest.

Fabian, finishing his appraisal, found it easy to understand that Tante Isabelle would approve of and enjoy Charles Boylston above any of Gervais' other friends "even if he was a Yankee." He was the ideal suitor for the daughter of the house, from a conservative and an aristocratic mother's point of view—wellborn, well reared, well educated, rich, personable and high-principled. If Cresside married a man like this, and continued to live close by, where her position and her prestige would be continually before the eyes of the Capital and the River families, it would more than compensate for Gervais' mésalliance. For Gervais' marriage would always remain a mésalliance in his mother's eyes, despite her reluctant liking for her daughter-in-law and Merry's own phenomenal adaptability and forebearance. Fabian had no delusions on that score; he was not deceived by the surface harmony which reigned at Belle Heloise. Isabelle d'Alvery would never be satisfied until the pomp and circumstance of the Estrades had been restored, and she was counting on Cresside to do this.

Counting vainly, Fabian reflected, shifting his observant glance from Charles to Cresside as he hesitated over a knight's gambit. The Bostonian meant no more to her than he did; he felt sure of that. Cresside, herself so vital, would demand some essential element of vigor which Boylston lacked. That is, if ever again she demanded, or accepted, anything from a man. There were women, Fabian knew, who could not care, as Cresside had once cared for Sylvestre, more than once in a lifetime; and this was all the more likely to be true after a tardy and tragic discovery that the bounty they offered with such prodigality and pride had been taken carelessly or deceitfully. *I'm rather sorry for Boylston,* he thought, abandoning the gambit, and advancing his queen. *But if he weren't such a thoroughgoing polecat I'd be sorrier still for Sylvestre. Not because of what he's done to Cresside, though that's scummy enough, Lord knows. I can't even look at the girl without having something turn over inside me at the sight of her eyes. But because of what he's done to himself. He got a glimmer of it on his wedding day, when he stood looking at her after she was hurt; he'd have given whatever his substitute is for a soul if he could have married her then, instead of Regine. But he didn't really know what frustration can do to a man, through the years, once he's sold his birthright for a mess of red pottage. Some day he'll find out, and then God help him! No, damn him, I hope God doesn't help him, or man either. I hope he gets everything that's coming to him. But I wish Boylston had something coming to him too, something good, because he really is the right kind of people. And I wish Cresside. . . .*

The door of the Garden Room opened, and Preston and Pascal came out, looking refreshed and expectant. Cresside laid down the scraps of fine linen and narrow lace which she was whipping together.

"What about some claret lemonade before we start to the cemetery?" she inquired. "I think you'd find it very refreshing. Nonsense, of course it isn't any trouble to make—in fact, I have it half made already. I'll get Selah to bring it right out. . . . Do you want to see your fellow Yankees' graves, Charles, or are you going to sit here until the rest of us get back? I think Merry'll be down again any minute now. Gervais generally goes out to see how the hoe gang's coming along, as soon as he gets up—Sance is a good overseer, but Gervais doesn't think he keeps the hands' work quite up to the good old Army standards, and we're having a lot of trouble with Johnson grass; so Gervais is out in the field most of the time, too. But Merry comes back to the patio to do a little light gardening before supper. Perhaps you'd like to help her."

"I would, some time. But today I'd like immensely to go with the rest of you to the cemetery, if you don't mind."

"Oh, I don't mind! I suppose it isn't just the thing to say 'The more the merrier' when you're going to a graveyard. But please consider that I've expressed the proper equivalent."

The expedition proved a complete success from everyone's point of view. Cresside first led the way through the wicket gate beyond Angus Holt's garden into a narrow *allée,* bordered on one side by mulberry trees and on the other by elderberries. She stopped for a moment, looking up at the delicate flat clusters of small white flowers which were just beginning to fall.

"We make wine out of those elderberries," she said. "I reckon we'll be making more than ever now. We don't make mulberry wine because there aren't any mulberries. According to Creassy, those are all 'he' mulberry trees. So, of course, they aren't any more good than other males without normal co-operation."

The corners of Fabian's mouth twitched, and Preston and Pascal both chuckled. Charles Boylston smiled, politely but a trifle forcedly, and Cresside, making a slight *moue* at Fabian, went on towards the cemetery without further frivolous remarks. Beyond the *allée* the rustic bridge, to which Fabian had referred earlier in the day, spanned a little gully, on the other side of which the ground widened to form a spacious grove, permeated with the sweet scent of new mown grass. The greensward was studded with beautiful trees, pecans for the most part, though there were a few cypresses and flowering thorns among them; their trunks were wreathed with vines, their branches draped with moss. Above the dense growth of thickets, the levee was plainly visible. But the River Road itself was concealed by the shrubbery, so that the line of verdure remained everywhere unbroken, and seemed to reach upward towards the sky. The veterans gazed about them in amazement and awe.

"I never saw a more beautiful grove, me," Pascal said. "You wouldn't think there was all this space, either, between the road and the cane fields, would you, now? Is it much further to the cemetery?"

"But Mr. Tremblet, this *is* the cemetery! Any number of Yankee dead are buried here—dozens of them died in that smallpox epidemic, and some were killed in battle besides. We don't know whether most of the graves were never marked, or whether the markers disappeared —Creassy says only the officers' graves had tombstones, and that the cypresses were planted to mark the others because it was hard to get marble; but that's just Negro hearsay—no one in the family seems to have been interested enough to learn the truth about it. Anyway, there are only four stones here now, and they have no inscriptions on them—they're plain gray marble, very small and simple. But someone must have tried to beautify their surroundings once—there's a big bush of bridal wreath beside one of them, and trifoliata beside the others. Come, I'll show them to you. They're all on the other side of the grove, not far apart from each other."

Walking silently and slowly, the men followed her. They saw the sheltering trees before they saw the stones, the bridal wreath already past its snowy bloom, the lemon trees already laden with hard green fruit and wreathed with scarlet trumpet vines. While the others stood watching him, Fabian bent over, trying to discover some mark or symbol which would betray the identity of the men whose humble headstones were so pitifully blank. But his search was futile. He straightened up, breaking off a branch of the strange tree which had fruit and thorns on the same bough.

"There ought to be a record of these men somewhere," he said. "The War Department must have been functioning when they were here, at least after a fashion, and I shouldn't be at all surprised if Madame Lucien Estrade managed to keep some kind of a plantation diary, during her husband's absence in the war. It would have been entirely in character. . . . You've never come across anything of the sort, Cresside?"

"No, never."

"Well, I'm going to see what I can dig up. It might be interesting. Meanwhile, let's pretend we know who these men were. . . . Ummm! Over here would be Colonel McIvor—second generation Scotsman— never let a Sunday newspaper come into the house—if they had Sunday newspapers in those days, always prayed his men into battle, but couldn't pray himself out of the smallpox, poor old devout devil. He'd have hung Jeff Davis to a sour apple tree fast enough, if he'd had his way. And his wife had one black silk dress and no children —a dress that would stand alone. Hail and farewell, Colonel. . . . Next to him would be young Lieutenant Jem—short for Jeremiah— Hawkins, the best dancer in Cincinnati, pride of the Burnet House cotillions, if they had cotillions. A gay young rake of a bachelor, was Jem, but paying court to the daughter of the bank where he clerked. And he sang tenor around the campfires—just befo-o-o-re the battle, mother. Next to him—well, let's see, that'd be a New Englander, the kind you used to read about selling wooden nutmegs. Had a captaincy in the state militia, and kept a country store in South Scituate, Mass. Wife's name was Hepzibah, of course, and they had nine children, all conceived without taint of sin, regardless of how much sand the old boy used to put into the sugar. Lord, how he hated to give up the store and go off to the wars—with all those government contracts he might have got hold of; but it wouldn't have looked right, giving up his militia commission that way. Wonder if Hepzibah married again. Bet she did. Imagine her introducing his nine stepchildren to the new mister. . . . And finally, over here, is the one real fanatic, a sort of junior John Brown, a black abolitionist who took the sword in one hand and a copy of *Uncle Tom's Cabin* in the other and went out to set the black man free. Calvin Cromwell Stafford was his name —and it's a good thing he didn't survive, for he'd have been the loudest carpetbagger in Dixie if he had, holding down a job as collector of customs at Savannah and burning a candle in front of a picture of Thad Stevens, till he got himself elected to the Senate where

134

he'd have voted for the impeachment of Andy Johnson. Well—here they are. *De mortuis nil nisi bonum*. They were men of courage and they died far from home. May their rest be ever peaceful. . . ."

None of the others had stirred while Fabian was speaking. Now, for a moment no one spoke. Cresside stood looking at him intently, her enormous eyes fixed on his face, her lips quivering slightly. At last Pascal broke the spell which had been wrought partly by the place itself and partly by Fabian's fantasy.

"I could sit here listening to you all night, me. But I think, maybe, if it's convenient for you, Mr. Fabian, we ought to be getting back to town. My granddaughter, she doesn't like to have me late to supper, and——"

"Of course not, Pascal. It's high time I was on my way, too. Thanks no end, Cresside, for bringing us here."

They went briefly back to the patio, where they found the twins, refreshed by food and sleep, again happily installed in their cradle, and Merry, as Cresside had predicted, "doing a little light gardening." Charles Boylston decided to stay on and help her with this, but the others made their farewells, leaving good-by for Gervais, who was still in the field. As they approached Hathaway Hall, Fabian suggested that the two old men might like to drive through the short semicircular *allée* which separated the house from the road without concealing it; and at their eager assent, he turned in among the trees. Instantly he heard someone calling his name, and looking up, saw Regine, as usual dressed in white, standing in the gallery above them.

"Fabian! Oh Fabian! Won't you please stop!"

He halted the car and called back to her, mimicking her appeal.

"Regine! Why Regine! I didn't intend to, but of course I will, if you make a point of it. Are you badly in need of help? Is the house on fire or something?"

"Of course I'm not in need of help and of course the house isn't on fire. I want to see you, that's all. Wait, I'm coming down."

Regine came gracefully down the curving steps to meet them, one hand resting lightly on the railing of the balustrade, the other caressing the rose at her breast. She was wise enough to adapt the grotesque fashion of the times to her own type, rather than to follow it slavishly, and in spite of her short-skirted, long-waisted dress, she managed to produce a picturesque effect. Her greeting to Fabian was charmingly coy.

"I'm glad I finally succeeded in attracting your attention," she said with a little laugh. "I saw you every time you went by this morning: first alone, evidently on your way to Belle Heloise; then going back to town, with Gervais; finally returning again, with Gervais and these two gentlemen. Mr. Tremblet? Mr. Vicknair? I'm delighted to welcome you both to Hathaway Hall. Won't you all come in where it's cool and let me order you a drink?"

"We've had so many drinks at Belle Heloise that I don't know whether we can hold any more. But we can try," Fabian said agreeably, following her lead up the stairway. "Anyway, we'll be glad to come in. Sorry I didn't see your previous signals—also that I haven't managed to get out here before. I don't seem to have been anywhere lately. Everyone at Belle Heloise has been calling me to task on that score. . . . Well, travel must agree with you, Regine. You look like a million dollars."

"It's probably my new Paris clothes," she said with another little laugh. "But as far as that goes, I don't see how travel could help agreeing with me, when it was made under such ideal conditions! Do you? I want to tell you all about the garden party at Buckingham Palace, and our motor trip through the Dolomites, and our villa at Cannes—oh, everything! But let's get comfy before I begin."

She opened the front door and her visitors followed her into the vast hallway, flanked with Corinthian columns and further embellished with a wide tinted cornice of elaborate plaster work simulating magnolias. As they progressed past the entrance to the White Ball Room, disclosed in all its magnificent emptiness, Preston cast a surreptitious and triumphant glance at Pascal: he had been right after all; there was nothing in the relatively simple style of decoration at Belle Heloise that could be compared to all this grandeur. But once they were seated in the room at the left of the front door, he did not feel so certain. It was not sunny and inviting, like the patio where they had spent the day, and neither did it have the dignity of the more formal apartments at Belle Heloise. Evidently the Hathaways, in their preoccupation with preserving the White Ball Room for great ceremonials, had neglected both homeliness and harmony in their living room. It was commonplace and cluttered without being comfortable, and it bore the imprint of no special personality. Preston remembered Pascal's remark that the folks who owned Hathaway Hall did not live in it enough, and that this was bound to show up, in any house; this room looked as if people simply occupied it occasionally, as they might have occupied a hotel room without ever actually inhabiting it, and without even taking the trouble to keep it tidy. Strange that a beautiful young lady, who looked so much like a fashion plate herself, should be satisfied with a parlor of this sort, Pascal reflected; and then decided that after all, perhaps the young lady was more concerned about being beautiful herself than about making her habitation beautiful. He was sure that Mrs. Gervais d'Alvery felt just the opposite, though she was certainly lovely looking, too, much lovelier, when you came right down to it, than this young lady—friendlier, simpler, sweeter, somehow. He didn't know just why, but he didn't take to this young lady the way he had to Mrs. Gervais d'Alvery. . . .

"So you've been spending the day at Belle Heloise," Regine went on. She did not say anything more about getting a drink for them, or summon anyone else to do so; instead, she picked up a large fan from the littered center table, and wielded it languidly and gracefully, her rings and bracelets sparkling with the movement. "I've been rather expecting the d'Alverys to drop in and welcome us back. But we haven't seen any of them yet. How are they?"

"The young couple and their offspring are all flourishing. And Tante Isabelle has certainly staged an astonishing comeback. But Cresside still looks pretty puny, as Mrs. Randall would put it."

"Why, I had no idea she wasn't well! We never corresponded as schoolgirls, so I didn't think it was strange I didn't hear from her while I was abroad. But then, I wasn't paying much attention to letters from anyone, except mamma. And, of course, I wasn't far from her at any time. You know she came to Europe on the *Paris* Line the week after Sylvestre and I sailed on the *France,* and she stayed at the Berkeley while we were at Claridge's. Then when we went to Cannes, she went to Nice, and so on. She'll be so sorry to have missed you this afternoon—she's gone to play bridge at the Graces'. . . . Why, *cher,* I didn't hear you come in. Fabian's brought some friends to call on us—Mr. Tremblet and Mr. Vicknair."

"How do you do?" inquired Sylvestre impersonally. "Nice of you to drop in." He shook hands, rather limply, with the three callers, and apparently oblivious of the invitation in Regine's upturned face, took some dog-eared magazines off an oak rocker and drew it up beside Fabian. Like Boylston, he was immaculately dressed, though unlike the Bostonian, he wore his spotless white linens with an accustomed grace. But there was nothing about him to indicate the preoccupied planter. Indeed, his appearance suggested the gentleman of leisure who had been able to devote the entire day to keeping cool, rather than the harassed landowner who had just returned to the house for a hasty shower and a quick change before dinner. Mrs. Hathaway had long entrusted the supervision of the plantation to her manager, Grover Blood, whose personal reputation was unsavory, but whose professional efficiency had gone unchallenged, in spite of his predilection for wine, women and song. Mrs. Hathaway did not like changes and apparently Sylvestre had been only too glad to follow the line of least resistance and allow Blood to continue shouldering the responsibility and doing the dirty work around the place. "Did I hear you saying something about Cresside as I came in?" he went on, lighting a cigarette and, as an afterthought, tendering the opened case to his callers. "That she wasn't well?"

"Yes. Possibly you may recall that she had a pretty bad fall the day you were married," Fabian remarked, declining the proffered cigarette, but lighting one of his own.

"Of course, we remember! You don't really think we'd be so stupid as to forget that, do you, Fabian?" Regine broke in, before Sylvestre could answer. Again she laughed, and this time Pascal realized that one of the reasons he did not like this young lady was because of her laugh. It was tinkling, but it was tiresome. "We didn't know it was serious, though," Regine continued. "That is, we knew she was hurt, but we didn't realize she was injured. Why, all the family came to our wedding, that very same afternoon!"

"Yes, I know," Fabian said drily. "That is, everyone but me. I figured I'd be the least missed, and apparently I was right—you'd even forgotten I wasn't there, Regine! But I stayed behind with Dr. Champagne. Of course, we knew it would upset your entire program, if one usher dropped out at the last moment, so Gervais decided he ought to come anyway, as long as there wasn't anything he could do for Cresside at that stage—she was under a pretty powerful opiate by then; and you may be sure that whither Gervais goeth, there Merry goeth also, if he wants her to, and he did. Besides, of course, it was a great treat for her to see a beautiful wedding like yours—I'm sure she'll always enjoy going to beautiful weddings. She'll get a vicarious thrill out of them that will partly make up for the one she couldn't get out of her own stark marriage ceremony, worse luck! As to Tante Isabelle, I wouldn't have put it past her to come here that day if there'd been a broken neck instead of a broken back to cope with at Belle Heloise. She'd made up her mind it was to be her first public appearance since her widowhood, and when Tante Isabelle makes up her mind, she doesn't stop for hell or high water."

"What do you mean, a broken back? Cresside didn't *break* her back, did she?"

"She broke a couple of vertebrae. You don't have to break all of them, you know, to suffer the tortures of the damned. She was in a plaster cast for about six weeks, and after that in some kind of a brace. She had to stay in bed for months and months. She's up and around now, but I'm not so sure she ought to be. She doesn't look like herself at all, even yet. She is nothing but skin and bone and eyes."

"Why, poor, poor Cresside! We had no idea . . . Of course that explains why the d'Alverys haven't been to see us. We'll go down to Belle Heloise right away."

"It might be a good plan to wait until the road dries out a little. The seepage is pretty bad this year, and there's no point in running the risk of getting stuck in the mud, if you don't have to." Fabian turned from Regine to Sylvestre, changing the subject without preamble. "By the way, how are your crops coming along? There's a rumor going around that you've got mosaic disease here at Hathaway Hall."

"Well, some of the leaves on the new growth do look a little mottled. But I don't believe it's anything to get excited about—anyway Blood thinks it isn't. . . . Did you say Cresside'd been in bed for a year?"

"No, I didn't say she'd been in bed for a year. I said for months and months, but it must have been darn close to a year, at that. . . . You don't seem to be taking this mosaic disease very seriously, Sylvestre. Have you been getting any of the bulletins the Government's sending out?"

"Yes, I've been getting them. But to tell you the truth, I've thrown most of them into the wastebasket and turned the rest over to Blood," Sylvestre said impatiently. "The Government's always sending out bulletins about something. It must use up tons and tons of paper that way—not to mention millions and millions of the taxpayers' money."

"Maybe. But it'll also cost the taxpayers of Louisiana millions and millions if this thing spreads."

"Why, Fabian, what makes you bring up such a gloomy subject in the course of a social call? I never knew before that you were this kind of a terrible killjoy! What do you know about sugar, anyway? You're not a planter. You're nothing but a lawyer."

Obviously it was impossible to keep the lovely young lady out of the conversation for more than a few consecutive minutes. Perhaps, Pascal reflected, that was another reason he did not take to her. He had never liked women who were too talkative. Now, Mrs. Gervais d'Alvery was different. She just put in a pleasant word here and there. To be sure Miss Cresside had more to say; but when she talked there was some point to it, and she did not interrupt either; she spoke in turn. Pascal had never liked women who interrupted, particularly women who interrupted men. Anyway, he was getting a little tired; it had been an exciting day, and a long one. Besides, he knew his granddaughter would be cross if he were late to supper. Not that he needed any supper, after the bounteous dinner he'd eaten, not to mention the claret lemonade which he'd drunk when he woke up from his nap; but he knew his granddaughter would expect him to be prompt at table just the same. He was relieved when he saw Fabian rise, and the thought crossed his mind that Fabian did not care any more than he did for women with tinkling laughs and the habit of interrupting, no matter how young and lovely-looking they might be.

"Yes, I know," Fabian was saying. "I'm nothing but a lawyer, and, of course, Sylvestre's had all kinds of experience with sugar. Well, we must be getting along. Give my regards to your mother, Regine. Nice to know the family's in residence again. I always hate to see a fine old place empty, and there are so many empty places along the River Road already, worse luck! But I'm glad that one of them, at least, is coming back to its former state. I mean Hackberry Lodge, the old Surcliffe Plantation, that Charles Boylston's bought. You've met him, of course? No? Why, that's too bad. But you're bound to the first day you go to Belle Heloise. He haunts the place, more than any ghost ever did."

"Oh, Fabian, please don't talk about ghosts! I'm simply terrified of them. What do you mean, he haunts the place?"

"Nothing frightening. You don't need to be terrified, Regine." Fabian paused a moment, glancing from Regine to Sylvestre and then at Regine again. "He's taken a terrible tumble for Cresside, that's all.

And Gervais and Tante Isabelle have both gone to bat for him. I only hope Cresside has sense enough herself to know a good fellow when she sees him."

CHAPTER X

"Mis-ter Speak-er! Mis-ter Speak-er!"

"The gentleman from Pointe Coupée is recognized."

"I move you, Mister Speaker, that the Committee on Federal Relations be instructed to report forthwith on the resolution ratifying the Federal Suffrage Amendment."

For hours on end—or so it seemed to Gervais d'Alvery—nothing had happened in the somnolent House, now so suddenly electrified. The very atmosphere of the Chamber had been dormant, and the members in that state of torpor for which heavy dinners, warm weather, and complete indifference to legislative routine were about equally responsible. A few insignificant measures were being passed in perfunctory fashion. In each instance, the clerk read the full text of a bill in a rapid monotone; then the Speaker rapped with his gavel, mumbling something unintelligible; finally the clerk called the long roll of a hundred and eighteen names and members responded almost mechanically. Gervais, looking lazily about, was convinced that probably no one within earshot of Tallieu's monotone and Walker's occasional mumble cared whether or not Bienville Parish acquired another justice of the peace or whether a certain Julie Becassine were permitted to sue a levee board for the recovery of twenty-eight dollars damages to her property.

An overtone of sibilance was added to the pervading drone by rows of determined ladies, seated on either side of the amphitheater, who whispered to one another as unremittingly as they fanned themselves. Outstanding on one side were Mrs. Lydia Wyckliffe Holmes, the Misses Badley—Nan and Daisy—and Miss Mittie Alden; they were all looking daggers at the ladies on the other side, whose leaders were Mrs. Ruffin Pleasant, wife of the ex-governor, Miss Jean Gordon of New Orleans, and Mrs. Goldenberg. The animosity of these glances was returned in kind, for "Miss Lyd's" crowd favored ratification of the Federal Suffrage Amendment, now requiring favorable action from only one more state. Mrs. Pleasant's group, on the other hand, advocated a Suffrage Amendment to the State constitution only. Ostensibly everyone favored woman's suffrage; the method by which it could best be obtained was the only acknowledged issue. But no one was deceived by this pretext. The Anti-Ratificationists were actually Anti-Suffragists as well, and everybody realized that Ferd Claiborne,

140

the member from Pointe Coupée who had so startled the House by his outburst, must have something up his sleeve: what he was saying and what he really wanted were indubitably two entirely different things.

The Ratification Amendment had long since been referred to the Federal Relations Committee, whose chairman, Scott Wilkinson, a young Shreveport attorney, was temporarily away. In his absence, Jules Dreyfous, a short, baldish, scholarly hardware dealer from New Iberia, and an ardent ratificationist, bustled to his feet to take up the Claiborne challenge. Gervais rather admired Dreyfous, who had long made superior wines for his home table, and who continued this practice as placidly as though the National Prohibition Amendment had never been passed; but on the suffrage issue, Gervais saw eye to eye with Claiborne. The latter, one of the handsomest men in the legislature, was an attorney, a planter, and a professional politician; yet he found time to raise his own strain of fighting cocks, of which he was inordinately proud, and to import from Arabia an occasional blooded stallion for his stables. Claiborne's conservative views regarding women's place in politics were wholly in harmony with those of Gervais. According to his tenets—and according to those of practically all South Louisiana sugar planters—a lady had privileges, rather than rights, and the sordid business of voting was not among them, whatever the rest of the country might think. To be sure, Gervais had been repelled, rather than attracted, by the *obiter dictum* of Representative Jules Carville, from Iberville Parish, to the effect that if these ladies who were demanding suffrage only had a dozen children apiece, like his wife, they would be so profitably occupied that they would stop worrying about political equality. This was beyond the point, as Gervais saw it; it was not a question of how many children a woman had; it was a question of her superior and secluded sphere in life that was at stake. Claiborne's clamor for recognition, suddenly shattering the somnolence of the House and silencing the buzzing of the women, roused him from his doze into immediate and eager alertness. Glancing around again, quickly instead of lazily this time, he realized that Claiborne must have made a count of noses and particularly of absentees, coming to the conclusion that he had enough votes among those still present to postpone action on the Federal Resolution indefinitely. Gervais was more than ready to follow Claiborne's lead.

"We have had this measure before us for five weeks now," the member from Pointe Coupée was continuing vociferously. "Such delay is wholly unreasonable. The House is entitled to dispose of the matter and get it out of the way."

"Mister Speaker, I rise to object. In the absence of the Committee Chairman, no action should be taken."

Dreyfous, still on his feet, spoke insistently, but endeavored to maintain an attitude of composure and dignity despite the uproar which surrounded him. The clamor for recognition had become general. Everyone was trying to talk at once, everyone was trying to shout everyone else down, no one was listening to what anyone else was saying. The partisan ladies had ceased to whisper to each other and to fan themselves; they had become a part of the general pandemonium. But this subsided as quickly as it had arisen. The Speaker, somehow making himself heard above the hubbub, ruled that the Clerk should inform the Chairman of the Federal Relations Committee on his return that it was the desire of the House to have this resolution reported out at the earliest possible moment. This left matters precisely where they had been before, yet somehow each side indicated by the bearing and demeanor of its members that right had triumphed over the forces of evil and that a notable victory had been won. The two cohorts of fanning ladies on opposite sides of the amphitheater no longer glared at one another; frankly, openly, each gloated over the defeat of the opposition. The House settled back to its earlier languor.

"The Governor would like to speak to you for a moment, Captain d'Alvery, if it's convenient for you to leave the Chamber just now."

Gervais looked up to see Stanley Ray, Governor Parker's secretary, standing beside his desk. He smiled, suppressing a sigh of relief.

"It's perfectly convenient," he said. "In fact, for the last hour I've been trying to think of a valid excuse to get away. Ferd Claiborne has just stirred up a little excitement, and I'd begun to hope for better things; but it was nothing more than a flash in the pan. Let's go."

He rose and followed Ray up the aisle. As he went through the nearest gate intersecting the low railing which separated the amphitheater from the rest of the Chamber, he nodded pleasantly to its guardian. But the thought crossed his mind, as it had so often before, that the three "doorkeepers" did not really earn their eight dollars a day. It did not require much effort on the part of anyone to get past them, and their sole occupation seemed to consist in opening a gate any legislator could go through without assistance. Here was another example of the countless practices which struck him as needlessly extravagant, another contributor to the general irritation which made him glad to get away from the Chamber. He went rapidly down the great iron staircase curving gracefully around the central pillar which supported the stained-glass dome; still more rapidly across the black and white tessellations of the main rotunda and into the Governor's office, where, as usual, a loose blade in the ceiling fan was rattling inescapably. *Strange that no one ever seems to think of having that damn blade fixed.* Gervais said to himself, by no means for the first time; *if I had to stay here long, it would drive me crazy. So would the color of the carpet as far as that goes; if I hadn't seen it I'd say only a snake could be such an evil looking green. . . .* But he was comfortably aware, as these thoughts passed through his mind, that he would not have to hear the blade or see the carpet for long. The door leading from the Governor's outer office to his private sanctum was open, as always, for it was a point of pride with Parker that this should never be shut, and Gervais entered the inner room without formality.

He found the Governor ensconced at the massive desk which had once allegedly belonged to Maximilian of Mexico. Except for a brief interval at lunch time, Parker had been there since early morning, for it was another point of pride with him that he never reached the Capitol later than eight o'clock. Now, at five in the afternoon, he was still fresh and alert, and he greeted Gervais with a pleasant briskness.

"Good morning, Captain. How are things shaping up at Belle Heloise?"

"Almost too well I suppose. Somehow it doesn't seem right not to be able to complain about the way things are going on a plantation."

Parker chuckled. "Better take advantage of that feeling while you can. You won't have much opportunity to do it. By the way—" he swept a shirt-sleeved arm towards the window in the Norman bay where his desk was placed—"How do you like the way we're cleaning the State House grounds? Regular snake-hole when I took over."

"Looks fine, Governor. You can see the figurehead from the old battleship *Louisiana* now."

"Well—we do what we can. I'm bringing in some gold fish for the fountain down there, too. However, I didn't invite you down here to talk to you about landscape gardening. What I wanted to discuss with you very seriously, Captain, if you'll permit me to lay my side of the case before you, is the constitutional convention bill of Representative Chappuis. I am told you have expressed yourself as favoring submission of the new constitution to the voters. Is that correct?"

"Well, yes, I suppose so. I think I might subject myself to a good deal of criticism if I voted that the people had to accept a new constitution whether they liked it or not."

"That's the usual and plausible argument, but it won't hold water, Captain. No constitution can be written which doesn't offend some one in one or another of its provisions. In order to vote against that one provision, the people must vote against the whole document."

"But that still doesn't answer the argument of those who always talk about the dear people, and what sort of a fix will I be in if I run for re-election and my opponents raise the shout that I'm the one that refused to let them vote on the constitution?"

"The answer to that is simple enough. Let the people elect as delegates to the convention only those whom they can trust to write a constitution which need not be submitted to popular vote when it is finished. There can be no objection to that—no matter what old Gilbert Dupré from St. Landry says to the contrary. He'll be a delegate to the convention himself, you mark my words, even if we pass it without the submission clause."

Gervais nodded thoughtfully. "I guess that might be made a point, all right," he agreed. "I'd like to think it over though, and talk it over, too, with Fabian d'Alvery. He's my attorney as well as my cousin and I've got a good deal of confidence in his judgment. I was planning to stop by his house anyway before I started home this evening. I want to see if he can't suggest something we planters could do that might induce the Equalization Board to loosen its stranglehold on sugar. I don't for the life of me see why they should be hanging onto it like grim death now that all the other commodities that were controlled during the war have been released."

"Why, that's easy. Because it's the simplest to regulate. The situation would be different if the sugar refineries were scattered from one end of the United States to the other instead of being confined to a few seaports. . . . Well, Fabian might be helpful, though I don't see how anyone here can be; but I'd also be glad to have you talk the other matter over with him. I've a good deal of confidence in his judgment, too."

Dismissed as informally as he had been welcomed, Gervais went out of the East door into St. Philip Street, where he came face to face with his mother-in-law. Mrs. Randall had evidently just completed the "grocery shopping" which was one of her principal diversions, for she was carrying, with an air of triumphant weariness, a large string bag full of knobby packages; some dusty greens protruded from one of these, a fowl's yellow feet from another. Her dingy street clothes were vaguely suggestive of the gray wrappers she wore in the house, and her limp hat did not wholly conceal her untidy hair. For the thousandth time, Gervais marveled that such a drab creature could have borne and reared a radiant being like Merry; the flame which illumined the girl must have been struck from some other spark. Reluctantly, because the antipathy between them was still mutual, he stopped and saluted the drab woman.

"Good afternoon, Mrs. Randall. I'm glad to see that this heat apparently isn't too much for you. Just the same, that bag must be pretty heavy. Better let me get my car and run you home."

"I wouldn't want to take you out of your way, seeing as how I'm still able to walk," Mrs. Randall responded. "Leaving the Capitol early, aren't you, Gervais?"

"I'm on my way to see Fabian about something for the Governor," Gervais answered, chagrined because he felt compelled to acknowledge her implied rebuke by explaining his actions. Then, seizing upon the chance of changing the subject, he added hastily, "By the way, if you have any influence with Miss Mittie Alden, I wish you'd pry her loose from the Suffrage bunch that's rooting for my opponents."

"Miss Mittie's got a mind of her own," declared Mrs. Randall. "She don't need the Governor nor anybody else to tell her what to do. Anyhow, I'm glad to see the old maids sticking up for themselves. Most married women just go around saying amen to their husbands. 'Fraid to do anything else, I suppose."

"If you mean to imply that Merry's afraid of me—" Gervais began.

144

"No, Merry ain't afraid of you, I'll say that much for her. Just the same she hasn't got a mind of her own any more. She's wax in your hands," Mrs. Randall retorted, quoting from the latest thriller with which she had beguiled her leisure. "If she hadn't been, she wouldn't have married you as fast as if there'd been reasons why she had to, and she wouldn't be in the family way from one year's end to another. She can't even get out to see her own mother, tied down like she is. She's got a baby in her arms and under her apron both, instead of just one or the other, like in the old saying. Well, I must be getting along. Miss Mittie'll be looking for her supper when she gets in from the Capitol and I have to cook it for her. *She'll* stay to the end of the session all right and she'll have a right to be hungry."

Having shot this parting bolt, Mrs. Randall walked triumphantly away, one shoulder sagging under the weight of the string bag. Gervais, irritated at his own annoyance, walked on down St. Philip Street and made a series of left turns into Somerulos Street. It was only a short walk, and the sidewalks were abundantly shaded by trees in full foliage. But the day was very warm, and when Gervais reached Fabian's well-ordered little house, its quiet and coolness were so amazingly refreshing that he went out of his way to compliment Carmelite on her extraordinary talents for keeping his cousin comfortable. She hoped she knew how to do things right for her white folks, she said, civilly enough; but her tone seemed to imply that her master was more felicitously and intelligently served than his visitor, and she added, without any amiable discursiveness, that he would find Mr. Fabian in the garden with Belizaire. This did not mean that Fabian was reclining in an arm-chair with a book in his hand and a drink at his elbow, while his dog dozed beside; it meant that he was down on his knees weeding the walks and flower beds, while Belizaire spun around snapping at bugs and chasing butterflies. However, Fabian immediately arose, cheerfully dusting off his hands, and saying it was high time he called it a day. Should they stay outdoors or go inside? And what would Gervais like in the way of a drink? Not that it would be as good as he would get at Belle Heloise, since Cresside was not there to mix them. . . .

Inside, Gervais said, because it was so wonderfully cool there; and a gin rickey, if there were any of the real stuff in the house. Fabian assured him that there was, mixed the drinks with adroitness, and listened patiently to everything Gervais had to say about the Governor's theories on the constitutional amendment and the sugar planters' troubles on account of official control. He thought Parker had the situation sized up right, he said; he hoped Gervais would side with him against submitting the constitution to a popular vote. He would like to be helpful but he did not know, offhand, that he himself could do much about the Equalization Board; he thought the men in Washington—Gay, Rogers and the others—were probably bringing all possible pressure to bear. It was a good thing Louisiana had a sugar planter in the Senate, and after all, this man had introduced a bill on sugar equalization that was due to come up for approval any day. What, exactly, did Gervais think could be done at this end? Gervais did not seem to know, and Fabian renewed the drinks, waiting patiently for his cousin to bring up some other subject, the first two apparently being exhausted. But for some time Gervais sat rather moodily, speaking fitfully and inconsequentially, and declining to be diverted by Belizaire's persistent antics.

"I seem to sense a slight malaise, as Tante Isabelle would delicately define it," Fabian remarked as Gervais finally rose to take his departure, after what seemed to his cousin like somewhat aimless procrastination. "Nothing really wrong, is there?"

"No, of course not. But I just had an encounter with my mother-in-law and you know how that always affects me. Besides, the Equalization Board does get my goat, and I do get fed up with it all at the Capitol."

"What, so soon?"

"Yes, so soon. This struggle over suffrage is just a wrangle among a lot of termagants. Lord knows how they ever got any he-men into their cat-fight. The worst pain in the neck is that so-and-so Tack Evans, from Caddo. He's hand in glove with the opposition, and he's buzzing around the Capitol most of the time, laboring under the delusion that he's aiding and abetting Mr. and Mrs. Ruffin G. Pleasant. He'd like to make a hit with them, because he thinks Ruff might get to the U. S. Senate one of these days. But he doesn't really care a damn about suffrage one way or another."

"Well, you should worry about Tack Evans. He isn't a member of the legislature."

"No, but he might as well be, as far as I'm concerned. And there are plenty of members who do get my goat. Take that screwball from along the Texas border, for instance, Brother Ellery Scobell. He started out as a sharecropper, and he's still not so far from where he started. He's labored to get into the legislature so that he could have the dipping law repealed, and he actually goes around with two ticks in a nickel-gripper purse. He's always coming up with queer laws himself, too, though it's the ticks that he's got his heart really set on. I believe those two devils, Happy Sevier and George Perrault, egg him on to introducing most of them—the bachelor bill, for instance, and the one subsidizing a lone oarsman to row out to the middle of the Mississippi and pick up driftwood——"

Gervais was interrupted by a hearty laugh from Fabian. He himself snorted and went on.

"I'm glad you think it's all so amusing. Maybe you wouldn't if you had to sit there and hear it for hours, day after day."

"Listen, Gervais. You better develop your powers of endurance, not to mention your sense of humor. There's still a long, long trail a-winding before you reach the Mansion."

"Who said anything about wanting to get to the Mansion?"

146

"No one. But I rather gathered that was the eventual objective, in the back of your mind. Or was it the United States Senate? Or one after the other in swift succession?"

"Some day that vivid imagination of yours is going to get you into trouble, Fabian. I'm not a professional politician, any more than I was a professional soldier. I'm a sugar planter, first, last and always. The only reason I wanted to go to the legislature—and you know it—was to see that our agricultural interests got more and better representation than a few sharecroppers like Scobell and you lawyers were giving them."

"All right, all right. Stop weeping about it. You'll be showing your legs to the jury, next. This blues-singing of yours is a new line, especially as there can't be much wrong with the plantation either, now that sugar's hit twenty-six."

"No, but there may be, any time, if that god-damn mosaic disease starts to spread. Hathaway Hall is too near Belle Heloise."

"Yes, I've always thought that way about the place myself," Fabian responded. "But after all, there aren't any signs that the disease is spreading, are there, as yet?"

"No."

"Then what's eating you, for God's sake, besides the astounding discovery that all your fellow legislators aren't silver-tongued orators and selfless philosophers?"

"Nothing. That is, nothing to speak of. Except that Merry doesn't seem quite like herself."

"There, now, we're getting somewhere at last. No wonder you're upset. What seems to be the trouble?"

"She's had to start weaning Sybelle. That was to be expected, under the circumstances. But she's worrying, and when she's upset, I am too, it's so unlike her."

"Can't Dinah come to the rescue?"

"Well, that's just the point. Dinah took over Vail almost from the outset. Merry had enough for one, but not enough for two. Now she's afraid if Dinah tries to take on two she won't have enough either. Then both babies might suffer for it. Merry can't make up her mind whether to risk it, and to start giving them each one bottle a day, so that the amount could be increased if necessary, or to put Sybelle on cow's milk altogether and let Vail go on with Dinah until the hot weather's over. She's obsessed with the idea that she may not be fair."

"Can't Dr. Champagne make the decision for her and relieve her of the responsibility?"

"Oh, he jokes and says Vail is such a husky specimen that he'd probably get along all right if we started feeding him syrup and rice right now. But then he always adds very pompously that in a case like this a doctor can't lay down the law, that it's a question for the young mother—or the young father—to decide. And Lord knows I'm not an authority on the care and feeding of infants."

Gervais' voice had grown increasingly edgy as he went on. Fabian looked out of the window and drummed on the table with his fingers.

"As a matter of fact, I don't believe the syrup and rice are necessarily a joke," he said at last. "They're pretty well standardized, down on Bayou Lafourche. I wouldn't know, of course, exactly how early in life they make up an accepted diet, but I imagine there must be lots of cases when the kids are pretty small. Families down there usually run about a baker's dozen, and I've often noticed two or three youngsters crawling around the same gallery who seemed to be pretty much of an age. There must be plenty of cases where other young mothers get caught the same way Merry has."

"I don't care for that expression, Fabian. Especially as it's incorrect. Merry wants to have children."

"Sorry. As a matter of fact, I wasn't referring to the same phase of the situation that you were. I meant caught on the horns of a dietary dilemma, not involuntarily prolific. Though at that I should think two pregnancies within a year might try the tranquility of any woman, even Merry."

"I still don't care much for the way you're talking. These first kids are coming along pretty closely together, but I'm not anticipating the establishment of one of those Bayou Lafourche families you've been talking about. Four or five youngsters would fill up the place very satisfactorily, and I'd like some chance to have Merry to myself. So I think I can assure you the next ones will be further apart, especially if we get a boy for a Christmas present."

"You're in a hell of a hurry for another son, aren't you? No, don't tell me again that you don't care much for the way I'm talking. At the risk of further rebuke, however, I can't help asking, if you want to have Merry to yourself, why on earth you don't take her off somewhere, before it's too late again? She's never had any kind of a nice trip, as far as I know, not even a wedding trip. And I should think a change of scene might do her no end of good, just now—change her train of thought, too, and stop her worrying. It wouldn't have to be a long trip to do the trick—you and she could simply get aboard the *John D. Grace* some Thursday evening after the legislature adjourns for one of its week ends, and spend the time between sessions in New Orleans. You could blow yourself to a swell suite at the Grunewald and take Merry shopping. I haven't seen her wearing anything yet a modern girl would recognize as real jewelry. I saw Regine the other day and she was simply strung with it. Besides, you know that Billy Pereira would be tickled to death at the chance to show you a tall time."

"If you were married, and had two semi-invalids on your hands, besides twins and a pregnant wife, you might find that little pleasure excursions like the one you're outlining aren't so easy to arrange. In fact, I wish you would get married, if only to try out the practicability of putting all of your pleasant little theories into practice, as I said

148

before. . . . Incidentally, Merry'd never consent to taking a trip and leaving the twins."

"To the tender care of Cresside and Dinah? For three days? I dare you to ask her!"

"All right. I will ask her. And I'll drop in tomorrow, just to tell you that you were wrong."

"Don't bother. You all keep badgering me about not coming out to Belle Heloise. I'll be down for the day Sunday, and we can work out the details of your belated wedding journey then."

Fabian arrived to find the place unwontedly silent. The dogs barked briefly when he drove up, but for once they seemed uninterested in picking a quarrel with Belizaire, and wandered aimlessly off again. Amen did not come forward to take the car, and after parking it himself, Fabian went into the house and drifted through the downstairs rooms without finding anyone. The pleasant patio was empty, too, except for Miss Larcella, who was stretched out in a sunny spot, the latest litter of kittens dozing contentedly beside her. But as Fabian started up the outside stairway, leading from the platform by the Garden Room to the rear of the upper gallery, he met Cresside coming down, her finger on her lips.

"Hello and hush!" she said softly. "Come on back to the patio—unless you'd rather sit among the relics in the drawing room. But anyway, don't come upstairs. Dinah and I have just succeeded in getting the twins to sleep, after their customary ceremonial visit to *maman,* and I don't want to go through that struggle again. They seem to feel, even if she doesn't, that formal calling went out of vogue with the war, and they resent being thrust into starched dresses, and all the rest of it. Besides, between teething and weaning, they're fussy anyway."

"Where is everyone else?" Fabian inquired, turning to go down the stairs at her side.

"Well, *maman* is in her boudoir, and I believe Lucie is rearranging her hair and washing her off, where it shows, with Florida Water. She takes her daily constitutional in the pergola again now, and of course, such violent exercise ruffles her locks and brings on profuse perspiration. Dinah is watching over the twins and Lou Ida is getting dinner, rather rebelliously. I don't know whether you'll have anything fit to eat or not. All the other servants, except Lucie and Dinah, have gone to a big baptizing and Lou Ida wanted to go, too. Some of the hands from the quarters are prominently featured in it. In fact, nearly everyone who belongs on the place is down by the riverside breathing the odor of sanctity. I expect some of the most trifling niggers are coming out of the water this minute, shouting 'I seen de Lord! Glory Halleluiah'!"

"Are Gervais and Merry down on the river bank lending dignity and distinction to this gathering?"

"Oh, no. They're attending High Mass at St. Agnes'. You and I are the only apostates of the family, Fabian."

"So Merry goes to St. Agnes' with Gervais now, does she?" Fabian asked, without commenting on Cresside's last statement.

"Sure. That was a foregone conclusion, wasn't it? That she would, I mean. In spite of all her mother's assertions, I think she's already practically forgotten about the Reverend Mr. Hawkins and the Sunday School she attended regularly from childhood. It's only a matter of time before she'll be received into the tender arms of Mother Church. She never even questions anything Gervais wants her to do, apparently. Not that I'm criticizing her wifely docility. Merry's a grand person, and she's got plenty of backbone, too, except where Gervais is concerned. No one realizes that better than I do. . . . What can I get for you? A julep? A Sazerac?"

"Either or both, by and by. I don't know a more beguiling Hebe than you are, Cresside—your ambrosia is one of the chief attractions of Belle Heloise, as far as I'm concerned. But the day's still young. Can't we just sit down and talk for a few minutes, while you drink to me only with your eyes?"

"Yes, of course, if you will pledge with yours." She dropped lightly into one of the chintz-covered chairs, and Fabian, drawing another close to it, lowered himself awkwardly into it. "Perhaps I'd better warn you that I may use my eyes to glare at you, however," Cresside continued. "And that my conversation may take on a pretty acid tone. I understand you're responsible for relegating me to the role of the traditional competent old-maid aunt."

"Never! What made you think so?"

"Didn't you suggest to that fool brother of mine that Merry might actually like to breathe a little freer air for a change? He hasn't quite said you did, in so many words, but I know he never would have thought of it himself, and he did let out that he'd been seeing you on legal business, the very day he casually brought up the matter."

"So they are going to take a trip?" Fabian inquired, with obvious amusement, but without either denying or accepting Cresside's charge.

"Oh, sure! The *John D. Grace* has orders—and what orders!—to stop here Thursday night; and the royal suite has been reserved at the Grunewald—you know, the one Charlie Chaplin occupied when he was here. And letters dispatched to all our most prominent kith and kin in New Orleans, the ones who have big houses, big cars and big doings."

"I'm very glad to hear it. Merry'll have a lot of fun. Incidentally, so will you, with a free hand during her absence. I haven't done anything to cry *mea culpa* for. I might even suggest it would be a good idea if you took a trip yourself, a little later on. You've stuck pretty closely to Belle Heloise, too."

"Well, your first idea wasn't so bad. But don't make a habit of getting these inspirations. You might develop into a sort of Mr. Fixit.

I haven't the slightest desire to go away on a trip."

"Well, so long as that's true . . ."

"It is true. Hark, I think someone else is arriving! Probably Charles."

"Is it as easy to guess as all that?"

"Oh, yes. He practically lives here. And he has ideas about trips, too. Only his are different from yours. He thinks I ought to take them with him."

"Then they're not different from mine. I'd thought of that myself, too. He's a good fellow, Cresside."

"Yes, I know. But my ideas *are* different."

"Mind letting me in on them?"

"I think some of your earlier fancies are better than this latest—the one about the competent old-maid aunt, for instance."

"Listen, I'm willing to stand back of everything I did say about that trip for Merry. But not back of a single thing I didn't say—or back of anything I didn't think, either. And I never in the world thought of you as an old-maid aunt, Cresside, in spite of your competence—and you're a darn sight more competent than you like to let on. Because you couldn't be a traditional spinster—no matter how hard you tried."

At the sound of an approaching car, heralded by the barking dogs, Cresside had risen, and before there was time for footsteps to echo through the long hall, she had reached the door leading into it from the patio. But Fabian had risen too, almost simultaneously, and now, despite her fleet-footedness, he was almost abreast of her. She swung open the door and slipped through it, half turning to speak to him from the other side.

"Then you have no idea how hard I *can* try, Fabian," she said. There was a slight note of mockery in her voice, but it still sounded carefree, almost gay, as it had ever since his arrival. He had enjoyed every minute he spent with her, for she seemed more like her old self than at any time since her accident. Now, suddenly, there was a change. She did not go forward to meet the expected visitor, but stood so still that she gave an effect of rigidity; her laughing lips stiffened into a hard line, and her big eyes narrowed to half their size. Silhouetted in the doorway, she looked as if she had been transfixed. The sight was the more alarming to Fabian because it was so completely out of character; he had never seen Cresside frightened, and he would have asserted, unequivocally, that there was nothing which she feared. He opened the screen door abruptly, calling her by name and stretching out a reassuring hand. But the seizure was as brief as it was violent; she had almost recovered before he reached her. For an instant she gripped his hand convulsively; then she went quietly through the long hall towards the front entrance, where, instead of Charles Boylston, Regine and Sylvestre were standing.

"Darling!" Regine exclaimed, anticipating any greeting from Cresside. "We just couldn't wait any longer to see you, so we came here, straight from church. How *are* you? Oh, hello, Fabian! Are you spending the day here again?"

"No, I'm not spending the day here again," Fabian answered. "I came out to collect on a bet, and then I just stayed on for a while. But I understand it isn't the best time for visitors—the servants have all gone to a baptizing and the twins are teething. So I'm starting back into town any minute."

"Well, we can't stay but a minute ourselves. We left Regine's mother at Hathaway Hall, and she's expecting us right back. But as Regine said, we thought——"

Sylvestre's inconsequential remarks trailed away without coming to any definite conclusion. Regine, who had thrown her arms rapturously around Cresside and kissed her excitedly, released her with apparent reluctance, and then, still clasping her hand, but holding her at arms' length, regarded her with playful but close attention.

"Now stand still and let me look at you," she ordered. "A little bird told me you were nothing but skin and bones and eyes and I want to see for myself. Why, I think you look wonderful! You'll never have to worry about dieting, with a figure like that! And your eyes are gorgeous. I don't wonder you keep the countryside spellbound—oh, I've been hearing about that, too! Now let's come and have a nice cozy talk, just you and I—the kind we used to have at slumber parties, don't you remember? Fabian, why don't you take Sylvestre into the library and tell him some more about that queer blight you think's affecting our sugar—the Midas disease, was that what you called it? Cresside and I want to be by ourselves, because we've got lots more interesting things to discuss than sugar, haven't we, honey? And we don't want any more men around while we're doing it, do we, darling?"

"I'd be very pleased to take Sylvestre into the library," Fabian said. "At least, if that's what Cresside would like me to do. You haven't given her a chance to tell us yet, Regine."

"Why, I know Cresside a lot better than you do, you saucy creature! She always wants to do exactly the same thing I do, when we're together. You don't seem to realize what intimate friends we are, Fabian, or how long we've been parted! We've got to catch up."

"By all means, take Sylvestre into the library, Fabian," Cresside said. Now that she finally had a chance to speak, her voice was as cool as her cousin's, and as collected. "Perhaps you'll get a drink for him—as you said, not very hospitably, the household's slightly upset today; but I know I can depend on you to stay long enough to do the honors." Without having once looked directly at Sylvestre, she turned from Fabian to Regine. "We do have a lot to catch up with," she said. "And first of all, I'm sure Merry would want me to show you the twins, as she's not here to do it herself. I believe she and Gervais were going to Mrs. Randall's after church—that's why they're not home yet. But, of course, *maman* is, and this is one of her good days. Why don't we go upstairs instead of sitting in the parlor? Then she can see you, too, and I'll have Dinah bring the twins into her boudoir."

"Ah was jes' fixin' to bring 'em down to you, Miss Cresside, while Ah helps Lou Ida get dinner. They's woke up, and they's fussin' some again. Can't nobody quiet 'em like you can."

This unexpected announcement came from the stair landing. Dinah, huge, composed, competent, was standing there, a baby cradled on either capable arm, against her ample bosom. She came unhurriedly down the steps, a snowy *tignon* framing her dusky face, her full skirts brushing against the carpet as she descended. Beside her, on the white plaster wall, a long cashmere shawl, centered with scarlet, hung in place of a picture. Behind her, in its niche, stood the ancient Spanish statue, with tall sprays of cape jasmine rising from the silver vases on either side of it, and vigil lights burning before it. For a moment, nobody spoke; something about the sight silenced even Regine temporarily. Then Cresside went forward to meet Dinah, and Fabian saw, with an immense wave of relief, that the smile which had left her lips had come back to them. Only it was not mocking any more, or gay either; it was triumphant.

"I'll be glad to take them, Dinah," she said quietly. "You may give them to me here. Then you can go right on out to the kitchen and help Lou Ida. I know she needs you." Cresside slipped a hand under Sybelle's downy head, and lifted her gently, while the beautiful blonde baby smiled engagingly. "Hold her for a minute, will you, Fabian?" Cresside asked. "If you're going to be a steady customer of the house, you'd better begin learning how to take care of babies. I think perhaps we might all go out to the patio after all—the day cradle's there." She deposited the girl twin skillfully in Fabian's inexperienced but willing grasp and turned back to Dinah. Vail was already beating the air with chubby fists, and a broad grin of welcome, which disclosed two brand-new teeth, illumined his rosy face. He bounded up and down with irrepressible vigor, and as Cresside took him from Dinah, he gurgled with glee. She held him high and close to her, his dark hair touching hers, his big blue eyes level with her own.

"What do you think of the heir to all the d'Alverys?" she asked. And this time, when she spoke, she did look at Sylvestre.

CHAPTER XI

THE OPPORTUNE ARRIVAL of Gervais and Merry created an almost immediate diversion. Why, she had seen Sylvestre and Regine at St. Agnes', sitting on the Gospel side, in front, Merry exclaimed. If they had only said they were coming to Belle Heloise, she and Gervais would have driven right out themselves, instead of stopping by to see her mother. They could have done that later. Was somebody getting drinks for them? Had they been upstairs to see Madame Mère? Didn't they think the twins were adorable?

Her poise instantly eased the tension which Regine's chatter had only intensified, and carried the visit through to a more harmonious end than the beginning had indicated as possible. But she did not suggest that they should stay to dinner, or urge them to linger when they rose to take their departure after a rather brief call. Gervais went with her to the door when they took their leave, and hardly waited until they were out of sight to give her an exuberant kiss and a hearty hug.

"My, but you handled that beautifully, honey!" he said enthusiastically. "I've been dreading the Tremaines' call ever since they got back, knowing it was on the cards, and wondering how we'd get through with it. But you made it seem smooth as silk. I reckon I'll just have to make good as a politician after all—you'd be wasted as the wife of a mere planter!"

"I'm not wasted as *your* wife, whatever you do, darling. . . . What became of Fabian? He didn't slip off, did he? Of course, I meant to ask him to stay to dinner, as soon as Sylvestre and Regine had gone."

"Oh, he's sure to be somewhere around! I think he'd just stay anyhow, whether you asked him or not. He knows perfectly well he's welcome. Don't worry about him—he'll turn up directly. Come on, let's get out of our church clothes and into something cooler."

They started up the stairway, arm in arm. Before they reached the landing where the Spanish statue was enthroned, Merry paused, releasing herself, and called to Cresside: was she with the twins? Were they all right? Sybelle was in the day cradle on the patio, almost asleep, Cresside called back. She had Vail herself. He was fussing a little again, but he was all right. Both babies were all right. . . .

"I'll bet anything she's walking him up and down in her arms, the way all those new books Dr. Champagne has given us say you mustn't," Gervais muttered, speaking at the same time that he stopped to genuflect, in his customary casual way.

"Yes. I think she probably is. But it doesn't seem to do him any harm and he loves it. You know what Dinah says—'Cain't nobody quiet him like Miss Cresside.' Sometimes I think Dinah knows more about babies than the man who wrote those books."

Merry genuflected also, more respectfully and formally than Gervais. He put his arm around her again.

"Maybe you're right. You usually are," he said. "And who's getting to be a darn good little Catholic, too, I'd like to know?" he added in a pleased voice. "Didn't I tell you that everything would work out, if you'd just marry me? And it has, hasn't it? That time *I* was right!"

"Yes," Merry agreed. "You were. It did work out. Everything's perfect, Gervais—our life at Belle Heloise and now this lovely trip we're

154

going to have together, and next winter the new baby and all——"

They went on to their own room still happily embraced, and oblivious, as they so often were, of everyone in the world but each other. Momentarily they had forgotten about Cresside. But their surmise concerning her had been correct, at least in part. She was walking up and down with Vail in her arms, though she was not doing it, as they had pictured her, on the patio. She had gone into the Garden Room, carefully closing the door behind her. It was not until after she had done this that she saw Fabian writing, with his back to her, at the flat-top desk which had come out of the old custom house in New Orleans.

"Why, hello!" he said, turning around, but without rising. "Am I in the way or anything? If I am, I'll clear out. It doesn't upset me though, if you just want to change the baby's diapers. I figured I had a little spare time before dinner. And I thought I'd dash off a note to Happy Sevier, while I had the chance. He's gone back to Tallulah, now that vacation's on, and I'm thinking of spending a few days with him on the plantation."

"Good idea. . . . And you're unexpected but you're not *de trop*. And of course it wouldn't upset me to have you here while I changed Vail's diapers. What do you take me for—a prewar prissy? When it comes to that, I wish you wouldn't talk like one yourself. But, as a matter of fact, Vail's dry, by some miracle. He's wakeful though. His teeth hurt him. I want to get him to sleep and this is the quietest room in the house."

It's also the most detached room, Fabian said to himself. *She was trying to get away and pull herself together, after an upsetting experience, just as I was, though I hope she doesn't realize that. And, of course, I'd have to stumble into the place she wanted to be. Now I can't very well clear out unless I make it pretty pointed that I know what's the trouble with her. I certainly take the blue for clumsiness.* He turned away again, looking out of the window to Angus Holt's pleasant garden, only vaguely conscious, in his distress, of the glossy sago palms and prim brick-bordered flower beds. But presently he became aware that Cresside had spoken the truth. She really did not mind having him there; in some strange way his presence was soothing to her. She had sought solitude, but what she actually needed was the sense of comfort and support that springs from sympathetic companionship. The realization that he could give this to her was both surprising and rewarding. He sat very still, without trying to talk to her, but watching her with increasing, though unobtrusive attention. She was walking slowly up and down, holding the baby closely to her breast and singing to him as she walked. It was years since Fabian had heard the old Negro melody:

"Little David, play on yo' harp Halleluiah!
Little David, play on yo' harp Hallelu.

One day, one day Ah was walkin' 'long,
Yes, Ah heard a reason f'om on high,
Say go in peace an' sin no mo'
Yo' sins are forgiven an' yo' soul set free.

Little David, play on yo' harp Halleluiah!
Little David, play on yo' harp Hallelu.

Ah pluck yo' feet
Out de miry clay
An' sot 'em on rock ob eternal age;
Where de win' may blow
An' de storm may rise
But de gates ob hell
Shall neber prevail.

Little David, play on yo' harp Halleluiah!
Little David, play on yo' harp Hallelu."

The verses went on and on punctuated by the refrain, while Fabian listened and watched. Every now and then the baby's eyelids drooped, only to fly wide open again; every now and then he raised his downy head and looked belligerently around him, with a sudden yell. He was fighting sleep with the same stubbornness that all the "mule-headed" d'Alverys displayed, when they declined to accept a given situation. Cresside continued to walk and to croon, but Fabian could tell both from her step and from her voice that she was getting very tired. He rose from the desk.

"Couldn't I carry him for you, a little while?" he asked. "You could go on singing, you know. But you could do it sitting down."

"Yes, I could. All right, take him. Thanks, Fabian."

Fabian could not remember when he had held a baby, except for the instant that he had taken Sybelle at Cresside's bidding, earlier that same day. Momentarily, he felt terribly awkward; but as he walked up and down with the mutinous infant in his arms, the sensation changed. He was gratified to find that Vail did not seem to resent the transfer, but almost immediately cuddled down, with a resigned sigh; his eyelids drooped and did not rise again. There was something about the feeling of this warm, relaxed little body, pressed close to his own, that affected Fabian poignantly. So this was what it was like to have a child in your arms, even a child that was not your own! It stirred you to a deeper sense of responsibility and protectiveness than any other human experience—unless it might be the experience of guarding your own child. . . . And that child's mother. Profoundly moved, Fabian looked across at Cresside over the baby's nodding head.

"The inevitable recognition of proper authority, accorded to one male from another," he said, speaking lightly because he did not dare speak otherwise. "This kid knows he can put it over on you, but that he can't on me. I'm a fierce old cousin, not a doting aunt. Just call me in hereafter when you want a slight show of discipline, will you? Meanwhile, now that I've got him to sleep, tell me what to do with him next."

"You could take him out to the patio and put him in the double cradle with Sybelle. That's where he's supposed to sleep, of course. But I'd really rather keep him here—the less he's moved around, the less danger there is that he'll wake up. Suppose you lay him down on the bed. I'll sit here and watch him, to make sure he doesn't fall off."

"Right. I'll sit here beside you and watch him, too."

Cautiously, having deposited Vail on the four-poster with great care, Fabian pulled up two chairs, placing them side by side near the bed. For a few moments he and Cresside sat quietly looking at the baby, without speaking to each other. Then Fabian put out his hand and took Cresside's.

"Listen," he said. "Apparently Sylvestre gave you an awful shock by coming here today unexpectedly. Anyway you acted as if he had."

"I know I did, and I'm sorry. But I got hold of myself right away. I don't think anyone but you noticed that I was shot to pieces."

"I don't think Regine noticed. I'm almost sure Sylvestre did, though. I know this is one of those things that's a lot easier to say than to do. But if I were you I wouldn't ever give him the chance to see you shot like that again."

"I'm not going to. I know I can't keep out of his way. I realize he's a near neighbor now, that the Hathaways are old family friends—oh, all the rest of it! But just the same——"

"Just the same, I hope you'll hang on to yourself the next time."

"I've just told you, I'll try. But why, specifically?"

"Because you've given him a jolt, too, and I don't know how he'll react to it—perhaps by trying to 'talk things over,' which I know is the last thing in the world you'd want to do. Up to now I think he was laboring under the comfortable delusion that you and he had just fitted naturally into the postwar scene, and what either of you may have said or done was merely part of the picture. I don't think it ever occurred to him that the very sight of him would hit you like that —as if you'd suddenly seen a spreading adder. Well, I know you're not afraid of snakes, but you get the idea. I mean the way most girls would look if they did."

"I'm not afraid of snakes, but I do loathe liars. And that's what Sylvestre is—a damn dirty liar! He told me he loved me when he didn't. That's the only thing I'm holding against him. But it's plenty. Because I believed him. I wasn't just going in for heavy petting on general principles. I know you think that's part of what you delicately call the postwar scene. That and bathtub gin. But he knew I believed him when he said he loved me."

"I know it, too, Cresside. And I never sized you up wrong. But——"

"I told Gervais he wanted to marry me, and I honestly thought he did. It wasn't until afterwards that I found out he'd been engaged to Regine all the time, that I didn't really mean anything to him. But after I'd started lying, I couldn't stop. I had to go on and on. He made a dirty liar out of me, too!"

"He lied to you, and you lied about him, because you loved him, but that didn't turn you into a liar, Cresside. I'll grant you Sylvestre is a liar, and lots besides that you haven't called him. But I won't grant that you are. I won't let you call yourself that."

"You won't let——"

"No. And I won't let Sylvestre make your life miserable either. But you have to help. You mustn't give him the satisfaction of seeing he can upset you, and you mustn't get him to wondering why he should, so much. If you do, he'll try to find out. You'll have to pretend when you see him it doesn't mean a thing to you, one way or another. And presently it won't. You'll take it in your stride, the same way you've always taken things a lot harder than that."

"You're telling me this just to give me a lift."

"No, I'm not. I'm telling it to you because it's true. You don't think I'd lie to you, do you, Cresside?"

"I know you wouldn't. I know you never lied to anyone about anything that mattered."

"Well, then——"

He smiled at her and pressed her hand. But he did not try to say anything more, and neither did she. They continued to sit side by side in silence, watching the sleeping baby, their mutual sense of recaptured tranquility and new-found companionship merging into deep contentment. They were still sitting there when Dinah quietly entered the room and said that she would watch to see that Vail did not fall while they ate their dinner, which was now ready. There was nothing about her imperturbable and respectful manner to indicate that she had experienced any trouble in finding them or that their joint vigil surprised her. They went out together to join the others leaving Vail in her safekeeping.

CHAPTER XII

FOR SEVERAL DAYS after Fabian's warning, Cresside watched guardedly for Sylvestre. But as time went by and she neither saw him nor heard from him, she gradually became less apprehensive. Besides, she was preoccupied in many other ways; she was helping Merry and Gervais with their preparations for departure, and taking over more and more responsibility for the twins. By Thursday evening, when the whistle of the *John D. Grace*, sounding from upstream, heralded its imminent arrival, she joined, with her customary appearance of gaiety, the little procession starting for the steamboat landing.

Considerable bustle attended the d'Alverys' departure: Amen headed the procession, wheeling a barrow piled high with bags, which he intended to place, personally, in the cabins reserved for his white folks, as he had no confidence in "steamboat niggers." He was followed by Dinah, wearing the costume she reserved for great occasions; but instead of carrying a twin on each arm, as usual, she propelled them in a perambulator veiled with a lace-edged mosquito bar, for at the approach of dusk, the mosquitoes began to swarm in a vicious cloud. It was because of these same pests that Merry and Gervais, who came next, carried nothing but mosquito whips of slit palmetto, which they flourished constantly. Following the prospective travelers came Madame d'Alvery in the elaborate wheel chair which she now used when she went about the plantation, beyond the pergola. It had a top shaped like a gigantic parasol, and the billowing fringe with which this was edged helped to keep off the insects; so did Lucie, who walked beside Selah as he pushed the chair, and who wielded a large fan, for Madame d'Alvery did not exert herself to the extent of using a mosquito whip. Fabian and Cresside brought up the rear, adequately armed, but somewhat neglectful of their weapons, because they were both trying unsuccessfully to keep Belizaire in line.

The five Negro roustabouts who made up the steamboat's deck crew were already standing by the gangplank as the procession went over the crest of the levee, and, entirely uninhibited by the presence of quality, they began to call out eager invitations to Dinah. A trip to New Orleans would not cost her a cent, they assured her; they had space and to spare for the likes of her. The only response which Dinah condescended to make was brief and disdainful: she had a man of her own, not no River trash neither, and she wasn't leavin' him, right now; when she did travel with her white folks, they'd be paying her passage. While this exchange of compliments was taking place, the captain stepped forward—a burly man badly in need of a shave, who wore a yachting cap on the back of his head, but whose informal attire did not otherwise even suggest a uniform. Tugging at his straggly mustache, he wanted to know whether Captain and Mrs. d'Alvery had dined already. If not, perhaps they'd join the rest of the passengers, who were having steamboat hash in the saloon right now. . . . Oh, very well, then! Probably they'd like to see their cabins, first thing. Afterwards he'd be very glad to have them go up in the pilot-house, if they'd care to. It was nice and cool there and they'd get a good view of the River. . . . Nonsense, they were not to mention it.

Merry was enchanted with the prospect of going to the pilothouse, and it was the exuberance of her thanks which evoked the captain's disclaimer. He turned away, slightly embarrassed, to give an order

159

to the mate, and Merry, experiencing her first misgivings about leaving the twins, now that the separation was imminent, bent over to kiss them tearfully, while she murmured final admonitions to Cresside and Dinah. When she looked up, she saw that the group at the gangplank had been enlarged; Sylvestre and Regine had joined the others. Sylvestre, looking rather sulky, was carrying a large beribboned basket, and Regine immediately enveloped Merry in one of her comprehensive embraces.

"Darling!" she exclaimed. "We've had such a hectic day we were afraid we couldn't get here, but we were determined to tell you good-by, and somehow we made it. And look!—I brought you a *bon voyage* basket. Of course in one way it seems absurd to see your friends off when they're only going as far as New Orleans, but after all, if that's the extent of their travels, why then you know it seems important to them anyway!"

"Yes, it does seem important to me," Merry answered. "It seems very exciting. The basket's beautiful, Regine! And the captain's so nice! He's asked us to go up to the pilothouse!"

"Oh, that!" Regine said, with a slight shrug of her pretty shoulders. "Why that's nothing but a little dark room with a bench on one side of it! And you don't see anything when you look out except the River, and the landings at the stupid little places where you stop. Now on an ocean liner, when you go up on the bridge, and see the big harbors as you come into them—Plymouth and Le Havre and on the way home, New York—why, that really *is* something! Of course, mamma and Sylvestre and I were shown every courtesy on ocean liners. We sat at the captain's table and went to his quarters for cocktails, and naturally we were invited up to the bridge, too. It was the most beautiful day, the morning we came into New York, and we saw——"

"How long are you going to be gone?" Sylvestre asked, turning to Gervais and handing him the basket, as Regine went on and on. Though he had not given the effect of interrupting her, since she was talking to Merry, she immediately interrupted herself in order to answer.

"Merry says they're coming back Sunday night on the Gulf Coast Limited," Regine announced. "She says they have drawing room A. She's actually excited about that, Sylvestre! I've been telling her that you and I never dreamed of traveling without a drawing room—except, of course, in Europe, where you have to take *compartements* on the *wagon-lits*. But then we always had two connecting ones, with a lavatory between, so it was even more spacious and convenient than a drawing room. The European trains are so much better than ours, aren't they?"

"The ones I traveled on weren't," Gervais retorted. "They had accommodations for *40 hommes, 8 chevaux,* and believe me there wasn't anything very spacious or convenient about that arrangement."

"Why, Gervais, you sounded a lot like Fabian the way you said that! I didn't know you ever got so sarcastic! Of course, I wasn't talking about war conditions, I was only trying to describe——"

Her patter was drowned by the whistle blaring the signal for departure; by the twins, whose behavior so far had been exemplary, but who now howled with fright at this loud and sudden sound; and by Belizaire, who whirled around in circles, barking sympathetically. She clapped her hands over her ears with a playful gesture, backing away from the gangplank; then, after a brief pantomime designed to exact pity for her helplessness in the midst of such pandemonium, she linked one arm affectionately in her husband's, and began waving a lace-edged handkerchief with her free hand. Cresside and Dinah, firmly grasping mosquito whips, were already lifting the twins from the perambulator to soothe them, and calling out reassuringly to Merry, who had turned, halfway to the boiler deck, in a way which seemed to indicate that she could not bear to leave after all; while Gervais, speaking reassuringly also, propelled her on her way.

"They'll be all right in a minute," he said. "I reckon maybe we ought not to have brought them down to the landing. I forgot all about that darn whistle. And it's past their bedtime anyway. But Cresside'll have them quieted in no time. Come on, honey, we mustn't hold things up any more—there's been a delay as it is, stopping the boat on purpose for us. Gosh, but it's a relief to get away from Regine's everlasting gabble, isn't it? She goes on like a Swiss music box. I'd like to dump this damn basket of hers overboard—we haven't any place to put it or any earthly use for it. Wouldn't you know that Dizzy Dora would come to a grubby little barge with a thing like this? Let's raffle it off at the ship's concert for the sailors' orphans. And now that that's settled. . . . Where would you like to go first? To see our quarters, or straight to the pilothouse?"

Merry decided in favor of the former. These were tiny cabins, containing nothing except a single berth and a bowl and pitcher on a small wooden stand, and opening directly on the narrow middle deck, surrounding the dining saloon in a semicircle. A breeze from the River swept through them, cooler than any which reached Belle Heloise from May to November, and infinitely refreshing after the heat of the day; and in themselves, they were not uninviting: the coarse linen sheets on the bunks were very clean, and the well-painted shutters were carefully screened. But Merry's happy face clouded a little when she saw that there was no communicating door between her cabin and Gervais'.

"We're going to be really separated, aren't we, darling? For the first time!"

"Well, it isn't a very serious separation, you know. I can walk out of my door and into yours without much trouble—and I will! But there aren't any double beds on steamboats, worse luck, not even on luxury liners like those Regine keeps bragging about—perhaps that special feature doesn't seem as much of a disadvantage to her as it does to you! So you think you'll really miss me, do you?"

"You know I will. It does seem as if we could have managed somehow, in one cabin."

"Take my word for it, we couldn't! If we could have, do you think I'd have got two? Don't forget, I'm going to miss *you!* . . . Well, now that you've inspected our *suite de luxe,* suppose we go on up to the pilothouse."

Merry was more than willing. But as they stepped out on the narrow deck, they found their passage blocked by almost the last person whom they would have expected to find among their fellow passengers. Luigi Tramonte, wearing "store-bought" clothes and a turquoise stickpin in his plaid cravat, had just emerged from the cabin beyond Gervais', and hastened towards them, beaming broadly.

"How you do, *Capitano!* How you do, Mis' d'Alvery!" he said heartily. "So you going to the city, too? Now, ain'ta that a nice surprise, we meeta like this!"

"Well, it's a surprise to us, too, Luigi," Gervais answered. "I generally travel by train, now that the old side-wheelers are gone. But Mrs. d'Alvery thought she'd enjoy the River trip. Do you take the *John D. Grace* often?"

"At first I take him only once a year," Luigi replied. "Now I take him two, three, maybe four time. I no can get alla I need for my trade in Baton Rouge. I gotta go to the city, but it don't costa so much. I gotta relations there, I staya by them. Mike Montagino, he'sa live back of Marrero, him and me is cousins. He gotta nice farm, too. I ride into town every morning on his vegetable truck. One very fine truck, but he can afford it. He's a make-a plenty money on his farm with four girls and five boys already, and soon his wife have new bambino, make-a ten to help. He gotta nice house, too, plenty room for company."

"That must make things pleasant for you, Luigi," Merry said.

"Ver' pleasant and ver' cheap, too, Mis' d'Alvery," Luigi assured her. "Mike he's gooda fellow. I think maybe he make-a me fine price on his old truck. He got new one, now."

"So you're thinking of getting a truck next, are you, Luigi, instead of saving for the fancy grocery store?"

"No, no, *Capitano.* I sava for fancy grocery store alla time. But if I have truck instead of cart, I make-a more money, and then I save-a more, too, see? Anyhow, I talk to Mike about it. I got plenty time to talk to him and buy what I got to buy. I buy plenty julery wholesale this trip, and Netta, she helpa me pick 'em out." He paused for breath, his jovial face taking on greater animation than ever. "You seen my Riccardo, but you ain't never seen my Netta, no, *Capitano?*" he inquired. "She don't go with me on the cart. She stay home, cook, clean, sew for me and my Riccardo. But always she comes to city with me. She's ina there with Riccardo right now. I bring her out."

162

He turned back to his cabin, and for a few minutes the sound of an unintelligible but heated argument came to the d'Alverys' ears. Apparently Netta was reluctant to present herself to her husband's patrons, and he was insistent that she should. At last he emerged in triumph, with his wife on his arm. Her face was downcast, her manner bashful; she could hardly be persuaded to look up, and as she understood very little English and spoke less, conversation with her was necessarily limited. But in spite of these disadvantages, there was something very appealing about her. Only her unkempt hands, their roughness and redness accentuated rather than mitigated by her many rings, betrayed the rigor of the labors she had always performed; otherwise she gave the impression of a contented and cherished woman, rather than a hard-working one, retaining in maturity, to a surprising degree, the loveliness she must have had as a girl. Besides the rings, she wore an abundance of other jewelry, strings of coral, and cameos in heavy settings which represented considerable value, and great golden loops hung from her pierced ears. Her beautiful black hair was piled high on her graceful head in a crown of heavy braids, and confined with a tortoise-shell comb. Her dress, subtly suggestive of a peasant costume, set off her trim figure to great advantage, and her skin had the mellowness of a ripe peach. The few words that she was persuaded to utter were spoken in a voice that was sweet as well as shy, and the only time that she raised her head, she revealed magnificent eyes and red lips parted in a hesitant smile over fine small teeth. Luigi regarded her with bursting pride throughout the difficult interview, and when she prevailed upon him to permit her return to their cabin, he insisted that the d'Alverys should come too, and take a look in at the door.

"Looka see, our cabin alla same like yours!" he said proudly. "And looka see Riccardo, whata good boy!"

The good boy was sitting up in the berth, still wide awake, but perfectly placid, and smiled an unembarrassed greeting to the visitors. Obviously he had inherited none of Netta's timidity, and his English was better than Luigi's. His mother helped pick out the jewelry when they went to New Orleans, he told the visitors, with a little prompting from his father; but he helped pick out the toys. He and papa were beginning to carry toys in the cart now, just a few; but when they got their truck, the old one that Cousin Mike was going to let them have now that he had bought a new one, there would be room for lots and lots of toys.

"That's right, Riccardo," Luigi said delightedly. "Next time we come to Belle Heloise, we bringa toys to the twins, don't we? We bringa doll to Sybelle for a present, then maybe the *Capitano* buy a ball for Vail! Now you go to sleep, that's a good boy!"

"*They* seem to be managing all right in one cabin," Merry murmured, after she and Gervais had finally succeeded in taking their leave of the Tramontes without hurting Luigi's pride by doing so too abruptly. "How do you suppose *three* of them can?"

"Oh, I suppose Netta curls up at one end of the bunk and Riccardo at the other! And that Luigi sleeps on the floor. And I don't believe any of them worries too much about washing. Perhaps I ought to say I'd be glad to sleep on the floor for the sake of sharing a room with you. But after all, you and I aren't Italian immigrants, and the sad fact remains that the reason Luigi's doing it is financial, not amorous. He wouldn't think of spending money on two cabins. . . . Obviously he's making money though," Gervais added thoughtfully. "The next thing you know he'll have a whole fleet of trucks and that fancy grocery store, too. Not to mention a house of his own that will knock the daylights out of his cousin's. But that's not our little red wagon! Come on, let's go up to the pilothouse."

It was even cooler in the pilothouse than it had been on the cabin deck and at first it was very quiet. Evidently none of the other passengers had been invited to sit there, for Merry and Gervais had to themselves the bench Regine so contemptuously described. The pilot, a spare angular man in civilian clothes, nodded to them as they came in, but did not speak; he stood staring out into the deepening dusk, smoking a pipe and spinning his wheel with a nonchalant ease oddly at variance with his general awkwardness. After the boat was well under way, headed downstream towards Plaquemine, a variety of sounds began to drift up from below decks—the clatter of crockery negligently handled as it was washed and put away; the occasional clang of the fire doors leading into the boilers, as these were slammed shut; the rhythmic puff of the blower fan, almost as though the boat were drawing labored breath; voices of passengers who had finished their steamboat hash and were now seated on the forward deck, talking. But all these sounds seemed to come from a great distance, they were all indistinct and unfamiliar; Gervais and Merry, conscious of an alien atmosphere, spoke to each other in hushed tones, and only occasionally. Once Gervais addressed the pilot.

"Is it all right if I smoke a cigarette?"

"Sure."

Without elaborating on this statement, the pilot relapsed into the silence that had hitherto engulfed him. Eventually it became so oppressive that Merry and Gervais did not speak either. Gervais' cigarette made a tiny point of light in the enveloping darkness, but no other was visible except an occasional beacon until they came within sight of Plaquemine. Then the blaring whistle sounded again and the boat turned, backing water, to make the landing below the locks. A powerfully built, pleasant-faced priest, wearing a travel-stained cassock, disembarked alone, and a rubicund groceryman standing by a mule-cart was apparently the only white person who had come to meet the boat; but half a dozen Negro girls, dressed in flimsy blouses and bright-colored skirts, were evidently awaiting its arrival with eagerness. Far from maintaining the attitude of contempt with which Dinah had regarded the roustabouts, they immediately opened an exchange of extremely broad jokes with these ribald deckhands, as the men began to carry boxes of groceries down the gangplank, depositing them near the waiting mule-cart.

"Don' yo' want a fella with a strong back fo' liftin' boxes, gal?"

"Huh! Strong back fo' liftin' boxes don' mean nothin'.'"

"Dat ain't what 'em gals on Rampart Street tells me, and dey done got you skint a mile fo' looks."

"Maybe dey is got me skint fo' looks, but dey don' know real mens like Ah does. Dem po' N'Yawlins folkses, dey don' never see no real mens like us has got on Bayou Plaquemine."

"Real mens! Some po' ol' cotton chopper, dat's all you's ever got."

This interchange of civilities did not seriously hamper the process of unloading, which was enlivened rather than hampered by it. The mate stood idly by, ostensibly to hurry the process, occasionally giving vent to a phrase or two of listless profanity, and then left the crew to go its own way, while he occupied himself with the placement of some timbers, on which to drive off the two Ford "phaetons" whose disembarkation he proposed to handle personally. The roustabouts, their heads grotesquely draped with gunnysacks which fell shawl-like to their shoulders, kept moving back and forth between the crest of the levee and the boiler deck, with the strange gait which was neither a walk nor a trot nor a shuffle, but which was so peculiarly their own. The boat's electric searchlight played upon their figures, etching them out vividly in the long oval of radiance it threw upon the sloping grassy backdrop of the levee, and their shadows, shifting grotesquely about the sward, seemed bent upon a weird dance of their own. The roustabouts did not continuously banter with the bold little hussies who were so ready to jest with them. Some of them chanted, in a singsong as eerie as their gait, and as peculiarly their own:

"We got these twenty boxes to unload."
"Yes, Lord!"
"Twenty boxes offen de steamboat and up on de levee."
"Yes, Lord!"
"Pile gettin' smaller, boys, time to rest is comin' fast."
"Yes, Lord!"
"Only three more boxes left, boys. Oh, possum and cornbread!"
"Yes, Lord!"
"Jes' one mo' time——"
"Yes, Lord!"

The chanting and "coonjining" came to an end only when the unloading was finished. The soap and breakfast food, the salt and canned goods, were all on the crest of the levee then, and the rubicund grocer, having signed the waybills handed him by the mudclerk, was supervising the removal of the commodities he had purchased; the mule-cart began to move slowly down the ramp on the landward side of the levee. The mate, having directed the adjustment of the timbers to form rails, in a way that was satisfactory to him, was trying to drive the first of the two Ford phaetons up the levee. It did not have power enough of its own to make the grade, and he was obliged to call the roustabouts, who were now resting from their labors, and joking again with the little hussies, to come and push it. The second phaeton behaved better; it bucked successfully over the crest and rolled triumphantly down the other side. With the disposal of the phaetons, the stop at Plaquemine came to a logical close. Blaring out one more whistle blast, the boat backed into the stream and floated off into the night; only the beacon lights, upheld by their tripods, pierced the profundity of the darkness.

"Have coffee?"

The taciturn pilot's abrupt question, suddenly shot out of the silence, was startling out of all proportion to its importance. However, both Merry and Gervais managed to answer in the affirmative, and the pilot leaned towards a speaking tube attached to the wall, and addressing some unidentified personage below decks, called imperatively for refreshments. An untidy mess boy promptly appeared carrying a tin tray, set with thick white cups, a battered sugar bowl, and a can of condensed milk.

"Take cream?"

Merry and Gervais said that they would; the coffee was very bad and the condensed milk did not improve it, but the travelers swallowed it somehow, feeling it would be ungracious to reject the pilot's expression of hospitality. Fearful lest he might repeat it, however, Merry said that she was beginning to get sleepy, and that she thought it might be a good idea to go to bed. They went carefully down the gangway, finding most of the cabins, including the Tramontes', already in darkness, but the saloon was still brightly illuminated. The captain, the mate and the mudclerk, together with three male passengers, were now having a game of penny ante, in which they were agreeably absorbed. None of them even looked up at the d'Alverys' approach; but, almost simultaneously, a sound of scuffling and sudden oaths, followed by a sharp outcry came from the forepeak. The mate, himself swearing vociferously this time, vaulted up and shot out of the door. As he tore past them, Merry shrank back, grasping Gervais' arm.

"What's happened?"

"Some kind of a sudden quarrel among the roustabouts. A knife fight probably."

"They—they won't get killed, will they?"

"No, of course not. The mate probably has the fighters separated by now. He's used to dealing with that sort of thing—it happens often enough."

"But why should it?"

"It might be over a dice game—but most likely it's about one of those little hellions we saw on the levee. Even white men fight over

166

perfect ladies, sometimes, you know. Come on, honey, let's get to bed. There's nothing to worry about."

She did not feel entirely reassured, but she did not want to seem silly either, so she smothered all further expressions of anxiety and withdrew, reluctantly, to her cabin. In spite of her happiness with her husband, there were still occasional moments when he made her uncomfortably conscious that she lacked experience and sophistication. She knew he did not do this deliberately, but she could never wholly suppress the pangs of regret that she did not, in every way, measure up to his standards; and she stood for a while in the doorway of her cabin, after Gervais had gone unconcernedly into his, wondering, against her will, whether the passage of time would intensify or eliminate the difference between them.

The turmoil on the forepeak had died down quickly, as he had predicted it would, and the interrupted quietude now seemed even more profound than before. The same alien quality in the atmosphere which had hushed her speech in the pilothouse overwhelmed Merry now; so did the unfamiliar attributes of the various landings which, at intervals, continued to interrupt the progress downstream. The blare of the whistle, the churn of the waters, the "coonjining" of the roustabouts were repeated again and again. At Bayou Goula a woman disembarked who was wearing a widow's veil of rusty crepe and clutching a large black reticule of well-worn leather; an elderly man, also dressed in mourning, had come to meet her, and an old-fashioned fringed surrey, with an emaciated white-haired Negro in the driver's seat, was waiting for her. At Whitecastle the departing passenger was a much harassed mother, whose three fretful children importuned her incessantly, and whose husband called to her angrily from the shore, for God's sake, would she make those kids shut up. Merry speculated about these other travelers, whom she had never seen before, and would probably never see again; evidently they were all plain people, in even more moderate circumstances than hers had been before she married. All through the night such people would be getting off at landings along the way—Burnside, Donaldsonville, Convent, Vacherie, Lutcher, Edgard. By morning there probably would be no one left on the boat besides Gervais and herself and the Tramontes. Now that the glorious days of steamboating were over, not many through passengers used the River. To most persons these local stops represented convenience as well as economy. Very few went by the River for pleasure. But Merry was glad Fabian had suggested the *John D. Grace* and that Gervais had fallen in with the idea, regardless of his scoffing remarks to the effect that sternwheelers were in the same class as towboats. She was getting a great deal out of the trip; experiences like this would increase her fund of worldly knowledge, and for Gervais' sake she craved this.

At last she closed the door of her cool little cabin, and climbing into her bunk between the coarse clean sheets, slept peacefully until a "high-yellow" girl appeared at her bedside, carrying a red-copper tray set with morning coffee. Merry could not help wondering rather idly whether this might not be the hussy over whom the roustabouts had fought; the girl had a triumphant look, and she lingered in the cabin with such an expectant air that Merry guessed she was eager to be questioned about something. Thanking her for the coffee, Merry handed back the cup half emptied, saying that she preferred to wait until she could drink hers with her husband, and adding that she did not need any help with her dressing. The high-yellow girl departed with seeming reluctance, tossing her head and clattering the china. Merry bathed conscientiously from the bowl and pitcher, supplementing the inadequate supply of water with cologne from a little wicker-covered bottle her mother-in-law had given her, and talcum powder from a gaily decorated can. Then she dressed with the utmost care in her crowded quarters. But she felt vaguely dissatisfied with the results, as she looked in the small blurred mirror hanging over the washstand. She had never used make-up and it did not occur to her to do so now; but she wished she might look her very best when she met Gervais' New Orleans friends for the first time, and she could not help believing that somehow she might have achieved better results if she had been in a less primitive place. She experimented with her curls, but they fell stubbornly back in their accustomed waves, and she had no better luck with her blouse, which already needed pressing, though it had been spick and span when she had left Belle Heloise the evening before. Finally, unable to think of any other preparations or improvements she might make, she went on deck.

She saw no sign of Gervais and Merry decided not to wake him, as it was still very early. Luigi and Riccardo were not in sight either. But Netta was already standing beside the rail, gazing with obvious interest at some cargo ships which had formed part of the World War fleet but were now tied up in a "graveyard." On the other side of the River a fourmaster, stately even in abandonment, seemed like a great adventuress absorbed in reverie over the magnificent gallantries of the past. Merry had never seen one like it before. She spoke excitedly to Netta, indicating it.

"Look at that sailing vessel, Mrs. Tramonte! She must have been beautiful once, don't you think?"

Netta nodded, smiling assent. She seemed a little less shy than the evening before; her eyes were no longer downcast, and she responded more and more readily to Merry's exclamations of delight, as each bend of the River disclosed some new spectacle: the towering grain elevator, with a little freighter flying a Norwegian flag drawn up beside its conveyors; the long low cotton warehouses, drenched in the morning radiance; the spotless liners of the Great White Fleet and the dingy ships from Brazil, respectively discharging bananas and coffee; the Chalmette refinery, looming up in the distance. Finally she spoke, slowly but resolutely, on her own initiative.

"I think Napoli more pretty. But I lika New Orleans best."

"I hope I'll see Naples some day. It must be very beautiful. But I don't believe, myself, that I could enjoy anything more than this. I'm glad you like New Orleans best, Mrs. Tramonte. Is it all right to ask you why?"

"In Napoli very poor. In New Orleans maka much money."

The reply seemed conclusive. Merry, her eyes on the distant silhouette of the sugar refinery, made no immediate attempt to answer it. Netta asked a question herself.

"Your man—he maka money in New Orleans, too, no?"

Merry laughed. It was a laugh of contentment and security and pride, and Netta understood it as such.

"I think my husband's going to *spend* it there!" Merry said. "I think we're going to have fun, spending it together!"

CHAPTER XIII

THE *John D. Grace* had almost reached the Bienville Street landing when Gervais joined Merry on deck. He glanced swiftly around the wharf and almost instantly located a swarthy but extremely handsome young man, whose modish attire and slight swagger made him outstanding in the crowd.

"There's Billy Pereira now!" he said. "That lad who looks like a prosperous Spanish *elegant* and damned proud of it!" Then, as Billy Pereira looked up with a dazzling smile, doffing a very fine Panama hat, Gervais called out, "Hello, Don Guillermo! So this is New Orleans!"

"Hello, yourself!" Billy called back. "Hello, Mrs. d'Alvery! I'm sure enough grateful to you both for getting me up to see the sunrise. Quite a sight, isn't it? I'd almost forgotten. . . . And speaking of sights, give a look at my new bus, over yonder by the vegetable truck, will you?"

"Not that glassed-in Locomobile showcase!" Gervais followed the exclamation with a whistle. "Man, what bank have you robbed? Or are you just showing off the state of the coffee market?"

"Oh, the boys at the Boston Club paid for that—they thought I had mice in my paneling when I offered to bet on Parker in the election. I hope it didn't teach them a lesson—I'd like a private Pullman of my own—and the city election comes in September. Pretty smooth bus, though, isn't she?"

The Locomobile was certainly very smooth, and the vegetable truck parked beside it—also the latest model of its type—proved to be the one of which Luigi's "relation," Mike Montagino, was the very proud possessor. After the simple processes of landing, the d'Alverys and Tramontes exchanged introductions to their respective hosts, who were both slightly staggered by these, then they all parted with mutual expressions of good will, and Billy Pereira continued his agreeable small talk as the Locomobile turned into Canal Street and rolled smoothly along towards the Grunewald.

"I've got you a slick suite. I'm sure you'll like it, for it's really a knockout. We were all tremendously sorry that you wouldn't stay with us, but we understood this was a sort of belated bridal fling. Mother's counting on you for dinner at the house tonight, though, and she's asked a few friends in to meet you. Tomorrow I thought we'd take in the regatta from aboard the *Suzette III* and follow that with the dinner dance at the Yacht Club—unless there's something else you'd rather do, of course. And Father wants you both to come and look over the office—we've just finished remodeling the whole building. Three-thirty's a good time, because everyone knocks off for a cup of coffee then and you might enjoy having it with the rest. But, of course, you'd be more than welcome whenever you could fit the visit in with your other plans."

They had no other special plans, Gervais said, in a gratified voice, while Merry listened with breathless excitement; they would be more than pleased to fall in with all of these. Of course, Gervais wanted to call on his broker, Mr. Garfield, the first thing, to find out just how much of his sugar was sold and how substantial his credit was. If the news proved as good as he expected, he was going to take Merry to do some very special shopping after lunch, and they would drop in to the office for coffee as soon as they had finished it. Meantime, while he was conferring with Mr. Garfield, he believed Merry intended to look up some clothes. If either Billy's sister, or his mother, would take her to the best places, of course that would be extremely helpful. . . .

The pleasant plans speedily developed into delightful engagements. Billy's sister, Mary Ellen, called for Merry before she had time to unpack, and whisked the visitor away in her own smart yellow roadster, for an "orgy of squandering," as she herself described it. Breathlessly, almost unbelievingly, Merry bought clothes for the maids, for the twins, for the new baby, for Madame Mère, for Cresside, for herself. Remembering Cresside's generosity, when she had come to Belle Heloise as a dowerless bride, she took special pleasure in selecting an unusually smart outfit for her sister-in-law. She was going to insist that Cresside come to New Orleans in the very near future, and have "an orgy of squandering" with Mary Ellen, too. Merry even began to wonder whether Cresside could not be persuaded to consider

Billy Pereira as a suitor, since unfortunately Charles Boylston did not seem to be making much headway.

Gervais was lunching with Mr. Garfield at the Boston Club, so Mary Ellen took Merry to Antoine's, where two other girls, both pretty as pictures and smart as paint, joined them in the Mystery Room. Much of their conversation centered on recipes for homemade gin—"aged in the bathtub, all of five minutes"—and other expediencies brought on by prohibition. Some of it, however, was devoted to new dance steps, new bridge rules, and conjectures as to prospective carnival queens; and one of the girls was preoccupied with the romance of Mary Pickford and Douglas Fairbanks which had "thrilled her to pieces." Merry felt rather relieved when Gervais, looking very well satisfied with life, came breezing into the Mystery Room while blue flames were leaping from the *cérises jubilées* in process of preparation and said he was ready to take her away.

"You had a good time, didn't you, honey?" he asked, struck by the fact that she was rather silent, as they turned into Royal Street.

"Ye-es. They were all just as nice as they could be. And so attractive! But Cresside would have fitted in better than I did, Gervais."

"Look here, you haven't let those empty-headed flappers wear you down, have you? I thought you'd find them highly amusing! Which reminds me, I've got something on my mind I want to talk to you about, when we get back to the hotel. But first we're going to do that very special shopping. Here, this is where we're headed."

"Here" was a fashionable jeweler's, where they were evidently expected, for an unctuous clerk immediately came forward, calling Captain d'Alvery by name, drawing two chairs up to a glittering showcase, and saying that Mr. Straus would be down in just a minute. While they awaited his arrival, Gervais outlined the purpose of their errand, hitherto unexplained.

"Mr. Straus is the head of this firm, honey. I telephoned him from Mr. Garfield's office and said we'd be in. I had very cheering news from my old broker—my credit balance couldn't very well be better. So while we're waiting for Mr. Straus to come, I want you to start looking around for an engagement present and a wedding present and the present you had coming to you when the twins were born. Don't ask Mr. Straus how much anything costs. Just tell me what you want."

For a moment she could not answer him. Her eyes brimmed over with tears, which she rarely shed, and her lips, usually so firm, trembled uncontrollably. Gervais would never have believed that jewelry would mean so much to Merry, of all persons. He had not even taken Fabian's hint very seriously at first, and now he hardly knew whether to be pleased or piqued, because the suggestion had proved so felicitous. He did not understand that Merry's emotion was caused less by the prospect of possessing ornaments which almost every man who could afford it gave to his beloved, than by the long delayed discovery that he really wanted her to have these tangible proofs of generous devotion.

"Why, Merry, don't look at me like that!" he whispered, amazed in his turn. "If I'd known you were going to take it this way, I'd have warned you beforehand. Come, don't let these people in the store see you cry!" He squeezed her hand, surreptitiously, and leaned over the showcase, putting his head close to hers. "Listen, we'll look at these things together. Of course, the engagement present must be a ring. The only question is what kind."

A diamond solitaire, Merry managed to say, though speaking tremulously; she knew that lots of girls thought these were old-fashioned now, but that was what she had always wanted. . . . Why, they were not in the least outmoded, the unctuous clerk hastened to assure her, and Mr. Straus, appearing just then, genially corroborated the statement. Of course, that was what Mrs. d'Alvery had in mind, wasn't it?

With the new solitaire already sparkling on her left hand, Merry began to finger the strings of pearls now laid out on a black velvet pad for her inspection. It was evident that Gervais felt a pearl neck-lace was the proper gift for a bride, just as she felt that only a solitaire was exactly right for an engagement present. The chosen string, complete with a diamond clasp, was soon hanging around her neck, and a bar pin having been selected as the third item on the list, she fastened it slantwise to the front of her dress, in the same way she had noticed Mary Ellen wearing one at luncheon. She would feel conspicuous stepping out into the street again, she said, half in jest and half in earnest; she was afraid people would turn around and stare at her, she sparkled so. But she thanked Mr. Straus very graciously for his help and took her departure without too much apparent self-consciousness. Her eyes were brimming and her lips tremulous again as she passed through the door. But she regained her composure without admonition this time, and the call on the senior Pereira passed off with complete smoothness and great satisfaction to all concerned.

The coffee-importing house was handsomely located in a beautiful old building ornamented, on the outside, with exquisite grill work which had been carefully preserved, and appointed, on the inside, with furnishings which represented the highest standards of office equipment. Immediately beyond the front door was a large round table with a black marbleized top, to which small swinging basins, uncomfortably suggestive of dental-chair attachments, were fastened at regular intervals. At this table a bronzed, crisp-haired man was sitting, dipping, with a long-handled spoon, into some small tumblers which were arranged in front of him, making a strange sniffling sound as he put the spoon in his mouth, and then spitting out the brown liquid to which he had only just helped himself. This man, Gervais explained to Merry in a hasty undertone, was a professional "coffee taster"; the little tumblers contained coffee which he was sampling—"cupping," the process was called. The coffee beans in small pans, from which the beverage in the tumblers had been made, would be accepted or rejected according to his verdict. Gervais did not have time to go into further details, for he and Merry were almost immediately swallowed up by the group of clerks eagerly pressing around the urn which dominated a small cupboard directly behind the testing table. A smiling, white-coated Negro was deftly dispensing coffee from this urn, and the clerks who crowded around him, after accepting their brimming cups and glasses, began darting in every direction, intent on reaching their favorite spot to sip the fragrant brew. Merry tried to edge in among the other girls, excited at the prospect of sharing this pleasant experience with them; but before she reached the urn, Billy opened the door leading from some secluded sanctum in the rear, and hastened towards her and Gervais.

"Hello, there! Father wants you to have coffee with him in his office. Why didn't you bring the Missus straight in there, without waiting for me to come out, Gervais?"

"Well, she was getting a great kick out of it right here. So was I, for that matter! I'll say you've done a smooth job of remodeling. I'd hardly know the place, it's so changed since the last time I saw it. That's a fine fresco, too!" He nodded towards the wall, which was adorned by a highly colored painting of coffee-gathering peons, but as Billy did not seem disposed to let Merry linger any longer in the crowd, Gervais followed his host from the open offices to one that was completely enclosed, where the elder Pereira—almost as slim and quite as elegant as his son—was awaiting his guests.

"Well, Gervais! Well, young lady! Merry—that's your name, isn't it? I'm not going to stand on ceremony with a pretty girl like you. How do you like our quarters here, Merry?"

"I think they're fascinating. I never dreamed there were places like this in New Orleans—I thought they only existed in Rio de Janeiro, or Bogota, or some other exotic city. It's a sort of story-book place, Mr. Pereira—especially this room!"

She looked around her with unconcealed admiration. The modernistic atmosphere of the outer offices had been carefully excluded from this one. It was sheathed in mellow paneling and furnished in richly embossed leather and intricately carved wood. A fine old portrait hung over the marble mantel, and rows of beautiful books, bound in half-calf, filled the shelves of a handsome secretary. The outstanding ornaments of the room, however, were the coffee cups scattered about it, ranging from exquisite gold and silver "miniatures" in glass cases and tiny after-dinner coffee cups, to large costly specimens in Spode, Crown Derby, lusterware and other priceless porcelains. Mr. Pereira, observing the appreciation with which Merry's eyes rested on these treasures of his, addressed her with increasing cordiality.

"I'm delighted that it pleases you so much, my dear young lady,

173

delighted . . . Yes, we've managed to preserve this room pretty much as it always was—basically, I mean, basically. Of course, we've added the little nicknacks I saw you looking at, ourselves. . . . If you ever run across anything that would fit well into my small collection, don't fail to let me know. Now which are you going to have—iced coffee or hot coffee? Jerry's waiting to take your order."

The smiling Negro who had been presiding at the nickel urn was now standing in the doorway, beaming more broadly than ever. Merry said she would take hot coffee, thereby going up a peg further in the old connoisseur's estimation. More or less monopolizing the conversation, and directing it towards her, he went on chatting volubly.

"So you didn't realize how successfully we could compete with Rio de Janeiro or Bogota when it came to an exotic atmosphere? You must persuade your husband to bring you to New Orleans often, my dear Merry, and learn better, you really must. What is there about your part of the state that makes people so loath to leave it? Once they get there, they stay on and on. Now take that handsome young man who had a vague idea he'd like to learn the coffee business—I mean Sylvestre Tremaine. He's the son of two of our oldest friends; in fact, you'll meet his parents at our house tonight. I'd have been glad to push him straight to the top, if he'd only shown the slightest sign of applying himself to the work. But no, his mind was wandering off all the time in the direction of the River Road—well, perhaps I ought to say in the direction of a lovely young lady who lives there. Anyway, he wasn't of any use to me. I finally had to tell him I thought he'd do better in sugar. I hope I wasn't a poor prophet."

Merry looked at Gervais questioningly, uncertain how she ought to reply. He caught the glance and answered for her.

"I'm afraid you were, sir. Sylvestre won't ever make a planter. His place is riddled with mosaic disease right now, and he isn't doing a blessed thing about it."

"Well, well, I'm sorry to hear that. But I suppose one must make allowances for these young husbands. They can't help being pre-occupied. Can they, my dear?"

Merry did not feel equal to discussing this either. She was uncertain whether to say Gervais had never neglected his work for her, or whether to permit the inference that he was so passionately in love with her that their plantation suffered from neglect. She was glad when Gervais took up the ball for her a second time, and gladder still when an inconspicuous gesture of his prompted her to give the signal for departure. The chance mention of Sylvestre Tremaine had clouded her enjoyment in the Pereiras' unique establishment.

She was also slightly disappointed at finding that the Pereiras did not live in the French Quarter, which she had somehow taken for granted, but in the new "development" at Gentilly, which Gervais explained to her was a corruption of the French Chantilly, adding that a highway leading from there to Versailles, the old De La Ronde

174

"No, I didn't forget. There wasn't time. But we'll take time now. . . . I've been thinking for a long while, Merry, that I'd like to do some restoration at Belle Heloise."

"Restoration?"

"Yes. You know those small empty buildings back of the Big House? Of course they're in a terrible state of dilapidation now, but they're not too far gone to restore, and I'd like to do it. They balance the *pigeonniers* in front—nearly all the old places had some sort of a symmetrical design. One of those buildings used to be a storehouse, with a room at one end that my grandfather and great-grandfather used for an office. My father never cared to spend much time in an office, so he let the whole storehouse fall to pieces. But I'd like to rebuild it—we really need one—and revive the office custom. There really isn't enough space upstairs for me to spread out my private papers—the ones I don't care to keep in the sugar house; there's going to be less and less as our family grows. And, of course, *maman* would shudder at the very thought of having me put the parlor or the library to any useful purpose!"

"I think it would be wonderful for you to have an office of your own, and to use it the way your grandfather and great-grandfather did. . . . What about the other little building?"

"Why, that was the *garçonnière*—all the unmarried sons of the family slept there, in the early days, after they got away from their mothers' apron strings, and all the bachelors who came to the house as guests. My father stayed in it for months and months before he was married, and then he and my mother lived in it until her parents died." Gervais paused for a moment, recalling, with his usual reluctance, the story of Philogene's strange wedding night. He had never told it to Merry, and he did not intend to do so now, but he could not help thinking about it. "Of course, then it ceased to be a *garçonnière*—as a matter of fact, Cresside and I were both born in it. But it never was kept in really good condition after the War Between the States, and when my father and mother didn't need it any more, they let it disintegrate, like the office. They thought it represented just one more needless expense."

"But you don't?"

"No. I'd like to rebuild it. I found the old plans, tucked away at the back of the bottom drawer in the plantation desk, not long ago. I didn't say anything to you about them then, because I wasn't too sure how I was coming out for money. But after my talk with Garfield this morning, I feel justified in going ahead. Of course, I'd have to modify the interior a little to put in modern plumbing and so on. But the general effect would be the same as it used to be." He paused again, not because of an unpleasant recollection this time, but to give emphasis to his next question. "How'd you like to have a little house of your own, honey? A little house where you and I could be by ourselves? Don't you think that would be fun?"

"Fun! I think it would be heavenly! But are you sure——"

"Yes, I'm sure. I didn't spend the whole morning in Mr. Garfield's office—I talked to an architect for half an hour, too. He says he's sure I can find someone in Baton Rouge to do the job, but that if I can't, he'll undertake it himself, whenever I say the word. And I'm willing to say it tomorrow morning, if you'll give the plan your blessing."

"Gervais, I don't think I can stand it, if you keep springing surprises on me like this! First all that beautiful jewelry and now a little house of our own! Have you got the plans with you? Can you show them to me?"

"Yes, they're in my suitcase. Wait a sec, I'll set the tray down outside, and we can spread them on this table."

Merry bent entranced over the mottled sheet of paper, brittle with age, which kept curling up at the edges until she weighted down its four corners with toilet articles. The original plan showed three large rooms downstairs, with three dormers above; the rough sketch which the architect had drawn from these indicated that one of the downstairs rooms could be divided to provide for a bathroom, a small dining room and a kitchen. The other ground floor rectangles were labeled "living room" and "master's bedroom," each with a fireplace, those representing the dormers "baby's day nursery," "baby's night nursery," "baby's bath and linen closet!" Merry looked up questioningly.

"It's lovely, but it isn't very large," she said. "There wouldn't be room for all of us, would there? We wouldn't take Dinah and the twins with us?"

Gervais picked up the plans, and rerolling them neatly, placed them back in the metal tube from which he had taken them. "Well, I don't know," he said slowly. "What do you think? I'm afraid it might be pretty crowded for them and Philogene, too, and we'll have him almost as soon as the house is done. We'll have to get a second nurse anyway, and the twins and Dinah are pretty well fixed where they are. Maybe it would be better to leave them in the Big House. But we don't need to decide that right now. Come on, honey, we've got to dress. I'm afraid we've run a little too close to the wind as it is."

The telephone on the little table between their beds rang as he spoke; the doorman was calling to say that Miss Pereira was waiting for them at the Baronne Street entrance. They dressed with frantic haste and dashed downstairs in record time, breathless with apologies. It didn't matter at all, Mary Ellen said, smiling at them from her yellow roadster. They had plenty of time, if they made it snappy; but perhaps they had better shove off now. . . .

They sped out Canal Street towards the cemeteries, whose white tombs rose like tiny marble houses along well-ordered streets; then they turned across the New Basin Canal to the dusty shell road and continued until they passed the huddle of road houses that fringed a little park along the Lake Pontchartrain wall. Skirting this, they get used to it in no time." But as he spoke a cannon boomed without warning, and Merry jumped, stifling a small scream.

"The five-minute gun," Mary Ellen said soothingly. "That gives them a chance to jockey for position—knowing that they have five minutes before the race will start. They've all got stop-watches. When I'm in one of the Skipperette races I always think this is the most exciting moment, because usually, at the finish, the boats are too far apart to make it thrilling."

The *Suzette* had been headed for a bobbing metal buoy when the five-minute gun sounded, and by the time the starting gun boomed its message, she had reached a point well along the triangular course. Merry took the second report more calmly than she had the first, but she was confused by the huddle of sails weaving in and out at the starting line.

"They're all going in different directions," she said in a puzzled voice. "Why don't they all go the same way, if it's a race?" she turned appealingly to Mary Ellen, who obligingly made a diagram designed to clarify the mysteries of tacking into the wind; but the sketch which her hostess drew so easily seemed very complicated to Merry and after a moment she laid it down.

"It's too much for me," she said apologetically. "But the little ships are beautiful. . . . Where's Billy now?" she added, fearful lest she might have sounded unappreciative.

"He's on the starboard tack," Mary Ellen replied absently, her attention now centered on the approaching flotilla. "Wait till he comes about. You can tell how they stand on the race by the order in which they'll round this buoy. And the same way at the next buoy, and so on. There go the first ones—damn! I think that's Ed Pinac. Billy'll be fourth. Yep—there they go!"

Again the *Suzette* got underway, heading this time for the buoy at the lakeward apex of the triangular course, and, for three laps around the triangle, her passengers watched the progress of the race. Finally the cannon boomed again, for the first yacht had crossed the finish line, with Eddie Keep at the tiller. Merry was on the point of offering condolences, when Mary Ellen clapped her hands delightedly.

"Our Willum's an easy second, children!" she cried. "And that keeps him right up there at the top of the standings. Let's take a little turn around the lake before we go in, Daddy, and give Merry something of a trip. You know how Billy is, he won't want dinner for ages yet. First they'll all go to the bar and sail the race over again. And then somebody'll start a dice game, and finally the showers and all. If we go in now we'd just have to sit around and hear the rocking-chair fleet tell about the races they used to sail in the *Calypso* or the *Skimmer*. We can kill a couple of hours better out here."

Mr. Pereira nodded indulgently and gave the necessary orders. Soon they were running eastward past the distant, feathery trees at Citrus and Littlewoods, and sounding the siren imperiously for the drawbridge in the railroad trestle spanning a narrow point in the lake. Then, after a tempting glimpse of Fort McComb in the distance, they turned about. The pastel twilight was deepening over the lake now, and the water was smooth as glass, for the wind had died with the sunset. Beacon lights were beginning to wink along the shore, and from the Yacht Club beamed a strong white shaft of radiance. Merry leaned back in her comfortable chair, contentedly breathing in the soft air, her pleasure no longer marred by perplexity. She was genuinely sorry when they cut past the breakwater to the wharf again, but she was getting tired, too, though it was still only the edge of the evening, Mary Ellen told her afterwards, as they "freshened up" at the club. The crowd was going to meet for dinner on the broad screened gallery built out over the water, and afterwards there would be dancing inside, with ship lanterns for lights. And Billy would want to show Merry the trophy case, with the lovely Lipton Cup that formed the centerpiece, and the photographs of past Lipton teams and famous old yachts. . . .

Somehow Merry braced herself to see it through, and afterwards it all became a glowing memory. But she was almost frantic with fatigue before the dance ended, and when Gervais reminded her that they had promised to meet Mr. Sullivan on the roof of the Elks' Club, she looked at him with entreating eyes and gave a little groan which she made no effort to suppress.

"O.K., if you're sure enough all that tired we'll go back to the Grunewald. But Sullivan's important to me politically, Merry."

"I forgot about that. I reckon I can keep going another hour or so. That would be enough to show we appreciate his invitation, wouldn't it?"

"Plenty. And we can sleep late again tomorrow morning, you know."

It was indeed very late when they woke after their gala evening— so late that the Jesuit Church, where there was a twelve-ten service every day in the year, was the only one where they could still possibly get to Mass. Gervais made this announcement, without much enthusiasm, from the bed which was effectually separated from Merry's by a telephone table to which a large metal lamp was immovably affixed. Sitting up herself, so that her view of her husband would not be wholly obstructed, Merry saw that he was still lying on his back, with his arms thrown over his head and his eyes half closed.

"Is it far from here?" she inquired, tossing her curls back from her forehead and reaching for her dressing gown.

"No. Just across Baronne Street. At that, I don't know if we could make it, by twelve-ten."

"We can try, can't we?"

"Oh, I suppose so! . . . You're not going to end up more Catholic than the Pope, are you, Merry, after that good Baptist upbringing of yours? Dragging me out to church when I'm still half dead with sleep?"

"I'm not dragging you out. I thought you wanted to go. I thought you told me all Sundays were 'holy days of obligation' and that unless you were prevented by illness or some other emergency——"

"Oh, hell! I suppose I did tell you that! But I didn't realize you were going to be such an apt pupil. Give me a kiss, anyway, before you force me to get up, without any mercy, after a tall Saturday night."

He smiled at her invitingly, still making no move to rise. Merry slid out of her bed and sat down on the edge of his. He put his arms around her.

"Happy, darling?"

"You know I am."

"Love me a lot?"

"You know that. too."

"I need to have you say so, about once in so often, or I'm not easy in my mind."

"I thought things were supposed to be the other way around. I thought it was wives who complained if they weren't reassured on that point often enough, not husbands."

"That's just the popular fallacy. I feel terribly in need of reassurance right now, Merry."

"All right. I love you. I love you more than tongue can tell. But I'd love you a lot more if you'd stop acting like a spoiled child. You don't really need any reassurance; you only want me to keep on flattering you until it's too late to go to church."

"It'll serve you right if the epistle is that one about wives being subject to their husbands. It'll inspire me to demand more docility. I'll get even with you for this yet."

He grumbled, under his breath, until they were actually in their pew, and afterwards in the taxi which they took down to Esplanade, where they dined in state with Madame Omer Estrade, an elderly cousin of Madame d'Alvery's, whom she greatly resembled. But considerable merriment was mixed in with his mutterings, and Merry knew that he was not really angry, that he was only teasing her in the way that amused and delighted him. All the other Estrade relatives still living in New Orleans had been bidden to meet them, and again Merry was somewhat overpowered by the importance and dignity of the company in which she was expected to hold her own. The Estrades were all extremely civil to her, but they could hardly be termed cordial; they talked on and on among themselves, while course after course was served, about people and places of which she had never heard, apparently oblivious that they were excluding her from the conversation or indifferent to this fact.

"I really believe, Euphrozine, that Lolotte received more presents for her First Holy Communion than any child I ever knew. Not that this surprised me—a little angel, if ever there was one. I could not

183

control my emotion when I saw her going up the aisle of the Cathedral, wearing her white veil, with her hands folded in prayer and her eyes fixed on the altar. I felt as if any moment she might be taken from us and transported to heaven."

"You have reason, Anzolette. My sentiments were the same. But speaking of veils, and of gifts, did you realize that there were more than twenty yards of rose-point lace in Coralie's bridal costume and that she received almost a thousand wedding presents? Those flounces on her skirt, which she inherited from poor, dear Eugénie, were simply priceless, and Vincent de Laune gave her the most magnificent *parure* of diamonds and rubies I have ever beheld. She did not wear more than half of it at her wedding, for fear of parading too much splendor. But she showed the complete set to me privately, so I know whereof I speak. Nevertheless, had she been my daughter, I should not have approved the match. Of course, the de Launes are very well connected. But they have never been on terms of intimacy with the d'Alverys. And I have heard it said that old Hyacinthe de Laune, Vincent's grandfather——"

"Yes, yes, I know that story, too. We can only hope there is not a word of truth in it, for Coralie's sake. It would be terrible if her children . . . And if I'm not mistaken, she is already *enceinte*——"

"She was, but there has been a disappointment. Now she must repose herself indefinitely. First, of course, to recover from this present crisis and secondly to avert similar calamitous episodes. I trust she will be warned by the experience of Justine, who declined to listen to advice from me or anyone else. It is no secret any longer, I suppose, that she has now had a series of mishaps and has had to abandon all hope of a child. I am not surprised that Roland has sought consolation elsewhere."

"Yes, and I hear he has lost heavily at the races besides. Did you not tell me, Dominique, that Roland had not once backed a winning horse this season?"

While this went on Merry sat for the most part in silence, tasting superlative dishes and sipping vintage wines, though Gervais, no longer in a teasing mood, adroitly contrived to bring her into the conversation now and then. The afternoon was already far gone when the Estrades finally filed solemnly from the somber dining room to the sumptuous drawing room, where coffee and liqueurs were served amidst a lavish display of bric-a-brac, marqueterie, gilt-framed mirrors, crystal chandeliers, family portraits and brocaded furniture; and while these refreshments were being passed, fresh cohorts of visitors began to arrive. These, it appeared, were not close relatives like the dinner guests who still lingered on; but they were kin just the same. Merry, whose own family was small and detached, had never before visualized such a circle as this, complete, compact and self-sufficient; she had never before listened to such endless and satisfied discourse on trivialities.

"I cannot understand how Dieudonné ever consented to the sale of Trianon! To be sure, it was in terrible disrepair, and he was so heavily in debt that he could not possibly have repaired it. But I should have let it fall down around my shoulders before I should have sold it to Yankees! Protestants from Chicago!"

"I do not think I even know their names, Simeon."

"North. I have never heard of any Norths in Louisiana. They are doing the place completely over—ten bathrooms, among other superfluous luxuries. Dieudonné is taking Melisande over the Lake. He says he is going to look for a small place at the Pass. I do not see how he could ever have peace there, using the money he got from Trianon to buy a place in Mississippi!"

"Mr. LeBreton offered to send Bertrand on the Grand Tour with his two sons, but René has declined to let him go, very wisely, I think. There is no reason why Bertrand should leave New Orleans. He has never created even the smallest scandal. And with René's practice ready made for him to step into, the way it is——"

This was still going on, with no signs of stopping, when Gervais rose, saying they would not have time to pack, unless they returned to the hotel immediately. Upon hearing this announcement, the relatives apparently ceased to regard him and Merry as outsiders, for they immediately gathered around, making long farewell speeches and sending interminable messages to poor Cousin Isabelle, who was such a patient sufferer, and dear little Cresside, who must be quite a big girl by now, and the sweet, precious twins, who must without fail be brought to New Orleans. As a result of these tardy and prolonged courtesies, the travelers caught their train with only one minute to spare, and Merry stretched out thankfully on the hard little sofa in drawing room A and slept most of the way to Baton Rouge. When she came briefly to herself from time to time it was to hear Gervais teasing her again.

"I'm sorry that party wasn't more comprehensive. I missed about six families, all told, and they average ten to the family. My great uncle Theodore wasn't there, for instance, and only four of his daughters. He's quite deaf, so that everything you say to him has to be repeated several times. Then there's my second cousin Elaine. She has a slight impediment in her speech, so it's difficult for you to hear *her*."

"Are you trying to tell me what I've been spared, or what I've still got ahead of me?"

"Oh, what you've still got ahead of you! And we didn't even let any of the d'Alvery connections know we were going to be in the city. I'm afraid they'll be very much annoyed when they find out we were there—of course, some of the Estrades will tell them. The d'Alverys are much the more numerous of the two families, because there's Fabian's branch and my branch, too."

"Oh, Gervais, please stop! I'm too tired to hear about any more relatives, Estrades or d'Alverys either!"

"Glad to be getting back to the peace and quiet of the old plantation after all, are you, honey? Perhaps you'll be satisfied to stay there now, instead of wanting to run all over the countryside."

"Why, I always was satisfied to stay there! Who suggested this trip, I'd like to know?"

"Not me. Fabian. Blame it all on Fabian."

"*Blame* it!"

"Then you did like it, in spite of the relatives?"

"Oh, Gervais, I've adored it all! You know I have! But can't we talk about it tomorrow? I'm so sleepy!"

Amen met them at the station with the olive-green Buick, which had been one of Gervais' recent purchases. The boy seemed glad to see them, but his grin was less expansive than usual, and though he adequately answered the questions which were put to him, he did not volunteer any remarks. Yes'm, Miss Merry, the little twinses be's doin' fine; seems like dey done get more and more pert every day. Yassuh, Mr. Gervais, Madame and Miss Cresside dey was all right, too. After that, he did not say much, and for the most part, the drive along the River Road proceeded in silence. They passed a few parked cars, with engrossed occupants, and Gervais remarked to Merry, the edginess coming into his voice, that this sort of thing seemed to be on the increase all the time—and if the neckers got more numerous, somebody'd better hang red lanterns along the levee, both as a traffic safeguard and a trade-mark. Little else had been said when they swung into the driveway, now embowered by crepe myrtle in full bloom; emerging, they caught the first glimpse of the illumined colonnade, framed by moss-draped oaks.

"Do you know what this driveway always makes me think of? The approach to the sleeping beauty's palace!" Merry said, rather hesitantly. Gervais sometimes teased her for her fantasies and she was still a little shy about expressing them. But this time he was attuned to her mood.

"I see what you mean. It does give you the feeling of approaching a place that's enclosed and secret. But there was more of a wood, wasn't there, surrounding the sleeping beauty's retreat? And all sorts of brambles and thickets for Prince Charming to hack his way through, not just privet and myrtle. I don't remember the details. But my father used to read the story to me, in French—'*La Belle au Bois Dormant,*' the name of it was. That old fairy-story book must still be around somewhere. We'll have to dig it up."

"Yes. Besides finding out whether the Belle Heloise driveway looks like the enchanted wood, we can get ready to read aloud to the twins, when they're a little older."

"To the twins and to Philogene, too."

He pressed her hand fondly. He was in high good humor, happy to be home again. The trip had been a great success, but no hotel was comparable to Belle Heloise in comfort, no other diversions equal to those it afforded, no other occupations so congenial as those intimately connected with the land. He would have a good sleep in his own big bed, with Merry in his arms, not separated from her by a silly little glass-top table with a telephone on it; and early the next morning he would be out to see Sance and Plauché, before starting for town in time to have a cup of coffee at Izzy's and find out what was going on, so that he would be informed when the legislature met. The Chappuis bill for a Constitutional Convention was to be up for a vote any day now, and old Judge Dupré from Opelousas was all set to unlimber his heaviest oratory against its nonsubmission feature. . . .

Selah was standing at the door, vaguely apologetic and slightly disheveled, as usual, but more purposeful of expression. He did not help Amen with the bags, but hung about while his son dragged them slowly up the stairs, as if intent on getting something off his mind.

"Good evening, Selah. Glad to see you. Amen says everything's gone along fine since we've been gone."

"Ah don' know what he say. Ah know what Ah thinks."

"Well, what do you think?"

"Madame, she ain't seemed so well. She been mighty worried and uneasy. Yesterday she never left de bed at all. She be's waitin' up for you, Mr. Gervais. She wants to see you befo' you retires."

"All right. I'll go to see her as soon as I look in on the twins."

"She did say, Mr. Gervais, effin she could speak to you *alone*———"

"*All right* . . . Good night, Selah."

"Good night, Mr. Gervais. Good night, Miss Merry."

"And now what do you suppose has happened?" Gervais muttered, as he and Merry went up the staircase. "That's a great message to send me by a servant—not that I suppose you care."

"No, of course, I don't care. Why should I? It's natural for a woman to want to talk to her children alone sometimes—I'm sure I shall! And nothing much can be wrong—you worry too much, Gervais! Come see the cherubs with me and then I'll start undressing while you go in and talk to Madame Mère."

Gervais had declined, from the beginning, to have the twins sleep in his room: it was one thing, he had said, grinning, to share it with a pretty girl like Merry, and quite another to turn it into a family dormitory. So the big bedroom back of his had been made into a nursery; the shutter door between the two could be opened or closed at will, and Dinah had her own cubbyhole just beyond. Though the twins still used the double cradle in the patio during the daytime, they had now graduated to separate beds upstairs, and slept in beautiful rosewood cribs, representing some of Mallard's finest craftsmanship, with elaborate mosquito bars depending from the testers lined with tufted satin. Merry and Gervais did not raise the mosquito bars, nor light the gas in the room; they tiptoed in very cautiously, and peered silently at the sleeping infants. From the first, they could hear the babies' quiet even breathing, and as their eyes became accustomed to the dim light filtering in from the hall, they could see the two plump, quiescent little forms, stretched out in complete relaxation and repose. The babies did not stir at their visitors' approach, but quiet as they were, Dinah heard them and appeared at the doorway leading into her own quarters, still fully dressed.

"Dey's done wonderful," she whispered proudly. "Vail, he done cut another tooth, but it come through easy like nothin'. An' Sybelle, she likes her bottle jus' fine. She done stop her fussin' right away after she didn't see you no mo', Miss Merry. Ah reckon it was a mighty good thing you went to Nyawlins. Ah's glad you's all two back, sho' nuf, but Ah promise you, Miss Cresside and me, we can take care of dem twinses without nobody help us, no time. Yes, *Ma'am.*"

She was still gloatingly surveying her charges when Merry, completely satisfied as to their welfare, went through the shutter door to her own room and Gervais crossed the hall to his mother's apartment. Selah's statement that Madame d'Alvery was "waiting up" for him had misled him. He had expected to find her in her boudoir, but instead she was propped up against the big square pillows in her great four-poster, the white counterpane drawn up smoothly over her old-fashioned nightgown, as it had been on the night when he had tried to talk to her about Merry. The memory of this interview still rankled, in spite of its apparently felicitous consequences; he did not like to be reminded of it in any way. But he made a genuine effort to speak cheerfully and courteously, as he gave his mother the customary respectful though impersonal kiss.

"Well, *maman,* we've had a fine trip," he said. "I'm sure Merry'll tell you all about it in the morning. She can give you details about shopping and parties better than I can. But Selah said you wanted to speak to me about something tonight—alone. What's on your mind?"

"I have reason to be very much disturbed about Cresside, Gervais."

"Why, what's the matter with her?"

"I suppose you would say there is nothing. I feel there is a great deal. And I think we may have to take drastic steps."

"I can't somehow see myself taking 'drastic steps' as far as Cresside's concerned. I never did have much success along those lines, you know. And I certainly can't do anything unless I learn in which direction I'm supposed to move."

"Charles Boylston has come very faithfully to see us in your absence, Gervais. And he has talked to me very earnestly. Of course, he told me long ago that he desired to marry Cresside—in fact, he paid me the compliment of asking my permission to address her." Madame d'Alvery's tone implied that through this act alone Charles Boylston was entitled to a superior place in her esteem, since it set him so far above the rank and file of mannerless modern suitors. "But now he has told me, with great distress, that he is making no headway. Cresside does not even take his proposals seriously. She does not seem to appreciate either his affection, or the very great advantages that the alliance he proposes would bring with it. She declines to listen to him. She even laughs at him."

"I could have told you all of that long ago, and so could Merry. But I still don't see where the drastic steps come in. I like Boylston immensely—under all the circumstances, I don't know anyone I'd rather have for a brother-in-law. But I can't hypnotize Cresside into falling in love with him, or lock her up in her room on bread and water until she consents to marry him whether she loves him or not."

"Then you had better persuade her to go away somewhere. Perhaps a European trip would appeal to her. With the sugar situation what it is, we could afford to give it to her and no doubt we could find some discreet relative of ours who would accompany her."

"You know as well as I do that I couldn't get Cresside on an ocean liner unless I gave her knockout drops. I know it's the classical custom to send a girl to Europe when you want to break up a love match. But this is the first time I ever heard of doing it to foster one. She certainly won't marry Charles Boylston if you get her halfway around the world from him."

"I am not suggesting that you should send her to Europe to get her away from Charles Boylston. But I am suggesting that unless you can persuade her to accept the protection she would have as his wife, you do so in order to get her away from Sylvestre Tremaine."

"Sylvestre Tremaine!"

"Yes. Charles Boylston has not been the only visitor since you and Merry went away, Gervais. Fabian has also been here very constantly—so constantly that I almost had the impression he was watching for something to happen. It did happen after he left here Saturday night."

"*What* happened?"

"I am trying to tell you, Gervais. I wish you would not display so much impatience, no matter how you may feel. He and Cresside apparently had a very pleasant evening together. I joined them for dinner, and they started a cribbage game immediately afterwards. Later, I came upstairs, and when Fabian left, I heard them laughing and talking on the gallery. I think Cresside went out to his car with him, and watched him drive away. Sylvestre was apparently watching for him to leave, too—he must have been somewhere on the place already. Because Fabian had hardly gone when Sylvestre called softly from the garden to Cresside, who was still on the gallery."

"And then you listened?"

"Gervais, I must ask you not to speak to me as if I were an eavesdropper or a spy. The windows were all open. I could not help hearing. Of course, Cresside was taken completely by surprise. Any other girl would have cried out, in alarm. But you know that she is not easily frightened. She spoke to Sylvestre in a controlled way, but very coldly. She told him to leave at once, and never to come back again without his wife. I cannot repeat the exact words that she used."

"You don't need to. I have a pretty good idea what they were anyway.

189

But I don't care much for this vicarious information. I still feel——"

"I do not need to have you instruct me in propriety of conduct, Gervais. I should not have taken advantage of the open windows, nor should I be repeating this to you now if I did not think the occasion demanded it. Sylvestre was not violent in any way. He did not try to touch Cresside—indeed he promised her, vehemently, that he would not, and I believe he kept his word. But he reiterated that he had to talk to her. He said that he had waited and waited for his chance, and that now Regine had a severe headache, that she had taken a sleeping draft and asked him not to disturb her. So he had seized the opportunity, in spite of the unseemliness of the hour. He implored Cresside to tell him——"

"What did she tell him?"

"Nothing. She spoke to him coldly a second time, and then she walked to the front door, came inside, and locked it. It is the first time, as far as I know, that the front door of Belle Heloise has been locked since the War Between the States."

"That's rather beyond the point. The point is that the time had quite evidently come to lock it. I don't for the life of me see why you're worrying about Cresside and why you think she ought to be sent away if she doesn't get married. It seems to me that she showed a good deal of sense and spirit—more than I'd have given her credit for, a few years ago. And incidentally, I think she can handle this situation better than anyone else can do it for her. I suppose you think I ought to step into the picture now, and go after Sylvestre with a gun, figuratively if not literally. But I can tell you that if I did, I'd only make things a darn sight worse than they are already."

"I am not suggesting that you should go after Sylvestre with a gun, and I admit that Cresside did show sense and spirit. But the aftereffects were very serious, and her conduct since then has been extremely strange. I am very sure, Gervais, that she did not sleep at all last night. She was extremely pale this morning, and she has been very silent all day."

"Has Fabian been here again?"

"No. Before he knew when you were leaving, he had invited those two queer old men—the derelict veterans he has so inexplicably befriended—to spend the day with him. He said he did not want to disappoint them. Besides, to do him justice, I must say he undoubtedly felt that there was no special reason why he should return. Cresside was happy and tranquil when he left her last evening. Certainly he could not foresee that Sylvestre would try to reach her late at night, nor had he any reason to suppose that she would be upset today. But she has been, still further."

"For God's sake, how?"

"Regine was here this morning, without Sylvestre. She spoke of last night's headache, and said it was no better when she woke today; so Mrs. Hathaway and Sylvestre went to church without her. But after they had gone, she felt so nervous that she did not want to stay in the house alone except for the servants—at least, that was the reason she gave for coming over here. Cresside was obviously disinclined to talk to her, especially by herself; she brought Regine to my boudoir. Regine's manner was very hysterical, Gervais, and her conversation very indelicate. Both were entirely unbecoming a lady."

"Perhaps by now you're not so sorry you didn't get her for a daughter-in-law, after all. I'm only surprised that this is only the first time you've noticed she hasn't any self-control. But what happened, specifically?"

"She said she would not have minded the headache, if there had only been a chance that it was one of the first indications of pregnancy; but she knows it was not. She said Sylvestre was very resentful—that is the word she used, resentful—because there were no prospects of a child. While they were abroad, she went on, he was just as thankful as she was that 'they didn't get caught.' I am still quoting, Gervais. But since their return, he feels differently, especially since he has seen the twins and learned that Merry is already *enceinte* again. This has apparently given him a feeling of frustration. He reproaches Regine and she retaliates by asking him why he is so sure their childlessness is her fault—that it may very likely be his. I gather that there have been scenes, that these recriminations go on and on. She threw herself about and wept while she described them."

"The darn fool! How did you finally get rid of her?"

"Cresside did that. Very adroitly and courteously, I must admit. She succeeded in convincing Regine that it would be much better if she were at home when her mother and her husband returned from church, and also managed to calm her before getting her out of this house. Naturally, I did not hear everything they said after they left my boudoir, but I could hear Cresside's voice, and it was very soothing—almost sweet. I should hardly have recognized it as hers."

"Well, Cresside's voice has changed a good deal this last year—not that it's the only change either. But we still don't seem to be getting to the point of all this."

Madame d'Alvery raised herself slightly on her pillows, and smoothed the already even sheet with her white fingers. Then she looked up at her son with smoldering eyes.

"The point of all this is that after Regine left, Cresside seemed to withdraw further and further into herself, looking paler and paler all the time. Charles came in and stayed for several hours; but Cresside was completely distrait all the time he was here; she did not even take the trouble to badger him. And after the twins were in bed she went out. It is the first time she has done so since they were born. She told me she was going, but she did it tersely, with her hand already on the door, and when I called after her, she was gone. She has not come back. I have no idea where she went or where she is now."

PART IV

The Bastard Grain

June 1920–December 1920

"A successful sugar planter must possess knowledge or information of many types. He should be an agronomist, a chemist, a mechanical engineer, a surveyor, a veterinary surgeon, a banker (or at least enough of one to know how to get funds for making and saving of a crop!) and finally a lawyer to keep out of the bankruptcy court; but I say above all he should be an optimist and always ready with the encouraging thought of *'l'année prochaine.'* He should be one who loves to see the earth turn from the share and the tender shoots of cane mark the long brown rows. He should love to see the fields when they lie like a sea at calm, under the summer sun, and when autumn comes, to see the skillful cutters top and fell the standing cane and cast the purple stalks in even piles ready for the wagons. He should love to hear the sound of rustling leaves and ringing steel above the song of the workers, weird and wild but full of melody. It should fill him with supreme contentment to realize that inside the factory the furnace fires glow and the engines turn endlessly; that the massive rollers crush out the liquid sweets; that the amber juices dance and foam and the machines revolve with lightning speed, until at last emerge the pure and sparkling crystals, finished product of twelve long hard months."

—Adapted from a speech made by Honorable Edward J. Gay at Houma, Louisiana, before the American Sugar Cane League, which was taken from the memorial address delivered by Honorable Theodore Wilkinson in the House of Representatives, eulogizing Senator Gay's grandfather.

The Bastard Grain

June 1920–December 1920

CHAPTER XIV

CRESSIDE STARTED DOWN the driveway without any definite plan of action. She did not want to go anywhere or do anything in particular. But she desperately desired to get away from the house, which had seemed, all night and all day, to be closing in on her like a prison. She did not dare stay on the gallery or in the garden, for fear that Sylvestre would suddenly appear and accost her again, as he had the evening before. The grounds, already shadowed by approaching dusk, seemed to harbor some even more mysterious menace; she had always ranged freely through them, but now she was afraid of something indefinite and none the less threatening because she visualized it vaguely. The idea of escape obsessed her to such a degree that she was unmindful of destination; her mother had not exaggerated in saying she left so swiftly that she could not be stopped.

All the servants except Dinah and Lucie had the evening off, as they usually did on Sunday; therefore, Amen was not in watchful attendance as she sped through the colonnade and across the lawn. She backed the first car she saw out of the shed that served as a garage and turned it into the driveway. A cardinal was poised on the near-by Ligustrum, and at Cresside's approach he began to dart through the foliage, a scarlet streak weaving in and out of the glossy green. Behind the great oaks which dominated the west side of the Small Yard the sky had the rich color of molten gold, and the Spanish moss, floating from the branches of the trees, looked like gray lace draped against its splendor. Ahead of her the pink plumes of the crepe myrtles made a radiant arch. But she was blind to all this familiar beauty. Despite the roughness of the twisting driveway, she forced the car ahead. Then, having reached the highway, she jammed on the brake, and, for the first time, paused to consider which direction she should take.

Fleetingly, she thought she might go straight to Charles Boylston and tell him she would marry him after all, and the sooner the better. She knew that if she went back to Belle Heloise with the news that she was engaged to him, most of her problems would be solved. But she dismissed the idea almost as quickly as she conceived it. Charles Boylston was not the sort of man to whom a girl, even a girl with whom he professed to be deeply in love, could rush with a declaration like that. He would be startled, even somewhat shocked, if she appeared, unaccompanied, at his bachelor establishment; and his amazement over such a breach of etiquette would temper his pleasure in seeing her. He would receive her courteously, but not ardently, and he would certainly indicate that he assumed only some grave emergency, quite unconnected with her own attitude towards him, could possibly have brought her to his door at such an untimely hour. Moreover, under no circumstances would he wish their marriage to be precipitate or unpretentious. He would want an engagement, first formally announced at some suitable function, and next sufficiently prolonged to admit proper preparation for an elaborate trousseau, an impressive wedding and an extended trip. He would feel it fitting to present Cresside to all his Boston relatives during their engagement, and later he would want them all to come to Louisiana for the marriage ceremony. No doubt—though he said so little about his family—he had an unmarried sister or cousin, grim and passé, whom he would expect to have a member of the wedding party, and who would elicit no enthusiasm whatsoever among the ushers. Probably he would also dwell on the obstacle presented by Cresside's religion; she was sure no Boylston had ever married a Catholic, and that only the presence of an eminent Archbishop as the officiating clergyman would make Charles and his family feel that he was not condescending a little in a social sense. Cresside felt unequal to facing all the complications which she saw crowding in upon her in connection with Charles Boylston. She did not want to arrange any ceremonies or start any arguments or raise any issues; she only wanted to find understanding and sympathy and refuge, as she had found them that afternoon in the Garden Room, with Fabian. . . .

She turned the car abruptly to the right and swung up the River Road towards the capital, wondering how she could have possibly been so stupid. Of course, it was Fabian whom she wanted to see; of course, he was the only person in the world who would understand and help. He would be pleased and not shocked to have her come to his house, and even if he were surprised, he would not show it. He might receive her rather gravely, instantly realizing she had sought him out for some special reason, or he might ease the situation by cracking one of his wry jokes; but it would be all right either way. And there would be no ulterior motive in his welcome; he did not want to marry her, he had never thought of her in that way. Fabian had been in love with Merry, but Cresside felt sure that was the only time.

She also felt sure that he was not in love with Merry any more, and that this was actually less because, as a man of integrity, he would not have allowed himself to look at his cousin's wife with covetous eyes, than because he had gradually made the discovery that she did not represent his ideal after all. Quoting, as he did so easily and so aptly, he had once said something to Cresside about the type of girl he liked best—

> "A creature not too great and good
> For human nature's daily food"——

Of course, he did not add that Merry *was* too great and good, and Cresside knew that he admired her sister-in-law immensely and was devotedly attached to her; but the inference was there just the same. Fabian, whose own life was singularly blameless, had infinite tolerance for the weaknesses and misdoings of others. Though naturally there were limits, Cresside said to herself, wincing a little. Well, that was beyond the point. The point was that he would be glad to see her, that he would help her, that he was not in love with her. She knew, now that she realized Fabian was the only person she wanted to see, that she was still as incapable of facing desire as she was of facing ceremony and controversy. Charles Boylston had never told her that he desired her, he had never tried to take her in his arms; but naturally he would, as soon as she consented to marry him. And she did not want to hear his voice shaken with passion, she did not want him to touch her. . . .

She had already passed the cemetery which she had so successfully cleared, and was now approaching Hathaway Hall. As its white immensity, luminous in the twilight, towered before her, she pressed down on the accelerator and sped on. Unbelievable that only a little over a year before she had been in and out of that house as freely and gaily as she went in and out of her own. Regine had then been her most cherished intimate, and Sylvestre, "the old family friend" of the Hathaway family, her own accepted suitor. Now Regine and Sylvestre were husband and wife, with strife between them already, and she herself was estranged from them both, worse than estranged from Sylvestre. She listened to Regine's chattering and complaining, when she could not escape from it, with contempt untinged by pity; she did not think even Fabian was sorry for this vapid girl who had brought trouble to herself as well as to everyone else, and she marveled that she could ever have found anyone so silly and selfish good company. She was even slightly ashamed because she had. But she did not dwell on shame, in thinking of Regine, as she did in thinking of Sylvestre. How in the name of heaven could she ever have loved a man like that—shallow, indolent, sensual, insincere? Why had she failed to see him, in that radiant, long ago Easter moonlight, as she saw him now in the deepening dusk?

There was no answer to these poignant questions and there never could be. Cresside tried not to ask them of herself, and usually she succeeded. But the sight of Hathaway Hall, once so familiar and inviting, now so strange and sinister, had inevitably raised them. She tightened her lips and straightened herself in her seat; she had not realized it would tire her so much to drive a car. Her back hurt and her arms ached; but she had almost reached town now. Just beyond the batture, on her left, was The Willows, where she had gone so often with "the gang," and sounds of revelry were coming from it. She had heard indirectly that it had been raided several times, and that this had only served to increase its popularity. It seemed as strange to her that she should have found The Willows and its habitués exciting as that she should have loved Sylvestre Tremaine. Probably it still facilitated the same cheap thrills that it always had; but she would only find these offensive now. She would not even be able to talk the same language as the gang, though once everyone had said she had the best "line" in the Parish. It was queer what solitude and suffering could do to a girl—solitude and suffering and shame. You did a lot of thinking when you lay in bed month after month, with an injured back. You thought things *through*—things that mattered. But you lost your line. You lost your gang. You lost a good deal more than that too. . . .

She left the River Road and turned into a narrow uneven side street that crossed the railroad track. Four or five dilapidated Negro cabins were scattered along it, their dusty yards and narrow porches overflowing with impoverished but cheerful humanity. Kerosene lamps, shining through the open doorways, revealed further activities inside: groups gathered around rickety tables, drinking and dicing, women in rocking chairs, holding babies to their bared bosoms, girls wearing bright dresses and held closely embraced. Someone was playing a harmonica, someone else was singing, two or three couples were dancing, and a little boy was plucking white blossoms from a laden bush near a disreputable outhouse. The street, though obviously served by neither electric power or sewerage, was within the city limits, and the people who dwelt there were subtly different from their country neighbors, who lived such a short distance away. Cresside had often been told that it was unsafe for a girl to go among them alone, especially at night. But she felt no fear of these Negroes. On the contrary, she rather envied them their undemanding lightheartedness, and slowed down to watch them. She thought they all seemed happier than she was, and marveled at their merriment, seeing their squalor. . . .

She did not have far to go now. Approaching Fabian's pleasant little house from the rear, she passed his garden first, bright with zinnias and gladioli. Then, as she turned the corner, she saw that his car was drawn up before the front door, and that he was on the point of getting into it, accompanied by Tremblet and Vicknair. She called out to him, stopping her car——

"Oh, Fabian! Hello, there! Wait just a minute, will you?"

He looked up, calling cheerfully back to her. The dusk was deepening into dark now, but the light from a street lamp fell on his face and as she went towards him she could see that he did not look either annoyed or astonished, but quietly pleased. She had kept telling herself that of course he would, but when she saw that he really did, a great wave of relief rushed over her.

"Good evening, Mr. Tremblet. Good evening, Mr. Vicknair," she said agreeably. "Was Fabian just getting ready to take you home? Please don't let me keep you, if he was. . . . But you wouldn't mind if I waited till you got back, would you, Fabian? I wanted very much to see you for a few minutes, if I could."

"Of course I wouldn't mind having you wait," Fabian answered. He spoke cordially and simply, as if it were the most natural thing in the world that she should come to see him. "Here, take the key. Carmelite went home a couple of hours ago and Belizaire's in there all alone. He'd be delighted to have your company. But I'm afraid you'll have a rather long wait. You see, I'm taking my guests across the river to Port Allen."

"It's this way, Miss Cresside," Pascal broke in. Now that she looked at the two old men more closely, she saw that their faces were pinched and anxious, and there was a quaver in Pascal's voice that she had not heard there before. "We got a telephone call, us, saying our friend Max Stoetzner was mighty low. He had pneumonia last winter, and he's never got his strength back. Every so often he's had sinking spells, and they've got worse all the time. Now he's bad off."

"We only got the message a few minutes ago," Preston took up the recital which Pascal, apparently, was unable to continue. "Pascal's granddaughter, she telephoned us here—the call came to her house first. So Mr. Fabian said he'd take us to Port Allen. It isn't as if Max was just ailing. It's like Pascal says. He's bad off."

"You wouldn't care to come with us, I suppose, Cresside, instead of waiting here for me?" Fabian asked quietly. The question was entirely unexpected. Cresside looked from her cousin to the two old men in momentary bewilderment.

"Why, yes," she said finally. "Yes, I'd be glad to go. That is, if I wouldn't be in the way. I wouldn't want Mr. Stoetzner to think I was intruding."

"Mr. Stoetzner hasn't any relatives. I'm afraid he's going to be pretty much alone through this bad spell except for these two friends of his. I think they'll agree with me that you wouldn't be in the way and that you might be helpful."

"We'd be proud if you'd come with us, Miss Cresside," Pascal and Preston said, almost in unison.

"All right then, I will. Would you like me to drive, Fabian?"

"No, thanks, I think maybe you've done enough driving already for a girl who hasn't handled a car in over a year. Come on, let's get going."

He had not answered her curtly, as if she had offended his pride by her reminder that he disliked driving and that it was not easy for him.

She knew he appreciated her thoughtfulness, but he was thoughtful, too. He could see that driving was far more of a strain for her than it was for him, that while he was awkward and uncomfortable in the driver's seat, he could manage all right and she should not try. Without any protest she got in beside him, folding her hands in her lap and looking straight ahead of her. She could not tell him any of the things she had meant to say, now that the two old men were with them. But that did not seem to matter much. She had been reassured already by the welcome and now she was comforted by his nearness. It was strange that such a crippled body could transmit such a feeling of strength and security. He smiled across at her.

"I take it you told Tante Isabelle you were going out."

"Yes. But I didn't say where. Because at the moment I didn't know myself."

He smiled, a little wryly. "You speak as if it were of no special consequence, just so she has the principal item of information. I'm afraid Aunt Isabelle won't look at it that way. But there's nothing we can do about it at the moment, without a telephone. It's more important for us to be on our way than to relieve her mind."

They were already over the crest of the levee and going down the long ramp towards the ferry landing. The *City of Baton Rouge,* tied to the shore as an "emergency," was nevertheless brilliantly lighted. The *Louisiana,* which was in service, and which was also strung with small sparkling lights, had reached midstream on her eastward passage and was puffing comfortably towards them. Cresside gazed first at one and then the other for a long time, finally turning to Fabian.

"I've always loved a lighted ferryboat. And it's a long time since I've seen one."

He nodded again. "Now that you've made a start, you'll be getting out more. There's no reason why you shouldn't see one as often as you like. We can come down here and look at them together, whether there's any reason for crossing the River or not. I like to see them, too, especially when the water's so smooth you get a perfect reflection, and when there's a crescent moon in an amethyst sky, the way there is tonight. Do you wish on crescent moons over your left shoulder, Cresside?"

"I used to."

"Well, here's a good time to begin again."

"I was never one to wish on moons, me," Pascal announced from the back seat. "But I always spit when I see a hearse. There's one right ahead of us now. I kinda wish there hadn't been, seeing that we're going to Port Allen because Max has had this bad spell. Not that there's any connection, of course." He spat, guardedly, out of the rear window. "Some say you ought to spit when you meet a nun, too. But I don't hold to that. All the nuns I ever saw were fine women. They didn't bring bad luck to anybody."

"It's just as well to be on the safe side, though," Preston suggested, also spitting guardedly.

The hearse went clattering over the planks and rounded the curve of the open deck. Fabian made a sign to the collector indicating that he did not wish to park directly behind it, and swung his car into the open space at the bow. Most of the other passengers were leaving their automobiles and going off for soft drinks and chocolate bars, but Pascal and Preston huddled together and talked to each other in undertones.

"Wouldn't you like to get out for a minute, too?" Fabian asked Cresside. "You can see the moon and the reflections on the water better by the railing than you can from the car."

"Yes. I'd like to very much."

They got out, passing a wide-shouldered Negro who sat hunched up, busily scraping a long horn with a piece of glass. Fabian stopped and hailed him.

"Hello, Willie!" he said cordially. "The way you're working, that horn ought to be super-duper, by the time you've finished the job. You must be making it for the head beater himself."

The big Negro looked up with a grin. "Why, hello, Mr. Fabian!" he said in a pleased voice. "Ah ain't seed you in a dog's age. You belongs to come across the ferry about once in so often, whether you's got any call to or not. Us misses you when you doesn't. No, this here blowin' horn ain't for no head beater. But Ah's gettin' me twenty-five bucks fo' it, and Ah's bound to give 'em his money's worth. He's that Yankee genman what's bought de place down near your kinnery on de River Road."

"Well, I'll hope to hear it blowing some day myself then. Mr. Boylston's a friend of mine—he might very well ask me to hunt at his place. And he's a good fellow, too, Willie. He just hasn't caught on to our ways yet." Fabian nodded in a friendly manner and went along further down the bow, with a hand under Cresside's elbow to guide her. "That's quite a character," he explained. "Willie Swan, his name is. Most of the boys around here call him 'Ferryboat Bill'—not to his face though. He's one of the firemen on this ferry. But he'd rather make hunting horns than do anything else. I don't suppose there's anyone around here who can touch him at that sort of work. Did you see those scraps lying on the bench beside him? He collects little pieces like that and fits them together as skillfully as a cabinetmaker does fine wood. Then he polishes and carves them and fines them down so that they'll have just the right texture to give a rich tone. When he started out, he'd take any old cow horn he could pick up and tinker with it. Presently he was doing such wonders that he began to get orders from all over the world."

"That's swell, isn't it? I'm glad he's had such good luck."

The rejoinder was adequate enough, as far as the actual words went, but they had been spoken in a voice that was almost expressionless. Fabian saw that this was not the moment for an attempt to rouse Cresside's interest in Ferryboat Bill or in anyone else. He must first give her a chance to tell him what was on her mind. They had reached the railing and were standing side by side, looking out at the sky and the river, and casually, as he had placed his hand under her elbow a few minutes earlier, he now put his arm around her shoulder. This time her response was immediate. Instead of dreading to have him touch her, she suddenly realized she had been hoping he would. Now that he had done so, his arm felt as if it belonged where he put it and she was not afraid of anything he might say to her either.

"I'm sorry I couldn't get out today," he remarked. "Did you have any other company?"

"Yes. Charles came to dinner and stayed most of the afternoon."

"And no doubt behaved all the time like a *parfait gentil* knight?"

"Oh, yes! If you can think of a stuffed shirt in armor. . . . When I decided to go out tonight, I thought first of going to see him."

"Well, I'm rather glad you didn't. Not just because I'm gratified you came to see me instead, though of course I am. But because I'm afraid Boylston may not be at his best if you burst in on him unexpectedly. I have an idea he doesn't care for dropper-inners."

"Yes, that's what I thought, too. I bet we're thinking exactly the same things about him."

"I bet we are. He's a good fellow though, Cresside, as I told Ferryboat Bill. Don't make any mistake about that."

"I'm not making any mistake—at least not about that."

"All right, just so you're sure of it. . . . Any other company?"

"Yes. Regine came over this morning, while her mother and Sylvestre were at church. She was trying to get over a bad headache. At least, I don't think she was trying very hard. She cried and carried on. She said Sylvestre was disappointed because he didn't have a child."

"That's a pretty common disappointment, Cresside."

"Yes, I suppose so." She turned away from the River and looked at Fabian; his face was noncommittal as well as grave and his voice had been unusually expressionless when he spoke. But something sharp, like a knife thrust, went through her when she heard it. So that was one of the reasons Fabian was bitter! Because he hadn't fathered a child, because he thought he never would! He was all over being in love with Merry, but he wasn't all over being a cripple, he wasn't all over. . . . And Sylvestre, who was strong and young and handsome, and who could have practically any woman he wanted, was only disappointed because. . . .

"I assume you managed to get rid of Regine and her weeping and wailing without too much trouble," Fabian said, still speaking without much expression in his voice.

"Yes. As a matter of fact, it really didn't take very long. I think she wore *maman* down more than she did me."

202

"And that's church? You haven't any nev. item beyond the fact that Charles is a shade too conventional and that Regine isn't the least bit pregnant?"

"Yes, I have. Sylvestre came last night, Fabian, after you left."

"I see. . . . Can you tell me about it?"

"There isn't much to tell. Regine had taken a sleeping powder, and he thought . . . He frightened me, Fabian, because he came on me so unexpectedly. But he didn't hurt me. I've got to be fair. He only said he had to talk to me—*had* to."

"And what did you do?"

"I didn't give him a chance. I locked the door in his face."

"I see," Fabian said again. "Well, I don't think he'll come back, Cresside. I don't think you've got a thing to worry about. I'm mighty glad you came into town though. I was tickled to death to see you myself and I believe you're going to be no end of comfort to these old men. Because I suppose their friend is going to die. You realized that, didn't you?"

"Yes, I realized that as soon as you asked me if I'd come along."

"We don't have much trouble understanding each other, do we? Look, we're almost across. We've got to get back to the car."

He took his arm away from her shoulder and put his hand under her elbow to guide her and steady her. It felt as if it were in exactly the right place there, too. And she knew there was nothing more they needed to say to each other.

The little house on the outskirts of Port Allen, at which they finally stopped, was no larger than the Negro cabins Cresside had passed on the narrow side street crossing the railroad track. But instead of being characterized by squalor permeated with good cheer, it was characterized by tidiness permeated with tragedy. Everything about it was orderly, from the flower beds in the pocket-sized yard and the scalloped edging of the wooden roof over the tiny porch, to the center table in the front room, which was covered by a yellow plush cloth, and which supported a china vase, a Bible and a photograph album. A corpulent woman, her uncorseted body a shapeless mass of flesh, but her face gentle and sympathetic, met them at the door.

"I'm Mrs. Hartzberg, a neighbor," she said. "The doctor had to leave on a confinement case, but he said he'd be back as soon as he could. He thought he'd get here in time." She paused to give significance to her last statement. "There's nothing anyone can do, when it comes to that. Poor Mr. Stoetzner's sinking fast. You're the friends he asked for, aren't you?" she added, looking at Pascal and Preston; and, as they nodded, she turned to Fabian inquiringly.

"I'm Fabian d'Alvery and this is my cousin Cresside," he explained. "Mr. Vicknair and Mr. Tremblet were at my house when the bad news was relayed to them, so we took my car and came over. . . . Do you happen to know what brought on Mr. Stoetzner's attack?"

"Well, sir—" she hesitated, looking at Cresside as if uncertain whether she ought to go on. Then, deciding that this was one of those rare young ladies who could face tragedy without hysteria, she continued, "Of course, fifteen dollars a month isn't so much to live on. You don't get so much fuel and food for fifteen dollars a month."

"But Max had his savings, besides his pension!" Pascal broke in. "He could have drawn on those. He always said, him, that he had enough to manage with the two together in any emergency. Didn't he, Pres?"

"I don't know as I ever heard him say he had enough," retorted Pres, unable to agree, even at such a moment as this. "But he did have savings, yes. He could have drawn on them."

"He did have savings," Mrs. Hartzberg repeated. "But he put them all into Liberty Bonds, so there'd be more money to fight the Huns. Because he came from German stock it made him feel that he ought to do more than most in his circumstances. Of course, he could have got his money back again, most of it anyhow, but he didn't want to. He was stubborn that way. He wouldn't admit this was any emergency, so he tried to live on his pension. I reckon there was a good many times he just sat around in a cold room without bothering to fix himself anything to eat. He could have come and sat in our kitchen just as well as not, if we'd only known. We always manage to have a good fire, and enough to eat, such as it is. But he was certainly one to keep to himself. He didn't go to church or belong to any organizations, and he didn't have much truck with his neighbors except me and my husband. He never let on he felt puny until he had the second of these spells, and by that time the weather was coming warm and I thought he'd be all right through the summer. But I reckon you don't get over any sickness too easy when you're in your eighties. You keep getting weaker anyway from old age. At least that's what the doctor says. He says it's nobody's fault, and that the old man could have been took with these spells even if he'd had all the money in the world. But I feel real bad. I never realized what it would mean when he couldn't work in his garden and raise vegetables."

"I'm sorry you didn't, Mrs. Hartzberg, for of course we'd all have been glad to help. But I know you've done the best you could. . . . You'd like us to stay here, wouldn't you, until the doctor gets back?"

"If you please, sir. And I'm going home for a while if you can spare me. I haven't got supper for my old man yet and he works on the railroad. I don't want him to leave for his shift hungry." She hurried away and Fabian turned to the two old men.

"You'd like to go in and sit with him, wouldn't you?" he asked. "Cresside and I'll stay in here. But please call us if you need us."

Pascal and Preston tiptoed into the bedroom, leaving the door open behind them. Cresside could see a shrunken form on the clean narrow bed, a pointed face with closed eyes and a lifted chin, and hands unlike any others she had ever beheld in both coloring and texture—

yellow and waxlike and inanimate. She tried very hard not to shrink from the sight, and not to stare at it either. She watched Pascal and Preston draw two straight-backed chairs up to the bedside, and saw them bending over the dying man, who roused himself briefly, recognizing them and speaking to them; then he drifted away from them again, muttering something wholly unintelligible, and relapsing into silence, broken only by heavy uneven breathing. Cresside resolutely looked away through a second open door into the kitchen beyond. She could see a small well-blacked iron stove, with a bright tin tea-kettle placed precisely over one of the lids, and clean red and white dish towels hanging from a rack overhead. The place did not look comfortably cluttered, like most small kitchens; no currents of warm air and no appetizing smells issued from it; it looked cool and vacant and disused. Somehow it hurt her to see it, almost as much as it had hurt her to see the emaciated form on the bed, and again she looked away, her eyes traveling this time around the tiny parlor where she and Fabian were sitting on either side of the center table covered with yellow plush. A cuckoo clock hung on the wall, and every fifteen minutes a tiny mechanized bird darted out of a little door and screamed; she was so startled the first time this happened that she wondered why the sick man was not roused from his lethargy, but gradually she grew accustomed to the sudden noise of the clock herself. The sounds that drifted in from outdoors, through the window opened to the warm June night, were harder to bear. People were walking up and down the street, gossiping, quarreling, lovemaking; they were unmindful, as they passed by this bare little home, of the pitiful old man who lay breathing his life away inside it. Some tipplers, exchanging smutty stories, broke into raucous guffaws; two angry girls, disputing a suitor's favor, began to call each other vile names; a Negro, strolling lazily along with his arm around his sweetheart, broke into husky jubilant song.

> "Oh, what a night to go co'tin',
> Oh, what a night to make love.
> Some little white clouds wuz a-floatin'
> High up in de blue skies above.
> De stars wuz a-winkin' an' blinkin'
> An' de moon wuz a-shinin' so bright,
> An' I wuz so happy jus' thinkin'
> Of my gal on dat wonderful night."

Cresside tried to close her ears to the melody and the sound of kisses and shrill giggles which followed it and to focus her distracted mind on the room where she and Fabian were sitting. Besides the cuckoo clock, various other small carved wooden objects were neatly arranged here and there: two miniature bears, a bowl with a fork and spoon lying slantwise across it, a chalet with isinglass windows which she thought was probably a music box. On either side of the cuckoo clock were photographs of men and women in Bavarian peasant costumes, encased in black oval frames, and on the mantelshelf a picture of Max himself, taken before he was wounded at Donaldsonville. While Cresside was looking at this she heard him speak for the first time, intelligibly, though with obvious effort.

"That uniform I had made on purpose for the dedication of the Albert Sidney Johnson Memorial in New Orleans—it's hanging in my closet. It's just as good as it ever was."

Max did not tell his friends how he wanted it used. However, they knew and they reassured him, telling him they would find it, that they would get it that moment and show it to him if he wanted them to. But he had already relapsed into his coma. Cresside looked down at the floor. She was blinded by the tears in her eyes, but she could see that though it was bare, it was scrubbed white. She kept on looking at it until she had regained her self-control, and then she glanced up and saw that Fabian had stretched his arm across the table, that he was reaching for her hand. She put hers out, gripping his hard.

"He—he was in want!" she said in a horror-stricken whisper. "Not somewhere over on the other side of the world—right here in Louisiana, a few miles from the place where we live ourselves, in comfort and luxury."

"Try not to think about it that way, Cresside. He kept what he wanted most—his pride."

I wonder what you want most, Cresside said to herself, momentarily forgetting Max Stoetzner and thinking only of Fabian. Then, remembering what he had said on the ferry about a common disappointment, she believed she knew. Fabian and Sylvestre, otherwise poles apart, were united in one supreme desire. Each wanted a son, a child who would bear his name and appear in his image. Except that, of course, the child Fabian wanted would not be crippled, but strong and whole as the one in Sylvestre's vision. Surreptitiously she studied Fabian's face, wondering why she had never before realized how vivid and appealing it could be when it lost its look of somber bitterness. *We've all taken Fabian too much for granted,* she thought; *his deformity, his loneliness, his kindness, everything about him. We've shown him we depend on him but we haven't shown him we care for him. We haven't done anything to make him forget his deformity or alleviate his loneliness or repay his kindness. But we can begin, if it isn't too late. It is too late, though; we can't make up to him now what he's missed. I can't make up to him for anything. There's nothing in the world I can do for Fabian. . . .*

"I want you two boys to stop quarreling." The labored voice of the dying man suddenly broke the oppressive silence. "I want you to promise. I wouldn't rest easy in my grave if I thought you were all the time bickering, there beside the monument, and me not around to stop you."

206

"Why, we don't quarrel, us. We haven't quarreled in a long time. Have we, Pres?"

"No, not since I don't know when. Fabian don't hold with no quarreling neither, and we're at his house a lot now."

Fabian did not hold with quarreling. He held with pleasant, peaceful things like books and flowers, a bountiful table, a quiet house; and he shared all these with his friends, men who weren't of importance in the state, men who were poor old derelicts like those in the next room. He had no one else with whom to share them; his nearest relatives were distant cousins; his father and mother were long since dead; he had never had any brothers and sisters. He never would have a wife and children. He had his friends and his flowers and his servants and his dogs. That was all. And there was nothing Cresside could do about it. . . .

"There's money put by for funeral expenses. That means the notices, too. And I want them to have good wide black borders. It wouldn't hurt any to have them posted up in Addis the same as Port Allen. Maybe Plaquemine and Baton Rouge, too."

"We'll get them, Max. We'll have them put on all the telegraph poles and all the lamp posts, too."

The heavy silence descended again on the pitiful little house. This time it remained unbroken until the arrival of the doctor, a drab elderly man, shabby and stooping. It was plain that he was almost dead on his feet.

"I'm sorry I've been gone so long. It couldn't be helped. A hard birth—high forceps. I was afraid I was going to lose the child, but now I think he and his mother will both pull through. . . . Mr. d'Alvery, isn't it? Reynolds is my name. Good of you to come. But I'm afraid there isn't anything either of us can do here."

The doctor shook hands with Fabian and then with Cresside, saying it was good of her to come, too, apparently with no feeling of interest or curiosity about the circumstances of her presence or Fabian's. He went on into the bedroom, closing the door behind him, and asking Pascal and Preston to stand back, with a brusqueness that was a mark of fatigue rather than insensibility. For a few minutes no further sounds reached the little parlor. Then the doctor came back into it again, looking more exhausted than ever.

"Well, he's gone, poor old fellow. His friends are all broken up. I was fond of him and I'll miss him, too. But that's a doctor's life—first birth, then death, then birth again. I've got to go to another woman in labor tonight. I'd like to speak to you first though, Mr. d'Alvery, about funeral arrangements and so on—alone if I could. Perhaps the young lady wouldn't mind sitting out in the car for a few minutes."

The wait seemed very long. Cresside sat still, with her hands folded quietly in her lap again, and her head bowed. She was dimly aware of

207

the doctor, going out, and a little later of another man, going in— a slight mulatto, dressed in black, who moved very quietly. But neither man spoke to her or appeared to notice her. Mrs. Hartzberg returned, walking heavily; apparently she did not see the girl sitting in the car, for she too went by without a word. Cresside felt terribly alone. She tried not to cry, but she could not help it. She wept, thinking about Max Stoetzner, and she wept thinking about Fabian. She did not weep thinking about Sylvestre Tremaine, for the simple reason that she had forgotten all about him. . . .

At last Fabian came out and got into the car again. He did not speak to her either, but his presence gave her the same sense of solace and security that it had before. As he leaned over to turn on the ignition, she asked an astonished question.

"Aren't we waiting for Preston and Pascal?"

"No. I'll come back for them in the morning and see if there's anything else I can do at the same time. But I've got to get you home before Tante Isabelle has fits and, of course, they'll sit up with their dead friend."

"Of course. It was stupid of me to forget."

She began to think of the night her father had died, when the house had been so suddenly hushed of the gaiety which had been such an integral part of him that it persisted to the very end. She remembered that her mother, clasping a great crucifix, had lain down on her huge white bed, refusing to rise, and that the stricken servants had gone about lighting candles in a dim room and massing flowers beside a still form. Except when he was relieved by Fabian, who was grave and quiet, it was Gervais who had watched ceaselessly by Philogene's side, so shaken with grief that he could not speak; and at intervals Cresside, sobbing too, had sat with her brother, while a solemn priest recited the prayers for the dead, and various black-robed relatives, and innumerable acquaintances whose presence seemed to her intrusive, came and went, holding handkerchiefs and talking in low unnatural tones. Only Fabian, who had come now and then and put his hand on her shoulder, without saying anything, had been of real comfort. But before all this happened there had been an interval when she was sent away just as she had been tonight. It was not entirely clear to her why, but she remembered that the strange, somber man who had spoken to her then bore a subtle resemblance to the mulatto who had gone through Max Stoetzner's gate. As if he were reading her thoughts, Fabian clarified them.

"The undertaker's there now. I don't know whether you noticed him when he went in—a nice-looking mulatto. It was a surprise to me to learn that there was an undertaker in Port Allen—I thought you and I would have to see about getting one over from Baton Rouge. But the doctor says this man is very highly thought of locally, and that he prepares nearly all white persons for burial here, as well as the dead of his own race. He seems very gentle and soft-spoken. He's lived all his life in a little house right by the cemetery near the ramp and perhaps that makes him feel at home with dead people. I think he'll make everything as painless as possible for those poor old codgers. But what he has to do is gruesome enough at best. You can't get away from that."

"No, you can't. It's terribly gruesome, Fabian."

"Well, try not to think of it. Think about something else."

"I can't seem to."

"Of course you can. Think about the cane coming up all along this road. Think about the fight going on in the Capitol. Think about the twins playing on the patio."

She tried obediently, finding it unbelievably helpful when Fabian suggested she should stand in the bow with him again while they were crossing the ferry. The sickle moon had set, but in the still river the lights from the city beyond were reflected in columns of radiance. They were so beautiful that Cresside was glad the boat pursued a U-shaped course, instead of going straight across, so she could watch them longer. Fabian put his arm around her again, and kept it there after they got back into the car and until they were within sight of his house. Then he made a commonplace remark.

"If you'll get into your car, Cresside, I'll trail you out to Belle Heloise. I'd ask you to come in and have a drink and a sandwich first, but it's pretty late. I'm afraid Tante Isabelle will be mighty worried about you—Gervais and Merry, too, if they're home by now, and I think they must be. You better have the drink and the sandwich after you get home."

"All right, I will. Thanks, Fabian, for everything. I'm sorry to put you to so much trouble—all that extra driving."

"Nonsense, it isn't any trouble. And look here, you must get it out of your head that I mind driving. I don't—not that much."

The stars were very bright and the outline of the road and of the levee was clear; there was nothing menacing or mysterious about the grounds at Belle Heloise when Cresside, closely followed by Fabian, turned into them. The house, coming suddenly into view beyond the avenue of crepe myrtles, was still brilliantly lighted, the colonnade dazzling and luminous in the frame of oaks. As the dogs began their inevitable barking, Cresside thought, resentfully, that Gervais would be out in a minute, that she would have no chance to say anything more to Fabian. To be sure, she had said very little to him anyway, not half what she intended, but she had held the feeling that she could. Now the chance was over. . . .

Fabian got out of his car, slamming the door. He was not even trying to keep quiet. He was telling the household that Cresside was back, and that he had brought her home. But as he helped her out of her car, surprisingly, he put his arm around her again after all.

"You're not sorry I took you, are you?"

"No, I'm glad you did. Not that I was any use."

"You were all kinds of use. Preston and Pascal will never forget that you were willing to go—and that you did. A woman's almost as necessary in a death chamber as at a birthing, even if her purpose there isn't quite as obvious. . . . Look, you're not going to worry any more, are you?"

"No."

"Is that a promise?"

"Yes."

"Cross your heart and hope to die?"

"Yes."

"All right, then—you can go to bed now, like a good girl . . . Oh, hello, Gervais! Did you have a good trip this go round? . . . Why no, I don't see any reason why you should have worried. If you think I've brought Cresside back too late, I'll go in and apologize to Tante Isabelle. But hell, I took it for granted you'd know she was all right if she was with me. And you wouldn't have expected her to be with anyone else, would you?"

CHAPTER XV

Although she herself had succeeded in gaining a stranglehold on her family through pseudo-invalidism, Madam d'Alvery was inclined to view the bodily infirmities of others with contempt rather than sympathy. She did not dislike Fabian, but she had never accorded him a position of importance in the family circle: his deformity, in her opinion, inevitably signified a general lack of stamina, and to her a man without vigor was also a man without consequence. Cresside's constrained behavior, precipitate departure and prolonged absence had seriously shaken her, and gradually her anxiety had turned into anger. She deeply resented Fabian's casual rejoinder to Gervais' indignant greeting of the truants, which, like everything that had previously transpired, she heard through the open windows. In spite of the untimely hour, she sent Lucie downstairs to summon Fabian to her bedside, and as he did not immediately appear, she repeated the request, somewhat peremptorily. When he finally came, looking tired but unconcerned, and carrying a highball in each hand, she was still further offended.

"Hello, Tante Isabelle," he said, setting the glasses down on her night table and pulling up a chair. "We were just pouring out our drinks when you sent for me, and I hoped you wouldn't mind if we went on mixing them before I came up. I thought you might like one, too. Gervais said you wouldn't, but I brought it along anyway. The

210

rest of us sure needed them. Apparently Gervais and Merry have been painting the town red in New Orleans. They're pretty much all in, especially Merry. And Cresside and I have just come from a deathbed. It's been a rather devastating experience for her."

"I have not the least idea to whose deathbed you are referring, Fabian, or why Cresside should have been present at such a spectacle. I have myself been greatly perturbed by her mysterious absence, and I think you will admit I am entitled to an explanation of it. Since you are apparently responsible, at least in part——"

"Yes, I know. But I thought, under the circumstances, perhaps tomorrow would do just as well." While he was speaking, the tall clock in the hall began to strike in its sonorous way, echoing through the bedchamber, and immediately afterwards the tinkling tune of the parlor timepiece came faintly towards them. "I should have said, later today," Fabian continued. Madame d'Alvery's drink was still untouched, and without urging her a second time to take it, Fabian picked up the second glass and began sipping from it, deliberately. "I still think that would be the best plan—it's pretty late, Tante Isabelle. However . . . you already know that Cresside was upset when she left here and you know why. I do, too, because she told me. She felt she had to talk to someone. Almost everybody needs some sort of a safety valve and I'm glad Cresside thought of me in that connection. I'd like to do anything I could to contribute to her peace of mind, especially as I'm very fond of her. I couldn't ask her to spend the evening at my house because I was just leaving it myself, in answer to an emergency call. So I asked her to go with me and my old friends, Tremblet and Vicknair, to Port Allen. They got word that Max Stoetzner, the third musketeer in that group, was dying. Of course, it never would have occurred to me to take Cresside to Stoetzner's house, under ordinary circumstances. Just the same, I don't think the experience will do her any harm, in the long run. On the contrary, I think it may do her some good. It's already taken her mind off some other things that seemed to be worrying her."

He drained his glass and got up, pushing back his chair.

"Not that there's any reason why they should have," he said. "I've tried to tell her that. I don't know whether I've succeeded in convincing her or not, but if I haven't yet, I will, within the next few days. I'll be back for another chat with you, too, Tante Isabelle, as soon as I've seen that this poor old codger gets a decent Christian burial, so-called, and all that. But if I don't start home now, it won't be worth while going to bed at all. That's one advantage you have over the rest of us. You just stay there most of the time, which does away with a lot of bother. You're a mighty shrewd old lady in lots of ways, and believe me I know it. I take my hat off to you."

He smiled, lifting his hand quickly to his forehead and flinging it out, palm raised, in a gesture that was half deferential and half mocking. Then he nodded and left the room without further farewell.

Madame d'Alvery blew out the bedside candle which she still continued to use in preference to gas, and then lay still, slipping her rosary between her white fingers. But the movement was mechanical; there was no urge for prayer in her heart as she did it, only increasing resentment. Gervais and Merry did not come back to say good night. She heard them go to their room, more silently than usual, closing the door carefully behind them, and she chose to interpret this as another slight instead of giving them credit for trying not to disturb her. She heard Cresside and Fabian moving about downstairs, first in the lower hall and then on the front gallery. They were talking, but in whispers, as if they were guarding against the chance that their words might reach her ears; she strained these futilely, even as she raged against the suspicion of eavesdropping. Finally she heard the girl come back into the house alone, and then the lights went out, one by one, until Cresside's was the only one left.

Through the shutter doors dividing her room and her daughter's, Madame d'Alvery could see the girl's shadow. Cresside undressed wearily, as if the mere effort of stepping from her shoes and letting her slip fall to the floor were too great for her. But she did not turn out her light immediately after getting into her nightgown, as her mother had expected she would. Instead, she stood still for a moment, as if hesitating about something. Then she left her bedside and came slowly across the room, opening the shutter doors.

"Are you asleep, *maman?*" she asked softly from the threshold.

"No, I have not been able to compose myself. How could I?" Madame d'Alvery asked coldly, still fingering her prayer beads.

"Then may I come in?"

"Your request is rather tardy. I should have welcomed you more warmly several hours ago."

"Yes, I know," Cresside answered, unconsciously echoing Fabian. "Just the same, I'd like to tell you I'm sorry I went off at half cock the way I did. That is, I'm sorry as far as you're concerned. It was selfish of me, leaving you to worry about me all evening."

"I am glad you realize that at least."

"Of course I realize it," Cresside said, coming closer to the bed. "I'm darn tired, but that's exactly what I'm trying hard to tell you. I think you've got it coming to you. After all, you've got a right to know what I'm up to when I go out and you haven't any special reason to suppose that I mightn't be up to mischief. I'm not sorry I went, though. If I can do it without going into conversation on a lavish scale, I'd like to make that clear, too, before I go to bed. It might be a good thing for both of us if we understood each other a little better. I'm willing to do my share by trying to make you understand me. Then perhaps some time you'll do yours by trying to make me understand you. Not that you ever have yet."

She sat down on the steps beside her mother's bed. In her flimsy nightgown she looked even smaller and frailer than in her trim belted dresses. But she did not look frightened any longer. The expression on her pale face was self-possessed and resolute.

"I don't see why I've been such a fool about Sylvestre Tremaine," she said. "I don't mean, a fool to fall for him in the first place. We don't need to go over all that again. I mean by acting like such a sissy since he came back from Europe. I don't wonder you're sore at me. Suppose he does try to talk to me? I don't have to listen if I don't want to. I can keep right on shutting the door in his face, the way I did night before last. Suppose he does try to make passes at me? He can't get very far if I freeze right up, and I do that just at the sight of him. He couldn't touch me with a ten-foot pole. Fabian tried to tell me a while back that I oughtn't to give him the satisfaction of thinking he meant anything to me one way or another. I did try and I hope I put up a fairly good bluff. But it was just a bluff. I dreaded the very sight of him. I don't any more, though. He honestly doesn't matter to me, one way or another. He doesn't prove anything at all."

Madame d'Alvery was still silent, but she was no longer withdrawn. Her prayer beads had slipped unnoticed from her fingers. She made a slight gesture, but it was not towards recapturing the rosary; she suddenly felt impelled to stretch out her hands and smooth her daughter's dark hair back from the girl's soft forehead. Her habit of repression was too strong for her, and she did not do it. But Cresside had seen the gesture and sensed its significance. Unexpectedly encouraged, she went on almost boldly, forgetful of her fatigue.

"You know, *maman,* one trouble's been that every time I've seen him this spring, he's given me the feeling that I was stark naked. I don't mean the feeling that I was sitting around somewhere in his presence with nothing on but a nightie, the way I'm sitting beside you now. Or that I was in bed with him, the way Merry is with Gervais this minute—the way that means more than anything else in the world to them both. But as if I were publicly stripped of everything, not just clothes but decency, as if Sylvestre had done the stripping. As if he wanted to keep me exposed. It didn't seem possible to me, when we were with other people, that everyone who saw us together could help knowing what had happened. And when we were alone it didn't seem possible that he wouldn't make it happen again. The Sunday he and Regine came here together, I could almost hear her giggling and whispering, 'Why, Cresside, whatever do you mean, going around bare naked like that?' and when Sylvestre came by himself, night before last, I'd hardly caught sight of him before I felt as if he were fumbling with the fastening on my blouse so that he could get his hands on my breasts."

"Cresside, those are not the thoughts of a modest girl. Or the words," Madame d'Alvery said slowly. But she could not bring herself to speak severely. From out of a distant past, she seemed to hear another young girl, crying out desperately to her parents, *"Je ne peux pas me coucher avec ce cochon là, il veut m'enlever la chemise!"* That girl's desperation had been silly and groundless, the product of false shame and un-enlightened puerility; but the memory of it softened the haughty woman whose daughter had never before come to her in the night with whispered confidences. In Cresside's confession of her sensitivity, her mother recognized a kinship with herself, hitherto undivined.

"You're wrong. If I weren't modest, if that's what you call it, I wouldn't care if I was naked," Cresside retorted. "And I do. I care a lot. Isn't that what makes the difference? I mean, between being in love with a real man and being ashamed that you fell for a dirty welsher? If a girl's really in love, I don't believe she's afraid of being stripped. I think she's ready to be revealed."

"Perhaps you are right, Cresside. Yes, I believe that you are," her mother said, speaking still more slowly. She herself had never become ready for revelation; it was in her later relationships that her instinct had failed her, not in her first recoil; and that, she was beginning to realize, was because she had never really cared for anyone as Cresside would still eventually care for some one. Philogene d'Alvery had been the only man in her life, and he might have been her lover as well as her husband, if she had let him. There was no malice in his mockery, and though it was natural for him to be idle and aimless, it was also natural for him to be both tender and ardent. But she had persisted, first in her role of martyred maiden and later in her attitude as the unfortunate victim of a *mariage de convenance*. Philogene had been much in her thoughts during the days that Gervais and Merry had been in New Orleans. He had asked her to go there with him, shortly after their marriage, for a season of opera and a round of visits, and she had tartly inquired who would pay the bills for such a trip. It would not have cost much and she knew it; she was merely taunting him with his dependency. He knew that, too, and never asked her to go with him anywhere again; instead, once a year, he had gone off by himself, clothed in his outmoded but still dashing best, and spent several days at the Boston Club, hobnobbing with his old cronies there, at their expense. They were glad to see him and were never tactless enough to mention that he had neglected to pay his dues. When he returned to Belle Heloise, she had received him with reproachful chilliness that widened the breach between them. There would never be any such breach between Cresside and the man to whom, in time, she would want to be revealed. Mutinous and misguided as the girl had been, she was generous to the point of prodigality and some day her generosity would be her reward instead of her undoing. . . .

"Anyway, I'm fully clothed at last, mentally," Cresside was saying, breaking in on her mother's reverie and speaking more lightly. "You might say that I have on a chemise and a pair of corsets and under-drawers and four petticoats already—in fact, all the things you wore when you were a girl. Now I'm casting around for a set of steel

214

armor—the sort that has spikes on it. And what was that gadget girls wore in the Middle Ages, when their true loves went off to the Crusades and they didn't want any trespassing? The girdle of chastity it was called, wasn't it? Well, I'm going to have one of those, too. When I'm all fixed up like that, Sylvestre won't have a prayer of getting at me."

In the dim light which filtered through the door of Cresside's room, Madame d'Alvery could see that Cresside was actually smiling, in her elfin way. She hunched up her knees and clasped her arms around them. "Now that I'm sure I can keep him off, I can stop worrying about other people," she said cheerfully.

"Other people? What other people have you been worrying about, *chère?*" Madame d'Alvery asked, with unwonted gentleness.

"Why, no one special. Almost anyone. I haven't just been thinking about what Sylvestre might do. I've been worrying about what he might say to somebody else. Don't you think Sylvestre belongs to the breed that kisses and tells?"

"Try to put that out of your mind, Cresside."

"Yes, *maman,* but answer me. Don't you?"

Madame d'Alvery hesitated, but she could not escape the girl's earnest eyes.

"Perhaps. Yes, since you ask me, I cannot deny the possibility."

"All right then. That possibility's been an obsession with me. But I've just realized there's nothing he can tell that wouldn't hurt him more than it would me. If he were given to getting drunk all the time, that would be different—he might very well get chatty in his cups and say plenty that he'd never breathe when he was sober. But Sylvestre doesn't care about liquor, that is, not especially. Looping around isn't his idea of a thrill. It takes something else to give him that."

Cresside spoke with scorn. She looked straight at her mother for a moment, and then she rose from the steps and came closer to the bed, leaning her arm on the counterpane and her head on her arms. At first Madame d'Alvery was afraid that the girl might be crying, but presently she realized that Cresside was only relaxing. She had been very tired, but she had persevered and said everything she had started out to say; now she could rest. This time, almost unconsciously, Madame d'Alvery reached out her hand and began to stroke the girl's dark hair. She did not stop until Cresside looked up again.

"I thought that all through while I was sitting outside Max Stoetzner's house waiting for Fabian to finish talking with the undertaker," she said. "That's why I say I'm not sorry I went off this afternoon. I hope now that I've told you all about it you're not sorry either. I've been so close to the whole darn thing here, I couldn't see any of it straight. Now I think I do, because I got further away from it and because Fabian got me started on the right track, in another direction. I couldn't have started myself. But I can go on, if he helps me, and he's promised he would. Fabian's wonderful, isn't he, *maman?* I think we ought to be mighty proud that he's our cousin. He's the grandest person I ever knew in my whole life."

CHAPTER XVI

MADAME D'ALVERY LAY sleepless and thoughtful for a long time after Cresside finally went back to her own room; but the girl herself immediately fell into a deep and dreamless slumber. The shutter doors were still ajar; through either accident or design, she had failed to shut them, though it had never been her habit to leave them open, or Madame d'Alvery's wish that she should. Nothing about the two bedchambers suggested an intimate or fond association between mother and daughter; they might have been at opposite ends of the house, through the desire of both, as far as any closeness or connection was concerned, except that of architectural design. Now, for the first time, the wakeful woman remained poignantly aware of the sleeping girl's nearness and felt strangely assuaged by it; at the same time, a fierce new desire to protect and support her daughter surged through her proud constricted breast. When Lucie came in with her early morning coffee, she raised a warning hand and spoke in a whisper.

"Put down that tray and close the shutter doors. Miss Cresside got to bed very late and she was very tired. I don't want her disturbed."

"No, Madame, Ah ain't a-gwine disturb her."

Lucie moved soundlessly about the room, her expression as usual impassive and incurious. But still Madame d'Alvery was not satisfied.

"I wasn't referring only to closing the doors and making no noise while you are waiting on me. Don't take her any coffee till she rings for you. And tell Dinah not to count on having help with the twins from Miss Cresside this morning. I suppose Miss Merry will sleep late, too. Dinah will have to manage alone or you will have to help her."

"Yes, Madame. Ah done understan' 'bout Mis' Cresside de fust time. You knows Ah be's glad to help wid de twinses, too."

Lucie slipped a bed jacket deftly over Madame d'Alvery's shoulders, arranged her pillows and placed the tray in front of her. Then the maid went into the boudoir and dusted quietly until her mistress had finished her coffee; through the practice of years, she was able to time her return to the minute. Afterwards she waited respectfully for further orders, without making the inquiries or suggestions which would inevitably have come from Creassy.

"I shall remain in the bed until Miss Cresside wakes, Lucie. I believe she intends to go out with Mr. Fabian again—an old friend of

216

his has just died and he may need her help. I shall get up and go to the couch after I know her plans for the day. But I do not want to be in the midst of my toilette when she comes in to tell me what they are."

"Yes, Madame. Ah understands. And don't you worry none 'bout de twinses. Ah's gwine right now to help Dinah with 'em."

Lucie departed, taking the tray with her. Madame d'Alvery picked up her breviary and read the office of the day, conscious from time to time of the normal sounds made by an awakening household without giving them any real attention. Eventually she closed her book and went back to her prayer beads. But her thoughts were still on her child instead of her God, and every now and then her eyes strayed towards the old watch which had belonged to her father and which lay on the night table. It was after ten when she finally heard Cresside stirring, softly and intermittently at first, as if she were still so drowsy that she did not realize the hour; then with a startled swiftness. The girl pattered across the room, knocked lightly on the shutter doors, and swinging them open, stood disclosed on the threshold still in her nightgown, her small white feet bare and her dark hair tumbled about her pale face.

"Hell's bells, *maman,* do you know what time it is? Why didn't someone call me? I meant to be across the river by this time! And I've got to see to Vail first."

"Lucie is helping Dinah with the twins. There is nothing for which I require her at this moment. It had occurred to me that you would wish to go out again, and I am glad to dispense with Lucie's services, so that you can. But I thought you needed rest first, Cresside. I gave the orders that you were not to be disturbed."

"Well, I've sure got to get started now, if I'm going to be any use. Look, I don't know what time I'll be back today either. You're not going to worry again, are you?"

"No, *chère,* I am not going to worry again."

Within half an hour Cresside was already tearing down the River Road, and for the next few days she was home so little that Gervais hardly saw her. If he had been less preoccupied himself, with the activities of the hoe gang and the laying by of cane, he would have perhaps attached more significance to her absences and to the subsequent difference in her; but neither made any great impression on him. He learned, without attaching much importance to it, that she had helped Fabian with the arrangements for Max Stoetzner's funeral, after having previously been present at the aged veteran's death and later actively concerned with his surviving friends; and he saw that she was graver and more silent than usual. But he assumed this was only a passing phase, caused by a strange and stark revelation. He did not sense the fact that though she had been sobered by the circumstances of Stoetzner's death, she had been steadied and strengthened by some other experience at the same time.

He did observe that as the summer wore on, Fabian was at Belle

217

Heloise more and more, and that he and Cresside were spending a good deal of time in each other's company; but he noticed it without curiosity or interest. The corn was being gathered now, the hay harvested; the remodeling of the *garçonnière* and the storehouse had begun. He had more than a hundred hands at work in the fields, besides the carpenters, masons, plumbers and electricians in the yard. These men required an enormous amount of direction, and he had little enough spare time on his hands, even for Merry, far less for anyone else; he did not connect the change in Cresside's bearing with Fabian in any way.

For the most part, she still remained on the plantation, giving a good deal of time to the twins, not a little to the supervision of household activities, especially the seasonal one of preserving fruit. This had begun with the ripening of the dewberries in April and the figs in June; now the laden pear and plum trees would soon require stripping, too. It was hard for Merry to stand over a hot stove and Cresside did not mind; someone had to supervise Lou Ida, and she was the logical one to do it. But when Fabian came out to Belle Heloise after office hours, she was never too busy to stroll through the garden and grounds with him, and when he suggested they should go as far as the batture and spend the evening there, she consented to this, too. There was no reason why Lucie should not continue to help with the twins, Madame d'Alvery said, when Cresside first consulted her; she herself required nothing until bedtime. The girl leaned over to kiss her mother good-by, and afterwards Madame d'Alvery rose from her couch and went out on the gallery, watching her daughter and her nephew until they disappeared among the crepe myrtles of the driveway. Later she suggested to Gervais and Merry that it was high time Dinah began training another nurse in her own expert ways, so that the newcomer would not be wholly unfamiliar with them when the expected baby was born. A girl from the quarters, named Lethe, who was the eldest of a large family, and who had shown herself both skillful and tender in the care of her younger brothers and sisters, was brought to the Big House and the twins took to her kindly from the first. Until the time came when Philogene would need his nurse, there was no reason why Cresside should not come and go more freely.

The walk to the batture was not long or hard. This widened gradually from a strip of hard white sand, which lay beyond the levee directly in front of the house, to a densely wooded triangle about half a mile distant, comprising over three hundred acres. At some points a stretch of sloping ground separated the woods from the sand, and this had long been a favorite daytime picnicking place because it was shaded without being too densely overgrown. The hard sandy strip, on the other hand, besides being used for a bathing beach, had often been the scene of evening "beer and shrimp" parties, organized to entertain visiting celebrities, and of moonlight dances, more informally arranged for the entertainment of younger guests. Shrimp were plentiful in the river along the batture; Amen always put out a dozen or more shrimp boxes off the bank early in the spring, baiting them with corn meal and cottonseed cake, and often the catch continued good until November. There was excellent fishing, too, both in the river itself and in the barrow-pit where the batture began to widen; lines were set out in the river each evening and drawn in each morning, heavy with catfish and gaspergou. The barrow-pit fishing was not done with set lines but in person, with poles, and game fish, such as perch, trout and sac-a-lait constituted the catch; the sport which this furnished had always been a favorite locally, and so had swimming. There were two bath houses back of the beach, and, in the water, a place was roped off by means of stakes driven into the river bed, to mark the limits of safety for all but the most experienced swimmers. Because of the river's changing course, it was necessary to realign the zone every year, and though Selah had formerly taken charge of it, Amen had now succeeded his father in attending to this task, too.

Before going to war, Gervais had usually spent a good deal of time on the batture himself, helping Amen with the shrimp boxes and the set lines in the early mornings, picnicking and swimming and dancing in the evenings. He had kept a couple of skiffs tied to the bank, and not infrequently he had rowed across the river for an outing in Plaquemine, with Cresside and Sylvestre and Regine making up the party. Plaquemine was a pleasant prosperous little town; there was an old saying that it had only four streets but at least one millionaire family on every one of them—the Schwings, the Wilberts, the Gays and the Sherburns. With so much wealth to draw on, it was sophisticated for its size, and the outings had always been lively and amusing. They had ceased, at least as far as Gervais was concerned, with his interest in Regine. This had never been founded on anything more substantial than her prettiness and her propinquity, and after he met Merry he was soon deeply attached to her; but as their "understanding" was unofficial and his mother's attitude an obstacle, he had never attempted to force an issue by bringing her out of town.

Since his return from France, he had hardly been down on the batture at all. It was not important to him, from the viewpoint of productiveness, and Merry's condition, both this summer and the summer before, had automatically precluded her from tramping over rough ground and, indeed, from practically all forms of amusement which the batture afforded. At first he had been too passionately in love to leave her, and later too preoccupied with plantation problems. Now, when he saw that his sister was beginning to spend considerable time on the batture again, his own dormant interest in it revived.

"You seem to be taking quite a little exercise again these days," he observed, rather tardily, one evening, as he met her on the stairs. "Back not hurting you any more?"

"Only off and on. I can take walks all right. And, of course, I can fish—that doesn't require much strength, mental or physical either, when you do it in a barrow-pit. I haven't tried any strenuous swimming yet. Just a little paddling around."

"Good. I'm glad you're having some fun at last. Glad Fabian is, too. I'd been trying for a long time to get him out here more. But he always put me off. Said he had a jealous mistress."

"You dirty liar! You know damn well Fabian never said anything of the sort!"

"Hold on, spitfire! He did say it. But he was talking about the law. You know he's strong on classical quotations. Well, apparently he's appeased his mistress, and it's a good thing. There's no reason why he should slave himself to death. He's got plenty of money, so he can afford to take it easy. I wish I were in his shoes."

"You'd like to be solitary and deformed and completely disillusioned, I suppose?"

"I said, hold on. Of course, I wouldn't like to be solitary and deformed—the disillusionment's a matter of temperament, not circumstances. But we won't argue over that. I merely meant I envied him his steady income. . . . You know, you've given me an idea, going back to the batture. I think I'd like to have a good old-time beer and shrimp party before the legislature closes. I'd ask the whole bunch and the usual hangers-on. None of the new members has ever been down here for one of these shindigs, and not many of the old ones— I don't need to tell you our father never bothered with politicians as such—he only asked the men he really had a liking for. Would you feel like helping me get up a racket of that kind? Or aren't you equal to it? I don't want you to do it if you aren't, but all my womenfolk seem to be disabled in one way or another."

"I'm not disabled any longer, and of course I'd be glad to help. I think you've got something there—that flea circus down at the capitol ought to get a great kick out of a Belle Heloise beer and shrimp party. And you better stir your stumps and give as many of that kind as you can while you've still got a free field. By the time you're really a big shot in politics, Sybelle will be down there dancing practically every night with her crowd, and you won't have a look-in."

"I'm sure not going to start worrying about what might happen seventeen or eighteen years from now. Whatever made you think of it yourself?"

She made a little moue and ran on up the stairs without answering him. She did not tell him, then or ever, that the evening before she and Fabian had been sitting on the sandy strip when the moon rose, and that while they were talking together about dancing, the subject of Sybelle had come up.

"Cresside, wouldn't you enjoy getting out more again?"

"I am getting out more again. We've been fishing twice this week, and we've brought supper with us both times. I could've stayed in the water longer tonight, but those darn shrimp kept nibbling at my legs. That's why I came in. Not because I was tired."

"I didn't mean going fishing and swimming with me. I meant getting out more with other people. Or having them come here. You used to go in a lot for dancing, Cresside. I hope you'll take it up again, as soon as you feel strong enough."

"I shan't, Fabian."

"Why not? You're a beautiful dancer. It would be a shame if you gave it up."

"No, it wouldn't. I have given it up."

"You're very foolish to say a thing like that, at your age and with your natural grace."

"If I don't ever say anything more foolish than that, I'll be doing pretty well. A darn sight better than I usually do."

"Look here, Cresside——"

He stopped. He could not quite bring himself to say, "Cresside, if I could only dance with you myself, I could cure you of this silly notion. But I can't, because I'm a cripple and so you'll have to cure yourself. You mustn't get too dependent on me, because there are so many limits to the ways I can help you. I wish there weren't, but there are. You must stand on your own two feet unless you let some other man help. But there are dozens who'd be only too glad of the chance, good ones, too. Why don't you let them have it?" She knew this was what he was thinking, but she was tongue-tied, too. She could not say on her own initiative, "Fabian, I don't need excitement and admiration any more; I don't even want it. I only need and want just what you're giving me now, comfort and strength and companionship. I'd rather go fishing and swimming with you, or just sit on the sand and talk to you, than go dancing with any other man, a man who isn't a cripple, who's strong and whole and handsome. You haven't forgotten, have you, that I did go dancing with another man who was like that and dreaded the sight of him afterwards, until you made me see that he needn't mean a thing to me any more, one way or another? Well, you don't suppse I want to have anyone else make love to me, do you, after that? You don't suppose I want to go through all that turmoil and anguish again?" Instead she waited a minute, hoping that after all he would go on, and when he did not, she said, "I reckon Sybelle will be the next d'Alvery girl to dance on the batture. She'll look lovely, too, if she's as pretty when she grows up as she is now. Can't you just see her on the white sand, with the moonlight shining on her blonde hair?"

"Yes. It'll be a beautiful sight. Some poor boy'll probably go straight off his base over it. But that's still in what's bromidically called the dirn distant future. I can see you much clearer and closer. Moonlight looks nice on dark hair, too, you know."

"Well, doesn't it show up enough when I'm sitting still, for the love of Mike?"

"No. It takes motion to really show it off. But I won't pester you about it, if you'd rather I didn't. . . . *À propos* of nothing, I've been meaning to tell you that I stopped in at Hathaway Hall a few days ago. I sat through half an hour of Mrs. Hathaway's pronouncements and Regine's giggling chatter and then I went out in the fields and had a little talk with Sylvestre."

"I didn't know he ever went out in the fields. I thought he was one of their lilies who neither toiled nor span."

"Oh, yes, he goes, every now and then. Of course, he lets Blood do all the dirty work, and it's plenty dirty, in more ways than one. But Sylvestre has to find some excuse for a means of escape. No man could keep on listening to that giggle indefinitely. He'd go nuts."

"Did you have an interesting conversation with him?"

"Very brief. But very much to the point. I don't think he'll be making you any more unannounced visits after dark when his wife's laid up with a headache. I mention it just in case you're still worrying about that."

"I wasn't. It was swell of you to go there, Fabian. But Sylvestre doesn't prove a thing to me any more, thanks to you. And I might add, thanks to *maman*. There were a few little matters I'd been brooding over and I tried to tell you about them. But believe it or not, I couldn't— they just weren't the sort of thing any girl says to any man. So I finally broke down and said them all to her, the night after Max died. I went to her room to apologize for rushing off the way I had, because, when I thought it over, I figured she had that coming to her. Then the next thing I knew, I'd started spilling the beans. I don't know who was more surprised, she or I. But it worked. We're getting on like a house afire now and I've got Sylvestre almost out of my system— not quite, but almost. Near enough so that I'm sure I'm going to."

"Fine. . . . You know, I don't believe Sylvestre and Regine are going to be at Hathaway Hall much anyway, Cresside. They're planning to start for Hot Springs pretty soon. And Regine said they might go back to the Riviera next winter. Once a planter gets the absentee landlord habit, it grows on him."

"And then what happens to the plantation?"

"You ought to know. You've seen enough tumble-down places around here. It doesn't take them long to disintegrate in this climate, once they're deserted."

"Mrs. Hathaway wouldn't let that place disintegrate. She's proud of it, whether Regine and Sylvestre care anything about it or not. And Regine used to have a complex about it, too. You know that she insisted on making her debut and having her wedding in that great empty White Ball Room. She's always thought it was the zenith of elegance. And she had practically a fixation on the gallery."

"Yes, but that was when she could get away from it whenever she wanted to, in the company of anyone she chose. Especially in Gervais' company. It's been getting less and less of a fixation since she's been tied to a man who doesn't want her and who's bored to death in the country. As for Mrs. Hathaway, she isn't a well woman, Cresside, unless I miss my guess. She's got a mighty queer color. Of course, I didn't mean to intimate, though, that Hathaway Hall was going to disintegrate right away. Blood's a mighty capable manager. But he's also a periodic drinker and his favorite potion's whisky mixed with chloroform. A combination like that can do plenty to a man's insides, if he sops it up for a week at a time every so often. At that I shouldn't be surprised if Blood came to an untimely end for another reason."

"You mean, one of his numerous lady friends might polish him off some fine night?"

"Yes. . . . There isn't much going on around here you don't know about, is there, Cresside, even if you did spend a year in bed? His little apartment at the rear of the Hathaway boarding house is quite a seraglio. Half the mulatto kids you see stacking cane around that sugar mill are his—there's hardly a trifling Negro wench on the place he hasn't had, and there have been two or three pretty ugly rows already—probably you knew that, too. Now Blood's started a new system of seduction with a succession of sisters—white girls this time, daughters of those no-count Renos that are squatting on the old Faith estate. He's got rid of Vina, the eldest, already, and passed on to Durice, the second one. But I think he has his eye on the third. Her name's Déette and she's a handsome little she-devil if there ever was one. Everything's quiet enough on the surface but I believe the situation's volcanic underneath."

"And you think when the volcano erupts the plantation will go, too?"

"I don't say it'll go. But I think it'll cease to produce sugar. And then presently the cane fields will be nothing but rough overgrown pastures, with cattle straying through them. Probably there'll be tenants of a sort in the house for a while, who let chickens and pigs and goats wander in and out through that fine basement—afterwards squatters like the Renos, who'll do worse and come to a bad end themselves. They'll disappear one by one and then the place will be left to the snakes."

"Unless someone else steps into the picture. Someone that cares."

"Yes, of course that might happen. If Gervais had married Regine, the way Mrs. Hathaway and Tante Isabelle planned, instead of marrying Merry to suit himself, of course the two places would eventually have become part of the same plantation. One of Gervais' children would eventually have been given Hathaway Hall. But the way things have turned out . . . You can't see Vail eventually living there, can you, Cresside?"

"No. I sure can't," she said shortly. Then, as if to mitigate her abruptness, she added, "But Sybelle might. She might fall in love, herself, with the boy you thought of who would be watching her dance in the moonlight, and he might be the new owner of Hathaway Hall, the one who had rescued it from destruction and decay, besides being a regular fairy-tale hero. Or don't things like that ever happen except in books?"

"No, I reckon they happen in real life, too, sometimes—to other people," Fabian said bitterly. Then as if he, too, were conscious of ungraciousness, he added, "But maybe Sybelle will meet a real Prince Charming—it's about time some girl had luck along that line, in this family. I know it won't hurt your feelings any if I say Gervais doesn't seem to be quite living up to the beau ideal of a hero, though fortunately Merry isn't on to him yet. And I like your vision of Sybelle dancing in the moonlight. I'm afraid I didn't sound as if I did. But I want you to dance, too, Cresside. Do it to please me, if you won't do it to please yourself."

She turned to him quickly. He was not speaking bitterly any longer. Great earnestness had crept into his voice, and, in the moonlight, she could see that his face was very earnest, too. She was amazed that it should seem important to him whether she danced or not. But she would have cheerfully walked over red-hot coals if she thought her doing so would mean anything to him. She felt a queer little catch in her throat as she tried to answer lightly so that he would not know how much he had moved her.

"All right. I'll do it to please you. Provided, of course, that you find me exactly the right partner. Come on, it's time we were going in."

Gervais had not the remotest idea that conversations of this type were taking place on the batture. But he was pleased when Cresside mentioned the shrimp and beer party again, at dinner the day after their meeting on the stairs, asking if he had thought of a date for it, and whether he wanted her to help in getting together the provisions. He would see to buying the beer and bread, he told her, outlining his plans to his mother and his wife for the first time. He supposed there were enough pickles in the storeroom; it would not matter if they used up all they had, since a new supply would be made so soon now. He would be grateful if Cresside would oversee the boiling of the shrimp, because he had more confidence in her than in Lou Ida, when it came to a question of seasoning with hot red pepper. He thought perhaps the following Wednesday would be a good time for the party, but he would let her know. How much notice did she need?

Oh, not a great deal, she said easily. If he had not looked in the storehouse yet, to see how many benches they had on hand, she would be glad to do that first thing. If there were not enough, she would walk over to the cooperage with Fabian when he came out that afternoon, to see about having some more made. The tables would be no problem, since there were always plenty of planks lying around here and there. ... A day or two later she asked him to go down to the batture with her, and showed him the setup already arranged on the sand—the planks lying across wooden horses to form long tables, with rough benches on either side of them, where the guests would eat, and a couple of smaller tables for the service of whisky, mineral water, Coca-Cola and ginger ale. Well, she seemed to have thought of everything, Gervais said in a pleased voice. If the good weather only held, the party was bound to be a big success. Everyone he'd invited had accepted, and everyone seemed pleased to be asked. The sample of boiled shrimp she had given him was tops, too. He had been right about her judgment regarding the hot red pepper. He hoped *maman* would not fuss over the smell of the boiling shrimp. It did have a way of getting all over the house. But, after all, it did not last long. . . .

There was no question about the success of the party. The guests, who had been invited for eight, began to arrive earlier than that, most of them in cars, but a few in old-fashioned surreys. A runway of planks had been laid across the ditch and they drove straight over the levee, parking their automobiles and hitching their horses on its river side along the batture. Almost without exception, they were neatly turned out in fresh seersucker and linen suits. But they readily followed Gervais' suggestion that they should take off their coats and roll up their sleeves; the discarded vestments were chucked into the vehicles the guests had just left, or draped over the limbs of trees. Prevailing differences in build and stature were disclosed in the course of this process. Taken by and large, the North Louisianians were taller, ruddier and more spare than the men from the Southern Parishes, many of whom were short and thickset, with black hair and olive complexions. Various local peculiarities of speech, quite aside from the French accent, were also noticeable; many of the North Louisianians stressed the final syllable of words ending in ent: saying government, accident, prevalent; the Cajuns repeated their personal pronouns, and added yes and no to the end of their sentences. Gervais' pet aversion, Brother Ellery Scobell, of the "two ticks and the nickel-gripper purse," was theoretically an uncompromising prohibitionist. So were most of the others from the northern hill Parishes; but they had accepted Gervais' invitation to the beer and shrimp party with the same alacrity as the southern Creoles, to whom, in most cases, the Eighteenth Amendment simply did not exist. Now the various members of these different factions were striding across the sand together, laughing and joking as they went. Charles Boylston, whose position as a neighboring planter and a family friend had indicated his inclusion on the list, but whose acquaintance among the other guests was limited, stood on the side lines, directing interested questions at Fabian, who had brought Belizaire with him and who was waiting until the dog quieted down a little before attempting to circulate.

"That's John Tanner of Shreveport just going up to Gervais, isn't it? I've met him, but I don't know those two fellows who are with him."

"Why, you must know Tack Evans, Charles. He's around everywhere these days."

"That's right, he is. I just didn't connect him with this particular crowd at first. But I remember now, I heard Gervais saying he was going to ask the 'hangers-on' as well as the members of the legislature, so Evans qualifies all right. What is he stewing about now? The pipeline bill?"

"Yes. Says if somebody doesn't watch them the Baton Rouge cutthroats will get in their dirty work and kill it. Huey Long, the other fellow Tanner's got in tow, says 'improper influences' are being used to defeat Tanner's bill."

"Huey Long? That pudgy-looking geezer with a loose lock hanging over his forehead and the diamond tie pin at his shirt under his bow tie? What does he prove, as Cresside would say?"

"Why, you must know that, too. He's one of the Railroad Commissioners. That doesn't prove so much in itself. But Long's smart as a steel trap. He'll go a lot further before he winds up. Look, Charles, we can't keep on standing over here as if we thought the rest of the crowd had leprosy or something. Belizaire seems to know that he's got to put up with these queer goings on now, and you ought to make it a point to know all these men if you're going to live in Louisiana. Come on and meet Long. I'm inclined to think he's more or less of a scoundrel, but he's a rather intriguing one."

They walked on towards the group standing around Gervais, and Fabian, shaking hands with the various men in turn, embarked on a series of agreeable introductions to which Boylston responded adequately. Everything was now in readiness for the guests; the boiled shrimp, still in the rough, were set out in big bowls that ran at intervals down the length of the makeshift tables. No dressing was served; the high seasoning of the water in which the shrimp had been boiled took the place of this. Fried chicken, piled in dish pans, was provided especially for those who might not like sea food; and between the bowls and the pans lay long loaves of bread, opened cartons of crackers, and plates heaped with pickles and mounds of golden butter. The beer bottles were packed in big tubs of cracked ice, and the guests helped themselves to the beer, throwing the drained bottles down on the sand; but Amen and Selah were stationed at the two small tables where the hard liquor and soft drinks were being served, opening bottles and mixing highballs. Some of the plantation hands had also been called in from the quarters to make themselves generally useful; they circulated among the guests, passing paper plates and suggesting refills, and when it began to grow dark, they lighted the gasoline torches, shaped like inverted saucepans and equipped with a piece of pipe at the bottom, which had been hooked to the trees beforehand. The legislators ate and drank prodigiously, peeling the shrimp and throwing the shells down on the sand among the empty beer bottles, as they did the chicken bones, in spite of Fabian's muttered warning about keeping these away from dogs. The long loaves of bread, the big mounds of butter, disappeared as if they had been spirited away; in an incredibly short time all that was left on the tables were empty bowls and boxes, a few broken crackers and a few spilled pickles. But the drinks held out.

By midnight the guests who had begun by talking about politics and agriculture were telling broad jokes and bursting into carefree song. The pipe-line bill and the repeal of the dipping law—another burning issue—were alike forgotten. Men who had been calling each other hard names on the floor of the legislature and secretly maneuvering to outwit each other were caroling with their arms about each other's necks. The party broke up to the strains of "Sweet Adeline" and "Give Me the Moonlight, Give Me the Girl, and Leave the Rest to Me," sung, in some cases, decidedly off key, but in all instances with great heartiness. The old-fashioned surreys and the model T Fords finally went bucking over the levee and up the River Road again, their occupants in a mood so mellow that the echoed evidences of it continued to float back towards the batture. Gervais, delighted at the success of his party, invited Fabian and Boylston to go up to the house with him for a final drink. They left the hands from the quarters to clean up the debris on the beach and put out the torches; but Selah returned to serve the highballs on a silver tray in the drawing room. Gervais' own room was in darkness, and he felt sure that Merry was already asleep; but seeing that a light was still shining in Cresside's, he called up to her. Wouldn't she come down and join them? They all wanted to thank her for the swell idea she had put into his head. Sure, she called back, she'd be there in a jiffy; she had always thought the best thing about a party was the fun of talking it over afterwards. Because of Charles her "jiffy" was a little longer than it would otherwise have been. Instead of appearing in a negligee, she got dressed. But for all that she made good time, and she was excellent company when she did arrive. Gervais could not remember when he had seen her in better spirits.

He told Merry so the next morning, adding that he was sorry that she had not been there to give the nightcap its final fillip; and during the next few days he took special pains to tell her the news items which he thought might possibly interest her, partly to guard against giving her the feeling that she had been left out of a pleasant group, in which she logically would have been included, and partly because he was beginning to realize how much of her enjoyment was vicarious these days. Her condition was already noticeable, and though she appeared to accept her disfigurement philosophically and sensibly, he knew that her natural shyness made her sensitive about it. She stayed close to the plantation, seeing only her family and her most intimate friends, and taking no part whatsoever in the activities connected with the legislative session. But she was pleased because he participated in them, and she loved to listen to his descriptions of the political picture and to his impressions of the main figures in it.

That violent oddity of an upstart, Huey Long, was going around making all kinds of loose charges, he told her. Long claimed that Parker had promised legislation should be passed declaring oil pipe lines common carriers and that this promise had been broken. In turn

Parker replied that he had made no pre-election promises, either to Commissioner Long "or to any other living man." . . . A number of hearings had been held and at one of these Long made the bald statement, of which Gervais had already told Merry, that "improper influences" were being used to defeat the bill introduced by Representative Tanner of Shreveport, which carried the provision Long was demanding. Finally there was a hell of a conference in the Governor's office, at which the major oil companies all had representatives, and which various other individuals, Long among them, had also attended. Two or three men had risen and asked Long in a threatening way whether he had been talking about them when he spoke of "improper influences" and he had instantly backed down and said he did not have them in mind. Later that same evening he had run into Tack Evans on Third Street, and spoken bitterly about the way high and mighty powers were picking on him. Gervais had seen Tack afterwards at Izzy's and Tack had passed the tale along.

" 'I'm just a poor boy from North Louisiana and all these millionaires have it in for me.' That was the sob story he tried to hand out. But Tack came right back at him. 'Poor boy, hell! You've got a diamond as big as a marble on your finger, and a bigger one on your shirt.'— You should have seen him at the beer and shrimp party, Merry! He had on his diamond tie pin then, though he had on a bow tie. It was fastened to his shirt under the bow. I don't think Charles is ever going to recover from the sight. . . . Well, that's just an aside. Tack's parting shot was priceless. 'By God, Huey,' he said. 'I'll bet you've even got diamond buttons on your drawers!' And Merry, it wouldn't surprise me if he did have! I'm telling you, the man's fantastic. But at that, he's nobody's fool. Fabian's right about him there."

The story about the diamond buttons on Huey's drawers was circulating freely through a delighted legislature the following day. But when the closing session came, it was rocking with laughter over another, and Gervais passed this on to Merry also.

"The two Badley sisters certainly pulled a fast one tonight, Merry."

"A fast one? Those two nice girls! Why, what did they do?"

"Well, you know they've been among the most ardent leaders of the Ratification Wing, and the last count of noses in the Senate showed that there were just enough votes to pass the State Suffrage Bill provided there were no absentees. But late this afternoon old Senator Louque of New Orleans decided that enough was enough and that he was going home without waiting for adjournment. In his absence, the anti-Ratificationists did not have enough votes to pass their bill, and Ex-Governor Pleasant rushed down to the railroad station to hold Louque in Baton Rouge by any means. But meanwhile the Badleys had got wind of the contretemps, and they went charging over to Louque's boarding house in that huge Studebaker touring car of theirs. Then they offered to drive him to Geismar so that he could overtake an earlier local which had already left and get him home at least an hour sooner than he would have otherwise. He very gratefully accepted, and while poor Pleasant was striding up and down the station platform, the picture of grim determination, Louque was speeding southward in luxury, guarded by those 'two nice girls'!"

For the time being, this was the last of Gervais' long leisurely stories, told for Merry's benefit; after the close of the legislature, he threw himself, with redoubled energy, into the execution of his plans for improvements on the plantation. A progressive young architect named Arnold Fletcher had recently settled in Baton Rouge, and had done a fine piece of work in restoring and modernizing the beautiful little house near town which belonged to distant kinsfolk of the Hathaways and which had been occupied by Prince Murat during his exile. Gervais had been so much impressed by this achievement that, with the approval of the New Orleans architect he first consulted, he had asked Fletcher to take charge of the restoration program at Belle Heloise, and Fletcher had accepted the commission with enthusiasm; it was not often that so important a project was entrusted to so young a man. He had thrown himself into the undertaking wholeheartedly and efficiently, and the dilapidated buildings had lent themselves to restoration and adaptation better than Gervais had dared to hope. The interior of the storehouse was now transformed to provide him with two offices, the outer one small and plain, but the other suggestive of a large luxurious library; a shower and a kitchenette joined these, still leaving some space for storage, and upstairs there were three bedrooms and a bath for male guests. The original *garçonnière* was even more attractive in its new form; it had taken on all the attributes of a charming cottage especially designed for the comfort and convenience of a young couple.

"We'll be all settled in our new home by the time the crops are laid by," Gervais told Merry. "That's when most planters go away on their vacations, because there's a month's leeway before the fall plowing begins. If it hadn't been for Philogene, we could have gone to Hot Springs ourselves—well, I reckon that wouldn't have been the best choice, with Sylvestre and Regine and Mrs. Hathaway spread all over the place. White Sulphur, maybe, or Asheville. You aren't disappointed, honey, are you, that you're tied down like this?"

"Disappointed! With a new house of our own to move into? We couldn't possibly have as much fun, on any kind of a trip, as we'll have doing that!"

She was entirely sincere in her statement; everything about the transformed *garçonnière* was a source of joy to her: the modern kitchen and bathroom, so much more attractive and convenient than the corresponding portions of the Big House; the large bedroom and the tiny dining room, which she had equipped charmingly and ingeniously from the stack of discarded furniture relegated to the attic; the sunny living room which she made brighter still with brasses and chintzes and gay prints. She had always scrupulously avoided making or even suggesting changes in her mother-in-law's domain; but this was her own, and her patient transformation of the rear gallery from a catch-all for rubbish to a pleasant and livable patio had given her a good preparation for a more ambitious undertaking. And she did not stop at the *garçonnière;* she showed the same resourcefulness and put the same care into the appointments of Gervais' offices, rescuing the dilapidated books which she found scattered under the eaves among the broken furniture, and arranging them on wide built-in shelves. Old pictures and old papers came in for the same solicitous treatment; the bare walls were soon adorned with long-forgotten portraits and engravings, and documents which no one else had ever taken the trouble to frame. Even Charles Boylston's impressive study could not compare with Gervais' library in atmosphere and distinction when Merry had finished with it. He was so proud of it that he promptly planned another party to show it off to his friends, and lent a willing ear to Fletcher's suggestion that now the first plans had developed so satisfactorily, they should expand their original program of restoration to include the quarters, the school-house, the overseer's home, and even the old cooperage, blacksmith shop and stables.

"Fletcher says there isn't a place on the River Road, not even Uncle Sam, that could compare with this if it were all put in proper order," he told Merry. "Not many of the plantations had even the quarters made of brick—of course, we had our own kiln here originally; and that mud wall type of construction in Lezine's house is disappearing fast. It would really be a shame not to preserve it. It's beginning to look as if we'd have plenty of use for the old schoolhouse, too. If we put it in order now, it'll be ready when the kids are old enough to need it."

He had an equally cogent reason for every proposed item of renovation, and every evening he pored, with increasing enthusiasm, over the blueprints which Fletcher submitted to him in rapid succession. Merry, proud of her own contribution to the improvements, shared his eagerness to go on with them. But with the greater caution of a girl brought up to count the cost of everything she had, she asked one or two anxious questions.

"Won't all this be pretty expensive, honey, if we go into it on such a lavish scale?"

"Yes, but it represents a good investment, too. It's poor economy to let a place run down the way this one has. Once it's in really good shape again, it won't begin to cost so much to keep up, in the way of constant patching and tinkering."

"I suppose it won't. But still wouldn't it be better to have the work done gradually? I mean, we've done the *garçonnière* and the store-house this year. Couldn't you do Lezine's house next year and the cooperage and quarters the year after that, and then the schoolhouse last of all?"

"And meanwhile let them get further and further out of repair? No, that's just what I've been talking about. I want to get them all in good order and keep them in good order. I keep telling you, it'll be economy in the end. Besides, I want this restoration work off my mind, so I can concentrate on the crops. As it is, I'm subject to constant interruptions, with all these carpenters and masons running to me every hour or so about this and that. After grinding begins, I'll have to be at the mill all the time; I can't stay at their beck and call. And next year, we are going to have a trip instead of a baby, no matter what we do or don't do to be sure we get it."

He grinned at her in his old engaging way. She smiled back at him, her anxiety assuaged by his assurance.

"I'm sure you know best, honey. And of course you know I'd love to see it all done myself. I was only wondering if there was enough money."

"There's enough credit, and that amounts to the same thing."

"Does it really? Hasn't the price of sugar kept on going down since July?"

"Well, yes. But not enough to get nervous over. Listen, Merry, you leave that part to me, and I'll take care of it. You've got enough on your mind as it is."

He picked up the blueprints and put them away, and he did not speak to her again about Fletcher's expanded program. But the work on it went steadily forward just the same.

CHAPTER XVII

ABSORBED AS HE WAS with his project of restoration, Gervais did not permit it to divert either him or his hands from the seasonal occupations of the plantation. The two types of work went forward together. By the time the storehouse and the *garçonnière* had become usable again, repairs on the cooperage, the quarters and the schoolhouse were already under way; after the corn and the hay were harvested, the ditches were cleaned, the wood brought in, and the land prepared for the next year's crop. The seed cane was hauled in mule carts from the fields where it had been cut to the fields which were ready for planting. Through the earlier part of the summer, all the field work had been done by men; now women and children followed after the mule carts, straightening the cane which the men had tossed from them, and laying it in six-foot rows the entire length of the field. They squabbled among themselves, and when the cane was not thrown straight, or the division of labor seemed unequal, this wrangling sometimes reached the proportions of a real quarrel. But often the Negroes sang, too. Gervais, riding over the headland, reined in his horse, and listened to the sound of their singing with a feeling of satisfaction comparable to the impulse which produced the song. Dinah's mother, Hester, who had a voice as powerful as her big black body, led the weaker women who followed in her wake and echoed her refrain.

> "Ah wants to be ready"—Hester sang—
> "Ah wants to be ready,
> Goin' to Jerusalem,
> Jes' lak John."

And all the others chorused:

> "Goin' to Jerusalem,
> Jes' lak John."

"I always did like that song," Gervais told Merry when he came in. "I like the sound of it and I like the meaning of it. 'Ah wants to be ready' too, honey—ready for the grinding season and for everything else that's ahead of us. I'm aiming to be, too—and that's more than can be said of everyone on the River Road," he added, rather self-righteously.

Merry glanced at him with a question in her adoring eyes, and he went on so readily that she guessed he had been hoping she would ask him to explain. "Alphonse Loubat was here yesterday," he said. "You know, the inspector who comes around every year to check the boilers, for the insurance company. He thought the safety valves would go through this fall all right, though he was just a shade doubtful about one of them. I told him I wasn't taking any chances. A new safety valve only costs about a hundred dollars, and I'd rather make a clean sweep of them all than to risk having anything go wrong. He said it was certainly a satisfaction to deal with a planter who had such a keen sense of responsibility, and then he added that it was too bad Sylvestre Tremaine didn't have a little more of it. It seems the boilers at Hathaway are in pretty bad shape, but Sylvestre insists he can't afford to do anything about them at present—and look at the money that family throws away, running around from one eastern watering place to another and all over the face of Europe! Between you and me, I believe Sylvestre bribed Loubat to pass the boilers."

"But if Loubat accepted a bribe, wouldn't he be just as guilty as Sylvestre, if anything went wrong?"

"Oh, I suppose so! But you'd naturally expect a planter to have higher principles than an inspector. After all, an inspector's only a petty official, with no standing or station to speak of, and a planter's a landed proprietor, personally responsible for the welfare and safety of all his employees. I know of one explosion due to a clogged safety valve which killed half a dozen persons, among them a poor Negro who was just patiently sitting on his cane cart, two hundred yards away from the mill, waiting his turn to get up to the carrier. He was hit by a flying tube, and his head was cut right off. . . . There, I ought not to tell you things like that, especially just now. Forget about it, honey. Lightning

232

never hits twice in the same place. There isn't going to be any explosion at Hathaway."

"But was this—did this terrible thing you've just told me happen at Hathaway?"

"No, it happened at Hackberry—years ago that was, long before Boylston took it over. You may be sure everything's in A-1 condition there now."

"But then if there *were* an explosion at Hathaway, it wouldn't be a case of lightning striking twice in the same place. It would be the first time."

"Oh, for God's sake, Merry, I've asked you before not to be so literal! I meant the general neighborhood when I said 'the same place.' I never heard of another explosion anywhere around here. I still don't think there'll be one at Hathaway, in spite of Sylvestre and his criminal carelessness. I was only telling you what Loubat told me."

Merry hesitated before replying. A few minutes earlier she was sure Gervais was waiting for an excuse to talk about Hathaway; now she did not know what he wanted her to do. But besides being horrified, she was reluctantly intrigued. More and more, as it came closer to her time, she was dependent on him for the news of the countryside, and the men and women who figured in it, both righteously and unrighteously. At first she had innocently taken it for granted that this rural region was always tranquil, and that everyone who lived along the River Road was hard-working and high-principled. Gradually she was discovering her mistake, especially in several conspicuous instances. She did not know as much about Grover Blood as Cresside did; nevertheless, rumors concerning him were so widespread that some of them had inevitably reached her, and these were lurid enough to rouse her curiosity. She finally ventured to ask another question.

"Hasn't Sylvestre's manager—Grover Blood, that's his name, isn't it?—any more sense of responsibility than Sylvestre? I should think he'd hesitate to take a chance on defective boilers."

"I wouldn't. You could class him in the same general group as the inspector. He isn't a property owner, and he's long passed the point of taking pride in someone else's property. He never did have any lofty ideals or even any especially humane sentiments. Just now he's all worked up over a girl. Of course, you've got to expect that sort of thing, on general principles, among white and colored both during the slack season that's just coming on. Haven't you noticed Amen mooning around? He's after Creassy, just when you need her most, too. And I'm pretty sure that our sugar boiler, Dupuy, is having a little affair with Seraphine, over at the boarding house. But Blood does these things on a different scale. Sance tumbled on a pretty tense scene in the manager's quarters, just the other day."

Again Merry felt that Gervais was waiting to have her inquire what he meant. She asked her next question with less hesitation.

"What sort of a scene?"

"Sance went to see Blood about breeding his mare. He didn't get any answer when he first knocked at the door of Blood's apartment— I don't know whether I've told you, but he's got quite a nice one, as such places go, fixed up on the second floor at the back of the Hathaway boarding house. Finally Sance tried the door and it wasn't locked, so he walked in. He didn't see anyone at first, but he went along into the next room and there he came full upon Blood in bed with Durice Reno. And this was about three o'clock in the afternoon! . . . Of course, there's nothing wrong about taking a siesta," Gervais added with a grin. "You know I like to do it myself, and to have a certain young lady with me at the time. But mostly men who feel a nap's incomplete without feminine company lock themselves in before they go any further."

"I don't think all that's funny. I think it's revolting, and I don't think you ought to compare——"

"Sorry, honey. I didn't mean to compare, only to explain. But, of course, it would strike you that way. . . . And this was just the beginning of the little episode I started to describe. Do you want me to go on or not?"

"I don't know. Yes, I reckon I do."

"Well, Blood finally roused himself enough to sit up in bed and curse, and just then someone else knocked on the door. Blood couldn't very well get up and go to it, because you see he didn't have much of anything on, and he couldn't nudge Durice and ask her to go, for the same reason. I'll say it must have been damn awkward. Here he was swearing at Sance for stumbling in on him, and he had to choose between having someone else, he didn't know who, do the same thing, or asking Sance to get out, shutting the bedroom door behind him, and stalling off the next visitor for a few minutes."

"And which did he decide to do?"

"He didn't do either, because the next visitor also got impatient and burst in, just the way Sance had. And this next visitor was Déette, the youngest girl in the no-count Reno family. She's just a child, but about as tough as they come—about as handsome, too, in a wild, pagan way. Durice is mighty good-looking, herself—all these worthless Renos are. The two sisters must have been quite a sight, together—Durice sitting up in the bed, with a considerable gap between the covers and her hair, and Déette swearing and stamping around in her dirty rags."

He paused, and for the first time since their marriage, Merry felt a swift thrust of misery. During the days when Gervais was in France, she had sometimes suffered such pangs. For all her simplicity, she knew that men, being only human, could not always withstand fleshly temptations, even when they tried, and that they did not always try when such temptations were not only almost inescapable but enticingly presented. Besides, though she had told herself and convinced the world that she trusted him completely, her own hold on the man she adored was then too tenuous to give her a sense of security. But never since he had so urgently entreated her to marry him and she had consented, had she doubted his wholehearted devotion. She did not really doubt it now. Nevertheless, for a moment she could not help feeling, from something in his voice, that he almost envied his overseer the stolen sight of that beautiful nude girl, and her wild wicked little sister. Reluctantly she realized that even the happiest marriage could not wholly change or subdue every primitive male instinct and craving, and she wished, desperately, that her own body were still beautiful, that maternity had not engulfed her so fast and so completely. Her anxiety and her regret were both ephemeral; the thrust of misery was nothing more than a swift stab, gone almost as quickly as it had come. But afterwards there was a little ache where the sharp pain had been, and every now and then she was conscious of it.

"Déette had been sent to get Durice," she heard Gervais saying now, the tone which had so disquieted her gone from his voice again. He was telling her a story, that was all—a shocking story, but a spirited one, which she had assured him she wanted to hear. "Déette said that Paw had been took bad, that he needed Durice to help nurse him. Vina, she wasn't no use to him, because she was in the bed herself. The quack she went to after Blood got through with her hadn't done such a good job. She was right sick, and if she died, there was going to be hell to pay. Durice had better watch out. If she didn't, she'd be in the same sort of trouble as Vina, and if that happened, there'd be shooting instead of doctoring. She was to come back with Déette, straightaway, or sick or well, Paw would get up and come after Blood with his gun."

"Do you mean to tell me that this—this girl stood there and said all those things to her own sister with those two men in the room?"

"Sure. And a lot more I haven't told you, too. Finally Blood laughed in an ugly way, and said Durice could go, if she was needed for sickness in the family, but that if she went, Déette had better stay and do for him; he was ready to bet a smart kid like her would be real handy around the house. At that point Sance couldn't stand it any longer. He said he'd never paid Blood any mind before, but he took hold of Déette and shoved her out of the bedroom, calling back to Durice that he would wait for her to dress and take them both to the Faith estate himself. I reckon there were some pretty harsh words exchanged between him and Blood before he left, but he finally got both girls away all right. I don't know how long Durice will stay at home, but I think Blood'll hesitate before he tries to lay his dirty hands on Déette again. For the next year or two anyway. Sance is good with a gun himself, and Blood knows it. It's time someone stood up to that scoundrel. I'm glad Sance had the guts to do it and I've told him so."

Gervais got up and walked to the window. A hard rain was falling, pouring in sheets from the shrubbery, overflowing the old sugar kettles used as garden ornaments and spattering on the ground. Gervais gazed gloomily out at the downpour, the scene he had just been describing already fading from his mind.

"This rain is going to raise hell with the planting," he said. "When you take a hundred people out of the fields, all at once, you get behind with it mighty quick. But Fletcher's getting along fine with the inside of the cooperage. I think I'll swim over there and have a look at the work. Anything I can do for you before I go out, honey?"

"You might see if you can find Creassy for me. She hasn't been here all evening, and she left quite a little pressing undone."

Merry was still eating two meals a day at the Big House, as Madame d'Alvery had expressed a preference for this arrangement, even though Gervais seldom came back from the mill for them. But Creassy continued to bring morning coffee to her mistress, and was theoretically on duty at the *garçonnière* for personal service at all times, except during the night. Until lately she had been faithfulness itself in her attendance, and therefore Merry had been inclined to view her recent derelictions leniently. But Gervais' quick temper was immediately roused by his wife's words.

"Didn't I tell you! She's off somewhere with Amen. I'll find her all right, and bring her back here in short order."

"Don't scold her, Gervais. You know how devoted she's been to me ever since we were married. It's only these last few days that I haven't been able to depend on her."

"Don't *scold* her? I ought to switch her! That's what my grandfather would have done, in a case like this. I'm sorry it isn't practical any longer. That's the only thing stopping me."

He turned up his collar, pulled his hat down over his ears and flung himself out of the *garçonnière* without even stopping for the customary kiss. The house servants, with the exception of Dinah and Lucie, were all quartered in a long plain building that stood at right angles to the Big House, behind the Satsuma trees. On the ground floor were a laundry, wine cellars and general storerooms; above them, a row of cubicles. Gervais strode off towards this building, his feet sinking into the soggy grass at every step, and then splashed through the puddles which surrounded the quarters. Throwing the door open, he called loudly, first to Creassy and then to Amen. Lethe, who was in the laundry, put down the frilled baby dress she was ironing, and came forward quietly, speaking in her usual gentle way.

"Ain't neither of 'em here, Mr. Gervais. Does you want somethin' Ah could do fo' you?"

"You can go to the *garçonnière* straight off and stay there till I find Creassy. You don't know where she is, I suppose?"

"No suh, Ah sho' doesn't. Ah ain't seed her since dinner time."

Gervais did not feel convinced that Lethe was telling the truth, but he knew that there would be no use in arguing the point with her. Besides, the culprits could not be far off. If it had been a pretty day, they would unquestionably have "taken the levee"; in this downpour, however, they would have been drenched to the skin before they could enjoy the delights of privacy. From the quarters Gervais went to the stables; but these were empty, too, except for one brood mare who looked at him, above the opening of her box stall, with large reproachful eyes. By this time his rage had mounted to such a pitch that he was ready to ring the plantation bell and institute a general search. Indeed, he actually started towards the mule shed with this drastic action in mind. But as he passed the chicken house, he caught a glimpse of color through an opening in it that did not seem to belong there, and almost instantly he connected it with Creassy; a smothered scream confirmed his suspicions. He stepped inside, and confronted the dusky lovers.

They had retreated as far as possible into a corner, but they were not wholly hidden, and realizing that they were caught they separated at once, and came forward, looking shamefaced, but speaking plausibly and simultaneously.

"Lou Ida, she say she need more aigs for trifle tonight. She done sent me out to de hen house to gadder dem for her, Mr. Gervais."

"Ah done come out here to help Amen, Mr. Gervais, caise Lou Ida, she in such a powerful hurry for dem aigs."

"More eggs for trifle! Hasn't she got half a dozen kids she can send after those, any time? You both better think of some better excuse than that for being here. Get out of here quick, you *trifling* wench! If you don't, I'm likely to shake you till your teeth chatter. And I'll do more than that, if you ever leave your mistress again, when she needs you."

"Yes, suh, Mr. Gervais, Ah's a-gwine fast as Ah can. But Lou Ida, she done send us out to dis here chicken house and dat's a fact."

Without stopping to pick up a single egg or cast a backward glance at Amen, Creassy whipped out of the chicken house with unnatural speed, and ran through the rain, her apron over her head. Amen did not attempt to follow her; nevertheless, he began to edge cautiously towards the door. Gervais seized him savagely by the shoulder.

"Didn't I tell you when I first came home from France, you no-count nigger, that I wouldn' have you taking up with anyone on this place?"

"Ah ain't took up with nobody, Mr. Gervais, suh. Me and Creassy, us is fixin' to get married next week, or de week after at de lates'."

"Then how come you didn't mention it to me until I caught you here? Besides, don't you know Miss Merry can't spare Creassy right now?"

"You's allus in such a hurry, Mr. Gervais, suh, Ah doesn't have no chance to talk to you. An' Creassy, she gwine wait on Miss Merry jes lak she allus done. Gettin' married ain't a-gwine make no difference."

"Yes, she was waiting on Miss Merry this evening, wasn't she? And it won't make any difference, I suppose, when she begins to be sick herself?"

"Us ain't a comin' to de chicken house no mo', Mr. Gervais, Ah promises you dat. Ah reckon it was jes' de rain made us kinda restless. And Creassy, she didn't know Miss Merry needed her right now. She ain't a-gwine to be sick neither. No *suh*."

Amen's expression had changed while he was speaking. His face no longer betrayed fear of his master's wrath; it had assumed the look of injured innocence. Gervais, still seething himself, knew that he could talk until doomsday without getting anywhere. Amen's plausibility was impregnable. Nevertheless, Gervais made one last gesture of authority.

"She better not be," he said sternly. "That is, unless you want me to send you both packing. Of course, Mr. Blood might give you a job. But I won't have you around if you don't behave yourselves."

"Us doesn't belong to Hathaway, Mr. Gervais. Us belongs to Belle Heloise."

"Well, then, remember that. . . . If you and Creassy really want to get married, I shan't try to stop you. Very likely Madame will be glad to give Creassy her wedding dress. And I'll speak to Miss Cresside about some kind of a spread for you. But don't you bother Miss Merry about anything right now. And don't you forget again that if you belong to Belle Heloise you've got to act as if you did."

"No, suh, Mr. Gervais, Ah ain't a-gwine to forget. Ain't nobody forgits Belle Heloise and Hathaway, dey's different."

The look of injured innocence had faded into one of complete blankness. The Negro's voice, respectful throughout the interview, trailed slowly off into silence. He stood still, meeting his master's stern gaze with a vacant stare. But after Gervais had gone out, as Amen stooped to pick up the neglected egg basket, his thick lips parted in a slow smile and he began to sing to himself:

"Dere's no hidin' place down dere,
Dere's no hidin' place down dere,
Oh Ah went to de rock to hide mah face,
De rock cried out, 'No hidin' place,'
Dere's no hidin' place down dere.
Oh de rock cried out, 'Ah'm burnin' too,'
Oh de rock cried out, 'Ah'm burnin' too,'
Ah want to go to hebben as well as you,
Dere's no hidin' place down dere."

CHAPTER XVIII

WHEN THE GRINDING season opened that year, Merry was already so great with child that she found any exertion an effort. Nevertheless, she went with Gervais to see the blessing of the cane crop.

This ceremony always took place the evening before actual work began in the fields and in the factory. All the hands, clothed in their Sunday best, were lined up in long rows beside the field nearest the sugar house, with their carts, mules and implements. Minnie and her driver occupied the most prominent place, but all the carts were decorated with stalks of cane in honor of the great occasion. Everything was in readiness when the Archbishop, robed in full pontificals and carrying his crosier and a censer, began his walk between the rows, followed by lesser clergy; in their train came the "bossman," the overseer, the chief engineer, and various invited guests from town and from neighboring plantations. As he progressed, the Archbishop bestowed his blessing on everyone and everything he passed; he prayed that the workers might be industrious, the mules patient and enduring, the knives sharp, the carts strong, the harvest plentiful. The men stood with bowed heads until he had gone by; they held their hats respectfully in their hands and their dark faces glowed above their clean white clothes. The women, who wore fresh starched dresses, held their children close to them and hushed them if they pointed or asked questions. The Negroes at Belle Heloise were nearly all Baptists, but they held the Catholic Archbishop in very high esteem; they admired his regalia and his following and firmly believed that his blessing would insure a good crop.

Merry was also very much impressed with this ceremony, which she watched with her mother-in-law from a parked car, and somewhat overpowered with the responsibility of entertaining the Archbishop at dinner afterwards, which the rest of the family took easily, as a matter of course. The grinding season appeared doubly significant to her, when she had seen it ushered in with such solemnity; she understood its importance better than she had before, and her eagerness to learn all she could about sugar-making increased apace. Every day she walked over to the mill to watch the cane arrive, hoping that the more she saw the better she would understand the process which heretofore had baffled and mystified her.

The cane came in three ways: in the laden carts drawn by Minnie and Susan, Katie and Mattie, and all the other mules; in the open cars drawn by the funny little engine which pulled them along the narrow gage tracks branching into the various Belle Heloise fields; and by the Y. and M.V. trains, which hauled it in from the distant plantations which had no mills of their own. The Y. and M.V. trains did not especially interest Merry; but she was enchanted with the funny little engine, which bore the name LUCIEN ESTRADE on an oval plate above its fender, and which was equipped with a miniature headlight that gleamed in the darkness when the miniature train came chugging in after nightfall. All plantation engines had names, Gervais told Merry; sometime he intended to have a PHILOGENE D'ALVERY as well as a LUCIEN ESTRADE. And what about a MEREDITH RANDALL, she asked him laughingly. Well, perhaps a MEREDITH D'ALVERY, he said, but not a MEREDITH RANDALL. She was so completely a d'Alvery now that he had forgotten she was ever anything else. And though there was no condescension in his fond voice when he said it, Merry knew that the forgetfulness was intentional.

The October days were clear and dry and warm, and beside the shed where the cane was raked into the carrier the sunshine streamed down in dusty shafts. Usually the cane was brought in from the fields faster than it could be fed to the carrier, and lay in great piles all around it. Dust rose from it as it was dumped on the ground and again when it was lifted up. This dust looked like golden powder, sparkling in the sunshine.

Merry could not understand Gervais' passion for machinery. Only the great black spur wheels, glistening with lubricant, and the strong iron chains turning in endless motion, which she saw when she went inside the mill, were fascinating to her, and this was not on account of their power, but on account of their beauty. She was still confused when Gervais tried to explain their purpose and that of other machinery to her, and he did not encourage her to wander about the mill much these days, in any case. The steps leading from one level to another were very steep and many of them had no hand rails; the floors were slippery in spots with oil and water and syrup; much of the machinery was set in deep pits and the borders around these and the mill floor were often obscure. She might easily stumble or fall, and no one had time to stop and look after her. He would prefer to have her keep out.

But he was pleased with the interest which caused her to take her one walk in the direction of the sugar mill, and he hardly ever failed to watch for her, and to come and speak to her for a moment, when she stood looking at the cane while it came in, her head raised, as if she were breathing in the golden dust with delight, and sniffing the fragrance that poured out through the open doors. There was nothing like it in the world, this sour-sweet smell, redolent of the boiling juice and the lime and sulphur which were its clarifying agents. None of the flowers which bloomed so profusely at Belle Heloise—the cape jasmine, the sweet olive, the orange blossoms—gave forth a perfume comparable to it, in his book. When he saw Merry breathing it in with the golden dust, and knew that for her, too, this was becoming the supreme scent of the place, he was immeasurably proud and pleased. It had been the very breath of his nostrils ever since he was born; his love for it was as natural as it was for the land itself. But to Merry, only a year before, it had still been new and strange. Now she loved it, too, and this mutual love of theirs was one more mighty bond joining them together. Looking at her uplifted face, radiant with ripening maternity, he thought they had never been closer than they were now, not only because of the burden she bore, but also because the harmony of their bodies was finding constant expression in the harmony of their minds and spirits.

He never stayed with her long on these golden afternoons. Plauché, the chief engineer, and Dupuy, the sugar boiler, did not leave the mill at all during the grinding season; they stayed on duty for indefinite hours and snatched a little sleep as they could in small makeshift rooms, Plauché's on the mill floor and Dupuy's on the pan floor. Gervais was almost equally constant in his supervision; the days when he had come to have mid-morning coffee with Merry at her bedside were now only part of a rapturous past. He slipped from her side before daylight and did not come back to her until the last watch began at midnight, having hastily eaten his dinner and supper at the boarding house. She waited up for him, keeping the open fire burning brightly in their living room, and over the hot toddy which she had prepared, they talked together briefly, before he stripped off his clothes and fell into a dead sleep. And this talk was always limited and one-sided. "The Delco got out of order again today. Damn if I don't think the old-fashioned lanterns and flares were better. . . . There's been a choke on the crusher—too much cane fed to the mill," he would say in his edgy voice. "These things ought not to happen." Or, speaking still more irritably, "A chain broke on the cane carrier this afternoon and that meant a thirty-minute delay. Every delay of that sort means a loss of money, and with the price of sugar dropping the way it is, we can't afford to take any kind of a loss." Sugar was now selling at about thirteen cents, half what it had brought when he and Merry took their prodigal trip to New Orleans and began their extravagant program of restoration and expansion on the plantation. He did not tell her he realized now that he had plunged ahead too rashly, but she knew that the fear of financial embarrassment must be a constantly gnawing worry. He seldom asked her what she had been doing, and sometimes he did not go in to look at the twins for several nights running. Neither did he go anywhere else. Sunday was just like any other day for a planter during the grinding season, he told Merry, though formerly he had been meticulous about taking her to Mass. He played no poker, he asked none of his political cronies to the house, he did not go to Izzy's to seek them out. The mill and the fields constituted his world.

Even when Mr. Harding passed through Baton Rouge on his way to New Orleans, Gervais could hardly be persuaded to join the group invited to meet the special train at Anchorage and accompany the party of the President Elect across the river. Merry, for once overcoming her shyness and self-consciousness, had been eager to accept the invitation to membership on the Ladies' Committee which was to present Mrs. Harding with an elaborate floral offering and spend with her the brief period which her husband would allocate to the local politicians; otherwise Gervais might actually have declined to go. At least, that was what he said at first, insisting that the care of his crops meant much more to him than meeting any Black Republican. Later he seemed to derive considerable satisfaction in helping to plan the arrangements for the visit, and after it had taken place, in talking about the smooth way everything had run. It was his idea, for instance, that Fire Chief Bogan should be notified by telephone as soon as the ferry had left the

Anchorage landing; that the fire bells should immediately ring twenty taps and the whistles blow along the river, just as they always did on New Year's Eve. In that way everyone would know the train was coming and assemble at the depot ready to see the President Elect; it was important there should be no delay about this, for he could stop only long enough to greet the general public from the rear platform of his private car. Gervais was greatly gratified because all his ideas worked out so well, and because Merry had such a nice homey chat with Mrs. Harding. Personally, he was ready to admit he would never have believed that Harding had so much personal charm and such a distinguished presence, or that he could speak so soundly and convincingly. Gervais quoted the President Elect frequently, saying that he held exactly the same views.

" 'I like to think that one of the lasting things that came out of the Great War and the sacrifices which were made in that War was the wiping out of sectional lines'—that's what I like to think too, Merry. 'I have an abiding faith that great things are coming to America, and that the whole country is to share in this great achievement.' I'm glad I heard Harding say that. It's just what needs to be said. It can't be stressed too often."

The glow of his general satisfaction lasted a long time. However, the Harding visit marked the only departure from his rule that nothing should take him off the plantation and that no one should interfere with his work there. The year before it had not been like this. Gervais had made excuses, to himself and to Merry, to come home for his meals, to linger in Merry's company, to discuss their hopes and plans and to tell her—and show her—that he adored her. The crop had not meant so much to him as it did now. This was partly because it had been a better one, perhaps; the stand of cane was not nearly so good this year; the effects of the mosaic disease were showing up all too plainly. But Merry knew that his present preoccupation could not be wholly explained on these grounds or that of financial involvement, and sometimes, as she lay alone in the darkness, she would think longingly of the time when her husband had been so wholly her lover. She reminded herself that her advanced pregnancy had set limits on their intimacy, but this excuse was inadequate, too; it was a time for tenderness, now more than ever, even if it were not a time for passion. Honestly, as she was honest in all things, Merry admitted to herself that Gervais would have left her alone, even if there had been no imminent prospect of another child.

There had been no recurrence of the brief pangs which the vision of the Renos had roused; unfearful of the power of any other woman and too generous-hearted for jealousy, Merry had moments of panic because she knew that the land had reclaimed her husband for its own and that perennially it would continue to do so. In her loneliness she could not always suppress her resentment of this. But the bad moments came only during the long nights, when she was listening and waiting interminably for the whistle blasts to announce the change of watch. They never came when she stood in the dusty sunshine beside the mill, looking at the cane as it came in, and knowing that at any moment Gervais would join her. At these times she was conscious, as he was, of their kinship of interest and purpose, and of the tie which bound them together, strengthened because of this kinship. She knew, indubitably, that they were no longer dependent, as they once had been, and as lesser loves remained, on the satisfaction of the flesh. After the harvest was in and the child was born, the land would give Gervais back to her and she would be ready to receive him. Their reunion would be one of spontaneous gladness. She could afford to wait for it, in rapt anticipation, because the interval which marked their separation was in itself a fulfillment.

Most of the men who came and went while Merry watched the coming of the cane were familiar to her now, and they exchanged brief and friendly greetings with her as they hurried to and from the factory. "Looks like plenty of sugar in the cane, Miss Merry," Plauché would say in a satisfied voice. "The boss is bound to give me those new filter presses I want next year." Sometimes it was new juice pumps he mentioned instead; Plauché was always after more and more replacement, Gervais told her; but he was usually good-natured about doing without when he could not get it. Sance, on the other hand, had a violent temper. Sometimes he came dashing up on horseback to see what had become of his carts, and if these were drawn up in long lines, awaiting their chance to unload, he yelled at Plauché in unbridled rage. "Look here, Chief, what's the big idea playing hell with my work like this?" he bellowed at such times. "The whole damn cane-loading crew's had to stop." Then he would pull off his sombrero and add apologetically to Merry, "You must excuse me, Miss Merry; but I've got to have those carts in the fields. If I don't, I might just as well lay off every last one of my niggers."

Merry liked Lezine Sance and he liked her; usually she managed to say something soothing if noncommittal before she turned to greet Seraphine, who was apt to come by at about the same time, carrying a big armful of mish bread. Seraphine was the wife of Tiphane, the night watchman, and she operated the boarding house. "What are you giving the boys for supper tonight, Seraphine?" Merry would ask her. "Beef stew. But they're getting mighty tired of that. We'll be having cooler weather pretty soon, then I kin give 'em fresh pork. If any of the hogs should get out of the yard, don't you worry none about 'em, Miss Merry. They won't be botherin' you long." Seraphine would have her laugh in which Merry would join, and then she would lumber on, pausing once to call back over her shoulder, "Want I should send you over some hot cakes when I make 'em tomorrow mornin', Miss Merry? The new people who've just come in, they say they just can't get enough of my hot cakes." "No, thanks, Seraphine," Merry would call back. "I know they're wonderful, but you've got enough to do feeding the big crew you have now without bothering to send goodies to the Big House." There was jealousy between Seraphine and Lou Ida, and Merry knew better, by this time, than to fan it into flame. But with the insatiable hunger of healthy pregnancy she secretly yearned for Seraphine's cakes, which were better than Lou Ida's.

Besides the workmen who came and went, there were frequent visitors from outside. The young people of the locality had a fad for making up "sugar-house parties" and going in groups to the plantations up and down the River Road. The year before, such visitors had been discouraged at Belle Heloise because of Cresside's critical illness. Word of this had gone around and the sight-seers had considerably stopped at Hathaway Hall or Hackberry Lodge instead. Grover Blood made a great to-do about important visitors. He never failed to escort them through the factory himself, followed by a small black boy bearing coffee on a silver tray, so that the dignitaries could refresh themselves whenever they wished. But he was disdainful of lesser lights, and barely tolerated sugar-house parties, while Boylston, though courteous, was ill at ease—and showed it—with the free and easy youngsters who made them up. So the popular preference was for Belle Heloise, and now that they knew they were welcome again, the young people flocked back there. Usually they brought baskets with them, eating under the cane shed. Before going to the mill they stopped to snatch stalks of cane from the carrier and lay bets with each other as to who could chew it the fastest. The cane was tender and brittle and juicy; the boys peeled it for the girls, and some of the merrymakers showed surprising skill in making away with large quantities of it in record time. After they tired of this pastime, they went inside, taking tin cups with them from which to drink the sweet juice as it poured from the crusher; without such a drink, the visit would have been thought incomplete, and the more daring members of the party also carried hip-pocket flasks and added a jigger or two of whisky to the juice. If the visitors happened to be on good terms with Dupuy, they also brought loaves of mish bread and clusters of oranges, still on the branches of the trees from which they had been plucked, and pocketsful of pecans, trying to time their visit just when a strike was ending. If they were successful in this, and if Dupuy were in a propitious mood, he would put the foodstuffs on his paddle and thrust it into the boiling syrup; coated with this, the bread and oranges became sweetmeats of rare delicacy, to be savored at leisure, often by couples who retreated to obscure corners and did not join their companions until they were dragged from their hiding places, to the tune of a good deal of teasing. The group finally departed in high spirits, the sound of their laughter and singing floating back to the mill as the truck in which they were riding went jolting down the sugar-house road.

If there were friends of hers in such groups, as there often were, and if they arrived in the afternoon, Merry went with them into the sugar house. Miss Mittie came often on Saturdays, bringing riotous school children with her, and Merry tried to keep popcorn on hand for these youngsters; they loved to take it into the mill with them, crunching it as they rushed around, "popping" the paper bags afterwards. Hazel Wallace, who had worked with Merry in Goldenberg's store, was another familiar visitor. Hazel's fortunes were rising. She was Mr. Goldenberg's private secretary now, and she had a steady suitor, Al Ferrar, who worked in the advertising department. Previously Hazel had never come freely to Belle Heloise; she had always been a little overawed by the Big House and by Madame Mère, and she had not even made any attempt to see the renovated *garçonnière*. But by the stacked cane, with Al at her side, she was at ease and Merry was, too. Al gave one arm to Hazel and the other to Merry and they all entered the sugar mill together.

"Gosh, that looks just like a roller coaster, doesn't it?" Al exclaimed, watching the carrier as it sent the stalks endlessly on and on through the giant crushers which shredded the cane more and more finely, while the liquid poured from it in a waterfall to the juice pan below. A powerful Negro, wielding a long-handled wooden rake, stood by the juice pan skillfully keeping the flow unclogged, while a jolly looking little colored boy reached under the mill with a can on the end of a long pole and collected a cupful of juice. Having done this, he poured the contents of the cup into a numbered tin pail on a shelf near by and ran off with it toward some unseen destination.

"What are those buckets for?" Hazel asked, diverted from the roller coaster.

"Samples. That was one of our best sample boys. He's taking some juice into the laboratory to be tested. We can go there later on too, if you like."

Merry knew that Gervais would not mind having her walk around with Hazel and Al, because they would watch carefully and see that she did not slip. But Hazel was not interested in the laboratory. She had reluctantly taken a course in chemistry at high school and the very word laboratory still filled her with aversion. Merry made another suggestion.

"Then let's walk back to the furnaces where the bagasse is burned. I think they're a beautiful sight."

"Bagasse?" Al inquired in a puzzled voice. He had only recently come from New Jersey, and all the processes of the sugar mill were mysterious and exciting to him.

"Yes. That's what's left of the cane, you know, when all the juice has been squeezed out. For a long time people used to throw most of it away—they thought it was good for nothing except fertilizer, and Fabian still swears by it for his camellias and gardenias. Then they found out it made wonderful fuel. Come, let me show you. It goes into the furnaces from the top."

They walked on towards the rear of the mill, past the glistening black spur wheels which Merry admired so much and the fast-spinning fly wheels. As they advanced, she indicated a machine shop at their right, saying, with pride, that all the repair work was done on the place at a great saving of time and money. At their left a pile of rubberoid material, from which circles the size of a stove lid had been cut, cluttered the pavement at one point, and Merry explained that this stuff was sheet packing used in the engines, that some of the cylinders must have just been repacked and that there had not been time to pick up the leavings. They passed a tank, too, filled with frothy liquid, which Merry told them was raw juice. They had all agreed that the carrier reminded them of a roller coaster, but now they disagreed about the contents of this tank. It looked like the white of an egg, Hazel said, ready to go on a giant floating island; more like whipped cream, Al thought. Merry stood out for ocean foam. They stood discussing it and joking about it for some time, and then Merry reminded the others that they had started out to see the burning bagasse, and they continued their walk towards the rear, where three gigantic brick furnaces stood in a row. Above the iron doors near the floor level, a round opening showed in each; and through these the leaping flames and the falling bagasse were plainly visible. The bagasse fell fast, in a shower of tiny flakes, gilded by the light from the fire below; the flames became quivering streaks of crimson as they soared. The whole effect was magical but satanic in its splendor.

"Gosh!" Al exclaimed again, in sincere but inarticulate admiration. "Gosh, I never saw anything to equal that, not anywhere."

"There isn't anything to equal that, not anywhere," Merry said proudly. "Anywhere except on sugar plantations, of course. There's a shed in the rear where the surplus bagasse is kept, and you can see it piled up there, if you want to. But that's all it is, just a pile. I think perhaps I ought to have let you see the rest of the mill first, before I brought you to the furnaces. I'm afraid you won't find the tanks and the mixers especially thrilling either. Why not come back to the *garçonnière* with me for some coffee and some cherry bounce? You can have a look at the twins, too."

Merry kept cherry bounce as well as popcorn constantly on hand these days; freshly dripped coffee and homemade fruit cake were always in readiness, too, and usually pralines and new-salted pecans. Her manner of serving refreshments had not the spectacular quality of the notorious Mr. Blood's, but her hospitality was unstinted and spontaneous. It was something of a problem to get the pecans picked, she told Hazel and Al, as they all went towards the house; there were more than three hundred trees on the plantation, and the nuts, falling in the first cool wind, had to be gathered during the grinding season; so none of the hands from the quarters were free for the work. Fortunately the house servants liked to pick; they were allowed to do it on shares, and they were out in the grove every minute they could get. Cresside liked it, too; she herself picked and also supervised the Negroes, taking the twins to the grove in their big perambulator, and insisting that it was easy to keep them amused there. There was a full crop this fall, much better than last; Gervais had told Merry it was seldom this was especially good, two years in succession. The pecans looked beautiful, shining as if they had been coated with wax as they lay on the dark ground. Perhaps the next time Hazel and Al came out, they would like to go to the grove themselves. They were welcome to all the nuts they wanted. . . .

Hazel said they would be glad to pick pecans, pleased because Merry seemed to take it for granted they were coming again. But for the moment her attention was fully engaged with the *garçonnière*. Merry took her two guests through it from top to bottom, pleased beyond measure at their outspoken admiration of her success with interior decorating. Then, settling them before the living-room fire, she served the cherry bounce herself, in small ruby-colored glasses, and afterwards Creassy came in, bringing the coffee and fruit cake and nuts on a spacious silver tray. Dinah followed with the twins, who had just been brought in from the grove, their cheeks rosy from the crisp air; and Cresside dropped by for a few minutes, too, supplementing Merry's spread with a proffer of cigarettes, which Merry had forgotten, as usual, because she did not smoke herself. Hazel had always assumed that Cresside d'Alvery was very high-hat, because when she first came back from Convent, she had trained with such a fast crowd, and because since then she had kept so much to herself, until just lately. Not that the poor girl could help that, Hazel admitted tardily, when she had been laid up from such a bad accident; just the same it was a pleasant surprise to find her as simple and friendly as Merry, who did not put on airs either, now that she was Mrs. Gervais d'Alvery instead of Meredith Randall. Cresside had on a pullover sweater and a short woolen skirt, both somewhat the worse for wear, and her hair was all blown around because she had gone out in the grove hatless. Hazel would have felt she must apologize, if visitors had caught her looking like that, and she smoothed down the skirt of her spotless new beige afternoon dress and glanced at her matching pumps and handbag with a feeling of secret satisfaction. But Cresside did not even seem conscious of her old clothes and tousled hair. She sat around and smoked and chatted and drank coffee until she happened to glance at the clock, and said hell's bells, she had no idea it was so late. Fabian would be there any minute to take her to see Annette Kellerman in "What Women Love." He thought she ought to find out. Would the rest excuse her? It had been grand seeing Hazel again and meeting Al.

Merry had enjoyed seeing Hazel and Al, too, and when Gervais came in that night, she tried to tell him about their visit, over the hot toddy. But Gervais had a fresh worry. It was all he could talk about before he went to sleep.

"We had to slow the mill down today because the centrifugals couldn't keep out of the way of the pans."

"Why not, Gervais?"

"We're getting bastard grains in the sugar. There'll be hell to pay if we can't get rid of them."

"I don't think I know what you mean by bastard grains, *cher*. Have you told me about them before?"

"Probably not. We didn't have any trouble to speak of with them last year. In fact, I can't remember that we've ever had much trouble with them at Belle Heloise before."

"But what *are* they?"

He closed his eyes, wearily. "They're small-sized grains that appear in the masse cuite after the desired amount of granulation has already been secured. If you don't get rid of them, they clog the small holes in the centrifugals and the sugar just won't dry because the molasses can't pass out through these holes."

"But what causes them in the first place?"

"You're asking an awful lot of questions tonight, aren't you, Merry?"

"Only because I'm interested. Only because everything that troubles you or makes you happy is important to me."

"I know. It's extraordinary how quick you've caught on, too. I didn't mean to snap you up. Oh, you were asking me. . . . Well, the bastard grains might be Dupuy's fault. He may have been careless in graining the pan. Possibly he didn't take in enough grain to start the strike. That's the usual cause of this special kind of trouble. Then again it's possible that he and Plauché have been fighting——"

"But why should they?"

"Oh, no special reason that I know of. The sugar boiler and the chief engineer just seem to be natural enemies and Dupuy's always picking a quarrel about something. Plauché's naturally good-natured, as you know, but once in a while Dupuy gets his goat. If that's what happened lately, Plauché may have slowed down the water pump. That would have caused the pans to heat up and melt away some of the original grains. If the trouble does lie between Plauché and Dupuy and I can't get it patched up, I'll lose a lot more money."

He was not saying a lot of money, he was saying a lot *more*. So he was losing it right along, losing more than he could afford. And sugar had gone down another cent. For a moment Merry sat still, fingering her pearls. Then she folded her hands in her lap, looking down at her beautiful solitaire. She ought to have told Gervais in the first place that she did not want these baubles, she said to herself reproachfully. She ought not to have let him see how much it would mean to her to get away from the Big House, and have him to herself in the *garçonnière* either. But it would not do any good to tell him so now. The money advanced on credit was all spent, and they could not get it back. It would sound as if she were reproaching him if she tried to talk about it. Besides, she had begun to think about something else, something which perhaps she might speak of, and find out if her mind had reflected his, as it did so often.

248

"Strange, isn't it, that this problem should have arisen now, when you've never had it before?"

"Yes, it is." They looked at each other for a moment, both falling silent. Then Gervais got up and put his arm around her. "Don't you get to seeing symbols in everything, like the niggers do," he said. "Come on, honey, I'm dead on my feet. Let's go to bed."

As the season advanced, Gervais was able to take the grinding more easily in his stride, in spite of his varied worries. If the crop was not as good as the year before, at least the weather was better; that more or less evened things up. One warm mellow day succeeded another in leisurely succession. The Satsumas hung in golden balls on the orange trees by the house, and in Angus Holt's garden the golden cosmos and marigolds, flowers of all Saints, bloomed in riotous profusion. The leaves were turning, too, and the moss that draped the oaks shone in the sun as it did at no other season; Merry called them "the gold and silver trees." There was no rain and no frost. Labor was plentiful, for many returning soldiers had found no regular jobs awaiting them, and Gervais was able to enlarge his force of factory workers from their ranks. Moreover, women as well as men turned out in prodigious numbers and the fields were full of cutters; their bright garments dotted the landscape, their broad knives sang in the sunshine.

The improvements Gervais had made in the mill were contributing to higher efficiency, too. One day the shaft on the Walsh Feeder rake, which swept the cane from the cars to the carrier, suddenly snapped, and there was a long delay in consequence; but this was the only major breakdown. Merry sensed the lessened strain in her husband's manner and conversation. He was neither exhausted nor nervous when he came in at midnight, and he stopped speaking solely about mishaps and expense. Instead he would say contentedly, "The mill ran well today—no stops of any kind," and eventually, with still greater satisfaction, "The sucrose is fine, and we have the cane deliveries in grand shape."

"Couldn't you take things a little easier then?" Merry asked.

"I can't really let up until the whistle blows for the last time. But I thought I might take part of a day off, at least."

"That would be wonderful," Merry began. But he interrupted her.

"Perhaps you'd better let me finish. I didn't mean to spend it at home. I meant to go hunting, if you wouldn't mind too much."

"Why should I mind?" Merry asked. The mental vision of long hours with Gervais had faded as soon as it was formed. But she spoke staunchly. "Were you planning to go 'possum hunting with Cresside?" she asked. During the last few weeks Cresside, who was getting around more and more, had been out several times in mixed groups of six or eight, starting as soon as it was dark and spending most of the night in the woods. The girls as well as the men wore high-laced boots, corduroy breeches and heavy windbreakers on these expeditions and

249

carried flashlights and lanterns. They always took a black boy with them who wore a carbide light fastened to his forehead for the purpose of "shining" the 'possum's eyes and holding the bag into which it was put after it was shaken from the tree. They also took two or three dogs who first trailed the 'possum and eventually finished him off. Apparently the hunters spent hours at a time sitting around a camp fire while they waited for the dogs to find the trail, and wiener roasts, hot chocolate, and carefree and casual singing were also features of the night's entertainment. As Cresside described it all afterwards, it sounded very thrilling to Merry, who had never done hunting of any kind. But when she asked her interested question, Gervais answered her contemptuously.

"Lord, no! I outgrew that kind of sport years ago. I was thinking of going on a wildcat hunt. There's a Negro named Pinkie Baker who lives over on the other side of town, who's got the best hunting dogs around here, and every now and then he lends them to Parker. The Governor likes cat hunting. He doesn't always follow the run, but he enjoys listening to the dogs after the cat's been jumped. Parker's taking Pinkie's dogs and striking out to Boylston's early Saturday morning—the hunt going to start from there. The Governor's bringing Fabian along with him, and they'd be glad to stop by for me. Happy Sevier and Ferd Claiborne are going together in another car. And Harvey Lawrason's at Boylston's already. He's driven over from Livingston Parish and brought his own dogs with him, some in the car and some in a trailer—people really go in for hounds where he lives, near Denham Springs. . . . That'll make a party of seven or eight all told and it's a good crowd. I haven't seen Lawrason to amount to anything since I got back from France."

He was making no effort to conceal his normal masculine yearning for congenial male companionship. Merry did not let him down by voicing her equally normal feminine disappointment that he preferred to spend his first time off with these friends instead of with her.

"Parker's been out with Boylston two or three times already," Gervais went on. "It seems that last year when Boylston was hunting, he had a rather peculiar experience. Cresside said he'd told her about it. I don't know whether he told you, too, or whether she did."

"No," Merry answered, leaning over to refill the toddy glasses from a pitcher that stood on a hob by the fire.

"Well, his gyp Diana started a trail, and when he caught up with her, she was standing on her haunches, baying in front of a hollow tree with a big hole in it. Boylston asked her what she was doing, hunting 'possums when she knew he wanted to hunt cats! It's hard to believe, but you talk to these hounds just as if they were humans, and when you start out you tell them what you're after, and they don't trail anything else that day. He'd said 'Scat!' to Diana, the first thing after they'd left the house, and it wasn't like her to make a mistake. She answered him by sticking her head into the hole and when she took it out, her face was all scratched up. So Boylston looked in the hole himself, and sure enough, there was a big cat. He drew back mighty quick, and the cat jumped out and ran like mad, with Diana after her. Boylston says he doesn't know how he happened to look in the hole again, but he did, and there were four kittens! He took up two of them and nicked pieces out of their ears, and then he took up the other two and cut their tails off. Afterwards he called Diana back, so that the cat would have a chance to raise them. All this year he's been hunting the marked cubs. Of course, they're grown cats now. . . . What's the matter, am I boring you?"

Merry could not bear to see the suffering of any living creature, or even to hear about it. She had flinched when Gervais had mentioned the mutilated kittens, and the happy expression on her face clouded. But she knew there was no use in telling Gervais, or any other born hunter, how she felt. Even Cresside, who was so phenomenally kind to the twins, felt no compunctions about killing doves.

"No, you're not boring me," she said quickly. "I think that's a very interesting story, Gervais. Has Charles caught any of those marked cubs?"

"Yes, he caught one when he was hunting alone, and one the first time Parker went out with Pinkie's dogs. Now he wants to round up the others, and I'd like to be there when it happens."

"Naturally you would. I'm glad Charles has invited you. I'm glad you feel you can go," Merry said, again filling the toddy glasses from the hob.

It was a little earlier than usual when he left her two mornings later, but she was accustomed, by now, to having him slip away in the darkness, without a word or a caress. She knew that his silent departure signified neither negligence nor indifference, but a genuine desire not to disturb her; and usually, though she was aware of his leaving, she drifted back to sleep again almost immediately. Now she had been vaguely wakeful and restless for some time already. She snuggled down among the pillows, after the car had rattled over the cattle gap and the dogs had stopped barking, but she could not seem to get comfortable. For a few minutes she continued to shift her position, with increasing discomfort. Then a sharp dagger-like pain shot without warning through her vitals and trailed away into numbness.

"It can't be that," she said aloud, in bewilderment. "It isn't time yet—not for two weeks at least." But she turned over, and tried to switch on the electricity. Evidently the Delco was out of order again, however, so she lighted her bedside candle, and looked at the little clock standing on the night table beside her. It was exactly four o'clock. She lay down again, without extinguishing the candle, and kept her eyes on the moving hands. At twenty minutes past four the dagger-like pain stabbed her again, harder this time. Instead of leaving her numb, it left her spent. She gave herself a few moments to recover from it;

then, putting on felt slippers and a warm woolen robe, she lighted the lamps that were kept in readiness for emergencies, setting one in the window, and taking a lantern, started for the Big House. It loomed darkly before her, surrounded by eerie black trees, and above them the stars had a far frosty look. It was colder than it had been any night during the fall.

"That's why I'm shivering," she told herself, as she hurried forward. "I'm not frightened, I'm just cold. There's nothing to be frightened about. I'll be all right as soon as I get to Dinah. She said it wouldn't be bad this time."

Merry did not deceive herself. She knew that it would be bad, that it had to be. There was no escape from the dreadful hours which lay ahead of her. But she also knew that she had the strength and courage to meet them undefeated, that no woman's life was full and complete without them, any more than it was full and complete without the hours of rapture which had come before them. Remembering these, she found that she could go on. The third pain, like a vicious auger, boring its way through her body, smote her as she reached the gallery. She seized the newel post of the outer stairway, and gripped it hard, smothering a scream. Then, clinging to the railing, she continued to mount the stairs.

CHAPTER XIX

WHEN GOVERNOR PARKER and the two cousins arrived at Hackberry Lodge, the other men were already gathered around a log fire in Charles Boylston's paneled study, smoking and drinking small blacks. All of them, except Happy Sevier, who had on his old army breeches and puttees, and Boylston, who as usual looked as if his whipcord were the recent creation of a London tailor, were wearing high boots over ordinary well-worn trousers. Harvey Lawrason, the wealthy lumberman from Denham Springs, was outstanding in the group. Though slightly stooped, he was so immensely tall that he still towered over all the others, and his huge bony hands had an unmistakable look of power. He had light sandy hair, and light eyelashes which looked so short that even a casual glance from his pale blue eyes had the effect of a stare. Though he was essentially a man's man, numerous women had figured prominently in his life, and current gossip centered around a pretty widow in Baton Rouge; but hunting was his real passion. He had a background of considerable culture, but it suited him to talk as if he were utterly unlettered, and he was a teller of tall tales, introducing most of them with the strange expression,

"Which-I-God"! and speaking in a high drawling voice. He was in the midst of a story now.

"Those Walkers of yours look all right to me, Charlie, but I want to see 'em in action. Which-I-God, you can't tell nothing about a dog by looking at him! You take Martin's Choice. There ain't a setter that's worth his salt that don't trace his blood back to him, one way or another, and yet, he was the sorriest looking bird dog that ever nailed a covey down wind. He had a tail a big rat wouldn't have been ashamed of, and a pinched-in face, but Lord-in-the-mountains! what a nose and bottom! That dog could run his legs off to the elbow and still go after birds. I mind the time Sam Cannell brought him to our little old field trial in Clinton. Well sirs, I got a thick-headed brother-in-law that thinks he knows all about bird dogs—I ain't apologizing for him; a man ain't responsible for what his sister marries. He used to pay a mint of money for his dogs and brag of what world beaters he had in his kennels. So me and Sam rigged it up how he was going to take Martin's Choice over to my brother-in-law's and offer to sell the dog to him for five dollars. 'Course, everybody knows Martin's Choice was open champion that year, and five thousand dollars couldn't have bought him. Likely his owner would get more than that out of stud fees. Well sirs, we did it. And my brother-in-law give that sorry-looking pup one disgusted look and says, 'Take that thing off my property, whatever it is. You claim it's a setter all right, but it looks to me like it got a sight of muskrat blood in it. Go on, take it out of here, whatever it is, it might be catching.' Well, it just goes to show, there was somebody who thought you could tell all about a dog by looking at him, turning down a chance to buy the national open champion for five dollars."

While Lawrason drawled on, without commanding undivided attention, a drowsy, slatternly, colored girl, who had on a cloth with flapping ends fastened loosely at the back of her head instead of the customary neat *tignon,* was passing the coffee in a haphazard way. A man's jacket, thrown across her shoulders, partially covered her dingy woolen dress; but she looked cold as well as sullen, and Fabian felt sorry for her. He spoke to her kindly as she stopped to serve him.

"Pretty early to be up on a cold morning, isn't it, Tilda?"

"Sho' is, Mistah Fabian. Don't seem like it's worth while for us'uns to bed ourselves, iffen us has to stir agin so soon."

"We've got to get started early if we're going to hit a trail by daybreak," Boylston said, rather sharply. The remark was addressed to Fabian, but it was obviously aimed at Tilda, who gave her master a resentful glance as she shuffled off with the tray. Boylston paid his servants higher wages than anyone else on the River Road; but he had never learned to make them like him. "I don't want to hurry any of you," he said, speaking this time to the company at large. "But I think if you've finished your coffee, we ought to be on our way."

The guests gathered up their caps and guns and went out into the yard, where the darkies and the dogs were waiting for them. Pinkie Baker's four black-and-tan hounds—Hayes, Crook, Beulah and Fox—had been left in charge of George Dyer, the Governor's chauffeur, when Parker himself went into the house with Fabian and Gervais. The trailer which Lawrason had brought over from Denham Springs, filled with redbones, was parked close beside the Governor's car, enabling Simeon, Lawrason's man, to pass the time of day, more or less obscenely, with George, whose own conversation was less lurid but who was not above listening. Amos Palfry, Boylston's driver, who had brought out his master's purebred Walkers, tightly tethered, stood a slight distance away from them. Swung over one shoulder he had Ferryboat Bill's handsome horn, which was his insignia of leadership, and which he wore with great pride; and while he waited for the expedition to get underway, he kept admonishing his dogs. Two younger Negroes, Cass and Willie, who also worked for Boylston, and usually went hunting with him when he had a sizable group at Hackberry Lodge, were also standing in the yard, discussing the relative merits of the different types of sports common to the countryside.

"Ah sho' wish dis here was a 'coon hunt us was goin' on, 'stead of a cat hunt."

"Uh, not me. Ah likes cat huntin' fust rate. Squirrel hunts and 'possum hunts, 'ems for ladyfolks much as menfolks. Don't even no dogs go along, squirrel huntin'. How comes you don't like cat huntin' well as 'possum huntin', Willie?"

"Can't eat no cat, can us? Don't get de hides to sell, neither—bossman keeps 'em for hisself to stuff and den feeds de meat to his dogs. Ain't no better eatin' dan 'possum, nor squirrel neither, and dey keeps de pot full pretty near all through de cold. Ah don't mind havin' ladyfolks on de hunt neither. Leastwise Ah don't mind havin' Miss Cresside. She plumb game on rough goin', and Ah seed her shine four 'possums all in de one night. Now Miss Regine, dat's different. Ah can do without ladyfolks like her jes as well as you can."

"Reckon it's Miss Regine done set me against ladyfolks huntin'. Ain't never forget dat night she come out in de woods in dem little high-heeled slippers of hern 'stead of de tall boots Miss Cresside got sense enough to wear. She kept a gettin' stuck in de swamp and a hollerin' after de res', 'Oh, wait a minute! Oh, please come back and get poor little me'!"

Like most Negroes, Cass had a considerable gift for mimicry. He mocked Regine's silly way of speaking so effectively that the other darkies all turned around to listen, grinning with appreciation, and some of them snickered under their breath. Willie grabbed his companion's sleeve.

"Yo' hush yo' mouf, nigger, lessen yo' wants to get us into bad trouble. Don't yo' know Miss Regine done stole Miss Cresside's beau? Ain't none of de d'Alverys forgive her for dat and ain't never goin' to.

254

And dere's Miss Cresside's brother settin' right inside de house dis minute, lak as not to come out while you's talkin'."

The warning had not been given a minute too soon. Just then the door of the house was flung open, and Boylston and his guests came out. Cass and Willie straightened up quickly and came forward respectfully and somewhat shamefacedly. Lawrason, who missed little connected with an outing of this type, glanced at them shrewdly. Then, with his foot on the running board of his own car, he called out to Dyer.

"Good morning, George! How's Beulah today? Hear she didn't do so well on her last hunt."

"Dat's right, Mr. Lawrason, she sho' was confused. But she don't do dat once in a blue moon. Ain't no better trail dog anywhere, 'ceptin' old Hayes, of course. He's got 'em all beat. But you're goin' to see Beulah doin' fine today, too."

"We won't see any of them 'doin' fine' unless we get started pretty soon," Boylston remarked. It always irked him to have his guests stand around, chatting and joking with the Negroes when it was time to be off. "Come on, boys, let's go."

The circle broke up slowly, with some final discussion as to the best division of the guests among the different automobiles. Boylston went with the Governor this time, Gervais with Claiborne and Lawrason, the trailer, packed with barking redbones, in charge of Simeon, attached to their car. Fabian and Happy Sevier followed in one of Boylston's cars, and Amos with Cass and Willie and the Walkers brought up the rear in another. Their route took them over the headland, past the ruins of an old Confederate fort, and the road, cut by the cane carts, was very rough, so that they had to proceed slowly towards the bluffs where they were bound. A little light was beginning to show in the dark sky, paling the stars, but revealing the order and richness of the fields, some already planted with the next season's crop. Parker, peering out over them with his keen, beady eyes, complimented his host on his achievements.

"You've done wonders with this plantation, Boylston. I know the state it was in when you took it over. What yield are you getting to the acre this year?"

"About fifteen tons. Not as much as last year, due to this damn mosaic disease."

"Yes, I'm afraid that's going to play havoc all over the state, and I know it's beginning to show up along the River Road already."

They were leaving the headland, and at a signal from Boylston George stopped the car. They got out near the edge of a field covered with a brownish plant which was just going to seed. Parker stopped to pull up a handful of it.

"Lespedeza!" he said enthusiastically. "So you've got that, too! Nothing like it for cattle and pasture land, in my book! You can't do better than increase your acreage of this, Boylston."

"I'm planning to, Governor, next year."

Parker selected a stalk of Lespedeza from the handful he was still holding and began to chew it reflectively, in much the same way that he chewed tobacco. The two men walked on together towards a pasture overgrown with Cherokee rose, scrub oak and briar thickets, flanked by tall bluffs, where the reddish soil was partially covered with straggly trees. A white frost which gleamed in the pale light coated the bushes and the patches of grass which showed between them; this would disappear with the day, but meantime it gave an effect of eerie loveliness to a scene which in any case would have been peculiarly enticing to the men who had come there.

"Here's the place where Amos saw the cat tracks two days ago," Boylston said. "He'll be along in a minute, but your car makes better time than the rest, Governor." While he was speaking, however, the second car swung into sight and he added, "Here come Claiborne and d'Alvery, though. Claiborne's quite a character, isn't he?"

"I'll say he is. And he has some damn original ideas about the duties of a game warden."

Parker spoke rather drily, and as the others got out of the car and came nearer he called out, "Ferd, could you by any chance spare me some of those birds you've got in your cooler?"

"Birds? I don't get you. What birds, John?"

"You get me all right. I'm talking about those becs my old friend Surget was caught with last week. Somebody took them away from him, but no one's heard what happened to them after that."

"Oh, hell, I'm sure they were preserved for a noble purpose. I'm here to defend Ferd on that score," Fabian said pleasantly. The cars had all arrived in the pasture now, and he had come forward in time to change the drift of a dialogue which had begun to take a serious turn. An angry flush was spreading over Claiborne's face and Parker was no longer speaking jestingly. "Look, we're not any of us here in our professional capacities this morning, are we?" Fabian went on. "We're just so many hunters, and it looks to me as if we're in for some damn good sport."

As he spoke, he motioned towards Simeon, who was just getting the redbones out of the trailer, and to Cass, who had already taken the Walkers from Boylston's car. All these dogs were still held in leash, but Amos now walked over to the Governor's car, releasing old Hayes and Beulah and turning Crook and Fox over to Willie. With the two trail dogs leaping joyously around him, Amos next began to kick vigorously at the bushes, shouting "Scat!" as he did so. Instantly Hayes and Beulah rushed off into the dark thickets, while the other hounds strained impatiently at their leashes, pulling their drivers around over the rough rime-covered pasture. For a few moments the hunters, now ready and eager for action, remained motionless and alert, listening attentively. Then the sound they had been awaiting came to them through the stillness: old Hayes was giving tongue, his deep voice loud and triumphant.

256

"Good for him! He's hit the cold trail in record time!" Lawrason exclaimed. "We're off, aren't we?"

The leashed dogs, freed at last, were already tearing after their leaders, their drivers whooping them on. The other men immediately plunged into the brush after them, and for the next thirty minutes pushed forward with perseverance, "cold trailing" the cat which had fed along the way during the night. The ground was very rough, and Fabian and Happy especially found it hard going. But the thrill of pursuit, even more than the cool, crisp air, was a powerful stimulant; they were all tingling with it, and in their excitement, they were almost unaware of the impediments to their progress, though they hardly spoke to each other as they first forged forward. But when the dogs, who had been snuffing the scent as they scurried along with their noses close to the ground, raised their heads and began to bay, the hunters turned to each other, proudly identifying their own.

"What's the matter with Mort, Harvey? I haven't heard him sound off yet."

"Listen! There he is now!"

"There goes my little red bitch, Molly, giving tongue, too!"

"That's Hayes, Pinkie's prize hound again! I'd know him anywhere. There's not another dog in the state with that deep bell-like voice."

"Right you are. I'm here to tell you there's no better sport than hunting with him. Just the same, Fox is my favorite."

The light, filtering in through the trees, was brighter now. The men could see, more distinctly, the robin feathers left on the trail, remnants of the cat's final feast before settling down to sleep, and they were pressing ahead with redoubled vigor and enthusiasm. The dogs had begun to circle around a briar patch flanked by a huge fallen log, their voices rising in chorus, and the hunters were all hurrying towards it, when Gervais froze in his tracks, shouting a warning to the others.

"Look out! I swear I smell a cottonmouth! Yes, there he is, right alongside that log!"

As he spoke a thick brown-and-black moccasin, curled up under some fallen leaves, opened its deadly white mouth and then, sluggishly uncoiling itself, slithered away among the bushes. It was gone before most of the hunters were more than half aware of it. But Gervais fell back a little, glancing uneasily at the thickets around him and several of the dogs, getting the same nauseous scent, recoiled too, as they shrank away, while others snapped at the rustling leaves, breaking the chorusing circle.

"Mr. Gervais, he's done got dem dogs upset," Willie said to Cass in a contemptuous undertone. "He's gwine to have snake jitters all mornin' hisself, too. Iffen dis here had a been a 'possum hunt now, and Miss Cresside had been along, she'd had old Mr. Cottonmouth kilt before he could a got away. Ah tells you again, Cass, Ah likes 'possum huntin' de best, and Ah likes for de ladyfolks to be along, iffen it's de right ladyfolks. Ah seen just as good spo't an' better 'possum huntin' dan we seen on dis cat hunt yet. Ah don't find no fun just a plowin' and a plowin' t'rough dese blackberry bushes all day. Iffen us'd been 'possum huntin', us'd a had a couple of 'em treed by now."

"Us's a goin' to have dat ole one-eared cat treed plenty soon now too, big boy. Come on, can't you hear de bossman callin' you?"

The hunters were dividing. From now on the hunt would be even more strenuous than it had been before. The "cold trailing" was over, and the "hot trailing" beginning. The cat, though the hollow log had been located as its bed, had made a swift getaway at the approach of the dogs; but they had lost less than a minute and they were now off in close pursuit, Amos whooping them on more vociferously than ever. Lawrason and Claiborne had followed along after them, without waste of time, and were already crashing through the brush. Boylston and Gervais were still standing near the log, the former because he was too punctilious to leave any of his guests unceremoniously, the latter because he was still shaken by the "snake jitters" of which Willie had shrewdly suspected him. Fabian, grasping the cause of his host's indecision, lowered himself slowly to the log and nodded pleasantly to Boylston.

"This looks like a pretty good stopping place to me," he remarked. "I'll have the rest of my fun sitting down and listening to the dogs, taking it easy while the rest of you wear yourselves out. What about leaving Willie here with me, Charles? You don't really need him, do you, with the other drivers you've got? I wouldn't mind having a good fire to toast myself by. Anyone else staying behind?"

"I am," Happy Sevier answered. "Hard enough to get this far. Pushing a cat's too damn strenuous for me. You've got the right idea, Fabian."

"That's my viewpoint, too," Parker said quickly. His decision to remain with the two friends was announced with such a promptitude that it seemed to take them out of the cripple class and place them among his preferred companions. As Gervais and Boylston disappeared, he walked in a leisurely way over to the log, took out the plug of tobacco which he always carried in his pocket, and, as usual, bit off a corner of it and rolled it deliberately around in his mouth before he went on with what he had to say.

"I don't know whether you two are especially interested in the Constitutional Convention we're going to have next spring," he remarked at length. "Personally, I hope it's going to do great things for this state. You've already heard me speak about my plan for the development of the University, Fabian. The Convention ought to give a good deal of time to a program for that. And with the River Road the way it is, most of the time, I'm sure your cousin would agree that the creation of the State Highway Commission would be a mighty good thing, too."

"He sure would. But if the Convention didn't do a thing but recast that darn suffrage article he'd be ready to say it hadn't met in vain."

Parker laughed. "Oh, I've got that on the list, too. But the reorganization of the judiciary's much more important. I don't need to tell either of you two young lawyers that the Louisiana courts are in a bad way. I've watched the election of delegates with a good deal of anxiety— a lot's going to depend on the kind we get. I'm not worrying about the representatives from this Parish—Carruth Jones and Eugene Cazedessus are both all right. But what do you know about this young lawyer from Lake Charles—Sam Jones?"

The Governor was off on his pet topic. He continued to talk politics with the two young lawyers, beside a cheerful blaze which Willie kept feeding with dry branches, while intermittently muttering to himself that he wished he were 'possum hunting instead of cat hunting. Meanwhile Gervais and Boylston went on, soon catching up with the others. One of the young dogs had already jumped a rabbit, Lawrason told them, and that had caused a delay. Now the cat had evidently got into a thick place, for it was just "babbling around," as Amos described its maneuvers. At all events, the hunt was temporarily more or less at a standstill, and the men, now all drenched with sweat and pretty well winded from their exertions, were not sorry for a short breathing space, though their enthusiasm was still unabated. Lawrason enlivened their wait with another characteristic story.

"Parker don't never fail to make the gracious gesture, does he? Like he did just now, I mean. No, Which-I-God, I take that back. I heard of one time he wasn't so gracious. Tack Evans was tellin' me about it. Parker's nobody's prissy, but he don't like smut, not even in stories. Well, you all know that. Anyway, the Governor and Tack and a couple of newspapermen were on their way to Alexandria to some damn meetin' or other, and they stopped overnight along the way at one of them little two-story hotels without any elevator, and the bedrooms, if you could call 'em that, all in a long row on the second floor. The bellhop, who was puffing along after 'em with the bags, was a funny lookin' midget, not a boy, you understand, but a queer little ol' dwarf. When he set Parker's bag down, just before he started to unlock the door, this midget tugged at the Governor's coattails and says in a hoarse whisper, 'Does you want a lady tonight, sah?' Tack said it was somethin' to see the Governor standing there grim as they make 'em in his pepper-and-salt suit, with an expression on his face that could have froze hell fire. If some little ol' dwarf had tried to pander to the Archbishop of Canterbury, when he was in full pontificals just ready to go to the Cathedral, it would have been about the same thing."

This time Lawrason's story met with a gratifying response. The hunters were now in the midst of a forest, dense, for the most part, with oak and gum trees and heavy with palmetto and other underbrush; but it was studded here and there by gum ponds and patches of grass where cattle had grazed, and intersected by small creeks. The men finally reached one of these streams, after their first two delays, only to find that the trail had been broken again. The dogs, who were all hot and tired by now, were baying around a tree at the water's edge, in a state of disorder and confusion. Amos, quieting them as he glanced around with an experienced eye, pointed to a long limb overhanging the water.

"Look-a-here, Mr. Boylston suh, de cat done crossed de creek on dat limb for sure. Dat's how de dogs lose trail. Come on, you no-count hounds, you's gwine swim across dis creek wid old Amos. Us a-gwine find dat one-eared cat yet."

He strode into the water as he spoke, the dogs, eager and excited again, swimming around him, straining up the bank on the far side of the creek, and springing forward once more. Only old Hayes failed to join the rest of the pack. For some moments he remained in the water, lapping it up with calm enjoyment, and splashing around in a leisurely way. The hunters, who were still standing under the long-limbed tree, watched him with varying degrees of anxiety.

"At this rate he'll never pick up the trail again, and there's no telling whether Beulah can get it without him. They're a grand team as trail dogs, and old Hayes is all right alone. But Beulah isn't."

"Don't worry, Charles. Even if Hayes falls down on the job, Mort won't. Nor Molly either."

"Old Hayes ain't a-gwine fall down on no job, Mr. Lawrason. He's full of fat and he gets mighty hot, runnin' lak he's been doin'. Soon as he cools hisself, he'll pick up dat trail again, right quick. You's a-gwine to see. You'll have your cat most any minute now."

While Amos was still speaking, old Hayes, after pausing to take one last drink, climbed slowly up on the opposite bank and went over to the driver, wagging his tail and lifting his head. Then, as if he were glad to get back on the job again, now that he had shown his gratitude in the driver's confidence, he shot off in a different direction from the other dogs. The hunters, fording the creek in their turn, began crashing through the woods once more, to be arrested almost instantly by the renewed sound of his baying, mingled with shouts from Amos.

"Which-I-God, he *has* got that stinking cat!" Lawrason exclaimed. "Fast work! He must be somewhere in this clump of oaks."

The hunters tore their way along, closing quickly in around the tree where old Hayes was standing guard, baying with all his might and main at the base of a heavy grapevine which climbed the oak. But the other dogs were nowhere to be seen, and though it was now broad daylight, the men were not rewarded by the expected sight of a crouching cat, glowering at them from amongst the branches. Boylston spoke to Amos with the sharpness of disappointment.

"Old Hayes must have told us a lie this time. There's no cat in that tree."

"Sho' dey is, Mr. Boylston, suh. You don't see it, but it be's dere."

"We'd see it if it were there, all right. That tree's too clean to hide anything."

Claiborne had spoken sharply, too. Every bloodthirsty instinct was now fully roused and the seemingly false summons was a sorry slacking of the morning's excitement. Without deigning to answer his master's guest, Amos called old Hayes to him and asked Boylston to step back, while he himself began to shake the ropelike grapevine. As it vibrated and swung away from the tree, a ball of moss above it suddenly seemed to become animate, scattering strands of it fell to the ground. The rest, violently rent apart, disclosed an enormous cat which leaped from its hiding place and hit the ground with almost incredible speed. But Boylston was quick, too. Before it could reach cover in the underbrush, he raised his rifle and shot. At the same instant old Hayes sprang forward and pounced upon its tumbling form. It gave a vicious snarl and clawed futilely in the air. Then it rolled over and lay still—a huge, wicked, magnificent beast—minus one ear.

For a moment Amos stood still, savoring his moment of triumph; then he turned to Boylston, whose face, stripped of its customary control, was lighted with atavistic satisfaction, and quietly asked whether they were to go on with the hunt. But everyone was agreed that after the dramatic capture of "one-ear," pursuit of another cat could only end in an anti-climax. The lust to kill was now assuaged; the inevitable letdown had followed. Amos was instructed to call in the other dogs, and after blowing his horn and allowing them to "wrastle" the cat for a moment, he took it from them to save its hide, and slinging it over his shoulder, started back towards the pasture with unconcealed satisfaction. Indeed, everyone's return to Hackberry Lodge was marked by high good spirits. Most of the men, delighted by the success of this hunt, were already planning another. Without much difficulty, Lawrason was persuaded that he might as well remain over the week end, and there was some rather broad joking about his ulterior motives for remaining near Baton Rouge, which he took in good part. . . . The hunt had covered at least fifteen miles, Boylston thought; what did he mean, fifteen? Gervais corrected him; it wasn't really much over five; it just seemed longer; poor Charles, he was just a tenderfoot still when it came to scrambling through briar patches. Maybe Gervais could outwalk Charles, but at least Charles didn't have snake jitters, Fabian remarked in a dry aside. . . .

By the time they had reached the house, they were deep in a discussion of the relative merits of different hunting breeds, and this went on while they made their way, without formality, to the dining room, and attacked the hearty breakfast awaiting them. They were all ravenously hungry by this time; the huge platters of pork chops, ham and eggs, and country sausage, were soon emptied; the tall piles of hot cakes and hot biscuits, the great mounds of hominy grits melted away. But Tilda, now clad in a formal and immaculate uniform, re-filled the coffeepot again and again, and it continued to circulate as the argument went on and on. It would seem clear enough, from the morning's performance, that Pinkie's black and tans were peerless, Parker contended. Well, he would still stick to his redbones, Lawrason said. Look at the muscle of them and the size! Mort tipped the scales at nearly seventy pounds. And then that rich russet of theirs—where could you match it? It gave color to any hunting scene. He'd never heard that size and color were what made a good hunting dog, Boylston remarked. Why, Lawrason himself had rambled on and on about Martin's Choice early that very morning! Now Walkers were smaller than redbones, he was willing to grant that, but they were better shaped and better proportioned and they were a good deal more intelligent. He would never forget a dog he had owned when he was still with the Middlesex Hunt. While he was riding to hounds he had dropped his crop, and after the kill, Patrick, this dog of his, had gone back over the course by himself and retrieved it. He had come into the house, carrying the crop in his mouth, just as they were all sitting down, in their pink coats, to the hunt breakfast, and laid it on the rug at his master's feet. Patrick had been the talk of the county for weeks afterwards. . . .

"Well, I reckon that was right smart for a dog, up in Massachusetts," Lawrason drawled. "But I'm here to tell you, we've got hogs over in Livingston Parish smarter than any of your Yankee hounds. Why, I had a hog once that was so smart he'd go to the crib and fetch some corn and put it by a log. Then he'd lie down and wait for the chickens to come along and eat it, and he'd catch them, one by one, and eat them. Naturally this was a razorback hog. Those razorbacks never need to exert themselves any. Which-I-God, this one's nose was so long he'd be standing on that log where he'd killed the chickens, and dig for roots with his nose in three feet of water."

The laughter which greeted this sally was echoed by the honk of a horn sounding in the driveway. Boylston, already absorbed in the effort to cap Lawrason's tall tale, paid no attention to the sound until Fabian touched him lightly on the arm and motioned towards the window. Boylston looked up in surprise.

"Why, it's Cresside!" he exclaimed, jumping up and hastening through the door. Fabian, stiff from his morning's exertion, rose and followed him, walking even more awkwardly than usual. Boylston's other guests turned in their places to see the girl get out of the car, greet her host and her cousin excitedly, and come swiftly back towards the house with them. She had on a red jacket and skirt, and a small red hat was pulled down over her ears, after the fashion of the moment; but her black hair bushed out irrepressibly underneath it, and her manner was very gay. She stopped on the threshold of the dining room and waved a buoyant greeting.

"Hello, everybody!" she said. "No, please don't get up. Of course, I'm not here to stay. All you mighty huntsmen will have to excuse me for breaking in on you like this, but I'm out with a search warrant for my brother. . . . Gervais, you've got a son."

262

"Which-I-God, another?" Lawrason said incredulously, as Gervais, pushing back his chair, rushed over to his sister and began to ply her with imperative questions. Cresside laughed and held up her hands as a signal of her helplessness to cope with his outburst.

"Yes, another!" she said gaily. "That's what I meant, of course. Three children in eleven months is going some, isn't it? Hold on, Gervais, I can't tell you everything at once. Yes, Merry's doing as well as could be expected, and the baby boy weighs nine pounds, all quite in the best tradition. We've had what you might call a hectic morning though, I can tell you—no one but you needed to go cat hunting for excitement, Gervais! Merry came in to get Dinah about five, and then Dinah woke me and I woke *maman*—a regular merry-go-round! Hang it, I didn't mean to make a lousy pun like that! We sent Amen into town posthaste for the doctor, but good old Champagne was off on another case, and of course it didn't occur to Amen that he might go and get someone else! He just left a message and came on back to Belle Heloise. Naturally we sent him off again, with ants in his pants, but by that time we knew we'd have to manage as well as we could without him. And were we glad the good old acetylene was still functioning in the Big House and that we weren't dependent on that damn Delco! I sure do hand it to Merry, Gervais. She never once lost her nerve, and if you think most girls wouldn't have, without a doctor or a nurse, or even a husband in the house. . . . And she didn't make any mean cracks or do any moaning and groaning because you were off hunting while she was having her baby. . . . I have to hand it to Dinah, too. She's my choice for a midwife, makeshift or not, anywhere, any time. And *maman* stood up to the whole thing like a Trojan, too!"

"I know you'll excuse me if I dash off." Gervais turned to Boylston, his flushed face wreathed in smiles, and wrung his host's outstretched hand, while the others crowded around him, slapping him on the back, and heartily voicing their congratulations. "We weren't expecting this for at least a couple of weeks yet, or of course I wouldn't have been here, and there'd have been a nurse on call in the house. But I can tell you I'm pretty proud of my wife just the same. There's nothing she can't take. Come on, Cresside, you can tell me the rest on the road."

"Have you had anything to eat yet this morning, Cresside?" Fabian inquired.

"Why, no, I reckon I haven't. But that's all right. I hadn't even thought of it."

"Why don't you stop long enough to snatch a cup of coffee anyway? Gervais can go along in your car and I'll take you home."

"Good idea," Gervais said jovially, answering for his sister. "Look, I must get going. But I hope you all stop on your way back to town, and have a drink with me to make Philogene's hair curl—that's his name, of course. So long."

Gervais flung himself out of the door, followed by the redoubled congratulations of his friends, which were now rising to a chorus of shouts. Cresside sat down in his place and reached for his cup.

"This is all right, isn't it, Charles? That is, I believe it was Fabian who asked me to stay, and after all this is your house. But everyone was making so much noise I couldn't half hear."

"Of course it's all right. I'm very much honored at having you here. I was trying to tell you so, but in the midst of all this hubbub. . . . Wait, I'll have Tilda bring you some fresh coffee."

He spoke courteously, but with a slight constraint in his voice. *Something's wrong,* Cresside said to herself, feeling half amused and half angry. *Is he annoyed because Fabian came to my rescue, before he thought of it? No, that can't be it. Maybe he's shocked because I stayed. He mightn't recognize Fabian as a chaperon, and he thinks all these other men will be surprised because I'm lingering on. When I've been up for hours and taken a long cold ride, without getting anything to eat, not to mention having helped deliver a baby! If that's the trouble, he's even more of a fool than I've thought he was. And he thinks he's such a man of the world! The rest understand all right. They're my kind of people.* Aloud all she said was, "Don't bother, Charles. This is plenty hot. I'll have some more as soon as I get home anyway."

"But I want you to let me send for some fresh. And I really think you ought to have some toast, too. Some toast and some soft-boiled eggs. How long do you like your eggs cooked? About three minutes?"

"No, I don't like them boiled at all. I like them scrambled with hot red peppers and okra. I don't like toast, either. I like cakes and cuite. I said don't bother, Charles. I've almost finished already."

She knew that she sounded ungracious and she was annoyed with herself now, rather than with Charles, whose air of formality had changed to one of concern. She realized that she ought to question them about the hunt, to show interest in their outing and enthusiasm at the result. But she could not bring herself to do it. She was too unhappy. She had come in so joyously, openly glad to be the bearer of good tidings, secretly proud of her own share in meeting a hard situation. Now all the radiance was gone from the morning. She took one more long swallow, pushed back her cup and rose, the men rising with her. She looked at them with a comprehensive smile.

"I'll be seeing you all at Belle Heloise pretty soon, won't I?" she asked, with forced cordiality. "Me, I'd better be running along to get that hair-curling mixture started. Fabian thinks I'm a pretty good barmaid. I hope you'll all agree with him." Then, tardily remembering that Gervais and Fabian had gone to Hackberry Lodge in the Governor's automobile, she turned to Parker in genuine confusion. "I'm terribly sorry, Governor Parker," she said. "I'm afraid I've been assuming too much, and that Fabian has, too. I forgot he didn't have his car here, and I'm sure he did, we were both so excited. Will it really be convenient to have me tag along?"

"It'll be more than convenient; it'll be delightful," Parker said instantly. "In fact, your arrival has marked the pleasantest part of the cat hunt for me. I didn't suppose, when I stood listening to the dogs baying, that I'd be hearing something so much more thrilling within a couple of hours. I don't know of any better news than the assurance that the old River families will be carried on. But it's high time I was getting back to my office, and I know you're needed at Belle Heloise. I'm ready to start whenever you are, Miss Cresside."

"I'd like very much to take Cresside home myself, if you'd let me, Governor," Boylston began. The constraint was completely gone from his voice now, and he spoke with unaccustomed eagerness. But the cordial invitation came too late, in the aftermath of the awkward moment when he himself had been so ill at ease as to cause Cresside's discomfiture and to make everyone else aware of the strained atmosphere. The girl shook her head, and linked her arm in Fabian's.

"You ought to give me a chance to say which I'd rather do," she answered, speaking gaily again. "And when it comes to a choice between you and the Governor, you ought to know which it would be, Charles. My head's completely turned by flattery from such a high quarter. I'm not planning to even look at any lesser light than a congressman, from now on."

CHAPTER XX

WHEN GERVAIS' GUESTS crossed the cattle gap at Belle Heloise, they found Amen waiting to direct them: *the Captain says, please gent'e-men, will you all go on to de garçonnière? Dey's keepin' de Big House quiet as dey kin caise Miss Merry an' de new baby, dey's sleepin' now; Madame, she be's restin' too.* They nodded, returning Amen's broad smile, and having circled the Satsuma trees, where a few golden balls still hung, parked their cars near the house servants' quarters and walked through the formal garden. Cresside ran ahead of the others, snatching off her red cloche and shrugging out of her jacket as she went; but as she dashed into the living room, she saw that Gervais had already succeeded in organizing his forces without her. The room was decorated with red roses and Chinese holly, the fire lighted, and steam was rising from the little brass kettle on the hob beside the hearth; Selah was standing beside an improvised bar, while Creassy hovered helpfully near him. Hot toddies and highballs were circulating in no time, and the convivial atmosphere which had characterized the hunt breakfast became increasingly jocose. But by this time most of the men were disinclined to linger indefinitely over their drinks; they

265

would have to make it short and snappy now, they told their beaming host. Governor Parker wanted to get back to the Capitol, Happy Sevier to his wife, Lawrason to the merry widow of the moment and Claiborne to his office, and they confessed this with varying degrees of frankness. Fabian did not indicate or express any special reason for haste, but having gone to the hunt with the Governor, he logically left Belle Heloise with him. Only Boylston continued to stand by one of the built-in bookcases, fingering the mellow volumes with obvious appreciation. The servants removed the glasses, mended the fire and left, and still he did not turn. Finally Gervais, who was beginning to fidget, asked rather abruptly to be excused.

"You don't mind if I go back to the Big House, do you, Charles? Of course, everything was fine when I last looked in, just before you all came, but I want to have another look——"

"Go right ahead. Merry said something about finding a first edition of *Jorrock's Jaunts and Jollities* in the attic, and I've been trying to locate it. So far I haven't had any luck. But perhaps Cresside will help me."

Cresside, after exerting herself to be helpful as long as this seemed necessary, had stood for a few minutes with her back to the fire, hitching up her short skirt in the rear, so that the warmth of the flames would toast that portion of her person thus exposed to it. This was a fairly general practice among the girls whom Charles had met locally and it was enjoyed entirely without self-consciousness, but it had never ceased to seem shocking to him. He had avoided looking at Cresside as long as she stood in this position, thus engaged. But now she had sunk down on a big sofa by the fireplace, and was sitting with one foot tucked under the other knee and her head thrown back against the pillows. Her eyes were half shut and she was smoking a cigarette. She looked comfortable, drowsy and detached, and she answered without stirring.

"Find the darn book yourself. I've had enough activity for one morning. . . . I'll stay here and keep Charles company though, Gervais, if he wants me to, so that his search won't be a lonely one while you're away gazing at your offspring."

Gervais did not give her time to change her mind, which he knew she was quite capable of doing, where Charles was concerned. He hurried from the room, and presently the sound of his impatient footsteps was swallowed up in distance. The servants were still washing dishes in the kitchen, but the living room was very quiet. Cresside continued to smoke without speaking, and only the flames made a small cheerful murmur. Boylston removed another leather-bound book from a shelf, turned its yellowing pages, and put it back again. He repeated this process until the kitchen clatter subsided and the back door closed behind the departing servants. Then he came over to the sofa.

"I don't care a hang about *Jorrock's Jaunts and Jollities,* either," he said. "I've got first editions of that and Surtees' other book, *Handley Cross,* myself. I just wanted to talk to you. I never have a chance."

"You've got a chance now. The book hunt sounded pretty phony to me, right along. I thought you might have something on your mind. I only hope it isn't too far on the serious side. Me, I'm sleepy."

"It's very serious. I hope you'll wake up and listen. And I'd appreciate it if you wouldn't badger me while I'm trying to talk."

Cresside opened her black eyes wide and looked at him with mock gravity. Her expression was quite as trying as a badgering tone.

"Don't, Cresside," he said, almost pleadingly. "I'm in deadly earnest, and I wish you'd try to be, for once. There's nothing funny about what I'm going to say."

"Sorry, Charles. I didn't know you were really so upset. What's the matter?"

"You thought I wasn't glad to see you when you arrived at Hackberry Lodge this morning. I was. I was very glad. But when you came bursting in with your good news, I was so upset for a moment that I couldn't help showing something was the matter. I want to apologize, first of all, for giving you the wrong impression."

"Oh, forget it! I thought you were mildly shocked because I came to your house, and that if you couldn't take it, under the circumstances, you were an awful prissy. But I wasn't offended, or upset, myself."

"I'm very glad. But I want to do more than apologize. I want to explain."

"It isn't all that necessary. Why do you bother?"

"I've just told you, because I want to. I'm jealous of your brother's good fortune, so jealous I can't seem to stand it."

He spoke with gathering intensity. Cresside, who was accustomed to hearing him talk in a calm and measured way, and to whom the change therefore seemed more portentous than it would have in most men, answered with unusual coolness herself.

"You'll have to, won't you, if there's nothing you can do about it? Lots of other people do, anyway. One of the finest men I ever knew reminded me, not so long back, that childlessness was a pretty common disappointment. And I shouldn't think, in your case, that it had to be a permanent one. You've got almost everything most women would want."

"I don't seem to have enough for the only one I want," he said bitterly. And as she did not answer, he went on, "Besides, it isn't a mere question of childlessness. It's a question of general disappointment and disillusionment."

Cresside still made no reply. It was all too obvious that Charles Boylston was determined to unburden his soul, and though she could not prevent this, she was equally determined not to encourage it.

"Probably you've wondered how I ever happened to land in Louisiana," he went on vehemently. "I've never discussed the reasons why I left home, because they were too painful. I didn't come here with any set purpose of becoming a planter in the first place. I was just trying to get away from Boston and everything connected with it."

"Well, I can understand that," Cresside murmured.

"Cresside, won't you please stop taking that tone? Of course, I wasn't trying to get away from Boston as a place! I'm very fond of it. I was trying to get away from tragic associations with a girl I had known all my life. Our families had been friendly for generations—they lived in the same block on Beacon Street and had adjoining properties on the North Shore. She went to Miss Winsor's at the same time I went to Noble's, and she came out when I was a junior at Harvard. We always saw a great deal of each other and everyone took it for granted that sometime we would be married. Our engagement was announced the week I graduated, the day before the Beck Hall Spread."

Cresside could not keep the corners of her mouth from twitching. She knew, from Charles Boylston's voice, that what he was saying really had some sad significance for him; nevertheless, the way in which he coupled "tragic associations" with the Beck Hall Spread seemed to her ludicrous in the extreme. However, she managed to suppress a second flip remark.

"But no date had been set for the wedding," Boylston continued. "We both took it for granted that we would have a long engagement. I entered law school the next fall and Dorothea went abroad to study at the Sorbonne. Then I decided that I didn't care to go on with my course, and I bought a very nice year-round place near Hamilton. I always had plenty of money; one of my grandfathers left me his entire fortune direct. So I wasn't worried about making a living. But Dorothea didn't want to stay in the country all the year round; she didn't care for horses and dogs, either. I thought I'd better give her time to get used to my general idea."

"Neither of you thought about trying some kind of a compromise?"

"I didn't, and if she did she never mentioned it. Merry didn't suggest any sort of a compromise to Gervais, did she?"

"No, but he didn't buy a new place out of a clear sky without consulting her; he already had one that he'd inherited, with all its obligations. Besides, he offered Merry a great deal more than she'd ever had before, materially speaking. I think she regarded Belle Heloise as something straight out of a fairy tale—in fact, I'm not sure that she still doesn't. I gather that you and Dorothea had about the same sort of background and about the same amount of opportunity, only different tastes. That might make a lot of difference. You weren't presenting her with a pleasanter kind of life. You were trying to present her with the kind that seemed to her deadly dull."

"Didn't Merry wait for Gervais all the time he was abroad, even though they weren't formally engaged?" Charles demanded, ignoring Cresside's suggestion. "Wasn't her behavior exemplary throughout that time?"

"Yes, but I think Patient Griseldas like her are pretty rare, in this day and age. Merry's the exception that proves the rule—to almost everything. Besides, I don't quite follow your line of thought. You started out by telling me that you and Dorothea had both agreed on an indefinite engagement, which doesn't sound to me like such a mighty passion to begin with, if you don't mind my saying so. And now you've apparently switched around to something else. You're not trying to tell me, very delicately, are you, that Dorothea finally got tired of this long engagement, and being human after all, stooped to folly?"

"That's just what I'm trying to tell you. And I see you intend to treat it as something humorous to the very end!"

He turned away from her abruptly and walked towards the door. Genuinely contrite, Cresside sprang up and ran to him, putting her hand on his arm.

"I'm sorry, Charles," she said penitently. "I didn't mean to hurt your feelings, truly I didn't. I know it must have been an awful blow if this girl you'd expected to marry for such a long time went back on you. You're right, Merry wouldn't have done a thing like that. No girl would, who was worth her salt—that is, if she were sure the man really loved her. But don't you think that perhaps, when you didn't urge her, she got the idea you didn't care, and this snake in the grass convinced her that he did, and so——"

"She came to my house and asked me to release her," Charles said hoarsely. "She'd never come there alone before, and I was so glad to see her—I thought she was going to say she was ready to marry me, and everything. And instead of that, she'd come to say she wanted to marry someone else. I didn't realize she'd even seen anyone else— oh, you know what I mean! I thought she was absolutely true to me in every way. I told her that I'd never heard of such nonsense, that I loved her dearly, that of course I wouldn't release her. And then she said that I'd have to—she said she was going to have a child."

Cresside's fingers, which had been lying lightly on his sleeve, closed quickly around his arm.

"I'm terribly sorry, Charles," she said, speaking still more contritely than before. "That must have been a knockout blow. I don't wonder you feel as if you'd been cheated. I don't wonder you've been embittered. But after all, Dorothea must have loved this other man very much, or she wouldn't, a girl like that——"

"You're not defending her, are you?"

He swung around and snatched at her hand, suddenly facing her again. Unconsciously Cresside backed away from him a little.

"No, I'm not defending her," she said in a startled voice. "But I still think she thought you didn't love her any more, and that this other man did. It must have been terrible for her, too, having to go to you like that and tell you what she did. . . . Let go my hand, please, Charles, you're hurting me."

"You'll have to forgive me," he said, releasing her instantly. "I wouldn't hurt you for the world, you know that, Cresside. . . . And, of course, you realize I don't love Dorothea any more, as a person. I've never seen her alone since that night, never wanted to. I stayed around until she was married, so that nothing would look queer; in fact, I was one of the ushers at her wedding. Then after a little I traveled rather aimlessly, and I was gone so much that eventually I sold my place in Hamilton. Everyone thought I acted very well and that Dorothea treated me very badly, but no one guessed just how badly. . . . Her baby died when it was born and that gave color to the report that it was premature. I haven't thought of her for years except as a symbol of everything I've missed. She shattered my life completely—the life I had then. That's why I had to get away from everything that reminded me of it. And one winter when I was in Florida, I motored over to Denham Springs for the hunting and met Harvey Lawrason. He told me about Hackberry Lodge, said it could be had for a song, asked me why I didn't buy it, for the fun of the thing. I've never regretted it. I found a new life here, better than the one I left. But still it's terribly incomplete, terribly lonely, bound to be, the way it is. If I only had any assurance that some day it would be different, if I only had any hope——"

"You will have, some time, Charles."

"Is that a promise, Cresside?"

He tried, gently this time, to take her hand again, and again she retreated, speaking in her startled voice.

"No, of course it isn't a promise," she said. "A promise of what? It's just a statement. Nothing is ever hard all the time, for anybody. It can't be, in the nature of things. . . . I'm very much touched, Charles, that you wanted to confide in me. I feel very much honored. And I'm sorry I was so flip—I honestly didn't realize at first how deeply you felt. I will, another time. But I'm afraid I've got to ask you to excuse me now. You see, a day like this, there's a lot to be done, and I'm the logical person to do it. Stay here and read for a while if you feel like it, why don't you? I'll look in on you again, by and by. But meantime I've got to run over to the Big House."

She ran so fast and so blindly that she collided with Gervais, who was returning to the *garçonnière* at a more leisurely pace than the one at which he had left it. He took her by the shoulders and regarded her laughingly.

"Hold on, hold on!" he said. "What's your hurry? Come on back to the *garçonnière* and have another drink. Merry and Philogene are both asleep and incidentally so are the twins. 'All is calm, all is bright.' There's not a thing that needs doing at the Big House."

"In that case, I think I'll take a short walk on the levee. I want to get some air."

"Didn't you get enough air, going all the way to Hackberry Lodge and back, for Pete's sake?"

"Well, I got some. But I want some more."

"Look here, you and Charles haven't quarreled again, have you?"

"No, we haven't quarreled exactly. But he's trying to propose again, by a new method. He's been telling me all, and I've been a very unwilling listener to the history of his past. He's upset, and he's succeeded in upsetting me, too. I want to get away from him for a while, and he hasn't the least idea of going home. I'm sure he thinks that if he keeps hammering away, eventually I'll give in and marry him. But I never shall, never, never, never!"

Her voice broke in something suspiciously like a sob. Gervais regarded her curiously but more sympathetically than usual.

"Look here," he said again. "You're all worn out. You've had a hell of a time yourself this morning. I didn't want to ask you to do anything more, because I know you've done two or three people's work already. But if you really do want to take a walk, would you mind going to the cemetery instead of along the levee? I'd like very much to have some flowers put on our father's tomb today. I suppose you'll think I'm a sentimental fool, but I can't help feeling——"

"I don't at all. I'd like very much to do it. I'll go and pick the flowers straight off. So long, Gervais. And see if you can't get rid of Charles gracefully, within the next hour or so, won't you? I can manage to stay away that long, but I don't want to find him here when I get back. You can tell him I've gone to bed, exhausted, without hurting your conscience too much, can't you?"

She stopped to get a flower basket from the tool shed at the rear of the Big House and went on to Angus Holt's garden, her pace now less suggestive of flight, but still rapid. The first white camellias were just coming into bloom; two of the smaller trees were already laden with beautiful blossoms, waxen against the glossy green of the leaves. She gathered a dozen or more, selecting some that were still only half open, bell-shaped buds and others that were already full blown, resembling roses and daffodils in formation, but infinitely more delicate; all were fragile and flawless. Nothing needed to be added to these—they were in themselves a perfect offering. She arranged them carefully in the shallow basket, so that they would not bruise each other, and started down the River Road, her sense of haste and panic already assuaged.

The cemetery never depressed her. Like most Creoles, she felt very near to her dead, and could linger among their tombs with a sense of peace and communion, not only on All Saints' Day but at any time and season. As a child, she had been accustomed to joining the groups making leisurely visits to the family lot, taking her toys and her lunch with her and playing contentedly for hours. Lately she had preferred to go alone; but the feeling of ease and familiarity still lingered. Entering the cemetery now, she went quietly past the chalklike rectangular

271

blocks nearest the road, the uneven tiers of crumbling red brick and the pretentious mossy monuments, towards the little Gothic chapel which marked the resting place of the Estrades and the d'Alverys. But as she approached it, she saw that she was not alone in the cemetery. A man was sitting on the slab adorned with the small recumbent lamb. He was half hidden by the simpering female figure in marble which dominated the Hathaway lot, but Cresside instantly realized who he was. For a moment, she stood stock still. Then, bracing herself for the meeting, she went on, calmly confronting Sylvestre Tremaine.

"Why, hello!" she said casually. "What on earth are you doing here?"

He rose from the slab and came up to her. His attitude, when she first caught sight of him, had been one of extreme dejection. Now she saw that his handsome face was stormy and somber. He neither smiled nor held out his hand.

"Nothing," he said shortly. "But I have to get off somewhere, every once in so often, and this morning a cemetery exactly suited me. . . . Very convenient for a suicide and I was practically on the verge of that. What are *you* doing here?"

"Just bringing flowers, as you see. To put on my father's tomb. We try to do that fairly regularly, on general principles. But this morning there was a special reason. We've got a new baby at Belle Heloise and his name is Philogene."

"A new baby already!"

"Yes, already. He's a little ahead of time, but he's a fine big boy just the same. Mother and child are not only doing as well as could be expected, but very nicely indeed, thank you."

"Gervais is getting more than his share," Sylvestre said moodily. "Those twins are fine-looking children, especially Vail. I'd give my eyeteeth for one such youngster."

"Well, you'll probably have one sooner or later. Most people do. But don't let's talk about it. I've heard a lot on that subject already this morning, and enough is enough."

She nodded, still casually, and moved along towards the chapel again, apparently unconcerned because Sylvestre had moved forward, too. He opened the wrought-iron gate of the railing surrounding the Estrade lot, and waited for her to enter. Then he hesitated.

"Could I help you fix the flowers? I'd like to, if you'd let me."

"Thanks a lot. But I can do it all right alone."

She unlocked the chapel and went in, closing the door behind her. Sylvestre continued to stand by the gate, swinging it absently back and forth, until it seemed to him Cresside had been gone an abnormally long time. Irrationally worried, he went to the closed door and knocked.

"Cresside, are you all right? What on earth are you doing there all this time?"

"Of course, I'm all right. I'm arranging the flowers, that's all. I'll be out in a minute."

Her voice was muffled but composed. After another wait, so long that Sylvestre felt almost irresistibly impelled to tug at the closed door she came out with the empty basket on her arm, relocked the chapel, and started serenely out of the lot without speaking.

"Cresside," Sylvestre said desperately. "I wish you wouldn't act this way—as if I just weren't here at all."

"Well, you're not, as far as I'm concerned."

"But I am. You can't accuse me of forcing myself on you this time. I hadn't the remotest idea you were coming to the cemetery when I did. Now that we have met though——"

"I'm not accusing you of anything. But there's nothing I want to say to you either. At that, I did say hello."

"There are any number of things I want to say to you. I've wanted to say them a long, long time."

"If you're bound to talk to me, I suppose you will, and I can't very well help hearing you, as long as I'm in this cemetery. After all, you've got just as much right to come here as I have. You came to your family lot and I came to mine. Now that I've been there, I'm going straight home."

"It isn't my family lot. It's the Hathaway family lot. And I wish to heaven every Hathaway was in it!"

He spoke with passionate bitterness. Cresside, making no answer, walked quietly on.

"You wouldn't blame me either, if you knew the life those two women lead me," he said savagely. "It's a hell on earth. And they hate me as much as I hate them. That's my only hope of escape. I think sooner or later Regine will leave me, in a fit of rage. If she does, I may have a chance."

"If you've got to talk, I wish you wouldn't talk about your wife and your mother-in-law, especially like that. And I don't know what you mean by chance."

"I mean a chance to get free, of course. If Regine would only give me the least pretext, I'd get a divorce like a shot."

"She won't. You can't get a divorce just because your wife loses her temper, Sylvestre. Especially as you've probably given her all kinds of reasons for doing it."

"I can get a divorce for mental cruelty in some other state, if I can't get one in Louisiana. I will, too, if this goes on."

"And where will that get you?"

"Why, I just reminded you. Then I'd be free."

"I still don't get the point."

"Yes, you do. You're only pretending you don't. You know that I'm crazy about you, Cresside, that I always have been. You know I realize what a damn fool I was when I let Regine——"

"I know you're crazy. You can stop right there."

"But Cresside, you did love me, you loved me a lot! You can't have got all over it so soon! I haven't. I want you more than I ever did!"

"Well, that's just your tough luck then. Because I don't love you any more. I have got all over it. It took me quite a long while, and it wasn't an easy process. I might remind you in passing that you didn't do anything to make it easier. However, we'll let that go."

"But Cresside——"

They had already passed the pretentious mossy monuments and the crumbling brick tiers and were now approaching the chalklike rectangular blocks, which were in full sight of the River Road. Involuntarily, Cresside gave a small sigh of relief.

"You better go back to your stone slab," she said. "I told you I couldn't stop you from talking to me in the cemetery, but I didn't say anything about letting you walk home with me. If you had that in mind you'd better dismiss it, along with some of these other quaint ideas of yours. Listen hard, Sylvestre, I want you to get all this straight: Regine isn't going to let you go, because she hasn't got anyone else in sight, but even if she did, that wouldn't prove a thing, as far as I'm concerned. I wouldn't believe you if you swore on the Holy Bible that you wanted to marry me. I was a damn fool to believe you once, but at least I'm not such a fool to believe you again. And if I did believe you, and you could marry me, that still wouldn't get you anywhere. Because I don't want to marry you. I wouldn't have you if you were the last man on earth. I hate and despise the very sight of you and I wish to heaven I never had to see you again, even at a distance. I thought I had all the snakes cleared out of this cemetery. But I see I was mistaken. I see there's one I haven't got rid of yet."

PART V

"Some Precious Instance"

December 1920–August 1921

"Nature is fine in love: and where 'tis fine,
It sends some precious instance of itself
After the thing it loves."

—Shakespeare: "Hamlet," IV, c. 1601

PART V

"Some Precious Instance"

December 1920–August 1921

CHAPTER XXI

As THE END of the grinding season approached, the fear that the drop in the price of sugar might be more than temporary became a sad certainty. In December it was down to ten point five; in January it hit eight cents even, the lowest price in five years. At this unpropitious moment, Fletcher, who had shown great nonchalance on the subject of statements while the restoration work was still going on, sent in a bill for the entire amount due him. Gervais had understood that this could be paid in easy installments over a long period, but it now appeared that Fletcher wanted the whole sum at once, and it was a staggering one. When Gervais asked Mr. Garfield, his New Orleans broker, to advance it against the next year's crop, Mr. Garfield replied, in an unusually brief and formal letter, that this was entirely out of the question; ten thousand dollars was the largest sum with which he felt justified in supplying Captain d'Alvery at the moment and he was really stretching a point to do that. Fletcher's acceptance of the ten thousand was anything but gracious. He would be willing to give Captain d'Alvery ninety days in which to settle, he said, since there had evidently been a misunderstanding about the installments; but he had paid for the labor and the materials himself, while the work was in progress, and that had been a considerable strain on his own resources. He was sure Captain d'Alvery would understand. . . .

"Unless I have some kind of a windfall pretty soon, I'll have to get Bisbee to let me have it," Gervais told Merry resentfully, tossing Fletcher's letter over to her as she sat peacefully propped up on pillows in her bed, nursing Philogene, who was thriving on his food as the twins had done beforehand.

"Are you expecting any kind of a windfall?"

"Well, no. But that's not saying I might not have one."

"And you're sure Mr. Bisbee will let you have the money?"

"I don't see why not. I went out of my way to be nice to him when he came to this Parish as a stranger. And there isn't a bank anywhere around better fixed than the Cotton Factors' National. . . . I don't have to go to Bisbee right off anyway. I can wait a couple of months at least, and see if something doesn't turn up, as I said. But meanwhile, there's no getting away from the fact that I'm not much in the mood for reviving an old-fashioned celebration."

The year before, he had been urged by both his overseer and his Negro hands to stage the celebration to which he had just referred. He had declined then on the grounds of Merry's imminent confinement, for the grinding season came to an end almost immediately before the birth of the twins. Now that Philogene was already safely in the world, however, and was proving to be such a lusty child, the request had been renewed and he had found no excuse which would prevent him from consenting to the celebration. In his grandfather's time it had been the custom, both at Belle Heloise and at many other plantations, for the "bossman" to give his men a feast the day that grinding was over. The last carts to come in from the field were always gaily decorated with cornstalks and flags, and even the whips and the mules' harnesses were ornamented with a few festive leaves. The Negroes were paid in full on this day, and as many of them had worked overtime, they were "nigger rich," as the saying went. The *vincanne,* made of undistilled rum and fermented cane juice, had been "cooked off" and set aside in great barrels beforehand. Now it was liberally dispensed to the Negroes from the corn shed, and added considerably to their high spirits. As the last cane went into the crusher, the men gathered around it, and, with hearty and prolonged cheers, flung their hats into it, too; the battered homemade palmettos, ground up with the stalks, were jokingly said to add something special to the flavor. After the final long blast of the whistle, announcing the end of the sugar making, the Negroes produced a chair suitable for such a grand occasion, and looked around for their "bossman," who made a show of hiding. When they found him, they overrode his mock objections, and installing him in the seat of honor, bore him first around the mill and the quarters, and finally around the Big House, at the head of a procession of a hundred or more; and as they marched they sang the songs which they had composed on purpose for the occasion. Finally they deposited him on the front gallery, and clustering around him, waited for him to rise and address them. In his speech he always praised them for the hard work which had made the good harvest possible, thanked them for their faithfulness, and invited them to go "around to the back" to the "feast" of meat, bread, cheese, cake and red wine that had been prepared for them. Afterwards they returned to the quarters and continued their revelry far into the night, singing, dancing and love-making.

Most of these pleasant customs had continued. The carts were still decorated, the hats still tossed into the crusher, the whistle still blown, the *vincanne* still served, and there was still revelry at the quarters. But the triumphal procession, the flowery address, and the "feast" back of the Big House had long since been abandoned. It was originally Lezine's idea that Gervais could profitably and pleasantly make a special occasion of his homecoming after the war by reviving them, and all the Negroes were in hearty accord with this. Because of the inevitable delay in carrying out the plan, Gervais had rather hoped they might forget about it. But their long wait had only served to increase their eagerness. Gervais could not go back on his promise now.

"Cresside's all for the celebration, too," he said, leaning over to insert a finger in the baby's fist, and smiling again as he saw the tiny hand close around it. "She offered to go to the attic and try to find some of grandfather's clothes that I could wear. I believe she's up there now. I wouldn't put it past her to come down with complete outfits for all of us. I'll say this for Cresside, when she really gets her teeth into anything, she doesn't let go until she's done a thorough job. . . . I'd like to know how you feel about it, though—does it strike you as a tremendous bore or an awful effort? If it does, we'll call it all off again. You know I wouldn't be sorry for the excuse."

"Yes, I do know. But wouldn't it be a mistake, Gervais, to disappoint all our people a second time, when they've set their hearts on this? And I think Cresside has the right idea. If we're going in for the celebration at all, I believe we ought to do it up brown. Of course, women enjoy fancy dress more than men do—I know that. But you'd be so wonderful in the role of Lucien Estrade, that you ought to be able to stand the strain, for once."

He muttered something unintelligible, but she could tell from his expression that the idea of impersonating his grandfather was beginning to catch his fancy. He picked up the satiated baby, who was already half asleep, and sat down by the bed with his small son in his arms.

"If we go in for costumes and all that," he said, "we'd almost have to make an event of it, for ourselves, I mean, as well as the Negroes. And we couldn't ask some of our neighbors without asking all of them. What I'm driving at is, we couldn't invite Charles unless we invited Regine and Sylvestre, too. So far we've never been caught quite this way—to give the devil his due, I think Sylvestre started for Hot Springs a week earlier than he intended on purpose to relieve me of embarrassment when I had my beer and shrimp party. But he's home now—they all are. He's made a point of saying he was sticking around until the end of the grinding season, though heaven only knows why—he almost never goes to the mill. I naturally don't care a damn whether his feelings are hurt or not, but I don't want Regine to go around telling everyone Hathaway's been slighted, and starting the whole Parish wondering why."

"I don't think Cresside would mind at all if you invited Sylvestre and

Regine, honey," Merry said reassuringly. "I'm almost positive she isn't sensitive about them any more. But why don't you ask her, straight out?"

"Ask her what, straight out?" Cresside called from the living room. "Look here, don't you think it's about time, after all the holy wedlock you've enjoyed, that you two woke up and took notice when someone else comes around? I banged the outside door when I came in on purpose. . . . Never mind, though, for the moment. Just see what I've found!"

She came into the room staggering under an unwieldy armful of old clothes, and slinging them down on the bed, began to sort them and hold them up for inspection. She had found the suit of elegant gray broadcloth which Lucien Estrade had worn at his wedding, and any number of quaint costumes that had belonged to the various ladies of the family. She herself wanted to wear one of their mother's dresses —a bright plaid taffeta. Of course, that went with a later period, but after all, they weren't trying to be too technical about all this. She was going to take a black brocade that had belonged to Evaline Estrade up to *maman* right now and see whether she wouldn't fall for it. Cresside would come back after a moment to find out if the bridal finery fitted—there was a second day dress—a lovely changeable silk— that would be just the thing for Merry, too. . . .

"By the way, what were you thinking of asking me, when I came in?" she paused to inquire, with her hand on the doorknob again. Merry and Gervais exchanged glances and Merry answered for both of them.

"Gervais wondered how you'd feel about having him invite the Tremaines to the celebration. He thought it would be rather pointed if he didn't."

"Sure it would. Go right ahead. I don't care who's invited. Except that I wish sooner or later we could have one party sans Charles. I'm completely fed up with him, and seems like I'm never going to get shed of him. But I know we have to have him this time, worse luck. I only hope he doesn't show up in the uniform of a Yankee officer commanding the First Massachusetts Regiment."

"Cresside's very unjust to Charles," Gervais muttered under his breath, as the door closed behind his sister. "I've never known him to say or do a thing that wasn't tactful. Why on earth should she drag in anything as far-fetched as the uniform of a Yankee officer, in his connection?"

"I don't know. He just rubs her the wrong way somehow. But after all, let's be thankful that if she won't fall in love with Charles, she isn't in love with Sylvestre any more. That's something."

"Yes, that's something," Gervais agreed. He gave the sleeping baby back to Merry, and taking off his own coat, picked up the elegant gray broadcloth. "I reckon we can go right ahead and make plans," he said, slipping into it and shaking it down over his shoulders. "I'm

280

beginning to get into the spirit of the thing myself. It isn't as if it were going to cost us much. Of course, if I had that to worry about, it would be different."

He walked over to the cheval glass and surveyed himself with satisfaction. Lucien Estrade's coat fitted as if it had been made for him. But he had to wait a minute before Merry looked up and admired it. She had begun to reread Mr. Garfield's letter and the tone of it troubled her. It required a real effort for her to dismiss it from her mind.

However, at the time of the celebration she seemed in high spirits. The second day dress, which Cresside had found for her, was a little too tight; it had been made to fit a slender bride, and Merry was full-breasted, as became a nursing mother; besides, she had put on a little extra weight, which she carried well, after each confinement. But Cresside, who was so handy with a needle, had helped her to let the dress out, and it suited her admirably. Merry looked very lovely as she stood on the front gallery, between her mother-in-law and her sister-in-law, welcoming the guests. The fitful winter weather had moderated, after a hard freeze, and the day was as warm as summer. Tulip-shaped, magenta-colored buds were tipping some of the bare branches on the Japanese magnolias; here and there scarlet branches of flowering quince blazed among the greenery. Angus Holt's garden had been dotted overnight with purple pansies; the paper-white narcissi, which encircled the oak trees studding the Small Yard, were unfolding in a sudden bloom; and their fresh, provocative perfume scented the balmy air. Regine was exulting in the mildness which had enabled her to wear an elaborate costume which she insisted had once belonged to her idol, Empress Eugénie, and which Sylvestre had bought for her in Paris, paying some fabulous sum for it. Its complete unsuitability for plantation wear, at any period, did not trouble her in the least; she had even gone so far as to insist that Sylvestre accompany her to the party in the guise of Napoleon III, imperial and all. The fact that his costume could not by any stretch of the imagination be considered authentic, and that his silly little beard seemed perpetually on the point of coming unglued, did not trouble her either. She was still chattering volubly when the sound of shouts and singing announced the approach of the triumphal procession, and when Madame d'Alvery's withering glances failed to silence her, Merry put a gentle hand on her arm.

"Let's all watch and listen," she said. "You know I never saw or heard anything like this before, Regine. I don't want to miss a single trick."

Regine, who had cornered Charles Boylston, continued to chatter as if she had not heard the request. Sylvestre, touching her arm in his turn, less gently than her hostess, spoke to her with unconcealed annoyance.

"Didn't you hear Merry?" he asked sharply. "Hush up, can't you?"

"Hush up yourself! You know how I hate to be interrupted! Can't

281

you see I'm right in the middle of a story Charles is just dying to hear?"

"I can see you're right in the middle of a story fast enough, but that's chronic. I'm not so sure Charles is dying to hear it."

"Perhaps you'll tell me the end of it later on, Regine," Charles said. "I'd like to hear it very much. But as Merry says, it would be too bad if we missed something because we were absorbed in a story, and all your stories are absorbing. I've never seen a procession like this either, and I've been looking forward to it."

He smiled persuasively as he spoke, and his tact was more effective than either Merry's pleading or Sylvestre's brusqueness. He was looking even handsomer than usual, too, in old-fashioned, bottle-green hunting togs, in no way suggestive of a Yankee's uniform. Regine, accepting his courteous attention as a personal tribute, thought Cresside was a fool not to snatch at him, and resolved to tell her so at the earliest opportunity. But there was no immediate prospect of such a chance. The procession was already in sight, winding its way through the grove between the schoolhouse and the Big House. Four huge Negroes, all black as the ace of spades, were carrying the massive chair on which Gervais was enthroned. He was in high good humor; his expression was jovial as he waved his gray beaver gracefully above his head while advancing. The bright winter sunshine gave an added sheen to his pearl-colored clothes, and the contrasting colors and quality of the Negroes' jeans accentuated the elegance of their fit and finish. Sance, Plauché and Dupuy walked directly behind him, wreathed in smiles and attired in their Sunday best. Back of them came the plantation "band," made up of instruments owned and played by Negroes on the place, and consisting of four harmonicas, three banjos, two guitars, and a violin. The musicians, playing entirely by ear, did this remarkably well. After them marched the long double file of field hands in their bright cottons. Some of them carried broad sugar knives in their hands, others long stalks of tasseled cane over their shoulders; all of them were singing—their own song, the one they themselves had composed on purpose for their own supreme festival. They sang it with the zest of natural high spirits; but the *vincanne* in their stomachs and the money in their pockets raised these to a still higher pitch:

> "Ah is so glad us done got thru at de lastes'
> Ol' Satan thought he had me boun' de fastes',
> But he miss mah soul an' he cotch mah sin,
> An' give me a chance for to work an' win,
> Now Ah's free from satan an' Ah's free from sin.
> Ah is so glad us done got thru at de lastes'.
> Oh happy day, happy day,
> Us done got thru at de lastes'.
>
> De bossman's glad an' so is us,
> Ain't nobody gwine for to fret or fuss.

Caise times is good an' day won't git wuss—
Sugar makin's done, and us got our pay
Oh happy day, happy day,
Us done got thru at de lastes'."

The procession had almost reached the gallery. Merry, at a pre-arranged signal, detached herself from the others, and moved forward to meet her husband. As the bearers set down his chair, amidst a chorus of cheers and a round of applause, he stepped towards her and held out his hand. Then they turned and walked together to the demilune of mellow brick which formed the front steps. When they turned again to face their family and friends on the gallery and their people clustering around this, Gervais put one arm around her neat waist and held up the other to command attention.

"I don't want to make a speech," he said. "But in behalf of this lady and myself, I do want to say just a word of welcome to our guests and of appreciation to our workers. I want all our friends who've come out from town and all our neighbors along the River Road to hear me tell our people how grateful I am to them for the faithfulness and industry that made the grinding season which has just ended such a big success. This is a great day at Belle Heloise, and we want everyone to join us in celebrating it."

The applause on the gallery, the cheers from the marchers, broke out again. Everyone was in a mood to enjoy even the most trite remarks, especially when these were spoken with the ease and grace Gervais managed to give them. He smiled engagingly as he went on.

"The crop really is in," he said. "Of course, Sance, over there, said it never would be, if the rains kept up. But it is, in spite of Sance, who's a hopeless pessimist."

Everyone looked in the direction of the overseer, cheering and applauding him now; and he grinned sheepishly but delightedly. "And Plauché said we wouldn't have sugar worth the name, if I didn't get him those fancy new filter presses he's been talking about since God knows when. But we have. We've never made better sugar at Belle Heloise than we have this fall. And Dupuy said the old water pumps wouldn't hold out, and that we might all be blown from here to kingdom come if the new ones I'd ordered didn't get here at the beginning of grinding. Well, those pumps came in just last night—they're down at the depot at Baton Rouge now, so they ought to be ready for us to use next year anyway, unless we have as much trouble getting them set up as we had getting them here by express. But even if we do, I reckon we'll be able to hitch along some way, just as we have this year, in spite of Dupuy!"

Attention shifted from the overseer to the chief engineer and the sugar boiler, and Plauché and Dupuy accepted the "bossman's" ribbing and the hearty tribute of the entire gathering in the same abashed but gratified manner as Sance. Gervais saluted each of them in turn and continued in a slightly more serious vein.

"Most of you know that originally we planned to have this party last year, to celebrate my return from France, and most of you know why we didn't. Well, it's a good thing we put it off, because now we can have a double-barreled celebration. I feel I have every cause to rejoice because I came out of the hell I'd been through in France, and got back, safe and sound, to the beautiful home I love so much. I'm deeply touched and honored by your feeling. But I know you'll agree with me that there's an additional cause for rejoicing. Since I came back, three children have been born in this house—two boys and a girl. This means that as far as we can look ahead we don't have to fear that sometime Belle Heloise will be neglected or fall into alien hands. I want all my people to take a look at their future 'bossman' and his brother and sister today. I hope they'll feel happy, when they do, to think that some day their children will be working for him, just as their grandfather's children are working for me, helping to carry on the tradition of Belle Heloise. I hope they'll tell me that they are!"

He glanced towards the front door, and as it swung open, Dinah and the twins came out of it. Vail and Sybelle were now so big that it was almost impossible for her to carry them both at once. But Vail was already beginning to toddle, and, clutching her hand, he managed to make the grade, though his movements were somewhat impeded by the voluminous stiffness of the old-fashioned dress into which he had unwillingly been thrust. Sybelle, similarly attired and enjoying it, crowed and gurgled in Dinah's arms; and close behind them came Lethe, cradling Philogene, slightly resentful at the interruption of his slumbers, and clad in a long lacy christening robe and a tiny close-fitting lace cap. At the sight of the babies the tumult around the gallery increased; the Negroes burst into prolonged shouts and loud exclamations of enthusiasm. They could not wave their hats, since these had all been cast into the crusher in accordance with immemorial custom; but they waved their bandanas instead. Gervais took each of the babies in turn and held it up for the guests and the Negroes to see. Then he signaled to the nurses to take their charges back into the house, and put his arm around Merry again.

"I notice that my family got more applause than my speech," he said, the engaging smile still on his face. "That's fine, that's the way I want it to be. It's a great family and I'm not a great speech-maker. That's one of the reasons I'll never get very far in politics. I'm no orator and no statesman. I'm just a plain planter, just your friend and neighbor, just your 'bossman.'" And as a murmur of dissent began to rise and swell, he held up a hand for silence. "That's all I have to say to you," he said. "But Lou Ida's spent nearly all her time, these last few days, getting ready for this celebration. I think we all better find out what she has for us."

With a few final cheers, the Negroes reformed their processional and started around to the rear of the house. Merry and Gervais, from their station at the front door, motioned to their guests to leave the gallery and come into the dining room. A large silver bowl, filled with frothing eggnog and surrounded by silver goblets, stood at one end of the long mahogany table; at the other an immense coffee urn rose above a circle of tiny porcelain cups, ornamented with the Estrade crest; the intervening surface, covered with glistening damask, was almost hidden by an endless array of fruit cakes, biscuits, sandwiches, pralines and salted pecans. On the sideboard stood two silver champagne buckets, with fragile and beautiful Venetian glasses between them. Madame d'Alvery seated herself behind the eggnog, inviting Mrs. Hathaway to serve the coffee. Merry, Cresside and Gervais circulated among the guests, supervising Selah, Creassy and Lucie, and accepting congratulations on the great success of the celebration. The babies were briefly brought back and made the rounds of their delighted admirers again. On the surface the atmosphere was carefree, gay and permeated with the spirit of lavish and traditional hospitality. Only here and there a comment was made or a question asked which indicated some underlying disturbance.

"I never drank better champagne," Melvin Bisbee murmured to Charles Boylston in his pinched voice, holding his bubbling glassful of golden liquid up to catch the candlelight. "I'll say this for our host—he knows how to carry on in the grand manner. But lately I've heard rumors that things weren't going so well with him," Bisbee continued, in a lower tone. "I hope that isn't true?"

It was a question rather than a statement, but Boylston did not choose to regard it as such. He regarded the banker with a frosty look in his blue eyes.

"I don't discuss business matters with Gervais," he said, after a marked pause, in a voice as cold as his glance. "I come here because I enjoy the d'Alverys' society. They've always been extremely kind to me. I believe they're rather unusual in that respect, as far as outsiders are concerned. Most Creoles keep a closed corporation."

"Yes, yes, quite so. I am not unmindful of Captain d'Alvery's many courtesies to me. And, of course, I know nothing about sugar. But I understand that this year's crop has been more or less of a failure, in spite of all the satisfaction expressed at today's celebration."

"It isn't quite as good as last year's. That is, mine isn't. As I just said, I don't know so much about Gervais', and he's rather preoccupied at the moment, so I wouldn't think it was the best time to find out. Why don't you ask Tremaine about his?"

Boylston turned away, rather pointedly, and walked over to Fabian, who was sitting alone at the moment, except for Belizaire, upon whose nose he had just placed a sponge drop. Madame d'Alvery had never allowed either Snow or Cornet to come into the house, and she frowned sternly on all visiting animals. But Fabian, nonchalantly observing that was no way to run a plantation anyhow, had serenely continued to bring his dog with him on all occasions, and lately his aunt had refrained from invidious remarks on the subject. Today she had actually stooped and patted Belizaire on the head and Fabian was now pressing the advantage gained by putting him through a few tricks. Having balanced the sponge drop, he gave the order "Say grace!" and the spaniel immediately put his paws on the chair beside his master and buried his long sensitive nose in them. There he remained motionless until Fabian exclaimed "Amen!" Then he leapt in the air, snapping at the sponge drop with avidity.

"You certainly get away with murder in this house," Boylston remarked, sitting down beside Fabian and handing his empty glass to Selah for a refill. "I wonder what would happen if I appeared here with one of my Walkers. Well, I don't begrudge you your privileges—I'm glad enough to be here under any circumstances. The South certainly survives at Belle Heloise. . . . Incidentally, Gervais tells me that the next party is to be a christening. I'm glad to hear it. I remember feeling disappointed last year that there was no celebration when the twins were baptized, because this house is such an ideal setting for a ceremony of that sort. Of course, Cresside was still incapacitated then, though."

"Yes—but hasn't she staged a grand comeback?"

Fabian glanced across the room, and Boylston followed his gaze. Cresside was standing by the fireplace, engaged in lively conversation with Harvey Lawrason, who was visiting at Hackberry Lodge again, and who was obviously enjoying himself immensely. The quaint plaid dress, with its full skirt and tight bodice, was extremely becoming to her, both in color and in style, and unlike the changeable silk which Merry was wearing, it had required no alterations, for Cresside was still slim as a reed. But her look of gauntness and emaciation was gone and her sparkling eyes were no longer black-ringed in a haggard face. Framed by the ornamented marble mantel, with the glowing firelight for a background, she made a picture that was not only vivid but enchanting. Instinctively Boylston rose and took a step in the direction of the hearth.

"I want to show you another trick of Belizaire's," Fabian suggested. "I think it's about his best. Wait here just a sec, will you, Charles?" He rose, too, but instead of going towards the fireplace, limped out into the hall, his dog at his heels. Presently he returned, and reseating himself, addressed Belizaire as quietly as he might have spoken to a child. "I left my cigarettes out there," he said. "Go get them for me, will you?" And when the dog bounded off, to return with the package in his mouth, Fabian added, "Oh, but I forgot the matches, too. . . ."

"Very diverting," Boylston said a little drily, as Belizaire returned triumphantly a second time. "But after all, there's no reason why I should concede that Harvey's also a privileged character, even if you're willing to." He nodded and sauntered on towards the fireplace, and Fabian, after looking at him quizzically for a moment, returned to the

286

dining room. Madame d'Alvery and Mrs. Hathaway were still sitting at their posts, though the demands for refills were now few and far between, and the guests had scattered informally through the parlor, library and music room. Fabian drew up a chair and sat down by Mrs. Hathaway, who forestalled any remark he might make by a rather captious one of her own.

"Fabian, tell me whether you do not agree with me. I have just been saying to your Aunt Isabelle that while this celebration has been delightful, on the whole, I feel that part of Gervais' speech might well have been omitted. Of course, I have in mind his reference to the security of this plantation."

"'As far as we can look ahead, we don't have to fear that Belle Heloise will be neglected or fall into alien hands'? Is that what you mean, Mrs. Hathaway? Why, I thought that was one of his best lines! I wrote it for him myself."

"There was nothing the matter with the line, as you call it, in itself. But it was based on the fact that three children have been born here within the last year. In view of the fact that Regine and Sylvestre are childless, and that we are all so deeply disappointed because of this, I think Gervais would have been more tactful if he had made no such reference to it in our presence."

"Well, I don't know. My view was that he was talking primarily to his people, rather than to his guests. After all, this was the Negroes' celebration. The rest of us were only onlookers. Don't you agree with me, Tante Isabelle?"

"Completely, Fabian. You analyzed the situation exactly as I did—in fact, I said the same thing to Mrs. Hathaway before you came in. Naturally, all of us here would be extremely sorry if there were never an heir to Hathaway. But that cannot prevent us from rejoicing that we have been so greatly blessed at Belle Heloise."

She rose, and Fabian immediately went over to her and offered her his arm. She smiled at him with unaccustomed graciousness as she took it.

"I think we may safely join the group in the music room now," she said. "Unless, of course, dear Mrs. Hathaway, you would prefer the group in the parlor, or the one in the library. But I believe we are to have some spirituals before the party breaks up and the music room always seems the most appropriate place for that. Besides, Dinah has taken the twins there, at Sylvestre's suggestion—he said he wanted to get better acquainted with them. But we must not leave him indefinitely to their mercies—at this time of day, when they begin to get tired, they are sometimes riotous also, especially Vail. . . . If anyone desires more coffee or eggnog, Selah may take it around as he is still taking champagne. I believe my son is planning to make quite an occasion of that also. Of course we shall count on your presence for that too, *chère*."

CHAPTER XXII

Philogene's christening was indeed a great event, but it marked the last of the entertainments reviving the traditional hospitality at Belle Heloise.

A few days after it took place Gervais received a letter from Arnold Fletcher, saying that he would greatly appreciate another payment of ten thousand dollars on account. He had not forgotten that he had agreed to a ninety-day delay for full payment; but it did so happen that he was unusually pressed himself, and he was sure Captain d'Alvery would be glad to accommodate him with this small sum. A year earlier, Gervais would readily have agreed that ten thousand dollars was a small sum; but it did not look that way to him now, and he was sure, from Garfield's latest communication, that it was futile to look for further advances from that quarter. Ruefully, he went to Bisbee and asked him for the money, and without apparent hesitation, Bisbee let him have it on an open note. The transaction was so much easier than Gervais had expected, despite the confident way in which he had spoken about it to Merry, that he tried to tell himself there was no reason why he should worry any more: if Bisbee would let him have that much without formality, he would let him have a larger amount with satisfactory collateral. He allowed Fletcher's ninety-day limit to pass without mentioning it and without undue concern; and he felt safer still when the deadline went by and the architect did not immediately send him a reminder that it had. Then he was suddenly and rudely shaken from his sense of security.

One pleasant Sunday in April, Melvin Bisbee came out to Belle Heloise. He had been meaning to pay a party call ever since the christening, he said—in fact, he had two or three party calls on his conscience! He certainly always had been entertained like royalty on the River Road! He went first to the Big House, where Madame d'Alvery received him graciously, saying she was sorry Cresside was out, but that Merry and Gervais were fortunately both at home; she would send Selah to the garçonnière immediately to let them know they had a visitor. Meantime, she and Mr. Bisbee would have a glass of port together while they awaited the arrival of coffee and the other members of the family.

The call passed off agreeably, but tepidly. Gervais and Bisbee discussed the recent decision, made by two members of the Railroad Commission in the absence of the third, granting an increase in rates to the Cumberland Telephone Company. This action had apparently precipitated a major political battle, for the absent Commissioner happened to be that firebrand, Huey Long; he had immediately issued a volcanic statement to the press, charging that his colleagues had pre-

288

judged the case and sold out the public; he added that Shelby Taylor, one of the other Commissioners, had promised him faithfully to vote against the increase. Recriminations were now bitter on both sides, but Huey had the louder voice and there were signs that his voice was becoming increasingly powerful. The "poor boy from the country, who wore diamond buttons on his drawers," was making himself more and more of a nuisance.

Madame d'Alvery and Merry took very little part in this conversation, but as neither objected to the role of listener, there was no awkwardness because of this. They continued to sip small blacks and to eat little frosted cakes with composure while Gervais and Melvin Bisbee discussed Huey Long. It was not until Bisbee rose to leave, and inquired rather tardily for the children, that Merry got in a word edgewise.

"Wouldn't you like to see them? We'll have them brought in if you would."

He was either oblivious of the eagerness in her voice or indifferent to it. He had never been especially interested in children or intimately associated with them, and the two recent celebrations at Belle Heloise, with which the three youngest d'Alverys had been so closely connected, had already taxed his powers of expressive admiration. He shook his head with attempted archness, his pinched voice cracking a little as he answered.

"Suppose I postpone that pleasure until my next visit? It's such a pretty day, as you say around here. I've been hoping that Captain d'Alvery would ask me to take a turn in the fields with him before I went back to town. And, unfortunately, I haven't time for both today."

The last thing that Gervais desired was to take Bisbee "for a turn." The fields were grassy because of excessive rains, and the cane had come in to a very poor stand. The young growth which should have been so fresh and green was already streaked with yellow. Bisbee, who was originally a Hoosier, might not grasp the exact significance of all these telltale signs, but after all, now that he had reached the standing of a prominent banker in a sugar Parish, he must have learned what most of them meant. Gervais explained that the ground was very wet and that he was afraid his visitor might find the going rather rough. But it appeared Bisbee had come prepared for this; his rubbers were in the car. He said good-by to Madame d'Alvery and Merry and went out to get them. . . .

A week later he wrote to Gervais and asked for collateral on the open note. Of course, he explained, this was only a formality. But since the loan had been made, the board of directors had met and decided that they must observe such formalities more rigidly than in the past, owing to the general financial situation. . . .

Merry had seen Gervais lose his temper many times by now. But she had never seen him as angry as he was on receipt of this letter. He

289

strode up and down their pleasant little living room, shouting and swearing.

"He came out here on purpose to spy, the dirty sneak! He pretended he was making a social call, and all the time he was just snooping around to see what the prospects were for a good crop!"

"They're pretty bad, aren't they, Gervais?"

"You're damn right, they're bad! But that doesn't excuse Bisbee. I ought never to have let the bastard inside this house! I ought to have seen his stripe from the beginning."

Merry listened, silent and miserable, as Gervais ranted on and on. Her own career in the business world had been brief and limited; but her good sense told her that however reprehensible Bisbee's conduct might have been as a friend, as a banker he was only acting with proper prudence. However, she was wise enough not to voice this opinion. She waited until the worst of Gervais' anger had spent itself, and then she asked one or two cautious and hesitant questions.

"You can let him have the collateral, can't you, honey?"

"Yes, of course I can . . . Some kind of collateral. I don't at the moment know just what."

"Is there some other bank you could go to that wouldn't ask for it?"

"Of course there must be—but I wouldn't know which, offhand. I've done all my business with the Cotton Factors' National for years. If they treat me like this, then——"

"What about Fabian? Would you mind asking him to help you?"

"I'd mind like hell. He's kept telling me, ever since I got back from France, that I ought to try a different kind of seed cane—as if there *were* any different kind I could try! The land's worked out, that's what's the matter."

"Wouldn't it help if you raised two or three kinds of crops, instead of one?"

"Oh, it's supposed to! You must have been listening to Fabian yourself, Merry. You don't know anything about land. Of course, it's possible to raise cotton and rice. I don't need to tell you that—you've seen them both growing here and there along the River Road. But if I tried to do that, I'd raise the cost of my overhead without any assurance that those crops would do better than the sugar, and it's hard enough to keep one complicated set of machinery paid for and in order without trying to tackle two or three. If you're a millionaire, like Boylston, it doesn't matter about the cost of your overhead, and when one crop fails you can take it in your stride and wait for another. That's why he can afford to dabble around in every sort there is."

She was afraid he was going to say, *If Cresside would only marry Boylston, everything would be all right. She could ask him for the money I need, and he'd give it to her. After all, she has an interest in Belle Heloise and he'd want to protect his wife's property.* As a matter of fact, the words were already on the tip of Gervais' tongue; something in Merry's expression stopped him from saying them.

"We've had a series of unbelievably bad breaks in the weather, too," he said. "First days and days of rain, then a long stretch of drouth; first a heat wave, and then one freeze after another. Not just one season either—year after year. There's nothing any human being can do about that. It's an act of God—or the devil."

"But Fabian *could* help you, couldn't he?" persisted Merry, not to be diverted.

"Oh, he could, all right. Fabian's very well off and he doesn't spend anything except on those damn camellias of his. He hasn't got anything to spend it for—it isn't as if he had three or four hundred thousand dollars' worth of machinery to keep up and more than a hundred hands to pay and a big family to provide for. One dog doesn't cost much, and Belizaire's his only interest, except his garden and that little insignificant house."

"I shouldn't be surprised if he gave away a lot of money to people who need it, in a quiet way, and he's always seemed very interested in his family, and very kind, to me."

"Now get this straight, Merry. I'm not asking Fabian for money. We're not quite in the class of deserving paupers even yet. And I won't have him coming here all the time, knowing I'm in debt to him, and feeling uncomfortable every time I look him in the face."

Again she had the wisdom to be silent, instead of asking what he did intend to do, if he could not go to his broker or to another bank and would not go to Fabian. But she lay awake most of the night, worrying; the next morning Philogene was fretful, because she did not have enough milk for him. Then the following day still another letter came in from Arnold Fletcher, and this one tersely called attention to an account past due and abruptly demanded the balance owed for the work of restoration.

It was so long since Merry had been to town, or even spoken of going, that Cresside was taken completely by surprise when her sister-in-law, who had never learned to drive a car, asked her for a ride. However, she managed to answer in her usual casual and cordial way: sure, she said, she had thought of going in herself, anyhow; it would be fun to have Merry along. About what time? Right after Philogene's three o'clock feeding, Merry answered. She did not add that Gervais would be out in the fields then, but something about the flushed, almost frightened look on her face suggested to Cresside that he had not been told of the plan, and that there was some special reason why Merry did not want him to know about it. Cresside asked no further questions, but she regarded Merry covertly during the course of the ride, and what she saw moved her to sympathy. Merry's expression was still as sweet as ever, her features as faultless; but some sort of a blight had fallen on the bloom which had been her greatest beauty. The slight excess weight, the slight weariness of carriage, the slight look of dowdiness caused by ill-fitting and outmoded street clothes—none of these could quite account for this faded look. *That fool brother of mine had done this to her,* Cresside said to herself savagely; *I don't know how or what, but somehow and something. I'd like to wring his damn neck. That's all any man's neck is worth, wringing; almost any man's neck,* she added to herself, with one swift and tender mental reservation; and she wanted desperately to say aloud, *I'm sorry, Merry. Is there anything I can do to help?* Instead. as they neared town and she slowed down the car, she merely waited for Merry to tell her where to go.

"Oh, I forgot!" Merry said in confusion. "Would it be convenient for you to take me to the store? If it isn't, just drop me at the first corner."

"It's perfectly convenient for me to take you anywhere you want to go. But you'll have to tell me which store."

"Oh! I forgot!" Merry said again. "I meant Goldenberg's. We never called it anything but 'the store' when I was working there. Of course it was silly of me not to think——"

"It wasn't silly. It was perfectly natural. I'm the dumb one, not to understand right away what you meant. About how long do you want to be there?"

"I shouldn't think more than half an hour. But I want to go over to my mother's for a minute afterwards, and I'd like the walk. Why don't you meet me there, any time you like, just so I get back before six?"

"Right. Let's say five-fifteen, so that we won't run too close to the wind."

"But what are you going to do in the meantime? Won't it be awfully dull for you, waiting around?"

"Oh, I can always count on a date at the Confederate Monument, you know! Or I can go to Fabian's house and play with Belizaire. I might even drift into Fabian's office and read law. You know there's no telling to what lengths the modern girl will go."

She was off with her usual gay salute, and Merry went through the revolving doors and entered Goldenberg's store. She had hardly set foot in it since her marriage, and she had not once returned to Mr. Goldenberg's office after resigning as his secretary. She had no sense of ease and familiarity as she took the elevator to the sixth floor, and her feeling of strangeness tightened the lump which already constricted her throat, and made the hollow at the pit of her stomach seem deeper. The slatternly but cheerful colored girls, who had formerly run the elevators, and who had never failed to greet her with a grin, had been replaced; the new operator was a young man who wore his smart uniform as if he had grown accustomed to similar clothes in the Army, and he held himself with military precision and aloofness. But as Merry went through the Department of Rugs and Draperies, and saw the scatter rugs cluttering the aisle as they always had, she stooped down and put them in their proper places, folding them neatly. This trivial service, performed almost instinctively, made her feel more at home again. However, when a lounging clerk, after regarding her with a disapproving air, came haughtily forward and asked if he could show her something, she flushed and answered with acute embarrassment.

"No, thank you. I used to work here, and I straightened the scatter rugs whenever I went down this aisle. It seemed natural to do it again, that's all. . . . I'm on my way to Mr. Goldenberg's office."

"Have you an appointment?"

"No, but I'm sure he'll see me, if he's there."

"He may be in conference. Of course, you can ask his secretary."

"I'm going to. She's an old friend of mine."

She turned under the pulsating red arrow, and went past the steel lockers, the freight elevator, the adjustment bureau and the fire escape to the cubbyhole at the end of the glassed-in cubicles. Hazel was typing busily, but Merry saw a small diamond twinkling on her left hand, and guessed that Mr. Goldenberg might soon be looking for a secretary again. Hazel jumped up in a startled way when Merry spoke to her.

"Why, Meredith Randall! What on earth are you doing here? Why didn't you let me know you were coming, instead of just walking in on me like that?"

"I didn't have any way of letting you know. I decided to come very suddenly, and you know we haven't a telephone. . . . Is Mr. Goldenberg in, Hazel?"

She ought to have asked for Al before saying anything else, she realized after she had spoken. But her nervousness had added to her sense of urgency. Now that she had made up her mind what she was going to do, she did not want to postpone the evil moment; she wanted to have it behind her. Hazel, though a little disappointed by Merry's directness, was unresentful; she had not forgotten how cordial Merry had been to her and Al when they went to the sugar house. She rose immediately.

"Yes, he's in. I'll tell him you're here. I know he'll be glad to see you."

She went into the private office, leaving the door open behind her. Merry could hear her speaking to Mr. Goldenberg and his cordial and instantaneous rejoinder. He came to the threshold himself with an outstretched hand.

"Why, Mrs. d'Alvery, this is a great pleasure. How are you? I haven't seen you in a long time!"

Again the lump in Merry's throat tightened. Gervais had never invited the Goldenbergs to Belle Heloise himself, and when she had first suggested doing so, he had answered vaguely that it wasn't just the best time; later, when she pressed the matter, he had said rather shortly that he did not think his mother would particularly care to have the Goldenbergs at Belle Heloise, and as it happened, he shared her viewpoint, for once. The fact that Mr. Goldenberg must be aware of this viewpoint made her mission all the harder now. Merry's hands had grown terribly cold, and her voice shook a little as she answered.

"Yes, I know. I don't get in town very often. But I came today on purpose to see you."

"I'm very much honored. Won't you sit down and tell me what I can do for you?"

She was thankful for the seat, but she was not sure things were any easier because he realized this was not a social call, that she would not have come if she had not wanted to ask a favor. The situation, stripped of all pretense, became horribly bald. She stood a moment to gather her forces, fixing her eyes on the glassed-over desk, which she saw was still adorned with the bud vase, the picture of Mrs. Goldenberg, and the small neat calendar in a frame of tooled leather. Then she looked up and faced Mr. Goldenberg.

"My husband's in trouble," she said. "Bad trouble. He doesn't know which way to turn. I've been trying and trying to think of some way I could help him. Finally I thought of coming to you and telling you all about it. Gervais doesn't know I've come. I'm afraid he may be very angry when he finds out. It's the first time I've ever kept anything from him, and, of course, I'm worried about that, too. Just the same, I thought it was better not to let him know until afterwards."

"I'm very glad you thought of coming to me. I'm very much honored," Mr. Goldenberg said again. "Is this trouble of your husband's financial?"

"Yes. He spent too much money last year. He made a great many improvements on the place because he thought that would be a good investment, in the long run. And anyway, sugar was so high that he had every reason to feel he could afford what he was doing. Then the price of sugar fell—of course you know that. And now the new crop is a failure—the cane is riddled with mosaic disease. His factor won't advance him anything and the bank he's always gone to won't lend him anything."

"I'm very sorry to hear that he's had such difficulties and that they've made you so unhappy. Was there any special way you thought I could help?"

"Yes. I remembered that you were a director in another bank. I used to transcribe letters about loans for you sometimes, you know. I'm sure you have a great deal of influence with the other directors. I thought perhaps you might be willing to bring up the question of a loan to Gervais at the next board meeting."

"Yes, I would be willing." At the unhesitating reply a great wave of relief engulfed Merry, leaving her assuaged but limp; the dreadful tautness, the dreadful sensations of cold and choking were gone; but now she wondered how she could summon the strength to say anything more.

"Of course, I can't tell you how the other directors would feel about the matter," Mr. Goldenberg went on. "And even if they were willing to make a loan, I don't know whether your husband would be satisfied

294

with the terms of it. They might seem pretty harsh to him. Money's very tight these days, I'm sorry to say."

"I realize all that. I know we have to go ahead just a step at a time. But if you proposed a loan, we'd have taken the first step, anyway."

"Very well, Mrs. d'Alvery. I'll propose the loan at the next meeting of the directors. It's on Monday."

He drew a small pad of scratch paper towards him and picked up a pencil.

"I'll have to ask you a few questions," he said. "Not that your answers will affect my promise—it's merely that I need more information than I have. How many acres are there on your plantation?"

"Gervais always speaks about arpents. I think there are around three thousand. An arpent is a little smaller than an acre, isn't it?"

"Yes. . . . And how many tons of cane, approximately, did the plantation produce last year, Mrs. d'Alvery? Do you know?"

"Nearly forty thousand. Of course the year before was much better."

"I'm taking it for granted that since you're suggesting this loan you would be willing to sign a paper waiving your homestead rights? Is that correct?"

"I am not just sure what you mean, Mr. Goldenberg. But, of course, I'd be willing to sign anything to get Gervais the money he needs."

Her voice did not tremble any longer, though she felt so tired. It was firm and eager. Mr. Goldenberg raised his searching, bloodshot eyes and looked at her with admiration.

"I'm afraid your husband is going to need a very large sum, in order to clear up the indebtedness for the improvements he has already made and to meet the running expenses of getting in the new crop," he explained. "In order to mention some figure, let us say a hundred thousand dollars, though perhaps he will not need quite that much. If the bank advanced him any such amount, it would have to take a mortgage on the property. There wouldn't be any other way to handle the transaction. So you would have to waive your own rights in the plantation, the rights you have as Captain d'Alvery's wife. You acquired these, automatically, when you married him, you know."

"I suppose I did. I never thought about it though. You see, Mr. Goldenberg, I married Gervais because I was terribly in love with him— I didn't think about money or anything else. I'm still—I still love him so much I'd do anything I could for him. My rights don't matter. But it matters a lot to have him happy."

Mr. Goldenberg continued to look at her searchingly as she spoke. His admiration increased with his appraisal.

"I can see that you are absolutely sincere, and perhaps, as an old friend, you'll permit me to say, whether Captain d'Alvery is in financial difficulties or not, I consider him a very lucky man," he remarked gently. "But do you think your mother-in-law and your sister-in-law will feel the same way about it that you do? Of course, they have rights in the property, too, since it is inherited."

"I'm sure Cresside would feel the same way that I do, Mr. Goldenberg. She and Gervais quarrel a good deal, but underneath it all they're very fond of each other. And Cresside's a grand person, generous to a fault. I know she'd want to help. .... Of course, my mother-in-law's a grand person, too," Merry added loyally, but a little hesitantly. "I wouldn't dare speak for her until I've talked with her. You see, I'm very ignorant about money, Mr. Goldenberg, and I didn't realize, when I thought of asking you to arrange for a loan, that the bank would have to take a mortgage on Belle Heloise. I do happen to know that Madame Mère has a very strong feeling about mortgages. I've heard her say so, a great many times."

Uncomfortably, Merry remembered certain scenes between Gervais and his mother. Madame d'Alvery, from the first, had opposed his plan of restoration. There was plenty of room for them all at the Big House, she insisted. François and Adela Estrade had raised ten children in it without feeling crowded, despite the constant presence of various indigent relatives who made visits of indefinite length, as Philogene d'Alvery had begun by doing. And besides all the elderly aunts and uncles and cousins, Angus Holt had lived there for years. Madame d'Alvery saw no reason for rebuilding the storehouse and the *garçonnière* to create more living space, still less for restoring the cooperage and the blacksmith shop. She was ready to concede that machinery must be safe, if it were in use, but she would rather have seen the mill shut down than equipped with installations which were not paid for. "It is better to have a leaking roof that is your own roof and that no one can take away from you, than one that is watertight and mortgaged to someone else," she said repeatedly. It was her favorite example of a property owner's only sound position. Merry knew that nothing would ever change this viewpoint, for Madame d'Alvery had tried, far more forcefully and persistently than Merry, to stop Gervais' reckless expenditures. But after all, she had not succeeded. Now that money had already been spent on the leaking roof, so to speak, something must be done about repaying it.

"I'll talk to Madame Mère," Merry said, meeting Mr. Goldenberg's bloodshot eyes squarely. "I'll let you know what she says. Of course, it wouldn't be fair to ask you to present this question to the directors and then find that the family wouldn't consent to a mortgage at all. I'll come back to see you again, sometime before Monday, Mr. Goldenberg. Or else Gervais will come himself. And—and thank you. I can't tell you how grateful I am to you. But I think you know. I hope there'll be something I can do for you sometime that will mean as much to you as this means to me."

Merry walked up Third Street to the Boulevard with feelings of mingled relief and dread. She had accomplished the first part of her mission, and this had lifted a load from her heart. Mr. Goldenberg had been generous in every sense of the word—generous and considerate and understanding, as she had thought he would be, for all this was entirely in keeping with his character. Yet before she went to him, she had not been able wholly to suppress a little forking fear that he might betray some natura resentment because she waited until she was in trouble before seeking to renew their acquaintance, that his reception of her might be cool and his manner distant, so that the petition, difficult enough at best to put forward, would be repelled at the outset. Now that fear was lulled, but she still had her husband to face, and she knew that this second ordeal might be harder than the first. However, she realized that she must try to compose herself before seeing her mother, whose antipathy to Gervais had increased, rather than abated, with time. If Merry's agitation was evident, Mrs. Randall would seize upon it and ferret out its source. Resolutely, the girl forced herself to walk slowly, breathing in the sunny air, looking at shop windows as she went along, and trying to divert her thoughts both from the interview which had just ended and the interview which was still ahead of her. As she passed the Confederate Monument, she saw that Pascal Tremblet was sitting alone on the bench in front of it and stopped to speak to him.

"Good evening, Mr. Tremblet. Where's your sidekick this fine day?" she asked, as he rose to greet her. But even before he answered her, she knew that her question had been ill-timed. His pinched face had a stricken look, and the gnarled hands clasping the old cane were quivering.

"He's not so well, him, Miss Merry," Pascal said slowly. "He didn't come out to meet me yesterday, so I went to his grandson's house, and I found him in the bed. He said he'd be up again today for sure, if it was pretty weather, and you couldn't ask for prettier weather than this, now could you? But like you see, he isn't here."

"Perhaps he'll come later on. Perhaps something has detained him," Merry said, trying to speak convincingly.

"No, ma'am, I'm not trying to deceive myself. He hasn't come because he isn't able to. Likely he won't ever be, again. I'll be all alone, me, pretty soon."

"Please don't say that, Mr. Tremblet! . . . Have you spoken to Fabian?"

"Not yet, Miss Merry. But Miss Cresside, she stopped by the Monument a while back, and she said she'd do it for me. I'm looking for him to come by almost any time now."

"You're right in counting on Fabian, Mr. Tremblet. He'll do everything he can for you and your friend. I wish I could stay with you until he comes, but I'm on my way to see my mother, and I have to get back to the plantation to feed my baby at six o'clock."

"Yes, Miss Merry, I know how it is. Don't you worry any about me. I'll be all right. I'll just sit here and wait for Fabian."

She went on her way reluctantly, a fresh worry added to those that already burdened her; but she found her mother too preoccupied with her own troubles to notice the unconvincing quality of Merry's determined cheerfulness. Mrs. Randall was rocking back and forth in her little sitting room, sniffling suspiciously, and she did not even look up when her daughter came in. Merry, who was used to such experiences, stooped to kiss her and spoke to her affectionately.

"Hello, Mother! Aren't you going to tell me you're glad to see me? I was ever so glad that I had a chance to come into town!"

"Well, it's nice you've got something to be glad about. Everything's looking pretty black to me, right now."

"Why, what's the matter?"

"Miss Mittie's lost her job, that's what's the matter. I don't know what's going to become of her or me without her salary."

"Lost her job!" Merry echoed in dismay. "What happened?"

"She got suspicious when the principal didn't say anything to her about next year. All the other teachers had been told they'd be kept, that they'd get formal notices saying so a little later on, same as usual. She didn't hear a word, so she made inquiries. And she found out she was being fired for disloyalty."

"Disloyalty! But Miss Mittie's the soul of loyalty! No one could possibly think she was disloyal."

"I don't know what anybody thinks, but that's what the State Superintendent says. Some of the women in that Suffrage crowd she goes with would like to see him lose his own job, because they don't think he's fit for it. He claims Miss Mittie's been one of those working against him. That's disloyalty, as far as he's concerned."

"But *was* she?"

"I don't know, Merry. Miss Mittie won't talk about it herself. All I know is, after this month, she won't have anything to live on, except what she's saved, and that's mighty little. What can a teacher save out of her kind of pay? She can't get a job anywhere else in Louisiana either, when she's been fired in Baton Rouge on account of trouble with the State Superintendent. And she can't go back East. She couldn't qualify to teach there any more. She hasn't tried to keep up with all the newfangled Yankee notions. She's just drifted along, like we do in the South. She never thought she'd have to do anything else."

Merry listened to her mother with a sense of mounting disaster. It was not the first time she had heard of a teacher's displacement on some pretext for which politics were really responsible. Besides, she knew that her mother spoke the truth: Miss Mittie, conscientious and intelligent as she was, had always openly expressed her contempt for modern schoolroom methods, and those expressions would count against her now. Under all these circumstances, it was unlikely that anyone would be able to intercede for her successfully, or that she would be able to re-establish herself, on her own initiative. And without the money from Miss Mittie's board and lodging, Mrs. Randall herself would be almost penniless. The long postponed moment of her mother's dependence on her, which Merry had foreseen when

Gervais urged her to marry him, had come at last, and somehow she must cope with this, too. But she could not force her tired mind to do so immediately. She continued to sit beside her mother, silent and appalled, while Mrs. Randall went on sniffling and rocking, until she heard Cresside honking outside. Then she rose and went slowly towards the door.

"Just a minute!" she called to her sister-in-law. Cresside called back that there wasn't any hurry, to take her time. Just the same, Merry knew that she must not linger. Philogene would be hungry, Gervais would be annoyed, half a dozen things might have gone wrong during her unannounced absence. She put her arms around Mrs. Randall's bony shoulders and hugged her hard.

"Don't feel so badly, Mummy," she said soothingly, calling her mother by the name she had not used since childhood. "Miss Mittie'll be paid for one more month, whatever happens. You and she can both manage that long. And before the month's up, I'll think of something I can do to help. I don't know what it'll be, but something. I've got to go now, because my baby needs me even more than you do. But I know you need me, too. I'll come back in a few days and we'll talk this over again."

CHAPTER XXIII

As SHE WENT down the steps of her mother's house, Merry decided that she would say nothing about the trouble which had befallen Miss Mittie until she had thought out some way of relieving it. But on the way back to Belle Heloise, she did tell Cresside about her talk with Mr. Goldenberg. She felt that if she were armed with her sister-in-law's support regarding the mortgage, she would be better prepared for the inevitable battle ahead of her, and she was not disappointed about securing this.

"Merry, I do hand it to you for spunk," Cresside said heartily. "I told you that the night you came to Belle Heloise and again the morning Philogene was born, but now I'm ready to tell the world. I know it took guts for you to go to Mr. Goldenberg like that. Of course, I'll put the old John Hancock anywhere he wants me to. And I'll do what I can to make *maman* and Gervais see the light of day. I don't suppose I'll get very far with your beloved husband. But we better start right off by reminding him that if he has this money from the First National, he can tell Fletcher to go straight to hell, and that he won't have to dig up any collateral for Bisbee. He can pay for the restoration straightaway, and clean up his open note, too, writing a sweet little missive to the effect that of course it isn't due for months yet, but that it gives him great pleasure, etc. If he's smart, he'll manage to wedge in a line saying he didn't think of 'formalities' between friends, and that he's sorry Bisbee didn't see it the same way. That ought to give the old skinflint the idea that he won't be coming to Belle Heloise any more, and believe me, he'll be sorry, and too late. He was lapping up atmosphere along with champagne, and writing bragging letters about both of them back to Peoria, or wherever it is he comes from."

"You always know just what to do, Cresside. I wouldn't have thought of beginning by reminding Gervais he could get rid of Fletcher and Bisbee straight off. I think that's just the way to handle him. Can you think of an equally good way to get around Madame Mère?"

"I haven't yet, but I'm working on it. Just give me time."

The evening did not start off too propitiously. Merry and Cresside had never left the plantation before at the same time, and though Dinah and Lethe had done the best they could with their charges, the twins had sensed the withdrawal of authority and Philogene the absence of his most important source of supply. Vail had fallen down and cut his knee; Sybelle had stuck the corner of her bib into her eye; Philogene had been howling at the top of his lungs for nearly an hour. While Cresside rushed off to get iodine and boric-acid water, Merry hastily unbuttoned her dress, and within a few minutes comparative quiet and order were restored; but it was impossible for either girl to answer the questions about the afternoon satisfactory until the children were in bed and dinner over. When Gervais started back to the *garçonnière,* however, Merry detained him.

"I want to talk to Madame Mère and you together," she said. "I want Cresside to stay in the room while I'm doing it, too. Let's all go into the library, shall we? I've told Lethe she must listen for Philogene, that I wouldn't be back right away."

The session which ensued was stormy from start to finish. Gervais was almost as angry because Merry had been to Mr. Goldenberg without consulting him as he had been over Mr. Bisbee's letter about "formalities." He spoke to her as he had never spoken before, and the flush of embarrassment with which she had begun to tell him of her mission faded to pallor deeper than Cresside's while she listened. Her lovely natural color did not come back at all that evening, and she had to keep biting her lips to keep from crying. But she could not be cowed, though her husband and her mother-in-law, joining forces for once, declared over and over again that they would never mortgage their ancestral home. Even the taunt that only an outsider would have made such a suggestion, and the reproach that the Estrades would turn over in their graves if they knew of it, failed to move her; and at that point Cresside succeeded in coming to her rescue. She had not thought of going to Mr. Goldenberg herself, she said; but that was only because she did not know him well enough to ask favors of him: she thought it was darn lucky for them all that Merry did. As far as being an outsider went, she was just as much of an Estrade as her mother, and just as much of a d'Alvery as Gervais, too; and she was all for the mortgage. If their ancestors did turn in their graves, perhaps they would wake up and find out that things had changed a good deal since their day, on the whole for the better; but whether they did or not, their descendants might just as well face facts. What did Gervais want to do? Let Fletcher and Bisbee start telling all over town that he was bankrupt?

They parted, completely at odds, and without reaching any definite decision, when Merry had to return to the *garçonnière* to give Philogene his final feeding for the night. Gervais did not speak harshly to Merry again; he ignored her as completely as if she had not been present. He did not lie close beside her with his arms tenderly around her when he went to sleep; instead, for the first time, the width of the bed divided them and it was symbolic of the greater gulf separating them spiritually. Merry lay wide-eyed and wretched, thinking of her mother's troubles as well as her own and longing to creep over to her husband and beg his forgiveness for having offended him; but she resisted the impulse with the same firmness that she had resisted the attack which had preceded his withdrawal. Morning found them no nearer together, either figuratively or literally, than they had been the night before, and the strained silence between them lasted for several days. Merry knew she had done everything she could and said all there was for her to say. But Cresside kept hammering away at her brother, whenever she saw him, and in the midnight talks with her mother, which had now become habitual, she continued to speak on the subject, less caustically but no less insistently. On Saturday morning she confronted Gervais as he was mounting his horse, and asked him if he were planning to call on Mr. Goldenberg that afternoon.

"I sure am not," he said abruptly. "What gave you the idea that I might?"

"Well, you know the directors' meeting is on Monday, and you also know that Merry promised to give him some kind of an answer before then. She agreed to go herself if you didn't and I think she's done her share in trying to get you out of this mess already. It's taken a lot out of her. I wouldn't put it past you not to mind that, but don't forget it's taking a lot out of Philogene, too. Maybe you haven't noticed that Merry's going around looking more and more like a ghost and that Philogene's howling his head off from hunger."

"So what?"

"So that if you're not going into town today, I think I will. I can go to see Mr. Goldenberg myself. I can tell him that *maman* and Merry and I are all very much in favor of the mortgage and that we hope he'll be able to arrange it. After all, we control the greater part of the property, among us."

"You can't lie to him like that. *Maman* isn't in favor of the mortgage."

"Damn right she is. She wasn't to start with, but she is now. Go ask her yourself if you don't believe me, you dumb Dora."

Gervais tied his horse and strode off towards the Big House, without answering Cresside. His mother received him reproachfully but calmly.

"Certainly Cresside told you the truth," she said in a cold voice. "What possible reason could she have for lying to you? I feel exactly as I always have—that it is far better to have a leaking roof that is one's own, than a whole one on which someone else has claim. But since in this case you have already repaired the roof with someone else's money, your creditor must be reimbursed. We cannot repudiate our just debts, Gervais." It was exactly the line of argument on which Merry had counted, but Cresside had facilitated and expedited the process of deduction. "Cresside also consulted me about going to see Mr. Goldenberg herself, in case you declined to do so," Madame d'Alvery continued. "I gave my consent to that, too. Naturally, she would ask Fabian to escort her if she made such a visit, so that the family would be represented by one of its male members."

"You don't mean to tell me that Fabian knows all about this mess, too?"

"I have an idea that Cresside may have given him some inkling; they went to see Pola Negri together last night," Madame d'Alvery answered imperturbably. "After all, Fabian was bound to find out about it sooner or later, and Cresside was the best person to tell him. He has always been very fond of her; I do not need to remind you of that. I believe he told her that he would keep the afternoon free until he learned, definitely, whether she would need him or not."

Eventually, Gervais and Cresside went into town together, after a second passage at arms which left them both angrier than the first. She had better learn to hush her mouth and mind her own business, he told her. She would, Cresside retorted, when he stopped spending money like a drunken sailor; maybe he could get away with squandering his wife's and his mother's and his children's, but she wasn't sentimental about her share. . . . He thought things had come to a pretty pass when every female d'Alvery was ready to accept money from a Levantine. They weren't accepting money from a Levantine, Cresside replied bluntly; they were going to borrow it from an American bank, if they were lucky. And since a Hoosier Baptist like Melvin Bisbee, who had been lugged out to Belle Heloise by Gervais without consulting anyone, wasn't willing to help them do that, she thought they were darn lucky that a German Jew, who was a friend of Merry's, was willing. . . . Anyway, he would thank her to leave Fabian out of it; if he had wanted Fabian to know, he would have told their cousin himself. Was thazzo? Well, she had wanted Fabian to know about it so she had told him herself. And that was that. . . .

The recriminations went on and on, but in the end it was Cresside who wore her brother down. Impudently, she suggested that as Fabian would be waiting around for her, she might as well ride into town with Gervais when he went to see Mr. Goldenberg; he could let her off at Somerulos Street before going on to Third; there was no use using up gas for two cars when one would do. He froze into haughty silence after his outburst, as he had before. But this did not affect Cresside in the same way as it had Merry. His sister rejoined him after midday dinner very smartly dressed, and wearing just enough make-up to complete her general air of jauntiness. As they rode along, she made a number of wisecracks, apparently unconcerned because he gave no sign that he had heard her, and when he left her in front of Fabian's house, she waved to him gaily from the gate.

"Give my best to Mr. Goldenberg," she said pertly. "Tell him I'm sorry I didn't get to see him myself this time. I've been dying to, ever since you told Merry he looked like a Levantine. I haven't the least idea what a Levantine is, but it sounds intriguing. I suppose we'll be having him and Mrs. Goldenberg to our next dinner party though, and I'll see him then. That is, if he'll come. I wouldn't, if I were in his place, but maybe he'll take a charitable view of our shortcomings, for Merry's sake."

Fabian, who had been watching for her, opened the front door in time to hear her farewell remarks to her brother, and greeted her with a quiet chuckle.

"Hush up and come on in," he said. "What'll you take to celebrate your victory? I see that among you, Tante Isabelle and Merry and you got Gervais completely whipped down. I knew you would. He can win medals and all that in a World War. But there's no hero living who could stand up long against a gynarchy like the one that's getting established at Belle Heloise."

"I haven't the least idea what you're talking about," Cresside said, grinning. "You're as bad with your gynarchy as Gervais is with his Levantine. I wish you'd use words a poor girl can understand. You're right though—Gervais's whipped down at last. It's taken nearly a week and a great deal of moral suasion, but it's done. . . . I'd like a julep, of course."

"I thought you would, and I thought you'd be here about this time, bringing Gervais in chains with you. So it's already made and in the icebox. I'll go and get it for you."

He returned from the kitchen with two beautiful frosted goblets on a silver tray, offered Cresside a cigarette, and sat down on a sofa beside her, with Belizaire at his feet. For a few minutes they sat smoking and sipping their drinks without speaking, enjoying the companionable silence. Then Fabian made a pensive remark.

"I've been wondering, since you spoke to me last night, if there weren't something I could do to help out. I don't mean by lending Gervais money. Of course, I'd be willing to do that, but I know he'd hate it like hell. I really think Merry's plan is a lot better, anyhow.

303

Gervais'll work to pay off that mortgage to the bank as he never'd have worked to pay back a relative who'd loaned him money 'informally.' But I've got another idea."

"Feel like telling me what it is?"

"Yes, in a general way. I'd rather not tell you the details until I see how they work out. But briefly, I think I might go back to Washington. I don't know whether you remember I went there about a year ago when Gervais got all hot and bothered about the Equalization Board. I made some contacts then that I think might be still more useful now. Anyway, it would be worth trying."

"Right away?"

"No, I couldn't go right away. I've got two or three cases coming up that I can't very well leave. And I want to watch the Constitutional Convention fairly closely, too—Reid and Pleasant are readying a hell of a fight to boost the Severance Tax and I've got a couple of oil companies among my clients, thank God. But I could go late this summer— that is, I could if I knew what to do with Belizaire. He ran away the last time I left him, and Carmelite was almost beside herself."

"Would you trust him to me?"

"I'd trust anything I had to you, of course. But wouldn't he be an awful nuisance to you? You've never had a dog, and a dog's a lot of fun, but a lot of work, too. . . . Snow and Cornet don't count," Fabian added scornfully, reaching out to put his hand on Belizaire's waiting head as he spoke.

"I know they don't. I've always wanted a dog—I mean a real dog— of my own."

"Then why in hell didn't you tell me so?"

"I don't know. Why should I have told you so?"

"Because I'd have seen that you had one."

"Well"—she flushed a little, and spoke with unwonted earnestness. "I don't think I ought to have one of my own," she said. *"Maman* wouldn't like it, and she's put up with a good deal from me already. It isn't fair to worry her with anything else. Besides, the twins take up a good deal of my time. I don't believe I'd have enough to look after a dog, too, right now. Perhaps when they're older. . . . I'd like for Vail to have a dog, a real dog. Every boy ought to. And I'd be awfully happy if you'd lend me yours, while you're away."

"Well, you may be sure I'll be awfully glad to do it. It's a bargain. How about another julep?"

It was not until the following week, after the Board of Directors had reported favorably on the loan to Belle Heloise, and the necessary documents to provide this had been duly signed, that Merry spoke to Gervais about her mother. She was not waiting for a favorable opportunity, as far as his need was concerned, since she had ceased to hope for this; but she wanted to be sure one disaster was averted before she tried to deal with another. When all the papers had been passed and

304

the money was actually in the bank, she again invited a general conference as the family left the dinner table.

"Perhaps Cresside has told you already that I went to see my mother the same day that I went to see Mr. Goldenberg," she said, looking from her husband to her mother-in-law after they were all seated in the library. "Anyway, I'm sorry to say that I found her very unhappy. Our friend and lodger, Miss Mittie Alden, has been unjustly discharged by the State Superintendent of Schools. Of course, that means that her salary'll stop, when school closes. She won't have much of anything to live on after that, and neither will my mother."

"Gosh, but I'm sorry, Merry!" Cresside exclaimed, while Madame d'Alvery murmured something vaguely though politely sympathetic, and Gervais looked hard at Merry without saying anything.

"When Gervais asked me to marry him, I told him just how poor we were, Madame Mère," Merry went on, turning to her mother-in-law. "I said that the time might come when I'd have to take care of my mother again, just as I did when I worked for Mr. Goldenberg. I'm afraid it's come now. She doesn't own the little house she lives in, because she couldn't meet the interest on the mortgage, and it's in such bad repair that I don't believe she could get another lodger who would help her meet expenses, the way Miss Mittie has. My father didn't provide for her in any way before he died, and of course my brothers' pension money went to their wives and I haven't been able to give her much, these last few years." Merry did not speak resentfully; she made a simple statement of an unfortunate fact. "My mother's depended on the money she's been getting from Miss Mittie to keep her going," Merry concluded.

"I think it is greatly to your credit, Merry, that you have such a sense of responsibility to your mother. But it is not clear to me just what you want to do for her."

"Why, *maman,* it must be! It's plain as print! Merry wants to invite her mother to live at Belle Heloise, and Miss Mittie, too, just the way your relatives and Angus Holt used to live here! Papa, too, for that matter! A darn good idea I should think!"

"Be quiet, Cresside, for a moment, and let Merry speak for herself. . . . Is that what you had in mind, *chère?*"

"Yes, Madame Mère, it is. . . . And I'll never forget that you called me *chère* when you asked me, feeling the way you do about the mortgage, too!"

Merry's words ended in a sudden sob. She leapt up and walked quickly across the room; then she knelt down and buried her face in her mother-in-law's lap. Madame d'Alvery looked at her son over the girl's bowed head.

"Since you have insisted on providing so many extra living quarters on this plantation, you are hardly in a position to complain if they are used, Gervais," she said. "I certainly shall not do so. . . . Merry, my dear, I beg of you not to weep. You should have been spared this unhappiness, and you would have been, had I known sooner that the need you describe existed. Cresside is right. The situation is similar to many that have prevailed before. . . . I suggest that we offer Mrs. Randall and Miss Alden the rooms above your office and library, Gervais. These would seem to me the most practical for their purposes, and the pleasantest, because of the little kitchen. They will have more privacy in the remodeled storehouse, and more independence, than anywhere else on the place—though, of course, we will make it clear that we shall expect them to join us for meals at the Big House whenever they feel inclined. We will also make it clear to Miss Alden that in the near future she can be very helpful to us, by teaching the children. Personally, I shall be glad to see the old schoolhouse in use again. And as far as I am concerned, your mother is welcome to whatever we can offer her, Merry. Shall we consider the matter settled? If so, I should like to have a game of bridge before I retire for the night."

CHAPTER XXIV

"I've LEFT SOME old trousers of mine in the dog house. When Belizaire finds them, he'll know I'm coming back. And I'll put him in the run before I leave. If I don't, he'll break away from you and follow the car. In fact, you'll probably have to keep him in the run or on the leash all the time, for a few days anyhow, to prevent him from making off."

"There isn't any shade in the run. I won't be able to leave him there through the heat of the day. Can't I take him into the house?"

Fabian shook his head. "There are too many doors. You might think you had every screen locked, and the next thing you knew he'd be out of one of them that a servant had inadvertently opened. You can take him into your own room, or on the gallery outside of it, once in a while, if you really want to. But I wouldn't make a practice of it. Pretty soon you'd be a slave to him, and heaven knows that's the last thing I want. Better keep him tied up in the patio. And let Amen lead him back and forth between there and the run and take him for a walk twice a day. Don't you do it. Belizaire's strong enough to pull you right off your feet. You might get a bad fall that way, and hurt your back."

"I don't believe I would. But I'll try to do just as you said about everything, Fabian."

They walked slowly out towards the run, Belizaire following with dragging steps. Several times he stopped entirely, looking reproachfully from his master to his newly appointed guardian. Fabian spoke to him,

306

first coaxingly and then sharply, but his habit of obedience was not strong enough to bring about submission to the unwelcome orders. He was finally pulled bodily into the run, and prevented from escaping only by swift maneuvering in closing the gate after him. He immediately sat down on his haunches, and, lifting his head, began to howl, loudly and dismally, as if he were in dire distress and terrible pain.

"That's nothing," Fabian said reassuringly. "He always does that when I leave him in a strange place. He'll stop after a while, when he gets accustomed to his new surroundings."

"But this isn't a strange place. You've brought him here dozens of times."

"Yes, but I've always stayed, too. And I've never shut him up before. . . . Well, there's no use in having the agony long and drawn out. So long, Cresside."

"So long. And good luck!"

She had been half hoping that he would kiss her good-by before he went to Washington, though there was no reason why she should expect that he would. He was not demonstrative by nature and they had never been classified by relationship as "kissing cousins." On the rare occasions when he had taken her hand or put his arm around her shoulder, this had never seemed like a caress; it had been merely a gesture made to signify protectiveness and restore confidence. Cresside had no delusions on this score. But she had always welcomed these gestures, and increasingly through the summer she had found herself longing for them; there was something about them that not only imparted a feeling of security, but which filled her with supreme contentment. If an impersonal touch could do this, it seemed reasonable to assume that a kindly kiss could do even more. She stood watching Fabian out of sight, feeling frustrated because she had not found out whether her assumption was correct.

She had no leisure at the moment to brood over this unduly, however, as it was almost time for the twins' supper. They ate this in the patio now, sitting in high chairs on either side of a small table. Though they were enveloped in sizable bibs of turkish toweling, securely tied around their plump persons, their enthusiastic but bungling attempts to feed themselves required considerable guidance: the silver mugs which they seized needed steadying to avert overflows; the short-handled spoons which they dipped into their porringers had a way of emptying themselves before reaching the hungry pink mouths. Dinah always sat between the twins on one side of the table, turning watchfully from one to the other; but Cresside, who could forestall accidents more quickly, usually sat on the other side. Long before their supper was finished, they had begun to be sleepy, and if their naps had been curtailed for any reason, fussy as well; it took tact and patience to slip the final mouthfuls down, and afterwards to get the twins settled for the night. Merry was busy with Philogene at the same hour, so it was also Cresside who helped Dinah sponge off Vail and Sybelle, get them into their nightgowns, and tuck them into their cribs under the enveloping mosquito bars. By the time all this was done, Selah had almost invariably announced dinner, and she had barely time to freshen up hastily herself. After dinner, Merry and Gervais sat for a few minutes with Madame d'Alvery; then if there were no guests they went back to the *garçonnière*.

It was now tacitly understood that Mrs. Randall and Miss Mittie would come to Belle Heloise as soon as their money gave out. But they were still managing somehow on St. Napoleon Street, so the family program was as yet unaffected by the complications which their presence would eventually entail. Cresside remained with her mother until Madame d'Alvery retired; then she generally read for an hour or two before going to bed. Fabian had never asked her if she found the evenings at Belle Heloise long and empty; but he had asked her a number of times whether she had read this or that which he had recently enjoyed, and upon receiving a negative answer had given her the book in question, carefully marking the passages he had especially liked. She had read practically nothing as a girl, except the "literature" required in the English courses she took at Convent, all of which she heartily hated, and the more salacious current novels, which occasionally came up for discussion in "the gang," and which were theoretically banned in the house. Now she was becoming tardily aware of a great treasure house to which she could retire at will, sure of respite and refreshment.

When she finally put down her book, on the night of Fabian's departure, she realized that Belizaire was still howling woefully. She went out doors and stood close to the run, speaking to him in comforting tones; but she did not dare to open the gate and go inside for fear that he would slip past her and rush off in hopeless pursuit of his master. Momentarily, she succeeded in calming him; but as soon as she stopped talking to him, or moved away ever so slightly from the run, he began to howl again. While she hesitated, wondering what she had better do next, Gervais called to her from one of the windows of his room.

"For heaven's sake, Cresside, stop puttering with that hound and go to bed! If I'd known you'd make such a fuss over him, I wouldn't have let Fabian leave him here! Or if I'd known he was going to raise such a racket either! I haven't had a wink of sleep yet and neither has Merry. Pretty soon he'll wake up the kids, too, and then there'll be hell to pay."

"Well, he hasn't waked them up yet, and I don't believe he will. And it isn't late, so you and Merry haven't lost much precious sleep. Fabian said he'd probably quiet down before long and I reckon he will. But he's lonesome."

"*Lonesome!* He's a disturber of the peace. Go back to the house, can't you? If you start disturbing it, too, that'll be the last straw."

With a few parting words of encouragement and comfort to
308

Belizaire, Cresside left the run. She was reluctant to leave her charge, and she was not greatly concerned about her brother's loss of sleep; however, she was still hopeful that Belizaire would eventually quiet down, and it seemed puerile to start an argument with Gervais in the middle of the night. She herself tossed and turned for a long time; but her wakefulness was due less to the dog's continued outcry, drowning the sorrowful note of a mourning dove, than to her distress over his misery; she could close her ears to it, but not her mind. Before dawn she was up and dressed again, feeling she could stand it no more. She longed to let Belizaire out, to take him for a walk herself; but remembering Fabian's final words of admonition, she resisted the temptation, and sat waiting for Amen to come and release the prisoner, forgetting that she was down hours earlier than usual and wondering what made the boy so late. When the unconcerned but good-natured Negro finally appeared on the scene, still yawning, and cautiously inched his way into the run, slipping on the leash before Belizaire could elude him, Cresside went into the Garden Room and sat down at the old Custom House desk.

"Dear Fabian"—she wrote——
"Belizaire misses you very much. So do I. This is the first time I've ever thought I'd rather be a dog than a girl, but now I do. Because a dog can get up on his hind legs and tell the world just how he feels and a girl has to keep quiet about it. I want to cry, too, and I know I mustn't.

As ever,
Cresside."

She read the letter over two or three times, sat staring out at the garden for a few minutes, read the letter again, and tore it up. Then she went out on the patio and waited for Amen to bring Belizaire back from his walk. Lucie passed her as she went up the outside stairway with Madame d'Alvery's breakfast tray, and briefly bade the troubled girl good morning in her usual incurious and respectful manner. She did not indicate, by either word or look, that she was surprised at seeing her young mistress downstairs before early morning coffee had been served. But a few minutes later she returned with a second tray, and set it down on a small wicker table by Cresside.

"Thazza mighty fine dawg of Mr. Fabian's," she remarked. "Cain't none of us say his name though, to call him or make of him. Bellie, that'd be easy. But it don't jes' sound respectful to Mr. Fabian."

"I don't think he'd mind at all. And I think Belizaire would come if you called him that. You can try anyway."

"Yassum—Ah's fixin' to bring you some mo' coffee right soon."

Lucie was followed after an interval by Dinah, bringing Vail. The twins still spent most of their waking hours on the patio, much of the time in a large play pen, from which they were occasionally released for more freedom of action. Vail could walk very well now, and

309

often succeeded in getting out of bounds, unless he was carefully watched. Sybelle tagged after him with more uncertain footsteps but she already lisped a number of words, while Vail stubbornly declined to say more than two. As these were "Auntie" and "Dinah," however, they sufficed to meet his every requirement; Gervais not infrequently remarked that Vail would grow up a near-mute, unless Cresside and Dinah stopped catering to him so slavishly. . . .

Dinah put Vail into Cresside's outstretched arms now, before going back upstairs for Sybelle. The girl tossed him up in the air two or three times, while he shouted with glee, and then put him on her knee to "ride a cockhorse," a performance in which he heartily co-operated. But when she tried to hold him in her lap, he wriggled away from her. Vail demanded boisterous amusement; if he did not get it in one way, he sought it in another. He succeeded in squirming out of Cresside's grasp, but instead of heading pellmell towards the lawn, he scrambled over to Belizaire, and looked questioningly but joyfully first at the dog and then at Cresside.

"Nice doggy," Cresside said encouragingly. "Pat him, Vail. Look, this way! That's it! Can't you say doggy, Vail?"

"Auntie," Vail responded promptly.

"No, no, not Auntie. Doggy! Sybelle can say doggy, Vail."

"Auntie," reiterated Vail, with characteristic stubbornness.

"My, but you're a mule-headed little boy! I don't know what's going to happen to you when you grow up if someone doesn't teach you to mind."

Cresside looked at him with doting admiration as she spoke. He had always been a beautiful baby and he was already beginning to show promise of becoming a very handsome child. He was very large for his age, sturdy rather than chubby and amazingly strong; he handled heavy and unwieldy playthings with complete ease, and when he was angry, flung them a considerable distance. His coloring was striking; he had very red cheeks, very blue eyes and very black hair. As his hair was completely straight, it presented a problem: Gervais thought it should be cut like a big boy's, but the other members of the family insisted he was still too young for this, so it was left long and stuck out, rather wildly, in every direction. Cresside and Dinah had both spent endless hours trying to curl it and smooth it but to absolutely no avail, and its natural disorder was further increased by Vail's habit of running his stubby fingers through it. He did so now, as he continued to look from Belizaire to Cresside.

"Doggy," Cresside repeated, patting Belizaire's upraised head and stroking his long ears. Vail eyed her roguishly and began to chuckle.

"Auntie," he said again.

Cresside chuckled herself. She and Vail were laughing together, each enjoying the other's merriment, while Belizaire, momentarily cheered, began to wag his tail, when Selah came out on the patio.

"Dat peddler man done come, Miss Cresside," he said. "Him an' his little boy. Dey ain't come in no cart dis time, but in de reddest truck ever been on dis road. De little boy done brung a present for Miss Sybelle, he say."

"Ask him if he won't come out here, Selah. Dinah'll be down with Sybelle any minute now."

As it happened, Dinah, with Sybelle in her arms, emerged from the hallway at the same moment that Selah opened the kitchen door for Luigi and Riccardo to pass through. The peddler and his son were both attired in their best, and Riccardo was carrying a long cardboard box with great care under one arm. As they approached the baby girl and her nurse, he mutely held this box out. Luigi hastened to explain the nature of the offering.

"Gooda morning, Miss Cresside," he said, "My, my, whata beautiful bambinos! Thata boy, soon he be big like-a my Riccardo. But the leetla girl, how she's look just like-a dolly, with the yellow curls, the pink cheek and oh! sucha beega eyes! Looka now, Sybelle, see whata my Riccardo bring you! Maybe you think you a-lookin' on yourself in the glass!"

Helpfully, Luigi whisked the lid off the box. Inside lay a huge flaxen-haired baby doll, elaborately dressed in fine muslin and lace ornamented with pink satin ribbons. The doll's waxen eyelids, heavily fringed with dark lashes, were tightly closed; but when Luigi tilted the box, so that her position became upright, her eyes flew open. Watching Sybelle, to see if she appreciated this miracle, Luigi then fumbled under the frills for some hidden contraption and immediately the doll began to bleat, "Mam-ma—Mam-ma!"

"Mam-ma!" echoed Sybelle, thoroughly entranced.

"That'sa it!" Luigi exclaimed. "Thisa dolly bambina say Mam-ma justa like you! Go to sleep, justa like you! Wear pretty clothes, justa like you! She all for you, Sybelle. Riccardo bringa her to you from Nawlins. Take her out the box, Riccardo, so Sybelle cana see!"

"Suppose we sit down," suggested Cresside, "and put the doll on the table. Then Sybelle can see it better, and touch it, too, if she wants to. But we must be careful she doesn't break it. What a magnificent doll that is, Luigi! Much too beautiful for a baby to bang around. We'll have to keep it in a safe place until Sybelle gets older."

"You wanta keep it safe, you keep it safe, but the dolly isa for Sybelle. We got a fine stock of toys now, but this dolly no come-a out no stock. Riccardo got this dolly justa for Sybelle. Ain't I got right, Riccardo?"

"Yes," agreed Riccardo, without much enthusiasm. Now that he had delivered the doll, a weight was lifted from his mind, and his gaze was no longer focused on the puzzled baby girl in the nurse's arms, or on the pleasant young lady who had invited his father to sit down; he was looking around the patio in search of other attractions. As he caught sight of Belizaire and Vail, his flagging interest revived, and he tugged at his father's arm.

"Look, Papa!" he said. "There's a nice black dog. Can I go over and pat the dog, Papa?"

"Now you listena me, Riccardo, you never come here to pat no black dog. You come here to give a dolly to leetla Sybelle."

"But I did give her the doll, Papa. Can't I go over and pat the dog now?"

"Do let him, Luigi," urged Cresside. "That's Fabian d'Alvery's dog, Belizaire. He's very kind to children. You see Vail's made friends with him already."

"That ain't what he come here for."

"I know, Luigi. But let me take him over there for just a minute. I'll bring him right back."

She offered the little boy her hand, which he took willingly, and led him to the further end of the patio, where Belizaire was chained to the stair landing, with Vail still squatting beside him. "I've been trying to make Vail say doggy, Riccardo," she said. "But I haven't had any luck. Perhaps if you say it, he'll try to copy you."

"Doggy," said Riccardo obligingly. "Nice black doggy." He patted Belizaire, staring at him covetously, and reiterated his greeting. Vail looked at the intruder with a belligerent expression, but he neither moved nor spoke until Cresside turned to lead the reluctant Riccardo back towards the table where the others were sitting.

"Auntie," he called after her imperiously. "Auntie!"

Cresside hesitated, biting her lip and looking apologetically at Riccardo. "I'll have to go back and get him, if we're to have any peace," she said. "He'll be howling at the top of his lungs in another minute. Run along to your father, without me, Riccardo." Then as he complied, she retraced her footsteps, picked up the heavy child and returned to the group gathered around the table with him in her arms. Dinah's expression remained respectfully blank while this went on. But Cresside knew that the nurse, like the peddler, whose astonishment at such indulgence was undisguised, felt she should have left the refractory child where he was or made him walk. With an obstinacy equal to Vail's, she continued to clasp him closely to her, hitching him a little higher on her shoulder. "Selah says you've got a beautiful red truck, Luigi," she said irrelevantly. "I'd like to see it, if you'd show it to me."

"Sure I show you my truck, Miss Cresside," Luigi said proudly. "We carry plenty things now. You remember when I had just Johnny Crooks—stage planks—sauerkraut candy—alla kinda stuff like-a that? All on my back, too, in a basket? You remember my cart, too, maybe yes? Now I got kitchenware—fancy dress goods—julery in thata cart, also my fruit anda candy? Now I gota crockery—ready-made clothes— home furnishings—toys—objects ofa piety—I got a real store now, an' he's all in my truck! Better as whata you find on Bayou Lafourche, and the onliesta one on the River Road!"

He led the way around the East wing of the house with exultant

312

footsteps, his son at his side, Cresside with Vail and Dinah with Sybelle following after him. The red truck was parked near the entrance to the butler's pantry, with all the importance of a fire engine, and a number of little pickaninnies from the quarters, not to mention quite a few of their elders, were gathered around it in awe and excitement. Luigi had not only repainted it, since purchasing it from his prosperous cousin, Mike Montagino; he had so materially altered the body that he had succeeded in converting it into a caravan. It was completely enclosed, except for sliding doors on the side and small windows at the rear, which permitted an inviting view of the interior. This was filled to the last inch with an amazing variety of staples and knick-knacks, all arranged with such neatness and precision that despite the crowding and the small space, there was no confusion. Cresside regarded it all with almost as much enthusiasm as did the pickaninnies.

"Why, Luigi, I never would have dreamed anyone could do such wonders with an ordinary old truck! This is enchanting. People couldn't help wanting to buy everything you've got when you've made it all so attractive!"

"Well, now, you picka out one leetla toy for that beega boy you got, also one for new bambino, too," Luigi said expansively. "I make-a special price, justa for you. I wanta you should tell the *Capitano* so soon like he come in. My truck ain't all what I got. I gotta my fancy grocery store, too! Whata you think for that, heh?"

"Luigi, you haven't! Where is it?"

"Well, it ain't a fancy grocery store yet, Miss Cresside. It's justa leetla old building on Lafayette Street. But I get me gooda trade bimeby, account she's close-a by the ferry. Nota no rented place. I buy— for casha money, too. She's a gonna be fix up with plate-glass window, showcase, everything."

"Marvellous. I'll bet your wife is crazy about it, too."

"You betcha, sure. We got our house in back of the store and now she don't got to take so mucha care for Riccardo no more, account he's agoing to school soon. We do alla work ourself, save-a plenty money thata way. You tella *Capitano* so soon like he come in from the field, no, Miss Cresside?"

She promised faithfully that she would, and as she watched the gaudy truck swing out of sight, with Riccardo sitting up very straight beside his father and Luigi manipulating the wheel with a flourish, she told herself laughingly that she could hardly forget such an amazing piece of news; the rate at which the peddler was forging ahead was nothing short of staggering. She sat thinking about him and the little son of whom he was so proud for some time after she had gone back to the patio. But Gervais, who did not come in until after the twins had been put down for their naps, and who found her busily engaged in brushing Belizaire's tangled coat, greeted her in a way which put her

313

immediately on the defensive and drove the morning's pleasant interlude from her mind.

"I hadn't any idea you'd spend the entire time Fabian was gone dry-nursing his pooch. You've never shown much interest in our own dogs. In fact, I've heard you say dozens of times you didn't see how anyone could go dog crazy, like Fabian."

"That was a long time ago, before I'd seen much of Belizaire. And I've heard *you* say, dozens of times, that you didn't see why we had specimens like Snow and Cornet in the first place, that we ought to get some *real* dogs at Belle Heloise. I agree with you, for once. I'm going to ask Fabian if he can't get us a puppy, the next time Belizaire sires a litter. Vail has noticed him already. He and Sybelle are nearly old enough now to start playing with a puppy."

"They'd have a fat chance of playing with a puppy if you sat and fondled it all the time, the way you're fondling Belizaire."

"Well, naturally I wouldn't. In the first place the puppy wouldn't need to be tied up. This would be its home and it would be chasing around, having a great old time. It wouldn't be confined and pining for its master, like Belizaire—I've never seen a human being as lonely as that poor dog. In the second place, I wouldn't worry about a puppy the way I'm worrying about Belizaire. It would be ours, and if anything happened to it, that would be our own hard luck. This is entirely different. Belizaire's all Fabian's got."

"Oh, come on! Fabian's got as good a practice as any lawyer around here. He's got a very tidy patrimony, too, besides what he earns. And he's got the best cook in Baton Rouge and one of the most distinctive houses."

"Oh, for the love of Mike! I mean all that *matters.*"

"Well, if you'd ever done half the worrying about cash, in your whole life, that you've done in the last twenty-four hours about that noisy beast, you'd know it matters a good deal to a man if he doesn't have to worry about it. Fabian's sitting pretty—a darn sight prettier than I am right now, with sugar dropping further and further down every day and money getting tighter and tighter all the time."

"Maybe if you didn't spend so much you wouldn't have to worry so much."

"You talk as if I'd been throwing money to the four winds. I only did what practically every other planter did last year when sugar went up to twenty-six—increased my acreage, improved my machinery, put my whole place in apple-pie order. It didn't seem like extravagance to any of us—it seemed like a sensible investment. How could we tell that sugar would drop to ten before the crop was in and keep right on dropping? We weren't to blame for the drop. If you'd ever bothered to keep informed about current conditions you'd know price fixing was responsible for that—price fixing and a market flooded with Cuban sugar."

"I suppose you cleared up all the back debts on the place, didn't you, before you started in on your little improvements? You might as well come clean, Gervais. You can't fool me. You're not satisfied without putting on a big show—Fabian is. His house is cute, but you could get the whole of it into one wing of Belle Heloise. And at that he hasn't got a real home because he hasn't a wife and children. A man can't call a house a home no matter how cute it is if there's no one to welcome him when he gets there at night except a cook and a dog."

"Of course he can, if that's his idea of a home. It is Fabian's. He could have had a wife if he'd have wanted one, easy enough. There are plenty of girls who'd be only too glad to marry him for his money and his position."

"And as if Fabian would want a girl who'd marry him for that! As if he weren't shying off all the time for fear some damn gold digger won't try to do that very thing! Plenty of those babes look as if butter wouldn't melt in their mouths, and they have a line you could hang clothes on! Fabian doesn't intend to get fooled, so he's always on guard. Naturally he's terribly sensitive. You men who are all looks and mighty few brains don't seem to know what it does to a man's pride when he thinks a girl wouldn't want to look at him, much less touch him. He gets the idea *anyone* who married him would be doing it for money because there couldn't be any other reason. And you think Fabian could have got married, easy enough, if he had wanted to! To a girl worth having! What about Merry? She didn't want him, did she, with all his money and position? Didn't you ever hear of a burnt child fearing the fire? What about a burnt man then? You darn fool! You make me sick and tired!"

Cresside jumped up and rushed to the Garden Room, slamming the door behind her. Gervais stood looking after her, with even more perplexity than annoyance. It was a long time since he had heard her lapse into the sort of expressions she had just used, and it gradually dawned on him that only resentment or rage would have made her revert to them. Obviously she was very angry, though the cause of her anger remained a mystery to him. He was also surprised at her disturbingly shrewd observation about Fabian and his way of life; he had never given her credit for analyzing any character or situation with such thoroughness and thoughtfulness. He considered following her, first with the idea of arguing and then with the idea of apologizing. But eventually he decided that nothing would be achieved by argument, and that he did not owe her an apology. He went out to the fields again, dismissing the matter from his mind. But he unwillingly faced it once more when he came back, to find Charles Boylston installed on the patio beside Cresside, who in turn was seated near Belizaire, with her perpetual "baby sewing" in her hands and an obstinate expression on her face.

"Hello, there, Gervais!" Boylston said. "Come here and see if you can't do something with this stubborn sister of yours. I can't. She used to say, every time I asked her to go out with me, that she couldn't leave the twins. Now she says she can't leave Fabian's dog. I never did think she had much of an alibi—after all, Dinah was always here and Merry never left the twins but once—for three days. Now I can't see that Cresside's got any alibi at all. Fabian couldn't have expected her to sit and hold Belizaire's paw all the time he was gone himself."

"Maybe I know as much about what Fabian expected as you do. But we won't go into that. If my alibis don't hold water, I'll give them up and spell things for you in words of one syllable. I'd have done it long ago, but believe it or not, I was trying to let you off easy. However, the truth is that I don't want to go out with you, that I never did and that I never shall. When you've thought that over, you might decide whether it isn't a waste of time for you to come here quite so much."

Again she jumped up, and disappeared into the Garden Room. Belizaire strained at his leash and whined as she slammed the door behind her. Charles Boylston looked at Gervais in extreme bewilderment.

"I honestly don't know what I've said or done to upset her so much. I'm terribly sorry."

"You needn't be. You didn't upset her—she was upset already. She lit into me this morning, and she has me foxed, too—I can't imagine what's got into her. I'll say this for Cresside, she's flip, but she isn't very often downright rude, like she's been today. Everyone except Merry calls me 'edgy,' and I reckon I am, sometimes. But I never thought Cresside was."

"She isn't. Of course, she wisecracks about almost everything, but this is different. She can't really mean that she doesn't want me to come here. . . . Can she?"

"Of course not. She's going through some kind of *crise des nerfs*, Lord knows what for. Come on, let's find Merry and have a drink."

Cresside reappeared at suppertime, indisposed to eat and abnormally silent, but completely controlled, and very courteous in a chilly way. After supper Merry proposed bridge and Cresside joined the others, agreeably enough. Whatever the cause of her *crise des nerfs*, it had not affected her game; as usual, she played her cards swiftly and skillfully, covering her partners' mistakes without criticizing them, and capitalizing on her opponents'; she won every rubber. But she did not move from the bridge table when Boylston began his farewells, and after seeing him off, Merry and Gervais made a dash for the *garçonnière* without going back to the Big House, for it had begun to rain. They discussed Cresside's strange conduct for a few minutes before settling down for the night; but as usual when they were alone, they dismissed vexing subjects easily, in their preoccupation with each other. When they were almost asleep, Gervais muttered drowsily that he was thankful the hound had stopped howling at last, and Merry, with equal drowsiness, murmured she was thankful he was getting used to his

316

quarters. Neither of them suspected that these had been abruptly changed.

For Cresside had lain, a second night, listening to the dog's lament, sounding above the note of a mourning dove, and this time she had decided that she could not stand it. Before, Belizaire had been lonely, but as far as creature comforts were concerned, he was well off; now she knew he must be drenched through and through, that part of his wretchedness should be laid to his dripping condition. She slid out of bed, put on her slippers and bathrobe, and without turning on any lights or making the slightest noise, crept through the twins' room to Dinah's cubbyhole. Then she groped quietly around in the dark until she touched Dinah's substantial shoulder.

"Hush!" she said softly. "The twins are all right—don't wake them up. But it's pouring cats, dogs and billy goats. I can't leave Belizaire out in all this rain. And Mr. Fabian made me promise I wouldn't try to take him out on the leash by myself. Will you come and help me get him in, Dinah?"

"Ah sho' will, Miss Cresside. You step out on the rear gallery, please ma'm, and Ah'll come to you right away"

Dinah in deshabille was even more majestic than in the picturesque clothes which she wore in the daytime. She presently appeared, wearing a voluminous crimson robe and a *tignon* which matched it. She had brought the flashlight that she always kept by her bedside, and she held it steadily before her as she advanced. Then she put her arm around Cresside, supporting her while they went down the stairway to the patio and across the soggy grass to the dog run. Belizaire was already crouching by the gate, apparently aware that deliverance was at hand. He submitted with docility to the leash and trotted quietly after his rescuers as they retraced their steps across the lawn, up the back stairway and through the rear gallery. When they reached the door leading into the upper hall, Dinah paused.

"What does you want to do with him now, Miss Cresside?"

"I'm going to take him into my room, of course."

"He's mighty wet. He's gwine ter drip all over your pretty rugs. If he lays down on one of 'em, he's gwine ter leave his shape there."

"I don't care about my pretty rugs. I'm going to have him where it's dry. . . . Let's get some bath towels and rub him, and let's try to be quiet so we won't wake *maman*."

"Ah ain't a-gwine make no noise. You climb back onto de bed, Miss Cresside, while Ah gets you another nightgown. You's done got soaked to de skin yourself. Ah'll do de rubbin' after Ah gets you fixed up. But Lordy! Dat dog's shaking himself dry dis minute. Look how de raindrops goin' all over the floor, lak Ah tol' you. Bellie's gwine be all right, but your carpet, it ain't never gwine be de same again."

"Please stop worrying about the carpet. And please rub Belizaire anyway, even if you do think he's all right. I'll write a letter while you dry him. I won't get out of bed again."

Cresside had raised her arms while she was talking, and Dinah had deftly slipped off the drenched nightgown, swiftly drying the girl's slim body before slipping on another gown that was soft and fresh. Then she took a larger towel, and getting down on her knees, began to rub Belizaire, singing softly as she did so:

"Ol' Mr. Owl was settin' on a limb,
He looked at me, Ah looked at him,
Says Ah 'Mr. Owl, Ah's always heard
Dat you is a mighty wise ol' bird.
Now dere's sumpin' dat Ah craves to know,
Does de one Ah love, love me or no?
Won't you tell me dis, Mr. Owl? Please do'!
But ol' Mr. Owl jes said 'Whoo-oo-oo'?

Says Ah 'Mr. Owl Ah done axed you
Does de one dat Ah love, love me true?
You ought to know, you is so wise.'
But ol' Mr. Owl jes blinked his eyes
An' turned his head fus' lef' den right,
Den flew to a limb plumb out of sight.
So Ah axed again 'Is mah true love true'?
He jes flapped his wings an' said 'Whoo-oo-oo'?"

While Dinah sang, Cresside sat up and wrote, taking a pad and pencil from her bedside table, and looking over, between every other word, to see if Belizaire were still submissive.

"Dear Fabian,
It is raining very hard tonight, and I could not believe that you would really want me to leave Belizaire out in the run through such terrible weather. He might have drowned. No, I suppose dogs don't drown, do they? But he might have caught pneumonia. So I have brought him into my room. I did not take him on the leash by myself. Dinah helped me. She is rubbing him with a big bath towel now and presently he will be nice and dry, and then he will lie down on the rug by my bed and go to sleep. I shall be awfully glad to have him. It will not be so lonely for him or for me either. Night is the loneliest time, isn't it, when you are missing someone?
As ever,
Cresside."

She put down the pad and pencil and looked over at Belizaire again. Dinah had finished drying him, and he was stretched out contentedly in a characteristic position, his hind legs widely separated and laid flat on the floor, so that he looked almost like a rug himself. He gazed up at her with large grateful eyes and made little grateful sounds in his throat. After Dinah had left and the room was completely dark again,

318

Cresside could still see his eyes, glowing through the darkness; she could still hear the little sounds in the stillness. She was happier than she had been at any moment since Fabian had left. But by and by she reached out for the little pad that lay on the bedside table and tore off the sheet of paper on which she had written. Then she tore this into many small pieces. After that she lay for a long time looking at Belizaire's glowing eyes and listening to the small sounds he made which mingled with the notes of the mourning dove instead of drowning them as his dreadful cries had done. By and by he went to sleep. He put his head down on his front paws and closed his eyes and everything was quiet. But Cresside lay and watched and listened just the same.

If they had not brought him in out of the wet, Cresside and Dinah said to each other, two days later, they would have thought that Belizaire had caught cold in that hard pelting rain. But since he had been brought in and well dried, since he had stopped crying for Fabian and seemed so contented in Cresside's room, they could not understand what ailed him. He grew more and more listless; he could hardly be cajoled into going out with Amen; he could not be tempted into eating anything. When he finally refused to drink water, Cresside told Amen to put on his leash and get him into the car; she was going to take him to the vet, and she thought Amen had better come along. Belizaire lay unprotestingly at her side while she drove up the River Road at top speed; and he was equally apathetic when she got him into town, crawling across the sidewalk and cowering in a corner of the strange-smelling little office where he finally landed. The veterinarian, who was very busy, and who had only one rather bewildered assistant to help him attend to the heterogeneous collection of animals which unhappy owners were crowding upon his attention, said he did not think there was much the matter; however, Miss d'Alvery would have to leave the dog for an examination. How long? Oh, for several hours at least—overnight would be better. . . .

"I don't think Mr. d'Alvery would want him to stay overnight." She remembered what Fabian had said in the first place, when he had gratefully accepted her offer to care for Belizaire: that dogs often picked up diseases when they were put with other animals, that he was thankful to have his in the run at Belle Heloise by himself. On the other hand she did not want to offend this doctor, who represented her only possible source of authentic information and scientific helpfulness. "It's ten o'clock now. Suppose I come back for him at one?"

"Very well, Miss d'Alvery. I can't give you the results of any blood tests by then, I'm afraid. But you can get those tomorrow, if you prefer."

Cresside patted Belizaire's head and told Amen to stay where he was, with the vague idea that he might in some way mitigate the dog's depression. Then, leaving her car parked, she walked around to the telegraph office and hastily wrote out a message, handing it to the clerk and leaving the building before she could change her mind about sending it, as she had in the case of the two little notes.

"Mr. Fabian d'Alvery
Willard Hotel
Washington, D. C.

Belizaire is sick and I am very much worried. Please come home as soon as you can.

                                        Cresside."

Having sent the telegram, she did not know exactly what to do next. Finally she decided to go and sit in Fabian's garden until it was time to call for Belizaire again. As she turned off Third Street, she saw Pascal Tremblet and Preston Vicknair on the bench near the Veterans' Monument. Pascal's fears about his friend had fortunately not been realized. Preston had recovered from his temporary indisposition, and the two old men were apparently deep in argument. She went over and spoke to them and they both jumped up, greeting her with delight.

"Why, good morning, Miss Cresside! It's not often we see you in town. How are the little twins?"

"They're very well, thank you, and so is their baby brother. But Fabian's dog, Belizaire, is sick. Fabian left him with me when he went to Washington himself, and I'm terribly worried. I came into town to bring Belizaire to the vet's."

"Worms, most likely," Pascal said. "They take the life right out of a dog. Has he howled, Miss Cresside, like he was in pain?"

"He's howled, but only at first, from loneliness. Since he's been sick he's been very quiet."

"Then it wouldn't be worms," Preston announced, authoritatively. "Mr. Fabian must have looked out for worms anyway. But you take fleas, they suck a dog's blood. I saw that dog scratching, the last time I was at Mr. Fabian's house, and I wanted to ask him then, did he have his dog defleaed regular. But——"

"Fleas!" interrupted Pascal. "Fleas wouldn't hurt him none. Fleas is natural to a dog, Miss Cresside. Don't let Pres pass off any nonsense on you. But mosquitoes, they might get him down, if he was bitten enough. Did you leave him out nights?"

"At first I did. That's what Fabian told me to do. But since we had that hard rain the other night, he's been sleeping in my room. . . . I didn't know so many different things could be bad for a dog. But I did know he oughtn't to catch cold and I did know he was lonely. He misses Fabian terribly."

"Well, Miss Cresside, I reckon it ain't only his dog misses him. I was saying to Pres, just before you came along, that this wasn't the same town, with him gone. You see, we sorta got the habit now, going to his house. He's asked us more than ever, since Max died. We were counting up how long it was since he left, and we couldn't hardly believe it was less than a week. Seems more like a month."

"I thought I'd go and sit in his garden while I waited for the report on Belizaire. Wouldn't you like to come with me? I'm sure Carmelite will give us all a cool drink. As far as that goes, I'm sure she'd be glad to give you your dinner, if you'd like to have it."

"We wouldn't like to intrude when Mr. Fabian was away, Miss Cresside."

"Nonsense! You wouldn't be intruding. I'm sure he took it for granted you'd keep on going there, just the same, whether he was there or not. But anyway, I'm asking you now."

Fabian's house and garden seemed very empty without him and his dog, but otherwise the pleasant atmosphere was unchanged: the garden was full of flowers, sunshine and sweet scents; the house was quiet, cool and orderly. Carmelite was moving around the kitchen with calm efficiency. Of course, she could give the gentlemen their dinner, she said, a little haughtily, as if hurt at the implication that there could be the slightest doubt of it; but wouldn't Miss Cresside stay and have it with them? Cresside hesitated for a moment and then called the veterinarian. There was a long wait before he came to the telephone, and she pictured him, still harassed in the turmoil of his office, trying to escape from one anxious patron in order to attend to another; but he finally reminded her, rather curtly, that he had said in the beginning that he would like to keep the dog under observation, and that the longer it was left with him, the better. He had already taken its temperature and this was 104°; not that this was anything to worry about in itself.

Cresside went back to the kitchen more worried than ever. But she told Carmelite that she would be glad to stay for dinner, and when it was ready she took her place quite naturally at the head of Fabian's table. The two old men were also completely at ease. Cresside played fantan with them after telephoning the veterinarian, getting out the cards from the corner cupboard where Fabian always kept them and setting up the card table in the same place that he did. In order that Carmelite might not be diverted from her cookery, Cresside had mixed the drinks, too, with her usual skill, serving them on a silver tray lightly overlaid with summer lilac and maidenhair fern, in frosted silver goblets with a ginger lily pierced by a slender tube of green glass on top of each. Then finding that Carmelite had not picked fresh flowers that day, she went out into the garden and did so herself, decorating the dinner table and the living room. She had never done this at Belle Heloise; that had long been her mother's province, rightful however neglected; now it was Merry's, joyfully improved. Cresside could not presume on either. But here there was no one else to do what she had done. She was surprisingly happy in doing it and touched beyond measure when Pascal, always the more voluble of the two veterans, finally put into words what both felt so strongly.

"It's nice to have you here, Miss Cresside. Not that we don't still miss Mr. Fabian. But you seem to belong here, too. Now if we could just have you both——"

"But you can, of course. I'll come and play hostess any time you like. I'm sure Fabian wouldn't mind at all. Not that he needs me. He's a wonderful host himself."

"Yes, of course. But a house seems that much more homelike when there's a lady in it."

He was saying something of the same thing she herself had said to Gervais, Cresside realized, though she had been talking about the effect of a wife, and naturally these two poor old men were not thinking of her in that light—only as Fabian's cousin, who was substituting for him as well as she could at the moment, and who might occasionally supplement his hospitable gestures in the future. But except for the corroding anxiety about Belizaire, she felt curiously content, as she sat after dinner, pouring the coffee, measuring the brandy, and listening to the garrulous veterans as they rambled on. She knew she had made them happy, and she was happy herself in feeling that she "belonged," as they had put it, in this pleasant little house, that she fitted so easily into the pattern, that it became her to be there. . . .

The veterinarian was reassuring when she returned to his office; he felt certain there was nothing much the matter with her cousin's dog, he told her; undoubtedly just a touch of distemper. He would give her some medicine to take home with her, which she should administer three times a day; he had already given the first dose. Amen, who had sat patiently in a corner throughout her long absence, now led Belizaire back to the car, and they drove down the River Road again in the peaceful twilight. Cresside was still conscious of the unwonted contentment which had come to her in Fabian's house; but as the evening wore on, she became disquieted again. Belizaire, instead of lying quietly on a rug, retreated under her bed, and stubbornly stayed there. The bedstead was built so low, that slim as she was, Cresside herself could not creep under it; she could only lie down beside it, begging Belizaire to come out. But her powers of persuasion were inadequate; he rolled over, and then lay, limp, prostrate and unresponsive, his black form swallowed up in the darkness of his hiding place. She called first Amen and then Dinah, to see if they could accomplish what she failed to do, but though they tried, perseveringly, their efforts were as futile as her own. Finally she dismissed them, and lay down on the rug herself. If she got into bed she would not be able to see Belizaire, and though she did not suppose it would make any difference, she felt impelled to keep watch and to listen for his breathing. Over and over again she thought that this had stopped. But very early in the morning he moved slightly, and a little later he crawled towards the foot of the bed and lay down again. The knowledge that he was still alive filled her with thanksgiving, but it did not assuage her fears for the future. She raised herself on her knees and stretched out her arms across the counterpane. Then she buried her face in its overhanging folds.

"Please God," she prayed. "Please don't let him die. He's all Fabian's got, and Fabian trusted me with him. I've done the best I could for him, but I reckon I just don't know how to take care of a dog. You'll have to help me—" She stopped, not because the prayer came haltingly, for it was as spontaneous as a child's, but because she was sobbing. She waited until she could form words again, and then she went on. "If You let Belizaire get well, I won't ask for anything else. Not anything. But please help me to do this one thing for Fabian."

She stopped again, no longer inarticulate with tears, but confused when it came to bringing such a prayer to an end. To her present shame, she had not said, in a long time, any of the prayers she had been so carefully taught; she had not gone to church, she had observed no periods of private devotions, and she had always managed to elude the austere priest who had baptized the twins and who had come regularly for years to hear her mother's confessions and say Mass in the invalid's room. So she had almost forgotten the printed patterns. And in any case, none of the prayers she had learned before would have helped her to word the one she was trying to utter now; no pious mother, no catechism, no missal supplied formulas to use in such a case as this. She was not even sure it was proper to pray for a dog, in the eyes of the Church, or certain Fabian would have approved her petition. For Fabian called himself an unbeliever. He had been reared, like herself, in a Catholic household, baptized and confirmed; during his parents' lifetime, he had gone regularly to confession and communion. But that was a long time ago. Since then he had not merely neglected the sacraments, as she had; in his moments of bitterness and gloom, he had denied them. And after all, this was his dog for which she was praying. Had she any right to invoke Divine aid in the face of his possible resentment? She thought possibly Father Navarre, the saintly man whose aid Gervais had invoked at the time of his hasty marriage, might have been willing and able to give her wise and sympathetic counsel. But Father Navarre had not remained in Baton Rouge; he had gone back to his native swamplands, to the humble trappers and fishermen and moss gatherers who loved him and whom he loved. Probably he had forgotten all about her by now. Increasingly sorrowful and increasingly perplexed, she went on groping. "I know this is just a dog, I know there aren't any prayers to fit. But somehow he's made me want to pray again, and You know I haven't in a long time. So it ought to count for something. Because if he gets well it will give me faith again. Not just to beg either. To worship too. . . ."

The anxious hours of the next day followed each other laggingly. Amen and Selah came upstairs in the morning and moved Cresside's bed; then they lifted Belizaire up and helped her to give him his medicine, while Dinah stood watchfully by, ready to help, too. But

Belizaire did not try to resist; he still lay limp and apathetic. After he had been dosed, he was put on the upper gallery, so that he would not be able to crawl out of reach again. But this was apparently a needless precaution; he stayed quietly on the clean white bath mat that Dinah spread out for him. Cresside sat beside him and Lucie, in her usual incurious way, brought trays to her there. Nobody suggested that she should do anything else, and nobody told her she was silly to sit all day beside a sick dog; indeed, one by one, her mother and Merry and Gervais came and sat with her, talking to her in lowered voices, as if they were trying not to disturb Belizaire. Madame d'Alvery told Cresside the story of a pet she had owned when she was a young girl. It was a story Cresside had never heard before and which she would have believed her mother incapable of telling, for it revealed secret stores of tenderness which her daughter had not supposed she possessed. Then before she left the gallery, she bent down and ran her white, ringed fingers gently over Belizaire's wasted body.

"I do not think he has fever now, Cresside. I think his medicine is helping him."

"I hope so. . . . You don't know, do you, *maman,* whether Amen has come back with a report from the doctor?"

"I believe he has. I believe Gervais will come and tell you about it. Try not to grieve so, *chère*. And tonight, get some sleep."

"I'm going to sleep here. Amen's going to move out my chaise longue. I couldn't stand having Belizaire crawl under the bed again."

"No, it might be better as you have planned it. *Bon soir, chère.*"

"*Bon soir, maman.*"

The news which Gervais brought in soon afterwards was unalarming. The veterinarian had found a slight infection in Belizaire's blood stream, and he believed that certain injections might be advisable. However, as this treatment was rather drastic, he suggested waiting for the return of the dog's master before trying it. Meanwhile, he was sure Miss d'Alvery was doing everything she could.

"And you are, you know," Gervais went on. "You couldn't have done more for Belizaire if he'd been a baby. When it comes to that, no one could do more for a baby than you've done for the twins ever since they were born. You're a steadfast little cuss, Cresside."

"I just happen to care for babies. And—and dogs. In spite of what you said."

"I'm sorry I said what I did. By that I mean I'm sorry for several things I said. I know you don't think I've got much sense. But, at that, I've got sense enough to realize that I'm just as lucky in my sister as I am in my wife."

"Thanks for them kind words. But you didn't need to tell me that, just because Belizaire is sick."

"I didn't tell you that just because Belizaire is sick. I've been meaning to say so for a long time. But I'm not very good at saying things like that. Fabian's the orator of the family."

Merry came to see Cresside while Gervais was still on the gallery, and for a few minutes their talk centered on the children. Cresside was not to worry because she had not done as much as usual for the twins these last few days, Merry said. They were getting along finely. It was time they learned to manage without "Auntie's" constant attention anyway. They imposed on her, especially Vail. . . . Cresside remonstrated at this statement, but she was too tired for much argument, and after a few moments Merry signalled to Gervais that they had better go. When they left Cresside, they both kissed her. She could not remember when Gervais had kissed her before. He was as undemonstrative as most brothers, and therefore it meant all the more to her that he had kissed her now. But not nearly as much, she thought, after Gervais and Merry had gone away arm in arm, as it would have meant if Fabian had kissed her before he started for Washington. She lay for a long time, staring out into the starlight, thinking about the kiss he had not given her and wondering why she could not put it out of her mind. Eventually she went inside and undressed. After she had slipped into her nightgown, she happened to think of a thin negligee which she had never worn, and without rhyme or reason she felt she would like to wear it now. She had chosen it because it was so quaintly cut, like an old-fashioned wrapper, and yet so cool and dainty. It was made of pale blue silk, trimmed with tiny tucks and rows of featherstitching, and it had little frills of narrow Valenciennes lace at the neck and wrists. She took it from the shelf of her armoire where it had lain indefinitely under a pile of filmy modern lingerie, and after she had put it on, she realized she had wanted to wear it because it was the sort of dressing gown that Fabian would have liked, if he ever noticed such things, or saw them. Still thinking of this, she returned to the gallery and lay down on the chaise longue which Amen had carefully placed beside Belizaire's mat.

Belizaire seemed to be resting quietly. She put out her hand and touched his head. He did not respond by looking up at her, but he made the slight movement which was so reassuring to her, and finding that by lying on her side, she could continue to touch him, she nestled down, still caressing him. Except for the gentle wail of the mourning dove, the night was very still. Little by little, its quietude seemed to steal into her troubled heart. She was no longer terror stricken. She knew she had done all she could. She could possess her soul in patience while she continued to await the answer to her prayer. Praying again, she drifted off to sleep. . . .

It was the movement of Belizaire's head beneath her hand which awakened her. She felt that before she heard any sound. Then she was dimly aware that the sick dog was struggling to his feet, that a car was coming into the driveway, and that there was some connection between the two. She sat up, listening and looking around her, still more than half asleep. There was a little light in the sky, enough to show it pale and luminous against the dark trees. She could see

Belizaire, too, no longer an indefinite black shape, but a clear-cut creature, suddenly alert. Through some strange chance, the other dogs were not barking; but the car had stopped, and someone was skirting the lower gallery with cautious footsteps. She swung herself off the chaise longue and ran to the railing, Belizaire staggering along beside her. As she reached it, she heard Fabian's reassuring voice.

"Hello, there. I thought you might be outside and I was looking for you. I got your wire and gathered you wanted me to reach here as soon as I could. Can I get in? And may I come up? I'll try not to wake anyone else."

"The front door's unlocked. Of course you may come up. I'm thankful you're here."

"Well, so am I. I'll be with you in just a minute."

He continued to move slowly and quietly, but she could hear him coming closer—into the house, through the lower hall, over the stairs, through the upper hall, to the door of the front gallery. Then he opened this noiselessly and came out. Belizaire gave a weak bark of joy, and crept up to him, fawning at his feet. As Fabian leaned over to stroke the dog, Cresside went toward him, too.

"Fabian," she said and stopped. "Oh, Fabian, I'm so glad you've come home." Her thankfulness welled up in her throat, choking her. For a moment she could not say anything else. But she saw that Fabian was no longer bending over Belizaire, but standing straight and looking at her intently. She made a great effort and managed to go on. "I don't know what happened to him. I must have failed to take good care of him somehow. But I'd have given my right hand if this hadn't happened, when you trusted me with him. I know he's all you've got."

"I haven't got you, by some miracle, have I?" Fabian asked, and took her in his arms.

CHAPTER XXV

So A KISS was not merely a weird tremulous thrill, that made you throb and tingle as it pierced you through and through. It was not merely a signal of mysterious danger, which beckoned an invitation while flashing a warning. It was not merely the blossom on the tree of knowledge of good and evil, burgeoning into bitter fruit. It was home after exile, safety after danger, joy after sorrow, fulfillment after frustration—all that and so much more besides, for which there were no words. When Fabian lifted his head at last, Cresside looked up at him with such wonderment that her joy was veiled by it.

"I didn't know a kiss could be like that," she whispered. "Of course, I've been wishing, for a long time, that you would kiss me, but I didn't realize why. I only——"

"Well, I didn't know a kiss could be like that either," Fabian replied, interrupting her. "If I had, you'd have been spared all that wishful waiting, because I simply couldn't have held out. It's been hard enough as it was. Why didn't you give me some sort of a hint? You must have known I'm not any good at guessing. And you must have known that was what I desperately wanted to do."

"But I didn't! I'm not good at guessing either! Once I guessed wrong and since then——"

She stopped short. Fabian put his arms around her again, but this time instead of raising her face eagerly towards his, she bowed her head.

"What's the matter, darling?" he said. "You don't mean to tell me that one was enough, after all? I thought that was just a sample! Come on, your hair's nice, just as soft as silk." He ran his hand over it again slowly and tenderly. "But I can think of something a lot nicer," he added. "Why Cresside. . . ."

She had begun to cry. She was doing it so quietly that Fabian, observant as he was, had not instantly realized it, and she was trying hard to stop. He spoke to her very gently.

"I thought you were so happy, Cresside. There, I know you were. And that made me happy, too. Don't you want me to be happy?"

"Yes. More than anything in the world. But——"

"There aren't any buts. Look, what do you say we go down to the Garden Room? I'm afraid we'll wake Tante Isabelle if we stay here, and I don't want to do that just yet. Besides, I think some good strong coffee would go down well, don't you? I've got a thermos in my car— or I can make some fresh, while you dress. I suppose you have to dress. I wish you didn't though. Whatever it is you're wearing, it's a knock-out."

She looked up, her eyes still wet, but her tremulous lips curving into a hesitant smile. "I put it on because I thought you'd like it," she said shyly. "That is, of course, I didn't have any idea you were going to see it, but I thought it was the sort of thing you would like if you did see it."

Fabian laughed. "Well, you certainly guessed right that time. But at that I reckon you'd better put on a dress if you're coming downstairs. We don't want any of the servants drifting into the Garden Room and jumping to rash conclusions which unfortunately would be incorrect. After all, I'll have plenty of future chances to see you in an outfit like that, and mighty soon, too. I'll give you a little more time than Gervais gave Merry—I mean a little more than he gave her at the last minute, not more than he gave her all the years he was dawdling around. But I shan't give you much. You could get ready to marry me sometime the latter part of next week, couldn't you?"

"Fabian, you don't mean that, do you? You don't want to *marry* me?"

"I most assuredly do. I thought you'd gathered that much anyway. And I gathered that you wanted to marry me. This hasn't been a case of 'Love me, love my dog.' It's been just the other way around. I don't see how you could be so upset about Belizaire, if you weren't pretty fond of.me. You weren't trifling with my young affections, were you, just now, when you kissed me?"

"I—Oh, Fabian, you know how much I care! Don't—don't joke about it. You know I'd do anything on earth I could for you. But I can't do that. I can't marry you."

"Darling, I won't joke if you don't want me to. It just seems natural when I'm so happy, that's all. But I won't let you talk nonsense either. Of course, you're going to—a week from Saturday or two weeks from Monday, just as you prefer. But not a day later than that. Look, I'm going to take Belizaire down to the kitchen with me. I'll bet I can get him to drink some milk while I make the coffee. I'll meet you in the Garden Room in fifteen minutes."

It was considerably longer than that before Cresside joined him. When she did, she found the door into the Garden Room wide open and the first rays of morning sunshine gliding into the room, through the lacelike pattern made by the tiny leaves of the green vines creeping across the windowpanes. Obviously Fabian had taken time to go out into the garden, for there was a vase of fresh flowers in the center of the Custom House desk, which he had set like a table, with service for two. The inkwell and blotter had been removed to the top of the bookcase and supplemented by a white cloth, serviettes, silverware, porcelain, steaming coffee, hot milk, sugar, buttered toast and fig preserves. Chairs were drawn up on either side, facing each other, and Belizaire was stretched out, matlike, beside one of them. Fabian, with a napkin over his arm and one of Lou Ida's aprons tied around his waist, was standing behind the other. He pulled it out with a flourish.

> "Ma'amselle, s'il vous plait,
> Le dejeuner est pret . . .
> Le café est bien chaud,
> Le pain grillé est beau"—he chanted.

Then, after she was seated, he whisked off the apron, threw down the napkin, and took the place opposite her. "I like two lumps in the morning and a real half and half mixture," he told her. "Not black, the way I take it the rest of the time. You'll pour it out for me, won't you? You might as well get into practice."

"Fabian, I told you——"

"Yes, and I told *you*. We'll discuss that after breakfast. But let's get something inside of us first. Listen, Belizaire is going to be all right.

328

He's drunk nearly a pint of milk already. I think part of the trouble was just that he was pining for me. He always does that when I go away. Flattering, but inconvenient. I don't know what the devil to do with him when I have to leave him. Well, of course, that's probably going to solve itself automatically. He'll get more and more used to you. Except that generally when I go away, you'll go with me."

"Fabian——"

"Eat some of this toast I made, won't you? I think it's good. You haven't asked me yet how I got along in Washington. Don't you want to hear?"

"Yes, of course, but——"

"I think I had pretty good luck. You remember that when I went before, it was primarily to see if there were anything I could do to change the position of the Equalization Board, but of course I was concerned about the general sugar situation, even then. Senator Gay was helpful in all sorts of ways. Among others, he got an appointment with Houston, the Secretary of Agriculture, and I went to see him with Gay. The Secretary was co-operative, too. He said he'd assign the best man he had for such kinds of work to making experiments in new types of cane. The best man he had was a scientist named Brandes who'd had a lot of experience in Argentina before coming to the Arlington Bureau."

"Yes? And what then?"

"Well, I don't want to go into too many details. It's all right for you to say you're not bored, but we've got lots of things besides sugar to talk about this morning. The gist of the whole matter is that I went to see Brandes just as soon as I got to Washington last week, and he let me bring some Java cane back with me. It comes in three varieties and it's done well in Argentina. Brandes is confident it could do well in Louisiana, too, because Argentina's cane fields are about as far south of the Equator as Louisiana's are north, and the soil's similar, as well as the climatic conditions. I've got a few stalks of these three varieties in my suitcase. And that suitcase is in my car, which as you know is parked outside the butler's pantry right now."

"So that——"

"So that I want that ham-headed brother of yours to plant that Java cane right out here, back of Angus Holt's garden, and see what happens. Of course, I don't know anything about sugar, but it's my guess that if nothing goes wrong, those three or four stalks will produce six or eight stalks each by next fall. Then those could be replanted, and by 1923 there ought to be enough cane to plant three whole rows, one of each variety. After that—well, I reckon we're getting too far ahead of the game. For the moment, I only want to be sure that Gervais plants everything that's in my suitcase—except the shirts and socks!—right where he can keep his eye on it."

"Couldn't you and I plant it ourselves?"

"No, I think Gervais better do it. Not that I don't like the suggestion that we should do things together. And not that you haven't pleased me no end by taking an intelligent interest in this, considering all you've got on your mind anyway. But there are lots of other things for us to do, honey."

While they were talking, Cresside had taken a few swallows of coffee and crumbled a small piece of toast on her plate. Fabian asked her three times to refill his cup and helped himself to four pieces of toast, spreading them lavishly with butter and fig preserves. After he finished, he poured the leftover milk into a saucer and offered it to Belizaire, who began by sniffing at it disdainfully but ended by drinking most of it. Then Fabian stacked the dishes on a tray and carried them back to the kitchen. Through the open door leading into the patio, Cresside could hear him talking to Lou Ida, who evidently had just come in. But when he returned he shut the patio door behind him.

"I don't think anyone's going to disturb us here," he said, and Cresside knew that he must have told Lou Ida, in that quiet way of his which was so much more effective than Gervais' storming, that he did not want anyone to disturb them, and that no one would risk incurring his disfavor by doing so. "So I'll stop joking now. By way of beginning to be serious, I might tell you I'd like it very much if you'd walk into my arms again."

She had been standing by one of the windows, where the tiny leaves of a clinging vine wove their delicate pattern, engaged in tracing the lacy design with a hesitant finger. Now she turned and faced him squarely. It was obvious that she was making a great effort to speak calmly, but he could see her clenching and unclenching her small hands while she spoke.

"Fabian, I can't. I didn't think, that first time, how you'd take it. I didn't think of anything, except that I was thankful you were back, for Belizaire's sake, and overjoyed because my wish had come true. But my wish didn't go any further than a kiss. One kiss."

"Your conscious wish. But there must have been some subconscious wishes in the back of your mind, too, Cresside. You couldn't have kissed me like that if there hadn't been."

"Well, I—I reckon there were. I—I care a lot for you, Fabian."

"Couldn't you stop using that word 'care' and say 'love' instead? That's what you mean, isn't it?"

"I suppose it is. I suppose I do love you. Yes, I know I do. But honestly, I never thought of it like that until this morning. I've only thought that it meant a lot to be with you, because everything that happens while we are together seems natural and pleasant and comforting. We never seem to bore each other or get on each other's nerves. And we seem to understand each other without any explanation. I don't know how to say it, but there's been a sort of effortless harmony."

"You're saying, very beautifully, that we've loved each other for a

330

long time. Because everything's seemed that way to me, too, Cresside. Didn't you know that was the way it seemed when a man and a girl fell in love with each other?"

"No, I didn't. I thought when a man and a girl fell in love with each other they were after something else."

She spoke scathingly. Without taking any apparent notice of her tone, Fabian came over to the window and put his arm around her shoulder, easily and impersonally, as he did on the ferryboat.

"Well, of course they are, sooner or later," he said, speaking in his quiet way. "But if it's later instead of sooner, they gain a lot, in the long run. I'm glad you used the word harmony, Cresside. It almost makes up for having you shy away from the word love. After you'd found out that there was mental and spiritual harmony between us, you guessed that there might be physical harmony, too. Well, now you know that there is."

Cresside stood very still, so still that she seemed to become remote and rigid. Fabian's arm slid easily from her shoulder to her waist and held this fast. Involuntarily she relaxed in his embrace, gradually losing her detachment.

"Don't make any mistake about this," he said steadily. "When I asked you to marry me, I wasn't thinking of good companionship. We'd keep on having that, of course—without any barriers, without any separations. But we'd have much more than that. You'll never know what it meant to me, Cresside, when I first began to realize my deformity wasn't repulsive to you, that there was something else about me that made up for it. Because you're so lovely that any man in his senses would want to have you, if he could. You're not going to tell me I can't, are you?"

"I can't say anything else, Fabian."

"Why, darling? Can you tell me?"

"I'll try. But I don't know how to begin."

"I think I can help, if you'll promise not to be hurt by anything I'll say."

"I can't promise you that. But I know you won't mean to hurt me, that you won't any more than you can help."

"All right. Has your refusal to marry me anything to do with Sylvestre Tremaine?"

Again something about her stillness suggested attempted withdrawal. This time Fabian did not try to recapture her. After a long pause she answered, speaking steadily herself.

"Yes. It has a lot to do with Sylvestre. He didn't want to marry me, Fabian."

"You're wrong. He'd have given his right hand to marry you."

"When it was too late."

"That's his hard luck—his lasting hard luck. He's going to covet you vainly all his life, Cresside."

331

"But he didn't always. Not vainly, Fabian. He got what he wanted. All he wanted. Almost without the asking. Because I wanted it, too. That's what I thought love meant then."

"Well, you know better now."

His calm rejoinder failed to check her passionate outburst. She went on vehemently, the words coming with a rush at last.

"What good does it do me to know better now? What good does it do either of us? If I'd dreamed you were falling in love with me, I'd have shut you off, the way I shut off Charles Boylston. But I didn't. I thought you were just being kind to me. And sometimes I thought you'd guessed. We've been so close, in so many ways, I didn't see how I could keep a secret from you."

"You couldn't. I did guess."

"You did!"

"Yes, of course. The day you had your bad fall."

"The day I had my bad fall! Why, that was the day Sylvestre and Regine were married! More than two years ago!"

"Yes, it's a long time. I've wanted to marry you for a long time, too."

She twisted suddenly around, staring at him unbelievingly. He slackened his hold on her waist so she could turn easily in his arms, but not enough to risk having her break away from him.

"Why, you couldn't! You couldn't have wanted to marry me if you knew!" she gasped.

"But I did. I still do."

"Fabian, you're not going to pretend you don't mind!"

"I'm not going to pretend anything. I do mind. But I don't mind enough to let it make any difference about wanting to marry you. I've told you twice already this morning that I'd like to marry you next week. If you were in love with Sylvestre, that would be different. But you're not. You loathe the very sight of him. When it comes to that, you never really were in love with him, any more than I was ever really in love with Merry. I think we were both awfully lucky that we've got a second chance. So I wish you'd let me go right now to Tante Isabelle and Gervais and tell them to start getting ready for a wedding. They must be awake by this time."

"Fabian, please stop talking about getting married next week. And please let go of me."

"I won't stop talking about getting married. But I'll let go of you if you'll promise not to run away."

"All right. I promise. But I don't feel as if I could stand up any longer. I feel as if I've got to sit down."

"I'm sorry, darling. It was terribly selfish of me, not to realize that you'd be getting tired. But it's been so wonderful, holding you this way."

He released her, kissing her half-hidden cheek as he did so, and then pulling the two chairs away from the desk and placing them

332

side by side. When she was seated in one of them, he drew the other still closer and sat down himself, taking her hand in his.

"Is that better?"

"Yes, it is better—not that I didn't think it was wonderful to have you hold me that way, too. And I wasn't getting tired exactly. But my knees were beginning to give way and I had a queer feeling in the pit of my stomach."

"Is it gone now?"

"No, not quite. . . . There's something else I've got to tell you, Fabian."

"There's nothing else you have to tell me. You didn't need to tell me about Sylvestre. I knew it already."

"Yes, but I wasn't sure you did. You wouldn't have thought I was playing fair, would you, if I'd married you without telling you?"

"No. But you always do play fair. Of course, you'd have told me sooner or later. You didn't need to agonize over Sylvestre though, this morning, when we were both so happy. You could have told me any time before we got married."

"Fabian, we're not going to get married. It isn't just a question of the past—of Sylvestre. It's a question of the present—of Vail."

"Of Vail?"

"Yes, I can't leave him. He's mine."

She had met his eyes, squarely, all the time she had been speaking. Now she drew a deep breath that ended in a sigh, and gripping his hand convulsively, hid her face on his shoulder. He reached over and gathered her into his arms again.

"I have a feeling we can talk about this better if we're closer together," he said tenderly. "I'm going to hold you on my lap. There! Are you comfortable, darling?"

"Of course I'm comfortable," she answered, in a strangled voice. "That isn't the point. Didn't you understand what I said to you, Fabian? Merry isn't Vail's mother. I am."

"Yes, I understood. But it wasn't a shock to me."

"You haven't known that all this time, too!"

"I've thought so. And it's been a mystery to me how anything like that could be so thoroughly concealed. It's been a mighty well-kept secret. Would you feel like letting me in on it? On the details, I mean. Don't if you'd rather not——"

"But I want to. Of course, some people are in on it already—*maman* and Gervais and Merry and Dr. Champagne, besides the trained nurses and the upstairs servants."

"What about the priest who baptized the babies? Wasn't it the same sourpuss who comes to hear Tante Isabelle's confessions, about Lord knows what?"

"Yes. But I'm almost sure he didn't catch on. Anyhow, the inscription on the baptismal certificate's mendaciously in order—'Malcolm Vail, legitimate son of Meredith and Gervais d'Alvery'—Merry showed it to me afterwards to reassure me. I wasn't at the ceremony—still couldn't lift my head—and later, when the sourpuss, as you correctly call him, said he'd like to come in and see me before he left, I had Creassy tell him I was asleep. I've always avoided him, so my message was quite in character. I think most of the house servants must have guessed, but you know how jealous they all are about shielding their white folks. They've been wonderful—everyone's been wonderful when it comes to that. Most of the credit belongs to Merry, though."

"To Merry! Why?"

"It was her idea—that the babies could be passed off as twins. When she found out about me and realized that they were due at the same time, she suggested it. She said she was sure we could carry it off. You see, my bad back had put me out of circulation anyway. Besides, I don't need to tell you how isolated this place is in midwinter—it's a wonder Dr. Champagne managed to get through, considering the state of the River Road! As a matter of fact, Vail and Sybelle *are* twins. That is, they were born the same night. I was taken sick first, but I was sick a lot longer than Merry."

"I'm sorry you had such a terrible time, darling. I was afraid you did. You looked like a ghost for months."

"Oh, but that wasn't just the long labor! I really did hurt my back. I hurt it badly. Everything they said about that was true. I was in a cast, I did have to wear a brace. I was in bed for months on account of my back. But I would have had to stay there anyway. I had pernicious vomiting. I'd begun to have it before I got hurt and I couldn't have hidden it much longer. Of course, Dr. Champagne discovered it right away."

"Cresside, you've been through nearly every sort of hell there is. But I'm going to make up for some of it. I'm going to help you forget about it once we're married."

"But I can't marry you, Fabian. That's what I keep trying to tell you. And I'm trying to tell you, too, how wonderful Merry was. She kept encouraging me. The others didn't. Not even the doctor. You see, they all thought it would be a blessing in disguise if I lost the baby. They hoped I would. Some of them even. . . . I don't need to tell you about that, do I, Fabian?"

"No, you don't need to tell me about that."

"Well, but Merry said I was right to want to go through with it. She said she was sure I could. She told me if I could stand having a hard time physically, she'd keep me from having a hard time otherwise. She convinced the others she and I were right, she made them carry on, she taught them to play their parts without a hitch. I don't see how I could have held out, Fabian, without Merry."

"You would have, some way."

"I don't know. . . . I didn't go downstairs from the day I hurt my back until Vail was three months old. The horrible nausea lasted all the time I was pregnant, and then afterwards, of course, it took me a long time to get my strength back. But nothing that happened to me did Vail any harm. All my vitality went to him. Dr. Champagne said sometimes it happens that way. Vail weighed more than Sybelle when they were born and I nursed him, too, long enough to give him a good start."

Cresside was not speaking in a strangled voice any longer, but in a tone of fierce triumphant pride. Fabian bent his head so that his face touched hers, and clasped her more closely in his arms.

"You couldn't have done all that, darling, no matter how much Merry helped you, if you hadn't had tremendous courage and endurance yourself. If Vail ever finds out that you're his mother, he'll be mighty proud of you."

"But he mustn't ever find out! It would kill me if he did! We've taken every precaution that he shouldn't! Who'd do such a cruel thing as to tell him?"

"I don't know. There are about a dozen people in on this secret already, aren't there? Well, there's an old saying that it's no secret that's known to three. Sooner or later there's almost bound to be a leak. I don't mean an open scandal—I think you're fairly safe from that. But some kind of an allusion to an old mystery—accidental, probably, rather than malicious. For instance, Vail might overhear a private conversation between persons who would have bitten out their tongues rather than betray your secret. But you've got to face the possibility that your son may know the truth, just the way you face everything else, Cresside."

Again he pressed his face to hers and tightened his embrace.

"Except that hereafter I'm going to help you face that—and everything else," he said. "But no matter how much I help, I can see it would be hard for you to leave Vail. I can't imagine why I didn't think of that before, because I've kept threshing over this whole situation for months now. Of course, you know I'd be more than glad to have you bring him with you. But that would be a dead give away, that would set tongues wagging. You can't undo everything you've done so far."

"Of course, I can't. So, of course, I can't marry you either."

"That doesn't follow at all. As a matter of fact it would be a good thing for both of you if you left him."

"A good thing! If I left my own child!"

"You don't want him to know he's your own child. You just said it would kill you if he found it out. Well then, naturally you want him to believe Merry's his mother. You want him to believe you're his aunt. I should think that would be easier all round if you weren't in the house with him. As it stands you monopolize Vail, Cresside, you can't help it. You always have. And he turns instinctively to you for everything he needs and wants. You feed him, you bathe him, you get him up in the morning and put him to bed at night, you sing to him and play with him. The first word he said wasn't mama. It was auntie. He doesn't say mama yet. If you leave him, he cries for you, if he's angry you pacify him, if he's ailing, you soothe him. I've never seen the slightest sign that he relied on Merry, or that he missed her when she wasn't around; I've never heard him chortle with glee when she appeared. Wouldn't it be a good thing to start changing all that before he gets much older? Answer me honestly, darling."

"I don't know. Yes, I suppose it would. I hadn't thought of it that way before."

"Well, won't you? Of course, you'll miss Vail terribly at first, if you leave him, and he'll miss you, too—for a few days. But it won't take him any longer than that to get used to a change if you go while he's still a baby. And remember you wouldn't be far from him anyway. You could come and see him whenever you liked. I suppose in the natural course of events you'd be at Belle Heloise every day or two, while I was at the office. And he'd look forward to your visits pretty soon—his aunt's visits. He wouldn't ever think of you as the mother who went off and left him—he'd think of you as the aunt who came to see him. He'd grow up believing Merry was his mother, the way you want him to, unless there were some mischance. And if there were, you'd still be near enough to explain. He'd grow up as Gervais d'Alvery's first-born son, as Sybelle's twin, as little Philogene's elder brother. All that would mean a lot to him, Cresside, now and when he's older, too."

"Yes, I know. It's what I've wanted for him, it's what I've tried to get for him. Only I thought I'd be here, too."

Her voice was trembling uncontrollably again. So were her hands. Fabian held these fast in his.

"You will, whenever it's best that you should," he said reassuringly. "But it isn't best all the time. Please believe me, Cresside. It isn't best for the boy and it isn't best for you. You oughtn't to live the rest of your life as the outlier of the family circle, in the aftermath of a tragedy. You ought to have a home and a husband of your own and children you could acknowledge as your own. You'd be happy yourself if you did, and you'd give a lot of happiness, too." He stopped, halted by his innate reluctance to voice his own desperate loneliness and his own overpowering need. But he knew now that he must do more than admonish her as a mentor; he must appeal to her as a lover. "You don't seem to know what it would mean to me to have you for my wife," he said urgently. "You don't seem to know what it would mean to me to have you for the mother of my son. But the truth is it would mean everything in the world. You've told me that you love me and I believed you. If that's true, don't you love me enough to marry me?"

SUGAR PLANTATION
RECORD AND ACCOUNT BOOK

No. 2

SUITABLE FOR A FORCE OF 120 HANDS, OR UNDER.

BY THOMAS AFFLECK

PART VI

"Please Oh Jesus"

EXTRACTS FROM GERVAIS D'ALVERY'S DIARY

1921–1927

"He planted, bought land, engaged in sports, and watched with a careful eye the inhabitants of his quarters. He religiously kept a diary in which he recorded the work of the plantation, the events of the day, and even his most private thoughts."
—From *"Plantation Life in the Florida Parishes."*...As Reflected in the Diary of Bennet H. Barrow.

PART VI

"Please Oh Jesus"

EXTRACTS FROM GERVAIS D'ALVERY'S DIARY

1921–1927

CHAPTER XXVI

Aug. 20, '21. Heavy thunder showers in night. Clearing before day-break. At Fabian's insistence planted samples of cane he brought from Washington in his suitcase. This is the so-called P.O.J. 234, initials standing for Proefstation Oest Java—an outlandish name for an alien product in which I have no confidence. Foresee it will be butt of much derision. Fabian knowing nothing about sugar can't be convinced soil is worn out and that this experiment is just an empty gesture. Never saw him so stubborn about anything, however, and had to shut him up somehow. Personally I have more faith in new emergency tariff bill for which Ed Gay in Senate and Whit Martin in House have done so much. Without their efforts sugar would not have been included on dutiable list and if it can only stay there we may have prosperity yet. Mrs. Randall and Miss Mittie came to see Merry yesterday, admit now entirely out of money, have decided to move into storehouse Sept. 1st. Mrs. R.'s attitude rather that she is conferring favor than that we are granting one, fear endless complications. Charles here for supper, Cresside actually civil to him. She looks better and seems happier than any time I can remember, hope she is coming to her senses at last. Philogene cut his first tooth today, weight 20 pounds stripped.

Sept. 10, '21. High winds. Storms threatening but fortunately passed by. Cane developing as well as can be expected considering diseased condition. Luigi Tramonte celebrated opening of his new fancy grocery store this evening. Philogene still teething, slight fever, Merry unwilling to leave him, but L. having made great point of our coming I went with Cresside and Fabian. Found surprisingly large crowd assembled, among

339

them "College" Cangelosi (now very prosperous, joked with Fabian about Victory Loan speech F. made to deaf mutes), Mayor Grouchy, Father Gardino, Police Officer Tony Lango and numerous customers including S. T. and C. B. Also several queer old men who tipped their hats when they came in but afterwards replaced these and kept them on, several buxom matrons with teen-aged daughters who went around introducing girls to everybody, numerous pregnant and nursing mothers, etc. Eating and drinking continuous, part of counter used for bar, large wooden tubs with mixer's ice behind it, unlimited quantities homemade wine and beer, also large glass bowls filled with Johnny Crooks, stage planks and sauerkraut candy, doubtless to recall L.'s first source of success. Door open from store, where men mostly remained, into house where women congregated. Riccardo standing beside door offered each guest upon entering paper flower, drenched with strong perfume. Table in dining room also decorated with paper flowers (which apparently Netta takes pride in making), covered with coarse lace cloth, laden with bottles of vermouth, Lacrima Christi, Asti Spumante, huge platters of chicken and spaghetti, also various Italian sweetmeats, *pignolate, muscardini, rocotta,* etc. Netta much bejeweled as usual presided in dining room, situated between up-to-date kitchen leading into store and garish living room beyond. Luigi beaming, telling everyone days when he had to "study to make a nickel" now over and he can "afford to put on dog." From present indications think he will probably end by putting on too much.

Sept. 20, '21. Continued good weather but cane not quite up to July promise and that none too good. A rather dull, dragging day at the State House, especially when Governor Parker appeared before the Agricultural Committee meeting over which I presided in the absence of the chairman, to raise hell about the Cameron Parish farmers not being reimbursed for the cotton they were not permitted to plant. Hope nobody goes after mosaic disease that way. Mrs. Randall and Miss Mittie now settled in upper part of storehouse. Constant coming and going during settling process has robbed me of all sense of peace and privacy in my office. Mrs. R. having discovered *maman* takes daily constitutional when able has decided it is her prerogative to do same though I do not think she ever heard of constitutional before coming here. Fabian came out early evening; stayed till midnight. Called on Mrs. R. and Miss Mittie in storehouse, as they declined to have dinner with us. Brought Cresside present of cocker puppy named Maud sired by Belizaire. Made astounding statement he and C. are engaged and talked to *maman,* who took it calmly, for hours on subject. C.'s behavior as usual extremely baffling. Denies engagement but upon being pressed admits attachment, so things look worse than ever for Charles after all. C. seems as delighted with puppy as if F. had given her diamond necklace.

Oct. 3, '21. That loud-mouthed draft dodger from Shreveport, Huey Long, surrendered to the Sheriff at the courthouse this morning after Governor Parker had sworn out two charges of criminal libel against him day before yesterday. Long had distributed to all our desks in the House sometime before we met a typically crazy mimeographed circular that I understand he typed and mimeographed himself up in the Railroad Commission offices the night before, saying that the Standard Oil Company controlled Parker, dictated his policies and made him distribute patronage at its orders. Apparently all that's based on is the appointment of Hunter Leake's son to be superintendent of Charity Hospital in New Orleans, and I believe one notarial commission issued to my fellow Representative Teddy McGiehan of the 4th Ward. This will put Father's old friend Judge Harney Brunot in an awkward position since, I am told, he will hear the criminal charges without a jury so that he will be unable to pass the buck to anyone else. For my part, they can put Long under the jail instead of in it.

Oct. 7, '21. Sudden cold spell; cane ripening rapidly. Shall have to start grinding ahead of schedule if it continues to mature at present rate. Everybody so interested in legislative investigation of Jefferson Parish Sheriff and the Giant-Yankee World Series that no one paid much attention today to a motion to draft impeachment proceedings against the entire Railroad Commission—Huey Long, John T. Michel and Shelby Taylor. Those three had it hot and heavy in the House last night, calling each other liar till the rafters rang. Tonight Fabian actually did bring Cresside diamond necklace, putting it on at dinner table in front of us all, kissed back of her neck when he fastened it. C. neither mocked nor repulsed him but sat very still, hands trembling, tears in her eyes, then after a few minutes excused self and left table. F. remained seated through meal, made himself unusually agreeable, told *maman* she had better begin to make plans for a wedding, which *maman* seems perfectly willing to do. Disappeared immediately after dinner, apparently knew where to look for C., brought her to *garçonnière* for nightcap around eleven. I feel sure F. is wasting time and effort, Merry does not agree with me, have avoided discussing subject with *maman* as have no desire to start useless argument.

Oct. 31, '21. Weather unseasonably warm. Cane too green in consequence. Sugar down to 6.9 cents. Don't see how we can hang on if this keeps up. Continual trouble with bastard grains in spite of every care. Bringing *masse cuite* to higher temperature and adding more sugar has failed to eliminate them. Finally had whole mixture pumped back to pan floor, completely remelting and recrystallizing. Lost six hours in process. Beginning to believe Merry's superstition justified. Semmes Walmsley and his crowd now up in Kansas City are going to try to get our Legion Convention for New Orleans next year. Hope to attend if he succeeds, as I have not been to New Orleans for any kind of

341

outing since Merry and I went June of last year. Rumor circulating that Mrs. Hathaway has cancer but that she will not consent to operation. Have not paid much attention to it owing to preoccupation with our own troubles. Creassy has had second stillborn baby, mourning general in both quarters and Big House. Feel genuinely sorry for her and Amen.

Feb. 15, '22. Sugar now down to 6.40. Impossible to cover cost of harvesting at this figure. Continued rain has kept work at standstill for nearly a month. Apparently over at last. Low temperature welcome, has stopped sprouting of seeds in windrows. Spring planting should be completed by end of month. Daily constitutionals taken by *maman* and Mrs. Randall continue to be source of strain which gets on my nerves. Mrs. R. persists in starting walk at one end of pergola at *maman's* habitual hour for starting at other, so they meet by sun dial in center, bow and pass without speaking, *maman* very busy with her beads and Mrs. Randall with her Bible. Believe *maman* would willingly unbend if Mrs. R. were not so openly hostile. Miss Mittie very helpful generally with children, however, and has already taught Vail some of his letters from the plantation bell. Fabian out this evening as usual, announced he was starting unexpectedly for Mexico on Monday in behalf of client who has large interests in silver mine near Taxco, State of Guerrero. Possibility that something may also develop in tin as side issue, big commission apparently in offing. Wish I had his luck. F. urged Cresside to marry him immediately and go with him to Mexico City for honeymoon. She declined as I knew she would but appearance indicates she has been crying since he went home.

April 22, '22. Stalks of P.O.J. planted back of Angus Holt's garden have all survived winter well and are now sprouting. As I foresaw, most planters of my acquaintance maintain scoffing attitude and say initials mean "Poor Old Jones," but I'm beginning to think skeptics may be wrong and Fabian right about eventual success of experiment. Young cane up to fair stand everywhere, field work in active progress, fields tolerably clean. River very high, however, threatening floods. May be necessary to divert labor to strengthening levee which would have material effect on crop. All levees in this district are now patrolled, men stationed every half mile. This evening Lou Ida served hot dewberry pie with whipped cream for first time this season. Luscious dish. Girls will start making jam tomorrow as bushes along River Road are now laden with berries. These are certainly our biggest *lagniappe* crop. Fabian writes he is going to Bolivia via Vera Cruz, Yucatan and Panama, then down West Coast. Purpose of trip to secure services of Bolivian tin expert for his client as interests have developed along desired lines. Urges Cresside to meet him in Mexico City and marry him there and has written to all the rest of us stressing advantages of such a plan and saying that surely one of us could arrange to accompany her. F. knows quite well that I cannot leave plantation at this season and that Merry cannot leave the children at any season. Preposterous to assume that *maman* could make the trip.

May 10, '22. Cloudy. All levees remain intact and river here checks only slight rise in last 24 hours. No new weakness has been reported on either side of river for several days and I'm beginning to think worst is over, but we have sure gone through perilous period in last few weeks with constant rains intensifying flood danger and difficulty of pushing work on levee fast enough. Break at Medora narrowly averted, another at Mark prevented only by timely warning of guard and quick collection of 200 men who went immediately to work. Service on local Red Cross committee organized for relief in addition to my own work and personal responsibilities has kept me humping night and day and even menace of crevasse has not kept my mind wholly off financial troubles, for interest on mortgage is due next week. Shall have to ask *maman* for money from her private funds in order to meet it. Hate like poison to do this and fear I have taken my feelings out on Merry. Her attitude remains calm and cheerful about everything. She is so sure we will come through all right in the end that I cannot help deriving some courage from her attitude. Sight of *maman* and Mrs. Randall silently pacing back and forth in pergola, respectively engrossed in beads and Bible, still constant source of minor irritation to me, however, and I feel Cresside should recognize fact Fabian is orphan one of his chief merits. His old friend Preston Vichnair died yesterday, Cresside helping with funeral arrangements as she did in case of Max Stoetzner.

June 19, '22. Finally making some headway about grassy condition of fields caused by excessive rain and lack of attention during high stage of river but now evident we shall be at least three weeks late in laying by. I am getting more than I bargained for in this legislative business. All they are talking about now is horse racing, anyway. What with the regular session of 1920, the long special session of last fall, and the present regular session, I am being swamped with politics. This will be my last term unless I change my mind, as I probably will. I suppose the Governor feels the same way, in view of that mess at Amite in the trial over those six Italians for the third time on the murder charge. But Parker promised those people if they would refrain from violence against the six, he would see that the courts took the proper course. Luigi Tramonte out to see me. Much excited over trial. Claims Italians never get a square deal. F. writes from Bolivia he will be back in Mexico next month. Again urges Cresside to meet him there and to everyone's amazement *maman* has offered to go with her. Think C. is wavering after all. Wonders will never cease.

Sept. 21, '22. Nights cool, days dry and warm. Three pieces of P.O.J.

originally planted back of Angus Holt's garden have now increased to six stalks and are ready for replanting. Reasonably sure we shall find a better name for them than Poor Old Jones. Vail and Sybelle at last on mend after terrific siege with measles caught Lord knows where. All possible complications. Dr. Champagne says Cresside's devoted nursing largely responsible for satisfactory recovery and she frequently expresses thankfulness that disease struck week before instead of week after she was planning to go to Mexico. Philogene in midst of light case naturally caught from others. No anxiety concerning his condition. Merry and I are curiously awaiting next move of Fabian's, due back end of month. Cresside has used children's illness as pretext for refusing altogether to see Charles.

Oct. 7, '22. Cloudy, showers, cooler. Dove hunt back of levee yesterday great success, hundreds of them flying into barrow-pit just before sundown. Beautiful sight and wonderful shot. High-speed sport, lucky I took my automatic. Doves came in so fast lead had to be greatly increased. Crowd came back to house with me for supper. Plan announced in morning paper to extend present city limit of Baton Rouge through amendment to charter by Governor with advice of Attorney General. City has doubled in size since last extension, showing real progress in our capital. Children now entirely recovered from measles, lively as crickets, but Fabian has not yet returned from Mexico. No direct word from him in several weeks, but his client writes he has been quite ill and this has caused delay. Can see Cresside is extremely anxious about him, evidently in her concern for Vail she overlooked fact Fabian might also need her. Maud's first litter of puppies born late last night after supper party had broken up. Cresside acted as solicitous midwife but everything went well. Three males, one female. None black, which will be disappointment to Fabian, as he keeps hoping to get one that will look like Belizaire.

Nov. 20, '22. Cloudy and cool. Letter from Parker now in Washington expresses satisfaction over conferences with Harding on alleged interstate Klan activities and hopefulness for help from Department of Agriculture in making grounds of new University veritable botanical garden. Have just discovered that Cato has been using cart borrowed ostensibly to haul stove wood to his cabin after knocking off work to take sugar out to back of purgery and make profitable sale to bootlegger. Difficult to discipline properly considering his value to me. Fabian appeared unexpectedly from Mexico, looks badly but seems in good spirits, warmly welcomed by Cresside who now unreservedly admits engagement. So Merry wins again. Obviously C. has greatly missed F. and lately been much worried about him besides. Went with them to find *maman* who was walking in pergola, where Fabian by confronting her and Mrs. Randall simultaneously forced them to recognize each other's existence, another triumph for him. F. says he has

344

received cable announcing death in Penang of his late client and our former neighbor Mary Surcliffe who obtained legal separation from Englishman she married but has nevertheless traveled over world for years on British passport taking enormous quantities of luggage and much valuable jewelry with her. Penang police do not know what to do with body or property, yet so far have declined to deal with any other officials, claiming lack of authority. F. who is named as executor foresees many complications.

Dec. 19, '22. Colder but fair. Frost to coast. Temperature 24 to 28 in the north between sugar and trucking region. Went quail hunting early this morning, returned with full bag which will go well for Sunday breakfast. Hope to get in another hunt New Year's Eve day. Smallpox has developed in city jail, new Parish jail opened on Tuesday, prisoners from other jails will be brought to Baton Rouge. Parker returning to city Sunday, states he will not try to deal with complex situation in Highway Commission, precipitated by resignation of Buie, until more pressing work is done. Complications foreseen by Fabian regarding Mary Surcliffe's estate seem to be increasing. Will cannot be probated in Penang because this was not M.'s legal residence. English solicitor F. has consulted by cable gives cheerful information it cannot be probated in London either because of insufficient property and doubtful residence there and does not see how it can be probated elsewhere either! F. is inclined to take less gloomy view and meanwhile has applied for probate of will in Baton Rouge. Penang police, who finally had to do something, cremated poor M. thus eliminating problem of shipping body.

Jan. 5, '23. Cool and cloudy. Izzy advertising he will serve wonderful $1.00 dinner on Sunday, 12 noon to 9 p.m. Shall try to persuade Merry to go in to town with me for that much of an outing after Mass. Great excitement hereabouts over alleged masked-band outlawry in Morehouse Parish and specifically over the kidnapping and alleged slaying of Watt Daniel and T. F. Richards, whose headless bodies were found in Lake Lafourche. Fabian has obtained probate Mary Surcliffe's will in Baton Rouge, also through Goldenberg have got bank here to persuade Penang police to turn M.'s jewelry and other property over to Dutch bank there pending his arrival on scene, as he has decided to leave immediately taking one of Dollar Line boats which circumnavigate globe stopping at 21 ports Penang among them. This time does not request but demands that Cresside go with him and I believe she will consent. She has devoted much time lately to making Pascal Tremblet's last days comfortable and happy, he passed away peacefully yesterday so the story of our own Musketeers has ended.

Feb. 6, '23. Cresside and Fabian married in parlor this afternoon, Merry's condition providing ample excuse for very quiet wedding.

Family and servants only persons present. However, to please *maman* C. wore beautiful old brocade dress from Evaline Estrade's trousseau instead of traveling outfit as she had originally intended and looked lovely. Vail and Sybelle, acting as attendants, did remarkably well, Vail carrying ring on cushion, Sybelle holding bride's bouquet of camellias from Angus Holt's garden. C. and F. left immediately after ceremony for New Orleans where they will take CRESCENT LIMITED for New York City, embarking next week on *President Harrison* of Dollar Line for first lap of round the world trip. Leave-taking inevitably painful but tactfully curtailed by F. V. keeps asking for C. but not unhappily and Miss Mittie's doing a fine job with him. She and Mrs. Randall attended wedding and Mrs. R., after weeping copiously, actually spoke to *maman* so I hope ice is broken at last, indoors at least, though C. and F. will have a chilly ride for mantle of snow covers most of Dixie and colder weather is coming up tonight. More than 400 cases of flu in Baton Rouge which, according to telegram just received from George Favrot, has been ranked as 7th port in U. S. by Shipping Bureau. Status due entirely to shipments from here by Standard Oil. Wish to heaven I had some share in this prosperity.

Mar. 17, '23. Baby girl born 4 a. m. I have insisted on naming her for her mother, but am using French form, Joyeuse, to avoid confusion. M. had her usual easy time, but poor baby got cold welcome as far as weather is concerned, for she arrived in a killing freeze, the latest we have ever had at B. H. First time I have ever known old saying to prove false that after leaves appear on pecan trees spring is really here and all danger of freeze is over. Weather predictions are for still another within next 24 hours, followed by heavy rains. Cold has effectually set back crop, and I am much concerned about stubble. Radiogram received from Fabian and Cresside who had just left San Francisco for Hawaii after delightful trip through Canal with brief stopovers at Havana and Panama.

May 20, '23. Nothing but rain rain rain since April 1st, and rainfall now so heavy that all fields are flooded and all rows flat. Grass has obtained tremendous advantage for shortage of labor gone to Standard Oil has made it impossible to fight this successfully even in brief intervals between rains when field work could be done. Impossible to meet interest on mortgage even with *maman's* help and shall have to borrow more money or risk losing place. Immediate need $20,000 which I believe Goldenberg will let me have to protect original loan as I doubt if he could get $100,000 for plantation as market now stands. Outlook is sure dark but Merry continues to be calm and confident and keeps finding new ways to cut corners and reduce expenses all without complaint. Mrs. R. acting more and more like a human being which is another mercy as is excellent health of all three children. Vail still asks for Cresside but less and less frequently and is devoted to

Miss Mittie. Just received long letter from Cresside written in Penang where Fabian has succeeded in straightening out Mary Surcliffe's tangled affairs before worst of heat has set in. C. still feels China most interesting of countries of which they have had brief glimpses. Now that chief (admitted) purpose of trip is accomplished C. and F. are planning to retrace their steps slightly to visit Sumatra and Java then continue to Ceylon dividing time until fall among mountain resorts where they can be cool and comfortable. Obviously no financial embarrassments for them and I gather no prospects of increase in family either.

Aug. 1, '23. Checking my ditches today during intervals between downpours, find main canal caved in, several lateral ditches stopped up. Have everybody including teamsters diverted to work there and will have to keep the men doing this for several weeks. Charles and I went sounding for loggerhead turtles in swamp back of plantation this evening, Amen paddling pirogue. Came back with 6 altogether, the largest measuring over 3 ft. in length. We shall have turtle soup from now on as long as we want it and shall have lots of meat to give away besides. Delicious food, no one could ask for better, perhaps we can get our minds off the rain for a few hours if we invite in some friends to share it with us. Have suggested this to Merry, as it is a long time since we have had any company, and she is now making plans for an informal party.

Sept. 1, '23. Creassy has at last given birth to healthy baby whom she persists in calling Dumps, why I don't know, probably she doesn't either. So little cash on hand I was hard put to make expected present but have managed by giving up a 5 dollar gold piece I have carried for luck ever since I can remember. Rains have now lasted five months and we have the sorriest looking crop seen on this date at B. H. Stubble particularly poor as I foresaw. Cane not already laid by abandoned to work out its own salvation in combat with grass. Goldenberg sent for me today. Told me client whose name he will not divulge had tried to buy mortgage on B. H. at discount. Board of Directors has declined to accept offer because it would involve considerable loss to bank but he has warned me time may come when such loss might represent lesser of two evils in opinion of Board. Have promised Merry that if this happens I will appeal to Fabian for help but personally am so completely discouraged am almost ready to let place go rather than struggle any further.

Sept. 11, '23. Rain still continues unabated. That earthquake in Japan must be something dreadful. Thankful Fabian and Cresside got safely out of there last spring. I hate to think of all those people being killed, and yet, somehow, I never could bring myself to trust any Jap I ever met. Three candidates have formally announced today for the Gov-

347

ernorship. Our own Henry Fuqua from whom I have bought practically every piece of hardware at Belle Heloise, Dudley Guilbeau from Opelousas, and that unbelievable clown Huey Long, who was 30 years old on August 30th, and celebrated it by getting drunk and announcing for Governor. The gossip is Parker will support his own Lieutenant Governor, Hewitt Bouanchaud. I'm going to run again, but for the Senate this time. Naturally I'll support our Baton Rouge candidate, Henry Fuqua. Luigi Tramonte out early evening with his son Riccardo, remarkably handsome boy, to whom both Vail and Sybelle appear to have taken great fancy. L. says this will be his last trip down River Road as he has now hired a man to drive his truck. Encouraged by success with fancy grocery store in Baton Rouge he is opening branch establishment in Opelousas.

Dec. 25, '23. Grinding finished yesterday with no celebration beyond lighting usual Christmas bonfires on levee. Lord knows there was nothing to celebrate as far as sugar is concerned. Yield was low at outset of grinding and continued so, campaign has lasted only 44 days altogether. Believe I will plan a snipe hunt for Sunday to get my mind off my troubles. Dr. Champagne here today to see children who now all have chicken pox another obstacle to Christmas festivities. Apparently there is a Santa Claus, however, because as matters stand I'm already good as elected. A good thing R. J. did not run, as he likely could have pinned back my ears, which might have been the best thing that could have happened to me. The Klan issue is making the campaign unusually bitter. Cable of holiday greetings from Fabian and Cresside. They are spending Christmas season in Holy Land which apparently surpasses their every expectation, but Cresside is "not well." I wonder?

Jan. 15, '24. Fair, light freeze. There will have to be a run off between Bouanchaud and Fuqua. Bouanchaud led in yesterday's primary, but most of the Long vote will go to Fuqua, who is, therefore, almost certain to win. Long got a surprising vote, however, more than 70,000. I think this looks ominous. My own election was fairly one-sided. Charles very helpful and friendly throughout campaign. Still sorry I did not get him for a brother-in-law. Children all well. Phil and Joyeuse coming along nicely, both getting better looking all the time though neither is a beauty like Sybelle. She and Vail will be four years old tomorrow. Small party planned to celebrate. Vail suggested we invite Riccardo Tramonte which of course I declined to do. He certainly takes strange fancies. Maud has produced another fine litter of puppies but no black ones among them. Unusual piece of luck today. Killed an alligator 9 ft. 4 in. long with 3d shot. Distributed almost 300 lbs. reddish coarse-grained meat in quarters.

April 15, '24. Generally fair. Cooler. Letter today from Fabian and Cresside, now leaving shortly for home as they are "expecting" in mid-summer. However they have spent several weeks in and near Naples and in Rome. Met Luigi Tramonte on Third Street yesterday and he stopped me to say he had also heard from C. and F., telling him they had looked up his people, tickled to death with this attention. He now owns two trucks and is opening branch store in Lafayette as one in Opelousas is doing so well. He had just come from bank where I gathered he had made substantial deposit. I was on my way there to arrange further extension of mortgage and borrow money to pay interest. Am certainly getting deeper and deeper involved all the time, nevertheless cannot help feeling increasing interest aroused by our experiments is hopeful sign. Busy all day with visiting planters from west side who have heard about remarkable progress we are making with our experiments in P.O.J. and who asked to look at cane and examine tests we are making.

July 1, '24. Interest in our experiments with Java cane continues to increase, several hundred planters from all 11 sugar parishes having now visited Belle Heloise to see what we are doing, and derision with which our efforts were first greeted is now obviously on decline. Negroes beginning to refer to P.O.J. as "Please Oh Jesus." Personally feel designation much more apt than "Poor Old Jones." Must admit Fabian shows considerable forebearance in not saying I told you so, but he is so overjoyed at birth of baby daughter and Cresside's satisfactory convalescence after long hard pull that his mood is mellower than I have ever seen it before. After some discussion child has been named Frances Isabelle after first owner of B. H. and *maman,* who is making much more of her than she ever did of any of my children. These are all delighted with their little cousin and behaved very well at christening, of which Fabian made quite an event for a self-labeled agnostic, though I have not heard him saying much about that either of late.

July 27. Need of rain very widespread and acute. Anxiety as to outcome of crop is universal and justified, cold and backward spring and abnormally dry summer having both affected it disastrously. No longer any hope of retrieving lost ground, even if plentiful rains should come now. Wish I could afford one of the new Buick motors which really do have "every feature to please customer" as announced by company, but I might as well wish for the moon. The poor old '20 bus will have to carry us around a while longer. Just heard of Rand's discovery that snails cause root rot; this may provide hopeful future if we can control snails, though whole picture looks pretty black. Lack of pasture and drinking water for cattle constitutes serious menace. Dr. Champagne here today to see Merry, who is not doing so well as on previous pregnancies, reports Mrs. Hathaway's days undoubtedly numbered. Operation was unsuccessful because too long postponed and great suffering is apparently inevitable during final stages of disease. *Maman* planning to visit her regularly and seems genuinely saddened by impending loss of old friend but I am much more concerned about Merry who should have more care. Creassy preoccupied with Dumps and expecting another baby herself no longer of much use to Merry, as I foresaw when Creassy and Amen got married. C— will not even help with preserving as she and A— both subscribe to old superstition that fumes from boiling fruit and sugar bring on miscarriage, in fact she lays her last mishap to these— Amen who describes C's condition as *"comme çi, comme ça"* also neglecting his work for me, far more interested in thriving through surreptitious business he is doing in love powders, conjures, etc. Seems to be succeeding Luigi Tramonte as most popular peddler among Negroes on River Road though with different set of wares, and whole thing started when drummer passing through happened to drop a dream book and a circular of charms which Amen picked up.

Sept. 15, '24. Mrs. Hathaway died of cancer this morning, *maman* went to make visit of condolence, found Cresside already there making herself generally useful, apparently quite without self-consciousness. Funeral tomorrow, Fabian will be one of pallbearers and so shall I. Feel unable to refuse, but am not sorry Merry's condition provides excuse for non-attendance. Continued drought. Parched fields present pitiful appearance. Red rot and root rot both prevalent, Rand's discovery that snails cause latter made too late to save this season's crop. Unless we get relief from drought fall planting useless because of dry ground. Nevertheless increasing numbers of planters continue to come here to see our cane and examine our tests in P.O.J., and I find there is widespread study of experiments being started by Office of Sugar Plant Investigations and reports on successful efforts made in other sugar-producing territories to meet same prices Louisiana is facing today. This intelligent interest is naturally very gratifying, but I get the biggest lift of all from the Negroes. It really does something for me every time I hear that chant of "Please Oh Jesus" in the fields.

Nov. 1, '24. In spite of continued drought have gone ahead with fall planting, not knowing what else to do. Have decided to start grinding what cane we have, Lord knows not much. Hathaway shut down, no planting, no grinding, Tremaines away for indefinite absence. Looks like beginning of end there. Hackberry also shut down, but think Charles will stage comeback since he has the money to lose, but says he won't butt his head against a stone wall any longer. Believe he is not sorry to get away too, and his manager, Seaver, is the right sort and will look after everything in the owner's absence, which is more than I can say for Blood. River Road almost deserted now except for us. Not enough interested in national election Tuesday to take my mind off my own troubles. I shall vote for Davis, of course, but hope Coolidge gets in, of which there is very little doubt. This is the first national election in which women play a part. Merry can't get out to vote and naturally *maman* did not even register, but Cresside says she will go to the polls as often as she can talk men into letting her do so. Fabian apparently still enjoys her persiflage more than I ever did.

Nov. 20, '24. Hurry call to Big House, Merry taken suddenly in labor. Did not stop to wash syrup off my hands before going to her room, she saw these still dripping, cried out she hoped no son of hers would ever be a sugar planter. Utterance wholly unlike her, doubtless due to shock of pains which came abnormally hard and fast. Everything soon over, and though badly torn by rapidity of birth M. is now resting quietly after tearfully telling me how deeply she regrets her outburst. We have another fine large boy, are naming him François Estrade after first owner of B. H. but shall probably call him Franchot. Wish prospects of supporting large family now have were somewhat brighter but outlook could hardly be worse. Predicament of planters acute. 1920 hit us with a lead pipe and 1923 stuck a knife into us but 1924 has blown us up with dynamite, and terrible as it is, the drought won't keep us from high water next January, so I'm thankful the Levee Board down in New Orleans is getting busy on a spillway below the city. Maybe that will teach the rest of our people and the people in Washington some sense, especially Ransdell, who still clings to the "levee only" theory of flood control.

Dec. 15, '24. Finished grinding today, again no celebration, even less cause for it than last year. Campaign lasted only 38 days. Acreage planted to sugar has been steadily decreasing. Nevertheless am amazed to find from records that more than 2,000 planters have visited B. H. this year to see our experiments and I realize that our general standing in State has never been higher. Too bad our financial status cannot compare favorably with this unexpected prestige, but Merry insists it will yet. Franchot thriving. Other children devoted to him, but Merry failing to recover her strength and slight operation may be necessary to repair damage done at baby's birth. Fear we shall not have a very merry Christmas this year, though I have succeeded in purchasing a radio for Merry, which she greatly desired. Unfortunately the New Orleans stations do not come in clearly, though we have no difficulty with other parts of Louisiana much further away. Vida Pelayo, one of our Baton Rouge girls, has been crowned the most beautiful coed at L.S.U. Wish Merry were well enough to do the honors for the family, but have asked *maman* and Cresside to attempt them in her place. Charles has invited me to the camp he has acquired in the marsh below Lake Arthur for duck hunting during the holidays and

351

Merry insists I should accept invitation on account of valuable contacts with other guests. However, much as I should enjoy it I hesitate to go, partly because I do not think I should leave home just now and partly because I do not feel I can afford high stakes at poker games which I know will actually occupy more time than shooting.

Mar. 27, '25. Cloudy, showers. Stalks of P.O.J. now ½ to 2 feet high. Whole field of this now planted next to field of native cane, cultivation and fertilization exactly same, but looking down rows, striking difference between two immediately evident. Native cane shows pale dotted line, P.O.J. thick green line. Also stubble of new varieties much thicker, more uniform and taller in growth than plant cane of old varieties, remarkable showing. Two-year-old stubble of P.O.J. has amazing growth, indicating heavy harvest. Row of two-year-old stubble of old variety left alongside test piece does not show a single sprout. Still feel Fabian is most forebearing not to say "I told you so!" and am thankful for Frances Belle's opportune appearance on scene for my sake as well as his.

April 15, '25. Fair. No change in temperature. Experimentation in connection with disease- and pest-elimination work now well under way. At suggestion of Dr. R. D. Rand, am making tests with dichlorbenzene to see if it will not destroy snails causing red rot. If this does not do trick, we will try something else. Also making studies of other tests and fungus growth. Laboratory costing $7500.00 paid for by sugar industry will shortly be erected. Have placed 52 acres at B. H. at disposal of Dr. Brandes' dept. In this tract will be tried canes evolved at Canal Point and imported varieties to see if they will produce well under Louisiana conditions. Work has already begun, 200 varieties have been received and are being closely watched. Most have already indicated unsuitability for Louisiana conditions, but several have possibilities. P.O.J. has now been distributed in limited amounts to leading planters throughout state, selling for $110 a ton as against $5 for ordinary cane. All this will be used for seed plots throughout sugar parishes and resulting seed should permit cane to be planted on commercial basis next year. Sylvestre back at Hathaway, Charles at Hackberry, both apparently ready to go on again now I have proved it can be done. Seaver has kept Hackberry in good shape but Blood has let everything run *down* at Hathaway while running *round* himself with those Renos.

Sept. 22, '25. Cloudy. Everyone is looking forward to cooler weather after steamy days. Objections are being raised to new types of cane because these are smaller in diameter and have thicker fiber than old types. Do not feel these objections valid, as tonnage is there, new cane being considerably taller than old, and sugar content is there, as proved by figures. After all, it is sucrose we are after, not geometrical proportions. Granted new cane may be harder than old to crush, this problem has been met in Puerto Rico and Argentina, so believe we could meet it here. At worst, it only involves minor mill changes including installation of knives ahead of crusher. Miss Mittie has opened up old schoolhouse and started Sybelle and Vail with regular lessons, Phil of course tagging along after them. It seems good to see old building in use again and I don't believe children could have a better teacher. Mrs. Randall now as devoted as *maman* to all of them but especially to Joyeuse and Franchot who of course need her most. Merry is right, things do have a way of working out.

Nov. 15, '25. Wakened from sound sleep last night by loud roar, jumped out of bed, as I was rushing out of doors met Plauché who said everything o.k. at our factory but feared long-expected accident had occurred at Hathaway. Joined by Sance and Dupuy, drove down River Road and into *allée* top speed in pouring rain, could not see anything at first as place was in darkness except for glimmer of flashlights and torches used by workers searching in wreckage, but could hear Negroes wailing and shouting above escaping steam. Eventually came up to mixed throng surrounding entrance to mill, met Blood coming out who told me about casualties, which include two poor little darkies carrying midnight lunch to their father, a bagasse burner, seriously injured along with several others. Five deaths altogether. Boiler shell had gone through roof of factory, landed on top of cane pile. Most horrible catastrophe I ever heard of in this wretched business. Asking for Sylvestre, was told I would find him in office, went there to offer assistance and found him frantically looking for insurance records. Just like him, thinking of his miserable dollars instead of worrying about poor devils burned to death because of his criminal negligence and of their bereft families. Naturally said I would finish Hathaway crop at Belle Heloise, but this will not give work to all Sylvestre's hands, much less cure the injured or bring dead back to life. Home at 4 a.m., found Merry waiting up for me with hot coffee. Bet Sylvestre is catching hell from Regine right now instead of having sympathy and support with which I'm blessed.

Nov. 19, '25. Sylvestre here today on return from New Orleans, greatly upset because insurance company denies claim, referring him to letter written in July canceling boiler policy until installation of new valves. S. admits receiving and ignoring letter, got no sympathy from me. Father of two little children who were instantly killed has now died of burns himself, leaving widow and three other children whom I shall find ways to befriend though with Hathaway crop as well as my own to look after I'm hard pushed. Sylvestre and Regine leaving immediately for Europe to spend rest of winter, Blood in charge again, hell to pay.

Feb. 11, '26. Partly cloudy, rising temperature. Fabian and Cresside have gone to New Orleans for Momus Parade, opening Carnival season, will probably remain there several weeks as F. insists C. should have change and relaxation after devoting year and a half to baby tending. Merry has now spent six years in this way without respite and is beginning to show it, but she still insists she is all right and I can still see no way to make things easier for her. Don't know what we should have done without Mrs. Randall and Miss Mittie after all.

Feb. 26, '26. Fair, warmer. Jack Frost arrived as scheduled Fri. night and left thick white covering which dissolved in sun early Sat. a.m. Beautiful sight. Great excitement in quarters over Cato who "died" in current epidemic of flu which has hit us all but without exciting results except in his case. He had been growing steadily weaker after hard bout, then lost consciousness and was laid out in his funeral clothes by relatives who had been watching him all night. We have had many curious wakes at Belle Heloise but never one equal to this, for some 6 hrs. later he suddenly surprised mourners by coming to and thanking his lucky stars he had managed to rise up in time to tell them he wasn't dead after all. Believe they regard his recovery with mixed emotions as plans were already under way for elaborate funeral which some of them would undoubtedly have enjoyed. Amen taking great credit for Cato's cure, insists it is due to his charms and he has gained much added prestige as medicine man.

March 16, '26. Recent cold snap still unabated, light winds. Never have felt so much like giving Vail a good thrashing as I did today. Luigi Tramonte tactless enough to bring Riccardo out here with invitation for twins to take part in St. Joseph's day celebration, helping to trim altar and remaining to eat at Saints' table, Sybelle impersonating Blessed Virgin and Vail St. John. I naturally refused to let them do this, whereat Sybelle burst into tears and Vail was downright mutinous, saying he and S. would ride their ponies to town if they could not get there any other way. Seems Cresside made initial mistake in taking them to see this display on St. Joseph's day last year, and they were entranced with fancy foodstuffs, decorated candles, elaborate bouquets and all other paraphernalia of this fantastic Italian celebration. So the Tramontes promised them that they might take part in it this year. To make matters worse, I can see that both Cresside and Fabian think I am unreasonable in not indulging their whim, but I have got to put a stop to this childish infatuation somewhere or there's no telling where it will end.

May 11, '26. Fair and colder. 1926 session of legislature began yesterday. Devoted strictly to routine business except for election by acclamation of Clark Hughes of Bossier Parish as Speaker House of Representatives. No other candidates. Senate and House both ad-

354

journed early. Governor's message, read today, refers to sugar planters' plight by saying "whatever can be done to help and strengthen our fellow citizens of the sugar district in the great disaster that has overtaken so fair a portion of our beloved state, I feel sure will be cheerfully done." Wish I shared his conviction. Ancient game of lobbying already in full swing, a number of prominent women among those moving about Capitol working both for and against Mothers' Pension Bill. Went to Ferd Claiborne's camp on False River for fish supper with entire Senate Committee on Conservation. Caught last ferry back from Port Allen, after very hilarious party. Ate 10 *sac-a-lait* myself well washed down with cold beer and did not begin to stow away as much as many of my companions. Some discussion of pending bills but conversation centered mostly on Long's latest antics which are getting under everyone's skin and on Richard Byrd's feat in reaching pole by airplane.

June 23, '26. Partly cloudy. Laying by crop, find Sance has been careless in plugging quarter drains. Will get him to ride down each cut with me to show him drains not properly cleaned out. Don't see how the fool expects to save crop this grinding, should we have another rainy season like that of '23. Neglecting work on plantation for duties at Capitol which are riding me. House killed luxury tax but will reconsider tomorrow due to change of one vote. As it stands calls for 10% tax on all forms of tobacco, cosmetics off. Cresside has been wisecracking about this, but general political situation does not predispose me to much levity. Long continues his clowning, renting Community Club pavilion for purpose of holding public meeting to discuss Watson-William and Chef—Rigolete bridge proposition only one of his innumerable freakish and extravagant gestures. He has repeatedly attacked Highway Commission and present state administration for stand on this bridge question but has now come in for his share of attack. Charges being hurled that he has made thousands of dollars from the blood of workingmen under present Accident Compensation Act. Fine fishing in barrow-pit now, took Vail down there with me about 4:30 Sunday, caught 6 bass before sundown, but lost biggest one which would have weighed at least 5 lbs. Vail caught 2 himself, came home proud as punch, and had Lou Ida fry them separately for his supper and Sybelle's.

July 17, '26. Summer resort weather still prevails, cool mornings and evenings. Largest number of laws ever enacted at session of legislature will become effective on 28th, i.e. 20 days after adjournment. President of City National Bank has come out with this statement: "If a sugar planter when approaching my institution for a loan could show me that he is trying to carry out the practices of seed selection and thus guarding against root rot and mosaic infection, as the University Sugar Experiment Station is doing, he would find my bank in a receptive mood." As this is exactly what I am doing it ought to facilitate extension of my notes, and in view of the fact that it is now almost impossible for the majority of Louisiana sugar planters to negotiate new loans, this statement should prove most significant to those who have doubted wisdom of my ways and should also act as inducement to many to attend field-day meeting at University Sugar Station on 20th. This evening Amen brought me 6 frogs he caught last night with his own gig, never tasted anything better in my life than the legs, though as usual I had great difficulty persuading Lou Ida to cook them. She still insists they jump out of the pan. Have decided to go on a frog hunt myself tomorrow night and try my own luck, so I took my hip boots in town today for patching and got additional batteries for my flashlight.

Aug. 27, '26. Trying hard to stagger back on my feet after another knockout blow which has hit thousands besides myself. Wednesday weather bureau ordered area to take every precaution in view of hurricane advancing out of Gulf to East Louisiana and Thursday storm hit us hard. Miraculously Baton Rouge emerged with only minor injuries—roofs lifted, trees uprooted, poles down, windows and doors smashed, etc. All Ill. Cen. trains New Orleans-Hammond under water, country around Port Allen deluged. Many roads impassable, but Fabian got out here yesterday a.m. to tell me he and Cresside were o.k. and to report conditions generally and today I got to town myself. 5 known dead, several missing, property worth millions destroyed. Morgan City apparently faced hardest hit, virtually wiped out and farmers between B.R. and Hammond still fearful Amite River will overflow and flood their land. Cotton crop in north badly damaged, corn everywhere stripped and laid flat, pecan crop virtually destroyed, acres and acres of cane hopelessly flattened. With reappearance of sun, however, P.O.J. has straightened itself up and shows every sign of surviving. Believe last remaining skeptics will be convinced by this spectacle and even that attitude of Federal Loan Bank towards planters may undergo change. This time Merry is the one saying I told you so and has gone out in the fields with me to look at extraordinary sight of upright rows gleaming in evening light. We sure have cause for thankfulness which few others around us possess and I am not unmindful of this in spite of general discouragement.

Nov. 20, '26. Temperature moderating but cloudy. Cato's eldest son, Rush, went to work today as water boy. This is his first job and he is very proud of riding on the wagon and distributing buckets. Went deer hunting in the Morley swamps last Sunday, left Belle Heloise at 2 a.m., drove down River Road halfway to New Orleans, then went into swamps about 9 miles back of Blind River by boat. Placed on stand just before daylight, very tiresome as I could not

356

smoke or shoot the black squirrels I saw in trees. Two bucks killed that day, but neither driven over my stand. Hard walk back to boat, stepped in hole and went up to my shoulders in icy water. Like to freeze to death before I finally got home.

Dec. 14, '26. Temperatures all over South have tumbled sharply last 24 hrs. In and near Baton Rouge it is cool and cloudy. Lowest point of production in 60 years but upward swing seems in sight at last. Fabian and Cresside driving to New Orleans this week end for the reception being given at the Orleans Club by Mrs. Syms for her daughter Marie Louise and will probably stay over for the Airy dinner in honor of L. O. Broussard's little girl Betty. She was at Belle Heloise a good deal during her uncle's attendance at the Constitutional Convention five years ago. It is hard to realize she has grown up. Wish Merry and I could go with C. and F. but it is still out of question for us to spend money on pleasure. Merry cannot leave children anyway and I have had no diversions either this year for even my bird hunting has failed me. 'Possum hunts with Amen have constituted my only amusement, Lord knows not much of one.

Apr. 15, '27. Good Friday. *Maman* insisted on going to town for 3 hr. service against my advice for though high winds of early morning had much abated before noon and levees are holding around here heavy rains continue and news that Plaquemine locks have caved in indicates serious situation. Sandbagging has brought about quick results but with water at new maximum almost 2 feet in excess of that in 1922 we must expect further trouble.

Apr. 25, '27. Weather bureau predicts 48.5 feet water at Baton Rouge by May 18 which by far shatters all previous records. Plans being made here for emergency. Red Cross appeal to be announced. Committee of 8, myself among them, named as result of conference when all civic and commercial organizations and Parish and city government representatives met last night. Secretary Hoover and Maj. Gen. Jadwin, Chief of Army Engineers, arriving at Memphis last night on way South, outlined plans of relief and announced all resources of Federal Government were at command for stupendous work ahead. Sure hope we can regard this as a literal promise. Known deaths in Mississippi Valley floods now exceeds 60. Thousands of refugees are in peril on levees, knolls, housetops and in trees. Property damage likewise is increasing as additional plantations are inundated and more towns are flooded. No telling when our turn will come as sand boils have already begun to appear and I do not know whether we can continue to control them though Cato showed great courage and forethought in sandbagging a small one which he discovered near ditch on side of levee on returning to quarters after day's work there. Am beginning to realize all previous troubles insignificant compared with present danger of losing our home.

April 29, '27. Herbert Hoover and James Fieser, National Director of Red Cross, arrived in Baton Rouge last night to confer with officials here on Mississippi flood-relief work. Left B.R. at 11 this morning for Vicksburg after viewing operations and conferring with Ex-Governor Parker whom he has appointed director of situation. Of course, I feel he could not have chosen a better man for the job. Hoover himself shows no disposition to mingle informally with local workers and to get our views which is disappointing to many of us but we all recognize his ability as an executive and his public statements are reassuring. In the latest one he says: "Louisiana needs some help from Federal Government and from American Red Cross. Whatever is needed, whether from the Government or from the Red Cross, we shall go to the limit of our governmental responsibility to supply it." Again I hope this may be considered as a literal promise but doubt it.

May 10, '27. Crest of flood rapidly moving south from Vicksburg area, situation here becoming more acute hour by hour with 5 ft. rise reported along stretch of embankments. Approximately 1000 square miles already under water according to statement issued by Army engineers. Water going steadily over top of dyke, all schools and stores closed in Big Bend area of Bayou des Glaizes, entire population either isolated or evacuated. Hoover and Davis, Sec. of War, arrived early Sunday morning by boat from Natchez and after a number of conferences at some of which I sat in, left by auto for New Orleans. Authorized State Farm Rehabilitation Committee to proceed with loans for purchase of seeds up to $50,000. They will return Wednesday and I hope authorize funds for further relief work. Am patrolling levee myself during late shift, fearful of monkey business from west side, unable to keep from thinking what it will mean if there is a crevasse between Baton Rouge and Belle Heloise, though house will stand anything except direct break. Merry supervising work in kitchen, coffee made by bucketsful, sandwiches by basket for men on the levee. *Maman* praying constantly before Spanish statue, keeps Vail and Sybelle beside her there as much as she can. Cresside tried to get V. to town but he would not go, stoutly maintaining his place was here with me, pretty good for 7. Could not help feeling proud of him myself and C. did not insist when she saw how he felt. Sybelle also begged to remain, she and V. never willingly separated, but C. has taken three younger children. House servants standing bravely and efficiently by, quarters paralyzed by fright, women and children removed to bluff for safety, taking shelter with kin in cabins there. Sance and I have had great difficulty getting men on levee to fill sandbags, not enough leaders among Negroes themselves to insure sufficient teamwork, so I have got to keep going come what may.

May 14, '27. Yesterday flood waters charged through two crevasses in Big Bend area relieving pressure on levees between Belle Heloise and Angola. If river does not rise in next 24 hrs. I believe we are safe but do not dare bank on this yet. Patrol still continuous, National Guard taking charge where Charles and I, both deputized, leave off, as Blood has passed out of picture on one of his tears and Sylvestre as usual in case of emergency is off on a pleasure trip. *Maman* says she has made vow of votive offering if we are delivered, still spends most of her time praying in front of Spanish statue but now occasionally leaves stairway to pace back and forth on gallery looking at land or to go to attic where she watches river from windows. Merry still on constant duty in kitchen, do not see how she stands up under the strain, Sybelle and Vail have learned to make sandwiches and are helping her, neither one the least frightened and both exceptionally well-behaved. Cheers me to see them and to realize that whatever else I lose I shall have a great deal left with such a family.

May 30, '27. Fall of river continues steadily, danger point for our region now definitely passed. Sandbags still in place on levee and patrol continues but less intensively so. National Guard has been able to extend area under its supervision and I have been relieved. Hoover to tell story of flood in radio talk from New Orleans tonight, will leave immediately afterwards for Washington to confer with President but will return next week. Provision of additional capital was most important object of his visit and he hopes to obtain national subscriptions which will at least equal state subscriptions. Slept 12 hrs. on end last night. Today Fabian came out bringing back younger children, all well and happy and glad to be home again as we are to have them. Later F. and I went in his car to swamps west of Port Allen. Unique experience for beyond lay area 45 miles wide and 150 miles long completely inundated. Extraordinary sight included fences festooned with moccasins wrapped around wires for miles on end which of course was most repulsive feature of scene to me. F. and I fished for black bass from running board, came back with catch of 60, averaging 3 pounds. On return found *maman* in bed in state of complete collapse which did not surprise me and I must give her credit for keeping up and about as long as emergency lasted. Merry delighted with reunion of family and still shows no sign of going under, though I suppose we must look for let down sometime and no woman could stand what she has forever.

June 12, '27. Perfect summer day. Took *maman* into town today so that she could fulfill her vow of making thank offering for our safe deliverance from flood. She has given up some of her finest old jewelry to do this, which means there will be less for Sybelle and Joyeuse, as I shall never be able to get them anything comparable to the Spanish heirlooms; but I could not bring myself to find fault with her. I realized how she felt when I went out into the fields for the first time after the flood and saw the cane on which all our hopes for the future are based rising fresh and green all around me. I knelt down between the rows and thanked God it was still safe and prayed that it might come into its own this fall. I have faith that my prayer like *maman's* will be answered, and if anyone had found me on my knees in the field I should not have been ashamed though naturally I did not mention it to anyone. Only wish I felt as hopeful about the flood-control situation as I do about the sugar situation. Hoover has just left here after another brief visit in course of which he met with our local committees in Senate chamber. He had long discussion regarding details of financing operations which most of us felt should be comprehensive enough to cover a year's period. Hoover, however, says these problems will have to be met when they are reached and that the current plans were only for immediate present. Beginning to feel he does not realize how far-reaching problem is and this causes me grave concern. Partially reassured by report Senate Commerce Committee and House Flood Control Committee at present in St. Louis declare control of greater Mississippi flood waters a national problem to be solved by Federal Government. Also by fact that at Flood Control Conference called by mayor in Chicago Secretary of War assures hearers President is for flood control.

July 30, '27. Generally fair. More and more concerned about flood situation. Louisiana officials have presented formal request to National Government for federal funds to repair levees as local boards have no more resources for obtaining money but so far these petitions have met with no results. Not unnaturally our poor people who are going back to water-soaked, mud-caked homes and ruined crops are looking to Washington for help but so far none is forthcoming and editorial in today's issue of *State-Times* has urgently called on Coolidge to act, while Governor Simpson has sent lengthy telegram calling for Special Session of Congress for emergency appropriations. Evidently trip made by Hoover to Rapid City in order to confer with Coolidge has been without results that will help us at present for he is reported to have told the President that though immediate general aid was necessary to help flooded areas, reconstructing levees and rehabilitating homes, he thought all this could be cared for at regular session. Evidently his definition of immediate is different from mine. Splendid showing made by Java cane at this point most helpful in taking my mind off these worries, as is health of children and their general development, all as good as I could wish. Cresside has been out daily functioning with usual efficiency while Merry has been laid up after at last submitting to slight operation indicated ever since Franchot's birth. Glad to say her convalescence is proceeding satisfactorily though slowly for she did not seem to have much reserve strength. No one realizes better than I how severely all her resources have been taxed. No man ever had a more loyal, loving and courageous wife.

Aug. 19, '27. Fair and cooler. Saw Fabian in town this afternoon, asked him what he thought of his great friend John Sullivan now. It developed into quite an argument. F. dislikes Huey Long as heartily as I do but said Sullivan had just as much right to back him for Governor as John Parker, Ruffin Pleasant and J. Y. Sanders had to get their crowd of has-beens together in support of as stiff a stuffed shirt as Riley Wilson. I told him Riley Wilson was at least a gentleman. He retorted that Huey Long could at least play with alphabet blocks without guidance, and between an honest dunderhead and a capable rascal, there wasn't much to choose. I must confess I was not deeply impressed with Congressman Wilson on the one occasion when I met him, but that does not warrant Fabian in charging that "we half-baked amateur Warwicks were driving a lot of people to vote for what would be potentially the most vicious influence in the public life of this state." At this point both of us realized that we had completely overlooked the fact that Governor Simpson is himself a candidate, and in the laughter over this ridiculous situation our quarrel was forgotten. This does not mean however that I shall forget the blatant banners inscribed EVERY MAN A KING BUT NO ONE WEARS A CROWN and Huey's clowning at the so-called "Peoples' Convention" and the ridiculous inference that Wilson was to blame for flood conditions drawn from Huey's statement, now in everyone's mouth, that "Wilson has been in Congress fourteen years and this year the water went fourteen feet higher than ever, giving him a flood record of one foot of water per year."

Nov. 2, '27. Fair and cold. Merry and I in New Orleans to participate in official welcome by Mayor and Members of Council to first sugar made in Louisiana from P.O.J. cane. Our first outing together since 1921. Several bags of raw sugar itself will be sold at auction at Sugar Exchange today for benefit of New Orleans Community Chest and flood sufferers in Lafourche Parish. Four girls riding on float presented Mayor and Members of Council with small bags of new sugar and Mayor responded with greetings emphasizing vital importance of new stimulus given sugar industry of Louisiana through advent of P.O.J. cane. Mayor and Members of Council were also presented with samples of new cane itself taken from huge collection of stalks with which float was decorated. The cane to be auctioned at Sugar Exchange is our own produced at B. H. This is a great day for us. Tide has really turned and better days are ahead. The Negroes will have to start a new chant. They don't need to say Please Oh Jesus any more. We can say Praise Our Jesus instead.

PART VII

"Bloody Monday"

March 1929

~~~~~~

" 'Bloody Monday' brought one of the most frenzied scenes in
Louisiana. . . . records."

—Harnett Kane: "Louisiana Hayride"

PART VII

"Bloody Monday"

March 1929

CHAPTER XXVII

"I ought to have known better than to have let your husband exhaust himself like this, Mrs. Tremaine. I can't tell you how sorry I am."

"Oh, please, Mr. Gayland, don't give it another thought! He'll be all right in the morning. I'm sure he will. And it isn't your fault anyway."

"But it is. We didn't get in from the Club until nearly three! He can't have had more than two or three hours' sleep! I shouldn't have planned a guinea hunt the day after the dance—especially for a guest who'd spent the previous day climbing all over the sugar mill and riding through the fields. Your husband came down here for a vacation. He didn't come for an endurance test!"

Roger Gayland, the personable manager of the Central Santa Catalina, lifted his wine glass and hastily tossed off a drink. He was genuinely concerned about this extraordinary guest who had excused himself from the dinner table when the meal had progressed no further than mango cup and black bean soup, on the plea of extreme fatigue. A number of extra guests had come in by track car from neighboring centrals, the women in pretty filmy dresses, the men in white linens; the evening promised to be a festive one, with bridge and dancing later on. Meanwhile, the table, decorated with scarlet hibiscus blossoms floating in a silver bowl among small lighted candles which floated too, was beautiful to behold; and the dinner itself was worthy of the best efforts which Anunciata, the Gaylands' mountainous and inspired cook, could put forth. Pargo almondine, roast suckling pig and guanábana ice cream were all scheduled to follow the mango cup and the black bean soup; and the only peer Anunciata had in the preparation of these typical Cuban delicacies was the head chef at the Jockey Club in Havana. Gayland had felt, with reason, that Sylvestre Tremaine was bound to be impressed with such a feast, and to compare it favorably with the one at which they had met. And here he was, fading out of the picture, before the colors in it were even set, so to speak!

The Tremaines were new acquaintances of the Gaylands. The capable manager and his pretty wife, Laura, were extremely popular with the American colony in Havana, and the last time they had gone into town, they had been introduced to the vacationists from Louisiana at a dinner which Sidney Wade, a member of the Consular staff, and himself a Louisianian, was giving for them in one of the elaborate private dining rooms of the Club. The Tremaines were themselves the owners of a fine sugar plantation on the Mississippi River, Wade had told Gayland—at least it had once been a very fine plantation, though he was afraid Sylvestre Tremaine had let it run down since taking nominal charge of it, when he married Regine Hathaway. Sylvestre was an Orleanian who did not know anything about sugar then and had never learned anything since, though somewhat belatedly he seemed interested in trying. Gervais d'Alvery, the owner of Belle Heloise, the next place from the Tremaines' on the River Road, had made quite a name for himself through some successful experiments with Java cane; it really had begun to look as if the sick industry of the South were about to revive, largely through his efforts. At all events, Tremaine's pride had been pricked by the sudden *réclame* of Belle Heloise, which Hathaway might have had just as well, since soil and climatic conditions were identical on the two plantations. The Hathaway fortune, into which Tremaine had so advantageously married and which was in consequence available for investment, was far more substantial than the d'Alverys' and had nowhere nearly as many drains upon it. Therefore Tremaine had decided to look around himself, through the West Indies and Central America, to see if he could not find some adaptable improvements. That was why he and his wife had come to Cuba this year, instead of going to Europe. They were great travelers—possibly that was one of the reasons the plantation was not doing so well. Anyhow, they were going on later to Puerto Rico and Jamaica. Regine Tremaine was rather silly, but she was easy to look at. Sylvestre's mother and Sidney's had been friends all their lives. The Consul would greatly appreciate . . .

Roger Gayland nodded understandingly over his liqueur and acted on the hint with promptitude. He hoped the Tremaines weren't going to hurry in and out of Havana, tourist style, he said to Sylvestre, as the two sauntered side by side after dinner from the private dining room to the private gambling rooms which adjoined it. They really ought to see something of Cuba, while they were about it. Of course, it was as trite to say that the capital wasn't the country, here as anywhere —but it was also as true. The highway which Kaiser was building through the center of the island was still only under construction, of course; but it was finished as far as Matanzas, and if the Tremaines did not have a car of their own with them, he, Gayland, would be delighted to send a company car for them. The central he managed, Santa

366

Catalina, was just the other side of Matanzas, and they would pass a number of other pleasant places on the way, Central Soledad and Central España among them, where they could drop in and look around. The managers of nearly all of these places were Americans, and they were always delighted to see people from home. The Tremaines needn't be afraid of primitive living conditions—the *casa de viviendo* was really very comfortable. What did Mr. Tremaine think of the idea?

Sylvestre thought very well indeed of it, and said so, his handsome blue eyes fixed on the roulette wheel. It was very kind of Mr. Gayland to suggest it. Of course, he would have to ask Regine, but he was sure she would be delighted. He felt more secure in saying this than he usually did, in making similar statements about his wife, who was becoming more and more captious with time. But she was genuinely enchanted with Havana—with their beautiful tiled suite overlooking the harbor, with the bars and shops and clubs, with the Consul's attentions. She had been effusive in her admiration of the private dining room where they had just feasted—the distinctive drapes, the needlepoint chairs, the baroque glass, the wild orchids which formed the centerpiece. By the time she had drunk two Daiquiris and two Cuba Libres, she was giggling and gushing almost uncontrollably, and her enthusiasm had increased with each course. Later on, after she had consumed innumerable glasses of champagne flavored with fresh pineapple, she would have consented to almost anything. Of course, by and by, when the effects of all these beverages were beginning to wear off, she might berate Sylvestre for dragging her off into the country, when she was having a little fun at last and forgetting all her troubles. But he did not think so. He thought that life on a Cuban central would present enough novelties to keep her satisfied, for a few days at least. He glanced in her direction, decided that nothing would be gained by consulting her at this stage anyway, and agreeably accepting Gayland's invitation, concentrated again on the roulette wheel.

Regine put on the indicated show of outraged dignity because he had acted "high-handedly" in neglecting to refer the matter to her; but as a matter of fact, she was as much pleased as Sylvestre by the Gaylands' proffer of hospitality, and hastened to pronounce every attribute of the central "too romantic for words." She applied this description to the double avenue of palms which in typical Cuban fashion led respectively to the sugar mill and to the manager's home, adding that a single *allée* of oaks, leading to a plantation house, would never seem adequate to her again. She applied it to the *casa de viviendo,* which was comfortable and rambling, with high ceilings, bare walls, tiled floors, and a succession of lofty rooms which all led into each other and into a central patio. She applied it to the carved mahogany furniture, made on the central by dexterous local carpenters, to the iron grill work ornamenting the long windows, and to the inlaid tables and trays, patterned of various native woods, which were scattered at random about the house. She applied it to the oxcarts used instead of mule teams to draw cane in from the fields, to the costumes worn by the different *comparsas* at the annual fancy-dress ball of the employees in the central and to their performance of the danson, the conga, the rumba and other dances. Finally she applied it to the guinea hunt which had proved so exhausting to Sylvestre, but from which Regine had returned, after the better part of a day in the saddle, still as fresh as when she had started.

The strange part of it was, she now reminded her host, that Sylvestre had not seemed at all tired when they first came in. She recalled to Mr. Gayland that while they were in the patio for tea, Sylvestre had shown no signs of fatigue. Later, when they had gone back to their rooms, he had dawdled a long time over their mail, which had come in while they were out hunting, and she had been slightly surprised, because there really was not much of it. In fact, upon inquiry, he had told her there was no special news in any of it, just a letter from Sidney Wade, saying he had written to his mother that they and the Tremaines had met, and enclosing the letter she had sent in reply. She was very pleased at the renewal of the old family friendship, she wrote enthusiastically. Probably Sidney had forgotten, but she and Mrs. Tremaine had often made up picnic parties together when their children were small, spending the day with them "over the Lake" or in the Pearl River woods. To refresh his memory, she was sending him a snapshot of Sylvestre that she had taken on one such occasion. Sidney had sent on the snapshot along with the letter, and Sylvestre, at Regine's request, had shown them both to her. She thought it was terrible, the way poor little boys had been dressed, twenty-five years ago, in those stiff piqué sailor suits that would stand alone, there was so much starch in them. The idea of taking children on a picnic in clothes like that . . .

She had dismissed the snapshot, readily enough, after one glance at the white piqué suit. But Sylvestre had looked at it for so long that she finally asked him what he saw in the funny old thing, and he had put it back into the envelope, and said he thought he would take another shower. She had gone into her own room for a little nap, and when she went back to his, lo and behold! he was looking at the picture again. This time she thought he acted a little nervous. He glanced in a queer way from the picture to a bag that was standing in a corner, and then back at the picture again. She wasn't interested in either one, and she didn't see any reason why Sylvestre should be. Anyhow, it was dinner time by then, and she could hear the other guests beginning to arrive. So she had told Sylvestre to come along and——

"You don't suppose he could have had a slight heart attack, do you?" Roger Gayland inquired, at last managing to get in a word edgewise, and speaking with genuine anxiety.

"Goodness, no! There's nothing the matter with Sylvestre's heart. He's never done anything to strain it."

"I'd feel easier if you'd let me call a doctor. We've got a very good one, right here on the central."

She shook her head and effectively put an end to the argument by turning to the man on her other side and beginning a long breathless story with no particular point. In the end, Roger Gayland prevailed—"spoiling everyone's evening for nothing!" as Regine pettishly put it. The slim, suave young Cuban medico could find nothing the matter with Mr. Tremaine beyond fatigue and indications of slight nervousness. He prescribed a sedative, said there was no reason why Mr. Tremaine could not continue his journey, and bowed his unctuous way out. . . .

Regine and Sylvestre had not shared a room, from choice, for some time, and one of the aspects of their visit to Santa Catalina especially pleasing to Regine was the spaciousness of the apartments which had been assigned to them. She went to bed, after her disappointing evening, without speaking to her husband, and the next morning she had finished her coffee and cuddled down for one more snooze, when he came into the room, fully dressed, and looking considerably more purposeful than was his wont.

"Good morning," he said. "Do let me thank you for all the tender care you gave me last night. I don't suppose there's one man in a hundred with such a solicitous wife."

"Oh, for goodness sake! I knew there was nothing the matter with you. That silly little doctor said so himself, didn't he? I don't know just what kind of an act you were trying to put on, but whatever it was, it was a damn poor one, if you ask me. And I might remind you for the 'steenth time, that I don't care very much for your brand of irony, especially the first thing in the morning."

"I'm delighted to hear you're not worried about me. Because if you were you might think I was unable to travel, and then we'd be held up here for several days. But that silly little doctor, in whom you have so much confidence, said that I could, you know. And I'm going to. I've been quite busy on the telephone while you've been asleep. I find we can get passage back to New Orleans on the *Heredia,* sailing tonight. Wade's been very helpful about the reservations and Gayland's kindly offered to drive us into town himself. We can have one more dinner at the Jockey Club before we leave, if you like."

"You must be stark raving crazy! Why, the Gaylands invited us for two weeks and we've only been here four days! Besides, we've got passage from Santiago to Kingston on the nineteenth."

"You mean we did have. I've cancelled it. We're going straight back to Louisiana. I've been recalled by very urgent business."

"You dirty liar! You never did a stroke of work in your life! You've invented this just to spite me. You saw I was having a little fun at last, and you made up your mind it shouldn't keep up. If you're going back to New Orleans tonight you can go alone."

"I can't think of any arrangement that would suit me better. I'll call Wade and tell him I don't need the suite de luxe after all, that any old kind of a cabin will be all right. Shall I tell Gayland you'd like to stay here? Or will you come along back to the Sevilla Biltmore?"

In the end, of course, she went with him, mutinous, sullen and abnormally silent. He made no effort to conciliate her, and throughout the trip they hardly spoke to each other, except in public. Shortly before they landed, however, Regine remembered that her jewelry, which as usual had been left with the purser for safekeeping, had not been reclaimed and that Sylvestre had the receipt for it. She tried the door between their cabins, and to her amazement and indignation, found it locked. Banging on it, she angrily demanded admittance.

"What do you mean, locking me out like that? Let me in this minute, you louse!"

"I'm busy right now. What do you want?"

"I want to get in. Never mind whatever else I want."

Sylvestre made no reply, but Regine could hear a faint noise that sounded as if he were handling something that rustled. Mystified now, and increasingly provoked, she began to bang on the door.

"If you don't let me in this minute, I'll go to the purser and have him break open the door."

"I advise you not to do that. I think you'd find you'd made a great mistake. Especially as by the time you got him here, he'd find the door unlocked. I'll be ready to open it very shortly."

Regine, still raging, was now aware that her rage was futile. The mysterious sound of rustling continued a few minutes longer, then stopped abruptly. Sylvestre opened the door and confronted her calmly.

"What can I do for you?" he inquired with cold politeness.

"You can refrain from locking your door in the future. After all, I'm your wife."

"I don't have any chance to forget that, worse luck."

"And incidentally, you can go and get my jewelry out of the safe. I hadn't thought of making the purser a present of it."

"I have it here for you. I got it the first thing this morning. I didn't need to be reminded of that either."

His tone implied that her relationship to him was comparable in significance to some trifling commission. She snatched at the leather box which he ceremoniously handed to her and flounced out of the cabin, slamming the much discussed door after her. They did not see each other again until it was time to go on deck, and Regine, watching her husband like a cat for some sign to explain his extraordinary behavior, noticed that he moved with a strange stiffness utterly unlike his usual easy grace. He continued to walk in this way while they passed through the customs and went on to his parents' house. But this was one of the places where separate rooms had never been offered them, and where both had hesitated to suggest such an arrangement; the great connubial guest chamber, gloomily furnished in marble-topped black walnut, assigned to them in the Tremaines' old-fashioned house on Esplanade, did not even have a private bathroom, and without giving grave offense, they could not go on to Hathaway before the next day. For the next twenty-four hours, they were condemned to intimacy. Having accepted this fact, Sylvestre was placed in a position where he was automatically obliged to satisfy at least part of Regine's curiosity.

"Look here," he said, as his mother's retreating footsteps assured him that she was on her way downstairs, "I've got to let you in on a secret, because I can't help myself. But if you breathe a word of it to anybody, I'll choke you."

"I'm not interested in your stupid secrets. I don't care whether you tell me or not."

"Well, you seemed to, a short while back. Anyway, it doesn't happen to be the sort of secret you have to tell. It's the sort where seeing is believing."

Without saying anything further, Sylvestre began to unfasten his trousers. Regine, watching him with reluctant curiosity, saw in amazement, as these slipped to the floor, that Sylvestre's legs, from his knees almost to his ankles, were encased with stalks of sugar cane. He sat down on the sofa, and began to detach these, sighing with relief.

"I can tell you I've been pretty darn uncomfortable for the last few hours," he said. "Not that I suppose it matters to you. But I couldn't have gone around with those things strapped to my legs, the rest of the day, to save my skin. Now listen. You know all the hullabaloo Gervais has created by getting that Java cane started at Belle Heloise and on to the market. Not that any of the credit is actually due to him, of course. It was all Fabian's idea. But birds can fly and so can I. There were some wonderful varieties of cane at Santa Catalina, kinds that have never been tried out in this country. I didn't see any reason why Gervais should beat me out at a game that two can play, and I didn't see any reason either, why I should lose time by letting my find pass through two or three years' tests at a Government Experiment Station. So I just picked a few stalks of cane that afternoon we were out in the fields, while you were raving over the oxen, and brought them into the house with me. Neither you nor anyone else took the slightest notice while I did it. I put the cane in my bag and got it to Havana all right that way. But of course I couldn't leave it there for those snooping customs officials to find when they went rummaging through my luggage and report me to the agricultural authorities. So I strapped the stalks to my legs. I know plenty of people who smuggle liquor in this way, and that gave me the idea."

He paused, long enough to add weight to his next words. By some miracle, Regine, unwillingly fascinated, for once did not interrupt him.

"I've been pretty careful to keep quiet about all this, so far, because I didn't propose to have you babbling to someone aboard ship, '*in strictest confidence*,' what your smart husband had done. I thought at last I might actually have pulled off something you'd be proud of, or like to pretend you were, anyway. Now that we're through the customs and I haven't been reported, it doesn't matter so much whether you know. Anyhow, as I said, I couldn't have stood going around any longer with those things strapped to my legs. I had to take them off. And thanks to mother's quaint conviction that all married couples like to share a room, I had to let you see what I was doing."

He drew on his trousers again, picked up the pieces of cane, and replaced them in the bag where they had previously been secreted, locking it and setting it down in a corner. Then he turned back to Regine, with a satisfied smile on his face.

"Well, that's that," he said. "I'll plant those stalks myself, tomorrow evening, right back of the house at Hathaway, where I can keep my eye on them. I'll beat Gervais at his own game yet!"

"And what about that old photograph you kept looking at? What's that got to do with this smart plot of yours?"

"I don't know what you mean."

"Oh, yes, you do. I mean that photograph of yourself, at the tender age of six or thereabouts, that Sidney Wade's mother sent him, and that you got all hot and bothered about."

"I didn't get hot and bothered about it. As a matter of fact, I threw it away. I didn't even think it was worth keeping."

"You acted as if you did when you first got it. You acted as if you were pretty excited about it, for some reason. I thought that was one of the mysteries you were going to explain."

Regine's final remarks were addressed to a retreating figure. Sylvestre was already in the upper hall by the time she had finished speaking. He called back to her from the stairway.

"Some day that vivid imagination of yours is going to get you into trouble, Regine. Come on down as soon as you can, will you? Mother's signaling to me that dinner is ready."

CHAPTER XXVIII

SYLVESTRE HAD LIED to Regine so many times, about so many different things, that from an ethical point of view the small circumstance of having lied to her about the photograph did not trouble him in the least. However, he was concerned that she might either find it during some absence of his, no matter how securely he hid it, or catch him again in the act of inspecting it, and he was extremely reluctant to let her know he attached any special importance to it, or to have her wonder why.

Since Mrs. Hathaway's death, the second story at Hathaway Hall had been entirely closed off. When they were there, Regine and Sylvestre occupied a suite on the ground floor in the ell, which was almost as large as the main part of the house, and which jutted out at right angles from it, back of the stairway. Both had two rooms and a bath to themselves, and with this spacious arrangement were very little in each other's way, even with their growing reluctance to be together. Sylvestre entered his wife's boudoir almost as seldom as he entered her bedroom; but she occasionally wandered into the apartment which he called his study, though he had never used it for anything which justified such a designation. Regine did not care for reading or sewing or any branch of housekeeping; neither did she care for gardening or outdoor sports. Therefore, from sheer boredom, she was restless. She was also innately curious and innately suspicious, and because of these traits, she watched her husband far more closely than a less inquisitive and more trustful wife would have dreamed of doing in her place. Sylvestre was acutely aware of both her attitude and her habits; this awareness served to make him doubly uneasy now.

He considered the possibility of embarking upon some chemical experiments, real or pretended, and reopening a suite of the closed chilly rooms on the second story, which had never lost its air of emptiness and death, for this serious purpose. A laboratory could logically be locked against intrusion and accident, when it was left for the night; and the location of the one he visualized, at the end of a long uncarpeted stairway and upper hall, almost automatically precluded any noiseless approach to it. But if he spent most of his time in this remote second story, he would not be able to watch the smuggled cane with the closeness he considered advisable. He had set it out himself, as he had told Regine he intended to do; but instead of putting it back of the house, according to his original plan, he planted it directly outside his study windows, clearing a small piece of ground on purpose to receive it, and fencing it in with wire. Reluctantly, he had told Blood how he had secured the alien stalks and what he hoped to do with them. He knew that Blood had always resented his presence at Hathaway, and cherished no desire to further his interests there; in his turn, he heartily disliked and distrusted his manager. But after all, he could not sit at his desk all the time, looking out of his study windows, and the Negroes on the place were all more accustomed to taking and heeding Blood's orders than his own. Besides, they, too, had always resented his presence, and they had never forgiven him for the explosion. Instinctively, they had laid the responsibility for this at his door, and Blood had not hesitated to throw out various hints in their presence about the "bossman's" negligence, so that it had become the subject of widespread and continued gossip among them. They considered him directly responsible for the casualties resulting from it, and their hatred of him was the more intense because it was smothered. Sylvestre had overheard fragments of their talk from time to time, and although these were always quickly hushed in his presence, he knew that they constituted a menace to his authority. He watched for his manager, and when he saw Blood jogging past the house on his plantation pony, called him over to the newly planted patch.

"I'm trying a little experiment here, Blood," he said with elaborate carelessness. "You might be interested in it, too. That mound's planted with cane I brought back from Cuba with me."

"Is that so?" Blood inquired, tonelessly. If he really did feel any interest in his superior's experiment, there was nothing in his voice to indicate it. He did not inquire how Sylvestre had managed to get the cane past the agricultural authorities, and he hardly glanced in the direction of the little patch. He simply sat on his horse, waiting for Sylvestre to go on.

"Yes," Sylvestre proceeded, finding this harder than he had expected. "I think I've got something there. I believe we may be able to start something at Hathaway Hall that'll turn the limelight away from those swelled-headed neighbors of ours, after a while."

Blood continued to sit on his horse without saying anything. Sylvestre went on more and more awkwardly.

"But, of course, we've got to get under way first. I wasn't able to bring a great deal. I don't need to tell you it's important that nothing should happen to those few stalks. Please give orders to the yard man to leave that corner alone. Of course, I'll tell him myself, but I want you to tell him, too. And tell him and all the other hands that they've got to keep their kids away from the lawn around the Big House. The place is overrun with a pack of hoodlums most of the time. If they got in behind that wire and trampled that earth down there'd be hell to pay."

"All right, Mr. Tremaine. I'll speak to Jonah and I'll give the children a talking to. Was there anything else?"

"No, there's nothing else right now."

"Good evening, then."

"Good evening."

Sylvestre went back into the house feeling resentful as well as vaguely uneasy. There was not a little jealousy mingled with his distrust of his manager; he envied Blood both his unquestioned authority and his untrammeled existence at the rear of the boarding house. Blood was the real master of Hathaway, indoors and out; men were afraid of him and women submitted to him. Phronsie, Jonah's "high yellow girl," was one of several comely mulattresses on the place that Blood had ruthlessly taken; Jonah had never dared protest against his daughter's violation, and the girl, apparently, had accepted it without either struggle or shame. Many of the "wild hoodlums" that Blood controlled so easily were his own children; there was a harsh parental quality in the ease with which he handled them. And then there were the Renos, those beautiful, savage sisters, "fighting fierce" before the advances of every other man, but catering with the utmost compliance

374

to Blood's sensuality. Once when Vina was leaving the boarding house, in a rage because Durice was threatening to supplant her, Sylvestre had come upon her unexpectedly as she was swinging through the grove at dusk, and had tried to detain her. She had broken away from him, taunting him and reviling him, and then she had run like a deer straight back to her unhallowed and invaded hideaway. The memory of this meeting still made Sylvestre writhe. He had been unwise, to say the least, in trying to meddle with his manager's paramour. Probably she had told Blood about the encounter, and if so, Blood must inevitably have despised him for his weakness, while resenting his trespassing. Either he should have left the girl alone altogether, or he should have gone ahead with what he tried to start.

He tried to excuse himself for the first mistake on the ground that the wild, graceful girl, running freely through the woods at dusk, with her long unbound hair streaming out behind her, had been a sight to rouse desire in any normal man. It was easier to do this than it was to find excuses for the second mistake. He told himself that his failure to take her was based on his reluctance to coerce her; but he knew that this was only partly true. If he had coveted her uncontrollably, he would have found a way to keep her, either by cajolery or by force; to his own chagrin, he found that he did not so covet her. Sometimes his senses were momentarily stirred and sometimes he succeeded in stimulating them; but neither sensation was lasting or overpowering. He had managed to sneak away to a few famous bagnios in the course of his European travels, and had derived temporary satisfaction from such experiences; but it was always shortlived. His marriage, as far as he was concerned, had been a fiasco from the beginning, though he had succeeded in meeting Regine's requirements as a bridegroom. He had managed to act with sufficient urgency at first to permit the tearful resistance and show of shocked surprise which he knew she would wish to enact; afterwards, with the sympathy and self-abasement to which she thought her altered state entitled her; and eventually with due appreciation for her sacrificial attitude towards his gross male nature. As a matter of fact, his desire for a child had long been his one incentive for approaching her, and lately she had begun to complain, not of his demands, but of his neglect, for his pretense of passion had worn thin. There was only one girl whom he had really wanted to have and to hold, and through his own folly, he had lost her.

He went slowly up the stairs, after his tantalizing encounter with his manager, thinking neither of Grover Blood nor of Vina Reno, but of Cresside d'Alvery. He was still thinking of her two hours later as he continued to sit in the bare room, which he visualized as a laboratory, and in which he had found at least temporary isolation. He had scarcely seen her since her marriage and it was not in the image of the tranquil and secure young matron, encompassed with loving-kindness, that he saw her now, but as the high-spirited, uncontrolled girl, straining to escape from a cheerless house and revolting against everything that represented an established and hateful order. But even this desperate mood had not been sufficiently strong to explain her impassioned surrender or to excuse the advantage he had taken of her inexperience and her recklessness. Her very sensitivity had been her undoing; she had been deeply devoted to him as well as madly in love with him; that was why she had scorned to question his trustworthiness or to count the cost of her prodigality.

The realization of what this had meant to her in disillusionment and in suffering had come to him with slow relentlessness, gathering force with time. Sylvestre had always been sensual and shallow, but he had never been deliberately vicious; Fabian was right in saying that Sylvestre had begun by laboring under the comfortable delusion that he and Cresside fitted naturally enough into the postwar scene, and that whatever they had said or done was merely a logical part of that picture. His first regrets after jilting her were largely selfish; he found Regine's frivolity, vapidity and sentimentality a sorry substitute for Cresside's blitheness, courage, and unquestioning love. It was not until he saw her stricken, on his wedding day, that sympathy was mingled with his mounting sense of frustration and unwilling bondage. Even then, he felt no special compunction for what he had done. He was appalled when he saw her lying broken in body though still dauntless in spirit, on her great white bed and resentful because she would not let him stay with her in her extremity. But it did not occur to him that her accident was one for which he was either directly or indirectly responsible. It was not until he came upon her unexpectedly, in the hallway at Belle Heloise long afterwards, that he began to realize how completely her love had turned to loathing and to wonder why. Later on, each time she repulsed him, his bafflement, like his longing, increased almost unendurably, and he redoubled his efforts toward putting together the pieces of the puzzle which had so long foiled him. Now, at last, he thought he saw the complete pattern. What a fool, what a consummate fool he had been, not to realize from the beginning what had happened to Cresside, not to recognize a resemblance which now seemed to him so startling, not to know, instinctively, that he actually had begotten the son of whom he had long despaired!

It was all clear as day to him now. Of course, Cresside had really fallen from the ladder; of course, she had really hurt her back. But why? Regine "felt faint" every time it suited her purpose to do so; but Cresside had always been as scornful of such attacks as she was impervious to them; and then, without warning, she had fainted dead away. Sylvestre was an only child, and he had no close relatives and few intimate friends of his own age, so he had heard fewer intimate discussions of feminine symptoms than most young men. Even so, he knew the simple fact that sudden overpowering faintness was one of the first unmistakable signs of pregnancy. True, no one else had apparently given a thought to the possibility of some underlying reason

376

for Cresside's disastrous vertigo—no one except her doctor, who must instantly have discovered the cause of it. But then, no one else suspected—or so he vehemently told himself—that he had become Cresside's lover two months earlier. He alone could have connected her collapse with that brief, secret interlude of passionate enchantment under the Easter moon.

If he had only done this as he stood looking down at her when she lay so small and helpless in her great white bed! Perhaps then it might not have been too late, perhaps he might still have had his only love and his only child! Some spark had passed between them as they gazed at each other; perhaps she had counted on him to guess what she would not tell him; perhaps if he had not failed her in divination, as in everything else, she might have forgiven him after all. It was not until she turned away that she had said, "This is your wedding day, Sylvestre. Regine will be waiting for you." If he had only said first, "Cresside, it's my wedding day, and it's yours, too. It's you and I that belong to each other, not Regine and I. Her vanity will be hurt if I leave her, nothing else, so she'll get over it. Her love isn't a vital part of her, the way yours is of you. I don't deserve to have you forgive me, but can't you, out of that boundless love? I'm not much of a man, but I might be, if you'd help me to begin over again." If he had only taken her tenderly in his arms and summarily sent for a priest, she might not have refused, point blank, to repeat her marriage vows after him. He remembered, and cringed at the memory, how she had said to him, that other time, "It's just the same as if we were married, isn't it, Sylvestre? Because we're going to be, as soon as we can, because we love each other as much as if we were already." And how he had answered, with his mouth and his breast on hers, "Of course it's just the same. A few words mumbled by a priest don't make any difference, any more than a few words printed on a diploma." She had not questioned his logic then, but afterwards—a long time afterwards—she had spoken of the matter again. She had said, "It isn't just a few words, after all, is it, Sylvestre? It's what they stand for. In the marriage service and on the diploma, too."

Poor, reckless, loving, bewildered girl! Underneath all her flippancy and all her flouting, her confusion and her desire, the dependence on basic standards, the capacity for eventual straight thinking, were still there. That was why she might have relented at the eleventh hour. She had neither wanted nor expected to be a light-of-love; she had wanted and expected to be his wife. And certainly she would have been appalled at the thought of branding an innocent child. And he had left her, without a struggle, to expiate a sin that was less than half hers, to shield their son from the stigma that was his inescapable heritage.

The stratagem which had saved them both and blinded even the child's own father to the truth was, after all, relatively simple, Sylvestre now saw. Gervais' marriage and his sister's seduction had been almost

377

simultaneous; their children, begotten and conceived at the same time, would normally be born at the same time, too, and meanwhile, Cresside's injury was explanation enough for her seclusion. The doctor, of course, was utterly trustworthy, and up to the limits of their capacities, the servants were, too. If ever there were a leak, it would almost certainly be accidental, and obviously, the d'Alverys had ceased to expect any such accident. If any of them had feared, in the first place, that he himself might guess Vail was his son, these fears must have long since been dulled by his own crass stupidity. He thought of Cresside as he had seen her standing on the stairs, the first time he had gone to Belle Heloise after his marriage. "What do you think of the heir to all the d'Alverys?" she had asked him, holding up the beautiful blue-eyed, black-haired boy for him to look at. Such a superb bit of bravado could never have been staged without a complete sense of inviolability, when he startled her by coming on her suddenly at night, she had lost this sense; she had been afraid that by her defiance, she had roused his suspicions. She had thought he had meant to question her about the child, to force the fact of its fatherhood from her. Women were much more conscious than men of procreation as a part of passion, perhaps because it was they who inevitably proclaimed it to the world. He still had not thought of Vail as his son when he sought her out; he had thought only of her as his lost love, for the very sight of whom he yearned inexpressibly. In telling her that he had to see her, he had meant no more than that; it had really seemed to him that if he did not, his already empty and aimless life would be utterly unbearable.

It was at the festival celebrating the close of the grinding season that he had first become acutely aware of Vail. Hitherto he had subscribed, when he thought of it at all, to the unobservant masculine theory that all babies look alike. But during the lengthy periods when the three small d'Alverys were being paraded for the admiration of the guests he could not help noticing that they did not look in the least alike. It was natural that Philogene's countenance should be nondescript, since he was still an infant in arms, and therefore Sylvestre could not logically compare it to Vail's. But twins, even non-identical twins, usually bore at least a family resemblance to each other, and here were two as different as dawn from dusk. Not only in regard to coloring either; they were entirely dissimilar in both form and feature; and though both were admittedly fine physical specimens, Vail was the more advanced and the more provocative of the two. Sylvestre played with him until Dinah took him away and for a long time afterwards he was haunted by the thought of it. But between the abrupt cessation of festivities at Hathaway Hall and his own frequent absences, he did not see the child again at close range for a long time and gradually he forgot about him.

The next encounter, when it came, was wholly unexpected. Sylvestre had stopped in at Tramonte's fancy grocery store to get some of the antipasto for which it was increasingly famous, when he caught sight of two small black-haired boys, one of them evidently a few years older than the other. They were partially hidden by hanging strips of garlic and rows of beautiful cheeses, and were seated at a table in the rear of the shop, with a lovely little blonde girl between them and a spotted spaniel at their feet. Both were absorbed in large platefuls of spumone and neither seemed to notice his presence; but after eyeing them attentively for a few minutes, Sylvestre walked back to the table.

"Hello!" he said, addressing the younger boy. "Aren't you Vail d'Alvery? And isn't this pretty little girl your sister Sybelle?"

The pretty little girl smiled engagingly, showing small pearly teeth and delightful dimples. She nodded a friendly reply and then glanced down at her plate, archly, rather than shyly. The little boy looked up, swallowing a spoonful of spumone before he answered. Something in the expression of his big blue eyes sent a strange shiver through Sylvestre.

"Yeah," he said at last, unconcernedly. Then, as if eager to correct an oversight, Vail added, "And this is Riccardo Tramonte. He's my best friend just now."

The little Italian instantly slid from his seat and held out his hand politely. "I'm glad to meet you, sir," he said. "Won't you sit down? I'll get some more spumone right away."

These damn Dagoes teach their children better manners than we do, Sylvestre thought to himself resentfully. Aloud he said, "Thanks very much, Riccardo. I'd like to, if I wouldn't be butting into your party. . . . Aren't you and Sybelle a long way from Belle Heloise, Vail, all by yourselves?"

"We're staying with Aunt Cresside. She always lets us come here and have spumone with Riccardo. He comes to have dinner with us first, except when he's in school."

"I see. Well, that sounds like a very pleasant arrangement. Is this your dog or Riccardo's?"

"She's mine."

"She's a very nice looking little dog."

"You bet she is. Uncle Fabian's dog, Belizaire, is her daddy. Uncle Fabian says none of Belizaire's puppies is ugly."

"What's her name?"

"Maud."

"Isn't that a rather queer name for a dog?"

"I don't think so. I think it's a swell name for a dog. Maud used to belong to Aunt Cresside. But when she went around the world she gave Maud to me. Belizaire stayed with us, too."

Vail put his partially emptied saucer down on the floor and Maud began to lap up the remains of the spumone with avidity. Riccardo, emerging from a door at the rear of the shop, again addressed Sylvestre with extreme politeness.

"This is Mr. Tremaine, isn't it?" he said. "Mama says, won't you come into the dining room to eat your spumone? I'm sorry my father isn't at home, too. He's in Hammond, opening a new branch store."

"How many branch stores has he now?"

"This'll make four. And he has six trucks. . . . Shall I tell mama you'll come in, Mr. Tremaine?"

"Yes, if you and Sybelle and Vail will come with me."

Riccardo picked up the saucer which Maud had effectively emptied, and held open the door at the rear of the store, ushering his guests into the kitchen beyond, where Netta was waiting to welcome them. She was now frankly forty, and as she had never made any effort to curb her enjoyment of macaroni, ravioli, gnocchi and other substantial food-stuffs, her figure was beginning to look full rather than rounded; in places her dark cloth dress, no longer suggestive of a peasant costume, seemed about to burst at the seams. But her beautiful brown eyes still gave distinction to her pleasant face, and her glossy black braids, still unflecked with white, formed a crown of glory for her well-shaped head. Moreover, the plainness and gracelessness of her clothes were almost startlingly relieved by the fine diamonds she was wearing, both in the long lobes of her pierced ears and on her roughened hands. She regarded all the children with a beaming expression and held out her arms to Sybelle, hugging her ecstatically, while Maud circled around them, barking in a joyous tone. Then, releasing the little girl, Netta put her arm affectionately around Vail's shoulder, while she nodded her greeting to Sylvestre.

"Howdado, Mr. Tremaine, howdado!" she said amiably. During the years while she had been gaining weight she had been losing her painful shyness, and her manner, though properly deferential to an important customer, was entirely self-possessed. "Won't you come-a right along into the dinin' room, please? We goin' to have-a leetla party, everythin' alla ready. Verra nice you come-a, too."

She led the way, not without unmistakable pride, through a spotless kitchen, where, Sylvestre noticed in passing, the equipment was far more modern than at Hathaway Hall, to a dining room furnished in golden oak, and hung with highly colored lithographs of saints and martyrs surrounding a large framed crucifix. The religious note was accentuated by a similar gilt crucifix and some small plaster statuettes which stood on the mantelpiece, but slightly relieved by two large tinted photographs in oval frames, one of Luigi incongruously clad in full dress so ill-fitting as to suggest rental, the other of Riccardo in a blue serge sailor suit, with a ribbon dangling from his hat. Netta had retained her predilection for paper flowers, and a multi-colored bouquet of these ornamented the center of the lace-covered table, which as usual was heavily laden, this time with small spicy cookies, covered with pink and white icing, little crescent-shaped pies filled with fluffy cream cheese, and numerous other delicacies which were new to Sylvestre, as well as the spumone and fig newtons with which he was already familiar. Sybelle clapped her hands with delight as she looked at the display, and then rushed back to Netta for another hug before wriggling into her seat.

"Oh, Mrs. Tramonte, you're the *nicest* lady! You've got my own favorite set of dishes out for me again! But why didn't you tell me we were having *viscotta* and *cassate* before I ate so much spumone in the store? You know they're my favorites! I won't have room for half as many as I want!"

"Now, now, you have-a plenty room, Sybelle. Mr. Tremaine, please, you sita here, side-a Sybelle? We leta leetla boys sita other side. What you wanta first? You ain'ta had spumone yet at all, better you begin witha that. Take-a leetla glass wine, too. Luigi, he have-a good luck with his wine this year. Zinfandel grapes, they verra, verra nice for wine."

She began to fill glasses and to heap plates, still conversing without self-consciousness or restraint. The two boys, stuffing themselves contentedly and slipping occasional tidbits to Maud, who crouched expectantly beside them, did very little talking as the feast progressed; Riccardo occasionally contributed a brief remark, but Vail seemed completely indifferent to such amenities. Sybelle answered sweetly and softly when Sylvestre spoke to her, but Netta, to whom she was obviously much attached, absorbed most of her attention; she rose repeatedly to embrace her hostess again, or to murmur words of affection and appreciation in Netta's willing ear. Sylvestre, liberated from conversational effort both by Sybelle's preoccupation and Netta's volubility, and more and more arrested by Vail, studied the child, who was seated directly opposite him, with increasing attention. Some time elapsed before Sybelle roused him from this scrutiny by making a startling request.

"I'll burst if I eat any more, Mrs. Tramonte, truly I will. Couldn't I play with the crucifix a little bit now?"

"Sure you cana play with him alla you wanta, Sybelle. Geta the crucifix down from the mantel for Sybelle, Riccardo."

Riccardo rose, and reaching for the gilt crucifix which stood between the statuettes, placed it proudly in front of Sybelle. Now that he could observe it more closely, Sylvestre saw the image was hung with various miniature utensils, representing the implements associated with the crucifixion—a sponge, a spear, a ladder, a lantern, a scourge, a hammer and so on—and that all these were detachable from the central figure and those which surrounded the cross. Gravely, Sybelle began to move these miniature utensils from one position to another, while Netta sat helpfully beside her, offering an occasional suggestion, and making small pious sounds under her breath. Vail had risen at the same time as Riccardo, and taking a sheriff's badge and a B-B gun from the sideboard, had gone into the living room. Obviously, the crucifix did not hold his interest; but Riccardo continued to linger on the threshold, manipulating a lasso with considerable skill, and glancing every now and then towards Sybelle, as if to determine whether she were appreciating his performance. Sylvestre, after watching this by-play with amusement for some moments, thanked Netta for her bounteous hospitality, and excusing himself from the table, also went into the living room and approached Vail, who had somewhat inconsistently added a belt, a bowie knife and a red bandanna to his sheriff's badge, and was taking aim at various gaudy but otherwise inoffensive ornaments.

"What on earth are you doing, Vail?" Sylvestra inquired, more and more intrigued.

"Nothing," Vail answered, once more allowing an interval to elapse before saying anything at all. Riccardo again stepped into the breach.

"We're going to play stagecoach after a while. Like in the movies. Vail's practising. Sybelle's the one who gets rescued. Mostly I'm the bandit chief and Vail's the sheriff. But sometimes Vail's the bandit and I'm Sybelle's father. Except when papa's here. When he's here, he acts, too. He's grand."

"I should think he might be. . . . I'd like very much to watch you two boys play stagecoach."

Again he looked at Vail expectantly, and this time Riccardo waited for his friend to answer. The reply, when it finally came from the desired quarter, was anything but cordial.

"We're not going to play stagecoach right away. Sybelle always wants to play with the perfume bottles after she gets through playing with the crucifix."

"The perfume bottles?"

Sylvestre was still looking at Vail, but as he was obviously uninterested in continuing the conversation, Riccardo was finally forced to do so.

"Yes, the bottles with the perfume mama uses on her paper flowers. When they're most empty, she saves them for Sybelle. Then Sybelle fills them up with water, and goes around sprinkling things."

"I see."

"And next she dresses up in some old shawl of mama's and some big old comb and fancy stuff like that."

"I see," Sylvestre said again, though this time he was not so sure that he did. Momentarily, he wondered if Gervais and Merry realized how much time the twins spent with the Tramontes when theoretically they were with Fabian and Cresside, and whether Sybelle's prattle had ever disclosed her status as Netta's petted darling and Riccardo's heroine of high adventure. But after all, it was none of his affair, and he was far more interested in Vail, who was certainly no prattler. He made another attempt to draw the little boy out.

"If you and Sybelle are going back to your Aunt Cresside's after you get through playing stagecoach, Vail, I'll be glad to wait for you and walk around to Somerulos Street with you."

"We're not going back there. Aunt Cresside's coming here to get us after a while. She's going to take us home in her new car that Uncle Fabian gave her. It's a knockout."

382

Vail opened the door leading from the living room into a small gallery, and with Maud at his heels, ran down the steps into the back yard. Riccardo, abandoning the lasso after one more backward glance at Sybelle, whose attention was still evenly divided between his mother and the crucifix, again made the appropriate gesture which Vail had neglected to supply.

"Do you want to come out, too, Mr. Tremaine? You could look at the rabbits and the chickens. I take care of those. We've got a garden and an orchard."

"What kind of an orchard?"

"Well, we've got a chestnut tree, cherry trees and fig trees. We have bay trees and Grand Dukes, too."

"I'll be glad to come with you. I had no idea there was so much land behind the house. That's a fine kitchen garden you've got. It looks as if you had nice neighbors, too."

Sylvestro's eyes wandered past the fruit trees and the coops and runs where the white chickens and brown rabbits were confined. He could see rows and rows of rich green vegetables rising above well-weeded ground and beyond them several neat well-located cottages. The entire scene was one of plenty and unostentatious prosperity.

"Yes. Those houses belong to papa. . . . I think I'll feed my rabbits now, if you don't mind, before Vail and I play in our mine."

"Your mine?"

"Yes, sir. We've got a mine over yonder behind the Grand Dukes. We keep our pretend treasure in it. That's fun."

"I reckon it must be. I've never been much good at pretending I had something when I didn't. . . . Vail's over there already, isn't he? I haven't seen him for the last few minutes."

"Yes. Vail don't like to wait."

"And do you two boys let Sybelle dig for treasure with you?"

"Well, sometimes she comes and watches. We wouldn't let any old girl hang around, but it's different with Sybelle, because Vail's her twin. Anyway, she's not like those other old girls. She's all right to have around. And you could stay, too, if you want to."

Sylvestre hesitated. He was terribly tempted to remain, to see what would happen if Cresside found him there talking to Vail when she arrived. In the end he dismissed the idea, partly because he was actually ashamed of it, and partly because Vail himself gave him so little encouragement to remain. Something about the little boy's attitude towards him seemed actually antagonistic. He rode out of town, obsessed with this thought, and with the strange notion that he had been looking at his own double, in miniature. It was absurd, he said to himself; no man knew what he really looked like; anyone could have black hair and blue eyes and a ruddy skin. But when he reached Hathaway Hall, he locked himself in his bathroom, and stood for a long time, staring at himself in his shaving mirror.

He went on telling himself it was absurd to imagine a resemblance, and then reflected on other resemblances which he had found or fancied. He had seen married couples who had grown to look like each other, especially after they had lived together a long time; he had seen adopted children who resembled their parents. But after all, such resemblances were largely those of expression. This was different. He wished he knew exactly what he had looked like when he was Vail's age. . . . And then, a few weeks later, he had found out.

It was fantastic that a faded old photograph, received from a comparative stranger on a remote Cuban central, should have clarified a mystery and explained an attraction which had baffled him for years. But it was also true. Sitting in the one broken, straight-backed chair which remained in the bare, second-story room, Sylvestre took the snapshot from his pocket and scrutinized it carefully for the hundredth time. That was Vail's tousled black hair which his own mother had never successfully slicked into place, that was Vail's sturdy form undisguised by the stiff piqué suit, those were Vail's big clear eyes relentlessly staring into his own. "The heir to all the d'Alverys" was actually his own heir, bone of his bone, flesh of his flesh, begotten under an Easter moon, born in a locked chamber on a bitter winter night. And he himself, during the secret travail of his child's mother, had been basking on the warm sands of the Riviera with the simpering fool he had chosen to marry in her stead!

It was too late to think of that now, he told himself bitterly, while still wincing at the thought. But a man did not have to act like a fool or cad forever, merely because he had once played the part; he could profit by his past mistakes, he could retrieve his lost ground. . . . At least there was a well-established theory to that effect. But reviewing his own problems from a practical angle, Sylvestre saw no way in which he could solve them. How could he possibly prove that Vail was his son? The d'Alverys had safeguarded the child and his mother at every turn. And granting for the sake of argument that he could prove it, what would the revelation of such a secret accomplish? Nothing except to tarnish the good name of the woman he loved and to stigmatize as a bastard the boy who could never belong to him. He could not marry Cresside now, he could not acknowledge and legitimatize Vail. He was doomed to stand helplessly aside, while another man encompassed his own lost love with tenderness and devotion, and his own child grew to manhood under a name that was not his.

Out of the chaos and resentment in his wretched mind, only one clear and comforting thought emerged: sooner or later Vail was bound to discover the truth, and conceivably, once this had happened, some chance encounter between father and son might bring about mutual acknowledgment of their relationship. Sylvestre realized that Vail adored Cresside; every reference the child made to her revealed the love and harmony between them. Consequently he would inevitably begin by despising the man who had brought such suffering and shame upon her, and—judging from Vail's conduct at the Tramontes'—

384

there was apparently an instinctive antagonism to combat besides. Nevertheless, or so Sylvestre tried to tell himself with conviction, all close kinships had definite claims upon those bound together by ties of blood, and were possessed of hidden strength to enforce them; however reluctant Vail might be to admit that he knew Sylvestre was his father, eventually he might be persuaded or impelled to do so; and once this had happened, Sylvestre was hopeful that he himself might extenuate his wrongdoings, emphasize his repentance, and win his son's consent to occasional secret but intentional meetings. If he could do this much, he would try to be satisfied, since he knew only too well that it would be the utmost to which he could look forward. But even the admission of the hidden bond between them would in some measure assuage his broken spirit and alleviate the loneliness of his childless existence.

As he persistently dwelt on the idea that Vail would ultimately acknowledge their relationship, Sylvestre told himself that if the boy did not make the eventual discovery until he, too, had committed some hotheaded act of folly, he would judge his father less harshly than if he still regarded him through the uncompromising eyes of blameless youth. But this thought did not bring much consolation with it. In the first place, Sylvestre knew that he could not classify the seduction of Cresside tolerantly and simply as a hotheaded act of folly. It had been nothing of the sort. It had been a crime blasphemously committed in the name of love. In the second place, it did not in any way gratify him to think that Vail might inherit his weak traits instead of Cresside's strong character. He was proud because the boy looked like him, but he honestly hoped that the resemblance between them was only skin deep. In the third place, he felt he could not possess his soul in patience much longer; the sooner the showdown came, the better he would be pleased. Therefore, far from hoping that Vail's conduct would help to bring about a rapprochement between them, Sylvestre tried to conjure up ways through which, by his own present prowess, he could induce his son to think more leniently of his past sins. Any number of worthwhile men—so ran the specious argument he was preparing—began by frittering away their time, marrying for money, and living incontinently. But as they grew older and wiser they turned their talents to good account and became exemplary husbands and fathers. He would call upon Vail to observe the splendid rehabilitation of Hathaway Hall under his supervision—the rehabilitation which he had just begun by the introduction of the smuggled cane, and which his fond fancy already depicted as having reached remarkable heights by the time this imaginary conversation could take place. He would demonstrate his extraordinary patience and forebearance towards his tiresome and exasperating wife, and his blameless conduct as far as all other women were concerned. He would invite his son to come to him for the little favors which perhaps, under the circumstances, Vail would hesitate to ask of Gervais d'Alvery, but which he, Sylvestre, would be only too glad to grant, and with the little problems to which possibly Gervais did not have time nor inclination to listen. Of course, Gervais d'Alvery had always been a fine fellow, one of the best, and he had now become a very substantial citizen as well. But after all, he had a large family; he had to divide his attention among five children, which was very different from lavishing all his affection on one; and his existence was further complicated by his political duties, and by the financial worries which, though now greatly lessened, were still something of a burden. Sylvestre, on the other hand, with only the plantation to consider, had any amount of leisure and any amount of money, both of which were entirely at Vail's disposal.

I don't want your money. I don't want your advice. I don't want anything to do with you. Hathaway isn't yours, it's your wife's, and I don't want anything to do with her either. I don't want her wondering what's become of you, if you sneak off to see me on the sly, and finally ferreting out the reason you do it. I certainly don't want to go to her house. She was a false friend to my mother, just as you were a false lover. Suppose you are my father? Well, that's my hard luck. Suppose you would like to be with me? Well, that's yours. I can't help the fact that you got me. But I can keep away from you, most of the time, and I'm going to.

Sylvestre would gladly have given ten years of his worthless life if, after all his specious arguments, this did not still seem to him the inevitable retort. He tried to change it, or at least to soften it, as it came echoing back to thwart him and mock him, but without success. In imagination he continued to see the future Vail standing before him, ruddier and sturdier and older than the little boy at the fancy grocery store, not only alien and antagonistic now, but accusing and condemning. . . .

Someone was coming up the uncarpeted stairway and down the long hall. The bare boards creaked under the advancing footsteps, and to Sylvestre there was something eerie about the sound; it was like the weird noise attributed to the uneasy ghosts which allegedly prowled through haunted houses at night. Annoyed with himself for entertaining such a nonsensical idea, Sylvestre slipped the snapshot back into his pocket, pushed the broken chair against the bare wall and went to the door. Regine met him on the threshold.

"What on earth are you doing up here all by yourself?"

"Just looking over the premises. I'm thinking of rigging up a laboratory here, if you wouldn't object."

"What good would that do?"

"I might make chemical experiments here, the way Gervais d'Alvery does at Belle Heloise."

"I thought it was that cane you brought in fastened to your legs that you meant to experiment with."

"Well, there's no reason why I shouldn't do both, is there?"

386

"No, except I don't see how you can keep your eye on that cane if you stay up here much."

This was exactly what Sylvestre himself had feared, while endeavoring to dismiss his anxiety as absurd. But he answered sneeringly.

"You didn't expect me to sit and watch it all day, out of my study window, did you?"

"It might not be a bad plan, if you really want to keep an eye on it."

"I've put a fence around it. I've told Blood that Jonah's to let it alone and that the kids are to stay out of the yard from now on."

"Well, evidently Blood hasn't hurried about relaying your orders. Anyway, one of Phronsie's children has climbed over your silly little fence and is squatting down there in the dirt, picking the eyes out of the stalks. I just thought maybe you'd like to know."

Instead of simpering, as usual, Regine spoke with malicious triumph. Sylvestre pushed past her, and swearing under his breath, tore down the stairs and out of doors. A plump little pickaninny, dressed in calico, was seated squarely in the middle of the new plot with a small spade beside her, her beribboned head bent over an obviously congenial task: she was digging her small blue nails deep into the tender young stalks which she had just uprooted and plucking from them the tiny eyes which formed the seed for future shoots. Sylvestre swooped down and slapped her hands hard. Then he picked her up and shook her with all his force. Her head was bobbing back and forth on her shoulders and her eyes bulging from their sockets when he finally set her down.

"You come along with me," he commanded. "I'm going to take you straight to your mother and tell her to whip you to within an inch of your life, you devilish little brat!"

"Ah ain't done nothin', Mr. Tremaine," the child whimpered, trying to draw away from him. "Ah was jes' playin' in de yawd wid my spade lak Ah allus does."

"Well, you're not to play in the yard any more, you hear? If you do, I'll whip you myself, and it won't be within an inch of your life, either. I'll sure enough kill you. Come on now, you can't get away from me. You needn't think you can."

The child's whimper had risen to a wail by the time they reached Jonah's cabin, where his two daughters, Phronsie and Meme, also lived with their respective broods. It was one of the pleasantest and tidiest on the plantation. Flowers bloomed profusely in its tiny yard, clean clothes flapped perpetually from a line hung between two chinaberry trees beside it, and only one harmless old feist wandered aimlessly among the fluttering fowl which surrounded it. The children playing on the small gallery were well-dressed and looked well-fed; no doubt Blood saw to it that they should be, Sylvestre thought savagely, recoiling from the unwelcome thought, which had just struck him, that the little girl he was dragging after him was probably his manager's daughter as well as Phronsie's. However, the realization of this did not prevent him from speaking harshly to the child's mother, when she lifted the hanging cloth from the open doorway and came out on the gallery.

"Flail this little hellion till she remembers to keep her damn paws off the plants in my garden," he commanded harshly.

Phronsie regarded him thoughtfully before answering. She was neat looking herself, like her children, and she was extremely pretty besides. Her figure was slight and graceful, and her skin was golden rather than brown. Both her neck, which was completely bare, and her arms, which were bare to the elbow, looked firm and warm against her thin white dress. Her hair was parted in the middle and braided closely around her shapely head. She looked more like some of the lovely East Indians whom Sylvestre had seen during the course of his travels than like a Louisiana Negress. The children on the gallery came crowding up to her, and she caressed them, smiling while she hushed them. Her composure was complete. Resentfully, Sylvestre recognized the fact that he could not frighten her or even hurry her.

"Ah sho' sorry she been bad, Mr. Tremaine," Phronsie said at last. None of the Negroes had ever paid him the compliment of calling him Mr. Sylvestre; they liked to show that, after all these years, they still considered him an outsider. "Most generally, Minta she's a right good little girl. What you been doin', honey, to worry de bossman?" Phronsie went on, in her gentle pleasant voice.

"She's been digging up my new cane," Sylvestre said vehemently. This time Phronsie answered so quickly that her reply was almost an interruption.

"Mus' be a misconviction somewheres. Ah doesn't ever let mah young 'uns go out to de fields, Mr. Tremaine."

"I didn't say anything about the fields. This is a very special kind of cane. I planted it in the yard myself, right by the Big House. I told Mr. Blood that the children were to be kept away from there, and that Jonah wasn't to do any weeding around there either. Mr. Blood promised me he'd see that my orders were carried out straight off. And the first thing I know, here's this brat of yours right in the middle of my patch, destroying my seeds."

"Ah sho' is sorry, Mr. Tremaine," Phronsie said again. "Minta's sorry, too, ain't you, sugar? She ain't gwine do it no mo', Ah promises you dat. But you has to excuse her dis time, please suh."

Phronsie smiled down at her little daughter and stroked the child's hair reassuringly. Minta had finally succeeded in wriggling out of Sylvestre's grasp and was clinging to her mother, regarding her accuser with frightened and reproachful eyes. She was even lighter than Phronsie, Sylvestre noticed, now that he had a good look at her; and, quickened to the consciousness of such things, he saw, or fancied he saw, a marked resemblance to Blood's gross countenance in her small features. Curse it, he would never get anywhere, with this lay of the land! He muttered something that was still wrathful and that was meant to be threatening as well, and then he strode off, bent on hurrying back to his desecrated cane and finding out how much damage had actually been done. In his haste, he almost ran into Jonah's other daughter, Meme, who was advancing towards the cabin with a large basket on her head, and who was either unable or unwilling to change her course when she saw him coming. Meme had the sense of perfect balance which enabled her to carry such burdens with grace and ease and she walked freely and firmly; but she was several shades darker than her half sister, and she had none of Phronsie's inescapable charm. Blood had never bothered her, and she had been genuinely devoted to her husband, the poor Negro who had died from burns after the explosion, and to the two children who had been instantly killed while happily carrying their father his lunch. Now she was pathetically loyal to the memory of all three. She still wore the dingy black in which she had persistently draped her spare frame from the beginning, and she seemed to take no comfort in her remaining children, who were left in the care of their aunt while she worked at the boarding house. She never smiled and seldom spoke, but she brooded perpetually, and little by little a sinister expression had crept into her lackluster eyes. When she finally glanced in Sylvestre's direction, the look she gave him was one of such thinly veiled hatred that he veered away from it, and hurried on without saying anything to her except good evening. He had meant, when he went to the cabin, to speak sharply to Jonah as well as to Phronsie. But somehow Phronsie had thwarted him and now Meme had upset him. He would not have put it past her to connive with Amen, the rising "medicine man" who had begun life as the d'Alverys' yard boy, and "put a conjure" on Hathaway. Of course, there was nothing in these silly tricks and primitive beliefs. Nevertheless, he had not liked the look of the funny little bundle of string, feathers, and miscellaneous rubbish which he had found on the gallery that morning. . . .

He was relieved, on approaching the new cane patch, to find that the damage wrought by Minta was, after all, relatively slight. Most of the eyes were gone from the two stalks which she had dug up, but the others were undisturbed and intact; he could still count on plenty of seed with which to carry on his experiment. He replaced the earth and smoothed it down again with mingled hopefulness and relief, when Blood came up and spoke to him with unaccustomed civility.

"Phronsie's just been over to the boarding house to see me, Mr. Tremaine. She's very sorry for the accident, and so am I. In a way, I feel to blame for it. I did speak to Jonah, right after I saw you early this evening, and cautioned him about letting the mound alone. And I've put the fear of the Lord into most of the kids already. But I hadn't got around to Phronsie's and Meme's. I meant to go over to the cabin later on . . . I told Phronsie you're right, that Minta ought to be switched. But she's so frightened already from the shaking and scolding you gave her that I really don't believe it's necessary. I don't believe you could bribe her to go near that cane patch again."

Sylvestre noticed that the manager did not say, "Minta will have to be switched," only "Minta ought to be switched." But he decided that after all it was better not to press the point. Doubtless Blood was correct in saying that he himself had already given the brat a wholesome lesson.

"Well, I hope you're right," he said shortly. "Still, I don't intend getting another scare like that. You'll have to put two or three of the older boys to watching that mound in shifts, during the daytime. I don't suppose there's any danger that one of the kids will walk in his sleep and start digging up the cane by moonlight, so there'll be no need of keeping up the watch at night. But I can't sit and stare at the patch out of my study window all day."

This was the second time he had said that now, he realized, and the thought had been running persistently in his head before he put it into words. At this rate he would be going off his base pretty soon, over a half-dozen stalks of stolen and smuggled cane. And yet, of course, it was not the half-dozen stalks of cane themselves that counted; it was what they represented, what they might mean to him in the future. Cresside had reminded him how much some trivial thing could mean, long ago in the moonlight. *"It isn't just a few words after all, is it, Sylvestre? It's what they stand for. In the marriage service and on the diploma, too."* Those stalks of cane represented the ultimate triumph which was to help him redeem his past sins in his son's eyes. He did not intend to let anything happen to them. Not even if he actually must sit and watch the place where they were planted out of the study window. . . .

"You sure can't, Mr. Tremaine," he heard Blood say in a conciliatory way. "Don't you worry about that though. I'll get hold of a couple of trustworthy boys. I'll attend to everything. I'm just as interested as you are in having this experiment succeed and taking those stuck-ups at Belle Heloise down a few pegs. Well, good evening again." The manager walked away, his self-assurance obviously restored. He was apparently well satisfied—almost too well satisfied, his employer thought—with the interview, and Sylvestre resented the ease with which it had been carried off by his manager; but after a final survey of the cane patch, he partially dismissed it from his mind and walked slowly up the curving stone steps that led to the gallery and across this to the house. It had been an unusually warm day, and probably that was the reason his head had felt hot all afternoon—that and the fact that the cursed brat, and her smooth-spoken slut of a mother and her old black witch of an aunt had all got under his skin. When it came to that, not only his head felt hot. He felt hot all over. But he could fix that. He would go in and take a shower. It was almost dinner time anyway.

He went into his study, looked out of the window at the mound, and walked on to his bedroom. He had been a fool to wear a tweed suit on a day like this, whatever the calendar said. He would get into Shantung or seersucker straightaway. He took off the offending coat, the creation of a famous London tailor, and hung it over a chair. Next he unbuttoned his vest, laying his watch and chain on the table beside him. Then he decided to take one more look at the faded old photograph before he got into the shower. He reached into the pocket where he always kept it and it was not there.

CHAPTER XXIX

HE STOOD PERFECTLY still, the perspiration with which he was dripping changing to cold sweat. He was bathed in it, as he had been only once or twice before in his life, when he was recovering from a long illness but still very weak; it produced a sensation of debility so extreme as to verge on helplessness, and this time it was accompanied by a feeling of great constriction. His heart was no longer in the right place, but midway down his throat, and his hands were numb. He tried to reach for his handkerchief, to mop off the worst of the sweat, and at first his fingers merely twitched, refusing to function. He went through a period of ineffectual misery which seemed to him endless, while the lump in his throat continued to grow larger and larger. At last, however, he succeeded in wiping his face and in rummaging through his pockets. But afterwards the cold sweat poured out of him more profusely than ever. The search was futile. The photograph was nowhere to be found.

He slipped hurriedly into his clothes again, trying to figure out, while he did so, where and when he could have lost it and how he was going to recover it. He certainly thought he had put it back into his pocket when he heard Regine coming along the uncarpeted hall; but he had done this so hastily that the picture might conceivably have fallen out because it was not far enough in. He groped his way upstairs again, peering around him as he went. It was getting dark and there were only a few inadequate lights on the second story. It was hard to see anything in the dusk, and there was an eerie quality to the dimness and emptiness, just as there had been to the sound of Regine's footsteps when she came over the bare floor. He jumped when he heard her calling to him now from below.

"Sylvestre! Where on earth are you?"

"I'm upstairs. What do you want?"

"Dinner's ready. Micah's looked everywhere for you. Why did you go upstairs *again,* for heaven's sakes?"

For the first time, he felt bitterly sorry that he had lied to her about the picture. If he had only refrained from telling her he had torn it up, he could say, quite casually, that he had mislaid it, and that as Mrs. Wade wanted it back again, he was hunting for it so that he could send it off. Of course, that would not explain why he had attached enough importance to it himself to carry it around in his pocket for ten days; but at least it would not be nearly as awkward as to confess that he had never destroyed it, and to try to justify his falsehood. Under the circumstances, his safest course lay in saying nothing at all, at least for the present, and throughout dinner he maintained a stubborn silence in the face of Regine's persistent curiosity. He could not eat, but he managed to sit still until she had finished; then he walked out onto the gallery and down the steps leading into the yard, while Regine continued to pursue him with her fretful questions.

"Why don't you speak to me? Where are you going now?"

"I haven't anything special to say to you. I've got to go out for a few minutes. I won't be long."

"But *why* do you have to go out?"

"Good God, Regine, do you want an explanation every time I walk across the yard?"

He strode away, increasingly angry not only with Regine but with himself. He did not see why on earth he had put the photograph in a small leather traveling frame by itself, instead of among the papers and notes in his billfold. If he could have said he dropped his wallet, and set everyone searching for that, the chances were at least even that when and if it were found, it would be returned to him unmolested. But the little picture frame was a single one with an open face; the first person who looked at it might easily see the same resemblance that he had. To be sure, Regine had not done so, but then she had barely glanced at it, and she had been more intrigued by the queer clothes than by the child's features depicted in it, which was typical of her. If she saw it again, however, she would inspect it more closely, searching for the clue to her husband's interest, and very likely she would discover it. She had seen Vail almost as often as he had, which was not very frequently, to be sure, but enough for her to put two and two together, once her suspicions were aroused. As for Blood, he had probably seen a good deal of the little boy. The d'Alvery children rode their ponies on the levee, visited the family tomb in the cemetery, played with the little pickaninnies from the quarters, and ranged freely up and down the River Road. Considering the proximity of the two plantations, the common interests of the two and the surface friendliness between the overseer at Belle Héloïse and the manager at Hathaway, it was inevitable that Blood should have run into Vail over and over again. Besides, after the explosion, while the Hathaway cane was taken to Belle Héloïse for grinding, Blood had been there every day, and doubtless the little d'Alverys haunted the sugar house, after the habit of their kind. Probably Blood had already noticed the telltale likeness; probably he was only waiting for the chance to put his conjectures to the best use. The photograph would give him just such a chance. As for the Negroes, they seemed to have a sixth sense about such things anyway. Phronsie, whose child he had just manhandled; Meme, who held him accountable for the hideous death of both her husband and children, had far more reason than Blood to wish him ill; if their suspicions were backed by evidence, they might make deadly use of it.

Sylvestre had taken a flashlight with him when he went out, but conscious that Regine was watching him from the gallery, he did not dare to use it. He scuffled along the grass, cursing the inadequate starlight. As he approached Jonah's cabin, he began to move more cautiously; lights shone from within it and he could hear sounds that seemed to come from the gallery, even before he could see the outline of figures; someone was crooning a lullaby and someone was strumming a banjo. Probably Phronsie was singing to Minta to soothe the child after her fright and Jonah was playing the accompaniment. It was quite possible that Blood had gone back there; Sylvestre remembered that the manager had said he intended to visit the cabin that evening anyway, even before the disturbance created by Minta. He always did these things brazenly, so secure in his place as "head beater" that he was indifferent to the scandals he constantly created. And Durice Reno was too fearful of the menace personified by Déette to risk losing him to her sister, as Vina had lost him to her, through a tempestuous display of jealousy.

When Sylvestre came close enough to the cabin to see, though still indistinctly, that four persons were seated on the gallery, he stopped; and while he hesitated about going on, he heard a car drive into the *allée,* and saw its lights go off in front of the stone stairway. Apparently he and Regine had callers; if he did not put in an appearance presently she would begin to call him, thus proclaiming the fact that he was prowling about the grounds for some unexplained purpose. Feeling more thwarted than ever, he went slowly back to the Big House, still scuffling as he went. He realized now that he could not find the photograph that night, that he would have to try again in the morning, and meanwhile someone else might come upon it accidentally. Fortunately, Regine was a late riser, and thanks to the arrangement of their rooms, she would be none the wiser if he were up and about by daybreak. He was generally a late riser also, and his appearance on the grounds at an early hour would inevitably be a source of surprise to the servants. But that much of a chance he would have to take. He must find the photograph. He must—he must—he must. . . .

The urgency of this possessed him. He was still terribly hot, still intermittently bathed in that awful cold sweat, and his head had begun to ache, too, so badly that it stupefied him. The loss of the photograph was still all too clear in his torpid mind; but he took in only the general drift of conversation. His callers were two old friends from New Orleans, Ray Tucker, now a member of the legislature and Fred

Snell, an habitual hanger-on, and both were in a state of extreme excitement. Apparently the House of Representatives had been a scene of wildest disorder that evening. The Speaker, John Fournet, had ignored the demand of Representative Cecil Morgan of Caddo to speak on a point of personal privilege. Morgan had stayed on his feet, shouting, "I have in my hand an affidavit that the Governor has tried to procure the assassination of a member of this House!" and the Speaker had ordered the Sergeant-at-Arms to seat Morgan. But three of his fellow members had formed a human barrier around him, and the entire legion of Long sycophants and paid goons had not been able to shout him down. Amidst the outcry, however, Fournet had recognized the ostensible motion of Cleveland Frugé, one of Long's floor leaders, to adjourn. This would have meant the end of the special session, blocking any effort to impeach Long. Fournet had made out that he was putting the motion, and opened the voting machine, and without regard to the plain fact that no real vote was being recorded, had declared the House adjourned. Thereupon a free-for-all fight had developed, which reached unimaginable proportions. Representative Sayes' forehead was laid open, while other legislators piled on top of each other in the bull-ring yelling and swearing . . .

"The worst nigger brawl you ever saw couldn't compare with it," Tucker declared, with an enthusiasm which he evidently expected his host to share. Sylvestre, who had not heard more than half of the dreadful details, tried to put some show of interest into his reply.

"It must have been some fight. How did it end?"

"Well, in the end Mason Spencer called a voice roll and it stood seventy-two to six against adjournment. Huey's in for impeachment now, sure as shooting. By the way, I suppose you realize that no one's worked harder for it than that next door neighbor of yours, Gervais d'Alvery. He and Huey never did get along, and ever since that Standard Oil tax came up they've been fit to tie. D'Alvery hasn't lost a chance to get in his licks. I wouldn't like to be in his shoes if Huey ever gets out of this hole."

"Gervais is usually able to look after himself pretty well."

"He'll sure as hell get a chance to fix Huey's clock if the House puts in an impeachment resolution tomorrow, like they say they're going to do. Huey'll be tried by the Senate, and Gervais has one damn big vote there now."

"Can't people talk about anyone but Long in Louisiana nowadays?" Sylvestre burst out irritably.

"He'll do big stuff unless they impeach him," Snell replied. "If that happens, you won't be hearing of him so much. We only thought you'd like to hear the news. Looks like nobody's going to bed in Baton Rouge tonight. The whole town's standing around in the middle of Third Street till yet, and the newspapermen have already christened the day 'Bloody Monday'; the moon's red all right and it's my guess this is only the beginning of trouble. But if you want to talk about something else. . . . Where have you been keeping yourself?"

"Well, we've only just got back from Cuba. We've traveled a good deal lately, you know. And when I'm home, the plantation keeps me pretty busy."

Even to Sylvestre, this sounded inane. The plantation had never kept him busy, and Tucker must be aware of this; everyone knew that Grover Blood was the real master of Hathaway. But Sylvestre could not think of anything else to say. His headache was getting worse; his temples were throbbing now, and another wave of cold sweat had drenched him. He wished Tucker and Snell would go home and leave him in peace, so that he could hunt for the photograph again. No, damn it, he couldn't hunt for the photograph again until daylight, but he could lie quietly in the dark trying to figure out where he had dropped it. Of course, before he went to bed, he would look out of the window and make sure the Cuban cane was still all right. He had almost forgotten about the cane, in his worry about the photograph. Almost, but not quite. If Tucker and Snell would only go. . . .

"Well, we better be pushing along," Tucker said at last, tardily sensing a lack of cordiality. "There's likely something fresh a-stirring in old Red Stick by this time. . . . But why don't you come in to Izzy's some night and have a snack with me and some of the boys? We've got a good crowd—you ought to get in with it." He shook hands, looking at his abstracted host more attentively than before. "You're O.K. these days, aren't you, Sylvestre?" he inquired, with a touch of solicitude. "I mean, you're feeling all right? You look sort of peaked to me."

"Of course he's all right," Regine interposed, answering for him. She did not have a headache, but she, too, had found the conversation hard to follow, besides being deadly dull. Her distaste for the discussion of any political question amounted almost to a mania, and her contention that all men in public office were either boors or crooks had so far successfully separated her husband from many of his youthful cronies. She did not propose to let the garrulous Mr. Tucker and his vulgar associate, Mr. Snell, get the idea they were welcome at Hathaway Hall, thus late in the day. She hoped they had seen the significance of her failure to offer them drinks. "He is dreadfully busy though," she went on coyly. "I know you've all got the habit of thinking that Gervais d'Alvery's the only planter on the River Road who ever accomplishes anything, but you're wrong. If it wasn't a deep dark secret, I could tell you something——"

Somehow Sylvestre succeeded in shutting her off, by leading the way into the hall and talking himself, more volubly than at any previous point in the evening, as he attempted to usher the callers out. But the door into the White Ball Room was open, and as they went past it, Tucker asked if Snell, who had never been at Hathaway Hall before, could have a look at it. Sylvestre obligingly lighted the gas, revealing the vast apartment in all its glacial splendor, and the two visitors stepped inside on the slippery floor.

"Nothing to touch it, anywhere around here," Tucker remarked with gratifying admiration. "Don't use it much though, do you?"

"No, just for weddings and funerals. We've had one of each in the last ten years, that's all."

"Maybe you're about due for one or the other again then," Snell remarked jocosely. Regine, who had quickly rejoined the group, looked at him with unconcealed contempt.

"I'm afraid I don't think that's very amusing, Mr. Snell," she said freezingly. "Besides, my husband seems to forget that when I was a girl we often had balls in this room and that I made my debut in it. I'm very proud of it and I have a great deal of sentiment about it. We have forty rooms in this house and the White Ball Room's my favorite. Mr. Tucker's right in saying there's nothing around here to touch it. So, of course, we don't use it indiscriminately. We keep it for occasions of real importance."

"Well, you'd call weddings and funerals important, wouldn't you now, Mrs. Tremaine?"

The impossible creature seemed bent on being offensive to her. She turned and walked back to the living room without another word, holding her head very high. When Sylvestre returned there himself, a few minutes later, he confronted her with unconcealed rage.

"You sure were the gracious lady throughout that conversation," he said furiously. "I haven't got so many friends left—you might at least be civil when one of them bothers to look me up. And that doesn't mean you need to go around shooting off your mouth, either. Do you happen to remember that I said you weren't to tell, or even to hint, about that little experiment of mine?"

"Oh, yes! I remember all right! But I reckon I can speak if I want to. . . . I didn't tell anything, anyway."

"You would have, if I hadn't shut you up. And you may find I'll do it more forcibly next time."

"Is that so? Well, you listen to me, Sylvestre Tremaine. . . ."

She followed him into his room, still haranguing him, and she did not leave him until he had told her, three times, for God's sake to clear out, each time speaking more roughly than before. He extinguished the gas, went over to the window, and looked down at the mound where his cane was planted. The starlight was brighter now, and he could see it clearly. If only it did not look so much like a grave! he thought, with an involuntary shudder; a place where hopes were buried, not revived. The involuntary comparison depressed him, and the depression only deepened when he forgot the cane again in his concern about the photograph. His temples were still throbbing, and when he pressed his cold, wet hands against them, instead of relieving the pain, this made it worse. Tucker must be right. He probably did look peaked; he certainly felt like hell. He'd hardly ever been ill in his life and of course he wasn't ill now; just the same, something must be wrong. If he could only find that photograph, he'd feel better. If he could only be sure no one else had found it. . . .

He woke to find himself sitting on the sofa, still fully dressed. He went and looked at the mound again, and then he relighted the gas. It was two o'clock in the morning, four hours to go before daylight. He got out of his clothes and took the shower which he had abandoned in the afternoon; but it required such an effort to do this that he did not even try to dry himself. He lay down on his bed, naked and exhausted, and fell into another stupor, which was troubled by dreams this time. He was searching, searching everywhere for the photograph, but he could not find it. And he was looking for it in such strange places—all the places where he and Cresside had been together. First The Willows and the levee and the cypress grove where they had been when they were in love with each other. Then the hallway where she had turned on him with such loathing and the cemetery where she had told him she would not marry him if he were the last man left on earth. He kept begging her, in these dreadful dreams, to help him with his search, and she kept scornfully declining to do so. And after all, he could not blame her for that, since, of course, she would not wish to be confronted with the likeness that would help him to prove Vail was his son as well as hers. But he pleaded with her, and finally tried to catch her, and when he did that she disappeared and everything was dark and he had to search blindly and alone. . . .

At last he woke again, and this time his head was clearer, though it still hurt him unmercifully. Daylight was just filtering into the room, and he jumped up, remembering that there was not a moment to be lost, that he must find the missing photograph at once. He pulled on his shirt and trousers, discovering that this required an effort, too; however, his sense of urgency drove him forward and presently he forgot his weakness. He did not put on his shoes, but this was only because he knew he could move more noiselessly without them; if he did not find the photograph on the stairs, or on the second story, he would come back for them before he went outdoors.

He went up the stairs one at a time, panting, and scanning every inch of the floor space. He was relieved to find that he could move so noiselessly, that his painful progress was not marked by any of those eerie sounds he had heard the evening before. He stopped for breath, when he reached the second story, and wiped the sweat from his face with his shirt. Then he crept along again, still carefully scanning the floor. At last reaching the room at the far end of the hall which was his destination, he saw, with some surprise, that the door was slightly ajar. He could have sworn that he had closed it the night before as carefully as if some priceless treasure might be hidden there—as he now knew that indeed it might be. But the latches on old doors were unreliable; often you thought they had caught firmly, only to discover afterwards

397

that they had sprung open again. With no fresh feeling of concern, he leaned against the jamb, resting for a moment before he swung it wide. Then he cried out in fear and in fury. Regine, clad in a white dressing gown, was standing in the center of the bare room, an evil expression on her beautiful face.

CHAPTER XXX

FOR A MOMENT he stared at her stupidly, too dumbfounded to believe his eyes. Then he sprang towards her, clutching her arm.

"What are you doing here?" he demanded roughly.

"The same thing you're doing here, I reckon. Haven't I got as much right here as you have? After all, this is my house."

Ordinarily he would have made a stinging retort to her last statement. This time he did not even hear it.

"What do you mean by the same thing I'm doing here?" he demanded, still more roughly.

"Oh, I know you think I'm a simpleton, but at least I'm not a congenital idiot! I realized when you came back here last evening there must be some special reason for it. Of course, I didn't know what the reason was, but I thought perhaps you were hunting for something you'd lost and were worrying about. When you went scuffling around outdoors afterwards I was pretty sure that was it. I was pretty sure you hadn't found it, too, because you acted mighty jumpy all the time those men were calling. So I figured you'd come back to look for it just as soon as it was light again. I guessed right, too, didn't I? But you see your poor silly little wife had the same idea. And she got here first."

"And what good do you think that did you?"

"Plenty, maybe . . . Let go my arm, Sylvestre, you're hurting me."

"I'll hurt you a lot worse if you don't answer my question this minute."

"Oh, I'm not afraid! You wouldn't dare!"

She laughed, and at the taunting sound, his last remnant of self-control deserted him. His head had been throbbing before; it was pounding now. But his thoughts, which for a long time had been so confused, were suddenly clear, and his strength, which had streamed away from him, came surging back. At all costs, he must first find out how much Regine knew or guessed, and then he must silence her. It would be easy enough to discover whether she had the photograph, for she was obviously wearing nothing but a nightgown under her sheer negligee, and she had only soft heelless slippers on her stocking-

398

less feet; there was no way in which she could conceal anything about her person. But she might conceivably have hidden the photograph somewhere else, if she had been upstairs long enough, though it would take some ingenuity to do it, in such a barren place; and the action, on the face of it, would seem pointless. Her instinct would naturally be to take her booty away with her.

Moving with inescapable swiftness, Sylvestre released his hold on her arm, but immediately seized both her hands, pinning them in one of his. She strained away from him, screaming, but her struggle and her outcry were both ineffectual; he was far stronger than she was, and there was no one else within hearing. All the servants slept out; and tardily remembering that they would not come on duty for two hours yet, and that consequently there was no chance of rescue, Regine next tried vainly to bite her assailant, while he rummaged in the pockets of her dressing gown, shook it free from its fastenings, and finally stripped it off her. Then, forcing her to the floor and dropping on one knee, he tore off her slippers, and shook these. She was trying to kick now as well as to bite, but he continued to dodge as he ran his questing hand over her again and again, from head to foot. There was nothing whatsoever on her beautiful body but the filmy nightgown. It was futile to search any longer.

Sylvestre took hold of her feet with his free hand, gripping them as relentlessly as her hands. Pinioned like this, she could not struggle against him. He leaned over her and spoke to her savagely.

"Tell me what you've done up here, you hellcat!"

"Don't you wish you knew, you damn brute!"

"I'm giving you one more chance."

"What do you mean, one more chance? You can't keep me here forever."

"No, but I can kill you, and I will if you don't answer me."

From the moment that he seized her, Regine had been furious, and her rage had mounted with his violence. But until this moment she had not been frightened. Sylvestre's manhandling, though it bruised her body and outraged her dignity, had not really shaken her sense of fundamental security. She had always possessed the stronger will of the two, and she had bent him to it, when and as she wished; over and over again, she had made him pay for the slightest show of resistance, and all the time he was searching her, she had been sustained by the vindictive thought that she would take rich revenge for this insulting treatment. Now there was something about his flushed, distorted face that sent a shiver through her. She had never before seen that menacing look in his gorgeous blue eyes, or that rigid expression on his weak handsome mouth. Instinctively, she shrank away from him, bracing herself against the floor.

"I haven't done anything. I'd only just come here myself when you got here."

"You lying little bitch! You were gloating, not five minutes ago, because you'd got here first."

"It was just a bluff, Sylvestre, truly it was. I didn't really have anything to gloat over. I was provoked with you because you wouldn't tell me what you were doing up here or why you went out last night. It's natural for any woman to be curious about her husband, especially when he acts the way you do, shutting up like a clam and streaking off by himself all the time."

The sharp bravado had all gone from her voice. It had sunk to a dragging whine, but it did not appease the frenzied man who was holding her down. Gripping her hands and feet more firmly than ever, he bellowed at her.

"What in hell did you imagine I was looking for?"

"I didn't know. But I really did think you'd lost something. I wanted to find out what it was."

"Well, what did you find out?"

"I didn't find out anything, Sylvestre. I realize now it was all a mistake, that you haven't lost anything, and that you weren't hunting for anything. I'm sorry I've made all this fuss. I won't ever do it again."

"You're damn right you won't. You won't ever have the chance."

The look on his face was not merely menacing any more, it was actually murderous. And he was no longer crouching beside her. With one of his swift, unpredictable movements, he had released her feet and sprung on top of her, so that he could keep her prostrate while straddling her body and still have both hands free. These hands had suddenly become abnormally strong, and they were moving rapidly towards her throat. Regine's whimper rose to a scream again.

"Oh, don't—don't—don't! I'll do anything you say, but don't treat me like this! I can't bear being hurt so, I can't stand——"

"If you don't tell me what you've done with that photograph, I'll strangle you. I give you two minutes to decide. One of them's almost gone already."

The clarity of his thoughts had long since been swallowed up in frantic determination; the pounding in his head had become a tumult, the confusion in his mind a chaos. At first he had realized he must not give himself away by referring to the photograph until he was certain Regine either possessed it or knew its whereabouts. He had adroitly avoided any mention of it. Now he had completely forgotten the necessity of such precaution in the deadliness of his purpose. He was impelled to force Regine to speak or to silence her forever. His lapse was his undoing. Regine's wits were sharpened by desperation and the wording of his threat indicated a last chance of escape. It did not take her two seconds to seize upon it.

"I'll show you, Sylvestre, if you'll let me up."

"No, you won't. You'll tell me, lying right where you are."

"But you can't go and get it while you're holding me down like this. And I don't think I can explain exactly. I wedged it in— Oh, it's terribly complicated. You know it isn't easy to hide anything in a bare room like this, Sylvestre."

It had suddenly dawned upon her that perhaps fear and rage did not wholly account for her husband's horrible behavior. His skin had a mottled, poisonous look and madness was mingled with the menace in his eyes. She remembered his collapse at Central Catalina, the increasing strangeness and secretiveness of his conduct ever since. The fainting fit which the Cuban medico had dismissed so lightly might have been the first sign of some serious derangement after all; probably Sylvestre was feverish and delirious now and such symptoms might account for a great deal. The possibility did not rouse the slightest sympathy for him, but it did suggest that cunning and patience might work wonders. When she saw him looking around, vainly trying to locate a possible hiding place, and felt his hold on her slacken slightly, she was doubly confident that her guess might mean her salvation. But after a moment's hesitation, he disappointed her.

"You'll have to explain. And if you don't lie still while I'm looking, I'll come back and knock you down again. I'll knock you *out*. I'm going to be sure you've told me the truth before I let you go. I know what a damn liar you are."

"Oh, Sylvestre, how can you be so cruel to me! I won't try to get away, I won't lie to you. But——"

"I said, two minutes. I think they're about up."

His transfigured hands were creeping closer to her throat. She screamed again.

"I put it back of the mantelpiece when I heard you coming. There's a little crack between the shelf and the wall."

Jumping up, he rushed across the room to the fireplace and saw that at least part of what Regine had said was true: the mantel did not fit closely to the side of the room; it was conceivable that a small thin picture might have been slipped between the marble and the wall; but there was nothing in sight. He turned furiously back to Regine.

"You *are* lying to me! The crack's there, but the picture isn't."

"It must have fallen down inside. You can see that the crack's big. Maybe you can pull the shelf away further, if you try."

He grasped the heavy mantelpiece with both hands and tugged at it. But apparently the crack was an old one, for the shelf seemed securely settled in its present position. Its immobility maddened him still further. He tried to shake it, stopping every now and then to see if the crack had widened and to glance in the direction of Regine to make sure she had not moved. When he saw that she was still prostrate and motionless and that he had made no impression whatsoever on the crack, he attacked the mantel with redoubled fury, and presently, when he stopped shaking it, it was only to glare at it with increasing intensity. Realizing that his attention was at last thoroughly diverted, Regine cautiously raised herself to a sitting position. Then, watching him closely as she did so, she silently got up, and putting one bare foot softly before the other, began to tiptoe across the floor.

She had almost reached the middle of the room when the marble shelf suddenly gave way, falling forward with a loud crash amidst chunks of cement and clouds of pulverized plaster; and as Sylvestre sprang over the wreckage, and bent down to examine the yawning space behind it, Regine saw her chance to slip through the door, which was still ajar. In another minute, she would have gained the hallway and with it her freedom; with so good a start, she could have outrun her captor, even if he had missed her then. But a puff of wind, wafted through the open window, blew the door to just as she reached it. Startled by the sound, Sylvestre looked up, and the next instant he had pounced upon her.

"So you thought you'd get away! Well, you can think again! And I shan't let you off so easy this time. This time you'll really get what's coming to you!"

He tried, without success, to throw her as he had done before. She had managed to get her hands behind her before he reached her, and without holding them in his grip, it was harder to force her down. He grasped her around the waist and shoulders, grappling with her, but she managed to keep her footing. All he could do was to force her further and further backwards, until they were nearly to the window which he had so carelessly left open the evening before. Then as he pressed her against the sill, he gave her a quick shove. With one last terrible scream she toppled over and fell.

Sylvestre watched her hurtling through the air and heard the thud of her body on the ground, his befuddled brain clearing again. Then everything was still. He had not really meant to kill her, only to frighten her into telling what she knew and what she had done. But if the fall had broken her neck, as he believed from the stillness it must have, he would not be sorry. No matter how little she knew, it was too much. He realized now the fatal mistake he had made in asking her what she had done with the photograph. If she had not known before that the photograph was in existence, she knew it afterwards, and, out of revenge for his abuse, she would have been spurred on to make vicious use of her knowledge. Only death could silence her effectively, and therefore he hoped she was dead. In a minute he must go and make sure. Meanwhile, he must think out his wisest course of action. He had no mind to hang for murder. And he still had not found the photograph.

He left the window, picked up the fallen dressing gown and slippers, and looked carefully around the room. It was still completely empty, except for the broken chair and the rubbish on the floor by the fireplace. He went over to the mantel and examined it with the utmost attention. The photograph was not there, and it could not possibly be hidden anywhere else. So Regine had made up the story about slipping it between the mantel and the wall, lying to the last as she had lied from the beginning and as he had always lied to her! Involuntarily, he thought of an old German saying which Cresside, who was surprisingly good at languages, had often quoted to him: *"Zwischen uns sei Wahrheit"*—let truth be between us two. There would have been truth between him and Cresside if he had only allowed it, for she, at least, had passionately desired it; there had never been either the will or the attempt for it between him and Regine. But he could not blame her for this last lie. All the responsibility for that lay at his door. He had terrified her and enraged her, and then, while he was frantic with fury himself, he had given away the secret which he could not trust with her. She had slyly taken advantage of him, and now she had paid for this with her life.

Holding the dressing gown over his arm and the slippers in his hand, he went out of the room—purposely leaving the door ajar this time—down the stairs and through his apartments to Regine's, which were back of the ones he occupied. There was a bay window in her bedroom, similar to the one in his study. He looked out of it and saw Regine lying on the ground beside the main part of the house from which the ell they occupied jutted at right angles. He did not go outside, for though it was very dry, he did not intend to take the risk that his footprints might show in the soft ground. Moreover, though the quarters and all the outbuildings were on the other side of the Big House and at considerable distance from it, he did not intend to have some stray Negro, passing by on a chance errand, catch sight of him bending over his dead wife's body. For he was positive now that she was dead. She had not stirred since he had looked down on her from upstairs.

He folded the dressing gown, laying it across the foot of her empty bed, and placed her slippers neatly beside it on the floor. Then he went back to his own room and walked over to the bay window there. The mound beneath it was undisturbed, and it no longer suggested a grave to him. Instead he seemed to see the tender stalks which he had planted pushing up from it and quivering slightly in the soft breeze, their color clear and beautiful, like the color of jade. Sylvestre considered the mirage with relief and satisfaction, telling himself that his cane was safe and thriving and that in due time he and his son would together enjoy the fruits of his enterprise, undisturbed by any alien presence.

But first he must find the photograph, first he must explain Regine's death, first he must get rid of this damn headache and these damn sweats. It was hard to decide with which of these attempts to begin, especially as his strength was streaming away from him again. But he believed that in spite of his returning confusion he had finally thought out the best course to pursue. He took off his shirt and trousers, put on his pajamas, and went back to bed, lying there quietly until he heard Micah, the butler, and Jinny, the cook, stirring about in the kitchen. Then he reached for the old-fashioned bell pull which hung under the canopy, and tugged it hard three times. This gave Micah's special signal, and though the butler had never served his master with that special type of alacrity which betokened genuine respect and admiration, he appeared with reasonable promptitude. As he opened the door, Sylvestre spoke to him querulously.

"Where in hell have you been all this time?" he said. "Hereafter one of you niggers has got to sleep in the house, so I can get hold of you if I want anything. As it is, I might die before any of you came around—you're later and later all the time getting to work. I've been sick as a dog all night. I tried to call Mrs. Tremaine and I couldn't make her hear me. Then I tried to get up and walk across the floor and I fainted. It was all I could do to get back into bed. Tell Mr. Blood to send someone into town for Dr. Champagne straight off. I believe I'm a dangerously ill man."

CHAPTER XXXI

ACTUALLY, SYLVESTRE DID not believe anything of the sort. But Dr Champagne had hardly looked at him when he made the same observation mentally.

The physician's arrival at his patient's bedside had been greatly delayed, and he reached it in a state of much perturbation. He was a man full of years and wisdom, and his long and varied experience as family physician to half the countryside and coroner of the Parish had made him almost impervious to surprise and shock. He knew that something must be radically wrong when he found Phronsie standing at the entrance to Hathaway, with the unmistakable air of being stationed there to waylay him; but he naturally assumed that the message she had been told to give him concerned Sylvestre. He was speedily informed of his error.

"Please, doctor, Mister Blood say, will you come round to de side ob de house, back ob de ell, befo' you goes in to see Mr. Tremaine? Dey's been a mighty bad accident dere."

"What kind of an accident, Phronsie?"

"Miss Regine, she's a layin' on de ground, right outside de dinin' room. Looks lak she done fall out ob de window upstairs."

"Hasn't she told you herself how she got hurt?"

"No, suh, she ain't said nothin'. Looks lak she cain't."

"You mean she's too badly hurt to talk?"

"Yas, suh, dat's what Ah means. Looks lak she done broke her neck."

"You're not trying to tell me you thin' she's dead?"

"Yas, suh, Ah is. Mister Blood, he say, wasn't none of us to tetch her till you get here."

Dr. Champagne opened the door of his car and motioned Phronsie in beside him. As usual she looked tidy, calm and lovely; neither her voice nor her manner betrayed the slightest agitation. The physician had occasionally observed Negroes who seemed to gloat over a catastrophe, when their affections were not involved; but usually, in the case of close connection with a tragedy, like the present one, they grieved openly and sincerely. Phronsie's composure struck him as abnormal. He continued to ask questions as he drove rapidly up the *allée.*

"You've spoken twice about Mr. Blood. What about Mr. Tremaine? Is he too ill to take charge?"

"Yas, suh. Us done tol' him about Miss Regine layin' on de ground with her neck broke and he don't do nothin' but thrash around in de bed, and say he wish he had a broke neck hisself, 'stead of a splittin' head. Don't seem lak he takes nothin' in. Leastways, Mr. Blood, he thought——"

"Who found Miss Regine? How long ago did all this happen?"

"Micah, he jes' natcherly happened to look out ob de dinin'-room window when he was a passin' through dere. He say he don't know what made him. He'd been through de dinin' room three-four time already dis mornin', without seein' nothin'. Mr. Tremaine, he done ring his bell to tell Micah to have Mr. Blood send for you, and den he ring it agin to ax had Mr. Blood sent, and Micah, he hadn't never looked out ob de window, goin' back and fo'th to Mr. Tremaine's room. But bimeby he jes' natcherly——"

"And then he called Mr. Blood immediately?"

"No, suh, he done called Jinny de firstes'. She come and she see Miss Regine layin' on de groun' with her neck broke and she scream and scream——"

Dr. Champagne decided that, in her own quiet, collected way, Phronsie was gloating after all. At all events, it was clear that she could not be hurried in acquainting him with the complete sequence of events, and they had already reached the Big House. He parked his car in the driveway, picked up his bag, and hurried around to the side of the building, Phronsie following close behind him.

Before he saw anyone else, the sound of voices reached him. For the most part these were awestruck and subdued, with only an occasional shrill or strident note. Strangely enough, no one seemed to be sobbing. As he rounded the ell, he came upon a cluster of Negroes encircling a spot which they effectually concealed, and so absorbed in gazing at it, and in muttering to each other, that only two or three of them glanced in his direction as he approached. But Blood had obviously been watching for him. The manager, who was standing a little apart, talking with the Chief Engineer and one or two other men whom

405

Dr. Champagne did not recognize, detached himself from this group and came forward hurriedly.

"I'm sure glad to see you, doctor," he said earnestly. "This is bad business."

"Very bad. I must hear all you know about it as soon as possible. But I've got to get to Mrs. Tremaine first. Stand back, boys."

With Blood at his side, he pushed his way through the circle and knelt down beside the lifeless figure on the ground. The Negroes watched him fixedly, but the murmur around him suddenly ceased, to be followed by a deep hush; not one of the onlookers stirred or spoke while his expert hands performed their grim task. Regine was lying as she had fallen, in a crumpled heap, and in his determination that nothing should be done until the arrival of the doctor, Blood had not even covered her. The lovely body, the long soft hair, the flawless face, were all unconcealed; but the eyes were staring, the posture grotesque, and rigor mortis had already set in. The Negroes shuddered as they gazed at her. It was only a moment before Dr. Champagne looked up, speaking with stern authority.

"She's been dead several hours," he said. "You did right not to move her, Blood, until I got here. But I want to get her into the house now. Fetch me a sheet and something we can use for a stretcher. And send one of your boys for the sheriff—he'll have to be in on this, too. The others better go on about their work now."

Murmuring again, the Negroes began to move away, many of them with backward glances. Blood, having given the requisite orders, remained with the doctor, awaiting the arrival of the stretcher and the sheet. Without further questioning, he began to volunteer additional information.

"I couldn't help this ghastly delay, doctor. Micah didn't discover the accident until after Bart had started to town for you."

"Phronsie told me that much. And that he and Jinny just stood and screamed, at first. Perhaps you'll go on from there."

"They tried to get Mr. Tremaine up, and they couldn't. Then they went over to the other side of the house and yelled till they made Jonah hear them. He came for me. Micah was afraid to stay here without Jinny, and Jinny was afraid to stay without him; so neither of them would come. They were scared stiff as it was, what with a raving maniac in the house and a corpse on the ground outside. I got here as fast as I could. There wasn't any doubt in my mind that Mrs. Tremaine was dead, from the moment I looked at her, though, of course, I don't know enough about such things to guess how long before that she'd been killed. But she was cold when I touched her, so I reckoned it was quite some time. I'm glad I did the right thing, not moving her. It seemed sort of heathenish, leaving her there on the ground. But I figured that until a coroner——"

"As I said before, you did right. But as you said before, this is a bad business. And we're still a long way from the bottom of it. I'll

406

be thankful when the sheriff gets here. . . . Well, here come the boys. Let's get this part over with, anyway."

Leaning over, he lifted the dead woman himself, laid her gently down on the shutter which served as a stretcher, and covered her carefully with the sheet which the men had brought. He had never cared for Regine Hathaway, as he had cared for Cresside d'Alvery; but after all, he had brought her into the world, as he had all the children in the great houses along the River Road, and he had always retained the feeling of intimacy with her and responsibility for her typical of old-fashioned family physicians towards their life-long patients. It was appalling to him that she should have met an untimely death in such a horrible way. He walked silently beside the stretcher, with a heavy heart and a troubled mind, and when the small procession reached her room, he again lifted her up, and placed her carefully in her own bed with the same gentleness which he had shown in laying her on the shutter. Then he dismissed the two bearers and turned again to Blood.

"There's nothing more either of us can do here at the moment. Of course, nothing should be disturbed in the bedroom until Mason's seen it. But somebody ought to stay here. What about Phronsie? She seems a good deal more intelligent and collected than Jinny."

"She is. I'll get her straight off. I told her to wait in the kitchen to see if she was wanted."

"Good. I'll tell her what little I have to say, and then I'll go in to see Mr. Tremaine. I'd rather you didn't leave the house either, Blood, until Mr. Mason's been here. You can stay in the library and let me know when he arrives, if I'm still with Mr. Tremaine then."

Sylvestre was apparently unaware of the physician's presence for some moments after Dr. Champagne had entered his room. He was lying on his back with his eyes shut, breathing heavily, and he neither moved nor looked up when Dr. Champagne spoke to him softly and laid a quiet hand on his shoulder. His face was terribly flushed, his skin hot to the touch through his sleeve. The doctor spoke to him a second time, and a third. At last he rolled over, "thrashing about the bed," as Phronsie had said, for a few minutes, and afterwards muttering something unintelligible under his breath while he stared at the doctor. Then he closed his eyes again and relapsed into immobility and silence.

The doctor felt his pulse, which was racing, and took his temperature, which was a hundred and four. Sylvestre made no resistance while his wrist was held and the thermometer was placed under his arm, but he did not rouse again either, and he seemed equally oblivious of the stethoscope's passage over his chest and of the thumping administered to his abdomen. Having examined him as thoroughly as possible under the circumstances, Dr. Champagne regarded him gravely and at some length; then he went back to the library and spoke to Blood, who was sitting on the sofa with a half-emptied glass of whiskey in his hand.

"Better lay off that for a while yet," he advised. He had often been called on to treat the manager during one of Blood's periods of abandonment to corn and chloroform and he had no delusions about what would happen, once Blood was really started on a drinking bout. "We've got a very sick man here. You'll have to send another boy to town to bring out a nurse. But I can't wait for her to get here to have help with him. I need it right away. Is there anyone on the place who could give it to me?"

"No one but Phronsie and Durice. You've seen for yourself what both of them can do, when I'm having one of my own spells. But I don't have to tell you Phronsie can't be in two places at once. And I don't know how you'd feel about having Durice at the Big House."

The manager did not speak either defensively or apologetically; he simply made a statement of fact, and, to the doctor's relief, his voice was clear and steady as he did so. Evidently the half-emptied glass of whiskey in his hand was his first, and he had set it down without argument at the doctor's suggestion. "I'll get another boy on his way straight off," he said, rising. "And I'll send Durice over at the same time, if you say so."

"Send her, by all means. Mr. Tremaine mustn't be left alone for a minute. I'll stay in there with him until Mr. Mason gets here. Then I'll probably have to leave long enough to go over the ground with him. Tell Micah to watch for the sheriff while you're out on your errands. He ought to be able to do that much without having the heebie-jeebies."

The doctor walked back to the threshold of Regine's room, observed Phronsie sitting quietly and respectfully at the bedside, and himself returned to Sylvestre's, where Durice, looking strangely subdued, presently joined him. He gave her a few simple instructions, telling her to call him instantly if the patient should rouse, and then he went hurriedly upstairs, passing quickly through a succession of great empty rooms and not stopping until he came to the one at the rear, with the open window and the fallen mantelpiece. Even here there was nothing to detain him, because neither of these provided a fresh clue to the mystery; he had already seen, from the outside, that the window was open, and the heap of rubbish on the floor had no conceivable connection with Regine's death. After an absence of only a few minutes he returned to the sick room and sat down, considering the different aspects of the baffling situation while he continued to watch his unconscious patient, and trying to focus his attention on the living rather than on the dead for the moment. He regretted that he lacked the necessary equipment for a blood test, but he did not feel at all sure that even if he could have made it, this would have helped him to recognize Sylvestre's symptoms. He remembered that the Tremaines had just returned from Cuba, and that they had been traveling extensively through the West Indies and Central America before that; it was entirely possible that Sylvestre had picked up some obscure tropical disease which was known only by hearsay to most general practitioners in Louisiana, and which he himself had never treated. Presently he decided that as soon as he got back to town he would telephone New Orleans, and summon a specialist for consultation; he felt increasingly sure, as he continued to watch the sick man, that there was no time to be lost in pursuing such a course. But he could not start back to town immediately; he must await the arrival of Mason. He began to worry about several other patients whom he had not seen yet that morning, to whom he had not even telephoned, and to whom he could not telephone from this isolated place. There was an old man with double pneumonia, a young girl whose appendix had burst before he could operate. They were both as badly off as Tremaine. . . .

"Please, suh, Mister Mason done come. He done look aroun' outside already, and say ain't nobody to leave de place. He tell me to find out where does you want he should go nex'?"

"I'll come right away. I want him to go straight to Miss Regine's room with me."

Dr. Champagne rose with a sigh of relief. He and Mason were fast friends, though their mutual acquaintances had always been somewhat puzzled by their congeniality. The doctor, who was paunchy, stooped and careworn, came of a distinguished family, and might have made a great name for himself as a specialist in a large city if he had not honestly preferred a general practice among his own people. The sheriff, young, slim and alert, was a product of "catfish town's" worst slums. He had climbed rapidly through his own efforts to his present position of prominence and responsibility and he was ambitious to go further. His entire record was creditable to him, and the fact that he had kept his office clear of graft had won him the regard of the community. Since he was likeable as well as honest and able, he got on well with almost everyone; but the elderly physician was one of his few intimates. They not only trusted and respected each other; they were extremely fond of each other. Dr. Champagne felt as if part of the heavy burden he was trying to carry was already lifted by Mason's mere presence. He greeted his friend in much the same way that he himself had been greeted by Blood, while they shook hands gravely.

"I'm thankful you're here at last. We've got an ugly situation on our hands."

"Suicide?"

"I'm afraid so. Of course, maybe it's just a hideous accident. But what would Regine be doing upstairs at daybreak unless she went there with suicide in mind? The second story isn't used, never has been since her mother's death. And even if she went up there, why should she perch on a window sill and topple off it?"

"She wouldn't. I think I'd dismiss the comparatively comfortable theory of an accident. But would she have any motive for suicide?"

"None that I know of. But obviously her neck was broken by a fall from that open window."

"Evidently but not obviously. You haven't thought of murder?"

"I've thought of it, of course, but I couldn't account for that either. Who would go upstairs looking for Regine at such an hour in the morning—even suppose someone wanted to murder her, and I don't see why anyone should. She wasn't overburdened with sense and she could be pretty tiresome, but she wasn't the sort to stir up violent enmity."

"You say the second story hasn't been used for years. Have you been up there this morning?"

"Yes, I've just come from there."

"Well, suppose you go again. Suppose we go together. By the way, the colored boy who came in to get me—Bart, I believe his name is—says Tremaine himself hasn't appeared at all so far. Claims he can't get out of bed."

"That's correct. He's unconscious. He's a very sick man."

"You're sure of that?"

"Of course I'm sure of that. I assume you want to see him for yourself though. Come on in."

They went back to Sylvestre's room together. He was still lying on his back, still breathing stertorously, his face mottled, his body inert. Mason, who was by no means squeamish, underwent an overpowering feeling of revulsion as he looked at him. Turning away from the bedside, he beckoned the doctor to follow him into the hall.

"I reckon he's out of the picture all right. Anyway, he and his wife were on pretty good terms, weren't they, as far as you know?"

"Yes, pretty good. I wouldn't have called them an unusually devoted couple, but they seemed to get along as well as most married people I've come across."

Mason nodded, smiling a little grimly. Like the doctor, he had suffered his disillusionments on that score, and no longer took them too seriously. "You don't suspect the manager or any of the sugar-house staff, I suppose?" he asked. "When Blood's drunk there's no telling what he'll do, and the mechanics at a mill take their tone from the man who runs it."

"I know that, but Blood's cold sober this morning and I don't need to tell you that except when he's on one of his tears, he's as level-headed as they come. Besides, it's all to his interest to have Regine live; as long as she was the owner and nominally in control, he could do what he pleased; she never interfered with him and neither did her mother before her. He always has resented Sylvestre's presence though, I know that. I'd be a good deal more suspicious if he'd been the one to fall out of the window. Well, that's beyond the point. Blood's shown remarkably good sense and good management about everything and the men under him are all a pretty good sort right now—there was a thorough house cleaning among the staff members after the explosion. I wish he'd got rid of his women, too, but I'll say this for him, he knows how to handle them. He had Phronsie waiting at the gate for me and she's watching Regine now. You've just seen Durice for yourself."

"Yes, and she still looks more like a whore than a ministering angel to me," Mason remarked, his smile growing even grimmer. He leaned against the newel post of the stairway and spoke reflectively. "However, that's not saying she looks like a murderess. And I'll grant that Phronsie's quite remarkable in her way. I think we can dismiss the women on the place. None of them would have had the physical strength to drag Mrs. Tremaine all the way upstairs and down a long corridor, let alone to pitch her out of the window. But a man might have. And it isn't just a mill that takes its tone from a manager; it's a whole plantation. The hands on this place haven't got too good a name either. I've been sent for more than once to settle rows of one kind or another, and some of them have been pretty ugly."

"I know that, too, but I haven't the slightest reason to think this accident was the result of any kind of a row. None of those you've been called to settle was connected with the Big House in any way— I don't know a place where that's more remote, in every sense, from the quarters." He drew up a chair and sat down. Apparently Mason, who was young and strong, did not mind standing indefinitely; but he himself was beginning to feel his age and the incidents of the morning had affected him, personally, far more deeply than they had the sheriff. If they were to go on talking this thing over, he would have to get off his feet. "We can check and see if there was any sort of a disturbance here last night, but even if there were, that wouldn't prove anything to me," he went on.

"No, it wouldn't prove anything, but it might indicate something. And there could have been a murder without a row. I just mentioned rows to remind you of Hathaway's general character."

"I don't need reminding. I've been called out here, too, after those rows were over, to patch up the rioters. And I've already admitted murder may have been done this morning. But supposing a man could have been able to drag Mrs. Tremaine upstairs when a woman wouldn't, why should he? It doesn't stand to reason, when it would have been so much easier to get rid of her some other way."

"No reason except that a fall from a window would look more like an accident. But if I know anything at all about Mrs. Tremaine, she would have fought like a tiger if she'd been attacked. Any signs that she had been?"

"Of course there were some bruises. But not more than could have been caused by her fall."

"What about her clothes?"

"She didn't have anything on but a night dress. That wasn't either torn or stained. Her dressing gown was folded across the foot of her bed and her slippers were on the floor beside it, just as if they'd been neatly placed there by the maid who got her mistress' things ready for the night."

"I may be getting you all wrong, Doctor, but everything you say sounds to me as if you weren't very eager to have me push my inquiries. How about it?"

The doctor did not give a direct answer. Instead he spoke as if he were thinking out loud. "Of course I want justice done," he said slowly. "But I don't want to get some poor nigger in trouble by casting suspicion on him when I'm convinced he's never been near the house. I've seen too much harm come from charges of that sort. And I don't want to stir up a family scandal either. I've also seen too many of those. It's my honest belief that Regine Tremaine committed suicide, though I don't know why in the world she should have. And, of course, there's just the thousandth chance that she may have been a sleepwalker, though I never heard that she was. In that case her self-destruction wouldn't necessarily have been deliberate."

"In other words you don't want her death laid to anyone else's door?"

The doctor brought out his direct answer at last. "No, I don't, Mason. I'll go further than that—I'll say I hope very much you'll feel you can report that her death was accidental."

They exchanged a long look of mutual understanding. Then the sheriff turned away, jiggling his watch chain.

"Well, if that's the way you feel about it, I reckon I shall, too, in the end," he said reflectively. "But as a matter of form, I'll have to talk to Blood and at least two or three of the other men and go over the premises pretty thoroughly. And, of course, I've got to take a look at Mrs. Tremaine."

Retracing the steps the doctor had already taken, they went up the stairs and down the long corridor together into the room at the rear. At the sight of the fallen mantelpiece, a gleam of fresh interest came into Mason's observant eyes.

"What about this, Doctor?"

"Well, what about it?"

"Marble mantelpieces don't fall down by themselves, do they?"

"No, but we don't know how long since that one fell down. And I can't see any connection between a fallen mantelpiece and a suicide or a murder—at least not this time. Regine hadn't been hit with a heavy slab—there'd be marks of it if she had and there weren't."

"Just the same, I'm going to question the Negroes. Bound to, on the face of that. I'll begin with the house servants."

Micah and Jinny were still cowering in the kitchen; they had not dared to creep away to their own cabin, and neither could anything have persuaded them to go into the front of the Big House. When the doctor and the sheriff approached them, they looked at each other instead of at their callers, and their expressions were stubborn as well as terrified. Evidently they had taken some sort of council together and decided on a course of action in case they were hard pressed at any point. Mason spoke to them reassuringly.

"Don't look so frightened. I haven't come to arrest you. I only want to ask you a few questions."

"Us doesn't know nothin', Mr. Mason, suh. Ain't no use to ask us no questions."

"You can tell me which of you does the sweeping in this house, can't you?"

"Us helps each other, Mr. Mason, suh. Us doesn't never try to do it alone. It's a mighty big house to sweep, you can see dat."

"Yes, I can see that. . . . Well, if you help each other, then you both ought to be able to tell me why neither of you cleaned up that mess on the second floor, the last time you were sweeping up there."

Again the two servants exchanged glances. "Us ain't seen no mess on de second floor. Us don't know what you means by dat mess," they said almost simultaneously.

"All right. Then perhaps you can tell me how long it is since you've swept up there."

"Us disremembers, exactly, Mr. Mason. Mought be some time back, mought be jes' a few weeks."

"I'm sure Mrs. Tremaine must have been particular about having the house kept clean. I'm sure you must have had some regular day. for sweeping."

"No, suh, us hasn't, not since Mis' Hathaway done died. Mis' Hathaway, she done make us clean de whole house good every Friday. But po', po' Miss Regine, don't seem lak she ever cared wuz de house clean or not. She lak'd everything round her person nice and pretty, clothes and sheets and de lak ob dat, but she didn't care nothin' 'bout no ole empty second story, no, *suh!* Oh, po', po' Miss Regine! Ain't ever gwine hab nothin' pretty round her no mo', after she be's laid in de grabe."

As if controlled by unseen springs, the Negroes both suddenly sat down on either side of the kitchen table. Jinny, putting her apron over her head, began to wail, while Micah ejaculated, "Save us, please Lord!" at intervals which he apparently judged to be appropriate. Mason, addressing them somewhat more severely than before, said they had better try to search their memories, as he might want to question them again. Then he turned to Dr. Champagne, the grim smile twisting his lips again as he started across the room.

"That's like what my wife calls trying to sew with no knot in her thread," he remarked. "Just the same, I think that fireplace has some connection with this business and I've got to go on trying to find out what it was. I believe I'll go over to the boarding house next."

"Please, sir, I think Mr. Tremaine's waking up. He may be just talking in his sleep, but anyway he's muttering to himself, so I thought I'd better let you know. You told me to come for you if he roused."

Durice Reno was standing in the doorway, her bearing alert, her expression self-important. The doctor barked out a brief word of commendation, but neither he nor the sheriff stopped to question her; they hurried away together while she stood looking after them with a quizzical expression in her mocking green eyes and a half smile on her full red lips. Micah and Jinny, cutting their lamentations short, rushed upon her.

"What he done say, Miss Durice?"

"Plenty. But I ain't telling what. Leastwise not now. I can't stop to talk to no niggers. I got to get back to my patient, ain't I?"

The house servants had always treated her with the unique type of contempt reserved by Negroes for the persons whom they considered poor white trash. This was her chance to take revenge. She sauntered slowly away, shrugging off their importunities, and re-entered the sick room on tiptoe. Dr. Champagne, who was slightly deaf, and who was already bending over the bed, did not look up. But Mason, who was standing near him, wheeled around and spoke to her sharply.

"That'll be all for the moment, Durice. I'll call you if you're needed."

She turned reluctantly, debating whether she might possibly see or hear something more if she lingered near the keyhole; but the sheriff's manner did not encourage her to do this. She decided that he was quite capable of flinging the door open at any moment, and that if he did so, and found her there, he might deal with her harshly. He was no doddering old softie, like the doctor, as she knew from previous unpleasant experiences. She went on to the library, where she picked up a movie magazine, and began to turn its pages in languid interest. Nothing that had ever happened in Hollywood could compare, in her opinion, with what was happening at Hathaway right now. . . .

Her suspicions in regard to the sheriff were quite correct; he made sure that no eavesdropping was taking place before he returned to the bedside. But the doctor had momentarily forgotten the very existence of Durice, for the first word he caught when he leaned over Sylvestre had been "Cresside." It was mumbled indistinctly, and it was followed by a long interval of silence; but eventually it was repeated as part of an incoherent sentence. The doctor, startled by this unexpected and ominous reversion to a long-buried secret, took Sylvestre's hand and tried to speak soothingly.

"Cresside isn't here, Sylvestre. She's never been here, you know. You mean Regine, don't you?"

"No, I don't mean Regine. I mean Cresside. I want to speak to Cresside d'Alvery."

His voice was suddenly firm and forceful. He opened his eyes and looked at the doctor, his dull gaze clearing.

"If she isn't here, you'd better send for her. There's something I want to tell her."

"Very well, I'll send for her. But just in case she can't come, suppose you tell me what you wanted to say to her. I'll be glad to give her the message."

"Why in hell should I tell you? What are you doing in my room?"

"This is Dr. Champagne, Sylvestre. You know me, I'm an old friend of yours. I'm in your room because you're sick, and because I hope I can help you to get better. You can tell me anything you'd like to have Cresside know. I'm an old friend of hers, too."

He had often found that if he spoke to a delirious person as if the man were rational, it helped him to become so. He hoped that this might happen now, and he also hoped that he might be able to divert Sylvestre's thoughts and words into some other channel. He glanced towards the sheriff, but Mason was still standing near the door, watching the entrance while listening intently to everything that was being said; the doctor could not catch his eye and signal to him that he, too, could be spared for a few minutes. Dr. Champagne had no reason to suppose that Mason had ever possessed the slightest inkling, until this minute, that Cresside d'Alvery and Sylvestre Tremaine had ever been anything but agreeable and casual acquaintances. If Sylvestre could only be sidetracked, Cresside's secret might still be guarded and others might be disclosed. He tried a new approach.

"Did you want to tell her Regine had been hurt? Of course, she'd want to know that, they were such old friends. I'll see to it that she does. She'll be very sorry."

Sylvestre gave a short guttural laugh ending in a snort. The sound was ugly and unnatural. But his answer showed that he had understood the question.

"No, I wanted to tell her that Regine couldn't hurt her. You can tell her that if you like yourself, since you're such an old family friend. You can tell her I fixed Regine so she can't do any more mischief. She's done plenty already. But I've put a stop to that."

"How, Sylvestre?"

"Why, I pushed her out of the window! I don't mind telling that to an old family friend. She lied to me and I put a stop to her lying. The only trouble is, I didn't find where her cache was first. I tried hard enough. She said it was behind the mantelpiece so I tore that down. But there wasn't anything there. The damn dirty lying little bitch——"

He became increasingly profane and increasingly incoherent. For a few moments the doctor continued to question him, patiently and adroitly. But the effort was futile. Sylvestre had relapsed into his coma. There was a long silence. Then Mason crossed the room quietly and stood beside the doctor's chair, putting his hand over the back of it.

"Well, that's that," he said briefly. "At least you don't think he was just raving, do you?"

"He was raving, but I think he was telling the truth, too. I think he did kill his wife. I think he imagined she knew something or had something that might injure someone else, and in his fevered state——"

"Then he could have got out of bed, early this morning? He wasn't too sick after all?"

"He must have been, by all the standards we know how to set. But sometimes a man with a deadly purpose has a strange spurt of strength."

"It won't last though, will it? He's going to die, isn't he?"

"I don't know what to say. I might be mistaken again. I told you before he couldn't have gone upstairs. But he did. He tore down a heavy marble mantelpiece and pitched a strong, active young woman out of the window. However, if I weren't afraid of guessing wrong again, I'd say he couldn't live till night."

"I reckon you won't guess wrong again. I reckon one of the reasons you guessed wrong before was because you wanted to. We all do that sometimes. . . . No need for me to send in my report straight off. We can wait twenty-four hours and see what happens. If he does die. . . . That was Mrs. Fabian d'Alvery he was talking about, wasn't it? She's a fine woman, one of the best. And Fabian's always been a mighty good friend of mine. If Tremaine dies. . . . Well, I still don't see why we couldn't report an accidental death. Hell, it's some kind of an accident, isn't it, however you fall out of a window? I'll just forget about the boarding house and the quarters, for the present anyway. I'd better push along to town and see if I can get that nurse of yours on her way out here, so that you can get on to your other patients. I suppose you'd like to have me drop in at the undertaker's, too. Anything else I can do?"

The doctor appeared to ponder. "Relations aren't any too cordial between Hathaway and Belle Heloise," he said finally. "All the same, the d'Alverys and the Tremaines used to be pretty good friends and they're still near neighbors. If we could get Merry d'Alvery over here, it would help a lot. I've seen her before in an emergency, and she's good. Anyhow, I think it would be just as well if you took time to go over and have a short talk with Gervais about what's happened. He'll be getting some kind of news through the Negro grapevine, and he'd better have a straight story."

"Right. It won't take me five minutes to run over there. Perhaps I could even bring Mrs. d'Alvery back with me."

As the sheriff went out of the front door, he noticed that a long spray of white flowers had already been attached to it. The gallery was empty, but at the foot of the curving stone stairway a little girl with cream-colored skin and neat braids was standing, clinging to the wrought-iron railing. She looked up at Mason expectantly.

"Hab Mr. Tremaine done died?" she asked.

"No. Mrs. Tremaine died, I'm sorry to say. But Mr. Tremaine's very ill. You mustn't make any noise."

"Ah ain't gwine to make no noise. Mr. Tremaine, he cain't get out ob de bed, can he?"

"He sure can't. I just told you, he's very ill."

416

Mason got into his car and started for Belle Heloise, intent on reaching there as quickly as possible. Halfway down the driveway, he encountered a tall, spare Negress, dressed in rusty black, so deeply engaged in conversation with a Negro whom Mason recognized as Amen, the "medicine man" of the River Road, that she did not even hear the approach of the car. Mason tooted his horn, and Amen seized her by the arm before she looked up, startled, and jumped out of the way. Ordinarily, the sheriff would have stopped to speak to the pair, but for the moment he was in too much of a hurry because of other matters that seemed to him more pressing. At the entrance, he met Merry, turning into it, and put on his brakes abruptly.

"I was just coming after you," he said with relief. "Dr. Champagne hoped you'd be willing to come, and that Captain d'Alvery would be willing to have you."

"I want to do anything I can. Gervais isn't home, but I know he'd feel the same way about it. He started into town early, on account of this fight at the Capitol—an impeachment resolution's being introduced in the House some time today and the Senate is in session, too. Of course, he hadn't heard, before he left, that there was trouble at Hathaway. But Sance went over to see Blood about something, and came straight back to me. And the quarters are humming with all sorts of blood-curdling rumors already. I hope the facts aren't quite so bad."

"I'm afraid they are. But I'll leave the Doctor to give you his version of them. I've got to get to town as soon as I can. I'm thankful you're here to stand by, Mrs. d'Alvery."

He wheeled his car around and disappeared at top speed up the River Road; Merry went on towards the Big House. She, too, saw Meme and Amen talking together; but like Mason she was in too much of a hurry to stop, so she did not hear what they were saying to each other.

"Ah ain't never ax yo' to put no conjure on Miss Regine, Amen. Yo' done wrong."

"Ah never did put no conjure on Miss Regine, Meme. Ah done put it on Mr. Tremaine, jes' lak you say."

"But Mr. Tremaine, he ain't dead. Onliest thing 'bout him, he be's sick."

"He's gwine be worse, you mark my words, Meme. Dat conjure Ah put on him, Ah ain't never know it to fail. De white folks, dey gwine to say he died ob a fever. But Ah knows better. Don't yo' heah dat death bird a-singin' in de tree? Death birds don't sing for pussons dat's daid already. Dey sings for pussons dat gwine die."

"Effin it works, how much Ah got to pay yo' fo' your conjure? Ah's poor, yo' knows dat."

"Ain't got to pay me no money at all. Jes' got to let me keep dat little ol' picture yo' showed me, what you done pick up on de path side ob your cabin."

"Pooh! Dat's easy."

"Sho' it's easy. Well, looks lak we'd better not stay here too long a talkin'. Yo' be's pickin' some mo' flowers, Meme. Gwine to need 'em pretty soon for a double funeral."

They parted, both well satisfied with their talk. Meme went on slowly up the *allée* and joined her little niece, Minta, who was still standing in an attitude of expectancy on the stone stairway.

"Hab Mr. Tremaine done died yet?" she asked, even more eagerly than she had asked the same question of Mason.

"No, honey chile. But he's mighty sick lak."

"He couldn't get out ob de bed and cotch me then, could he?"

"No, sugar, he couldn't cotch you now."

Meme walked on towards the garden, and soon her arms were filled with beautiful white flowers. Minta, after wandering up and down the garden paths for a few moments, turned back. Presently she was squatting down, contentedly, on top of the mound under Sylvestre's study window, spading up the stalks of cane which were left in it, and picking the eyes from them, one by one.

She was still sitting there, humming contentedly to herself, when Merry came to the window, half an hour later, and pulled down the shades.

CHAPTER XXXII

MRS. HATHAWAY HAD never invited her nieces, the Misses Wilhelmina and Gwendolen Murdock, to Hathaway Hall. She had always regarded her elder sister's marriage to a Pittsburgh industrialist as a mésalliance, and no visits were exchanged between the two families from the time it took place. The marriage culminated in a divorce, which, if anything, made a bad matter seem worse, for Mrs. Hathaway held equally rigid views on both subjects; and these views had not changed when Mrs. Murdock died, leaving two grown daughters. They wired their aunt, asking if she and Regine would not attend their mother's funeral; but the reply was an uncompromising refusal. Several years later, when her own mother died, Regine made no corresponding gesture; she had never been aware of her cousins as individuals, and she saw no reason why she should belatedly burden herself with their presence. But after the double tragedy at Hathaway, Dr. Champagne, acting on Fabian's advice, himself wired to the Murdocks, and they arrived in time for the spectacular ceremonies in the White Ball Room. Afterwards they naturally lingered on for a few days, to recover from the fatigue of their hurried journey and the strain of the funeral rites; and before the question of their return to Pitts-

Merry was still sitting beside her mother-in-law, turning all this over in her troubled mind, when Vail came in to ask, did she know it was six o'clock and wasn't she going to read aloud that evening? She left immediately with him for the *garçonnière*, where the younger children were waiting for her; and though she continued to think about the newcomers with misgivings, she did not mention them again to her mother-in-law and Madame d'Alvery did not bring up the subject either. Several weeks elapsed before she saw the Murdocks again, and when their next meeting took place she was inclined to feel sorry for them rather than critical of them. Wilhelmina, the elder of the two sisters, came over to Belle Heloise to say that Gwendolen had been ill for some days and that she had become deeply depressed; they would both be more grateful than they could say if Mrs. d'Alvery would drop in to see her for a few minutes. Merry, whose sympathies were easily roused, and whose conscience smote her because she had neglected a sick neighbor, volunteered to drive back with Miss Wilhelmina immediately and her offer was eagerly accepted. She found the invalid still in bed, but propped up with pillows and obviously glad of company; and sitting down between the two sisters, she listened to their joint lament, and tried to put in an occasional encouraging word.

Plantation life, it seemed, was by no means all that their first fond fancy had pictured it; they had not dreamed that the mere mechanics of living would be so difficult. In the first place, the servants were slovenly and stupid; the Misses Murdock did not for the life of them see how their aunt and their cousin had ever put up with them. After the first week, they themselves had decided to dismiss Micah and Jinny and replace them with well-trained, hard-working substitutes; they had been informed, before they started for Louisiana, that it was as easy as anything to get niggers to work for you down there. One of their friends, who had spent some time in the Deep South herself, had actually said that all anyone had to do was to stand on the levee and shout and the darkies would come running. But they had discovered, to their sorrow, that this was far from being the case; they would either be obliged to keep Micah and Jinny after all, or have nobody in the house at all. And since the servants knew this as well as they did, and were also deeply resentful of the unsuccessful effort to oust them, these worthless creatures were now slacker than ever and insolent as well. Miss Wilhelmina had even had hard work to persuade Micah to serve afternoon tea. . . .

"You know, I don't believe he ever did it before," Merry said consolingly. "You probably wouldn't have had so much trouble if you'd suggested coffee. And I'm afraid your friend must have been thinking of the 'good old times' when she told you about standing on the levee and shouting; it isn't all that easy any more. So far, we've been very fortunate at Belle Heloise, but I don't know how long we shall be. We can see quite a difference in the new generation that's just coming up. For instance, Amen, who was the yard boy when I was married, thinks he's much too good for that job now, though his father, Selah, is very proud of being our butler. And Lethe, the younger children's nurse, can't be compared with Dinah, who took care of both my husband and his sister when they were little and came to me when the twins were born. I don't think we ought to blame them too much. I think they're groping for something they haven't found yet, that they don't know how to find, and we haven't helped them much, I'm afraid. . . . I imagine there's a little extra difficulty at Hathaway, too, because some of the Negroes around here are afraid of the place, or pretend to be. You know how superstitious they are, and when a double death occurs under rather strange circumstances. . . . Well, of course I'd be glad to have a little talk with Micah and Jinny myself if you'd like to have me. I take it for granted you offered them higher wages than Regine was paying them—they always expect that from Yan—from Northerners. I know Charles Boylston was up against the same thing that you are, but I was able to straighten that out, so perhaps I can help you, too. . . . Is there anything else I can do for you?"

They would be no end grateful if she would speak to Micah and Jinny, the sisters hastened to assure her, and they were sure she could help them in other ways, too. The plumbing kept getting out of order, and it seemed to be practically impossible to get anyone to come out from town and fix it; perhaps she knew of somebody? The cistern was not anywhere nearly large enough, either; it had not run dry yet, but it showed signs of doing so, and Micah had assured them, as if he were really rather pleased than otherwise about it, that very frequently it did; then it would be necessary to "switch over" to the well water, which turned everything it touched brick red.

"All our linen will be ruined," moaned Miss Wilhelmina, "our beautiful embroidered linen! And I suppose we shall look like Indians when we get out of the tub! Micah says that when the cistern runs dry he has to tote all the water for dish washing from the old sugar basins out back, and that he doesn't know whether he'll be able, this year, he's got 'Arthuritis' so bad. That's what he calls it, Arthuritis. Jinny is complaining, too. She says every time she raises her arms, it gives her such a swimming in the head that she feels faint. She says she's sure she's coming down with heart trouble, and that if she does, she'll have to get a lot more rest than she's having now. As if she wasn't loafing most of the time, as it is!"

"The cistern won't run dry as long as the spring rains keep up," Merry assured them, deciding it was better not to resume the subject of Micah and Jinny. "I'm afraid if there's a drought this summer you may find the water situation quite a problem though. We all do. But every time I ruin a towel or get out of a tub looking like an Indian, I see something that makes up for it. Don't you? I'm sure there isn't any place in the world, for instance, where the flowers and the trees and the birds are as beautiful as they are on the River Road. I'd miss those a lot more, if I didn't live where I could see them all the time, than I do a little water once in a while."

The Misses Murdock were not able to look at it just that way; an abundant water supply was simply one of the commodities which was taken for granted in civilized communities, like Pittsburgh. So, incidentally, were mail delivery and telephone service. They had never even inquired, beforehand, whether they would have these; and then to find, on the very outskirts of the state capital, within a few miles of the state university, too. . . .

"Gervais feels just the same way about all that as you do," Merry told them. "He's working on it, too, but I don't know whether he'll get very far. You see, he isn't on the best of terms with the present administration, and that makes quite a lot of difference—more than it ought to. About the road, too. I know that's in terribly bad shape. I've never seen the sand boils worse than they are this year."

The road was indeed in bad shape, the Misses Murdock agreed vehemently—so bad that it discouraged visitors from coming to Hathaway and they found it very hard to drive over themselves. This meant that they got out very little, for so far they had not been able to secure a satisfactory chauffeur. Neither Jonah nor Micah had ever driven a car, which was another unpleasant surprise; they had taken it for granted that every handy man about a place could drive nowadays. And it appeared that none of the other Negroes could be spared from the fields just then, which seemed to them a queer way of running a big place. They would have thought that surely one—but they had talked and talked to Mr. Blood about this and it had done no good. And he was too busy to take them any place himself. Their first impression was that he would prove very obliging, but they were sorry to say. . . .

"Work is very heavy on a plantation, almost all the year around," Merry reminded them. "When you've lived on one a while, you'll realize that, and you'll get used to the isolation. In fact, you'll like it." She did not want to discuss Mr. Blood, or the lack of visitors at Hathaway Hall. She thought the less said about the manager the better, under any circumstances, and she was very much afraid that the Murdocks had not made a sufficiently favorable impression to encourage a continuation of visits, now that the first curiosity of the countryside had been assuaged. "We don't have a chauffeur either," she went on. "And I don't drive to town very often myself. I'm not an especially good driver, because I learned too late, so I don't enjoy it; and then of course five small children keep me pretty busy! But I do go sometimes. I'll be glad to stop by for you and take you with me, the next time. And I'll try to be more neighborly. I feel terribly to think I've neglected you while you've been sick, Miss Gwendolen. I hope you won't be again, but if you are, you must let me know straight off. . . . Dr. Champagne has taken good care of you, though, hasn't he? He's the soul of faithfulness—the roads are never too bad for him to get through to his patients! I don't see how he does it always, but he does."

Dr. Champagne had been out only once, Miss Gwendolen said, bridling a little. He had not seemed to grasp the gravity of the case, and in any event, both she and her sister were agreed that he evidently had not kept abreast of the times. They preferred a more up-to-date physician. To do Dr. Champagne justice, he *had* seemed to grasp this phase of the situation, and had recommended a young practitioner named Dr. Leonard Manners. Dr. Manners was exactly the right type: he had such ⌒ pleasing personality! He was so gentle and sympathetic! But unfortunately his services were in such great demand that he could not get out on the River Road every day. The Murdocks were not surprised at his popularity; but it did make things hard for them, because, with the servants so slack and everything—well, it had been a trying period. They were beginning to feel doubtful whether they could continue to live at Hathaway Hall after all. . . .

"Oh, you mustn't feel that way about it," Merry said in genuine distress. Nothing that had occurred in the course of the call had caused her to like the Murdocks any better than she had before; but she was concerned because their first favorable impressions had not lasted and because she herself had done nothing to make these more enduring. "You'll get used to all the little inconveniences, really you will. I know, because I did myself. You'll feel, after a while, that nothing could induce you to live anywhere else."

"Possibly we might, Mrs. d'Alvery, if there were anything to offset the little inconveniences, as you call them. In our case, birds and trees and flowers aren't enough, as they seem to be for you. You see, we've always been used to a very delightful and sophisticated society in Pittsburgh, and nothing ever happens on the River Road. . . ."

"When she said that, I had hard work not to laugh," Merry remarked, in telling Gervais about the call afterwards. "Here they are living in a house where there'd been a mysterious suicide before they got there, and since they've arrived, their manager's driven one girl off the place and taken on another, creating a scandal all over the countryside. I wouldn't call that so uneventful, would you?"

"Not exactly. But I don't think your new-found friends were completely candid when they complained that nothing ever happened on the River Road. I think what they really meant was nothing has happened the way they wanted it to."

"What do you think they wanted to have happen, Gervais?"

"They want to get married," Gervais said bluntly. "Do you suppose they'd worry all that much about the plumbing and the cistern and the telephone if they had someone making up to them? They told you themselves they'd feel differently if they had anything to offset these little inconveniences. Their white-pillared ante-bellum house doesn't mean a thing to them unless it can be coupled with romance with a capital R—quite aside from the fact that they've reached the age where they'd be a little anxious and eager anyway. I should think you could have guessed that, from the way they talked and acted, that Sunday they were here to dinner. I'm sure *maman* did."

"Yes, I know she did. She spoke to me about it then. But I think maybe you and she are a little too hard on them, Gervais. I think——"

"No matter what you think, I know. They came down here to get married, because they hadn't succeeded in Pittsburgh and they felt maybe they'd have better luck in a new field. They were ready to go to almost any lengths in their hunting, too. Of course Charles would have been the perfect answer to their maiden prayers. But Charles saw through them just as well as I did—he's about to start off on another trip, did I tell you? He's getting so he's away almost as much as the Tremaines used to be—I'm not sure how much of this is flight and how much is just growing restlessness—he wanted to get married, too, you may remember, but certainly not to anyone like the Murdock sisters——"

"You're exaggerating, Gervais. He couldn't marry the Murdock *sisters* very well, if he did want to, now could he?"

"All right, all right! As I've said to you a good many times before, don't be so literal!" He did not speak irritably, in the way he so often did when he made this accusation, but laughingly and teasingly, putting his arm around her and drawing her close to him. "Either one of the sisters. There's not much choice between them, when it comes to that. If he had, he wouldn't have run into any of the difficulties and delays that I did."

"Difficulties and delays! I married you the very day you asked me!"

"The very day I asked you for about the 'steenth time! Well, we won't go into that. What I was saying was that poor Charles had to run so that he wouldn't get knockout drops in his coffee when he was making a neighborly call, and wake up to find himself in such a compromising position!—and place!—that, being a gentleman, there'd be nothing he could do except make straight for the minister's."

"Which sister do you think would have given him knockout drops and dragged him off to her room?" Merry inquired, finally entering into his lightness of mood.

"I think they'd have flipped a coin. Or maybe they'd have fought it out, tooth and toenail, to the death, leaving the spoils to the survivor. Because it's certain that they've both been after him. And it's also certain that now they'll do the next best thing, as they see it. Unless this young doctor they're trying to get into their clutches comes across, they'll both go out for Blood, and I'm not making a bad pun either."

"Gervais! You shouldn't joke over a thing like that!"

"I'm not joking any more. I'm in deadly earnest. And I shouldn't wonder if Blood fell for it in the end."

"Why, that would be horrible—for a nice woman to marry a man like that!"

"Honey, I don't see why you go on thinking they're nice women. They're horrible women. It would serve them right—either of them right—if Blood did consent to a marriage."

"But Gervais, have you heard what the Negroes are whispering about Blood now?"

"You mean that when Durice wouldn't go, he took a whip to her? Yes, I've heard and I think it's probably true. But I don't think that would stop either Wilhelmina or Gwendolen. Some women actually get a thrill out of a man's cruelty. Look here, you're getting all white around the gills. You can't even stand hearing about anything of the kind, and Franchot's just like you that way, do you know it? We've got to get him over it somehow—it won't do for a boy to be so squeamish. Sometimes I've thought—but never mind about that now. And let's forget about those next-door neighbors of ours for a while and think about ourselves instead. I might go so far as to make love to you if you'll give me a chance. I haven't in quite a while. I mean you haven't . . ."

This conversation left Merry still more troubled than the one with her mother-in-law. The Murdocks reminded her of her promise to take them into town when she next went herself, and she kept it; but she did so unhappily, and after that she made excuses, both to herself and to them, about going in again, and similar excuses about visiting them: her family seemed to take up all her time; she had never found housekeeping so hard; she was not feeling very well for some reason. . . . Miss Gwendolen recovered from her illness and both sisters came frequently, on their own initiative, to the *garçonnière*. They were never invited to dine at the Big House again, and Madame d'Alvery and Gervais avoided them pointedly; but Merry continued to suffer their presence, and, once in a great while, to return their visits. No one else went to Hathaway now, no one else sympathized with the strangers' isolation and disillusionment. She knew that if she deserted them, they would be utterly alone, and her kind heart contracted at the thought of such desolation. . . .

Then, late in August, she received a letter, delivered by a smirking Negro, which filled her with fresh consternation.

"Dear Mrs. d'Alvery:

I am writing to tell you that Mr. Grover Blood and I were married very quietly this morning and that by the time this letter reaches you we will already have left Hathaway on our honeymoon. I would have asked you to be a witness at our wedding, but I realized that I would only embarrass you by doing this, because of course I know from the way they have acted that your mother-in-law and your husband have both tried to keep you from being my friend. I feel that they have been very unjust and unkind, though perhaps I should not say this to you; but so has my own sister, as far as that goes. She was not present at my wedding either, and she is now packing to go back to Pittsburgh for good. No doubt you will hear from her soon, too, telling you her side of the story, for she thinks she has one, though I don't. I am glad she is leaving, as she has shown that she is utterly unfitted for plantation life and there would have been no peace while she was around; but of course I could not put her out as long as she was co-owner of Hathaway and I have had a time with her. Fortunately I have enough money from my mother's estate to buy out her interest in the plantation and I shall do so immediately. I expect to be very happy now that I am married to the man of my choice and I hope that when I return from Hot Springs you will resume the visits which have always meant a great deal to me—that is, if you can do so without having your mother-in-law and your husband make you uncomfortable about them. You might tell them for me that my husband's background is just as good as any of the River families', and they had better recognize this for I intend to have them. It is not his fault that his parents lost their place during Reconstruction and that he has had to earn his living on other people's plantations. Lots of splendid men have done just the same thing without having to contend with all the prejudice that he has; but from now on he will have everything that he wants, for I have plenty of money to show the world, which I shall do. The time will come when Hathaway will be recognized as the finest plantation on the River Road; of course it should have been long ago, but evidently no one had enough spirit to make it. I have, as everybody will soon find out, and in my future position of prominence, I shall not forget that you were nice to me when I came here as a bereaved stranger and did not treat me like the dirt under your feet.

Yours with affection and appreciation,
Wilhelmina Murdock Blood."

News of the fresh upheaval at Hathaway had already reached Gervais when he came in to dinner. Merry interrupted his vehement arraignment of everyone and everything on the place by showing him the letter she had received.

"I still feel sorry for the poor woman," she persisted. "I feel sorry because she's been so unhappy here, because she realized no one liked her, that she didn't fit in. I feel sorry she's married that horrible man in desperation. Perhaps if we'd all been a little more hospitable to her she wouldn't have done it, because she wouldn't have been so lonely. Now she's got nothing but misery to look forward to. She's quarreled with her only sister and presently her husband will begin to abuse her, and she'll be a hundred times worse off than she ever was before.

That letter's the most pathetic mixture of bravado and resentment and gratitude that I ever read."

"Good God, we didn't *ask* her to come down here, did we? I'll bet she never would have left Pittsburgh if she hadn't been just as 'isolated' there as she was here—that kind of woman never has any friends no matter where she lives. You may be able to work up some pathos out of the situation, but it's more than I can. I don't want you going over there, Merry, you hear? You've no call to help a thwarted angry old maid you hardly know pack her trunks while you listen to her lamentation, and you certainly haven't any call to welcome back the bride and groom. Christ, when I think of that man Blood lording it at Hathaway! Not because he was the manager, mind you. Now if it were Seaver who'd made a rich marriage, I'd say good luck to him. But Blood's just about as low as they come."

"I know he is, Gervais, and I understand how you feel. All the same, I'm going to help Miss Gwendolen get off. Just think how humiliated and abandoned the poor woman must feel, all alone in that big house, except for those sullen servants! Getting ready to go back to the place she left so triumphantly, thinking she had such a bright future! I won't be making a social visit, Gervais—you might object if I were, but I won't be. I'll be performing an ordinary act of Christian charity."

Gervais continued to vociferate, but Merry quietly persisted in the face of his opposition; she had done this from the beginning, when a matter of principle was involved, and though Gervais could make such a course doubly hard for her, and usually did, he could not swerve her from it. She spent the greater part of the next two days at Hathaway Hall doing everything she could to ease the departure of Miss Gwendolen, who was first hysterical, then vituperative and finally overwhelmed by the course of events. At last Merry took the wretched woman to the station and saw her comfortably installed in a Pullman seat which she herself had taken pains to secure. As the train pulled out, Miss Gwendolen pressed her face to the window for one last look at her only friend. Then she covered her eyes with her black-bordered handkerchief. She had resumed her heavy mourning for her departure, and Merry's last impression, like her first, was of a grief-stricken figure.

The newly married couple was absent for several weeks, for the wedding trip was extended to include New York, Washington and several fashionable resorts. During the interval Merry continued to go periodically to Hathaway Hall, supervising the servants and cajoling them into getting it swept and garnished against the return of the bride and groom. She did not let her charitable impulses carry her so far as to welcome them in person on the occasion of their homecoming; but she did see that everything was in perfect order, that the house was decorated with flowers and that the icebox was well stocked with food. It was hard for her to do all this, not only because of Gervais' continued opposition and her mother-in-law's expressed disapproval, but in the face of the antagonism which her presence roused at Hathaway itself. Merry had never before been conscious of ill-will among any of the Negroes, but she was conscious of it now; she knew they felt she was "siding" with the woman they all hated and regarded as an interloper, more than ever now that this outsider had married their own substitute for a "bossman." They blamed Wilhelmina Murdock, not Grover Blood, for the marriage, and they blamed Merry for giving it countenance. The same feeling pervaded the factory and the boarding house. Déette Reno had not been dispossessed from her quarters, and it was freely predicted that Blood would go on spending most of his time there. Déette heard the predictions with satisfaction, and smiled evilly to herself. . . .

The day after the honeymooners' return, Merry received a second letter from Wilhelmina, delivered, like the first, by a smirking Negro, and this time tied to a small package. The bride was very much touched at the evidences of Mrs. d'Alvery's thoughtfulness which had greeted her on her return. She had thought of Mrs. d'Alvery, too, in the course of her trip, and had bought her a little present which she was sending herewith. She hoped Mrs. d'Alvery would like it, and that they would be seeing each other very soon. The bride had bought quantities of new clothes, too, which she would like to show Mrs. d'Alvery, and instituted various changes on which she was eager to get Mrs. d'Alvery's opinion—or now that they were to be neighbors for keeps, might she say Merry's? And she was, always, most affectionately. . . .

Merry opened the small package with misgivings, to find a diamond wrist watch embedded among layers of soft cotton in a satin-lined box. Her misgivings mounted as she recognized its value. Gervais would certainly protest against her acceptance of such a gift, and yet she could not return it without giving grave offence. She was beginning to see more and more involvements as a result of her single-hearted kindness, and momentarily, she almost wished that she had followed Gervais' advice and left the Murdocks severely alone. But at the same time she knew that she could not, conscientiously, have acted otherwise than she had. When Cresside came out to Belle Heloise, later in the day, she confided her perplexities to her sister-in-law, finding her, as usual, a ready and sympathetic listener. But on this occasion, though Cresside was ready to lend all possible support, she was not as encouraging as usual.

"The whole thing's a mess. If Blood would only run straight, or something like straight, it might iron out, after a fashion—not that he and his bride would ever be accepted by the people they'd like to have for friends, but they wouldn't be completely ostracized by everyone. Of course, he won't run straight though. And you know as well as I do by this time, Merry, that the old River families will stand for a lot from their own black sheep, but they won't put up with much

431

from outsiders. Wilhelmina's goofy and Blood's rotten. You could try from now till doomsday, and you still couldn't make *maman* and Gervais feel any different about them. I know you meant to do the right thing, but you're just letting yourself in for more and more trouble. You see for yourself how it works out."

"You don't think I ought to go there at all?"

"I know it's mighty awkward all around, Merry. Heaven knows you've had enough trouble with Hathaway already, trying to walk a tightrope all the time Sylvestre and Regine were there. And that was nothing to what you're up against this go-round. I'm beginning to think the Negroes are right, that the place does have some kind of a curse on it. Well—since you've gone as far as you have, I believe that if I were you I would call once—in the daytime, when Blood's sure to be out in the fields. I'll go with you, if you like. And I should think you'd have to keep the watch. Suppose I ask Fabian about it though. You don't have to tell Gervais you've got it, this very day, do you?"

"No-o," Merry said so doubtfully that Cresside knew that even this temporary concealment would distress her; and in the end it was agreed that Merry should tell him while Cresside was still there, so that she would not have to bear the brunt of his displeasure alone. As usual, Fabian was helpful in pouring oil on the troubled waters. He did think that perhaps Merry had leaned over backwards in her efforts to be nice to people who did not deserve it, but after all that was her way, and a good way, if you took your religion literally, like she did. Certainly she would have to keep the watch, but in thanking Mrs. Blood for it she had better try to discourage further gifts and further obligations. And certainly she should call once, in the daytime, as Cresside had suggested. He felt sure that the call would be returned in the same way. Personally, he did not think that Blood would try to push anything, from a social standpoint; he was too shrewd for that. When he was sober, there wasn't a shrewder man anywhere around. If he would only stay sober. . . .

Taken by and large, Fabian's conclusions were a good deal like his wife's, and their temperate views of the situation seemed to be justified, at least for the moment. Nothing untoward occurred in the course of the call which Merry and Cresside made together. The bride, who was beautifully dressed, received them with effusion and insisted on showing them her trousseau and her newly appointed apartments. She was obviously extremely conscious, and smugly so, of her marital state, and made numerous intimate references to "Grover"; but she gave vent to no resentful comments on the general attitude of the countryside, and uttered no threats concerning the future. Tea was elegantly served by an imported maid who had been added to the household staff, and when the calls were returned, as they were after a suitable interval, Mrs. Blood's new Rolls Royce was driven by an English chauffeur, impeccably uniformed. She appeared at church

432

in the same style, and other evidences of lavish living became apparent day by day. Arnold Fletcher, the same architect who had precipitated Gervais' financial difficulties, was called into consultation at Hathaway Hall, together with an outstanding interior decorator and an outstanding landscape gardener. Presently the place was swarming with workmen; the huge white façade glistened with fresh paint, the neglected grounds resumed a semblance of their original formality. In so far as she could fulfill her purpose in making Hathaway the finest place on the River Road by spending money upon it, the new Mrs. Blood was doing so. All the outward and visible signs of supremacy were there; only the inward and spiritual grace was lacking.

Nevertheless, as the autumn advanced, the splendor in which the bride lived became less and less solitary. Though Cresside and Merry did not call a second time, other visitors came more and more frequently to Hathaway. Wilhelmina actually appeared at the *garçonnière* one afternoon with the triumphant announcement that the Governor had been to her house the night before.

"He came after the servants had left for the night," she went on to say, "and he had his bodyguards with him. My, but they're a lot of huskies, aren't they? The Governor pounded on the door with that loaded cane they say he always carries. I thought the house was coming down. Grover got a pistol out of his dresser drawer himself, before he went to let them in—of course he didn't know who was there. Of course I didn't either and at first I tried to keep him from going downstairs. But he doesn't know fear. He told me not to be silly and went straight along, and I was so frightened that I just cowered under the bed clothes, shuddering. Then I heard Grover saying, 'Why come right in, Governor—*this is* an honor'! And next I heard Mr. Long asking for whiskey."

"You don't mean to say you thought it was an honor to have Huey Long come to your house in the middle of the night, battering down the front door and demanding whiskey!" Merry exclaimed.

"Well, after all, Merry, you know the Governorship's a great office in any state. I was wondering whether I oughtn't to get up and dress, so that I could welcome Mr. Long myself. But when Grover came back to our room for the keys to the cupboard where we keep most of our whiskey, he told me to stay where I was. Then he muttered something about not getting out any of the old stock, that Long was so drunk already he wouldn't know the difference, whatever he served. But right after he went back to the living room I heard the Governor roaring, 'Christ, this must be what you use for your own toots, Blood! I don't water my drinks with chloroform to take away the taste. I want some of your real stuff, and I want it god damn quick'!"

"And you still felt his visit was an honor?"

"Well, I do think he expresses himself rather crudely, but he has force, and personally I greatly admire force in a man. Next I heard him saying, 'I'll bet you I can smell out something better than this myself'! and he started to the wing where the downstairs bedrooms are. We've never slept there because——"

"I shouldn't think you would."

"But I always keep them in perfect order. I'll say this for myself, I'm a model housekeeper, even if I do have those lazy niggers to contend with all the time. Pretty soon I heard a shout and a crash. It seems Mr. Long went right up to the first bed he came to and pulled down the mosquito bar. Grover told me afterwards that he said, 'Jesus, no one sleeps under those things any more! No one but a'—well, I can't say the words he used—'like you. I'll bet you've got something or somebody hidden in that bed, you . . .'"

"I know what the words are, Wilhelmina, but I don't like to hear them, so I'm glad you didn't repeat them. I'm glad he didn't find anything after all that vulgar commotion, too."

"Well, of course, there wasn't any *one* hidden in the bed," Wilhelmina said, a trifle sharply. "But Grover *had* put some of our finest whiskey under the mattress on account of the servants. The Governor acted as if he thought it was a great joke, finding it. The men all went back to the living room after that, and sat around for hours."

"Drinking?"

"Well, naturally Grover had to drink with the others," Wilhelmina retorted, speaking sharply again. "But the Governor never lets any of the bodyguards touch a drop. Anyway, he stopped shouting and storming after he got what he wanted, and grew more and more genial. He says he knows he can find a place for a man like Grover, that my husband could be very valuable. And if he gets an official position . . ."

It was quite clear that Wilhelmina Blood was thrilled and gratified by this episode, that she did consider even such an intrusion an honor when instigated by the Chief Executive of the state, and that the prospect of being affiliated with the all-powerful Long machine impressed her greatly. Pending this advancement, she began to make club connections as well as church connections, and her generosity, in both directions, was conspicuous. To be sure, the bridegroom did not appear in the increasingly pleasing picture, and the captious might have complained that there was something wrong with it for this reason. On the other hand, he created no fresh scandal. If he continued to visit the boarding house and the quarters, he did so after dark, and with none of his former bravado. If he drank, he did so in extreme moderation. The grinding season began auspiciously, with a full crew in the fields and excellent organization in the factory. Sance, who had managed to maintain amicable relations with Blood throughout the crucial period since the manager's marriage, as he had on many less critical occasions, brought favorable reports to Belle Heloise of the situation at Hathaway. There was a lot of new machinery at last; there was a fine crop coming along; Blood was handling everything just right. There wasn't a better man, in his line, anywhere in the Sugar Parishes. What if he did carry on? What if he did know on which side his bread was buttered? Hell, that was his affair. He knew his job. . . .

Gervais listened, grudgingly, to his overseer's praise. Then, late one Sunday night, Sance came to the *garçonnière,* and told a terrible story, white to the lips . . .

Merry knew that catastrophe had befallen, as soon as she heard the overseer's knock. She got out of bed and wrapped a dressing gown about her. Then she waited, shivering, until Gervais came back into their room, shutting the door behind him as if he were trying to close it on some kind of horror. He took hold of her shoulders, gripping them hard, and tried twice, unsuccessfully, to speak to her.

"Tell me quickly, Gervais, what's happened. Has one of the children——?"

"No, the children are all right. All the family. All our people. It's at Hathaway."

"What's at Hathaway?"

"Another accident. The explosion wasn't anything compared to this. Or the suicide. They've got Blood away, they've had to, he'd have been torn to pieces if they hadn't. It won't be safe for his wife to stay either. You'll have to help her now. I shan't try to stop you this time."

"Of course you won't. You wouldn't have before, if you'd understood how I felt, or how much she needed me. But you haven't told me yet, Gervais——"

"It's so ghastly I don't know how to tell you. It's always so hard for you to listen to horrors."

"It is hard. But if it's something I ought to know, I'd rather hear it from you, Gervais, than anyone else. Please tell me."

"Blood went on another tear Saturday night. The servants say it started with words at the Big House. Blood and his wife quarreled."

"Yes, Gervais. I know you were afraid they would sometime. Go on."

"So he left her and went to the boarding house. Déette's still there. At least she was still there——"

"Yes, yes, Gervais. Go on."

"They drank and drank, almost all night. They shouted out loud that they were celebrating their reunion. Everyone in the boarding house heard them. There's no mystery about what happened this time."

"What did happen?"

"Suddenly he turned on her and drove her out. Cruelly, the way he had Durice. He told her to go and get Durice. He said he wanted her sister back again, that he was tired of her. And at last she started. She was so drunk she didn't know where she was going. He was so drunk he didn't know anything had happened after she left. No one thought it was queer she didn't come back. Everyone thought she'd slunk home, like both her sisters before her."

"Where had she gone, Gervais?"

"She'd wandered out to the mill yard and climbed into the carrier."

"But she couldn't have, Gervais. A dozen people would have seen her and stopped her. She couldn't have climbed into the carrier when it was going, anyway."

"It wasn't going. That's what I'm trying to tell you. At Hathaway they shut down the mill Saturday night to clean it and don't start it up again until Sunday night. There's no one around outside except the watchman after it's closed. He wasn't anywhere near the carrier when she climbed into it, dead drunk. She was still drunk when it started again."

"Gervais, you're not trying to tell me——"

"Yes, I am, that's just what I'm trying to tell you. The crusher feeder saw her when she came over the top, but he couldn't stop the carrier then. She was ground to pulp, right before his eyes——"

Suddenly he realized that she could not stand any more. She was shaking all over and the horror which he had made her visualize was reflected in her eyes as she stared at him. Then with a sharp intake of breath she buried her face on his shoulder. He put his arm around her and bent his head to touch hers.

"There," he said. "There. Don't, Merry." His voice was quiet and gentle, as if he was speaking to one of the children. "It's a hell of a world, some ways, and horrible things happen in it now and then. Take it easy for a few minutes—you'll feel better if you do. But as soon as you can pull yourself together, I want to get you to Hathaway."

"I couldn't go. I wouldn't be any use this time."

"Yes, you would. You're needed badly and you've always told me that being needed meant more to a woman than anything in the world except being loved. Didn't you mean it?"

"Yes, when I said it. But——"

"This is the time to prove it then. Because it's the only time you'll have a chance, as far as Wilhelmina Blood's concerned." He waited a minute and then he spoke with inescapable finality. "If you don't help her now, you never can," he said slowly. "She can't stay on the River Road after this. It's the end for her at Hathaway."

436

PART VIII

"Visited on the Children"

Summer 1930

~~~~~~

"For I the Lord thy God am a jealous God, visiting the iniquity of the fathers upon the children."

—Exodus XX:5

"Visited on the Children"

Summer 1930

CHAPTER XXXIII

For the first few years of his life Belle Heloise was Vail d'Alvery's world, and to him it seemed perfect and complete.

In this world were shady groves, where you could play hide-and-seek, and wide stretches of open lawn, where you could race with your brothers and sisters; a garden that was always bright with flowers waiting to be picked for Mummy and *grand'mère* and Aunt Cresside; a big friendly house, with a sweet-smelling kitchen where Lou Ida was always making good things for you to eat when you were hungry, and a big bedroom where it was always still and dark when you were tired and needed to go to sleep.

The house was filled with kind people, white and black both, who wanted little boys to be happy, and the Small Yard was alive with kindly creatures, too. Nostar, Vail's pony, was the largest and most important of these. Vail had thought beforehand that he wanted to have a pony with a white star on its forehead; but when it arrived at Belle Heloise, as a present from Uncle Fabian and Aunt Cresside, though it was the most wonderful pony Vail could imagine, it was jet black all over. So Vail named it Nostar. Sybelle, Vail's twin, had a pony, too, named Twinkle, because that name went so well with Nostar. They rode all over the Small Yard and the levee together, and when Daddy went with them, over the headland, too. Phil, who was eleven months younger than Sybelle and Vail, did not have a pony yet. When he went with them he still rode with Daddy, on the front of the saddle.

Next to Nostar and Twinkle, Maud and her families were the most cherished adjuncts to Vail's out-of-doors world. The families were new and different every year, and there were always a few days of heartbreak when the beautiful puppies were given away. But Maud, another present from Aunt Cresside and Uncle Fabian, was Vail's very own. Mummy and Daddy had both promised him faithfully that she would never be given away and the certainty of this was his greatest comfort when the puppies went. Maud was a lovely little spotted spaniel with great pleading eyes, who followed Vail wherever he went and slept on his bed at night. She had only one bad habit: sometimes she chased the white ducks which waddled back and forth at will through the Small Yard, fluttering up, once in a while, to perch on the rims of the old open sugar kettles now used as garden ornaments, or to paddle through the rain water with which these were filled. Once she had killed two of the golden ducklings that mysteriously appeared one morning, waddling after a proud mother duck, and then Daddy had made Vail whip her, and had actually said something about sending her away after all if she did not do better. But she had done better, and the heavy load which weighted down Vail's heart at the thought of life without Maud was lifted again.

In addition to the ponies and the dogs and the ducks, there were all sorts of little wild creatures that helped to people Vail's world. There were little brown cottontails which went leaping through the garden to the grove, so fast that Maud could not catch them, and squirrels which scampered down the boughs of one tree and up the branches of another. There were carpenter bees that Vail loved to shoot with his air rifle, lying on his back for hours at a time in the sunlight, watching the bees at their work of boring the wooden framework of the gallery, and aiming at them just as they plunged into the holes they had made. There were funny little lizards which changed their color from green when they were on the grass to brown when they were on the garden path. Once in a while there was a snake, too. Vail almost stepped on one, zigzagging over the stone steps leading into the patio, when he went to let Maud out the last thing at night, one time when her puppies were very young indeed and needed her all the time. He had shrunk back, frightened for a moment, but he knew he must take care of Maud, whatever happened, so he had gone out of another door, and when he came back, the snake had disappeared. Afterwards he told Aunt Cresside about it, because he felt he had to tell someone, and Daddy did not like to have anyone even speak of snakes. Aunt Cresside had praised Vail and said he had done just right, that snakes nearly always slithered away if you left them alone, and that he must not let them or anything else spoil his world, which was so beautiful. He promised her he would not and he never had, after that.

Besides riding horseback on the levee, Vail and Sybelle spent a great deal of time sliding down it. A levee slide was made of two or three barrel staves with flat pieces of wood nailed at each end, and at each corner of the footpiece a string, tied to use like a rein. The twins sat solidly on one end of the slide and put their feet firmly on the other, grasping the strings and guiding the slide with these; and before they started down the levee bank, they greased the under side of the staves to make them good and slippery. Vail did not believe that the coasting up north which Miss Mittie, their teacher, told them so much about, could compare with levee-sliding for fun. It was the most fun of anything they did, especially when Vail and Sybelle sat on the same slide, as they liked to, though each had one.

A great deal of Vail's time was spent playing games. One of those he liked best was played in the autumn, when he and Sybelle and Phil all helped to pick the pecans in the grove and spread them out in the sun to dry. Even Joyeuse and Franchot, their younger sister and brother, tried to pick pecans and join in games almost as soon as they could toddle. Vail would pick up double handfuls of the nuts and say, "Old horse, old horse, who wants to ride him?" The other children all tried to be the first to shout, "I'll ride him!" Next Vail would ask, "How many miles?" Phil usually made the mistake of saying a great many; it was Phil's way to talk big about everything. Then he would lose because he had to pay Vail the difference in pecans, between the number he had guessed and the number Vail actually held. Sybelle did better. She considered carefully, tipping her golden head first to one side and then to the other while she talked; she also watched the size of the pecans and compared these to the size of Vail's hands. So very often she won. Then she held the pecans while the other children guessed. Of course, Joyeuse and Franchot did not know much about counting; they were just as likely to say ten as three. But they liked to play and Vail liked to have them.

They all played other games, too, like "Jack in the Bush" and "I'll Cut Him Down" and "How Many Licks?"; and Vail and Sybelle helped with the plums, in the summertime, just as they did with the pecans in the fall, gathering the plums as soon as they turned yellow and learning how to ripen them in meal. They learned a great many useful things, like that, little by little, so that they would know how to take care of Belle Heloise themselves some day, when Mummy and Daddy were old, the way *grand'mère* was now, and did not want to be worried any longer; and from the Negroes they learned all sorts of sayings and stories, which were fun listening to, whether they were really true or not. For instance, Selah told Vail that if he would hold a penny in his hand while the New Year's whistles were blowing, he would have plenty of money for the next twelve months, but that if he wanted sure enough greenback money, he must also eat cabbage and hogshead and black-eyed peas for dinner New Year's Day. And Amen told him that the yellow butterflies which came winging over the levee by the hundred, early in the spring, turned into shrimp by and by, and that it was really butterflies they were getting when they crossed the batture to empty the boxes which had been tied to stakes in the river shallows near the bank. And Dinah told him that the reason the lightning bugs could gleam in the darkness was because they made their homes in the "sparkfire wood" which was scattered through the swamps, and could draw on its hidden flames whenever they wished. She said that the lightning bugs stored up fragments of these flames in their own bodies, and released these as they wished, by pushing their bodies out while they flew. She also said that the children must not stay out too late in the evening, or wander too far from the Big House, because, if they did, the lightning bugs would lead them astray, into briar patches; she could tell many a tall tale of disobedient children who had been so misled. Miss Mittie, who called lightning bugs fireflies, the way people did up North, said this was all stuff and nonsense, and Vail was inclined to listen to her instead of Dinah, because he liked to stay out after dark. When he stole out and stood beside the levee at night it was hard for him to tell sometimes where the ridge of this ended and the skyline began, and which were fireflies and which stars against the velvety blackness. But it delighted him to try, and he learned a lot that way, about the sights and sounds and smells of the country at night. Apparently the fireflies retreated to their homes in the "sparkfire wood" and stayed there all winter, for he never saw them then; but they came out in the early spring, at the same time that the wayside hedges were sweet with honeysuckle and blue iris and spider lilies began to bloom along the River Road. He picked bunches of these flowers to take back to Dinah for peace offerings, so that she would not scold him for staying out late or threaten him with the briar patch; and then she was placated and told him more stories, about the roadside flowers and how they got their names, and he learned all that too.

Of course, there were sure enough lessons, too, out of books, which were bothering sometimes, though they did not actually spoil anything. But most of the lessons were not *too* bothering except during the first drowsy spring days. And Miss Mittie, who seemed to know how children felt about that, did not keep Sybelle and Vail and Phil in the old schoolhouse very long at a time when it began to be warm and sunshiny and inviting outdoors. She got them to their desks early in the morning, but when she saw their eyes straying from their primers to the open windows where the wasps were buzzing, she said, there, that was enough, they could make up for lost time some rainy day. And off they went to ride the ponies and romp with Maud and do all the other wonderful things that were beckoning them outdoors.

Often Miss Mittie came with them. Once Aunt Cresside had shown her how, she tied pieces of meat on strings at the end of short poles, and day after day sat patiently for hours, while they trotted up and down the banks of the big drainage ditch back of the house to catch crawfish. Sybelle or Phil would carefully lift one of the short poles, to raise the bit of meat to which several crawfish clung with fatal greed, and Vail would scoop them into his net which he then emptied into a big bucket. (The crawfish and the tempting sunshiny weather came at about the same time.)

Miss Mittie also helped the children to harness the big black grasshoppers which came along later in the year, and which everyone except Miss Mittie called devil horses, because they had first been brought to Louisiana in the horse feed of the Yankee soldiers who had made so much trouble at Belle Heloise before most of them were buried in the graveyard beyond Angus Holt's garden. Miss Mittie, who had begun life as a Yankee herself, could not be expected to feel the same way about the devil horses as the rest of them did; but the children overlooked this, because she was so helpful in the matter of harnessing.

The harnesses were made of thread, and the carts the devil horses drew were made of match boxes, and the stables where they lived were made of shoe boxes. Miss Mittie helped make all these things, after Aunt Cresside had shown her how, and explained that when she was a little girl, she and Daddy had driven devil horses themselves. She told the children that they had also gathered driftwood for the Christmas bonfires on the levee, and hunted quail eggs on the ditch banks along the rough roads, when their father drove over the headland in his top buggy, taking Daddy and Aunt Cresside with him; then afterwards the quail eggs were hatched under the hens in the chicken house. Vail and Sybelle gathered driftwood, too, and learned to mix it with roseau reeds and pile it around tall central poles which were placed on the levee just before Christmas; then on Christmas Eve they went up there to help light these piles, and to listen to the crackling of the roseaus, which sounded exactly like the fireworks they set off on the Fourth of July. So it was really like having two celebrations in one. And they hunted quail eggs sometimes themselves, but not very often, because Daddy did not usually drive a buggy when he went over the headland. Usually he rode horseback, taking Phil in front of him on the saddle. But sometimes, when Mummy said she would like to see the stand of cane, too, Amen got out the old surrey, and they all piled into it. That gave the children their chance to hunt quail eggs and very good fun it was, too.

Once Vail asked *grand'mère* if she had done all those wonderful things when she was a little girl, and she said no, because she had no one to play with, and it was not much fun, levee-sliding or picking up pecans or fishing in the ditch, or driving devil horses, or hunting for quail eggs alone. But Vail had plenty of people to play with. Sybelle and Phil were both fine playmates, and Joyeuse and Franchot were pretty good, too, and would be better still when they grew a little bigger. They were there to play with all the time and other playmates were there off and on, among them Barry and Nellie Pereira, who came up from New Orleans with their father and mother every now and then, to stay at the Big House. Still another was Riccardo Tramonte, whose father had a magnificent store, right near the ferry, and a whole fleet of motor trucks besides, which carried provisions all over the state, supplying smaller stores which he owned also. Vail liked Riccardo even better than he liked Barry and Nellie, though Daddy and Mummy did not seem to like him so well. They never invited him and his father to stay to dinner, much less to spend several days, the way they asked the Pereiras. This was puzzling to Vail, because if he had been allowed to have his way, he would have asked Riccardo to Belle Heloise every Sunday. Riccardo could not have come other days in any case, because he went to a big school, where he was already in the fifth grade, and on Saturdays he played games, not just marbles and pitch and toss, but important games like baseball. In the summertime he went traveling, down the River to New Orleans, and all over the state in his father's trucks. One summer he actually went to Italy to see his grandparents, and brought back some coral beads for Sybelle and a Sorrento paper cutter for Vail. (Mummy would never let Sybelle wear the beads, though they were ever so pretty, but Vail kept the paper cutter in his desk and used it all the time.) Riccardo was three years older than Vail, and it was Vail's greatest ambition to be like him in every way. Sybelle agreed with Vail about Riccardo; she also thought he was very wonderful, and she was always delighted to see him when he came to Belle Heloise. But then, Sybelle agreed with Vail about almost everything. Lou Ida said it was because he was her "litter brother." Litter brothers always meant more to their sisters than ordinary brothers, like Phil and Franchot, or so Lou Ida said anyway.

Besides the Pereiras and Riccardo, of course there was also Frances Belle, Aunt Cresside's little girl, who came to Belle Heloise almost every other day. She would be a fine playmate, too, when she got a little bigger. She was a very nice little girl, though she was not quite as pretty as Sybelle. Vail was sure no one else was as pretty as Sybelle. She had beautiful blonde curls and blue eyes and the softest, pinkest cheeks in the whole world. Phil and Franchot and Joyeuse had brown hair and brown eyes and clear pale skins. Vail's cheeks were very red and his hair was jet black and his eyes were blue, not a soft sky blue like Sybelle's, but a deeper, brighter color. They were big, except when he squinted them up, which he did sometimes when he could not see very well. He could see the print in his primer all right, but in some of the books Daddy kept at his office, the print was very small, and when Vail tried to read it, he squinted up his eyes.

Vail and Sybelle had almost finished their primers now, and soon they would have first readers, which had pretty big print, too, though not quite as large as it was in the primers. Miss Mittie had the first readers put away in her desk already, waiting for them, and they were very excited about this. Every now and then they asked her to lift the lid so they could see the readers, which had beautiful red covers and which were tucked away in a corner, beside Miss Mittie's pencil box. Phil had not got very far in his primer yet; he would always rather play than study, not just on warm sunshiny days, but any time. Miss Mittie tried to scold Phil because he was so lazy, but no one ever scolded Phil much, and Daddy did not even try. Daddy had taught them all their letters, on the plantation bell, before they began with

444

their primers in the schoolhouse, and when Sybelle and Vail did especially well, he let them ring the bell afterwards. But he let Phil ring the bell whether Phil did well or not. He even let Phil blow the whistle when grinding was over.

One day, just before the end of grinding, Vail and Sybelle and Phil all managed to get into the purgery together, when no one was watching. There were big barrels of *vincanne* in the purgery, ready to serve to the hands as soon as the final whistle blew; but the children had never had any, though Phil had teased and teased for a taste. Phil seemed to think—and Vail and Sybelle agreed with him—that *vincanne* was probably just as good as *cuite,* which was mighty good indeed; when it was cooked up high, it was as good as pull candy. The *vincanne* was disappointing after all, and Uncle Fabian, who came out with Aunt Cresside and Frances Belle and found them all three very sick and sleepy-feeling in the purgery, said something about stolen fruit not being the sweetest after all. Uncle Fabian spoke pretty sternly to them for sneaking into the purgery and for stealing the *vincanne.* No one had thought of looking for them there until he did, and Mummy and Aunt Cresside were frightened because they were so sick; and Uncle Fabian said, and meant it, that they ought to be ashamed of themselves for making their Mummy and their Aunt Cresside so unhappy. Daddy scolded Vail and Sybelle a little, but he did not scold Phil at all. He said he thought it was funny to see the little tyke tipsy.

They never went back to the purgery, because they really were sorry —at least Sybelle and Vail were—that they had made Mummy and Aunt Cresside unhappy, and anyway, there were lots of other places in the mill that were more interesting than the purgery. One of these was a small square room on the pan floor where a Negro named Cato spent endless hours shoveling sugar and singing spirituals as he shoveled. Cato was an enormous man, whose coal-black body, bare to the waist, was always glistening with sweat. He wore white cotton pants, with a pocket on each side, and from these pockets hung huge handkerchiefs, one bright red and the other bright blue. He took these out of his pockets from time to time and wiped the sweat from his brow and his body, but it came right back again, in little shining beads. The rest of the time he shoveled sugar, which was piled so high that it looked like a big snowdrift, or so Miss Mittie said. Of course, the children themselves had never seen a snowdrift, but she had shown them some pictures of these, in a geography book they were going to study by and by, and they agreed with her. Miss Mittie also had a glass paperweight, representing a snow scene. If you turned it upside down, and then put it right side up again, little glittering flakes would fall from the top of the paperweight on the tiny houses and trees underneath it, and presently everything would be white and sparkling. The children loved the paperweight, which Miss Mittie had brought with her from Salem, Massachusetts, to Baton Rouge,

Louisiana, many years before, but it was not big enough to remind them in any way of the endless piles of sugar which Cato shoveled. Daddy told them that this was crystal sugar, and that it kept going down a shaft that led from the small square room to the granulators, which would complete the process of making it into the beautiful white sugar for which Belle Heloise was famous. Daddy used pretty long words sometimes.

The children never tired of watching Cato, or Betsy Ann, the little old white mule that went round and round outside the sugar house, her traces fastened to a long pole, her bridle to a slender wooden cross bar attached to this. She propelled a little mill which a sample boy fed with cane from carts and which extracted juice from the cane stalks. Daddy explained to the children that the cane ground by Betsy Ann's mill was not the cane they raised at Belle Heloise; this went directly into the carrier from other carts. It was cane brought to Belle Heloise by planters who lived elsewhere, and who were paid according to its sucrose content. The juice from the cane for Betsy Ann's mill was kept apart from the other juice and taken to the laboratory for testing. In this way Daddy could always be sure that the other planters were getting just what they should for their cane.

"Betsy Ann represents the first step in the chemical analysis of the cane," Daddy said, using big words again. The children nodded, their eyes on Betsy Ann, who was still faithfully and patiently going round and round. Her labors seemed as endless as Cato's.

Vail remembered the first time he had ever noticed Betsy Ann especially, because it was then he had asked Daddy if that little white mule was the one the men called Minnie. Vail had heard the men saying that Minnie was a very fine mule, with plenty body, and he thought this must be the one they were talking about, because it would seem to him that she would need plenty of body to turn the mill so endlessly. But Daddy had laughed, saying no indeed, Minnie was the best mule they had, worth lots and lots of money, and she had to be kept for work in the fields. Vail must watch, the last day of grinding, for the gayest cart that came in and its lead mule. That would be Minnie and her cart, because the men took more pains with these, and had more pride in them, than in any others. Betsy Ann was just a poor old broken-down mule, who couldn't do anything harder than turn the little mill.

"That looks hard to me though," Vail said pityingly, still thinking how endless Betsy Ann's labors were.

"But it isn't—not nearly as hard as the work Minnie does. . . . Look, Vail, you'll probably be a planter yourself when you grow up, and, of course, Philogene will. It isn't too soon for you to begin to learn about mules, to recognize good ones and poor ones. They're very important on a plantation; they represent a big investment."

There Daddy went, using long words again. But Vail was really interested and he tried to look as if he understood.

"Don't ever forget how much the mules mean to the men who handle them," Daddy continued. "Once you've given a pair to one man, don't ever try to shift and give it to another. There's likely to be a killing if you do. There was a killing at Hathaway, just last week, because Mr. Tremaine took a pair away from his man Jam and gave them to another man named Kish. He didn't know any better." Daddy spoke with scorn, and Vail, who somehow had never cared much for Mr. Tremaine, nodded with real understanding this time. He was sorry a man had been killed, partly because he was naturally kindhearted, and partly because he knew that the Negroes at Hathaway had no graveyard of their own, as they did at Belle Heloise. Even the few who strayed from the plantation came back to be buried, and he wondered what the poor people at Hathaway did when they died, since there was no proper place for them to go afterwards. He would have liked to interrupt and ask Daddy, but Daddy did not like to be interrupted. "Mr. Tremaine says a mule's just a hybrid with no pride of ancestry or hope of posterity," he went on, using such long words now that Vail could hardly follow him. "He's a great one to talk about that. . . . Well, he's lost a man and it serves him right. I don't want you losing any men or any mules either, Vail. I want you to feel responsible for them. And another thing: that responsibility means taking care of the mules when they're old. Of course, it costs something to feed them, and money's more important to a good many planters than anything else. I hope it won't be to you. I hope you will feel the mules have earned their right to a comfortable old age. At Belle Heloise we've always felt it was even worse to send a mule away from a plantation where she'd lived a long time than to shift her from one driver to another. I've seen a mighty tough overseer beg a planter, with tears in his eyes, not to sell the old mules who'd outlived their usefulness. . . . See here, you look as if you were ready to cry yourself. There's nothing to cry about. I'm not going to sell any mules, and I'm sure you're not either. Run along, and find Sybelle. You know about Minnie and Betsy Ann now, and which is worth the most. By this time next week I expect you to know the name of every mule on Belle Heloise, and the name of every driver."

He did not do quite as well as that, for there were a great many mules on Belle Heloise, dozens and dozens of them, or so it seemed to Vail. But he learned to know quite a number of them and he learned which were teamed together: Fuzzie and Florence, Martha and Mary, Clara and Agnes, Sarah and Sophie. He noticed that these were all ladies' names and asked about that. Then he learned that on Belle Heloise, as on the best plantations, only mare mules were used. Of course at Hathaway it was different. Mr. Blood used horse mules, such as Floydie and Major, Sam and Bill. He learned which men handled the mules, too: Roden, Monk, Temps, Orange, Neeley. He learned that four mules were attentively driven with one line in the fields, but that when only two, in tandem, were attached to the empty cars which had previously brought cane to the carrier on the plantation railroad, they were hardly guided at all. After an "empty" was unloaded near the mill it was detached from the miniature train, and a Negro snapped the chain of his tandem hitch to it. Next the mules hauled it around a sharp V curve to the other side of the mill. At first the car seemed heavy and the long iron chain attached to it was taut. But as the pull progressed, the chain slackened. Then the driver told the mules to go on, and he himself draped his legs around the long iron chain and went to sleep. He did not need to watch the mules, because they knew the way as well as he did, and the sharp curve did not bother them at all. They took it at an easy gait, and the driver continued to sleep until the "empty" had rounded the factory and reached the place where it was picked up to go out into the fields again.

All this was intriguing to Vail. He did not stand hour after hour in the dusty sunshine, patiently watching the carriers come in, as Merry had stood, that autumn before the birth of Philogene; he scampered about from one part of the plantation to another. But every now and then he stopped long enough to see something of special interest and soon there was almost no process on the plantation with which he was not familiar, no aspect which did not stimulate him or satisfy him. He knew that the reason dirt was brought from the batture and put in the bottom of the furnaces was because this would keep the bagasse from sticking. He knew that the purpose of lime was to make the impurities in the raw juice settle, so that these could be removed from the rest, and that blackstrap molasses, the leavings of sugar making, was fit only for cattle. He knew that the little magnifier, which he sometimes saw Dupuy using, was provided so that the sugar boiler could watch the grains in the syrup and get exactly the right amount, and he also knew that the old man really preferred to use his fingers for testing, and that he often did so on the sly. He loved to listen to the men singing inside the factory, to the sound of the engines growing louder and louder as he went up the sugar-house road and skirted the mill pond, and to the trip of the automatic which measured the exact weight of each bag, as the finished sugar poured down from the granulators into the open bags standing on the sugar scales. He loved to stick his fingers into these bags, hurrying to get as many tastes as he wanted before the bags were sewed across the top to close them, and trundled away to the vast storage warehouse or to the freight cars drawn up on a track behind the mill, waiting to take Belle Heloise sugar away. He loved to see the black chimneys looming up against a blue sky that had little fleecy white clouds racing across it, and the still golden sunsets behind the moving branches of the shadowy trees. He loved to watch the great bonfires of burning shucks and rubbish, and the flaming radiance which transfigured the façade of the sugar house after nightfall, with the dark derricks etched against it in bold relief. He was very conscious of colors, and once he asked Aunt Cresside if she had ever noticed the way the sky changed, over the

448

stack, just at sunrise. It was a queer pinky blue at first, then lemon yellow, then orange, then a flaming red slowly spreading beyond the stack at either side, all across the horizon. Aunt Cresside said no, she never had seen all that, but she would like to, and she would come out to Belle Heloise the very next morning on purpose. So they stood for a long time together watching these wonderful color changes in the sky. It was a very happy morning for him, because though he loved to stand before the stack at sunrise by himself, he found it gave him even more joy when Aunt Cresside was there with him.

But best of all he loved to ride on the funny little engines which pulled the open cane cars through the fields at Belle Heloise to the sugar factory. In a general way, the men spoke of these engines as the "dummies," but they all had special names of their own besides. There was a very old dummy named LUCIEN ESTRADE, and two newer ones, a PHILOGENE D'ALVERY and a MEREDITH D'ALVERY. Vail thought it would be fine if there were one named CRESSIDE D'ALVERY, too, for Aunt Cresside, and another ISABELLE D'ALVERY for *grand'mère,* and he told Daddy so. But Daddy said they could not afford to have any more dummies just now, and that Vail had better be satisfied with three, which was as many as there were at Hackberry Lodge and more than there were at Hathaway.

Of course he was satisfied, Vail answered hastily, clambering up on the steps of the dummy and pulling Sybelle up after him, before Daddy could change his mind about letting them have their promised ride. They had wanted very much to get on at this special hoist, because it was the furthest from the scale house, and that would mean the longest possible ride. But John, the engineer, and Joe, the fireman, had been muttering about the heavy load they had already, and saying maybe it wasn't the best time for the chilluns to ride the dummy. John and Joe had both succeeded their fathers in the positions of trust which they now held, and they were both training young relatives—John his eldest son, Joe his youngest nephew—to succeed them by and by. Meanwhile they realized they could not be too careful.

Once he and Sybelle were actually aboard the dummy, however, Vail knew that John would not put them off. He would tell them to stand back from the boiler, braced against the tender, and he would try to speak very severely. But if they begged him, he would let Sybelle ring the bell and Vail blow the whistle, just before the dummy started, and this was almost as much of a privilege as it was to ring François Estrade's great plantation bell or to blow the mighty whistle at the mill when grinding ended. So Sybelle tugged at the bell pull with all her might and main, and Vail blew as hard as ever he could, and then they were off, leaving Daddy behind at the hoist, sitting on his horse, with Phil in front of him on the saddle.

Another bell they liked to ring was the one on the *John D. Grace.* That was even more of an adventure than ringing the bell on the dummy because it involved a much more exciting excursion. The

John D. Grace did not stop at Belle Heloise very often, and neither did any other steamer, though in the wonderful old days, which they persuaded *grand'mère* to tell them about sometimes, all the beautiful side-wheelers had stopped there regularly, both for passengers and for sugar. But when the *John D. Grace* did stop nowadays, Vail and Sybelle were sometimes allowed to go aboard, in charge of Miss Mittie, and ride down the River as far as Gardere Landing, where Daddy met them with the car or Selah with the old surrey, to take them back to Belle Heloise over the River Road. And meantime they always had steamboat hash in the saloon, which tasted so much better than Lou Ida's cookery, and went up into the pilot house to help steer the boat, and blow the whistle and ring the bell. The captain was a very kind man, always joking and laughing, and they found out that the pilot, though he did not say much, was kind, too, inside.

Lezine Sance, the overseer on the plantation, was another very kind man, and on rainy days, when they could not play outdoors, Vail and Sybelle loved to go after school to the house near the quarters where Lezine lived with his mother, a funny old lady with hardly any teeth, who always wore a white cap and who did not speak much English. Their house was one of the first buildings ever put up at Belle Heloise and was unlike any other on the place, though there were many similar to it further down the River Road, around St. Gabriel and Geismar and Union. The children found this house fascinating. Its walls were made of adobe, formed from a mixture of mud and moss and supported by hand-hewn timbers placed crosswise. Construction of this kind was called *briqueté entre poteaux* and was very sturdy and lasting. The walls in the front room, which was Madame Sance's special pride and joy, were tinted dusty pink, and her best furniture was arranged neatly all around them—the commode and the armoire and the four-poster she had brought there as a bride, when she married Lezine's father. The bare floor was made of wide planks kept very clean, and two old rockers, with a low wooden bench between them, were always drawn up on either side of the hearth, whether the fire was lighted or not. When her housework and gardening were done, Madame Sance sat in one of the rockers and knitted, and every now and then Lezine came in from the fields and sat for a few minutes in the other. He was a very devoted son and took pains to keep his mother company in this way. The children sat on the low bench, side by side. Lezine told them how the crop was coming along, and Madame Sance told them stories about her girlhood in St. Gabriel where she had lived with her parents and eleven brothers and sisters in another house that was *briqueté entre poteaux*. One of the reasons she had consented to marry Lezine's father was because he could promise her a home like the one she had always lived in; otherwise she might have hesitated to go so far away from her family—all of fifteen miles. According to her, life on the River Road was not half as exciting as it had been when she was young, and the purpose of most of her stories was to prove this. But to Vail it seemed very exciting indeed, and she was one of the persons who helped to make it so.

Madame Sance always offered the children coffee, asking them whether they would rather have it black or white, and they told her white, because they were not supposed to drink strong coffee yet, though they both liked it very much already if it had lots and lots of sugar in it. Dinah had begun to put a little coffee in their morning milk, about a teaspoonful to a cup, when they were four years old, and this had gradually been increased, though they still did not have the half and half mixture which Daddy and Mummy and *grand'mère* drank for breakfast, nor were they allowed to drink second and third and fourth cups, like their elders. The first time Madame Sance offered them coffee, as far as Vail could remember, she had not only asked whether they would like it black or white, which they understood, but also whether they would rather eat it or drink it, which they did not understand. Then they had watched her and discovered that she dipped large pieces of mish bread in her cup and sucked the coffee from these and that this was what she called eating it. So after that they told her they would eat their coffee too.

Vail could sit for hours, passing a good time listening to the stories Madame Sance told and "eating" the coffee she gave him; but even she was not as fascinating to him as the tall quiet Negro they called "Honeybee" Crock. In the spring bees often swarmed at the side of the house over Angus Holt's garden; you could see them whirling through the air and hear them droning; then presently they began to get inside. *Grand'mère* was not afraid of them, the way Franchot was, but they annoyed her. She was wakened in the morning by the noise they made and when she saw them circling round her room and hanging from the tester of her bed, she said it was time to send Amen for Honeybee Crock, who lived in a cabin a piece up the River Road. Then Honeybee Crock would hasten down in his model "T" Ford and stand under the window of *grand'mère's* boudoir, beating on a dishpan with one of Lou Ida's big kitchen spoons. Presently the bees would start flying out of *grand'mère's* window and swarm on one of the low-hanging limbs of the mimosa tree; Honeybee Crock said they did this partly because they liked the noise he made and partly because they liked him. When a large cluster had formed on the limb, Honeybee Crock stopped beating the pan and began to talk to the bees, whose droning became softer and softer. Then at last he took them in his bare hands and put them in a special hive which he always had with him and carried them away. They never stung him; they were glad to go with him. After that the bees did not bother *grand'mère* any more that year; but Vail always waited and watched for the time when Honeybee Crock would come back again the next spring.

For a long, long time, these people and these pleasures sufficed to make Vail d'Alvery's world perfect and complete. Then it began to enlarge, and at first this expanding sphere seemed just as beautiful and even more exciting than the smaller one had been.

Instead of seldom leaving the plantation, he began to go more and more often to town. One evening, shortly after his seventh birthday, he heard *grand'mère* telling Mummy and Daddy, rather severely, that he and Sybelle had now reached the age of reason, whatever that might mean, and that it was high time they had religious instruction, beyond the prayers she and Mummy had taught them and the Bible stories told them by Miss Mittie, "a Protestant from Massachusetts" as *grand'mère* called her, in a queer tone of voice—why, Vail did not know. He could dimly remember that when he was very, very little, a sour-faced priest named Father Martin had come regularly to Belle Heloise to hear *grand'mère* confess and celebrate Mass in her room; but later on, after she was not so puny any more, she often went to church in town and Father Martin's visits became more and more infrequent. When she suggested that he should begin coming regularly again, to teach Vail and Sybelle their catechism so that they could prepare for their first Holy Communion, Vail did not think much of this plan; he remembered Father Martin as one of the few unappealing figures peopling his pleasant world. Therefore, he was very much pleased when Daddy said no, rather shortly, they would get the kids to town somehow for instruction, and soon after that Vail and Sybelle began to go to catechism classes at St. Agnes'.

The catechism classes themselves were not so much, Vail privately thought; but he did not say this, because he could see that Sybelle really enjoyed them, and because Daddy made such an effort to get them to town, in spite of all there was to do on the plantation in springtime, and because *grand'mère* was so gratified that Vail and Sybelle were being properly prepared, at last, for their first Holy Communion. But the trips into town which these classes involved were simply swell. They were made in the new Buick that Uncle Fabian and Aunt Cresside had given Daddy and Mummy for a Christmas present after the faithful old one had practically fallen to pieces; and when a catechism class was over, Vail and Sybelle always went to visit Uncle Fabian and Aunt Cresside, who took them back to Belle Heloise later on, in their own car. By the time the period of instruction had passed, and the first Holy Communion had been duly celebrated— Sybelle looking like a little angel in her floating draperies, Vail very self-conscious in his stiff white suit—the visits to Somerulos Street had become a habit. So these went on and on, during the next two years. And in the course of these visits, Vail and Sybelle did all sorts of things they had not done at Belle Heloise. They went to the movies. They went to Luigi Tramonte's fancy grocery store. They went to the Capitol and saw Daddy sitting in the Senate chamber.

All this was great fun and very exciting. But once in a while something happened that made Vail feel uncomfortable instead of joyous, and raised the first doubts in his mind about the perfection of his expanding world.

For instance, there was the time that Betsy Ann died. All through the grinding season she had gone patiently round and round outside the sugar house, her traces fastened to the long pole, her bridle to the wooden cross bar, propelling the little mill which a sample boy fed with cane stalks and which extracted the juice from these. She had never stopped until the final load was in. And then, when Monk went to unfasten her, she had fallen where she stood. Vail had been standing near by, watching her until the last minute, as he always did, and hoping that Monk would let him lead her away to the mule shed. He hurried over to her and knelt down beside her.

"She's all tired out," he said wrathfully. "It's too hard for her, going round and round like that. I'm going to ask Daddy to give her something easier to do next year."

"Won't be no need, Vail." Monk had knelt down beside the little white mule, too, and was touching her with understanding. "She tired out all right. She through. Ah done hear, plenty times, 'bout mules and folkses, too, droppin' right in they tracks, but this here the onliest time Ah ever seed it."

"What do you mean, she's through?"

"She daid. Ain't you never see no daid mule alyin' on de groun' befo'?"

No, Vail had never seen a dead mule before, or any dead creature, to think of it as such, for the things you ate did not count, even those that men brought home when they went hunting. The sight was almost more than he could bear, for he had loved Betsy Ann and she had been a part of his life as far back as he could remember, so he stayed with her as long as they would let him, and when they came with a cart to take her away, he asked if she were being carried to the colored cemetery, and if he couldn't go, too, and see the funeral. Aunt Cresside came along just then and explained that mules were not buried in cemeteries, and that it would be better for Vail not to try to stay with Betsy Ann any longer; and for the first time in his life he broke away from her and went up on the levee all alone except for Maud. He did not want even Aunt Cresside to stay with him during the first hours of his grief over Betsy Ann. It was not that he was ashamed to have her see him crying. It was only that he had to be by himself for a while.

Then, there was the time that Mr. Tremaine had come butting in at the fancy grocery store, just when Vail and Sybelle and Riccardo were having such a good time eating their spumone. If Mr. Tremaine had had any sense, he would have known they didn't want him hanging around. And still he had stayed and stayed, asking tiresome questions, until Vail wished he could tell him just where to get off. Mr. Tremaine had spoiled the whole afternoon, butting in like that. Vail was glad when he heard Daddy telling Mummy, not long afterwards, that Mr. and Mrs. Tremaine had gone to Cuba, that very likely they'd be gone all spring. Daddy went on to say it was no wonder everything at Hathaway was going from bad to worse, and Vail gathered this was because no one looked after Hathaway properly, the way Daddy looked after Belle Heloise. But even then Vail was guiltily glad Mr. Tremaine had gone away. He did not want Mr. Tremaine hanging around, whatever happened at Hathaway.

Afterwards his feeling of guilt about Mr. Tremaine increased, and with it his feeling that everything was not right in his world. Because Mr. Tremaine did not stay long in Cuba, and just a few days after he returned to Hathaway, he died, and people said it was because he had caught a bad tropical fever. At least, most people. Vail heard Amen talking to some of the other Negroes about it, and Amen said it wasn't nothing of the sort. But when they asked him, what then, he wouldn't tell. He started to, and then he saw Vail and stopped.

Of course, it was not Vail's fault that Mr. Tremaine had gone to Cuba, he knew that. But he had been so glad to get rid of him, that when Mr. Tremaine died, it gave him a queer feeling in his stomach, even worse than when Déette Reno was killed in the crusher a few months later. He would have supposed, beforehand, that if anyone had told him he would be rid of Mr. Tremaine for good, he would have said that was grand. And it was not grand. He tried to tell Aunt Cresside how he felt about it, and for the first time, he found it hard to talk to Aunt Cresside. That was another thing that made him feel something was wrong. And for a long while, he looked in the opposite direction every time he went past Hathaway Hall. He hated the sight of that big blank empty house. He hated the thought of it. He hated everything that reminded him of Mr. Tremaine and he had never hated anything or anyone before in his life. . . .

The following summer he came across someone else whom he hated. This was a queer little man who stood beside him back of the Senate rail when he and Sybelle went there with Aunt Cresside to watch Daddy, who was talking with all the other men listening to him. The little man had small sharp features, a thin pointed nose, and little rat ears that were set very close to his head. He had oily black hair which came down over his little rat ears, because he needed a hair cut, and he clutched a big umbrella all the time. He offered Vail some gum, which Vail declined, though ordinarily he would have accepted it with avidity; he was very fond of gum, but grand'mère considered the use of it an extremely vulgar habit, and none of the children at Belle Heloise were allowed to have any, out of respect for her views. Therefore, they habitually welcomed every possible chance of getting it elsewhere. But Vail, who was not usually any more observant about such matters than other small boys, noticed that the little ratlike man had grimy fingernails and clammy-looking hands, and he shrank from putting anything in his mouth that such a repulsive creature had

454

touched. The man gave a funny little laugh, which sounded to Vail something like a rat's squeal, when Vail refused the gum; and then he made one or two remarks under his breath, using very nasty words. Vail had heard some of the words before, in the sugar house and the quarters and the fields, but they had not sounded so bad in those places as they did here in the Senate chamber, and he hoped very much that neither Aunt Cresside nor Sybelle would hear them. But evidently Aunt Cresside did hear them, for she glanced across Vail at the little ratlike man, and presently she said she thought perhaps they had better be going, she didn't believe anything more that was exciting would happen in the Senate that day.

The little ratlike man was still standing beside them, clutching his umbrella and muttering nasty words under his breath. When they reached the rotunda Daddy joined them and said, hello there, he'd seen them going out, and how would they like to come across the hall to Chris's cigar stand for a coke. Of course, they all said that would be grand, and it was. There was something about drinking a coke under the big stained-glass dome that made it taste better than it did at home. Vail and Sybelle made theirs last as long as they could, but finally Aunt Cresside said, for heaven's sake, hadn't they sucked the bottles long enough, and how about coming over to the house for a few minutes. And Daddy said swell, cokes were all right as far as they went, but they didn't go far with him. He could still top them off with mint juleps and he would, whenever he had a chance. He had to see a man for a minute and after that he'd be right over to Somerulos Street.

By the time he got there, Aunt Cresside had the juleps ready and some more cokes for Vail and Sybelle, and Uncle Fabian had just come in from his office, so Frances Belle had climbed up on his lap and was asking funny questions and was awfully cute. They were all having a grand time, and Vail was hoping that Daddy wouldn't think about going home for a long while yet, when Aunt Cresside began to ask questions herself.

"Gervais, have you ever noticed a queer little ratlike man, clutching an umbrella, in the crowd back of the Senate rail? He's been there every time that I have lately. He sat beside us today."

"I reckon you must mean Sammy Mudge. Yes, I've seen him. He's always hanging around when Long's on the floor, or when anything's going on that Long wants to have watched."

"He looks to me like a foul creature. What does he prove?"

"Well, he's on the pay roll as a State Highway Policeman, but as far as I know he's never done anything but pass by twice a month and pick up his check."

"He must do something the rest of the time."

"I suppose he must, but I wouldn't know what it is. He's more or less of a mystery. You're not the first person who's been curious about him. Some people figure he's got a dagger in the handle of that umbrella he clutches all the time, but that's just a rumor. He's never been seen with Long, but there's probably some kind of a body buried between them."

Vail did not like to hear about bodies being buried. He had heard a great deal of that kind of talk, when Mr. Tremaine died of the bad fever and Mrs. Tremaine fell out of the window, and Déette Reno was killed in the crusher, and he hoped he would never hear any more. Involuntarily he wriggled a little in his seat, because of the queer feeling in his stomach. Daddy saw him and drew the wrong conclusion, which was something Daddy did more often than Aunt Cresside.

"These kids are getting restless, Cresside. You run them ragged, taking them here, there and everywhere. I wouldn't bother, if I were you. They can't understand what it's all about, over there at the Capitol. Why don't you just let them stay in the yard? Well, time I got them home now anyway. I'll be seeing you. . . ."

Daddy did not say anything more about Sammy Mudge on the way home, and Vail hesitated to say anything himself, because once Daddy dismissed a subject, he did not like to have someone bring it up again. But Vail kept thinking about the horrid little ratlike man, and a few days later, to his surprise and disgust, he saw him again, this time at Belle Heloise.

It was one of those pretty evenings when Miss Mittie was lenient about lessons and Vail had left the old schoolhouse early, and was on his way to the stable to saddle Nostar and Twinkle. Sybelle was not quite through with her sums, which she could not do as fast as he did his, but in a few minutes she was coming to meet him, and they were going up on the levee together. Vail was hurrying, so that he would have both ponies ready by the time she joined him, and he almost ran into Sammy Mudge, who was standing near the old brick stable, half-hidden by the shrubbery clumped around the tall arched windows and talking to Amen, who seemed to be much interested in what he was saying. They both jumped a little as Vail came running up, but Sammy Mudge spoke to him straight off in a way that was meant to be pleasant.

"Why, hello!" he said, grinning in a toothy sort of way. "If it isn't the little fellow who doesn't like gum—unless he's changed his mind. If he has, I've still got plenty. We were just talking about you, sonny."

"Hello," Vail said curtly. He gathered that Sammy Mudge expected him to respond to this second suggestion about gum, and to inquire what the two men were saying about him; but with characteristic stubbornness, he did neither. Instead he swung along towards the stable, intent on getting away from the "foul creature," as Aunt Cresside had called him, and wondering why Amen should have anything to do with him.

"Say, sonny, what's your hurry? Come on back."

Vail went on without turning. But when he reached the stable door, he hesitated for a moment, and then, instead of going in, he ran across the back of the Small Yard to the *garçonnière*, where he found Merry sitting in the living room with Franchot on the floor beside her, playing with his blocks. The little boy jumped up joyfully at the sight of the bigger one and flung two thin little arms around Vail's waist.

"Come build houses for me, Vail. Build me a sugar mill, like the last time."

"Sure I will, Franchot, after supper. I'm going riding with Sybelle right now and I want to see Daddy first. . . . Has Daddy come in from the fields yet, Mummy?"

"Yes, dear, he's in the office."

"Is he by himself or has he got men there?"

"I think he's alone. What's the matter, Vail?"

"Nothing. I just want to see him."

Franchot sought, somewhat clamorously, to detain him, but after repeating his promise about the toy sugar mill, Vail freed himself and ran out again. Gervais, who was just leaving the office, waved a greeting to him.

"Hello there! Through school already?"

"Yeah. Sybelle and I are going up on the levee. . . . Daddy, do you remember that man we saw in the Senate, the one who holds the umbrella?"

"Sammy Mudge? Sure I do. What made you think of him?"

"He's out beside the stable, talking to Amen. He tried to stop me when I went by."

"What do you mean, he tried to stop you?"

"Well, he said for me to come back. But I didn't want to talk to him. You didn't invite him out to Belle Heloise, did you, Daddy?"

"You're darn right I didn't. I'm glad you told me he's here, Vail. I'll have a word with Mr. Sammy Mudge myself. You go ahead and get ready for your ride."

Again Vail hesitated at the stable door. Now that Daddy was there too, he did not want to get away. He wanted to know everything that happened, because it might be exciting. But he knew, from Daddy's expression, that this wasn't Daddy's idea, and he had learned from experience that it was a good thing to respect Daddy's ideas. However, the stable door was wide open and so were all the stable windows, because it was such a pretty evening, and as he saddled the ponies he could not help hearing what Daddy was saying to Sammy Mudge and Amen. He hoped and believed that Daddy would not mind this, because he was not eavesdropping on purpose. . . .

"Hello, Mudge. Quite a ways off your beat, aren't you?"

"I have to do my work on the Highway, you know, Captain d'Alvery."

"Belle Heloise isn't a highway."

"Well, I was inspecting the River Road. You know, well as I do, it's got to be watched when the river's up."

"First time I've known the Highway Commission to worry much about it. Anyway, the river's not up."

"It's rising—at least we got a report that it was due to rise. So the Engineer said for me to come out and have a look. I never knew when I left town that the water in my radiator was low. Must have sprung a leak or something. So I just dropped in to get her filled up. Nothing wrong with that, is there? And now your boy here's got me all fixed ——"

"You'll be on your way again? Good. Sorry he gave you the trouble of walking all the way back to the stable. There's a pump right by the Big House."

There was a brief silence, broken only by the sound of hurrying footsteps. Vail knew that Sammy Mudge must have scuttled off, leaving Amen alone with Daddy. Then he heard Daddy's voice again, even colder and sterner than it had been before.

"I didn't see any water can either. I thought I'd let that pass, because I wanted to get rid of that rat more than I wanted to stand here listening to his lies any longer. But I think you better tell me why he really came here, Amen."

"Ah doesn't know, suh, hones' Ah doesn't, Captain. Ah done give him his water already. Right out ob de pump too, jes' lak you say. De can is settin' right dere now, you can see it fo' yo' ownself. But after us done fill de radiator, Mr. Mudge, he say he never wuz to Belle Heloise befo', he lak to take a little walk aroun' de place——"

"You're darn right, he's never been to Belle Heloise before. What's more, he isn't coming here again. Better get that straight, Amen. Think you have?"

"Yes, suh, Captain. Ah has it good 'n' straight. But——"

"But that still doesn't explain why he should have wanted to take a little walk around the place. Or why you should have let him, without asking me first. Or why you should have been hiding in the bushes, whispering to him. Or why he should have tried to stop Vail."

"Ah di'n' think you'd mind effin he took a little walk around de place, Captain, and us wasn't hidin' in no bushes, us wuz jes' restin' after de walk. An'——"

"Come clean, Amen. You can't put me off with that kind of talk. You'd better tell me what you've really been up to."

Instead of answering directly, Amen began to whine in a different key. "Must be some misconviction, suh. You allus suspicions Ah be's cuttin' up when Ah isn't, lak de time you fin' me and Creassy in de chicken house."

"You're god-damned right I'm suspicious. I know you've got some of the niggers along the Road believing you're a conjure doctor, you no'count, trifling, nappy-headed fraud, and you've just about broken

458

your daddy's heart, carrying on the way you have. There's never been a better man working on this place than Selah, and that's saying plenty, too. We've always had good people working for us at Belle Heloise. You're the only really sorry one I could name."

"Captain, Ah swears to God——"

"You can stop right there, Amen. I never knew you to say you swore to God that you weren't getting ready to tell the damndest lie you could think of. I told you I wanted to know what Sammy Mudge was doing on my place, and you know it. Quit stalling. You better come clean right now if you know what's good for you." ·

"He come to git water, lak he say, and den we done took a little walk an'—oh, please, suh, don't lay hold ob me dat away! Yo' hurts me, yo' hurts me bad! Ain't nothin' mo Ah can say. Mr. Mudge he jes' axed me wuz yo' all good friends with Mr. Sylvestre and Miss Regine when dey wuz alive."

· "All right, we're getting somewhere now. I'll let go of you after you've told me the truth. What did you say when he asked·you that?"

"Ah say, yo' wuzn't friends exactly, leastwise Ah disremembers ever seein' yo' all ever actin' lak yo' wuz friends. Ah done hear though, a long while back, things wuz different."

"What was different?"

"Dat yo' and Miss Regine wuz friends, but dat yo' didn' want to be friends no mo' 'count ob Miss Merry. An' dat Miss Regine she took on 'caze she wuz mad an' den she done stole Miss Cresside's beau away from her an' marry him."

"You told Sammy Mudge all this dirty gossip about your own white folks?"

"No, suh. Yes· suh. Le' go mah arm, please, Captain, suh. Ah never meant no harm, Ah wuz jes' passin' de time ob day, lak us duz sometimes——"

"Listen to me now, Amen, and get this good. I don't aim to say it again. If ever I hear of you talking to strangers about the d'Alverys or any of their kinfolks, or if ever I hear of you and that bastard Mudge even being seen together, I'm going to kill you. You wouldn't be able to run far enough or fast enough to get away from me. . . . I ought to give you a hiding right now, but I'm afraid if I started, I wouldn't stop till I did kill you sure enough. You know me, Amen. You know I'm not just making talk. Mind now, the next time there'll be no questions and no talk—just one awful dead nigger, and that'll be you."

Again there was a sound of scurrying footsteps. Vail stood still, a new kind of fear gripping at his heart. He had heard Daddy speak loudly and harshly a good many times when he did not understand what it was all about, but he had never before known him to say he would kill anyone, and the threat gave Vail the same queer feeling in the pit of his stomach that had come there once or twice already, only now it was worse. He wanted to get out of the stable, and he wished

Sybelle would hurry up and come, so they could go for their ride; her sums must have taken her longer than she expected. . . .

At last he decided not to wait for her any longer, but to build the toy sugar mill for Franchot after all; Sybelle would come and look for him in the *garçonnière* anyway if she did not find him in the stable. He hitched Nostar and Twinkle in their stalls and started back across the yard, walking slowly, and glancing over his shoulder once or twice to see if Sybelle were coming after all. There was no one in sight, but pretty soon he heard sounds from the *garçonnière*: Daddy was still shouting, and Mummy was begging him to hush, the way she did when she was trying to soothe him. But this time Mummy sounded unhappy herself, which was very unlike her. She did not raise her voice, but still it did not sound the way it usually did.

"I know it's dreadful, Gervais, but please try to tell me about it quietly. I'm so afraid someone else will hear you."

"There isn't anyone else around to hear me. Don't you suppose I know? And don't you suppose I know that if Amen told Mudge that much, he told him a lot more? Don't you suppose I know that rat is Long's stool pigeon? Don't you suppose I know he's been sent out here to dig up dirt?"

"Please, Gervais! Please be careful. And please don't be so upset. There's no dirt Mudge could dig up here now. There's nothing Amen knows."

"No dirt? Nothing Amen knows? I'll bet there's nothing he doesn't know! There's been a leak somewhere, there always is. Creassy's always known and Amen's wormed it out of her some way. He's told Mudge everything he knows and Mudge hotfooted it back to Long with the news! I'll bet Long knows by now that Sylvestre Tremaine was Vail's father!"

CHAPTER XXXIV

SAMMY MUDGE LEFT Belle Heloise exceedingly well pleased with himself and his achievements. To be sure, Captain d'Alvery's inopportune appearance had given him a few moments of acute uneasiness. But nothing had come of this after all, to Sammy's intense relief. Placing his umbrella carefully beside him on the seat, and settling back in his car with a good grip on the wheel, he prepared to enliven the long drive to Maringouin with a mental review of the recent successes which had followed a long series of failures.

This was by no means the first time that Sammy had been summoned to a secluded hide-out, deep in the swamps near Maringouin:

a "camp" to which Huey Long retired at intervals, ostensibly for mental relaxation and strenuous physical exercise. A few of his boon companions generally accompanied him to this sylvan retreat, which was reached by one of many obscure logging roads transecting the region, and it was presumably the society of these cronies which afforded him the mental relaxation; a wood pile in the rear of the house—a weather-beaten cabin rising on stilts above a relatively high piece of cleared ground—suggested the wherewithal for strenuous exercise. But Sammy Mudge had never found His Excellency engaged in making the chips fly. Instead it was his experience that after he had passed the armed guards who were stationed along the logging trail, he would be met in front of the shack by Clovis, the wizened and toothless caretaker, with whom he would exchange a brief greeting. After that Clovis would disappear inside, where Huey was invariably ensconced, and announce the arrival and identity of the visitor. Sometimes this announcement met with an immediate response, and sometimes it was repeated over and over again before it was acknowledged in any way; but the acknowledgment, when it came, varied very little in form.

"All right, all right! Tell the son-of-a-bitch to wait."

The interval which followed was generally a long one, and Sammy Mudge became very tired before it was over. No one ever asked him to sit down, and though he leaned on his faithful umbrella, this did not give him as much support as he might have wished. No one ever offered him any refreshment either, and he was always hungry and thirsty after his tiresome ride; a bottle of beer and a sandwich, or even a coke and a cracker, would have helped a lot, especially on those occasions when he had failed in his appointed mission and knew he was in for a dressing-down. Now that at last he had succeeded beyond his fondest hopes in ferreting out the facts concerning a secret scandal, he did not need a stimulant as much as usual; but it was hard for him to control his impatience as he stood leaning on his umbrella and waiting for Long to appear. He was eager to tell his story, produce his evidence, and receive his reward. . . .

He had begun to feel that he had passed the point of endurance when the Governor of Louisiana emerged from the shadow of the doorway and crossed the narrow gallery of the shack, scratching himself as he came. His appearance was even more bizarre than when he had first startled the state by his eccentricities, and the insolence of his manner and bearing had become more obvious with the years. His hair was tousled above an unshaven face, and he wore nothing but pajama pants and bedroom slippers, the scantiness of this attire accentuating the ungainliness of his body. Without the slightest sign that he had even seen his faithful henchman, he squatted down on the steps, called over his shoulder for a cup of coffee and then sat staring straight ahead of him till Clovis brought it. Having consumed it, still with no sign of recognition to Sammy, he called in the same loud tone of voice for a cigar, and after getting this, sat chewing it without lighting it for some minutes more. Then, without warning, he turned and roared at Sammy Mudge.

"Find out anything?"

Sammy jumped and then swallowed hard, in his effort to collect himself quickly. But he did not allow his great moment to escape him. He managed to answer promptly and adequately.

"Sure I found out something."

"All right. What?"

"Well, d'Alvery's still mighty short of cash. He's paid off some of his notes, but there's a lot of 'em on call yet. They come to around a hundred and fifty thousand——"

"Jesus, what I got to contend with! Ain't every mortgage in this state recorded so any fool can go and look at it? Ain't I got a bank examiner with a tongue in his head? Every nigger on the River Road knows d'Alvery's hard up."

"I just mentioned the money like in passing, Governor. I heard a lot of talk about that along with the rest, and so naturally——"

"What do you mean, the rest?"

"The rest I found out about the d'Alverys. While I was down on the River Road, inspectin', I run out of water for my radiator and——"

"I don't give a good god-damn about your radiator——"

"All right. . . . One of them twins at Belle Heloise ain't a twin."

"What do you mean?"

"That boy ain't no twin of that girl and he ain't Gervais d'Alvery's boy."

"Who you been talking to?"

"Well, I been talking to Durice Reno, that old blister of Blood's, for one. And I been talking to that conjure nigger they got on Belle Heloise. You see——"

Long jumped up, ran his hands impatiently through his tousled hair, threw his half-chewed cigar into a puddle and sat down again. "Listen! Will you for Christ's sake come to the point?" he shouted. "So you've talked to some whores and some niggers and you can prove by them the d'Alverys took in a baby and raised it for one of theirs! You mean it was the Captain's kid by some other woman?"

Sammy smirked toothily. "Better'n that, Governor. This is his sister's kid."

"Why, you crazy weasel-head, his sister's married to Fabian d'Alvery. She'd be raising her own children if that was her boy. Anybody would know that much; anybody except maybe you."

"No, Governor, it's like this: you take some time back she used to go with that guy Tremaine at Hathaway and she got hooked. So when the baby was born d'Alvery and his wife covered up for her on account it was born just about the same time as d'Alvery's little girl; they made off like Mrs. d'Alvery had had twins. But only one of the kids was hers, the other one, this boy, was his sister's."

Long dropped his head between his shoulders and stared fixedly at the ratty little man as though trying to hypnotize him. Sammy shifted his umbrella nervously from one hand to the other and finally broke into speech. "Honest, Governor," he began placatingly. "I'm telling you how——"

"Shut your damn-fool face! Here I am working night and day trying to do something for the people of this state and I got to rely on dumb half-wits like you for what little help I need." He suddenly straightened up like an uncoiled spring. "If I have Joe and Tony take you out in the middle of that swamp and leave you there, you reckon you could ever find your way out? Well, that's what I got a good mind to do."

"But Governor——"

"Don't you 'but Governor' me. What the hell are you trying to do, get me shot? Get me run out of Baton Rouge?"

"But look, Governor, I even brought you this snapshot I bought off that conjure nigger at Belle Heloise. It's a picture of this kid's daddy when he was a kid himself, and it's the spittin' image of that boy like he looks today excusing his clothes."

"Give me that god-damn thing." Long snatched at the photograph, tore it into fragments without looking at it, and threw the pieces at his retainer. "You and your 'I thoughts,'" he snarled. "I can send out in that swamp and get varmints that are smarter than you, yes, and that smell better. If there was any use explaining. . . . But what the hell. I could make more dough talking to the side of this house. If I don't have you killed, you think you got sense enough to keep your trap shut? Because one way or another it's going to be kept shut."

"Sure, Governor, sure. I only tried to do what you wanted."

"You better try to do what I don't want. Maybe you'll get it right that way. Get back to Baton Rouge and don't let me see you again till I send for you." And as Sammy, crestfallen but obedient, started off, Long shouted, "Wait," and turned towards the shack. "Got those things wrapped up, Clovis?"

A muffled but affirmative answer came from within. "All right. Put 'em in a box and bring 'em out here," Long directed. Then, turning to Mudge again, he went on, "Couple of fish and a soft-shell turtle. Take 'em in to Joe King at the Heidelberg. Tell him to put 'em on ice for me. Think you've got sense enough not to get to Baton Rouge with a dead skunk instead of these catfish?"

"Sure, Governor, I'll take 'em right to the hotel."

"And call up Oscar and Jesse and tell 'em I want to see em here first thing tomorrow morning."

"I'll telephone straight off soon as I've given Mr. King the fish."

The wizened caretaker had reappeared, carrying a long box, and handed it silently to Mudge, who stowed it away in the rear of the car. Sammy, somewhat cheered by this new evidence of trust, got in himself and leaned out of the window.

"So long, Governor. Count on me. I'll see to everything."

He disappeared down the rough road between the watchful guards. Long looked after him, a quizzical expression on his pudgy face, as he stood scratching himself luxuriously. Then he turned back into the house.

The details of this scene were, of course, unknown to Gervais. But his assumption that Mudge had "hotfooted" it to Long became a certainty two days later, when he received a curt note summoning him to see the Governor the following morning at ten o'clock. He handed it to Merry, on returning from the Capitol that evening and, lighting a cigarette, began to pace restlessly up and down the long room, awaiting her comment.

"He's sent for you before, hasn't he?"

"You know he has. I told you about the offer he made me."

"Then mightn't he just want to make you another?"

"Merry, you're guileless, but you're not all that guileless. There isn't but one Lieutenant Governorship and I've turned that down already. It would have meant a lot to me, too, not just in itself, but as a stepping stone. I'd have jumped at it, if I could have had it on the level. But there's nothing else he could offer me at the moment, even if he wanted to, and you may be damn sure he doesn't. This time he's got it in for me."

She came up to him and put her hand tenderly on his arm. "I wish you wouldn't take all this so hard, honey," she said. "It troubles me when I see you worried. What difference would it make if Long did have it in for you?"

"Plenty. You don't seem to realize, Merry, how much I care about going ahead, politically. Not just for my sake, either. For yours and the children's. I'd like to see you all in the Mansion, I'd like to take you all to Washington——"

"But I thought you loved Belle Heloise better than any place in the world. You said when you came back after the War that you never wanted to leave it again."

"This isn't a case of what I love. It's a case of what I accomplish. And I just said, not only for myself——"

"I'm sure I'm happier at Belle Heloise than I would be in the Mansion or in Washington, Gervais. I'm sure the children are better off here, too. It's a wonderful place for children. They're all thriving, they're all happy. . . . At least they're nearly always well, they're nearly always lively. Of course Franchot isn't quite as strong as the others and I've been a little troubled about Vail these last few days. He hasn't seemed like himself."

"I haven't noticed anything. What do you think's the matter?"

"Well, he's hardly talked at all, for one thing."

"There's nothing unusual about that. Vail never talks much."

"No, but he talks some, and when he's silent, he's still companionable. This is different. He's acted as if he didn't want to talk to anybody. He hasn't eaten much either."

"Probably needs a good dose of castor oil. Why don't you give it to him?"

"Because I don't think there's anything the matter with him physically; I think he's got something on his mind. Miss Mittie went back to the schoolhouse yesterday for something she'd forgotten and found him there poring over a dictionary. She's been trying for a long time to teach him to use one without the slightest success, so naturally she was startled at finding him absorbed like that, and anyway, it isn't like him to stay indoors after school hours—he always wants to get out and run around, you know that. Miss Mittie asked him if she could help him find what he wanted, and he shut up the dictionary and went off without answering her. Later on I saw him riding on the levee, but he was alone—I never knew him to start off before without Sybelle, and she felt terribly. It was all I could do to comfort her. He won't play with the other children either and you know how kind he's always been to them."

"I still think castor oil's your answer. Vail's never tormented Joyeuse and Franchot, I'll say that for him; just the same he's always been stubborn and contrary. Dose him and then leave him alone. He'll come around all right. Anyway, don't worry me about him just now. I've got enough on my mind as it is. . . . Another thing you don't seem to realize, Merry, is that this isn't just a case of losing out, politically. It's a case of fighting probable blackmail and everything that goes with it. I've always told you we'd have to face the music sometime. I reckon that time's now."

"And you still think it wouldn't help to tell Fabian?"

"Tell Fabian? That Long's fixing to spread smut about Cresside?"

"Fabian might be able to stop him. He's pretty powerful, you know, after all, in his quiet way. At least I should think it would be worth trying."

"I don't. I know it's the last thing on earth I ought to try."

As a matter of fact, he did not dismiss the suggestion quite as abruptly as his words and manner indicated. Lying sleepless beside Merry during the long night, he considered the question from every possible angle. But in the end, he found that his viewpoint was the same as it had been in the beginning; and it was still unchanged the following morning when he met his cousin accidentally in the lobby of the Heidelberg Hotel. Fabian, whose cynical outlook on life had been greatly tempered by his happy marriage and triumphant fatherhood, greeted Gervais with a genial grin.

"Hello there! What's your hurry? Come on into the coffee shop and tell me what's cooking at the Capitol while we snatch us a small black."

"I'd like to, but I haven't got time."

"What's the matter? The legislature doesn't meet till eleven, does it?"

"No, but I've been summoned to the clown prince's presence."

"Where, at the State House?"

"No, in his highness's suite up on the tenth floor."

"Better take him tribute in the form of strawberries and cream. They tell me he's a sucker for that."

"It's an idea. I think I'd know just where to put 'em, too. But I don't believe they'd do the trick this time."

"What's it all about?"

Gervais shed his lightness of manner. "I wish I could honestly say I didn't know," he said rather ruefully. "But I think I do. The way matters stand we're out to beat that bond-issue scheme of Long's with its sixty-million-dollar slush fund. It squeezed through the House by one vote, but with Cyr on our side in the Senate, Pike Hall and Boone and John Caffery are all set to talk it to death in as fine a filibuster as ever was put over."

"I know, everybody's talking about that on the streets."

"Well, I think the crazy bastard is going to threaten me to bring me around to his side." Gervais lowered his voice. "Believe it or not, he's already offered me the Lieutenant Governorship in the next election. I bet John Fournet would give birth to a litter of goats if he knew it. But naturally I turned it down."

"And now you figure it will be the straight iron fist with no velvet glove? What the hell could he possibly threaten you with?"

Gervais hesitated, thinking again of what Merry had said about Fabian and aware that his cousin suspected he had not spoken with complete candor. Then he shrugged his shoulders impatiently. "Who knows what the maniac has in his mind?" he muttered and turned hastily towards the elevator. "See you in church," he called back as he entered the cage and the mirrored doors slid shut.

A swart thick-shouldered man was pacing up and down the hall near a wide door which shut off two rooms at the end of the corridor into a single suite. He gazed at Gervais impassively as he approached.

"All right, Joe. You can tell his Nibs I'm here," Gervais informed him.

Without a change of expression, Joe turned and knocked on the door. It was opened by a muscular young man with close-cropped blond hair. He was coatless and thus exposed a well-filled shoulder holster. "It's the Senator," Joe announced.

"Yeah, sure," agreed the guard. "Come in here, Senator. The Governor's taking a bath. He'll be right out."

This prediction was almost immediately verified as Long, wet and glistening, stepped from the bathroom onto the thick-piled rug of the parlor, toweling himself briskly. "Sit down, Senator," he urged. "Hope

466

you ain't as fussy as that Admiral who like to got me shot for treason because I never had nothing on but my pajamas when he come up to see me."

Gervais chuckled. "No, I'm not fussy, Governor," he assured his host, accepting the proffered chair.

"You know," Long said, toweling himself more slowly. "It's a funny thing. You take when I was a kid up in Winnfield, folks thought if you took one bath a week that was a plenty. Now you got to bathe every day. No telling what they'll think up next."

Gervais accepted this bit of social philosophy without attempting to elaborate on it. "No use beating about the bush, Governor," he said. "You wanted to see me about something."

"That's right," agreed Long. He turned to face the bedroom. 'Murphy, bring me my socks and drawers," he called.

"Well, here I am," suggested Gervais.

"What I wanted to talk to you about was this program of mine for helping everybody in this state. Now we give 'em the free schoolbooks, even though they went to the Supreme Court of the United States to try and stop me, and we got the good roads started, but we got to keep the work going. You know folks need jobs. I expect you've heard about that crash that Wall Street rigged up on the country. We pass this bond-issue bill and that'll help everybody. It'll give us the roads, and the Lord knows that the people of this state need 'em, and building the roads will give jobs to people that ain't got 'em."

"Governor, my mind's made up about that," Gervais said unsmilingly. "I haven't changed it since we talked the other day."

Long, who had put on and laced his shoes, rose from his chair, stamped his feet tentatively and called to the bedroom, "Where the hell's my pants?" Then he turned to Gervais. "You know there's more ways to kill a cat, Senator, besides choking it to death with cream cheese," he said slowly.

"Meaning just what?" Gervais asked.

"Meaning I tried to show you how we could help each other, but you wouldn't listen. This time I'm telling you you better help me out on this bond-issue bill."

"Governor, are you threatening me?"

"I most assuredly ain't. If I was a mind to threaten, there's a couple of stout boys with guns to back me up, so you don't need to bow your neck any."

"Suppose you say in plain English just what you're after."

"All right. What would you say if I was to tell you that I know plenty about what's been going on at that plantation of yours?"

Well, I knew that was it all the time, Gervais said to himself. *I knew it was coming and here it is. It's no surprise, so it ought't to be a shock either. But it is. A thing like this always hits you harder than you figure it's going to, when it finally comes, no matter how well prepared you think you are for it.* Aloud he only remarked stiffly, "I'd say that blackmail was a little out of line among the duties of a Governor."

"Who's blackmailing anybody, d'Alvery? Listen, you're a silk stocking. I'm a country boy from Winn Parish. I got every big corporation in the state and every big newspaper and every crooked politician fighting me. The way that John Sullivan double crossed me, do you think I'm going to ask Emily Post what fork I should use when I'm fighting back? I got the common people of this state to study about. They're the ones trusting me. They're the ones crying for these roads and I aim to see them get 'em. You got one vote that I need. John Parker could get a vote out of you whenever he wanted to, just by talking to you. Well, I guess I ain't got his highbrow winning ways, the kind you take to, and when I offered to dicker with you the other day you wouldn't listen. So, if there's ary a way under the shining sun I can buy that vote out of you, or club it out, I aim to do it."

"Do you really think, Governor Long, that you or anybody else on earth could bribe me or club me into doing something dishonest?"

"What's dishonest about giving poor people roads?"

"The dishonest part is handing you sixty million dollars that you'll use to line the pockets of your special friends, if not your own directly, for the control of every election in this state during the next ten years."

Long suddenly chuckled. "Do you for true think I'll take ten years to spend that dough?" he asked.

"Certainly not," retorted Gervais. "I was talking about the control— if somebody doesn't shoot you first."

Long snorted. "Somebody'll have to shoot it out with a lot of boys that'll be shooting back before he ever shoots me. But that ain't either here nor yonder. . . . Ever think of resigning from the Senate?"

"No, never."

"Well, you might."

"And if I don't?"

"Well, if you don't, and if you don't dicker either, some of the things I know about what's been going on at that high and mighty plantation of yours will be put to use. And before you say anything to that, you might stop and think what it'll mean to you and all your kinnery."

Gervais rose and crossed the room without replying. Then with his hand on the door knob, he turned. "Sorry, Governor, no sale," he said coldly. "Pop your whip any time you choose. But don't forget that once you have popped it, it'll be my turn."

CHAPTER XXXV

In spite of Gervais' contention that nothing was the matter with Vail, Merry remained unconvinced. However, she was secretly almost as much disturbed over her husband's break with Long as he was himself, and the lesser anxiety was swallowed up in the greater one. She continued her efforts to tempt the little boy's appetite, and she gently reminded him, several times, that he was hurting the other children's feelings by his unreasonable refusal to play with them. But she did not make repeated attempts to draw him out, and having won his confidence, to comfort him, as she would have done if she had been less anxiously absorbed. Vail, sensing her preoccupation without understanding the reason for it and increasingly hurt and perplexed, withdrew further and further into his protective shell.

Much of the conversation which he had so unfortunately overheard was still incomprehensible to him. But one fact stood out inescapably: Sylvestre Tremaine, whom he had always hated with all his might and main, was his father. The man whom he still habitually labeled as Daddy had said so, angrily and positively. It was obvious that he resented the relationship as much as Vail himself, but it was also obvious that he was sure of it. And automatically this not only meant that the man Vail called Daddy was not really his father after all, but that Sybelle was not his twin, Joyeuse was not his younger sister, Phil and Franchot were not his brothers and Mummy was not his mother.

All this was so staggering that at first he did not grope beyond it. But presently the question which was its inevitable sequel crossed his troubled mind: if Mummy was not his mother, who was? Certainly not Mrs. Tremaine, for if she had been, he would have lived in that great blank house at Hathaway with her and her husband, instead of at Belle Heloise with Daddy and Mummy—that is, with the d'Alverys. But even if she were not, even if Mr. Tremaine had been married before to some lady who had died, it seemed strange to Vail that Mr. Tremaine had not insisted upon having him live there anyway. Vail knew that men wanted and expected to have their children live with them, at least in all the cases he could think of. There must have been some special reason why Mr. Tremaine did not want him. Or Mrs. Tremaine. He remembered the reluctant and often cruel stepmothers in the fairy stories he had read. That must have been it: his own mother had died, and Mr. Tremaine had not wanted him, or else Mr. Tremaine had been afraid that his new wife would be unkind to him; so they had fixed it up that he should live with the d'Alverys. Just the same it was funny that Mr. Tremaine had never come to see him at Belle Heloise and that he should be called Vail d'Alvery instead of Vail Tremaine. . . .

He was turning over these strange things in his mind, sitting all alone, except for Maud, on the River side of the levee, so that no one would see him from the Road, when, for no reason at all as far as he could see, he remembered something Amen had said: "De d'Alverys ain't never forgive Miss Regine for stealin' Miss Cresside's beau." After he remembered that, he kept on thinking about it. He had heard Daddy—there, it was no use, he couldn't call him anything else—and Uncle Fabian, too, teasing Aunt Cresside about Mr. Charles Boylston, who used to live at Hackberry, down the River Road, and who still came back there once in a while. When they teased her like that, they spoke of Mr. Boylston as her beau, and she did not seem to mind, though she did not joke about it the way they did. But they had never teased her about Mr. Tremaine, and now that Vail thought of it, he remembered that the only time he had ever talked to her when she had not been glad to talk to him in return, was the time he had brought up the subject of Mr. Tremaine. He was sure Amen must be mistaken. He did not believe Mr. Tremaine had ever been Aunt Cresside's beau. If he had been, Daddy and Uncle Fabian would have teased her about that, too, once in a while, and she would have laughed when she listened, the way she did when they teased her about Mr. Charles Boylston.

Vail had practically convinced himself that Amen was mistaken, finding considerable comfort in the conclusion, when he remembered it was this very statement of Amen's which had made Daddy so furious that he began to talk about killing. And afterwards, when Daddy was talking to Mummy, he had said, "Amen *knows*. There's nothing he doesn't know." So it must have been true after all. Daddy was angry because Amen *knew* and because he told what he knew. And this was that Mr. Tremaine had once been Miss Cresside's beau and that Miss Regine had stolen him away from her. It wasn't a joke the way it was about Mr. Charles Boylston. It was a disgrace. People weren't supposed to joke about it; they weren't even supposed to know about it. He had always thought Aunt Cresside was the loveliest lady in the whole world, lovelier even than Mummy, and he knew that Uncle Fabian thought so, too. Uncle Fabian had been her husband for a great many years, and another thing they joked about was the fact that it had taken her a long while to make up her mind to marry him. But some time, even before this, that hateful man, Mr. Tremaine, had been her beau. Daddy was so ashamed of this that he had threatened to kill Amen for speaking of it, and Aunt Cresside must be ashamed of it, too, or she would not have refused to talk about Mr. Tremaine herself. . . .

Vail finally left the levee and walked slowly home with Maud at his heels, the puzzle still unsolved. It was supper time already, and everyone else was at the table; he could hear voices coming from the

470

dining room as he approached the house, and without stopping to wash his hands, he went through the pantry and slid silently into his seat. He fully expected to be scolded, as *grand'mère* was very particular about punctuality at meals, and it was one of those minor matters in which Daddy always sided with her against Mummy. But neither *grand'mère* nor Daddy said anything to him about his tardiness now or even appeared to notice his arrival. They were too busy talking with each other.

"I confess I was surprised at Mr. Goldenberg's call, Gervais. I have always thought he showed remarkable delicacy of perception in recognizing that your transactions with him were confined to business. It is strange that after all these years he should have come here to make a social call."

"Do you remember the Sunday afternoon when that skunk, Bisbee, came out here to make a social call and what happened afterwards?"

"Yes, very well. But surely you do not imagine——"

Daddy laughed, but he did not sound as if he thought anything was funny.

"I don't visualize Goldenberg as a skunk, if that's what you mean. His stripe's different from Bisbee's and he's done the best he could for me. But I think he's probably been put in a damn awkward position himself. Probably he came here to tell me about it, hoping it would be a little easier all round than if he sent for me to come and see him. It would have been, too. I'm sorry I missed him."

"What is this awkward position to which you refer, Gervais?"

"Well, I know that an examiner went to the Citizens National Bank this morning, dead drunk, and started a fearful row. After he'd spent an hour or so in general hell-raising, the President decided it was about time to telephone the Governor and find out what it all proved, as Cresside would say. He did find out."

"Find out what?"

"That Huey wanted the bank to extend some of the notes it meant to call, and call some it meant to extend. He said, if it didn't, he'd have all the state funds on deposit there withdrawn. The Citizens National's in pretty good shape, as banks go these days. But it can't afford to lose those state funds."

"And yours would be among the notes the Governor wanted called?"

"Not a doubt of it. He warned me he was getting ready to club a vote out of me, if he could. This is the first blow."

"But what can you do to save the situation, Gervais, if your assumption is correct?"

"I can't tell you right now, *maman*. I don't know yet myself."

Daddy's voice had begun to be edgy. He did not like to have *grand'-mère,* or anyone else, ask him so many questions. Mummy, who had not said anything so far, spoke now, and there was something

471

the matter with her voice, too. It did not sound edgy, but it sounded very unhappy.

"Mr. Goldenberg came over to the *garçonnière* after he left the Big House, Gervais. He talked to me, too. I haven't had a chance to tell you."

"Well, suppose you wait and tell me a little later on."

Mummy opened her lips and closed them again without making any sound. *Grand'mère* spoke severely.

"Gervais, I should also like to hear what Mr. Goldenberg said to Merry."

"All right. I didn't say you couldn't. But I don't think the table——"

"Selah will not come in again, Gervais, until I ring for him. And fortunately all of this is over the children's heads. . . . Vail, stop pushing the food around on your plate that way. Why don't you eat your supper properly?"

Grand'mère was not eating much supper herself, as far as Vail could see, and neither were Daddy and Mummy. He was tempted to say so, but decided it probably would be better not, so he took up his silver mug and tried to sip some milk. That was easier than gulping down rice and beans. Mummy looked from *grand'mère* to Daddy as if she could not quite decide which one to mind, and then she went on and said what *grand'mère* wanted her to.

"He told me what you thought he'd come to tell you, Gervais. The Governor has threatened the bank and Mr. Goldenberg can't do anything more as a director because the bank can't afford to lose those state funds. You guessed right about that. But Mr. Goldenberg told me something else, too. He said he'd be glad to make you a personal loan. If he did that you could pay off the notes, couldn't you?"

"You mean he'd take over the mortgage himself?"

"That's what he'd have to do, isn't it? I didn't understand exactly how it would work out, but I knew he was trying to be kind and helpful. I knew——"

"And I can tell you what I know. I do understand how it would work out. The Goldenbergs would be the real owners of Belle Heloise instead of the d'Alverys. And if you ask me, that's the way the old Shylock meant to have it work out, from the beginning!"

"Gervais, how can you be so unjust? He's distressed, really he is, about the bank. But he says——"

"I don't want to hear any more about what he says. I've heard too much already. And I'll tell you something else myself: if that wily old Levantine ever gets hold of Belle Heloise, it'll be over my dead body!"

Daddy flung down his napkin and jumped up from the table. Mummy sat very still, and Vail could see that she was crying. *Grand'-mère* sat very still, too, but she held herself bolt upright, and there were no tears on her cheeks. She did not say anything until Daddy had stalked out of the room, and then she reached across the table and took Mummy's hand.

"You must not be so distressed, *chère*," she said. "And you must not reproach yourself, or let Gervais reproach you, for going to Mr. Goldenberg in the first place. Of course, he is not a person whom I should have expected to meet socially, in the old days. But I agree with you he had no ulterior motive in arranging the loan to begin with, and that his purpose in coming here today was kind."

"Would you mind as much as Gervais, Madame Mère—having him take over the mortgage?"

"Yes. I should mind very much. I have kept hoping we could regain a clear title to Belle Heloise ourselves and this arrangement would mean shifting our obligation from an institution to an individual. Any possibility of alien possession is alarming to me, as you know, and this is not only a matter of family pride. There are the children to think of now. We must safeguard their future."

Grand'mère glanced around the table, looking at them all in turn. She had apparently not paid them much mind before that, but Vail knew she always noticed a good deal, whether she seemed to or not. Franchot was half asleep already; he had pushed aside his bunny plate, and was resting his thin little arms on the table and his tousled brown head on his arms. Joyeuse and Phil had finished, too; they were surreptitiously playing cat's cradle behind the cloth. Sybelle was still eating, quietly and daintily; her head was turned away from *grand'mère* but Vail knew that she was listening, as carefully as he was, and that later on, if he would give her the chance, she would talk to him about everything they had heard. . . .

"I do think of them," Mummy was saying. She was not looking around, like *grand'mère*. Her eyes were still on her plate, and her voice still had that unhappy, strangled sound. "I think of them all the time—at least when I'm not thinking about Gervais. I worry about them all the time, too. Gervais thinks I never worry about anything, but that's because he's a man. I worry because there's so much I can't do for either him or the children, no matter how hard I try. Gervais needs a heap of money to pay his debts and keep this plantation running, and they're going to need a heap, too, for a good home and a good education and a good start in the world. I know how important Belle Heloise is to them. The good home isn't any problem as long as we've got this, but it would be if we lost it. And even with it I don't see how on earth we're going to give so many of them all the advantages they ought to have."

"Hush!" *grand'mère* said warningly. But it was too late. Vail had been so concerned, since he came in to supper, about Daddy and Mummy, that he had forgotten all about himself for a few minutes. Now he remembered his own troubles again, and these began looming up before him, larger than ever. When *grand'mère* finally gave the signal to leave the table, and Sybelle asked eagerly, what about playing jackstraws, he said, go ahead and play with Phil, if she wanted to; he was going out and he did not want her tagging along either. But instead of going out, he went up to his room and sat for a long time fingering the piggy bank that stood on his dresser, between the picture of Aunt Cresside, riding an elephant in Ceylon, and the battered brush and comb which he always neglected to use unless someone came along and made him.

For some time now Vail had been given an allowance of a dollar a week, and he had been taught, out of this sum, to save money for contributions in church, deposits in the piggy bank, and presents for the family and the servants; he had also been allowed to spend money from it on movies and candies and marbles and similar items. He had always been very proud of this allowance, and had managed it fairly well, keeping accounts in a little ruled book which Miss Mittie recognized as part of his equipment for satisfactory progress in arithmetic. Aside from planning how to use his allowance, he had never thought much about money. But he remembered that several times, no matter how carefully he planned, he had not had enough to get or do the things he wanted, and if Daddy advanced him small sums on such occasions, it was always harder to balance his little ruled book afterwards, and in the end he had to go without more than in the beginning. So he understood that something like this was worrying Daddy and Mummy now. Daddy was troubled because he had spent more money than there really was on things he wanted, which evidently worked out badly for everyone, and Mummy was troubled because there would not be enough money to give so many children all the things they were going to want. She would not have needed so much if there had not been so many children. She had said so, before *grand'mère* had hushed her up, and Vail could see for himself how that would work out. It must take a lot of money for five children, more than twice as much than if there had been only two children. And even if there were four instead of five, that would help some. It did not seem fair to him that Daddy and Mummy should have to keep on spending money on a boy who was not theirs after all, when they had two boys of their own, and two girls as well.

He kept thinking about this before he went to sleep that night, and afterwards he dreamed about it, in a confused way. The next morning when he waked up he was not sure, at first, just how much he had heard at the supper table and how much he had dreamed, but he talked things over, very cautiously, with Sybelle, making her happy by seeking her out, of his own accord, for the first time in several days, and afterwards some things were clear to him, because Sybelle, who had listened to every word, just as he supposed, knew exactly what had been said at the table. But there were still other things which were not clear to him, and he kept on thinking about those. He could not see yet why he had always lived at Belle Heloise

474

if Mr. Tremaine was his father; he could not understand why Aunt Cresside would not talk about Mr. Tremaine if he had been her beau and why Daddy wanted to kill Amen for doing so; he could not guess who his mother had been. . . .

Sybelle had seemed so pleased because he had gone out of his way to find her, and had been so helpful about untangling dreams from things which had really happened, that finally he decided to seek her out a second time and see if she could help with these other problems, too. He found her sitting under the mimosa tree in Angus Holt's garden, all dressed up clean for the evening in a white dress and white socks, the big bow on top of her golden head bobbing a little as she bent over a book in which she was apparently much absorbed. Vail thought he had never seen her look so nice, and it came over him that though he had treated her badly these last few days, he loved her better than anyone else in the world, except his Aunt Cresside. The realization that she was not his twin after all, or even his sister, smote him afresh.

"Hello, there," he said carelessly. "Gee, you read lots, don't you? I wish I could read that much. I've got so many other things to do, I can't."

"It's too bad," Sybelle said understandingly. She did not dispute the greater demands which a boy would naturally have upon his time, but yielded the point with feminine tact and feminine graciousness. "I wish you could read this anyway," she went on, eager to share her pleasure with him. "It's grand. It isn't one of our own books that we got Christmas. It's a book I found in the library."

She spoke somewhat smugly. The children were not supposed to take books from the library without permission, and as a matter of fact, not many books were casually left around there; most of them were kept in locked secretaries. Evidently Sybelle had "put something over" on their elders, and felt pleased about it, rather than guilty.

"What's the book about?" Vail inquired, without going into the ethics of the situation. He really did not care much, but he wanted to make up to Sybelle for treating her so badly, and he could see that she wanted to talk about the book.

"A foundling," Sybelle said, still smugly. "I adore stories about foundlings, don't you?"

"I don't know. What do you mean, foundlings?"

"Well, sometimes they're princes in disguise, of course. I like those best of all. But this one isn't. It's just about a poor little baby whose own father and mother didn't want it."

"Why not?" Vail inquired, pricking up his ears. He had not dared to hope this would be so easy.

"Well, his father was a very wicked man who did something queer to his sweetheart."

"What do you mean, something queer?"

"I don't just understand. But she was terribly ashamed of it anyway. And afterwards she had a baby and she didn't want anyone to know."

There was a slight pause. Then Sybelle whispered a hesitant question.

"Vail, do you know how babies come?"

"Yes," Vail answered abruptly, flushing as he did so and thinking about Maud.

"I wish you'd tell me."

"Well, I won't."

"All right then, don't. But anyway, I think what happened in this book—the queer thing, I mean, had something to do with the baby coming. Does something queer happen, Vail? You might tell me that much."

"It isn't queer exactly. But——"

"Well, but Mummy and Daddy weren't ashamed of having babies, Vail. They were pleased. And Uncle Fabian and Aunt Cresside were pleased about Frances Belle. Terribly pleased. I think you're a meanie not to explain. And I think from something this book said, that whatever happens, it's all right if you're married, but if you're not ... Listen, Vail." Sybelle picked up the book and began to spell out loud. "Do you know what i-l-l-e-g-i-t-i-m-a-t-e means? That's what this baby was. He wasn't just a foundling, he was an i-l-l-e-g-i-t-i-m-a-t-e child. In lots of places they call him a bastard, too, and it seems to mean the same thing. I've heard the men on the place talk about bastards, especially black ones, haven't you, Vail? But I don't believe they meant the same thing that this book does. I never heard them say that a black bastard was an i-l-l-e- —what's the matter, Vail?"

"Nothing. I've got lots to do, that's all. I can't stand here all day, talking about some fool book you've read and waiting for you to spell out long words."

"But Vail, I thought you wanted to hear. I thought you said you wished you had more time to read yourself. I thought—Vail, please come back!"

Vail had wheeled suddenly away from her and was running through the garden towards the wicket gate that led to the Yankee cemetery. Sybelle threw down her book and ran after him, but the grass had not been cut that spring and it was tall and thick. She stumbled on some stones which were hidden by it and fell down, tearing her pretty white dress and barking her dimpled knees. When she got to her feet again, whimpering a little with pain, Vail had already crossed the cypress grove. Sybelle saw him plunging into the bushes beyond it and after that she lost sight of him.

So she never knew that he had flung himself down on the grave shielded by the strange tree where flowering thorn and bitter fruit grew together, and that he was crying as if his heart would break.

CHAPTER XXXVI

WITHIN A FEW HOURS of its appearance, reports of the outrageous scene at the Citizens National Bank were spreading like wildfire through the capital and the state. Hardly a man came into Fabian d'Alvery's office that afternoon who talked about anything else. This was by no means the first evidence of the Governor's high-handed methods in punishing people who got in his way and rewarding his faithful followers; but it affected more men in each group, and it hit harder and closer than anything that had happened in Baton Rouge before. The city seethed with resentment, rage, fear and excitement.

When Fabian started home, he was still undecided whether to mention the occurrence to Cresside immediately, or to wait until she spoke of it to him, of her own accord. It would not take her long to realize that her brother would be affected by the disgraceful contretemps; she had known about the loan from the beginning, and Gervais had never made the slightest secret of his enmity for Long. Fabian, who always liked to think things through before speaking of them to anyone, and who seldom acted with haste, finally decided to sleep on the matter, at least; if Cresside had said nothing by the time he left for the office the next day, he would broach the subject. Momentarily he had forgotten that they were to entertain out-of-town guests that evening, some agreeable people named Townsend whom they had met in the course of their travels, and who were now breaking a transcontinental trip in New Orleans. The Townsends had written ahead suggesting that they should come up to Baton Rouge on purpose to see the d'Alverys, and the response had taken the form of a cordial invitation. When he remembered this, Fabian realized that their friends would probably have arrived before he reached the house himself, and that the conversation would almost automatically be slanted towards past pleasures which they had all enjoyed together, and not towards some local fracas of which the less said the better to outsiders who might still be unaware of Louisiana's political disgrace.

His assumption proved correct. He found Cresside seated at ease on the garden terrace with the four Townsends grouped around her, listening lazily while her enthusiastic visitors recalled the details of a day they had all spent together in Cintra, and saying excitedly that none of the gardens they had seen there surpassed the d'Alverys' in charm. It was true that this had become increasingly beautiful with the years. Shortly before his marriage, Fabian had bought two lots which adjoined his own, torn down the ramshackle little houses which had long been an eyesore to him, and surrounded the entire area with a high brick wall. Previously his shrubs and flowers had been planted in a haphazard manner, even his cherished camellias

477

being stuck in here and there every which way. He had enjoyed working in his garden, and it had reflected fostering care, but it had been without orderly design. When he called in a landscape gardener to help him make it worthy of his bride's reception, the combination of this expert's knowledge with his own money and eagerness had worked wonders. Soon flagstone walks were bordered with bright-colored flowers, shrubs were clumped for effectiveness, a lawn formed a wide unbroken expanse of emerald green. At one end there was a lily pool, at the other a fountain rising above the statue of a smiling child, and in the center a sundial recording the radiant hours. The enclosure became one of infinite harmony and peace.

Fabian had been amply rewarded by Cresside's appreciation of his efforts and his thoughtfulness. She quickly came to share his delight in his garden and to pass a great deal of time there; it was her preferred place for resting and reading, for playing with Frances Belle and Belizaire, for spending long quiet periods with her husband after his day's work was over. It was also her chosen center for entertaining. When the camellias were at the height of their bloom, she gave small garden parties almost every week. Wearing an exquisite pastel-colored dress and carrying a large shallow basket over her arm and a pair of long shears in her hand, she would lead her guests proudly from one beauty spot to another, and as they progressed, she would clip the choicest blossoms that they passed and lay these tenderly in her basket. Later on, after coffee and drinks on the terrace, each of the guests was given a little flower-covered tray to take home, the different varieties carefully divided to produce the most charming effect—alba plenas on one tray, Magnolia Floras on another, Pink Perfections and Purple Dawns on still others. Fabian nearly always joined Cresside on these occasions, making the rounds of the garden with her and calling her attention to the perfect blooms that she had missed. He experienced a deep satisfaction from having her entertain in this way, so adequately and graciously, yet with such tranquility and simplicity. He told her so, and touched by his feeling about it and his way of expressing this, she created more and more occasions for hospitality of this type. Everyone in Baton Rouge considered it a compliment to be asked to one of Mrs. Fabian d'Alvery's garden parties, and invitations for house guests were eagerly sought and highly prized.

The camellias had been gone for months now, of course; their falling petals had made small circular carpets on the grass beneath the laden trees, some snowy, some rosy, some flaming. Cresside loved them better when they lay like that than at any other time, she said, though they were past the point of picking then, and there was an interval between parties before the azaleas were at their height; after those came successively the daffodils and iris, the roses and gardenias. In the interval she and Fabian kept the garden to themselves and their child and their dog, cherishing it more and more all the time.

Later in the season, like this, only a few roses remained, and only the gladioli and zinnias were at their best; neither Fabian nor Cresside cared as much for these as they did for the earlier flowers. But the guests from the north had never seen such gladioli and such zinnias in the course of all their travels, and kept saying so. Besides, the grass was still like green velvet, and the pool was covered with lilies floating among their pads and the fountain trickled softly through the evening quietude. All these aspects of the garden enhanced its loveliness and deepened the peace with which it was permeated. Fabian could not bring himself to speak of crassness and calamity in such an atmosphere.

After they reached the dinner table, he decided that this was not the time nor the place either. Carmelite had always been a superlative cook but it had taken Cresside's guiding hand to supply a setting worthy of her masterpieces, and Cresside's piquant presence to add the final touch of charm to a feast. The lace-covered table was set with shining silver, fragile glass and precious porcelain; it was lighted with tall tapers and decorated with exquisite flowers; and as Fabian glanced across it at his wife, he thought that she herself had never looked lovelier than she did that night. Without being beautiful, in the sense that Merry was beautiful, she created a greater effect of beauty. Fabian knew that this effect was only an illusion, but he also knew that it was the reflection of an inner radiance which was real. By encompassing Cresside with tenderness and devotion he had done far more than give her present happiness. He had made her feel that her security was impregnable; he had effaced the very memory of past pain and danger. The restless and riotous years, like the years of shame and suffering, were all behind her now. Her life was one of walled gardens and candle-lighted rooms, of quiet, well-ordered days and nights beatified by close communion with a man who loved her and whom she loved. . . .

The dinner progressed, smoothly and delightfully, from the perfect soup with which it began to the perfect pudding with which it ended. The Townsends continued to recall the pleasant excursions which the d'Alverys had shared with them, and to express the hope that they might have similar experiences in the future. Why not, Fabian said, looking across the table again and seeing that the suggestion was pleasing to Cresside; they had not liked to leave their little girl for any length of time, so since her birth they had not traveled much. But presently she would be old enough to travel herself—oh, not around the world, perhaps, but certainly as far as Europe. He had been intending to look up those castles in Spain where the early de Alverez had lived before they crossed over into Southern France and became d'Alverys instead. Spain was a very pleasant place; for the matter of that, Southern France was a very pleasant place, too. They could probably find a suitable villa in Pau where Frances Belle could be installed with a competent and trustworthy governess, and which he and Cresside could use as a center for their side trips. He had always wanted to spend at least a week in Carcasonne, and to go from there to Nimes and Arles and Avignon. Was that the sort of excursion the Townsends would enjoy, too?

Exactly, they told him with enthusiasm, and after dinner was over and Frances Belle had come in to make her curtsy and say good night, Fabian set up a tilt-top table and spread motor maps of Europe on it. When these were finally folded up and put away, everyone was astonished to find how late it was. A tray laden with soda siphons and excellent liquor was brought in and put down where the maps had been and Cresside mixed the drinks which Fabian passed. But the Townsends did not linger over these. It had been a wonderful evening, they said, but if they did not go then they never would. Well, they'd keep in touch with the d'Alverys about the French trip —next summer ought to be the very time. Good night, good night. . . .

Carmelite and the house boy who had been added to the small but efficient domestic staff had already left for the night. Cresside and Fabian took the drinks and the ash trays out to the neat quiet kitchen themselves, gave the living room the final touches which would leave it orderly for the morning, looked in on Frances Belle to see that she was sleeping quietly, made the rounds of the outside doors to make sure that these were locked. But as they reached the one leading into the garden, Cresside opened it again.

"Let's go out for a moment more, shall we? It's such a lovely night!"

They stepped out on the little terrace. The starlight was very soft and the tapering forms of the trees were reflected in dark shadows across the smooth lawn. Not only the fragrance of flowers but all the subtle scents of summer were in the air. Cresside slid her hand into her husband's.

"You know what I've been thinking all evening, Fabian?"

"Sure. I'm the world's champion mind reader." He laughed and leaned over to kiss her hair. "Don't encourage me to talk nonsense by doing it yourself. You know crystal gazing isn't in my line. Tell me straight out."

"I've been thinking that no one has the right to be as happy as I am."

"Why not?"

"I don't know. Perhaps because there's so much misery in the world."

"We all get our share of it sometime," Fabian said. Then, because he did not want any words of his to remind her about the share she had had, he added hastily, "Don't forget that if you're all that happy, you make me mighty happy, too."

"Do I really?"

"You know it, don't you?"

"I hope so . . . Yes, I do know it."

480

"And you really are all that happy?"

"Yes, really. You know that, too, Fabian."

"Because I built this garden for you, and buy you Venetian glass and sapphire bracelets and plan trips for you?"

"Don't joke about it. You know those aren't the reasons."

"I don't know anyone who can afford to joke about it any better than we can, do you, Cresside?"

"No. You're right. We can joke because we're so safe."

For a long time after she had gone to sleep, he lay thinking of what she had said, but no anxiety permeated his thoughts. He knew that he had made her happy, he knew that he had given her security. But still he was not satisfied. He wanted to make her happier still, he wanted to safeguard her still further. The instinct to please her and protect her had always been as strong within him as the instinct to possess her, and now it had become a driving force. For in his possession of her he himself had found not only great joy but complete fulfillment. By accepting his love and bearing his child she had vindicated his starved manhood. He could never sufficiently requite her.

She stirred slightly in her sleep, stretched out her arms and found his waiting to receive her. She seldom spoke at such moments; words were superfluous in the harmony that prevailed between them. But this time she began to murmur drowsily, her lips already against his.

"Fabian, I want to say something to you."

"You can say anything you want to, darling. You know that."

"No. This is hard."

"Well, if it's hard——"

"But I want to. We've been mighty happy, Fabian, like we said this evening, but we could have been happier still."

"I couldn't."

"Yes, you could, and so could I. If I hadn't always put Vail first."

Fabian did not answer. Cresside caught her breath, but the sigh did not end in a sob, as he was afraid it might. It ended in swift tense speech.

"Even the night we were married, I was thinking about him. I was worrying for fear he wasn't all right, that he wouldn't be, unless I was at Belle Heloise to take care of him. Every time I thought of his asking for me and not finding me, it nearly broke my heart. I missed him so it seemed as if I couldn't stand it. No matter where we went or what we did, I kept yearning for him. And you knew it. You can't deny it."

"I shan't try to deny it, darling. But I never held that against you. I expected it. I knew it was bound to happen."

"Perhaps you thought I'd feel like that for a little while. But I don't believe you thought it would last. I think you hoped that after a little while you'd come first. Didn't you?"

"Perhaps. Yes, I suppose I did. But I've never held that against you either, Cresside—that you couldn't put me before Vail. You've given me so much——"

"If I'd put you first, if you'd known you were first, you'd have let me have another child."

"No, I wouldn't have, Cresside. I've told you, and I meant it, that I'd never let you suffer like that again. It isn't as if you could have children the way Merry has them—a few hours of discomfort, a few minutes of pain, and then everything all over. I can't stand that long-drawn-out agony of months. I've reproached myself for letting you have Frances Belle—I knew what you'd been through with Vail. But I wanted a child of my own, and so I was selfish enough to let you give it to me. But I'm not selfish enough to let you do it again."

"You wanted a *son* of your own. You haven't got him yet."

"I'll never get him. I couldn't love any son more than I do Frances Belle."

"How can you tell unless you have one?"

"We've been all over this before. Do we have to argue about it again, Cresside?"

"No. I don't want to argue with you about anything. I didn't start out to do that—I don't ever mean to. I only started out to tell you that you do come first now. You have for a long time. I wasn't sure you knew it. Did you?"

"No. I'd begun to hope so. But I wasn't sure."

"I want you to be sure. I'm telling you so you will be. And there's something else I want to tell you, Fabian: I know now that you were right about Vail all the time, that he's better off where he is, without me. I've never owned up before that I'd changed my mind about that. And I've changed my mind about being too happy. I'm going to revel in my happiness from now on, because you say it makes you happy, too. I want to do everything in the world I can for you, Fabian."

Daylight was already filtering into the room when she fell asleep again. But Fabian did not go to sleep. He lay looking at her, his heart welling up with fresh tenderness and new determination.

"I'll keep her happy," he vowed to himself. "I'll keep her safe. If anyone ever tries to hurt her again I'll kill him, so help me God."

CHAPTER XXXVII

ONE OF CRESSIDE'S hard and fast rules was about telephoning Fabian at his office. The poor man had no time to himself, she sometimes said gaily; his working hours belonged to his clients and his leisure hours to her; but at least neither intruded on the other. She made such a point of this non-intervention that any departure from it was disquieting to Fabian; if his secretary told him that Mrs. d'Alvery was on the wire, he leapt to the conclusion that Frances Belle had come down with diphtheria or that Carmelite had inadvertently set fire to the house. When he picked up the receiver, the day after the Townsends' visit, in response to his secretary's summons, it was with the knowledge that something equally calamitous had happened.

"Is anyone in the private office right now, Fabian?"

"No. You can say whatever you want to and I'll try to answer."

"I've just come from Belle Heloise. Gervais'd already gone to town, because he's bound not to miss a moment in the Senate Chamber, with this filibuster going on, come hell or high water. But I gather he's pretty well shot to pieces. *Maman* and Merry certainly are, anyway."

"What's the matter?"

"All Gervais' notes have been called. Didn't you know? Merry seemed to think you might."

"I was afraid they would be, when I heard about the rumpus at the bank yesterday. I meant to speak to you about it. But there didn't seem to be a good chance yesterday evening—or last night. And you were so sound asleep when I left this morning that I didn't want to disturb you."

There was a brief silence. Fabian knew that momentarily Cresside's troubled mind had reverted to the pleasant evening with their friends and to their own intimate hours of rich and rewarding communion. His thoughts had constantly wandered in the same direction all the morning, and he had made no effort to control them. He was glad to feel that Cresside was also dwelling on their mutual happiness

"I hadn't heard anything about the rumpus at the bank from anyone else," she finally continued. "The Townsends came early, and before that I was busy, getting things ready. You know how it is."

Fabian did know. He realized that the smoothness with which his pleasant household ran was due in no small measure to Cresside's skilled and patient management, and that the degree of perfection it had reached was by no means accidental. Cresside went out very little, and though she was hospitable, she preferred to invite her guests at stated times, for definite occasions like her pleasant garden parties, than to have them dropping in at any and every hour of the day. In like measure, she did not call up her friends unless there was some special reason for it, and she discouraged idle chatter over the telephone on their part.

"Merry says Mr. Goldenberg went out to Belle Heloise yesterday afternoon and offered to take over the mortgage," Cresside went on. "She thought it was mighty decent of him and I do, too. But Gervais doesn't look at it that way and *maman's* taking it pretty hard, too, though she's nicer about it than Gervais. She would be, of course."

"Yes, of course . . . You'd like me to see Gervais, straight off, I suppose?"

"I'd like you to send some kind of message to him, straight off, if you don't mind. And then go on out to Belle Heloise as soon as you can leave the office and stay until he gets home. Meanwhile you can talk to *maman* and Merry. At least, I'm taking it for granted you can. I'm taking it for granted there's something helpful you can say to them."

"You bet there is. Don't worry about it, Cresside. Anything else?"

"Yes. There's something the matter with Vail, too, Fabian. He hardly spoke to me and he got away from me as soon as he could. Merry says he's been acting up for about ten days now. But he seemed all right to me, when I've seen him before."

It was Fabian's turn to pause for a moment. *So Vail's found out,* he said to himself. *Well, I always knew he was bound to, sooner or later, but I hoped it wouldn't be this soon. If only Cresside hasn't guessed that's what's the matter . . . and if only a lot of other people haven't found out, too—* Aloud, he said quietly, "I wouldn't worry about that either. All kids have their off times, you know. I'll have a talk with him and find out what the trouble is. I reckon I can fix it up all right. I've got to meet a client at the Heidelberg for lunch but I'll go out to Belle Heloise straight from the office, like you suggest. Don't wait supper for me."

"I'll have a bite with Frances Belle when she has hers. Then I'll have another with you when you get home—in the garden."

"Right. So long, honey . . . By the way, you're still happy, aren't you?"

"Yes, now that I've talked to you. That was all I wanted. I know everything's going to be all right now."

Fabian hung up the receiver and reached for a pad of scratch paper. For a moment he sat drawing small geometrical designs on it. But only for a moment. Then he tore off the ornamented top sheet, and wrote five words on the next one, which he slipped into an envelope and addressed to Gervais.

"How much do you need?"

His departure for Belle Heloise was unavoidably delayed. It was late afternoon when he reached there, and the Big House was preternaturally quiet. Evidently Selah had gone out to the servants' quarters, for no one met Fabian at the door, and he wandered through the downstairs rooms without finding anyone. Then he went outdoors again and stood beside the wing where Madame d'Alvery's boudoir was located.

"Are you there, Tante Isabelle?" he called. "May I come up?"

"If you please, Fabian. I was half expecting you."

He found her, not enthroned as usual, on her sofa, but sitting in a
484

large Turkish chair by the window, looking down on Angus Holt's garden. She turned as he came in, and though her dark eyes met his with their usual dauntlessness, he could see that her natural pallor had a gray tinge. He put his arm around her and kissed her.

"Why put in the half? You ought to have been wholly expecting me, after what you told Cresside this morning. You ought to have known I'd get here as soon as I could."

"I hoped you would, Fabian. I sent Lucie away so that we could talk privately if you did. But I have ceased to expect very much of anyone."

"Nonsense, Tante Isabelle. You know I'm bound to be around. Don't talk like a tragedy queen, making her last great speech, upstage, before she kills herself. Talk to me like an affectionate mother-in-law. What were you looking at so hard when I came in?"

"The green rose. You know about the green rose, Fabian."

"Yes, of course. But why were you staring at it so?"

"I was thinking, Fabian, that I should hate to have it tended with alien hands. It is so uniquely our own. I have never given even a slip of it away."

Her own hands trembled a little as she spoke, though her voice was still firm. The so-called "green" rose was one of such extreme delicacy that its translucent white petals reflected the verdure of its foliage and actually seemed tinged with this color themselves. The parent plant had come from a Sevillian courtyard, and the same bride who had brought the Spanish statue to the house, had planted this rose herself at Belle Heloise, long before the advent of Angus Holt. In planning his garden, however, he had given it a place of honor, and the rose had always retained this. Madame d'Alvery was right in calling it unique; there was not another like it in any garden on either side of the River Road. It dominated the sago palms and palmettos, the false indigo and monkey grass, like a princess; even the camellias and Creole lilies looked stiff and common beside it, and the other roses lost their importance. Fabian knew that to Madame d'Alvery it was the symbol both of family tenacity and of family superiority. He did not minimize all that it meant to her.

"Well, I hope you never will," he said, speaking more lightly than he felt. "I sure don't see any reason why you should—unless, of course, you feel like giving slips of it to your granddaughters some day, so they can plant it in gardens of their own and carry on the tradition. I know I'd admire to have one in the Somerulos Street garden, as they say up north, but I understand how you feel about it. . . . Look, I sent Gervais a message this morning, and asked him how much he needed to get clear. Everything's fixed up, or going to be. If you're sitting here worrying for fear some lady friend of Long's is going to start cutting your green roses, or even that Mrs. Goldenberg's going to, you can stop right now. Incidentally, though, Mrs. Goldenberg's a mighty nice old lady, almost as nice as you are."

"Do you mean to tell me that you have assumed the mortgage, Fabian?"

"Hell, no. I just paid off the notes, that's all. Gervais and I can straighten out the details later."

Madame d'Alvery's hands were still trembling. Fabian drew up a chair beside her and took them in his own.

"Listen, Tante Isabelle," he said, "don't you start getting any false ideas about this. I didn't mind letting Gervais flounder along alone just so he didn't hurt anyone but himself while he was doing it. I'm afraid I didn't even mind so much as I should have when he hurt Merry in the process. I figured she'd married him with her eyes open, for richer, for poorer, for better, for worse, and that she ought to be able to take what was coming to her. She has, too. I hand it to her. She's taken it darn well, she's a good soldier. . . . I didn't mind so much whether he hurt you either. You were pretty hard on poor Uncle Philogene and I figured it might be good for you to have a taste of your own medicine. Well, you are hard, but you're a good soldier, too. I hand it to you as well as Merry. All of which is neither here nor there. The person I don't want to have hurt and don't intend to have hurt is Cresside. And it would hurt her like hell if she thought Vail wasn't going to stay on this place."

Madame d'Alvery's hands had gradually ceased to tremble, but she did not try to speak. She continued to look at Fabian in silence, her gaze not only unflinching but intent.

"I haven't a son of my own," Fabian went on. "I don't expect o have one. So I've got to give Cresside's the place mine would have had." Fabian had never before spoken of Vail to his mother-in-law as Cresside's son, but now he did so in a matter-of-fact way, as if the reference were one which was natural between them. "That isn't too hard for me, either," he went on. "Vail's a great kid—any man would be proud to have him for a son, or even in place of a son. I'm going to see that he gets everything that's coming to him—at Belle Heloise and elsewhere. And, incidentally, I don't intend to let Gervais forget that for all practical purposes his white-headed boy, Phil, isn't the 'heir to all the d'Alverys' as Cresside had the guts to call Vail, the very first time she showed him off. Gosh, if I hadn't been in love with her before then, I sure would have after that. And what she says, stands. Where is the little tyke, by the way? I want to have a talk with him this evening, too."

"I have not seen him since dinner time, Fabian. And he hardly spoke to anyone then. If you can get him to talk with you, it will be more than any one of us has been able to do, for a fortnight now."

"And it hasn't occurred to any of you to wonder why?"

"Merry has worried about him. But she has been even more worried about Gervais. Surely, Fabian, you do not think—after all these years —after all our care——"

For the first time, fear leapt into her brave eyes. Instinctively, she tried to rise. Fabian put a detaining hand on her shoulder.

"Better let me try to find out first, Tante Isabelle," he said gently. "If he does know—and I'll bet my bottom dollar he does—then somebody else does, too, besides the original conspirators. I'm also willing to bet that none of them gave the secret away. And whoever that somebody else is, I can probably deal with him better than you can, if you don't mind my saying so. But first I'm going to find Vail. Sit down again and go on looking at your green rose in peace. No one else has got a prayer of picking it."

Fabian waved to his mother-in-law from the doorway, with his old gay gesture, and went on through her bedroom to the upper hall, calling Vail as he did so. The chamber in front of Madame d'Alvery's, which had once been Cresside's, was now restored to its original state as a guest chamber; Henry Clay had always slept there when he visited Belle Heloise, Zachary Taylor, Judah P. Benjamin, and a host of other dead and gone celebrities. Now it had the *soigné* air of being kept in readiness for their worthy successors. The room across the hall from it, which had been Merry's bridal chamber, had been assigned to Sybelle, when it was judiciously decided that she and Vail were too big for joint occupancy of their original nursery directly behind it; but Vail had continued to sleep there. Receiving no response to his call, Fabian pushed open the shutter door and went in.

Some indefinable quality of the room's emptiness roused his suspicions. It was abnormally neat, for one thing. Like most small boys, Vail habitually scattered his possessions about and neglected to pick them up again. Now the room was completely uncluttered. Even the bureau was bare. Cresside's picture was gone from its place.

Fabian went back into the hall, closing the shutter door behind him, and walked thoughtfully down the stairs. He could hear Selah moving about in the dining room, setting the table for supper, and enticing odors were stealing subtly from Lou Ida's kitchen. Fabian had originally intended to go to see Merry as well as Madame d'Alvery, but now he decided against it. He felt reasonably certain that all the children, except Vail, were with her in the *garçonnière,* as he knew that she conscientiously tried to read aloud to them for an hour every evening. He did not want to talk to her about the notes unless he could see her alone, and he did not want to risk rousing suspicions which were possibly still non-existent, by asking questions about Vail. He decided to follow his hunch, and strike off down the River Road.

He had not gone more than two or three miles before he caught sight of the little figure for which he was watching. Vail was trudging along the road, carrying a small suitcase, which he kept shifting from hand to hand, as if it had already begun to seem very heavy. Maud was following at his heels, not leaping about him and snapping for bugs or nosing excitedly in the grass as she usually did, but dragging her feet reluctantly. Every now and then she stopped entirely, cringing and curling herself into a dejected crescent. When she did this Vail stopped, too, setting down the suitcase and leaning over his dog to encourage her in a voice of false heartiness. Fabian watched him for a few moments without trying to catch up with him; then he quickened his pace, and putting on his brakes, leaned out of the window and spoke casually and carelessly.

"Hello, there, Vail! Looks like we're going in the same direction. Want a lift?"

Vail did not answer immediately and Fabian did not try to hurry him. He waited as if it were quite natural for the boy to take his time.

"No, I reckon not," Vail said at last. "Me and Maud were just out for a walk."

"I'd be glad of your company a piece down the road. I've got a long ride ahead of me, and I'll have to take most of it alone. You could have your walk with Maud, going back."

Again Vail considered his answer at length. "All right," he said finally. "If it would keep you from being lonesome—" Without explaining his small suitcase, he lifted it into the car, involuntarily sighing with relief as he did so. Then he signaled to Maud, who jumped up with her first sign of joy, and climbed in himself. Afterwards he sat staring straight ahead of him with the suitcase at his side and Maud in his lap.

"It's a nice evening to be out on the road," Fabian remarked, after a considerable interval. "Let me know if I'm taking you too far though. You'll have quite a walk back."

"You don't need to worry about that, Uncle Fabian."

"I wasn't worrying. I was just calling your attention to it. I know it's hard sometimes, to keep track of distances. It's a far piece from Belle Heloise."

"Yes. But maybe I ought to tell you, Uncle Fabian. I didn't mean to go back to Belle Heloise tonight."

"I see. Well, I thought you might be spending the night with friends, when I saw your suitcase. But afterwards, when you said you were just out for a walk with Maud——"

"That wasn't exactly true, Uncle Fabian. I took Maud with me, because I figured she was mine and I had a right to her. Of course, Nostar's mine, too, but I didn't know just how I'd take care of a pony. Now a dog like Maud doesn't take up any room. She sleeps with you."

"That's right," said Fabian encouragingly.

"And she eats the scraps off your plate."

"Yes, but, of course, when she's going to have puppies she needs more than scraps and she oughtn't to get too tired walking, either.

488

I'm hoping we're going to get that little black clown in the next litter. It doesn't seem as if we could miss again. The new family's due in a few weeks, isn't it?"

"Ye—es," Vail said doubtfully. He had temporarily forgotten the prospect of the new family and the possibility of the little black puppy for which Fabian had watched and waited so long. Obviously the reminder was not especially welcome.

"I won't let her walk too far at a time," he said rather hurriedly. "And I'll give her lots of scraps. Just the same a dog isn't so much trouble as a pony. A pony's got to have a stall. And it's got to have oats."

"That's right," Fabian said again, without pressing the subject of the puppies.

"And I didn't know just where I was going to find the stall and the oats. I'm not going to spend the night with friends—at least not that I know of. But I thought there'd be some place——"

"Yes, of course, anyone along the Road would be glad to put you up. Except now that Hackberry's closed there aren't any houses very near. And naturally the folks would like to know where you were. They might worry if they didn't, don't you think? Not that you can't take care of yourself all right. They know that. It's just the way fathers and mothers have to worry, that's all."

"Yes, but——"

The stubborn little mouth had begun to quiver. He waited till he stopped choking. Then he went doggedly on.

"But Daddy and Mummy aren't really my father and mother. Did you know that, Uncle Fabian?"

"Yes, Vail, I knew that. I've known it a long while. I knew you'd find it out some time, too."

"Well, so I don't think Daddy and Mummy would worry the same, do you, as if they were really my father and mother?"

"Yes, I think they would. I think they might even worry more. Because they're responsible for you to your real mother. They promised her they'd take good care of you, if she'd trust you to them and let you live with them. They persuaded her that she ought to—that is, they helped me to persuade her. I felt just the same way about it, you see. And if you went away, no telling where, they'd be afraid she'd think they hadn't taken good care of you or that they hadn't made you happy."

Vail did not answer.

"She would too, you know," Fabian went on. "She trusted you to them because she thought it was best for you to live at Belle Heloise and best that everyone should think that they were really your father and mother. She'd be terribly upset if she found out you'd run away. She'd believe she'd made a mistake, after all."

Vail still did not answer.

"It's this way, Vail: a long time ago, someone made your mother

489

very unhappy. So ever since then, all the rest of us have tried to see that she wouldn't ever be unhappy again. We didn't think it was fair that she should be. I still don't think it's fair that she should be. And if she got upset about you—well, that would make her unhappier than anything else in the world, because she loves you more than anyone else in the world."

Vail swallowed hard. "I didn't know that," he muttered. "I thought maybe—" He stopped, partly because it was so hard to go on and partly because he did not know how to go on. Fabian finished his sentence for him.

"You thought maybe no one would care if you ran away?" he said. "Why, you couldn't have, not if you'd really figured this thing out. I don't believe you even tried. If you had, you'd have known that everyone would have cared. For instance, poor little Sybelle's probably crying her eyes out this minute, wondering where you are. I'll tell you why I think you ran away. I think something happened at Belle Heloise that made you feel badly and you thought maybe you'd feel better somewhere else. Didn't you? You were thinking mostly how you felt yourself, not how anyone else felt. Weren't you?"

"Gee, Uncle Fabian——"

"I said *mostly*. I know you thought there'd be a difference between real fathers and mothers and make-believe fathers and mothers, the way they'd worry, but just the same——"

"I reckon you're right, Uncle Fabian. I reckon I did think mostly if I could just get away——"

"We all think that once in a while, Vail. But we're always wrong about it when we do. The only way to make a hard thing any easier is to lick it. Not to run away from it. Once you've licked it, then it never seems so hard. The way for you to lick this feeling you've got is to go back to Belle Heloise and stay there. And if you want to do a really thorough job, you'll never let on what you found out, because it wouldn't do you any good and it would make everyone else feel worse. . . . How did you find out, by the way?"

"Well, Sammy Mudge came to see Amen. They were hiding in the bushes by the stable, whispering, when I went to saddle Nostar."

"I see. So then——"

"So then they tried to make me stop, but I wouldn't. I went and told Daddy Sammy Mudge was there. And he was awful mad. He sent Sammy Mudge away, and then he gave Amen an awful bawling out for tattling on his own white folks. I heard because I'd gone back to the stable to finish saddling Nostar and Twinkle. I didn't listen on purpose. Sybelle and I were going for a ride."

"Sure you didn't listen on purpose. And what happened next?"

"Next Daddy went back to the *garçonnière* to tell Mummy about it. He shouted at her, the way he does when he's mad. She tried to make him hush because she was afraid someone would hear him. I
490

did hear him. Franchot had asked me to build blocks with him, and when Sybelle didn't come to the stable to go riding——"

"Yes?" Fabian said encouragingly.

"I went back to the *garçonnière,* too. At least I started. And Daddy said Amen must know everything. He said Amen must know Mr. Tremaine was my father!"

It was no use. He could not help choking now, no matter how hard he tried. He blurted out his final words between sobs, and then he tried to wipe his eyes and nose on his sleeve, before leaning over and burying his face on Maud's faithful little body.

"I hated him, Uncle Fabian," he said in a smothered voice. "I hated him worse than anyone I ever knew, except Sammy Mudge. The way Daddy hates snakes."

Fabian brought the car quietly to a stop. "Look here," he said. "There's no use getting further and further from Belle Heloise when we've got to get back there, the sooner the better, too. But I want you to come up on the levee with me a few minutes first. I think it'll be easier to have a good talk there than it is here, don't you? And I want to have a talk with you, Vail. I want to set you straight about two or three things before we start back."

Without protest, Vail clambered out of the car. As he stumbled up the bank of the levee, he snuffled several times, and wiped his eyes and his nose on his sleeve again. But by the time he reached the ridge he had stopped. He sat down, drawing Maud into his lap once more, and stared at the river, as he had previously stared at the road.

"It's this way," Fabian said, lowering himself clumsily to the ground beside Vail. "I wanted to tell you I hated Sylvestre Tremaine, too. I reckon we'd find that we felt the same way about lots of things, Vail, if we had a chance to talk them over. I hated him just the same way you do, the same way your Daddy hates snakes. That's a good way to put it, and you're not the first person to do it. There are some people who are a lot like snakes and Sylvestre was one of them. Sammy Mudge is another. But Sylvestre Tremaine is dead. He can't do any more harm with his coils and his poison. And Sammy can't either. There are ways of taking the fangs out of snakes even while they're alive. Did you know that?"

"No," Vail said, looking up with sudden interest.

"Well, there are. So forget about Tremaine and don't worry about Mudge. I know how you must feel having Tremaine for a father, but forget about that, too. I don't know how you'd look at it, but I'd be mighty pleased if you'd try to pretend that I was your father. Just to yourself, I mean, and when you and I are together. Because, you see, I've always wished I were."

"Gee, Uncle Fabian——"

"I've wished it for two reasons, Vail. First, because I think you're a fine boy, because I'd be mighty proud to have a boy like you for my son. I've got the nicest little girl in the world, I wouldn't trade her for any boy I ever saw, but I'd have been awfully glad to have a boy, too. Every man wants to have a son—you'll find that out for yourself some day. So let's pretend I have, and that it's you. Shall we? Good, let's shake on it!"

Vail extended a grubby little paw and Fabian shook it hard. Then he went on holding it.

"I'm going to talk to you now as if you were my son, Vail, and as if you were grown up. The second reason I wish you were mine for true is because I love your mother so much. When a man loves a lady a lot, he wants her children to be his children, too. He's sorry when they're not. So I'm sorry about that and she is, too. But it's grand for me to know that even if I couldn't be your father, you could have the loveliest lady in the whole world for your mother. . . . Haven't you always thought your Aunt Cresside was the loveliest lady you ever knew?"

"Yes," Vail muttered.

"Well, you thought right, because she is. And you know now that she's your real mother, don't you?"

"Yes."

"You and I'll talk about all this again some time soon. You needn't be afraid to ask me anything you want to, and I think I can explain lots of things to you, so you'll feel better about them. I'll explain why Aunt Cresside didn't want you to know she was really your mother and why you mustn't ever let her know that you've found out. But now we've got to get back to Belle Heloise, where she wanted you to stay. And we've got to keep mum about this. Because it's our secret now. Right?"

"Yes, Uncle Fabian."

"Good. Come along. Maybe you'd give me a hand while we're going down over the bank. It's hard for me to manage alone, where the walking's rough. I'm going to count on you to help me over the rough places, Vail, when we're out together, after this."

When Gervais swung into the driveway at Belle Heloise that night, the Big House was already in darkness, but he saw that a light was burning in his office as well as in the *garçonnière*. He went first to his own living room, where he found Merry waiting up for him.

"Fabian's still here," she said, in answer to her husband's unspoken question. "He said he wanted a word with you before he went back to town. He's waiting for you in the office. Oh, Gervais, isn't it wonderful that he could help you—and that he did?"

"I can tell you that better when I know just how many strings there are attached to his *beau geste*. But I'll grant you it's reprieve, anyway."

"You're not going to talk to Fabian like that about it, are you?"

"Don't worry. I didn't me n to imply the reprieve wasn't a godsend.

I'm prepared to pay for it, in cash or in kind. I was only trying to tell you I knew I'd have to."

He left her, crossed the narrow strip of lawn which divided the small twin buildings, and entered his outer office. This was dark and empty. But the door was open into the large inner room which Merry had made so characteristic of a luxurious library, and Fabian was sitting in a Morris chair beside the big desk.

"Hello," he said without getting up. "How's the filibuster going?"

"Fine. There's not a chance of getting that bond-issue bill through the Senate."

"Even without your vote?"

"What are you driving at, Fabian?"

"You told me yourself, the other day, that with Cyr on your side, Pike Hall and Boone and Caffery were all set to talk it to death. I should think they could talk just as well with you on the plantation as in the Chamber. Maybe better. And I don't believe any one of them would go back on his word."

"I said, what are you driving at?"

"Just this: I think I know now what Long had up his sleeve when he sent for you the other day. Never mind how—it's too late to go into all that tonight. We can take up the details some other time. I don't know how far he'd go, or how fast he'd move, to carry out any threats he may have made—personally, I believe there are some limits to what he'd dare do. But he sure didn't lose any time getting his bank examiner to the Citizens National, and I think we'd better beat him to the draw before he tries anything else. I drafted a letter while I've been waiting for you. It's lying there on the desk. If you'll sign it, I'll take it in with me tonight and see that it's delivered the first thing in the morning."

Fabian nodded towards a single sheet of paper lying on the center of the neat blotter. Gervais picked it up and read it through at a glance. Then he flung it down on the desk again.

"If you think I'm going to let that dirty son-of-a-bitch frighten me——"

"He's frightened you already, hasn't he?"

"Not into quitting. I'll fight him to the last gasp. If he gets licked on this, he's through. All I've got to do is to hang on to the end of the ession and then——"

'Then, if he's licked, he'll start all over again and win out some other way. The time to stop him was then years ago, and none of us had the guts, or the brains, to do it then. We may think we've got the guts now, but they won't do us much good without the brains, and we sure haven't got those. Maybe we can find some new way to fight him, but it'll take time to figure that out. And it's a sure thing we can't lick him the old way. You're through in politics, Gervais. You might just as well face it. But you've still got the plantation for life. At least you can have it if you want it."

"He suggested the same course you'd like to have me follow and I told the dirty bastard I'd be damned first. I told him he could pop his gun whenever he wanted to and that when he'd done that, then it would be my turn. Do you really suppose I'm going to let him think——"

"It's a long lane that has no turning. I'm not saying I don't hope you'll have a chance to get back at him yet, some day, that I won't help you every way I can. All I'm saying is I care a damn sight more for my wife's happiness and my own peace of mind than I do for your career and a large part of my wife's happiness is dependent on feeling the world believes Vail's your eldest son—and that he has a right to everything that means—now and in the future."

"You said yourself you didn't believe Long would dare——"

"I don't. But I'm not taking any chances. As I said before, you're through with politics but you've still got the plantation for yourself and your heir. You don't owe me a red cent, Gervais. But I'm going to have your signature on that letter before I leave this room."

The Governor of Louisiana, running through his morning mail, chuckled and turned to the only visitor he had at the moment, who happened to be one of his purchasing agents. "Listen to this letter I got here from that lily-livered silk stocking, Gervais d'Alvery," he said. " 'I find that the interests of my plantation demand so much of my time under present conditions that I cannot also do justice to my duties as a Legislator. I therefore ask you to accept my resignation as Senator from the 20th Senatorial District, effective immediately.' "

Long laid down the letter with a laugh. "It's a funny thing about d'Alvery," he said. "I was talking to him a few days back and kind of hinting we knew all about his many troubles, meaning I would maybe fix his clock so he'd lose his plantation, and, lo and behold, he jumps up and makes a regular Little Rollo-Lord Fauntleroy speech thinking I meant something else. Never mind what right now—I might tell you some time later. But he needn't have worried. I might've taken a chance on him, but that crippled cousin of his, Fabian d'Alvery, is one man I don't fool with. He's mighty quick on the trigger, I've found that out already. Well, good riddance, that's all I can say. I have a hunch that things are going to start coming my way right soon."

"The Sweetest Story Ever Told"

May 1936–December 1936

... "Little by little and stitch by stitch,
The girl is put in her proper niche
With all the virtues that we can draw
For someone else's daughter-in-law,
A girl to be kind to, a girl we're lucky in,
A girl to marry some nice Kentuckian,
Some Alabaman, some Carolinian—
In fact, if you ask me for my opinion,
There are lots of boys in the Northern sections
And some of them have quite good connections——"

"The Sweetest Story Ever Told"

CHAPTER XXXVIII

"HELLO, AUNTIE! I heard Uncle Fabian had gone to Washington again, so I came by to see whether you and the kid wouldn't like to go to the Plaquemine Sugar Festival with me."

"Why hello, Vail! I think that's a grand idea! But are you sure we wouldn't be in the way? Isn't there someone else you'd rather take?"

"No, I'm sure there's no one else I'd rather take. You're still my best girl, Auntie. Come on."

Vail put a stalwart arm around Cresside's slim waist, hugging her hard and kissing her soft cheek resoundingly. He had never gone through a period of self-consciousness about demonstrating affection; he embraced Sybelle and Joyeuse spontaneously and warmly, unembarrassed even when Gervais told him, somewhat derisively, that he was the only d'Alvery who had ever kissed his sisters without being bribed or badgered into doing it. But he could afford to take the jibe good-naturedly, for his worst enemy could not have accused him of effeminacy. At sixteen he was already taller than either Fabian or Gervais, and so powerfully built that, lacking the typical weediness of adolescence, he would have looked like a man, except for his tousled black hair, the youthful glow of his skin, and the immaturity of his carriage and manner. He was an unusually striking and attractive boy, just as he had been an unusually striking and attractive baby; but he had not yet learned to carry his height or control his strength, and his clothes always looked outgrown, outworn, and unsuitable. Cresside ventured to smooth back one of the unruly locks which fell over his forehead, because she knew Vail would regard the gesture as caressing rather than critical; but she did not dare to straighten his flaming necktie or button his loosened shirt. He would have taken it from her, as he did so many things that he took from no one else; but she realized that he was touchy, that he did not like to have anyone fuss over him, and she refrained from presuming on his fondness.

"Your lessons for tomorrow are all done, I suppose?" she asked, turning towards her bedroom from the hall where they had been standing.

"You lie, Auntie. You don't suppose anything of the sort. But you're wrong. As a matter of fact they are done—for once," Vail retorted. "Where's the brat? Should I collect her while you're fetching your bonnet and shawl?"

"She's in the kitchen with Carmelite, making gingerbread men. She's getting to be a very enthusiastic little housewife. But she'll drop her cookie-cutter like a shot when she sees you. She doesn't hesitate to tell everyone—including your brothers and sisters, I'm sorry to say—that you're her favorite cousin."

Cresside smiled over her shoulder at Vail, who grinned in return, and went on into her bedroom. Though they were crowded in their little house on Somerulos Street, Fabian and Cresside were both attached to it, and had never seriously considered leaving it. They still slept in the square bedroom back of the library, with Frances Belle in the tiny one behind it, which had been created when part of the second ground-floor chamber was partitioned off into a bathroom. After she got bigger, she could move to one of the two dormers, which were surprisingly pleasant—after she got bigger or after she was displaced by a little brother, Cresside sometimes added. But Fabian never mentioned the little brother and he occasionally said, rather curtly for him, that Frances Belle would have to be a good deal bigger before he would consent to having her sleep upstairs.

Cresside sat down in front of her dressing table, applied fresh make-up discreetly, and fluffed out her dark hair under a blue hat. Her happy marriage had caused her to bloom. There had never been a rift between her and Fabian, or a cloud as large as a man's hand darkening their home; she had come to embody this harmony and tranquility and at thirty-five her face was softer, her figure more feminine than at eighteen. She had kept her slenderness and her style and she had no white hairs and no wrinkles. Vail often told her that people would really think she was his best girl instead of his aunt, while they were among strangers, if she did not develop a middle-aged spread or try out a henna rinse, and she was always secretly delighted when he teased her in this way. She had a few acquaintances on the West Side, but not many, and it pleased her to think she might be mistaken, if not for Vail's sweetheart, at least for an older sister, at the Plaquemine Sugar Festival. Taking off the blue hat, which she decided was a little old-fashioned, she slipped out of her dress, too, and changed quickly into a fresh gay print that made her look younger than ever, and a flower-wreathed straw which matched it. When she went back to the hall which divided her bedroom and the library from the drawing room and the dining room, she found that Vail and

Frances Belle had already gone out of the house and were waiting for her in the car. They called to her gaily and she joined them.

All three could sit together in the front seat without crowding. Vail admittedly took up more than his share of the space, but Frances Belle was a slight, elfin child, prettier than her mother had been at the same age, but otherwise very much like her; she took up no room at all, to speak of, and Cresside took up very little, so that evened things up, Vail declared, hoisting himself in behind the wheel. He had not been driving a car long, and the only one available for his use was an old rattletrap which Gervais had discarded; but the boy handled it well and kept up a stream of high-spirited conversation as they drove along.

"This ought to be a good show today. You've heard the name they've given the pageant, haven't you?"

"I don't think I have, Vail. I haven't heard much of anything about the Cane Festival."

" 'The Sweetest Story Ever Told.' Dad thinks that's silly, but I think it's keen."

"Well, he would, you know, Vail. Humor has to be of a very high order to appeal to Gervais. But I agree with you. I think it's a good title for this particular kind of pageant—it isn't designed primarily for the intelligentsia. Do you know anything about this sweet story?"

"Oh, it's supposed to trace the history of sugar from the time when this 'was shrouded in the mists of antiquity' up to the 'moment of its present high development'! There'll be eleven floats. This pageant's in addition to the regular Festival parade, by the way. It's something new this year. . . . The maids for the queen's court of honor are being chosen differently, too."

"Are they? In what way?"

"Well, you know last year and the year before they were sponsored by the different plantations, and named after them—Margaret Supple was Miss Catherine, Margaret Hecht, Miss Saint Delphine, and so on. But this year the schools have been invited to select the maids."

"Which schools?"

"Well, mostly high schools from the different parishes, but some academies, too. I'm sorry Grand Coteau wasn't one of them. Syb ought to have stood a good chance of being picked for a maid, and she'd have got a great kick out of it."

"Do you think Sybelle's happy at Grand Coteau, Vail? I wasn't happy at Convent—I was glad when I heard it had closed down."

"You're darn right she isn't happy. But that wasn't the big idea. You know the folks wanted to get her where she wouldn't run into Rick Tramonte. Daddy and Mummy could stop him from coming to the house, but they couldn't stop him from walking the levee. And when we took the victrola down to the batture, for sand dances, he always showed up. . . . Maybe you don't know it, but Syb's a riot when she dances in the moonlight."

"I do know it. I've known for a long time she would be. Your Uncle

Fabian predicted, years ago, that something like this would happen. I wasn't sure it had happened to Riccardo Tramonte, though. No one came right out and told me before why Syb was sent away to school."

"Well, I reckon we can't blame it all on the batture. Syb and Rick made a getaway once and of course that would have to be the night Dad took it into his head to come down on the beach. When he found out they'd gone to one of those bootleg shindigs at Hathaway he was fit to be tied. They'd never done it before and I don't believe they ever would have again. Neither of them runs with the 'hotcha' gang that goes there. But they were bound to cut loose sooner or later and they had a bad break, picking the time they did. Dad acted the heavy father—if anyone ever told him those went out with the War he didn't listen. But he couldn't very well lock Syb in her room and poke bread and water through a shutter door. So he thought Grand Coteau was the next best answer."

Cresside did not reply immediately. She knew that Hathaway had succeeded The Willows as the popular "hot spot" on the River Road, but she had never previously discussed the matter with Vail. Quite aside from her own personal feeling about it, there was something uncanny in the current vogue among riotous students for taking their own band and their own liquor to the deserted house, and dancing, by guttering candlelight, in the White Ball Room from dusk until dawn. The abandoned plantation was posted and theoretically trespassers were prosecuted; but so far no serious attempt had been made to break up the outlawed parties which had begun when prohibition was still nominally in force and had continued to flourish since its repeal. The thought of her lovely young niece in such a setting, under such conditions, was appalling to Cresside, and she realized, more keenly than ever before, how her own rash conduct at The Willows must have affected her family. But she was wise enough not to voice any censure of either Sybelle or Riccardo to Vail. Instead she spoke gently, suppressing an involuntary sigh.

"Sybelle's awfully young, Vail, to be falling in love."

"Aw, come clean, Auntie! You know being young isn't the lowdown on that. If she'd gone overboard for somebody like one of those Pereira boys, Dad would have said buh-less you my chee-ild—I mean my children. But Rick won't ever be anything but a Dago peddler's son to them. It don't matter his father's one of the richest men in Baton Rouge, even. Say, you got to go to some of the football games with me this fall, Auntie, and see him in action. He was the hottest sophomore fullback L.S.U. ever had, and made All-Southern."

"I want to go to the football game, too," piped up Frances Belle, speaking for the first time.

"Right. We'll all go to the football games, sugar. That is, if I'm here."

"What do you mean, Vail, if you're here? I thought you told Fabian you didn't want to go to Princeton."

"I did tell him so. Look, Auntie, I've been meaning to talk to you about this for quite a while. Wait till I steer Leaping Lena down the levee and on to the ferry. Then we can get out and stand in the bow."

Cresside opened her lips and then pressed them together again. Because finances were admittedly still in a bad way at Belle Heloise, it had been natural for Fabian, as the rich relative of the family, to offer to help meet the expenses of Vail's education, and equally natural for him to suggest his own alma mater. However, Vail had stubbornly but gratefully declined. He never could make the grade at one of those swell Eastern colleges, he said, a little ruefully; he wasn't in their class. Now with Uncle Fabian, it was different, because he *was* in their class; and it was damn white of Uncle Fabian to suggest sending him. But he thought L.S.U. was more like it, for him. Phil would be ready for L.S.U. the same year he would, because Phil was smart, just the opposite from him. He thought probably they better stick together. That is, if he could manage to make the grade at all; his latest marks hadn't looked much like it. . . .

"Vail, I want a coke," Frances Belle said shrilly, breaking in on Cresside's recollections.

"Sure you do. So do I. So do you, don't you, Auntie?"

"No, thanks, Vail. You and Frances Belle go get yours. I'll wait for you here."

They had already come over the clattering gangplank, paid the collector, and swung into line with the other cars. Now they got out of theirs together, Frances Belle darting off towards the soft-drink stand on the upper deck, with Vail in rapid pursuit, and Cresside walking slowly to the bow. Hunched up in front of her was the same wide-shouldered Negro she had first seen while crossing the river with Fabian sixteen years before. He looked almost exactly as he had then, except that he was thinner; bent over a horn in the making, he moved a shard of glass back and forth along the rounded surface, as though he were still engaged on the same task that had busied him then. She stopped and spoke to him.

"Good evening, Willie. Remember the first time I saw you on this ferry a long while ago, when I was with my cousin Fabian d'Alvery before we married? That was our little girl who went by just then."

Ferryboat Bill looked up, grinning. "Proud to see you again, Mis' d'Alvery. Do Lord, think how de time go by! Don' seem possible you could have a gal-child big as de one Ah just see. De boy look fine, too. *She* got no beau already, have she?"

"Oh, no! Why, she's only eleven. That was Vail d'Alvery."

"Sure enough? Well, Ah still says Ah don' see where de time go to. Me— Ah's makin' blowin' horns till yet, lak you sees. Dis here ram's horn done been sent me to fix up all de way from Afriky."

He held it up so that she could get a better look at it. It was beau-

501

tifully polished, and somehow it reminded her of the Shofar which she and Fabian had seen in a synagogue at Jerusalem. She paused long enough to admire it, recalling with poignant happiness that joyous period in the Holy Land. Then she went on, with a pleasant good-by, her anxious thoughts already reverting to Vail. Was he unhappy at Belle Heloise, she asked herself wretchedly, and strainir g at the leash to escape? It certainly was not beyond the realm of possibility. She had been terribly unhappy there herself, and so had her father before her, Philogene because he never belonged to the place, and she because she never conformed to it. Perhaps Vail, who did not really belong or conform either, was beginning to be vaguely conscious of this, vaguely restless and rebellious. They must take up the question of Princeton again, and not only for Vail's sake, but for Fabian's, too. Fabian, with no son of his own, would be happy to have at least a foster son there. . . .

"I didn't upset you, did I, Auntie? I didn't mean to. There's nothing to be upset about." Vail had come back and was standing close beside her with his arm around her, just as Fabian had stood when they first crossed the ferry together. Other memories crowded in on Cresside, but she detached her mind from those centering on Fabian and listened intently to Vail. "It's only that I've had a pip of a job offered me, and I think maybe I'd rather have that than go to college anywhere. Naturally if I could help Phil, I'd stay with him, like I was going to in the first place. But Phil needs me like a cat needs two tails. He's got so many friends that I've got to pry him loose from them all the time, or I'd never see him myself. Everybody likes Phil."

"Everyone likes you, too, Vail. You've got lots of friends yourself."

"Sure, I've got lots of friends. But it isn't the same. You know that just as well as I do, Auntie."

"Who offered you this job, Vail? What kind of a job is it?"

"Mr. Pereira, the last time he came to Belle Heloise for the week end. It's a job in his coffee-importing house. He said twenty-five dollars a week to start, just as soon as I got through high school and a steady raise every year. . . . Why Auntie, what's the matter?"

Cresside had suddenly dropped her purse. As Vail retrieved it and gave it to her she answered him with obvious effort.

"Nothing's the matter, really. I'm upset at this sudden idea of your not going to college. And it just so happens that a long time ago I knew a young man who went to work for the Pereiras and they didn't get along very well. Perhaps you wouldn't, either."

"I don't see why not. The Pereiras are grand guys. It must have been this fellow's own fault if he didn't get on with them. Who was he anyway?"

"Perhaps it was his fault," Cresside admitted, disregarding the last question. "But Vail, you've taken me completely by surprise. I never heard you say you were interested in learning the coffee business. I thought you were interested in being a sugar planter. I didn't dream you thought of leaving Belle Heloise—unless you went away to college, of course, but then you'd come back. I'd miss you very much if you went to New Orleans. It may be very selfish of me, but I can't help hoping you won't."

"But Auntie, I wouldn't be nearly so far away from you if I went to New Orleans as I would if I went to Princeton, and you never said a word about my doing that! I could come home from New Orleans week ends, and I could see you then, couldn't I? Anyway, Belle Heloise is just bulging with boys. One more or less wouldn't make any difference. Honest, now, do you think it would?"

"Of course it would," Cresside said unconvincingly. "It would make a difference to your family and it would make a difference on the plantation—you're needed on the plantation."

"Auntie, Phil wants to stay on the plantation and Franchot wants to stay on the plantation. And some day we'll all want to get married and have families of our own. Do you think there'd be room for us all at Belle Heloise? Somebody would have to be the boss—and that wouldn't go so good with the others."

"But you're the eldest. If anyone goes, it ought to be one of the others."

"I don't see why, when they're interested in sugar and I'm not."

"But you *are* interested in sugar! You wanted to come to this Festival today. You were more interested than any of the others. None of the others took the trouble to come. I don't believe they even thought of it."

"No. But you see——"

Cresside looked quickly up at Vail. He had been talking to her very earnestly but now, to her astonishment, he looked a little sheepish. He seemed on the point of explaining something and then to be bashful about it. Nothing could have been more uncharacteristic of Vail. And as she looked at him again, Cresside saw that he himself had straightened the tie and buttoned the shirt which she with such difficulty had forborne from touching. His unruly hair had been neatly slicked into place, and as the breeze from the river ruffled it slightly, he raised a preternaturally clean hand and smoothed it back.

"Why Vail!" she exclaimed involuntarily. "You didn't have any special reason for wanting to come to the Festival, did you? I mean, there wasn't any special *person* you thought you'd see here? Or was there?"

"Vail, I want an Eskimo Pie," piped Frances Belle. She had kept quiet for a long time, during a tiresome conversation from which she had been excluded, but now she could stand it no longer. She seized his hand again, dragging him once more in the direction of the soft-drink stand and speaking to him urgently. "If we don't hurry we won't get it before the ferry lands," she said. "Come on, please, Vail!"

They were on the road between Port Allen and Plaquemine before

503

Cresside got the answer to her question. Something had deterred her from repeating it, and she had almost decided Vail was determined to ignore it, when he broached the subject again, of his own accord.

"You asked me a while back if there was any special reason why I wanted to come to the Festival," he said with rather unconvincing nonchalance. "Well, of course I always like to see the Plaquemine–White Castle ball game at Athletic Park—they have darn good teams for places that size. And I like to eat at Breaux' Restaurant. That gumbo they have— Boy! That's something."

Cresside waited patiently for Vail to come to the point.

"And this year a big motorcade is coming up from St. John Parish— all the cars with banners and stuff showing what plantations and factories they come from. And the Governor and Mrs. Noe are coming. I reckon they must be in Plaquemine already. We're kind of late."

As if he could hardly wait to see Governor and Mrs. Noe, both highly familiar and completely unexciting spectacles in Baton Rouge, Vail pressed his foot down on the accelerator and took a firm grip on the wheel.

"Usually there are quite a lot of pretty girls there, too," he went on, reverting to the tone of unconvincing nonchalance in which he had begun. "The maids sure do look right cute wearing their gingham dresses and carrying their sugar-cane bouquets. Until now they've been rather on the grown-up side though—some of them as old as twenty, I reckon. But now that there's been this idea of high-school kids——"

"Is one of your school friends a maid in the Festival?" Cresside inquired guardedly.

"You mean from Baton Rouge? No one from the high school; there's a girl from St. Joseph's Academy and quite a few from the sororities at L.S.U.—but of course they're old," Vail explained. "Most of the smoothest ones come from other places, like Breaux Bridge and Abbeville and New Roads. There's a girl from New Roads that's a knockout. She's smart, too. She's the winner of one of the prizes the committee offered for the best essays on sugar growing. Gosh, if I was as smart as that girl, I wouldn't have anything to worry about. I could go to Princeton, like you and Uncle Fabian want me to."

"What is this girl's name?" Cresside inquired, still guardedly.

"Susannah. Most of the crowd call her Sue, though."

"Susannah what?" asked Cresside, refraining from asking what crowd, though this was the first time she had heard of a crowd from New Roads in connection with Vail.

"Susannah Prescott."

"Any kin to the Baton Rouge Prescotts?"

"No. She's a damn Yankee," Vail chuckled. "Her folks come from somewhere in New England—Connecticut, I reckon. Or maybe it's Vermont. It doesn't matter—one of those little states," Vail continued with Louisianian loftiness. "They're some sort of kin to Charles Boylston. I thought he might have told you about them. I met them through him."

"No, he hasn't told me about them. I haven't seen much of Charles Boylston lately."

"Well, I've always thought he had a crush on you. I always thought Uncle Fabian cut him out," remarked Vail, with the disconcerting penetration of the young. "Not that I'm sorry, though. Uncle Fabian's worth a dozen Charles Boylstons. Some Yankees are darn nice just the same."

"Have the Prescotts bought a place in New Roads?" inquired Cresside, dropping the subject of Charles Boylston.

"Yes, one of those nice old houses near Parlange, facing False River. You must know the one I mean. It used to have a queer German-sounding name. But the Prescotts have changed it. They've renamed it Salome."

"Salome!"

"Yes. That was the name of one of Sue's great-grandmothers. You wouldn't believe it, but she saw the name herself, in some little country burying ground where the Prescotts used to have their family lot. Salome Church, this lady's name was, and she married a man named Shadrach Prescott. Sue says she came near being named Salome herself. Her father wanted to, but her mother stood out against it."

"I should think she might."

"It makes a nice name for a place, don't you think?"

"Yes, I think it makes a nice name for a place."

"Mr. and Mrs. Prescott want you to come and see them at Salome," Vail announced. "You and Uncle Fabian both, of course. I reckon you'll meet them today. They'll be coming to Plaquemine with Sue." He slowed down and slipped one of his hands briefly into Cresside's. "If they ask you to go to see them, you'll say yes, won't you, Auntie?" he asked, and his voice was no longer casual; instead there was a note of entreaty in it. "Of course I would have told Mom about Sue," he said, "except that she is so upset about Syb and Rick already. I knew she'd say I was too young, too. . . . I oughtn't to have told you you were still my best girl, Auntie, because you're not any more. Sue's my best girl now, that is, I want her to be. The reason I want to get a job is so I can start earning money myself and be independent. And I wanted you to come to the Festival so that you could see her."

"Vail, please stop at the drugstore so we can get a banana split!" begged Frances Belle.

CHAPTER XXXIX

VAIL WAS RIGHT; they had been a little late in getting started. When Frances Belle demanded the banana split, he spoke impatiently to her for the first time.

"Good Lord, we haven't got time to go to a drugstore now! It isn't half an hour since you had a coke and an Eskimo Pie. Those ought to hold you for a while. We've got to get this car parked somewhere, if we can find a place for it. The town's jam-packed full already."

Frances Belle continued her clamor while Vail circled anxiously about, and Cresside tried to quiet her, with forced patience but without satisfactory results. She knew that her efforts would have been more successful if she could have concentrated on the fractious child instead of the impatient youth. But she was hardly conscious of what she said as she attempted to quiet her little daughter; in her distracted state it was all she could do to keep her voice under control. She had been so pleased because Vail thought of sharing his outing with her, so flattered that he kept up the joking pretense that anyone would take her for his best girl, so sure that she represented the paramount interest of his life; and after all, he had not brought her to Plaquemine because he wanted her to have a good time; he had not come to watch the sports or listen to the speeches or associate with sugar planters. He had come because he wanted to see a pert little Yankee who was inappropriately established at New Roads, and he had brought his Aunt Cresside along, so that she would make the suitable and gracious approach towards acceptance of this girl and her family. It was ridiculous, it was incredible. Vail was much too young to be serious about a sweetheart. Why, he was only a few years older than Frances Belle, who kept squirming around and shrilly demanding some form of food every few minutes! Vail's general behavior was almost equally immature. And yet—and yet— Startled as she was at the turn of events, she must not forget to be fair. He had not shut her away from an experience that was vital to him; he had asked her to share it, he wanted her to share it. He had not spoken of it to Merry, but he had revealed it to her. And he had not done anything discreditable, he had not shown himself untrustworthy in any way. This girl who had caught his fancy might be an outsider, but apparently she had background and breeding, she probably behaved herself; and Vail was courting her openly, not only willing but eager to have both her family and his witness his suit. Suddenly a great wave of relief engulfed her, sweeping away the haunting dread of years: that some day he would do what his father had done and be what his father had been. She looked towards him with eyes that were bright with tears, but they were tears of thanksgiving. . . .

506

"I reckon we can just squeeze in here," Vail was saying in a voice of triumph, as he indicated a narrow alley which by some miracle had been overlooked. "Come on, let's get going. I'm afraid we'll just have to stand anywhere we can find a place, to see the parade. You don't mind, do you, Auntie? Afterwards I'll see that you get a good seat somewhere." Oblivious of her inner turmoil, he was still concerned for her comfort. "That's the L.S.U. Band you hear, sugar," he went on, speaking good-naturedly to Frances Belle again in spite of his haste. "A hundred and sixty pieces they brought over. Makes you feel proud of the old home town, doesn't it, to think they can furnish all that many? It's heading the parade. The drum major's Llewellyn Williams. That white outfit of his is pretty smooth, isn't it?—and he sure swings a wicked baton. We'll see the floats in a minute. Here, stand in front of me, both of you. I'm wide enough to keep off the crowd and tall enough to see right over you."

The bystanders on the curb in front of the Hotel Silber had made room for them, and they wedged their way in between a tall rawboned young farmer wearing a plaid shirt and a battered fedora, and a corpulent woman in rusty black, whom Cresside recognized, after a few minutes of trying to place her, as Mrs. Hartzberg, the kindly neighbor who had befriended Max Stoetzner in his extremity. Presently they were chatting like long-lost friends, discussing, with enthusiasm, the details of the parade which was now progressing triumphantly down the street. Following the band and preceding the floats came a large contingent of plantation overseers, mounted on their sturdy cobs. These men, living the year round in the saddle, rode not only with the accustomed ease which might be taken for granted, but also with an effect of unity which would have done credit to any cavalry. Vail, who was an excellent horseman himself, gazed at them with mingled admiration and regret.

"Sance ought to be there," he said in a voice of disappointment. "He can ride with any of them. If Syb had been home she'd have got Dad to let him come. Syb can do almost anything with Dad—at least she could until the hullabaloo about Riccardo. Now Phil's the white-haired boy. And he wasn't interested in this show, for some reason." Vail followed the overseers with his eyes until they had turned the corner, clattering out of sight. By that time it was too late for him to get a good look at the first float, representing the creation of sugar by a celebrated magician at the request of an Indian Rajah. Frances Belle, greatly intrigued by the brilliant colors and fantastic costumes with which this float was embellished and filled with curiosity as to their meaning, nudged him in the ribs, avid for information.

"What are those men doing there? Why do they wear clothes like that? What are they saying to each other?"

He tried to explain, but the first float had gone past before he succeeded, those portraying the successive introduction of sugar into China, Persia and Egypt were already lumbering past, and Frances

507

Belle had begun to ask questions about these. The Crusaders appeared, establishing their sugar routes across the Mediterranean; Columbus, bringing it to Santo Domingo; Etienne de Bore discovering modern granulating methods, and Frances Belle's curiosity was still unappeased. On the final float a group of Negro hands was gathered around a mammoth plantation bell. Obviously delighted at having become the center of attraction, they grinned expansively, showing their dazzling white teeth and responding jovially to the applause of the crowd.

"Our hands belonged on that float, too," Vail said, turning from Frances Belle to Cresside and speaking in the same regretful way in which he had referred to Sance. Evidently the fact that Belle Heloise had not figured in this Festival was preying on his mind, and suddenly Cresside realized that this was because he would have been proud if the Prescotts could have seen it represented, and been properly impressed with its importance and prestige. "That bell doesn't begin to be as big as ours," he went on. "The inscription on it isn't so hot, either. I can't even make it out." And then Cresside seemed to see her father standing by the great bronze bell which was so eloquent a memorial to Thiac-Maignon, the Creole artisan who had cast it, and to hear the first Philogene drawling, "*J pour joie, A pour amour, P pour passion, R pour ravir, T pour tempter, I pour ivresse, E pour extase—dis donc, Cresside, a tu compris?*"

She did understand now, but she had learned in a hard school, and when she was Vail's age she had not known at all. A fresh pang shot through her heart at the realization that he must learn it all too, and that such knowledge never came easily. She had been thinking of the Prescotts as interlopers on the Southern scene; now she saw that in the supercilious New England way they might consider Vail easygoing, ill-groomed and unscholarly. As a background, Belle Heloise did not loom as large as it once had; even its rightful heir would be no great match for a girl of wealth and position. And Vail was not its rightful heir. But for Fabian's intervention he would not have been its heir at all. Though, of course, the Prescotts did not know that, must never find that out. . . .

"Let's drift over to the Knights of Columbus Home," Vail proposed restlessly. "That's where the queen and her ladies-in-waiting were supposed to watch the pageant. The rest of the bunch will most likely be somewhere around. Anyway we can find out. I reckon we can get through the crowd now. Would you feel like trying, Auntie?"

"Of course I feel like trying it. I'm still a pretty good walker, you know, Vail, in spite of my advanced age, and the Home's only about a block away."

"Advanced age, my foot! You don't look a day older than those coeds!"

He put his hand under her elbow and they "drifted" along to the Knights of Columbus Home. But apparently they had delayed too

508

long. The balcony was already deserted. Disappointed, but by no means disheartened, Vail suggested that they should go on.

"I reckon the only thing to do is to keep milling around until we find someone we know. There's going to be a concert on the Community Club grounds and the queen's parade is going to wind up there. Then the girls will go straight on to the ball. We're certain to see the Prescotts at the Community Club."

"I'm hungry," Frances Belle announced. "I want my supper. I'm tired of walking around. Can't we have supper somewhere, Vail?"

"You must have a tapeworm, kid. You don't do anything but eat," Vail retorted. But he did not speak crossly. Instead he looked at Cresside inquiringly. "It might not be such a bad idea, you know," he said. "We could go to Breaux' Restaurant and just sit there until it's time for the concert. Sit and eat too, of course. Other people might think of doing the same thing."

The sidewalk was clearing now, and their progress was fairly rapid. Leading the way, Vail dove down three or four steps to a half-hidden entrance into a channel-like café with a lunch counter at one side of the narrow space. Beyond this counter, the space widened somewhat, and tables were scattered about where, Vail explained, "the twenty-five-cent lunches were served." Here he paused, looking quickly around, and then hurried forward again towards still another section of the café, divided from the "twenty-five-cent tables" by a step and a railing. Almost immediately he turned to Cresside in triumph.

"Oh, Auntie, there they are now! Mr. and Mrs. Prescott, I mean! At the first fifty-cent table. . . . Why, how do you do, Mrs. Prescott? How do you do, sir? Mrs. Prescott, this is my Aunt Cresside, Mrs. Fabian d'Alvery. And this is my little cousin, Frances Belle."

His voice rang with pride as he presented them. Cresside acknowledged the presentation graciously, and Frances Belle, quickly remembering her manners, hastened to drop a quaint curtsy. In return they were greeted with cordial civility. She and her husband had just started their tea, Mrs. Prescott said; of course Mrs. d'Alvery and Vail and Frances Belle must join them. Only she knew they would rather have coffee. She hadn't lived in Louisiana long, but she had lived there long enough to know *that!* Extra chairs were quickly drawn up to the table and the toast and fig preserves which had accompanied the tea were promptly supplemented by heartier fare. Frances Belle became speedily absorbed in a double sundae, and Cresside, drinking her coffee in slow sips, appraised the Prescotts with decreasing anxiety, perfectly well aware that they were likewise appraising her. They were gentlefolk, there was no doubt of that, even gentlefolk of considerable distinction—a little on the stiff side, perhaps, but that was understandable. Both were tall and slim and fair, with that subtle resemblance to each other which long and harmoniously married couples often attain; seeing them in a crowd, Cresside would have taken them for brother and sister rather than for husband and wife, and as she observed them more closely she saw, or fancied she saw, that they resembled Charles Boylston, too. They were both courtly, if reserved, of manner, and they were both dressed in beautifully tailored clothes, more appropriate for city than plantation wear, in Cresside's opinion, but undeniably fashioned by a master hand. Mrs. Prescott was wearing no ornaments but her engagement ring and a brooch at her throat, but these jewels, like her clothes, were exceptionally handsome. Vail, though he spoke both to Mr. and Mrs. Prescott with more obvious respect than Cresside had ever seen him display towards his elders before, did not seem overpowered by them; indeed, he apparently knew them well enough already to be comparatively at ease with them.

"I've been looking around everywhere for Sue, sir. I thought she'd be at the Knights of Columbus Home."

"No, only the queen's ladies-in-waiting and the two previous festival queens watched the parade from the balcony with her. All the other maids sat on a platform in front of the Catholic Church."

"I wanted her and Auntie to meet each other. Do you know where she is now?"

"She's just gone to some friend's house to dress. You know the girls are wearing colonial costumes this year instead of gingham and I imagine they're getting great fun out of it—I never knew a girl who didn't! But of course Sue must meet your aunt later on. . . . You're staying for the ball, I hope, Mrs. d'Alvery?"

"I'm afraid that would mean keeping Frances Belle up too late," Cresside began. Then seeing Vail's expression of consternation she added hastily, "But I suppose that wouldn't hurt her, for once. Yes, we'd be glad to."

"Then you'll see Sue in all her glory at the Community Club. Perhaps we can sit together. . . . We've been hoping, Mrs. d'Alvery, that something would bring you and your husband to New Roads. Don't you ever come over to False River?"

"We haven't been there in a long time. But we'd like very much to call on you. Is Sunday a good time? Fabian's in Washington today, but that's unusual. He's nearly always at home and at liberty on Sunday."

Sunday was a *very* good day for them, Mrs. Prescott declared. Indeed, they were trying to continue their lifelong custom of making a feature of their Sunday breakfasts and asking their friends to share these, at noon instead of nine: that and the pitchers of fruit juice on the sideboard were the only innovations. They served baked beans, brown bread, codfish balls, apple sauce, doughnuts and coffee, just as they always had.

"It sounds wonderful," Cresside murmured appropriately, not without some inner qualms concerning the codfish balls. But the Prescotts were playing up nobly, and for Vail's sake she was determined not to let them down. It presently transpired that they had served these

510

Sunday delicacies not only in Boston, or thereabouts, as she had more or less taken for granted, but pretty much all over the world. Mr. Prescott had been for a long time in the American Foreign Service, though he had now retired and spent most of his time tinkering with inventions; he had served in such divergent points as Lisbon, Port-au-Prince, Cairo and Helsinki. Looking at them more closely, Cresside saw that both he and his wife were considerably older than she had at first supposed; Susannah must have been born when they were far past their youth. Was she an only child, Cresside wondered, remembering that Vail had not mentioned any brothers or sisters. Mrs. Prescott answered her unspoken question.

"Our one ewe lamb is taking to Louisiana like a duck to water," she said. Then laughing a little, she added, "There I go, mixing metaphors again! My cousin Charles is always teasing me about that." The conversation turned, naturally enough, to Charles Boylston, and Cresside and the Prescotts were still talking about him when Vail reminded them it was time they started to the concert.

The Community Club was on the same street, but it was several blocks away, near the locks, where Bayou Plaquemine flowed into the river. Frances Belle's footsteps were lagging before it was reached, and though she had ceased to clamor for food, she was obviously tired and sleepy. Cresside suggested that it would be better if she kept the little girl at the rear of the grounds and urged the others to go forward without her; but it was soon obvious that the only seats left were in the back row of the roped-off space. The Prescotts and the d'Alverys sat down side by side and listened, with uniform politeness but varying absorption, to the performance of the State University Band.

The music was surprisingly good, and the band members made a gorgeous showing in their purple and gold uniforms. But in spite of her best efforts, Cresside's attention constantly wandered from them. She was watching the street for the first glimpse of the parade and straining her ears to catch the sound of the other band which would accompany it. Vail, she knew, was even more impatient, and he showed it. The Prescotts remained completely calm, applauding at all the proper intervals, their eyes fixed on the gold and purple uniforms. If it had been her daughter who was shortly to appear as a figure of fantasy, she could not have been so serene, Cresside thought, glancing down at the drowsy child nestling at her side. It would be only a few more years before Frances Belle would be as old as Susannah, taking part in festivals, going to balls, finding her first suitor. Her heart failing at the thought, Cresside pressed her little daughter more closely to her side. . . .

The band was playing "The Stars and Stripes Forever," which was apparently its final selection, and the parade was coming at last. The strains for which Cresside had been listening became audible, faintly at first, but gradually growing louder and louder. The red flare of torches appeared in the distance, and presently the Negroes who carried them came into view, their white coats and white kerchiefs ruddy with flickering light. The Negroes were in high spirits; they sang and whistled, exchanging jokes with their cronies among the spectators, and occasionally interrupting their march to execute a few dance steps. In their wake the first float, golden and gleaming, swung into sight, drawn by four fine black horses, whose harnesses had been wrapped in gold cloth. In the center of the float a masked girl, adorned with the jewels of a Carnival Queen, was shown stepping from the crystal circle of a hemisphere. She wore a golden crown and carried a golden scepter, and two other girls, also gorgeously dressed, bore her golden train. The float moved slowly so that there would be time for the queen to bow and smile in every direction, acknowledging the applause of the crowd; but after it had passed the Community Club, the parade accelerated its pace. The light from the torches was fitful, bringing some of the floats into bright relief and obscuring others; Cresside's impression of the majority was confused. She saw Father Time encircled with girls dressed in pastel shades, all so young and pretty that they had no cause to fear him, and failed to catch the symbolism of the display. She saw a water wagon—one of the great barrels on wheels used in the cane fields—surrounded by laughing Negroes, as the plantation bell had been, earlier in the day, and this seemed to her significant and appropriate. A horn of plenty trundled by, overflowing with animated sugar bags. Then a great sugar bowl, with a charming head peeping from it and others peeping around it, swung into sight, and Vail clutched her arm excitedly.

"There's Sue! In the sugar bowl! Look, Auntie! Isn't she a knockout?"

Cresside murmured, "Lovely, darling!" with convincing enthusiasm, but the float had gone on before she had received more than a fleeting impression of shining silver and fair young faces; and after these had disappeared, Vail was no longer interested in the parade. He wanted to get into the hall before all the best seats were taken, as they had been at the outdoor concert. As it proved, he was right in urging his companions to hurry and in propelling the sleepy Frances Belle himself. The Community Club was packed already, and it took some maneuvering to get a good look at the stage. This had been ornamented with a backdrop representing the façade of an ante-bellum plantation house, with a columned entrance and long French windows. Patches of young cane were scattered realistically over the foreground, and at one side, under a clump of trees, the queen—who had apparently been whisked in through a side door—was seated, still masked, on a large thronelike chair, her maids of honor hovering attentively near her. A string orchestra had been playing while the audience was gathering, but now a slight, kindly-looking man mounted the platform and held up his hand for silence.

"Ladies and gentlemen," he said. "It is a great pleasure and a great

512

privilege for me, as the Mayor of this city, to welcome you to the third Louisiana Sugar Cane Festival. I think those of you who have attended our first two festivals will agree that this year Plaquemine has surpassed all its previous efforts. This evening you have beheld a representation of the sweetest story ever told. You must have thrilled, as I did, at the splendor of that magnificent historical pageant. And while its spell was still strong upon you, another parade has magically unwound before your wondering eyes—a parade led by the Queen of the Festival, enthroned on a golden float, and followed by other sumptuous floats proudly bearing as their burden the loveliest maids from every sugar Parish in this State, come to do honor to our own."

The Mayor paused to take breath and to await applause. Relieved on both scores, he continued with increasing fervor as he approached the climax of his peroration.

"But up to this moment, ladies and gentlemen, you have been denied the privilege of meeting these lovely young ladies. In the case of the Queen, even her identity has been withheld from you by means of a mask. In the case of the others, while you have been able to gaze on their charming countenances, you have not been informed of their names or the location of their homes or the educational institutions which have chosen them as representatives. It is now my proud prerogative to introduce to you this bevy of beauty, beginning of course with their Sovereign Lady. Queen Sucrosa III, I command that you unmask, revealing yourself to this gathering as none other than Miss Genevieve Kearney of New Roads!"

Again applause resounded, spontaneously this time. The Queen, accepting the Mayor's hand, stepped from her throne to acknowledge it; and as it went on and on, she made a graceful, deprecatory gesture, signifying that it was time to stop, and glanced towards her ladies-in-waiting as if to say it was their turn now. They were both Plaquemine girls, whom the Mayor had known from childhood, and at some length he traced their family background and cultural development and paid due tribute to their charms.

"At this rate, it will be midnight before we get to dance," Vail muttered, creasing his yellow program and uncreasing it again. "The old geezer must be wound up. The introduction of the maids was supposed to start at nine-twenty and it's way past that now."

"Not much past, really," Cresside told him in a whisper. "I think the Mayor's almost through anyway. And he's enjoying himself so much! You shouldn't resent it if he rambles on a little. Besides, think how proud the families of those girls must be. They're drinking in every word he says."

"Well, I'm not," Vail said tersely. "I want to see the maids have some kind of a chance. I want——"

"Hush, darling! He really is through with the ladies-in-waiting. Now he's signaling to someone else."

A pretty girl had appeared from the wings and given her hand to the Mayor, who presented her to his audience as Miss Katherine LaCour, representing the Innis High School. She curtsied gracefully, crossed to the other side of the stage, and went down the runway, where she was met by a young man who had been patiently standing there for some moments, obviously awaiting some kind of a cue, and they took their places in a semicircle of reserved seats in the front of the hall. Before Miss LaCour and her escort had moved aside, the Mayor was introducing another maid and another young man had stepped eagerly forward to escort her to the semicircle. The fourth time that this process was repeated, Vail stirred in his seat and half rose.

"What's the matter?" Cresside asked, still in a whisper.

"Nothing. I reckon it's time for me to be moving towards the stage, though. It'll be Sue's turn any minute now."

He went carefully past her and the Prescotts, nodding and smiling a little self-consciously, and edged his way along the side of the hall, moving with his usual boyish awkwardness and holding his head with an air of assurance which Cresside felt certain must be assumed. He had said nothing about this part of the program, which was evidently the prelude to some sort of a fancy dance, nothing about Susannah's selection of him as a partner. For it must have been a selection; this orderly progress could not be impromptu; it had obviously been planned with great care. If Vail had not been shy about disclosing the role which he was to play, he would have talked about it, as he had about other features of the Festival; and suddenly Cresside felt a pang of pity for him. It meant so much to him, this meeting with Susannah, and it might mean so little to her! Vail was young to be hurt. . . .

"Miss Lydia Dupuis of Breaux Bridge, representing the Cecilia High School," the Mayor was saying. "Miss Nancy Barker of Plaquemine, representing St. Basil's Academy—Miss Beulah Butte of Reserve, representing the Leon Godchaux High School. . . . Miss Susannah Prescott of New Roads, representing St. Joseph's Convent. . . ."

Holding her breath, Cresside watched the wings for Susannah's entrance. She saw a slim girl who held herself very erect, and whose brown hair was parted smoothly in the middle. Her eyes were gray, her eyebrows and eyelashes almost black; they made a striking note of color in her otherwise pale little face. She had a small straight nose and a firm but shapely chin. At first she gave the impression of being very demure; but when she smiled and acknowledged her introduction, she showed bewitching dimples and her lashes curled coquettishly down over her delicate cheeks. The curtsy she made was accomplished and graceful and the colonial dress which she wore was obviously no festival costume, hastily put together for the occasion from sleazy material; it was made of rich cream-colored grosgrain and trimmed with ivory-tinted lace. Cresside guessed that these warm shades might be the result of antiquity, that both dress and lace had

514

once been snow white and that they had served as the bridal finery for one of Susannah's great grandmothers, perhaps the startlingly named Salome Church. But whoever its original owner, Susannah wore it well; the tight pointed-bodice and plain elbow sleeves became her; the voluminous skirt made her trim waist look all the smaller. Only over the bosom it did not fit her; her ancestress must have been fuller breasted than she was, probably because Salome was older than Susannah when she wore it and had already lost Susannah's appealing immaturity. Even in colonial times, girls as young as Susannah did not marry. Or did they? Did they do it sometimes even now? Cresside looked at Susannah with fresh apprehension and reluctant admiration, as the girl walked slowly down the runway to meet Vail. After that, Cresside saw nothing clearly until the Royal Dance was in progress, and Vail and Sue were circling the hall among the other maids and their escorts.

They danced easily and well together, as if they had done it before and were accustomed to each other's ways. But there was far less appearance of abandon in their movements than in those of most couples on the floor. Many of these were already cheek to cheek; others were releasing each other to execute fancy steps, and then flinging themselves into their partner's arms again, more closely embraced than before. Vail's steps and Susannah's were in perfect unison, but he held her lightly, and she continuously gave the effect of insisting on her identity, rather than merging it with his. For the most part she danced in silence, her head slightly bent, and Cresside was more conscious of the girl's smooth brown hair and its white part than of her highbred little face. But every now and then she looked up with the arch expression for which Cresside was already beginning to watch, and said something which obviously pleased and amused Vail very much, for he threw back his head and laughed whenever she did so. Something about this carefree interchange of merriment struck Cresside as inexplicably poignant. She looked away from the dancers, belatedly turning her attention to the Prescotts.

"I understand now why Vail was so upset when I said perhaps we wouldn't stay for the dance. He's very fortunate to have your lovely little daughter for a partner. She's easily the most charming girl in the group."

Briefly, and not too emphatically, Mr. and Mrs. Prescott disclaimed their right to the compliment, commenting favorably on Vail in return: he had so much vitality, and at the same time, so much stability for a boy of his age; and he was almost outrageously good looking! That special combination of coloring—very black hair, with bright blue eyes and ruddy cheeks—was most unusual. The Prescotts were eager to see his twin; they had heard that she was really a beauty.

"Yes, there's no doubt of that. But don't expect her to look like Vail. She's as fair as he is dark and has wonderful blond ringlets instead of a straight black mop like his. I don't know whether you remember Mary Pickford in her prime—well, Sybelle's a little that type. The younger children are delightful too, especially Philogene. He's generally considered the flower of the family. But I mustn't run on like this about my young relatives: . . ."

Her eyes wandered towards the floor again. All the girls, wearing their quaint colonial costumes and dancing with the natural zest of youth and high spirits, made a pleasing picture. But she had spoken the truth when she said that Susannah was the most charming in the group. While Cresside looked at her with renewed intentness, half hopeful, half fearful of finding some flaw, the music came to a slow stop. Lingeringly, Vail's arm began to slide from Susannah's waist, and as if slightly intolerant of his procrastination, she freed herself, in the same light easy way that she had danced, and started across the floor with Vail following her. When she reached the side, she faced Cresside with her bewitching smile, holding out a small shapely hand.

"I'm so glad you came to the Festival with Vail, Mrs. d'Alvery," she said. Her voice was cool and pleasant, like her parents', and she spoke with complete poise. "And is this Frances Belle? What a sweet little girl! No, please don't wake her!"

Susannah bent over the sleeping child, smoothing back a stray curl. "I've been wishing I could meet the rest of Vail's family, ever since he brought Phil to see me," she went on, straightening up again. "I hoped Phil would come to the Festival, but Vail says he wasn't interested. I'm afraid I didn't make much of an impression on him. But he did on me. I've kept telling Mother and Father that they might as well make up their minds that Phil's my fate, because I have. I'm going to wait for him to grow up."

CHAPTER XL

As THE D'ALVERYS approached the little house on Somerulos Street after taking the last ferry, Cresside saw, with surprise, that the lights were on in the library and realized that Fabian must have come home unexpectedly. Her joy at the thought of seeing him was tinged with regret because she had not been there to welcome him, and she ran swiftly up the steps, leaving Vail to follow with Frances Belle in his arms. The little girl had slept soundly throughout the drive home, and she did not stir when Vail lifted her out of the car. Fabian opened the front door and greeted his family with mock reproof.

"Deserting me, are you, Cresside? Stealing your aunt, eh, Vail? What's the big idea?"

"The idea was to introduce me to Mr. and Mrs. Prescott of New

Roads and their daughter Susannah," Cresside answered with something of her old drollery. "But the Plaquemine Sugar Festival was the medium for this auspicious presentation. We've seen two parades and a coronation and a ball and we've listened to three bands. We're pretty much all in now, but we'll tell you about it tomorrow. Good night, Vail. Just shift Frances Belle over to her father, will you? I think I can get her undressed without waking her. Thanks for taking me to the show. I've had a swell time. And by the way—I think Susannah's a grand girl."

Muttering an incoherent word of appreciation, Vail kissed her good night and sauntered down the walk. From the gallery Cresside watched him as he got back into the rattletrap car and slammed the undependable door so that it would shut. Then she waved to him a last time and went back into the house with her husband as Vail bucked off down the street. Consequently she did not see him turn the car around and start back into town instead of proceeding towards the River Road. He did not stop until he had almost reached the ferry again. Then he drew up at the little house behind the Fancy Grocery Store where Luigi and Netta, in spite of their mounting prosperity, had continued to live, and where they had taken it for granted that their only son would continue to live with them, instead of in barracks or at a fraternity house, while he attended the University. A few lights were still burning inside, and beyond the open window, Vail could see Riccardo seated at a desk. He whistled, giving a special signal that had been understood between them for years. Riccardo immediately jumped up and came to the door.

"Hello, there! What on earth are you doing out at this time of night?"

"Hello yourself! I've been to the Plaquemine Sugar Festival. What are you doing *up* at this time of night?"

"Studying. The finals are getting too darn close for comfort."

"Hell, you should worry. You haven't got a mark below A minus all year."

"I'm not worrying. But I don't want to get anything lower than that next year either. . . . I haven't been studying all evening anyway. Just off and on. I've been reading that new book of John Gunther's, *Inside Europe*. It's keen. You ought to read it yourself, Vail, and find out what's going on over there. You haven't got the first idea."

"I got plenty to do, just trying to keep track of what happens right on the plantation. Dad can't look after everything. . . . What else you been doing while I've been out dancing?"

"Sounds sort of like the ant and the cricket, the way you put it. I've been listening to Paul Sullivan's broadcast. Do you know what? He's sure we're in for another war."

"You're crazy with the heat. Or else he is. The last one was the war to end all wars."

"That's what you think."

"It's what everyone thinks, isn't it? I know that's why Dad went."

"I reckon it's what everyone thought in 1916. I don't know that so many people think that way any more. What does your father say about the occupation of the Rhineland?"

"Nothing much. Something about how France and England could have stopped it between them but maybe they didn't think it was all that important or they would have. He said a lot more about——"

It had been on the tip of Vail's tongue to say, "About the Italian invasion of Ethiopia," but he stopped just in time. Riccardo, either oblivious of the slip or pretending to be, swung open the screen door.

"Come on in, why don't you? If we're going to settle the future of the world we might as well do it sitting down."

Vail did not wait to be asked a second time. There was nothing on earth he liked better than to stay up till all hours arguing with Riccardo on weighty matters which neither of them understood very well. When he did not return from an evening's outing, it was assumed that he was spending the night on Somerulos Street. Occasionally this was the case, and as no one ever brought up the question, he did not feel it necessary to disclose that far more frequently he was spending it at the Tramontes'.

"I could do with something to eat," Riccardo announced, latching the screen door. "How about you?"

"I sure could. I haven't had anything to speak of all day."

"I thought they had good food over in Plaquemine."

"Maybe they do somewheres. We couldn't find anything," Vail declared shamelessly, forgetting how recently he had chided Frances Belle for her unbridled appetite.

"Well, we had a man-size hunk of roast for dinner. Must be a lot left. Let's see anyway. Don't make any more noise than you can help. Father has to get off to Lafayette around five tomorrow morning—I mean this morning. I don't want to wake him and Mother."

The two boys tiptoed to the immaculate kitchen and switched on the lights. The huge white refrigerator loomed enticingly before them. Opening it, they extracted the substantial remains of a twelve-pound beef roast, cut off thick rare slices, and made themselves bulky sandwiches. Reinforcing these with three-fourths of a chocolate layer cake, half of a dewberry pie, and two bottles of milk, they returned to Riccardo's bedroom and spread the feast on his desk in the midst of his books and papers.

"How was the dance?" Riccardo inquired, sitting down, his mouth full of sandwich.

"Swell. Aunt Cresside liked Sue a lot, too. At least she said so, and she's all set to be nice anyhow. The hitch will come with Mom and Dad and *grand'mère*. Especially *grand'mère*."

"How come?"

"I never knew it to fail. A fellow's family always says, why yes, of course she's a very nice girl, but still she isn't exactly the *sort* of girl that——"

Vail grinned, speaking in a mocking falsetto. Riccardo failed to return the grin.

"Anyway, they don't stop you from taking her to a dance. They can't, so long as her folks let her go. Now you take Syb and me, we can't even get to go to a dance together."

"I know. It's a dog-gone shame."

"I thought maybe I could take her to the junior prom this year. But I've just got a letter from her saying no soap."

"Gee, I'm sorry, Rick. If it was my say-so, she'd go with you, you know that. Anyway, it's a cinch no one can keep you from taking her to the senior ball. You're sure to be Colonel of the Corps next year, Rick, and if you choose Syb for Sponsor of the Regiment——"

"What do you mean, if? You know good and well I'd choose her. I chose her for one of the Battalion Sponsors this year, but all it got me was I had to choose over again—my big fat cousin Drina Montegino from New Orleans."

"Just the same I don't think even Mom and Dad would try to keep Syb from being Sponsor of the whole Regiment."

"I do. Besides, I may not have any say about it. There's nothing so certain about me being Colonel."

"Well, you're a Major already, aren't you? If you can get to be a Major when you're a junior I don't see any reason why you can't get to be a Colonel when you're a senior."

"You seem to overlook the little detail that there are four Majors and only one Colonel."

This was so undeniably true that Vail did not attempt to deny it. Instead he devoted himself to the dewberry pie, having by this time devoured his share of the sandwiches.

"Anyhow, I've got one thing coming," Riccardo said after a reflective pause. "At least I think I have. I'm almost sure Father's going to give me a boat for a graduation present."

"Gee, that's swell. What kind of a boat?"

"Well, naturally I want a Gar Wood. I don't know whether it'll be a light cruiser or just a speed boat."

Vail whistled. The Fabian d'Alverys had always been extremely generous to him, but none of their gifts had begun to reach the proportions of a Gar Wood boat, nor did he know anyone besides Riccardo whose parents would have thought of giving graduation presents on such a scale. "I should think a speed boat might hold you for a while, you lucky bum," he said enviously.

"Yeah. But if I got a light cruiser then you and I could maybe go up north and bring her down the river ourselves."

"Say, that would be the cat's whiskers, wouldn't it? How long do you reckon it would take us to make the trip?"

"Oh, we ought to allow a couple of weeks. Might as well look around a little while we're about it. And maybe after we got the boat down here we could work it so as to take the girls out on it sometimes—Sue and Syb."

"Yeah, maybe we could. Especially if we could get Aunt Cresside on our side."

"You think your Aunt Cresside's tops, don't you?"

"You bet I do. There's nothing the matter with Mom though, or your mother either."

They went on talking about the new Gar Wood and all the uses to which he could be put while they finished up their food and undressed. There were two cots in Riccardo's room and one of them was always in readiness for Vail; he kept a pair of pajamas under the pillow, an extra shirt in the bottom bureau drawer, and a toothbrush of his own in the bathroom. They gave him an extra feeling of "homeyness," even when he neglected to use them, as he very frequently did; while a hidden package of razor blades was a still more beguiling feature of his visits to the Tramontes'. He had not as yet achieved a razor of his own, as his need for one was still not urgent or even obvious; but he experimented with Riccardo's, once a week or so, to his own great satisfaction. Tonight, however, he suddenly felt very tired, so he dropped off his clothes and got on to his cot without a single superfluous motion. He was almost asleep when Riccardo, who was much more meticulous in his habits and therefore took longer to get to bed, spoke to him again.

"You know, I've been thinking, Vail. If there is a war, I'll get into it right away."

"How do you figure that out?"

"Because when I graduate I'll be a reserve officer with a Lieutenant's commission. I won't have to wait for a draft or anything like that."

"Hell's bells, Rick, you talk as if you *wanted* us to get into a war."

"No, I don't want us to get into a war. But if we *do* get in——"

"Oh, for crying out loud! You've got war on the brain. You better stop listening to Paul Sullivan and reading John Gunther."

"Well, you'd better read *something*. You'll forget how if you don't. Did you see Mussolini's statement about Ethiopia in the *Advocate*? Didn't that get a rise out of you? Because if it didn't, it sure as hell should have."

So Rick was ready to talk about Mussolini after all, and maybe he was right about another war, at that. If there really were one, of course Vail would want to go himself; he did not read books and listen to broadcasts, foretelling one, the way his friend did. But he had always been a ready listener to the accounts of Lucien Estrade's dramatic feats on Beauregard's staff and of the exploits in France which had led to the winning of Gervais' medals and the death of the two uncles for whom he himself had been named; he had always hoped that sometime he himself could exceed their triumphs, and make the family even prouder of him. He had also seen numerous thrilling movies depicting the glories of war which had inspired him with the fancy of sharing these in the hero's role; and since he had met Susannah, this idea had taken a firmer hold on him. It was gratifying to imagine her following his triumphs from afar, keeping his picture in uniform on her dresser, weeping when she saw his name in the casualty list, welcoming him on his well-decorated return with open arms. Vail dwelt on these pleasing pictures with renewed satisfaction, driving down the River Road the evening after his excursion to Plaquemine. He was alone, for Philogene and Jerome had stayed in town to go to the movies with some of their own special cronies and Franchot had been ailing the last few days. So there was no chaffing and clattering going on, and he could think things through by himself, as he had always liked to do. He believed that Rick was right about most things. Every time he went to the Tramontes' he firmly resolved that he would read more, that he would study harder, that he would strive to be more like his idol. But he was no sooner back on the plantation than this absorbed him again. He resented the hours that he was obliged to spend in school, without spending extra hours buried in books after he reached home. He did not want to study, even after it grew dark. It was one thing sitting up half the night, once a week or so, talking to Riccardo; but if he sat up late every night, he was too sleepy, mornings, to get up at daybreak and ride out over the headland. And that was what he loved to do above everything else in the world. He might talk about going into Mr. Pereira's office to learn the coffee business, because he was flattered that he had been offered the job, and because he was not sorry to impress Aunt Cresside with its importance. He might even feel he had better accept it, because there were so many of them at Belle Heloise and because he would need more money than he could get at home, as his rightful share, if by any chance he should happen to want to get married some day. On the other hand, he might decide to go to Princeton after all. He did not really object to it because it was a highbrow Eastern college; he could make the grade if he tried, and reluctantly he admitted to himself that perhaps he ought to, on account of Sue. There could be no comparison between the eligibility of a suitor who had gone to Princeton and a suitor who had gone into the coffee business straight from high school. But in his heart of hearts he knew that he would never willingly leave Belle Heloise for any reason whatsoever, that it was almost as much a part of him as his hands and feet. All the aspects of it which had meant so much to him as a child meant even more to him now.

He was nearly home again, and something within him quickened at the realization of this; but as he approached the desolate expanses of Hathaway, he deliberately looked in the other direction. It was

521

a habit he had failed to outgrow. He himself had never been to any of the "bootleg shindigs" which were responsible for Sybelle's banishment, and he shared the aversion which the local Negroes had for the place, though without superstition. It had never been inhabited or planted since the hideous accident which had cost Déette Reno her life and banished Blood in order to save his skin. Blood was now managing a sugar factory in Mexico with conspicuous success, and Wilhelmina, who had long since divorced him, spent most of her time wandering aimlessly over the Continent from one watering place to another, much as the Tremaines had once wandered. The Negroes who had worked on the plantation had been only too glad to leave; some of them still lived in the scattered cabins along the Road, raising small patches of cane and vegetables themselves, or working at Belle Heloise when extra hands were required; others had moved into town, "bettering themselves." Micah and Jinny were profitably installed in the household of a Standard Oil magnate; Jonah was the janitor of a school; Meme ran a small café identified with the sign STRICTLY COLORED. Phronsie had gone over to the West Side, where she had achieved a more ambitious establishment, more alluringly designated. Under the twinkling legend MISS PHRONSINA'S HOUSE OF JOY appeared the further caption COME IN AND PLEASURE YOURSELVES. There was evidence to indicate that this admonition had not gone unheeded. But Minta had been sent off to an excellent school and from there she was going to a colored college. Later on, she was going to be a teacher herself.

The deserted cabins at Hathaway were only part of the desolate scene which Vail so deliberately avoided. The looming façade of the Big House was no longer white and gleaming; it had taken on a grayish tinge, and though this was only from lack of paint, the result was eerie, especially in a dim light. The garden and lawns which had formerly been so elegantly patterned had long been overgrown with rank grass and weeds, and thickets were closing in on the once productive fields. Wilhelmina Blood had been trying for years to sell the place, but without success. There was no market, any longer, for houses and plantations of that size. A new order of things had brought about a different way of living and the River Road had been shorn of its unique importance as a thoroughfare by the new airline highway, which cut straight across country, instead of following every bend of the Mississippi, and reduced the distance between Baton Rouge and New Orleans by nearly thirty miles. Besides, locally, nearly everyone except the riotous students shared Vail's feeling about Hathaway.

He continued to look at the levee now, until he had rounded the bend in the road which marked the boundary between Hathaway and Belle Heloise; then, joyously he turned back to his own land. The hoe gang which had been cleaning the fields were just leaving these to go home, and the hands were singing as they swung away towards the quarters. The cane was already shading the rows, and Vail thought, with satisfaction, of the old saying that if the fields were green by the first of May, the crop was assured. He knew that this saying was not infallible, that if the next months were so rainy that the hoe gang could not work regularly, the Johnson grass would get ahead of the men and there would be the devil to pay. But if this did not happen, and nothing else untoward occurred, the cane would be as high as the fourth bars of the old-fashioned fences by the Fourth of July. Then the crop really *would* be assured.

He hoped nothing would happen to it this year, for Dad's sake. Dad had been through a long siege of bad luck, and it was time he had something better coming to him. The plantation was a part of him, too, and he suffered with it and throve with it, just as Vail did. Except for his family and his hunting, it was almost his only interest now. Vail had been too young, at the time of his foster father's retirement from politics, to grasp many of its implications, but he did know that there had been a bitter disappointment connected with it, and that since then Dad had tried to make the plantation compensate for everything else. He was highly regarded, not only as the virtual savior of the sugar industry in the state, but as a progressive planter who did not rest on his laurels but who continued to experiment in new methods and to improve old ones. He had met with marked success in both directions; frequently he was asked to deliver addresses and write articles on the cultivation of sugar cane, and he was also called into consultation at various agricultural experimental stations, including the one in Washington. Though all this gratified him, to a certain degree, he was not essentially a writer or a speaker and he had wanted to go to Washington in a different capacity. His failure to do so had embittered him. He looked and acted older than he was, and it was only when he went hunting that he seemed to shed his cares and his age.

The year before he had gone, at Charles Boylston's invitation, on a hunting trip to Alaska, taking a train to Seattle and a boat to Juneau, before starting back into the hill country. Harvey Lawrason of Denham Springs, who came more and more frequently to Belle Heloise now that Hackberry Lodge was closed most of the time, had been his fellow guest on this occasion, for Mr. Boylston never did things by halves, once he got started. He had even told Gervais he would be glad to invite one or two of their former political associates, if the Captain thought it would do any good. Charles thought it might; now that Huey Long was dead, politics were going to be different in Louisiana: for instance, there was Happy Sevier, who had always been a good friend of his; Happy was now a member of the legislature, and might very well become quite a power there. But Gervais smiled rather wrily, and replied that it was Charles' party, and that of course, the host must do as he pleased. As far as he personally was concerned, however, he did not care about trying to get in touch with anyone who had not first made an attempt to get in touch with him. He thought they would have a much better time if only the three of them went, as originally planned. So it had been decided that way, and the expedition was a great success. Gervais had sent back numerous snapshots, showing himself with a formidable growth of beard, and standing proudly beside a Kodiak bear he had killed. The bear's head had been mounted and placed over the fireplace in his study, supplanting a family portrait, while the fur had been made into a rug to be put in front of the hearthstone. And Gervais had actually come home with the beard, even more bushy than it looked in the snapshots. Afterwards he had given a big party, inviting all the educators and sugar men who thought highly of him as a progressive planter, and for a time the atmosphere had been very jovial. But he had pointedly omitted from this gathering all acquaintances with political connections, and presently he had sunk back into his old bitter state.

Vail had been delighted that Dad had had this fine trip, and with Sance to help him, had shouldered the responsibilities of the plantation in Gervais' absence, as he always did during the briefer periods when Gervais went to Washington and elsewhere. He did a very good job for a boy of his age; he was flattered at the confidence shown in him and tried to deserve it; but he could not help feeling sorry that the trips Dad took were so seldom the sort in which Mom could share. When Uncle Fabian went anywhere, he took Aunt Cresside with him; sometimes Frances Belle went along and sometimes she was sent out to Belle Heloise while her father and mother were gone; but in any case, Aunt Cresside shared in all Uncle Fabian's pleasures and opportunities. Of course Vail understood that Mom did not like hunting or sports of any kind, and that while Dad did not mind this, the way he minded that Franchot did not like them either, he nearly always chose a hunting trip when he went anywhere for pleasure and this automatically debarred Mom from going too. Of course Daddy could not take her to Europe and Hawaii and Peru, just like that, the way Uncle Fabian took Aunt Cresside; there was not money enough and there was the responsibility of too many children. But he could have taken her to Washington once in awhile and to New Orleans fairly often. *Grand'mère* and Granny Randall and Miss Mittie could have looked after the family while he did that. Mom was only a little older than Aunt Cresside, maybe three or four years, but there were times when she looked almost as old as *grand'mère*, whose face did not have a line in it even yet, and whose figure was still her great pride. Mom loved her husband and her children and her home devotedly, and she never complained because it did not ever seem to occur to Dad that she might have welcomed a few outside interests and diversions; but Vail felt they would have given her a great lift, and that she would have looked younger and felt gayer if she could have had them.

524

Before Sybelle had been sent away to Grand Coteau, on account of Riccardo, Vail had usually managed to have a ride with her on the levee after they got home from school; now he spent this period with Sance or Plauché, doing whatever was indicated at the season. After supper he generally played some kind of game with Joyeuse and the younger boys before he went reluctantly back to his books for an hour or two. The youngsters were all very good at games, and showed so plainly that they were pleased because he played with them that he was flattered by their outspoken gratitude and admiration. Besides, the games gave him a good excuse for putting off the lessons, and in his mind there was only one choice between the two.

On Saturdays and Sundays he spent even more of his free time with the youngsters. He taught them all to swim in the river and to ride on the levee; he took them fishing in the barrow pit and squirrel hunting in the woods back of the plantation—at least he taught them all to swim and to ride, and he took all of them except Franchot hunting and fishing. It made Franchot sick to see a fish squirming on the hook, and he cried the first time he saw a squirrel, which had been frisking and barking only a few minutes earlier, lying dead on the ground. The others all made fun of Franchot when this happened, but Vail had stood up for him. He was a good shot for his age, and he liked to go fishing as well as anyone; but he had not forgotten how he felt when Betsy Ann died, and he knew that in a sense Franchot loved all free wild creatures the same way he himself had loved Betsy Ann.

"Leave him alone!" Vail had said fiercely to the others, as they crowded around Franchot, jeering. "If this isn't his idea of a good time, it isn't, that's all." Vail took up the dead squirrel and tossed it away where Franchot would not see it. "Come on, brat, let's you and me go home. There's lots else to do, besides squirrel hunting. I'd rather ride on the levee myself, any day. What say we go for a good long ride straight off?"

Vail had a real horse now, because he had outgrown Nostar; but Nostar was still alive and well, and though he was getting stiff and slow, Franchot rode him and loved him. Maud had died at a ripe old age several years earlier; but before she died, she had produced not only the coal-black puppy which Uncle Fabian had wanted so long, but a replica of herself, which Vail loved almost as much as he had loved her, and which he named Maudie after her. He said that from now on there would be a Maudie at Belle Heloise, just as there was always a Minnie. The current Maudie went racing along the levee when Vail and Franchot rode there, nosing the ground and snapping for bugs, just as her mother had done before her. She was an integral part of the plantation, too.

This last winter Vail had not spent as much time with the youngsters as before, first because he had taken on more responsibilities during the grinding season and afterwards because he had gone to

New Roads on so many week ends. Groups from the Baton Rouge High School frequently started out on a Friday evening over the fine paved highway now connecting Baton Rouge and New Roads and reaching Jim Jarreau's camp in time for supper. This supper consisted of perch, trout or sac-a-lait fried in deep fat along with little cornbread balls, called hush-puppies because it had once been the local custom to quiet the dogs which gathered around, begging for fish, by tossing the fried cornbread to them. The girls and boys who came to Jarreau's ate prodigiously of these homely delicacies. After supper there was always dancing in the adjacent pavilion, connected with the bar, sometimes to the music of the gaudily colored juke box at one end of the hall, sometimes to the strains of a hillbilly band, imported for the occasion. Groups from the New Roads schools also came to these suppers and these dances, and it did not take long for the two "crowds" to get together, especially as many Baton Rougeans had relatives living along False River and vice versa. Often the Bouanchauds or the Kearneys gave house parties and then the "gang" from Baton Rouge stayed over until Sunday for more dancing and for various kinds of sports.

The Saturday night dances were different from any others: whole families came to the "night spots" from the surrounding countryside, some on foot, some in wagons, and some in broken-down cars. They were seldom seen seated around the tables, though occasionally they brought food with them; more often they got to dancing with the least possible delay, refreshing themselves from time to time with beer which they drank direct from the bottles, standing at the bar or on the dance floor. Even nursing mothers found the exigencies of their condition no deterrent to their enjoyment; they carried their babies in their arms while they danced and permitted them to feed at will. The babies were in no wise upset by this casual treatment either; they evidently drank in a love for dancing with their mothers' milk. As soon as they were able to toddle, they began to dance themselves, taking to it like ducks to water; and the older they grew, the more proficient they became. The patriarch of a family danced with his great grandchildren, and his wife knew all the latest steps. The high-school groups did not mingle much with these family parties, but they liked to be in the same hall with them, vicariously sharing their pleasure; there was a general feeling that nothing was quite so much fun as the Saturday night dances on False River.

The young people also hunted quail on horseback during the winter week ends, riding pinto ponies from Glenwood plantation, where they usually went for at least one meal with Trammel Harrison and his wife, who had been Miss Josie Glen. They fished off Lawrence Bizette's wharf, where chairs were provided for their comfort, and if the fish did not bite very well near the wharf, then they hired boats from Oliver Guillaume and went fly-fishing or casting. They went speed-boating too, as several of the local boys had craft of this kind and it was exciting sport, especially by moonlight. On Sunday mornings many of them got up early and went to Father Savouré's little church at Lakeland, because he was their favorite priest; then they resumed their fishing and boating and hunting until it was time to start back over the new highway again. Very often as they went bucking along towards town they sang the song which was such a favorite among the local children that some of their elders, who had not admired Huey Long, said sarcastically it must be part of the school curriculum:

> "They call him a crook, but he gave us free school book,
> Tell me what's the reason they shoot Huey Long?
>
> Huey Long in his grave, while we riding on his pave,
> Tell me what's the reason they shoot Huey Long?
>
> Huey Long dead and gone, Louisiana left alone,
> Tell me what's the reason they shoot Huey Long?"

Vail sang this song along with the rest of the crowd, as he did "You're the Top," "The Music Goes Round and Round," "Moon Over Miami" and numerous other favorites of the moment. Most of them he hummed or whistled at home too, but he was careful never to include "What's the Reason They Shoot Huey Long?" in his solos. He knew that Dad hated the very mention of Huey Long's name, and that in some vague way the Kingfish had been responsible for his political disappointment and his subsequent bitterness. Vail did not have very much to say about the excursions to False River in any case; their significance to him soon centered around Susannah Prescott, and he was not ready to talk about her yet. He had not outgrown his childish habit of taciturnity, and none of his elders tried to force his confidence or restrict his freedom; it was taken for granted that he could come and go as he pleased and that he would want to go more than he did when Sybelle was at home, because he missed her companionship. But until he told Cresside about Susannah, when they were on their way to the Plaquemine Sugar Festival, it had not occurred to any of them that he had already found another companion who meant even more to him.

Vail had first met Susannah at Jarreau's and after that once or twice at the Triple Arch and the Island Queen; but her parents did not allow her as much latitude as most of the local girls were permitted. If she went to a fish supper with her friends, Mr. and Mrs. Prescott went, too; and althought they sat at a separate table, they made their restraining presence felt just the same. They required their daughter to leave the Friday evening dances at ten-thirty and they did not let her go to the Saturday dances at all, once they had seen the young mothers dancing and nursing their babies at the same time; moreover, they always took her home themselves. But at the Bouanchauds' house and at Glenwood she was not quite so strictly chaperoned, and Vail was everlastingly grateful to Miss Josie for giving him his long-sought chance to see Susannah alone.

He dwelt on this episode now as he swung into the driveway and came in sight of the Big House at Belle Heloise. Most of the crowd had assembled, as usual after Sunday dinner, in the huge chamber back of the parlor at Glenwood; it was the favorite gathering place. But Susannah did not care for it. She did not make this too obvious, because she was too well-bred; just the same she managed to convey the impression that she had never been accustomed to sitting in bedrooms in mixed groups, and that she would a little rather not. She lingered behind in the parlor and Vail lingered too. Several of their fellow guests called to them, but Miss Josie glanced at them and went on without them to the huge chamber which was dominated by two enormous four-posters.

"They're having a good time where they are," she said. "Why not just leave them alone for a while?"

Susannah had seated herself on an old horsehair sofa, crossing her small feet in front of her and folding her slim hands in her lap. She did not say anything at all; she simply sat there, looking composed and contented and very, very pretty. Vail, who had never cared for noisy girls, found himself liking her better than ever when he found she did not immediately start in on some pointless chatter. He seated himself at the opposite end of the sofa, feeling comfortable and contented too. The silence between them was not awkward; it was companionable. But eventually he was moved to break it.

"This is a nice place," he said. "I like to come here."

"Yes. I do, too."

"You live in a pretty nice house yourself, don't you?"

"I think it's nice."

"I'd like to see it sometime, if I could."

"I'm sure Father and Mother'd be very pleased if you'd care to come and call."

"Sure enough? You think I could come this evening?"

"I don't know why not. I don't think they have any other engagement."

"Maybe I could take you home. Then if it was all right, I could come on in. Were you planning to go home with anyone special?"

"No. Just anyway it happened."

Mr. and Mrs. Prescott did not insist on taking their daughter home themselves after she had been to parties in private houses during the daytime. But in return for this concession, it was understood she was to remain with a group. She did not "date," she was not "going with" anyone—in fact, Mr. and Mrs. Prescott considered both these expressions, and the practices they described, extremely vulgar.

"Do you think your father and mother would mind a lot if it would be with me? I mean, without anyone else along?"

Susannah raised her eyes and considered him carefully. This was

528

not upsetting to Vail either. He preferred a girl who thought things over, the way he did, to one who jumped at the chance of going anywhere, anytime, alone with a boy. Besides, she had beautiful eyes, and when she raised them he had a really good look at them; usually they were half hidden by her long black lashes.

"Don't you have to take some of the crowd back to Baton Rouge in your car?" she inquired at length. She had learned to speak of the "crowd" since coming to New Roads though she had never done so when she was going to the Winsor School in Boston.

"Yeah. But I'll have plenty of time to come back and get them. They'll be whooping it up for hours yet."

A sudden burst of merriment from the bedroom served to confirm this statement. Susannah rose, smoothing down her skirt.

"All right. Let's go and tell Miss Josie good-by straight off, shall we? Unless you'd like to stay longer, of course."

A month or two earlier she would have said, "Let's go and say good-by to Mrs. Harrison now, shall we?" Vail was impressed with the progress she was making towards talking like a regular human being, and he thought her idea of immediate departure excellent. He hastened to the door at her side.

"I'll bring Leaping Lena right around," he said enthusiastically. "Thanks a lot, Susannah."

That was all there had been to it, except, of course, the ride between Glenwood and Salome. This would have been wonderful if she had only sat beside him on the front seat of the old rattletrap car, with her hands folded in her lap and her eyes veiled again. But that was not all there was to it. In order to say something, Vail had told Susannah about the current Maudie and asked whether she liked dogs, too. After thrilling him beyond words merely by saying that she did and listening politely to his praise of Maudie, she had gone on to tell a very exciting story.

"I have a dog now, too. I never had one before, but this German Police was on the place when we came, so Mother let me keep him. His name's Major."

"That's a nice name for a German Police."

"Yes, I think so. He's a very gentle dog and he has a strange story. A wolf is in love with him."

"A wolf! In love with a dog! I never heard of such a thing!"

"No. I never did either. Would you like to hear the strange story?"

"You bet I would."

"Well, you see, Mr. McPherson, the man who owned Salome before we did, brought a wolf there that he had caught while he was hunting once in North Louisiana. It was a young lady wolf, a gray timber. He kept her caged at Salome for about two years. Then he decided to set her free again. She ran off into the woods, but every night she came back and stayed with Major. She does still."

529

"Gee, I'd like to see her."

"You can, sometime. She never hurts anyone, but she's never been caught again either. She comes to see Major and then she runs off to the woods again. Mr. McPherson kept hounds, too, and every once in a while after he set the wolf free he used to invite his friends to Salome—Voralberg its name was then—for a wolf hunt. Of course he locked up Major beforehand, because, if he hadn't, Major would have tried to protect the wolf. But the men set the pack of hounds after her and then they followed themselves in cars from different points on the plantation. There are old cattle paths all around the place that have been made into good roads. Sometimes the chase lasted so long that they went as much as two hundred miles—not straight, of course, but in circles amounting to that much. But the wolf had so much more endurance than the hounds that finally she exhausted them and won out, and the very next night she would come back to Major again."

"Does your father have wolf hunts, too?"

"No. But Mr. McPherson kept on having them for five years and still the wolf never stopped coming. But she's still very wild. She's never 'softened' for anyone but Major. She's never had any cubs either."

Vail was tremendously intrigued with this whole story, which he thought even much more exciting than the one about Romulus and Remus. He was also curious about the conduct of the wolf with the police dog when she was in heat, but he decided, rather quickly for him, that it would not be suitable to ask Susannah questions on such a subject or discuss it with her, at least until he knew her a little better. In any case, they were already turning into the driveway at Salome and afterwards there was only time for a brief stilted call in the formal drawing room before he had to go back to the crowd. At least, that was all there had been time for that day. Since then he had been to Salome a number of times, and once Phil had gone with him. . . .

For a moment the image of Phil at Salome rose up to disturb Vail's happy memory. Phil had been instantly at home there, as he was every place. He had not minded the formality of the drawing room, or the restraining presence of Mr. and Mrs. Prescott, or the precision of the service at supper, for which Susannah's parents, unbending for the first time, invited the two boys to remain. It was because of Phil, not because of Vail, they had done that. Vail had never made them laugh, the way Phil did, he had never asked them easy questions or told them funny stories. They had taken an instant liking to Phil, that was clear enough; they had urged him to come to Salome whenever he felt like it. But Phil had neglected this golden opportunity, never going to Salome a second time. He had his own crowd, which preferred the Amite to False River; and the next week end when Vail, trying hard to be fair, asked him to come along, he said hell no, he had other

530

fish to fry besides those you could get at Jarreau's. He did not so much as refer to the Prescotts' kindness.

So Vail had gone thankfully back to Salome by himself, and Susannah, after asking briefly for Phil, had amazed and delighted Vail by inviting him to be her escort at the Plaquemine Sugar Festival, for by that time she had written the prize-winning essay and had been chosen to represent St. Joseph's Academy. And now he had told Aunt Cresside and Rick Tramonte all about her, and was eager to tell Mom and Dad and *grand'mère,* too. . . .

Maudie came bounding out to meet him as he put up his car in the shed and continued to leap along beside him as he entered the Big House. It was nearly always quiet there, in "first evening," when Mom was still in the *garçonnière* and Dad still in the fields and *grand'mère* resting, and there was something very pleasant about this abiding peacefulness. Today it was even quieter than usual, for with Phil and Joyeuse both in town and Franchot in bed, there was no one around to make any noise. Vail was very sorry for Franchot, the poor kid was sick such a lot. He decided to go over to the *garçonnière* straight off and see if he could do anything to help pass the time for the little boy; but first he would get rid of his books, for a while anyhow. He was on his way to his own room with them when *grand'mère* called him.

"Is that you, Vail? I should like to speak to you for a minute before you go out again."

He went willingly enough into the boudoir. His grandmother, who was as usual enthroned on her sofa, indicated the Turkish chair beside it.

"Did you have anything you meant to do just now, Vail?"

"I thought I'd see if Franchot would like to play checkers or something, that's all. Do you know how he's feeling?"

"He is better. Suppose you stay with me a few minutes first."

"All right."

Vail sat down in the Turkish chair and waited. He did not have to wait long.

"Your Aunt Cresside came out to dinner this noon, Vail. She told us that you had taken her to the Sugar Festival in Plaquemine yesterday."

"Yes, I did. I thought she got quite a kick out of it, too. Didn't she speak as if she'd had a good time?"

"She spoke of meeting a family named Prescott, from Boston, distantly kin to Charles Boylston and now living in New Roads."

"Well, I thought she liked them, too."

"Apparently they are persons of some background, in their own way. I have always liked Mr. Charles Boylston, Vail, I believe you are aware of that. I see no reason for assuming in advance that I would not like his kinsfolk. But I am surprised you have never told us before of this new acquaintance, since apparently it is important to you."

"I didn't know it would seem important to you, *grand'mère*. If I had, I'd have been glad to tell you about it."

"It is important to me also."

"Well, there really isn't a lot to say. Except there's a girl I like and I reckon Aunt Cresside's told you that already."

"Yes. She told me this girl was very lovely to look at, that she carried herself and conducted herself with great dignity. I could see that she was most favorably impressed with everything about her and I was inclined to be favorably impressed also, until your Aunt Cresside mentioned something she had said at the end of the evening which seemed to me rather lacking in restraint."

Vail thought for a minute, trying to isolate one speech of Susannah's from all the others. "You mean the joke about Phil?" he finally asked. "Why, Aunt Cresside didn't take that seriously! She couldn't have. It didn't amount to anything. You mustn't take it seriously either, *grand'mère.*"

He rose and walked over to the window. He did not want to talk about Susannah any more just then after all. He had been glad to, until the subject of Phil had come up. He was slightly ashamed because he found this so irritating, but there it was.

"Just hearing about Susannah isn't enough," he said. "I want you to invite her over here—with her father and mother. I reckon Aunt Cresside's told you that, too. She promised me she and Uncle Fabian would go over to New Roads for one of the Sunday breakfasts the Prescotts have, and then I thought we could ask them all to Belle Heloise for Sunday dinner. Let's wait and talk about Sue after that, shall we? I really have a lot to do right now." He looked out of the window, and then he smiled, as if he had thought of something that pleased him. "I'll tell you what, *grand'mère,*" he said. "I'll bet you dollars to doughnuts that when you see her you'll say here's a girl, at last, good enough for the green rose!"

CHAPTER XLI

The INDICATED EXCHANGE of civilities between Belle Heloise and Salome began almost immediately.

The Sunday following the Sugar Festival, Fabian and Cresside called on the Prescotts and the call was promptly returned. An exchange of invitations next ensued, with Cresside taking the lead by asking the Prescotts to a garden party, and at the garden party Gervais and Merry, Vail and Philogene were all present. Waiving formality, the Prescotts proceeded to invite all the d'Alverys to Sunday morning

532

breakfast, even though Gervais and Merry had not yet called—a departure from precedent which, as far as the Prescotts were concerned, represented a real landmark. Only Madame d'Alvery and the younger children were missing when the family delegation set out for New Roads to attend this time-honored festivity; and a week later the two clans came together in full force, when the d'Alverys entertained the Prescotts at Belle Heloise.

By this time Sybelle, having returned from Grand Coteau, was home again for her summer vacation, and helped to welcome the guests. Charles Boylston, who had briefly reopened Hackberry Hall, was included in the Prescott group; and the Pereiras, who were weekending at Belle Heloise, relieved the family atmosphere. The household servants, scenting a budding romance and reveling in the prospect, outdid themselves to impress the Yankees and the city people with the sumptuous fare and skilled service to which their own white folks were accustomed. The codfish balls and baked beans, the brown bread and apple sauce served by the Prescotts on their blue Canton ware were meager indeed compared to the shrimp and oyster gumbo, the turkey with corn-meal dressing, the okra and rice and spoon bread, and the puff pudding which Lou Ida excitedly prepared and which Selah served with dignity on the Sevres plates which had been painted to order for Evaline Estrade with the complete history of Evangeline. Madame d'Alvery, wearing all the ancestral jewels she still retained after fulfilling her votive offering, presided in regal fashion at the head of a table covered with old lace and set with ancient silver. Gervais, resuming his neglected role of genial host and expansive man of the world, played this again to perfection. Merry, clad in a new and becoming dress which Cresside had chosen for her, looked young and lovely again, and Cresside herself was, as usual, the personification of chic and charm. Fabian, almost as familiar as the Prescotts themselves with the distant parts of the globe where they had lived, conversed about these with understanding and ease, and the poise which Sybelle had acquired at her convent school enhanced her artless graces. Mrs. Randall contrived to be unusually agreeable and Miss Mittie contributed several New England witticisms. Indeed, the only members of the family group who did not endeavor to create a favorable impression and signally succeeded in doing so, were Frances Belle and Philogene.

Frances Belle was restless. She did not like to sit for such a long time at the table, keeping still while a lot of grown-up people she did not know talked about a lot of things she did not understand. She wanted to jump up and run around and she wanted to talk herself. Moreover, though she was fond of food, she did not want it all at one big meal like this, either; she wanted to have some of the things she liked best for dinner and the rest at intervals during the afternoon. Her instinct told her that Lou Ida would not want any chilluns running in and out of the kitchen after this feast was finished; she would want to go back to her own quarters and rest her feet and discuss the Prescotts with the other servants. Frances Belle also resented her separation from Vail. It was tacitly understood that she was always to sit beside him when she came to Belle Heloise, and here he was placed between Susannah Prescott and Nellie Pereira while she herself was wedged in between Franchot and Barry Pereira. Franchot did not talk much because he was not feeling very well, and though she knew she ought to be sorry for him on this account, she was feeling too sorry for herself to have much sympathy left over; and Barry Pereira never talked much to anyone except Joyeuse, who was sitting on his other side, telling how crazy she was about her chemistry course. Frances Belle grew more and more silent and sullen and then she began to pout. Finally she got up from her seat and whispered first to her father and then to her mother, who looked at each other and said, all right, if *grand'mère* was willing, she might be excused now. Mr. and Mrs. Prescott, who missed no detail of her behavior, told each other afterwards that they simply could not understand why Mr. and Mrs. Fabian d'Alvery, who were such charming, cultured persons themselves, had not taught that horrid little girl better manners.

Philogene's conduct was even more reprehensible; he was worse than restless, he was rebellious. He had already made plans to go with his own crowd to Amite when he was informed that he was expected to be on hand for the Prescotts. At first he had flatly declined to do any such thing; it had taken an admonition from his father, much sterner than those Gervais usually gave Philogene, to bring him around; and though he had stayed at home, because he had been forced to, it was with the mutinous resolution that he would show that prim, stuck-up little Yankee Vail had such a crush on just what he thought of her anyway. Susannah, who had been secretly fearing that she would not have a chance to talk to him, was overjoyed to find that though Vail was on one side of her, Philogene was on the other. But her joy was short-lived; Philogene displayed none of the fascination which had so captivated her and her parents on the occasion of his one visit to Salome. He answered her in gruff monosyllables when she spoke to him, and spoke about nothing at all of his own accord; and as soon as dinner was over, he mysteriously disappeared, and was seen no more for the rest of the evening.

When Mr. and Mrs. Prescott referred to him, in the course of the drive home, in the same disparaging way that they had spoken of Frances Belle, Susannah quickly defended him. She did not believe he was feeling well. Someone had told her Franchot was not, but she thought that was a mistake; she thought it must be Phil instead. He had given up other plans in order to be home that day; he had told her so himself. Well, he would not have done that unless he had meant to be pleasant, now would he? Yes, she did think Madame d'Alvery was a very fine looking old lady. Yes, she did like both Mr. and Mrs. Fabian d'Alvery and Captain and Mrs. Gervais d'Alvery, and she did think Sybelle and Joyeuse and Franchot were all very nice. But she still liked Phil the best. She had told him she hoped he would come over to New Roads the next time Vail did, and he had said he wasn't sure, he thought he might be going to Amite, but he would come if he could. She believed he would come and that the next time he would be feeling all right again.

While the Prescotts were discussing the d'Alverys, the d'Alverys were equally busy discussing the Prescotts. Sybelle told Vail, very sweetly, that she thought Sue was lovely and that she did not wonder he was crazy about her; but a minute later, her lips began to tremble and when he asked her cripes, what was the matter, she asked him if he didn't wonder she felt badly to think the whole family would break their necks, like this, to be nice to his girl and her family, when Riccardo and his parents were never asked to the house for so much as a cup of coffee, and when she hadn't got to go to the junior prom. Here she had been home just a few days, and Dad and *grand'mère* were already saying they thought it would be a good plan for her to make a nice long visit to their kin in New Orleans and Mummy was not saying anything; so probably she would have to end up by going.

"I wish I could do something to help, Syb. You know I think Rick's a grand guy. You know I don't want you to go away again. I've missed you like hell all winter."

"You've gone over to New Roads nearly every week end. I don't believe you missed me over there."

"Yes, I did. That is, I knew it would have been even more fun if you'd have been along. Look, Syb, I'm going to try to work something. I'm going to see if we couldn't fix it so Rick could go along to New Roads the next time I do, and you, too. You don't have to start making those visits right off, do you?"

Sybelle shook her head, her brimming eyes overflowing. "It's no use, Vail. You know the Prescotts wouldn't invite Rick to their house either, and that's where you really want to go, when you talk about New Roads, isn't it? I'll just have to wait. But I can tell you one thing. I'll never look at anyone else, not if I live to be a thousand. And I can tell you another. Just as soon as I'm of age, I'm going to elope. Rick says now he won't let me, but maybe by that time he'll be just as whipped down as I am now!"

She sat down on the bench beside the refectory table and turned her head away, so that Vail would not see that she was crying, even though she realized that he knew it. Ordinarily he would have sat down beside her and tried to comfort her. But now, hearing approaching footsteps, he merely put a steadying hand on her shoulder and spoke in a warning voice.

"Hang on to yourself if you can, Syb. Someone's coming."

As he spoke, the door from the hall into the patio was thrown open, and Mr. William Pereira came out, rubbing his hands together and smiling with an air of great heartiness. He had put on considerable weight with the years, and his phenomenal prosperity had increased his inherently cheerful outlook on life. At the moment he was replete with good food and good wine and he had found his fellow guests excellent company. He could not have been in better humor.

"Well, well!" he said jovially. "What are you doing, off here by yourselves? Not badgering your sister about her boy friend by any chance, are you, Vail?"

"No, sir, we were just talking. I was telling her——"

"Don't you let him try to put anything over on you, young lady," Billy Pereira persisted. "You're in a position to give back as good as you get, these days. And this is the lad who tried to persuade me that the reason he wanted to go into the coffee business was because he wasn't interested in sugar! Well, now we know what he *is* interested in, don't we, Sybelle?"

"I reckon I didn't explain just right, sir. What I meant to say was——"

"Oh, I know what you meant to say and what you meant to keep up your sleeve, too! But the cat's out of the bag now all right. Well, I seem to be getting as much mixed on my metaphors as Mrs. Prescott does. . . . Have you noticed whether Sue's inherited that from her mother Vail?"

"I don't think she has, Mr. Pereira. But anyhow——"

"Anyhow it wouldn't matter if she had? Suits you right down to the ground, eh, just the way she is? Now I tell you what, Vail. It never does any harm to look around a bit. That's what I'd do if I were you. I wouldn't let this little Yankee have the satisfaction of knowing you'd fallen for her, hook, line and sinker. I'd keep her guessing. I'd let her worry. It's good for girls to worry. Why, look at Sybelle here, worrying her head off, and she was never prettier in her life!"

"If you don't mind my saying so, Mr. Pereira——"

"But I do mind. I'm giving you good advice and I'm telling you you ought to take it. Just the same, I'll say this too, Vail. Now that I really know what your interests are, I'll make you a better offer— thirty a week instead of twenty-five, whenever you care to start. Any young couple ought to be able to manage on thirty a week. You could, couldn't you, Sybelle, if you had the chance?"

There was seemingly no end to Mr. Pereira's joviality. Sybelle and Vail continued to writhe under it, while he went on and on. Meantime the "small fry" had all gathered in the parlor around the old piano, and were singing vociferously to the accompaniment of Joyeuse:

"Va-il d'Al'ry, so they say,
Goes a-courtin' ev'ry day.
Sword and pistol by his side,
Susy Prescott for his bride!"

The strains of this song, which none of the singers seemed to find it tedious to repeat, penetrated easily to the patio. Vail could feel his face flushing and his temper rising; if it had not been for Sybelle, he would probably have "blown up." But he did not want to risk adding to her discomfiture, and at last the ordeal ended. The small fry deserted the piano and rushed out into the yard for a game of croquet. The Pereiras announced that they must allow for a brief stop at Hackberry Hall on their way to New Orleans, and Charles Boylston departed to prepare for their coming. Cresside and Fabian went home too, deciding that was the best place for Frances Belle, who was still sulking. The members of the immediate family had the Big House to themselves again, and assembled in the library to enjoy a quiet evening and talk over the day.

"I like those people," Merry said, unequivocally. "I like them all. I'm glad we've met them. I hope they'll come to Belle Heloise very often."

"That man Prescott's nobody's fool." Gervais also spoke without hesitation. "Vail, you said he was a retired diplomat, and I had an idea he was just sitting around on his hands these days. But it seems he tinkers with machinery all the time. He's had two or three inventions patented already. Now he thinks he's on the track of something that'll revolutionize cane cutting. I suppose it would be too much to hope that anything would come out all right in this wretched business——"

"The P.O.J. came out all right."

"Yes, I grant you that, Merry. But with all these governmental restrictions on acreage and marketing that we've got now, we're almost back to where we were before we started those experiments. Just the same, it would help if we could solve some of our labor problems by machinery. That problem's bound to get worse instead of better. Those strikes they're having in France are just the forerunners of what we've got to expect here."

"That child spoke excellent French," Madame d'Alvery interposed. "Her parents' was good but hers is better—*vraiment, de l'academie!* I was interested in her account of the False River dances. They have evidently made quite an impression on her and she describes them very well. I used to go to dances in New Roads occasionally when I was young, Gervais—more often than you and Cresside ever did, I think."

"Did you, *maman?* I never heard you speak of it before."

"Possibly not. . . . I also went once to a dance in a public hall in Back Brulé with your father shortly after we were married—Doiron's, I think the name of it was."

"Tell us about it, *grand'mère,*" Sybelle urged, with genuine interest.

"Well, the hall was just a rough structure divided into two rooms, a large one for dancing and a small one where the children who were brought along could be put to sleep, some in beds and some on quilts spread out over the floor. In the larger room there were benches surrounding the wall where the older members of the community sat and watched the dances. The local girls were in *robes de style* made of flowered cretonne, identical as to cut but different as to design. They had all provided their escorts beforehand with enough material for blouses to match their dresses; hence it was easy to tell which young men and which young girls were interested in each other."

"That's not so hard, ever," muttered Vail, whose spirits were beginning to revive.

"A violin and an accordion furnished the music and the party opened with the lancers," Madame d'Alvery continued, without appearing to notice his interruption. "Only those in costume were allowed to take part in this, though outsiders were welcome to look on and join in the subsequent figures. But of course my husband wished to participate in every dance, and knowing beforehand of this ruling, he had insisted that we go provided for it. So I had a very lovely *toile de Jouy* made on purpose for the occasion and we danced with the others. I remember that the refreshments consisted only of Creole gumbo, baked sweet potatoes and black coffee—a rather extraordinary menu, but I must admit that it tasted good."

"I'll bet it did," Vail said, thinking of the gumbo at Breaux' Restaurant in Plaquemine.

"My husband enjoyed it so much that he wanted to make up a party again the following summer. Of course it was impossible at any other time of year."

"Why, *grand'mère?*"

"Because such expeditions could be undertaken only when the dirt or plank roads were passable and it did not take too long to go with a horse and buggy—remember we had no 'pave' then and no automobiles. So we made our plans. But the next summer my poor little baby was only a few months old and I could not leave him. My husband suggested that I should take him, after the fashion of the Back Brulé women—which I gather is still the fashion in the countryside around False River."

Madame d'Alvery paused in her recital and smiled. Her family, who had never before heard of the expedition she had just described and who had never known her to tell a story in this vein either, waited, with suppressed astonishment, for her to continue.

"It was the sort of jest he enjoyed," she said. "Indeed, I do not think he would have been in the least nonplussed if I had taken him at his word. But I could never unbend as he did. . . . I lost my poor little baby shortly afterwards, and then of course I did not dance again, at Doiron's Hall or anywhere else. But I believe I still have that *toile de Jouy* dress put away somewhere, though I have not seen it in a long time. I shall ask Lucie to look for it. I recall that the pattern was made up of rose garlands and blue lover's knots against a cream background. Possibly Susannah might be interested in seeing it or even wearing it, if costume dances are becoming general again. I believe, Merry, that

538

it would compare favorably with the dress she wore in Plaquemine, from what Cresside told us of that."

"I'm sure it would, Madame Mère. I'd like to see it myself."

"Well, we will look it up. Susannah would set it off very well. She has been taught to stand and sit properly, which is something, in this day and age. You really must speak to Joyeuse, *chère*. She sprawls over everything. When she sits with her knees spread apart and her toes turned in, as she does half the time now, it is almost more than I can bear. I suppose it is what comes of sending her to a public school. And does she have to wear socks and sneakers, except for sports? After all, she is thirteen now, and unless I am very much mistaken, Barry Pereira is beginning to be *épris* with her. It is ridiculous, but it appears to be true. If she is old enough to have a beau she is old enough to act like a young lady. Well, as I was saying—the little Prescott really does act like a lady. She even enters a room with grace, which in my experience is rare in the young. I notice that she does not wear socks and sneakers. I must say she is very suitably dressed. Very stylishly, too. You may be sure everything she has comes from Paris."

It was some hours later before Fabian and Cresside spoke about Susannah. They had gone to bed early, almost as soon as Frances Belle, for they were unaccountably tired, and Fabian had fallen asleep almost immediately. He woke to the realization that Cresside was also awake, and guessed that she had not slept at all. He reached out his arms and drew her towards him.

"Anything the matter, darling?" he asked gently. "You're not worrying about Vail, are you?"

"Yes, I am."

"But you knew this would happen sometime."

"Yes. Sometime. But not when he was only sixteen."

"Most boys have crushes as young as that, Cresside. I know I did. Not that it got me anywhere."

"That's what I'm worrying about, mostly. He's so young to be hurt."

"There's no certainty that he will be, is there?"

"No, but I'm afraid he will. I'm afraid this isn't just a crush. I'm afraid it's the real thing. And I'm selfish, like most women. I'm not ready to lose him so soon. I didn't think I would."

"Well, there's one person you'll never lose. You know that, Cresside. Doesn't it help at all?"

"Yes. I do know that. And it does help. A lot."

She put her face close to his in the dark and kissed him. Then she lay very quiet in his arms. They were still around her, holding her and supporting her, when she finally went to sleep.

CHAPTER XLII

Vᴀɪʟ ᴡᴇɴᴛ ᴛᴏ ʙᴇᴅ, the night after the momentous gathering of the clans, in a glow of happiness. The day had seemed perfect to him from beginning to end and only one regret crossed his mind: he wished he had told his family about Susannah Prescott months sooner; as it was he had wasted a great deal of time which might have been far more profitably spent. But even this regret was short-lived. He was too elated over the satisfactory present to dwell with disappointment on the wasted past, especially as he foresaw an increasingly rosy future. Now that Susannah had come once to Belle Heloise, he was sure she would be coming right along; she would be there for the swimming and fishing and the sand dances that summer, and in the fall for hunting. Sybelle would ask her to slumber parties, and they would sleep in the very next room to his, which was an exciting thought, just in itself; they would get to be close friends, the way girls did when they sat up whispering to each other half the night and this would create another bond between him and Susannah. Of course Sybelle would also go with him to New Roads, and he would find a way to get Rick there, too, whatever Rick and Sybelle might say about it themselves. Suppose the Prescotts were just as unreasonable about peddlers' sons as the d'Alverys? Rick had managed the sand dances and if he could do that he could certainly manage Jarreau's. . . .

In these rosy dreams Vail failed to consider the eventuality that though Susannah did come to Belle Heloise several times during the early part of the summer, it was neither Sybelle's company nor Vail's for which she showed a marked partiality, but Phil's; and that though the twins were frequently asked to Salome, Phil was always included in these invitations. Then in August Mrs. Prescott found that she could not stand the heat in Louisiana any longer, and departed for Bar Harbor, taking Susannah with her; to make a bad matter worse, when she rejoined her husband in November, she left Susannah behind with Boston relatives, to resume her studies at the Winsor School. It appeared that Mrs. Prescott had been disappointed in local scholastic standards; she had also felt that possibly Susannah was going to more parties than were good for a girl of her age and that it would be better for her to remain in the North most of the time until after her formal debut at the Chilton Club. When that had taken place, Mrs. Prescott would be delighted to have her daughter enjoy a carnival season in New Orleans, under the right auspices; indeed, she thought they might take a house there for part of one winter. At all events, Susannah would not forget how kind and cordial everyone in Baton Rouge and New Roads had been to her and would

540

look forward to seeing her Louisiana friends again in due course of time. . . .

Vail accepted the first of his own disappointments fairly philosophically. He was as ready as anyone to admit Phil's superior attractions—the easy grace, the quick wit, the fluent speech, the laughing ways which he himself lacked. Phil had never gone through an awkward age, mentally or physically; he danced well, he talked well, he wore his clothes well. There was a harmony between his brown hair and his hazel eyes and his delicately tanned skin which was less striking but more pleasing than the violent contrasts in Vail's coloring; even more pleasing, many persons thought, than Sybelle's exquisite blondness. Phil and Joyeuse looked and acted very much alike, and Franchot would have shared this beguiling resemblance if his sensitive little face had not been so thin and pointed and his bearing listless instead of gay. Vail could understand why Susannah should have found Phil better company in many ways, and he did not begrudge his brother her preference for sharing superficial pleasures with him; Vail felt that somewhere deep within her she must instinctively feel that he really counted to her for more in important respects, because she counted so tremendously to him, and that presently the superficial pleasures would not matter. He thought, since he knew beyond any shadow of a doubt that she was destined to be his sweetheart, she could not help finding it out too, sooner or later.

Phil's own attitude towards Susannah was responsible, in no small measure, for this absence of active jealousy. He soon ceased to avoid her or to treat her rudely, but he accepted her favors instead of seeking them, and there was a little condescension mingled with his carefree affability. If he and Susannah became separated from the others in the course of a sport which they all shared, such separations were either accidental, or maneuvered with great delicacy and adroitness by Susannah herself. Phil never instigated them. His attitude towards her was exactly like his attitude towards Nellie Pereira, and Nellie's methods were a little less subtle than Susannah's. Phil took the line of least resistance with girls, and since Nellie made it more difficult to resist than Susannah, she saw more of him. And she was a very pretty girl, too. Vail counted on Nellie to divert Phil more and more as time went on. This confidence helped to quiet the pangs which might otherwise have tormented him.

However, he found it much harder to reconcile himself to Susannah's indefinite removal from the scene. In her absence, the week-end outings to False River completely lost their allure for him and even the diversions he had always most enjoyed at Belle Heloise began to seem dull, flat, stale and unprofitable. He came in for a good deal of teasing, which he took good-naturedly at first, but more and more touchily as time went on and Susannah did not even answer his letters. Fabian was the only person who succeeded in reasoning with him during this period or even in persuading him to talk about his troubles.

541

"You know, I've always thought the only kind of girl who was worth having was the kind that was hard to get," Fabian said one day, apropos of nothing in particular, when the two were sitting on a log, resting during a dove hunt. "It took me five years to persuade your Aunt Cresside to marry me. First I had to get her used to the general idea and then I had to give her long breathing spaces between proposals. You just can't hurry that sort or badger them. It takes time and it takes tact to get them in the end. Your Aunt Cresside admits herself that if I'd tried to pull anything fast on her, everything would have been all over."

It had always been tacitly understood between them that they should refer to Cresside as Vail's aunt. This time the reference had other implications for the boy, in any case.

"Five years!" he exclaimed in outspoken dismay. "What on earth did you do with yourself all that time? I should think you'd have gone nuts.'

"Not at all. I was too busy."

"What doing?"

"Making money, for one thing," Fabian said practically. "I knew I'd need plenty if I had a family later on. I don't think your Aunt Cresside's ever gone without anything she wanted. I don't intend that she ever shall. Or Frances Belle either. But I had several other interests besides raking in shekels—my camellias, for instance, and Belizaire. And I did a lot of traveling in connection with my law practice. I learned to speak Spanish and I met some very interesting people and saw some very beautiful sights."

"Didn't you ever get low in *your* mind?"

"Lord, yes! Everyone gets low, every so often. And I didn't have anything definite to bank on, for a long while. There wasn't any reason why I should have had—then or later, as far as that goes. You'd know that, just to look at me."

Fabian had never referred to his deformity since the first day he had asked Vail to help him down the levee bank, and Vail seldom thought of it himself, unless it was directly called to his attention. Fabian had too many other attributes which were more arresting.

"All the same, I managed to hang on to a forlorn hope for two years," he continued, smiling as if certain recollections of the period were not altogether unpleasant. "And after that it wasn't so hard because the hope wasn't so forlorn. I'll admit the courtship seemed to me more like an endurance test than a romance, almost up to the last. But that was worth waiting for. And so were all the years we've had together since."

He picked up a dry stick and poked reflectively among the fallen leaves, the happy smile of reminiscence deepening. Then he dropped the stick, brushed some stray twigs off his knees, and put his hand on Vail's shoulder to steady himself as he rose.

"Time we were getting back, I reckon," he said. "They'll be looking for you at the Big House and for me on Somerulos Street—seems pretty good to have supper waiting and someone glad to see you when you get in, doesn't it? Fact is, I think that's about the best part of the hunt We might go out again next Sunday, though, unless you've got something better to do."

"No. I haven't got anything better to do."

"Well, for the love of Mike, don't talk about it in that tone of voice, even if you haven't. But look here, Vail, you're beginning to go stale on this place—it's time you got off it for a while. You'd better take a quick trip to Europe with us this summer."

"Gee, that would be swell, Uncle Fabian, if Dad could spare me——"

"Of course he could, during the slack season. We'll take a fast boat—might as well be the *Normandie*—and go wherever you say for a few weeks—France, England, Italy. Afterwards—see here, I don't want to run the subject of Princeton into the ground, but——"

"I've been meaning to tell you. I've decided to go after all, that is, if you still want me to and I can get in."

"Of course I still want you to and of course you can get in—at least you can if you really put your back to it and do some sure enough studying between now and next June. I even suggest that we cut down on all this Sunday hunting, much as I enjoy it—a good deal of work can be crammed into long week ends, as your friend Rick could tell you. By the way, I was glad to hear that he got his Colonelcy. I thought he would. I'm picking that lad to go straight on and up. But don't forget I'm picking you to do the same."

With his usual deliberation Vail turned this conversation over in his mind before he began to act upon it. But not long after it took place his correspondence with Susannah changed in both volume and character. Instead of plying her continually with rambling and reproachful letters, he waited for one of her own brief and infrequent missives, and after allowing a week or so to elapse, answered it in kind. He was working hard as hell, he told her, between school and grinding. His chemistry course was a caution, at least he thought so, though that brat Joyeuse simply ate up anything of the sort. She spent every Saturday fooling around the laboratory at the mill, at least when she could get the head chemist to let her. He was at the mill till all hours himself, as they were mighty short-handed. He hadn't been to New Roads in over a month, so he didn't have any news for her about the crowd. He hadn't even been hunting, because he was too busy week ends. But his Dad was planning a squirrel hunt in the Atchafalaya swamp back of Port Allen to celebrate Phil's birthday, and of course he was going to take time out for that. The whole family was going, even Franchot, who hated hunting, as she knew. But Franchot wanted to please Phil, especially when Dad had gone to all this trouble, and Mr. Lawrason was coming over from Denham Springs, too. Mr. Lawrason didn't go in much for squirrel hunting as a rule; he always wanted to use his dogs, so cat hunting was more in his line; but he was making an exception this time, on account of Phil's birthday. After that they would all be too busy in what spare time they had getting roseau reeds ready for the Christmas bonfires, so she mustn't be surprised if she didn't hear from him straight off again. He sent her his best. . . .

Susannah read this letter with more attention than she had given any he had sent her in some time, and answered it fairly promptly, for her. But several weeks went by before she heard from Vail again, and she had actually begun to watch for a letter. When it finally came, she found it contained only a few lines:

> "Dear Sue:
>
> This is just to say I was glad to hear from you, and that I would have written sooner except that Franchot is very sick and I can't seem to think of anything to say but that, because it's all I've got on my mind. I wish to heaven we'd never gone on that damn birthday hunt, and I don't feel right now as if I would ever want to go hunting again, though I suppose some day I shall. I will tell you what happened later on, that is, if you want to hear. Meanwhile you must not think it was Phil's fault or Dad's that everything went wrong and you must excuse this measly little note.
>
> Yours,
Vail."

The hunt to which Vail referred with such bitterness began under very pleasant and auspicious circumstances. Harvey Lawrason arrived at Belle Heloise on the eve of Philogene's birthday, bringing with him his trailerful of dogs, as if he hoped that the nature of the trip might be changed at the last moment. However, he took the announcement that the plans stood for a squirrel hunt with hearty good nature, and after an excellent supper, while everyone else sat around the fire listening to him, embarked on a series of typical tall tales. Gervais, who was in rare good humor, rallied him by saying these were not up to his usual standard, however.

"Which-I-God, a funny thing happened last week to a nigger I knew up in Tangipahoa Parish. Quit this nigger's name was. His ma named him that because he was the tenth to come along in twelve years and she figured it was quittin' time for her. But she had another one after all, and named him Golast, and he was. Well sirs, as I started to say, this nigger Quit went out in the woods to chop, and his wife, Silky, toted his dinner out to him in a bucket, just like she always done. 'Bout the time he knew she was coming, he drove his wedge into the top of an old block, and then he sat down on it himself, to rest a mite while he waited for her. She see him settin' there when she come along, and he had a grin on his face, too; she was a mighty good cook, and he always looked forward to them dinners she brought him. But when she hollered, 'Hello, Quit'! he didn't answer her, and after she got up close to him, she could see he was dead. The pressure of the wood in that block had drove the wedge up through his body, right where he sat."

"You say this happened to a nigger you knew up in Tangipahoa Parish, Harvey?"

"Yes sir, just this last week."

"Well, it's a funny thing, but my father told me that same story, about a nigger down here on the River Road, when I wasn't more than five years old. I wouldn't go looking for any more stories in Tangipahoa, if I were you, Harvey—they're stale. Fact is, I think that's one Parish I'd steer clear of anyhow, if I were you. The men up there don't stand for any fooling, when it comes to their womenfolk. They shoot mighty quick. And with tastes like you've got——"

"Which-I-God, I got the same tastes as any man, ain't I? Only difference is——"

"If you're planning to get off at four in the morning, I think the children ought to start for bed early," Merry said, rather hastily. Franchot was snuggled up on the sofa beside her, half asleep already, and she ran her hand lovingly through his hair. "This little boy seems to be coming down with another cold," she said. "He's been sneezing all day. I believe he's a bit feverish now, too. I think perhaps he'd better not go after all."

"But Mummy, I want to."

"You know you don't like squirrel hunting much, honey. Remember that first time, when Vail brought you home——"

"Aw, I was just a baby then." Franchot was wide awake again now, and hastening to defend himself. He spoke almost too eagerly. "Course I like squirrel hunting—leastwise I'm going to, soon as I get used to it. Besides, this isn't just any old squirrel hunt, right on the plantation. It's a real trip, way over to the other side of Port Allen. And it's Phil's birthday party. Like he had a cake and everything, only different."

"We're going to have a cake too, anyway, after everybody gets home. You could help me put the candles and the lettering on, if you stayed here."

"Merry, it's no wonder that boy's a mollycoddle. You pamper him like nobody's business. Right at the very time when he's beginning to get over his silly willies about hunting."

"There's a phobia of your own, Gervais, you've never got over."

"Good God, Merry, are you trying to compare a natural antipathy for poisonous snakes with squeamishness about the mere sight of blood?"

"About needless killing? And calling it sport? Yes, I am."

They were on the verge of one of those heated arguments which roused Gervais to quick and violent rage and transformed Merry's characteristically gentle and yielding attitude to one of stubborn resistance. Their love for each other was still strong and vital after all

545

these years; but they had never achieved the complete harmony which existed between Fabian and Cresside, and a struggle of wills, like the one which was now beginning, completely disrupted the pleasant atmosphere. Vail, who was always acutely uncomfortable during such scenes, rose and edged over to Franchot, throwing a persuasive arm around his shoulder.

"You heard what Mom said about getting to bed, brat. Come on, let's go. I thought maybe you'd sleep in my room tonight. Then one of us would be sure to wake the other up on time."

"I thought Phil was going to sleep there."

"Well, he is. But hell's bells, there's room for all three of us, isn't there?"

It was the first time Vail had made such a suggestion, and Franchot was thrilled at this admission into the fellowship of his older brothers. He was still more excited when he really did wake up first. He had been restless all night, partly with the fear that he would oversleep, and partly because his cold, which seemed to be getting worse, made him uncomfortable. But in his elation over the chance of rousing both Vail and Phil from their profound slumbers, he forgot his aching head and sore throat; and when Vail asked him, during their hasty breakfast, how was the cold this morning, he said truthfully enough that he felt fine, he thought it was gone. Gervais, noticing his flushed cheeks, asked him the same question and received the same answer. Well, the flush was probably due to excitement, then, Gervais decided, not without reason; for Franchot's apparent exhilaration lasted during the drive to Port Allen and over the old logging roads behind it. The woods which the hunters soon entered were the dismal type of low cypress, where quantities of gaunt black "knees" projected from pools of stagnant water and the scattered gum trees were already bare of leaves; and as the ground became increasingly soggy, they got out of their cars, and started to separate into groups of two. It had originally been Gervais' intention to keep Phil with him, and send Franchot off with Vail; but proud of the little boy's sudden staunchness, he made an abrupt change of plan.

"You tag along with me, son, and I'll show you some real sport. Before the day's over, you'll forget you ever thought you didn't want to hunt. Listen, do you hear that blue jay? He's warning all the other creatures in the woods that someone's coming. We have to keep mighty quiet for a few minutes."

There was a period of profound silence. Gervais stood with his arm around Franchot's shoulder, waiting. Then a flock of crows circled overhead, calling harshly and interrupting their flight to swoop down towards one tall tree after another.

"They've found an owl," Gervais whispered to Franchot. "He was asleep, but they waked him up. Now they're chasing him from tree to tree, pecking at him."

"Will they hurt him?"

Gervais could feel Franchot flinching as the child asked the troubled question. He answered nonchalantly.

"Not to worry about. Just watch, Franchot, and I'll show you lots of other interesting things. You must keep your eyes open in the woods and your ears, too. That's a Lord God you hear now."

"A Lord God?"

"Yes, a very large woodpecker with a big topknot. You can't see him though. He may be as much as half a mile away. He gets on a hollow stub in a swamp and raps away at it. 'Log God' is the old English name for him. That's how come the colored folks got it changed around to 'Lord God.' Some of them even call him 'Papa Lord God'!"

Franchot listened attentively. Nothing about the deliberate beat of the woodpecker's rapping suggested pain, and the longer he stood still, the longer the evil moment of killing could be postponed. Presently he heard another sound, this time one that was vaguely familiar.

"Isn't that a catbird, Daddy?"

"No, it's a cat squirrel. I'm not surprised you thought it was a catbird, though. They sound a lot alike. He must have seen some of the others in our party. We'll wait here a minute or two longer and give someone else a chance for the first shot."

The delay added to Franchot's sense of reprieve, but he was chagrined at having mistaken the cat squirrel for a catbird. He had often watched squirrels in the woods back of Belle Heloise and had learned a good deal about them. He knew that when they were feeding on cypress balls you could hear them a long way off, just as he had heard the woodpecker a few minutes before. He could even recognize two distinct sounds—the noise the squirrels made while they were gnawing the cypress balls with their teeth and the noise the pods made after these had been emptied of seeds by the squirrels and were dropping in a light patter on the dry leaves which covered the ground. He knew that after a squirrel had finished with one ball, it would scamper to a limb from the crotch of the tree where it had been feeding, and begin searching for another seed pod; and that after it had eaten all it wanted, if nothing happened to disturb it, then it would start playing with two or three squirrels. It would race round and round the trunk of the tree, flipping its bushy tail in the air, and sometimes it would even leap from one tree to another, which was still prettier to see. On the other hand, if it caught sight of a human being, it gave three or four short, sharp barks close together, thereafter moving very quietly, to keep the tree between itself and its probable enemy, and then "freezing." Since Franchot knew all this, he felt he should also have known enough not to mistake a bird's note for a squirrel's bark. He was grateful to Gervais for making light of his error and eager to atone for it. So instead of seeking further reprieve, he assented with apparent willingness when Gervais suggested it was time they were getting on with their hunt.

For some moments more they kept together, moving quietly forward. They heard two shots, close together, and then, after an interval, a third one further off. The others were beginning to get their squirrels, Gervais remarked; possibly they had come across a wood duck, too. But it was squirrels they were really out for this go-round. And it was about time for Franchot to start looking for them himself. How about this point for a stand? It looked pretty good to Daddy because there was a clear vision of the upper limbs all around. He was going further on himself, but he would be within easy calling distance if Franchot wanted him—only, of course, no one shouted on a hunt unless there were a darn good reason for it. But he knew Franchot realized that. He would come back after a while, whether he were called or not. Meantime Franchot was on no account to leave his stand. If he wandered off he might get lost for true. Well, so long and good hunting!

Franchot did not voice any objection when Gervais suggested leaving him; but after his father had disappeared among the trees he was a little frightened by the stillness and the solitude. These woods were not like those back of the plantation, which he knew and loved so well; they were darker and more dismal, and their strangeness, as well as their gloominess, was disquieting. The crows had ceased their circling and cawing and the woodpecker no longer rapped against his hollow stub. No more shots rang out in the distance either. The silence was complete. But it was not a tranquil stillness; there was a queer tensity to it. Standing watchfully at the point of observation where his father had placed him, and conscientiously watching the upper branches for the squirrel he was expected to shoot, Franchot was conscious for the first time since early morning that his head was hot and his hands cold and that his throat was really very sore.

He was still gazing steadfastly at the trees, when his attention was diverted by a strange sound in the distant underbrush. For a time he tried to disregard it, but as it continued, growing a little louder as if it were getting closer, he turned in the direction from which it seemed to be coming and peered with a feeling of mounting fright into the tangle of underbrush. At first he could see nothing; then he became dimly aware of moving branches, and of a strange horned creature which was causing this motion. Something enormous and terrifying was unquestionably coming towards him. Franchot dug his feet more firmly into the ground, bit his trembling lips and fired.

The shadowy creature leapt into the air and then charged wildly forward, knocking against the trees which obstructed its path. Franchot dropped his shotgun and screamed. Then he shrank back towards the swamp, overwhelmed with shame and terror. The scream had been involuntary, and he was appalled because he had not managed to suppress it; he knew that while he might have shouted in an emergency, the scream would be unforgivable; he had lost his last chance of proving he was not a sissy and a 'fraid cat. And he had no idea what

548

long days and nights of watching and nursing, of hoping and despairing, that followed the birthday party. She sat, dry-eyed and composed, at the funeral, and stood, still dry-eyed and composed, by the open grave. But when Gervais tried to put his arm around her to support her there, she drew away from him; and when he came into their room that evening, she was still wearing the veiled hat that she had worn to the cemetery, and she looked up at him over an open suitcase.

"I was coming to tell you, in just a minute," she said steadily. "I'm going to spend the night with Cresside and Fabian. Perhaps several nights. I'm not sure what I'm going to do after that. Except that I'm not coming back here."

"Merry, you're completely unstrung, you're completely shattered. No wonder, either. But you don't know what you're saying. You couldn't."

"Yes, I could. I do. And I'm not unstrung. I'm not going to argue with you this time either, Gervais. But I'm going."

"Merry, I've never needed you so much in my life as I need you now. You can't fail me now."

"I never have before, have I, Gervais? You'll have to give me credit for standing by, without complaining, through thick and thin for nearly eighteen years."

"I do, Merry. I never could have pulled through myself without you. I can't go along without you now, either."

"You'll have to, Gervais."

"You've got three other children of your own and a foster child. They all need you, too. They can't get along without you, either."

"Vail's almost a man now. He can look after himself and Phil, if you can't, and if Fabian and Cresside don't—but they will. Your mother can look after Sybelle and Joyeuse, at least until we can work out something better. I don't know why we've always treated her as if she were an old woman. She was under fifty when you came home from the war. She isn't really old, even yet. And she's strong as steel."

"She didn't do such a good job of looking after Cresside, you may remember, Merry."

"Well, my mother's here, too. That is, I don't suppose you'll turn her out, even if I do go. Or Miss Mittie, either. I think I've earned their keep."

"Merry, how can you be so unjust? You know your mother's welcome, that she always will be, and Miss Mittie, too. But they'll be lost without you, we all will. It's been you who's given us courage, who's given us hope, who's given us strength. Don't take all that from us now. We can't survive if you do."

For a moment he had a faint hope that she might waver. Instead, she turned away from him without answering, and continued to pack the open suitcase.

Vail had a very sweet letter from Susannah in answer to the one he wrote her telling her that Franchot was ill and that he couldn't think of anything else. A few weeks later he had another, telling him she had just heard about Franchot's death, and that she wanted to let him know how very, very sorry she felt for him. If there were anything at all that she could do. . . .

There was nothing that Susannah or anyone else could do for Vail just then. It was one of those times, of which Fabian had warned him before there would be many, when he had to fight his way through alone. It did not make it any easier for him to know that Gervais was fighting through it alone, too.

CHAPTER XLIII

NEITHER FABIAN nor Cresside tried to reason with Merry or even to talk with her the night after Franchot's funeral, and they managed to make Frances Belle understand that Aunt Merry was very unhappy and very tired, too, and that she must not be worried. The little girl was feeling very badly about Franchot herself, so she understood that part; but she did not see why Aunt Merry was coming to Somerulos Street for a rest, instead of just going to bed at the *garçonnière*. However, an unwonted firmness in her parents' manner warned her that it was not the time to disregard their suggestion, and the more she glanced at Aunt Merry on the ride back to town, the more she realized that something dreadful must be the matter. Because Aunt Merry not only looked very sad and very tired; she had changed so much in all sorts of ways that she did not seem like the same person any more. She seemed like a total stranger.

After they got home, and Aunt Merry had gone to bed in one of the little dormer guest rooms, Frances Belle called her mother and talked to her about Franchot, and asked if Aunt Merry looked the way she did because he had died. Cresside said yes, and then she tried to add a reassuring note.

"I think perhaps Dr. Champagne will come to see Aunt Merry in the morning, darling, and give her something that will make her feel better. Perhaps she'll feel better anyway, after she's had a good sleep."

"She didn't look as if she were sleepy to me, Mummy. She looked queer. Had she gone to sleep, when you came downstairs?"

"No. But I hope she will pretty soon. I hope you will, too. Good night, honey."

"Mummy, I don't feel sleepy either. I feel sort of frightened. I wish you'd stay with me."

"There's nothing to be frightened about, darling. But I'll stay with you, if you want me to."

Cresside lay down beside Frances Belle and gently stroked the little girl's head and back. For a long time Frances Belle tossed restlessly about, but little by little she was quieter, and finally her even breathing betrayed her drowsiness. Cresside waited until she was sure Frances Belle was sound asleep before she herself moved from the bed. Then she tiptoed back to her own room, where she knew Fabian would be waiting for her.

"Frances Belle's upset," she told him in her troubled voice. "We oughtn't to have taken her to the funeral. She's too young to see that sort of thing."

"Is she upset over the funeral or is she upset over Merry?"

"Well, both, I suppose. I'm upset about Merry myself. Aren't you?"

"I'm concerned. But let's not worry too much until we see how she is in the morning. Things do have a way of working themselves out if you give them a chance."

"They take a long while, sometimes. And this is so out of character. Merry's always faced everything like a good soldier before."

"Perhaps that's why she can't face this. There's always a limit somewhere. But I confess I wouldn't have expected it of her either. . . . Well, as I said before, let's wait and see what happens in the morning."

There had still been no sounds from the dormer bedroom when Fabian left for his office the next day, and both he and Cresside hesitated to run the risk of disturbing Merry if she were resting at last. However, at ten o'clock Cresside went upstairs with a tray and knocked on the door, so lightly that the rap could not possibly have roused Merry if she had still been sleeping. But she answered immediately.

"Come in. I'm not asleep."

"Have you been awake long?"

"I'm not sure. I think so."

"Well, why didn't you call me when you first waked up, Merry?"

"Why should I, when I didn't want anything?"

"Because of course you wanted something. You always want coffee as soon as you wake up."

"You mean I always did. I don't any more. But I'll drink some if you'd like to have me, Cresside."

Merry sat up in bed and accepted the tray from her sister-in-law's hands, pouring out the coffee and drinking it clear, in slow, small sips. But she did not unfold the napkin in which the rolls were wrapped, nor even appear to notice anything on the tray except the coffee, and presently she set the cup down.

"Thank you," she said. "Cresside, I've been thinking . . . I believe I'll go and see Mr. Goldenberg."

"Today?"

"Yes, today. I don't want to put it off. I'm afraid if I do I won't go and I believe it's the best thing I *can* do."

"I hoped you'd stay in bed today, Merry, and rest. I hoped you'd let me send for Dr. Champagne and ask him to give you a strong sedative. If you could have a good long sleep——"

"I don't want a good long sleep. I want to do something. I want to get things settled."

"I know Mr. Goldenberg's always been a mighty good friend to you, Merry. But do you think that just now——"

"Yes, just now, more than ever."

Cresside took the tray and turned towards the door. She was afraid that whatever she said might be wrong and that therefore it was probably better to say nothing. At the same time she did not feel she could let her sister-in-law make the rash move which was evidently in her mind without at least trying to stop her. She set down the tray on a small table and went back towards the bed.

"Merry," she said with great earnestness, "I know what it's like to be desperately unhappy myself—you realize that, don't you? I know what it's like to feel trapped with despair, just the way you do now. I would have been trapped, too, if you hadn't helped me. Well, it's my turn now. You must let me help you. I believe I can, if you'll only give me a chance. I won't urge you to go back to Gervais if you feel you can't. I won't talk to you about your duty to your husband and your children. I won't try to stop you from seeing anyone you choose or doing anything you think best, if you'll just wait until you're physically and mentally fit to do it. But you're not now. You're a sick woman—very sick. I'll play fair with you. I won't send for Dr. Champagne unless you tell me I may. But I want you to play fair with yourself. You won't be doing it, if you try to get out of bed and go downtown today."

"I'm not sick. But I am desperate. I've got to find a way out of my despair. I can't do it lying in bed. And no one can do it for me. Not even you, Cresside."

"But you said Mr. Goldenberg——"

"I said I wanted to see him. That's all. And I'm going to."

She pushed away the covering and swung her feet over the side of the bed. Cresside made one more effort.

"Then let me call him up and ask him to come here, Merry. It's a lovely mild day. You can sit on the terrace and talk to him. I promise I won't let anyone disturb you."

"We've none of us ever invited Mr. Goldenberg to come and see us at home before, have we? I should say this was a mighty poor time to begin. Besides, I'd rather see him at the store. It would seem more natural to me. And this is a business call, anyway."

"Well, would you let me call up and make sure he's there, and free? I'd hate to have you make the effort for nothing."

"He's always there and he's always free, as far as I'm concerned. You don't suppose Hazel would try to keep me from seeing him, do you? She's still his secretary, you know. She had the good sense to

554

keep her job, after she married. Of course, she never had any children."

It was worse than useless to argue with Merry; Cresside saw that at last. She picked up the rejected breakfast tray and left the room, heavy-hearted.

Merry was right; she had no trouble in penetrating to Mr. Golden-berg's private office. She was followed by curious glances as she went through the store, for her deep mourning made her conspicuous, and something in the expression of her pale, set face was also very arrest-ing. However, if she were conscious of the attention she was receiving, she did not betray this. She seemed oblivious of the strangers who stared at her, and she barely acknowledged the greetings of acquaint-ances, but went steadily on to the little cubicle where Hazel was typing, in her old easy, methodical way. Hazel was in the middle of a paragraph when Merry approached, and nodded without looking up, waiting for a good stopping place before rising to greet the unidentified caller. That was a habit of long standing, too, and heretofore Merry had always respected it. But this time she interrupted.

"Hazel," she said impellingly, "I want to see Mr. Goldenberg right away."

Hazel jumped up so quickly that she struck the release on her machine and sent the carriage shooting across to the other side. "Why, Merry!" she stammered. "You frightened me! You're the last person in the world I expected to see!"

"I didn't mean to frighten you. Mr. Goldenberg's in, isn't he?"

"Yes, he's in. I'll let him know, straight off, that you're here. . . . Merry, I want to tell you that I'm terribly, terribly sorry for you. I think it's the saddest thing I ever heard. I nearly cried my eyes out yesterday, at that poor little boy's funeral. I wish there was something I could do for you."

Hazel's sympathetic eyes filled with tears again. Merry looked at her without any sign of emotion.

"There is. You can tell Mr. Goldenberg I'm here," she said briefly, and leaned over to straighten a paper.

Neither Mr. Goldenberg nor his office had changed in any notice-able respect since her last visit. He rose to greet her, gravely and quietly, and then he sat down again and regarded her, still gravely and quietly, with his shrewd, bloodshot eyes. He did not express any surprise at seeing her and he did not offer her condolences or ask her questions. He waited for her to say whatever she wanted to tell him, and meanwhile his gravity and quietude were reassuring to her, as they always had been. She did not feel hurried about speaking to him, and she looked around the office, taking in its familiar details, while she prepared to do so. The thermos jar, the bud vase and the picture of Mrs. Goldenberg were still in their accustomed places. Merry remembered now that Mrs. Goldenberg had died some time before, and wondered, fleetingly, if Gervais would keep her picture beside him for years after she was dead. No, of course not. Men did not cherish the pictures of women who left them, only the pictures of women who stood by until they died. She was not standing by and unfortunately she was not going to die. It was Franchot who had died. . . .

"Mr. Goldenberg, I've always found I could talk to you very candidly about everything that matters a great deal to me," she finally heard herself saying. "I came and told you when I wanted to get married. I came and told you when I was afraid we'd lose Belle Heloise unless you could help us keep it. Now I've come to tell you that I've left Belle Heloise and my husband."

"I'm very sorry to hear that, Mrs. d'Alvery."

"I knew you would be. But still I thought you'd understand, if I told you why, and I want to."

"I shall certainly try. And when I said I was sorry, I did not mean for a moment to pass judgment. You realized that, I hope. I only meant it seemed a pity you should be disappointed in anything that meant as much to you as your marriage, or your home. I should have said that of all the women I have ever known, there was never one to whom both meant so much."

"They meant everything. I was willing to give up everything else for them. At least I thought I was, a long time. I *did* give up a great deal."

"I am sure you did. No woman could have done so much for her husband, or preserved her home, in the face of great difficulties, the way you did, without making tremendous sacrifices."

"I did make tremendous sacrifices. I loved Gervais so much I sacrificed my pride, and married him when I knew his mother would have done everything she could to keep me out of her house. Then over and over again I sacrificed my will and my judgment, so that Gervais could have his own way. The few times I opposed him we quarreled bitterly, and I dreaded those quarrels; so I avoided them as much as I could. Besides, I *wanted* him to have his way, even when it took him from me. It took him further and further all the time. I didn't realize it would, and I don't believe he did, either. I've got to be just. At least I've got to try."

"I am sure you would never be anything else, Mrs. d'Alvery."

"I don't know. I don't think it's right for a woman to talk like this about her husband, to anyone. But I've got to talk to someone. I've kept still just as long as I could. I can't stand it any longer. I tried to talk to a priest, but I couldn't do that. You know I wasn't born a Catholic. I only—" She bit back the words "I only became one because I knew it would mean so much to Gervais that I convinced myself I believed what he did." But she might just as well have said them, as far as Mr. Goldenberg was concerned. "I can't seem to get much out of the confessional," she went on lamely. "It isn't that I mind the principle, I think that's wonderful. I looked forward at first to laying my problems before someone wise and righteous, in complete confidence and candor. But there's always a long line of people waiting in a church, every one of them in a hurry, and the priest seems to be in a hurry, too. I can't pour out my soul when there's that sense of pressure and haste."

"No, I can see that would be hard for you."

"Of course this time a priest would have come to me. But I've been disappointed and thwarted so many times I couldn't risk it again. And I couldn't talk to Cresside, because she's one of the family. Naturally, it would be easier to talk to a woman than to a man, all things being equal. But as it was——"

"You know I have always been very much honored by your confidence. You know I'm very proud that you regard me as your friend."

I've got so few," Merry said in a low voice. "You see, all these years that I've lived at Belle Heloise, I've hardly seen anyone but my family, and I've hardly been off the plantation. I went twice to New Orleans when I was first married, but that's about all. I didn't mind, for a long while. I didn't care whether I ever saw anyone except my husband and my children. Gervais and I were very close at first. Very —very happy. And he enjoyed everything we did together as much as I did. But while I was having children so fast, he got out of the habit of doing things with me. There wasn't money enough to do much anyway. And then gradually he got out of the habit of talking things over with me, too, except the things that went wrong. Presently we weren't sharing anything except our troubles. No pleasures. No viewpoints. No ideas. Gervais expected me to make the best of the hard times, and I expected that, too. But I didn't expect that after the novelty of marriage wore off he'd prefer to have all his good times without me. I didn't expect he'd find his only serious interest in politics and crops, and his only diversion in hunting. I didn't expect he'd never ask what I wanted to do and where I wanted to go or what I thought or how I felt. I didn't expect that when I lost my lover I'd also lose my companion and my mainstay."

As she went on speaking, her voice became increasingly unsteady. She paused, hoping to bring it back under control, and again Mr. Goldenberg waited quietly for her to go on.

"I heard Regine Hathaway say once that all a man wanted anyway was someone comfortabl to sleep with," Merry said at last. "I flared up and told her that he wanted a great deal more than that, *in his wife*. I said if that was all he wanted he didn't ask a girl to marry him, he didn't offer her his name and his home and his position, he didn't choose her for the mother of his children. I thought——"

"And you were right in thinking so. You say you want to be just to your husband, and I believe you. So in spite of your feeling that he has failed you, I beg you not to imagine——"

"I'm not imagining anything. I know that he wanted someone to

557

keep his courage up, just as much as he wanted someone comfortable to sleep with. More, after a while. So I tried to do that. No one will ever know how hard I tried. And what happened in the end? He wasn't satisfied with having me sacrifice for him; he wanted to sacrifice the children, too. He needed someone to bolster his courage all the time, and yet he called our poor little boy a coward. He drove that child to his death, badgering him and hounding him. If it had only been me instead——"

She bowed her head and for a long while she did not even make any attempt to go on. But this time Mr. Goldenberg reached over and took her hand firmly in his.

"You are being very unjust right now," he said gently. "When you recover from the shock of this terrible experience, you yourself will be the first to admit it. Captain d'Alvery loved that little boy just as much as you did. He wouldn't willingly or consciously have hurt him for the world. But every father tries to develop manliness in his son. That's what Captain d'Alvery thought he was doing—all he thought he was doing. Harvey Lawrason's been here to see me too, Mrs. d'Alvery. He's another good friend who talks to me confidentially. Perhaps you've never seen it, but there's a very tender side to Harvey's nature. He's completely shot to pieces himself over this. He says none of them had the slightest idea the child was sick before they started on that fatal hunt. And as for the 'blooding,' he's seen that done over and over again, and never knew a man to think of it as anything but another episode in a day's sport. He admitted it's pretty rough sometimes—said he'd seen a shirt torn right off a young hunter's back and his whole body smeared with blood, over and over again. And once the deer's entrails draped around the hunter's neck, and its stomach put on his head for a cap——"

"On a child? A delicate, sensitive, twelve-year-old child?"

"Lawrason didn't say. No, I suppose not. Boys as young as that don't often shoot a deer—after all, Franchot only did it by accident. But your husband wasn't thinking of him as a delicate, sensitive, twelve-year-old child, Mrs. d'Alvery. He was thinking of him as the son he'd been afraid was going to grow up a milksop, who turned out to be a good sport and a fine shot, after all. He was so proud of the boy that his pride swallowed up everything else. He didn't think straight and he didn't see straight. He'll never get over that, as long as he lives. I'm so sorry for you that I can't find any words to tell you how sorry. But if you'll forgive me for saying so, I'm sorrier still for your husband."

"Mr. Goldenberg, if I'd thought you'd say that to me——"

"I had to say it, because it's true, and some day you'll realize that, too. But I know you can't do it now. No one could expect you to. And I want to do anything and everything I can to help you over this hard period. I've been trying to think how I could, all the time we've been talking, but so far I haven't succeeded. Could you suggest anything yourself?"

"I'd be very grateful if you'd let me ask you one or two questions."

"I wish you would, if that would help."

"You've spoken to me about Harvey Lawrason, you've defended my husband yourself, and said that he did. But would you have done what Gervais did?"

"No. Probably not. But your husband belongs to a great Creole family and I'm only an emigrant Levantine who's made his own way in the world."

So he calls himself a Levantine, Merry said to herself, surprised that her tragic thoughts could be diverted, even for a moment. *He isn't ashamed of it. Of course, there's no reason why he should be, but I've always supposed he was. I'm sure Gervais thought so, too.* Mr. Goldenberg went on talking while she pondered in amazement.

"I didn't say that sarcastically, Mrs. d'Alvery. And I wasn't trying to disparage great Creole families or extol poor Levantines, either. But every class and every race have the faults of their virtues as well as the virtues of their faults, their correlative weaknesses and strength. Prowess is an essential quality in men of your husband's breed; sensitivity isn't. It's the other way around in mine. But don't forget it was just that sort of essential quality which made you fall in love with him —prowess and vitality and magnetism and grace. You didn't fall in love with him because he was gentle and wise and subtle and long-suffering. If you'd been looking for that in a man, you'd have fallen in love with Fabian d'Alvery instead of Gervais d'Alvery."

"Both d'Alverys!"

"Ah, but Fabian isn't an Estrade, too! His mother was a Lassiter, wholly unrelated to his father. She came of a very different strain. And Fabian's a cripple, not a physical paragon, a scholar, not a warrior. He's seen more and suffered more than Gervais ever did—or could. He's learned more—he's got a greater capacity for both suffering and learning. But as I said before, none of that made you love him. The kind of man you were impelled to love was also the kind of man who wouldn't know how unhappy he was bound to make you or how cruel he'd almost inevitably be to a little boy who was more your child than his."

"Then in spite of everything I've said, and the way you know I feel, you think I ought to go back to him?"

Mr. Goldenberg appeared to consider, and while he did so Merry realized, with mounting gratitude and in spite of her agitation, that they had been talking for a long time already and yet he had given no sign of preoccupation or haste, though he was an extremely busy man. If she could only have talked to a priest like this! . . . She was grateful to Hazel, too—there had been no inopportune telephone calls, no distracting taps on the door. Only a very zealous and a very efficient secretary could have guarded her employer and his visitor like this.

"Yes," Mr. Goldenberg said at last, "I do think you ought to go back to your husband. I'm afraid I may hurt your feelings again; nevertheless, I'm going to remind you that while you sacrificed a great deal for him, he's done a great deal for you, too. He did offer you his name and his home and his position, he did choose you for the mother of his children. The name's ancient and honorable, the home's beautiful and historic, the position's not only secure but outstanding. Lots of people pretend to scoff at advantages of that sort; but the only persons who really take them casually, and who can afford to, are the ones who've always had them. You're very honest, Mrs. d'Alvery, so I'm sure you will be willing to admit you *hadn't* always had them."

"Yes, I am. But——"

She almost added, "I don't think they're really all that important." But she could not do it because, as Mr. Goldenberg said, she was too honest to pretend. And she was also withheld by the sudden poignant realization that they were supremely important to him, and that the knowledge he himself could never obtain them, for all his wealth and his power, was bitter to him. "Do you think that if a man gives a woman a great name to share and a handsome house to live in and a prominent social position to maintain, she ought not to expect anything more of him?" Merry inquired, substituting the question for the statement she had so nearly made.

"No. But I think they ought to go a long way in making her recognize her obligation to him," Mr. Goldenberg answered imperturbably. "Especially when he gives them to her gladly and proudly, as your husband has, and not grudgingly, as so many husbands do. And I think his personal conduct should also have great weight with her. As far as I am aware, Captain d'Alvery has never given you the slightest cause for complaint on this score. Gossip travels fast in a place like this. I should almost certainly have heard if he gambled recklessly or drank to excess, or if he humiliated you by improper conduct with any other woman."

"No, he doesn't—he hasn't," Merry said quickly.

"Well, then, human nature being what it is—" He broke off, looking at her with a smile which, oddly enough, had in it something of the whimsical quality of Fabian's. But it lasted only a moment. He shook his head and sighed. "I wasn't trying to argue with you," he said almost sadly. "I was only trying to make you see the whole picture, at least as I see it. And it seems fairly clear to me. But I know you won't go back to your husband, in your present frame of mind. Perhaps you can't. Perhaps it seems like such an impossibility that it really is an impossibility. If it were feasible for you to do whatever you wanted, what would you choose to do, right now?"

"I'd go back to work. I'd like my old job with you. Of course I know I'm terribly out of practice, that I couldn't qualify for it any more. So please don't think I'm asking for it, indirectly. But it's what I'd like. I can't live up to the d'Alvery standards. I've tried and I've failed. I'm sorry, but I'm not as ashamed as I was before you made me see what those standards really are, the way you did just now."

"You could get back into practice. You've done typing for your husband right along, haven't you?"

"Yes. I've always handled the correspondence and the accounts. He's never had a secretary since we've been married."

"You mean he's never had a paid secretary. There, I shouldn't have said that. Well, there's no question that you could qualify, as far as ability goes. But I wouldn't take you back into this store, Mrs. d'Alvery."

"You wouldn't? Not if I were really good enough?"

"No. Because I'm not going to be the one to give the whole Parish the chance to say that a girl from St. Napoleon Street tried to cross the tracks to the River Road and couldn't make the grade after all."

Merry flushed and bit her lip. Before she could frame an adequate retort, Mr. Goldenberg went on.

"But that doesn't mean I couldn't give you a position elsewhere, if you really want one, and I can see you're in earnest about that. Besides, you've convinced me that a complete change would probably be the best thing in the world for you. And it so happens I have a good many interests outside of Baton Rouge, though I don't say much about them here. As a matter of fact, I'm the principal stockholder in two very large New York stores. I'm in a position to add anyone I wish to the personnel in either. I'd be very glad to add you. But not in a secretarial capacity."

"I couldn't qualify, in any other capacity."

"You're a very attractive woman, Mrs. d'Alvery. But if you'll forgive me for saying so, you're not nearly as attractive as you easily could be." He looked at her, not unkindly but appraisingly, with his far-seeing eyes, and Merry, for the first time in years, felt acutely conscious of the lost trimness of her bearing, of her casual coiffure, and of her unmanicured hands. But almost immediately came the comforting realization that Mr. Goldenberg was right, that the effect of her figure would be very different in better-made clothes, that her neglected hair was still beautiful in itself, and that with a little care and attention her hands might be beautiful, too; it was only because she had lost interest in her appearance when she thought Gervais had that it had ceased to be a credit to her. "You were one of the loveliest girls I ever saw," Mr. Goldenberg went on, impersonally. "You could be just as lovely now, in a different way—not with that first elusive freshness which is never recaptured, but with the mellowness of maturity. If I'm not mistaken, you're still under forty. You could be almost irresistibly charming, if you cared to make the effort. I'd like very much to see you do it. . . . Incidentally, how is your French?"

"Why, it's—it's fair. I didn't know much when I married, but I started talking it right away, with my mother-in-law, because I thought that was one thing I could do to please her, and she taught me a good deal. She's insisted all the children must grow up bilingual. She's taught them, too. And we very often speak French at meals and read it aloud. . . . What makes you ask?"

"I was wondering whether a position on my Paris staff would interest you. The two New York stores I mentioned both have offices there, and we keep several representatives in France all the time, besides our seasonal buyers. We would easily use another."

"You'd send me to Paris!"

Her voice was very like a sick child's who had suddenly been offered a sojourn in fairyland. Mr. Goldenberg did not fail to notice this. Nevertheless, he answered in a matter-of-fact way.

"I'd be very proud to have you in my Paris bureau. I think, after you'd learned the ropes, you might easily become its directress. The present one's over sixty, though she doesn't look it, and she's been saying for some time she wished we'd give her an assistant whom she could train to take her place, eventually. I believe you'd be the very person. That is, if you're sure you'd be happy so far from your family, in the long run."

"But I've told you——"

"Yes, I know. I don't think you'd mind the separation from your husband—for the present. And it might be a good thing for both of you. But what about your children? Could you leave them?"

"Franchot was the one I couldn't have left," Merry said, her eyes filling with tears again. Then she went on, at first using much the same words she had spoken to Gervais the evening before, but gradually changing her line of argument.

"Vail's almost a man. He's always been independent and self-sufficient. And Phil's his father's white-headed boy. Gervais can easily be father and mother both to him."

"I wonder. Boys' mothers mean a great deal to them—often more than their mothers realize, I believe. Mine was the most powerful influence in my life, even more powerful than my wife. We came up together, the hard way. My father'd been killed in one of the Turkish massacres when I was a baby, so there were just the two of us, and part of the upward climb was pretty rough. By the time I married, the way was easier. And ease isn't what always keeps people close together, in spite of what you think now, Mrs. d'Alvery. Sometimes it is sharing troubles and hardships that counts for the most."

Momentarily his eyes rested in thought on the framed photograph of his wife; then he glanced at Merry again, and this time his gaze was less impersonal than when he had told her, a few moments before, that she had been a very beautiful girl and that she might still be a very beautiful woman. Merry remembered the shrewd, shriveled little old lady whom she had met when Mr. Goldenberg invited her into his office to see the Victory Loan Parade, and also the large effulgent woman wearing satin and pearls and sables, and she understood why a man like this would have felt closer to his mother than to his wife. At the same time she wondered why the realization that Mr. Golden-

562

berg was a tremendously wealthy widower should suddenly have made her vaguely uncomfortable, and why she was so self-conscious now under his glance when she had not been self-conscious at his words.

"I really don't think I mean all that much to Phil," she said, a trifle hurriedly. "Besides, he's self-sufficient, too, in a different way. He's so popular that no one person means a great deal to him, not even in his family. Sybelle's different; but it's Vail she's dependent on, rather than me. As long as she has Vail, she's satisfied. And just now, I think she and I might be better apart. There's been a little friction over her first suitor, and I think perhaps if we were separated for a time. . . . She could visit me once in a while, couldn't she?"

"Certainly. Whenever you liked. Besides, you should come back to this country at least once a year, to keep in touch, anyway. And possibly you'd like to take your younger daughter with you. Joyeuse, her name is, isn't it? That would be perfectly feasible, from my point of view."

"Oh, Mr. Goldenberg, you've made everything seem so natural and easy—and *right!* I haven't words to tell you——"

"Don't try. You haven't asked *me* to tell *you* much of anything, by the way—what your salary would be, or your living conditions or anything of that sort. Would you feel five thousand was fair to begin, with trans-Atlantic passage furnished twice a year and some kind of an additional expense allowance for incidental travel and other items? I should think you could manage on that, but I'm not sure. You'd have to spend a good deal on clothes, especially at first."

Again his eyes wandered over her appraisingly. But this time she was not embarrassed because she did not even notice the searching gaze.

"Manage on five thousand!" she gasped. "With travel expenses besides! Why Mr. Goldenberg, I've never had five *hundred* a year to spend on myself! If I had five thousand I could help at home, too. I could——"

"You see you're already beginning to think of helping at home," he said, rather drily. "No, you shouldn't try to do that. You'll need to spend at least that much on yourself, if you're to fill the position I have in mind acceptably. You'll need not only good clothes; you'll need a suitable apartment, and a car, and efficient servants. You'll need to go about quite a little, too, visiting picture galleries and museums and chateaux; a great many of the best fashion ideas have come from such sources. And then you'll have your young daughter with you. She'll need to go to a good school, to have travel advantages, too. No, I don't think five thousand and expenses will be enough. I think you had better start with seventy-five hundred. And I'm sure you won't make the mistake of supposing for a moment that this offer is philanthropic. I'm expecting you to earn every cent of your salary. I'm confident that you're going to."

He did not actually rise, but he made a slight movement which indicated to Merry that he would like to have her do so, that he considered the interview over. As she got to her feet, still too dazed for adequate speech, he made one more suggestion.

"You know now that you can get away any time you wish," he said. "You have the prospect of financial independence already. I believe that after a little while you'll find that your new interests and your provocative surroundings will help you to overcome your grief. So if you will permit me to say so, I think you should try very hard not to do anything at present which you would regret afterwards. Under normal circumstances you have great self-control and great dignity. I know it will be hard for you to do what I am going to suggest, but I hope you will not find it impossible. I hope you will now go back to your sister-in-law's house and permit her to send for Dr. Champagne, as she wished to do earlier this morning. I feel sure he will prescribe a sedative and tell you to stay in bed for a few days. After you have had this much needed relaxation, I think you should talk to him candidly, telling him much that you have told me, and I am convinced he will say you are desperately in need of a complete change and a long rest—in the sense that any release from strain is rest. Then you may tell him about my offer, and he will almost certainly advise you to accept it. After that, I think you should have an equally frank talk with your husband, and that you should ask Dr. Champagne to talk with him, too. Captain d'Alvery may oppose the plan at first, but I do not believe he will do so for long. I think he will realize that if you stayed at Belle Heloise, in your present condition, you would soon have a very serious nervous breakdown—so serious that you might never recover from it. I am less sure that he will realize his only hope of getting you back lies in letting you go, but perhaps he will. At all events, I think you should stay quietly at Belle Heloise for a fortnight or so while you are making your preparations for departure. Don't let anyone outside the family get an impression of flight, or of rupture. If you follow my suggestion, it will be very simple to say, afterwards, that you have gone away for a rest cure, and later on, that you developed interests, while abroad, which led to an independent career. So many women have these nowadays that you could do it, too, without causing any comment, provided you go about it in a way that seems logical, and provided the career is important enough and pursued far enough from home. I do not need to tell you that the executive director of a Paris office would occupy a very different position, in the eyes of the world, than a stenographer in Goldenberg's store on Third Street. There would be no question, in the former instance, that you had been unable to cross the tracks. On the contrary, the general opinion would be that you had done it so successfully that you had been able to go much further than the River Road."

He held out his hand, and Merry took it mutely. She did not ask him how he happened to know she had already left Belle Heloise and had gone to Somerulos Street. At the moment it did not even occur to her to wonder.

"I have been assuming all this time that eventually you would want to come home for good," Mr. Goldenberg said. "I hope and believe you will. But if for any reason you decide, in the end, on a divorce, of course Paris is an excellent place to get one. Several very able lawyers are among my acquaintances there. I will see that you meet them socially, at once, so that if you feel you need them professionally later on, the way will already be paved for you. In fact, I can probably arrange an introduction in person. Mrs. Goldenberg and I always used to go to Paris every year. She bought all her clothes there, and I laid the foundations for the present office. Since her death, I have not been back. But I have been thinking for some time that I ought to go regularly again."

PART X

Letters to Susannah

Spring 1937–Autumn 1943

"Off we go, into the wild blue yonder
Climbing high, into the sun.
Here they come, zooming to meet our thunder,
At 'em boys, give 'er the gun!
Down we dive, spouting our flame from under
Off with one hell of a roar,
We live in fame or go down in flame
Nothing'll stop the Army Air Corps!"

Letters to Susannah

Spring 1937–Autumn 1943

CHAPTER XLIV

Belle Heloise
May 26, 1937

Dear Sue:

I was very pleased to get your letter telling me about your school and everything and reminding me it was quite a while since I had written you. I know it is but I did not feel much like writing for a long time after Franchot died and Mom went away. (I suppose you know she had a bad nervous breakdown and as she couldn't seem to get well at home or in a sanatorium, Dr. Champagne decided that perhaps a complete change would help and she has gone to Europe, taking Joyeuse with her, which of course leaves another hole, though we were all glad the kid could have such a swell chance.) It's been pretty grim here at Belle Heloise ever since, and I didn't go to New Roads or anywhere else all winter, so I don't know what's been cooking. I have just kept plugging along trying to get better marks than I have so far, because I know if I don't I won't have a prayer of getting to Princeton, which I have now decided to do if I can. I wish now I hadn't gone to school for so long just to eat my lunch.

Last week my friend Riccardo Tramonte graduated from L.S.U., so I broke down and went to the military commencement and it was quite a show. Eighty-nine cadets got their Lieutenant's commission and Colonel Hill, the Commandant, administered the oath of allegiance to them after the graduation ceremonies. There was the traditional flag raising which is always one of the main features of graduation morning and there was also a regimental parade in the a.m. Then a review in the late p.m. and of course the military award program in the gymnasium. Rick got the highest award of all, the L. Kemper Williams saber, which is given annually to the best cadet officer. Colonel Williams, who is past president of the Reserve Officers Association, presented the saber in person. It is a knockout and I got about the biggest thrill of my life when Rick accepted it from him. Syb went to the exercises and a concert in the Greek Theatre with me and took part in the dress parade, but *grand'mère* would not let her go to the senior dance, on account she is in mourning, even though she had been chosen Regimental Sponsor. At least *grand'mère* said mourning was the reason. Me, I can't see how it would have been any worse for her to wear a party dress than her sponsor's special uniform, or how it would do Franchot any good now to make Syb miserable, and that is what *grand'mère* did and Dad too, not to mention leaving Rick high and dry for the dance. I would not stand for it if I were in their place and I don't know how much longer they will either. She and Rick have thought a lot of each other ever since they were kids; of course I realize everyone says that is just puppy love, but I think sometimes you can tell right from the start no matter what age you are. I reckon you can guess why I feel that way about it so I won't go into it all again.

Rick has gone abroad now, the lucky bum. The Tramontes invited me to go along and Uncle Fabian and Aunt Cresside invited me too, but I figured I had better stick around here a while longer. I'll be gone soon enough anyway and the house seems pretty empty already to Syb without having anyone else lighting out of it.

To answer your question, Phil is fine. He has been pitching on the high-school baseball team sponsored by the American Legion all spring and Baton Rouge has won games with Bogalusa, Hammond and Slidell, which gave us the District Championship, though we lost afterwards to New Orleans in the State Finals. Of course Phil went there to play and has been there twice besides to stay with the Pereiras who have shown him a tall time. They gave a dinner at the North Shore Club that he said was simply the cat's whiskers, boiled crabs and turtle soup and sheepshead salad and everything. *Grand'mère* doesn't seem to mind having Phil play around even if he is supposed to be in mourning.

Well, as I said before, there is really no news so I will close. As ever

Your affectionate friend,
Vail d'Alvery.

Belle Heloise
July 21, 1938

Dear Sue:

Well, what do you know? I got into Princeton after all and I'm coming East around Sept. 1st, maybe a little sooner. Uncle Fabian and Aunt Cresside are planning a trip to New York and New England then and this time I have decided to accept their invitation and go along. That is the slack time on the plantation anyhow and besides a few weeks here one way or another won't make much difference when I'm going to be gone all winter and they will mean a lot to me. We thought we might take in Bar Harbor somewhere along the line as we shall be motoring. Will you please let me know how late you will be in Maine yourself and whether your family would have any objections if we turned up? Of course we would stay at a hotel and we do not want to put you out at all but gee, it is nearly two years now since I have seen you and it sure would be swell if I could, at least I think so.

We had quite an epidemic of graduations in the family this spring because Phil got through high school too, and Syb finished at Grand Coteau. Phil has decided to go to Tulane instead of L.S.U. as long as I'm not going to be here, at least he said that was the reason but I'm beginning to think the d'Alverys are mighty good at alibis. He has been itching to get away from the plantation for a long time and he is crazy about New Orleans so Tulane is a logical choice, though I should think he would rather go into the R.O.T.C. which is just starting up there than to take the regular college course, but naturally it's his business, not mine. I wouldn't be so sure the Pereiras wouldn't have something to do with it, what I mean is Mr. Pereira and Barry went there, not just that Nellie will be going to Newcomb next year. I think Dad is disappointed but he has been very decent about it as he is about most things. I don't think he's caught on yet that Phil isn't interested in sugar and I hope he won't for a long time. He's had a good many knockout blows as it is.

Syb is going to stay at home because *grand'mère* doesn't believe in college for girls and I don't believe Syb cared much about going anyway. *Grand'mère* and Dad both hope she can be a Maid at Carnival this next year, she would have stood a good chance of being Queen of Comus if Dad could have spent more time in New Orleans and kept in with his relatives and important friends, the way Uncle Fabian has. There won't be any question about Frances Belle when she comes along because Uncle Fabian and Aunt Cresside have an apartment at the Pontalba now and go down there a lot and Frances Belle is meeting everybody and everybody likes her. But Dad has never been able to afford to do anything like that and he has let all his best contacts slide except for the Pereiras and of course they have Nellie to look after first. He talked to me about it and said he was sorry about Syb, he had always hoped and expected she would be a Queen but somehow he had let the chance for it slip just like so many other things. I'm afraid he feels he has been a failure but there is no reason why he should really because he is a grand person. I told him I was sure Syb wouldn't care about being a Queen anyhow, and that was the truth because I don't think she will. All she cares about is marrying Rick and I reckon it is just as well he stayed abroad, that is, if Dad and *grand'mère* are going to keep on along the same lines. Rick is studying for his Master's at the Sorbonne. Mr. and Mrs.

Tramonte are so proud of him they can hardly see straight, of course they were always but this is just the cat's whiskers as far as they are concerned. I go to their house once in a while to spend the night just like I did when Rick was home; it gives them a chance to talk about him, of course I might add it gives me a chance too.

Well, let me know about Bar Harbor as soon as you can because it really would be swell if I could see you there as I said before.

With my best,

Vail.

Blair Hall
Princeton University
January 12, 1939

Dear Sue:

Of course I was very much interested to get your letter saying you were going down to New Orleans for Mardi Gras. Yes, I do remember hearing your mother say she thought it would be a pleasant experience for you. Of course it is just my hard luck I won't be in Louisiana when you get there, but you will see Syb because she is going to spend three months with our Estrade cousins who live on Esplanade and take in the whole show. I think things are going to be all right for her, about being a Maid I mean, but naturally all that is supposed to be a deadly secret right up to the day of the ball.

I am surprised Phil didn't answer your letter, I reckon he's busy studying for his mid-years, or maybe as you say he never got it any way, though just Tulane ought to reach him all right. His complete address is Kappa Alpha Fraternity House, Tulane University, New Orleans.

This is a grand place, wonderful teachers, a swell bunch of fellows, beautiful grounds and buildings. I wish you would come and see it, perhaps you will some day. I am majoring in American history, as that is what Uncle Fabian wanted me to do, and don't think I made any mistake. However, I may as well confess I seem to be getting a lot more out of the Civilian Air Pilot's Training for which I signed up right after I got here than I am anything else. I am by no means alone in this feeling, for the whole college is air-minded and there is a Flyers' Club where nobody talks about anything else. However, not knowing how much interested you are in subjects of that sort, if at all, I won't go into details about my course right now.

As ever,
Vail.

Belle Heloise
September 4, 1939

Dear Sue:

I would have written before but I have spent most of my time lately listening to the radio at the Tramontes' and expecting every minute to hear Rick say, "Well, what did I tell you?" but he hasn't. He sure left Europe in the nick of time, apparently the people who are caught over there haven't a notion of how or when they can get home. Rick was really itching to stay, so he wouldn't have minded if he had got caught, but after all he has been gone a winter and two summers already and all this time his father has been counting the days until he would become a junior partner—the business is a big one now, mostly wholesale, and Mr. Tramonte's getting on in years, so he really does need help. Besides it looks an awful lot like Italy would go in with the Axis later and the Tramontes are going to take it mighty hard if that happens. Personally I think it's just as well none of them is in Naples right now because it's a cinch they'd have a tremendous row with their friends and family about Mussolini if they were.

Now that Rick is back in Baton Rouge to stay—unless we get into this war ourselves which he still says we will—there has got to be a showdown about having him at Belle Heloise and I'm going to have a try at thrashing the whole thing out with Dad and *grand'mère* after supper tonight. I have only got ten more days at home before I go back to college and naturally I want to see all I can of Rick during that time as I shan't get another chance until Christmas, and I don't propose to keep going to his house and never asking him to mine. Besides even if Dad and *grand'mère* won't consent to a formal engagement I want them to at least admit there's an "understanding" between Rick and Syb, because there is, whether D. and G. like it or not. When you come right down to it there's not the slightest reason why S. and R. shouldn't get married straight off except the family is so mule-headed about it. Rick is getting a fine salary and earning it too, and Syb has had plenty of chances now to find out whether there might be anyone she would like better and there isn't. Some ape is always bobbing up that she met when she was at Grand Coteau and the River Road gets blocked with cadets coming out from L.S.U., not to mention all the old fogies who gave her a whirl when she was in New Orleans last winter and want to keep on doing it. And they just aren't there as far as she's concerned. If a girl cared for me like she cares for Rick I'd be right in the seventh heaven. Of course I don't mean any old girl. I mean a very special girl and you know who.

In one way I'm sorry to have a showdown just now with Dad because he has had another big disappointment which he has taken rather hard. You know that the place next to ours, Hathaway Hall, has been vacant for a long time and has got terribly run down. Mrs. Grover Blood who owns it has been trying to sell it for ten years because there were lots of reasons why she didn't want to live there herself but neither did anyone else. Well, this summer a Mr. Trevers, a big shot from Monroe, got really interested in the place and made Mrs. Blood a good offer for it. Then he found out that the sugar act of '37 would prevent him from marketing anything but syrup and he wanted to market sugar—at least he could have marketed sugar from ten acres but what would that amount to when he would have had nearly 3,000 under cultivation? You see this fool law provides that only mills that were in operation when it was passed would be given the marketing quota and that this would be based on the amount produced then and as Hathaway had been closed down for nearly ten years, Mr. Trevers couldn't get any quota. So finally he got all hot and bothered and said he would have to withdraw his offer. Mrs. Blood took the case to court and Uncle Fabian did everything he could to help her, but there was no soap. She stayed with us while she was trying to make a go of things, and she and Dad kept talking evenings about what was the use, you couldn't win in the sugar business whatever you did. Then one of these junk agents came along right out of the blue and said there was a big demand for American machinery in Mexico and offered Mrs. Blood $50,000 for the machinery in the Hathaway mill and she took it. The machinery cost close to $350,000 so that meant a $300,000 loss but she said it was better than having the mill stand idle forever and she was sick of the whole thing anyway. All this week the wreckers have been tearing things up at Hathaway, and Dad has gone over there every day and watched them, and said well, that was the end of sugar raising at one more place on the River Road and as far as he could see he might as well let the wreckers come here and gut our mill too. Of course that was all nonsense because we were operating full blast in '37 and the only way we had been hurt by that law and the other one those ginks up in Washington passed two years ago and then repealed was that we had to plow under part of our cane and burn up some more. Naturally that was pretty bad but not bad enough to get us to the point where we would let some Mex who would sell sugar back in the U.S. at a big profit have our machinery for a song. If Dad had only gone to Congress like he should have I bet he could have stopped all this foolishness and he would have been a lot happier about everything. Mom was the only person who could talk Dad out of these moods he has now. She was always so cheerful and sure everything would turn out right in the end, until she broke down all of a sudden. I guess she had just taken it too long. Now there is no one to fill her place with Dad or the rest of us as far as that goes. But we thank our lucky stars she didn't get caught in this European jam anyway. She has had a swell job in Paris for two years now which she has enjoyed very much, and it has been fine for Joyeuse too; but she had quite a lot of piled-up leave so she decided to let her assistant go to the fall openings and spend her leave in Latin America. You see her work has to do with fashions and that sort of stuff and she thought it would be a good plan for her to see the native costumes in Peru, Bolivia, Guatemala, Mexico and what have you, to get new ideas. She had seen most of the picture galleries, etc., in France which is another way she gets ideas, but not the ones in Italy, so she and Joyeuse went down to Naples, stopping along the way to look at pictures and finally took one of those high-toned Italian ships that go straight to the west

574

coast of South America and landed in Valparaiso. Now that she's got there she naturally wants to make the most of it, especially as she can't do her job in Paris while this war is going on and wants to run things in New York till the shooting's over, once she gets organized for a good start.

Well, I hope I haven't bored you with all this talk about family matters and about sugar, but you see I feel as if you were one of the family, at least you know I wish you were and as far as the sugar's concerned I care a lot about that too and I'm going to be a planter no matter how many laws these ginks pass, or how many quotas they fix or how many acres they make us plow up and burn over. I never could be anything else, come hell or high water, and I shall hang on to Belle Heloise even if it is the last plantation to raise sugar on the River Road. I would rather die myself than have it gutted and deserted like Hathaway. Down deep in his heart I know Dad feels the same and maybe I can have some influence with him because we are the only two left with this feeling except *grand'mère*, and it is different with an old lady than with a man. Maybe she thinks it isn't but I know it is. Phil has finally told Dad that he doesn't want to stay on the plantation which of course was another blow. He wants to go into business with Mr. Pereira instead. I thought of doing that myself for a while but it was not because I wanted to. It was because I thought maybe that would be the quickest way to make money. If I had a grand girl just waiting to marry me like Rick I might be thinking more about that, but as it is I'm not, and even if I were I know now I'd have to manage and so would my wife on what I could make at Belle Heloise because this is where I am going to stay.

As ever,
Vail.

Blair Hall
Princeton University
May 28, '41

Dear Sue:

I have just done something that seems mighty important to me so I hope it will seem that way to you too. Anyway I want to tell you about it.

I think I wrote you I was very disappointed because I was not old enough to register in the draft last fall, I thought it was tough luck to miss it by just a few months and I decided I would not wait for the second registration if I could help it. Ever since I came up here I have been hearing and seeing a lot that has made me feel Rick was right when he said we were bound to get into this war, though I couldn't see it while I was still in Belle Heloise. (Somehow the idea of war doesn't hit you very hard in a place like that, it always seems so peaceful, but when you get right down to it there was plenty going on there in my great-grandfather's time.) Rick was right when he said there was going to be one in Europe and I didn't believe him when he first told me that and now I realize my mistake. With Yugoslavia and Greece both conquered things are moving mighty fast and there's no telling which way they'll move next. Well anyway, yesterday when I read Roosevelt's proclamation announcing an unlimited state of National Emergency something snapped inside of me and I sent in an application for enlistment in the Army Air Corps as a flying cadet. Of course my civilian pilot's training is going to come in mighty handy now, as I've already taken two phases (primary and secondary) and have a total of nearly 90 hours in the air. So I'm not especially worried about the flying cadet examination and I'm hoping very much to get into action right away but I don't believe I'll have much chance of making one of the summer courses, it's so late already. If I don't I'll go home as soon as I've taken my physicals; I have to go into New York for those—90 Church Street. Well, I don't suppose the address makes any difference to you, but somehow even that's exciting to me.

As ever,
Vail.

P.S. By the way, I don't think I wrote you before that Rick was called to active duty in Feb. He had received a notice from the War Dept. several months before saying he would be and asking if there were any reason why he would need a deferment. Of course there wasn't, and he reported to Camp Shelby at Hattiesburg, Mississippi. He's crazy about it there and naturally his letters make me even crazier than I was already to get going myself.

Belle Heloise
Sept. 10, 1941

Dear Sue:

Well, here I've been practically all summer, just as I was afraid I might be, and nothing much has happened so there has been no point in writing. I've been busy with the usual chores on the plantation and I've managed to get over to Hattiesburg several times to see Rick. Once I even managed to take Syb with me and Rick has been home for one short leave too. Of course Syb and I haunted the Tramontes' house while he was there, and Dad did not ask too many questions about what we did when we went into Baton Rouge evenings. We were supposed to be at Aunt Cresside's when we were not going to the movies or what have you, but I think he suspects we were actually at the Tramontes', and though he has never invited Rick out here himself, he hasn't kicked up too much row when I've asked Rick to stay to dinner or something on my own. Dad's calmed down all sorts of ways since Mom left and looks and acts lots older than he is, and I honestly believe if it wasn't for *grand'mère* he'd stop putting up a fight. But she eggs him on, every chance she gets. If she only knew it, she's making a big mistake, because it's the fact that Dad's seemed more ready to let nature take its course that's made Rick and Syb willing to let things slide a while longer hoping he'll see still more reason and give them the kind of wedding and send-off they really want. But every time *grand'mère* gets up on her ear, they think maybe they'd better take the shortest cut out of all this nonsense, which of course they could do perfectly well.

I've kept hoping that the next time I wrote I could tell you Mom had come home, because it didn't seem like she could stay in Latin America forever, and anyone would think two years would be plenty to learn all there is to know about quaint costumes and things like that. She has been back to the United States once and her route was right through New Orleans, but she didn't get a stopover to come home. I think that was just the last straw as far as Dad was concerned, because when it happened he had to stop pretending she wasn't well enough to come and face the fact she didn't want to come. He'd kidded himself along just as far as he could. She did invite Syb and Phil to visit her in New York and they both went and had a grand time. I went in from Princeton too, once or twice—it was term time for me while she was there, though Phil was having vacation from Tulane—and she took me out on the town too. We went to all the best shows and restaurants, etc. Mr. Goldenberg who owns the big department store on Third Street in Baton Rouge was there one evening too and was also very nice to me. He happened to be in New York on business. I don't know whether you know he owns two big stores in New York too, and that these maintained the Paris bureau Mom directed till the war broke out. Not that there's any reason why you should. Anyway he dropped in to see Mom and we all went to see "Lady in the Dark" and to the Oak Room at the Plaza afterwards. Mr. Goldenberg didn't seem to have any trouble getting reservations. Mom has a suite at the St. Regis and she was looking like a million dollars. I never realized before what a knockout she was or at least could be. She has an office in Rockefeller Center and a big staff and it's all mighty smooth. And she certainly isn't sick any more though there wasn't anything put on about that when Dr. Champagne said she was. She was good and sick for a while. But not for nearly as long as Dad tried to think. I don't mean he wanted her to be sick, I only mean . . . Well, I reckon I'm getting all balled up and I'd better stop trying to explain. But anyway, what I'm slowly getting at is, this summer Joyeuse wrote she was all fed up with Latin America and wanted to come home. She said Mom didn't need her any more than a cat needed two tails, and was Dad willing she should take the next plane she could get a seat on. Of course Dad cabled her he was and we all went down to meet her. I'm sure he thought right up to the last moment that when Joyeuse got off that plane Mom would get off too, that they were planning to surprise him. And then Joyeuse got off alone after all. She is just as smart as paint, you'd never recognize her as the leggy little somebody she was when you last saw her. She's only 18, but she seems older than

Syb in lots of ways and has she got a line, in three languages at that! She's going right into the junior class at the University, can you beat it? I had no idea they taught so much at those foreign schools as she's managed to pick up. She's planning to major in chemistry and physics and to spend all her evenings and week-ends in the laboratory at the sugar house as soon as grinding begins. I think Barry Pereira has different ideas about the way it would be nice for her to spend her week-ends, but that's neither here nor there. He hasn't got the field to himself by any means though. I think poor Dad is in a daze with so many boy friends cluttering up the scene, but I'll say this for Joyeuse, she knows how to handle them all mighty well. I reckon she learned more than languages in the course of her travels, and she gets no end of airmail letters from all over the place, addressed in big bold masculine hands. Well, I should worry about Joyeuse. Syb's the one I've got on my mind.

Speaking of Barry Pereira, he got a great kick out of his ROTC training and is all fixed up now with a commission of Ensign in the Naval Reserve, so he's in the same sort of position that Rick is, generally speaking, in case we get into the war—ready to jump right into the fight the minute it starts. And here I am still waiting around to hear from that application of mine.

I gave Phil your message and he said to give you his best too. Of course he'll have to register early next year and I suppose he'll be drafted right after that. I still don't see why he didn't go into the ROTC when he had such a good chance at Tulane, and he still doesn't see it my way, in spite of Barry Pereira and everything and we've stopped talking about it because we both seem to get hot under the collar when we try.

Well, I reckon this is all the family news for the present and I've written you again as if you really were one of the family and will repeat I wish this were true. You've told me you wanted to think it over and I've tried not to hurry you, to give you all the time you needed, but don't you honestly feel you've thought it over enough now? Couldn't you possibly say yes and let me come to see you before I start back to College?

Honey, if you only could, it would mean everything in the world to me.

> Yours ever,
> Vail.

> Blair Hall
> Princeton University
> Nov. 2, 1941

Dear Sue:

Well, I seem to be off to a flying start at last and I don't mean to make a bad pun either.

As you know I was pretty discouraged not hearing a word all summer or for two months after I got back here. But yesterday evening I got a notice from the War Dept. telling me my application had been accepted and instructing me to report immediately to the recruiting officer at the P.O. Building in Trenton. Of course I hot-footed it in the first thing this a.m. and my orders are to start immediately for primary school at Cimarron Field, Oklahoma City, so please address your next letter there. I understand I'll be there until Jan. and then get sent on to Enid, Oklahoma, for basic training which comes next—that is if I can make the grade. I also understand they don't allow cadets much time out for writing love letters but you can bet I do love you and that I shall never stop trying to get you to marry me whether I keep on saying so every few days or not. There is no time to enlarge on that now either though as I have to pack.

Yours ever,
Vail.

Cimarron Field, Okla.
Jan. 5, 1942

Dear Sue:

This is only to say hello and to wish you a good year coming up. The schedule here is mighty stiff, just as I expected, and there isn't much time for letter writing. However, since you say you'd like a description of the place, here goes!

This field is about 25 miles out of the City located on very flat plains. The buildings are quite attractive—white frame construction decorated inside with a scheme inspired by the Indian tribes around here. We sleep in double-deck bunks and the food is super. There's a huge stone fireplace in the recreation room with Indian relics all around it which would be a grand place to spend hours of ease if we had any. The flying field is sod-covered with a wind tee separating the right and left traffic patterns in the center. These are the main items that occur to me right now though I suppose I could think up a lot more if I had the time. Maybe they'll suggest some questions to you and if they do I'll gladly answer them, probably from Enid as I expect to be pushing off for there pretty soon now unless there's some sort of a last minute slip-up.

I have had a note from Dad saying that he and Harvey Lawrason and Charles Boylston have all written to the War Department for questionnaires to fill out. I didn't see it—I don't get much time for reading either—but it seems there was a general notice in the papers asking men who had served as officers in the First World War to do this if they felt inclined. Dad had already written offering his services and had got a polite acknowledgment, nothing else; but now he hopes the questionnaire may lead to something. I wouldn't be surprised to see him get into active service yet before Phil does, or me either, and all I can say is, more power to him. I like to see the old boy showing some spirit again. It's the first time he has in a long while but now he's like an old fire horse rearing to go again.

Well, time's up, so I must sign off, with my best as always,

Vail.

TELEGRAM

ENID, OKLA.
MARCH 15, 1942

MISS SUSANNAH PRESCOTT
NEW ROADS, LOUISIANA
MADE THE GRADE ALL RIGHT. LEAVING IMMEDIATELY FOR ADVANCED SINGLE ENGINE TRAINING AT LAKE CHARLES. SORRY NOT TO SEE YOU EN ROUTE BUT SHOULD HAVE BETTER LUCK DURING NEXT TWO MONTHS AS I SHALL BE MUCH NEARER YOU. MY BEST AS ALWAYS.

VAIL.

Gerstner Field, Lake Charles, La.
April 3, '42

Dear Sue:

I was ever so pleased to know you got the note that was attached to the handkerchief-sized parachute I released when I went over Salome on my last navigation flight. I jazzed the throttle and waggled my wings too, but I knew there wasn't much chance you'd realize who it was, since I couldn't let you know beforehand I was coming and ask you to be on the look-out. It was a grand flight, the best I've had so far. It was such a clear day that visibility was really unlimited and of course I was delighted to see the cane coming up to such a good stand. False River was beautiful from upstairs and Salome stood out so plainly I almost felt as if I could reach down and touch it or you. I wish I could have.

Realizing it was so uncertain whether you'd get the little note, I didn't put three things in it that I wanted especially to say. The first is that I can't tell you how glad I am you're back in Louisiana at last. I began to think you were going to stay in Boston the rest of your life and of course I couldn't help wondering whether there might not be some special attraction keeping you there. Second, I've got some good news: I get one week-end off while I am here and this next one's it. Of course I'm heading straight to Belle Heloise and by the time you get this or very soon after your mother'll be having one from *grand'mère* asking if you won't all come over and spend Sunday with us. And please remember that we mean it and that we want you the worst way.

Third, I'm going to ask if you won't come to my graduation on the 20th of May. Uncle Fabian and Aunt Cresside are coming and bringing Frances Belle and Dad is bringing Syb and Joyeuse. It's even possible that *grand'mère* may come, so you see you'd have plenty of chaperones—worse luck, but I know your father and mother still go in for those in a big way. Of course if you like I will ask them too and I really think they might find it rather interesting because the school here is going to put on quite a show when its first graduating cadets finish training and get their wings. I'm tickled pink to be in this first class. Just a year ago this place was a rice patch out in the country; now it is a fine flying field with any number of red-roofed, gray-shingled buildings, streets, planes, officers and enlisted men who keep it humming day and night. It makes you realize we do things in a big way in the USA—even in the South, whatever you Yankees say, once we get going and have a reason for it! Well, I won't write any more details because I hope you'll soon be seeing it yourself. Let me know when you're coming and how many so I can make reservations at the Majestic.

As ever,
Vail.

P.S. Yes, Phil was drafted all right and sent to Camp Beauregard for processing. Now he's at Fort Bragg, near Fayetteville, North Carolina. You're right: I don't see why you don't hear from him direct. Rick's still at Shelby but doesn't think it'll be long now. Gosh, I wish he and Syb could have got married before he pushed off. I don't need to add I hope I can. Harvey Lawrason has got another questionnaire from the War Dept., more complete than the one that came in first after he and Dad and Charles Boylston all wrote in January. So he has answered it and is eagerly awaiting developments. He went over to Belle Heloise to tell the family about it, incidentally regaling them with his usual tall tales. This time he told one about a man who lived up near Denham Springs, and who had said he hoped there wouldn't be any mourning at his funeral; instead he wanted his friends to get together and celebrate in a big way. Well, according to Harvey, he died, and the celebration took place just as he wanted. But all the guests, including the officiating clergyman, got so high that the next day no one could remember where they'd buried the corpse and they haven't found him yet. I wish I'd been around myself to hear good old Harvey telling this story and saying Which-I-God every few minutes. There's no one tells a story just like Harvey does or such stories either.

Dad and Charles haven't had a second questionnaire yet, but Charles heard that a procurement officer for the Army Air Corps was to be in New Orleans on his way East from Dallas, so Charles went down to see this man and Dad went at the same time and tendered his services to the Commanding Officer at the Port of Embarkation. So they are also eagerly waiting to see what happens next.

Dear Sue:

Of course I was interested to hear that you had stopped off at Fayetteville to see Phil on your way North, and I agree with you that your parents have made a lot of progress towards a more enlightened viewpoint about chaperones and am glad you could take advantage of it. Just the same I'd like to have got the good of this change of heart myself and I sure was disappointed that you didn't get to Lake Charles. You see, I'd counted on having you pin my wings on for me, and though I was glad to have Aunt Cresside do it, if you couldn't, still it wasn't quite the same. Most of the fellows had their girls pin their wings on after the exercises but there was one quite interesting exception to this: Colonel Schauffler, who made the graduating address, pinned his own wings, which he had won 25 years before, on his son, who was one of my classmates, and who is now here at Harlingen too. The Colonel made a good speech, telling us we had been fortunate in having the preparation we needed to go out into the world and fight and now we were the best-trained men, not only in the USA, but in the world. He "reminisced" as he called it, a little, and said that when he was training he was in the air only two hours before he got his license, and that General Billy Mitchell, who did so much to make it possible for us to get our flight training, was up less than that. Even when Col. S. made his first flight over the German lines in 1917, he had been up only 12 hours. I know we're lucky in having so much better preparation all around, but at that I wish it didn't take quite so long to get into action for I sure am rearing to go. However, there are rumors that next year the course is going to be a lot longer, so I suppose that instead of griping I ought to thank my lucky stars that I got in when I did.

To get back to the graduation, it was held in Recreation Hall and was mighty impressive. The Chaplain who delivered the invocation called it the first milestone of the post and invited us to pause there. After that he got going on the Pilgrim Fathers and I didn't quite see the connection or follow him very well, but I'm sure you would have. The stage looked swell, all fixed up with flowers and plants, and we marched across it to receive our wings and personal congratulations from Col. S. to the tune of war planes overhead, so it was all very military as well as very festive. Col. S. also presented the class with a song which he and his daughter wrote, so you see he was quite the big shot of the occasion. The name of the song is "Happy Landings, Army Air Force" and it was printed on a large white drawing board where we could all see it, and illustrated too. The hall was chock-full of the pilots' families and friends and I sure was glad to have so many of my people there. I think they got quite a kick out of it too, especially Aunt Cresside. Dad got a snap shot of her taken while she was pinning on my wings which I am enclosing just in case you'd be interested. Of course I never told her I really meant you to do it. I missed Mom too, so things weren't quite perfect, I don't suppose they ever are. I don't know though—that very afternoon one of my classmates, Marion Henderson, was married in the Post Chapel. His girl and her mother had both come down from North Carolina, his father assisted the Chaplain in performing the ceremony and his mother and brother were there too. I reckon he thought things were about perfect, I know I would have in his place.

I was unexpectedly sent to Matagorda to finish my gunnery practice; now I have been shipped down here as tow-target pilot and don't know how long I'll have to stay before I get across. Rick made it all right, not long after I last wrote—left San Francisco as a First Lieutenant in his Infantry Division and is now "somewhere in the Pacific," the lucky bum! Charles Boylston has started on his way too as he was ordered to report to Harding Field for physicals two weeks ago, then commissioned Captain in the Air Force straight from civilian life and sent to Miami. (His service in the First World War was in Infantry, but that doesn't seem to matter!) He had just 9 days at Hackberry before starting off, but Seaver has really run their things for years and done it mighty well, so that doesn't matter so much. Harvey is foaming at the mouth because he has got no further than a 3rd questionnaire, this time from the procurement officer in New Orleans, and according to Dad arrived there breathing fire and brimstone over the delay which he doesn't like any better than I do; but I think he'll be getting somewhere pretty soon. Dad has been in New Orleans himself for two months now, on duty at the Port of Embarkation with the rank of Captain, but has applied for transfer to the School of Military Government at the University of Virginia, as he thinks the course there might lead to something for which he is better fitted. I don't know just what will happen to the cane crop this year with neither of us at Belle Heloise and a lot of the hands gone too, for the draft has caught up with some of the Negroes and others have left to take big-paying jobs in town. However, Sance is still on the job though he's getting pretty old now and I know he will do the best he can and Uncle Fabian has given me one of your father's harvesters for a combination birthday and Christmas present, which of course is going to make a huge difference too.

My duties as tow-target pilot here consist almost entirely of flying an AT-6 equipped with a reel on which cable is wound to pull up the flat flaglike tow-target. An enlisted tow-reel operator rides in the rear seat of the airplane and it is his job to attach the tow-targets and play out the cable through a hole in the bottom of the fuselage. The work is apt to be rather monotonous as it consists in flying from the field to the gunnery ranges which parallel the Texas coast north from Brownsville—a distance of approximately 50 miles. After we reach the gunnery ranges we fly at a specified altitude from one end of them to the other, then turn around and fly back again. The training missions are accomplished by a group of 4 airplanes, one tow-target airplane and 3 firing airplanes, flying in formation as far as the gunnery range; then the tow-target plane starts up the range, playing out 6 or 7 hundred feet of cable to which the flag-target is attached and one of the firing airplanes makes passes at the target. In all cases the firing is towards the open water. Each of the gunners is using ammunition that is distinguished from the other gunners' by paint applied to the nose of each bullet before it has had a chance to dry completely, so when it passes through the cloth target a colored ring, red, green, blue, or what have you is left on the flag-target. When all the firing planes have completed their mission, the tow plane returns to the home base, releasing the target over the base where it is retrieved by a ground crew.

Well, that's enough shop for today.

As ever,
Vail.

Harding Field
December 10, 1943

Dear Sue:

This is Phil's twenty-first birthday and I sure wish we were together for it because he is already overseas, the lucky stiff. Somewhere in Northern Ireland, I think, but of course all we have is his A.P.O. number. If you thought my letters sounded discouraged before, I don't know what you will think now. I was sure I was going to get across after Harlingen, especially as I asked for overseas duty, but when my orders came through—well, just look at the top of this page and you'll see that it has taken me 13 months of the hardest kind of training to get as far as home. Of course, it's nice in a way to be near the folks and I can run out to Belle Heloise every evening, but I should hate like hell to have to tell my grandchildren one of these days that I fought the battle of the Heidelberg Baroque Room. Right now I'm taking what is called an indoctrination unit course along with about 600 others. I'm not going to explain that. It wouldn't interest you, and the less I talk or think about it, the better I feel.

I haven't the faintest idea how long they'll keep me here; probably until I trip over my long white whiskers.

Phil isn't the only one who's made it overseas. Believe it or not, Charles Boylston, after receiving Combat Intelligence training at the AAF Intelligence School at Harrisburg, is now somewhere in England with the Eighth Air Force. I bet even Harvey Lawrason beats me across. He's in Dallas now waiting for assignment—a Captain in the Military Police. I have a hunch he may get the snappiest berth of all. With the kind of luck he usually has I'd be an ace by this time. And what do you know? He got time off to get married before he went to Texas and the wedding was at Belle Heloise! Everyone thought he was

584

a confirmed bachelor though there was a pretty little widow in Baton Rouge he liked a lot and used to come over from Denham Springs to see. She lived in one of the Pentagon Building apartments and of course they're nice but they're mighty small, and she didn't have any kin, so *grand'mère* crashed through and offered her the parlor at Belle Heloise for the ceremony. Syb wrote it was a very pretty little wedding and Dad got up from New Orleans and gave the bride away. Since then Mrs. Lawrason has been in Dallas near her husband though she is coming back to Baton Rouge when he goes overseas. Gosh, some people have all the luck! *Grand'mère* is all set to keep on being nice to her though they never knew each other before. War does make a lot of difference in some people's feelings and I can't understand why it hasn't yet in Mom's. She is located in New York now for the duration and is doing awfully well, that is, financially. She writes to all of us except Dad and *grand'mère* and she would like very much to have either or both of the girls come and live with her but it just so happens they prefer to stay at Belle Heloise. Syb is working at the local headquarters of the Red Cross and Joyeuse is doing a swell job on the plantation and still making good enough marks to get by at the University. She is really running the laboratory as we do not have a graduate chemist left there now. The one we did have has gone to DuPont, and though the younger man who was working under him has stood by and is very capable and intelligent, he does not even have a high-school education. Two women, wives of men who are working in the mill, who are high-school graduates, are helping him, and doing the best they can too, but Joyeuse has taken charge of the whole outfit and they were thankful enough to have her. The others all work on eight-hour shifts, but she just plows right along, night, day, any old time. I don't see how she stands it, but she seems to thrive on it. (Incidentally, we haven't even got any sample boys left any more; sample girls have taken their place too!) All this is rather rough on her various boy friends, especially Barry, whose ship gets into New Orleans every now and then and who would naturally like to have her come down there while it is in port. But she says there will be plenty of time for all that, meaning I suppose dates, after the war is over, which shows she isn't very hard hit yet. Just as well, two in one family are enough even if they weren't as far gone as Syb and I both are.

To go back to Joyeuse for a moment, I don't know whether I ever told you she can run a tractor as well as any man I ever saw and I wouldn't put it past her to go straight out into the fields if the labor shortage gets any worse. The new harvester is working like a breeze, the crop will get in, and it's a good one.

As ever,
Vail.

P.S. Don't you think you could make it over here for just one weekend at Christmas time?

Dear Sue:

What do you know? Rick has been in Fiji! He has sent Syb some trinkets from Suva and she and I have both had long letters from him. Syb didn't show me hers—just read parts of it to me—which didn't surprise me much! But I think you'll be interested so I'm copying down parts of mine.

"Word came through today that we are permitted to say where we have been this last year and since this is the case I might tell you a little about it. Most of my time was spent in the bush but I got in to Suva three times and stayed at the Grand Pacific Hotel(!) which is reserved for officers only and where the servants are Indians. While there, was able to get a little beer and a good deal of Scotch whiskey which is about all they drink over here, owing to the British influence."

Well, from there Rick goes on to tell about some marriage customs among the Fijis which I reckon I better not repeat to you as I don't know just how they would strike you though I thought they were very interesting. If you think you'd like to hear them let me know and I'll put them in my next letter. After describing these quaint customs Rick goes on to rave about the beauties of the island, which however, apparently didn't make up for the discomforts, as he says: "Our biggest problem was encountered on patrols and routes into the interior and hell is a small word for the hardships of jungle country. At one time I stayed wet for 10 days. All of my equipment including soap, extra socks and what little else I carried were soaked during the first two hours. There is nothing harder than to have to lie down in a pool of water on a chilly night in wet clothes and try to get enough sleep to keep you plugging along the next day. When I finally emerged into civilization, such as it was, my shoes were in shreds and my clothes in ribbons. That was when I took five days leave in Suva. I had so much water in my system that all the liquor I drank did no good—the water neutralized it. But some of the dinners with the English resembled heaven. To go to their lantern-lit wood houses and eat off china at a table with cloth on it and have cold beer in the evening was anything but hard to take."

There was a lot more and I just ate it up but I've got to remember you've hardly met Rick and that you can't be expected to care what's happening to him the way I do, and besides he's only one of several who's having exciting experiences. Dad graduated from the School of Military Government at Charlottesville late in May, right up close to the top of his class, and was sent at once to Algiers for final indoctrination and training, alongside British outfits. Charles Boylston is "somewhere in Scotland," apparently at some air station. Harvey Lawrason has been in Rio and is now apparently in Bombay, but from his necessarily vague letters his wife gathers this is just a way-station to some even more exciting place. Everybody but me seems to get sent to exciting places.

I have finished the indoctrination course I mentioned in writing before, and am now one of 80 left here out of the original 600 who took it, the others all having been divided elsewhere, but of course I couldn't be one of those. However, if I can't be overseas I'm glad to be near home, and at least the work isn't monotonous any longer, quite the contrary. I have now begun to have first-hand experience flying P-47s in formation flights over Lake Pontchartrain. The last one I was in was not such a success as far as I was concerned. The weather closed in, one of those fogs boiling up from the Gulf, so I headed towards Lake Maurepas and started to follow up the Mississippi but got lost because the visibility was so bad. Finally I was led home by a combat returnee pilot who was out scouting the weather. Now I've been put up for questioning because I left the flight, and can only hope the quality of mercy won't be too much strained in my case.

As ever,
Vail.

Belle Heloise
September 18, 1943

Dear Sue:

The next date line will probably be the stockade at Camp Livingston where I will be awaiting execution for having mutinied. I don't know just how much longer I can take the battle of Third Street. I've about made up my mind to push one of our stone lions off his pedestal and take his place as being more of a contribution to the war effort than anything they've got me doing now. You've heard about our lions, haven't you? Nobody knows where they came from or how they got there. The day after Harding Field was opened, there they were. Incidentally, a cow was found in the swimming pool at the same time. Nobody knows how she got there either, but they got her out. She's probably gone the way of all hamburger stands by now, as she was real; but the stone lions have stayed on. They say that any time a virgin walks between them those lions roar. However, there's never been any kick about the noise. One of them has lost his lower jaw, though, so maybe he did try to roar once.

Otherwise it's the same old routine that I've written to you till you must be as sick of it as I am. Our squadron of P-47s is the hottest one in the entire Air Force. Maybe that's why they're keeping us here. Any time we get to Europe and Fatso Goering hears about it, the *Luftwaffe* will quit and the war will be over.

Phil is in England and no doubt has got hot and cold running girls in every shire. He's griping because his outfit missed the North African show, Sicily, Italy and all the rest of the good clean innocent fun in the Mediterranean. He should be in my shoes; then he'd really have something to gripe about.

As ever,
Vail.

Harding Field
October 15, 1943

Dearest Sue:

Well, they've come through at last—of course I mean the overseas orders. I've had final physicals, made my last will and testament and now I'm getting 10 days leave. After that I'm to report to the staging area and receive my equipment down to the last shoestring and razor blade. Then I'll be on my way almost any moment.

So this won't be a long letter. It's just to tell you the news and ask you again if you won't marry me. Not whether you'll think it over, this time. Whether you won't just do it, straight off. We could crowd a lot of happiness into 10 days, honey, if you would. I know there wouldn't be time for the kind of wedding you'd like to have. But does that matter such a lot, at least, if you care? You could wear that dress of your great-grandmother's that you wore at Plaquemine, couldn't you? And everyone would help you get ready. It ought not to take so long at that. Please try hard to say yes, and say it quick. Because of course 10 days are quite a lot, but we've got to make every one of them count. Please, Sue. Please, darling. If you only knew how much I love you and how hard I'd try to make you happy I'm sure you would.

As ever,
Vail.

"Hail the Conquering Hero"

Autumn 1943–Autumn 1944

The right is more precious than peace, and we shall fight for the things which we have always carried nearest our hearts—for democracy, for the right of those who submit to authority to have a voice in their own governments, for the rights and liberties of small nations, for a universal dominion of right by such a concert of free peoples as shall bring peace and safety to all nations and make the world itself at last free.

—*Woodrow Wilson: Address to Congress, April 2, 1917*

PART XI

'Hail the Conquering Hero'

Autumn 1943–Autumn 1944

CHAPTER XLV

"This is the next best thing, isn't it, Vail?"

"Yes, it's the next best thing. But you know it wasn't the next best thing I wanted. It was the very best."

"Hush! I'm afraid someone will hear you!"

"What difference would that make? I don't care if the whole world hears me. It's true. Don't you think, Sue, that even now—I've still got two more days. We could get married tomorrow. We could——"

"I said, please hush, Vail! People are staring at us."

"Let's get out of here then, and go some place where they can't."

He rose, pushing back his chair abruptly and signaling to their waiter. They had dined at the Court of the Two Sisters and stayed on for dancing afterwards. Between every dance Vail had proposed again, lightly and casually at first, more and more urgently as the evening wore on. Susannah was thankful he had suggested leaving at last. She had been on the point of doing so, a dozen times, herself, but she was trying hard to help Vail get all the pleasure he could out of these last days, and she did not want to suppress him or rebuke him, if she could help it. Now she had almost reached the breaking point.

She had answered his last desperate letter very gently. She wished she could say yes, she told him. He must not think it was because she would miss a big wedding, if she married him straight off; she knew things like that did not matter, when you really cared. But that was the trouble. She didn't really care—at least not enough to marry him. She thought the world of him and all of that. And he mustn't blame her father and mother. She had told them about his letter and they had both said they would be willing. They were very fond of him too. It was just that she didn't love him the way he wanted. And it wouldn't be fair to marry him when she didn't. But if there were anything else she could do . . .

Vail had gone to Cresside and Fabian after hearing from Susannah, and they had immediately invited the girl to spend a week with them at their apartment in New Orleans. She had accepted by return mail and had joined them there the following day. As there were only three bedrooms at the d'Alverys' apartment in the Pontalba, Vail took a room at the Monteleone and he had slept there for a few hours each night; the rest of the time he had spent with Susannah, who consented readily to every outing he suggested and proved herself a consistently adaptable and delightful companion. They had made the harbor tour on the *President* and returned to drink coffee at the French Market. They had dined in a private room at Antoine's and taken in the floor show at the Roosevelt. They had wandered through the French Quarter, window shopping as they went, and ended up at Pat O'Brien's after having their fortunes read in tea leaves. They had gone to the Fishermen's Mass at Our Lady Star of the Sea. And now they had been dancing, closely embraced, all the evening. But there had been no other close embraces, nor even a light exchange of kisses and an occasional lingering handclasp. Vail knew that if he started to kiss Susannah the kisses would soon cease to be light, because that kind would not satisfy him, and she knew it too. Through forebearance on his part and tact on hers they had managed, so far, to keep their association merry and casual. Now Susannah realized that it could not be kept like that any longer.

The interested eyes which had already made her uncomfortable followed them as they moved across the floor and left the restaurant. Now that he had outgrown his early awkwardness and brought his unruly locks under control, Vail had become an exceedingly handsome young man; his color was as striking as ever and he wore his uniform with dash as well as with distinction. Unhappily, Susannah realized there was not a girl among those who were watching them, unless in love with someone else, who would not jump at the chance of being with Vail. Because vanity was not among her failings, she did not consider the correlative probability that there was not a fancy-free youth in the restaurant who would not have been equally glad to squire her. Just as Vail had outgrown his awkwardness, she had outgrown her slight stiffness. Her flawless features had become softer and sweeter; she had infinite grace of bearing; everything about her was charming. Meeting an unusually bold glance, she flushed a little, bending her head and veiling her eyes in her old shy way. Vail caught the presumptuous look, glared at the offender, and held open the door for her.

"I reckon it was just about time we left," he said, reverting to the light and easy way of speaking which he had managed to maintain until that evening. "You were attracting altogether too much attention, Sue. All those stares had nothing to do with my inopportune proposals; they were wholly the result of your fascination. . . . All right, we'll skip it. Where do you want to go next?"

"I suppose I might suggest that you take me home."

"You might, but I hope you won't. I reminded you a few minutes ago that I had two days more. Now I'll remind you that's all I've got. You don't expect me to waste one of my evenings in the Pontalba Building, do you?"

"We could sit on the gallery. It's plenty warm."

"We could at that. It's not a bad idea of yours, Sue. I don't see why neither of us thought of it before."

Susannah made no direct reply. The d'Alverys' gallery was comfortably and attractively equipped with rattan furniture and potted plants; Cresside had managed to give it the same gracious atmosphere which characterized her walled garden on Somerulos Street, greatly as the two places differed in every other respect; but she had also screened it so effectively from the adjacent galleries that she had given it great privacy too. Susannah had deliberately avoided so intimate a setting for a tête-à-tête. Now she knew that the time had come for her to seek it because she could no longer postpone the moment of talking to Vail with great candor.

They went quietly through the paved vestibule and up the bare curving steps to the apartment. Shaded lamps still gave a subdued glow to the patio and drawing room, but the bedroom doors were closed, and the pleasant stillness suggested that no one had waited up for them. They went out on the gallery and through the delicate tracery of its ironwork looked down on Jackson Square. The old-fashioned street lamps shone brightly above their dark standards and the façade of the Cathedral caught some of their radiance and reflected it. Otherwise the Square was in soft darkness. The Cathedral clock struck midnight, and the notes vibrated and trailed off into silence. Then nothing happened to disturb this. Vail came closer to Susannah and put his arm around her.

"Sue!" he said imploringly.

"Yes. I want to talk to you, Vail. Let's sit down, shall we?"

She freed herself gently, but when he tried to take her hand, after they were seated, she did not repulse him. She spoke to him with great earnestness however.

"I've got to tell you, Vail, why I can't marry you, why you must stop asking me to. I hoped I wouldn't have to, but after tonight I know——"

"You don't have to tell me anything you don't want to. There's nothing you could tell me anyway that would change my mind. I haven't changed it in all these years, have I?"

"No. But you will now. I don't love you, Vail. I've kept telling you that all along and you wouldn't listen. Perhaps you'll listen if I tell you I belong to someone else."

"No, I shan't. Because if you were engaged to someone else you wouldn't be out here with me. You wouldn't have been running around with me all this week. You couldn't play any man a dirty trick like that. You haven't got it in you."

"I didn't say I was *engaged* to anyone else, Vail."

"Well, good Lord, you're not trying to tell me you're *married,* are you?"

He laughed lightly, and leaned over to give her the kiss she had so long managed to evade. She drew away from him.

"Yes, I am. That's just what I'm trying to tell you. I'm secretly married. I've been secretly married for nearly a year."

"I don't think much of your joke, Sue."

"It isn't a joke. It's gospel truth."

"You couldn't be married. No one would marry you and keep it a secret. No one would want to."

"My—my husband did, Vail. He wouldn't marry me unless I promised to keep it a secret. And—and I wanted him so much I didn't care what terms I married him on, just so I could do it."

"The dirty, thieving blackguard! The miserable sneak! The——"

"Oh Vail, stop—please stop! You mustn't talk about him like that! I'm—I'm married to Phil."

The soft stillness of the night had suddenly become electrified; instead of uniting them it tore them violently apart. Vail dropped Susannah's hand and leaped to his feet.

"You're—you're married to Phil!" he said hoarsely. "You've been married to him for nearly a year! No, you're not, you couldn't be! No Army chaplain would marry you secretly and no civilian priest either. Even if there were, you couldn't keep it a secret. If you went off together and registered at a hotel, someone would be sure to find out about it. Besides, you'd be using Phil's name now, you'd be getting part of his pay, you'd be living at Belle Heloise while he was gone, waiting for him to come back——"

"Vail, you don't understand. We were married by a Justice of the Peace. Phil—persuaded him not to let anyone know."

"You mean he bribed this damn rascal not to record the marriage?"

"Vail, please don't talk about it like that. It wasn't Phil's fault. It was mine."

"You'll have hard work making me believe that, Sue."

"But it was. You see, Phil knew I was in love with him. I don't mean he thought perhaps I might be, from the way I—from the way I ran after him. Because I did run after him. You know that. You've seen me do it, over and over again. But I mean I told him so, too. Of course I shouldn't have, but I did. And, the last time I went up to Fort Bragg, he said, hell, if I felt that way about it, maybe we better get in a week end together before he was sent overseas."

So that's what he did, Vail said to himself. *I reckon that's what Aunt Cresside has always been afraid I'd do sometime. I reckon she's dreaded that she'd find out, sooner or later, I was the same sort of blackguard my father was. And instead, it was Phil who did it. Phil, who'd always been the white-headed boy of the family. Phil, who's the overseas hero now, winning medals while I got stuck at one training camp after another. Well, he may be all that, but he's a dirty bastard just the same.*

594

He took Sue off to some filthy cathouse and registered under a false name and laid her. No. I'm getting this all mixed up. Phil's an officer and a gentleman, I'm the bastard. But I wouldn't have done what Phil's done. I've always loved Sue too much to mess around with whores, and Phil's treated Sue as if she were a whore herself. My sweetheart, who was going to be my wife. God damn him to hell . . .

"Vail, you don't understand even yet." Sue was speaking in a voice of desperate pleading. But she was not pleading for herself, she was pleading for Phil, who had done this dreadful thing to her, and suddenly Vail's hatred for Phil became a consuming flame. But she went on pleading. She even tried to take Vail's hand, just as many times he had tried to take hers, and this time it was he who snatched it away. "I told him I couldn't. I don't know why, but I just couldn't. Something inside stopped me. I know lots of girls do go off for week ends, nice girls too, and I don't blame them, if that's the only way they can be with the men they love and they're satisfied with that much. But I couldn't. I didn't. You see I didn't want Phil just for a week end. I wanted him for always. At least I wanted to know I had a right to him for always. So I said I was sorry, but I just couldn't. And then Phil made fun of me. He told me I was a sissy. And he told me I needn't be afraid, that he'd take care nothing happened to me. I didn't understand what he meant at first and then he laughed and explained I needn't be afraid I'd have a baby."

This can't be Sue who's talking to me, it can't, it can't. I thought she was going to be my son's mother. Hell, that's one of the things that's kept me loving her so! Any man would be proud to have her for the mother of his son, any man except Phil. No one but Phil would have acted as if she was some round heel in heat who mustn't get hooked, because, if she did, it would be awkward for him . . .

"By and by he stopped making fun of me and explaining things to me because he began to get angry. He said he guessed I didn't love him all that much after all, that I'd just been putting on a good act. And that was the worst of all, Vail. Because you see when a girl's in love she wants to do what a man asks her to for two reasons: first because she longs to make him happy and then because she wants to be happy herself. I mean, in belonging to him. I think lots of people forget that. They talk about girls 'yielding' as if it were some sort of a sacrifice. It isn't, not when they're really in love. It's what they yearn for more than anything else in the world."

I can't stand it if you go on talking like this, Sue. I'm going to war. I might be dead a month from now. I can stand the thought of that; the only thing that ever bothered me was I couldn't get across soon enough. But this is different. This is worse than being wounded; it's worse than being killed, sitting in this place where I meant to make love to you and hearing you say . . .

"But at last he said all right, if I was going to be stubborn about it, we would get married, if I'd promise to keep it a secret. We wouldn't go to a priest because it would take too long to get married that way. You see, I'm an Episcopalian, and he reminded me I'd have had to get my baptismal certificate and sign papers about my children's religion and promise all sorts of things before I could marry a Catholic, and Phil would have had to go to Confession and Communion and all that. I asked him if his father and mother hadn't managed to arrange everything very quickly, in spite of those obstacles—someone had told me about their marriage, you see, Vail. And Phil said yes, but that was a very special case, where the priest knew his father well and had great confidence in him and recognized that there was a real emergency. He said he didn't know any such priest, that the chaplain at camp was a tartar and that it was a Justice of the Peace or nothing."

Phil didn't know any such priest. Of course he didn't. No priest would feel confidence in Phil, the way Father Navarre felt confidence in Dad, when he said there was an emergency. The chaplain at Fort Bragg would know right away there was something wrong—chaplains wouldn't be any good, to the Church or to the Army either, if they didn't know such things. He would have sent Sue home to wait for the man who'd loved her for years only to find out just when he was starting off to war, that she was married to his brother. No, damn it, Phil isn't my brother. I'm glad of that anyway, even if it makes me a bastard. Thank God I didn't have a scoundrel and a sneak for a brother as well as for a father . . .

"So we went to the Justice's house. It was a horrid little place. But I didn't mind. At least I didn't mind much. Of course I'd always thought I'd be married in church and wear my great-grandmother's wedding dress, like you suggested, and that all my friends would be there, and that afterwards there'd be a reception with lots of flowers and a big frosted cake and champagne and presents. I thought there'd be a wedding trip to some lovely place. So I was a little disappointed because there was just a dingy little parlor with rubber plants in it and the Justice's wife and daughter for witnesses and then that terrible hotel."

"A horrid little place." An unshaven man, in his shirt sleeves, standing in one corner of a musty room mumbling words which should have been sacred and beautiful and spoken by a priest of God in a sanctuary. "A terrible hotel." A lousy dump, a pimp of a clerk, sneering at the soldiers who came in with a bottle under one arm and a whore on the other—sneering at them but accommodating them, in swift succession. With rooms where the empty bottles the last couples had left still stood on sticky tables, and the soiled towels still lay on the floor and the unhallowed bed was still unmade. Where the walls were so thin you had to close your consciousness to the carousal in the alley below and could not close it to the whoring in the next room! . . . And I had always planned to take Susannah to a cottage in the St. Tammany woods, where we'd be by ourselves among the clean and fragrant pines, under the friendly stars . . .

596

"We had to sit in the lobby, because there wasn't a vacant room. We waited and waited. I'll never forget the soldiers who came in or the girls who were with them—the ones who came in and the ones who came out. They seemed to be coming and going all the time. Just soldiers and girls—girls and soldiers—hardly anyone else. And the girls all looked just alike. They had queer battered hats with drooping feathers and moth-eaten fur collars on their coats. Phil looked at them and said, 'My God, even the whores are in uniform now'!"

Phil said this to Susannah, coupling her with those others, just as he had when he told her she needn't be afraid she'd have a baby. Susannah, who's always kept everyone at arm's length, whom I've loved for just that, more than I've loved her for anything else. She sat in that filthy lobby, wearing a trim little tailored suit and watched that drab procession while she waited to go upstairs and Phil said . . .

"Finally a sergeant came through the revolving doors and glanced around. He was alone and he didn't look like any of the men lounging in the lobby with their girls. He was very spick and span and had on white gloves and an initialed arm band. Phil saw him and muttered, 'My God! The M.P.'! I asked him what that would mean and he said to wait a minute, we'd find out fast enough. The M.P. went around stopping in front of all the men in the lobby, one by one. He spoke to them and after a minute or two some of them left the hotel. He didn't even look at the girls who were with the soldiers. Except when he came to Phil. Then he did look at me for a moment. But presently he turned back to Phil and said, 'Let me see your papers.' Phil reached into the pocket of his blouse and pulled out his pass. The M.P. inspected it carefully and then said, 'Report back to camp immediately.' Afterwards he went right on again, speaking to more men and Phil looked at me and muttered under his breath, 'Well, that seems to be that. We don't get our week end after all. Not this one, anyway. And it sounds to me as if we wouldn't be getting one for a long while. Unless I'm all wet, my outfit's pushing off ahead of time. Remember, you're not going to say anything about this little fling of ours till the war's over.'"

"You mean you haven't seen him since then?"

"No. He went straight back to camp and I didn't. I'd brought my bags in when I'd left that morning because we'd already decided we were going to be married. So the camp hostess wasn't expecting me, and after he'd made his rounds, the M.P. came back and looked at me again and asked if he could be of any service. Phil said, 'Thanks a lot. I'd be ever so glad if you'd take her to the station.' Then he said good-by to me right there and I didn't hear from him again for a month and by that time he was overseas. He'd been alerted right away, just as he expected. Of course he writes to me now, once in a while. But he's never said anything about our being married in any of his letters. I'm not surprised at that because I know the censor sees them and since Phil wanted it all kept a secret ... They all come addressed to Miss Susannah Prescott."

"You—you never went upstairs with him at all?"

"That's what I've kept telling you, Vail. We sat in that horrible lobby and waited and waited——"

For the first time her voice broke and she bent her head. So she did not see the swift change that came into his face, any more than she heard the thumping of his heart or sensed the great wave of relief which engulfed him. She was not even conscious of him. For a long time she sat pitifully still. Then she looked up again and went on unflinchingly.

"You know now why I didn't come to your graduation, Vail," she said. "And why I made excuses about coming to Belle Heloise and about having you come to Salome. I'd have loved being with you. I've always loved being with you. And I thought, just these last few days, it would be all right. I thought I could do that much for you. I didn't think it would be unfair to Phil——"

"Unfair to Phil! You talk to me about being unfair to Phil, after what he's done to you!"

He seized her hands again, this time holding them so tightly that she could not draw them away from him. "Look here, Sue," he commanded. "If you think I'm going to let what you've told me scare me off, you're making the worst mistake you've ever made in your whole life. You're not married to Phil. You're not married to anybody. That Justice might just as well be a bad dream as far as you're concerned. Forget about him. I'll see to him when I get home. Meanwhile remember you're engaged to me and don't take any more long chances."

"Vail, you know I can't be engaged to anyone. You know I *am* married to Phil. Everything's going to be all right as soon as he gets back, as soon as I have a chance to talk with him——"

"I'm going to have a talk with Phil myself, maybe sooner than he thinks, and I'll make it mighty clear to him what he's got to do next. I'm not going to spoil the rest of my leave telling you what I think of him. But I will tell you this much: if he ever gets in my way again, I'll know just what to do about that. And don't you ever say again that you love him. If you did, I might choke you. And I'd a lot rather kiss you. What's more, I'm going to."

CHAPTER XLVI

HE GOT his kiss, but afterwards he was sorry he had taken it, for he did not get one in return, and without response there was no reward. Susannah did not struggle against him, but she managed to withdraw

598

her real self so completely that he embraced only its image. When he released her, he instantly knew that the division between them was more than physical. The companionable warmth of her manner, which all the week had given him such a sense of well-being and ease in her presence, had suddenly cooled to one of complete detachment, and when she spoke to him, the friendly ring had gone from her voice.

"I'm sorry you did that, Vail. I'm sorry you've said what you have. I thought I could count on you to understand."

"I do understand. I'm going to make you understand too."

"You're not going to 'make' me do anything, Vail. Please don't ever use that word again, in speaking to me. I think we better not try to talk any longer—now, anyway. Good night. Good-by, rather. You're going back to Belle Heloise in the morning, aren't you?"

"No, not till afternoon. And I thought maybe you'd come with me, Sue. I thought we'd go by the River Road all the way. It's a beautiful drive. You've never taken it, have you? I want to show it to you. I've wanted to for a long while, and this is my last chance."

"I'm sorry, Vail. If you hadn't said I wasn't married to Phil and talked about being engaged to me yourself——"

"I won't, if you'll go home with me. I promise."

"I'm sorry, Vail," she said again. "I know you mean that now, but you might forget, if we took a long drive together. You might try to kiss me again."

"No, I won't, Sue. Look at me. If you'll only look at me, you'll believe me."

Involuntarily she glanced up at him. His eyes met hers squarely and steadfastly. For a moment she hesitated.

"Do you mean you wouldn't do it tomorrow and the next day, or do you mean you wouldn't ever do it again?"

"It would be easy to lie to you, but I won't do that either, Sue. I mean I won't do it tomorrow or the next day. Of course I'm going to have things out with Phil, as soon as I can find him. Of course I'm going to see that Justice of the Peace on my next leave—if I'd only known before what you've told me tonight, I'd have seen him on this one, even if it had meant giving up these days with you. If there were still time, I'd go to North Carolina now. But there isn't. I don't intend for a moment to give you up, though. The only thing I'm promising is that I won't kiss you again against your will, and that I won't talk to you again about marrying me until you're convinced yourself that you're free."

"But I don't *want* to marry you!"

"You will, some day."

He was still looking at her squarely and he spoke with complete conviction. Susannah's latent anger flared into sudden flame.

"You're making a great mistake. I'll never marry you, I'll never want to. I made a mistake too. I ought to have known enough not to come here. I ought to have known you'd act this way. I'm not going home with you, Vail. I don't want to see you any more. Don't try to see me again. Don't write to me either. I shan't answer if you do. Good-by."

"Aren't you even going to wish me good luck?"

She hesitated again. Her flash of temper was dying down, even more quickly than it had flared up. It was impossible to stay angry with Vail. He was not asking for her sympathy, he did not want that; nevertheless something about his complete singleheartedness was very moving. She not only wanted to wish him good luck, she wanted to tell him she would be hoping and praying for his safety and for his early return. She did not really mean she did not want to see him or hear from him again. She would have taken great pleasure in motoring up the River Road with him and spending the last day of his leave with him at Belle Heloise. She had always enjoyed his letters, and she knew they would be more interesting than ever, from now on, because his experiences would be so much more thrilling than ever before. She would have liked to take back what she had said. She would also have liked to kiss him good-by, as any well-bred girl would kiss a brother-in-law who was also an old friend and to whom she was genuinely attached. In fact, she had meant to do so. She had thought about it and even looked forward to it. But that was impossible, now that Vail . . . It was too bad.

"Yes, of course I wish you good luck," she said more gently. "The best in the world."

"Then you're wishing that I'll marry you. A safe homecoming in itself wouldn't mean so much to me, Sue. What I want is a safe homecoming to you."

She made a small deprecatory gesture. "You see, it's hopeless to try talking. Good-by again, Vail. And—well, the best of luck to you in everything else."

She moved away from the wrought-iron railing and crossed the gallery slowly. At the entrance to it she turned, and hesitated a third time. Then, without speaking again, she went into the house.

After he heard her door close, Vail went in himself and turned out the lights which Cresside had left burning for them, pausing a moment between each one. When the friendly drawing room and the pleasant patio were in complete darkness at last, he went down the curving stone stairway and along the paved entrance hall into the street. Somehow he knew that all the radiance had gone from the Square. But he noticed nothing else. Several late roisterers hailed him tipsily, but he did not hear them; several shadowy figures brushed against him, but he did not see them.

Everything that had passed between himself and Susannah seemed utterly unreal and fantastic. If Sybelle had secretly married Riccardo, Vail could have understood that; indeed, he knew it was only Rick's firm insistence that he would neither force his way into a family where he was unwelcome, or enter furtively into such a relationship, that had kept her from headstrong action. Joyeuse was also quite capable of taking matters into her own hands; she did not happen to be in love with anyone, but Vail was quite certain that if she were, she would not let anything stand in her way. Neither of the two, however, would have accepted a reluctant bridegroom, much less besought a lukewarm admirer to take her for his wife. That Susannah had done this was so utterly out of character that the whole procedure was inconceivable to him.

Mingled with his amazement was overwhelming relief. The fact that the opportune arrival of the Military Police had prevented the consummation of her marriage seemed to him nothing less than an act of God. Whatever Susannah said or thought, Vail knew that such a marriage could be annulled, and he was convinced that the time would come when she would be ready and eager to have it annulled. Somehow this must be done before she had a chance to commit another act of folly, this time one which would change her marital status—in other words, before Phil's first leave home. And as soon as she was officially free, he himself must persuade her to marry him without further loss of time. He did not question the possibility of this either. He declined to.

The bright expanse of Canal Street, stretching out before him, brought him to an abrupt stop. He had gone past his hotel without realizing it. Turning quickly back, he made a determined effort to come out of his trance, and even stopped to chat agreeably with one or two acquaintances as he passed through the lobby. After he got into bed, he tossed about restlessly for an hour or so; but he finally fell into a deep and dreamless sleep, and when he waked, the sun was streaming into his room. He fumbled for his wrist watch, then shook it to make sure it had not stopped the night before; the small luminous hands were pointing to eleven. He jumped up, shaved, showered and dressed in record time, and went down to the coffee shop, taking a thermos bottle with him. As he was finishing his breakfast, he asked the waitress to fill it and to put up a couple of sandwiches for him. As soon as these were ready, he checked out.

No use hanging around, with Susannah feeling the way she does now, he told himself conclusively. *Better have the extra time at home—I can use it all right. I won't go by the Airline though—I'd rather see the River Road alone than not see it at all before I leave. And it's a far piece from New Orleans to Belle Heloise when you take it thataway. I might as well get started.*

He had meant to say, at the garage, that he wanted his car washed, but as usual he had forgotten. Cresside often told him, laughingly, that no matter how many cars he had, or what make they were, they always looked and sounded exactly like Leaping Lena, which had long since given up the gasoline ghost. There was a good deal of truth in what she said. The jalopy of the moment had been new when rationing went in, but it had completely lost its original air of jauntiness, and it had developed a series of miscellaneous rattles with which no mechanic had ever successfully coped. Vail climbed in and waved a cheerful good-by to the attendant who had brought it around. Then he bucked rapidly away towards Claiborne Avenue. It was just one o'clock when he came in sight of the Huey Long Bridge, and swinging halfway around the traffic circle below it, saw the road home stretching out ahead of him. He actually forgot Susannah for a moment. He remembered only that this was his own countryside, that he loved it beyond any other part of the world, and that he would not see it again for a long time. Therefore, it never occurred to him that at this same moment Susannah, angrier than she had been at any time during the evening before, was engaged in futile argument with a telephone operator at the Monteleone Hotel.

"But Lieutenant d'Alvery can't have checked out. He told me himself he wasn't leaving till afternoon. Yes, I do want you to ring his room again. Yes, I do want you to have him paged in the coffee shop and in the lobby. You better try the garage too, he might have gone down there to see about his car. . . . All right, I will leave a message. Tell him that Miss Susannah Prescott would be very glad to meet him at Antoine's for lunch at one-thirty and that she'll drive up to Belle Heloise with him this afternoon. B-E-L-L-E H-E- oh, never mind! Just say, up the River Road. At least you must know how to spell that!"

Susannah was very seldom so rude to anyone. But then, she seldom had been so upset.

It was a perfect day, and Vail was not in a mood for haste. He wanted to loiter along, looking at every beautiful sight on the way, so that his memory of it would still be fresh and vivid when he was a long way off. Too bad he wouldn't be on hand for the celebration on St. Rosalie's Day; he and Rick had often gone to Kenner for the procession and the fireworks. They had always meant to test the malign powers of the famous tree at Poplar Grove too; but somehow they invariably lingered so long at Kenner that there had never been time for the notorious plantation ruins. There was no time now either; further on there was so much he wanted even worse to see. Just the same, the story he had meant to track down was curious. Nearly all the old houses along the River Road were supposed to be haunted; their ghosts were as much a part of their tradition as their gardens, and Vail knew that at Belle Heloise the two allegedly went together. But Poplar Grove was the only place he'd ever heard of where a tree, instead of a house, had been linked with the supernatural. According to legend, any animal left beneath it dropped dead. All nonsense, of course. But it would have been fun to take some decrepit old mule there and see what happened. No, not a mule, he thought hastily, remembering Minnie and Betsy Ann, nor a horse either, because of Nostar, and certainly not a dog. But there must be some kind of animal that didn't matter. And at Destréhan it would be fun to hunt for Jean Lafitte's buried treasure, much the same sort of fun it had been to dig in the Tramontes' back yard, when he and Rick were kids, with Syb sitting there watching them. After the war was over, he and Rick might ask if they could dig at Destréhan yet, just for the hell of it. He had meant to tell Sue about the tree and the treasure, if she had only come along. It would have been a relief to talk about nonsensical things like that, for a change. . . .

Still thinking about the legendary treasure, and the way he had hoped Sue would take the story about it, he slowed down before the entrance to the old plantation house of Destréhan, admiring the well-ordered verdant lawns and the sloping green roof of the gleaming white house which harmonized with its surroundings in such perfection. Here was one place, at least, which retained its original elegance; and Ormond, a little further on, was coming back into its ôwn. Its grounds still looked a little bare, but its red brick and white clapboards were glistening with fresh paint, and its wide wings stretched out invitingly beyond its slender colonnettes. Yet both Destréhan and Ormond in their prosperity lacked something which Belle Heloise in its shabbiness still possessed. Was it the love which a family could lavish uninterruptedly on a house from one generation to another which was missing? Destréhan House was now a club for an oil company. Ormond had recently passed over to new owners. Perhaps that was the answer.

Just above Norco, the site of another prosperous oil company, the River Road came to a dead end beside a sign announcing that trespassers on Government property would be prosecuted. Momentarily Vail, absorbed in other thoughts, had forgotten that this was the only indication of the approach to the vast Bonnet Carré spillway. He turned back and took the first side street to the Airline, remaining on it until he had passed LaPlace. He might as well drop in at Roussel's, he decided, since he was going right by it. He did not know a restaurant where the bartender made better old-fashioneds, or where the trim, white-uniformed waitresses served turtle soup and shrimp gumbo with more efficiency and dispatch. A Greyhound bus had drawn up at the entrance just before him, disgorging its hurried and hungry passengers; the bar, the counter, and the marbleized tables were all crowded; the jukebox was blaring out "Oh, What a Beautiful Morning," and every slot machine in the long row flanking the tables was rattling and ringing. *A fellow ought to have a girl with him in a place like this,* Vail thought; *if he does, all this racket and confusion are fun, because he and she are part of it. If he's alone, he's left out of it and feels a lot lonelier than he does on the open road. Of course, Antoine's is more Susannah's style; we could have had lunch at Antoine's and our drive too. But after all, she used to like Jarreau's; I don't see why she shouldn't like this too. I believe she would have.* For an instant his sense of desolation was so great that he thought of going out again without ordering anything. Then one of the trim waitresses came towards him, smiling confidently, and he said he would have a double old-fashioned, if she could make it snappy, and she said sure she could. She did, but while he was waiting, he managed to find a place in front of one of the slot machines, where he promptly hit the jackpot. Unreasonably elated, he told the waitress he might as well have turtle soup too, and it didn't matter whether she made it snappy or not. He wasn't in all that much of a hurry. He could wait until the bus pulled out. As a matter of fact, he lingered some time after that, savoring the familiar atmosphere. . . .

The Godchaux refinery was going at full blast, he observed, as he came to Reserve after swinging back on the River Road again; the imposing proportions of both factory and field, and the bustling activity which pervaded these, gave irrefutable evidence of the organization's prosperity. If the Godchaux could so signally succeed in this region, first as a family then as an organization, there was no reason that Vail could see why any other closely knit group could not do the same. Yet on the long stretch of road still ahead of him, the Colonial Sugar Refinery was the only other large plant of this kind left. Around Lutcher the fields were cultivated for shallots and the unique type of strong tobacco—perique—which was grown nowhere else in the world; but there would be no more sugar, except at the State Penitentiary Farm above St. Gabriel. Oh, sure, small patches here and there, to be sold to the big refineries for a bit of extra cash in the fall; but no real stand of cane till you reached Hackberry, which was run by a Boston Yankee. No sir, no real stand of cane grown by one of the old families till you got to Belle Heloise. . . .

He was no less puzzled than distressed by this. He knew all the explanations for it without feeling that any of them represented valid reasons. Surely some of the men who had once owned and worked this land could have clung to it and forced it to yield! Surely they could have kept their homes too, granted the same sort of effort and devotion! Only a few of the so-called Big Houses along this road had really been mansions; in most cases their proportions had been suited to families of moderate size and moderate means. The argument that they required armies of servants to maintain them, unlimited fuel to heat them, and vast fortunes to keep them in repair had no weight with Vail. Trepagnier and Esperance, two of the famous old houses which he had already passed, were "raised cottages," with their limited living quarters all on one floor; certainly they could not have been hard to run! Vail would have liked to know the unexpurgated story of their abandonment. St. Michael's convent baffled him in much the same way. Why should this great Gothic building, one of the earliest centers of the Sacred Heart in the Deep South, and for over a century a fashionable school for girls, stand vacantly forsaken amidst rank and straggly growth? Had these signs of disintegration already begun

604

when his mother went to school there? Could they have been at the root of her restlessness and rebellion?

Perhaps when he came back from the war he would find the answers to these questions—especially if someone else was sufficiently interested to help him search them out. But he made a determined effort to dismiss them from his mind now, reminding himself that he had not come up the River Road to fathom its mysteries or brood over its failures. He had come to watch the lovely light on the levee; the undulating effect of the road twisting around this; the peaceful cattle grazing there and the massed clouds overhead. He had come to see the lush vegetation, the clustering cabins, the Negroes loitering along, the old limestones which had once served as filters for the muddy river water. He had come to meet the great sugar trucks, shaped like assault boats, skeletal as they clattered past empty, menacing as they loomed up ahead, overladen, shedding stray stalks of cane in their thunderous progress. Resolutely, as his car swung up to the very doorstep of some house, he tried to close his consciousness to the knowledge that the reason he passed so close to it was because the road had been moved back again and again, when the river, cutting further and further to the east, had eaten away the land underneath the wide lawns which had once surrounded it. Several of these houses, more or less intact, were ornate examples of "Steamboat Gothic"; their cupolas, cornices, belvederes and balustrades still rose in bewildering array. But their shades were drawn and their galleries empty; evidently their owners had felt that without their elaborate grounds and the strutting peacocks, stone deer, fluted urns and latticed gazebos which had once adorned these, the multiple embellishments on the houses themselves had lost their effectiveness. Doubtless these property owners had left to dwell in surroundings of more suitable simplicity. Vail could understand such an action and the feeling which prompted it, and the blank look of the more showy places did not affect him as poignantly as the decay of those whose essential beauty was based on patterns which had survived the centuries. But after all, the period pieces reflected the mode and the taste of an era which had been not only prodigal but robust; this era was part of American history, and these houses the symbols of it. He could not help hoping they would not eventually go the way of the others. . . .

As he passed one great grove of moss-festooned trees after another, he was still less successful in ignoring their significance; he knew that these groves had once formed the setting for houses long since destroyed by flood or flame, and that whatever else might still be salvaged, these were gone forever. The bells hanging in separate scaffoldings beside the scattered Negro churches had once been the voices of plantations, just as the one cast by Thiac-Maignan for François Estrade still served this animate purpose for Belle Heloise. The bowl-shaped iron kettles used as watering troughs for stock in road-side pastures had once been part of the proud mechanics of sugar making. The rain-water cisterns, sprawling on short stilts beside houses still more squat, had once been sugar-mill boilers. He could not go a mile without confronting some fresh reminder that this region, once so rich that it was called The Grand Parade of the Deep South, was sinking further and further into desuetude; and with each reminder he resolved afresh, almost savagely, that once the war was over he would not rest until he had done his utmost to waken it to new life and new productiveness, and that Susannah should help him to do this. His love for her and his love for the land seemed more and more closely linked the further he went. . . .

At Burnside even the blacktop ended; from there on he would have only the dusty gravel road until he reached Belle Heloise. It had never been a matter of political expediency to improve this part of the route, though it was listed as a state highway. That was something else again: why should the old d'Alvery place not have blacktop going past it, if the old Bringier and Colomb places could? Vail resolved to find out, and having found out, to take action. He would certainly have his hands full, after the war. . . .

Suddenly it occurred to him that he was hungry, that the turtle soup he had eaten at Roussel's was all gone. But he still had the coffee and sandwiches he had brought with him from the Monteleone. As he went past the oil fields at Darrow, he knew he must be near the turn-off to Belle Hélène and decided to go and eat his supper on the steps of this magnificent deserted house. He had ceased trying to fight off his feeling of nostalgia about the vanished glories of the past; probably his mood was allied to the knowledge that without his efforts his own home would soon be a part of it. He watched for his turn-off, followed the dense growth of concealing shrubbery for a few hundred yards, and stopped his car beside the rickety gate where the noble mansion came into view.

It was not approached through an *allée* at the front, like so many plantation houses; instead the entrance was at the side, through the most beautiful grove of oaks that he had as yet seen. Only the leveled brick foundations remained of the outbuildings which had once stood at the west of the mansion, and these were so obscured by weeds that Vail stumbled over them as he walked along; but on the east, the picturesque shell of a narrow, two-story *garçonnière* and a square *pigeonnier* still remained. Above them loomed the Big House. Its upper gallery sagged sadly, but otherwise it showed no signs of serious deterioration. Its great square columns were still sturdy, its splendid cornice undamaged. Vail sat down on the crumbling pavement before the front door and looked out toward the river. A long sloping sweep of ground, which must once have been a terraced lawn, framed by magnolias, willows and water oaks, afforded an unobstructed view. The road itself did not show; it was swallowed up in the surrounding greenery. But if the trees on the batture had been cut, passing boats

would have been readily visible from the gallery. Vail could picture them as they must have looked in that proud past which had so absorbed him all day, and as they might still look in an even prouder future. Grudgingly he admitted that when it came to location, Belle Helène was unsurpassed; there was nothing elsewhere to compare with that splendid grove at the side and this superb open sweep in the front. The approach to Belle Heloise was restricted and confined compared to this.

A rosy sunset, suffusing the portico and the landscape with its radiance, gave added luster to their beauty. In this lovely light the ravages of neglect were lost and the most exquisite aspects of past perfection intensified. Vail forgot he was hungry, forgot he was tired, forgot he was disappointed and depressed as he continued to sit, looking out towards the river, and trying to remember what he had heard about this place which seemed so tinged with magic. He knew it had once belonged to a man of great prominence named Duncan Kenner, who had been Jefferson Davis's Minister Plenipotentiary on the Continent during the days of the Confederacy, and who had continued to merit such high esteem that even a "black Republican" like President Arthur had been impelled to appoint him to the United States Tariff Commission. But who owned it now, or why they did not inhabit it, Vail had no idea. He wondered about its name too. Someone had told him it was named for the heroine of Offenbach's opera, based on the faults and foibles of the Empress Eugénie. But that seemed to him unlikely, for eventually he recalled that its original name had been Ashland and the latter designation must have come long after the trivialities of the Third Empire had lost their vogue. Now that he thought of it, he did not know how Belle Heloise had got its name, and he was surprised that it had never occurred to him before that he should ask. He did not know of any d'Alvery or Estrade ancestress called Heloise, and if there had been one, he thought he would have. Perhaps some languishing lady, long dead, had read the romance of the scholar Abélard and his favorite pupil and had been so moved by it that she had chosen further to immortalize her. He would find out from his grandmother the next day, and write to Sue about it. Of course it was all nonsense for her to say he must not write to her. He would not clutter up the scene with letters, but he would write whenever he had anything special to say, and this was exactly the sort of thing that would interest her. She had been ever so interested in the origin of Salome. The origin of Belle Heloise, or Belle Helène, for that matter, should be equally intriguing to her. . . .

Some stray cows, turned out to pasture on the abandoned pleasure grounds, stopped to stare at him in mild wonder, and then meandered on again. Finally a Negro, riding past on horseback, reined in, sweeping off his tattered felt in an elaborate bow, and wished the visitor a civil good evening. Evidently he was some sort of a casual or voluntary caretaker. Vail got to his feet.

"Good evening. I hope I'm not trespassing. I was motoring up the River Road and I just stopped to eat my supper."

"Yo' doesn't want to buy Belle Helène, does yo', suh?"

"No, I've got a place of my own a little further up the river. At least my folks have—Belle Heloise."

"Ah done hear of it. An' Ah done hear it wuz a mighty fine place."

"We think so. I'm on my way there now. But I've always admired this one too, every time I've passed it, and I thought no one would mind if I stopped and ate my supper here."

"No suh, no one doesn't mind. Is yo' finished yo' supper now?"

The Negro was eyeing the untouched package of sandwiches covetously. It occurred to Vail that he really might be needy, though it was hard to imagine this, in such a land of natural plenty. He picked up the package and offered it to the Negro.

"Yes, I've finished. I had this much left over. Would you care for it?"

"Ah thanks yo' kindly, suh. Ah sure does. Ah hopes yo' passes dis way agin, soon an' plenty. Ah lives alone, up dis here road a short piece, and Ah was fresh outen anything to eat dis evening. Now Ah got me a nice supper. Ah's sorry yo' doesn't want to buy Belle Helène. Proud to of met up with yo', suh."

The Negro rode off, stopping to doff his hat in one more elaborate bow as he rounded the ruins of the *garçonnière*. Vail could not see beyond that. It was not "good dark" yet, but it was already "first evening"; dusk was closing in with the astonishing swiftness of regions where no long dim period prevails between the blaze of sunset and the splendor of night. It was logical that there should be no twilight here, Vail thought; the River Road was not a place of shadows, but of either darkness or light. . . .

He could, if he chose, take the cut-off between Geismar and Carville, and if he had not lingered so long at Belle Helène he would have done so, for from it branched off, obscurely and remotely, still another road that he loved, one unlike any other that he knew: a ribbon-like white strip, bordered on one side by a quiet bayou and on the other by tiny, tidy farmhouses that somehow seemed even quieter. He had always thought that some day he would find out who lived in those farmhouses, and how; their complete detachment, their almost uncanny tranquility had always baffled him. The ribbon-like white strip led to nothing but a peaceful pasture; it had no definite ending any more than it had a logical beginning. Yet for some mysterious reason families had dwelt along it for generations in such contentment that they had never cared to stray. He had thought that Sue might like to see this hidden byway too. He had meant to show it to her this very afternoon. But now it was too dark to see it in any case. He excused himself for not taking it on those grounds, and on the grounds that as this would be his last ride over the River Road for a long time, he could not afford to stray from it. . . .

It went on and on, twisting and turning with the river, and so narrow at many points now that two cars could not possibly have passed each other. But Vail met no other cars and saw almost no signs of life until the huge illuminated plant of the Leprosarium suddenly loomed up ahead of him. Its brilliant lighting, its concrete walks, well-pruned trees and freshly painted buildings gave it the air of an ultra-modern and uniquely prosperous little town, inexplicably located in a region where slackness, poverty, and an agreeably "do-less" existence were much more characteristic of village life. Only the high wire surrounding it betrayed it as a tragic enclosure, just as the inescapable rays of the searchlight, flashing from Monticello Farms, a few miles further on, marked that as a penitentiary operation. Vail passed them both without slackening speed; he hoped and believed that they were model institutions, and he could not miss them in the dark, as he had missed the picturesque paving stones taken from the old tombs at St. Gabriel. He had meant to show Susannah some of the old inscriptions and quaint names on those; but he had not meant to show her anything that would remind her of misery or crime. He did not wish to be reminded of it himself.

He was almost home now. Hackberry was the only plantation between Monticello Farms and Belle Heloise and at Hackberry he did slow down, reflecting that it would be courteous as well as pleasant to stop in for a farewell word with Seaver, who would be gratified with his visit, and who would give him the latest news of Charles Boylston while they sipped a nightcap. But the Lodge was in darkness, like all the other houses along the way, though the sugar mill was still lighted and noisy. Besides, now that he was so close to home, he felt as if he could hardly wait to get there. He pressed his foot down on the accelerator and went over the remaining stretch of road at unpatriotic speed.

The cattle gap rattled as the jalopy went over it. *I suppose I ought to have that fixed,* Vail said to himself. *But I don't believe I ever shall. Dad always said the noise it made was the first sound that told him he was home and that that was why he loved it. I do too. I'd miss it if I didn't hear it. Next he used to listen for the pigeons cooing and the dogs barking and watch for Amen lounging out to take the car. Well, the pigeons are gone and Maudie's the only dog and there isn't anyone to take the car. But I don't want anyone. Syb'll be waiting up for me. I've got her to watch for, and all the yard boys in the world aren't worth her little finger. And Maudie makes up for a dozen other dogs.* He was bucking forward through the crepe myrtles as he thought of this and swung past the iron gate leading to the yucca-bordered path and made the sharp turn that took him up to the right of the house. He saw it rising before him in all the loveliness of its lighted windows and galleries, its gracious symmetry, its uncluttered spaciousness, its welcoming warmth. Always it was beautiful in his eyes. But never half so beautiful as when he came upon it at night,

609

after making that sudden turn, and beheld it radiant above its dim lawns, among its dark trees. What did it matter if desolation reigned elsewhere along the River Road as long as this survived? He could not help what happened to other places; but this was his to preserve. He would have it and hold it not only against flood and fire, but against neglect, against sloth, against indifference, against carelessness and all other evils. . . .

Sybelle and Maudie were already in the open space beyond the colonnade. Before he was half out of the car Sybelle had her arms around his neck and Maudie was leaping around his legs. He disengaged himself, laughing.

"Look, you two, give a fellow a chance. You've got me pinned in, between you, and I want to get out of this car. I've been in it nearly all day." He kissed Sybelle heartily, gave Maudie a quick pat, and in mock desperation managed to slide through to freedom. But Sybelle linked her arm in his, and Maudie continued to leap upon him with joyous barks as they made their way across the gallery.

"I thought Sue was coming home with you, Vail!"

"I thought so too. But she said good-by to me in New Orleans."

"Oh . . . I was looking forward to seeing her. . . . I had the Henry Clay room all ready for her."

"That was sweet of you, Syb. But maybe it's better this way, after all."

"Well, if you think so . . . Joyeuse has gone to bed, but *grand'mère's* still awake, Vail. She thought Sue was coming with you too. She'd planned to give her a slip from the green rose. She's got it in a vase, by her bed."

"That's darn nice of her. She's never given one to anybody before, has she? I'll go and thank her."

"I think it would please her a lot if you'd have a snack in her room, too. I've got everything ready. We'll have time for our own visit in the morning, won't we?"

"Sure. We'll take time. Come on. Don't let's keep the matriarch waiting. This is pretty late for her, you know."

They went up the stairs together, past the Spanish statue, with Maudie close at their heels. Madame d'Alvery was listening for their approach; she turned her head on her great square pillows and looked towards the shutter door leading into the hall. When it opened, and she saw that Susannah was not there, she turned away again, in obvious disappointment, and looked fixedly at the slip from the green rose, rising from a vase on her night table beside the *vielleuse*. She had waited a long time to give this slip to just the right girl. And now it seemed the right girl had not come, after all. Vail saw the movement and understood it. He leaned over and put his hand on his grandmother's shoulder.

"I'm sorry that you're disappointed, *grand'mère*," he said. "I'm disappointed too. But you keep that slip where you can take good care of it. Some day Susannah'll be here to get it."

CHAPTER XLVII

It was still very early when Vail began to stir drowsily, and after half opening his eyes to the restful darkness, he closed them again and burrowed further down between the sheets. Maudie, who had welcomed him with rapture the night before and curled up contentedly at his feet when he went to bed, raised her head alertly for a moment, wriggled along at his side to lick his hand, and then, receiving no response beyond an absent caress, composed herself placidly for further slumbers. But Vail could not go back to sleep again after all. The realization that this was his last day at home had already pierced his semiconsciousness, and though he tried, for a little while, to drown it in dreams, he could not do so. When the first faint streaks of gray light stole into the room he flung aside the bedclothes almost impatiently, lifted the mosquito bar, and slid down from the high four-poster. Maudie immediately sprang up, and after a brief battle with the mosquito bar, which had always baffled and enraged her, freed herself, jumped down and stood expectantly beside him, wagging her short tail in a fresh access of hope and joy.

"Everyone else is still asleep, Maudie," Vail said, addressing her, according to his habit, as if she had been a human being. "We might as well start our rounds outdoors. We've got lots of space to cover before night."

"I'm not asleep. May I come in?" Sybelle called from the next room.

"Just a sec. Wait till I get my pants on. Sorry I waked you though, Syb."

"You didn't. I was glad when I heard you speak to Maudie. I'd been awake a long time—that is, more or less."

"Well then, I'm sorry about that . . . All right, come on in now."

Sybelle swung open the shutter door between their rooms, and he saw, in the slipper chair beside her bed, the doll which had been Riccardo's first present to her. She had persistently treasured this as an ornament since outgrowing it as a plaything, despite the merciless teasing of Phil and Joyeuse; and to Vail, Sybelle's stubbornness in this respect was typical of her tenacity in other ways. No one gaged as accurately as he did the deceptiveness of her apparent docility. She came towards him, digging her fists into her eyes and stumbling a little. Her face was still flushed with sleep and her blonde curls were tumbled around her shoulders; in her quaintly cut, rose-colored dressing gown she looked ridiculously young and almost unbelievably lovely. Vail put an arm around her to steady her, and she snuggled her head down on his shoulder and rubbed her face against his neck. He kissed her hair, and then smoothed it gently away from her forehead before kissing it again.

"You're a mighty sweet somebody," he said with great tenderness. "I wish Rick could see you, looking like you do now. It's too bad to waste all this on me."

"Nothing's wasted on you. Nothing's good enough for you. I hope you get the very best there is. Vail, I don't mean to pry, but didn't you get anywhere at all with Sue? What I mean is——"

"Sure I got somewhere with her. Look, what say you and I have breakfast together, as long as we're the early birds? I've got quite a lot I want to say to you and I didn't have much of a chance last night. It looks as if I wouldn't have another, either."

"I think breakfast's a fine idea. I'll cruise along and start the coffee dripping. Lethe and Creassy don't get here till eight-thirty."

"Doesn't *grand'mère* have her coffee before that?"

"Yes, but it's put in a thermos beside her bed at night, to save Dinah a trip over the stairs the next morning. Dinah's getting mighty old and feeble, Vail. She keeps saying, effin you and I don't hurry up, she won't never have no mo' d'Alvery young'uns to nuss, afore she gits buried alongside Selah and Lou Ida. She's faithful as they come, but her heart just isn't in taking care of an old lady the way it always was in taking care of a new baby."

"It wouldn't do to disappoint her in her declining years, would it? We'll have to see what we can do about it. . . . Well, to get off a highly original remark, times do change, don't they? Everyone used to have coffee in bed at Belle Heloise, and there were so many servants to bring it that they practically tumbled over each other on the stairs. Incidentally, I've been meaning to ask you, what became of Dumps? I thought she was shaping up pretty well, for a new house girl, that time I came home from Lake Charles."

"She was, but she decided to go to California and complete her education, or so she said. That's what Minta said too. I've heard they changed their minds and that they're both getting fantastic wages in a factory—seven dollars a day or something like that. Even allowing for exaggeration, I reckon they're making more than I ever could. I don't know whether you remember Minta, Vail—Phronsie's daughter. She was the prettiest little pickaninny on the River Road when you and I were children, and she's a beauty now. She could easily pass for white."

"And probably does, where she is now. Well, I don't know as I blame her for trying. . . . Look, we mustn't stay here jabbering like this if we're going to have any time downstairs. You have to be at the office by eight, don't you? I'll make the coffee, Syb. You've got to get into your uniform and I can go along to the kitchen just like I am, this last time."

He had everything ready when she joined him in the patio half an hour later, looking very trim and efficient in her neat uniform, with her golden hair tucked up smoothly under her stiff cap and her collar fastened close around her soft white throat. Vail regarded her appraisingly as she poured the coffee and passed the toast.

"You like this Red Cross work you're doing, don't you, Syb?" he inquired.

She considered the question before answering it. "Yes, I like it," she said at last, guardedly. "I wanted to do something to help along the war effort, and this seemed the most logical undertaking. I think I'm fairly good at it. Anyway, I try hard. But I don't love it the way Joyeuse loves the work in the laboratory at the mill. Do you realize how well she's handling that, Vail? There isn't another college graduate left there now, or any men. She's got just high-school girls to help her. But I believe Dad would say himself, if he were here, that it's never been better run."

"I'll bet he would too. And how about her morale? Is she keeping that up? I haven't had a chance to ask her this time, or to see for myself."

Sybelle laughed. Joyeuse and her "morale" constituted the pet family joke. On the occasion of his last visit to Belle Heloise before he started to sea, she had given Barry Pereira a somewhat indefinite promise that she would "try to wait for him." But she had none of Sybelle's single-hearted fidelity. Several young chemists at the Standard Oil divided her attention among them, and when her pretext of a common interest in laboratory work had worn rather thin, she took refuge in the contention that she had to do something to "keep up her morale" during Barry's absence, which, according to her, had now been "unreasonably long." The reminder that the war itself was dragging out to considerable length and that Barry would be among the first to regret this, had no visible effect on her; she continued to add to her list of eligible suitors and appeared to derive untroubled enjoyment from their attentions.

"Her morale seems to be getting better and better all the time," Sybelle said jestingly. "I don't know why it wouldn't. She has more and more men boosting it. I think it's rather hard on Barry, but after all, he knew what to expect—she's always been perfectly honest with him. Perhaps you could say something to her before you leave though —after all, there ought to be some limit." She glanced down at her wrist watch and gave a startled exclamation. "I've only got five minutes more, Vail," she said. "It's so good having you here, all to myself too, that I didn't realize how fast time was flying. You said there was lots you wanted to say to me. What, besides to ask whether I like my work?"

"I wanted to ask you how much longer you were going to let the family keep you from marrying Rick, hoping you wouldn't say, none of my damn business."

"I've never said that to you, Vail, have I, about anything? . . . I can't very well marry Rick, though, while he's out in the Solomons."

"Sure that's where he still is? I may be telling tales out of school, but his division's sure been through a terrific campaign and I've heard rumors it was going to be rewarded with a rest on Guadalcanal. You know that's taken shape as one of the large rear area bases now, and has all the comforts of home—pretty near all, anyway—tents and floors and all that."

He grinned and Sybelle tried to return the smile. But she shook her head.

"I'd be glad if I thought he was in a tent instead of a foxhole. But I wouldn't be any nearer marrying him."

"Well, I still don't know whether I'm talking out of turn. But there's another rumor going round that instead of getting sent to Guadalcanal, a few men are getting sent home. 'Secret missions' I believe the usual reason is. Steady there—I didn't say I thought Rick *would* be. I said I thought there was a chance he *might* be."

Sybelle gripped the table hard. Then she leaned across it and whispered.

"You won't give me away, will you, Vail?"

"You know I won't."

"If he does get sent back I'll marry him straight off. Even if I have to elope with him. If I have a chance like that, a chance I've hardly dared pray for——"

"Well, you may—and gosh, if I were only going to be here——"

"Yes, I know. You'd help me. You'd stand by. It's one of the reasons why I feel as if I couldn't bear to have you leave, Vail. Daddy's gone and Phil's gone, and even if they'd been here, they wouldn't have helped me. Daddy would have hindered me and Phil would have laughed at me. He wouldn't have understood how much Rick means to me, any more than Joyeuse does. I think maybe Franchot might have, if he'd lived—he was a sensitive little soul. But Phil and Joyeuse don't take love seriously, Vail, the way you and I do."

"I'll say they don't."

He spoke so harshly that she looked up at him in surprise. He pressed her hand and rose.

"I reckon we can't stretch those five minutes any longer, Syb," he said. "I'm mighty glad you told me what you have, though. You know I'm all for it. And whether I'm here to help you or not, you stick to it. You marry Rick as soon as he gets here, no matter how hard anyone tries to stop you. Don't elope either. Don't—don't do it as if you were ashamed of it. It'll mean a lot to him to have you act as if you're proud of it. I—I happen to know. You can carry it off if you make up your mind to. Have a real wedding, have a big party Mom will help you when it comes to a showdown. So'll Aunt Cresside and Uncle Fabian. You haven't raised enough hell about it so far, that's all the trouble. *Grand'mère's* the only one who'll put up a real fight to stop you, when you do, and if you can't get the better of one feeble old lady, you're not half the girl I think you are. Keep your chin up, Syb. Be a fighting lady. Remember I'm betting on you."

"I will, Vail. Thanks a lot. And there's something I want you to remember too."

"What's that?"

"That you're my litter brother. That I think more of you than anyone else in the world except Rick."

For a few minutes after she had left him, he continued to sit at the rustic table, smoking and playing with Maudie's ears. Then he stacked up the dishes and carried them into the kitchen, which was still empty. As a matter of fact, it had always seemed more or less empty to him since Lou Ida left it for the last time, and he was glad to leave it himself and go back into the patio. No other cook ever inhabited it as she had, filling it with husky song and fragrant vapors while she stood indefatigably at the stove preparing the hot cakes and beaten biscuits, the fried chickens and baked hams, the shrimp gumboes and crawfish bisques and turtle soups on which the family feasted. Creassy was skilled in her craft too, and Lethe plowed through a considerable amount of work during the course of a day; the d'Alverys still were better served than almost anyone else they knew. But there was more grumbling and less gusto than in the old days, less joyous pride in labors well performed, less love and respect for those who directed these. Vail had never laid any of Amen's shortcomings to Creassy's door, and he assumed the reason he did not care for Lethe as he did for Dinah was because Lethe had not been his nurse, and that therefore the same tie did not exist between them. But he did not deceive himself about the general situation at Belle Heloise or blame it all on the war. He knew that something vital and precious was disappearing from the place with its old servants and that the next generation would never know the fullness of experience which had made his own childhood so rich and warm because of them.

Almost as if he had called her, Dinah came down the outside stairway that led from the rear of the upper gallery to the patio. She still wore the full quaint type of dress which had always been her habit and she had never abandoned her tignon; but instead of moving majestically she now walked slowly and painfully, and he went forward to meet her and to take from her the tray which she carried with such difficulty and with such care. She spoke to him scoldingly, as she had always done, but he was not deceived by that either. He knew that Dinah was not really annoyed with him, that as a matter of fact she adored him, but that she saw no reason why she should not continue to admonish him, exactly as she had done when he was two years old.

"Yo' done wake up Madame with yo' chattering, yo' and Miss Sybelle," Dinah said reprovingly. "Don't yo' know dat po' old lady need her rest? Why yo' don't go set in de dinin' room eat yo' breakfuss?"

"Go on, Dinah, quit your fussing. *Grand'mère* couldn't possibly have heard us unless she was awake already."

"She ain't so well dis mornin', Mr. Vail. She worryin' herself caise yo' goin' away. She say yo' de onlies' one she got left. Po' little Franchot, he daid, an' de Colonel, he gone, an' Mr. Phil gone, an' now——"

Dinah began to rock back and forth, moaning. Vail set the breakfast tray down on the rustic table which he had just cleared and took hold of her arm.

"There's nothing for her to worry about, Dinah. Poor little Franchot's been dead a long time, so there's no use to start grieving about that all over again. And the Colonel isn't in any danger. As for Phil and me, that's just good riddance to bad rubbish. Besides, we'll be back again almost before you know it, bothering the life out of you, the way we always have. I'll go and remind *grand'mère* of all that in a minute. But I want to talk to you first."

"Yassuh, an' Ah wants to talk to yo' too. All right fo' yo' to say ain't nothin' to worry about, but Ah's tellin' yo' Ah's been hearin' all kinds of queer noises in dis house lately. Madame, she done hear 'em too. She ain't said nothin' but Ah knows. She done hear dat old ghost walkin' aroun', jes lak Ah has."

"I thought you told me a while back all the ghosts were at Hathaway."

"No, Mr. Vail, Ah don't never say *all* de ghostes is down to Hathaway. Is ghostes dere all right, but our own ghost, he don't never go away from Belle Heloise."

"What do you mean, our own ghost? I didn't know we had a ghost of our own."

"Sure you did, Mr. Vail. Yo' knows dat man what made de gardens and teach de chillun, he's our own ghost."

"You mean Angus Holt? I know my grandfather used to dress up in a sheet and try to scare everybody pretending he was Angus Holt. I know Phil did too, after Dad told him that story. I don't know anything else."

"Dey done cober up dey face wid de sheet when dey do dat, so no one won't see dey ain't no real ghost, an' dey don't say nothin' caise dey knows us can tell 'em by em's voices. De real ghost, he show his face an' he speak, too, when he git ready to tell bad news. Yo' po' granddaddy daid long time, Mr. Vail, and Mr. Phil, he gone away 'most two years now. Dey ain't walkin' in no gallery at Belle Heloise.

But dat ghost, he walkin' in de gallery 'most every night now. Don't mean nothin' good when he walk dere regular like dat, 'stead ob jes' once in awhile lak he generally do. Means he gettin' ready to show his face an' tell his bad news, one ob dese days."

"I'm sorry you didn't speak to me about him last night just as soon as I got home, Dinah. If you had, I'd have gone out and told him he'd got to stop disturbing my poor old grandmother and my poor old mammy. But it's too late now. I can't do it tonight, because I'll be gone myself. So you tell him for me, will you?"

"Lord sake, Mr. Vail, yo' knows Ah never talks to no ghostes! Ah covers up my head *good* wid de bedclothes when Ah heard dat ghost comin'. Ah hears him jes' de same, Ah can't help it, but——"

"Well, if you won't go out and talk to him I don't know what to suggest, but I reckon you better stop talking *about* him and listen to me for a few minutes. . . . What's this I hear about your getting tired waiting for some new babies at Belle Heloise?"

The mournful look faded from Dinah's face, and for the first time a glad light came into her old eyes when she looked at Vail, and a smile twisted her lips.

"Dat's right, Mr. Vail. Here's Miss Sybelle 'most an old maid already an' yo' 'most an old batch. Ah is worryin' 'bout it, Ah sure is."

"Well, you won't have to worry much longer. Because I've got a feeling Major Tramonte will be coming home pretty soon and that when he does you'll be having a wedding here."

"Yo' don't mean dat peddler man's boy, does yo', Mr. Vail? Caise Madame she ain't never gwine let my child marry dat boy an' neither me. My white folks, dey's quality. Ah ain't gwine nuss no babies what ain't quality babies."

"Now you listen to me, Dinah, and you get this straight. Unless you promise me you'll do everything you can to make Miss Sybelle happy while I'm gone, I'll come back and haunt you myself, dead or alive, worse than any ghost ever did. And the way to make her happy is to look after her when she gets married. Because she's going to get married and she's going to marry quality. I don't want to hear you saying any more about a peddler man's boy, you hear? I want you to start saying Major Tramonte right now and keep on saying it till you start saying Mr. Rick."

For a moment Dinah stood fingering her apron, her expression still mutinous. Vail put both hands on her shoulders.

"That's orders, Dinah," he said. "My last ones before I go away. I can count on you to carry them out, can't I?"

She looked up at him, the mutinous expression fading from her face and tears welling up in her eyes. She nodded her head slowly several times. Then she broke away from him and turned towards the stairs. He could hear her sobbing as she mounted these, even more painfully and slowly than she had come down. Her wretchedness was so heartfelt that it affected him poignantly. But sitting there, thinking about it, only made it seem the worse. Besides, there was still a great deal to be said and done, before he left the plantation. Vail went away from the patio himself, and strode out past the stables towards the sugar-house road; then, after a moment's hesitation, he decided to go to the overseer's house first and to the mill itself afterward. Sance still went home for his dinner, whenever he could; though his mother had long since died, his habit of getting back, as often as possible, to the quaint old house, was so firmly fixed that he never even tried to break himself of it. Vail thought that he might find his overseer there, alone; in that case, they could talk more privately and peacefully in the picturesque living room—unchanged, except that it had retained an atmosphere of emptiness ever since Madame Sance left it for the last time—than anywhere else about the place.

Evidently the same idea had struck Sance. At all events, he was standing in the open doorway, smoking his pipe, with an air of expectancy rather than the more characteristic one of haste. He had already finished his dinner, he said; but he hoped Vail would have coffee with him. Thanks, Vail would like to; they could talk while they were drinking; and forestalling the next questions, he added that he would take it black, not white, and that he would drink it, not eat it. It was pretty near his own dinner time; not that he ever had to worry about spoiling his appetite, but he thought this time it might not be such a bad idea to save up . . .

He grinned as he spoke, and Sance smiled back at him. But when they had their coffee and were seated opposite each other, on either side of the hearth, with the small empty bench between them, Sance could not keep his concern to himself.

"I'll do everything I can to save the crop, Vail. But we're getting behind already, and we haven't been grinding two weeks yet. I've been wanting to ask you how you'd feel about having some of those German prisoners on Belle Heloise. I don't need to tell you that's the way lots of planters are fixing to manage this fall, and with camps opening up at both Donaldsonville and Port Allen——"

"I'll tell you just how I'd feel. They may be good workers, and they may be the only ones you can get. But I'd rather lose the crop than have one of them set foot on Belle Heloise. The reason we're short-handed is because so many men, white and black both, who belong here, are trying to stamp out everything they stand for. Every time I think of the dirty bastards, I can't help saying to myself, 'Damn them, they're still alive, and they're still Nazis.' I won't have them doing our work on our place."

"Well, I can see your point. But just the same——"

"Wait a sec, will you? I've got some good news for you. Maybe when you've heard it, the picture won't look quite so dark to you. I had a chance to talk with my uncle about our problems here, while I was in New Orleans, and he authorized me to order three more Prescott machines."

"That's mighty generous of Mr. d'Alvery, and I appreciate it. Orders and deliveries are two different things, these days, though."

"I know that. But I've also been in touch with Mr. Prescott. He promised me he'd have one cane-cutting machine here by November first, and the other two soon after that. What's more, he said he could get us four extra carts. With that much surplus equipment, you'll be a lot better off than most of the planters who've taken on those damn prisoners."

"We may be, at that. I don't need to tell you that the best cane-cutting machine ever made doesn't clean cane as well as when it's cut by hand. We may have some pretty serious milling problems as a result of trying to substitute so much machinery for man power. Besides, it burns me up to think that though it costs more and more all the time to produce sugar, it's the only basic commodity that isn't bringing a better price than before the war. But hell! I reckon we can handle all these problems some way."

"That's the way to talk! Anything else you'd like to get off your chest before I go back to the fields?"

"Two of our boys who've been in the service have come home while you were in New Orleans, Vail. Maybe you'd like to have a word with them, too, before you leave."

"You bet I would. Which ones are they and what's your latest dope on them? Naturally I'd rather not let on I don't know."

"You knew that Cato's boy, Rush, was wounded in the landing at Casablanca last year, didn't you?"

"Yes, I knew that much. Is he one of those who's come back?"

"Uh-uh. He's quite the hero too. No, I wasn't making a dirty crack. I meant it. He was always proud of his work, even when he was just a kid, starting out as a water boy, and he'd got to be the best derrick operator I had in the yard when he went into the service. Well, the poor devil won't operate a derrick any more, for a long time, anyway. He may have to go back to driving the water cart. I reckon he could do that. I tell you, something turned over inside me when he showed up here one evening and just said he was reporting back to work—still in his uniform, mind you, with the Purple Heart and the African Campaign Ribbon and a Combat Star."

"Beat all his white folks to it, did he?" Vail asked, with a touch of envy. Then he added, ungrudgingly, "Well, more power to him! What about the other man? Is he a hero too?"

"I'm afraid not. He was discharged from Camp Rucker for mental derangement—couldn't stand the shock of crawling under live ammunition. But he showed up in a uniform too—not a private's, either—a Sergeant's. Afterwards, he got cold feet, because he heard someone on the Draft Board was on to him—cut his chevrons off and hushed his mouth. He's back on the mill floor as an oiler, and as far as I can see, he's doing as well as he ever did. That isn't saying so much and I wouldn't know how serious this 'mental derangement' really is."

Vail laughed. "I'll give him the once over and let you know what I think. And of course I want to see Rush. But I mustn't keep you any longer. So long, Sance! You know I'm counting on you. We've never lost a crop at Belle Heloise yet, and we're not going to begin now, either."

As Vail approached the laboratory, he could see Joyeuse standing by the window, gravely inspecting the precipitation of clarified juice in a test tube. The trim white uniforms she now habitually wore were very becoming to her; and the position in which she stood revealed to great advantage the lovely lines of her trim figure. Vail paused for a moment to enjoy the pleasing picture she made. But when she caught sight of him, she frowned and called to him impatiently.

"Just look what I'm up against!" she said, indicating the test tube. "It's all very well to talk about solving labor problems with mechanical harvesters. But everyone who gets off that line neglects to mention how much foreign matter is introduced with the cane. Leaves—grass—root dirt—"

"I know the labor problem can't all be solved by machinery, Joy," Vail said seriously. He had come into the laboratory, and now he stood beside her, watching her as she went quietly and efficiently on with her work. Her helpers had gone to the boardinghouse for their midday meal, but apparently she had no idea of stopping. "Those problems are eased though," he went on. "At least for everyone except the chemists. And with a chemist like you, the rest of us know that part of the problem's in good hands. I'm ready to leave it right there. I've got lots of confidence in you, Joy. Listen—I've been talking about problems, of one kind or another, all morning. Can't we forget about them for awhile, and go on up to the Big House? It must be almost dinner time and I'm hungry."

"Well, so am I, now that you mention it. There's just one thing I'd like to bring up myself though. You know that for years we've been using a line-drawing of the sugar mill on our bags. It's good, in its way, but it's rather static. I've been thinking, if we could have patterns printed on the bags instead——"

"What kind of patterns?"

"Well—centerpieces and doilies. The kind of thing women like to embroider for their dining-room tables. And fancy aprons—the kind they love to slip on over an afternoon dress when they're getting ready to entertain the weekly bridge club and might be caught by the first arrival without time to whisk the apron off. Women like that would feel they're getting a lot for nothing—material and pattern right along with what they'd paid for. They'd ask for Belle Heloise sugar instead of just sugar. The picture of the mill doesn't mean anything to them—they know they can't buy that. But patterns and cloth——"

"I think maybe you've got something there, Joy, certain female weak-

620

nesses being what they are—we won't discuss any of the others. Go ahead and try out your patterns. The dies won't cost much and they'd be your only expense."

"Not just doilies and aprons either," Joyeuse continued, much encouraged. "I think we should have dolls too—a pattern for a doll that would have to be cut out and stuffed, and patterns for two or three different dresses she could wear, after they were run up on the machine. I worked them all out to scale. We could label the doll with a name too—Belle Heloise, of course. You know Sybelle's always called the doll Riccardo gave her Belle Heloise. Little girls would get interested in our sugar as well as their mothers. I've got some sketches all made. I'll show them to you if you like."

"No, I'm ready to take your word for it that they're good."

"Just as you say. I didn't mean to unload anything extra on you, Vail. I can look after this part of the job and I will. You can depend on that, if it'll help any."

"You know it helps no end. But look, Joy, I wouldn't want you to get a lot of heroic ideas, and give up something that meant a darn sight more to you than chemistry and patterns, just because you promised me you'd stand by."

"I haven't any heroic ideas. It just so happens that nothing means any more to me than chemistry. The patterns are just a side issue, possibly profitable."

"Nothing—and no one?"

"Nothing—and no *one*."

She had disposed of the test tube and was washing up at the small neat sink in the corner. She did not turn around while repeating his question as a statement, lightly emphasizing the last word. But after she had dried her hands on a paper towel, she faced him with her sunny smile.

"Wouldn't two weddings in the family hold you for awhile?" she inquired. "I'll agree to that many. But if you're going to talk about more than that, you and I are going to have a row. Which would seem rather a pity, your last day at home. Come on, let's go eat."

It was evident to Vail, as he took Gervais' place at the table, opposite his grandmother, that a definite effort had been made to give his last meal at home a festive atmosphere. Joyeuse had not taken time to change from the crisp white uniform she habitually wore at the laboratory; but the three elderly ladies were all attired in what even a youthful masculine eye could recognize as "best dresses." Though Madame d'Alvery had never worn anything but black since her husband's death, she observed different degrees of elegance in fabrics, and today's costume was made of heavy grosgrain silk which rustled as she walked, and which was adorned with frills of rosepoint lace, fastened at the throat with a diamond and onyx brooch. In a stubborn effort to produce an effect as different as possible from Madame d'Alvery's perennial mourning, Mrs. Randall had long since abandoned her drab grays, and wore the brightest colors she could find; today's choice had been a sleazy rayon print with an emerald green background and a pattern of orange curlicues. Miss Mittie wore a genteel lavender silk and her mother's pansy pin.

With gratifying heartiness, Vail complimented them all on their appearance, admired the arrangement of flowers which formed the centerpiece, and praised each dish that Lethe presented to him. He did not think the *mirlitons* had ever tasted so good to him; he liked them split and stuffed, the way Creassy had fixed them that evening, best of all. The Satsumas were mighty sweet; it must have been an unusually good season for fruit—too bad there wasn't enough sugar to save it all, on a plantation at that!

After he had finished his chocolate ice cream, he continued to sit still, smoking one cigarette after another, and drinking his coffee in slow sips. He was thinking about Sue again, he could not help it; if she had only been there, how much she would have helped him through this hard meal! With her complete *savoir-faire* and her natural composure, she would have really eased the inevitable strain which his forced cheerfulness had only lessened a little. Another man at the table would have helped a lot too; he had never missed Gervais so much, and it was only because he hardened his heart against Phil, on account of Sue, that he did not miss the engaging young devil still more. He thought wistfully about Franchot too. Franchot would have been twenty now; if he had been there, he would have helped to counterbalance this ultra-feminine atmosphere. Vail supposed they would always think of Franchot as a frail child. But he might have outgrown the early delicacy, he might have been in one of the services himself by this time, if only——

Vail did not want to think about Franchot. He wanted to get off and be on his way to town. He glanced at his grandmother from time to time, to see if she would give the signal to rise, but through either accident or design she did not meet his eye, and he knew better than to take the initiative himself, at her table. He had heard her say more than once that a man who did not recognize the prerogative of the lady of the house in this respect was in the same class as a man who told his wife, in the hearing of others, that it was high time they left a party—to put it plainly, in the class of social pariahs. But Joyeuse had not inherited a taste for fine points of etiquette. When Vail began pouring out coffee the third time from the delicate porcelain pot which Lethe had put beside him, Joyeuse jumped up, pushing back her chair and turning to him instead of to her grandmother.

"I'm sorry, Vail, but I can't hang around any longer. My best helper at the lab is sick today, and I've got all her odd jobs on my hands as well as my own. You know I hope you get the best, and all that."

"Yes, I know. Well, go on keeping up your morale, but give Barry a break once in a while, if you can, without getting too much of a let-down."

"I'll think about it. So long, Vail."

"So long, Joy."

He rose to kiss her good-by, and instead of sitting down again walked around to his grandmother's chair.

"I know this isn't in order," he said. "Just the same, I'm going to remind you that it's long past your nap time. Dinah's been lurking around in the hall for the last half-hour, looking in at you accusingly. Of course you couldn't see her because your back was turned to her, but I could. I couldn't help it. She made up for your inattention by glaring and signaling at me. Would you like me to give you a hand over the stairs?"

"Not yet. I deplore the lack of manners Joyeuse shows, which is more or less habitual, and also the importunities of Dinah, of which Lucie would never have been guilty. But that is no reason why you should allow your last meal at home to be hurried. Sit down again, Vail."

"I'm sorry, *grand'mère,* but I'm afraid I can't. Of course I want to stop in at Somerulos Street on my way to the field, and time's getting short. I'll see you úpstairs and then I'll walk over to the storehouse with Granny Randall and Miss Mittie. I planned on doing that too, before I left."

Even Mrs. Randall's congenital pessimism could not prevent her from betraying her gratification at this attention. As she sat down in her small living room after their short walk from the Big House, she smoothed out the skirt of her hideous green and orange print and looked up at Vail with genuine affection.

"I appreciate the way you answered back to Madame d'Alvery just now," she said. "It isn't often anyone gets to put her in her place. You've always been mighty polite to me, Vail. I don't believe in flattery to the face, but as long as you're starting off to war and as likely as not won't ever come back, I don't suppose it'll do any harm to say you've always been my favorite grandchild. Far as that goes, I've always set more store by you than I did any of my own children. Your two uncles, the ones you're named after, never gave me a thought once they took up with those flighty girls they married, and neither of my daughters-in-law ever lifted a finger to help me, not even with their pension money coming in and all. I don't see them or hear from them from one year's end to another. Of course one of them lives in Natchitoches and the other in Harrisonburg and both those places are a far piece from here. But I'm not excusing them. They could drop me a postcard once in a while, and they could get to Baton Rouge someways, if they really wanted to . . . As for your mother, the less said about her the better."

"I wish you didn't feel that way, Granny Randall, about Mom, anyhow. Of course I don't know about the others. But she's invited you to go and stay with her whenever you felt like it, hasn't she? And doesn't she send you nice presents right along?"

"She knows I don't want to go skylarking around the country, at my age," Mrs. Randall answered, disregarding the second question. "Besides, I'm not talking about the way she's treated me. I'm talking about the way she's treated your father. If ever a woman deserted her husband, she did. And I don't trust that man she works for, I never have. I wouldn't put it past him to lead her into sin."

"Now, now, Granny Randall, let's not get out of line. You know that's a lot of nonsense—and not nice nonsense, either."

He turned conclusively away from Mrs. Randall. Everything that she said had been painful to hear. It hurt him to have her say that he meant more to her than anyone else in the family, when actually he was no kith or kin of hers. It hurt him to have her gloat over his real grandmother's humiliation at his hands, trivial as this had been. It hurt him to have her speak slightingly of her dead sons, whose Christian names he bore, and to slander her daughter, who had been his kind and loving foster mother. Some women seemed bent on hurting instead of helping as they went through life, he thought bitterly; and with fleeting horror, he wondered if Sue could possibly develop into one of these, after the inevitable disillusionment which was in store for her. He thought he had seen indications of such a trait in her mother, though in Mrs. Prescott's case this was always meticulously veiled in cool courtesy. . . .

Trying hard to dismiss such a far-fetched fancy from his mind, he looked towards Miss Mittie, whose rabbit-like nose was twitching painfully, and who was clutching a small round object wrapped up in crumpled tissue paper and tied with faded lavender ribbon, which he had an uneasy feeling might be a farewell present. Amen had already waylaid him to give him a charm, guaranteed to protect the wearer against "disease, death and disaster of every kind." Meanwhile the Negro recounted in a long rambling way, his feelings of faithfulness and devotion to the d'Alverys in general and Vail in particular. Vail had finally accepted the charm, but cut the sentiments short as civilly as he could. Of course, any offering and any declaration of Miss Mittie's would be very different; still he knew they might be a source of embarrassment.

"Miss Mittie, would you mind telling me what you've got in your lap?" he asked.

"It's something for you, Vail. I know you've always admired it. I want you should have it, to take along with you."

She stretched out a shaking hand and gave him the small round object. It was unexpectedly heavy. He untied the faded ribbon and parted the crumpled tissue, disclosing the old paperweight with the miniature snow scene.

"Why Miss Mittie, I can't take this!" he protested. "It's not like a present that came from some store! You brought it with you when you left Salem for Louisiana. You've treasured it all your life. You've told me your mother did too."

"I didn't want to give you a boughten present," Miss Mittie said stubbornly. "I wanted to give you that paperweight. It'll remind you of me when you're over in Paris, France, or wherever 'tis you're going. I don't want you should forget me while you're gone."

"Don't worry. I'll never forget you, Miss Mittie. I couldn't. You've been too good to me," he said gently. He could not tell her there was no possible way in which he could take a heavy, breakable object like a glass paperweight with him. It would hurt her too much. He knew that her offering had been not only loving, but sacrificial. He must find some way to dispose of the snow scene, without letting her know about it. He rewrapped and retied the package and put it in his pocket. "But thanks a lot, Miss Mittie. It was awfully good of you to give it to me. I *have* always admired it . . . I'm afraid I've got to be shoving along now. Maybe you'd give me a coke before I start, if you've got any in the house."

"When I haven't a coke for you, Vail d'Alvery, there won't be any cows left in Texas," Miss Mittie announced in triumph, scuttling off towards the kitchen.

There had been so many delays that it was late afternoon when Vail reached the little house on Somerulos Street. He whistled as he went up the walk, and Frances Belle came rushing out to meet him, looking pertly pretty in a smart lemon-colored dress. A young man followed closely behind her and held the door open for her. Vail had forgotten that some young man would almost inevitably be calling on Frances Belle at about this hour. He could not get used to the idea that she was grown up and it still irritated him.

"Hello brat!" he said casually. "What's cooking?"

"Nothing much . . . You know Punt, don't you, Vail—Punt, this is my cousin, Vail d'Alvery."

Punt, a red-headed, freckled young man with a pleasant face, whose surname remained undisclosed, greeted the newcomer with more civility than Vail felt inclined to show towards him at the moment. It was bad enough, in his opinion, to put up with all the young men who were eagerly engaged in helping Joyeuse keep up her morale, without running into any equally superfluous callers on Frances Belle, especially at such a time as this. He nodded in the general direction of the inoffensive visitor and asked a couple of curt questions.

"Uncle Fabian here?"

"No, he hasn't come home yet. He telephoned that he'd been unavoidably detained at the office."

"What about Aunt Cresside?"

"She's in the garden. She said, when you got here, to tell you to come on out there . . . Look Vail, Punt and I were just starting to a show. Mind if we go ahead?"

"No. But I hope Punt's got enough cash along to keep you in cokes. I never did."

"Oh, he saves up to show me a tall time, and you never did that. Will you be here when we get back?"

"I reckon not. I have to report at Harding Field in—" he looked at his watch—"fifty-five minutes."

"So long then. Happy landings!"

They kissed each other casually, and she darted off down the walk with her red-headed escort in close pursuit. Vail had always been fond of Frances Belle, but he had never cared for her intensely, or she for him, in the way he and Sybelle cared for each other. Funny, he thought, when she was really his half-sister and Sybelle only his cousin; and without being exactly offended he was somewhat surprised that Frances Belle should have taken his departure so nonchalantly. But then you could never tell about girls, especially girls with beaux, he told himself unoriginally, as he walked through the house and went out on the terrace. In the garden the trickling fountain made the only sound; but the chrysanthemums and cosmos were a mass of color and some of the early camellias were out too. Here and there the glossy green of their bushes was studded with the dark pink of the Daigaguira, the lighter pink of the Sarah Hasty, and the radiant white of the Neige Dorée. The latter were among Cresside's favorites and she had a shallow bowl of them on the table beside her. She was lying on a chaise longue with her hands clasped idly in front of her, wearing a white dress. Her face was very white too, and for the first time Vail noticed that she did not look young any more. She was as slender and graceful as ever, and she still had beautiful eyes and soft skin and infinite charm. But somehow the bloom was gone. She looked up at him and smiled.

"Hello, Vail."

"Hello, Auntie."

He pulled up a chair and sat down beside her. All day he had been trying to find time for everything he wanted to say—to Sybelle, to Dinah, to Joyeuse, to Sance, even to Miss Mittie. But now, when there were only a few minutes left, and he would have supposed, beforehand, that he would have tried to talk very fast, to make the most of them, he did not say anything at all. He could not think of anything to say and he knew he could not have talked in any case. He had a lump in his throat and the bones of his breast were too tight. He thought, if they did not loosen, something inside of him would be crushed. It had been hard, telling the others good-by, but it had not been like this. It wasn't hard now. It was impossible.

"Uncle Fabian isn't here?" he said at last. He knew Fabian was not there; Frances Belle had told him that her father was detained at the office. But he had to say something.

"No. He's very sorry. He said to tell you good-by for him."

Suddenly Vail knew Fabian had stayed away on purpose, that he had given them this chance to have their last few minutes to themselves and Vail was deeply touched. Then it occurred to him that Frances Belle had gone out for the same reason, not because she cared more about a date with Punt than a final visit with him, as he had so unjustly assumed. He tried to make amends for his mistake by a show of interest in her caller.

"Who is this fellow the brat's gone out with?"

"Punt O'Malley? He's the Master of the *McDougall*."

"I don't seem to place either one."

"He's a nice boy, Vail. His people aren't Baton Rougeans, they're Alexandrians—what your grandmother would call very respectable people." She paused and a fleeting smile of understanding passed between them. "But your Uncle Fabian and I think they're nice too. Punt's had a good education—graduated very young from Loyola and went straight on the river—apparently it was his one love, until he met Frances Belle. He's been here several years now, working for the Standard Oil. The *McDougall's* one of their boats. She used to tow petroleum products from the refinery here to Avondale and Port Chalmette. Now she's delivering bunker fuels and aviation gasoline to the Army and Navy in New Orleans harbor. Her Captain holds a Pilot's license as well as a Master's license and takes a Pilot's watch. Punt was pretty bitter for a long time because he couldn't get into the Army—I believe he has some sort of minor heart ailment that kept him out. He doesn't feel so badly about that any more though, because he's come to see he's helping indirectly. By the way, he's a great admirer of yours."

"Why, I never saw him before!"

"Yes you have, any number of times. But he doesn't stand out, in a crowd. You're his hero though. And now that he and Frances Belle——"

"You don't think it's serious, do you? That baby!"

"She's nineteen. How old was Susannah when you fell in love with her, Vail?"

"That was different."

"We all think so, about ourselves."

Silence fell between them. Vail guessed that Cresside was thinking, involuntarily, about her own girlhood and her own suitors, and with a fresh pang he realized that she could not have been more than nineteen when he was born. Probably she was remembering him as a baby, probably she was recalling the first parting between them and telling herself she was thankful she had not known then that a still harder one was ahead. He must say something, he must not let her know he read her mind. Again the words stuck in his throat.

"Miss Mittie insisted on giving me her paperweight when I left. Of course I can't possibly take it overseas, but I don't want to hurt her feelings. So I brought it this far. I thought maybe you'd hide it for me, someplace, till I get home, and then I'd take it back to her."

"You know I'd be glad to. Give it to me and I'll put it away for you."

He took the paperweight out of his pocket and handed it to her. She turned it over several times, watching the sparkling flakes falling on the miniature village. Then she put it down on the table beside her without speaking again. Vail knew he had to go on.

"I'll write you as often as I can, Auntie. But you mustn't worry if you don't get lots of letters. I don't suppose I'll have much time to write."

"No, I don't suppose you will."

She was not helping him at all. She was trying but the words were sticking in her throat too. He made a desperate effort.

"Auntie, you know I think an awful lot of Susannah. I'd hoped she'd marry me before I left. Well, you know all about that too, because I told you three weeks ago. If there's anything you and Uncle Fabian can do for her while I'm gone——"

"Of course, Vail. We'll keep in touch with her. She's a lovely girl. We're very fond of her ourselves."

"I'm worried about Syb too. If I only knew she and Rick could get married——"

"They ought to, of course. It's too bad they didn't, long ago. I'll do everything I can to help them, Vail."

"Thanks a lot. Well . . . I reckon I have to be going, Auntie."

"I know, Vail. I'll walk with you as far as the house."

He was thankful she was not coming any further, thankful that since he must say good-by to her he could do it in this beautiful and secluded spot which she had made so uniquely her own. She put her arm through his, and as he looked down at her, trying to smile, he saw something else he had failed to notice before: her hair was not like a soft black cloud any longer. It was in beautiful order but it was straighter and flatter than he remembered it, and there were gray threads in it. He had never thought of her as growing old and he did not want her to realize that he had noticed the first telltale signs of this now, so he was glad that she did not seem to. They went slowly across the terrace together, and she did not pause at all, on the way, or fall back, nor did she begin to cry, as he had been afraid she might at the last moment. Her face was whiter than ever, almost as white as her dress now, but it was composed. When they reached the door he looked at her and saw that her eyes were calm too. They were very bright, as if possibly tears were somewhere behind them, shining through, but these had not come yet and he knew now they would not until after he had gone. She looked at him with so much love glorifying her face that all the sadness was hidden, and he forgot that it did not look young any longer because something in it was far more beautiful than youth.

"Aunt Cresside," he said softly.

"Yes, Vail."

"There's one special thing I want to say to you before I tell you good-by."

"You can say anything you want to, Vail. You know that."

The words did not choke him any more. They came freely at last, just before he bent his head to kiss her.

"I've always wished you were my mother. Ever since I can remember. Ever since I was just a little boy. It's not that I don't love Mom too. But I feel so much closer to you. I feel as if we had always belonged to each other, as if we always would, whatever happens."

She closed her eyes. The blue-veined, translucent lids veiled them for a moment, the long black lashes fluttered on her white cheeks. But only for a moment. She opened her eyes again and looked at him with the same clear bright gaze as before.

"Thank you for telling me that before you went, darling."

"I had to. Good-by. . . ."

He could not add "Aunt Cresside" this time. He must not add anything else. But looking down at her he knew no more words were needed between them. Everything that counted had been said already.

The loading platform was packed to the last inch of standing room. The Colonel, gathering more than two hundred young pilots around him, had addressed them informally for the last time. He did not really make a speech. He merely thanked the pilots for their past co-opera-tion, urged them to maintain their high standards of discipline and wished them good luck. Then he stood watching them with a strange expression on his face as they swarmed aboard a troop train, a solid Pullman with a kitchen in the middle, which was drawn up alongside. The immobility of the train had a sinister quality. It looked like a long steel serpent, momentarily quiescent, but poised to strike when the unwary least expected it. Then, instead of striking, it began to glide slowly away, its evil potentialities still unrealized. As each car slid smoothly past him, the Colonel saluted again, the furrows in his face deepening, the lines in his mouth growing tighter and tighter. The train, still moving slowly and portentously, slipped further and further away from the quartermaster's warehouses fringing the field. The military band, stationed at the crossroads of the Texas and Pacific, played "Auld Lang Syne." Long before its strains died down in the distance, everyone on the platform had been lost to sight. Vail turned away from the window where he had been standing and went to locate his B-44 bag, which had been stowed in the ladies' room.

CHAPTER XLVIII

FOR SEVERAL WEEKS after Vail's departure, Sybelle waited, with determined hopefulness, for some word which would indicate that he had been right in his "hunch" about Rick. But when she next received definite word of her sweetheart's whereabouts, he was on Bougainville; the Thirty-seventh Division had joined with the Marines for the invasion of the last island in the Solomons still infested by the Japanese. If any of its officers had been sent to the United States on "secret missions" after the hard campaign in New Georgia, Rick was not among them. But the "rest" on Guadalcanal had materialized—so far, at least. Vail had been right; and during this welcome interlude Rick had been promoted again and was now one of the youngest majors in his Division. He had also received the Combat Infantryman's Badge, which, judging from the feeling with which he wrote of it, meant almost as much to him as his advancement in rank. Consequently, it meant almost as much to Sybelle, and nothing that Rick wrote, or that she read in the newspapers or heard on the radio, indicated that the Americans were, at the moment, engaged in offensive action. This naturally enhanced her peace of mind; and with the same patience and cheerfulness which had characterized her general attitude from the beginning, she went on with her Red Cross work, dropped in almost every day to see the Tramontes, devoted her evenings to Madame d'Alvery, and every night before she said her rosary and turned out her light, wrote a long letter to Rick, recounting the unremarkable events of the day and reiterating her expressions of changeless devotion.

As a matter of fact, she did have comparatively little cause for anxiety at the moment, so her serenity was not ill-founded, as she later learned. The first objective of the Americans had been an airfield, so this was built, as soon as a narrow strip of land had been conquered. Then the Division had settled down to the defense of this field, with patrols for reconnaissance their only offensive action. But the Japs, though cut off from their main supplies, probed constantly at the American lines, and in March they opened their all-out drive to throw the enemy off the island. They fought with fanatical fierceness, always attacking at night, and the Americans used flares, car lights and fires to illumine the tropical darkness, finally focusing searchlights on the clouds so that radiance would be reflected downwards. In the end their resourcefulness was rewarded: the attack was beaten off, the Japs retreating to the interior, and Rick's division began to prepare for its next major campaign, clearing a piece of jungle and training in this area to accustom itself to open country once more. But by the time the offensive had reached this stage, and long before Sybelle learned any of these details, the thrilling news had come through that Rick had been awarded the Bronze Star for "meritorious services during the preparatory training and combat action" both at New Georgia and at Bougainville; and almost immediately after the reception of these soul-stirring tidings, Madame d'Alvery had been subjected to one of the most grueling encounters in her entire experience.

She had wakened from her siesta feeling unusually refreshed and invigorated, and Dinah, after helping her dress and seeing her comfortably settled on her sofa, had gone downstairs to get the customary afternoon coffee. She returned almost immediately, without the coffee, and with an expression of mingled astonishment and dismay on her usually calm countenance.

"Dat peddler man done come agin, Madame," she said. "He ain't brung his boy with him dis time. He done come alone. He ain't come in no cart nor no red truck neider. He come in a big shiny Cadillac car, jes' lak de one Mr. Boylston got, only hit's bigger. He ain't gone round to de side neider. He come right up to de front do' and rapped with de knocker."

"Did you remind him that neither Colonel d'Alvery nor Miss Merry was at Belle Heloise and tell him that I never receive anyone except members of the family and very old and intimate friends?"

"Yassum, Madame, Ah sho' did. But he say, he knew dat all right. He want to see you, anyway—yassum. He come right along in de front hall while he a-sayin' it, too. He standin' dere now. Wasn't no way Ah could stop him."

"Very well, Dinah. Tell him I will come down right away."

Madame d'Alvery glanced swiftly into the glass to assure herself that her lace cap was set at the most regal angle, picked up her embroidered handkerchief, and descended the stairs with accustomed dignity. She had seldom seen Luigi Tramonte at the outset of his career, because he had usually gone only to the quarters in those days, and, on the rare occasions when he had come to the Big House, only as far as the patio. She had never encountered him since prosperity had put an end to his peddling, nor was she acquainted with any other individuals who might conceivably be classified with him. Therefore she had only the vaguest idea what to expect, and with considerable surprise, she saw that he was by no means unpresentable. He was dressed in dark, well-tailored clothes, and his snow-white hair, black brows and bronzed skin combined to make his appearance very striking. His figure had the solidity of advancing years, but it was by no means shapeless, and as she came closer to him she saw that his small ears, which lay very close to his head, were slightly pointed at the top, suggesting something faunlike in his nature or heredity. The rest of his features, however, had the fine coinlike quality not unrare among Italians, and his keen eyes met hers with no evasion or abashment. When she bowed, neglecting to hold out her hand, he did the same, and he waited, with no sign of discomfiture, for her to speak first.

"Good evening," Madame d'Alvery said, speaking in a tone of cold civility. To her own discomfiture, of which she was conscious with extreme annoyance, she did not feel certain how she should address him. Obviously she could not call this substantial citizen, who was a total stranger to her, by his Christian name; neither could she quite bring herself to call anyone whom she considered so completely her social inferior, Mr. Tramonte; yet the apparently inevitable omission disturbed her. "Dinah says you wish to see me," she went on, speaking more rapidly than was her habit in order to escape from her sense of inadequacy. "I gathered that the matter is very urgent. Will you tell me what it is?"

"Sure I tell you what it is, Madame d'Alvery. That's what I come-a here for. Sure it's verra urgent too. I have-a to talk to you about my Riccardo."

"Your son?" Madame d'Alvery asked still more coldly. "Is he in trouble?" she inquired, stubbornly refusing to admit even to herself that she was begininng to realize all too well the purpose of this presumptuous call.

"Riccardo ain't-a never in no trouble," Luigi retorted proudly. "You musta heard about my Riccardo, Madame d'Alvery, whatta fine boy he always been. Not a jus' now in de war. He leada his class atta school, getta plenty prizes, playa on alla the teams—baseball, football, basketball, everything. Alla same at University. Getta Kemper Weliams Saber, getta be Cadet Colonel—I getta ready to take-a him into business with me, soon like he finish. I didn't think about any war. Mighty gooda business, too, Madame d'Alvery. Ain'ta no better fancy grocery stores than I gotta—Baton Rouge, Hammond, Covington, Opelousas, Lafayette, Lake Charles, Donaldsonville, Thibodaux, two in New Orleans. I gotta lot of real estate too—apartment houses, office buildings, country places, alla things like that. I gotta everything to give my Riccardo a good start anytime. . . . Notta like my poor papa, have-a ten children, live-a in two rooms, worka in the fields alla his life, earna few lire a day. Riccardo alla son I ever got. But he's wortha ten to me, and everything what I gotta going to be his."

"I have heard that you have prospered, Mr. Tramonte, and that your son is a great credit to you. But I am still in the dark as to why you felt it was so imperative that you should see me this evening."

It had proved impossible to continue, indefinitely, to address her importunate visitor merely as you; reluctantly, Madame d'Alvery had succumbed to the indicated form of address. And she was beginning to be afraid that before long she would also be obliged to invite him into the parlor. She could not eject him forcibly from the house. She could not even turn around abruptly and leave him, without playing false to her own standards of civility; but neither could she confront him indefinitely, standing in the front hall, partly because she found their relative positions extremely awkward and partly because she had not the physical strength to maintain her own. She was amazingly strong for a woman of her years, despite the legend of fragility which she had managed to maintain with varying degrees of success; but she was not strong enough for that. Neither could she sit down without suggesting that Luigi Tramonte be seated also, for there was nothing in the hall on which she could safely sit. To be sure, an antique settee was located between the stairway and the parlor door, and opposite it, on either side of a long narrow table, were two chairs which matched the settee. All were exquisitely carved and inlaid with mother-of-pearl. But they were so brittle with age that they could hardly be moved for dusting, and then only with the greatest care. They had been relegated to the front hall for the very reason that no one ever stayed there, and that while highly ornamental and extremely valuable, they were completely useless. A sudden crash, attended by a precipitate fall, which would land her in an undignified posture, was the last kind of catastrophe that Madame d'Alvery desired. She could visualize no way in which to maintain her attitude of aloofness under such unpropitious circumstances. While she was pondering on her next step, Luigi abruptly jolted her from reflection into action.

"Sure my Riccardo greata credit to me," he said, speaking with increasing pride. "Verra, verra good son. Greata credit to his mamma, too. Gooda sons, they most generally gooda husbands. Greata credit to any family." Luigi paused long enough to let this statement sink in, but as Madame d'Alvery continued to confront him with a masklike expression, he shrewdly decided it was too soon to press this point, and went on to speak of Riccardo's other qualifications. "Greata credit to his school and his college. Greata credit to his country. How many boys you know, Major's when they make-a twenty-seven? How many boys you know getta Bronze Star for Meritorious Service?"

"I was aware that your son had won promotions very rapidly, Mr. Tramonte. But I still do not see—"

"Madame d'Alvery, you can't make-a me believe you're so dumb like alla that. You know my Riccardo love-a your granddaughter Sybelle. You know he always love-a her, ever since she was a leetla girl. You senda away to school so she couldna see him any more. You thinka my Riccardo not good enough for your granddaughter. Well, I don'ta say anything then, not for a longa time. I don't wanta my fine boy force his way, any place he ain'ta welcome—I tella him so, he feela justa the same—I thinka maybe he get over loving Sybelle too, maybe when she ain't a leetla girl any more, she treata him different, see, so he saya to himself, *I don'ta wanta no stuck-up piece like that for my wife. I wanta real woman for my wife, same-a my mamma a real woman.* But Sybelle, she ain'ta no stuck-up piece. She ain'ta no dolly either, like-a she looked when she was a leetla girl. She gotta pinka cheeks and beega eyes and yellow curls yet, but they don't make-a look like no dolly no more. She's a real woman. She's good enough for my Riccardo just like he's good enough for her."

"Mr. Tramonte, I must ask you to excuse me. I don't feel I can discuss my granddaughter, Sybelle, with you. If anyone is going to do that, though I cannot see the necessity, it should be Colonel d'Alvery, after he returns from overseas——"

"There ain'ta time to wait and wait like-a that, Madame d'Alvery—Sybelle and Riccardo, they waita too long already, causa the Tramontes they too proud to force-a their way places they ain'ta welcome. We done wrong to be so proud. Now you and me we gotta see Sybelle and my Riccardo getta married before he sent off to more Jap islands. I don'ta know the names of alla those islands, I can'ta pronounce them anyway. But I know they're a long way off. I know when my Riccardo gets way off in too many those places maybe he never comes back."

"We must not allow ourselves to think about it in that way, Mr. Tramonte. I have a son and two grandsons in the service myself, you know." Madame d'Alvery glanced from Luigi to the service flag hanging in one of the narrow many-paned windows flanking the front door, less because she wanted to look at it just then, despite her pride in it, than because she wanted to look away from Luigi. "I am confidently anticipating their return," she continued, with sincere conviction. It was really inconceivable to her that Gervais' name or Vail's or Philogene's would ever appear on a casualty list; she visualized calamities of this sort as occurring in other families, but not in hers. Lucien Estrade had come back safely after the War Between the States and Gervais after the First World War; in due time, he and her grandsons would come back safely from this war. "I think you should feel the same way about your son, if you will permit me to say so," she remarked, for the first time permitting the condescension in her voice to overcome the coldness.

"Well, I don'ta feel the same way about my son. You gotta son and a daughter, Madame d'Alvery, mighty fine son-in-law and daughter-in-law too. You gotta two grandsons and three granddaughters. If you lose-a one, even two, you gotta lot left. My Riccardo, he's alla I got. When you gotta just one boy, you can't helpa but think whata it would be like, if he didn't never come-a back from those places which I can'ta say— You can'ta help wanta he should getta bambino of his own before it's too late. You can'ta help but wanta he should be happy while he can. You can'ta help make up your mind he's going to be."

Luigi spoke with grim purpose and gathering intensity. In the course of each succeeding speech that he had made on the subject of his son, Madame d'Alvery had become increasingly aware both of the weakness in her knees and of the futility of her impassivity. With the same tardiness and reluctance which she had displayed in finally addressing him as Mr. Tramonte, she now invited him into the parlor.

"If you are determined to talk to me about your son, I think perhaps we had better sit down," she said. She was aware that never before in her life had she spoken so ungraciously to a guest, but she felt no compunctions on this score. The moment had come when she was obliged to admit the need of fortifying herself, both figuratively and literally; but she was doing this merely in self-defense. She was by no means ready to admit any of the usual obligations of a hostess, in the case of this ex-peddler who had first forced his way into her house and who now stubbornly pursued his preposterous arguments. She was certain that if Gervais had only been at home, he would have made short work of such presumption, and she had never longed more eagerly for her son's presence. But since she had been left alone in their aristocratic stronghold, she was determined that somehow she would protect and maintain its traditional inviolability. She led the way into the parlor without a backward glance or a welcoming gesture, and seated herself on one of the two stiff brocaded sofas which faced each other on either side of the hearth. A heavy rain was falling outside, and the room was gloomy, damp and abnormally cold; but she did not summon Dinah to kindle the fire or turn on the lights. Holding herself very erect, she faced Luigi, who had seated himself on the opposite sofa, and who also held himself very erect. Dinah had neglected to take his hat when he came in, and as long as he stood in the hall he had held it, somewhat uncomfortably, twirling it from time to time. Now he laid it on the sofa beside him and folded his arms, waiting for Madame d'Alvery to proceed.

"Let me try to make my position clear to you, Mr. Tramonte," she said with firmness. "Apparently it is important that I should, and I may say in passing, that when I speak of position I mean the family position. If my son were here, I am sure he would say the same thing to you that I shall. We both have a great regard for the family as a unit."

"That's a verra fine thing, Madame d'Alvery," Luigi replied, promptly and disconcertingly. "My wife, Netta, and my Riccardo and me, alla we feel the same way about our family. That's why I come-a to talk to you about my Riccardo and Sybelle. We alla know, we Tramontes, same all as you d'Alverys, when young folks wanta get married, old folks needa talk about it too."

"Yes, under normal circumstances. As a general thing, it is a very good plan for fathers and mothers and grandfathers and grandmothers of the two contracting parties to have an understanding about such matters, even before their children and grandchildren do. For instance, if Colonel d'Alvery and I had thought it would be advisable that Sybelle should marry the son of one of our neighbors on the River Road——"

"You ain'ta gotta so many neighbors on the River Road no more, have you, Madame d'Alvery? Just Meesta Boylston way down at Hackberry Lodge, eight, ten miles from here. And he ain't gotta no sons for Sybelle to marry. Faith Estate, those no-count Renos letta it burn to the ground after they bringa every kind of disgrace to it. Chelmsford and Cedar Grove, they been empty this long while back. Now Hathaway Hall too. I drive-a through the *allée* at Hathaway to the mansion when I come-a here to Belle Heloise just now. My my, does that place looka bad—columns rotting, railings missing, window; broken in, lawns alla growing up in weeds! Factry jus' a shell, and; machinery alla sold to Mexico, same-a like-a you fine people usta sella your poor slaves downa river. And that was-a fine place, finest on the River Road, when I first come-a here, carrying stage-planks and Johnny Crooks and sauerkraut candy in a basket on my back!"

Madame d'Alvery winced. But this was not wholly on account of Luigi's reference to his peddler's pack, gratingly as this fell on her ears, or even on account of his all too accurate description of the dilapidation of Hathaway Hall, which was an eyesore to her whenever she passed it. Though she shrank from the recollection, she could not now help remembering how she and Mrs. Hathaway had once planned such an alliance as she had just attempted to extol, and how their pride had indeed come before a fall and their haughty spirit before destruction. It was inconceivable that this shrewd self-made man did not know something of that sad and shocking story; indeed, as she swiftly thought over his statement, she was certain that his reference to Hathaway had not been accidental, and she was humiliated that he had scored so quickly and so effectively.

"Suppose we go back a little," she remarked a trifle hurriedly. "I am afraid you did not altogether understand me when I spoke of our family position. Or rather you interrupted me—unconsciously, I am sure. Doubtless you thought I had finished what I started to say. But I had not. What I was leading up to was this: both my son and I have the greatest respect for your industry and initiative, Mr. Tramonte, and I am sure that my dear daughter-in-law has, too. We are all aware, likewise, that you have every reason to feel extremely proud of your only son. Far from having anything against him personally, we admire his character and his patriotism. We can even understand why Sybelle as a child and as a young girl should have been so much attracted to him; he is very handsome, he has very good manners and he inspires confidence. But we cannot help feeling that as she grows older she will be happier with someone whose background is more like her own."

"Whata you meana by that, background, Madame d'Alvery? More money, better moral example, more family happiness than we Tramontes?"

Again Madame d'Alvery winced. It was an incontestable fact that while Gervais was getting deeper and deeper into debt, Luigi had been getting richer and richer, that while the d'Alverys were trying to conceal a corroding scandal the Tramontes had become more and more respected, that while the ancient walls of Belle Heloise had been almost rent asunder by discord, peace and harmony had prevailed in the little house back of the fancy grocery store on Lafayette Street. While she was groping for the right retort, Luigi went on relentlessly.

"You thinka maybe Sybelle don'ta get on with my wife? Never I see no young girl so happy like she is with my Netta. You thinka she go to better school, travel more, hear more good music, see more nice things?"

"No," Madame d'Alvery admitted reluctantly. Since she had insisted on sending her own son to Louisiana State University she could not logically complain because the Tramontes had also done this, or set Grand Coteau on a higher plane; neither could she claim that the aged and unprogressive Miss Mittie, who had been Sybelle's sole mentor until she was sent away, was a better instructor than the energetic and up-to-date young teachers to whom Riccardo's education had been entrusted in his tenderer years. On the subject of travel and general cultural advantages, the less said the better. She knew that the Tramontes had given their son a foreign trip nearly every year until the outbreak of the war, and that they had taken infinite pains to familiarize him with all the arts; she had heard Sybelle say, wistfully, a dozen times, that she wished she could go to the opera and the theater and the museums in New York, like the Tramontes, really meaning with the Tramontes.

"Then it's me, maybe? I don'ta speak such good English, no? Someone told me once, Pascal Tremblet I think, your papa he didn't speak no English at all till that Scotch tramp, whata you call him, Angus Holt, teacha him how."

"That's true, Mr. Tramonte. But it was because my father, and my mother too for that matter, were typical Creoles of the old school. All their people were Creoles too. French was their family language."

"Well me, I wasa Neapolitan, Italian wasa my family language. Whata the difference, Madame d'Alvery, except that I hada learn the English myself, alla same time I'm making money to take-a care my wife and bring up my Riccardo and start my fancy grocery stores? I didn't have no tramp come along to teacha me, I didn't have no nice house to live in while I was learning. But mostly, people understand me when I talk to them!"

He paused, but only long enough to take breath. Before the old lady, now thoroughly startled, could form a reply, he leaned forward, resting his strong, stubby hands on his knees as he did so.

"Maybe thata the trouble, maybe you thinka Riccardo not have nice enough house for Sybelle. I tella you something, Madame d'Alvery. I thought of that myself. Sybelle real woman like I said before, verra fine leetla lady too. Me and my Riccardo both know, ladies like Sybelle, they oughta have nice houses to live-a in. They oughtn't live back of fancy grocery stores, like me and Netta. So I don'ta go to Hathaway Hall today just to see him. I go to buy him for my Riccardo!"

Suddenly Luigi sprang from his seat, knocking his hat to the floor as he did so. To Madame d'Alvery, recoiling against the hard back of her brocaded sofa, he became an overwhelming, almost a threatening figure. With one hand he thumped his breast pocket, so hard that the result was a loud thudding noise. Raising his other arm, he shook his stubby forefinger in her face. Actually the gesture was only one of emphasis; but to her it had all the elements of a menace. She smothered a slight scream as she braced herself still more firmly against the sofa.

"I gotta the deed righta here in my pocket!" he shouted. "The Tremaines, whata they ever do for it? Leave-a it alla time for thata skunk Blood to raise-a hell instead of sugar! Geta themselves killed someway, leave it to a big fool Yankee woman don't know any better than marry Blood— These-a river families! I ain'ta gonna say anything against them, seeing my Riccardo marry into one. But I know whata I think, just the same. There, I'm saying more than I oughta. But we Tramontes, we alla know how to take-a care property. Ain'ta no place we ever owned ain'ta been improved. We'll improve Hathaway Hall too, make-a it like it used to be, Madame d'Alvery. It'll be just as nice a home for Sybelle as Belle Heloise was for Adela Ayela when her father gave it to her for a wedding present the time she marry François Estrade. We're going righta on with the same old family traditions you thinka so much of, giving fine places to our children for their wedding presents! I take-a the agent for that property right out to Hathaway with me today, I pay him cash for it— But the deed, thata made out to my Riccardo——"

While he was talking, Luigi had gradually ceased to beat his breast and shake his fist. Madame d'Alvery, still too startled to speak, drew a deep sigh of relief. Luigi, taking a long breath himself, leaned over and picked up his crushed and fallen hat. Then he brushed this off with his sleeve and deposited it carefully on the marble-topped table that stood near by. Afterwards he sat down on the same sofa as Madame d'Alvery.

"But they can'ta wait until Hathaway Hall's alla fixed up before they get married, Sybelle and my Riccardo," he said, with no trace of his former ferocity. "Sybelle, she'll have a nice time doing that, when my Riccardo's gone to one of those queer places I can'ta say the names of. It'll keepa her busy, give-a her something to think about while he's away. She'll be proud to have-a it ready for him when he comes back for good to go into fancy grocery business with me. She'll need plentya room for the bambinos, too, bimeby. But first— My Riccardo, he gonna have a shorta leave right away, Madame d'Alvery. I gotta telegram in my pocket, too, right alongside the deed—Sybelle, she came-a over to our house from the Red Cross before I starta out here. She gotta telegram too. She say she ain'ta gonna to wait any longer, no matter if the Tramontes are proud! It's better, don'ta you think so, our children have a nice-a wedding at St. Agnes' and alla their friends coming here for party at Belle Heloise afterwards, than they run off together and get married at Gretna? Tella me quick like anything, because you and I, we gotta make-a up our minds right now!"

CHAPTER XLIX

MEREDITH D'ALVERY had one of the pleasantest and most spacious corner suites at the Hotel St. Regis. From her drawing-room window, she could look far, far up Fifth Avenue, and there was no hour of day or night when this was not a thrilling and provocative sight. Her bedroom and bathroom were separated from the drawing room by an attractive foyer, and a white-tiled pantry led from this, completely equipped with a gleaming refrigerator, porcelain sink, and all the other accessories which made for comfort and convenience in serving everything from her own solitary but luxurious breakfast to a cocktail party for fifty persons. Not that Merry did the serving herself: she had an excellent maid, named Mabel, who took pride in being able to do everything that Mrs. d'Alvery could possibly require in the way of personal service, and when Mrs. d'Alvery wished to entertain, there was always the hotel staff, which was still excellent also, in spite of the war, to supplement Mabel's efforts. Merry entertained a good deal, and she nearly always did it in this spacious suite because it was so easy and agreeable that way. She did not need to lift a finger herself and yet she could almost create the illusion of being in a private house.

Of course she put in an active day at the office, at least from Monday through Friday, but her week ends were free, and she always took ample time out for luncheon because many of her most important connections were furthered in this way and through the evening parties at which she entertained so easily and agreeably in her suite. She could nearly always count on leaving the office by five, or five-thirty at the latest, and that gave ample time to be on hand for cocktails followed by dinner, or for a very elaborate high tea before the theater and midnight supper afterwards. Mr. Goldenberg had impressed upon her from the beginning that while he expected her office to be run efficiently, he did not consider that her usefulness to the store was limited to office hours. Not by any means. In a sense, she had a twenty-four-hour-a-day job. Some time during the twenty-four hours, she must naturally get the requisite amount of sleep, or she would not be fresh for her work; but the hours she was off duty could not possibly be uniform. He expected her to keep them flexible, according to the exigencies of the moment.

In this respect, as in every other, she had more than met his expectations. The New York center which she herself had organized, after the Paris branch had closed on account of the war, had been of even more value to the store than its predecessor. Merry had given it great prestige and brought great originality to it. Her South American sojourn had proved an extremely sound investment. As a result of it, she had built up a sizable clientele among Latin ladies, and wealthy New Yorkers appreciated the same unique touch that intrigued their sisters from the South. Mr. Goldenberg often told Merry that she had done more to further the Good Neighbor Policy than Nelson Rockefeller, and he was not speaking more than half in jest, when he said so, either.

The store was only a few blocks from the St. Regis, so Merry usually walked back and forth from her office. She had a car, and used it habitually on week ends. But the walk gave her a chance for exercise, which she needed and enjoyed, and an opportunity to see what other stores were offering. It also permitted the experience, which she had never ceased to find thrilling, of being part of the great crowd which streamed up and down Fifth Avenue. Conscious that her exquisite clothes could bear comparison with those of any woman she met, tingling with perfect health, intoxicated with the success of her career and the richness of her existence, her progress had such a triumphant quality about it that even in their haste, passers-by caught its contagion as they glanced at her, and went on their own way reanimated.

In the hotel itself, the doorman, the clerk, the bellboys and the elevator operators were all glad when they saw her coming. She had a pleasant smile and a friendly word for each. And when she approached her own suite, Mabel was always waiting to open the door and to greet her respectfully but warmly. Her mail was laid neatly on the desk, with a list of the telephone calls which had come in during the day meticulously beside it. The flowers that had been sent since she left for the office had been tastefully arranged, and the cards which had accompanied them were placed beside the letters and the list of telephone calls, with a notation to indicate whether they had come with the red roses or purple orchids. The clothes appropriate for the next engagement were already laid out in the bedroom. Always the right dress and the right shoes to go with it; if Merry were going out, always the right handbag and the right wrap too, and when the occasion indicated a hat, that was also in readiness. Mabel was very experienced, and she also had a natural flair for suitability in all things and on all occasions.

One evening early in April, the first pleasant warmth of spring, coming with a rush, tempted Merry to take her evening walk at a more leisurely pace than usual. She knew that before the next evening this pleasant warmth might be blown away by a stiff easterly breeze or engulfed in a cold driving rain, and that there might be no more warm pleasant days for a month; that was what very often happened, in New York. Involuntarily, as she loitered along the Avenue, looking in the shop windows and observing the most arresting details of the novelties worn by smart women, Merry thought of spring as it came to Belle Heloise, in January, with the last camellias and the first paperwhite narcissi; then with a veritable burst of bloom in February. Why, it had been spring there for two months already! She wondered whether the purple wisteria and the white Cherokee roses, which between them wreathed one of the oaks so completely that its own foliage was almost hidden, had been allowed to continue climbing over it, or whether they had been wrenched away from it at last. The d'Alverys had been warned, years before, that in time these would ruin the tree if they were not removed. But they presented a beautiful and unique sight every spring, and no one had wanted to forego the perennial delight. Another beautiful and unique sight was the fruit tree where part of the blossoms were pale pink and part deep crimson. No one had ever explained this phenomenon; no one had ever tried. Spring was not something you analyzed, in Louisiana. It was something you enjoyed. . . .

Well, you enjoyed it in New York too, Merry told herself, beginning to walk a little more briskly. The shop windows were full of new things, the women all had on new clothes, fresh asparagus and shad roe were appearing on the menus, Central Park had lost its bleak, dingy look, and there was a feeling of new life in the air. You were not dependent on a few clinging vines and some multicolored blossoms for joie de vivre; the city was full of it, even in wartime. Spending had never been more prodigal, prices never more exorbitant, pleasure never more extravagantly pursued. Merry was dining that night with Mr. Goldenberg at the Belle Meunière and she knew that the check for the tête-à-tête dinner would come to twenty dollars. They were going afterwards to "The Voice of the Turtle" and the tickets for that would be fifteen. Then if they went to the Oak Room at the Plaza for a nightcap, the evening's outing would run to fifty at the very least. And this was for a quiet evening's outing; a party for a dozen could easily have cost five hundred. What did it matter? Mr. Goldenberg had more money to spend than he knew what to do with. So, apparently, did everyone else. . . .

As usual, the doorman and the room clerk and the elevator boy all nodded to Merry smilingly; as usual, Mabel was waiting to open the door of the suite for her. It looked very attractive and inviting as she went in. The furnishings and ornaments, which she had picked up in the course of her long foreign sojourns, robbed it of the typical stereotyped hotel atmosphere. The flowers with which, as usual, it was lavishly adorned, gave it a festive appearance. It was a little too formal, a little too elegant, to be really homelike, but it revealed scrupulous care, impeccable taste and the domination of a sophisticated personality.

"Good evening, Mabel. Any special news?"

"Good evening, Madam. Mr. Goldenberg called to say he would come here for cocktails before dinner if that would be agreeable to you. He will assume it is unless I telephone him to the contrary. A telegram came in, just a few minutes ago. I called the office, but you had already left. I put it on top of your mail."

Telegrams, in large numbers, had been part of Merry's everyday existence for a long time now. She accepted their arrival without excitement, though Mabel had standing instructions to advise her immediately of any that came to the hotel during her absence, and if she could be reached, to open them and read them aloud immediately. However, since she had left the office before this one arrived, it was still unopened. She walked over to the desk and picked up the yellow envelope that lay on top of the neatly slit letters and carefully stacked cards, unsealing the flap. The message inside was so long that it covered two pages.

RICK ARRIVED SAN FRANCISCO TODAY ON LEAVE REACHING NEW ORLEANS FRIDAY—Merry read—HE AND I GETTING MARRIED NOON SATURDAY. HAVE CABLED DADDY WHO HAS CABLED BACK APPROVAL WITH HIS LOVE. MR. TRA-MONTE GIVING US HATHAWAY FOR WEDDING PRESENT RESTORATION AT HIS EXPENSE STARTING IMMEDIATELY AND I SHALL LIVE THERE WHILE THIS GOES FORWARD. WEDDING AT ST. AGNES RECEPTION AT BELLE HELOISE WITH GRAND'MÈRE'S CONSENT. UNCLE FABIAN GIVING ME AWAY, JOYEUSE MAID OF HONOR, FRANCES BELLE, NELLIE, SUE AND DRINA BRIDESMAIDS. ARRANGE-MENTS NECESSARILY HURRIED BUT GOING FORWARD SMOOTHLY. HOW-EVER IT IS BAD ENOUGH TO HAVE DADDY, VAIL AND PHIL ALL OVERSEAS WITHOUT HAVING YOU AWAY TOO. VAIL ALWAYS SAID HE WAS SURE YOU WOULD HELP OUT WHEN IT CAME TO A SHOWDOWN. WON'T YOU SELECT MY TROUSSEAU INCLUDING WEDDING DRESS AND TAKE CRESCENT LIMITED TOMOR-ROW AFTERNOON BRINGING EVERYTHING WITH YOU? WILL TELEPHONE YOU FROM TRAMONTES' HOUSE EIGHT PM EASTERN STANDARD TIME FOR YOUR ANSWER. PLEASE MUMMY BE READY TO SAY YES. NO GIRL FEELS HER WEDDING COMPLETE WITHOUT HER MOTHER. LOVE, SYBELLE.

Merry read the telegram twice, laid it down, picked it up again, and read it once more. Then she turned to Mabel.

"Please telephone Mr. Goldenberg and tell him I'm sorry, but I won't be able to go out with him this evening," she said. "I'll be glad to have him come for cocktails and stay for dinner too, if he will. But I'll have to be where I can wait for a telephone call. There's a family emergency."

"Very good, Madam ... Not bad news, I hope? Mr. Goldenberg is sure to ask."

"No, it isn't exactly bad news. But my elder daughter's fiancé is coming home on leave and she's decided to get married while he's home. She wants me to start South immediately. I haven't been there in a long time ... While you're telephoning, Mabel, you'd better call the head porter too, and see if by any miracle there's something to be had on the *Crescent Limited* tomorrow."

"Very good, Madam ... Would you be wishing me to go with you? Shall I ask the porter to get reservations for two persons, if possible?"

Mabel's efficiency had outpaced Merry's planning. She had not yet thought about taking Mabel with her. In her mind's eye she had been swiftly seeing again an exquisite wedding dress she had recently viewed at Jay Thorpe's, wishing enviously at the time it had been one of her own designer's creations, and involuntarily thinking that if it had been fashioned on purpose for Sybelle, it could not have been more suited to her. It was made of white marquisette with large hand-painted lovers' knots of palest blue scattered over the skirt, matching the clusters of forget-me-nots with which this was embroidered. The low-cut bodice was outlined with forget-me-nots too, the cuffs of the full bishop sleeves and the cap to which the floating white veil was attached were formed of them; the wide girdle was made of pale-blue taffeta. Merry realized her mother-in-law would protest that Sybelle should wear old satin and ancestral lace and that any touch of color was inappropriate for a virginal wedding gown; but she herself knew that this fresh filmy dress was more Sybelle's type than anything they could have dragged out of the attic, that the bows and forget-me-nots and girdle would match the blue of Sybelle's eyes and set off her blonde beauty to perfection. Merry hoped to heaven that this dream of a wedding dress, which was an exclusive model, had not been sold. It was too late for her to find out this evening. But she must have Mabel telephone, the minute the stores opened in the morning. . . .

She was tardily aware that Mabel was waiting respectfully for an answer. Now that her attention had been called to the possibility that her maid might accompany her, she realized that such an arrangement would have great advantages. Mabel's efficiency would be a godsend in such an emergency as this; furthermore, her presence would eliminate any dependence on personal service from the Negroes at Belle Heloise. Merry remembered how tenderly Creassy had ministered to her when she went to Belle Heloise as a bride herself, how much the faithful colored woman had loved her; but she also knew that Creassy had never felt the same towards her, after she left her home and her husband, and that she never would again. Quite aside from Mabel's greater efficiency, it would be a relief not to have Creassy's great dark eyes gazing reproachfully at her all the time. . . .

"Yes," she said at last. "Yes, I think I better take you with me, Mabel. Ask the porter to get reservations for two, if he can. And hurry! I've got to let Mr. Goldenberg know about my change of plan as quickly as possible, so that he can turn in the theater tickets."

Neither Mabel's manner nor her tone as she said, "Very good, Madam," again gave the slightest indication that the delay which had occurred was due to Mrs. d'Alvery's own preoccupation, and not to any failure on her part to move with alacrity. Merry went on into her bedroom, tossing her hat on the dressing table, and taking off the jacket to her tailored suit. This was Tuesday. If she did get the *Crescent* the next afternoon, she would not reach New Orleans until late Thursday night—only a few hours before Rick got there himself, less than forty-eight before the marriage ceremony. And evidently Sybelle was planning a large and elaborate wedding. How on earth could everything be made ready on such short notice? How could she buy an entire trousseau in one morning? And yet that was all she would have, for the *Crescent* left at two-thirty. Sybelle had given her no idea, either, where the honeymoon was to take place, what kind of clothes she would need for that. Oh, yes! And when it came to clothes, Mabel did not have the right kind laid out now. It was the first time this had ever happened. She was not dining in a restaurant and going to the theater afterwards; she was dining in her own suite, so that she could wait for Sybelle's telephone call.

Mabel came back to the room with an emerald-green hostess dress over her arm and matching slippers in her hand. "I'm sorry these weren't ready for you, Madam," she said. "But I prepared for the Belle Meunière and 'The Voice of the Turtle.' And since you told me you were dining in the suite, I've been on the telephone. Mr. Goldenberg says the change of plan is entirely agreeable to him, but since you are not going out he won't come until seven. I hope that will give you time to take a short rest, Madam. I am sure you must need it. . . . The porter is very sorry to say that at the moment the only reservation available on the *Crescent* is one upper. But he hopes to get something better. He has promised to keep right after the Pullman company. Meanwhile he is holding the upper. . . . Could you give me some idea, Madam, about how long we will be staying in Louisiana? So that I would know what to pack and how much?"

"You had better pack enough for a week, Mabel—well, perhaps for ten days. I should think we would be back on Monday the nineteenth at the latest."

She did not take time to rest. She bathed and put on the emerald-green hostess dress, and then she began to make lists of what Sybelle would need and what she herself would need, so that she could save time in the morning. She would not try to do anything about household linens until after her return. Even though Sybelle was going to start housekeeping immediately—and she did not really see how this was possible, in that ramshackle old house—the girl could borrow enough for her immediate needs from Belle Heloise, or probably—the thought was unwelcome but none the less persistent—from the Tramontes. Merry knew that Italians were good providers when it came to linen, as they were about many other things; probably Netta had dozens and dozens of beautiful hand-woven sheets and fringed towels stowed away that had never even been used. So she herself could concentrate on the question of clothes. Besides that dream of a wedding dress—and it simply *could* not be sold!— Sybelle must have quantities of beautiful lingerie, a stunning traveling outfit, at least two evening gowns, the usual basic daytime dresses and tailored suits. She herself must have a costume not only appropriate for the bride's mother, but arresting enough to cause comment. Merry realized it was important to cause comments about clothes, both Sybelle's and her own. It might help to divert comments of other kinds.

She tried not to think about these, as she went rapidly on with her lists. She knew that there would inevitably be awkward aspects to her return, no matter how objectively she treated this or how briefly she remained at Belle Heloise. Not that she felt any compunctions about going there. Her conduct, during her absence, had always been irreproachable; her right to her position there was still incontestable. She herself would have felt hurt if Sybelle had not wanted her at the wedding, and if anyone else, including her mother-in-law, thought it peculiar that she should return for this, after an absence of eight years, they could keep their thoughts to themselves or prepare for crisp rejoinders, just as they preferred. She did not propose to put up with any insolence, and when it came to aloofness, she could be aloof too.

"Mr. Goldenberg has telephoned from downstairs, Madam, to ask if he might come up."

"You said yes, of course, Mabel."

"Of course, Madam."

Even after all these years, Mr. Goldenberg had never shown the slightest familiarity in his association with her. In fact, it sometimes seemed to Merry as if he bent over backwards to avoid this. For instance, he might certainly have called her by her first name by this time, or at least Miss Meredith, as he had before she was married; but he still addressed her as Mrs. d'Alvery. He never came to her suite, or even to her office, unannounced. He had never mentioned Gervais to her, since the day of her frantic appeal to him after Franchot's death, when he told her so candidly he thought she was doing wrong to leave her husband, but that if she were determined on such a course, he would be glad to facilitate a career for her. The possibility of divorce, so lightly touched upon then, had never again been discussed. Merry knew that if she herself had broached this, Mr. Goldenberg would have assured her that he would make this process as painless and private as possible. She thought it was not inconceivable that if she did seek a divorce, and secure it, Mr. Goldenberg might afterwards ask her to marry him. But she did not feel by any means sure of it, in spite of his years of devotion. She knew he had very fixed ideas on the subject of loyalty in general and family solidarity in particular. . . .

"Good evening. What a lovely spring day this has been, hasn't it? Almost as pretty as a spring day in Louisiana. I don't know though. I doubt if anything is ever even 'almost' as pretty as that, anywhere in the world."

Mr. Goldenberg had given his hat and gloves to Mabel in the foyer, and now came into the tasteful, sophisticated drawing room, which was doubly attractive with the lights on. His remarks about spring in Louisiana constituted his first greeting.

"I thought of the same thing myself, as I was coming up the Avenue tonight. But then I decided I liked spring in New York better after all. I'm sorry I had to ask you to change our plans for the evening. Mabel didn't tell you why?"

"No, I'm sure she knew you'd want to do that yourself, while we had our cocktails."

Mr. Goldenberg smiled pleasantly at Mabel, who had already entered from the pantry with the silver shaker, glasses of embossed crystal, and caviar canapes on a Sheffield tray. Mabel's expression relaxed sufficiently to indicate that she would be very pleased to return the smile if she had considered that it would be respectful to do so, but that she knew it would not. She set the tray down in front of her mistress and returned to the pantry, where preparations for the service of dinner were already in progress. She knew that Mrs. d'Alvery liked to pour the cocktails herself, unless there were a large party.

"I had a telegram from Sybelle. Perhaps you'd like to see it yourself. At long last she's actually going to marry the one love of her life."

Merry did not mean to speak satirically, only lightly, but after she had spoken she realized that her tone had not been as tender as a mother's should be, under the circumstances. She handed the telegram to Mr. Goldenberg without further comment. He read it attentively, and handed it back to her.

"Why, I'm very glad to hear about this!" he said with obvious sincerity. "Those two have certainly been loyal to each other—they deserve all the happiness they can get." There he went, speaking straight off about loyalty; she was right, it was an almost passionate predilection on his part. But his next remark showed his concern for her. "It'll rush you a good deal, trying to do everything in one morning," he said. "But Miss Shattuck's very efficient. You've done an excellent piece of work, training her, and I hope you'll get the benefit of that now, through her help." Miss Shattuck was Merry's assistant at the office, and Merry was already counting confidently on her. "If necessary, she could follow you South, on Thursday," Mr. Goldenberg went on. "She'd still get there before the wedding. She could bring anything you directed her to secure, but that you didn't have time to select yourself. I think you could count on her good judgment and her good taste. You're taking Mabel, of course? And what about reservations?"

"Nothing available but an upper berth, so far. But I'm hoping there'll be something better in the morning, through last-minute cancellations."

"Of course there'll be something better in the morning, whether there are any last-minute cancellations or not." Mr. Goldenberg took a small pad from his pocket and made a brief notation on it. "I'll get in touch with you around ten and let you know just what. You'll be shopping by that time, of course. But I'll send you a message. . . . Perhaps you'd prefer I didn't stay with you this evening? I know you have a great deal to do."

"No, I'd like to have you stay. Mabel will attend to the packing, and I've finished making out the lists of what I need to get. There isn't anything more I can do until morning. It won't seem so long to me, waiting for Sybelle's call, if I'm not alone."

"In that case——"

They finished their cocktails, and at just the right moment Mabel reappeared to remove the tray. A table covered with a white cloth was wheeled in by a manservant, and immediately afterwards a small metal heater. The leaves of the table were spread out, the silverware arranged, the first dishes removed from the heater: clear turtle soup with sherry, so different from the rich thick turtle stew of Louisiana but almost as delicious. (Again that tiresome "almost"!) Mushrooms under glass. Broiled breast of guinea hen. Currant jelly. Broccoli hollandaise. "Tossed" green salad, about which there was no "almost" —it could not compare with Antoine's. *Milles feuilles* that were really excellent. All the appropriate vintage wines and finally a beverage that went by the name of coffee. Mr. Goldenberg drank his without comment or objection. Merry pushed her cup aside. The telephone rang . . .

"Yes, this is Mrs. Gervais d'Alvery. Yes— Hello, Sybelle! How are you, darling? Best wishes and all that! We seem to have a good line. I can hear you perfectly. Yes, I found it here when I got in this afternoon. Of course I'm coming. I'll do all the shopping I can tomorrow morning and Miss Shattuck will do the rest and bring the things South the next day. But it would help me if I knew what you need. I don't mean the wedding dress, I have that lined up already. But for your trip. No, I don't seem to be hearing you quite so well now. . . . Why, you can't, Sybelle! . . . You can't do that! . . . It's absurd, it's impossible! No, I won't try to argue with you over the telephone, but don't you understand . . . Operator, you've cut me off! No, we hadn't talked five minutes!"

For a moment she tried, vainly, to re-establish the connection. Then she gave it up. She turned to Mr. Goldenberg, the expression of her beautiful face distorted.

"They're not going anywhere on their wedding trip!" she exclaimed. "They're going straight out to Hathaway Hall! Sybelle says Mr. Tramonte has put a lot of people there to work already, and she is sure that by Saturday two or three rooms will be habitable. She doesn't see why they couldn't rough it there just as well as they could at some rented camp, and she insists they'll have a lot more fun doing it there, because it'll be their own home."

"Why, that's probably true, Mrs. d'Alvery. I should think it was a very wise decision on their part. Certainly Rick wouldn't get any pleasure out of further travel, after coming all the way from the Pacific! And certainly no one ought to do any unnecessary traveling now in any case. Don't you worry about Sybelle's comfort. I know Tramonte. He'll have done miracles by Saturday."

"Don't talk to me about miracles!" Merry's voice would have been sharp now, if it had not been shaky. "It seems this coming Sunday's the feast of St. Amico, and that the Tramontes always go to the shrine and march in the procession—you know that little chapel, made of zinc or tin or something, just below Donaldsonville! Some Italian built it as a votive offering because his sick child was cured by a stranger he decided afterwards was St. Amico. The feeling about it's fantastic—Luigi actually told me Netta would never have had a baby if she hadn't gone to that shrine and prayed plenty. Ever since Riccardo was born, they've never missed a year, celebrating St. Amico's feast. They march all the way from the shrine to the church in Donaldsonville. Luigi's always been one of the men who helped carry the statue of the saint, and Riccardo's done it too since he's been big enough! Luigi and Netta think it's another miracle that Riccardo's getting home safe and well in time for this celebration. He's going to be the main feature of it—at least, unless you count the statue! That's the way Sybelle d'Alvery's planning to spend the day after her marriage—going to a so-called shrine with a lot of ignorant Italians, and afterwards marching with them in a crazy procession and feasting the rest of the day! Can you still say you're glad she and this Dago peddler's son are getting married, Mr. Goldenberg?"

"Yes," Mr. Goldenberg answered. "Yes, I'm very glad. Even gladder than when you told me in the first place. I think you ought to be very proud of your daughter, Mrs. d'Alvery. She's willing to prove that she cares enough about her husband to respect the customs that are precious to his family. That means she's also proving that she's worthy of all the other brides in her family. Both sides of the family. Including the bride who grew up on St. Napoleon Street and succeeded in crossing the tracks to the River Road."

Merry flushed slightly and pressed her lips together without answering. Mr. Goldenberg went on talking pleasantly and calmly.

"It has never surprised me that Madame d'Alvery opposed first her son's marriage and later her eldest granddaughter's," he said. "After all, she has had a very restricted life and she is constitutionally a woman of limited vision. One could hardly expect her to grasp the advantages of such marriages to her own family, in either case. On the other hand, it has always surprised me that you should have tried to interfere between Sybelle and Riccardo. And it surprises me still more that you should refer to Riccardo, with great bitterness and contempt, as a Dago peddler's son, instead of speaking of him with pride and appreciation as an officer and a gentleman whom it is a privilege for you to welcome as a son-in-law."

"I'm sorry. I shouldn't have spoken as I did. But——"

"Suppose we do not try to discuss the matter any more just now. You must be very tired already and you have some hard days ahead of you. But I should be glad to talk to you about the situation at some other time. Possibly in Louisiana. I believe I'll see if I can't go down to that celebration myself. I've never attended the Feast of St. Amico. And I have a feeling that I'd be glad, all the rest of my life, if I saw Sybelle and her husband taking part in it."

CHAPTER L

MERRY DID NOT have to travel in an upper berth. Mr. Goldenberg reached her promptly at ten the next morning by telephone, to tell her that he had a compartment for her, and a lower in the same car for Mabel. He would call at the Hotel St. Regis a little before two and see her safely on the train. He would also bring a large lunch hamper, fully stocked. He realized that she probably would not have time to eat lunch before she left, and also that the dining-car service was now very inadequate, owing to war conditions. But she would be well supplied. She was not to worry over anything. Had she been able to get the wedding dress? Good! He was sure everything would shape itself satisfactorily in the end.

By the time she reached the station, it required considerable effort to conceal her nervousness and breathlessness. She had not slept the night before, and she had been going at top speed ever since the shops opened until returning to the St. Regis to get into the traveling outfit which, in accordance with custom, was already spread out for her. Mabel was dressed for the trip, and Merry's baggage was packed, strapped and tagged. She was taking the clothes she had bought for Sybelle in the containers that had been supplied at the stores, and Mabel tagged these also while Merry hastily changed. Then, after ringing for the bell captain, the maid brought a square box from the serving pantry and offered it to her mistress.

"Your corsage, Madam," she said respectfully. "Shall I put it on for you?"

The orchids were in a Max Schling box, as usual, exquisitely fresh and perfectly arranged. Mabel pinned them on the lapel of Merry's tailored blue serge and they started for the elevator. Mr. Goldenberg was waiting for them in the lobby, and said that the bags and boxes were already in the car. Mabel checked with the bell captain to be sure that none was missing and then they glided smoothly away to the station.

"I've arranged to have the head porter meet us and take us down in the elevator, the back way," he said. "You can get right on the train, Mrs. d'Alvery, and Mabel can give you your lunch at once, in the compartment. I know there's no service outside the diner any more, but you won't need it, with what I've supplied. If I may make a suggestion, I'd advise you to go straight to bed, and stay there until you reach New Orleans. I don't know when I've seen you look so tired. But Miss Shattuck's told me that you've accomplished wonders, that there's nothing left for her to do. That must mean you've been on the run all the morning, and you certainly will be, after you get to Louisiana. Why not have a good rest in the meantime?"

"I think I will," Merry agreed. Now that at last she had stopped hurrying, she realized how tired she was. "Thanks for everything, Mr. Goldenberg. I couldn't ever have made it if you hadn't helped, rounding off the rough corners."

"Oh yes, you could have. You can do anything on which you're really determined. But I'm glad if I've been able to be of some assistance. Good-by, Mrs. d'Alvery. As I told you, I may try to come to Louisiana myself. I've been away from Baton Rouge a great deal lately, and this is as good a time as any to go back. Unless some unforeseen difficulty arises, I'll see you Saturday; but in the church at Donaldsonville Sunday morning, anyway."

The lower berth in the compartment had already been made and the upper one folded back into place. Gratefully, Merry let Mabel help her undress, arrange her toilet articles, and serve lunch from the hamper. When the porter buzzed, Mabel went to the door and told him Madam was very tired and must on no account be disturbed, slipping a generous tip into his hand as she spoke. He brought more towels to supplement the already ample supply, looked about for possible papers to remove, and left with the fervent expression of hope that if the lady wanted anything she would please ring three times so that he would know it was her and leave whatever he was doing to come. The conductors had not yet been through, so Mabel said she would watch for them outside and forestall their entrance. She had the tickets in her handbag. She did hope Madam would have a good rest. . . .

To her surprise, Merry began to feel drowsy almost immediately. The reaction from the excitement which had kept her awake all night had already set in and she soon fell fast asleep. When she waked, the train was stopping jerkily at some station where lights were burning on the platform. She looked at her watch and realized with astonishment that they must have reached Charlottesville, that she had been sleeping for hours and hours! Charlottesville. . . . That was where Gervais had spent the entire spring of 1943! He had written her briefly when he had entered the School of Military Government, saying that most of the officers' wives were accompanying them there, that he would be glad if she would join him, and that he believed she would enjoy the experience herself. He thought that if they were together at a beautiful place like that, which had no associations whatsoever with Belle Heloise, they might achieve a reunion which would make them both very happy. She had answered the letter briefly and coolly: she appreciated his thought, but the spring trade was keeping her unusually busy; it would not be possible for her to leave New York just then. He had not written her since; when it came to that, he had not written her for a long time before then, either. The solitary letter must have been the result of protracted thought; it must have represented his last desperate appeal. She knew he would never make another. . . .

Why did she have to wake at Charlottesville, of all places? Why could it not have been Philadelphia or Atlanta, or any other place that she did not connect with Gervais? She rang for the porter, who appeared as if by magic, and who went to summon Mabel as if on winged feet. Merry ate a light supper, permitted Mabel to smooth her bed and turn her pillows while she herself prepared for the night, and then tried to sleep again. But she found she could not. She kept thinking about Gervais, who would not be at Belle Heloise to see Sybelle married. Their first baby—their beautiful little blonde girl who had seemed to them, as she soon also seemed to Riccardo, like the little princess in the fairy tale. The night of Sybelle's birth, her own normal and rewarding labor, the beginning of Cresside's secret and terrible travail—these were still vivid and enduring memories. How resourceful and reassuring Gervais had been all through that dreadful period, how co-operative with the doctor and nurses, how authoritative with the servants! The idea of presenting the cousins as twins had been hers, to be sure; but it was he who had carried the idea through to triumphant execution at a moment when she herself had been powerless to do so. And afterwards, how delighted they had both been with their own lovely child! How completely they had shared their enjoyment in her! The disappointment Gervais must have felt because his first-born was not a son—so soon assuaged, in any case, by the birth of Philogene—had never been voiced. And now that first-born was about to become a bride herself! Merry knew that while men were proud of their sons, their tenderest feelings were centered in their daughters. Wherever Gervais was tonight, he too must be lying awake, thinking of Sybelle, fearful lest some lack of gentleness might mar her bridal rapture, hoping against hope that her happiness with her husband might be lasting and complete. . . .

If Riccardo Tramonte himself could only have been disassociated from those dreadful parents of his! Merry could visualize exactly how they would look and act at the wedding. Netta would be literally strung with diamonds, Luigi would talk in loud boisterous tones, they would both drink too much champagne. It was bad enough to think of all this, and of having them receive the guests at Belle Heloise, with her mother-in-law and herself. But it was still worse to think about that ridiculous celebration the next day, and she could not help doing it as the train sped along. She was well-acquainted with the legend of the miraculous cure: an Italian laborer named Tony Musco, while returning from his day's work, had met a stranger who asked for a meal and a night's lodging, much as Angus Holt had done, in coming to Belle Heloise. Tony had hesitated, saying he had but little to offer at best, and adding that his home was a sorrowful one just then. His little boy, Lucien, was critically ill; the distracted father did not even know whether the child might not be dying before he himself reached home. However, the stranger quietly persisted. He was used to humble fare and poor lodgings, he said; and sometimes he had been successful in helping with just such cases as his prospective host described. As soon as he entered the Muscos' kitchen, he went to the child, whose crib had been placed there so that his mother could watch over him while she did her other work. Whatever ministrations the stranger performed were brief and seemed simple. But after the family and their unknown guest had gathered around the supper table, the little boy roused and asked for food, too. The next day he was well on the way to recovery. And as he sat looking at a dog-eared picture book, containing the highly colored prints of saints especially venerated by Italians, he pointed to one of these in great excitement crying, "Look, Mamma! There is the man who spent the night with us!"

His parents were easily convinced that the child was right—too easily, Merry said to herself, as she continued to think involuntarily of the story through the long night. By means of the most rigid economy they saved enough to build a tiny shrine; and as the news of the miraculous cure spread through the Italian settlement where they lived, money was gradually raised to import a realistic statue of the saint. It was given a place of honor in the shrine, which was eventually enlarged to form a small chapel. The local veneration of the saint became more and more general; and as an increasing number of cures were attributed to him, votive offerings of every description began to pour in—rings, bracelets, earrings, pendants, crucifixes. Their value was such that they could not be left scattered about in the shrine. A velvet stole was made to which they could be attached, and this was kept locked up in the Muscos' house, except on St. Amico's feast day, and shown only to the most honored visitors. But the Sunday after Easter it was draped around the saint's shoulders, and in all the magnificence of this adornment, he was placed on a float which was carried to the church in Donaldsonville. There he remained during High Mass, while his devotees heaped offerings around him. Then he was restored to his own shrine. But the celebration of the feast continued all the rest of the day, and its character became increasingly hilarious and decreasingly devout as it progressed.

Merry had visited this shrine once, long ago, with Gervais—indeed, now that she thought of it again, she remembered it was just before he had gone to the First World War, when they were not even formally engaged. It was he who had first told her the story of St. Amico, and half in jest, half in earnest, suggested that they should make an offering to him themselves. She had replied, also speaking lightly, that she did not think Protestant prayers would count for much, in such a place; and he had said, all right, he would make the offering by himself. But at any rate she might like to see the stole Tony kept in his house, with all the jewelry sewed on it. He had arranged for that, and secretly she thought that the Italian farmer, as well as the Italian saint, had doubtless benefited financially by the visit. Afterwards she had remembered it only as a pleasant outing which she and Gervais had shared until, some years later, Gervais told her that Luigi Tramonte, the peddler who came to Belle Heloise with stage-planks and Johnny Crooks, attributed the birth of his son to St. Amico. On this occasion, Gervais had made some slightly ribald remarks to the effect that Luigi's own persistent efforts to beget a son could possibly have something to do with it, and they had laughed over the story together. Later still, she had heard that some of Netta's most valuable jewelry had gone to adorn the stole, and that additional contributions of this character were frequently made by the Tramontes; also that they made a great point of observing St. Amico's feast day. But she had never given the matter serious thought, even during the period when she had been striving, like her husband and her mother-in-law, to break up the match between Riccardo and Sybelle. Now it forced itself upon her reluctant attention again. Why, in heaven's name, if Riccardo had to come home on leave and Sybelle must revolt against any further postponement of their marriage, did he come at just this time? Why could he not have come a month earlier or a month later? Or why, after waiting all these years to be married, could they not have waited two more days? The marriage in itself was enough of a blow to family pride. But to have the feast of St. Amico added to this! . . .

Merry finally decided that she could not stand thinking of it any longer. She rose, extracted some sleeping pills from her traveling bag, and took a double dose. Then she fell into a heavy drugged slumber, totally unlike her first natural, refreshing sleep, and did not wake again until two o'clock the next afternoon. They were just leaving Atlanta then, rather late, because they had been held up by a troop train, and Mabel had begun to be worried and had almost decided to go and see if anything were the matter when Madam finally rang. The coffee in the thermos was still hot, the carefully wrapped rolls still crisp; but Mabel could see that Madam was not especially enjoying her belated breakfast, and that she was further annoyed by the news that the train was late and losing more and more time. They would not be getting into New Orleans until midnight—until two in the morning—until four. . . . Finally the porter appeared with the information that passengers who preferred to remain in the train might do so, staying in the station until seven-thirty. Merry asked for a telegram blank and told Mabel to have the porter send a wire from Montgomery.

"I can't have my daughter hanging around that dreadful station, hour after hour, in the middle of the night," she said. "There's really no telling now when we'll get in. I don't see anything to do but to stay on the train. And that means we won't get to Belle Heloise until nearly noon on Friday! We won't have any time at all to prepare for a Saturday wedding!"

"I imagine the preparations are all very well in hand already, don't you, Madam? And it won't take me any time at all to unpack what you brought with you, once we're there. As Mr. Goldenberg said, please don't worry! I'm sure everything will be for the best in the end."

"Mabel, you said that just like a Baptist minister, condoling with a bereaved family. I ought to know. I was brought up a Baptist."

"I'm very sorry if I annoyed you, Madam. . . . Shall I take the telegram to the porter now?"

Merry was not annoyed with Mabel, specifically. But she was very much annoyed with the general situation, and the more she thought about it, the more this annoyance increased. To have the train hours and hours late, on top of everything else! To be obliged to spend another night on it! To be uncertain whether her wire would even get to Sybelle! She had sent it in care of the Estrades on Esplanade Avenue, assuming that was where her daughter would be staying, but she had neglected to inquire, during the course of their hurried telephone call, because she had been so upset. She did not dare take any more sleeping pills, for fear she would feel logy when she had to get up so early, and again she tossed restlessly about. She dozed a little after the train finally pulled into the L. & N. station a little after five, but she had not really slept soundly when Mabel came to call her, and she surveyed herself with great dissatisfaction when she was ready to get off the train.

"I look about a hundred," she said, half to herself and half to Mabel. "I don't believe my daughter'll even recognize me."

"You look beautiful, Madam, as usual. If I may say so, I've never been in service with a lady who had so much style. And when a lady has that, in addition to natural good looks . . ." Mabel's unfinished sentence implied that nothing could surpass this combination. "Here's another corsage for you, Madam," she added, producing an orchid and a pin. "The porter's kept it on ice for you. It looks just as fresh as when we left New York. I must say he's been very attentive. I've attended to tipping him, on the scale I thought you would wish. Shall I let him take the bags out now?"

In wiring, Merry had given her car number, and Sybelle was standing by the steps when her mother came out—Sybelle and a dark, extremely handsome young officer whose tunic was decorated with the Combat Infantryman's Badge, the Bronze Star and the Pacific Theater ribbon adorned with two battle stars. Rick's train had been on time, so he had reached New Orleans first! Wasn't everything wonderful, Sybelle exclaimed as she threw her arms around her mother, whom she seemed to recognize without any difficulty, in spite of Merry's fears. Now they could all go on to Baton Rouge together. Father and Mother Tramonte were also in New Orleans—of course they'd come down to meet Rick too. But they'd brought two cars, because Father Tramonte had plenty of gas, for his business, and there was never enough, at Belle Heloise! So no one would be crowded going back. Should they go over to the French Market for coffee first, or would Mummy rather go somewhere else? The Roosevelt, perhaps?

No, Merry answered hastily, she would really prefer the French Market. Besides, it would not take so long to get served there, and she supposed they ought not waste a minute if they could help it. Actually she was thinking about the Roosevelt when it used to be the Grunewald, of the suite Billy Pereira had engaged for her and Gervais when they came to New Orleans on the *John D. Grace,* of their irritation about the twin beds, of the stalactites and stalagmites in the Cave which later had so practically been transformed into the men's room, of John P. Sullivan and his powerful presence in those bright days of political promise and personal happiness. But her thoughts did not absorb her completely; she was a very competent executive now, she could observe quickly and accurately. She saw that her daughter was even more beautiful than she remembered Sybelle, and she saw how Riccardo Tramonte had managed to retain this radiant girl's love for so many years against such heavy odds. His good looks were different from Vail's, less striking without the strange contrast in coloring, but more classical; the Italian heritage was revealed here in its finest flower. He still spoke and acted with the slightly formal courtesy which had been so carefully instilled in his childhood and which had so set him apart from his rough-and-tumble American playmates, Vail among them. His smile came rather slowly, but it was still curiously gentle for a man who had been fighting and killing more than two years. He permitted Merry to take the lead in conversation, and Sybelle to make most of the answers, until the first excited greetings and exchange of news were over. But meantime he secured a table on the terrace at the Café au Monde, arranged curb service for Mabel in the shining Cadillac car, and indicated no resentment or embarrassment at being temporarily relegated to the background. After they had finished their coffee and doughnuts, which Merry enjoyed more than she would have liked to confess, he referred almost diffidently to their next plans.

"I'm going to drop off at my cousin's, the Montaginos, if you don't mind, Mrs. D'Alvery. It's right on your way, so that won't delay you at all. Then Sybelle will drive this car up, and I'll come along with my father and mother. It'll be about my last chance for a good visit with them, before I get married. I'm sure you'll have lots to talk over with Syb too. I'll be out to Belle Heloise this evening to see you both and pick up the car."

"But—" Merry protested. Surely Sybelle was counting on her fiancé's presence during the drive home! To her surprise, Sybelle seemed to understand and approve the plan.

"Rick and I talked it over together, Mummy, and decided this would be the best arrangement. He and I are going to have all kinds of time together, this next month. And I have got lots of things to say to you. It's been even longer since I saw you than since I saw Rick, and we haven't written to each other half so often, either."

Merry could find no further argument against an arrangement which seemed to have been settled before she was consulted, in any case. She sat on the back seat with Mabel, while Rick guided the gleaming car expertly through the traffic, with Sybelle beside him. The girl was neither unduly talkative nor unduly silent; she spoke to him from time to time, naturally and easily, as if they were resuming a pleasant conversation which had been interrupted only the day before. There was nothing strained or anxious in her manner, any more than there was in his. They were obviously completely happy in each other's presence, but they were not snatching greedily at long-delayed rapture, even now. Rick eventually brought the car to a stop before a very imposing residence in Metairie, where another exactly like it was already drawn up, kissed Sybelle without the slightest self-consciousness, and as she slid over into the driver's seat, asked Merry if she would not like to sit in front now. He made no suggestion that they should come in to see his parents or his cousins. But after helping Merry into the front seat, he stopped long enough on the curb to speak pleasantly to Mabel.

"I'm so glad you could come with Mrs. d'Alvery. I know how much help you'll be to her and Sybelle—well, and to all of us. And we all need you. There's lots to do."

"I am sure I am very glad if I can be of service, Major Tramonte."

Riccardo kissed Sybelle again, reiterated that he would be out that evening, and swung off up the walk. Sybelle started the car and drove away with such smoothness that Merry guessed this was by no means the first time she had handled it. The traffic was not heavy any longer, and presently Sybelle began to chat about wedding arrangements. Everything had gone very easily. They were going to decorate both the house and the church with white azaleas because that was the easiest thing to do right now, and really, nothing could be lovelier. She hoped Mummy approved the choice. Fortunately there were any number of chickens at Belle Heloise and plenty of shrimp on the market. So they could have two kinds of nice salad. Those would be the mainstay at the wedding breakfast. But Uncle Fabian had given them some champagne and there was still quite a lot in the *cave* too—she felt sure there would be plenty. Mrs. Trosclair in Plaquemine was making the cakes. No one, even in New Orleans, could make more beautiful cakes than Mrs. Trosclair. The Prescotts were going to bring them. Sybelle could hardly wait to see what Mummy had brought for her to wear. She knew everything would be beautiful.

"The wedding dress is a little unusual. I hope you'll be pleased with it, Sybelle."

"I know I shall. You have such perfect taste, Mummy."

Merry wished that Mabel had not been sitting on the back seat, where every syllable would inevitably be overheard. She had nothing to say against white azaleas and chicken salad, but she would have liked to take this first possible occasion to protest against participation in the feast of St. Amico. Sybelle went on with her happy chatter.

"We've opened up the *garçonnière*. Of course it's been closed ever since Daddy left, because we didn't need it, and it was just one more place to take care of. But we thought you'd rather be there."

"I'm sorry you bothered, if it was any trouble."

"Oh, it wasn't! It was fun. I love seeing it open again. It's had such a blank look ever since Daddy went away. Of course we wouldn't have wanted you to sleep out there all alone. But as long as you have Mabel with you——"

Sybelle turned around to direct her dazzling smile briefly on Mabel, and again the maid murmured she was only too glad if she could be of service. Merry was sorry she had not thought of saying she would prefer to have the *garçonnière* left unopened, that she would sleep in the Big House for the short time she would be at Belle Heloise. The *garçonnière* would have a blank look now, too. Its cozy and homelike atmosphere had been based on its ardent and intimate occupancy by herself and Gervais. When it had been deprived of this, it must indeed have looked blank. And Gervais had lived alone, in that blankness, for nearly six years. . . .

"You knew that Daddy had been quite sick, didn't you, Mummy? You didn't? . . . Oh, he's much better now," Sybelle added hastily, seeing Merry's startled look. "Of course if he weren't, Rick and I'd have planned to be married very quietly, instead of having this big wedding. He wasn't wounded; he caught something in Sicily. Naturally sanitary conditions are very bad there, and he didn't seem too well, even when he left Belle Heloise. Oh, nothing definite! But Daddy's aged a lot, so much more than you have, Mummy. You'd hardly know him. His hair's almost as white as *grand'mère's,* much whiter than Uncle Fabian's. He was invalided back to Africa for hospitalization. But now he's been sent to England. He's very happy about that. He thinks he's sure to run into the boys, one of them at least, sooner or later. I've had a cable from Vail, too. I didn't tell you that, either, did I?"

There were unlimited things Sybelle had not told her yet, Merry realized, wishing she did not find this news about Gervais so upsetting. She tried to ask the questions which would give her the greatest amount of information about him and everyone else in the least possible time, as they went speeding up the Airline. But the drive had never seemed so short. They were turning into the River

Road almost before she realized it and Sybelle was changing the subject, eagerly talking of something else.

"Don't you want to go into Hathaway for a moment, Mummy? I do so want to show you what's done already. Then you won't worry about my being comfortable there. And I'm afraid there won't be any time tomorrow——"

"Why yes, Sybelle, I'm perfectly willing to go there, if you want me to. But I really think I ought to say again——"

"Wait until you've seen it, won't you, Mummy, before you say anything?"

"Very well."

Merry remained rather pointedly silent until they swung into the *allée* at Hathaway. At least a dozen men were working on the grounds. Nearly all were elderly, and those who were not either walked with a limp or revealed some other physical disability; but obviously they were accomplishing wonders. The long rank grass had already been mown with a scythe; now it was being cut with a lawn mower and the edges of the driveway were being clipped. White paint was being applied to the dingy façade in sweeping if unskilled strokes. The center hall through which they went in had been thoroughly cleaned. Sybelle led the way proudly past the library and the White Ball Room, which were still closed, into the large dining room, where recent and thorough cleaning was again evident.

"We're going to use this for a general living room while we're camping out," she informed her mother. "And we're going to sleep in the little room off it, that must have been a children's dining room, or something like that, once. Just for now, I mean. Of course later on we're going to have one of the beautiful upstairs bedrooms. Look, Mummy, there's a lavatory right here and Mr. Tramonte's had a shower put in! The plumbing still works and so does the kitchen stove. It's really wonderful, after all these years. Oh, there's the new Coolerator! It looks just like an electric refrigerator, doesn't it? And tomorrow morning some more furniture's coming in!"

To Merry everything looked antiquated and barren and tasteless, but she could see that in Sybelle's eyes it was beautiful already, and as a matter of fact, she knew that it would be in time, and that meanwhile, it really was livable. Men and women were both working inside the house, under the capable direction of an enormous Negress with a beaming face, whom the girl presented to her mother as Be-a-trice Washington.

"Be-a-trice is going to be our cook," she told Merry. "She's just as good a cook as Carmelite. And she has a niece who's going to be the house girl. Where is Thuger, Be-a-trice?"

"She's hangin' things out on de line, Miss Sybelle, what she's washed good. Does yo' want Ah should call her fo' yo'?"

"No, not just now, thank you, Be-a-trice. My mother'll see her tomorrow. You'll both be over at Belle Heloise then."

"Us sho' will, Miss Sybelle."

"Isn't she something right out of a story book?" Sybelle whispered to her mother as they went down the beautiful curving stone steps, which, Merry noticed, had already been cleared of encroaching vines. "I have to be careful to call her Be-a-trice, though, not Beatrice. She says she'll leave if she's called Beatrice, because that isn't really her name. And Thuger comes from Sugar. That's what her folks called her when she was a little girl, but she couldn't pronounce her S's, so she called herself Thuger and now that's *her* real name. Father Tramonte got them both for me. He says it's all nonsense to say it's impossible to find servants any more. He says of course you can find them if you know where to look and if you offer them the right wages. He does know where to look and of course he offers the right wages. You see how it's going to be, Mummy, everything made just as easy and pleasant for me as it was for you."

"I'll admit that wonders have been done on this place already, Sybelle. But I'd still be happier if you were going to spend your honeymoon over at the Pass, or some place like that. And I've been wanting to talk to you about——"

"Can't we do it by and by, Mummy? I really think we ought to get home now. *Grand'mère's* been waiting for us a long time, and I want to see all the lovely things you've brought me before Rick gets out, and make sure the wedding dress fits and all that. . . . And you want to get settled in the *garçonnière*——"

Merry did not want to get settled in the *garçonnière*. Her dread of going there had been one of the main reasons why she had consented to stopping at Hathaway, and now she asked Sybelle if there were time to stop at the cemetery. Why, they would take time, Sybelle said; but perhaps Mummy would prefer to go there alone. She and Mabel would sit in the car and get a little better acquainted. Merry delayed as long as she could in the family lot, less because she wanted to linger there, once she had assured herself of the beautiful care given to Franchot's grave, than because the nearer she got to Belle Heloise the more she dreaded her arrival. It was far less strained than she had expected, however. Fabian and Cresside and Frances Belle were there already, awaiting her arrival; her mother and Miss Mittie had come over from the storehouse, so she did not have to see her mother-in-law alone. Besides, Madame d'Alvery's greeting left nothing to be desired; it was dignified, it was courteous, it was unreproachful. Again Merry felt, as she had felt in watching Sybelle and Riccardo together earlier in the morning, that conversation was progressing as if it had been taken up where it had been casually left off the day before. Only the underlying reason was different. In the case of Sybelle and Riccardo, their accord was so complete that it eliminated time and distance easily. In the case of her mother-in-law and herself, they had always been so far apart that more separation did not matter. Never, in all the years she had lived at Belle Heloise, had Merry been treated with more deliberate courtesy; never, not even when she came there as a bride, had she felt so completely like an outsider.

In spite of this feeling, which increased rather than lessened as the hours went on, the afternoon passed pleasantly and quickly. There were so many people in the *garçonnière* with Merry that she did not have time to brood over its blankness. Everything she brought with her was quickly unpacked and tried on, with repeated exclamations of delight. Sybelle said that the wedding dress with the forget-me-nots was just something out of this world; and how wonderfully the pale-blue dress for the maid of honor and the dresses of deeper blue for the bridesmaids blended with it! And what lingerie and laces! What hostess gowns and sports suits! Why, there must be just as much as ever to select from in the New York stores! Well, not quite, Merry said; but if you knew how to go about it, you could still manage to keep properly dressed. She was glad everything fitted so well. Mabel could make slight alterations very nicely, if necessary, but none seemed to be indicated. Instead she could start repacking Sybelle's things right away, except for what would be needed the next day. . . .

It was while Mabel was doing this repacking, with her usual skill and dispatch, that Merry noticed an unusual look on the maid's face. Her expression was not exactly mutinous; but somehow it had tightened and hardened. Merry took advantage of a moment when all the others had gone trooping into the little kitchen to get cooling drinks and she could speak to Mabel privately.

"Is anything the matter, Mabel?"

Mabel's expression grew tighter and harder. "Doubtless I should have expected something of the sort, Madam," she said, and her voice was tight and hard too. "But there seems to be no proper provision on this place for a personal maid."

"I don't think I understand. My mother-in-law's always had a personal maid. Creassy was mine until our old cook, Lou Ida, died, and then Creassy took her place, because I wasn't here any more."

"I am sorry to be obliged to remind you, Madam, that you are speaking of Negroes. I should not have supposed this would be necessary, in the case of a lady like you. Did you expect me to eat in the kitchen with them?"

"I'm afraid I didn't think about it at all, Mabel. I've had so many things to think of at once. But you don't have to, if you don't want to."

"There is no servants' hall, Madam. Only the kitchen and the butler's pantry. I went without my lunch, after that long train trip, too, when I was most uncomfortable, though trying my best to do everything for your comfort——"

"Well, I'm willing to do everything I can, in reason, for your comfort. You could have eaten in the *garçonnière* if you wanted to.

660

The kitchen here is ready for use. All the family, except myself, is out there now."

"I am willing to eat in this kitchen, Madam, since there is no servants' hall on the place, and since it is only a matter of a few days. But one of the Negroes must be instructed to bring my meals to me here."

"We're rather short-handed at Belle Heloise, for the moment, and we're getting ready for a big wedding on very short notice. Couldn't you get your own meals, and my morning coffee, the few days we'll be here?"

"I am a personal maid, Madam. Not a cook. You knew that when you engaged me. And I am sure you can't say, or any of my other employers either, that as a personal maid I haven't always given satisfaction."

Merry turned abruptly and walked out of the room, leaving Mabel in front of the open suitcases. Rick had just arrived with Drina Montagino and the drinks were ready; everyone else had gone into the living room to enjoy them. But apparently no one had thought of calling her.

"I'm sorry to bring up anything unpleasant at this stage," she said. She saw that the others had suddenly remembered her and that they were chagrined at their oversight. They were trying to make immediate amends for it by crowding around her with proferred chairs and glasses. "No thanks, not right now," she said, waving them back. "I just came in to ask if any of you would drive Mabel into town, so that she could catch the next train for New Orleans. I find she doesn't fit in here. She's an outsider. It's so unpleasant for her that she's going to make it unpleasant for everyone else, if she stays. No amount of efficiency could make up for that. We'll be much better off without her."

Of course they would be glad to remove the disturbing element from the scene, Fabian and Cresside hastened to assure Merry. That is, if she were certain . . . They gathered that she had grown quite dependent on Mabel, and some adjustment ought to be possible. . . . She was quite certain, Merry said crisply, and, within an hour, Mabel, who had made her life easy for her so long, had passed abruptly out of it, and Merry had sought out Creassy, who was already starting the preparations for a big company dinner.

"I've sent my maid away, Creassy," she began tentatively. Creassy sniffed.

"Does yo' mean dat po' white trash yo' done bring down wif yo' from de East?" she inquired, without pausing in the act of dismembering chickens for frying.

"Yes, if that's what you call her."

"Ain't nothin' else Ah kin call her. Our own white folks, dey know better dan to treat us lak dat po' white trash done. Anyways, Ah is yo' maid, Miss Merry."

"I was afraid I'd been gone so long that perhaps——"

"Shucks, Miss Merry, yo' knows better dan dat. When anyone comes to Belle Heloise, dey belongs here for always, no matter effin dey does go away, once in a while. Doesn't yo' think de Colonel, he's gwine to belong here, after he gits home from de wars?"

"Yes, but——"

"An' Mr. Vail and Mr. Philogene?"

"Yes, but that's different."

"Ah don't see no difference. Lethe, she can help wid de cookin'. Be-a-trice and Thuger, deys comin' over from Hathaway, too. My, my, don't it seem good, Miss Merry, Hathaway open again and quality fixin' to live in it? Us'll manage wid de work. What yo' need I should do fo' yo' right now, Miss Merry?"

"Well, for one thing, there's quite a lot of pressing to be done——"

"Yo' lay yo' dresses out on yo' bed, Miss Merry, lak yo' allus done, an' yo'll find 'em ready soon as yo' need 'em. Us is all mighty glad to have yo' back. Only trouble was, dat white trash yo' brung wid yo'."

Creasy's feeling seemed to be general. Rick and Sybelle had both been very courteous to Mabel, because it was their way to be courteous to everyone. But it appeared that even they had harbored doubts as to whether she would fit in. She seemed more suited to New York than to Belle Heloise. They were glad she had gone. Merry, secretly wondering whether the family did not feel that she too was suited to New York rather than to Belle Heloise, in spite of Creassy's reassuring words, tried hard to feel at home and failed. Supper was a rather hurried meal because the bridal party had to get into St. Agnes' for the rehearsal. Rick and Sybelle were both going to Confession at the same time, and wondered whether anyone else wanted to go too. Neither of them looked at Merry, specifically, as they said this, but she also did some wondering. Did they realize how long it was since she had gone to Confession? She did not see how they possibly could. But there was a short and slightly awkward silence, which Madame d'Alvery brought to an end by saying that since she was saving her strength for the wedding itself, she would not go to town that evening, and doubtless Merry would like to wait and go to Confession when she did. Perhaps Merry would rather not even go to rehearsal, when it came to that. She must be very tired, after her long journey and the trying scene with that impudent English maid . . .

Merry would not have supposed it could be possible for her to feel as grateful to her mother-in-law as she did at that moment. She would be very glad if they would excuse her, she said. After all, Cresside had told them she would be at the church that evening, she could attend to any last-minute details; and as soon as the jubilant bridal party had started into town, Merry went wearily back to the *garçon-nière* and climbed into the bed which Creassy had already opened, after removing the dresses that needed pressing. Merry had never slept in that bed alone before, and as she lay down in it now, the thoughts of Gervais, which she had been trying to dismiss ever since her train pulled out of Charlottesville, crowded relentlessly in upon her. It had been a shock to her to learn that he had been so ill, that he had aged so much, and that she had not even known of this; it was unexpectedly harder than she had foreseen, not only to occupy alone this room which he and she had shared, but to miss his familiar figure moving about the plantation. Was there, in spite of modern skepticism and modern evasions, a finality about marriage which was inescapable? This had not occurred to her before. But for the last twenty-four hours she had involuntarily dwelt on the thought. She ceased to worry about Sybelle and her daughter's share in the celebration of St. Amico because she was more and more concerned about her husband and her relation to him. . . .

She fell into a deep sleep at last and did not wake until Creassy touched her on the shoulder and spoke to her. Then she sat up with a start, to see that the shades had already been raised and the mosquito bar lifted, and that sunlight was streaming across her bed.

"Good gracious, Creassy, what time is it?"

"Don't yo' worry about de time, Miss Merry. Yo' was plum tuckered out. Yo' needed yo' rest. But Ah jes' figured Ah couldn't let yo' sleep no longer, effin yo' was to git to de weddin'. Here is yo' coffee, and Ah's gwine bring yo' somethin' else soon as yo's had yo' bath and got dressed. All de others, dey's finished a big breakfast and fixin' to go to de church."

"Why, it can't be all that late! But it looks like a beautiful day, Creassy."

"Yessum, Miss Merry. Such days is well accepted."

"That's what you used to say to me when I came here a bride myself. I remember how I loved hearing you. I'd never heard anyone say it before."

"Us all says it, Miss Merry. Thuger, she gwine be sayin' it to Miss Sybelle mighty soon. Yo' wuz a beautiful bride, Miss Merry, Ah wuz proud to wait on yo', and Mr. Gervais sure did set his eyeteeth by yo'. Now us had got us another beautiful bride and Ah hopes us gets two or three more. Can't be too many d'Alvery brides to suit me or too many d'Alvery babies comin' along to suit Dinah. No mam!"

Creassy departed, leaving Merry to drink her coffee and to think of the days when her maid had brought not only that first cup which she drank alone, after Gervais had already gone out into the fields, but also of that later mid-morning service, when he returned to their room, and they breakfasted in a leisurely way together. She remembered too the skill with which Creassy had kept the shuttered bedroom dark and quiet, that first summer, so that she could sleep and sleep, storing up the strength which had made Sybelle such a healthy happy baby. And now history was about to repeat itself. Yet not exactly. Sybelle's husband would not come in, every morning, to drink coffee with her, because after his short leave, he would be back in the Pacific somewhere, fighting. He would not be safely at her side. Sybelle was not as fortunate as she had been. Her husband had been with her always. It was she who had left . . .

Well, as if there were any time to be thinking about that! She pushed the bedclothes impatiently aside, made a hasty toilet, and hurried over to the Big House. She met Sybelle coming out of the dining room, where the last touches had just been given to the table festively prepared for the wedding breakfast.

"Oh, Mummy, I'm so glad to see you! I was afraid you wouldn't be here in time to help me dress, and of course I wanted you to, especially since it was you who brought me all those lovely things. Come on upstairs, quick! Joyeuse and *grand'mère* are dressing already."

"Then we have a moment to ourselves, Sybelle, and there are one or two things I'd like very much——"

"That time-honored 'little talk'? Now Mummy! You ought to know that went out before the First World War, along with the sort of brides who needed it!"

In spite of herself, Merry smiled. But she spoke seriously.

"No, I didn't mean that sort of a little talk. But I did mean another sort. I want to say——"

"You want to say again you don't think we ought to spend our honeymoon at Hathaway. Well, you spent yours here, didn't you, with *grand'mère* and Aunt Cresside right in the house? And I bet you were happy just the same! I should think the fact that Rick and I would have the house to ourselves, even if it isn't in perfect order, would a good deal more than make up for not having two other women cluttering up the scene."

"I realize it is too late for me to prevent you from going to Hathaway, Sybelle, and as I said before, I'm ready to admit that it has been made surprisingly habitable, under all the circumstances. But I do want to ask you, for my sake, not to go to that absurd celebration tomorrow."

"And I was going to ask you, for mine, if you wouldn't go yourself. Joyeuse is coming, so you wouldn't be alone. She realizes how much it would mean to me if my family were represented."

"*Joyeuse!* That hard-headed young scientist!"

"Yes. But she knows the Tramontes aren't hard-headed scientists. She knows they're very devout Catholics who accept miracles unquestioningly—well, credulously, if you want to put it that way. But she also knows how much it would mean to them, and to me, if some of the d'Alverys were at that celebration. The Tramontes are trying mighty hard to meet our standards. I think we might try to meet some of theirs. Because they've succeeded better than we have, so far. Not just by giving Hathaway to Rick and me, but by everything they've done. It's too bad you didn't go to the rehearsal with us last night,

Mummy, because they had a little party for us afterwards that was simply tops. And the loving kindness they've shown me—well, I couldn't talk about it without crying. We haven't time to talk about anything more now, anyway, and I've said all I can, all I'm going to. But I'll look for you tomorrow, Mummy. If I don't see you, something's going to be gone between us that we'll never get back."

Something's going to be gone between us that we'll never get back! Why did Sybelle have to say that, at the end of her strangely assorted remarks, part slangy, part stubborn, part exalted. The words kept ringing through Merry's tired but rebellious head even during the wedding ceremony, all through the reception, in the quiet and empty hours that followed the light-hearted departure of the bride and groom to the adjoining plantation. She was aware, with pride, that Sybelle was the most beautiful bride she had ever seen. Aware, with relief, that the Tramontes were impressive in appearance and dignified in manner. Aware, with satisfaction, that no function at Belle Heloise had ever passed off more smoothly and agreeably than this wedding breakfast. But all the time, through her awareness, she kept hearing those words: *Something's going to be gone between us that we'll never get back.*

She stayed in the Big House until the last jubilant guest had departed, until everything in the deserted rooms had been restored to its accustomed order, until Madame d'Alvery and Mrs. Randall and Miss Mittie were through discussing the details of the wedding and had gone wearily but elatedly to bed. Then she stepped out on the front gallery and looked down the walk towards the iron gate. It was still too early for the full bloom of the yucca which made the traditional bridal arch; but some of the amaryllis was already out, and Sybelle and Rick had followed the time-honored family custom of newly married couples by getting out of their car at the gate, instead of taking the sharp right-angle turn and driving all the way to the house. Merry could see her daughter yet, in her exquisite array of blue and white, and Rick in his uniform and his decorations, as they walked up between the scarlet lilies. They had stopped to kiss each other—first just inside the gate, then halfway up the walk, finally at the demilune in front of the house. Meanwhile they had been laughing and talking with each other and with the pretty young girls and the personable young men that followed them. Now they were alone, locked in each other's arms, exultant not only in their present rapture, but in the glad certainty that nothing on earth could prevail to lessen their love for each other. Merry had felt the same exaltation and the same glad certainty once, in her love for her husband, and now . . .

The front door opened, and Joyeuse came out. She had vetoed the suggestion of a tall evening at the Heidelberg with the bridesmaids and ushers, after the departure of the bride and groom. For

crying out loud, hadn't they made enough whoopee at the Tramontes'
the night before? She had, anyway. She was dead on her feet after
all this hullabaloo, and she had to get up early Sunday morning. . . .
She did not care any more about frills and furbelows than she did
about drinking and dancing. Merry saw that she had taken off her
bridesmaid's dress and put on a plain white smock, which she wore
with an air of ease and relief. She did not even care greatly about
any special person, beyond feeling moderate family affection, though
she had the d'Alvery gift of attracting young and old of both sexes
to her side. She was much more interested in her work. She would
be glad to get back to it, quietly, Monday morning. Meanwhile she
must keep her word to Syb and see what she could do with Mom.

"Hello there! Taking a look over the premises, now you can do it
in peace?"

"Yes. It's very beautiful here, Joy."

"It always was, if you remember. I reckon it always will be,"
Joyeuse said practically. "Have you made up your mind about tomorrow, Mom? Because if we're going to that shrine we have to get a
pretty early start."

"What time?"

"Well, the procession leaves the shrine at nine, so we have to be
there before that. I reckon it means a six o'clock call."

"Rick and Sybelle will have to get up at six tomorrow!"

"Yeah. Tomorrow. Not any of the other mornings while Rick's
home though. I reckon they know all about that good old French
saying: *'On se lève tard pendant la lune de miel.'* They've probably
enlarged on that to suit themselves: *'Et on se couche tôt.'* However,
that's beyond the point. Of course they could have spent tonight in
Donaldsonville instead of getting up at six tomorrow; but if you'd
tried that lately, you'd realize they were a lot more sensible to stick
to Hathaway. The hotel dining room's closed, and the First and Last
Chance Café is fourteen blocks away. Either they wouldn't have had
any bridal breakfast or they'd have to go a far piece for it. Well, we
should worry, especially as they didn't chance that. But we don't seem
to be getting anywhere, talking like this. I'm ready to hit the hay and
I should think you would be. Do I call you at six or don't I?"

"I'm afraid I couldn't make it, Joy."

"Of course it's up to you. Good night."

*Something's going to be gone between us that we'll never get
back.* Something *more*—Franchot's dead, Gervais is overseas, and
now Sybelle . . . Sybelle who's so loyal and loving, who's never let
anything come between herself and Rick and never will, who hasn't
spoken reproachfully or acted resentfully because I went away from
her father and away from her when they needed me so much, but
who says that now . . . Says it and means it . . .

Joyeuse had already gone into the house, she was halfway up the
666

stairs. In another minute she would have disappeared, because she never stopped to salute the Spanish statue. Merry ran after her.

"Joy, I think perhaps I can make it after all. I think you'd better call me at six."

Joyeuse came back down the stairs. She had been courteous to her mother ever since Merry's arrival, she had made no embarrassing allusions to the past or permitted any awkward silences to come between them. But hitherto she had given no sign of being glad to see her. Now she put her arms around her mother and hugged her.

"That's the spirit, Mom!" she said, her voice joyous, like her name. "That's the way for a great girl like you to crash through!"

Again it was a perfect spring morning, the kind that Creassy said was "well accepted." As Joyeuse and Merry motored down the River Road on the West Side below Donaldsonville, towards the shrine, they could see the sights and hear the sounds that always continued to proclaim spring so buoyantly. The thistle blossoms were pink and cream, and the levee was white with clover; cattle and horses and sheep were all grazing peacefully along it. Merry thought she had never seen so many calves and colts and lambs, frolicking beside their mothers. She said so to Joyeuse.

"I wish they didn't have so many cockleburs on them. Look at the tails on those poor sheep! I'd like to stop and pick the burs out."

"I noticed that Maudie still gets covered with cockleburs too, Joy. I tried to get some of them off her, the afternoon I came. But she wouldn't let me touch her. She growled at me."

"She won't, after you've been here a few days longer. You don't have to hurry back to New York, do you, Mom?"

"I ought to be back there by the nineteenth. I have a reservation out of New Orleans on Saturday."

"Oh!"

"But of course I could cancel it."

"Well, I hope you will. Hang around until after Rick's gone, if you can. Syb's going to miss him dreadfully at first. You could be a lot of help to her, fixing up the house. And she's sure she'll have a baby straight off. If she does she'll want you more than ever."

"I hadn't thought of all that. I'll see what I can arrange."

Joyeuse was turning from the highway into a narrow dirt road with small dilapidated houses on either side of it and a small zinc chapel at the end of it. Immediately in front of them was an open truck, laden with staring white plaster statues of St. Amico, which apparently were intended for sale at the shrine. Ahead of the truck was a bus, filled with jolly looking Negroes wearing uniforms and clasping brass musical instruments to their sturdy breasts. As Joyeuse drew up behind them, they jumped out of the bus, ranged themselves on one side of the road, and began to play "America the Beautiful" with great gusto. A considerable crowd had collected already. The larger part of it was outside the shrine, but the open door revealed an interior, lighted with dozens of candles, where all the stiff little wooden pews were occupied. American flags had been attached crosswise to the wooden supports of the little porch, and at the rear of the nave a toothless old woman was vigorously pulling a bell rope, mumbling as she did so, and occasionally turning towards the occupants of the nearest pews with impatient ejaculations; she was evidently annoyed because the procession was so slow in starting. Most of the congregation was kneeling in prayer, and paid no attention to her; but occasionally a pretty, smartly dressed young woman, who called her grandma, rose and endeavored to placate her. Occasionally also a worshiper left a pew to slip an offering at the base of St. Amico's statue, which had already been moved from its accustomed position near the high altar and placed on a float in the center of the aisle. It was adorned with the long velvet stole to which the previous votive offerings were fastened, and among them Merry could see the coral earrings and necklace which Netta Tramonte had worn as a young woman. Netta herself was seated in the front pew on the left with Luigi; Sybelle and Riccardo were beside them. It might have been a family group of long standing. Merry, feeling that all her sophistication was not proof against such a sight, and the feelings it had aroused, turned to Joyeuse almost helplessly.

"Do you think we have to go in?" she whispered.

"Yes, I think we do, just for a minute. I can see two vacant seats in that last pew. The procession's bound to start pretty soon, Mom. You won't have to stay there but a minute."

They went in, making all the proper motions—genuflecting beside the pew, crossing themselves as they knelt inside it, bowing their heads like the others; but it was Joyeuse who led in doing all this and Merry who followed. She did not try to pray; she could not. However, she knelt for a respectful period and when she rose from her knees she saw that the procession had already started. A cross-bearer was at the head of it. Then came the float on which the image of St. Amico was mounted, with Riccardo at the right of the statue and his father at the left, in front of the other men who were helping to carry it. They had already lifted the float to their shoulders, but Merry could still see the young officer's decorations, and his beautifully molded features above his burden. There was a new look in his eyes, joyous and rewarded and full of thanksgiving, and Merry knew that this look had come there because of Sybelle, not because of the saint. But he did not turn to look at his bride as he went down the aisle, carrying the sacred burden. He held himself very erect, facing straight ahead, and so did all the men with him. Though his exceptional grace and his military uniform made him outstanding among them, they were all good-looking men, Merry noticed, and all remarkably well-dressed. A second smaller float, on which statues of the Virgin and St. Joseph were mounted, followed after the first; this smaller one was carried by girls and women in white dresses, Netta and Drina and Sybelle among them. Two of the girls held up the procession long enough to wipe off the images with clean cloths before they started. Then they all passed from the shrine, accompanied by some smug-faced little altar boys carrying huge decorated candles, and immediately the sound of the bell was drowned in the music of the brass band. The pretty young woman, who, several times before, had tried vainly to placate the indignant old bell-ringer, now did so successfully. They hurried out together, in the wake of the altar boys, and the crowd that had filled the chapel and waited outside fell in line too.

"What is our next move?" Merry inquired, turning to Joyeuse. She felt that Joyeuse had taken charge, and she was glad of it; she herself had no sense of initiative at the moment, no sense of anything except unreality.

"Why, we just get back into the car and follow the procession to Donaldsonville. Then we sit through High Mass at the Church of the Ascension. There's nothing complicated about that."

As Joyeuse expressed this, it did not seem as if there were. But Merry still could not rid herself of the sense of unreality caused by the fact that she was following this procession and that her daughter and her son-in-law were taking part in it. She saw some of the cattle on the levee turn to look wonderingly at it as it passed, and stifled a small hysterical laugh; she felt just as she imagined the cows did. She saw clusters of Negroes, loitering in front of the cabins along the way, staring like the cows but smirking, too. She felt the same kinship with them. The band had run out of patriotic tunes and had begun to play jazz. Some of the women were dragging small unwilling children after them. One was nursing a baby as she walked. The day was beginning to grow warm, though it was still so early in the morning, and some of the men in the procession were mopping their streaming faces as they went along, panting audibly and giving vent to their feelings in language which could not, by any stretch of the imagination, be considered devout. But Riccardo, carrying more than his share of the heavy burden, was still going quietly and calmly ahead without turning or stopping, his bearing erect and calm. Merry had almost lost sight of him, in the distance. But she knew that the sunlight was still playing over the bright ribbons on his tunic and that the joyous exalted look still shone from his eyes.

By the time Merry and Joyeuse reached the Church of the Ascension, Mass was already under way. It had taken them some time to find a parking place, as all the space around the church was already occupied by other cars, except that pre-empted by the Negro band, which stood patiently awaiting the return procession. But an usher conducted them to seats which had apparently been held for them, as these were immediately beside the statue. It now stood in the center of the nave. The votive offerings on the stole glittered in the light that streamed down from the windows; the pile of crisp bills and printed prayers on the platform surrounding it was growing higher and more unsteady by the minute. Worshipers kept leaving their seats to bring others—a five-dollar bill clipped to an illustrated form-prayer or merely a humble scribbled petition. Merry watched the pews in front of her, hoping against hope that none of the Tramontes would do this, fearing unutterably that they might. At last, to her horrified amazement, she saw Sybelle slip out of the front pew and come back to the statue, a sheet of paper in her hand. She laid the paper on the pile, knelt down for a minute and then returned to the place where she had been sitting with the Tramontes. She did not look at her mother. But Merry could not help looking at the paper. The pile on which it lay was uneven, because it had already been heaped so high, and the single sheet was very light. Presently it was caught in the current of one of the large electric fans at the front of the church, as several others had been. It fluttered back and forth for a moment, and then fell to the floor of the aisle. Both Merry and the woman kneeling at the end of the pew in front of her automatically leaned over to pick it up. But Merry's hand reached it first, and still acting instinctively rather than voluntarily, she glanced at the words that were written on it.

"I am asking for a favor too, St. Amico," she read. "I want my mother. I need her. My father wants and needs her too. We all do. Please make her feel in her heart——"

Merry did not read any further. She folded the sheet of paper, and rising, slipped it securely under the growing pile which rose so unsteadily around the statue. When she had placed it so there would be no further danger that it might blow away, she returned to her pew and knelt down again. But this time she covered her face with her hands so that no one would see the tears which streamed from under her closed eyelids as she prayed.

In Sybelle's petition was epitomized everything she had known, but declined to acknowledge, since her return to Belle Heloise, everything she had felt and fought against feeling. Now she could no longer prevail against this knowledge and this emotion. She no longer wanted or tried to do so. Tardily she realized that she was a small part of something infinitely greater than the sum of all those present at this celebration, and for the first time since she had been taken into the Church of Rome, she understood the significance of its ritual and the meaning of its miracles. With the understanding came humbleness and contrition and overwhelming joy.

An hour later, when Merry went out of the church in the wake of the triumphant procession, she saw Mr. Goldenberg standing in the portal. He immediately started towards her.

"Don't look so surprised," he said. "I told you I was going to make it if I could. I didn't get here for the wedding, but I did get here for this service. And it was worth the effort. I don't know when I've been so deeply touched as I was when I saw the procession moving up the aisle of this church, with Riccardo Tramonte and his bride both in it. I congratulate you, Mrs. d'Alvery—on your son-in-law and on your daughter."

"Mr. Goldenberg," Merry said, and stopped. People were hurrying past them, but at any moment someone might pause and interrupt them. The band had already resumed its activities. It was playing "My Country 'Tis of Thee," in jazz. No time and no place could have been more inappropriate for an important statement. "Mabel didn't stay," Merry ended lamely. "She didn't fit in. So I had to send her back, the same day we got here."

"Yes, I heard. I hope you don't mind too much."

"No, I don't mind too much. I realized she was an outsider. I realize I am, too."

"Well, that's more serious. You'll have to do something about that, won't you?"

"Yes. I'll have to stay. I'll have to learn how to fit in again. Because I'm—" Suddenly the words came with a rush. "I find I'm wanted and needed here, Mr. Goldenberg. I've got to be with my own people. I can't go back to New York."

"I knew you never would, Merry," he said gently.

CHAPTER LI

MADAME D'ALVERY herself suggested having the party, early in the summer after Sybelle was married.

It was so long since they had given one, she said, that they would forget how if they did not do it presently. Of course it would not be the kind of party they used to have at Belle Heloise—the service and the foodstuffs were both lacking for that, not to mention the masculine company needed to enliven any festivity. But the *cave* still contained a few fine old wines, and, thank God, coffee rationing at least was a thing of the past—that *had* been a hardship while it lasted, not having it served nine times a day! The supply of festive linen was still adequate too, thanks to the way brides were outfitted in Madame d'Alvery's youth and her mother's and her grandmother's; the less said about present-day trousseaux the better, especially as neither Cresside nor Sybelle had given the family any time for preparation, and this unseemly haste, added to current shortages, naturally complicated a situation which she had been powerless to improve. For the party they would use one of her own damask tablecloths, monogrammed by the nuns. She had always thought that old silver looked especially well on plain damask, and certainly there was plenty of silver; there had been no pilfering Yankees in this war. As for the best porcelain, she had found most of that still unbroken when she last counted the plates, though some of it had been chipped, betraying the carelessness in handling that one must expect, now that Selah was no longer on hand to take care of it. But still, enough of the Sèvres service . . . She realized that the supply of flowers was low right now, but snow-on-the-mountains and Indian shot made an effective combination and there were still a few roses. Besides, they might even break off some branches of the luxuriant crepe myrtle for such an occasion, though usually she was opposed to taking anything from a tree . . .

"Do you think anyone is in the mood for a party, these days, Madame Mère?" Merry asked. "I don't. I know I'm not."

"No. But perhaps the mood would change. There would be no harm in trying."

"I don't know just what we'd serve at a party, either."

"My dear Merry, if you'll forgive me for saying so, you sounded very like your mother at that moment, instead of like yourself. I always used to admire your resourcefulness very much. I hope you have not lost it, during your protracted sojourn in large cities." Merry flushed slightly and Madame d'Alvery continued with assurance. "I do not think anyone has ever left Belle Heloise hungry yet and I do not think anyone ever will. We have every sort of fowl on the place and every sort of vegetable. We have butter and cream and eggs. Not that this is any special credit to us. Persons who live on plantations and do not have all that, should blame only themselves. On the other hand, I feel that guests who could not be satisfied with what we can offer would be very captious, under all the circumstances."

"We haven't any sugar," Merry said rather heatedly. "At least, we haven't any except the canning sugar, and we haven't a right to use that for a party."

"I agree with you, my dear Merry, and if the sugar situation were not so tragic, it would be humorous. When I think of the acres of over-quota cane Gervais was forced to destroy, when I think of the supplies, even from what we were allowed to produce, that were permitted to spoil in warehouses, because Yankees cannot be taught that sugar is a perishable commodity, it makes my blood boil. But surely we can squeeze out enough sugar for the coffee, and if not, Cresside will come to our rescue. I am afraid the real difficulty lies less with the commodities at our command than with your own disinclination for any kind of a celebration, Merry."

Madame d'Alvery had hit uncomfortably close to the mark and for a moment Merry was silent. She was not content to know that from latest official reports Gervais was recuperating satisfactorily from his wounds, that he had been awarded the Purple Heart, that before long he would be sent home, and that when he came he would come to stay. She needed to see him and feel him in the flesh, she needed to pour out her heart to him, bridging all the years of their separation, before she would be appeased. And until appeasement came, there could be no rejoicing either. But she tried, after gathering her forces, to answer with renewed spirit; recognizing that the antagonism between her mother-in-law and herself had never before been so great, or with so much reason, she declined to countenance it by bowing before it.

"When do you want to have this celebration, Madame Mère? On the Fourth of July?"

"Certainly not. I do not see any reason why we should celebrate the fall of Vicksburg, merely because professional politicians like to proclaim that there is no longer any North or any South or any East or any West."

For the first time in many months, Merry burst out laughing, heartily and spontaneously. Her mother-in-law regarded her somewhat superciliously until she recognized that Merry's objections to the party had been dissipated by this unforced and unfeigned evidence of gaiety. Then her own expression relaxed and she smiled in her turn.

"Now, not very originally, you will call me the last surviving unreconstructed rebel, I suppose," she said, still speaking rather loftily. "And remind me that persons, even in the South, think of the Fourth of July in connection with the Declaration of Independence, and not in connection with the fall of Vicksburg. However, since we seem to be exchanging reminders, let me recall to you the fact that to this day Vicksburg has never celebrated the so-called Glorious Fourth and I am not ashamed that I am still in sympathy with my kinsfolk there. Let us have the party on either the third or the fifth, Merry, and let us consider it a celebration of Gervais' wonderful escape and extraordinary progress towards recovery, and of the recognition his bravery has received. Suppose we start making out our guest list immediately."

It appeared that, after all, the celebration Madame d'Alvery had in mind did not run to large proportions. She wanted to ask Cresside and Frances Belle and Sybelle, all of whom she accused of neglecting her on account of their personal preoccupations, which she admitted was excusable in Sybelle's case but not in the others'. She also wanted to invite Mrs. Prescott and Susannah, whom she had not seen in a long time. She did not approve of the lengths to which Vail's courtship, which had begun so auspiciously, had now been prolonged. She felt as if there were some mystery about the procrastination, and she thought, if she could see the Prescotts, she might get to the bottom of the matter; she assumed they must have enough gasoline to make at least one trip from New Roads to Belle Heloise. Furthermore, she wished to ask Mrs. Harvey Lawrason, to whom she had taken a great and unexpected liking, and whom she called by her first name, which was Pearl. She had no other suggestions. She would be glad to have some from Merry, if her daughter-in-law had anyone else in mind. Naturally she expected that Miss Mittie and Mrs. Randall would join them; and she would be glad to have Fabian and Mr. Prescott also, though since they would be the only gentlemen, perhaps they would prefer not to come. . . .

"Punt O'Malley might be in town. He is, about once in ten days, you know."

"Punt O'Malley?"

"Yes. The master of the *McDougall,* Frances Belle's boy friend. And of course Joyeuse always has cohorts she can call in."

"I am not interested in Punt O'Malley, or in the cohorts, as you call them, around Joyeuse."

"Well, you weren't interested in Rick either, you know, and now you admit——"

"I really do not care to discuss this any longer at present, Merry. I find I am rather tired. We will have a dove party, and I shall be glad to have you add two or three more ladies, if you would care to. We will have Creole gumbo, and roast duck with pecan dressing and kumquat preserves, and rice and okra and green corn with peppers, and an aspic salad, and fresh peach ice cream, sweetened with saccharine. As I said before, I do not think that anyone will leave the table hungry."

There was certainly no evidence that anyone had. In fact, as the group moved from the dining room to the parlor, there was considerable murmuring about the folly of having eaten so much, even under great temptation. Mrs. Lawrason asked whether anyone would mind if she went into the Garden Room and removed her corset, a remark which was surprising to Madame d'Alvery, because she would not have expected a lady to make such a suggestion, and equally so to all the younger persons present, because none of them dreamed that such garments were still in existence, outside of museums. By the time Pearl returned to the parlor looking a little bulgy, but greatly relieved, the others were all grouped companionably, some smoking, some knitting, and one or two with tall glasses in easy reach. The effortless, inconsequential conversation, begun at the supper table, was still going on.

"I'd like to hear more about Colonel d'Alvery, Merry, if you'll tell me," Pearl said, drawing up the only vacant armchair and looking about for an ash tray. "Perhaps all the rest of you know the whole story already, but there was so little in the papers——"

"Well, you do know that he volunteered to go in with the Eighty-second Airborne Division on D-Day."

"Yes, but I'm not sure why."

"I'm not sure myself. But Fabian says he thinks the reason so many military government people were sent in with the invasion troops was because there was so much uncertainty about De Gaulle's temperamental marches and countermarches. According to Fabian's theory, Eisenhower wanted the issue of who was running what a *fait accompli* before any fuss could be raised."

"Sounds sensible to me. And then the plane he was in——"

"It was a glider. The plane that was towing it was shot down and the glider crash-landed behind the German lines. Gervais was hurt in the crash. But of course you knew that too."

"I know he was wounded, but someone told me it was he who organized the survivors and got them back to the American lines. I mean forward to the American lines. Well, anyway, through to safety. So he wasn't badly hurt, was he? I mean, he couldn't have done that if he had been——"

"He broke his left arm and three ribs. And he had what's called a spinal concussion. I'd never heard about that before, so I had to ask our new family physician, Dr. Jennings, to explain it to me. Of course we'll never feel he's infallible, the way we felt about good old Dr. Champagne; but I suppose he knows what he's talking about, in a case like this. It seems that with a spinal concussion several hours elapse between the actual injury and the first signs of it. Then there's bound to be a collapse. However, Gervais didn't give out till everyone in his party was safe."

"Aren't you terribly proud of him?"

"Of course I'm terribly proud of him," Merry answered quietly. But her heart was not so quiet. It pounded as she said to herself: *If I only knew how badly hurt he really is. Dr. Jennings says there are no serious aftereffects to a spinal concussion, that a patient's usually all right again in a few days, unless there are other complications. Of course we know there were the broken ribs and the broken arm this time, but we don't know that was all. I'm so afraid there may be other complications too. I'm worried on Gervais' account, and I'm worried on my own. I wouldn't be quite so much worried, if I only knew there'd be a chance to make up for these years we've lost through my fault. I'll try to think of all the reasons I have to be proud instead of all the reasons I have to worry. I don't need to think of just what he did on D-Day. That was enough, Lord knows. But he needn't ever have asked for a transfer to Charlottesville, he need never have gone overseas. He could have stayed in New Orleans as well as not. And he wouldn't. I've got that to be proud of, first of all. And I don't suppose he had to go into Sicily with the assault troops either. I'm sure he could have managed to stay in Africa longer, if he'd tried. He needn't have lived in the fields for weeks, camping in olive groves or anywhere he could. I've got that to be proud of, too. He wasn't a combat officer; he was a military government officer. He could have played safe, at least fairly safe. I don't suppose he would have been safe from disease, ever. I suppose he was bound to catch something, in the filth of those Sicilian towns where he finally went to do his own job. I suppose he was bound to be sent back to Africa for hospitalization, to be kept there weeks and weeks. And I didn't write to him then. I didn't send him a word that would cheer him through his long illness. I don't see how he can ever forgive me. There's no reason why he should. And now perhaps I'll never have a chance to tell him I'm sorry. Perhaps the next telegram that comes in will say——*

"He was attached to the General Staff Corps, in England, before the Norman invasion, wasn't he?" she heard Pearl Lawrason asking, still eagerly; and Merry answered, again quietly, "Yes, he went straight to England after he was discharged from the hospital in Oran. He said the English spring was beautiful . . ." *But that wasn't in a letter to me, she added to herself. That was in a letter to his mother. It might have been my letter, and it wasn't. I didn't get a letter until he was in a base hospital in France, after I finally wrote him that I was back at Belle Heloise. There were so many things he might have said in that letter, at least if he'd been able to write, and he didn't say any of them. He didn't say if a woman stayed away from her husband for eight years, she might as well stay away forever. He didn't remind me that I'd been the one to talk about heartlessness in the first place, and that it was his turn now. He didn't ask if his promotion and his medal were all I cared about. He just said:* "I've got something to get well for, honey, now that I know you'll be waiting for me when I get home, that I won't come back to an empty room." *. . . Dear Lord, if I only knew how much longer the room was going to be empty, because he isn't in it.* Her heart was pounding almost insufferably by this time and it had swelled so that it expanded far beyond its proper place. But somehow she managed to speak quietly once more.

"It's nice of you to be so interested, Pearl. But we mustn't talk about Gervais all the time. Especially since this is an old story to everyone but you, as you said yourself. What did you hear from Harvey last?"

"Oh, he's in Iran. India was just a way station," Pearl volunteered, so promptly that Merry knew that she should have asked sooner, that she should not have allowed her own thoughts to absorb her so completely. "I didn't know for a long time though. I finally wrote him that I could have sailed halfway around the world since I'd heard from him, and of course that's exactly what he's done himself—*more* than halfway around! On the whole he's been pretty good about giving me hints too. In one letter, written after he left Rio, he said, 'If it wasn't for hope we'd be pretty well lost,' and then I knew he'd been around the Cape. He must be somewhere near Basra now. You know the supply route for munitions and food to Russia runs from the Persian Gulf to the Caspian Sea. When his company got to wherever it is they are, the English were running through three trains a week, on the one railroad. Now they're running through fifteen a day. I'll tell the world that's some difference."

"I'll say it is!" Cresside exclaimed heartily.

"Yes, and they have an assembly plant for trucks, too. Those supplement the railroad. It's terribly interesting work. Harvey's crazy about it. And wouldn't you know, he gets in quite a little hunting on the side, too? He says the hunting's wonderful along the river beds in the Persian mountains. There are wolves and jaguars and foxes and boars. Once when he and some other hunters followed their game down to the plains, they found the natives trying to drive the wild boar off their rice fields with sticks. They didn't have anything else to do it with. So they were awfully glad to see the Americans. Harvey and his friends shot any number of wild boars that day. But he says the best sport of all is the gazelle hunting. He's seen as many as two or three thousand gazelles grazing at the same time and——"

She stopped suddenly. Here she had been running on about the hunting in Iran, and she ought to have remembered that the last time Harvey and Colonel d'Alvery went hunting together was the day poor little Franchot shot the deer by accident. She ought to have talked about something else, when Merry asked her to tell this group of women what she'd heard from Harvey. But she had thought of the wild boars overrunning the rice fields and the great herds of gazelles grazing freely on the highlands as thrilling and exotic; she had not thought of the tragic memories her stories might evoke. *I'm a damn fool,* she said to herself, thankful that the conversation was so general that she did not need to say anything aloud just then. But she continued to reproach herself. *I ought to have told them instead that the thermometer goes up to a hundred and seventy in the shade at Basra, or wherever it is Harvey's stationed, and we think it's hot here when it goes over ninety. We sit in a lovely dim dining room and still we talk about how hot we are. And Harvey's assembling trucks and loading trains, right out in that desert sun. We have juleps before dinner in silver goblets, coated so thick that you can scrape the frost off with your fingernail, and champagne comes out of a silver cooler so cold that the bubbles sting when they hit your tongue. And Harvey didn't have any ice at all for a long time after he left home, and then only a little, that couldn't be put in anything he drank because it was made from water coming out of infected streams. All he could do was to pack bottles in it, so that the beer inside wouldn't be lukewarm. He doesn't have any water even to wash with; in all that terrible heat, he can't take a bath from one month's end to another. These women who've all had baths before they came here, who drank juleps before dinner and champagne afterwards, don't want to hear about things like that! They've had a wonderful dinner too. How can I tell them the only fresh meat Harvey gets is bought from open shops where the lambs are strung up by their legs as soon as they've been killed, with their wool still on and the blood still pouring out of them? Presently the flies gather on them, so thick the wool's covered, and they look black instead of white. How could I talk about things like that? I couldn't! So I tried to tell them something that wouldn't disgust them. Besides, I couldn't tell them Harvey'd been awarded the Purple Heart, and it made me mad to think Merry d'Alvery felt she had so much more to brag about than I did. So I told them the best story I could and now . . .*

"Those gazelles must have been a beautiful sight, Pearl," Cresside was saying. "Fabian's always wanted to go to Iran and take me—Persia, he still calls it, of course. You've been there, haven't you, Mrs. Prescott?"

"Oh yes," Mrs. Prescott replied, in a tone that inferred she had been everywhere. Then she began to talk about the wonderful opportunity she had enjoyed in seeing the ruins of Persepolis, but Pearl did not pay much attention to her. Instead she looked gratefully at Cresside, and Cresside returned the smile. *She wanted to be reassured,* Cresside said to herself. *Poor Pearl! She was afraid she'd blurted out the wrong thing, and she was worrying over that. If she thinks of me at all in connection with this war, she says to herself:* "There's a woman whose husband's a cripple, who can't fight and whose only child's a young daughter, right here in the room with her." *She doesn't know about Vail. She doesn't know I have a letter he wrote me on D-Day, tucked inside my dress this minute, but that I haven't heard a word from him since. It was just like Vail to write me a letter on D-Day and the letter was just like him, too.*

"Dear Auntie:
    Everything is going well and according to plan. Don't worry about me because I'm fine and expect to stay so.
                                        As ever,
                                            Vail."

He didn't say: "If you never hear from me again, this'll show you I was thinking about you right up to the last." *Vail never says things like that. Why, even the day he left, he didn't say,* "I know you're my mother." *He knew he musn't. He only said:* "I've always wished you were my mother." *He isn't ashamed, so I don't have to be, any longer. I don't know how he found out and I don't care. I'm not afraid any longer either. I'm too happy because he said what he did to be ashamed or afraid either. He says just the right thing, always, neither too much nor too little. He isn't taciturn, like Gervais claims he is. A boy who is taciturn wouldn't have written at all. A boy would have had a sure-enough excuse, not writing on D-Day to anyone. Certainly not to his —Aunt. But Vail did write. He wrote on D-Day and the letter came through very fast. But nothing has come through since. And no one in the family has even thought that was anything to worry about, except of course Fabian, who understands, and Sybelle, who doesn't understand but who loves Vail very much herself. Everyone else is*

*thinking about Gervais and his wounds and his medal . . . No, I'm
wrong, Frances Belle isn't thinking about Gervais and his wounds
and his medal. She's thinking of that red-headed freckled young pilot
who's towing bunker fuels and aviation gasoline for the Army and
Navy to the ships in New Orleans Harbor. . . .*

The great clock in the hall struck sonorously, and immediately
afterwards the silly gilt timepiece under the *silene* on the mantelpiece
tinkled out its tune and for a moment the guests were silent, listening
to this. It was only nine o'clock now. Supper had been early, out of
consideration for Creassy and Dinah and Lethe, who were not much
pleased about the party anyway. But glancing at her daughter, Cresside
knew that Frances Belle, in spite of her surface civility, was already
restless, that she was counting the hours until she could see Punt
O'Malley again. *Frances Belle doesn't know how fortunate she is,
either,* Cresside thought. *She's resentful of every minute that she's
separated from Punt, though she knows he's coming back to her, safe
and sound, that she'll see him every few days. She isn't thinking of
wasted years, like Merry. She isn't self-conscious about saying the
wrong thing or jealous of anyone else's fame, like Pearl. She isn't consumed with secret anxiety, like me. . . .*

It was true that Frances Belle was not consumed with anxiety.
Instead, she was listening to the chugging sound of a boat going down
the river, waiting for it to whistle as it rounded the point beyond the
batture, and grappling with her first great temptation. She was trying
to tell herself that Punt hadn't really *asked* her to join the WAVES or
the WACS. He had only said that perhaps, as long as he hadn't been
able to get into the war, they might be glad some day if she found she
could and did; that when their children started asking them what they
had done, they might be ashamed if neither of them could say . . .
Oh, of course he was delivering high-octane gas for planes, he was in
an essential industry. If he'd been forty-eight instead of twenty-eight,
he wouldn't have minded—that is, he supposed he wouldn't have.
And he knew Frances Belle was giving blood regularly and working at
the USO, and that would have been enough, too, if she had been forty
instead of twenty. But as it was, he thought maybe some day their kids
would think it was queer, and that they themselves would be sort of
ashamed, or anyway embarrassed, trying to explain. . . .

I see what he means, Frances Belle was saying to herself, almost
petulantly, her ears cocked to catch the boat's whistle, which would
sound any moment now. *At first I tried to pretend I didn't, but Punt
looked at me, that straight way he has, and I was ashamed right then.
Because I did understand. I do. But I don't want to join the WAVES or
the WACS either. I don't want to be in a camp with hundreds of other
girls. I want to be at home with Mummy and Daddy, until I can be
with Punt. I'm sure they want me at home—they'd be all alone if I
went off and left them. Anyhow I don't want to go off somewhere
on the other side of the world among strangers. I just want to go*

*down the river with my sweetheart, the way he's promised I should
some day. I want to stand in the pilot house when he's at the wheel
and look down on it. The others may be satisfied to look at the River
Road, but I'm not. Even the peddlers don't travel on the River Road
any more. Nobody uses it to go between here and New Orleans—
everyone takes the Airline. Except for the few cars coming here and
to Hathaway and to Hackberry, you never see anything but the school
bus and a truck now and then and old rattletraps filled with Negroes,
until you get below Burnside. But it's just the opposite with the river.
It's crowded with craft of every kind, the way* grand'mère *said it was
when she was a girl, but there are more kinds now: old stern-wheelers,
pressed back into service; big new ones with huge, powerful engines;
long low cargo boats, fleets of tugs to push the steel barges, towboats
like Punt's. Yes, even submarines built up-river, trussed in wooden
cradles and floated all the way from Lake Michigan to the Gulf.
Cargoes are coming to New Orleans all the way from Minneapolis,
from Cincinnati, from Louisville and Memphis: coal and iron, cotton
and grain, oil and steel and flour. They're passing right by the house
this minute. The railroads can't handle all these and send them on their
way to war—the railroads or the old highways. But the river can. It
does. . . .*

Frances Belle could tell from the sounds she heard that one boat
had now rounded the point and that another was coming. So she
went on listening while the others continued to talk. She didn't like
sitting in her grandmother's parlor, straining her ears for the chugging
and whistling of a boat she couldn't even see. She wanted to be aboard
one, looking down on the river which had drowsed for so long, but
which had wakened to new life with the war. *I want to see it for
myself, the way Punt's made me see it at every season in every sort of
weather. I want to see it with the sun shining on it, and I want to see
it with the fog stealing over it, even though I know fog's its worst
enemy, worse than high water or high wind. Because you can still see
when there's a flood or a hurricane, but you can't when there's a fog.
Punt explained that.* "When the visibility's zero, kid, there's not a
thing you can do but make for shore with your compass and your
whistle. The whistle comes echoing back to you from the bank and
you can judge the distance by the sound of the echo. It sounds one way
when you're near the bank and another way when you're far from it.
You don't see how I can tell the difference? Gosh, that's easy! I can't
remember when I couldn't. But then I was just a kid when I first went
on the river. You have to be a deckhand three years before you're
even eligible for a pilot's license, and some men can't make the grade
then. We've got college graduates on the *McDougall* right now that
are still deckhands, that couldn't ever learn to pilot a boat no matter
how hard they tried nor how long. Then again we've got others who
never went beyond the fourth grade, but they're wizards when it
comes to handling a wheel. . . . Well, anyway, after you've been

a deckhand for three years, if the Master and the chief engineer will sign your application, you can take an exam; and if you pass it, you're issued a second-class pilot's license. You hold that for a year, and then, if you're good enough, you get to be a steersman; you're put in charge of the wheel. Finally after another year, if you're still doing all right, you can qualify as a full-fledged pilot. So it takes five years at least to do that. Hell, if you couldn't learn to guess how far you were from shore, by the sound of an echo, in five years, you never could, and I've been doing it for eight."

I don't want to be a WAC *or a* WAVE, Frances Belle repeated stubbornly to herself. *I want to stand beside Punt listening to that echo, and see if I can learn to tell how far we are from shore. I want to hear a whirlwind coming, too. Punt says you can hear it a long way off, that it sounds like a herd of cattle on the run, and that when a pilot hears that sound, he puts into shore as fast as he can. I don't know whether I want to see a flood. Punt says it's a terrible sight when you're up twenty feet or more above the land beyond the levee, and look down on the plantations and towns on the other side of it. He says it's a terrible feeling if you think what would happen if you lost control of your boat and went right through the levee and hit all those houses and churches and people and cattle. He says sometimes you can hardly bear to look at it, sometimes you can hardly bear to think of it. But you have to. That's part of being a pilot. So I reckon a pilot's sweetheart could stand it too. I'm sure a pilot's wife could. I could stand anything if I could only have Punt for my husband. But if I have to be a* WAC *and go off to the other side of the world, away from him, then I couldn't bear it, thinking there might be a flood while I was gone and he might lose control of his boat and go through the levee and kill people and knock down houses. If he really loved me he wouldn't ask me to be a* WAVE *or a* WAC. *No, that isn't fair. If he didn't really love me he wouldn't care whether our children would be ashamed of us some day. But perhaps we wouldn't ever have any children. I don't think I care much whether we do or not, if I can have Punt. I know I wouldn't want to have one right away, like Syb is going to and like Aunt Merry did. I'd rather be like Mummy. I wasn't born until after she and Daddy had been married a year and a half. And then they never had another. But Punt says "our children," so I reckon he wants to have several and he doesn't want them to be ashamed. . . .*

I wonder if Mr. Reynaud wouldn't let me go on the "McDougall" right now, without waiting for the war to be over and all. Punt'll be back tomorrow, I'm going to ask him then. I'm going to say: "Punt, let's get married and go down the river together. You know that room of yours you told me about all nicely furnished up on the Texas, way off from the crew's quarters? Couldn't we have that room for ours, Punt? I'd stay with you in the pilot house while you took your watch. I'm glad you still do that, even though you're the Master now. I wouldn't talk to you or bother you, but we'd look at the lights together —the ones beyond the levee and the ones on the river you said looked like stars, and at the real stars, too. There wouldn't be any fog that night, I know there wouldn't, or high water or high wind. It would be calm and beautiful and after your watch was over, we'd go to bed. And when we got to New Orleans you'd tell me about the different kinds of lights in the harbor—you'd show me which were the channel lights and which were the lights on the other boats that were navigating and on the boats that were tied up along the shore. They must be a beautiful sight, Punt, all those boats that are in New Orleans Harbor now, more than there ever were before—the men of war and the Liberty ships and the big French carrier that's in for repairs, the freighters and tankers, the towboats and harbor tugs and ferries too. I want to see them, moving back and forth across the dark waters, all lighted up, and lying at anchor too, on both sides of the river—our river. I want to hear the sound of the cranes on the ships being loaded, and the men singing and shouting while they work. I could go ashore after we got there, and wait for you, at the Pontalba, while the cargo was being discharged, if I were in the way. And then afterwards we would still have time to go to dinner at Antoine's, or just sit in Jackson Square for a while. Anything, so long as I could do it with you. Please, Punt, don't let's talk any longer about my being a WAVE or a WAC. Let's talk about having our honeymoon on the *McDougall*. I have just as much right to a honeymoon as Syb. And I'm not going to wait as long for mine as she did. I won't. I can't. I want to marry you, Punt, I wish I could marry you this very night. I can't stand it, staying in this stuffy parlor with all these dumb women who don't know how I feel, who just sit here smoking and knitting and jabbering about nothing!"

She could hear another boat now, not chugging or whistling, but puffing laboriously, as if it were having hard work to prevail against the current. *I can tell whether boats are coming upstream or going downstream already,* she thought. *If I can do that, I can learn about echoes too.* She pushed back her chair and rose, betraying to everyone the restlessness which Cresside had so long divined. Sybelle, who was not knitting gray socks but a pink baby blanket, looked up at her cousin with a questioning smile.

"Where are you going, Frances Belle?"

"Out on the upper gallery. I want to look at the boats passing by."

"You can't see anything but the funnels. As a matter of fact, the foliage is so heavy now, you can hardly see those."

"I don't care. I'll see what I can."

"You want me to come with you?"

"No, I feel like being alone for a while. But thanks, just the same."

That girl is no better mannered than she ever was, Mrs. Prescott said to herself. But Sybelle understood Frances Belle's mood and was not offended by it. After her cousin had left the room, she looked down again at the wool in her hands, her smile deepening. She was not

682

worrying about Rick just then. He was still on Bougainville, but it had been relatively quiet there since the Japs had failed in the all-out drive which they opened in March, hoping to throw the Americans off the island. After his brief leave, Rick had been transferred from the Infantry to the General Staff Corps. Now the operational officer had returned to the States on longer leave than Rick had been given, and Rick had assumed the full duties of the office, which he was amply qualified to fill. The wording of his citation, announcing that he had been awarded the Bronze Star, was proof positive of this. Sybelle knew every word of this citation by heart, and she repeated it softly to herself now, as she knitted and purled the pink wool:

"Riccardo Tramonte, Major, Infantry, United States Army, for the performances of meritorious services at New Georgia and Bougainville, Solomon Islands. During the preparatory training and combat action of both campaigns, Major Tramonte distinguished himself by a keen knowledge of the training methods required and superior tactical judgment which enabled him to make sound recommendations to the sector commander. His sound advice was based on personal reconnaissance into enemy territory, during which he was exposed to hostile observation and fire. His thorough plan for quickly reorganizing to repel further enemy attacks at Bougainville enabled unit commanders successfully to re-form their units only a few hours after the initial Japanese assault waves had been annihilated."

I'm so much luckier than Mother, Sybelle said to herself. *She'll never be able to think of Dad's decoration except in connection with his wounds. And Rick never got so much as a scratch all the time he was exposed to hostile observation and fire. I'm sure his mother's right. I'm sure he's under some special protection. She thinks it's St. Amico and I think it's God's very own. But what does it matter, as long as he has it? If he hadn't, he couldn't have come back here last spring. We couldn't have been married, we couldn't have had that perfect month together. I wouldn't be waiting for my baby now.* She continued to look down at the pink blanket and soon the smile which at first had merely curved her lips wreathed her whole face.

"How's the house getting on, Syb?" Susannah asked. "We saw the most remarkable change as we went by." Susannah had noticed the change at Hathaway, from the distance of the River Road, but she didn't seem to notice the pink blanket, though she was sitting within a few feet of it. Sybelle had hard work not to answer contemptuously; after all, the house mattered so little in comparison with the baby.

"Just fine! Of course everyone told me I wouldn't be able to get very far, trying to restore it right now. As a matter of fact, I didn't even try to restore the wing the Tremaines used. It was all falling apart, so I had what was left of it torn down. It was just an addition, anyway, that spoiled the lines of the original building, and we didn't need all that extra space. I'm furnishing that great empty White Ball Room to use as a double drawing room, and it's going to be lovely. I started out with that but now I've got all the ground floor rooms pretty well organized and I've made a good beginning upstairs. I did get discouraged at first, going into store after store, and having one snooty clerk after another ask me didn't I know there was a war on. Seven clerks asked me that, all in one day. I counted. The seventh time it was just too much. I said, 'Yes, I do know there's a war on. My father's in it and both my brothers and my husband. How many members of your family are in it?' The clerk stared at me in dumb amazement and mumbled something and then wandered off. But I walked after her. 'I'm going to have our own home ready for my husband when he comes back, too,' I said. 'I'm going to make it just as attractive as I know how, and I'm not depending on any essential war materials to do that, either. I'm going to have it ready for my baby, too. You're not carrying a soldier's baby by any chance, are you?'"

The others in the room were all staring at Sybelle in astonishment now. They had always thought she was lovely to look at, and they had always admired her amiable disposition; but they had never credited her with much spirit. The statement that she had so vigorously arraigned an offending salesgirl was startling to them. Besides, this was the first that Pearl and the Prescotts had heard of the expected baby, and as Sybelle had proclaimed her condition before it proclaimed her, this revelation was rather startling also.

"The clerk scuttled away like a rabbit after that," Sybelle continued. "I think she went to the rest room and stayed there all afternoon. Anyhow, I didn't see her again, and I was in the store for another hour or so. But I haven't been back there and I'm not going back. I'm not going to any of the stores where they asked me if I knew there was a war on. I'm going back to the ones that did the best they could for me, pleasantly, and acted as if they were sorry they couldn't do more. I've bought a good many things that way. My father-in-law told me to get everything I wanted and send the bills to him. I knew he meant it so I've done it. He's been a lot of help to me in other ways, too. I believe he knows every carpenter and mason and plumber in the Parish. Anyway, he's dug up all kinds of mechanics for me. They're mostly old or disabled and they don't work very fast, but they're getting things done by degrees. I think Rick will see quite a change when he comes back the next time, at least in the house and garden. I'm not trying to do anything with the factory or the fields yet. I'm waiting for Vail to help me with those. It's our idea—Rick's and Vail's and mine—that Hathaway and Belle Heloise ought to be run as one plantation, eventually. It can be done a lot more efficiently that way. I wonder why no one ever thought of it before."

Someone did think of that before, my dear child. I thought of it, and my neighbor, Mrs. Hathaway, thought of it. We planned an alliance between my son and her daughter; but her daughter stole my daughter's sweetheart, and my son went to St. Napoleon Street for his wife. So all our plans came to nothing, and that was a bitter pill for me to swallow. Now you've married the son of an Italian peddler, who's the only man we know rich enough to restore Hathaway— except perhaps Felix Goldenberg, and it wasn't Hathaway that interested him. And you're planning to run it with the help of Vail d'Alvery, whom you boast about as your "litter brother," and who isn't your brother at all, though you never found that out and never will. He isn't really the heir to Belle Heloise either; if it weren't for Fabian, he wouldn't have the right to run it, much less combine another plantation with it. Perhaps you think that wasn't another bitter pill for me. While Madame d'Alvery was pondering in this way she looked around with an air of satisfaction remarkable for its smooth deceptiveness and addressed the group at large in an agreeable voice.

"It is very pleasant to be having a party here again, even though it lacks the éclat of some of our previous gatherings," she said. "When I was a girl, we had a great many balls at Belle Heloise. My father always had the first dance with my mother and the second one with me; after that he danced once with each of the ladies present, beginning with the eldest and going on down to the youngest. Then he retired to the library and stayed there through the remainder of the evening, except for brief interludes when he returned to admonish the colored musicians. Finally, at one o'clock, he came in with a glass of whiskey in his hand. This was recognized as a nightcap and a signal for general departure. I never knew anyone to disregard it. Perhaps after the war we can begin having dances here again. Gervais might revive some of his grandfather's customs in regard to those, as he did in regard to the celebrations at the end of grinding season. I think he would play the part of the old-fashioned host extremely well." Madame d'Alvery paused to smile comprehensively at the ladies she had been addressing as a group, and then focused her gaze on Susannah. "We shall count on you to come over from New Roads, my dear, when we inaugurate such a series," she said. "You know I have never yet seen that beautiful dress of your great-grandmother's, which my daughter and grandson have both described to me so enthusiastically. I should like immensely to have you wear it at a ball given here."

"Thank you, Madame d'Alvery. I'd like that too," Susannah answered quietly. *My great-grandmother's dress,* she said to herself. *The dress I wore when I went to the Sugar Festival with Vail, the dress he wanted me to wear when I married him. Phil wouldn't go to the sugar festival. That was the only reason I asked Vail, because I couldn't get Phil. And Phil didn't care what I wore when I married him. It didn't mean anything to him, one way or another. The marriage didn't mean anything to him. Vail's right. It really isn't a marriage. Not just because Phil and I didn't go upstairs together in that horrible hotel. But because it wasn't sanctified, in any sense. A marriage can't be sanctified if a girl doesn't trust her husband, if she doesn't respect him. And I don't trust Phil or respect him either. How could I? He's never done anything to make me. He just attracted me, he just fascinated me.*

That doesn't last, if nothing else goes with it. It hasn't lasted—that is, I don't think it has. I don't think, if I saw Phil this minute, it would mean anything to me. There'd be that sparkle in his eyes I've always watched for, there'd be that quirk to his lips that's always been irresistible. But he wouldn't look me straight in the face, he wouldn't tell me the truth when he spoke to me. I ought to feel proud because he's done so well in the Army. He has done well, almost as well as Rick and Vail and Colonel d'Alvery and Captain Lawrason. But a girl can't go on feeling proud of a man in a personal way if he isn't proud of her. If he wants to keep their marriage a secret, if he doesn't want her to use his name or live in his home, she ends by thinking about him as if he weren't her husband at all, as if he were just another man she'd read about in the paper. I don't want to get any more letters addressed to Miss Susannah Prescott, New Roads. It doesn't matter what I see inside, because I've seen the outside first. Not that there's much to see inside either, or that I've seen anything he's written for a long time. I'm glad I haven't . . .

"How's Barry Pereira and what's he doing right now?" she asked, turning to Joyeuse. Not that she cared at all. But she didn't want to think about Phil any more, and she felt it might help if she talked about someone else.

"Oh, he's fine and he's been on what he calls the banana run ever since he went to Mobile and took command of the armed guard on that Liberty ship. He gets back to New Orleans every three weeks—that's a lot nicer, of course, than if his ship were in a convoy to Russia, gone for eight or nine months at a time. I see quite a lot of him, this way." *Too much,* she added to herself. *If he only wouldn't pester me so, teasing me to marry him, we might have fun together. I'd have time to do some of the things he wants to do. I'd make time. Now that I'm through college, now that it's the slack season on the plantation, I'm not all that busy. But we no sooner get going than he begins again:* "Joy, look what I've brought you. Joy, I wish you wouldn't act as if you thought I had leprosy or something—there's nothing fatal about a little pleasant petting. Joy, I've got the license right in my pocket." *I don't want his presents. I don't want his kisses. I don't want to be married to him. I just want to have fun. I can't see that Syb's having any fun, with that big tumble-down house on her hands and a baby coming and Rick over on the other side of the world. I can't see that Pearl Lawrason's having any fun, cooped up in that little apartment in the Pentagon, not daring to play the field any more, like she used to. I don't see that Mom's ever had any fun on Belle Heloise. She only began to have it after she went to Paris and Buenos Aires and New York. Maybe Aunt Cresside's had fun, but she waited a good long time before she got married. That's what I'm going to do. I'm not going to be swept off my feet by a snappy uniform, no matter what's inside it. I'd have to live with that a long while after the war was over.*

I'm going to be like Sue and have the sense to stay single. She doesn't look so well though, at that. She looks as if she had something on her mind. Or somebody. Not that I ever thought Vail got very far. . . .

"My dear Madame d'Alvery, this has been a most delightful evening. But Susannah and I have quite a long drive back to New Roads. So I'm certain you'll excuse us if we're the ones to break up the party. I assure you we do it most regretfully."

Mrs. Prescott had risen, and was crossing the room in her usual poised manner. Everyone else rose too, as she held out her hand to Madame d'Alvery, who spoke ceremoniously.

"I'm sorry to have you go. But you must come again soon. We have been seeing too little of each other lately. By the way, your kinsman, Charles Boylston, has been kind enough to write me several times. When a lady reaches my age, she takes such an attention as a great compliment. He seems to be enjoying his stay in Scotland very much. Doubtless he has written you about it, too?"

"Yes, but in very guarded terms. He is in command of the First Air Intransit Depot operating at some very large air base. I assume that in such a group as this, it is perfectly proper for me to say that much."

Mrs. Prescott glanced about her, as if to verify the accuracy of her statement, and the expression of everyone present seemed to confirm her right to confidence. Reassured, she continued in greater detail.

"He says it is an unforgettable sight when a vast number of planes, circling around in the mist overhead, are waiting for Control to give the signal which will permit them to land. The region where he is operating is extremely foggy, and often long delays occur on that account. Even officers of the highest rank may be greatly delayed in coming down, and as they have already flown the Atlantic, the problem of fuel becomes acute. Charles has moments of great anxiety."

Having said this much, Mrs. Prescott shook hands with Madame d'Alvery again and began a tour of the parlor, saying good night to each of the others in turn, her progress still marked by aplomb. She had almost completed her rounds, when a series of piercing shrieks, distant at first, but coming steadily closer, disrupted her ceremonious leave-taking. Cresside, who was nearest the door, moved hastily towards it, only to collide with Lethe, who charged into the room and rushed over to Madame d'Alvery, still screaming.

"Ah done seen him, Madame! Ah done seen him wid mah own eyes!"

"Be quiet, Lethe! What do you mean by this unseemly disturbance? Go back outside at once. I will come and speak to you in a minute."

"Ah doesn't dare go back outside, Madame. It's outside Ah done see de ghost. Dinah, she done tell me befo' she hear it, but Ah never did believe her till yet. She ain't never seed it anyways."

The woman was trembling uncontrollably. Her fright was obviously genuine. It had swept into the parlor with her, darting insidiously into every corner of the tranquil room. Madame d'Alvery spoke again, imperiously.

"I will go out with you, Lethe, and so will some of these ladies. Perhaps then we can convince you that you are laboring under a very silly delusion. . . . Was it in the patio that you thought you saw this apparition?"

"Yes, Madame. An' Ah ain't a-gwine back dere, not effen everyone on de River Road was to go wid me."

"Someone has been playing tricks again, the way Mr. Philogene used to play them."

"Who be's here to play tricks on us now?"

There was no plausible answer to the question. Madame d'Alvery pressed her lips together.

"Dat wuz de ol' tramp hisself, and yo' knows he don't never come back, lessen——"

"That will do, Lethe."

Madame d'Alvery walked firmly out of the parlor into the hall and through this to the patio, followed by her family, her guests and her trembling servant. Lethe had left the rear door open when she rushed in, and it still stood ajar. A light puff of wind blew towards them from the garden, making no sound. The patio was dim, silent and empty. Madame d'Alvery touched the switch by the door and light streamed instantly from the two electrified lanterns suspended on either side of the patio, flooding it with soft radiance. The dimness was dispelled. The silence and the emptiness prevailed.

"You see," Madame d'Alvery said quietly. "Go upstairs, Lethe, and wait for me. I want to speak to you alone. . . . Needless to say I am very sorry for this disturbance," she added, turning back to her guests. "I am afraid it will mar the memories of this evening, which I had hoped would be so pleasant for you. Good night, good night!" Her tone was one of dismissal. Neither the Prescotts nor Pearl Lawrason attempted to prolong their farewells. Cresside hesitated for a moment, but Frances Belle was tugging at her arm, and presently they left too, trailing Sybelle, who was taking Joyeuse back to Hathaway with her. Madame d'Alvery waited until everyone else had gone before she looked at Merry. Even then she did so very briefly, her hand already on the newel post.

"Sometimes we Creoles share our servants' superstitions," she said. "But you are not a Creole, my dear Merry. This scene must have been as distasteful to you as to any of our guests. Do not permit your mind to dwell on it. And do not feel that you need to come to my room with me. I can deal with Lethe better alone. Good night, *chère*. I am glad you humored me about the party. Except for this final diversion, I feel it was a great success." She went slowly on up the stairs without turning, and pausing merely to salute the Spanish statue. Only the *McDougall's* whistle sounding on the river broke the engulfing stillness.

CHAPTER LII

No, I'm not a Creole, Merry kept saying to herself the next few days. *Madame Mère doesn't need to keep reminding me of that. She never used to do it, either. I suppose the reason she does it so much now is that it represents a way of putting me in my place. But there's nothing wrong with my place. I'm glad I could make my own way in the world, I'm glad I haven't any of their silly old superstitions. I don't mind having a nigger act like a nigger, but when it comes to white folks. . . .*

She said this defiantly, and then still more defiantly she added: *Cresside needn't gloat, either, because Vail wrote her a letter on D-Day and Gervais didn't write me till the week afterwards. Vail was just going through some ordinary routine and Gervais was performing a great act of heroism. I've already heard that he wasn't seriously injured, and presently I'll hear he's all right again. I know Frances Belle thought, the night of that horrible party, that she was the only person in the room who hadn't the slightest reason to be worried about the man she loved. She was gloating too, because she sees that snub-nosed pilot of hers every few days, and because he's never any further away from her than New Orleans. All the others were talking one way and thinking another. Except me. I wasn't worried. I'm not worried now.*

She kept saying this, over and over, but eventually she found she could not go on talking so defiantly, even to herself. Then she whispered: *I am worried. I'm so afraid I'm not going to have another chance. And I must. That couldn't have been the end between us, that night after Franchot's funeral. We've got to have years and years together yet, or the rest of my life won't mean anything to me. I don't see how I could have thought that was really living, in New York. Life doesn't mean anything to a woman, unless she can share it with the man she loves. I've always known that, down deep in my heart. I was a fool to pretend I didn't.*

It seemed to Merry that there was no end to the days and nights that she kept saying all this to herself, over and over again. Actually, it was only a week or so after the party that Cresside came out unusually early, and breathless with haste. "I'm just a messenger," she said still panting. "If you had a telephone, I wouldn't be here. Gervais landed in New York this morning, and of course the first thing he did was to get right on the wire, the way they all do. He said to tell you he was fine, and not to think of trying to come East. Of course he's writing you more details. But he expects to be sent to La Garde right away. He'll call again from there. I reckon you'll have him home in a fortnight or so, Merry. I gathered that he was only going to La Garde for a final check-up."

"But Cresside, if he wasn't hurt any worse than he let on at first, wouldn't he have been hospitalized in England and then sent back to active duty on the Continent?"

"Well, he might have been hurt a little worse than he let on at first. Of course he couldn't go into details over the telephone. But he said something about 'battle fatigue.' Don't forget he'd been through a lot, even before the invasion—the Sicilian campaign, and that long illness and all. He sounded mighty cheerful to me, Merry. You know, I honestly believe, if he had to be bunged up, he'd rather be bunged up enough to justify him in coming home. He'll be so much happier here that he'll get well faster. Can't you imagine how he'd have fretted and fumed if he'd have had to stay in some damn Army hospital, instead of getting to Belle Heloise?"

Merry could imagine. She knew Gervais would rather be at Belle Heloise than anywhere else in the world and she began to consider carefully where he would be most comfortable. She was afraid the quarters in the *garçonnière* might seem cramped to him. The downstairs bedroom was good-sized, but there was no connecting room where a nurse could sleep, if it should prove advisable to have a nurse and possible to get one. Merry also realized that whether there was the complication of a nurse or not, it might not be feasible for her and Gervais to share a room, and certainly they could not share a bed, while he was in his present disabled state. Besides, it was in the *garçonnière* that their parting had taken place, in mutual anguish of spirit; if this were the scene of their reunion, it might arouse needlessly painful memories of the last time they had been together. After a great deal of reflection, she spoke to her mother-in-law on the subject.

"Madame Mère, I've been thinking that Gervais might like to have his old room back. Of course, the *garçonnière's* in apple-pie order, we could take him there at the last moment, if he preferred. But if he were in the Big House, he'd have a lot more space. And with the old nursery—I mean Vail's room—connecting with his, and Cresside's—I mean the Henry Clay room—across the hall, a nurse and I could both be near him, if it were necessary. And you would be, too. Naturally if Sybelle hadn't married, I wouldn't think of turning her out of her own quarters. But since she doesn't need them any more——"

"I had thought of exactly the same thing, Merry. But I had hesitated to suggest it. I was afraid you might feel I was trying to deprive you of the privacy you formerly enjoyed in your own small home, because I wanted to have my only son near me."

Madame d'Alvery spoke with the same cool courtesy which she had maintained ever since Merry's return. She had never once failed in civility towards her daughter-in-law; on the other hand, nothing like a real rapprochement had taken place between them. The gulf which had been bridged with such apparent ease in the early days of Merry's marriage to Gervais seemed impassable now. Merry also spoke with cool courtesy in replying.

"Then I'll begin organizing with that arrangement in view. Of course you'll tell me if anything I do is displeasing to you."

"I do not anticipate any such contingency."

The question was not raised between them again. But Merry mentioned her plan to Gervais almost as soon as their first greetings were over. The letter which arrived after the first telephone call revealed that there would not be time for her to get to New York before he was sent out of there himself, even if she disregarded his expressed wishes in the matter, and this was the last thing on earth she wanted to do. But she did go to New Orleans to await his arrival there, taking a room at one of the smaller hotels, because she knew that the Estrades' attitude would be exactly the same as Madame d'Alvery's, and consequently did not want to stay at the old family house on Esplanade. The next telephone call came through direct to her, and as Cresside had said, Gervais sounded extraordinarily cheerful: he was already at La Garde, the trip down had been very easy, he was feeling fine. Yes, honestly. He was only at the hospital for a final check-up. He didn't move around too easily and it tired him to sit up very long. But that didn't amount to anything. There was nothing serious or lasting about battle fatigue. He'd get his strength back in no time at Belle Heloise. And he'd been told he could go there by ambulance, in just a few days. Merry could go right along with him, if she wanted to. Meanwhile, what about coming down to the hospital? He was in a private room, they could have a good visit together. . . .

She was with him in fifteen minutes, sitting beside the narrow white hospital bed, holding his hand tightly in hers, partly because even this casual touch meant so much to her, and partly because she needed it to assure herself he was really there. His hand was not brown and strong any more; it was white and blue-veined, like his mother's, and so thin that it looked unnaturally long. Her clasp was firmer than his. She realized this and she knew he did; she also knew that the hand was typical of the whole man and that therefore it would be a long time before he was anything like his old self again. Because of this, and because neither of them could speak easily of his injuries, it seemed better to talk of unimportant things, like the arrangement of rooms.

"Madame Mère and I talked it over, Gervais, and we decided that perhaps you'd like to stay in the Big House, for a while anyway."

Again she outlined her reasons, omitting only the one which seemed the most cogent of all, as she had in speaking to her mother-in-law; again she reiterated that the *garçonnière* was ready, if he would prefer to go there. He listened quietly until she paused, looking at him in a questioning way.

"You're right, Merry. I'd better go back to my old room. I'd enjoy it, and it would be more practical all around—easier for the servants too, I suppose, and we've got to think of that, now there are so few left. In fact, perhaps we'd better close up the *garçonnière* until one of the boys needs it. It's on the cards that they'll both be getting married before too long. Of course Phil thought, when he went to college, that he didn't want to settle on the plantation. But he may change his mind. I sure hope he does. In that case, we'll let him have the *garçonnière* and turn the storehouse over to Vail, when your mother and Miss Mittie don't need it any more."

He seemed to consider the matter settled. It was not surprising that he did not care to discuss it long, for it obviously tired him greatly to talk for any length of time. Besides, the constant rumbling of the attic fan was sufficiently noticeable to create a disturbing element, and so were the frequent interruptions to which they were subjected. A Coca-Cola machine was just outside Gervais' door, and the officers who were ambulatory cases kept coming up to it to get drinks, instinctively glancing towards the open door at the same time. Some of them knew Gervais and came in for a cheery word with him. A pretty girl in civilian dress, wheeling a mobile wagon, approached in a sprightly way: wouldn't the Colonel like some magazines, or some cigarettes, or something? No, not right now, Gervais told her; thanks just the same though. He spoke more cordially than Merry could have, at the moment. She recognized that such incidents were unavoidable, and she realized that to many patients they must constitute a welcome diversion. But when a woman was alone with her husband for the first time in eight years! . . . She also wished that before closing the subject of the *garçonnière* Gervais had corrected himself and said "our room," just as she had corrected herself after saying "the old nursery" and "Cresside's room" in talking to Madame d'Alvery. She was further disturbed when the next question he asked stirred anxious thoughts which had lain dormant while her greatest anxiety was for him.

"By the way, when did you last hear from the boys, Merry?"

"I haven't heard from them in quite a long while. I was just going to ask you whether you had."

"No, I haven't either. What about Cresside? Hasn't she heard from Vail?"

"She had a note written on D-Day, and another about two weeks afterwards. That's all. She hasn't said anything, but of course I know she's terribly worried."

A nurse entered without knocking or appearing to observe Merry's presence, and thrust a thermometer into Gervais' mouth. He was obliged to wait until she had removed the thermometer and left, which she did as unceremoniously as she had entered, before he could ask the question which was the natural rejoinder to Merry's statement.

"Or Sybelle? He wrote to Sybelle once in a while too, didn't he?"

"Oh yes! Vail's always been very good about writing letters, until lately. It's Phil who never seemed to have time."

"Well, that's characteristic . . . Do you see anything of Susannah
692

Prescott these days? She certainly would have heard from Vail, if anyone did."

"I've seen very little. She and her mother came to a little party we had on the third of July—it was your mother's idea, Gervais, that we should have one."

"A very good idea too . . . And Susannah didn't say she'd heard from Vail, either?"

"No. She didn't refer to him in any way."

"Some sort of a rift there, do you think?"

"I wouldn't call it a rift, exactly." She stopped for a moment, another latent fear roused by her own words. There had been a rift between herself and Gervais, whatever they called it or avoided calling it. Dreading to dwell on this, she continued hurriedly. "Things haven't seemed to come to a head, that's all. Not that Vail hasn't wanted them to. He's never looked at another girl."

"Possibly he's found another now, more responsive, and that's what's taking up his time. . . . Well, don't worry about him, Merry, or Phil either. If anything were wrong, we'd have heard right away from the War Department."

"I know. Of course there really isn't any reason why I should worry about the boys. And anyway, now that I've got you home——"

She did not need to finish the sentence. Now that she had him home, every other fear was quiescent. She had her second chance, the chance she had prayed for but had not really dared to hope for. She was immersed in the effort of doing her utmost to deserve this chance. Her devotion to Gervais was selfless and complete. She thought only of what he wanted, of what he needed, of what might expedite his recovery. He stood the trip back to Belle Heloise remarkably well, and after that, though his progress continued to be slow, it was satisfactory, or so the doctors who saw him assured her; there was no real reason for anxiety on his account. By fall he would be able to get around a little again. . . .

"By the time grinding starts?"

"The middle of October? Well, possibly. But certainly by the time it's finished. And why should your husband worry or hurry about taking over? From all we hear, you've got a mighty capable young lady in charge at Belle Heloise."

It was true that Joyeuse was proving herself more and more efficient all the time. Actually, there was no reason that Gervais should take over, except that Merry felt sure he would be happier when he could. Not that he displayed any discontent or impatience, as it was. If the days seemed long to him, he never said so. He read the papers, he listened to the radio, he wrote in his diary. When Cresside and Fabian, or any of his old friends, came to see him, he welcomed them warmly. After he was able to walk about without assistance, he went to his office in the old storehouse for a little while every day and gradually the time he spent there lengthened. He conferred with Sance. His pride in Joyeuse increased obviously as he watched her in action. But his real interest centered in the mail. There was still no delivery at Belle Heloise, and gasoline was so scarce that it was impossible for Merry or Joyeuse to go into town every day. So Cresside brought it out on alternate days and came to the storehouse with it, whistling cheerfully to announce her approach. But weeks went on and still the word for which they were all watching did not come.

At last, when the suspense had begun to tell on them all, a form letter came through from the War Department with the news that Sergeant Philogene d'Alvery, serial number 38962548, had been slightly wounded in action on August tenth on the Danfront-Mortin road and was placed in an evacuation hospital awaiting transfer to a United States hospital plant in England. A surge of relief engulfed them. Inevitably "slightly wounded" not only meant that the injury itself could not be serious but that the removal of the boy to England would take him miles and miles from the danger zone. Their spirits received a further lift a few days later with the arrival of a very brief letter from Phil himself which indicated he had lost none of his graceless outlook on life, since he claimed his only worry was he would never be able to show the scar even after he got to the point where he could once more sit down in comfort. "Don't ask me where I'm going to wear that Purple Heart!" he concluded. And shortly after this communication came to Merry and Gervais, Cresside appeared at an unaccustomed hour, her face preternaturally bright. Another letter from Vail had come through at last, and it had wonderful news in it. She'd brought it out to share with them.

" 'Dear Auntie,' " she read aloud.

" 'I'm terribly sorry it's been so long between letters but I'm mighty busy these days. Of course I can't tell you where we've been or much of what we've been doing, except that our outfit and others like it have the big job of paralyzing communications. We've got things so that the Nazis can hardly expect to let a vehicle move on a highway or a train go out of the marshalling yards without some allied plane slamming it. It isn't like in the old days when we had the bombers to protect against fighter opposition. By the way, I got my first confirmed enemy plane the other day, an ME-110. Also I've caught my second oak-leaf cluster to the air medal, but think nothing of it. They're as easy to catch as the common cold, even in this climate. But as you'll see by the wording on the left-hand corner of this envelope, you should make a slight change in addressing your next letter.' "

She held up the envelope, speaking in a voice that rang with pride. "Look! 'Captain Malcolm Vail d'Alvery,' and so on and so on!" she exclaimed. "It's exactly like Vail to write about it all that way, isn't it?

694

'My *second* oak-leaf cluster! *As easy to catch as the common cold'!"*

"Take it easy, Cresside, or you'll bust," Gervais remarked. "Not that I blame you much. The boy's done damn well. . . . He doesn't say anything about having heard from Phil, does he?"

"No, he says he hasn't." Cresside resumed her reading, trying to conceal her feeling that the rest of the letter was a good deal of an anticlimax, as far as she was concerned. " 'I wonder if any of the folks have heard from Phil? I've been trying to locate him, but haven't had any luck so far. When I do, I'll let you know straight off. It might be some time though because most of our outfits have moved so fast and so far since the break-through at Coutance that I don't suppose even the staff knows from one day to the next exactly where they all are. Two letters about Dad—one from you and one from Mom—have come in this last week. I sure am glad the real hero of the family is staging such a swell comeback. Give him my best and tell him I'd be glad if he'd write me himself, but not to bother if he doesn't feel like it. We'll have lots of time to hash everything over when we're all back at Belle Heloise again.' "

CHAPTER LIII

EVERY MEMBER of the family shared Cresside's feeling of pride and triumph in this letter, and for a few days all thoughts centered on that, rather than on the form letter from the War Department. No further word came through from Phil, after his brief and rather ribald note, so they continued to assure themselves, without forced optimism, that he was all right. Then Cresside, who more than any other one person represented the most reliable and frequent source of information from the outside world, appeared with news of an entirely different character.

"It looks as if we'd have to get ready for another wedding," she remarked casually one afternoon, lighting a cigarette and dropping down in the Turkish chair beside her mother's couch.

"Another wedding!" Madame d'Alvery exclaimed. She had by no means recovered from the shock of Sybelle's, and she did not feel equal to facing another like it. Then she had a brief gleam of hope. "You mean that Vail's coming home on leave? That at last he and Susannah Prescott——"

"Nothing like that, I'm sorry to say. But——"

"Then has Joyeuse finally made up her mind to accept Barry Pereira?"

"No indeed. She's still completely absorbed in keeping up her morale.

At least as far as I know. You might hear about it first if she weren't. Anyhow, Merry'd know before I would. But my one ewe lamb has got her own way at last, like she usually does. I believe she's the stubbornest one of our whole tribe, and that's saying a good deal."

Cresside made the statement proudly rather than apologetically. Her mother, still preoccupied by the previous one, disregarded it completely.

"Frances Belle? But I did not even know she had a serious suitor, Cresside."

"Yes, you did, *maman*. At least I've told you so, a dozen times, and Frances Belle has brought him out here once or twice."

"You're not by any chance referring to that snub-nosed, freckled young Irishman who pilots some kind of a tug on the river, are you, Cresside?"

"Yes, I am, *maman*. Punt O'Malley. Only it isn't a tugboat he's on, it's a towboat. And he does hold a pilot's license and take a pilot's watch, but he's the Master. He's doing a very important type of work. I've explained all that to you before—at least I thought I had."

"You have explained nothing, Cresside, which would reconcile me to a marriage between Frances Belle and any kind of a river pilot. It seems as if all my grandchildren were bent on mésalliances."

"I wouldn't say that if I were you, *maman*. I don't think even you can say Vail didn't choose an aristocrat."

Cresside's voice was level, but its tone was slightly ominous, and the remark itself was too irrefutable for any attempted contradiction. While Madame d'Alvery, feeling that Providence was most unjust in calling upon her to face this fresh trial, sought for some short but divergent rejoinder, Cresside continued her attack along the same lines.

"As far as that goes, the Pereira family isn't exactly poor white trash, either, so you can't even confine your complaints to your grand-*daughters*. If I'm not mistaken, there were Pereiras in Louisiana before either the d'Alverys or the Estrades got here, some of them holding pretty important positions, too."

"You know perfectly well that I was not referring either to the Prescotts or the Pereiras when I spoke, Cresside. But unfortunately there does not seem to be the slightest prospect of consummation, in either of those directions. What I meant was——"

"What you meant was that Riccardo Tramonte is a Dago peddler's son and that Punt O'Malley might be shanty Irish. I got you all right the first time, *maman*. But somewhere along the line you could be fair enough to admit that if ever there was a living embodiment of Prince Charming, it's Rick. I won't go into all his other fine qualities; I won't even dwell on the fact his father's a multi-millionaire. Well, I'll concede Punt isn't in the same class as Rick, when it comes to looks. But when it comes to character, he's got what it takes."

"Then I am surprised that he is not overseas, like the other young men we know."

"He tried desperately hard to get into one of the services. But some kind of a minor heart ailment kept him out." Cresside spoke with unaffected lightness, as she had in describing Punt's handicap to Vail; she really had no reason to believe it amounted to much. "So he's been doubly determined to make good where he is and he's succeeded," she went on. "He used to be one of the Master's assistants on the *McDougall*. But since the war, Punt's been promoted. The former Master was getting old and he didn't feel equal to the great responsibility which goes with the job now, so he asked to be relieved. You must realize that Punt wouldn't have been selected if his record hadn't really been outstanding. You don't suppose Fabian sanctioned this marriage without checking up on the boy pretty thoroughly, do you? Frances Belle's the apple of his eye, I don't need to tell you that. He wouldn't stand back and let her make a major mistake. Being Fabian, he'd have found a way to prevent it."

"And he has sanctioned it?"

"Yes. That's what I came out on purpose to tell you. Punt feels he isn't justified in asking for time off; he takes his job very seriously and he says he's not having any vacations till the war's over. But Frances Belle'd set her heart on a honeymoon aboard the *McDougall*, in any case. Punt's feeling for the river's contagious and she's caught it from him. So Fabian's been to see Mr. Reynaud, the Superintendent of Inland Waterways, and he's consented to let Frances Belle go down to New Orleans with Punt on the *McDougall's* next trip. It's contrary to the company's policy, and all that, but somehow Fabian's persuaded the powers that be to make an exception in this case."

"And when will this extraordinary honeymoon take place?" Madame d'Alvery inquired, with a sigh which she did not even attempt to suppress.

"Well, we're not sure. Generally the *McDougall* pulls out twelve to eighteen hours after she gets in, but no one ever knows exactly when that will be, or how long it will take to load the barges. Sometimes she leaves around ten in the morning. Naturally that would mean a very small early wedding. Other times she doesn't go out till evening. That would give us time for a larger one, with a reception in the garden, if we only had enough notice. But probably we won't have, so we can't plan on it. I'll let you know definitely as soon as I can, *maman*. Anyhow, it will be within the next three or four days."

Fabian brought the awaited message to his mother-in-law two evenings later. Outwardly she had managed to maintain her usual attitude of detachment and calm; but inwardly she had been greatly upset by the unconventionality of the entire proceeding. Frances Belle had been to see her briefly, but the girl had sat on the edge of her chair every minute, her readiness for flight adding to her grandmother's malaise. No, she didn't care at all about a white satin dress and a lace veil. Personally she thought her new tailored Shantung was a knockout, good enough for anyone to be married in, and Punt thought so too. Now Syb and Rick both went in for things like veils and receptions and all that in a big way, and that was all right with her, if they liked it; but she didn't care a hoot about frills like that, and neither did Punt. All they wanted was to get married quick and get away quick. . . .

Having delivered this uncompromising statement, Frances Belle made good the escape for which she had been prepared all along, and Madame d'Alvery heard nothing further until Fabian appeared and saluted her in his old gay fashion.

"Well, the *McDougall's* in," he said. "But this being Friday, she won't pull out until Monday, probably around eleven in the morning. So the youngsters are going to be married at an eight o'clock Mass and come back to the house for an hour or so afterwards. We'll have a real breakfast for a wedding this time, not champagne and chicken salad and ice cream around one o'clock in the afternoon."

"Fabian, I simply cannot understand your attitude towards this marriage. When I think that Frances Belle is your only daughter— your only *child*—and the plans you must have had for her——"

"Yes, of course I did. Of course Cresside did too. We've tried to give her all the so-called advantages. I think we have. She's had a good home, she's been to a good school, she's traveled a lot. If the war hadn't come along she'd have had an old-fashioned debut, and she might have been Queen of Comus along with it. She'd have been a golden girl and she'd have met a lot of gilded youths, none of them in the least like Punt O'Malley. As you say, I had my plans all pretty carefully laid. Nothing quite like a war for changing fashions, though, Tante Isabelle. And Frances Belle likes to do things the new way."

"She likes to do things her *own* way. When I think of how you and Cresside have spoiled that child, Fabian——"

"I'm still betting on her," Fabian retorted agreeably. "And it wasn't ever part of my plan, or Cresside's either, to stand in the way of her happiness. Punt O'Malley *is* her happiness. . . . Do you think you can make eight o'clock Mass on Monday all right, Tante Isabelle?"

In a resigned tone Madame d'Alvery said she supposed she could, and she did. The ceremony had more to commend it than she had anticipated. The members of Punt O'Malley's immediate family had come down from Alexandria and they were really quite presentable. As his four brothers were all overseas, he had asked one of his assistants on the *McDougall,* Rodney Campbell, to be his best man, and this young captain proved to be very personable and well-mannered. Frances Belle looked surprisingly bridal after all, wearing her white Shantung suit and a little white veiled hat. Joyeuse made a bewitching bridesmaid, and Sybelle, who sat with the Tramontes, really seemed to be growing more beautiful every day of her life. Considering the early hour and the short notice, it was amazing how many people were present; St. Joseph's was almost filled. Even the New Orleans relatives and out-of-town friends like the Pereiras and the Prescotts had managed to come. The d'Alverys maintained their prestige in the face of every disadvantage. Madame d'Alvery doubted whether any wedding in Baton Rouge that year had been better attended.

The first upsetting incident did not occur until the merry and informal wedding breakfast was almost over. The telephone rang, and though no one paid any attention to it at first, Rodney Campbell, who was making himself extremely agreeable to Madame d'Alvery at that point, excused himself and went in to answer it. When he returned to the dining room, instead of going back to Madame d'Alvery's side, he approached the preoccupied bridegroom, and after several unsuccessful attempts, succeeded in attracting his attention. Punt listened to Rodney's whispered communication looking a little blank, and presently, in turn, whispered to Frances Belle. She edged over to her father, who had taken the vacated seat in the corner beside his mother-in-law, and spoke to him in a voice that was none the less vexed because she managed to keep it low.

"Wouldn't this burn you up, Daddy?" she said. "You know Punt's orders were to report back to the *McDougall* at eleven o'clock unless instructed to the contrary. Well, he *has* been instructed to the contrary. There's been an unexpected delay in loading the barges. They've been short of space at the S.O. ever since the high water cut the bank right out from under one of the docks. That phone call was to say that Punt and Rodney weren't to report till seven this evening instead of at eleven this morning. We can't have this crowd hanging around all that time. Their drinks would die on them no matter how many you gave them, or else they'd be looping before noon. Can't you get rid of them some way, Daddy?"

"Of course I can. They don't need to know that Punt's orders have been changed. After all, only the immediate family was going to see you off, because of the company's rules against visitors at the plant. Make your get-away in about ten minutes, baby, just as you'd planned to do. But instead of going out to the plant, go to Belle Heloise and stay for a couple of hours or so. Then come back here and we'll have a quiet lunch and a nice afternoon. These things do happen, but they don't add up to much in the long run. You'll still be on the *McDougall* before dark, and there couldn't be a prettier time to start out."

"But I thought I was going to be on her right away. And the orders might change again. We can't go all that far from the telephone."

"I'm sure Rodney'll be glad to stick around and listen. If the orders are changed within the next two hours, he can come straight after you. The company's bound to give Punt a reasonable amount of time to get on his boat. Don't worry, honey! Remember I'll be here too."

Madame d'Alvery's uneasiness became greater and greater as she listened, with her usual faculty for overhearing whispered conversations, to the proposed changes in program. She was not troubled because the Standard Oil was grappling with difficulties in loading its barges; her concern centered wholly on Frances Belle and the girl's possible course of conduct during the delay. She was all too well aware that her granddaughter was not the sort of reluctant and unenlightened bride that she herself had been. Far from rushing back to her parents to escape her bridegroom, Frances Belle might insist that there was no reason why an entire day should be wasted, when her honeymoon was bound to be so brief at best. Instead of repeating the now historic declaration *"Je ne peux pas me coucher avec ce cochon là! Il veut m'enlever la chemise!"* she was quite capable of saying, in everyone's hearing, "Come along to my room, Punt—our room, I mean. There's no use hanging around in this crowd all day."

Again, however, Madame d'Alvery's worst fears proved groundless. Frances Belle revolted, on general principles, against authority and advice from every source but one—her father. His she not only accepted but respected. She returned to her bridegroom and whispered to him again. Her vexation was at least partially under control now, her voice softer, and the distance that separated her from her grandmother greater; though Madame d'Alvery strained her alert ears, she could not hear what was said this time. But a few minutes later Frances Belle came over and kissed her, and Punt said good-by to her very nicely too; then they made the rounds of the room. Frances Belle was not going upstairs to change her dress, because she was traveling in the same one she had worn in church; she was not tossing out a bouquet, because she had carried only a white prayer book. A shower of rice followed her as she went down the walk on Punt's arm, and the car in which they dashed off was decorated with the usual streamers and placards; but they made their escape very quickly and efficiently, and not more than half a dozen persons knew that there had been any change of plan. Neither Cresside nor Fabian gave any impression of wishing to speed their guests; coffee cups were refilled and fresh relays of waffles and sausages appeared. But within an hour or so everyone except Rodney Campbell, Madame d'Alvery, Merry and Joyeuse had left—even Sybelle, who at last had succeeded in getting hold of just the right electrician, and who had no idea of letting him escape her through lack of supervision. When she left, she took Mrs. Randall and Miss Mittie with her. The O'Malleys had to get back to Alexandria, the Pereiras and Estrades to New Orleans. After these general departures, Cresside suggested that in view of the early hour at which Madame d'Alvery had risen, not to mention the subsequent effort she had made and the fatigue and excitement she had undergone, she might like to take her siesta earlier than usual, in one of the dormer guest rooms. But Madame d'Alvery was adamant on this point; she did not wish to be absent when Frances Belle and—she pronounced the name with difficulty—Punt returned from Belle Heloise. Her attitude towards the marriage remained unchanged. But no matter how fatigued or displeased she might feel, she hoped she would never be uncivil to a wedding couple on their bridal day.

The corners of Cresside's mouth twitched slightly. She knew what was passing in her mother's mind, and though herself undisturbed, realized perfectly—since she also had no delusions about Frances Belle —that she must be prepared for almost anything. However, in exactly two hours, the bride and groom returned, neither one looking in the least self-conscious, and reported that they had spent the latter part of the morning with Gervais, who had not been able to come to the wedding. He had been mighty glad to see them, for he was all alone in his office, with nothing much to do; in fact, he had urged them to stay and have dinner with him; but they had said they would be back in two hours, so they thought perhaps they better. Had there been any further word from the company? No, none at all, Rodney Campbell reported, so he would cruise along now; he'd be seeing them at seven. Merry and Joyeuse also announced that they thought they had better be on their way; the unexpected visit from Frances Belle and Punt must have cheered Gervais immensely; but still he was apt to get very depressed if he were left too long alone, and they had been gone quite a while now. Again the advisability of a siesta, this time in her own room, was urged upon Madame d'Alvery, and again she was adamant. She had never been inside the Standard Oil plant, she reminded her family, and she had always wanted to see it. There was no telling when she would be permitted another pass, the company was so strict about such matters, since the war. She would lie down for a little while after dinner, but she would prefer to do so in Frances Belle's room; it would tire her too much to go out to Belle Heloise and return, and the stairs to the dormers were rather steep. She assumed that the others would spend the afternoon playing bridge. . . .

Again the corners of Cresside's mouth twitched, but she did not fail to sense Punt's wretched embarrassment or to catch the mutinous expression on Frances Belle's face. As usual, Fabian came to the rescue, making everything seem easy and natural.

"Very good idea, Tante Isabelle. I've been looking for an excuse to stay away from the office this afternoon. One of the worst old windbags I know is due there for a long recital of his troubles with the levee board. Shall you and I take the youngsters on for a set game, Cresside, and lick the daylights out of them? Or shall we give them a fighting chance by rotating?"

"Give us a fighting chance, won't you please, Daddy?"

She cast one last resentful glance at her grandmother before the old lady took her triumphant departure. Then she and Punt set up the bridge table on the terrace, and the game began. It was by no means one-sided, for they were all good players, and soon their interest in it was unfeigned; though Punt glanced surreptitiously at his wrist watch, now and then, the gesture indicated little more than meticulous attention to the passage of time, in connection with his duty. When Madame d'Alvery, still obviously triumphant, reappeared, the others were all intent on five hearts, vulnerable, doubled and redoubled, and no one looked up immediately. She had come out softly on purpose,

701

as she had long since learned that much could be gleaned from an unobtrusive entrance; nevertheless she felt slighted by such complete absorption. Fortunately Fabian became aware of her presence after a minute or two, nodded to her, and making a warning gesture to indicate silence, smiled pleasantly. As soon as it was evident that Frances Belle would gather in all the remaining tricks, he rose quietly and went over to his mother-in-law.

"That gives the youngsters game and rubber," he said. "Frances Belle's right—all they need is a fighting chance. With that, they can take mighty good care of themselves. Sit down, Tante Isabelle. We'll be having coffee straight off—or maybe it better be high tea. What time do you generally have supper aboard the *McDougall*, Punt?"

"At six, sir."

"Then if you don't report in until seven, isn't there a chance the kitchen will already be closed for the night?"

"I'm afraid there is. I forgot about that."

Again he looked embarrassed and unhappy. A late and more or less fruitless forage, undertaken to supply his bride with some kind of a sketchy snack so that she would not go to bed hungry, would have been the last straw. Though chagrined at the necessity of his new father-in-law's reminder, he was nevertheless thankful for it. And Cresside acted upon it immediately.

"Of course we'll have supper right away. We've had champagne on ice all day—ever since we found you two were staying. And I know Carmelite has shrimp salad, too. We'll just reinforce those two main items. Let's eat right here, shan't we? We'll pull up another bridge table and put the two together."

Champagne was Madame d'Alvery's great weakness, and as Fabian had contrived somehow to hoard a dwindling supply of Pommery Sec, she was presently in a much mellower mood. The little supper party progressed pleasantly, and by the time they had finished the compote of fresh spiced pears which represented the last of the reinforcements to the shrimp salad, Fabian forestalled Punt in checking on the hour, and announced that it was time they started for the plant. Then, ceremoniously, he helped his mother-in-law into the car drawn up behind the one which had been stripped of its telltale bridal adornment. But first he got in a word with Punt.

"You two go along by yourselves. Just park your car at the dock and I'll drive it back and put it in my garage. Mrs. d'Alvery will take her mother back in ours. By the way, though, I hope you're not going to keep on calling her that! Do you call your own father and mother Dad and Mom? You don't?—good! Now get along—we'll see you on the boat."

Punt and Frances Belle had already been on the *McDougall* fifteen minutes when her grandmother and her parents arrived. For a lady in her seventies, who had contrived to maintain an illusion of invalidism for more than half of her life, Madame d'Alvery had shown remark-able agility in getting up the steep gangplank from the pier to the *Slack Barrett,* from that across another gangplank to the *Amos K. Gordon,* and from that across still another to the boiler deck of the *McDougall.* But it was hardly surprising she had not been able to equal Frances Belle's speed in doing all this, quite aside from the fact that the girl had a head start. Before seeking out her granddaughter, Madame d'Alvery investigated the tiny open deck equipped with a few old-fashioned rocking chairs, the oval saloon with small cabins opening from it, and even peered into the kitchen. Cresside and Fabian, though satisfied with a more cursory glance, waited until she had satisfied her curiosity; then they helped her up the steps to the Texas. The door leading into the Master's cabin stood open: the wide metal bed, narrow metal clothes closet, small table and straight-backed chairs which constituted its entire equipment, were all visible. Frances Belle's beautiful little overnight case, its initialed suede cover neatly buttoned down around it, and her large square leather hat box stood on the floor beside Punt's battered suitcase. The muslin curtains at the small window, though rather frayed, had been freshly laundered, and the bare little room had the unmistakable atmosphere of recent and thorough cleaning. There was a bunch of flowers on the little table, and on the hooks attached haphazardly to the wall, some coat hangers covered with pink velvet and adorned with ribbon rosettes. Madame d'Alvery was conscious of the cramped conditions and the inadequate furniture; Cresside and Fabian were conscious of the cleanliness, the flowers and the new coat hangers. But before any of them could make any comment, Rodney Campbell, swinging out of the office beyond the bathroom with some printed forms in his hand, nodded to the group hospitably.

"Punt and Frances Belle are up in the pilot house already," he said. "Punt's taking the first watch—that'll let him off at midnight. You haven't met Ted Graham, the second mate yet, have you? Well, he's there with them now and they're all expecting you to go up. Hank Martin, Punt's other assistant who generally alternates with me going down the river, offered to make this trip too, so that Punt could be relieved entirely; but he said no, he'd never been down the river yet without standing his watch, since he got his pilot's license, and he never would. So instead I'm going to stay aboard all the time the *McDougall's* in port and he'll have that time free. Don't you want to see the office, while you're on the Texas? Punt won't be down again until long after you've left, and from the look of things I don't believe Frances Belle intends to leave him. But it's all right for you to go in there and poke around by yourselves."

Rodney grinned, and went off with his forms. Fabian, politely asking Madame d'Alvery if she felt equal to another flight of steps, and having been indignantly assured that she did, led her up the last companionway, after she had taken advantage of Rodney's suggestion that she should inspect the office first. Punt was already standing beside the wheel, his eyes fixed on the barges which a large crew of men were lashing to the towboat. Another young man, with an equally pleasant face and alert manner, who was standing near by watching too, turned at once to the d'Alverys and introduced himself before Punt could do it for him.

"I'm Ted Graham, the second mate," he said pleasantly. "I was mighty sorry I couldn't get to the wedding, but we've got a new baby at our house, and I don't have so much time with him and my wife. I knew you'd all understand. We're sure proud to have a bride aboard the *McDougall*. Miss Frances is the first one, as far as I know."

He looked at Frances Belle with a smile. She was already perched on the large settee elevated on an iron stand back of the wheel, and had taken off her veiled hat and the jacket of her Shantung suit. Her hair was lightly ruffled, and the blouse she had been wearing all day was rather crushed. She looked completely at home and at ease. All the impatience and vexation had vanished from her face.

"Isn't it wonderful up here? Look at that sunset, Daddy. I think it's the most beautiful sunset I ever saw—or perhaps it's just that we can see it better, without a levee or houses or anything like that in the way! And then the flares, and the lights coming on at the plant, and the Missouri-Pacific ferry right behind us! It's all just as I knew it would be, only a hundred times better!"

She slid down from her high seat to fling her arms around her father. The embrace was rapturous, but it was not clinging. She loved him better than anyone in the world except Punt, but she did not need him any longer. Now that she had shown him her proud place in the pilot house, she wanted him to go—her mother and grandmother too. Of course she had been wishing all day that her grandmother would go, and on their way out to the plant, she had made some very cutting remarks about the old lady to Punt. But there was nothing cutting about her manner now, because she was so happy. She did not kiss Madame d'Alvery good-by with quite the same fondness she showed in embracing her father and mother, but she gave her an affectionate kiss just the same. Madame d'Alvery was so mollified by it that she unbent noticeably on the way home.

"I was not as unfavorably impressed by that boat as I expected to be," she admitted. "And I must say that all those young men have very nice manners. As you reminded me, Cresside, the war has brought about many social changes. We can hardly expect a girl of independent spirit, like Frances Belle, to accept the same restrictions in her circle of acquaintances that I did. It may be just as well that she should not. Perhaps we were almost too self-sufficient at Belle Heloise in the old days."

"I'm glad you've come to feel that way, *maman*," Cresside murmured. "I'm sure Frances Belle would be very pleased if she could hear you say so."

At the moment, as Cresside very well knew, nothing Frances Belle's grandmother said would have mattered to her in the least, one way or another. Indeed, it would probably have taken a very strong reminder to make her remember that she had a grandmother. The glass enclosures of the pilot house had all been thrown wide open now, and a cool breeze was blowing through; it swept away the heavy heat of the day, and with this, the last vestiges of the day's petty irritations and annoyances. The walls presented practically no obstruction, since only a minor part of these was not adjustable to the weather. There was a small wooden space, at the right of the wheel, to which a clock, some fluttering forms and a few framed notices were affixed, but that was all. Even the notices were intriguing to Frances Belle, and the wording of one was especially arresting:

"ALERT!—it said in bold black letters——

Your Skill and Devotion Will

WIN THE WAR!"

Lettered less conspicuously, in one corner, were the words: "U.S. Dept. of Commerce," and Frances Belle realized that such signs were probably distributed by the hundred. But she knew there was none taken more literally than this copy, or placed where the man to whom its message was intensely personal and stimulating would have it more constantly before him.

The flame of the sunset was subsiding, but under the darker skies, the twinkling lights along the shores seemed all the brighter, and overhead the stars were beginning to come out. A searchlight was playing too, in a long shaft of silvery radiance from the pilot house to the barges. Punt directed this towards the different places where men were still working below. Every now and then he called to them through a megaphone which he took from the ledge of the wide window before him, where it was conveniently placed, and they called back, cupping their mouths with their hands. But for the most part he seemed to know, instinctively, exactly where the light was needed most. In her fascinated state, Frances Belle watched this phenomenon and all the others about her with such complete absorption, that though she heard the *McDougall's* whistle, as she heard other wonderful sounds which had suddenly ceased to be alien, she did not even realize that the boat had started until Punt turned to her, his hands still on the wheel.

"Well, we're off at last, baby," he said in a tone of relief.

"Really, Punt? Why yes, I can see we're moving! But very slowly, aren't we?"

"We'll be going faster pretty soon."

"And nothing can stop us now!"

"No, nothing can stop us now. We go straight through to Chalmette."

She drew a deep breath. But she did not try to talk. It was enough merely to sit on the high settee, watching Punt at the wheel, and beyond him, framed by the great rectangle of the open window, the river and the shore. They glided quietly past the city, and after that there were fewer and fewer lights as they went along, fewer and fewer sounds too. But somehow the scene became increasingly beautiful in the same measure that it became increasingly dim and tranquil. Frances Belle sat very still, content in the quietude, yet more and more alive to the fact that time was not dragging any longer, that one moment was crowding quickly upon another. Presently Punt's watch would be over. Presently he would leave the wheel and go down to the Texas. Presently he would turn out the last light in the little room and stretch out his arms for her in the dark. Then he would find her quickly and hold her closely and take her for his own. If she had not loved him so much, she would have been a little frightened because that was all so near now, and because strange poignant feelings were forking through her, coming harder and harder all the time. She looked at the clock on the wall beside the sign which said "alert," and it seemed to her that it was not merely ticking any longer, but whispering too: "In just a little while now, Frances Belle. In just an hour or two. You've always been a spoiled child, whimpering if you pricked your finger, sulking if you couldn't have your own way. Your father and mother aren't here now. Only your husband. That's very different. He won't stand for any whimpering and sulking. He's going to have his way." Under her breath she talked back to the clock: "I'm not a spoiled child any longer. I'm a woman married to the man she loves. I don't need my father and mother here to protect me from my husband. What's his way is my way too. How dare you talk to me about whimpering over a cut finger at the same time you talk to me about becoming Punt's wife?" Suddenly she felt that she wanted to prove what she was saying by going down to the little room on the Texas right away, so that she would be waiting for Punt when he came. If she did that he'd know she wasn't frightened, but ready and eager for his love. She slid down from her seat, and instantly he turned to nod and smile at her.

"You must go down to the boiler deck in the morning and look at the way we're lashed in between the barges," he said. "You can't see very well in this light. There are two directly in front and two on either side filled with bunker fuel for the Army and Navy ships. Those are all big barges. Then there are two smaller ones still further up in front, at the left, filled with aviation gas. Our bow fits right in between the first barge in front and the first two on either side, leaving little open triangles where you can see the muddy water churning around our bow. I think you'd like to see it. We call it the duck pond."

"Of course I'd like to see it."

"The best place to stand is right on the open deck where the rocking chairs are. You can go down there as soon as you've had your coffee.

I'll send that up to you around nine, when we have ours the second time. I don't want you getting up at five-thirty. That's when the bell rings. Breakfast is at five-forty-five."

"I'd love to have breakfast with you, Punt. But I won't get up then if you don't want me to."

"No, I don't want you to. I have to go right back on watch, you know."

"You don't get off till midnight and have to be back at six?"

"That's right. We have all square watches on the *McDougall*. Some boats have a dog watch, but we never have. We all like it better this way."

So he won't come down until midnight and he has to be back here at six, she said to herself. *We'll have just five hours and a half together tonight, so we can't waste any of it. I must go down right away, so I'll be ready for him . . .*

"We're almost to Estrade point," Punt was saying. "I'll show it to you when we get a little closer. I thought we might send a telegram to your folks too, as we go by."

"Send a telegram?"

"That's what old Don Ferguson, our chief engineer, calls the special blasts we blow just before we get to the Navy Supply Depot, which used to be the public cotton warehouse. You'll hear them tomorrow morning. He lives right near there and his wife listens for them, when she knows the *McDougall's* coming downstream. Then she gets into their car and starts for Chalmette. I've never known her not to be waiting at the Standard Oil wharf when we pulled in."

"We have signals something like that, on our plantation bell. . . . When you and I get settled in our own little house, Punt, you'll have to send 'telegrams' to me. I haven't had a chance to tell you yet: Mr. Tramonte said this morning he thinks he has just the right one for us—a four-room bungalow in one of his new developments."

"Gee, that's swell. And you bet I'll send you telegrams. But right now let's salute your folks at Belle Heloise."

He reached for the cord dangling above his head and pulled it vigorously three times. "We mustn't forget to ask them whether they heard that," he said. "I've an idea your grandmother will, anyway. She's probably still awake, thinking about you, honey." He looked as if he would have liked to say more if Ted had not been there too, but he had explained to Frances Belle that a second man always stayed in the pilothouse, in case of emergency, and that they would have no chance to talk privately while they were there. She understood the look and she did not resent Ted's presence; she knew Punt would tell her the rest by and by. "You want to start watching for the dredge below Missouri Bend," he went on. "You'll see it any moment now. It's out in the middle of the river, with a pipeline going into shore."

"What's it doing?"

"Making the ship channel deeper. That fills in, every high water."

"I thought maybe I'd go down and get unpacked. I haven't even taken my toothbrush out of my bag yet."

Because of Ted, she spoke with elaborate carelessness. But she knew Punt understood her, just as she had understood him, and she thought that probably Ted did too. He seemed to be the right sort.

"Not a bad idea," Punt answered, also with elaborate carelessness. "But wait just long enough to see that dredging outfit, baby. The pipeline's lighted, and the quarter boat. Then there are the range lights too, and a big blinking red buoy over at the left of the channel. It's a grand sight, and you wouldn't want to miss it. Look—there it is now!"

There was the pipeline to be sure, glittering like a jeweled chain slung halfway across the river. There was the quarter boat too, drawn up against the left bank, outlined by its network of lights. There were the range lights, silvery as the searchlight had been when it played over the barges, instead of golden like the jeweled chain and the network. There was the ruby-red buoy. Punt had been right in telling her she must wait to see all this; she looked at it with a deepening sense of enchantment. But finally the channel and the dredge were behind them. If there were nothing much to see after that——

"Run along, baby. I'll be seeing you."

Frances Belle went down to the Texas and busied herself by putting her most essential toilet articles in the bathroom, and by laying out her white mules and her white ensemble of satin and chiffon and lace. She had not been entirely truthful in telling her grandmother that she did not care a hoot about bridal regalia. Secretly she would have liked very much to surpass the splendor in which Merry had robed Sybelle, and she could not suppress a slight pang now, because if they had only known, beforehand, that the *McDougall* would not go out until evening, she might have had the same sort of wedding as her cousin. But at least nothing could have been more exquisite than the filmy nightgown and the shining negligee that she spread out on the bed now, white as snow, light as feathers, soft as her own delicate skin. After she had arranged them, she stood for a moment looking at them raptly. Then she laid her watch and rosary on the little table, after moving this from its position between the windows and placing it beside the bed, and, for a moment, surveyed Punt's battered suitcase with hesitation. She would have loved to unpack it for him, to lay out his pajamas for the night, his clean shirt and socks for the morning. But after all the suitcase was his, and he might feel she had no right to open it without permission. Besides, he might actually prefer to perform small personal services for himself; she knew her father did, but she had an idea this was because he was unduly sensitive about proving that he was able to do so. She must remember to ask Punt. It was stupid of her not to have done so before; and she must be sure to convince him, when she did so, that she had not hesitated because she was reluctant to perform such services for him. She was eager to do anything she could for him, no matter what.

She unfastened her skirt, hung it neatly over one of the padded hangers, then took off her blouse, stockings and negligible undergarments, extracting others from the ample supply in the square hat box, and putting those she had worn through the day in an embroidered laundry bag. Then she started the water running for a bath. It was unexpectedly murky, and for the first time, she noticed small enameled signs over both the tub and basin, announcing the State Board of Health had pronounced this water unfit for drinking purposes. She was afraid she really would not be much cleaner when she got out of it than she was already, but at least she would feel cleaner. She dumped half a bottle of rosy sweet-smelling salts into the tub, and then she lay in it a long time, forgetting that the water was murky, remembering only that it was cool and soft and scented and thinking of why she wanted to be so fresh and fragrant.

At last she dried herself with one of the coarse clean towels hanging by the tub, turned out the lights and pulled up the shades. The same fresh breeze that had chased the heat of the day from the pilothouse swept in through the windows now, and there was enough light from some unseen source to keep the room from total darkness. Instead it was merely dim and restful, like the river between Baton Rouge and Missouri Bend. Frances Belle was not as faithful or as meticulous about her prayers as Sybelle, and very often she found ready excuses for getting into bed without first getting down on her knees, and merely fingering her rosary while she drifted off to sleep; but tonight she really wanted to pray. However, she hesitated again for a moment. She felt that probably it was not proper to pray—just as she was. On the other hand, she did not want to risk getting the smallest smudge on her nightgown, and she might, if she knelt down in it. Then she felt ashamed. The little room had been scrubbed and scoured; it was no mere figure of speech to say she could have eaten off the floor. But in any case, nothing so trivial as the possibility of a little dust should deter her from giving humble and hearty thanks on such a night as this. She put on not only the filmy nightdress but the white satin negligee, so that she was wholly and beautifully covered; then she knelt down and poured out her soul in thanksgiving, as she had never done before in the entire course of her selfish little life. She did not try to follow any formula. She said what came spontaneously from her overflowing heart.

"Thank you, God, for letting me marry Punt. Thank you for letting me come with him on his boat, down his river, instead of making me go off to be a WAC or a WAVE. Teach me how to be a good wife to him. Because that's all I want, all I want in this world. Just to be with him, just to belong to him. Thank you again for giving me this chance. I'll do the best I can with it. Amen."

She rose and slipped off the negligee, placing it across the foot of the bed again. Then she lay down between the cool clean sheets, and again a trivial concern troubled her briefly, as when she considered unpacking Punt's suitcase for him. Perhaps he liked one side of the bed better than the other; some people did. She should have asked him that too, because of course he would not tell her without asking, if she happened to guess wrong. He was much more considerate about the comfort of others than she was. But hereafter, she would be considerate too. Not just because she had promised, because that was part of being a good wife and an agreeable woman, but because she wanted to, now that Daddy and Mummy and God had let her marry Punt and she had nothing else to wish for. And after all, there was no present problem; she must get over on the further side of the bed, because that was so near the wall of the little room that it was impossible to pass easily between the two. She would lie on the further side, and he would get in on the side where the little table was. . . .

She reached for her rosary and held it firmly, moving the beads resolutely between her fingers and moving her lips too, in the proper prayers, as she did so. But she could not think about prayers any longer. She had already said the one that really mattered, the one which came straight from her heart. Now she could think only of Punt, who would be coming so soon. She had looked at her watch, just before she put out the lights; it had been half past eleven then. She could not believe that less than half an hour had gone by since, so she switched on the light and looked at her watch again. Only a quarter of twelve? Why, that was impossible—the watch must have stopped! No, it was going, it was ticking away reassuringly and whispering to her, in the same way that the clock in the pilothouse had whispered, only this time there was nothing menacing about the murmur. Instead, the little watch was saying: "In just a quarter of an hour, now, Frances Belle. In just a few minutes. You made Punt very happy, coming down to get ready for him, showing him that you weren't afraid of his love, but instead that you were so eager for it that you could hardly wait. Now you've made yourself very lovely, with your fragrant bath and your exquisite garments. You're a beautiful bride. He'll open the door, and look down at the bed and when he sees you lying there, waiting for him in the dimness, he'll be happier than he's ever been in his whole life. Just as you're happier than you've ever been in your whole life. But presently you'll both be even happier."

The little watch went on, telling off the moments. But Frances Belle could hear other sounds now, besides its prophetic ticking. At first she was hardly conscious of them, because she was listening so intently to the watch; and though she slowly became more aware of them, they did not disturb her. She knew there were bound to be many sounds on the *McDougall,* besides the whistle and the bell, and that most of these would be unfamiliar to her. But when she heard startled voices and hurried footsteps, she sat up to listen. Something must be wrong. Then the hurrying footsteps and the startled voices died away in the distance. Whatever had gone wrong must have been almost immediately righted. Of course it would be, with Punt at the wheel. And presently he would tell her what had happened— that is, if he thought it would be worth while, considering all the other important things they had to say to each other. . . .

She heard footsteps again, slow ones this time, approaching her room. It was midnight at last. Punt's watch was over. He was coming to her, and she wondered briefly why he was walking slowly like that, instead of hurrying, as she had expected he would. Then she wondered why he knocked instead of coming straight in. It was strange that a bridegroom should stop to do that, a bridegroom who knew his bride had been waiting eagerly for him a whole hour.

"Come in, Punt. Come in, darling."

"I'm sorry, Mrs. O'Malley. It isn't Punt. It's Ted. May I speak to you for a moment?"

She reached for the white satin dressing gown and switched on the light. She was surprised and terribly disappointed. When she spoke again the joyousness had all gone from her voice.

"Yes, of course. Come in, Ted."

He swung open the screen and entered the room. Then, for the first time, she was frightened. There was something about the expression of his face . . .

"Punt's had a sudden heart attack, Mrs. O'Malley. He slumped right down beside the wheel."

"Where is he now?"

"He's still in the pilothouse. On the settee. Rod's with him. Of course I ran for Rod the moment Punt started to slump. But the boat got out of control for a moment."

"I knew something had happened. I'll come right up to the pilothouse with you. Is there anything I ought to bring with me?"

"No. You don't need to bring anything."

"I thought perhaps there was something special he needed, when he had one of these attacks. He's never said much to me about them, though. You'll tell me what to do when we get there, won't you, Ted?"

She was already out of bed, knotting the white satin dressing gown about her slim waist, thrusting her bare feet into the white satin mules. She did not wait for his answer, but ran out of the room and along the deck ahead of him. She could see Rodney at the wheel and several other men clustered around the settee as she went rapidly up the steps to the pilothouse. Rodney turned towards her, but the other men fell back at once. Then she saw Punt lying very still, his face white under his freckles. She hurried to him and took his hand, but it fell back on the settee beside him, with a little thud. She looked imploringly from him to Rodney.

711

"He fainted, didn't he, when he had the attack? A faint lasts a long while, sometimes, I know. But isn't there something we can do to bring him out of it?"

"No, nothing. . . . A faint does last a long while, sometimes," Rodney said gently. "But Punt hasn't fainted, Frances Belle. I know you'll be a good soldier, for his sake. Because he always was. One of the very best."

CHAPTER LIV

The nearest place where the *McDougall* could put in was Donaldsonville. When it reached there, Donald Ferguson and Ted Graham went ashore immediately and divided the necessary telephoning between them. Rodney stayed with Frances Belle while they were gone, and at first he tried to talk to her a little. Then he realized it would be better if he did not. She required no soothing, because she was not hysterical; she did not even cry quietly. She simply sat beside Punt, looking down at him in a stunned way. Once or twice she tried to take his hand. Then she folded her own hands, and looked at those. Rodney knew she was not seeing her hands or anything else.

By and by sounds of various kinds began to come from the dock, and the chief engineer and second mate reappeared in the pilothouse. Ferguson, who was a kindly-looking, white-haired old man, went over to Frances Belle.

"The ambulance is here," he said. "And we've got hold of your father. He and your mother are leaving the house right away—well, of course, they have left it by now. Don't you think perhaps you'd better go down to your room and dress, my dear? Then you can go right along in the ambulance. That's what you want to do, isn't it? You're to meet your father and mother by the station in Plaquemine."

She rose obediently, and returned to the little room on the Texas, dressing in the clean underthings and blouse which she had laid out for morning, and in the white suit and hat which she had worn for her wedding. She had not unpacked anything else, and it did not occur to her to do so now. But she did put the new velvet hangers in her hat box, and she lifted the flowers out of the vase on the table by the bed. When Ferguson came to see if she were ready, she spoke to him about the flowers.

"I thought perhaps I could take these with me, for Punt, until——"

"Yes, of course. You'd like to carry those yourself, wouldn't you? I'll have one of the deckhands come for the bags."

"Is it all right for me to take Punt's suitcase away too?"

"Yes, of course," Ferguson said a second time, rather huskily. "I
712

wish I knew some lady in Donaldsonville, Miss Frances, that I could send with you in the ambulance. But you see I live in New Orleans, so I'm not acquainted much around here, and neither are any of the others. If one of us could go with you, it wouldn't seem quite so bad either. But you see, until the company can send us another pilot——"

"I know. And I'd rather be alone, really. I wouldn't want some lady from Donaldsonville with me. And you are all mighty kind, but——"

He could see that she meant it. He went with her to the ambulance, and so did Ted, while Rodney stayed behind on the boat after saying good-by to her in the pilothouse. She sat very still beside the stretcher, just as she had sat very still beside the settee. The driver and his helper told each other afterwards that they had never seen a young widow who took on so little. Fabian's car was already parked beside the platform of the railway station in Plaquemine when the ambulance drew up there. He and Cresside were standing beside it and hurried over. Frances Belle got out to meet them, but she did not cling to them when they put their arms around her, any longer than she had when she was saying good-by to them a few hours earlier. Instead she asked questions, in a stunned way.

"What do we have to do next, Daddy?"

"We have to take Punt to a funeral home, darling. I think it had better be one in Baton Rouge. We've made all the necessary arrangements, subject to your approval. In the morning, we'll have to go on to Alexandria. Of course Punt's family will want us to bring him there."

"Yes. I suppose so. I wish he could stay in Baton Rouge, but I suppose he can't. I can stay with him, though, can't I, until . . ."

"Yes, if you want to, darling . . . That is, except for just a few minutes. Your mother and I'll stay too."

"If you don't mind, Daddy, I'd rather not have anyone else stay. Not even you and Mummy."

"Frances Belle—" Cresside began. But Fabian put a warning hand on his wife's arm.

"We won't stay in the room with you and Punt, darling, if you don't want us to. We'll just stay near, so that you'll know you can get hold of us, any time. And perhaps you ought to rest for a little while before we start to Alexandria, so you won't be too tired when we get there. If you'd go home and do that, by and by, Mummy and I'd stay with Punt while you were gone."

"I don't want to go home and rest, Daddy. I want to stay with Punt every moment I can. I won't be too tired."

Again Fabian quietly warned Cresside against argument, and presently they went on again. Frances Belle accepted without any protest all the arrangements they told her were necessary. It was not until her mother asked her an inevitable question, the next morning, that she spoke obdurately.

"If there's anything you want me to do about clothes, darling, I'm afraid I ought to be getting to it, right away. There isn't much time, unfortunately."

"Clothes?"

"Don't you want a black dress, Frances Belle, and a black veil? To wear to the fun—in Alexandria, I mean?"

"No," Frances Belle answered abruptly. "I don't want a black dress or a black veil to wear in Alexandria or anywhere else. I'm going to wear just what I have on to Alexandria."

"But—".

"Widows wear white, don't they, sometimes?"

"Yes, but not——"

Cresside could hardly say: "Not the same white they wore to be married in." So she stopped. But Frances Belle went on.

"I've got enough white dresses, in my hat box, to wear for the next few days. I don't know what I'll be wearing after that or what I'll be doing. But I do know one thing: I won't be staying in bed for two years, and I won't be going around draped like an undertaker's window all the rest of my life. That's not my idea of the way to show a man you loved him."

Cresside pressed her lips together. There were so many things that she could not say, or must not say, to Frances Belle. Again her daughter spoke for her.

"And don't worry, Mummy. I won't make that remark in front of *grand'mère* unless she drives me to it. And I don't intend to give her the chance to do that. She isn't coming to Alexandria, is she?"

"No, she isn't equal to the trip. That isn't put on either, darling. She really would have come if she had been."

"Well, let's be thankful she isn't."

"So would your Uncle Gervais and Sybelle," Cresside went on, again feeling it was better to disregard Frances Belle's remark. "But the doctor advised very strongly against it. However, your Aunt Merry and Joyeuse——"

"That's quite enough. I'd really rather it was only you and Daddy. But I won't say that either, Mummy. I won't say anything that will make you ashamed of me."

"I'm not ashamed of you, darling. I'm very proud of you. Your father and I keep telling each other how wonderful you've been."

They had every reason to feel continued pride. Nothing could have been more dignified and controlled than Frances Belle's behavior throughout the next few days, and after their return to Baton Rouge she went back to her own room in a matter-of-fact way, unpacked and put her belongings in order. There were no signs of the reaction which her parents had feared would eventually be inevitable. She did not collapse and she did not cry in their presence; neither did she refer, in any way, to Punt. She said she would rather not see any callers, and she did not eat very much, but she spent a great deal of time with

714

Cresside on the terrace and she went to the table as usual. In the evenings she talked with her father, collectedly, about inconsequential things. Then he came home one afternoon to find that she was not there.

"She went out a couple of hours ago," Cresside told him, reassuringly. "I was glad when she said she wanted to, Fabian. It'll do her good to get away from the house and have some exercise. She's been shut up here with you and me for a good while now. She's been in her own room alone a good deal, too."

"Yes, I know. And I know that part of the time she's been crying. But I know that part of the time she's been thinking things through, too. She didn't say where she was going, did she?"

"No, just that she wanted to take a walk, like I told you."

He smiled, a little uncertainly, and after that he himself sat with Cresside on the terrace all through the early evening. He was still with her when Frances Belle came back and found them there together. She went to them and stood between them, putting a hand on the shoulder of each.

"Daddy," she said, "Mummy." Then she stopped. Apparently she found it hard to go on, yet they both knew they must not interrupt her, but give her time to say what was on her mind, in her own way. "I hope you won't feel too badly about what I'm going to tell you," she said at last. "I've just done something you may take rather hard, but it was something I had to do. Not just something I wanted to do this time. I've applied for enlistment in the WAC's. If I hadn't been married I'd have had to ask your consent because I'm under twenty-one, but since I am . . . Of course I don't know whether my application will be accepted, or how soon, if it is. But I do think we won't be having many more evenings together. So we ought to make the most of those, don't you think so?"

CHAPTER LV

NEXT TO Frances Belle herself, none of the d'Alverys took Punt's death quite so hard as Gervais. Not that he had seen much of the boy. But he had liked immensely the little he did see, and it had seemed good to him, on general principles, to have a young and healthy male around again, on a family footing. He did not accord this status to any of the young men who so futilely pursued Joyeuse, partly because she herself declined to do so, even in the case of Barry Pereira, and partly because none of them, not even Barry Pereira, went out of their way to show her father any special courtesy or consideration. But

Punt had always been very different in this respect; he had made a point of dropping in at the storehouse, the few times he had been to Belle Heloise, and spending a quarter of an hour or so with the boss-man, talking about the war, the crops and the river. Gervais had already begun to feel that the young pilot was really one of them when the bride and groom came out to spend the morning with him, after their early wedding. The hours they had been there then strengthened and cemented this feeling. When Gervais was told, early the following day, that the boy was dead, the shock was severe.

He was alone a great deal these days, and possibly this was one of the reasons his mind continued to dwell on the tragedy which had been so startling and which still seemed so futile. But aside from the fact that his loneliness gave him too much time for brooding, he did not especially mind it. The solitude was restful and he was still very tired. He had tried two or three times to go out to the mill, which was running at full blast now, but this had resulted in such devastating fatigue that he had been easily dissuaded from making the effort. Joyeuse and Sance came to give him reports about the progress of grinding, and he took their word that this was satisfactory; he did not even try to see anyone else connected with the work very often. Cresside and Fabian and Sybelle came faithfully to visit him, but this was usually after supper, for they were all busy during the day. It took Merry a good deal of time to do the errands, now that she was obliged to go from store to store, in search of the simplest commodity, and Madame d'Alvery spent most of the afternoon taking her indispensable siesta. Gervais also rested after dinner, but not for long; he got up very late and went to bed very early, spending the intervening time in his office and lying down there. Nothing disturbed him. The old familiar quietude of mid-afternoon still descended on Belle Heloise.

It was during this interval that he usually wrote in his diary. There was not much to set down in it these days. "Nights cool and pleasant. Days warm and fair. No traces here of Florida hurricane which was, however, very bad. 11 employees of N.O. Port of Embarkation killed while taking tug to East coast, when all hands were lost in storm. This has personal meaning to me as I knew some of these men when stationed at P. of Em. Sybelle naturally concerned over reports about Leyte landings, as Riccardo's division is almost surely taking part. Sincerely hope she will get no bad news and somehow feel she will not. She certainly deserves happiness if any girl ever did. Little local interest in national political campaign, as re-election of Roosevelt and Truman seems virtually assured. Most of our people concentrating on defeating unconscionably long list of constitutional amendments without faintest notion of what's in them. Too bad we took all that trouble to write new constitution when Parker was governor, if two-bit politicians are going to tinker with it like this now."

He had often reflected that diaries were queer things: if you had time to write in them at length, it was because nothing was happening; when

716

you were doing things that were worth recording, you had no chance to set them down. He would not have bothered with the diary any more, except from force of habit; he did not suppose the boys would ever be much interested in a day-by-day account of the familiar happenings at Belle Heloise. Diary keeping, like letter writing, had passed out of the picture, probably for good. It had been different during the First World War. He had managed to write his mother regularly once a week then, though there had never been the same sort of demonstrative fondness between them that had always existed between Merry and Phil. It was certainly a long time since they had heard from that boy, and Vail might almost as well have left his infrequent letters unwritten too, for all there was in them, beyond the assurance that he was safe and well. Of course that meant a great deal. But not as much as if they could have received the assurance that Phil was making a good recovery and would soon be home. . . .

When Phil came home, everything would be different. The house would not be somber and silent any more; it would ring with laughter again. Joyeuse had a naturally happy disposition too; but she took life more seriously since she had become so intent on her work. Her father could not logically blame her for that, nor did he; if she had not stepped into the breach, there was no telling what might have befallen Belle Heloise, with all the male d'Alverys overseas. He had not forgotten the state in which he had found it, after returning from the First World War, and it had never been hard for him to visualize Lucien Estrade's mournful homecoming. He himself had Joyeuse to thank that the plantation was more productive than ever; but in order to make it so, she had sacrificed much of her light-heartedness and something of her femininity. Gervais could not help regretting that this had happened. In naming her for her mother, he had hoped and believed he was choosing not only well but prophetically. . . .

He thought of her mother too, a great deal, in these days. He and Merry were separated much of the time. The mechanics of running a household, far more complicated than in former years, occupied the larger part of her days, and he had not yet suggested that they should begin to share their old room again. He tried to tell himself—and he felt sure she was doing the same thing—that this was because he was still restless and that he did not want to disturb her; but he knew—and felt sure she knew—that this was not the real reason. He bore no resentment because she had left him when he most needed her, because she had not been wise enough to understand or generous enough to forgive in that great emergency; he knew she had never realized, and never would, that Franchot's death had been an even greater blow to him than to her and that his subsequent desolation had been greater too. It was simply not in her power to do this, and a man could not blame a woman for the limits of her powers, especially if he had been the one to try them past her endurance. He had rejoiced sincerely over her return, and he was glad to have her at Belle Heloise now; he still

717

loved her dearly and admired her greatly. But some vital element had gone with her the night after Franchot's funeral, when she left the room that they had shared so long and so intimately, and he was afraid that the loss of this element was permanent. Evidently a woman could return to her husband more easily than his yearning for her could revive. At first, after she left him, this yearning had been almost intolerable; he had managed to subdue it, with grim determination and untold suffering; in the end he had been so successful that nothing could rouse it again. He looked at her with grateful eyes when she ministered to his comfort; he thought of her with appreciation as she went efficiently about her many tasks while he sat idly by the fire. But he wanted nothing else that she could do for him, and any pretense that he did would have been an insult to the memory of the sincere and ardent passion through which they had so long been united.

Possibly this estrangement from Merry was the greatest single source of his loneliness and depression, he told himself, as he sat alone in his study one mellow afternoon in late October, alternately scribbling in his diary and staring into the fire. He was not an old man, only a tired and embittered one; when he recovered from his weariness, when he regained a more normal and cheerful outlook, perhaps he would stop feeling the way he did towards his wife. With a fleeting smile, he visualized the probable difference between Harvey Lawrason's homecoming and his own. Harvey's would certainly be boisterous and lusty. That pretty little widow—darn it, he didn't mean that; he meant Harvey's wife, Pearl!—would doubtless shortly present him with a baby, maybe more than one, and Harvey would become a doting father, telling long tedious stories at family parties about his children's cute sayings, instead of enlivening hunt breakfasts with his tall tales and his Which-I-Gods. Gervais had known many a man who had married and begotten his first son—or at least his first acknowledged son —when older than he was himself, and Merry was still a beautiful and desirable woman. Perhaps it was still not too late to begin again as they had first begun. But even as he told himself this, he knew it was too late, not because it would be physically impossible, but because it would be spiritually impossible. The cleavage between himself and his wife was too great to be closed by any mere act of union. Perhaps in time he would find some other way to close it, but just now he was too tired to try. He did not want to try. All he wanted to know was that his son was coming home again, safe and well. . . .

He must have finally dozed off, in the tedious process of trying to think of something to set down in his diary which would divert his mind from such thoughts as these, for he sat up with a sudden jerk, roused by the furious barking of Maudie in the patio. She had grown up there, like all the puppies, and for a long time that pleasant enclosure and the vine-covered expanse of ground immediately behind it had constituted her world; then this had gradually grown to include the flower beds, the stretches of lawn, the pecan grove and the woods beyond. Now that she was getting old, her world had shrunk again. She seemed content to spend most of her time in the patio, as she had in the beginning, just as he was content to spend most of his time in one room. Men and dogs were a good deal alike, after all, Gervais thought, going to the door of the office to see what could possibly be causing this unwonted commotion on a peaceful afternoon. Then he saw Vail, with Maudie jumping around him as if she had suddenly gone wild, and he too felt a pang of fierce incredulous joy, followed by a sense of suffocation and rigidity, so that for a moment he could neither speak nor move. After that he managed to hobble painfully towards the open door and to speak huskily.

"Vail d'Alvery! Where on earth did you drop from? Come here and let me see if you're real!"

"I'm real all right. How are you, Dad? Gee, but it's grand to see you. . . . Behave yourself, Maudie! I'm not going to run away."

He went quickly up to the door and flung both arms around Gervais, half in embrace and half in support. For a moment they clung to each other wordlessly. Then Vail drew back a little, meeting the welcoming amazement in Gervais' eyes with smiling reassurance.

"Why—why—you never wrote us you were due for leave, Vail!" Gervais exclaimed.

"Matter of fact, I didn't know myself I had enough combat hours, till I went to ask how soon I'd be able to apply, and found I was already eligible. . . . Let's come in and sit down, shall we? We might just as well get comfortable. I've got quite a lot to say to you."

"I should think you might have. How did you get here, and when? I didn't hear a car."

"No, I walked over from Hathaway. Aunt Cresside brought me that far. I burst in on her, too. I did try to telephone her from New Orleans, to tell her I'd take the twelve-fifty, but all the circuits were busy, and after I'd waited for them to get clear, there wasn't even time to send a wire. But she and I'd had a good visit before we started down the River Road, so she decided not to stick around while I was talking to Syb. She thought she ought to get back to Uncle Fabian as soon as she could. She says he misses Frances Belle terribly. Gee, that poor kid had a tough break, didn't she?"

"Yes, it was pretty tragic. Punt was a mighty fine boy, Vail."

"That's what Aunt Cresside thinks too. By the way, she said to tell you she and Uncle Fabian will be out right after supper."

"That's good. But she might have taken time to come over here to tell us the news, while you were having your visit with Sybelle, and gone back for you afterwards. Fabian could have done without her that long. And couldn't you have wired when you landed, wherever that was? Then you might at least have had some of your family at the station to meet you, even if you didn't have a brass band."

"Yes, she could have and I could have. But we both figured maybe you'd like it better this way."

"I still feel you didn't get much of a welcome and I'm sorry, because you had it coming to you. I know how dead the place seems at this time of day. You didn't have any more of a homecoming than Lucien Estrade."

"I'll bet Belle Heloise looked mighty good to him, just the same, when he came in riding Minnie up the driveway, and it looked pretty good to me, too, tramping along. I really didn't want to be bothered with anyone, just at first. And now I've got a chance to talk to you. I'm glad no one's bothering us. I hope they won't, for a long while."

Unobtrusively, without asking whether he would like it done, Vail had helped ease Gervais into one of the big chairs by the hearth. Although the day was sunny and mellow, it was warmer outside than in, and a small fire had already been kindled. Vail poked it expertly, put on another chunk, and lighting a cigarette, sat down opposite Gervais. Maudie immediately jumped upon his lap and began licking his face and hands. He looked at her, still fondly, but more critically than before.

"Why, you giddy old bitch!" he said. "You've been having another affair during my absence! When's the new family due, Dad?"

"In about two weeks. I'm afraid it may be the last one, Vail."

"Yes, it might, at that. I've been hoping to see her through one more accouchement myself, and there's no denying she's already a lady of a certain age, so I'm glad I've got the chance. Keep all the puppies, will you, Dad, or at least distribute them in the family? I wouldn't want to lose the strain."

"All right, Vail. I reckon Sybelle would take at least two and Cresside one . . . But you weren't thinking of puppies, were you, when you said you had lots to talk about?"

"No, of course not . . . Be quiet, you wench, or I'll kick you out. This is the bossman talking."

"You didn't hear anything from Phil before you left England, did you?" Gervais inquired. "We haven't had a word except the letter he wrote a week or so after he was wounded."

"Yes, I've heard, indirectly. That's what I wanted to talk to you about, Dad."

Vail tossed his cigarette into the fire and pulled his chair a little closer, speaking with extreme gentleness. Gervais looked up quickly, with sudden fear in his eyes.

"You mean he's worse? You can't mean . . . But we'd have had some word from the War Department!"

"Yes, under normal circumstances. In nine hundred and ninety-nine out of a thousand cases, I suppose. But these weren't normal circumstances. This was the thousandth case. I can't tell you this the way it ought to be told, Dad. I've just got to do the best I can."

"You can tell me whether Phil's alive or dead, can't you?"

"He's dead. At least, I haven't any proof of it. Nobody has. Nobody ever will have. That's why you haven't heard from the War Department. There wasn't any way you could be notified, officially."

As he spoke, Vail's voice had grown more and more gentle. Gervais continued to stare at him with mounting horror. Vail put Maudie quietly on the floor, drew his chair still closer, and laid his hand on the older man's arm.

"I know how horrible it is for you, hearing this, Dad. I know how much Phil meant to you. It's the hardest thing I've ever had to do, being the one to tell you."

Gervais made a small, futile gesture. Then he gripped the arms of his chair and turned his head away, his lips moving, as if he were about to say something. At last he managed to speak, in a voice so low that Vail could hardly catch the words.

"I want to hear all you do know."

"Well, it was only by accident I found out even that Phil had been wounded. It's a strange thing, too. If I hadn't run into Tony Dalton at the Town House that night it might have been a year or two before we ever found out what happened. Tony's one of the Air Transport Command boys that went through primary with me but never made fighter. He was evacuating wounded from France back to England—I mean those who could sit up in a transport plane and wouldn't have to be sent over by ambulance—so he told me about Phil and how he had brought him to this hospital plant that wasn't more than about one hundred and twenty miles from our base. He said Phil was laughing and cutting up like he always did all the way across. Naturally if Phil had been seriously wounded I'd have tried to see him right away, but we were due to be briefed for a pretty important mission that night, so I waited till it was my regular turn for a week-end leave before I went. Colonel Jackson lent me his jeep when I told him where I was going and why, and I took off."

Vail reached down absently to pat Maudie, who had cuddled up beside his chair.

"Well, there really isn't a hell of a lot more to tell you, Dad," he continued. "Just what I found out when I got there, which was that one of those God damn rocket bombs had hit the hospital about a week before. You know they weren't like the buzz bombs. Those gave you some warning, but the first anybody ever heard of a rocket was the explosion after it hit. I saw the crater. It looked as though you could have dropped a city block into it. I don't know how many of the boys in that hospital were killed. Matter of fact, nobody knows. The record room was gone along with one entire wing and most of the official personnel, so nobody knew who had been in the hospital and there was no way to check. About all that they could do was to take a list of the names of those who were still alive."

Gervais attempted to clear his throat. "Then there is still a possibility—" he began.

"I'm afraid not, Dad," Vail continued gently. "Tony Dalton knew Phil. They were at Tulane together and Tony couldn't have been mistaken. Just to make sure I looked him up afterwards and explained the situation. I asked him if there wasn't any chance that Phil might have gone from the airfield where Tony left him to some other hospital, and he said no, he was positive. In fact, he gave me the names of some of the other boys who had been with Phil and I got hold of one of them among the survivors and he told me Phil had been with them. I know it's pretty rugged to take, but you want the truth, and that's the way it is."

Gervais, his whole body bowed forward, stared at the floor. Vail rose and walked towards the fireplace where he stood with his back towards the grief-stricken figure in the chair.

"I'm afraid there's something else I've got to tell you, Dad," he continued without turning around. "I didn't try to see Phil because I was sorry for him. I wanted to see him because I had an old score to settle. I'd been waiting a long time to do that. I thought perhaps he might be sent home on convalescent leave after he left the hospital, and I had to thrash things out with him before he got back here." Again Vail waited, giving Gervais time to ask what his score might be, but when at length the latter spoke, he made no mention of it.

"You told Cresside and Sybelle all this before you came out here?"

"Not quite so many details. But I told them the main facts. It seemed logical to tell them first, because I saw them first. You don't mind, do you?"

"No. That was natural, as you say . . . Your mother doesn't know yet though . . ."

It was half a statement, half a question. Vail chose to interpret it as a question.

"No, she doesn't know yet. Syb said she was in town doing the errands. I'll tell her when she gets back, if you want me to. But I thought perhaps you'd rather tell her yourself. But I will if you want me to. *Grand'mère* and Joyeuse, too."

"I'd be very grateful if you'd tell your grandmother and your sister. I don't think I can talk about it much, for a while. But you're right. I'd better try to tell your mother myself. She's going to take this mighty hard, Vail."

"It won't be any harder for her than it's been for you, Dad. Not as hard, maybe. You'll be able to break it better than I could. I've done a rotten job, I know that."

"No, Vail, you've done the best you could. There isn't any easy way, or any good way, to tell a man he's lost his son, or a woman the same thing. But she's going to take this mighty hard. You see——"

He did not seem to realize that he was repeating himself. He struggled up, and Vail did not try to stop him, or even to help him, this time, as he stumbled towards the door, catching at the furniture to support himself on the way. For a long time he stood looking out into space, and Vail knew it was not the adjacent gardens which he saw, but the invisible cane fields. He was listening, too, not for some sound from the house, but for the clatter of the mill. At last he turned.

"The day Franchot was born," he said slowly, "I was in the factory, trying out a new set of centrifugals, and Selah came running out to get me. I knew it must be a hurry call, and I didn't even stop to wash the syrup off my hands before I went into your mother's room. She was suffering dreadfully, anyway, of course, and somehow the sight of my hands, dripping like that, was so revolting to her that she couldn't stand it. She'd always been very brave and very patient when she was in labor, before that. But suddenly she began to scream, and between her shrieks she cried out that she hoped to God no son of hers would ever be a sugar planter. Dr. Champagne told me she was hysterical with pain, that she didn't realize what she was saying, but she must have, halfway at least, because she told me afterwards how sorry she was. She may have forgotten all about it by now. I hope she has. But I haven't. It made a great impression on me. I wrote it down in my diary." He half-turned, glancing towards the bookcase containing the neat row of Affleck's Record and Account Books, almost as if he thought of looking for the entry in question. Then he seemed to abandon the idea and went on. "I felt terribly, not only because I'd carelessly added to her anguish, though that was bad enough; but also because ... Well, maybe we Creoles are a superstitious lot. But when you get to be as old as I am, Vail, I believe you'll feel the way I do: that sometimes it's dangerous to hope and pray certain things will happen, because very often the greatest sorrow comes with the answer to such prayers. Just as it has this time."

He stopped abruptly, recognizing too late the tacit disclosure in his words. Vail put out his hand again.

"It's all right, Dad," he said. "I mean, I'm mighty sorry you think Mom may remember what she said, and that you do anyway, whether she does or not. I know how you must feel, and how she will if she happens to remember, because she did get her wish. But of course it wasn't a real wish, just as the doctor told you and as she told you herself. Naturally I don't know much about such things. I shouldn't suppose though that any woman would have an idea what she was saying at a time like that. But on top of everything else, don't start worrying because you think you've given away something you didn't mean to have me know. I've known ever since I was nine years old."

"But how——"

"We could talk about that some other time, couldn't we? Of course I'll do just as you want. But it seems to me all I need to say right now is that I feel you've always treated me as if I were your son, that no real father could have been any kinder to me or meant any more to me."

"That means a lot to me, Vail, but——"

"And I'll do my best to carry on here, the way you'd have wanted your own sons to do it, if they'd lived. It won't be the same for you, or for Mom, of course. It can't be. But the girls won't ever know. The world won't ever know. And after all, Dad, I love this place."

"Yes," Gervais said, still slowly. "I know you do. And I've every reason to feel proud of you, Vail. Just as proud as I would have been of —of your brothers." He paused for a moment, but he did not correct himself. "This place has belonged to us a long time, though," he went on painfully. "And this is the end of a dynasty."

"But it isn't. Don't forget, Dad, my mother's a d'Alvery. So am I."

For a moment they faced each other silently and steadily. Then Gervais bowed his head before Vail's unflinching gaze and turned without answering, groping his way back to his chair. Vail spoke to him from the door.

"I reckon you'd like to be by yourself for a little while," he said. "I'll go along to the Big House and see *grand'mère*—she must be awake by this time. And if Joy isn't ready to lay off for the day, she ought to be. . . . There's a grand girl for you, Dad! And Syb's another—they'll both help us to hang on! I tell you this stretch of the River Road will really be something, when Hathaway's going at full blast again, as part of Belle Heloise. And maybe Joy could wheedle Hackberry away from Charles Boylston. He doesn't really want to live there any longer. . . . No, I've got a better plan!"

Gervais still did not answer. Vail knew that he was only half listening, that his thoughts were still sadly centered on his lost son, on the desolate hearthstone.

"If Mom comes in before I leave," Vail went on, "I'll tell her you specially want to see her. I reckon she always comes right here anyway though, after she's been out, doesn't she?"

"Before you *leave*—but Vail, you're not leaving!"

He was alert again, and alarmed. He knew he should have responded far more wholeheartedly to Vail's grave and moving declaration of gratitude, affection and abiding purpose; he should have given a ready answer to the boy's one touching appeal, instead of turning away from him without a word. Surely, at such a time as this . . .

"Oh, not for good!" Vail was saying now. "You and I've still got lots to go over, before I take off again. But there's someone else I ought to see tonight, if I can, and I thought maybe this wouldn't be such a bad time for me to slip away for a few hours. After that, I'll be sticking around for nearly a month. . . . The jalopy still runs, doesn't it?"

"Yes, it still runs. Joyeuse uses it all the time—that is, until her gas gives out. I don't know just what the present status of that is."

"Well, she won't be using it tonight," Vail announced briefly. "After all, it's still my car. Joy probably is fresh out of gas—it would be just like her to use all she had and trust to luck to get more—which she would. But I'll get enough coupons somewhere to take me to New

Roads. I can pay them back after I get my leave allowance. By the way, I'm going to try to persuade Susannah Prescott to come home with me. I won't bring her here—of course I know you wouldn't want me to do that, right now. But Aunt Cresside said it would be all right to take her to Somerulos Street. You don't mind, do you? I mean, on account of Phil? Because I want to have most of my thirty days at home but still I want to see as much as I can of Susannah. You must know how that is, Dad."

He was not hurt, he was not offended, he had not misunderstood. He was only going so that Merry and Gervais could have the evening to themselves, and so that he himself could see his sweetheart. For the first time Gervais looked back at the boy with something like a smile on his somber face.

"Yes, I know how it is," he said. "And if you'd rather have Susannah stay here, after tonight, we'll do our best to make her feel welcome. She was very fond of Phil herself."

CHAPTER LVI

VAIL STARTED for New Roads assuring himself that of course Sue would come home with him and forcing himself to believe it. But this required considerable will power. In the first place, he was terribly tired, and his fatigue in itself was depressing. In the second place, though he had done his best to treat the nature of his homecoming as briefly and lightly as he could in talking to Gervais, the only welcoming warmth of which he had been conscious had come from Cresside and Sybelle. It had been a grueling experience to face both Gervais' hopeless broken-heartedness and the rigid self-control of his grandmother. Moreover, Joyeuse had come in from the factory while he was talking with Madame d'Alvery, and when she heard about Phil, she had sunk down in a chair, bursting into unashamed tears. Her face, so bright and alert when she first caught sight of Vail, became suddenly swollen and blurred, and she sat huddled in a little crumpled heap, the trim lines of her figure effaced by her attitude of dejection. Presently she rose, and without speaking again, went off to the little room beyond the boudoir, where she had slept ever since no servant was available for night duty; it was so near that though she closed the door, Vail could still hear her sobbing. She and Phil had never been quite so devoted as he and Sybelle, but their mutual light-heartedness and kindred tastes had nevertheless formed an extremely close bond between them. It was natural that she should feel his death very keenly and that she should take the tidings of it as she had. It must have been terribly hard for her to hear them. It had also been terribly hard for Vail to bring them.

He did not dwell on the latter fact with self-pity, but with the argument that probably the consciousness of the sorrow his tidings had inevitably evoked had a good deal to do with his own overpowering depression, and that when the various members of his family had been given time to adjust themselves to their loss, he would recover from his sense of desolation. He hoped he was not lacking in sensitivity because he was relieved that he had missed Merry; he felt that one more interview, like those he had gone through already, would have tried him almost past the point of endurance. And yet, he now remembered that he had one more such interview ahead of him. If Susannah were stricken too, the spectacle of her grief would be the worst of all.

He was too essentially honest to pretend to himself that Phil's death was a heavy blow to him. His first feeling, in the aftermath of the rude shock he received in finding the bombed hospital, had been one of personal frustration and defeat. As he had forced himself to tell Gervais, he had not gone to find Phil out of concern, but out of anger, intending to browbeat him into signing a statement which would make it easy for Susannah to secure her freedom; and Phil had been mockingly elusive in death, exactly as he had been mockingly elusive in life. Vail could feel horror over the manner of Phil's death, but he could not feel sustained sorrow for it; he was too conscious of having been defrauded.

And now, at the end of this tortuous road, was he himself on the point of erring almost as grievously as the dead man for whom he had no charity in his heart? In his readiness to accept Phil's heritage as his own and to take Phil's widow for his wife, was he cheating too? Still trying to act and think with complete honesty, he did not evade the ugly question. But despite his fatigue, despite his depression, the answer which he was finally able to give himself was reassuring and convincing. It was his own heritage he was claiming, not Phil's, he who really loved the land left by their common ancestor, he who was willing to work it, guard it, preserve it, no matter at what sacrifice. Left to Phil, Belle Heloise would have suffered the same fate as Trepanier and Esperance and all the other tragic places that had been abandoned on the River Road. Phil would have wasted his substance in riotous living, he would have sold his birthright for a mess of red pottage, and in the end only desolation and decay would have been left. And what was true of the land was true of a woman. Phil had never loved her either. He had only briefly desired her, and even his desire had been artificially fanned into flame by her declared fascination. What kinship had such a cheap and ephemeral feeling with the devotion of years? How could Vail himself be robbing the dead of a prerogative which had never been either treasured or possessed?

He had already achieved this saner viewpoint before he reached the cemetery, and he stopped there long enough to make a brief survey of the family lot. It was in beautiful condition, and in the care lavished upon it, for which he rightly guessed Sybelle and Joyeuse were about equally responsible, he saw an ulterior motive, probably prompted by their grandmother: it must be kept fittingly prepared against possible need at any time. Well, he would do what he could to help, in these few days he would spend at home. Gervais and Merry would naturally wish to have a special monument for Phil, and, with All Saints' Day so near, to expedite the erection of at least a temporary memorial. Possibly he could take care of that for them. At all events, he could offer to. He was sorry that he had not stopped long enough to gather some flowers before coming there that evening, but he had not thought of it till now. However, only the gesture was indicated. The tomb where the first Philogene lay with the Estrades and Franchot's small solitary grave were both already adequately adorned.

As a child, Vail had been taken to visit the family lot frequently, according to Creole custom; but he had always hated the Hathaways' prickly lamb and simpering stone mourner, which he was obliged to pass in order to reach the Estrade tombs; and from the time he learned that Sylvestre Tremaine was his father, he had never voluntarily done so, until today. Now he stopped and looked resolutely at the two stones which completed the group in the enclosure so long avoided. The Misses Murdock had lavished a large sum of money upon these, doubtless feeling this to be appropriate, considering the handsome legacy which they represented. But in spite of the elaborate carving with which they were ornamented, the lettering on them was brief; obviously the heirs, with all the eagerness in the world, had found almost nothing to record. Vail looked at this lettering now, realizing the futility and emptiness of the two lives, which had been so much more closely interlocked at the end than ever before:

Regine Hathaway Tremaine
daughter of
Roger and Emma Hathaway
and wife of
Sylvestre Tremaine
Born April 20, 1900
Died March 26, 1929

Sylvestre Tremaine
son of
Hyacinthe and Jeanne Tremaine
and husband of
Regine Hathaway Tremaine
Born November 9, 1895
Died March 27, 1929

Nothing else! No record of achievement, because there had been none. No quotations of sentimental or sacred character, because even the Murdocks realized what a travesty these would present. In life, Regine Hathaway and Sylvestre Tremaine had been aimless, selfish and sensual; even in death they had not achieved anything that would give them character or stature. Vail wondered now why he had ever shrunk from a sight as meaningless as the graves of such nonentities. He knew that he never would again. He had reminded Gervais earlier that evening that he was a d'Alvery, but he had forborne from adding: "As much of a d'Alvery as either Franchot or Phil. Their mother doesn't belong to the closed clan, any more than my father did." The fact that he loved Merry and that she deserved his love had prevented him from saying this. But it was true. And now the physical fact of Sylvestre's fatherhood lost all its significance, in the vast pattern of the lives which it had been powerless to affect with any degree of permanence. . . .

Vail turned in at Hathaway a second time, unable to resist the yearning to see Sybelle again. As if she had been waiting for him, she came running out to meet him, and urged him to stop. No, he said, he was on his way to New Roads, and smiled. She smiled back, understandingly; then, with her usual practical thoughtfulness, asked if he was sure he had enough gas; she had some idea how Joyeuse used it up. Well, he could do with a couple of coupons, Vail replied, though that was not why he had stopped by; he had just wanted to see her again, she looked so good to him. She laughed, and went off to get the coupons. When she came back he told her he thought it would be a good plan if she could get over to Belle Heloise for a little while that evening; everyone there had taken the news about Phil mighty hard. Dad was completely broken up, and so was Joy. Of course *grand'mère* never flinched; but sometime, for that very reason, she would probably break, just as Mom had suddenly broken, in a different way, and this might be the time; there was no way of telling. He still hadn't seen Mom. If Sybelle could manage to be there when she got back from town, he wouldn't feel like quite so much of a shirker himself. Of course she could manage, Sybelle assured him. She had meant to go anyway. Poor Dad! Poor Joyeuse! Poor *Grand'-mère!* Poor Mom! But still, as long as they had Vail . . .

"I don't rate as high with the others as I do with you, Syb. There's no reason why I should."

"Of course there is. You ought to. And you will yet. You wait and see. Don't worry, Vail, I'll go right over."

It was extraordinary how much better he felt after these few words with Sybelle. He was no longer absorbed by doubt and dread. He could see, and savor, the beauties along the way: the columns and galleries of the Pentagon, snowy and symmetrical beyond the glossy trees which framed them and the soft lights which illumined them; the high tower of the New Capitol, reflected in the still lake which gave the hospital on the opposite bank its name; the tall twinkling units of the Standard Oil, amazingly imitative, in miniature, of Manhattan's skyline; the mighty arch of the great steel bridge, spanning the Mississippi, which flowed towards the Gulf with deceptive quietude; the level and serene countryside, extending on and on, all the way to False River; then deep set in the midst of its verdure yet fronting the glittering stream, one lovely and venerable plantation house after another: Oliva, Parlange, Austerlitz, Pleasant View, North Bend, River Lake—at last Salome!

He turned in between the sturdy entrance gates and wound his way quickly through the cedars bordering the drive, towards the hip-roofed house, standing four-square behind its hedge of Cherokee rose. No street sounds penetrated beyond the spacious enclosure shadowed by pecans and oaks, and the privacy of the place was assured by the luxuriant growth of these trees. Yet it lacked the hushed and hidden quality of Belle Heloise. Lights shone from the windows and from lanterns suspended in the gallery. Household sounds, apparently issuing from the kitchen at the rear, suggested that the evening's work, while progressing smoothly and pleasantly, was not yet finished. In the drawing room at the front someone was playing the piano and singing an old song. Before he saw her, Vail knew it must be Susannah. He had forgotten that she liked to play and sing, or perhaps she had never done so much in the old days. There was nothing remarkable about the performance now. Her voice was pleasing, but it had no great range or volume. Her fingers did not touch false notes as they slipped over the keys, but neither did they bring extraordinary melody and meaning from the instrument. The whole effect was amazingly picturesque and slightly plaintive. But perhaps it was the old song as much as the quaint setting which made it so:

> " 'Love me little, love me long,
> Is the burden of my song,
> Love which is too hot and strong
> Quickly runs to waste.
> Still I would not have thee cold,
> Nor too backward, nor too bold,
> Love which lasteth till 'tis old
> Fadeth not in haste.' "

Vail waited until Susannah had finished the song before he went up on the gallery. He did not want to startle her or interrupt her, and he could see her quite plainly from where he stood beside the hedge. Astral lamps were placed on the small circular shelves at either side of the keyboard; they did not give much light, but it sufficed to reveal Susannah, and beyond her, the dim lines of her parents' figures. They were listening to her, seated at the rear of the room, beneath some paintings with heavy gilt frames which faintly reflected the lamplight. Vail listened too, while he looked at Susannah with hungry eyes. Her face was lovely and serene, as it always had been, her hair still parted in the middle, as he remembered it, and drawn down on the sides so far that it almost covered her small ears. She had on a very simple blue dress, with a square-cut neck and elbow sleeves and she was not wearing any jewelry. When she finished her song she played a few disconnected chords, and then she rose from the piano and moved towards the front door, which led directly into the drawing room, for houses of the earlier Spanish type, like Salome, were constructed without hallways. It was almost as if Vail had called her and as if she were answering.

"I was sure I heard a car come in," she said. She seemed to be speaking to herself, rather than to her parents or to any visitor, expected or unexpected. Vail did not find it disillusioning because there was a logical, instead of a mystic reason, after all, to explain her coming. He was glad this was natural. He had always wanted everything between himself and Susannah to be natural, just as he had always felt that everything between them was inevitable.

"You did," he said, speaking very gently. He was still afraid that she might be startled. "It's Vail, Sue. I've come home."

"I'm glad to see you, Vail," she answered, just as quietly. "I've missed you. But not as much as if I hadn't always known you'd come sometime."

She moved across the gallery and gave him her hand. He did not try to take her in his arms. For the moment it was enough to have her come to him like that, freely and without fear, and to speak as if she too recognized the element of inevitability between them.

"I just came in this afternoon. I've got thirty days' leave," he went on, holding her hand fast. "I hoped you'd go back with me tonight, so I wouldn't miss any of the time I might have with you. I don't mean to Belle Heloise. I can't take you there just now. I mean to Aunt Cresside's."

"All right. I'll be glad to go. Come in a minute and say hello to Father and Mother while I put some things into a suitcase. They'll be glad to see you too."

"In just a minute. There's something I've got to tell you, Sue, before we go in, before you come home with me."

His hold on her hand tightened. She waited, silently, for him to go on.

"It's about Phil. I never said those things to him I told you I was going to say. I meant to. I found out where he was and went there on purpose to do it. And I couldn't. Because he was dead."

This time it was he who waited and she who tightened her handclasp. But she did not make him wait long.

"You can tell me about it on our drive," she said. "That is, everything you feel like telling. I suppose you've had to tell your family already today. It must have been awful for you, Vail, to be the one to bring such bad news. But you don't need to tell me anything more

730

than you want to. As far as I was concerned, Phil died a long, long time ago."

Because she did not ask any questions, because she was so composed yet so responsive, he found it easy to talk to her. Indeed, the words came tumbling out with such rapidity that at times they did not form coherent sentences. But Susannah understood even when they did not, and Vail, more and more aware of her understanding, talked on and on. He told her everything there was to say about Phil. He told her about his own work, its dangers and hardships, its delights and rewards. He told her about his feeling for the future, what he wanted to do and what he felt he must do if Belle Beloise and all it stood for were to survive. This time he did not see anything that he passed on the road; several times Susannah gently called his attention to a turn he had almost missed or a stop light he had failed to observe. He even went past the little house on Somerulos Street and shot along towards Nicholson Drive. As he halted the car, at Susannah's signal, and swung it around to its proper place in front of the old granite block, he laughed a little, half in relief and half in exultation.

"My, but that was a grand ride!" he said. "Do you remember our first ride, the one when you told me about the wolf that was in love with a dog? I thought that was about tops, then, but it was nothing compared to this. What it's meant to get all that off my chest! And to *you.* . . . How early do you think I might come in, Sue, tomorrow morning?"

"Whenever you like. I'll be glad to see you if you come early, but I won't be disappointed or disturbed if you come late. I think you'll find your father'll want to talk to you, tomorrow morning. Probably all the others, too. They'll be over the first shock by that time, there'll be a reaction. Phil meant a lot to them, but you mean a lot too. Syb's right about that and you're wrong. In a sense he represented their past, their tradition. But you represent their future, their new world. By morning they'll all realize that. I shouldn't be surprised if you didn't get away until late. I'll just sit and wait for you in your aunt's garden. It's a lovely place to wait anyhow. . . ."

Cresside and Fabian had both stayed up for them. There were highballs made of Irish whiskey, which, by some freak of taste, Vail liked better than any other kind. There were also lamb sandwiches, which were his favorite. He had forgotten, until the moment, that he had not eaten any supper, but Cresside had not overlooked the possibility. After the others were all settled on the terrace, she excused herself and went back to the kitchen. When she returned, she was bearing one of the light lacquered trays she had bought in Mexico, and on it were milk and salad and a big piece of apple pie. Vail devoured them all with healthy appetite and heartfelt appreciation. While he was eating, conversation continued in an effortless way. They talked mostly about Frances Belle, who was at Fort Des Moines now, and who wrote from there regularly. They thought she was happy there—at least happier than she would have been anywhere else for the present. She was hoping for overseas duty, later on—but meanwhile she was finding herself——

"I've put Sue in Frances Belle's room," Cresside said at last. "Perhaps she'd like to come and see if I've thought of everything she'll need to make her comfortable. You two male creatures can get along all right without us for a few moments. But why don't you stay too, Vail? The dormer guest rooms are both in order. I opened one of the beds and laid out a pair of Fabian's pajamas, just in case the idea appealed to you."

"I think it's a swell idea. You would be the one to have it, Auntie. There's no earthly reason why I should go all the way out to Belle Heloise tonight and then back here the first thing in the morning, using up gas."

"It was really your uncle's idea," Cresside remarked. . . . "Shall we go and have a look at your quarters, Sue?"

"Yes, and I think I'll say good night now, too. Shall we have a breakfast date, Vail? Nineish?"

"Eightish. I couldn't sleep till nine to save my soul. I've been on Army hours too long."

"You'll shed them easily enough. Carmelite comes later and later, and we don't say anything because it really doesn't matter, the way we live now, and she's still the best cook in Baton Rouge. You surely don't want to get your own breakfast, if you remember the sort she turns out. I'm backing Sue against you this time, Vail."

"The woman wins. She always does, I reckon. Good night, Sue."

Again she gave him her hand, and again he realized, with fleeting amazement, that he was not disappointed because she gave him no more. Everything that was happening since he had found her seemed to be forming a pattern, which must be slowly and carefully put together, but which would be perfect when all the parts were in place. He watched her leave with no sense of regret. It was good to see her and Cresside together, friendly and at ease. He liked to think she was going to sleep in Frances Belle's room, next to Fabian and Cresside, and that they had wanted to put her there. . . .

"You ought to be turning in pretty soon yourself." Fabian was speaking in his usual imperturbable manner. "You must have had a fairly rugged day. But we might treat ourselves to one more drink first." He refilled both his glass and Vail's, and settled back in his chair, as if he were in no special hurry to get up or to have his guest do so. "Incidentally, while we're alone for a few minutes, there's something I might say to you. Not that it's particularly important. I don't want to dwell on it now, and I don't want to bring it up again, unless there's some special reason for it, which I don't anticipate. But it just happens to be one of those things to which we tritely refer as 'something you ought to know.'"

732

"All right then. Shoot."

"I don't want you to feel as if you were stepping into a dead man's shoes in taking over at Belle Heloise. If Phil had wanted it, which he didn't, you could have stood aside and let him have it, if that was what you felt like doing, for sentiment's sake. But he wasn't the heir to it. I bought Belle Heloise when you were nine years old. It's belonged to me, to all intents and purposes, ever since then. Naturally I didn't want it for myself. I bought it for you. You're the heir to it."

"I don't understand——"

"Well, there's no use going into all the details right now. But it would have been lost to the family if I hadn't stepped into the picture. And I did this with two distinct understandings. First, the understanding that Gervais should get out of politics, straight off; he didn't know how to play them, and it wasn't healthy for any of us, having him try. Second, that you should always be recognized as his first-born, with all the rights and privileges that went with that. I talked the whole thing over, first with your grandmother and then with Gervais. I made it perfectly clear to them both what I was doing and why. Nothing was ever put on paper—except a few politely mendacious lines to the smart scoundrel who was the Governor of Louisiana just then, to the effect that the plantation required all Captain d'Alvery's time and that therefore he was resigning from the State Senate, the resignation to take effect immediately. We d'Alverys don't need documents among ourselves. We've got our faults, good and plenty. But I'll say this for us: we don't promise anything without knowing what we're doing and we keep the promises we've made without anyone to tell us we have to. Wasn't it Will Rogers who wouldn't ever sign a contract, because he said a man's writing wasn't any better than his word? Well, that's the way we feel about it too!"

Fabian's tone had grown increasingly light as he talked; he had never lost the touch of whimsicality which had always been one of his greatest charms. His movements had become increasingly clumsy and difficult as he grew older; but somehow no one who was with him ever noticed this, because his face and voice were so attractive and compelling. Vail did not think of it now as Fabian braced himself against the arms of his chair and hoisted himself up by holding heavily to these. He had put his arm around Vail's shoulder before the boy was really aware that he had risen.

"Belle Heloise is yours," he said with a strange triumphant tenderness. "I know you'll never do anything to remind Gervais of this, as long as he lives. But he's too sick and Sance is too old, to carry on much longer without having someone else at the helm. I hope you can start taking over before you go back to France. Of course Joyeuse has done a swell job. But after all, running a plantation's a man's work. I want to see a man doing it. Your mother always wanted you to have Belle Heloise, and I have too. I'm glad I could save it for you.

Now you've only got to get the girl to go in it. You picked out the right one, a long time ago. And I'm betting on you to do the rest, without any help from me."

CHAPTER LVII

"LET'S NOT stay in the garden, Sue. Let's go up on the levee. I've done everything I need to in the fields and factory today, so I'm not on call any longer. And it's a mighty pretty evening."

"All right. I'll be glad to go."

She answered so readily that it was evident she welcomed the suggestion as a means of escape. She had been really happy on Somerulos Street with Cresside and Fabian. But here it had been different, as she feared beforehand that it might be. She had not wanted to decline, when Vail asked her to spend the latter part of his leave at Belle Heloise; but she knew beforehand that she would feel like an intruder and an impostor in this house of mourning, and it had required all the tact and self-control she possessed to meet the ordeal with dignity and composure. There was so much she might herself have said about Phil and so little she could say, if his family were to keep the bright memory of him untarnished. Vail realized this, but so far there had been no chance to talk to her about it. He had been obliged to give a great deal of time to the plantation. Fabian had been right, as usual. Vail's hand was needed at the helm, and whatever he could do now would ease the burden of the others while he was gone, and prepare the way for the still greater tasks that must be undertaken after he came home for good.

The laboratory was now the acknowledged center of plantation activities because it was Joyeuse who directed all of these, while carrying forward her own chosen branch of the work with unflagging zeal. Vail had been tactful enough to visit her promptly in her workshop and to compliment her wholeheartedly both on her ingenuity in getting supposedly unobtainable supplies and on the remarkable administrative quality she had displayed. Somehow she had improvised an extra clarifier out of scrap material, and performed various other feats, scarcely less remarkable. Moreover, all the men working under her respected both her authority and her ability; it had been no small accomplishment for a girl of twenty-one to achieve such excellent discipline together with such good feelings and such productive results. The new dies had also been a tremendous success. Housewives everywhere were asking for the sugar bags from which they could easily fashion centerpieces and aprons with no extra cost, while their small daughters were clamoring for the Belle Heloise dolls. The "side issue" of which Joyeuse had made so light had already been a sound investment and with greater production ahead was bound to become an increasingly profitable one. Vail did not overlook mentioning this in speaking of the other contributions she had made. She was pleased with his praise and showed it; but she was not disposed to have him prolong it or to take more than her share of the credit. Sance really deserved most of this, she insisted.

"He did wonders with those new three-row flame cultivators, all spring and summer," she said. "I didn't know whether I'd better ask Uncle Fabian for them or not, Vail. Of course last year they were still in the experimental stage and I wasn't so sure they would represent a sound investment. Fortunately we didn't have to do much ditching anyway. But this year, with drought when we ought to have had rain and rain when we ought to have had drought, not to mention all the labor difficulties, I could see poor Sance was getting desperate. We could have got German prisoners all right. But he remembered what you said to him before you went away. In fact, it had sunk in pretty deep."

"I am glad it did. Because I meant just what I said and I feel even more strongly about that now." He looked at her gravely, and she knew he was thinking, as she was, of Gervais' tragic breakdown, of the wanton destruction which had cost Phil his life, and of Orange and Neely, the two young Negroes from the plantation who had been killed in combat, one shortly before his division left Tunisia, one just after the beginning of the Sicilian campaign. But neither of them said so, and after a moment Joyeuse went on, "I hated to see poor Sance so whipped down and finally I decided I'd go and have a talk with Unk. But he beat me to the draw. He showed up here the very evening I figured on going to see him and asked me, didn't I think we ought to give those new flame-cultivators a try, and would three be enough to start out with?"

"Well, that sounds like him. I suppose he didn't even make the suggestion, either, until he had those cultivators parked right in his yard?"

"No. And Vail, they've taken the place of a one hundred and fifty man hoe gang! We've cleaned all the cane and burned all the ditches with them . . . but you let Sance tell you about that. After all, that's where he comes in. Besides, he's been hanging around all morning waiting for you and he won't get anything done today unless you give him a chance to tell you about those cultivators, and the wage and hour control, and the muleheadedness of the Draft Board regarding essential industries and everything else he's got on his chest."

"I'm going to look him up as soon as I've asked you one question and given you the chance to tell me it's none of my damn business."

"I'll save you time and trouble by saying I haven't changed my mind about getting married any more than you've changed yours about German prisoners. Nothing—and *no one*—means any more to me than chemistry. Now clear out, will you please, Vail, and let me get along with what I was trying to do when you came barging in here! It was fairly important."

If only everyone on the place had shown the predilection Joyeuse had for brevity, he reflected, rather ruefully, he would have had more time with Susannah. But he must let people talk to him in their own way when they had waited so long for the chance, and when they would not have another chance for so long again. If the men with whom he was to spend his life after the war did not feel they had his considerate understanding as well as his authoritative supervision, he would never make a successful bossman.

With this in mind, he listened patiently while Sance told him that the past year was the hardest he had ever been through, and all the reasons for this feeling. But when the overseer had had his say, Vail had his too.

"I know you've been through a hell of a time, Sance," he said. "I don't blame you for worrying over reports from the labor agents that all transient labor has been diverted. I don't blame you for feeling sore at the Government for leaving industries like ours so few essential materials. In fact, I don't blame you for anything. On the contrary, I think you've got a lot of credit coming to you. You've done a swell job in the face of no end of difficulties, just as I knew beforehand you would. But let's talk about some other aspects of the situation for a change. I don't need to tell you that the world's sugar supply is down to an all-time low. You know as well as I do that there's a very short crop in Cuba, due to an unprecedented drought. You know as well as I do that Hawaii's bound to have reduced production because of most of the man power there has been diverted to servicing the Armed Forces. You know as well as I do it's the consensus of opinion that all mills and fields in the Philippines have been destroyed. In fact, you ought to know all this a lot better than I do—details, I mean. You sure have had a better chance to keep informed."

"That's correct, Vail. I also know that the sugar beet factories in Europe are mostly destroyed, and that the sugar beet production in the United States won't be more than sixty-five percent of normal. But so what? Except that lots of poor devils are ruined and lots more people are going to be hollering louder than ever for sugar?"

"Well, just add that Java is still in the hands of the Japs, and that therefore every sugar-producing region in the world's been directly affected by the war. It doesn't give me any satisfaction to think about all this disorganization and destruction—I know what it means to the planters and the consumers who are up against it just as well as you do, and I'm darn sorry for them. But I can be practical about the whole thing too. Because I also know what it's bound to mean to us. At least I think I do."

736

He stopped and looked at Sance questioningly, as if giving him a chance to supply the answer. But as Sance only looked at him with curious and respectful interest, Vail went on himself.

"Doesn't it mean that there won't be any more Government restrictions of acreage? Doesn't it mean that there'll be a ready market for all we can grow in Louisiana? Doesn't it mean that as soon as the war's over, sugar prices are bound to hit their proper level again?"

"Well yes, Vail, I reckon it does. And when you put it that way——"

"When you put it that way, you can't help realizing we're bound to prosper, these next four or five years, come hell or high water. If we're not going to be in a position to compete with any sugar producers you can name, anywhere in the world, I'd like to know the reason why. You better be getting ready to celebrate, Sance. Happy days aren't here again—not yet. But they're coming mighty fast. We've got to be ready for 'em."

After this conversation Vail noticed a gradual but unmistakable change in the overseer's manner. Sance stopped grumbling about the impossibility of securing essential materials and began to talk cheerfully about the elemental law of supply and demand. Vail knew that the time he had put into such talks and into personal supervision at the mill and in the fields was well spent; but this did not alter the fact that he had less for Susannah. It did not keep him from worrying, either, about other aspects of the situation on the home front with which he felt he could not cope so successfully, yet which he knew cried aloud for remedy.

The day after his return, he had gone nonchalantly up the stairs, carrying his B-44 bag, and swung open the shutter door to his room. To his amazement and confusion, he walked in on Merry, who was sitting in her slip by the dresser, combing her shining hair. She jumped up with a startled exclamation and reached for a dressing gown while he stammered out apologies.

"I'm awfully sorry, Mom. I hadn't the dimmest idea you were using my room. Where shall I put my things?"

"Why . . . you'd like to put them here, wouldn't you, Vail? It was terribly stupid of me not to think of that . . . terribly stupid of all of us. But our minds have been so full of Phil . . . You see, after your father went overseas, the *garçonnière* was closed, and then when he came home again, your grandmother and I both thought that perhaps he'd like his old room back again. So I asked him, while he was still at La Garde, and he said——"

"Yes, of course. Don't worry, Mom. Why don't I just take my stuff down to the Garden Room?"

"But you were born in this room! You've always slept in it! When you and Sybelle were separated, it was she who moved. You can't tell me you haven't any sentiment about it. *I'll* move this time! I'm just mad at myself because I didn't do it before you got here, because I'd ever let you find out——"

"Of course, I've got sentiment about it. But hell, I'm too happy to be home at all to worry about the place I'm going to spend the few hours I'll be dead to the world. What do you mean, 'letting me find out' for Pete's sake?"

She looked at him without answering, and then he knew. It was not the mere occupancy of his room which he had inopportunely discovered; it was the degree of estrangement between his foster parents. Gervais had gone back to his "old room," but Merry had not gone back to her bridal chamber; instead she had taken possession of the nursery. If she had not tried to explain, the arrangement might still have seemed natural and convenient to Vail. But it was one of those many unfortunate instances where the lady protested too much.

"You see, your father still sleeps very badly, and it makes him nervous to feel he's disturbing someone else; and since there's only one downstairs bedroom in the *garçonnière* and he still needs someone near him—that is, since he did at first, we both thought . . . But he really doesn't any more. Please don't take your bag to the Garden Room, Vail. I'll just move across the hall, to the Henry Clay room. That's plenty near enough now. We can leave the shutter doors open. And then, with you here, you can call me if your father should want anything and you should happen to hear him first . . . Unless you'd like to have the *garçonnière* for yours. . . . When he said he'd like to go back to his old room, your father spoke of the fact that someday you and Phil would both be getting married and that when that happened——"

"He'd offer the *garçonnière* to Phil? Come clean now, isn't that what he said, Mom?"

"I'm making things worse every minute instead of making them better. Of course he'd want you to have the *garçonnière* now that Phil——"

"But I don't want it. Not because Dad wouldn't have offered it to me, if Phil were still alive. But because I want to keep on in the Big House. Because when I get married, I want to bring my wife here. Not to one of the outbuildings."

Vail put an affectionate arm around Merry's shoulder and seated himself on the big bed, drawing her down beside him.

"It was different with you and Dad," he said gently. "You wanted a little home of your own, where you'd be by yourselves. I can see how you felt too. *Grand'mère* and Aunt Cresside cramped your style, and in the *garçonnière* you could do things your own way. But it just so happens that *Grand'mère* never has cramped my style, and I know she won't cramp Sue's either, when Sue makes up her mind to marry me. They get on like a house afire already. So that's that. But I still don't see, when you understand about my having sentiment for a room, and so on, why you and Dad didn't go back to the *garçonnière* that meant all that much to you. Suppose there wasn't but one downstairs bedroom, etcetera, etcetera? Couldn't you have turned the dining room into another one, temporarily, for the luvamike? You eat most of your meals at the Big House anyway—always have. I should think you and Dad would have liked to have breakfast together again in that one big bedroom, the way you used to, whether you both slept in there or not. And supper in front of the living-room fire, sometimes. Supper's mighty cozy, eaten thataway."

"I think your ideas are better than mine were, Vail. I wish I'd thought of all this too. I believe if I had, instead of suggesting the old room, that perhaps your father——"

"Well, you and he could still move into the *garçonnière*, couldn't you, if you feel like that about it? It hasn't tumbled down or anything —at least it hadn't the last time I looked. Not that I care a hang where I sleep the next few nights, as I just told you. But if you're hunting up an excuse, you can say I do. You can say I barged in on you, taking it for granted I'd have this room—that much is true enough, anyway. And that afterwards, I acted so disappointed, you really felt——"

"Your father knows how you act just as well as I do, Vail. He knows I'd be telling a tall tale."

"Well, maybe. But he'd let it pass if he thought you wanted him to. And I'll tell him myself, when I have a good chance, that I'm not moving to the *garçonnière*, married or single, now or ever."

Vail's attitude, gradually and divergently made known to Madame d'Alvery and Gervais by himself and Merry, gave satisfaction to both, but especially to his grandmother. She regarded him with increasing respect, and her liking for Susannah also continued to increase. Vail took over his own room at once, and though Merry hastily moved some of her belongings across the hall, it was understood from the beginning that Susannah was soon coming out from Somerulos Street to Belle Heloise, that when she did she would occupy the guest room immortalized by Henry Clay, and that therefore Merry's transfer there was only temporary, undertaken to give time for a permanent one to the *garçonnière*. Vail's suggestion about transforming the dining room into an extra bedroom was accepted, and presently, his foster parents were re-established, apparently to their mutual satisfaction, in their "own little home." Watching, with affectionate solicitude, this new adjustment to an old manner of living, Vail was hopefully confident that in time it might prove a happy and harmonious arrangement. With characteristic male reserve on such a subject, Gervais said almost nothing to him about it. But Merry, having once involuntarily betrayed more than she intended to, seemed to find it easy to talk to Vail about the problems which had so far baffled her, and did so frequently and at length. Finally she asked him point blank whether he had been able to "see her side" and to understand why she had felt impelled to leave his father.

"Yes, I think so," he replied rather hesitantly. "At least, I suppose men and women look at things differently, and then, if they belong to different generations, that's another handicap. But I know you are absolutely sincere, Mom. I know you felt you couldn't live with Dad any longer, when you left him. And I know that as soon as you felt you could come back, you did."

"But you do feel I was unjust to him?"

"You went away at a time when he needed you very much, Mom; you know that yourself. He must have felt that you were going back on him, badly. But I know you felt he'd failed you, lots of times before that, and that finally he'd failed Franchot, which hurt you still more. Of course, I'll never believe he really did fail Franchot—we've been over that before, and you said you'd talked about it to Mr. Goldenberg, too, so I hope we don't need to go into all that again. But perhaps, speaking from the viewpoint of an awfully young and inexperienced male, who doesn't even pretend to know anything at all about marriage, I might say I believe one of the reasons you and Dad came to a parting of the ways was because, in so many cases, the same things didn't seem important to you. I read in some darn book, that for a marriage to be really successful, things had to. But I don't see why. Not everything, anyway. I should think there would always be enough basic things that were bound to, so that lesser things wouldn't matter."

"But how would you divide the basic things from the lesser things, Vail?"

"Well, I've told you already that I really don't know anything about it. But I should think that if two people had the same standards about right and wrong, for instance, just that would help a lot. If they agreed on the way they wanted to live, the way you and Dad agreed about the *garçonnière,* I should think that would help too. And if they both wanted children, and got them, and cared a lot for them . . . Gee, I'm not saying any of this the way it ought to be said. But I don't see why it should make a woman unhappy because her husband wanted to go hunting, and didn't ask her to go with him, when she hated it anyway, if she knew all the time it would mean everything in the world to him to find her waiting for him when he got home."

"It wasn't just the hunting, Vail. It was——"

"Of course it wasn't just the hunting. I used that as one example of what I'm trying to get across to you, that's all. I shouldn't think money would matter either, which one had it, I mean, or how much or how little, if two people had something else that mattered more, like a common interest or a common purpose. And— Oh, I could go on forever, I reckon! But doesn't it boil down to the fact that most women set lots of store by things that seem trivial to most men, and the other way 'round? And that if they both can't recognize this and say, 'Well, what the hell! am I going to let that interfere with my being happy about something that counts a lot more?'—why then they seem to get into trouble, that's all."

Merry and Vail had been sitting on one of the ornamental iron seats in Angus Holt's garden while they were talking, and as Vail made his final statement, the door of Madame d'Alvery's boudoir opened and Susannah came out on the upper gallery. She had spent a great deal of time with the old lady—indeed, she had felt far more at home with her than she had with Colonel and Mrs. Gervais d'Alvery. But she had learned to tell when her hostess began to feel tired and needed to be alone with her beads and her breviary for a while, and very often this coincided with the time when Susannah herself felt she could not bear to stay shut up in a stuffy room any longer, that she must have air and exercise and freedom, and—she admitted candidly to herself—that she wanted to see Vail. Now she had seized upon an opportunity which seemed to offer itself.

"I think I hear Vail in the garden, Madame d'Alvery, and there was something special I meant to say to him before evening. Do you mind if I run out and call down to him, before he gets away?"

"Of course not, my dear. Go, by all means."

Susannah ran to the railing and looked down, past the old sugar kettle and the brick-bordered flower beds towards the garden seat. The mellow columns of the portico and the moss-festooned oaks framed her lovely face and figure. Vail regarded her with a delight which he made no effort to conceal.

"Hello there! What're you doing indoors, a pretty day like this?"

"Oh, I've been sitting on a cushion, sewing a fine seam. But I've finished my stint, and I thought I'd like to do something else for a change. Would I be in the way if I came down to the garden?"

"You might. This is a pretty small seat and Mom and I are both using it right now, like you see. But if you urged me, I suppose I could draw up another."

"No, don't, Vail," Merry said under her breath. "It's time I went over to the *garçonnière*. I was just going to tell you so when Susannah came out on the gallery. You and she sit here. I'll see you both later. And . . . I can't tell you how much you've helped, Vail, or how grateful I am to you. But I hope you know. I hope you'll see for yourself, when you come home next time, what a change there's been."

"I hope so too, Mom. Good luck! Tell Dad I'll be seeing him."

He had not begrudged the time he had spent with Merry, any more than he had begrudged the time he had spent with Joyeuse and Sance. However, he was glad she was going to the *garçonnière* now, that he was free at last to be with Sue for the next few hours. He had been able to accept the periods in which he was parted from her philosophically; but the longing for her and the need for her had been there all the time too. Now at last there was nothing more to detain him and fetter him, now at last his longing for her could be assuaged and his need of her could be met. Because this was so, he had spoken to her joyously, in asking her to go up on the levee with him. When she answered with such readiness, saying she would be glad to go, his own sense of happy release was intensified.

"That's good, because I'm mighty glad too . . . What about taking Maudie? Would you mind?"

"No. I'd like to take her."

At the word "levee" Maudie had already bounded towards the front door with hopefulness. Now she stood there expectantly, rolling her brown eyes, her beautiful head raised, her short tail wagging, her whole body quivering with excitement. Vail fondled her for a moment, smiling down at her affectionately, and then threw open the door.

"Oh, very well, Maudie, if you really want to——"

It was the time-honored signal which Fabian had always given Belizaire, and to which the descendants of that great sire still joyfully responded. Maudie shot down the walk which was bordered in springtime with the scarlet amaryllis and the white yucca, and waited for Vail to unfasten the iron gate leading into the driveway. Then she was off again, through the crepe myrtles, past the *pigeonniers,* darting across the road, wriggling under the wire fencing, scrambling up the levee bank. When she reached the ridge, she stood still, her distended body silhouetted against the evening sky, awaiting the coming of her master and his other companion. Maudie recognized a rival in this slim, lovely girl, who walked with such quiet assurance beside Vail; but she knew that he wanted the girl to be with him, and his wish was her law and his happiness her aspiration, for her love was sacrificial. If there were twinges of jealousy in her faithful heart as she watched the two young figures ascending the levee, she betrayed this disturbance by no outward sign. Instead, by her immobility, she gave the ultimate touch of tranquility to the peaceful scene. Over the west bank of the river, white clouds were lifted, plumelike, against the soft sky; on the further side of the road, stretching endlessly off into the distance, rose the tall green shoots of sugar cane still unharvested; beyond the levee, the strip of smooth sand widened to form the verdant batture. Above a few birds sailed idly back and forth, and, in the distance, some ranging lambs cropped the clover. But Maudie was closer than these other creatures, she belonged less to the landscape and more to the lover. He remembered her and rejoiced in her even at this poignant moment.

"Good dog! That's it, stretch out and lie still. We're not going any further right now . . . Unless you want to, Sue?"

"No. It's beautiful here. We couldn't find a better place."

They sat down on the ridge, where they could see the river on one side of them and the road on the other at the same time. Susannah gazed at them both in silence, and Vail, knowing that she was thinking of them too, and in connection with him, did not break in on her reverie. She was the first to speak, and that was only after a long time.

"You love it here, don't you, Vail?"

"Yes. I belong to it. Usually land belongs to a man. Here it's the other way round."

"I know what you mean. I think you're right, too."

"But I love you more, Sue. I said I'd never live anywhere else. But if you'd be happier in some other place——"

"It's not a case of being happier in some other place. You ought to know that by now. I could have easily loved Belle Heloise too. And the road and the river and everything that goes with them—the groves and the cane fields and the levee and the batture. But you see——"

"You thought you were going to live here with Phil. You can't get used to the idea of living here with me instead."

"It sounds terribly bald when you say it that way, Vail. But—yes, I suppose that is the trouble—the root of it anyway. I loved Phil so much—and then afterwards I despised him so——"

Her lips trembled. For a moment she could not go on. Vail put out his hand and took both of hers in his.

"Darling," he said. He spoke very quietly, and he did not try to draw her closer to him. But there was an inescapable firmness in both his voice and his handclasp. "I'm going to say something that may hurt you, but if it isn't said now, I'm afraid it'll rise up and hit us later on, and I'd rather have it behind us than ahead of us. Phil never loved you. Not even the day he married you. He was flattered, he couldn't help being, because you acted the way you did. I don't mean you were forward or anything like that, whatever you may say yourself. I only mean that you showed how you felt, in the loveliest sort of way. But that you hadn't really found out then, what it meant to care for a man. You couldn't have, because love has to be two-sided to be perfect and complete. And Phil never found that out. He got killed before he had time. If he hadn't been, if there had been time, he'd have found out eventually that he loved someone else. He must have had it in him to love someone. But it wouldn't have been you—Nellie Pereira, maybe. And that would have hurt terribly, Sue, a lot more than what I'm saying now, a lot more than it hurt when you humbled your pride before Phil's casual acceptance of your devotion, because you thought you could love enough for two. . . . You're not crying, are you, Sue?"

"No, I'm not crying."

"Yes you are. Are you crying because you think I'm unfair, or because you know what I've said is true?"

She did not answer immediately. But when she did, though her voice was low, she spoke clearly and courageously.

"Because I know what you said is true."

"Well, if you know it, can't you face it? You're made of strong stuff,

Sue—not just fine stuff, but strong stuff. That's one of the reasons I love you so much. Of course there are lots of others. Shall I tell you what those are too?"

He smiled down at her, adoration in his face. She looked back at him, tears still shining on her long black lashes, but a happier light in her candid gray eyes.

"Not—not just now, Vail."

"All right—just so long as it's only postponed. Because I like telling you. And some day I think you'll like hearing it. I think some day you'll find out you and I are the same sort of people, Sue. Much more the same sort than you and Phil. Not that I'm trying to pay myself compliments. But sometimes people just fit and sometimes they don't. I know you and I do, or will, exactly the way I know you and Phil never would have."

Again she was silent, reflecting, and again he gave her time to turn her troubled problems over in her heart. But he continued to hold her cool little hands clasped in his, and she was conscious of his strength and his control. However, she made one more protest.

"I shouldn't think you'd want a girl your brother didn't want, a girl who ran after him without getting anywhere."

"I want the girl I know is mine, the one my brother didn't recognize as his because she wasn't. And you never ran after him. Out of your great bounty, you offered him your love—all the love you could have given him or any man then. But it's nothing compared to the love you could give to me now, if you would."

"Vail, when you talk to me like this——"

"You don't mind listening, do you? You didn't know I could, did you? Well, I didn't either. I never talked to anyone like this before and probably I'll never be able to again. But I can talk to you this way because you really are my girl, and I've got to make you see that."

The smile that illumined his face with love when he looked at her was growing brighter and brighter. He pressed the little hands that he was holding so fast. They were not cool any longer; they had grown warm as he held them.

"No," she said. "I don't mind listening." She spoke with a strange new note of shyness and surprise. "I like to listen to you. I—you're wonderful, Vail, when you talk like this. You make me see things differently. Phil did hurt me, the way you said. I knew he'd have hurt me more and more, all the time. And instead of hurting me, you——"

She hesitated, and he waited, giving her time to go on. "I don't know just how to put it," she said at last. "Perhaps you won't be pleased with the only comparison I can think of. We've had an old Negro working for us at Salome, the surly kind—if he hadn't been that kind, we probably wouldn't have had anybody; but even with the labor shortage, no one else would take this man on. . . . Well, a little while ago, he had a sudden illness, and of course we did what we could for him. We got our doctor to take the case, and we bulldozed the nearest hospital into making room for him, and then as soon as he could be moved, we brought him to our house in an ambulance. Of course it's only what anyone would do——"

"It's only what anyone ought to do, but unfortunately everyone doesn't. Not around here, anyway. Go on with your story, darling. I'm interested in it. I've always liked your stories, and this is even better than the one about the wolf."

"It isn't much of a story, really. I was just telling it to you so that I could make a point. The first time I went to see this man in the hospital, he was hardly out of the ether, and no one else was staying with him, so I did, for a little while. And presently he mumbled 'Miss Sue, yo' sure is a post in my life fence. It wouldn't hab stood up without you.' I didn't catch his meaning exactly, and I didn't think it mattered much, anyway. After all, he was only half-conscious. But when he'd been brought back to Salome, and was all settled in his big clean bed, he said the same thing over again. That time I did pay attention. That time I did figure out what he meant."

"I can, easily enough. So what?"

"Nothing, except—that's the way I feel about you, Vail. You're a post in my life fence. It wouldn't stand up without you. I wouldn't even try to make it, because it wouldn't matter enough. It took me a long time to find out how much you meant to me, but once I did——"

She stopped again, unable to go on. This time Vail put his arm around her. "There, darling. That's all I needed to have you say. You've told me all I needed to know—now. We can start out together, on that. And after we've started, we can keep on. It isn't going to be easy traveling, Sue, on the River Road. It never has been. It's been so hard that most people have given it up. Those are the people who made a mistake, because for a while it looked easy, and they were disappointed and angry when they found out it wasn't. They've tried to take short cuts, they've lain down on their jobs, they've been failures and quitters and crooks. But we're not like them. Syb and Riccardo aren't either. They're made of fine stuff and strong stuff too."

"They'd like to hear you say that. Sybelle thinks you're wonderful, Vail. She's prouder because you're her 'litter brother' than she is of anything else in the world."

"Nonsense. She's prouder because Riccardo's her husband and she is going to have his baby. Just the same I'm glad she thinks she's got something to be proud of as far as I'm concerned. I'm glad she still likes to speak of me as her 'litter brother,' even if it is an old Negro expression that highbrows look down on. She learned it from our mammy, and Dinah's one of the finest persons that ever lived. The words have a special meaning when she uses them, too."

There was a subtle change in his voice. For a moment Sue thought that something had sobered him, even while he spoke of being happy. But she did not know what it could be, and presently she decided that she had been mistaken after all. Then she forgot about it. For Vail was looking at her again with eyes of love, and suddenly something stirred, deep within her, that she had never felt when she was with Phil. She was hardly aware of the secret fluttering before it had become a swift strong pang. This was not fascination, it was fate; it was not merely the yearning of the flesh, it was the soul's sincere desire. She caught her breath in amazement and incredible joy.

"What would you think of riding into town with me after supper to tell Aunt Cresside we're really engaged at last?" he asked. "Aunt Cresside and Uncle Fabian too, of course. We'll tell Mom and Dad before we go, and *grand'mère. Grand'mère's* got a present for you that she's waited a long time to give you. Oh, nothing much in itself! But it stands for a lot. Later I'll drive you over to New Roads if you like, and we'll tell your father and mother. But don't count on staying at Salome. I'm going to keep you with me till the last minute this time. Then while I'm gone you can be getting ready for that wedding you always meant to have, seeing if your great-grandmother's dress still fits and all that. Because on my next leave——"

It was his turn to stop. At a magic moment like this, when they were both gazing with such bright expectancy into the future, the very thought of referring to anything connected with a sordid and tragic past was repugnant. But the necessity still remained, and like the other reference he had known would hurt her, it was better to have it behind them than ahead of them.

"Of course we know you were never really married to Phil," he said. "And of course we know he's dead now, too. All the same, there hasn't been time to deal with that Justice of the Peace yet. A marriage can't be annulled in a minute, without any red tape at all. If you don't mind letting just one person in on your secret, I'm going to ask Uncle Fabian to attend to that matter for us— He'll understand. He'll help. There's nothing he can't do. He's always been just like a father to me. I've been mighty lucky that way, having him and Dad both——"

He spoke sincerely and without reservation. He had entirely forgotten the tombstone in the Hathaway lot and its significance in his life.

"Just for added security, I suppose we also ought to wait till the War Department has made an official announcement of Phil's death. I don't know how long that will take, but it might be as much as a year— I mean a year from the time the records were destroyed. But that won't seem so long, will it, Sue, after all the time we've waited already? Of course if it hadn't been for these complications, I'd have made you marry me the day I got back. Oh, I forgot! You told me I mustn't ever use that word, talking to you!"

"You wouldn't have had to make me, because I'd have wanted to do it. I don't care what words you use though, any more, Vail. Words don't seem to matter now."

"They don't, do they? But there's something else that does. I've always understood that when people get this far, if not long before, there's a very pleasant custom——"

He bent his head and she lifted hers. Encompassed by the river and its road, they stood, as countless other lovers had stood before them, indefinitely embraced. Maudie continued to crouch, patiently and contentedly, at their feet.